THE NATE TEMPLE SERIES

BOOKS 0–3

SHAYNE SILVERS

This is a work of fiction. Names, characters, businesses, places, events, and incidents are either the products of the author's imagination or used in a fictitious manner. Any resemblance to actual persons, living or dead, or actual events is purely coincidental.

Shayne Silvers

The Nate Temple Series: Books 0-3

The Nate Temple Series Boxsets Book 1

A TempleVerse Series

Formerly published as The Temple Chronicles Series

ISBN: **978-1-947709-24-9**

© 2017, Shayne Silvers / Argento Publishing, LLC

info@shaynesilvers.com

ALL RIGHTS RESERVED. This book contains material protected under International and Federal Copyright Laws and Treaties. Any unauthorized reprint or use of this material is prohibited. No part of this book may be reproduced or transmitted in any form or by any means, electronic or mechanical, including photocopying, recording, or by any information storage and retrieval system without express written permission from the author / publisher.

CONTENTS

The Nate Temple Series—A warning   1

OBSIDIAN SON (BOOK 1)

Chapter 1	5
Chapter 2	9
Chapter 3	13
Chapter 4	18
Chapter 5	23
Chapter 6	31
Chapter 7	34
Chapter 8	41
Chapter 9	47
Chapter 10	51
Chapter 11	55
Chapter 12	63
Chapter 13	65
Chapter 14	73
Chapter 15	76
Chapter 16	83
Chapter 17	87
Chapter 18	92
Chapter 19	97
Chapter 20	102
Chapter 21	108
Chapter 22	113
Chapter 23	119
Chapter 24	124
Chapter 25	128
Chapter 26	135
Chapter 27	143
Chapter 28	147
Chapter 29	153
Chapter 30	159
Chapter 31	166
Chapter 32	171
Chapter 33	176

Chapter 34	182
Chapter 35	188
Chapter 36	195
Chapter 37	197
Chapter 38	201
Chapter 39	205
Chapter 40	209
Chapter 41	214
Chapter 42	220

BLOOD DEBTS (BOOK 2)

Chapter 1	225
Chapter 2	231
Chapter 3	236
Chapter 4	241
Chapter 5	248
Chapter 6	252
Chapter 7	257
Chapter 8	269
Chapter 9	273
Chapter 10	282
Chapter 11	284
Chapter 12	292
Chapter 13	299
Chapter 14	313
Chapter 15	320
Chapter 16	330
Chapter 17	339
Chapter 18	344
Chapter 19	348
Chapter 20	357
Chapter 21	360
Chapter 22	365
Chapter 23	370
Chapter 24	378
Chapter 25	387
Chapter 26	393
Chapter 27	398
Chapter 28	403
Chapter 29	408
Chapter 30	414
Chapter 31	417
Chapter 32	421

Chapter 33	426
Chapter 34	434
Chapter 35	439
Chapter 36	442
Chapter 37	446
Chapter 38	450
Chapter 39	456
Chapter 40	458
Chapter 41	465
Chapter 42	470
Chapter 43	480

FAIRY TALE (PREQUEL #0)

Chapter 1	485
Chapter 2	489
Chapter 3	494
Chapter 4	498
Chapter 5	500
Chapter 6	504
Chapter 7	510
Chapter 8	514
Chapter 9	521
Chapter 10	529
Chapter 11	531
Chapter 12	533

GRIMM (BOOK 3)

Chapter 1	541
Chapter 2	548
Chapter 3	554
Chapter 4	560
Chapter 5	568
Chapter 6	576
Chapter 7	580
Chapter 8	585
Chapter 9	592
Chapter 10	597
Chapter 11	603
Chapter 12	608
Chapter 13	613

Chapter 14	618
Chapter 15	623
Chapter 16	631
Chapter 17	634
Chapter 18	637
Chapter 19	641
Chapter 20	644
Chapter 21	647
Chapter 22	653
Chapter 23	657
Chapter 24	661
Chapter 25	666
Chapter 26	669
Chapter 27	677
Chapter 28	686
Chapter 29	691
Chapter 30	696
Chapter 31	703
Chapter 32	708
Chapter 33	713
Chapter 34	715
Chapter 35	719
Chapter 36	723
Chapter 37	730
Chapter 38	735
Chapter 39	741
Chapter 40	747
Chapter 41	758
Chapter 42	764
Chapter 43	770
Chapter 44	774
Chapter 45	781
Chapter 46	784
Chapter 47	787
TEASER: SILVER TONGUE (TEMPLE #4)	797
MAKE A DIFFERENCE	803
ACKNOWLEDGMENTS	805
ABOUT SHAYNE SILVERS	807
BOOKS BY SHAYNE SILVERS	809

THE NATE TEMPLE SERIES—A WARNING

Nate Temple starts out with everything most people could ever wish for—money, magic, and notoriety. He's a local celebrity in St. Louis, Missouri—even if the fact that he's a wizard is still a secret to the world at large.

Nate is also a bit of a...well, let's call a spade a spade. He can be a mouthy, smart-assed jerk. Like the infamous Sherlock Holmes, I specifically chose to give Nate glaring character flaws to overcome rather than making him a chivalrous Good Samaritan. He's a black hat wizard, an antihero—and you are now his partner in crime. He is going to make a *ton* of mistakes. And like a buddy cop movie, you are more than welcome to yell, laugh and curse at your new partner as you ride along together through the deadly streets of St. Louis.

Despite Nate's flaws, there's also something *endearing* about him...You soon catch whispers of a firm moral code buried deep under all his snark and arrogance. A diamond waiting to be polished. And you, the esteemed reader, will soon find yourself laughing at things you really shouldn't be laughing at. It's part of Nate's charm. Call it his magic...

So don't take yourself, or any of the characters in my world, too seriously. Life is too short for that nonsense.

Get ready to cringe, cackle, cry, curse, and—ultimately—*cheer* on this snarky wizard as he battles or befriends angels, demons, myths, gods, shifters, vampires and many other flavors of dangerous supernatural beings.

Like any epic tale, Nate's journey starts out with a noble cause...

To find a cure for a reptile dysfunction.

Because dragons have come to St. Louis...

DON'T FORGET!

VIP's get early access to all sorts of book goodies, including signed copies, private giveaways, and advance notice of future projects. AND A FREE NOVELLA! Click the image or join here: www.shaynesilvers.com/l/219800

FOLLOW AND LIKE:
Shayne's FACEBOOK PAGE:
www.shaynesilvers.com/l/38602

I try to respond to all messages, so don't hesitate to drop me a line. Not interacting with readers is the biggest travesty that most authors can make. Let me fix that.

OBSIDIAN SON (BOOK 1)

1

There was no room for emotion in a hate crime. I had to be cold. Heartless. This was just another victim. Nothing more. No face, no name.

Frosted blades of grass crunched under my feet, sounding to my ears alone like the symbolic glass that one would shatter under a napkin at a Jewish wedding. The noise would have threatened to give away my stealthy advance as I stalked through the moonlit field, but I was no novice and had planned accordingly. Being a wizard, I was able to muffle all sensory evidence with a fine cloud of magic—no sounds, and no smells. Nifty. But if I made the spell much stronger, the anomaly would be too obvious to my prey.

I knew the consequences for my dark deed tonight. If caught, jail time or possibly even a gruesome, painful death. But if I succeeded, the look of fear and surprise in my victim's eyes before his world collapsed around him, was well worth the risk. I simply couldn't help myself; I had to take him down.

I knew the cops had been keeping tabs on my car, but I was confident that they hadn't followed me. I hadn't seen a tail on my way here, but seeing as how they frowned on this kind of thing I had taken a circuitous route just in case. I was safe. I hoped.

Then my phone chirped at me as I received a text.

I practically jumped out of my skin, hissing instinctively. "Motherf—" I cut off abruptly, remembering the whole stealth aspect of my mission. I was off to a stellar start. I had forgotten to silence the damned phone. *Stupid, stupid, stupid!*

My heart threatened to explode inside my chest with such thunderous violence that I briefly envisioned a mystifying Rorschach blood-blot that would have made coroners and psychologists drool.

My body remained tense as I swept my gaze over the field, sure that I had been made. My breathing finally began to slow, my pulse returning to normal, as I noticed no changes in my surroundings. Hopefully, my magic had silenced the sound and my resulting outburst. I glanced down at the phone to scan the text and then typed back a quick and angry response before I switched the cursed phone to vibrate.

Now, where were we...

I continued on, the lining of my coat constricting my breathing. Or maybe it was because I was leaning forward in anticipation. *Breathe*, I chided myself. *He doesn't know you're here.* All this risk for a book. It had better be worth it.

I'm taller than most, and not abnormally handsome, but I knew how to play the genetic cards I had been dealt. I had shaggy, dirty blonde hair, and my frame was thick with well-earned muscle, yet still lean. I had once been told that my eyes were like twin emeralds pitted against the golden-brown tufts of my hair—a face like a jewelry box. Of course, that was two bottles of wine into a date, so I could have been a little foggy on her quote. Still, I liked to imagine that was how everyone saw me.

But tonight, all that was masked by magic.

I grinned broadly as the outline of the hairy hulk finally came into view. He was blessedly alone—no nearby sentries to give me away. That was always a risk when performing this ancient rite-of-passage. I tried to keep the grin on my face from dissolving into a maniacal cackle.

My skin danced with energy, both natural and unnatural, as I manipulated the threads of magic floating all around me. My victim stood just ahead, oblivious of the world of hurt that I was about to unleash. Even with his millennia of experience, he didn't stand a chance. I had done this so many times that the routine of it was my only enemy. I lost count of how many times I had been told not to do it again; those who knew declared it *cruel, evil, and sadistic*. But what fun wasn't? Regardless, that wasn't enough to stop me from doing it again. And again. Call it an addiction if you will, but it was too much of a rush to ignore.

The pungent smell of manure filled the air, latching onto my nostril hairs. I took another step, trying to calm my racing pulse. A glint of gold reflected in the silver moonlight, but the victim remained motionless, hopefully unaware or all was lost. I wouldn't make it out alive if he knew I was here. Timing was everything.

I carefully took the last two steps, a lifetime between each, watching the legendary monster's ears, anxious and terrified that I would catch even so much as a twitch in my direction. Seeing nothing, a fierce grin split my unshaven cheeks. My spell had worked! I raised my palms an inch away from their target, firmly planted my feet, and squared my shoulders. I took one silent, calming breath, and then heaved forward with every ounce of physical strength I could muster. As well as a teensy-weensy boost of magic. Enough to goose him good.

"*MOOO!!!*" The sound tore through the cool October night like an unstoppable freight train. *Thud-splat!* The beast collapsed sideways into the frosty grass; straight into a steaming patty of cow shit, cow dung, or, if you really want to church it up, a Meadow Muffin. But to me, shit is, and always will be, shit.

Cow tipping. It doesn't get any better than that in Missouri.

Especially when you're tipping the *Minotaur*. Capital M.

Razor-blade hooves tore at the frozen earth as the beast struggled to stand, grunts of rage vibrating the air. I raised my arms triumphantly. "Boo-yah! Temple 1, Minotaur 0!" I crowed. Then I very bravely prepared to protect myself. Some people just couldn't take a joke. *Cruel, evil,* and *sadistic* cow tipping may be, but by hell, it was a *rush*. The legendary beast turned his gaze on me after gaining his feet, eyes ablaze as he unfolded to his full height on two tree-trunk-thick legs, hooves magically transforming into heavily-booted feet. The thick, gold ring dangling from his snotty snout quivered as the Minotaur panted, and his dense, corded muscle contracted over his human-like chest. As I stared up into those brown eyes, I actually felt sorry…for, well, myself.

"I have killed greater men than you for less offense," he growled.

I swear to God his voice sounded like an angry James Earl Jones. Like Mufasa talking to Scar.

"You have shit on your shoulder, Asterion." I ignited a roiling ball of fire in my palm in order to see his eyes more clearly. By no means was it a defensive gesture on my part. It was just dark. But under the weight of his glare, even I couldn't buy my reassuring lie. I hoped using a form of his ancient name would give me brownie points. Or maybe just not-worthy-of-killing points.

The beast grunted, eyes tightening, and I sensed the barest hesitation. "Nate Temple…your name would look splendid on my already long list of slain idiots." Asterion took a threatening step forward, and I thrust out my palm in warning, my roiling flame blue now.

"You lost fair and square, Asterion. Yield or perish." The beast's shoulders sagged slightly. Then he finally nodded to himself in resignation, appraising me with the scrutiny of a worthy adversary. "Your time comes, Temple, but I will grant you this. You've got a pair of stones on you to rival Hercules."

I pointedly risked a glance down towards the myth's own crown jewels. "Well, I sure won't need a wheelbarrow any time soon, but I'm sure I'll manage."

The Minotaur blinked once, and then bellowed out a deep, contagious, snorting laughter. Realizing I wasn't about to become a murder statistic, I couldn't help but join in. It felt good. It had been a while since I had allowed myself to experience genuine laughter.

In the harsh moonlight, his bulk was even more intimidating as he towered head and shoulders above me. This was the beast that had fed upon human sacrifices for countless years while imprisoned in Daedalus' Labyrinth in Greece. And all of that protein had not gone to waste, forming a heavily woven musculature over the beast's body that made even Mr. Olympia look puny.

From the neck up he was entirely bull, but the rest of his body more resembled a thickly-furred man. But, as shown moments ago, he could adapt his form to his environment, never appearing fully human, but able to make his entire form appear as a bull when necessary. For instance, how he had looked just before I tipped him. Maybe he had been scouting the field for heifers before I had so efficiently killed the mood.

His bull face was also covered in thick, coarse hair—even sporting a long, wavy beard of sorts, and his eyes were the deepest brown I had ever seen. Cow shit brown. His snout jutted out, emphasizing the gold ring dangling from his glistening nostrils, catching a glint in the luminous glow of the moon. The metal was at least an inch thick, and etched with runes of a language long forgotten. Thick, aged ivory horns sprouted from each temple, long enough to skewer a wizard with little effort. He was nude except for a beaded necklace and a pair of worn leather boots that were big enough to stomp a size twenty-five imprint in my face if he felt so inclined.

I hoped our blossoming friendship wouldn't end that way. I really did.

2

After the laughter died down, the Minotaur spoke, his shoulders relaxing as he assumed a less-intimidating posture. "I must thank you for testing me this night. I almost forgot *The Path*, and for that, I must ask your forgiveness."

I blinked. "Uh, forgiveness?"

He nodded, relaxing even more as he steepled his fingers before him in a prayer-like gesture. "I have been reading quite a bit lately on the Buddhist faith. Most intriguing. I can't fathom why I had never heard of it until recently." He appraised me pointedly. "I need not react to such an overtly negative offense. Karma will come back to visit you… quite severely, I would imagine," he sneered.

It took a few moments for my brain to process his words. "Karma? You're a *Buddhist* now?" I practically yelled in disbelief. "Come on! It was just a practical joke. You make it sound as if Karma will be gunning for me."

Asterion replied in a lecturing tone, his snout pulled back like Mr. Ed chewing a wad of peanut butter. "The severity of the Karmic retaliation is weighted against five conditions: frequent repetitive action; determined intentional action; action performed without regret; action against *extraordinary* persons…" He leveled a meaty thumb at his chest with a vain grin. "And finally, action toward those who have helped one in the past." He wasn't able to conceal his pleasure. "Having broken all five this night, I would say Karma's going to *destroy* you." I rolled my eyes and shrugged. The Minotaur must have noticed my lack of concern, so he switched gears. "My deepest condolences, but if this is about your parents' murder, I cannot aid you."

Before I could stop myself, the frozen ground around us vaporized to baking clay and cow shit in a fifty-foot radius—steam rising up in a heavy fog. I could smell the soles of our boots burning like fresh tarmac. "What?" I hissed.

The Minotaur's eyes widened. "You are the heir to the notorious Temple wizards who recently passed. Why would you seek me out again if not to find their murderer?"

"The evidence revealed no foul-play. What do you know?" I whispered, my voice like gravel as I tried to blockade the torrent of emotions that had so suddenly swelled up inside me—the emotions I thought I had successfully walled away. Until now.

"Nothing! But come now, Temple. You know better. Are you claiming that you do not know a way to kill someone without a trace? You are a wizard. That is child's play for your kind. When a wizard dies, it's either violent or from extreme old age. For two to die within moments of one another is beyond calculation. Even Hermes wouldn't bet on that."

I had checked the evidence myself. Repeatedly. He was wrong. He *had* to be wrong. Calming myself, I came back to the reason for my visit, dispersing my magic out into the night with a flick of my wrist. The ground remained warm, but no longer smoldering. "Word around town says you deal in antiquities. Is this true?"

The Minotaur hesitated, glancing at the ground in relief. "Says whom?"

I glanced behind me as I heard the distant sound of sirens on a nearby road. *Impossible.* They couldn't be following me. Perhaps some kid had been caught speeding on the back roads. I was just being paranoid. "*Who*," I corrected, turning back.

"Irrelevant," he muttered.

That rankled me. "It is not *irrelevant*. It's paramount! The rules of grammar are just as important as the rules of engagement in war. Without them, we are barbarians," I argued.

The Minotaur frowned pensively. "I will have to think on this."

"So, are the rumors true or not?" I pressed.

"Possibly. What do you seek?"

"A book."

"I know *many* books. Perhaps you could elaborate?" he replied, sounding bored.

I weighed my options. My client wanted this badly. Very badly. And so far, I had turned up nothing. This was the end of the road. The sirens were closer now, and the flashing red and blue lights limned the fringes of the field. Fuck. It *couldn't* be for me. I rushed onward, anxious now. "I don't know the title, but I can show you the symbol from the cover." I had to move fast in case the cops really *had* found me. Regardless, if they drove by, chances were good they would either recognize my car, or at least wonder why such a beautiful vehicle was parked outside a field on a deserted country road.

The Minotaur knelt down to the ground, waiting. I noticed that his necklace was really a set of prayer beads. I shook my head in disbelief—the Minotaur, a born-again Buddhist. I traced my fingers just above the grass, releasing a tendril of fire like a pencil to burn an insignia into the now dry earth. It resembled a winged serpent over a flickering sun that appeared to be burning out, or fading. The Minotaur was entirely still for several breaths, and then he glanced warily toward the sky. After a long silence, he unfolded from his crouch, scuffed up the ground with his massive boot, and whispered one word. "Dragons." His horns gleamed wickedly in the moonlight as he towered over me.

I blinked. *What the hell?*

"Dragons?" I glanced behind me as the sound of slamming car doors interrupted my train of thought, and I realized that the flashing lights were just outside the field, right by my parked car. Shit. I *had* been made. Time to wrap things up. As I stood, I saw a flicker of silver in the air as Asterion tossed something at me. I reflexively caught it to find a dull, chipped silver coin in my palm. A worn image of a man holding the legendary Caduceus—the healing staff of doctors everywhere—was imprinted on one side, but the other bore only a pair of winged feet. "Flip once to save the life of another, and once to save your own," the Minotaur recited.

I frowned. "Why give me this?"

"I do as commanded. The book you seek is dangerous. I was told to pass this relic on to the first requestor." He fingered the prayer beads thoughtfully, glancing once over my shoulder at the flashing lights.

"How long have you held this?" I asked hurriedly.

He answered a different question instead. "I have guarded the original version of the book you seek since I was put in that cursed Labyrinth, but I fear that copies might exist in the outside world. If they haven't been destroyed over the years. Humans are always destroying their cultures." He snorted, eyes briefly flaring in outrage. "Both the coin and book were entrusted to me by Hermes." My mouth might or might not have dropped open in disbelief for a moment, but the Minotaur continued. "If your desire for this book is strong enough, meet me here two days hence. We will duel at sunset."

"But you're a Buddhist now. Couldn't you…I don't know, just sell it to me?"

The Minotaur shook his head with a hungry grin. "Promises made, promises kept." I glanced down at the ancient coin in my palm, thinking furiously. "Oh, and Temple…" I looked up to see his boot flying at my midsection, so I hastily threw up a last-second shield of air. It deflected only the fatal portion of the blow. "Karma says *hello*. Don't *ever* cow-tip me again."

The force felt like…well, what I would have imagined a heel kick from the Minotaur would feel like. Then I was flying toward the pulsing lights. The Minotaur's guttural laughter stayed with me as I tumbled through the starry night, and then I landed chest-first in a moist pile of cow shit, sliding a few feet so that it smeared a perfect streak from chest to groin. I heard a surprised grunt, and then a knee ground me deeper into the cold grass, mashing the molecular particles of shit firmly between each individual fiber of my six-hundred-dollar coat.

Cold steel clamped around my wrists. "I got him, Captain! He came outta' nowhere!"

I couldn't help it. I began to laugh—hard—despite the lingering pain of Asterion's well-placed farewell boot. "Fucking Karma!" I bellowed between giggles.

"I think he's hopped up on something, sir. Probably mushrooms, judging from all this cow shit."

"Whatever," a new voice—presumably the Captain's—said. "Let's take him downtown. We have a few questions for him about his parents' murder."

I choked on my laughter.

3

The heavy steel door clicked open and a second cop entered the room, sauntering up to me with silent arrogance. I had time to notice a third young cop standing guard outside —nervously fingering his holster—before the door closed. The interrogation room smelled like cleaning solution and metal. I sat with my hands cuffed behind my back, wrists slightly chafed, smelling like cow shit.

I was a putrid stain on the great, pristine cog of bureaucracy that is the United States government.

I was also rightly furious. And my car was parked out in the middle of nowhere. I'd have to get Gunnar or someone to drive me out there to pick it up later. After I wrapped up...well, whatever this hot mess was about to become.

The cop already seated at the table watched me with an amused grin—as he had for the past twenty minutes. He was well-fed for a cop, his belly sagging over his weapons belt—which meant he was most likely a desk jockey and hadn't spent a lot of time chasing down bad guys. His cheeks hung heavy on his face, reminding me of a melting candle. In short, he was the perfect depiction of Buddha serving me a steaming dish of Karma. He hadn't shaved and he looked like the kind of guy who needed to shave twice a day in order to look presentable. I wanted to slap the smile off his face.

"Now that we're all here, Detective Kosage," I growled to the new cop, "The cause of death, as your officers informed me, was inconclusive. Are you reneging on that statement?"

Silver streaks started at the newcomer's temples to merge with his wavy black hair, and he was comically short and scrawny, but he still somehow managed to compose an aura of authority. A modern Napoleon. He hesitated at my knowledge of his name, but then he glanced down at his badge and simply nodded. Then he proceeded to sit down, setting a Styrofoam cup of burnt-tar coffee onto the table beside a manila folder.

It was a few hours until midnight, and my palate was not that of a refined Starbucks Barista. Coffee was coffee. I eyed it longingly.

"Mr. Temple," he began in a nasally voice.

"*Master* Temple," I corrected him with an icy tone of warning. The patriarch of our family had always been referred to as the *Master* Temple as far back as anyone could remember. In today's society, it sounded out of place and conceited, but it was a formality I was insistent upon pressing here. And the media ate it up since it sold headlines, so everyone knew of it. Choosing not to use it had been intentional on Detective Kosage's part.

He nodded. "Of course, *Master* Temple." There was no mockery in his whiny voice, just emphasis, as if he also appreciated the concept of respect. "First things first." His badge glittered in the fluorescent lighting. "Trespassing is illegal. You managed to pass the sobriety test, ruling out mushrooms, so what were you *really* doing out there? Hmm? Could our city's youngest billionaire really find nothing else to amuse him?" He looked genuinely puzzled, glancing pointedly at the putrid stain on my chest. "We could hold you for 24 hours, Master Temple. After all, I'm sure Mr...." He trailed off, shuffling some papers from his file to find the name. "Mr. Kingston would not be pleased with your uninvited exploration of his property."

"Are these really necessary?" I jangled my hands behind my back.

Detective Kosage's eyes squinted thoughtfully before nodding. "For now, yes."

I stared into his eyes, waiting a full ten seconds to see if he would change his mind. He didn't blink. I decided right then and there that I was going to have some fun with my current situation. Regulars—as we called non-magical beings—were terrified of the concept of magic being real. Especially since the media had recently started fueling the fires with stories of magic happening all over America. The debate was on everyone's lips. Was it real? Was it a hoax? Regardless, most Regulars were unable to comprehend the possibilities of things they didn't personally understand, and it was *so* much fun to capitalize on that anxiety. It was who I was. My charm.

"Alright, boys. Have it your way." I lifted my hands above my head in a languorous stretch, my wrists already free of the cuffs, as they had been for the last nineteen minutes. I set the cuffs on the table, sliding them over to the other cop, Detective Allison. "Here you go, Ali." I tried to mimic the smile he had given me earlier, waggling a small bobby pin between my fingers. "It's amazing what one can learn on the web. Now, I'm not sure how you were raised, but it is considered the height of impropriety to have a conversation without offering refreshment to your guest. Especially when the host has one. Unforgivably rude, actually." They blinked back at me in unison—the shock on their faces was as apparent as the cuffs sitting on the table—a pink elephant in the room.

As if on cue, the door opened, and the nervous cop I had only briefly seen entered with a steaming cup of coffee. He set it in front of me and then anxiously backed out of the room. I deduced that we were being recorded since my two jailers hadn't moved or spoken after my Houdini act. I had an audience. My smile stretched wider. *Even better.* Steam curled up from my cup. I invisibly cast a bit of magic into the coffee, dropping the temperature enough for me to down it in one gulp, which I promptly did. Their eyes widened, amazed that the drink hadn't scalded my throat. I let them wonder at that. "Much better, gentlemen. Now, what do you two want to chat about next? Your future careers? Politicians and the media can be bought, and I have a few extra bucks to grease some palms. Elections are coming up." I waited.

The detectives stared from my hands to the cuffs again in disbelief. Detective Allison responded first, rising from his chair with a furious growl, but Kosage slapped a dainty palm on his forearm, the authority plain. "Let's continue this discussion…professionally." He glanced back to the folder as Allison glared hatred at me for a moment longer. He finally sat down, the chair protesting his bulk with a loud squeak. I arched an eyebrow at the noise, my opinion plain. His eyes hardened, but he leaned back as Kosage read from a paper. "Let's talk about Temple Industries for a moment."

Temple Industries. The technology company my parents had started twenty years ago, headquartered in the thriving metropolis of St. Louis, Missouri. The company's fingers stretched wide, claiming over 3,000 patents (more than Microsoft) that ranged from software, to computer chips, and even to defense technology for the U.S. military. No one truly knew *everything* that the company concerned themselves with, just that they always seemed to produce the most cutting-edge technology. The company was vast, falling into the reputable *Fortune 500*. But I wanted nothing to do with it.

"It might be a very, very brief moment, as I have nothing to do with my parents' company. Other than owning a hefty number of shares," I added honestly.

Kosage stared back, eyes sharp. I kept my face blank. "Yes, well, the Interim President of the company, Ashley Belmont, is less than forthcoming about details of ownership. You're saying that you have no intentions of taking over the company?"

"Why would I?" I answered questions with questions when pissed off.

Detective Ali leaned forward. "Money," he growled hungrily.

I glanced from face to face for a long moment before leaning back into the steel torture device that doubled as a chair. "I assume that being clever and thorough policemen, you have already combed over my finances?" Kosage waited a moment, and then gave a brief nod. "Then you have no doubt noticed that I am already fairly wealthy from previous investments not limited to my shares in Temple Industries." Another nod. "Furthermore, that I run my own arcane little bookstore which brings me a *sufficient* annual income."

"Plato's Cave," Kosage answered with a wry grin at my financial modesty.

I nodded. "Have you also noticed that the stock in Temple Industries has dropped significantly since my parents' untimely…death?" The last word was hard for me to voice. Kosage blinked, reaching down for the coffee to cover his tell. "Ah, perhaps my previous assumption was too flattering. Not as thorough as you should have been. I have made no move to assume leadership of their company, and the value of that company has only dropped since the unfortunate death of the owners." I used my magic to dramatically dim the lights as I slowly stood from my chair. Kosage's own chair slid back as he hurriedly set the coffee back down to the table, glancing up at the lights with a frown.

Regulars. They were still scared of the dark, refusing to believe that magic existed, even when it happened right in front of their faces. They didn't know whom they were toying with. No one knew I was a wizard. They probably just thought the lighting system was faulty, but it had the desired effect. "You *better* not be implying that I had *anything* to do with their deaths," I hissed.

As I allowed the lights to brighten back to normal, Kosage swiveled his nervous, brown-eyed gaze back to me, no doubt wondering if he had imagined the lights dimming. "Of course not. Please sit, Master Temple." I didn't. He shrugged, regaining his composure, but Detective Allison remained on edge. Steel scraped the concrete floor as he scooted back to the table. "As I was saying, Miss Belmont says she will not speak to us until she has had a chance to speak with you. But you do not answer her calls. Then we get a pack of lawyers on our backs for questioning her. You can see our predicament. Things would be easier if we could simply talk to her. But why would she need to speak to you first unless you are indeed planning on taking over the company?" He was whining again.

I had no idea why she would want to talk to me, but I *had* been screening my calls lately. They were coming in from all over. Every news channel within a hundred miles had somehow found my personal cell phone number. I shrugged in answer. "Are you arresting me?"

"There is no need for such words. We're just trying to get to the bottom of this. We share the same goals, Master Temple. Finding the cause of their...death." He had hesitated on the last word, making it obvious that he had intended to say *murder*. "If you could please sit and answer a few more questions, we can get this over with in short order."

The Minotaur's words from earlier came back to my mind. The St. Louis Police Department had been the ones to tell me that the evidence at the scene had been inconclusive. They had been found dead in one of their laboratories with no signs of struggle, drugs, poison, or any of the usual clues that indicated potential murder. They had simply died—and within moments of one another. My father had been found with a minor but precise—almost surgical—perimortem gash on his wrist, but it hadn't been deep enough to be fatal, and there had been no blade in sight. The detectives had even declared it as self-inflicted around the time of death.

Temple Industries had been their life, and ultimately, their death.

I felt the barriers of my will weakening, the brick wall of restraint crumbling against the tides of emotion and magic inside me. "I do not have the answers you seek, *gentlemen*." I dramatically flicked a finger as if to shake off a drop of water, and a blast of frigid air beckoned to my command. The sole door to the room flew inward as if hit by a battering ram from the hall—the lock skittering across the floor to rest at my feet—and the temperature in the room dropped significantly. Detective Kosage's cup of coffee tipped over, splashing the steaming liquid towards his face.

I snapped my finger as the door rebounded off the inside wall, revealing the startled guard outside. His hand shook as it hovered near his pistol, and his holster's button latch safety was rattling in the sudden wind. The steaming mass of coffee froze into a chunk of brown ice an inch away from Detective Kosage's bloodless nose. Several frozen coffee-cubed drops bounced off his face and fell into his lap.

His chair slid back as his reflexes finally kicked in. Both of their eyes were wide now as they flinched from the door to me, panicked. I walked around him and Detective Allison on my way to the door. "I'll talk to Miss Belmont for you. Next time, don't bother with the cuffs. Just say *pretty-please*."

"What the *fuck*?" Detective Allison roared in shock. "How did he—" He cut off, his face pale with fear as he glanced from face to face. "Was that..." he hesitated, risking a nervous look towards the camera in the corner of the room before finishing his question, "*magic*?" He whispered it low in hopes that the camera might not pick it up.

I smiled, dimming the lights more dramatically this time as I leaned closer, whispering back conspiratorially. "Come now, officers. Don't tell me you still believe in *fairy tales*..." My grin stretched further, more menacing, and they each leaned away. "Answers can be dangerous...*All men should strive to learn before they die, what they are running from, and to, and why*," I quoted. "Seems like you have faulty lighting here," I added as an idle observation, frowning up at the lights.

Then I strode out of the room, leaving the words hanging like an axe over their throats. I had a client to meet. Then a well-deserved drink with some friends. I wasn't about to waste my time babysitting the city's men-in-blue.

4

I leaned against the cold brick wall of the diner, glancing at the sign hanging above my bookstore across the street through the light flurry of snow falling down to the ground in fat, heavy flakes. *Plato's Cave* was artfully painted onto the aged wood. I contemplated the events of the night as I waited for my client to arrive, trying to keep the wind at my back in order to avoid the sickly aroma of shit still painting my upper body.

The cops now thought my parents had been murdered. A week had passed me by since hearing the dire news. No prior health issues could have caused it. *Age* had been the predominant concrete answer.

But now I wasn't so sure.

First the Minotaur, and now the cops. I wondered what had made them change their minds. *Means, motive,* and *opportunity* were the three things cops looked for in murder cases, as my childhood friend—now an FBI Agent—Gunnar Randulf had told me.

The news of their deaths had wrecked me, but as an old Japanese friend from college had taught me long ago, *grieve fiercely for one day and then move on*. His ancestors had been Samurai, a hard-ass culture. So, that's what I had done. The first day I had been a mess, sticking to my store, needlessly stocking shelves, and staying busy without giving myself time to think.

The next day I had sealed the coffin on those emotions, following the evidence clinically, detached after my allotted one day of grief. Then my present client had called on me, giving me something new to focus on. I had poured all of my energy and attention into his request, ultimately leading to tonight's meeting with the Minotaur.

From time to time I obtained rare books for—as was most often the case—less than reputable clients with large bank accounts. I had a reputation for being able to find goods where others couldn't, and it had landed me a decent income. I had clung to my new client's request like a bloodhound—anything to ignore the pain inside me. But now the grief was threatening to come back as I discovered that the cops apparently hadn't closed the high-profile case. It wasn't their fault that their prime suspect was a rich, trust-fund heir. How many times had I seen a similar case go through the media?

And prove to be correct.

It made sense, but it was wrong. And infuriating. If I had learned of even one shred of evidence proving murder, I would have most likely gone vigilante, and killed them myself.

I hadn't been that close to my parents the last few years, but that was mainly out of stubbornness. As encouraged, I had double-majored in Physics and Philosophy at the age of twenty. But I had encountered an enchanting mistress while at college—*Books*. More accurately, the Classics: *Milton, Sir Arthur Conan Doyle, Dostoevsky, Dante Alighieri*, and a vast slew of philosophers. Not wanting to stand in my parents' shadow, I had started my own business, something more in line with both my talents and my interests.

Plato's Cave, my own Atlantis.

And I had been damn successful against the modern world of digital formatting, Kindles, iPads, and Nooks. It seemed that ancient books and classic volumes only increased in worth, and I had contacts that the rest of the world didn't.

Legends.

Many people thought of myth and folklore as either the very first fictional writings, or the incessant ramblings of inebriated authors. Nothing more. But my family and I knew better. We were wizards, and being such, were deeply entwined with those mythical races. For better or worse, the myths were all very, *very* real: Hermes, the Minotaur, Hercules, wizards—and as I had just been informed—dragons. The trouble was *finding* them. Because they didn't *want* to be found. They had lived their glory days long ago, and for the most part, remained reclusive.

But sometimes they decided to socialize again, causing the occasional sighting or other unexplainable carnage, and that was usually where wizards came in. We were the unofficial police of the magical community, or at least the wizards I had met seemed to lean in that direction.

But I had ways of finding those recluses, and a significant amount of charm that helped me win them over to help me unearth those old, withered, and forgotten tomes. Like I had with the Minotaur. Thinking of that encounter, I couldn't help but wonder why the hint of dragons had set him so on edge. I was pretty sure I would know if dragons were in my city: big, scaly, hungry, flying lizards, stealing gold and virgins? Didn't ring any bells.

I briefly wondered why the Minotaur had been prepared for my request thousands of years prior, and what Hermes had to do with it all. I idly fingered the coin in my pocket. Old books were like that, most often entrusted to an individual for life, and then passed down to a loved one upon their death.

On the upside, the original might be able to fetch more money from my client. If I could prove it was authentic. It wasn't like I could tell him, *Well, the Minotaur told me it was the real deal, and he just wouldn't lie about something like that. He's a Buddhist now. They frown upon lying.*

Frustrated by my unpunctual client, I thumbed open my pack of cigarettes, placed one between my lips, glanced around to make sure I was alone, and lit the tip of the cigarette with only a thought. No fancy hand motions, words, or lengthy process used at all. It had taken a while to hone my focus enough not to light my face on fire. The first few attempts hadn't been as successful.

My magic was an ever-present companion of mine. I had been told that I was more powerful than most—things that were quite difficult for other wizards came easily to me.

As a wizard, I saw the world through tinted glasses. A whole world of colors, vibrations, waves, and particles danced around me, and I knew how to tap into them; manipulate them to my desire with a thought. It was simply a part of me. I couldn't imagine it any other way. But I definitely knew I was a minority.

Content, I nestled my shoulders against the cold wall, bent my knee to rest my boot against the brick in an impromptu lean, and took a sweet, heavenly inhale. I needed it after recent events.

I exhaled the menthol smoke, thinking of a favorite quote I had read long ago. *Man, controlling Prometheus' gift of fire between two fingers...*Relishing the cool smoke, I was startled by a sudden voice from the alley beside me.

"Those things are bad for you. Cancerous, even."

Recognizing the voice, my pulse slowly returned to normal as I turned to face my client. People were rarely able to sneak up on me. "My body is a temple, and every good temple needs some incense now and again. Something you should learn. Like punctuality, kid."

My client grunted as he stepped out into view, lighting his own clove cigarette by the smell of it. The fragrance surrounded us like a soothing blanket as he puffed it to life. "The brightest candle burns half as long, right?" He exhaled another cloud of the pleasant-smelling smoke from his nostrils. He somehow made it look dangerous, like a bouncer flexing his muscles, or a cop cocking his pistol.

"Hypocrite," I muttered.

He smiled. "You smell...bad," he finally concluded.

"I shit myself earlier. Deal with it."

He frowned. "Does this happen often?" I glared back, and he chuckled before shrugging it off. "Did you find it?"

I studied my client, trying to figure him out. Dark, lanky hair hugged his scalp down to his jaw, and his eyes were dark enough for me to have never placed a color to them. I peered closer, but seeming to sense my curiosity, he glanced away. His harsh angular jaw and cheekbones made stark shadows in the dim light. Tight leather pants clung to his legs, and calf-high boots that looked like they belonged on a *Pirates of the Caribbean* set covered his feet. The leather smelled clean and sharp. His white V-neck Tee contrasted the tight pants, and a thick silver chain hung against his chest, peeking out from underneath the fabric.

He looked like a modern James Dean. He wasn't even wearing a coat and it was snowing. Rebel without a cause, all right. I suppose many would have found him roguishly handsome, and I, being comfortable with my masculinity, realized this with a slight twinge of jealousy. "Possibly," I answered. "I'll know for sure in two days." I noticed a new smell for the first time around my client—cold rocks, and...snakes. I know that neither of those things instill a familiar sense of smell to most people, but being a wizard, my senses were enhanced, and I could place associations to such things. I stored it away for later thought.

The boy—because he was younger than me—nodded. "Two days. That's perfect."

Unsure what *that* implied, I probed a bit. "Are you sure you want it? My contact seems to think it might be dangerous..." I paused significantly. "Which raises the price."

He flashed me an amused smirk, took another inhale of his cigarette, and then dismissively flicked away the ash. "Price is not an issue." He leveled his dark, black diamond eyes on me. The irises *were* black. No color whatsoever. "It's vital that you get it for me. And no later than two days. Sooner is better, but *definitely* not any later." He glanced around warily, even up at the nearby buildings. *Paranoid much*, I thought to myself. "Any other inquirers?"

That question stumped me. "No. Why?"

"Just curious. I presume that this still remains a secret between us?" I nodded. "I have your word on that?" he pressed.

I knew that there was more to this than he was letting on, and that he was definitely not your Average Joe. He was wary, but unafraid—anticipatory. I repressed a shudder at exactly who my client might be. Everyone had his or her secrets.

"I've already told you that you have my word, but it's just a book. Why the secrecy?" The words sounded hollow even to me. Books were not always *just* books. I've cracked a deadly spine once or twice in my day.

Like *Twilight*. Now *that* was deadly. The series had managed to turn normal adolescent girls into raving, hormone-filled psychopaths, intent on dating vampires, and *no one* would *ever* knowingly do something *that* stupid.

He ignored my question. "Good...It's nice to know that some still honor their word... So, I'll meet you two nights from now? Where is our next cloak and dagger rendezvous?" he asked, grinning. "I recommend somewhere not so near to your place of business, wizard." He hadn't known that appellation last time, or at least he hadn't revealed his knowledge.

I told him a place off the top of my head and he began to laugh.

"Interesting venue. Ever been there?" he asked. I shook my head, and he laughed even harder. "Okay."

"I don't even know your name," I said, ignoring whatever he found so funny.

His nose crinkled as he scanned the street, muscles tensing slightly. "It's better that way. My name is on too many lips already. It seems I have many..." he glanced around again, muscles growing tighter, "Fans. See you in two days, Temple."

Then he stepped back into the alley, and...disappeared, even to my senses. He was simply *gone*.

"Whatever," I muttered to the empty alley. I turned away, taking another puff from my cigarette, and my phone vibrated in my pocket. I glanced down, read the text, and then glanced across the street towards my store. I saw my two friends, Gunnar and Peter, leaning against the door, staring back at me. They were waiting for our monthly nightcap, as we had done for the last five years in order to maintain our friendship amidst diversifying careers and, well, life in general getting in the way. I stepped away from the wall and waved as I headed their way, eager for that drink.

5

Gunnar studied the dark alley behind me as I approached. "Nate," he murmured absently, still focused on the alley. I took another drag of the cigarette, and then stomped it out under a heel.

Gunnar was built like a house—tall and strong—and his skin was as pale as fine alabaster. His face was hard, with a double-cleft chin, but a thick, neat, blonde beard covered that up. Blonde hair brushed his jaws, looking expensively well-kept; he had been forced to use some bogus religious excuse so that the FBI wouldn't make him cut it short. Gunnar Randulf was descended from the Norse Vikings, his last name meaning 'Shield-wolf,' and he left a trail of broken hearts wherever he walked. But despite all the attention his looks gained him from the fairer sex, he seemed immune to the casual chase, instead searching for that one true love. It was like trying to find the perfect steak without ever eating meat before.

He was the worst wingman *ever*.

Peter, on the other hand, was a study in contrasts—handsome, but unremarkable. Tall and wiry, with bright blue eyes, he looked like every other Yuppie in town. They each wore slacks and a shirt, not having changed from their respective jobs before heading over to my digs. I had known them both since childhood, and we had been friends ever since. Peter, being a Regular with no unique powers, was definitely the odd ball out, but it hadn't affected our friendship at all. "Who were you talking to?" Gunnar's face was curious, still staring at the alley.

"Whom. Fucking *whom*! Is everyone illiterate?" I grouched. Peter chuckled. We were alone on the street.

"I sensed him...*sensing* me. Then he was gone. And he smells like shit," Gunnar added.

"Sorry, but the smell is all me. I had an accident."

Gunnar's baby-blues weighed me, but he ignored my obvious lack of hygiene. "*What* was he?"

If Gunnar couldn't even place what the kid was, then I had no idea. I shrugged. "A client. That's all I know. And they pay my bills. Sort of a *don't ask, don't tell* policy. You two ready for our Round Table?" Peter and Gunnar both nodded, but not before both peering over my shoulder again. Peter looked curious, but Gunnar didn't seem satisfied with my response.

"Of course," he finally grumbled. "It's our fifth anniversary, after all."

I unlocked the heavy oak front door, closing my eyes for a moment as I turned off my secondary alarm system—a fine mist of magic laced over the entire perimeter of the building. My friends, knowing the routine, waited patiently, although Peter studied me curiously, no doubt trying to see something of my magic. Peter had experienced its effects once, and wasn't anxious to see it happen again. The feeling of a thousand fire ants swarming your body left an impression, and very real bites. One reason for the secondary protection was the valuable and unique items stored inside, but the other was because I lived in the loft overlooking the front lobby—and what a lobby it was.

I had purchased the antique 1920's theater and performed a few minor renovations, redesigning the Grand Lobby into a bookstore with a more modern feel. Several steps led down into the store from the entryway. Six-foot-high, glass-walled dividers effectively sectioned the room into a maze of couches, bookshelves, and cozy reading spots, and a European coffee bar was tucked back against the wall.

But the convoluted maze was actually an extensive web of *Feng Shui* that a team of monks had helped me design. Modern, yet classic. Yin and Yang. Vintage movie posters, steam-punk paraphernalia, and vinyl records decorated the rough brick walls. It was the ultimate man cave.

Even though the place was empty at this time of night, it still felt homey and welcoming. The glass-walled dividers were covered with wax-pencilled graffiti in a variety of different colors—quotes, ancient passages from classic works, names, and brief artwork—a rite of passage granted to my frequent customers.

I led the way to the back stairs that climbed the old brick wall to my loft.

Two of the three theaters nestled in the back had also been revamped. One was packed with almost every type of gaming system ever designed. I had even acquired a team of beta-testers to try out games in the developmental stages. Hence, installing the coffee shop in the lobby. Nerds needed caffeine to function.

And my business was the Atlantis for nerds across the land—Nerdlantis.

The second theater was now a vast library where I conducted my more profitable sales with those premier clients of mine.

The third theater was on a need-to-know basis, and not many needed to know.

My glass-windowed loft overlooked the entire store, both front and back, as I had gutted the old projector room to create a home within a home for myself—a *Sanctum Sanctorum*. The stairs creaked as we ascended my modern castle-tower, reminding me of the Captain's prow of a ship, overseeing the activity of the crew below. I shouldered the heavy oak door open and headed back to the bar against the far wall. Settling down into a pair of couches inside the large open loft, my friends took off their coats, relaxing as I began to work. I discarded my own ruined coat, tossing it into a nearby laundry basket with optimistic hope that it could be salvaged. I placed three cups before me.

Absinthe was the chosen poison for this auspicious evening.

The licorice-fired spirit had been the favorite drink of visionaries throughout history, including Oscar Wilde, Vincent Van Gogh, and Ernest Hemingway. But I wasn't about to attempt Hemingway's famous *Death in the Afternoon* cocktail of chilled champagne and Absinthe. I chose the French Method instead—slowly dissolving a sugar cube with spring water into the alcohol below, drawing out the deeper flavors of the drink.

I bent to my task, the process of making the perfect drink now a familiar routine for me, as I listened to Gunnar and Peter's soft conversation. Salivating with anticipation as the thick aroma began to fill my nostrils, I placed several ice cubes into the drinks, set my creations atop a silver tray, and then carried them over to the table in the sitting area. I handed Gunnar and Peter each a glass, bowed my head, and then backed away onto my own aged Darlington Chesterfield couch. I snatched up the last glass, and reclined with a pleased sigh.

"What's new with you two?" I asked curiously.

Gunnar answered first, clearly excited, "I was given authority to put together my own field team. Special Agent in Charge, Roger Reinhardt, is letting me dance the gray area a bit with some of my recent cases since the traditional protocol hasn't been very successful. My…unique talents will be a benefit. Jurisdiction and red tape hold us back all too often, so he's turning a blind eye, as long as I produce results." He winked. "Off the record, of course."

I grinned. This was huge. "That's fantastic! You mean that recent crimes have been more in our field of expertise? Involving magic?"

Gunnar merely nodded, but his lips tightened a bit, apparently closed on any further elaboration of the subject. Perhaps Peter wasn't supposed to hear details. He shrugged. "It will most likely fizzle to nothing, but it was good to hear that some people are wise to the fact that they are helpless in solving some of the newer crimes. It's only in the preliminary stages right now, though. A temporary trial-and-error experiment."

Peter, sensing Gunnar clamming up, chimed in, "I've gained a bit of respect around the investment firm. They're letting me work directly with a new client, a new family in town with deep, deep pockets." To himself, he murmured something lower that I couldn't quite catch; thumbing a worn leather bracelet I had never seen before on his wrist. Odd. Peter had never worn any accessories. Was he in danger of becoming metrosexual? Something *was* different about him, now that I thought about it. But I remained silent, not sensing anything specific. "It might even be my big break."

"Then I propose a toast to you two," I raised my glass. They did the same, and we each took a deep drink. This was what our round table was for, setting aside a single night to speak of how we were attempting to impact the world. After years of hard work, it seemed my two friends were doing just that.

Gunnar opened his mouth to speak, but I interrupted him. "You almost got me killed tonight with your stupid text."

He frowned before answering. "I was going to ask you about that. Was that some weird autocorrect mistake in your response? It said you were in a cow pasture."

"No. That's what I typed." I sipped my drink and sighed in appreciation as my taste buds were overloaded with fennel and anise.

"Okaaay...That's not mysterious at all," Peter said, his eyes twinkling as he leaned forward.

Gunnar was still frowning. "So, barring creepy clients and cow pastures, how have you been?" he asked carefully.

I grinned over the rim of my aromatic drink. "Both of those are actually related. I just got busted from the police station. Apparently trespassing is frowned upon. As is cow-tipping."

Peter choked on his drink. "Pardon?"

Gunnar wasn't so polite. "*What?* You know they're looking for any excuse to give you trouble! You even said that you noticed patrol cars hanging around the shop. And why on earth were you *cow-tipping*? Could you find nothing else to entertain you on a Thursday night?"

"I needed information," I began, settling deeper into the chair. I spotted my first edition of *Paradise Lost* on the table beside me, and recalled the last passage I had read before retiring the tome: *Do they only stand by ignorance, is that their happy state, the proof of their obedience and faith...*

It reminded me of the detectives at the police station. It had been close to a week since I had read the passage, but I had an almost eidetic memory, so it was forever burned into my brain. A gift and a curse. I had never quite gotten used to how others couldn't do the same thing.

"How could you get information by cow-tipping?" Gunnar pressed, knowing there was more to the story. We had fallen into a strong friendship almost from the very beginning, and then upon discovering our unique similarities, the strands of friendship had only grown stronger. We each had one foot in a whole other world.

The world of magic.

Gunnar was a werewolf, able to change at a whim now, thanks to my parents' help long ago. As if sensing this, Gunnar idly thumbed the tattoo on his wrist—a gift from my parents. Werewolves normally couldn't control their change from one form to the other, but the tattoo served as a totem, allowing Gunnar to shift at will, no longer a victim to the cycles of the moon. Merely a thought or a finger on the tattoo would begin the transformation. White, snowy fur slowly began to curl up from Gunnar's forearm before he realized what he was doing. He removed his finger, closed his eyes, and the fur disappeared.

Peter watched with a distant, familiar envy. He was a Regular, just happening to fall into our lives back in school, and he had been there ever since. Despite having no powers, he was a good friend, and an even better man. He was one of the few people who knew our secrets. Even Gunnar's boss didn't know the truth, but he did know that Gunnar had an unusually high success rate for solving cases that other agents had deemed *unsolvable*.

The age of digital media had made the lives of our kind harder to conceal. *YouTube* had caught more magic on film than any number of cameras in the past. Even dismissed as hoaxes, a growing number of people throughout the world had begun to question this resurgence of magical evidence with some serious scrutiny. Luckily, they were mostly regarded as intoxicated conspiracy theorists. I feared to imagine what would happen once the lid finally blew on that subject. It would be the Salem Witch Trials all over again. Blood would flow in the streets, and the government would no doubt pass a litany of regulations and laws within weeks. I shivered at the thought, coming back to the question.

"I needed to speak with the Minotaur," I answered, taking another sip of the licorice fire.

Peter leaned even further forward. "*The* Minotaur? As in the one Theseus killed in Daedalus' Labyrinth? He's *real*?"

"Come now, Peter. You know better. Of *course*, he's real. Almost all the myths are real. But the Minotaur wasn't killed. True, he was *defeated* by Theseus, but he swore not to eat people anymore—the first monster carnivore turned vegetarian—so he was allowed to survive. He's still...*kicking* around, so to speak. And he's good at finding things. My kind of things." I still felt the impression of his boot on my stomach, despite my hastily thrown shield. I was sure it would bruise nicely.

Gunnar growled unhappily. "So, after cow-tipping him, why on earth did he agree to help you? He could have very easily killed you, you know."

I let the silence build until they were both leaning forward. "He's Buddhist now." No reaction. "Or trying to become one. I'm guessing I survived because he struck a deal with Hermes long ago." I fingered the coin in my pocket, but remained silent on that gift. "It has to do with the client you saw earlier. He's looking for something, and my other sources turned up nothing. The Minotaur was my last resource. He said I could duel him in two days for the item. Then the cops arrived. They must have been keeping tabs on my car."

"Well, it's not exactly discreet," Peter mocked.

I grinned back, showing my teeth. "Jealousy does not become you, Peter."

He grunted indelicately. "Did you find what you were looking for?" I nodded.

Gunnar looked relieved. "You risk too much, Nate. You have access to an almost limitless fortune, but you still risk everything for these pennies you get from clients."

"They aren't quite pennies," I murmured, thumbing the coin in my pocket.

"You know what I mean, Nate. Don't bandy words with me. I know you." He frowned. "I heard radio chatter on the way over here. I'm guessing it was about you getting snatched up by the police. What did they want?"

"Just more questions." I waved a hand, not wanting to continue that line of conversation. "About the company and everything," I lied.

Peter practically shook with excitement. "Have you finally decided to pick up the reins?"

"No. But apparently, everybody thinks I'm scheming to do just that."

Peter grinned. "You, scheming? They must not know you *at all*." I smiled back, nodding faintly. "Well, if you won't do it, why don't you hire me to help? I could apply some creative financing to increase your profits."

Gunnar suppressed a grin behind his glass, but remained silent.

"Your track record is not so great, Peter. I can't risk that with my parents' company. It's much too vast for anyone except well-experienced professionals. It's not a toy to pass to my friends. No offense." Peter's eyes smoldered, his hand idly brushing his new bracelet again. "Why do you think I haven't jumped in myself, Peter? It's too big, even for me."

Gunnar leaned back, stretching his feet. "Say that again. Your parents would roll over in their graves—" He cut off abruptly, his face paling. "Oh, God. I'm so sorry, Nate. It just slipped out. I didn't mean—"

I waved a hand to interrupt him, dampening my anger quickly. "No, you're right. But choose your words more carefully next time." Gunnar looked ashamed of himself. Good.

Peter finally broke the silence. "Still, Gunnar has a point. You don't want to stay in this shit-hole for the rest of your life. What about Chateau Falco? Are you going to sell it? You can't leave it empty. It's been in your family for what, a hundred years? You can't just let it go."

"261," I murmured. Gunnar and Peter glanced at each other for a moment, not comprehending. I rolled my eyes. "261 *years*. And I haven't decided yet. It is not for sale at the moment, but who knows? I haven't been there for a long time."

"But you are its new *Master*." Gunnar raised his arms to mimic a zombie. "*Master Temple, your wish is my command*," he mocked.

I rolled my eyes before whispering softly. "The place ...scares me. It's not just a home. It has secrets that even my parents kept close." I looked at them, a serious expression on my face.

"You're not scared of *anything*. Hence, Minotaur tipping." Gunnar grinned.

"Well, I am afraid of *that* place," I answered honestly.

They blinked incredulously, the silence stretching. Changing topic, Peter finally continued on, wisely sensing that talk of the mansion was off the table. "At least you could hire me as a consultant. I couldn't hurt anything."

Gunnar laughed aloud this time. I shrugged as Peter scowled at Gunnar. "Wrong. I can't *hire* anyone because I don't *work* for the company. I'm just an investor."

"You mean they didn't leave it to you in the will?" Gunnar stammered in surprise.

"Years ago, they asked me. I declined. Hence my fall from grace in their eyes. I guess they looked at me as God once looked upon young Lucifer."

Peter looked baffled, "I don't understand you." He glanced at Gunnar's tattoo pointedly. "You either, Wolf. You each have the gifts of gods, and you do nothing with them. Well, *you* go cow-tipping." He waggled a frustrated hand in my direction.

"It's just something we were born with, Peter. It doesn't make us gods. And we *do* use it. When necessary." Gunnar idly caressed the crescent tattoo on his wrist again. He had been wetting panties before girls even knew what it meant back in Junior High—the only student with a full beard and a tattoo. Smug bastard. He was easy to hate.

"But you wallow in filth rather than taking the world by the balls!" Peter argued.

"Easy, Thrasymachus. Might is not right," I said with a frown.

Peter slumped in defeat. "Listen, if you two are going to talk philosophy again, I'm out. No more circle-jerking Plato for me, thank you very much. I've got work in a few hours." He stood to leave, downing his drink with a frustrated sigh. Setting the glass on a side table, he paused as if remembering something. "Hey, did you happen to find that book I requested a couple days ago?"

I frowned. For the first time, my eidetic memory failed me. "What book?"

Peter turned to face me. "I left a note with Jessie. He's a new employee. Not one of your veterans."

"He never mentioned anything to me," I answered honestly. I had only spoken to the kid once. My store manager, Indie, had hired him. "Why the sudden interest in a book? I didn't even know you could read," I teased.

Peter looked hurt. "What, I'm not allowed to read every now and then?" he grouched. "I left him a note with the title. He said he would leave it on your desk." I glanced back to see a crumpled piece of parchment on my ornate oak desk.

"I haven't been in the office for a few days. Just coming here to sleep. I've had…a lot on my plate."

Peter and Gunnar both nodded, faces grim. "It's no big deal. Just a book a client asked me to find. The rich one I was talking about earlier."

I nodded, suddenly distracted by an odd sensation on my arms. "I'll take a look around tomorrow," I mumbled, rubbing my forearm curiously as I stretched my mind out like a web, searching for the cause of the distracting warmth. It felt like a blanket of steam.

Peter nodded, pocketing his cell. "Alright, gentlemen. I bid you—"

His mouth closed with an audible click of smacking teeth as I suddenly leapt to my feet without a word of warning. The warm sensation had cranked up a dozen notches, as if I was now standing before an open oven. I darted to the wall of windows that overlooked my shop, and then stared further out to the street. I had left two of the loft windows wide open for air circulation from the store below. The ice cubes clinked together in my glass as I stared hard, my skin pebbling with sudden anxiety. I felt my friends' eyes on me, but I couldn't peel my own away from the street. It had begun to storm outside, heavy snowflakes beginning to cover the cars.

I heard my voice before I consciously chose to speak. "*Once upon a midnight dreary, while I pondered, weak and weary…Suddenly there came a tapping, as of someone gently rapping, rapping at my chamber door...*" The world slowed as I abruptly sensed a presence that stood just outside the front door to my shop. Something powerful was waiting for me. The waves of heat intensified.

Long ago, with my mother's help, I had created what some Tibetan monks coined a *memory palace*, a vast mental library where each item—whether a statue, painting, cabinet, plant or even a book—held a specific piece of knowledge or past memory. My mouth moved in pace with my racing thoughts as they wandered through the dusty library, the imaginary walls of bookshelves racing into existence all around me. I held a book in my palms, but I didn't need to consciously focus on it. Merely holding the construct transferred whatever memories or knowledge it contained into my current thoughts.

Gunnar grumbled. "Eidetic showoff. What—" The bell from the front door chimed and a shadow slipped inside, interrupting Gunnar. I heard him draw his SIG Sauer 9mm pistol in a swift motion, but it was a distant, sensory feeling to me, my mind still focused entirely on Edgar Allen Poe. An appropriate black cloak was folded around a woman's shoulders like obsidian wings, the whites of her teeth seeming to glow as she stared up at me from the floor below. Her eyes were coals of fire, a glint of yellow reflected off them from the light behind me.

My voice was faint even to me as I continued the poem.

"*Then this ebony bird beguiling my sad fancy into smiling, by the grave and stern decorum of the countenance it wore...*"

Her voice hissed back the only acceptable answer. "*Quoth the raven, Nevermore.*"

6

My friends stood beside me, understandably alarmed. Each syllable of her words was laced with magical seduction. Emphasis on *magical*. "You must read a fair bit, Temple," she said.

Gunnar's eyes weighed me. "I thought you were the only one who read ancient crap like that. And how did she hear you?" he whispered.

The woman took several slow, seductive steps towards the main floor, swaying her hips deliciously. She made it hard to focus. "I hear many things, *Wulfric*. But be a good doggy, and speak only when spoken to." Gunnar's jaw dropped further. She continued without missing a beat. "What kind of bookstore do you run, Temple?" She picked up a copy of *Atlas Shrugged* by Ayn Rand from a display case at the bottom of the stairs. "This isn't even a first edition." A slimy, oily fire suddenly spread from her fingertips, smothering the priceless tome. "Oh, my mistake. It was." The book crumbled to ash in seconds. What the *hell* kind of power was *that*?

I was sure that Gunnar understood the ancient appellation she had given him, as he was very adept at his Norse heritage. *Wulfric* translated to *Wolf King*.

Treading carefully, I chose civility. Courtesy was a good bet when dealing with ancient magical beings—courtesy or raw power. Having chosen the latter with the Minotaur, I gambled on the former this time.

"We're closed for the evening, Madame. Pray come back in the morning, and I'll allow you to pay for the damage to my book."

"Hmmm...But a girl can't be too patient. She wants *what* she wants...*when* she wants it." She dropped her cloak, revealing her utterly bare ivory skin, unblemished, and perfectly contoured with pleasant curves. I tried to mask my surprise...and lustful admiration. I was confident that I had never seen a body look so good. "But I do know how to repay a favor, bookkeeper." Her hand crept down between her legs, skimming her round breasts on the way, her nipples instantly tightening. A small moan escaped her lips, and her eyes became glassy. My pants tightened instinctively, and her moan grew lustier, as if she had somehow sensed my reaction.

Her eyes came back to mine, and I realized for the first time that her pupils were not circular. Not human. They were horizontal slits, and her irises were a vibrant yellow. The exact same shade as the oily fire she had used to incinerate my book. Remembering that touch helped me regain focus like a cold shower would help a pubescent boy in grade school. "I am seeking a book. An ancient family tome, titled *Sons of the Dying Sun*. Find it for me, and your *payment* will be...*climactic*." She flashed me a devilish grin.

Her voice threatened to overwhelm me with more than mere words. She was using magic. Old, powerful magic. I felt mental fingers massaging the deeper, more primal areas of my brain, coaxing me to listen and obey her as she so adroitly caressed the pleasure centers. A quick glance at my friends revealed they weren't faring well with the battle for self-control. Their feet began to carry them to the doorway leading downstairs. I laced my own voice with magic, hoping to break whatever spell she was casting. But her power grew thicker, stronger. I decided to stop speaking polite Old English. "I will keep my eye out, but I am not a big fan of creepy, naked women showing up at my place of business...despite any contrary rumors."

She grinned again, her magic growing ever thicker, as if flexing, but I continued, silently halting her with every ounce of power I could muster. I felt my control slipping, wanting nothing other than to rip my clothes off and meet her downstairs for a quickie. Or a Longie. Whatever she would allow. I noticed sweat on my temples, and momentarily imagined her licking it away and I froze.

Fuck that.

I lashed out with my power, no longer playing defense, and cut through hers like a blade. It snapped back into her with force, causing her to stumble back and then glare up at me. Gunnar and Peter shook their heads dumbly, eyes dilated. My hands were shaking with the effort. "This is quite unprofessional, and I am, in fact, in the middle of a business meeting. Come back tomorrow and I will see what I can do for you," I managed, in what I hoped was a steady voice.

"A shy wizard. Very well. If you don't like an audience, I'm sure I could persuade them to leave for you," she whispered coyly. Her magic came back faster and stronger—the very air quivering. My friends sagged at the sudden onslaught. Jesus, she was *strong*! I had never practiced much mind magic, but hers terrified me. Without my help, my friends would become drooling sycophantic sex slaves, obedient to her every whim.

With a crack of power that made one of the window panes shatter, I broke her spell a second time, and my friends visibly stumbled as they were released. I let out a breath. Gunnar tossed his gun onto the couch, thumbing his tattoo in anticipation as he risked a glance at me. What *was* she? I hadn't ever heard of mind magic like this before, but apparently, I was strong enough to simply outmuscle her. That or I was damned lucky.

"We can chat in the morning, but for now, leave. Twice asked," I said.

"We *demand* your service." The tone of her voice was damned intimidating.

"Why do you need my help? Have you checked amazon.com yet?" I snapped, wondering who she had meant by *we*.

Her eyes tightened. "We want what is ours, and will tolerate neither thieves nor bystanders. I don't want to ruin the surprise, but I'm sure your friend already has an idea what we're willing to do to reclaim our property." She winked at Gunnar. His face slowly paled in understanding, as if he had just made a grim connection in his mind.

I used the only name she had offered. "You see, Raven, I'm not that good with demands. And right now, you're trespassing."

"*Raven*...I like it." She sniffed the air, and then froze. "Why does it smell like—" Then her entire nude form stiffened as if recognizing a scent. "*Him*," she hissed. "You gave it to him, didn't you? I will floss my teeth with your guts for this, Temple!"

I stared back, lost. "Um, what?"

"Don't lie to me!" she shrieked, her chest heaving. She must have mistaken my confusion for concealment. "So be it. I will just have to see for myself if your last scream resembles that of your father." The lights went out, and a menacing cackle erupted from the darkness.

My rage jumped at the unexpected mention of my father. *What did she know?*

Then all hell broke loose, and I quickly discovered that Karma is indeed a bitch.

7

Several of my glass-walled dividers imploded as she let out a feral cry that was entirely inhuman. As the carnage began, I distantly wondered about her creepy horizontal pupils, what they might signify, and whom she thought I had given her book to. I also thought of my father's last scream at her hands, and my magic responded, filling me like a pool of frigid water.

Gunnar beat me to the stairs, leapt into the air, and *shifted*.

That was the only way I could describe it, and even having seen it happen a hundred times or more, it was still a breathtakingly beautiful thing to behold. His clothes exploded around him, and a huge, white-haired wolf with long ivory fangs and ice-blue eyes landed gracefully at the base of the stairs a story below—the remnants of *most* of his clothes raining down like confetti, having been unable to accommodate him mutating into his full werewolf form. But over his white haired rear-end was a pair of *Underdog* spandex underwear. I blinked in surprise, momentarily frozen. *Underdog underwear?*

Peter hung back, clutching a liquor bottle in a shaky fist. But whether to drink or throw, I didn't know. Regardless, he was wise to hang back.

I did the opposite. I was directly behind Gunnar, tearing down the stairs three at a time, whipping up all sorts of nasty to dish out on this bitch. But all *my* power was invisible. No pretty shape-shifting for the wizard. No one could see all the beautiful raw energy surrounding me, dancing from my fingertips, awaiting my command like a one-man rave party. As I breathed in more power, my senses magnified. Smells contained tastes, my vision was sharper, able to pierce more of the darkness, and the tactile feedback of my fingers sliding down the mahogany stair rail was as euphoric as a lover's lips brushing an earlobe. But no one could see a damned thing for all my hard work.

The world was unfair. Gunnar had a fucking outfit, and he *still* looked cool.

"Sic her, Gunnar!" I yelled as I threw pulsing blue lights into the air around her, hoping to confuse her or ruin her night vision. Then I let loose a hurtling streak of fire towards her beautiful rack, hoping to mar her perfect nudity.

Her face began to stretch, her tongue momentarily elongating before a flicker of hesitation crossed her eyes and she returned to normal again. *What the fuck?* My fire struck the wall behind her, neatly slicing through a framed movie poster as she effortlessly sidestepped and unleashed a screaming yellow ball of her own fire at me. I ducked behind a divider, and the ball slammed straight through it, shards of wood and glass biting into my arms and neck. A particularly long sliver of glass sliced deep into my forearm, which instantly welled up with dark, thick blood. I grunted in pain as my whole forearm flushed with heat.

Oily fire rained down upon a table behind me, igniting a small stack of precariously balanced books. She was some flavor of shape-shifter, but with much more control than even Gunnar had. Freaky. And I still didn't know what kind of shape-shifter she was. A demon of some kind by the looks of it. That wasn't good. Demons were hardcore. But I didn't have time to call for backup, despite the rules. If it was a demon, I would deal with it and apologize later.

From the shadows, Gunnar abruptly appeared in his *Underdog* undies, shattering through yet another glass-walled divider to grab the woman by the throat. But his long ivory teeth snapped together with a loud empty *clack* as Raven dodged him and then used his momentum to throw him through yet another of my oh-so-expensive glass-walled dividers. She grinned, slinging balls of slimy fire from her fingers after Gunnar, but he was already gone, melting back into the shadows of my store like a wraith. The fire slapped into a window, the glass spider-webbing with cracks before finally shattering out into the street.

I gathered my will and threw a battering ram of force straight at her smiling face. She leapt impossibly high into the air to dodge my attack, but the force caught her feet, sending her cartwheeling into the shadows with a groan of pain. I heard an immediate growl, the snapping of jaws, and then a sharp, piercing whine. Then Gunnar flew directly into a brick wall, the impact knocking a cloud of dust from the rafters high above. He struggled to his feet with another whine, shook his head, and then let out a piercing howl of rage that made my forearms pebble with gooseflesh.

Now he was pissed. Gunnar's icy werewolf eyes latched onto mine and I took a reflexive step back, wondering if his head had been knocked loose enough to now see me as a threat. But he simply stared. I held up a finger, and motioned him to circle around the edge of the store. He slipped back into the shadows without any acknowledgement of my plan. I hoped he understood, because it would take both of us to take down this monster.

Raven cackled again. "Is this all you've got? And I had heard so many tales of the legendary Temples. You're putting up even less of a fight than your parents did." My vision went red so suddenly that I almost froze, thinking she had cast a spell of some sort on me.

But it was just rage, an emotion that I was very, *very* comfortable with.

Again, I wondered what she had to do with my parents' murder. Was she lying just to goad me? I shook my head. It didn't matter. Her blood was mine. She was close, just behind a bookshelf ahead. "It's time to end this farce," her voice cut through the darkness.

I calmly strolled around the bookshelf, coming face to face with the demon shifter. Her eyes glowed yellow in the flickering light behind me, her horizontal pupils momentarily halting my advance. She washed her hands together dramatically, more of the oily fire growing in her palms, the exact same color as her irises. Then she grinned, teeth suddenly needle sharp, and threw her hands out at me. I slammed a projection of my willpower into the approaching scream of fire, and her flames splattered over a sudden clear shield of air between us, exploding into droplets of fire like paint on a glass wall. The heat instantly bled through the shield, lightly burning my fingertips. I rolled away as I dropped the shield, and watched as the fire fell to the ground of my shop, burning weakly. She stared at me on the ground and shook her head, disgusted, like one would at a peripatetic cockroach on a kitchen floor.

Icy blue eyes trailed her every move from the shadows, but she didn't notice. I watched, clutching my arm in real pain, fingers wet with blood, and tried to look terrified, beaten, as I struggled to crawl backwards. Her grin stretched wider as she took a single step closer, hands dripping more fire, but her fingers were now scaled yellow claws.

Then my pet werewolf slammed into her with such force that her head snapped sideways, the breath flying out of her in a grunt before he hammered her into a solid oak bookshelf.

The bookshelf didn't even wobble as her head struck the aged wood with a solid *crack*, her eyes briefly rolling back into her skull as she collapsed to the ground. I climbed to my feet as Gunnar clutched her throat between his finger-length canines, his eyes glancing at me. I brushed off my arms and strolled closer, glancing around my store to assess the damage. Indie was going to be pissed in the morning when she came in for her shift. I sighed. At least we were alive. With a thought, I drew the cold moist air from outside and doused the remaining fires lest they destroy any more of my priceless books. I snapped a finger and lit the candles that were spread about the room, filling the space with a familiar glow.

I tied up my forearm with a shred of cloth from Gunnar's clothes lying nearby. At least I knew it wasn't his underwear. Glancing out the window, I noticed a few people standing near the diner, pointing anxiously toward my store. One of them was gripping a phone to his ear.

Great.

Peter had reached the bottom of the stairs but he stayed there. As I said, wise.

Then I leveled Raven with very angry librarian eyes. Her ample breasts heaved with fury as her eyes finally managed to focus on me. I felt her attempt mind magic again, but I shut it down, violently. She glared back.

"You don't stand a chance, wizard. You think you can kill me without catastrophic repercussions?"

"I did ask you to leave. Nicely," I grumbled.

Peter piped up from the stairs, full of conviction. "Twice!"

An odd look crossed her face, and she eagerly tried to peer past my shoulder, but Peter remained a safe distance away, out of her view. Maybe she was surprised to find a Regular here with me. But there seemed something *more* to her look. Unsuccessful, she turned back to me. "You think you stand a chance against us when even your parents failed? My sisters will *destroy* you." The words actually frightened me with their simplicity. She wasn't trying to threaten. She honestly believed it. Gunnar's eyes flicked back to look up at me, questioning, but not releasing pressure. What did any of this have to do with my parents? Before I could ask, she began to move. "None shall escape the eclipse!" she screeched.

The woman's hand became a web of yellow reptilian talons again, darting towards Gunnar's furred throat. I prepared a blast of air to pin her arm down, but I heard a high keening wail like a mortar shell racing towards me from over my shoulder. I ducked instinctively, just missing the streaking projectile of ice that abruptly slammed into the woman's chest. Frosty smoke trailed up around the top of the liquor bottle that was now wedged firmly between her breasts, leaving a frozen crater of icy gore. Her eyes glazed over instantly. I studied the wound for a few silent moments, looking for the swell of a breath from her chest, making sure she was dead. My gaze was thorough. She was gone.

After a minute, I slowly turned. Peter was nervously wringing his hands together. I didn't say a word, stunned speechless by his display of magic. Peter began stammering. "I didn't know if you guys saw it or not. She was going to slice his throat." Gunnar had leapt back just in time, barely missing the fatal swipe of Raven's talons.

Gunnar shifted back to his human form out of the corner of my eye, naked except for his Underdog undies. Imagine the actors in the movie *300*, and you'll understand my rage a bit better. I wasn't jealous.

I rounded on him. "Really?" I snapped, gesturing energetically at his ensemble. "Have you no *dignity*?" His face turned crimson.

"I haven't done laundry this week! Spandex is the only thing I've found that works on the fly without being shredded. Do you have any idea how embarrassing it is to run around naked looking for clothes after I shift? Besides, I think I look cool." He flexed proudly.

I groaned, waving a hand dismissively as I turned back to Peter. "And *you*! How long have you been able to use magic? Why didn't you tell me? All this time I thought you were just a *Regular*!" I roared, my legendary wizard temper rising to the surface.

He evaded my questions, backing up a step. "Look, there's a dead woman...thing," he corrected, "on your floor, damage everywhere, and I just saved Gunnar's *life*. I can't be here when the cops—" he hesitated with a shudder, looking forlornly at Gunnar as he realized a cop was *already here*. If an FBI werewolf counted as a cop. "I have to leave. If anyone finds out I was involved in this, I'm a dead man." His words rang deeper than mere legal trouble. He sounded as if he meant his last statement literally. "I'll lose my job. Our company can't afford any involvement in," he waved a hand, "Whatever this is." His eyes widened. "I think I left my...phone upstairs."

"No—" I began, but too late. He was already padding up the stairs. I had seen him put his cell in his pocket before the attack. Gunnar and I shared a heavy look.

Peter raced down the stairs after a few seconds and then aimed for the door, intending to go straight past us. "Peter..." I began, reaching out an arm to halt him, but he brushed me off.

"I guess it was in my pocket the whole time." He looked panicked, eyes darting around the room. "And you didn't read my note about the book yet?"

"I already told you I hadn't," I answered with a frown. Was he in shock?

"Oh, okay. Well, it's on your desk. Whenever you get a chance." He still looked nervous and confused. It had to be shock. "No time to chat, Nate. I'm gone."

"That whole 'might is right' conversation might be much more relevant now."

Gunnar chimed in. "Yes, and *Dead men tell no tales*. I *am* an FBI agent, Peter." He hesitated, glancing from me to Peter curiously. "And *whatever* you did, you didn't have to *kill* her. Murder is kind of a big deal."

He threw up his hands, exasperated. "But she wasn't even *human*!"

"Point for Peter," I said. "But still, magic is nothing to play around with. You need training. And, damn it, I am a *trainer*!" I added, hurt.

He fingered his bracelet as if seeking comfort from it. "It's pretty new to me, too. I promise we'll talk. But not tonight." He forcibly shoved past us and out the door.

Gunnar and I stared at each other for a moment, and then down to the nude woman. Sirens wailed in the distance, coming closer. "This doesn't look good at all. What do you want to do about it?" He waved a hand at our feet.

"I'm not sure. You think Clorox will clean up the blood? Or will it ruin the lacquer finish on the wood?" I asked, clueless. I was a bachelor, after all.

Gunnar furrowed a brow. "No, idiot. The body."

I blinked. "Oh. That's nothing." I strode to the satchel that I had hung at the door earlier in the day, and withdrew two silver pennies from a Crown Royal bag tucked inside. I knelt down and placed them over her eyes, but not before thumbing back the eyelids to catch another glance at her oddly horizontal pupils. "Huh." Gunnar made a similar noise behind me. What I was about to do wasn't exactly necessary, but I tried to do it whenever I got the chance. Last respects. I stepped back with a whispered, "*Requiescat in pace*." A low horn wailed, somehow far away yet also near. I felt it like bass in my chest. The body disintegrated into a yellow pile of ash before our eyes, and a ghostly hooded figure on a boat coalesced behind it, sweeping the pile out the door with a misty paddle as he glided past us. I looked up at Gunnar. His eyes were wide with shock.

"I thought he was just a myth!"

The Boatman glanced back, nodding once before vanishing. I waved amicably. "The Boatman of the River Styx is as real as any other fable you've encountered. Charon helps guide the dead to their final resting place. You just don't see many people making his job any easier. I try to make friends wherever I can." Gunnar just shook his head. "You off the clock, or on?" I asked, staring him in the eyes.

He didn't answer for a long while, weighing his options. "Off," he said finally. "But if this becomes relevant, I'll have to put the badge back on." I nodded in relief. "Got any spare clothes for me?" I nodded, flipping my head towards the loft above. Gunnar darted away, looking like a freaking idiot in his stupid underwear. I grabbed a dustpan and broom, cleaning up the broken glass and burned books as questions raced through my head. My forearm ached, but it could wait.

I wondered what was so important about her book request, and why she had been so damned impatient to get it. The denizens of the magical world knew my reputation, knew I could find things for the right price, so why had she been so impolite about it? She had acted as if *I* was the thief; selling it to some unknown person she apparently held a grudge against. And she had mentioned my father.

Gunnar appeared as I was dumping the dustpan into the trash behind the coffee bar. I was muttering to myself as he slowly approached. Wizards were known for their tempers, and Gunnar had seen some of my most flamboyant. Not wanting a repeat, he waited. Again, I surround myself with wise friends. That thought brought me back to Peter, and a question I didn't want to think about on top of everything else. *How*?

I glared at him. "Four—fucking—thousand—dollars. Each!" I bellowed, brandishing my broom like a sword at the destroyed dividers. Gunnar expertly leapt back with an amused grin.

"You're good for it," he mumbled.

I scowled back. "Not the point. And you know it. What the hell just happened?"

Gunnar grew serious. "Honestly, I have no idea. Have you pissed anyone off lately?" My glare answered his question. "I mean, besides the Minotaur." He paused. "Or the police." He sighed. "Anyone more than usual?"

I thought, and thought hard, before answering. "No," I paused. "But she did say that you might know what was going on."

Gunnar's eyes instantly grew guarded. "Possibly. I'll look into it and let you know in the morning when I pick you up for the…funeral," he said sadly. My shoulders sagged.

"My life sucks huge wang," I complained. Gunnar nodded sagely.

"Pick you up at noon?" he asked softly.

It was already three in the morning. "Whatever."

"Can you handle the cops? Just tell them it was a…burglary or something."

"Or something…" I replied testily.

I heard him ask one last thing, but I had already turned away. "Does your mind really store all that stuff you read, or did you just happen to read Poe lately?"

I didn't answer. My thoughts drifted away from my friend, lost in the unpracticed task of cleaning up the place. I barely noticed him leaving, or the bogus answers I gave the cops, but soon all was silent and I was back upstairs overlooking my wrecked shop, sipping a new glass of fiery absinthe. I spun the coin the Minotaur had given me earlier around a finger, thoughts questing for answers to the night's events. A gift from Hermes. I hadn't actually ever met any of the 'gods' before.

I grunted, pensive. But at least there were some positives. I now had three books to find—one for Raven & Associates, one for Peter, and one for my mysterious client—and one of those was already found, as long as I could beat the Minotaur in our duel. But I didn't want to think about the duel tonight.

I wondered what kind of shape-shifter Raven had been. I was almost positive she hadn't been a demon, despite her looks. As if sensing the risk, she had chosen not to reveal her true form. She had to have a reason. And a demon wouldn't have cared. My thoughts grew darker as I watched the snowflakes continue to fall outside the shop's windows, as numerous as the questions drifting through my mind.

"*Quoth the raven, nevermore,*" I mumbled, downing the last of my drink as I began to scribble out a note for Indie to read in the morning—a list of laborers to call for the expensive repairs to my shop, and a vague explanation of how it had happened.

8

Gunnar slammed down the hood of his car. Licorice-smelling smoke clouded up from the engine block, filling the air with a sickly-sweet aromatic fog.

"At least it's consistent," I offered.

"Shut up, Nate," he growled in warning. "If you hadn't made me drive out to that god-forsaken field to pick up your car, we might have made it to the cemetery in one piece." His shoulders sagged. "Tow truck will be here in a few hours. We can call a cab."

"Let's just walk. It's not far, and I could use the fresh air." I waved away a particularly heavy tendril of smoke creeping towards us. Gunnar nodded, following my lead. I immediately looked around a bit, acting conspicuously nervous.

"What?" Gunnar asked, tensing.

"Isn't there a leash law in St. Louis?" Murder shone in his eyes. "Never mind." I smirked and continued on. He'd been up all night, researching leads, seeing if it related to whatever Raven had been talking about. Apparently, several bookstore owners in town—and even across the river in Illinois—had been targeted over the last few days, some surviving, but most not. Gunnar hadn't elaborated on details yet. But I definitely wasn't the first bookstore owner to be targeted by her.

"Why are you so annoying this afternoon?"

I grinned. "Have you ever had Cuban *colada*?"

"Cuban...Is that some kind of drug?" He threw his arms up in exasperation. "Damn it, Nate. I'm an FBI Agent!"

"Down, boy. It's not a drug, but it probably should be. It's Cuban coffee. A form of espresso laced with sugar. Liquid Nirvana." I quoted my friend from Miami. "*Nunca comience un día duro sin una taza de colada.* Never start a tough day without a cup of colada."

Gunnar squinted, eyes bloodshot. "Where can I get some?" Whipping out a flask from my pressed suit coat, I passed it over. "You had some the whole time?"

"Of course."

"You're a real asshole sometimes, Nate. Capital A." I grinned in response. Gunnar's nerves steadied after a few sips. "This is really good." I held out a hand for him to pass it back. Instead, he slipped it into his own suit pocket. "You should probably get a flask like mine so you can carry it around when on the go," he said as he patted the flask.

"You should probably get a new car, like mine," I answered drily. "So you can, you know, be on the go."

His smile instantly turned stony. "Capital A."

After a short, silent walk, we entered the infamous Bellefontaine Cemetery—the final resting place for both my parents, and also every one of my ancestors who had come stateside since the 1700's. The cemetery had been founded in 1849, and we had had all of our pre-1849 ancestors transferred here from their previous graves shortly thereafter. William Clark—from the famous Lewis and Clark expedition—and even Mark Twain were buried here. Only the best for the Temple clan.

Before I had a chance to admire the beauty of the Bellefontaine grounds, we were assaulted. Camera flashes nearly blinded us. A red carpet had even been rolled out over the blanket of fresh snow, looking like a bloody smear. We were momentarily descended upon, shoved bodily by a gaggle of reporters, all shouting to be heard over one another.

"*Master Temple, is it true that you're taking over Temple Industries?*" one voice shouted. I wanted to burn the ground to ash, but instead, I chose civility.

Kind of.

I glared at a film crew standing nearby, staring down my audience of likely a few million viewers. "Greetings, carrion. Where there is a carcass, there will always be vultures. I hope you're all having a splendid feast on the decaying remains of two of the greatest minds St. Louis has ever known. Now, if you would be so kind…step. The fuck. Back." Cameras and microphones lowered. The ashen-faced cameraman looked sickly as his boss ordered him to cut the feed. I took a few steps before turning back to them. "Oh, and have a nice day." Then I was off again, feeling marginally better.

Towering monoliths, marble angels, and skeletal, ancient trees surrounded me as I strode deeper into the cemetery, colder on the inside than I felt on the outside. The wind was muted here, as if holding its breath in the presence of so many dead. Gunnar walked beside me, a wry grin on his face. "That was efficient, and polite."

"A cemetery is a convenient place to commit mass murder," I glanced at his badge, which was prominently displayed on his belt. "Hypothetically," I added.

Gunnar nodded absently, looking awed as we came into sight of the towering Temple Mausoleum, even though he had seen it before. It was the largest private plot in the cemetery, safe in a wide swath of fresh grass that ringed the entire perimeter, secluded from all other nearby graves. Of course, snow covered the grass now. Due to its sheer size, many at first mistook it for the caretaker's residence, but only until they came close enough to witness it in its entirety. It was nicer. And bigger. Much bigger. The marble colossus was astoundingly extravagant, having been built to house our first ancestors on this side of the Atlantic, and their descendants had pulled out all the stops, trying to recreate the more lavish mausoleums found in their former European homeland.

It was a study in contradictions, almost every culture fused together for its creation. Corinthian columns climbed two stories to hold the massive marble roof overlooking the cemetery. Marble sentinels of all sorts stood guard between each column: armed Roman soldiers, nude men and women entwined in coital ecstasy or less profane romantic embraces, Spanish Kings, Queens, and even Arabic scholars. Several gods and goddesses could be seen in the mix if one looked closely enough: Anubis, Zeus, Odin, Athena, and a few others from a spattering of different faiths.

I spotted a small group of executives and lawyers from Temple Industries milling just outside the door, obviously waiting to speak with me. Didn't I already have enough to deal with? Then I spotted a discreet hand gesturing to get my attention behind the trunk of a large tree beside the path. Weird, but definitely preferable to more talk of my parents' company.

I flicked open my pack of smokes, stabbed one between my lips, and lit the tip with a thought. I pointed emphatically at the swarm of suits near the entrance, my feet planted firmly, a maniacal grin on my face. "Gunnar, *sic 'em!*" Gunnar stared back at me as if I had finally lost what little sanity he thought I had been clinging to. With the perfect moment lost, I lowered my wounded arm and sighed. "I just need a moment. Stall them." Gunnar glanced around warily, obviously reluctant to let me out of his sight after last night's events, but he finally complied.

I walked aimlessly, waiting until no one was looking my way, and then darted behind the tree where I had seen the hand. "Hello, wizard," a gruff voice greeted me.

I assessed the speaker, who was decked out in full-blown soldier gear, but it was an odd combination of ancient leather armor and modern warfare apparel. He looked as rough as his battle-hardened leather, creases marring his eyes in vicious crow's feet. A crude scar cut across his jaw, and another ugly slash zippered the side of his neck. His eyes were a milky green, reminding me of absinthe. "Ah, hello, Sir Larper. You are correct that this is a field of death, but not the one full of battles you no doubt seek. I'm afraid the field where your brethren await is over at the Park of Carondelet," I said in an overly serious tone.

He studied me, measuring me up and down for a moment without amusement. "I'm from Brooklyn, idiot. We don't participate in Live Action Role Playing games." He had said *we*, even though he appeared to be alone. "Name's Tomas. I'm here to tell you that you're in danger. We're looking for someone, and we believe he came to St. Louis."

"I did have an unexpected visitor last night." His interest perked up. "She was naked, pale skin, dark hair, and naked. Oh, and she had yellow eyes." He frowned, but shook his head, not recognizing the description. "I guess I had to pay extra because of the eyes. Although she wasn't worth the money."

"Yellow eyes...That doesn't ring a bell, but be careful. Something big is going down here soon. Maybe real soon. Bookstore owners have been dying pretty nasty deaths. Watch your ass."

I nodded as he turned away, taking a pleasant pull from the cigarette as I watched him leave. "Oh, and she had horizontal pupils," I added casually. He stiffened, turning back to me.

"What?" he asked quietly.

"Judging by the arsenal at your hip, I think you know what she was. She mentioned having sisters before I killed her." I let out a stream of smoke. "Tell me."

He blinked. "You killed her?"

"Wasn't all that hard, really. Kind of a breeze," I lied.

The man weighed me with his eyes. "She never shifted, did she?"

Damn. "Well, she started to," I answered defensively.

The man began laughing, wheezing even. "Spoken like the pup that thinks he killed a mama bear, only to discover that it was just a cub," he laughed even harder, before my scowl silenced him.

"She didn't seem to appreciate a glacial liquor bottle to the heart very much, shifting or not. Now, what was she, and what is your stake in this?"

He reeked of military, or perhaps mercenary training. "Dragons have been rumored in the city, but we came here only to find one in particular. A man. A very dangerous man. I guess he could possibly have a group of lady dragons at his beck and call. It would make things...interesting."

"Oh...like, real dragons?" I asked weakly.

The man blinked as if I were daft. "Of course. But I guess they're technically were-dragons. Able to switch between human and dragon form at will."

I inhaled my cigarette again, thinking. "I've never encountered one before last night," I murmured. "So, what do they want?" Assessing his gear again, a new thought hit me. "Are you supposed to be some kind of dragon hunter?"

The man grinned darkly as he slipped me a business card with a number on the front. "Why, yes. *We* are." His eyes fixated halfway up a particularly tall oak. I followed his gaze to see a human form tucked back against the trunk, almost invisible. The figure nodded down at us, tipping a fedora with a grin, balancing what looked like a grappling gun in the crook of his shoulder. I suddenly wondered how many more men Tomas had in his employ, and why they were so wary. But Tomas was walking away, leaving me alone by the tree trunk as he spoke over his shoulder. "We're not sure what they're doing yet, but we're keeping tabs on 'em. We've also got our eyes on you, Temple." I looked back up where the sentry had been, but he was gone. Not a rustle of movement. Professionals.

Dragons again. So, that's what Raven had been preparing to shift into. Not a demon, but a were-dragon. But why had she stopped? Surely, she could have protected herself against us if she had simply shifted into her dragon form. What irked me the most was that I hadn't known that dragons could shift at all. I had always assumed that a dragon was just another big, scary monster, lurking in caves and guarding treasures. Not something that could go unnoticed in a large city. But if they could appear human...

Gunnar called out my name, probably noting Tomas' departure from the tree. I stepped back onto the path leading up to the Mausoleum. "Coming." I took another drag on the cigarette before snuffing it out on the path.

Gunnar tried to intercept me before the group of gnarled lawyers and ancient board members could swarm me, but failed. "Master Temple, my deepest condolences. I have been trying to reach you for the past week, but it appears your cell service must be unreliable," a stunning, tall redheaded woman spoke, stepping out from behind the group of geezers around her.

Despite the fact that she was significantly younger than her companions, I realized that not one of them had spoken a word to me. They watched the firecracker woman with respect and...fear? Her eyes were tight with stress, strain, and Corporate America-itis. But it did nothing to hide her beautiful cerulean eyes. I had heard of Miss Ashley Belmont before, but had never met her, and hadn't expected such a big aura from such a frail package—maybe 110 pounds despite her height. My parents had referred to her as their right hand. Maybe I should have started working for Temple Industries after all. I realized I was staring, so quickly fumbled for an answer.

"No, I just didn't answer your calls." The woman blinked in surprise, and I almost slapped my forehead with my palm. *Think first, Nate*, I chided myself.

Her response was whip-quick. "Understandable. I have been meaning to talk to you about—"

"I don't give a damn about the company," I growled, agitated at my misperception of her. The fairer sex had always been my kryptonite, able to instantaneously make me lose focus. She looked hurt at the interruption, but I barreled past her, closer to my linebacker, Gunnar.

"I was going to say *your parents*, Master Temple," she said softly. I slowed, glancing over my shoulder at her. Her long legs, wavy red hair, and secretary glasses seemed to shelter a cunning intelligence and...a rare compassion.

Gunnar stepped forward, "I'm honored to introduce Ashley Belmont, stand-in CEO of Temple Industries. It is very rude to keep a woman waiting, Nate. I think you owe her a minute of your *oh-so-precious* time," he said, leveling a judgmental glare at me.

The woman nodded appreciatively, tugging her Burberry coat closed about her. Damn it. Gunnar was right. "My apologies, Miss Belmont. What can I do for you?" I asked politely.

"To be honest, I'm not quite sure myself. The information is confidential..." She glanced pointedly at Gunnar, and the shining, silver badge on his belt. He didn't even blink, unsnapping the badge and tossing it to me. I turned to face her bright stare as it sailed at my face, using magic at the last second to stop the badge an inch from contact. I reached up, plucked it out of the air, and stuffed it into my suit's inner coat pocket. Luckily, none of the older gentlemen were looking at me.

"I don't see any cops," I said.

She dipped her head, not even blinking at the show of magic. Huh. Magic didn't impress her, which meant she was privy to my world. My parents must have shared things with her. Or she was a Freak, like Gunnar and I. "That's all well and good, but I'm afraid I can only give cursory details here. The location isn't secure." She flicked her gaze over to a man silently climbing down from a nearby tree. He wore the same fedora I had seen earlier. "Perhaps you could permit me to join you at Chateau Falco following the eulogy?" she asked softly, eyes returning to mine.

I nodded after a moment. I definitely didn't want to go to my parents' mansion, but I did at least owe her a discussion, especially after a week of radio silence. And it was the perfect location for such a talk. She was acting like the perfect daughter to my parents' last wishes, regardless of her bloodline, and I was acting like their spoiled son. "Consider the invitation offered, Miss Belmont. I have a few things to wrap up first. Perhaps this evening over refreshments?" she nodded in response.

"See you then, Master Temple." She glided into the Mausoleum on stiletto heels. Gunnar's eyes followed her like a dog watching a steak.

"Pretty impressive gal," Gunnar spoke beside me. I nodded distantly as I saw Peter inside the Mausoleum, frantically engaging Ashley—no doubt attempting to secure a job. She was courteous to him, but I could see the denial in her posture. A tough woman. It seemed my parents' company was in good hands. "Any idea what she wants to talk to you about?" I shook my head as I strode forward.

"No, but we'll find out soon enough." I handed the badge back to him. "Let's get this over with." I stepped inside the Mausoleum, ready to see my parents sealed away forever. I only hoped that I could also bury my grief this day. The wings of the building hungrily embraced me as I stepped inside the citadel of death that had marked the end of so many of my ancestors. If a building had emotions, this one seemed hungry, anticipatory.

9

I was in a foul mood after the funeral. I had stayed longer than anyone else, wanting to be alone with my parents one last time. Now, I was blessedly at peace, the only living soul in the building. A cab was going to pick me up in an hour. The service had been a blur, speeches from friends and associates causing many tears and tight throats, bringing back all the grief I had attempted to hide over the past week, but both my friends had been there for me.

Neither said a word, nor did they try to comfort me. They just remained by my side, twin guardians determined to keep me safe during my moment of weakness; rock solid men. Now alone, I wandered the main floor of the vast Temple Mausoleum, studying the private alcoves on either side of me which each held an elegant tomb and statue of a fallen ancestor. You would be surprised how many relatives could be found in a quarter of a millennium. Ornate benches sat before each tomb, the design dating back to the particular time period of the individual, or—as was most often the case—couple. A locked, glass-encased, leather-bound book rested on an elaborate pedestal before each tomb, sharing a not-so-short biography of each resident. A large fountain gurgled just inside the main dome-ceilinged nave, emitting a soothing, bubbling sound that was made all the more beautiful by the stained-glass windows shining down from high above.

Oh, and my parents had recently made the windows bulletproof.

They had upgraded the security of the family Mausoleum, installing security cameras, reinforcing walls, motion-sensors—which I assumed would be totally unnecessary in a building occupied by corpses—and what compared to a bank vault door on the main entrance. It was the Fort Knox of Mausoleums, but I had never understood, nor received an explanation as to why.

I glanced up at the back wall past the fountain. A large mosaic of tiles decorated the wall in a huge family tree, except the names of the relatives weren't on the branches; they were on the roots. Sapphires marked each woman, and rubies each man, their names etched deeply beside each gem. My name was the last and lowest part of the root system, having no other relatives to share the nutrient production for the massive tree.

I was the last Temple.

After perusing each of my distant ancestor's tombs, I finally came to the task at hand and turned around, retreating back towards the entrance to rest in front of the one tombstone I had avoided after everyone had left. The one now belonging to my parents.

My feet dragged as I reached the newest area of the crypt, and I sat down heavily on the firmly padded leather divan a few feet away from it. Ever so slowly, I looked up, and saw my parents staring down at me through lifeless marble eyes. Sadness threatened to overwhelm me now that I was alone, and I felt a heavy guilt that I hadn't spent more time with them in recent years. Now the chance was lost forever.

The funeral hadn't really been legitimate, merely an excuse for all the distant acquaintances and celebrities of St. Louis to come say last words. The real funeral procession, and the first goodbye, had been only a day after their sudden demise, and I had been the only attendee. Not even my friends knew of it. That was the day that I had called Charon to give them their last ride home, as I had done with Raven at my store last night.

The door leading outside opened quietly, and I looked up to see an elderly bull of a man step inside, tugging in a janitorial cart. "You shouldn't be here." I growled. "It's private property."

The man looked back at me with an unperturbed smile. "I've been here more times than you, Laddie." His Scottish brogue was thick. "I kept the place clean for 'yer father going on forty years now. I guess I work for you now." He continued pushing the cart inside, the 8,000-pound door closing behind him with a dull thud. Soundproof walls—yet another addition from my parents. Maybe they hadn't wanted to disturb the rest of the cemetery with their after-life parties once they passed on. Courteous of them, really.

"Well, if you work for me now, then get out."

"Not in my contract, Master Temple." He began mopping up the spotless floor.

"Cantankerous old bastard," I grumbled under my breath.

"Aye, Master Temple. That I am. Ye have a mouth like 'yer father." I blinked over at him, but he was engrossed in his work, so I let him be. He obviously had the code to get inside the mausoleum, so I trusted his story. I resumed my study of my parents. I thought of their deaths, and the lack of evidence the police had obtained from both the scene and the morgue. The facts flipped through my mind like a speed-reader on crack, but I came to no new conclusions. If Raven had been telling the truth, why had the dragons wanted them dead? Apparently, my parents had made some big-league enemies.

A hand brushed my shoulder, and I jumped, realizing that I had dozed off. "Better clean yourself up, Master Temple." He dropped a silk kerchief into my lap, crimson lines showing through some of the thin material. "Never let 'em see you sweat." I stared down at it, listening to the cart shuffle away behind me. I slowly unfolded the cloth.

A larger game is afoot. Beware of the coming Eclipse, my son.

I stood in a rush, thrusting a finger out at the old man to halt him in a tight cocoon of air as he neared the door. My magic wrapped around him like a straightjacket, one of his feet frozen in mid-air as if I had stopped time. "What's the meaning of this, old man?"

The janitor stared back from his invisible prison. "The name's Mallory, Master Temple, not 'old man.' I found that next to your father before the police arrived. You haven't been answering your phone, so I decided to meet you the old-fashioned way. Didna' want the Bobbies' to find it. Awkward questions, and such, no doubt."

Bobbies was an English term for Policemen. Without preamble, the janitor rolled his shoulders, and my spell simply evaporated as if it had never existed. He continued tugging the cart through the heavy doors, and then disappeared outside, the door thudding closed behind him. I remained frozen, unable to even wonder how the senior citizen had so easily disarmed my magic. My gaze shifted from the door to the kerchief, and then to my parents' tomb.

The message had been written in crimson ink.

No, not ink. Blood.

Then I was moving. I bolted outside, ready to interrogate Mallory further, but when I got there, he was simply gone. His cart sat just outside the door, but of him, there was no sign. I saw the cab I had called earlier idling just outside, waiting patiently. After a few seconds of bewilderment, I decided to lock up the mausoleum via the electronic keypad, and angrily climbed inside the vehicle. "Did you see an old man leave the building a minute ago?" I growled in response to his jovial greeting.

"Just you, sir." He answered with a frown. I looked back. The cart was gone. *What the hell?*

"Never mind. Plato's Cave in Soulard." I calculated in my head. 7.5 miles. "Get me there in eight minutes." He nodded eagerly as I flashed a fifty-dollar-bill at him. I leaned back into the worn leather seats, satisfied by the sudden adrenaline-inducing formula-one driving abilities of the cabby. I closed my eyes with a sigh, thinking. I now knew the reason for the odd perimortem gash on his arm. What had been so important that my father had wanted to leave a message in his own blood? And what did that have to do with the upcoming solar eclipse in three days? Wait, two days now. I hadn't even remembered the big event until reading the message on the kerchief. It just hadn't seemed important. There was a big convention of astronomers in town awaiting that very spectacle, but I'd be damned if I knew how it was connected to my parents' deaths. Something nagged at me, but I was too exhausted to worry about it.

I began preparing a plan to acquire—or at least look into—the book that Raven had wanted me to find. Not knowing what it was about, or why it was so important, I figured that finding it might at least protect some of my fellow bookstore owners around town. Perhaps I could barter with one of the dragon sisters she mentioned. Either way, it was better to have it in my possession than it remaining an unknown. I spoke a quick reminder into my iPhone, commanding the feminine intelligence queen to transfer it to my calendar in case I forgot later. I was meeting up with Gunnar in an hour to discuss the information he had dug up on Raven and her vague hints. He also had all the information on the latest bookstore attacks. Maybe if we kicked up enough dust we would find a trail.

The taxi screeched to a halt in front of my bookstore. I glanced down at my phone. Seven minutes. I threw him the bill and climbed out. He tipped an imaginary hat at me, and—much more responsibly this time—pulled out into the street, adhering to the legal laws set aside by the grand city of St. Louis.

10

My phone vibrated before I had taken two steps. "Temple," I answered.

"Hey," Gunnar replied, sounding grouchier than earlier. "My car died today."

That brought a brief grin to my face. "I know. I was there."

"No, it *really* died. It's going to cost twice what it's worth to fix it, so I will be a public transport kind of guy for a while."

"Well, at least there are a ton of babes on the public bus."

"Not in this town. New York, maybe, but not St. Louis."

I tried not to laugh. "Still want me to swing by?" I answered instead.

"Yes. I've got everything together now. You sure you want in on this?" He sounded guarded.

"Um, someone tried to…hurt us last night." I modified what I had been about to say. Police were kind of nit-picky about overhearing unreported murders. Even if it was in self-defense. "Pretty sure I don't have much of a choice." I hadn't told him about the dragon hunters at Bellefontaine Cemetery. Nor the kerchief from Mallory. It would have to wait. With newfound resolve, I mumbled a confirmation. "As much as I would like to catch a flight to Cabo, there's no getting out of it for me. I found out some information that might help us a bit."

"Maybe you *should* get out of town. The cops are already watching you."

I shook my head firmly. "I'm not running away from this."

"Alright." He sighed. "See you in an hour, then." I clicked the phone off, and shoved it in my pocket. I placed a hand on the heavy door to my shop and strode inside. Standing there for a moment, I let the building's heat wash over me. Plato's Cave was doing a brisk business for a Friday, despite the renovations as a result of Raven's visit last night. A few workers milled around the broken window leading to the street, the sound of hammers striking nails filling the air.

A stunning, tall young blonde hung near the register, her *Got Jesus?* Tee stretched much too tightly over her breasts. A cartoon depiction of our savior was waving a thumbs-up in the most inappropriate of places, but the fabric was long enough to remain decent. Barely. Her name was Indiana Rippley. Her eyes reminded me of glacial chips of ice, almost a neon blue. She was my second-in-command at the shop, my store manager, and was privy to more classified information than the other employees.

"Hey, Indie. What's happening?" She had started as a simple part-timer, but had rapidly forsaken her college degree to instead continue working for me at the shop after confronting some of the darker clients I sometimes entertained. Her skills at running a tight ship had proven necessary; she was smooth sailing where others would run in terror.

"Not a whole lot, Cap'n. Other than the...sudden remodel." She added with a curious brow, gesturing at the workers near the windows. I nodded back, not rising to the bait. "Game night tonight," she said, scanning a paper before her. "Gods of Chaos IV, if I'm not mistaken."

"You're never mistaken, Indie," I answered, rolling my eyes.

She beamed up at me, dancing up a bit on her toes, a pleasant jiggle making the cartoon Jesus dance a quick two-step on her shirt. "We got the store cleaned up after you left for..." Her face grew tight, suddenly reminded that I had just come from the funeral. "Need a drink? I'm on break in five," she offered, knowing I had been through a tough ordeal today.

"I'm fine, Indie. But thanks." All I really wanted to do was succumb to her offer. I had crushed on her for years, but I had never made that final leap to show her my true feelings, fearing the nuclear fallout if things went south.

"Okay." Her eyes were full of doubt. "I just want you to know that you aren't alone. If you need a shoulder to lean on, don't forget about us little people," she said with a friendly grin. Eye candy for sure, but she was a trusted friend, and extremely intelligent. Her IQ had been clocked at 187 on three separate tests—well above genius level. Harmless flirting had been a part of our relationship since we had met so many years ago, but it had never crossed the line into anything more. I was protective of her, and she of me. But I still found myself wondering if there could be more.

"Thanks. But I'm fine. Maybe next week I'll be ready to talk about it."

"You know where to find me, Cap'n." She was also the only employee who didn't always refer to me as *Master Temple*.

I leaned over the counter, whispering conspiratorially. "Any particular guests I need to know about?"

She glanced about, making sure no customers were near. "Nope. We're all prepared for the worst though." She discreetly slid open a drawer by her long, pale thigh, revealing an empty LockSAF PBS-001 biometric fingerprint pistol case. Every employee had one, and the necessary paperwork for concealment, happily paid for by yours truly.

Even with rubber bullets, the guns could impact a world of deterrence. Noticing that Indie wore a tight black pencil skirt, I tried not to imagine where she had hidden her weapon. She smiled sweetly up at me, as if sensing my unspoken question.

I leaned back, and nodded. "I just need to step up to my office for a sec, then I'm off again. You mind holding down the fort tonight? I'm not sure where I will be, but my plate is kind of full right now."

She glanced at the schedule, feigning a frown. "Well, I'll have to cancel my dinner plans, but if my employer doesn't mind compensating me for it, I don't mind. My date is kind of a douche anyway."

"You debutante!" I laughed. "You know I'm good for it. Rain check for next week, and I'll take you out for lunch so you can hear all the boring details."

She nodded. "Only if it's somewhere good."

"Your pick."

She clapped her hands, and I had to force myself to walk away rather than study the effects her sudden motion had on her anatomy. I climbed the stairs to my loft, unlocked the door, and stepped inside, expecting a cluster-fuck of a mess, but I was wrong. I had woken up late this morning, and had momentarily turned into a human tornado while looking for my suit. But the room was spotless.

A smile split my cheeks, and I strode over to the window. Indie was glancing up at me. I mimed a worshipful pose, recognizing her deft hand at cleaning up for me. She deserved a raise. Her smile grew wider as she waved back up at me, and then she returned to her duties.

I changed quickly and then scanned my desk for Peter's book request. Spotting the parchment, I shoved it into my pocket, threw on a comfy tee and a jacket, snatched up my Fendi satchel full of magical goodies—including the SIG Sauer X-five pistol Gunnar had gifted me—and locked up behind me. Curious, I approached Indie again. "Any reason I never got the message from Peter earlier in the week?" I waved the note at her. She frowned, obviously unaware, "Peter said he left it with Jessie." Her eyes instantly became guilty.

"He seemed like a good guy when I hired him. He's an odd duck, but he's still trying to learn the particulars for working for you. Want me to talk to him?" Her face was set in a frown, no doubt anxious to rectify this situation with a Defcon 1 approach. And you wonder why I was hesitant to risk our friendship for a chance at romance.

"No worries. Just see that it doesn't happen again. I have full faith in you, Indie. If you thought he was worth hiring, then I trust you." My voice grew darker as I picked up a pirate accent. "No need to make him walk the plank…yet."

She grinned back, nodding once. "Aye, aye, Cap'n!" she bellowed loudly.

From around the store, all my employees dropped what they were doing to salute in my direction; a chorus of shouts that startled the customers. "Aye, aye, Cap'n!"

I saluted back. "See you later, Ind—" She held up a finger, commanding my obedience. I frowned but waited. As slowly and deliciously as an exotic dancer, she raised an arm from behind the counter, dangling a white paper sack like the dancer would dangle a pair of panties. Her face glowed with pride. "You. Are. An. Angel," I said, snatching up the bag of freshly-brewed colada. She nodded before turning to a nearby customer, engaging them with her full attention.

Raise for Indie—*check*.

I headed outside and smiled at my car parked in front of the store. It had cost quite a bit to get the city to allow me to purchase the space as a permanent spot, but it was definitely worth it. After all, like my father always said, *money doesn't spend itself*. I gunned the engine with a throaty roar, and sped off towards Gunnar's office. *Time for answers*, I told myself.

11

I squinted at the screen. "Any way you can tighten up the pixels? It looks like an Etch 'n Sketch. By a blind amputee." I stared harder, cocking my head slightly. "Having a seizure."

"If you would just give me a damned second," Gunnar snapped. "We aren't all billionaires who can afford a year's salary on a stupid iMac. The neighbor's call only came in five minutes ago, and I tapped into the street cam three minutes ago."

I waited, sipping a shot of the still-steaming colada that Indie had given me. Dusk had begun to descend upon the city as I reached Gunnar's office. Being in one of the higher levels of the FBI building, I had a pleasant view of the city from my chair. Gunnar's fingers shot toward me—imploring—as I began to take a meditative sip. With a sigh, I poured him a shot of his latest addiction. He downed it, never moving his eyes from the screen.

I had created a monster.

As if fueled by the caffeine, his fingers flew across the keyboard in a blur. Moments later, the picture on the digital screen cleared, revealing a recognizable image this time. He clicked *play*.

A female in a long trench coat entered a downtown bookstore. Nothing scary about that. Then Gunnar jumped ahead ten minutes. The same woman walked out, the street slightly darker now. She dipped into an uninhabited alley and dropped her trench coat. As the garment fluttered to the ground, there was a flash of pale nudity, and then a long, red tail knocked over a trashcan before disappearing into the shadows. Gunnar was watching me. "Damn. Dragons again. Must be one of Raven's sisters."

"What, like *real* dragons?" He asked.

"Of course, *real* dragons," I grumbled, mimicking Tomas, the dragon hunter I had met at the cemetery. I explained his description of the shape-shifting dragons to Gunnar. "You're telling me this isn't the FBI's first sighting?"

Gunnar shook his head, leveling me with a frustrated look. "Third. One bookstore owner died of hypothermia, but the thermostat in his store was set in the mid-seventies. The other was found covered in infected blisters, oozing puss and bacteria. But he had been to the doctor a few days prior, and had walked away with an impeccable physical report. Neither of them makes any sense. Then this. But at least this one is still alive. It's my first case in charge of the new team I was telling you about last night, and I still wouldn't even know what we were dealing with if you hadn't just told me. Which is the whole *point* of the new team." He glanced around warily. "A team that is more capable of dealing with...*our* kind of stuff."

"We need to go check this out. Now." I stood, curious about the odd particulars of the other deceased victims.

Gunnar nodded. "Alright, I'll call my squad to swing by after we check it out. I kind of want you off the books for now," he added sheepishly. "But tell me what else you found out, and how."

"On the way," I answered. Gunnar snatched up a coat the size of a tarp before locking his computer and darting out the door behind me. "We'll take my car." Gunnar scowled. He opened his mouth to ask another question, but I held up a finger, motioning to the agents swarming all around us. He clamped shut, unhappy, but understanding. The elevator door whisked open before me and Gunnar's boss, Special Agent in Charge Roger Reinhardt, stepped out. He was also a large man, full of authority. He wore short-cropped dark hair, looking every inch the politician, but I knew he was good at his job. He knew how to play the bureaucratic games with the big boys. His eyes widened at the sight of me, quickly searching for my visitor's badge. I waved it at him so he wouldn't have a heart attack.

"Nathin Temple. My deepest condolences," he offered sincerely.

I nodded back, wordlessly stepping past him into the elevator. He turned to Gunnar. "Any progress on the attacks, Agent Randulf?"

"Working on a lead now." Reinhardt looked dubious, glancing at me. "He's under my protection," Gunnar continued. "His shop was broken into last night, just like the others, but the perp escaped. He might be able to identify the assailant."

Reinhardt still looked unconvinced but finally nodded. "Have you found any...*special* consultants yet?" Gunnar shook his head. Interesting. It meant that Reinhardt didn't know that *I* was a special consultant, which also meant that my secret alter ego as a wizard was still safe. Goody. "I'm taking a big risk with your task force, Agent Randulf. Consulting with alleged...*gifted* individuals to help us catch *gifted* criminals still sounds like some cheap Hollywood movie, but I have to admit that things are getting...weirder out there." He grimaced at that, as if it left a sour taste in his mouth. I tried to keep my face blankly innocent and aloof. "It still feels like making a deal with the devil. Don't make me look a fool." He studied me curiously for a few more seconds, sizing me up, and then he strode away.

Gunnar joined me in the elevator as I hit the lobby button. Music played in the tiny steel box as we descended, not speaking. It was a huge deal for Gunnar to lie about Raven escaping, even though the cause was worth it. It was also worthy of note to hear that Agent Reinhardt assumed that Gunnar was simply 'consulting' with other Freaks, and not that Gunnar was one of those Freaks himself.

"Consulting, eh?" I offered.

Gunnar glanced at me, eyes tight. "It's the only way…for now. We need a home run. Neither the local law enforcement, nor the FBI can handle this type of thing. That's why Reinhardt is allowing me to do this. He knows, even if he won't admit it, that the crimes in this city are growing beyond his scope of understanding. He saw one of the other videos. I thought he was going to faint when he saw the tail."

"Well, then. Time to roll the dice," Gunnar grunted as the doors chimed open. Exiting the secure building, we hopped into my car and drove downtown. I handed him the kerchief from my pocket on the way, explaining its origins.

He studied it critically, even sniffing it. A wolf thing, I guessed. "Mind if I run some tests on it?" I shook my head, paying attention to the road in order to bottle away the pain of parting with my father's kerchief. "The solar eclipse…Raven mentioned that too. Any idea what it means?" I shook my head again. "And you say you've never seen this old man before the funeral?"

"No. But he knew some pretty strong magic. My power slid off of him like rain, and then he simply walked out. His appearance could have just been a cover, but he obviously has access to Temple Industries, and my parents hand-selected each and every employee. He also knew the code to the Mausoleum. As far as I know, only three people knew that code, and two of them are now dead."

"Could he be one of the…dragons?" The word sounded tough for him to say aloud.

"I don't think so. He gave me a lead. I'm pretty sure that's out of countenance with the Evil Bad Guy Bible." Another thought hit me. "And he didn't have horizontal pupils." Snow was still piled up on the curbs from the night before.

"I almost forgot about that. Creepy." I nodded, glancing over at my friend; he was practically hugging the dash of the small sports car with his massive bulk.

"Her magic matched the color of her irises, and even her hand when it started to change into that nasty manicure job that tried to slice your throat. At least that's what caught the Dragon Hunter's attention."

Gunnar sputtered. "What? *Dragon* Hunter?" he demanded.

"Oh, yeah." I did my best to look apologetic. "Back at the funeral, I met a guy when I was having a smoke. He told me to *watch out*. Said I was in danger. Apparently, something big is going down soon, and his crew is hunting a particular dragon in town. A man. He said he was keeping tabs on the bookstores, so I'm sure we'll run into them again."

Gunnar opened his mouth to say more, but I cut him off. "We're here," I said, changing the topic as I pointed at the deserted shop doors. I pulled my car into a parking space, and we climbed out. Gunnar was staring at the store, so I studied his silhouette against a streetlamp. He looked like an ancient Viking, his Norse heritage obvious. Raising my gaze, I scanned the nearby buildings, appreciating the beauty of the old city. The courthouse loomed over us, powerful, resolute, and regal, her white climbing columns and vast marble façade intimidating and imposing. My gaze flicked over the top of the courthouse directly across the street from the bookstore, and I immediately tensed. "Gunnar..." I warned.

He followed my gaze in time to see a long red tail swinging gently in a gust of wind between two gargoyle statues atop the courthouse. He slowly turned to me, eyes surprised. "Well, that was easy. Want to go have a chat with her?" An expensive car pulled up behind mine, squeezing into the last parking space on the street amidst a blare of angry honking as they cut someone off. The driver remained inside, studying a map. Tourist.

I nodded to Gunnar. "Have you brushed up on any Dale Carnegie lately?"

Gunnar grunted, smiling as he brushed his tattoo subconsciously. *"How to Win Friends and Influence People...Yep."*

I decided to leave my bag of tricks in the car, feeling confident in my inborn power. Magic was fueled by emotion, and I had plenty of that. Tools helped wizards focus their powers, but I had enough power and control that I rarely needed a focus for doing things. Unless I was trying something completely new. But I wasn't planning on experimenting tonight. Plus, I had a werewolf to back me up. Besides, Peter had killed the first dragon with a frozen liquor bottle, and he was untrained. I would rely on sheer power, because I was fast and efficient at destroying things when I needed to. The only other thing I trusted to use was the handy-dandy pistol that I had stowed in the glove compartment, but heading into a federal courthouse with a gun seemed idiotic. There was nothing discreet about the weapon. Gunnar carried a small backpack with a change of clothes inside in case he needed to shift into his werewolf form.

We crossed the street and headed inside the beautiful stonework courthouse. The five-story pillars supporting the roof reminded me of the Greek Parthenon. The red dragon tail was no longer visible, but I knew it was up there amidst the stone gargoyles that guarded the roof's perimeter. Gunnar had to wave his badge several times as security questioned our entrance, but we were finally admitted. The guards waved us on, turning back to their duties.

We took the stairs two at a time—swift, but not fast enough to alarm anyone we might run into—our shoes slapping the cold marble as we continued up to the roof. We didn't encounter anyone else at this late hour, but kept our eyes to the shadows just in case. What if the dragon was back in human form? I decided to pay very close attention to the eyes of any person who came near me. Any horizontal pupils and I would have to neutralize them.

Why had she remained so close to the scene of her break-in? The emergency call from the neighbor had informed Gunnar that the owner was alive, but scared shitless. Understandably so. Perhaps the dragon was waiting on the storekeeper, seeing if he went out in search of her request. That would mean that he had offered up some information to her that had somehow spared his life. Interesting. I'd have to question him about it, if we survived our own encounter with the dragon. We climbed to the top floor of the building, and looking both ways, chose a direction in search of a roof exit. Windows lined the wall, allowing a splendid view of the city below.

Seeing no one around, I spoke, my heels striking the marble with each step. *Tap, tap, tap.* "So, tell me more about this strike-force you're putting together. I can't imagine many Freaks are in the bureau, so how much good could it do?" *Freaks* were how the few unenlightened individuals—like the cops—referred to us. No one had yet confirmed, officially, that we existed, but plenty of civilians already knew or at least had a very good suspicion. Crimes were simply becoming too 'unexplainable' with the new advanced technologies revealing truths that had historically been hidden under reams of paperwork. A Kentucky Senator was even demanding that all Freaks should furthermore be termed Wizards since it had to be our fault that they all existed in the first place.

Idiots.

Gunnar looked at me, saying nothing.

"Wait, you said hush, hush. Do you even have any jurisdictional lines? Are they just going to put up fliers in every police station in the country, seeing if any Freaks are stupid enough to move to the buckle of the Bible-Belt?"

Gunnar scoffed. "Of course there are lines. Like I told you, this is just a test run. Reinhardt knows weird stuff keeps happening, and that more often than not, we remain aloof to the criminals and their capture. This is merely a beta testing of an idea I whispered to him. He's a Regular, but a damned good agent. He has no idea what he was *really* allowing me to do. What I was really asking him. For now, I basically just have a wider line than the other agents. Instead of a razor-blade, I'm dancing on a steak knife." I pondered that. Crime was getting nastier each year, and while most of it was the normal, run-of-the-muck kind of crime, some of it *did* need a firmer hand. Guns were fine, but sometimes not enough, and all too often, red tape plugged up said guns.

"Can't hurt, I guess. Any recruits yet, or just *consultants*?" I mocked, scanning the glass walls around us for a roof exit. Gunnar said nothing, so I stopped and glanced back. *Tap, tap, tap.* The sound of heels striking the ground continued.

He pointed a finger at me, face suddenly ashen. "*Me?*" I stared back, dumbfounded. "Oh, no way. I'm not even a cop! I don't know diddly about all the minutiae that took you *years* to learn. I'm a terrible recruit." Another thought struck me. "And I don't even *want* to join! I've got enough on my plate, thank you very much." Gunnar continued staring, but I realized he wasn't pointing at me. He was pointing *behind* me. Then he abruptly shifted into his *Underdog* underwear-clad werewolf form, clothes exploding into shreds. I only had time to hope that it wasn't the same pair of underwear from the night before.

Tap, tap, tap. The noise continued, and this time I realized it sounded quite different from our heels striking marble. It sounded like something tapping on glass. I turned, and found myself facing a massive grinning red dragon, snorting fog onto the cool glass from her scaly visage outside. *Tap, tap, tap.* A giant talon let out a staccato drumbeat. I was momentarily reminded of a sadistic child tapping on a glass fish tank.

Then the glass exploded inwards, and a massive arm wrapped around my waist, tugging me out onto the windy rooftop. "Ack!" I yelled as the grip squeezed the air from my lungs. Muscles bunched around me as the world tossed and turned. I heard Gunnar howl—a piercing lament—but we were moving fast, and between being tossed about like the victim of a drunken operator controlling a Ferris wheel and not being able to breathe, I felt positively unpleasant. Which pissed me off. And being pissed off typically makes me a tad reckless.

Everything halted, and I abruptly noticed a sad statue on the roof from inches away, his face pitying my dilemma. Then my body was hoisted out over the city streets five stories below, the grip loosening enough for me to breathe. Cars flashed by beneath me, oblivious to my predicament. "Now that we're alone, I propose we have a little chat," a woman's voice spoke. I lifted my head to stare straight into the dragon's fiery red horizontal pupils, ignoring the blood pounding in my skull. I gathered my will, ready to unleash hell.

"Ah, ah, ah." The blood-red dragon's voice cooed as she released one of the talons holding me up above St. Louis' beautifully paved streets. My body dropped an inch and I squawked in alarm. "I just wanted to have a few words with you about a family book." Her voice was that of a phone sex operator, full of empty promises that one couldn't help but buy. "Oh, and also about my sister since she never came home last night."

Another talon loosened, dropping my upper torso entirely and leaving me to hang upside down by my knees. I couldn't help it. I laughed, overcompensating for my panic. "Your sister won't be coming home any time soon."

She cocked her head quizzically. "Start talking. Now, wizard." My pack of cigarettes fell out of my pocket, sailing down into the night.

And down, and down, and down.

I swiveled, quite composed, and pointed an angry finger at her. "That. Was. A. New. Pack. Bitch."

More glass burst outward from atop the roof, out of my immediate sight. Her eyes swiveled towards the noise with a hiss and tongue of flame.

I am not above sucker-punches.

A rumble of power began to build at her throat as she prepared a counter-attack at the noise. I summed up my will, calling on the wind this high up, and bulldozed the sad-faced statue that had shown me a moment of compassion. A cloud of dust and rock exploded out, but a big portion of the statue sailed true, slamming straight into her wide-open mouth as she was ready to let loose her blast. Napalm fire, unable to go anywhere else, splashed all over her crenellated head, bathing her in a sick wash of flames from snout to chest. She shook her head with a roar of pain and surprise. "Eat that!" I crowed, still hanging upside down. Then the fire died out from her scales, causing no lasting harm. Blood dripped freely from her scaled lips, thanks to my thrown statue, one tooth dangling by a thread of her gums before it too fell to the roof like the drops of blood.

The roof around her flared with the liquid fire. I heard a shout, but it wasn't Gunnar's voice, and then three sizzling blue and black spears sailed through the night towards my captor. She dodged two of them, sending them off down into the nearby park, and hopefully not into a wandering pedestrian, but the third slammed home, tearing a jagged hole in one of her wings and piercing her thigh. Blue sparks sizzled up from the wound and she roared in pain.

She took one shaky step, freeing her wing, and then glared at me. "It appears that your time is up." With a smile, she let go of my leg, and I fell.

Fast.

I realized I was going to become a nuisance to the street-sweeper on the morning shift. The dragon launched off the roof with a snap of wings, sailing away into the night sky. Gunnar—in his giant white-haired werewolf form—stared down at me from the roof, his jaws stretched wide as if howling. But the wind whistled in my ears as I dropped, so I couldn't actually hear Gunnar.

But I *did* notice a freaking black boomerang suddenly racing towards my face from another building across the street.

My scream was in no way similar to that of a frightened little girl.

The black boomerang unfolded into a trio of interconnected rubber balls attached to a net of rope. Apparently, *Spiderman* was watching over my fair city. The web slammed into me, and then the weighted balls swung around and around my torso until finally hammering into different sections of my body like a boxer working a heavy bag. One was about a hair away from permanently ruining my chances at continuing my family tree, and luckily none hit me in the face or I would have officially been Mike Tyson-ed. The force of the impact was strong enough to alter my trajectory directly into a window on the side of the building.

And then *through* the goddamned window.

The heavy glass didn't impede my entrance in the slightest, but instead exploded into a tinkling shower of shards before me into what seemed like a plush office. I bounced off a very sturdy bookshelf, and then slid face first onto a long, wide wooden desk, my face efficiently clearing everything off the top of its surface: a stapler, a jar of pens, a book, a pile of papers, a keyboard, a monitor, and at the very end of the desk sat a steaming mug of coffee. I squinted my eyes shut in anticipation, scrabbling desperately to try and brake with my feet, but they were all tangled up in the damned web.

Again, my shriek sounded in no way similar to that of a frightened little girl. I slid to a halt, my nose brushing the scalding mug. But it didn't spill. I tried to steady my breathing, and cautiously peeled open the only eye not squeezed shut from the web, staring at the room's sole occupant.

A man had wisely scooted back from the desk. He reminded me of Father Time. Older than old, but he was apparently still spry enough to dodge a sailing, web-encased, wizard who happened to burst through his fourth-floor office window. He glanced down at me, long, heavy caterpillar eyebrows frowning with disapproval. His unblinking stare exuded a heavy sense of authority and importance. Then I noticed his getup. A thin black robe settled around his shoulders, and I noticed a wooden gavel on a bookshelf behind him.

I gulped. "Your Honor," I offered. The rope web pressed my nose flat against my face, and another lifted my mouth into what would pass for a world-record hair lip.

Without a word, he reached over my face, carefully plucked up his coffee, and then stepped out of the room. *He has a damned good poker face*, I thought to myself as I heard pounding feet racing towards me from just outside the open door. Then a swarm of security guards burst into the room, guns leveled in my general direction as if anticipating a ninja to disappear into a cloud of smoke and throwing stars. The lead guard blinked, and then suppressed a grin as he tucked his gun away. "I don't think he's an immediate threat."

I squirmed angrily, hoping to unhook one of the balls on the web, but I merely succeeded in slipping off the desk to fall straight onto my back on the hard wood floor. Pain flashed in my side as the wind was knocked out of me.

"Thun of a vitch!" I wheezed through the web.

12

It didn't take long for Gunnar to sort out the mess and get me out of handcuffs. That's two times in twenty-four hours. Impressive, right? Gunnar had changed into his spare clothes, and no one had seemed to notice. At first, Justice Simpson hadn't been very pleased with my interruption, but after checking my wallet for identification, he had burst out laughing so hard that I actually blushed. His last comment still aggravated me as we stepped outside, past another set of chuckling guards. I flipped them off. "Pricks." I muttered, rubbing at the rope burns on my neck. They laughed harder.

Gunnar glanced over at me, amused. "He did say that you could *drop by any time*. Quite courteous of him, given the situation."

"I take it you're walking back to the office?"

Gunnar grumbled back, "Thought you might like a souvenir." He offered me one of the dragon's teeth that I had knocked out. It was almost as long as my pinkie.

"Nifty." I smiled back, pocketing it. A beautiful blonde woman in a tracksuit was walking across the street from us, and I swiped back my shaggy hair for a semblance of dignity. Gunnar followed my gaze, nodding his agreed approval. Her hair was cut short along her jaw so that the bangs formed wicked points near her chin, layered perfectly around her thin oval face. She grinned at my obvious interest, and I winked back. She giggled and began to change direction towards us, limping slightly as if she had sprained her ankle while running. God, girls giggling! What a delicious sound.

We climbed into my vintage car, waiting for the jogger to approach us, her dazzling white teeth reeling me in as her long legs brought her closer. She leaned into the window, studying us both. "Got a pen?" She asked in a breathless voice. I silently slipped her one. Her eyes were like almonds, and the smell of clean sweat quickly kicked my hormones on, which had barely survived the *Spiderman*-like assault. She furiously jotted down a number on my hand. No name. Her fingers were feverish. "Whom do I ask for when I call?" I asked with a grin.

"You'll find that out *if* I *answer*. Or *if* you even call." She grinned, and then turned to walk off her twisted ankle.

"Gold-digger." Gunnar complained.

"But I've got gold, so it's a win-win." I answered, grinning.

"Money doesn't make you happy..." He said, reciting the well-known adage.

I started the car, revving the gas into a throaty growl beneath my feet. "Well, it sure as shit doesn't make you sad either, Gunnar." He rolled his eyes, but couldn't mask his grin as I pulled out into traffic. A few seconds later, the car parked behind us also pulled out. Was it the same car that had parked behind me before we went into the courthouse? Was this what a tail felt like? I was too intrigued to be scared. I mean, I had just survived a joint attack by a wannabe *Spiderman* and a red dragon. What danger was a mere Regular?

"So, who saved your ass with that net launcher?" he asked solemnly.

"Spiderman?" I offered.

"Seriously, Nate. There are three possibilities. One, they were trying to catch the dragon, and missed horribly. Two, they were trying to catch you for some dark reason. Three, it really was our friendly neighborhood web-slinger saving your pathetic life. In that case, I might have my first recruit, even if he does seem to have poor character judgment."

I grunted my displeasure at his quip. "I like number three best, but I guess you should look into the alternatives since *Spiderman's* just a comic book character." I frowned. "Who was that other guy on the roof with you?" The car was still behind me, but further back.

Gunnar looked frustrated. "I'm not sure. He appeared out of nowhere, shot the dragon with that electric spear gun, and then he was gone. Maybe he was one of those dragon hunters..."

I nodded. "Mind looking into it for me? I have to swing by Chateau Falco."

Gunnar arched a brow. "Need backup?"

"Pretty sure that's one of the safest places in town right now. I'll call you after."

I pulled up in front of the FBI building and he opened the door. "My team should be finished with the bookstore in a short while, so I'll let you know what we find out later. See you soon, Temple. And watch your ass." The tailing car continued on past me. I was simply reading too much into things.

"That's what I have you for, sweetie." I winked. He shook his head and slammed the door with more force than was necessary. I continued on, still on schedule to meet Miss Belmont at Chateau Falco.

13

I waited outside the gated fortress of Chateau Falco. A tall, thick, stone and rebar-enforced wall surrounded the grounds, and an arcane Damascus steel forged gate impeded my path. A life-sized nude statue stood atop the wall to either side of the gate—a man and a woman armed for battle. It had been rumored that the cremated remains of our first ancestors to settle here had been used for the mortar. Before I could beep in on the intercom, a familiar voice emanated from the speaker. "Greetings, Master Temple. Your fortress awaits. Lowering the bridge now." The gate began to slowly swing inward.

"We live in the 21st century, Dean. People don't have bridges. They have gates."

He ignored me. "Bridge lowered, Master Temple. You can safely cross the moat now." Then he signed off. I sighed, shifting into gear and driving up the mile-long cobbled drive, passing lush gardens on either side of me. Well, lush for this time of year anyway.

After a few minutes of driving—because Dean, the Temple family's Chief of Security and Butler, didn't appreciate speeding, and was known to let the air out of the tires if one disobeyed; even if said one was now the current Master Temple—I pulled into the wide circular drive leading up to the courtyard. I parked, leaving the keys inside.

I didn't see any other cars, and wondered why for a moment, but then recognized Dean's skilled hand as I spotted tire tracks leading to a large remodeled stable. He had already parked the guests'—whomever they may be—cars in the stable in case of more snow or rain. Chances were that the cars were also being detailed by one of the family employees while inside. I shook my head wearily. I didn't belong in this type of atmosphere, which is why I had left several years ago.

The fountain in the center of the drive was off this time of year, but the stonework statues in the center were still spectacular. I leaned back, taking in the looming four-story structure before me. Built over two hundred years ago, each generation had added onto it, but none dared stray from the original colonial design. The old pile now stretched close to 17,000 square feet, containing two wings, two large libraries, twenty bedrooms, three kitchens, a theater room, a glass greenhouse attached to the side, and even a mediocre observatory.

I sighed, fingering the quickly-made leather thong that now held the red dragon's tooth around my neck. It was so sharp that it scratched my chest a bit, but it was a badge of honor in my eyes. A warning. I walked up to the massive front door with the Temple Coat of Arms emblazoned in the wood. A pinprick light studied me from a corner in the sheltered Porte-Cochère, blinking red with a motion detector. Beside it, a screen came to life to reveal Dean studying me critically. "Ah, Master Temple, please come in. Follow the guiding lights to come entertain your guests in the Master Study. All are here, as the Master has requested." I sighed, having requested no such thing. It was as I had feared. Whether I wanted it or not, I was the new Master Temple, and not just in name. The family mantle was like royalty—inescapable. I began to take a step. "Ah, ah, ah. Please remove your shoes, Master Temple." Then he signed off. Dean remotely unlocked the door before me, and I stepped into the dim house, a nostalgic grin on my face. Even after years of hiding from this place, it seemed we picked up right where we had left off.

It was comforting.

And disturbing.

I kicked off my shoes, and finding no others nearby, I placed mine just inside the door, and followed the trail of dim LED lighting embedded into the marble floors, escorted by the technology of the house as it led me down one hallway, and then another, and on, and on, wondering all the while who else might be here waiting to speak with me. Trudging on, I decided that my parents should have bought an electric golf cart for inside the house. Since it was now mine, perhaps I would act on the idea. I passed rooms of cabinets filled with odd bits and ends from archaeological digs, or acquired through auctions or inheritance from past family members.

The rooms I passed held a timeless quality even amidst cutting edge technology. But I didn't let my guard down. The beauty of the house was one of its many defenses. A sleight of hand. If one looked close enough, one would notice that some of the paintings always managed to be staring at the people in the room, no matter where they were positioned. And I'm not talking about the paranoia one gets when they *feel* like the pictures are watching them. I mean that they might literally be watching you. I shivered, moving on.

Despite the chill outside, the floors held thermal-controlled piping beneath the marble tile, heating the stone to a comfortable temperature underneath my socks. It's nice what money can buy.

Reaching a large stairway, I ascended, following the lights and continuing on for another few minutes until I reached my father's old study. I hadn't needed the lights to guide me, but it was a nice comfort, as well as an intimidating show of power for my guests. I took a deep breath before opening the door and stepping inside. The pleasant, aromatic whiff of frequent cigar smoke hit me first, and then the heart-wrenching memory of seeing my father behind the now-empty desk at the end of the room, smoking his precious Gurkha Black Dragon cigars.

One of his five hand-carved, camel-bone chests sat on a corner of his massive desk. Each chest of a hundred cigars set my father back $115,000. Half-a-million dollars to kill yourself, slowly. Hypocrite, I may be, but at least I wasn't as reckless about the cost. A thick glass window covered the entire back wall, but this night it was basked in the soothing glow of many antique lamps.

I immediately studied the people in the room, uncharacteristically wary after my recent adventures. Ashley Belmont stood to one side, speaking to an older gentleman who had his back to me. She smiled over his shoulder at me. I waved back. "Miss Belmont. A pleasure," I said. Her smile grew warmer.

The man beside her turned, smiling knowingly at me. "Nasty bit o' news about the courthouse this evening. One should be careful when dealing with dangers that might be attracted to blood in the water. But of course, ye know this already, Laddie." Mallory grinned, striding over and pumping my hand enthusiastically.

"How did you..." I began, and then slapped my forehead. He had been the one Gunnar saw on the roof. "You were the one tailing me. But why?" I was genuinely perplexed.

He discreetly pointed a thumb at a long-barreled spear gun leaning against the wall, but flicked his eyes over his shoulder, reminding me of Miss Belmont's presence. "Just making sure the Master Temple is safe. Did ye think I was only a janitor?" His grin was infectious. Reassessing the older man, I realized that he was rather stout, with thick, heavy forearms. Coarse, iron-grey hair covered his skin and knuckles, reminding me of an old-school sailor. An old man for a guardian, I grunted. But he had most likely saved my life tonight. Having seen my magic slide off of him at the mausoleum, I deduced that he was most definitely dangerous. Which was a good quality for a guardian.

"Well, thanks, I guess. You could have just told me, though."

"Not nearly so much fun," he answered. "But I do believe that be a discussion for another night, over a glass of scotch. You have business this night, Master Temple." He pointed a finger across the room, indicating a sharply dressed man standing beside Dean, Chateau Falco's Butler.

I walked over with a familiar grin, and bumped knuckles with Dean as he extended his hand for a professional handshake. He had served as our Chief of Security since I was a child, but vehemently denied all titles except Butler. He came from a very different time, when the term *Butler* was a highly-respected profession. Dedication, Loyalty, Honor, and Prestige were his lifeblood. "Pleased to see you again, Master

Temple." He was about chest height, and his eyes seemed to shine like Caribbean ocean water surrounding the black island of his pupils. "Bad hygiene is not indicative of a respected gentleman, especially the last heir of the renowned Temples. Do not disrespect yourself like this again," he said under his breath. I grinned back, shrugging. If I wasn't wearing a suit, I was slumming it in his eyes.

"I showered last night, Dean," I argued.

"Then perhaps the finer points of how to properly groom oneself need to be relearned after years of bachelor-hood," he droned, respectfully, of course.

I grinned even further. "I know just the women to teach me. Thank you for the reminder, Dean. I will practice studiously with them. Several times, to make sure I learn it correctly." Ashley made an embarrassed sound behind me.

Dean blushed. "Incorrigible. Completely incorrigible."

I smiled, patting his arm affectionately. He was family. I studied the last sharply dressed man out the corner of my eye.

He waited patiently, fighting the urge not to introduce himself and rudely interrupt my reunion with Dean. Years of training came back to me in the blink of an eye, the training of the European Courts; the cloak and dagger dance of smiles and knives, where winks could mean assassinations, and glares could imply life-long alliances; the dance that had been ingrained into each and every Temple child. I turned to him after a heavy silence, face utterly blank, letting him know that this was my home, and he was here by my choice, not the other way around. Seeing my obvious attention, he broke first, as was proper. "Greetings, Master Temple. My name is Turner Locke."

I nodded at him. "A pleasure to make your acquaintance, Mr. Locke. Be welcome in my home." Dean glided closer to the wall, blending in like a piece of furniture, trying not to disturb the Master and his guests, but ready to serve in any capacity I required at the drop of a hat. I studied Mr. Locke. "What firm do you represent?"

He blinked in surprise. "None, Master Temple. I worked exclusively for your father after our first interaction."

"Then you must be a very adequate lawyer, Mr. Locke. My father wasn't easily impressed."

He nodded humbly in answer. "May I ask how you knew my profession?"

"What other profession would deem to speak with me so urgently after my parents' deaths?" I smiled icily. "Now, what is the purpose of this mysterious meeting I apparently called everyone to attend? I abhor unknowns, yet here I find myself wading in a plethora of them." My tone filled the room. Speaking pompously could be helpful in situations like this, keeping the listeners wary. Their smiles lowered, and Mr. Locke gestured toward a semicircle of chairs before the desk. "If you could please take a seat, Master Temple, I have pledged to share your parents Last Will and Testament."

I groaned inwardly. On top of the funeral, this was the nail in the coffin, so to speak. It was so real now. They were dead. I was alone. I mustered my resolve so no one would notice my weakness. They each began to take a seat, and I paused, realizing there were not enough chairs. I began walking to the side of the room to pull up another, but Dean hissed for my ears only. "Master Temple!" He flicked a discreet finger at my father's chair behind the desk. I opened my mouth to object, and Dean revealed a serrated blade in his deft fingers. "Tires," was all he said. No one else appeared to notice. I smiled, nodding lightly as I approached the chair behind the desk with trepidation and an overwhelming sense of foolishness—like a nine-year-old child putting on his father's shoes. Slowly, I descended into the worn leather, waiting for someone to declare me an imposter. I fought to keep my face blank.

The three seated before me grew tense, watching me as if a rabid lion had been let loose in the room. Dean practically oozed with approval as he glided up a few paces behind me, in full view of the three subjects before his Master Temple. Jesus, I didn't belong here, regardless of what Dean thought. I tried to sound like my father. "Would anyone care for refreshments?" Each of their eyes cautiously settled on the drinks already sitting on coasters before them, but they didn't speak. "Ah, of course. Thank you, Dean."

My butler nodded as he set a perfectly weighted glass of scotch in front of me. I leaned back, taking a pleasurable sip, having no fucking clue what I was supposed to be doing. I could dance with the best of them when I knew the game, but my father's game made me look a fool. I felt as if I should know a different language for this. I decided to stop pretending. I didn't want to live in my father's shadow. I would simply be myself.

"Well, since I am the only one in the dark here, why don't we just cut straight to the point? You obviously want my permission to do something, or you're expecting me to tell you that I will pick up right where my parents left off. Well, I can quickly dissuade you of any false assumptions. I will *not* be taking over the company, and you will *not* use me as a phony symbol of the company to increase shareholder value. I am *not* my father. I am sure that Miss Belmont is fully capable of running Temple Industries, or she wouldn't have been promoted to her position. By all means, please finish your drinks in peace, and Dean will escort you out as soon as you are ready." I took a sip of my drink, and leaned forward, baring my teeth in a smile.

A heavy silence blanketed the room. Dean sighed disapprovingly, but I ignored it. Mr. Locke spoke up first. "If I may be so bold…" I waved a hand, setting my glass down for fear of shattering it in my clenching fist. "You remind me very much of your father, more so than you might believe. Please understand that what I am about to say comes word-for-word from your parents' lips. I have it written and notarized if you would prefer?" I didn't blink, burning him with my eyes, and very seriously contemplating a dangerous display of magic to quickly evacuate my guests. But remembering that Mallory was here, I chose against the latter, unsure if he would simply make me look like a pouting child.

"Proceed," I said.

He withdrew a closed envelope from his briefcase, broke the rather impressive seal on the outside, and handed a small letter from inside to each person in the room, including Dean. As he handed me mine, I unleashed a thought and it burned to ashes in my hand. "Not interested," I said coldly. Ashley inhaled sharply, leaning away as if I might bite. Mallory watched me with disapproving eyes, discreetly shaking his head.

Mr. Locke didn't even hesitate, reaching back into his bag to withdraw another letter. "How many copies do you have?" I growled.

He looked embarrassed. "Your father warned me of your...disdain for authority. I have brought enough copies to be sure that you read one in its entirety." I sighed in defeat, nodding for him to read it aloud. He held it firmly, his hand quivering slightly as he began to read:

Nathin Laurent Temple,

Please do not do anything rash, my Son. I have asked my good friend, Turner Locke, to read this aloud, as I am unsure of its safety in your hands at this emotional juncture. Mr. Locke has several copies in case this one happens to be destroyed prior to complete evocation.

Typical of my father.

Two items of importance must be discussed. I wish you to assume control of Chateau Falco, as we both know it cannot and must not fall into Regular hands. It is a legacy of our family, and must be preserved. Everything on the grounds has already been transferred into your name, and whether you sign the deed or not, measures have been taken, bribes paid, to see that my wish comes to fruition regardless of your wishes.

Mr. Locke has three rather small gifts to bestow upon you at this time.

Mr. Locke reached inside the envelope, and produced three small, plastic credit cards, each a different color. He handed them over to me. On the back of each was a post-it-note with a number...followed by much too many zeroes. *Small gifts*, but oh so big at the same time. My eyes grew large, but Mr. Locke continued.

The numbers are approximations, as you fully comprehend compounding interest.

Second point. If you do not assume ownership of Temple Industries, it will be sold, along with all of its patents, to a dozen competitors in China. This will create a massive job vacuum in the city of St. Louis, our founding heritage town, and a rather unhappy reaction from the Mayor, Senators, and Representatives. A letter has also been sent to the President of the United States, warning of this possibility. You will most likely be shunned by the entire city you live in, and Plato's Cave will no doubt drown in the bad publicity.

I regret informing you of my decision like this, but your mother and I wanted you to chase your own dreams while able. Temple Industries is much too vast to leave out of the family's control. It must pass on with you. We respect and applaud your decision not to join the company sooner, having time to pursue your own business with Plato's Cave. We couldn't be prouder of you, Nathin. You are the apple of our garden, and we hope you will always remember that. Try and bring your unique light to your new company.

Know that Chateau Falco was like a child to us all, witnessing many family secrets and stories never before uttered aloud. All one must do is listen to discover those secrets...

With all the love in the world,
Your Mother and Father.

Always the last word. Turner handed me the letter. A drop of blood stood below each name, and an elegant signature flourished beneath each name. They had even used the proper—if unusual—spelling of my name, rather than simply using *Nate*.

My eyes watered and my shoulders sagged. My voice was dry. He was right. Damn it. "Very well. I humbly stand corrected. This is much bigger than myself. I accept." The tension in the room evaporated. Ashley's shoulders sagged with relief, but I couldn't fathom why. I feared that I was about to drive Temple Industries in a new direction all right, and faster than anyone thought possible.

Straight into the ground.

I didn't know a damned thing about such a large company. I was just a bookstore owner. I was way out of my league. I turned to Ashley. "I expect you to maintain your position, doing what you already know how to do. I will help in any way I can, but you must understand that I'm really not equipped to wing this kind of thing."

She nodded, smiling sadly. "Of course, Master Temple. It will take time, but I'm not going anywhere. Temple Industries is my life. I will run it as if it were my own."

"I will hold you to that. I don't wish for my lifestyle to change now that I am CEO. For all intents and purposes, things will remain the same as before."

She smiled sadly, a tear falling onto the personal letter in her own hands. "Your father said you would say that. You are very much alike." She tucked her letter away, and I didn't have the heart to ask her what it had said. I wondered how close she had been to my parents. They had worked together every day. This must be the ultimate tragedy for her as well.

I shook my head as Turner finished reading his own letter. "What did you get? A Rolls Royce?" I asked snidely.

"Among other things..." Turner answered in a whisper. His eyes were bloodshot. "As with your father, I will always be at your service, Master Temple. Retirement or not." He straightened his spine, attempting to clear the remorse from the room. I nodded with a genuine smile of gratitude. "One more point of concern." I nodded, waiting. "I must ask that you refrain from any actions that might be deemed...*notorious* in your dealings with the police or FBI." I frowned. Word got around quickly. Or he was just remarkably well informed. "The CEO can't be seen to be involved in official criminal matters. It wouldn't be good for business. Could you manage this last favor?" I grumbled, but finally nodded to appease him. There was no way in hell I was backing off Gunnar's case, so I would just have to be discreet about it. "That includes private inquiries into your parents' deaths. The police can handle it. It is their job to do such, and we can't have you devoting your time to such matters. It would be seen as weakness to the shareholders. Especially any...unplanned meetings with judges." He added carefully. *Damn you, Mallory*, I thought to myself, but I finally nodded.

"In that case," I said, "I will need Miss Belmont's full cooperation with the police. I've been hassled lately by them in regard to the company and the future ownership. If you could please talk to them and have it all sorted out it would make things much easier for me to leave alone. Make it clear to them that my taking over the company was not a sneaky move on my part, but that it was the last request of my father. That I only just discovered tonight."

"Of course, Master Temple."

Dean piped up. "Well, if business is concluded, would anyone care for steak?"

Everyone politely declined, not interested in such a heavy meal on such heavy hearts. Mallory leaned closer. "Now that ye have a few nickels, Laddie, what ye gonna buy?"

A smile tugged at my cheeks as I thought of Gunnar. "I know just the thing."

14

It seemed we had many people in the St. Louis area on retainer for late hour transactions. It had taken one phone call, and only a twenty-minute wait for them to have everything prepared. It was good to be king. Now I was racing down the interstate well above the speed limit, dialing Gunnar on speakerphone. The car kept attempting to pair my phone with the built-in Bluetooth, but I kept declining until it devolved into a shouting match between the technology and me. Gunnar finally answered. "Hey."

"Gunnar! Where are you?" I bellowed, cool October wind roaring around me—the acoustics surprisingly adequate for a hardtop convertible. I cut someone off with a squeal of tires and furious honking.

"Should I turn on the news? Because it sounds like you're in a high-speed car chase," he answered.

"No cops. Yet. Listen, where are you?" I answered, enjoying the shit-eating grin on my face.

"Still at the office, why?" I checked the rearview mirror. Mallory was furiously trying to keep up with me, but American Muscle couldn't match the handling of my ride. Still, he was doing a fair job, cutting off the same guy I had a moment ago, causing another peal of blaring car horn.

"Good, good. Come outside. I'll be right there."

"Is everything oka—" I hung up, howling like a wolf into the wind.

I took the next exit, swerving across three lanes to take the turn downtown. I paid no attention to traffic lights, savoring every shade of red I blew through as only a thirsty vampire could appreciate, hoping to lose Mallory, but he doggedly pursued me. No doubt, he was going to chastise me, but I couldn't help myself. Seeing the building, I downshifted, and slid into a 180-degree spin, pulling right up against the curb. Gunnar was standing outside the door, staring at me with wide eyes, a hand on his gun. Two agents also stood outside, a forgotten cigarette raised halfway to one's mouth as he stared from Gunnar to my car. The smell of burnt rubber filled the air as I reversed—much more cautiously—to the curb in a nice, orderly parking job...facing the wrong way. I climbed out, brushing a hand through my tousled hair.

Gunnar trotted over. "What the hell is going on? You showed up like the devil himself was chasing—" He froze as my '69 Firebird skidded to a halt in the middle of the street, her throaty grumble soothing in the cool night air. Mallory leaned out the window, grinning like a teenager. "Bloody smooth lady, Master Temple! *Bloody smooth!*"

Gunnar stared from me to the old man in my car. "It's him! He was the one on the roof with us!" He stared at me, eyes still wide.

"I know. He works for me. Mallory, this is Gunnar. Gunnar, this is Mallory, the man who gave me my father's kerchief at the mausoleum." My friend looked as if his brain had shorted out. I capitalized on his moment of confusion. "You're going to love it."

His eyes snapped back to me, not comprehending. "Love what?"

"Only the best for my BF."

One of the agents burst out laughing behind us. I turned to him, smiling broadly. The other agent grunted, handing him a twenty-dollar bill. I shook my head, not understanding their transaction, and saw that Gunnar's face was beet red. "I'm sure you meant BFF, as in *Best Friend Forever*, and not BF, which means *boyfriend*." He growled, angrily glancing back at the agents.

I was quiet for a second and then burst out laughing, unable to restrain myself. After my laughter receded, I spoke louder than necessary, turning my mistake into a blade against Gunnar. "Whatever you say, sweetie. I just wanted to show you how much you mean to me." I tossed him the keys to the gleaming orange Aston Martin DBS, already walking towards the driver's seat of my own car as Mallory climbed into the passenger side.

Gunnar stared from the car to me, stunned. "For me?"

"Of course," I answered, climbing into my car. "My first act as the new president of Temple Industries."

The agents were shaking their heads in disbelief, their homophobia momentarily overcome by the sleek sports car. No doubt they would sell this information to the first reporter they could find, but I didn't care. They stepped up closer to the car, appraising her majestic curves. "You really into dudes?" one of them asked me.

"Read the tabloids and get back to me. I have somewhat of a reputation with the fairer sex." I winked, revving the engine.

The second agent chuckled. "That's putting it mildly. If I took your reputation literally I would lock my daughter away somewhere you could never find her."

I leaned out the window with a lecherous grin. "Maybe you should." His smile wavered a bit before the car regained his full attention again. "Pick me up at the Chateau in the morning, Gunnar, we have much to discuss." Then, before he could argue, Mallory and I sailed off into the night in a flurry of burning tires.

Mallory's cheeks were huffing. "You don't lead a boring life, Master Temple."

"Stick around for the next few days and you'll see just how right you are."

"My old bones won't be ready for sleep after such a thrill as this beauty," he declared, patting the dash affectionately.

I glanced at the time. "You mentioned a discussion over scotch." He gave an excited nod. "If we hurry, I know where we can find a different type of beauty to enjoy that scotch with us. She'll be more entertaining than the 50-year-old Macallan I have stashed away."

"Beauty, eh? Two ways to warm an old man's bones." He ticked off a finger for each. "A fine young lass, and Macallan. And I do feel a chill. Let's hurry." He buckled up, grinning.

15

An earthquake rattled my nightstand, the sound shredding what was left of my cerebral cortex. I managed to peel open one bloodshot eye to see that it was just my cell phone vibrating, and realized that I was in one of the guest rooms at Chateau Falco. My head pounded from the night's activities. Mallory apparently had a cast-iron stomach, and had put me to shame as he, Indie, and I shared one of my father's $17,000 bottles of Macallan Scotch. We had caught up with Indie just as she was closing up shop, and Mallory had effortlessly snookered her in to join us on our haunt.

"*I be an old man, but I amma' no dead yet. Would ye care to join us for a nightcap, my wee bonnie-lass?*" She hadn't been able to decline. We had stayed up late, sharing stories about my parents, how Mallory had been first to find their bodies and take the note from my father, his history with the family, and definitely Indie. A whole lot about Indie. Mallory had been infatuated with the stunning manager of my store, and she had eaten it up like candy. I briefly remembered vocally agreeing with Mallory on all points, enthusiastically sharing my interest in Indie, and shuddered. Had I said something I wouldn't be able to take back? Had I told her how I truly felt about her and possibly ruined our friendship?

Damn it all.

There was only one way to find out.

I seriously considered blasting my phone into oblivion, but managed a semblance of humanity, and answered. "Ow."

"Nate! You all right?" It was Gunnar, and he was—dare I say—giggling. "This car is *incredible*! You had breakfast yet?"

"Shhh..." I fumbled at the nightstand and almost knocked over a glass of water. Three Advil sat beside it.

God bless Dean.

I considered crushing the pills and snorting them. Gunnar interrupted my thought.

"I can't hear you very well. Must be the fact that I'm driving a *convertible!*" he bellowed, shattering my eardrums like a swarm of pygmies reenacting a Stomp concert in the auditorium of my skull. "I'll see you in a minute. I'm at the gate now." The sound lessened and I heard him speaking to someone else. Then, "Thanks, Dean! See you in a minute, Nate!" My phone beeped in my ear as he hung up, piercing my eardrum anew.

I fell out of bed, kneeling on the floor as I snatched up the pills and water. I guzzled them down and managed to stumble to my feet before I noticed that I was naked. The room swayed slightly, and I chuckled, realizing that I was still kind of drunk. I shambled over to a wardrobe, threw on one of the heavy robes from the closet, and carefully zigzagged my way to the bathroom. After four tries, I managed to tear open one of the packages of toothbrushes that were stored in each bathroom, and brushed my teeth from a fresh tube of AquaFresh, my favorite. I opened the door, and stretched my toes into the shag rug over the marble floor just outside the room, letting out a groan of contentment. Shuffling down the hall, I almost ran straight into Dean, who had no doubt been coming to warn me of the inbound intruder. He studied me with an amused grin. "Did Gunnar receive the gift well?" Dean asked.

"He giggled," I answered.

"Hmmm...a grown man, giggling. Inappropriate." He turned his back on me, clapping his hands together like Zeus casting twin thunderbolts. "Breakfast is served in the main kitchen!" he bellowed loud enough for all of St. Louis to hear. I heard a feminine grunt from the room next to me, and then a *thud* as said someone fell out of her bed. I smiled, glad that I wasn't the only one still intoxicated. Then Indie began laughing.

The door burst open beside me and Indie flew out of the room in a drunken stumble, eyes glowing brightly as she bumped into me. She wore only a silk robe, and it was apparently very, very cold in her room, according to the little protrusions threatening to tear the silk covering her chest. Her bare feet arched as she stretched out, wrapping her arms over my shoulders and collapsing into me for a totally indecent hug. She leaned back, still holding on, and beamed up at me. Her breath smelled of fresh mint, and she had washed her face. Her soft, wavy hair tickled my neck. I needed a cold shower, stat.

"That was so much fun! You've been holding out on me, Nate. We should do it again some time." I spied Dean squinting at me in disapproval from the staircase, as if I was contemplating corrupting Indie's virtue in the hallway.

I cleared my throat, and patted her back neutrally. "Too true." I glanced back at the stairs but Dean had already left. "Are you still...a little drunk?" She nodded, grinning wider. I brushed a hand through my hair. "Good. I hoped it wasn't just me. They should put a warning label on that bottle."

"I'd do it again. In a heartbeat." Still pressed against me, she patted my chest with her hand, mimicking my heartbeat. "Thump-thump," she said, giggling. She curiously fingered my dragon tooth necklace with a frown, but didn't say anything about it. "Let's go eat!" She dragged me down the stairs bodily, never letting go of my hand. Her eyes roamed her surroundings as we walked. "This place is so beautiful! Why do you live at the loft when you have *this*?"

I shrugged, catching her as we both stumbled and almost knocked over a priceless vase. She laughed, and then danced forward a few steps, spinning in a cute pirouette with her hands above her head. I jumped forward to catch her again as she almost fell. She stared up at me for several moments, complete trust filling her eyes. Neither of us turned away; we just stared. "Always there to catch me…" She raised a hand to brush my cheek affectionately, her fingers as smooth as the silk hiding her nudity. "But who do you have to catch you, Nate?" Her eyes grew sad, almost misty.

"Me strong. Need no help," I growled in a caveman voice as I tugged her back up.

She shook her head with a smile. "Maybe, but it doesn't always have to be that way. You deserve the world, boss." With a wink, she tugged me ahead again, leading me into the kitchen to find Dean serving three plates of eggs and bacon onto the large table. A fire was roaring in the fireplace, making the air toasty and warm. Indie's frozen form slowly thawed, much to my disappointment.

I wondered if I was reading too much into our drunken dance through the halls, or if I was really too obtuse to see it any sooner than now. Did Indie care for me, too? She tugged my hand to a nearby chair, plopping herself down with a grin. Her hair was a mess, but she somehow managed to look alluring, a natural beauty, nothing like the magazine covers. Her beauty was pure. I found myself glancing at her often. I noticed that the top of her robe hung loose, revealing an impressive expanse of rounded bosom. I felt her eyes turn to me and I quickly looked away. She stretched her arms above her head with an amused grin as she stared me in the eyes, knowingly. My face grew heated.

"How is Mallory?" Indie asked Dean, still smiling at me.

Dean glanced over a shoulder, slapping a kitchen towel over his neck. "He was up an hour ago, going to the gym, if I recall correctly."

Our jaws dropped in unison. He was working out? We were still tipsy, and he was working out. He was like eighty-years-old. Indie turned to me with raised eyebrows. I shrugged. "Bon appetite." I shoveled a fork in my mouth, groaning at the pleasant taste. I heard a chime, and Dean glanced down at his phone.

He punched something on the screen, and then spoke. "Come in, Agent Randulf. Just follow the lighted path, and you'll find us in the kitchen. I set out a plate for you." He typed a rapid staccato on his phone, no doubt illuminating the correct lights to guide Gunnar to the food.

I could vaguely see the video chat on the phone. "Thanks, Dean. I'll be right there." Dean clicked off the phone, and tucked it back into his pocket.

Gunnar appeared a few minutes later. "Hey, Nat—" He halted, seeing Indie. "And the plot thickens…" he said with a wide grin. "Good morning, Indie. I didn't realize you were occupied, Nate. I don't want to intrude on your breakfast." He was barely hiding his smile as he noticed Indie's silk robe, and my own heavier robe. She grinned wide, turning to face me expectantly.

"We had a few drinks last night. I mean, not just *us*. Mallory was there, too."

Gunnar grinned. "Oh? Where is Mallory now?"

Indie continued smiling, remaining silent as she glanced back and forth, egging Gunnar's false assumption on. "He's at the gym." I realized how lame it sounded after I spoke. "Shut up and sit down, Gunnar. Or leave. Whichever is fastest." He chuckled and sat down, sweeping up the third plate without shame.

Indie kept the guilty smile on her face, leaving me to the wolves. Or wolf, in this case. "How have you been, Gunnar?" Indie asked, immediately followed by a full body hiccup that didn't go unnoticed by any of the present males.

"I've been good, Indie. And you?"

"Great! We had such a fun time last night. We sampled some delicious scotch…well, more than sampled, I guess." She giggled at him, and Gunnar smiled back.

"Nate knows how to have a good time. Too much so sometimes, but he's a good man. He's lucky to have a friend like you around to keep him out of trouble."

She nodded, serious. "I know." They shared a smile.

"Thanks for that, Dr. Phil. You almost finished?" I growled.

Gunnar apparently wasn't. "So, moving on up, huh?" He waved a fork at the house in general.

"Part of the package deal from the surprise Last Will and Testament read to me last night. The same package that got you your new car." Gunnar nodded, a mixture of sadness at the reason, but mild happiness at the result. "I'll explain later," I said as he opened his mouth to ask another question. He nodded, tearing into his plate hungrily.

We ate in silence, the two of them grinning often, but remaining silent. I stood, set Indie's empty plate atop mine, and attempted to carry them to the sink. Dean swept past me like a shadow, snatching up the plates with a frown, and continued on to the sink, looking offended. He took his job very seriously.

Gunnar stood but Dean was faster, snatching up the plate with a derisive sniff. Gunnar merely shook his head, grinning. "Thanks. Ready when you are, Nate."

"Good. Let's saddle up. I'm just going to grab my things from upstairs." I wobbled, quickly regaining my balance. The food was helping, but I still felt the lingering effects of the nightcap. Wait, plural nightcaps.

"I need to change, too. I'll walk with you upstairs," Indie said.

Gunnar rolled his eyes; amused at implications only another man could derive from the statement. "Meet me out front when you're…finished."

Before I could hit him, he left through a different hallway, leaving Indie and me to walk upstairs in peace. Indie tucked an arm through mine, supporting herself, or me, I wasn't sure. After a few minutes, she spoke. "Nate…I had a wonderful time last night." I murmured my agreement and she smiled. "Thank you for letting me spend some private time with you. It meant the world to me. Ever since I started working for you, it's been harder and harder for me to make friends outside of the crew at Plato's Cave, and to them I am merely an authority figure. I work and then go home. It was nice to get out and have fun with…you."

"But you had a hot date planned," I argued.

"A lie," she answered softly. "I've seen too many weird things since meeting you to go on dates with Regular guys." And that was true. She had seen me do magic, and had spent time around some of the more dangerous private clients I dealt with. The curtain had been pulled back for Indie, revealing some truths about the world that would definitely make it difficult to cope in mundane normalcy, and I was only just now beginning to ponder those consequences she must be facing. "To be honest, I haven't been able to find anyone who really interests me enough to spend time with. I really enjoy working for you. But it's more than the secrets you keep. I think it's just you." She slowed to a stop in front of her room, not letting go. "I guess that I'm trying to say that you are probably the best friend I have. I don't want to push you or anything, but just know that I'm here for you. Always. In whatever capacity that you need. Whether as a friend, a confidant, or..." Her deep eyes studied me intently, her silence speaking volumes.

This was a line I had never thought we would cross. Indie was a knockout, and one of the most brilliant women I had ever met. Aside from appreciating both her beauty, and cunning skills as my store manager, I had forced myself to maintain a professional distance. "Is that why you let Gunnar think what he thought?" I asked softly.

She thought for a moment. "Maybe. Maybe not. He approved of his assumption, approved of *me* with *you*. That was a very special thing for me to realize. But on the other hand, my denial would have merely served to confirm his assumption anyway. So, I remained silent. It felt...nice." Her eyes crinkled in thought. "Like Gunnar said, you really are a great man, Nate. One of the last. I just want you to know that I have never felt about another man the way I feel about you. I...adore you, and couldn't imagine not having you in my life. It's hard to talk at work without sending the wrong impression. You have everything, but just know that you could have nothing and my feelings would remain the same. I'm lucky to have you as a friend."

"And I, you," I answered honestly.

She smiled. Then she leaned close on tiptoes, and kissed my cheek, holding her warm, soft lips against my skin for longer than necessary. "Thank you, Nate." My body reacted on its own, and I pulled her in close. She didn't resist. We stared at each other from inches away, tasting each other's breath. My heart raced wildly, my brain trying to logically sort my emotions. I found myself leaning closer, her silk-encased torso pliant against my desire. I knew, beyond a shadow of a doubt, that she craved my touch in a not so professional manner, and I craved to be touched by someone who actually knew me and cared for me. She was genuine—a rare find. Others saw the Temple heir, but Indie saw Nate. Just Nate. Her skin was hot beneath my fingertips, and her breathing grew deeper as she studied my face.

"Oh, Indie..." I whispered, my fingers shaking as they pulled her closer. "This is a line that cannot be uncrossed..." I began.

"Cross it if you wish it." Her pupils dilated with honest lust. "But know that you can have me however you desire. I know your heart better than anyone, Nate. You live a lonely life. I only want to see you smile. I only want to *make* you smile…"

I leaned in, resting my forehead against hers as I closed my eyes. I felt her lips softly brush mine as she whimpered delicately, her skin on fire now.

Then my fucking phone vibrated in the other room.

We both jumped back instinctively, my heart thudding with adrenaline as if a bucket of ice water had suddenly been dumped over my head. Then, in a twirl of silk, Indie skipped into her room, pausing at the threshold. "Think about it, Nate. I've made myself clear, I believe, and I am not ashamed to say it. Not to you. Never to you." She smiled coyly, untying her silk robe, and letting the two halves separate slightly, revealing an unbelievably toned torso. Her grin stretched as my genitals threatened to mutiny against my still-ringing phone.

"We'll talk. Soon," I promised. I took a step towards her door, trying not to look away from her eyes. I pressed my car keys into her soft hands, squeezing them closed. "Take my car. I can pick it up later. Can I do anything else for you before I leave?" Her eyebrows lifted as her gaze swept over my body from head to foot, and then to her own scantily clad frame, before returning with a hungry twinkle.

"Do you really want me to answer that, Cap'n?"

"Right. Time for me to leave before I fall victim to your feminine wiles."

"One must use the weapons available to her." She smiled.

I turned, instincts screaming against me, and I heard her sigh softly behind me. I glanced over my shoulder in time to see her robe billow to the floor of the hall, and her naked silhouette slowly strut out of sight as she went deeper into her room to change. I almost walked clear past my room. I glanced at the phone, and saw that it was Plato's Cave. I listened to the voicemail on speakerphone as I began to change, and a roiling ball of ice slowly built up in my stomach as the words crashed home.

"Nate, it's Jessie." The new employee Indie had hired. "I don't know how to say this, but…" He took a deep, nervous breath on the other end of the line before blurting out in a rush of forced air. "The shop was broken into last night. They did a number on your loft, but the rest of the store seems okay. Books were tossed from shelves, but I don't think anything is missing from the store. The third theater room wasn't broken into either. The cops are here. You should be, too. Call me when you're on your way, I guess." Then he hung up.

The dragons were playing hardball now. I sat down on the edge of the bed, wondering if they had broken into the store in pursuit of their precious book. If they thought I already had it they were grossly mistaken, but at least they thought highly of me. It was something to remember, a card to exploit later. Another thought hit me a second later. What if I hadn't picked up Indie last night? A chill ran down my spine at the possibility of her being kidnapped and used as leverage against me. If the dragons wanted an angry wizard, I would give them the angel of the Apocalypse. I finished changing, rounded up all my things, and flew down the stairs to meet Gunnar, trying to focus on anything other than Indie and my fucking shop.

Indie's scent remained close, replacing the last fog of the drink from last night with an altogether new high. A whole-body high. The high of future possibilities.

16

Gunnar grinned as he drove. "So," he began. "Indie looked pretty good. She also looked tired. You keep her up all night?" His beefy hands massaged his new leather steering wheel.

"You like the car?"

He shot me a stupid smile.

"Interesting, because they haven't sent out the title yet. One phone call, and I put the car in my name instead of yours. One teeny-weenie phone call, and your dream car becomes my demolition derby car. I'll drive it off a cliff and send you the *YouTube* video."

Gunnar grumbled back, but kept the smile on his face. "Fine. Just asking."

I watched the shop windows fly by past the car, still feeling on cloud nine from Indie's touch. "I think she likes me."

Gunnar scoffed. "And I thought you were a genius. You really are an idiot sometimes, Nate. Of course, she likes you. She's worked for you for, what, five years now? She's not staying around for the health benefits. More like possible fringe benefits."

"The health benefits are completely free to my employees."

"Oh, well maybe she is staying for the benefits, then."

"Forget it. Let's get back to business. We need to swing by my shop."

He frowned. "Why?"

"It was broken into and tossed last night."

His grip on the steering wheel creaked. "What?" he demanded in a low growl.

"I got a message from Jessie while I was changing. The cops are there."

Gunnar swerved across incoming traffic to take us to the shop. We drove in a brittle silence, both furious and nervous at the implications of dragons breaking into my shop.

He didn't even need to ask who it was. We both knew it was the stinking reptiles. Then a thought crossed his face. "Do all your employees have their paperwork in order? They're all packing, right?"

I waved a hand, looking out the window as we turned onto my street and I saw my shop swarming with flashing red and blue lights. "They're set. Don't worry."

He parked a safe distance away and we climbed out into unusually warm autumn air. My heels pounded into the now dry sidewalk as I prowled up to the caution tape surrounding my shop and home. I glanced at the surrounding rooftops, hoping to see a dragon that I could blow to smithereens. Nothing.

We halted as a cop held up an instinctive hand at our approach, not even looking at us. "Sorry, this is a crime scene. No shopping today." I didn't move; staring at his badge, imagining all sorts of frightening magic I could use to get his attention. Then I recognized him as the young cop who had been standing outside the interrogation room two nights ago, and grinned. Perfect. Before I could scare the bejeezus out of him a second time, Gunnar whipped out his badge. The rookie turned to us, then, and his jaw dropped as he all but leapt back a step upon seeing my smiling face. "M-master Temple! My God. Where have you been? Never mind. Get in there. The Captain wants to speak with you."

"I take that to mean Kosage?" The rookie nodded nervously. I stared into his eyes until he began to squirm, and then whispered in a dramatic voice as we ducked under the caution tape. "Thanks for the coffee." His legs all but quivered as I glanced back at him, wiping his forehead with his sleeve. I briefly wondered what he thought about the display of magic in the interrogation room the other night, but the thought evaporated as I stepped inside Plato's Cave.

Cops milled around everywhere, taking pictures and sipping coffee from my coffee bar, probably not even paying for it. Damn the pigs. The shop was a mess, but not nearly so bad as it had been after Raven's visit. I chided myself for not setting the wards last night when we had picked up Indie. Then I saw him. Our eyes locked together at the same time, but mine tightened in anger.

"Kosage. What happened?" I hissed, as if blaming him for the invasion.

"Ah, Master Temple. Nice to see you again. As you can see, your shop was broken into. It seems they just broke through the tempered glass window, which was quite a feat given their makeup. They practically would have had to shoot it in, but no one reported gunshots. I take it you live in the loft upstairs?" He asked, flicking his eyes up above. I nodded. He flipped open a small notepad. "Where were you last night between the hours of two and three in the morning?"

"At Chateau Falco."

"Can anyone vouch for that?"

I leveled my hooded wizard eyes down on him, pointedly mocking his short, delicate stature. "You've already tried that angle, Kosage. Be very careful. Don't dare accuse me without solid evidence." My threat rolled off his back like water on a duck.

"Speaking of *that angle*, it seems my notes were mistaken from our previous discussion." He flipped a page. Then another. "I quote. *I have nothing to do with my parents' company*. Seems that's changed now, hasn't it?" my eyes were coals, but he continued on. "Any known enemies who might have wanted to steal from you?"

I hesitated, sensing Gunnar's apprehension. "No. But I do have some very pricy merchandise. Was anything stolen?"

"Your employees are checking the inventory as we speak. But so far it seems like nothing was taken, although they put up one hell of a search."

I nodded, thankful they hadn't tried breaking into the third theater. My secrets would be over if they had succeeded in opening that door.

Kosage closed his pad, lifting his eyes. "We should be finished shortly. We haven't found any smoking gun, so to speak. And all your employees' paperwork for their firearms are up to date, so there isn't really anything else we can do. Do you have anything to add that might aid us?"

I glanced around the store, sensing all eyes on us. After a few seconds, I shook my head. "Nothing."

Kosage assessed me for a few seconds, but then shrugged. "Thank you, Master Temple." He began to turn away, but stopped. "I see you are spending time with the FBI. Might I ask in what regards?"

Gunnar's hackles raised territorially, but I spoke instead. "You may not."

"Interesting. I think we'll be keeping our eyes on you over the next few days. For your own safety, of course." His smile was slimy. "Parents murdered, making you the new CEO of Temple Industries, which you seemed to lie to me about. Bookstore broken into while you are conspicuously absent, but nothing stolen. Escaping handcuffs without permission. Arguable assault when you departed the interrogation room. And playing with the FBI, but..." he looked me up and down. "No credentials to that effect. Those things could give you some trouble down the road, Master Temple. There's already blood in the water. No point in thrashing about."

"I think your work here is done. Pack up. Now." He turned to look at me then, a hint of anger in his eyes at the loss of face in front of his men. I smiled.

"You heard him, men. Pack up." He slowly turned to face me, clasping his hands behind his back. "I've got my eyes on you, Temple. If I hear even one whisper of your name at another crime scene, things will get ugly. And I know just the judge to call. I believe you met him last night." His smile stretched wide at my reaction.

"Make sure you wear your high heels if you want to step onto my level," I smiled politely. His face morphed into a murderous scowl before he left.

My employees slowly materialized from around the store, watching me carefully as if they felt that they had somehow failed me. "You were all hired for your unique qualities, your ability to roll with the punches. Show that to me now, and get this place up and running within the hour. Business as usual."

"Aye, aye, Cap'n!" they crowed, soothed by my subtle compliment.

"Anyone seen Jessie?" I asked aloud after a few seconds.

"He left after he called you. Had to get to class or something," I heard someone answer. I grunted.

"Alright. I need to head out with Gunnar. You guys got it from here?" The only answer was the bustle of work as they began cleaning up the store like a team of pixies. "Oh, and can one of you call that window guy again?" Someone laughed before answering an affirmative. Then I whisked out the door with Gunnar on my heels.

"Nothing fazes you, does it?" he asked as we climbed into his car.

"It wouldn't change anything. I've heard that you can either choose to smile or cry about problems, but either way, it doesn't change the fact that they still happened."

He was silent for a spell as he pulled out into the street. "Wise words. Who told you that?"

I smiled as I stared out the window. "Some Amway guy." The buildings whizzed past me, threatening my unsettled stomach. The cops would now be breathing down my neck at every turn. And the dragons had crossed a very dangerous line. It was time to take off the gloves. "Smiles and cries...either way, it doesn't change what I'm going to do to them when I see them next," I whispered.

"Within the limits of the law, of course," he said slowly. When I didn't answer, he continued. "Right, Nate?"

I traced my fingers along the magical auras drifting unseen around me, spinning them around my fingertips like a silk ribbon in the wind, imagining what horrors I could cause with my power. It felt more vibrant than usual, stronger. I shrugged noncommittally. "Sure, Gunnar. Sure…"

17

We were silent for a while as Gunnar drove, pondering the day's events. "What have you got?" I finally asked him.

Gunnar's face became stony. "I had a technician run the kerchief. It was human blood, and it was a match to your father. He had his blood on file from the...murder."

I nodded, letting out a heavy breath. I hadn't doubted it, but it was still a lot to take in. Gunnar handed me the kerchief sympathetically before continuing. "Well, a lot of people are coming into town for the eclipse event. All the hotels are practically full, so no luck on your dragon hunter friend."

"Plural. He said *we*. He's got friends."

"Irrelevant. Did you hear me say that every hotel is full? I need more information if you want me to find him."

I fished out the card the dragon hunter had given me. "Does this help?"

Gunnar scowled back, snatching the card from my fingers. "Tomas Mullingsworth." He blinked. "Have you tried simply calling him?"

I nodded. "Late last night. No answer. Think you can find him?"

"Yes, but you could have given me this last night, Nate."

"I was too busy buying you this Aston Martin. Want to guess how much it costs?"

"I'd rather not. Then I might feel like I'm indebted to you."

"Oh, you *are* indebted to me for this." I showed him my teeth. "Besides, I have so much going on right now that it kind of slipped my mind. I have to keep my participation in this out of the media. A request from my lawyer. And now the cops will be sniffing around my every move after the break-in." Gunnar nodded, looking pissed.

"And there's all this other stuff to focus on. I mean, Peter, a closet wizard, asks me to get him some bullshit book for a client, a dragon attacks me at my shop, then I go to my parents' funeral and receive a message from beyond the grave by a creepy old man, wizard, bodyguard, and then I was attacked *again*. And apparently, some Spiderman-wannabe has gone rogue, teaming up with these dragons, or dragon hunters." Another thought came to mind and I groaned. "And *tonight*, I'm supposed to duel with the Minotaur in some shit-infested field over a dumb book about—" My mouth went dry as I recognized the connection. Everything had happened so fast that I hadn't even thought about it. "Dragons..." I finished.

Gunnar glanced at me, making sure I was all right. "Huh. That's the kind of thing that we in the Bureau call a *clue*." He turned left at the light and continued on, the Aston Martin purring as he downshifted. "Still no idea who this client is? Or *what* he is?" I shook my head. "Seems pretty sketchy that he wants a book about dragons that is dangerous enough to warrant risking your life for, right around the time that a group of dragons is also seeking a *book*. One that they say belongs to them. One that they're willing to kill for. Then a group of dragon hunters arrive, saying they are hunting a rogue dragon." He was quiet for a moment. "How much is this book worth?"

"Fifty-thousand-dollars."

Gunnar swerved the car a bit, stripping a gear in the process. "I need a new job."

"You can fight the Minotaur if you want." I smirked.

He considered that for a moment. "I think I could take him."

My eyes widened, and then I began to laugh, deep belly laughs. It felt remarkably good after all the recent drama. "You? Take the *Minotaur*? An immortal monster? Do you have any idea how many innocents have died by his hand? Theseus was the only one to ever defeat him, and he was lucky, having help from the goddess Ariadne with her ball of thread to help him navigate the Labyrinth."

Gunnar was quiet for a time. "I'm guessing a ball of thread won't help us, right?"

I smiled. "No. No it won't. But then again, he's Buddhist now, so maybe we'll just have a nice political debate or something."

"Probably not, Nate."

"Yeah. Probably not." I had no idea how I was going to fight the Minotaur. I had magic out the Wahoo, but Asterion knew that, and was probably ready for it. I was just going to have to wing it. This book could give me answers about my parents, or my kid client might know something. Either way, I had to win. That settled, I took several deep meditative breaths, trying to banish my anxiety. The sound of Gunnar's scanner going off with a squawk almost made me jump out of my skin. "I think I just peed a little," I said, glancing down at the seat. "Not a lot."

Gunnar shook his head. "Gross." He fiddled with the radio, hit a button, and then spoke. "Agent Randulf, here."

Gunnar's boss answered, voice garbled. "Looks like you got another one just over the river. Owner found dead this morning after the neighbors heard a loud ruckus last night." Gunnar sighed wearily, and asked for the address. Reinhardt gave the store name, and forwarded the address to Gunnar's GPS unit. It blinked at us a few seconds later, instantly blaring directions at us in a feminine English accent.

"Alright. I can get there..." he smiled. "Pretty fast." He down shifted the car with a metal click, and the engine tried to tear free from the frame as we launched around an old blue-hair driving in front of us. Agent Reinhardt signed off with some jumbled response that couldn't be heard over the engine.

"It's just over the river," I noted, watching the GPS. "In Illinois."

Gunnar's teeth showed through the smile. "Which is what the FBI calls *jurisdiction*. This is the second attack across state lines, confirming our authority. We can kick the local police out easily this time." He looked over at me. "Which is a good thing, considering Kosage's got a hard-on for busting you. I wonder what you did to piss him off so much..." he trailed off, curiously.

I chuckled. "I spilled his coffee in the interrogation room."

Gunnar rolled his eyes, not believing a word of it. "I'm sure that was it." I leaned back in the seat, enjoying the G-force pull of the car as Gunnar broke every speed limit sign we passed. Street signs blurred past, then Interstate signs, and then I was staring out at the Mississippi river as the rails of the bridge whizzed past me.

My phone rang in my pocket. I plucked it out, glancing at the screen. Peter. "Just the man I wanted to talk to," I answered, reproachfully. Gunnar scowled silently.

"Yeah, listen. We should probably talk. You free now? I wanted to talk to you about that book." The line was quiet for a moment. "I think I wrote down the wrong title."

"No time now, I'm running errands with my new chauffeur." Gunnar's knuckles cracked on the steering wheel in disapproval.

"Oh. Well, where are you? Maybe I could meet you?"

I glanced out the window. "Not likely. Heading into Illinois to talk to someone near the warehouses just over the Eads Bridge."

There was a silence on the phone. "Okay. How about tonight? At the Cave?"

"Sure." I glanced at my watch, thinking of my schedule with Asterion, and then if I survived, the book exchange with my client. I also wanted to swing by the Expo Center to see if anything seemed off at the eclipse convention that was starting tonight, like maybe a group of dragons murdering the attendees. Maybe I could squeeze Peter between everything. If I wasn't dead. "How about nine? I might be a few minutes late."

Peter answered quickly. "Sure, sure. Just leave the security down so I can wait inside. It will be cold outside tonight."

"Fun fact. Seeing as how I know magic, I seem to recall a way for the cold not to bother you. Just a simple spell for a *wizard* to teach another *wizard*. Might be something that, if I were just learning how to use magic, I would have sought out another wizard to teach me," I growled.

"I know, I know. We have a lot to discuss. My client is really pestering me about this stupid book. He'll pay whatever you wish," he added the last quickly. He didn't realize that money was no longer a motivator for me. Looking at the sticky notes attached to the cards I had been given had surprised even me. That many zeroes made things confusing.

I hesitated before speaking the truth. "What's the new title? I have to know that if you want me to help you. And how much is it worth?" I asked curiously. Having studied his note yesterday, I had soon found that I already owned a copy of the unremarkable book at Plato's Cave. It was even in my personal collection in the loft, not downstairs in the shop. But now he had fudged the title. Nothing was ever easy.

He paused, speaking into the background. "High five-figures." I repeated his answer aloud. In the span of a week, I could make six-figures by selling two books. Gunnar grunted in disbelief, shaking his head. "I'll tell you the title tonight."

"Okay..." I frowned. "You realize I can't find something if I don't know what it's called, right?" Peter sighed on the other end. "And I'm not doing anymore favors until we have a nice long chat about your new ice cube making ability," I added.

I could feel Peter tense on the other end. "Okay, okay. See you at nine."

I hung up. We drove on in silence, Gunnar glancing at me now and then, but saying nothing. So far, I had accounted for two of the three books that had been requested of me. Now, just one, thanks to Peter's inability to write down the correct title of the book his client wanted. It should be simple enough to find though. If it was in any way similar to the original request. The important one was the odd book the Raven lady had asked me about, *Sons of the Dying Sun*. I pondered several possible sources, my mind distant from the sounds of traffic trying to avoid the British sports car. But that book would have to wait until after my duel with Asterion.

"Is that the first time you've talked to Peter since...?" He waved a hand at the air, implying the attack two nights ago. I nodded. "What do you think it means?" he asked carefully. "Wouldn't you have known a long time ago if he had..." he searched for a word, "the ability?"

I looked over at him, thinking. "Perhaps." I turned back to the window, feeling his eyes on me. "But perhaps not. It's not exactly a science. Some come into it early, with training and foreknowledge, like me. With others, it might take a traumatic experience for it to manifest." I was silent for a minute, thinking hard for an explanation. "Have you heard those stories about mothers who were suddenly able to lift a car off their trapped child? Or those who survive an un-survivable accident, and have no idea why? Most often, those are people like Peter apparently is. It hits them all of a sudden, and they don't quite understand it. Then they normally hide from it, unable to explain what they remember, because they don't want to sound crazy."

Gunnar stared hard through the windshield, cutting off a motorcycle with a sharp swerve. "But Peter didn't seem too surprised by his reaction."

"No," I said softly, growing angry. "No, he didn't. Which either means that he already knew or that he's much more cool-headed than we thought. Since being around us his whole life, maybe it was an awakening for him. He had wanted it for so long, and then, suddenly, there it was. He was no longer the outcast. He was just like us. Maybe his joy overrode his shock."

Gunnar spoke as we exited the highway into a seedy warehouse district just off the bridge. "It seemed more like the former to me. Cool-headed doesn't sound like Peter." I nodded, fury barely contained. "But then why didn't he come to you? I mean, you are one scary, talented wizard, and he never told you." His words trailed off as he waited for me to speak. I remained silent, anticipating our *talk* tonight. I would get my answers then.

Gunnar drove through a warren of dilapidated warehouses, glancing at the GPS every few seconds for our turnoff. A large truck pulled out in front of us, laden with construction rubble, and a smeared, dented sign that read NOT RESPONSIBLE FOR FALLING DEBRIS. Gunnar was glancing down when the back of the truck suddenly flew open. I yelled and Gunnar slammed on the brakes by reflex, then he saw the contents, and we both hesitated.

Stone gargoyles filled the back of the truck, but it continued moving down the street, blocking us from passing him. The driver must not have realized that the door had come loose. Gunnar swerved to the side, trying to get the driver's attention in his side mirror. The driver must have remained aloof to our honking, because Gunnar cursed and pulled back behind the truck, resigned to follow behind him until our turn.

We were still going the speed limit when I thought I saw one of the gargoyle statues move.

18

I leaned forward, holding my breath as I studied the huddle of lifeless gargoyles staring at us from the back of the truck. They were all demonic statues of some kind, but were each subtly different. Some had wings, and some bore weapons, or massive claws. But none moved.

As I began to relax, one of them blinked, turning its hideous head to stare straight into my eyes amidst a puff of dust and crumbling gravel that cascaded down its torso. "No fucking way," I whispered, my forearms pebbling.

Gunnar looked over at me. "We'll pass this schmuck in a minute or so, and then we can get to the crime scene," he said, attempting to sooth my impatience.

I shook my head and pointed. "The gargoyles. They're alive."

One of the gargoyle statues snapped out its wings, and Gunnar jolted as if he had been Tasered. "What the hell?" he exclaimed, slowing down. The gargoyle shook out its wings. Then it turned to look directly at us, curious. Gunnar went still. "Nate...?"

"I know, I know! I'm thinking!" I argued, keeping my eyes on the waking statues. It looked like someone had raided the wrong house, getting more than they bargained for. These statues weren't planning on staying in the garden for the owner's pleasure. I tried to recall everything I knew about gargoyles. I remembered that they could wake, but only for short bursts, turning back and forth from life to stone for mere seconds at a time, but only if they were strong. Really strong. Which explained the stories about people waking up the next morning and swearing that their statues were in a different spot than the night before. And it usually had to be night for them to have the kind of power needed to do so. Or if something traumatic had happened to them. Like suddenly being moved from their home. Shit. My hopes were that these statues would look around a bit, and then turn back to stone. Content. Not angry and vengeful. Yeah, right.

"Just stay calm. Don't do anything to startle them. Don't slow down, and don't speed up. Since we're staying the same distance away from them, they might just fall back asleep."

Gunnar nodded slowly, shifting only his eyes to me. "Okay. You're taking this pretty calmly. Has this kind of thing happened to you a time or two?"

I nodded. "At Notre Dame. But that was at night when they are known to have enough power to wake. I've never seen one come to life in daylight. It's kind of against the rules. Things can be believed at night, explained away as just a trick of the dark. Day time makes it all too obvious, and we Freaks need our secrecy."

"You're preaching to the choir. But how are they awake now, then?"

I explained my theory about a traumatic shift in their home, but even I wasn't so sure. These gargoyles hadn't fallen back asleep yet, and a couple more woke up while we were talking, flexing long-unused muscles. "What are the odds of this many bad things coincidentally happening to you in such a short span of time?" he asked.

"Not high." Another statue woke in a crack of stone and dust. They began looking at each other curiously, silent conversations traveling between their eyes as if asking *so, now what?* Several of them began to smile as if they had an idea. "Technically, a wizard could raise them, but he would either have to be close, very powerful, or have some kind of tie to these specific statues. I haven't heard of any wizards on this side of the river, but I guess I can't discount the possibility…"

As one, all of the statues turned to stare at us, cocking their heads like a cat spotting a laser pointer on the floor. Another gargoyle's wings snapped out, knocking the head clean off of one of the others. Okay, friendly fire was a good thing. "If nothing startles them, then they should just fall back asleep. I think. Just keep pace with the truck." Gunnar nodded, focused on a goal.

Then the truck swerved abruptly, and the driver honked his horn furiously as a car cut across the intersection just ahead of him. The gargoyles crouched, reacting defensively. We hadn't seen any other cars on this street, so the statues focused on the only sign of life near them.

Us.

I could see the hatred as they stared at us, and then they leapt out of the moving truck, landing in the street like a group of paratroopers in a war zone—eyes wary, and claws out. Gunnar swerved as one of the gargoyles drew a club strapped to his back and swung it at our car. The tip of the stone club screeched down the passenger side of the vehicle. "I am *definitely* going to sue that driver!" Gunnar bellowed.

"You can't. His truck said that he wasn't responsible for falling debris." Gunnar turned murderous eyes on me. I almost yelled for Gunnar to floor it so that we could get away, but then I thought about these monsters loose in the city, left to do as they pleased. "Gunnar, stop the car! We have to stop them!"

He pulled the emergency brake, spinning the car in a 180-degree turn so that we were facing the huddle of gargoyles. "Damn it, Nate! How the hell are we supposed to fight them?" He wasn't scared, just genuinely asking what we were supposed to do. "I won't damage my car by running over them." He folded his arms defiantly. I rolled my eyes. Drama Queen.

"The heads. I think if we can take the heads, they'll become inanimate again," I said, mind racing.

Gunnar cocked his SIG Sauer and climbed out of the car. Before they could move, his gun roared, blowing the head off the one with the club. I arched an eyebrow at him. "He scratched my car," Gunnar growled.

"My mother always said that a pistol is the Devil's right hand." I grinned. Gunnar smiled back, showing teeth.

Then they began to break up, moving on us like well-trained predators. But they weren't expecting a wizard and a werewolf to crash their party. They were just looking for a little entertainment. If I had my way, the entertainment would be completely one-sided, leaving only a whole truckload of gravel behind.

I suddenly had an idea. Something my parents had briefly taught me, but that I had never actually toyed with on my own. I guess this would have to count. I yelled to Gunnar. "Cover me, but no matter what you see, make sure you don't shoot me!"

Knowing my penchant for odd statements, Gunnar just nodded, popping off a few more shots at one of the more demonic-looking gargoyles. I took a deep breath, and instantly found the calm reservoir of power deep inside me. It actually helped clear my head a bit from the hangover. I waded into that power like it was a hot spring, allowing the tension to ease out of my muscles. I knew it took only seconds, but in my mind, it felt like an hour. Once relaxed, I began drawing that reservoir into me, through me, and then projected it over my skin in stone armor, doubling up over the most vulnerable areas. It was easier than I remembered. My skin felt like ice as the armor encased every section of my body, efficiently transforming me into a mobile, rock version of myself—Gargoyle Nate.

Once satisfied, I opened my eyes back to the real world. The gargoyles had taken no more than a few steps. Gunnar was efficiently picking off legs and heads where he could, but I knew it wouldn't be enough. There were close to a dozen of them. I glanced down at my stone hands in wonderment, twisting them this way and that.

To any passerby, I most likely looked like a human statue. Except that I wore clothes, and I could move. Neat, huh? I felt like a mannequin, and I knew that if I looked into a mirror, my face would still be there, but cast in stone. I could move without impediment, but with this armor I could take just about as much damage as one could dish out, but each hit tore off some of that shielding, so it was only temporary.

I turned to look at Gunnar. His eyes shot wide as he looked from me to the statues, and then he began to laugh. "That is so cool! Why do you bitch about my power when you can do *that*?" he asked, cracking off another shot to send one of the gargoyles down permanently.

I shrugged and turned back to the gaggle of gargoyles with a grin of my own. "Play with me?" I asked one who was warily approaching me, unsure whether I was ally or foe. It cocked its head in confusion. I reached out, grabbed its throat, and crushed the stone in my fist. The head toppled to the ground with a heavy thud. I pointed at one of the winged gargoyles. "You're next." The gargoyle let out a dusty roar, wings snapping out as if preparing to fly away.

Not today.

I rushed the gargoyle, batting down one of its wings as it crouched to take to the air. The wing shattered under my fist, knocking the beast off balance, then I punched it straight in the nose, knocking it clean off. The gargoyle stumbled, preparing to defend itself, but I kicked it in the chest so hard that its head flew off from the abrupt whiplash. The body skidded into the last few gargoyles, knocking them down like bowling pins. "Strike!" I roared.

Gunnar's gun blasted until two straggler gargoyles died at his feet. He was panting as he jogged towards me. I didn't wait. I dove into the pile of gargoyles like a wrestler, trapping a leg here, an arm there, until I found a hold. An arm bar tore off its appendage completely, and then I punched its throat until I felt pavement on the other side. A blow to the side of my head made me see stars for a few seconds, and then Gunnar's gun blasted off the sucker-punching gargoyle's head from only inches away. My ears rang, and I could feel some of the stone sliding off my face where I had been hit, leaving naked, vulnerable skin underneath. Gunnar noticed immediately.

"We need to finish this fast, before your armor fades completely." I nodded back, but was picked up in a bear hug from behind. I kicked out with my heel and connected with the gargoyle's knee, shattering it so that he fell down. As my feet touched ground again, I angled my head to protect the soft skin, and head-butted his nose with the back of my skull. He fell back immediately, tottering on his one good leg. I turned, crouched, and superman tackled him down to the ground. Gunshots continued as I pummeled the statue until only dust remained of his neck.

All was silent. I looked up to see Gunnar scanning the area. "I think that's all of them," he said. "But we need to get out of here before someone shows up and starts asking questions. I'll tell the cops that we drove by here when we heard the shots, but saw only broken statues in the road. Can you do something about your...appearance?" he asked with a wry grin.

I nodded, climbing to my feet as more pieces of the armor slid off of their own accord. With little effort, the rest of the armor began cascading down my body like falling roof tiles, crashing to the road in piles of slate. After a few seconds, I could feel the wind on my skin again, and rubbed it for warmth. The stone armor had been cold. I was now covered in dust like some vagrant homeless person. "I might get your car a little dirty."

Gunnar shrugged. "Nothing to be done about that." He checked the car for damage, but other than the first scratch, it was surprisingly unharmed. As we pulled out,

Gunnar spoke. "That wasn't too bad. But it's too much to be a coincidence." He paused, face thoughtful. "Someone is gunning for us, but the question is who? The dragons?"

I nodded. It was either the dragons or there was a third player in the game. Gunnar was right. It was just too unlikely to be a coincidence, but I couldn't imagine who else it could be, or why they would use such an obscure way to take us out. I mean, they were dragons. Why wouldn't they just eat us? Or burn us? Gunnar interrupted my thoughts.

"This might be a bad scene, Nate. You up for it?" I grunted affirmation, watching the warehouses pass by us as Gunnar finally found our destination. We pulled into a parking spot just outside a trio of flashing police cars.

"Put on your party dress. It seems all the boys showed up for this one. Let's crash the ball, shall we?" I said. Gunnar grinned, opening his door, and strutting like a peacock as no less than a dozen Illinois police stared open-jawed at the brilliant Aston Martin parked just outside the tape. The severe contrast of such a specimen in such a seedy district was perfectly satisfying.

"It's nice having a billionaire as a friend, you know that?" he laughed. With a nod, we strode towards the barricade like gods among men. At least, that's what Gunnar looked like. I hoped to establish the same sense of self-confidence as I followed behind him, covered in dust and gravel. A billionaire vagrant for a friend, more like it.

19

We were quickly past the horde of police officers and into the shop, thanks in no small part to the fear of uncertainty behind their eyes as they glanced from the towering Norwegian FBI werewolf in their midst, to the gleaming sports car parked a dozen yards ahead of them, to the dusty and dirty celebrity billionaire civilian in tow. They lifted the tape for us to enter. "Need backup, Agent Randulf? It's pretty...disturbing."

"Not necessary. Give us a few moments in private." The store was in shambles. Paperback and buckram books decorated the floor, torn open to leave loose pages lying about like the useless guts of an eviscerated animal. Fury smoldered deep down inside my stomach, as if I were looking at heaps of dead children lying about the room instead. Books *were* my children. It was sacrilegious.

Hundreds of spiny, silver needles covered the scene, as if a dozen chrome porcupines had exploded in a last act of martyrdom against the written word. Glancing about, I noticed that the needles were embedded into the walls, bookshelves, tables, and even through one of the side windowpanes, shattering glass out onto the street. Kneeling, I spotted faint droplets of blood on some of their tips.

Gunnar was still, scanning the small shop from the center of the carnage: the calm eye of a hurricane. Then he stiffened. I turned to follow his gaze, and I couldn't help but take an involuntary step back. On the far wall, the owner of the establishment hung six feet off the ground, crucified by much larger silver stakes at each appendage. Some of the wounds had shed more blood than the others, staining the wall in a viscous smear as it made its way down to the floor.

For instance, the one spearing the man's genitals into the brick wall had bled the most, conveying that it was one of the first inflicted.

I shuddered at the thought, remembering my close encounter with the net-launched web the night before that had almost made me permanently sterile. Gunnar arched a brow. "Pretty sick. Who carries around a bunch of stakes to hammer a person into a wall?"

I pushed back the emotions that were screaming for me to run away, and stepped closer to the body. It was riddled with tiny silver needles as well, like a bad advertisement for acupuncture. He had not died easily. I climbed onto a nearby table and studied the large stakes. After a moment, I glanced back at Gunnar. "They weren't hammered into him," Gunnar scoffed, stepping closer.

"Then how in the hell were they—" He blinked, noticing the polished, rounded edges of the stakes. No hammer marks marred their surface. I reached out and tentatively touched the cold metal.

My mind immediately crumpled, folding in on itself in utter defeat. I was falling, falling down into a black abyss with no one to catch me, and I was screaming with no one to hear me. Indie's words came back. *Who's there to catch you, Nate?* My subconscious immediately answered. *No one. No one cares enough to catch you. You're all alone. Who are you to fight something this strong? You don't stand a chance. You should just leave it all alone and go back to your shop.* I was terrified, completely terrified, and I was still falling into the blackness, a blackness like a thousand dying suns...

Something struck me across the face like a bitch slap from Jesus. I grunted in shock, my head instantly clearing up as everything came back into focus. I wasn't falling. I wasn't alone. That hadn't been my thoughts. I realized that I had fallen down from the table, and that Gunnar was holding me protectively on the ground. "Nate! You okay? What happened?"

I grunted, fumbling my shaky arms to hold myself up. He let go and slid back a few feet, watching me nervously. My eyes watered from the blow, and my head rang, but I wasn't angry with him. He might have just saved my sorry ass. I looked back up at the body and felt my breakfast ready to come back up, so I quickly turned away, breathing deeply. Hangover *plus* dead body *equals* projectile vomit. "They were," I shivered convulsively for a second, the fear trying to overtake me again. I managed to take a breath and try again. "They were cast at him. Thrown."

Gunnar looked from me to the man spread-eagled on the wall. "Cast? Thrown? Do you have any idea what kind of precision that would take?"

I nodded. "Positive. And to hold his," I studied the man. "190-pound weight into a brick wall required unbelievable force." I turned to face him. "This was a dragon, for sure. The same mind-magic as the Raven tried to use is present here. Except much stronger. Instead of lust, this one used fear. Unparalleled fear. She mind-fucked me just by touching the metal, and that was, what, twelve hours later?" Gunnar nodded, remembering the details from the cops outside. "I can't imagine what this man experienced before he died. He didn't even deal in the type of circles that would come close to what Raven asked me for." Studying some of the book covers on the floor, I growled angrily. "History. He was a fucking history book dealer. Nothing even remotely spooky. They must be getting desperate."

Gunnar nodded, eyes darting to the body again. "Another dragon. With silver stakes..." He sighed hesitantly. "Your ball."

I stared, momentarily confused. Then it hit me. Silver stakes were anathema to a werewolf. To hear that one of these beasts harnessed such weapons was beyond scary, even for me, but to Gunnar it was deathly so. "I didn't think of that. I guess this one's on me." Gunnar nodded slowly. "You know, our partnership feels one-sided, Gunnar. I'm handling all the nasties while you read reports. Very bureaucratic of you."

He grinned weakly, but seemed unhappy about it. "But I'll be there for motivation. From a distance. With a wall between us." He glanced at the brick wall holding up the body. "A couple walls between us, but I'll be there, cheering you on with a megaphone, you little dragon-slayer, you," he said unashamedly. As a werewolf, Gunnar could handle a world of pain, but he wasn't immortal. One stake to the chest and his world would end in a blazing eternity of pain. Or so I had read. Not a simple death for a werewolf, more like a Dante's Inferno, seventh circle of hell, type of death.

"Gee, thanks," I muttered. I looked at the corpse one last time and then spoke to Gunnar. "Mind if I send him off?" Gunnar shook his head. I didn't bother with the coins, but spoke the words, filling them with my power. "*Requiescat in Pace.*" The familiar wail of a horn rumbled deep inside my chest, and Charon drifted out of nowhere to pluck the victim's soul away from the body, laying it down in his boat as he continued on, nodding once at me in gratitude before he slipped out the front door. Of course, the cops outside saw nothing. They were blind to beings such as Charon. And Charon only took the *souls* of Regulars, as opposed to taking the entire *body* like he had with Raven.

Gunnar shook his head, and began taking pictures of the corpse in situ, various angles, and close-ups. Cop stuff. Me, being utterly deficient at police procedure, decided to go peruse the items in the store, verifying and cataloguing the victim's selection. Had the owner's loving fingers brushed off that particular buckram cover recently? I used my toe to flip over several books, glancing here and there at loose pages. The wind howled through the broken window, hungry to be the first to explore the virgin building's insides, and then abscond with the equivalent of a pair of panties for its conquest—in this case, a collection of pages from the destroyed books.

I sat down in a clear area of the floor amidst the chaos, quieting my mind, and drew a mental circle about me, lacing it with power. I needed to think. One by one, I blocked out my senses. First, sound; the fluttering pages, the incessant clicking of Gunnar's camera, the general creaking of the building, the muffled voices of the police outside, and then the wind. I closed my eyes to kill visual feedback. Then smell, and then touch. Next came sensations of a rather difficult-to-explain nature: the sense of life lingering in the room from Gunnar and me, the sense of death from the corpse on the wall, and then the overwhelming sensation of love that stained every article in the room. It covered everything: the books, the tables, the windows, and even the walls.

The owner had dearly loved his establishment, not looking at it as merely a potential source of income, but as a living being, demanding all the requirements for life.

Nourishment from books, care from the owner, praise from sales and contented customers, and vitality from the elements that were the store itself: the wood, windows, floors, insulation, stairs, furniture, and even the pot of coffee on the back table. The place was alive, and to think clearly, I needed to first empathize with that sense of life and then discard it.

Finally content, I floated in blackness; completely at peace. I had to fight my mind in order to remind it that this was nothing like the blackness I had just experienced from touching the silver stake. This was a peaceful tranquility with no sense of falling or fear. I managed it, barely.

In my mind, I folded myself comfortably into a wingback chair that was suddenly floating in the emptiness. Then, as if it were the most normal thing in the world, I flipped on a Tiffany lamp sitting on a stand beside me. It was dark in my imagination, both literally and emotionally. I whipped out an aging leather journal, and began jotting down notes. All the information I had acquired over the last week that might be relevant to the dragons or my parents was splashed onto the journal, all in question form, and then I took a calming sip of a Mint Julep sitting on the table beside me, contemplating anything else I might have missed. Satisfied, I set the journal down in my lap, and finished my drink, enjoying the cooling freshness of the beverage. I glanced down at my writing, thinking calmly.

Dragons. Dragons were searching my city for a family book, *Sons of the Dying Sun*, killing anyone who got in their way, allegedly even my parents. My father and Raven had both mentioned tomorrow's solar eclipse, which had attracted thousands of tourists to the convention center where speakers had arrived from all over the world to discuss the science, physics, and even mystical extrapolations of such an event. Some kid client wanted me to find a book that also had something to do with dragons. Dragon hunters had a mark on a particularly dangerous dragon they believed to be in town. My shop had been broken into, and I had just survived a random hate-crime by a truckload of gargoyles while driving to the scene of another dragon attack. Maybe that last one was just my luck...

I couldn't think of any particular dangers surrounding the eclipses in history, so what was so important about this one? Perhaps when this scene was finished I could go do some research on dragons and eclipses. To be honest, I knew nothing more than your average idiot about them. Arcane master of knowledge and wisdom, a wizard should be, but there were simply too many myths and fables to study to know them all before one might encounter them in the real world. I wasn't one of those librarian warrior Grimm brothers. I needed ammunition.

That settled, I spent the rest of my solitude pondering possibilities of tonight's encounter with Asterion. How would a reformed Buddhist want to duel? What would it consist of? Good old-fashioned arm-wrestle? Political debate? Chess? Surprisingly, none of these seemed appropriate.

I came back to myself to find Gunnar finished with the scene.

He was flipping through a particularly old book without interest, restless. His heightened sense of smell had to make this place exceptionally unpleasant. He saw me move and placed the book down, waiting for me to speak. I stretched out my legs, careful of any silver needles, waiting for the feeling to come back from my meditation. After a minute, I stood, and he spoke, "We have to find this book soon if we want to stop the killing."

I stretched my calves languorously. "I think I know a way. A way that might actually get us ahead of them. But it might skirt some grey areas with the law," I added the last bit carefully.

Gunnar studied me for a long while in silence. "How about I have my men do their job, and pretend I didn't hear whatever you just said. You can be on your merry way, and do whatever it is you feel like doing while they work this scene. In a couple hours, we will have a chat, and perhaps we'll have information to share with each other."

My eyes widened. Gunnar was a stickler for protocol, and here he was, urging me to do whatever would get us results. I simply nodded at him. "Good idea. Why don't you drop me off at Plato's Cave, and I'll call an old friend?" He nodded, turning his back on the scene, and heading out of the building. I followed behind him like a good little sidekick. In some cases, it could be helpful to have a cavalry behind you like the FBI, but in many other ways it slowed them down, making them impotent to perform as agilely as was often necessary when dealing with sociopathic Freaks.

20

The Illinois cops watched us as we left, already being bombarded by FBI agents parked nearby. They didn't seem in the least bit upset about passing off the responsibility of this particularly grim crime scene. They seemed elated in fact. "Agent Jeffries," Gunnar called to one of his men. A slim, rough, Midwestern looking man came up to us obediently. He reminded me of Chuck Norris. An American good ol' boy.

"Yes, sir?" His voice was light but gravelly, with a faint Texas twang.

"Take over for me. I'm going back to HQ to look into some other leads on this sick bitch."

"Yes, sir. You found out it was a woman?" Jeffries asked.

"Yep," I answered for Gunnar.

Jeffries shot me an appraising glance. "You must be Nate—" he corrected himself. "*Master* Temple." It wasn't mocking, merely obliging a deluded person their wishes. I nodded, maintaining eye contact. My face was still grim from the crime scene. He studied me harder. "How are *you* possibly going to help us catch this...bitch? Pay her off?"

I smiled back darkly. "Kill her, maybe. But definitely not catch."

He looked surprised, turning from me to Gunnar. "Pardon?"

Gunnar maintained his poker face, but I knew he was just as surprised, so I elaborated. "I assume that your men have an idea what we are dealing with? The *real* story, not the politically correct report? And also about my...specialty?"

Gunnar nodded. "They saw the video with the tail, and were briefed last night. They don't know about your specialty though." Gunnar grinned. "But word circulated pretty fast about how my *boyfriend* bought me a new car." Jeffries smiled.

I chuckled. "Okay. Catching her will be impossible. She breeds fear into all of those near her. This crime scene is more than twelve hours old, and when I touched one of the stakes I simply collapsed, overwhelmed with panic. I'm sure I don't have to tell you this, but make sure you have gloves in there, or else things could be difficult."

"Why in the hell did you touch a stake? You could have ruined crucial evidence!" Jeffries said, furious.

I waved a hand dismissively. "The dragon that attacked here was silver. Not grey as in color, but silver, as in the precious metal."

"Okay. How does a civilian possibly expect to help us catch a..." he paused, as if not believing he was about to say it out loud. "Silver dragon?" I couldn't blame him. I mean, dragons. *Come on!*

I waggled my fingers dramatically. "Remember, kill not catch. It's my forte." Doubt was still plain on his face, so I glanced around me, judging the proximity of the other policemen. "You trust him for a little show and tell, Gunnar?"

Gunnar smiled with amusement. "Light petting, only."

I could have called a ball of fire. I could have summoned a miniature whirlwind. I could have made him freezing cold. I could have done so many things, but not many knew my secret, and with the cops, that was a cover I hoped to maintain as long as possible.

Instead, I merely trapped him in icy wires that none around us could see. I extended my hand, offering for him to shake it. Jeffries couldn't move, his eyes wide. "My, my, such a lack of courtesy among men these days. Really, Agent Jeffries, it's considered the height of impropriety not to shake an offered hand."

The tough man's eyes widened further. To me, it looked like when you went out and bought a Christmas tree, and they wrap it up nice and tight in that plastic net so that you can fit the monstrosity on top of your car, but I was the only one who could see the fine threads of barbwire-like cords. His mouth opened and closed wordlessly as he struggled for a few more seconds before giving up. "You...you're a—" he glanced about cautiously to make sure we were alone. Point for him. "Wizard," he whispered finally.

I let him go, nodding as if he had commented on the weather.

He shivered again, but his composure wasn't broken. "So, the stories are all true. If you can do that without even trying, then I am not ashamed to say that the idea of this...dragon's magic overpowering you scares me shitless."

"I play for keeps, Agent Jeffries. Which means I'm not going to risk a capture. I'll just make sure this bitch dies quick, if I have any say about it."

Jeffries nodded, but glanced to his superior. "He's obviously got...secrets, but he's still a civilian. How are we going to describe the outcome if we end up...killing her? I don't think there are even rules about this kind of thing..."

"Statistically speaking, you can get away with murder," I said quietly. They both stared at me, slightly horrified. I shrugged.

Gunnar finally spoke, pointing a thumb at me. "He's one scary fuck, that's for sure. But you leave me to handle Agent Reinhardt. This is the whole point of our new team.

We must step out of the lines...but only when we have to. I'd like to keep my conscience as clear as possible." He turned a decisive eye to me. "We are not assassins."

Agent Jeffries glanced from Gunnar back to me, studying me curiously. "How have you kept it a secret for so long? You are famous. Does anyone else know?"

"Several people, but if anyone finds out prematurely, let me just say that I'll know exactly who leaked the information. And what I just did was only...foreplay."

He blinked. "Are you threatening a federal agent?"

I touched my chest innocently. "Who, me?" I made my glare heat his face. Literally. To him, it must have felt like an oven door opening from inches away. He staggered back with a surprised grunt. My smile never wavered.

"Okay, okay. I'll play nice. As long as you do too." I nodded. I didn't know what steps I could or could not take without ruining things, so I merely trusted Gunnar to keep me out of the frying pan when it came to the red tape.

"Just make sure I toe the line according to your procedures. I wouldn't want to mess anything up. You trust me to be scary, and I'll trust you to make sure I'm as...*bureaucratic* as possible." The word tasted foul on my tongue.

"Bureaucratic is not a word you're familiar with. Not at all."

I motioned for them to follow me over to Gunnar's car. Jeffries spoke up once we were out of earshot of the other cops. "Why don't you tell me what your attacker looked like so we can put out a description to the local law enforcement?" Wise advice, but totally impossible for me to reveal since we had killed her. We had to keep that secret or face jail time, or at least a trial, and I didn't want to air out my dirty laundry to these pristine officers. I also didn't want to go to jail, or see Peter go to jail for simply protecting Gunnar.

With magic.

Fuck. This was getting complicated. Withholding information while trying to pass out crumbs to help them. I wanted to help, but I was just out of my depth. I was not a team player. At least not as big of a team player as you had to be to be a part of the varying police branches. But I had to say something.

"We won't be seeing her any time soon. She jumped a boat out of town after our encounter and said that her sisters would finish off what she had started." There, all true statements, sandwiched between a fuck-load of emptiness.

Agent Jeffries watched me with cop eyes. I fought not to look guilty, opening up my power to calm me, slow my pulse, and ease my breathing. "Just tell him, Agent Jeffries. He won't shut up if you don't, and it would just be more embarrassing for him."

"Gee, thanks, Gunnar." I had no idea what was going on, so I waited.

Agent Jeffries' eyes were harder than before. Like brittle diamonds. "Sugar-coated lies. My favorite," he said.

I blinked. "Pardon?" I asked. "You would fucking *dare* to—"

Gunnar laid a hand on my arm, smiling. "Wait, Nate. Just hear him out."

I folded my arms across my chest, checking my power so that I wouldn't blow Agent Jeffries across the parking lot. "Okay, what's so funny, Gunnar?" I finally asked.

"Tell him the color of the car is black." I frowned, but complied.

"Lie," Agent Jeffries said softly.

"So, his IQ is higher than 24," I spat.

Gunnar sighed. "Say anything then, true or false, and hear what Jeffries has to say. Tell me if he's right or wrong."

Okay, I'd bite. I had a killer poker face. "I just inherited seven billion dollars."

Agent Jeffries didn't even hesitate. "Lie."

Gunnar looked startled at my statement, but arched an eyebrow in question.

"He's right. It was eight." They both stared back, dumbfounded. "Let me try again," I said, determined.

"Wait a minute. You inherited eight *billion* dollars last night?" Gunnar whispered violently. I just nodded, trying harder to trip up Agent Jeffries. He leaned back on the hood, concentrating.

"I voted for Obama."

"Definitely a lie."

I dug deeper. "My parents were murdered."

Agent Jeffries stared back. "You aren't sure."

Was this a power or was he just damn good at reading people? I opened my mouth for one more, but Gunnar had regained his composure, and interrupted me. "He can sense lies." I started to protest, but Gunnar held up one big Viking hand. "I'll prove it." I grumbled, leaning back on the car, too. Gunnar was silent for a time, but when he spoke, it was a doozy. "I'm a werewolf," he said, smiling as if it were a game.

I jumped up. "Whoa, whoa, whoa. Sounds like Gunnar lost his *fucking* mind there for a second. Excuse us, Agent Jeffries, but I think we'll be leaving now."

Agent Jeffries slowly turned to Gunnar, face serious, not hearing me. Was Gunnar trying to lose his job? I didn't know anyone who had blatantly outed themselves like this before. I know some had been caught shifting on video, but this was a first for damn sure. "True," Agent Jeffries finally whispered.

I looked from one to the other, wondering if I had just become Gunnar's new source of income. He was fucked. No one would keep a known werewolf on the books. The *first* admitted werewolf in the government, at that. Gunnar took a step towards Agent Jeffries. "Trade for trade. You told me your secret, so I told you mine. Only fair," Gunnar said calmly. "And there is a group of crazy bitches hurting innocent people in our town. But now, more importantly, do you still trust me?" He set his shoulders, and used a hand to lift Agent Jeffries' jaw so they locked eyes. What would Gunnar do if things went wrong? I didn't even know what the FBI would do when they found out. Would they just fire him, or hunt him down like a criminal...like an animal?

"You don't even have to ask the question, Randulf. Of course I won't tell. You've saved my ass more than a few times, and I would never forget that."

"That might be enough for Gunnar, but not enough for me," I said protectively.

Jeffries abruptly drew a knife and sliced his finger before I could even react. Then he did the impossible. I felt the hum of power instantly surround him in a small circle.

He knelt with one knee up, touched his forehead with the bloody finger, and then licked it clean. "I swear that I will never betray you, Gunnar Randulf, or Nate Temple."

Shit. He knew more than just how to sense lies. He knew a bit of arcane ritualistic magic. The circle snapped shut like a rubber band, and I knew that he would never be able to break his oath.

Over time, people had begun to assume that the ritual Jeffries had just performed was merely a formality, and had decided to simply trust another man's word, his honor. But it had begun here, with this ritual, when one literally swore an oath that could not be broken. Gunnar arched a brow at me, surprised. I nodded back. "He's telling the truth. He literally cannot betray either of us now. No matter what." My voice sounded dumbstruck, and I didn't even care to hide it.

Gunnar smiled down at him. "Thank you, Jeffries, but it really wasn't necessary."

Jeffries nodded. "It was for him." He pointed a thumb back at me as he stood, tucking the blade away into a pocket.

"Well, he does know how to make a fucking point. I can't do anything but trust him on this now, because there's no way for him to renege on his oath. Where did you learn that, Jeffries?"

"My parents," was all he said. Looking to Gunnar, he continued. "All this time I thought I was the only Freak around…It's good to know that I'm not alone. I can't wait to work with you two, even though he's a civ," Jeffries said with a grin at me.

"A civ who can kick some serious ass when necessary," I argued.

He nodded back. An agent was walking our way now, obviously intent on interrupting us. Jeffries spoke, "I need to get back to the scene."

Gunnar nodded back. "You do that. I'll be on my cell. Get back to me as soon as you hear something. We'll chat later." Jeffries turned to intercept the agent.

Gunnar looked at me and shrugged at the look on my face. I silently climbed into the car, saying nothing. He started the car and began to pull out from the curb, heading deeper into the seedy warehouse district. We drove in silence for a time.

Then the skin between my shoulders began to itch as if I were being watched. I glanced out the window, but blew it off as simple weirdness from the conversation I had just experienced, and the brief attack by the gargoyles. Gunnar finally broke the silence. "Did you really inherit that much money?"

I turned to him, thinking. "What time is it?" I asked.

He glanced at the dash and then told me.

"It's increased by about half a million by now, then." Gunnar stared at me, eyes lifted in confusion. "Interest," I added as I looked back out the window. Gunnar was silent for a time.

"Nate?" I heard him ask.

"Yeah?"

He was silent for a few seconds. "You said there were nicer cars than this…"

I rounded on him, blinking in disbelief. "Are you really about to *bitch* about not getting a *nicer* car?" I bellowed. We were about a mile away from the scene in a deserted stretch of vacated warehouses, probably converted to crack houses, now.

He shook his head and opened his mouth to answer, but the back of the car suddenly shuddered, and the whole back windshield blew into the car, raining pebbles of glass over both of us as the car began to skid, the sound of screeching tires mingling with the tinkling of broken glass. When Gunnar and I stopped screaming and he'd regained control of the car, I turned back to see what had hit us. Gunnar merely gunned it, screaming, "No fucking *way!*"

A silver dragon was chasing us down the street, long neck stretching her beautiful chrome head no further than a yard away as she kept up with us going sixty miles an hour. Her silver scales slid and writhed against each other like a computer technician's wet dream. "Hello, boys…I think you might know where to find a book I was hoping to peruse," she purred, not even out of breath.

"*Deceptacon!*" I yelled, frantically saying the first thing that came to mind.

She let out an erotically sensual peal of laughter that tightened my pants with the thrill of dark sex. Fantasy dark sex. The kind that only belongs in the back of the mind where one knows they will never actually act upon it. The thrill and danger of pleasurable pain.

I was too startled to break her wave of fear and power. She had caught me off guard, and now I felt like I was drowning in that dark pleasure-pain. Nothing I could do but ride it. Gunnar and I had already lost. She was just too powerful. Then Gunnar snapped me out of it with another strong Viking slap to the face. His eyes were wide as I came back to myself. "Do something, Nate!" Gunnar bellowed, panicked afresh at my choice of words combined with the mountain of werewolf kryptonite on our bumper.

I was our only hope, as long as Gunnar could keep us away from her claws and jaws, I was free to battle this legend in the seedy warehouse district of East St. Louis.

21

Two times in two hours was simply not acceptable. I'd had enough near-death experiences in my life to know that I didn't particularly enjoy them. Now, having *overcome* all those past scenarios was definitely preferable, but it was getting ridiculous how many times I found myself in them. And the baddies always got bigger, stronger, and meaner while I seemed to remain the same.

Totally unfair.

Her power swamped me like a lead blanket, making me shake and break out into a cold sweat as I struggled to grasp hold of my power that was screaming defiantly deep inside my core. She was simply too strong to battle solely within the mind. I idly wondered how old she was, and how many decades or centuries she had to perfect her talents. *How many centuries I have been alone*, her thoughts invaded my own, meshing together seamlessly. *It's hopeless. Just give in. I can take away all the pain in the world, so that you only have to live with me. No more responsibilities, no more fear of death, no more stress. I will protect you. Why would you want to fight someone who only wanted to help you?* Another slap from Gunnar snapped me out of it, almost unhinging my jaw.

I reacted instantly, using my fear and the pain to do something, anything that would help get us out of here. I whipped up a wall of razor-thin air, hoping to slice her ankles off, or at least trip her up so that maybe she ran into a building. I cast it out the rear windshield like a trip wire, about a foot off the ground. It caught her immediately, and she let out a very human shriek of pain and rage, momentarily shattering her onslaught of mind magic.

My magic cut into her huge reptilian feet, tripping her up expertly, but after her first roll over a random parked car—squashing it beyond oblivion—her wings caught air and she gracefully regained control. She landed back on her feet easily and resumed her pursuit; some yards further back from us, but still too close for comfort. At least she had a slight limp. She let out a roar that shattered windows in the blur of warehouses. Car alarms began squawking within a full block. We had to be going eighty miles an hour, but she was still keeping pace. I had to think of something. I extended my shield of power over both Gunnar and me, hoping to protect us from her magic before it caught hold.

Using magic to protect myself like I had with the stone griffins wouldn't keep Gunnar safe, and I was reasonably sure it wouldn't do much to impede her anyway, so I had to think outside the box.

I spotted a street sign racing towards us and instantly knew what to do. Our only choice if I could pull it off. "Gunnar! Get onto the Eads Bridge!"

He turned to me, eyes wide. "No. There are too many innocent drivers up there! Whatever you're going to do, do it here. It can't be worth the risk to go up there!"

I wanted to scream as she let out another roar behind us, making Gunnar swerve a little, startled. I grabbed the wheel and turned us onto the on ramp with a screech of tires, before Gunnar could argue. "It's our only chance! Stay near the rail and I'll take her out!"

Gunnar was forced to regain control of the car, but he spat out a curse in my direction. "How many will die with your plan, Nate?"

"I hope none. I really do, but it's our only chance. She's too strong."

My phone rang, making me jump in surprise. Not recognizing the number, I hit the speakerphone out of habit.

"Really? A fucking *phone* call? *Now*?" Gunnar yelled over the sounds of his offensive driving.

I ignored him, speaking urgently. "Temple. Kinda busy. Who is this?" I glanced back behind us, hoping the dragon took the bait. She let out a roar of pleasure at us directing the chase to a place with so much potential for collateral damage—so much more fear to feed on from innocent drivers—but I was sure I caught the faintest hesitation in her features, just like Raven in the bookstore. Then it was gone and she was chasing us anew.

The voice of the car chose that moment to go haywire from the impact of her first attack against the rear end of the vehicle—frightening us all over again. "*Door ajar, door aja-ajaarr.*" Then the voice garbled, and a fizzle erupted somewhere behind the dash. Car horns blared around us as Gunnar swerved back and forth, zipping nimbly between them.

The voice on the phone was bubbly. "Wow. Okay, you *do* sound busy. Are you in a parade or something? I didn't know anything was happening today."

"Facts! Speak faster or I'll hang up!" I screamed against the wind tearing through the open windows.

As we careened through traffic, I was glad to see that we were out of the dragon's reach. Then she swiped a car into the median with a powerful backhand and I cringed.

The driver stared at the dragon, frozen in utter disbelief. I noticed he was alone in the car, and was grateful. No kids in the backseat to worry about.

I take solace wherever I can.

The car thankfully skidded without flipping airborne, but that seemed to only infuriate the dragon more. "Right, right. Sorry," the voice on the phone apologized.

Our car's voice momentarily interrupted her. "*Low fyool. Locate the nearest fyooling station at your earliest conveenience.*" The sexy British female voice had begun to transform into a demonically possessed version of the childhood *Speak and Spell* toy. "*Now entereeng Soulard. Your destination on riiiight—*" It grew worse by the second.

The phone spoke again, sensing the press of limited time. "Oh, I didn't realize you had *company*. I work for you. I'm Abby. Miss Belmont informed me to tell you that when we were inputting your personal information into the system, a private video feed popped up into a queue for you to watch. One of the security cameras, as far as we can tell. The system will not allow us to access it. If you could swing by here and check it out, Miss Belmont would appreciate it. I think it's from the room of..." her voice grew soft. "The attack."

I blinked, momentarily forgetting the chasing dragon behind us. "The attack on my parents?" I asked, punctuated by another dragon roar in the distance.

"Yes, Master Temple. When can we expect you?"

"Um. In an hour or two, hopefully."

Gunnar interrupted, snatching my phone. "Right. Thanks. Bye." He tossed it back to me, glaring. "First, dragon. Then company. People are going to die if we don't stop her. Do something. Soonest." I nodded, shaking my head free of the sudden emotions as I numbly pocketed the phone. A security feed from the room of my parents' deaths. That might hold one of those elusive clue-thingies. Another roar startled me back to the present.

Glancing back, I saw the dragon inhale sharply, so I quickly prepared another volley of power, using my sudden emotion for energy. I had seen the red dragon do a similar thing when she had been about to let loose her napalm fire on the roof. I used the same tactic, hoping they hadn't shared war stories. I let fire roil inside me, drawing heat from anywhere and everywhere, willing it into existence until I could see it clearly in my mind. I saw cars on the opposite side of the highway slowing down as I drew the heat from their engines, even seizing some of them to an abrupt halt, much to their sudden panic.

Or maybe they had just stopped to stare at the freaking dragon tearing after us.

I shook my head, building the fire hotter and hotter, our own car slowing down. "Nate! What are you doing? We're slowing down!"

"Shut up, Gunnar!" I screamed as the power threatened to burn my blood to ashes. I had never called this much fire before, and I knew that I was at my limit, or possibly even beyond it. When the pain began to make stars in my eyes, I let it loose like a rocket launcher. It slammed into her snout just as she began to spit silver spears into another car. The fire halted most of the silver, slamming it back down her throat, causing her to slam down to the ground on all fours, sliding across the concrete highway, her talons clawing into the asphalt like a hot knife through butter. Our car abruptly tore forward, compensating for the floored gas pedal as I stopped pulling the heat from the engine. Gunnar swerved around another car, honking and screaming at them to get out of the way.

They obliged in sheer panic.

I turned back to see the dragon retching a car-sized lump of steaming silver onto the road like a cat with one of those vile hair balls they seem to be able to produce at the worst possible moments. She shook her head once and then launched into the sky. A state patrol car slammed into the pile of silver before the cop could dodge it, no doubt racing after us for help, and the car instantly flipped up into the air, somersaulting wildly. I imagined the screams from inside.

Was he a family man? Was he close to retiring, or was he maybe a new rookie on the force, hoping to change the world? I sensed the dragon's pulse of power, and realized she was toying with me again. I steeled my resolve, blocking out the cries in my own head as the cop died. There was no question. If he hadn't died from the first impact, the height and speed of the second impact with the road would surely finish him off. He was already dead. I swallowed the lump of guilt, blocking the dragon's power of fear from my mind.

But before the cop car could strike the ground, the dragon swooped down and caught the wreckage in a snatch of talons, sharply banking away to continue her pursuit beside us over the churning river on the other side of the bridge's rails. I stared into the driver's side, hoping to see the cop alive, knowing the odds were against him. If I did what I was about to do, he was going to die anyway. One life to protect so many others. It was a sacrifice that made a small part of me die inside, but I had no other choice. Gunnar roared in fury next to me, partially shifting form so that huge, beefy, wolf arms gripped the steering wheel as he spotted the cop car dangling over the Mississippi River Levee.

"Nate! Do something!" I nodded, still searching, hoping the cop was still alive. Then an elbow punched through the window, and…it was a fucking girl! Not a mature, battle-hardened woman of the force, but a young, and small, beautiful female cop. She was suddenly leaning out the shattered glass, firing at the dragon's underbelly without the slightest fear. First Spiderman, and now Wonder Woman.

The dragon let out a shriek of furious pain, and then looked into my eyes as we sped alongside her. She smiled broadly at me, and then dropped the car into the icy river, smiling as she ate up the surprise and fear for the cop's life tearing through my eyes. The cop would die in the frigid water of the Mississippi River because I hadn't acted sooner.

Not today.

I yelled incoherently as I half leaned out of the open passenger window, ignoring the broken bits of glass. I heard the cop scream as she fell several stories down into the dark water. Pedestrians on the walkway were running in panic, screaming in disbelief. The city was about to discover that their beloved Temple Heir was a wizard.

And I didn't give one.

Flying.

Fuck.

I called the weather to my command like a cloak, drawing every molecule of water from every cloud within a mile, and then I reached even further. I had never been that great with weather, but it was all I could think to do. She was made of metal, and I was betting that she hadn't passed swimming lessons as a young dragonling.

The weather responded instantly, water slamming into the vacuum I had created in the dragon's chest. Every crack in her body, every millimeter of space between scales, was suddenly filled with water, weighing her down dramatically. Then I did the opposite of what I had done a few minutes ago. I simultaneously withdrew all heat from her body, and cast the frigid temperature from the river below into those same water molecules, freezing them instantly. She faltered as ice abruptly creaked in her every joint, preventing her wings from working properly, and then she fell.

Fast.

"Temple!" Her bellow of rage was impressive, but the splash of her massive body hitting the river was even better. Sweet vengeance, thy name is Temple. Water splashed up so high that we could even see it from above the bridge. Gunnar slammed on the brakes, and we bolted out of the car—now sitting sideways on the highway—kicking down one of the maintenance fence doors that separated the pedestrians from the roadway. We leaned over the river and watched the bubbles until they stopped, and all that was left was the cool waves of the Mississippi welcoming the dragon to her new permanent residence at the bottom of the river.

Gunnar pointed urgently off behind us, and I saw the cop floundering weakly in the water a hundred yards back. I thought she would have been further away, and deader. Relief flooded over me as I saw a nearby boat pull up to her and toss her a preserver. She was alive, and the dragon was dead. I collapsed to my knees, crying out in relief, unable to hold myself up. I heard the screech of tires, and then metal slamming into metal where our car was parked. A beautiful ball of fire blossomed up over the Aston Martin. Then the world went black as I passed out from exhaustion.

22

I woke in the back of an ambulance, wrapped in cheap blankets, near the riverfront. I was freezing cold. Draining oneself with as much magic as I had thrown about today had killed wizards before, but somehow, I had survived. My thoughts were sluggish, but I saw Gunnar talking to another police officer who was also wrapped in blankets, skin visibly steaming underneath, and it all came back in a blink.

I stumbled out of my ride and attempted to walk over to the two of them. Cop cars were everywhere, red and blue lights strobing around us. I had been out for a while, judging by the height of the sun. Then another thought hit me and I tripped, barely catching myself. Temple Industries was awaiting me, and so was the Minotaur. A cop instinctively reached out to assist me but then hesitated, uncertainty and fear obvious on his face. I scowled at him, and he frowned sheepishly, lowering his eyes.

Gunnar and the other officer had noticed my approach and were striding towards me. Gunnar hissed at the officer who had shied from touching me. "How dare you? He almost died saving Officer Marlin and countless others from a murdering sociopath, and you can't even reach out a hand to keep him from falling down on his face? Is that the kind of thanks St. Louis has to offer?" His chest was heaving, and I almost fell down again as his rage suddenly coursed through me like electricity. My skin was buzzing, and my equilibrium wavered as my skin suddenly felt on fire.

"No, sir. It's just that Captain Kosage said...and the stories about what he did...I was scared to touch him. They say he called down the power of a god to battle a silver demon. I'm not a religious man, but others ran to the nearest church as soon as they could. They're calling him Archangel, or one of the Four Horsemen. He battled a devil in the middle of a high-speed car chase...and won." He looked at me. "I'm sorry, Master

Temple, it's just that...whatever you did scares me. I don't want to risk my family by being too close to you. Or my job, when Kosage hears about all this."

The other officer, Officer Marlin, I presumed, stepped up next to me and wrapped a delicate arm under my shoulder in thanks, supporting my sudden dizziness. She was short, maybe 5'5, and stunning. Her straight, dark, almost black hair would have ended just below her breasts if it hadn't been tied back. Her thin face was perfect for it. Her bright green eyes were fiery with a hidden power that I could only guess at, and were big enough to drown in. "Now that I'm here, what are your other two wishes?" I mumbled, feeling slightly giddy from the sudden warmth and power that had filled me upon seeing Gunnar.

She laughed delightedly and my heart melted. Girl's laughter just flat did it for me. Her teeth glowed white as she grinned, "I like him." Her fingers squeezed my shoulder affectionately, and it was as if the pressure broke something inside me, and then my body coursed with even more energy and power, refreshing me like a long night of sleep followed by a healthy breakfast. Her faith wrapped around me like a giant oak tree trunk for support. I felt stronger, more awake.

What the hell? How was I sensing others' emotions, and how was it fueling me? The petite officer spoke again, the blanket making her look frail and delicate, but I sensed there was more to her. "Well, I, for one, am grateful for his help. Never hurts to be friends with an archangel. You should be ashamed of yourself, officer."

The man's shoulders shrugged in defeat, but he turned and began walking closer to a small crowd of police officers. Then I felt my perception of the world abruptly jolt, like I had experienced only a few times before, and I grew instantly nervous. *Not again...*

A man suddenly darted out of nowhere with a purse tucked under his arm, and slammed straight into the departing officer. He fell, dropped the purse, and a slew of jewelry spilled out across the grass. The stunned cop reacted quickly, cuffing him, and then a man and woman burst onto the scene. "He stole my purse! Thank god you caught him!" She latched onto her boyfriend in relief. Gunnar and I stared at each other in disbelief as the cop carted the man off to a nearby squad car, the couple in tow behind them.

"Odds are never that good. He's either the stupidest criminal in the world, or god is looking down on us," Gunnar said softly. I nodded, but suddenly felt very aware of the power high I was experiencing. The last time I had felt a shift like this, some very strange things had happened around me. Odds had run wild. Things that would have never happened naturally suddenly did. Things like this. Was it happening again? Had I reached a new power plateau, distorting chance all around me? I shrugged, not speaking my fear.

Instead, I glanced down at Officer Marlin beside me, changing the topic. "I'm glad I could help, but I seem to remember that boat saving you, not some archangel. I am no hero. I did what anyone else would have done, and a better man would have done it sooner without risking your life."

She was tiny—and dare I say cute—as she shot me a reproachful grin. When

Gunnar stepped closer, the odd energy sensation tripled—filling me up like an overflowing teacup. I shook my head, studying my body for clues to this new power. I knew my body better than most people know their own, having studied the relationship between it and my magic over the years, but I came up with no alternative theories. It was happening again. I had reached a new plateau, and it was feeding off those magical beings around me—namely Gunnar and Officer Marlin—as it matured. But that meant she was...

"Whether I think you are an archangel or not is my own business, not yours. I know what I saw. You were glowing with...power?" She fumbled at a choice for words. "And you saved all of us. There's no telling what that..." she glanced at Gunnar for the correct word. Gunnar gave it, face serious. "*Dragon* would have done if you hadn't slain her." She let out a light laugh, and shook her head. "If you aren't a dragon-slaying hero, then you're a Savior Archangel. Pick your poison, but you're one of the two. I'd be honored to join you and Agent Randulf here in your next dragon slaying. But please, call me Tory."

I shook my head immediately. "You almost died today. We can't risk anyone else. Especially Regul—" I cut myself off, feeling like I had almost dropped a racial slur.

"It's okay, say it. Regular. But I think you'd be surprised..." She stepped back from me for a moment and reached out to Gunnar. My werewolf friend sighed and withdrew a bent piece of metal from behind his back, handing it to Tory. The petite bombshell took it, frowned for a moment, and then placed one of her dainty fists on either end of a long, straight segment of the bar. She lifted her eyes to mine, watching me with a grin, and began to bend the metal perfectly in half, not an ounce of strain crossing her face. It bent like a twisty tie at the grocery store. My eyes widened in surprise and her smile stretched wider. "I am no *Regular*, Master Temple."

I remembered her shattering her patrol car window with one blow of her elbow, and realized that in most cases it wouldn't have been possible for even a much larger man. Maybe adrenaline would help, but most would need a cushion to protect their elbow joint from permanent damage, or would have to take several attempts to shatter it so efficiently. She had made it look simple, easy. And she also showed no signs of an injured elbow.

She tossed the bent metal bar into the nearby grass. No one but us had seen it, as they all seemed preoccupied with the random thief they had just caught. "Agent Randulf offered me a job with his new team, although he didn't tell me what the team was called..." She glanced curiously at Gunnar, but the werewolf's face remained stoic. "He just told me what the goals of his team are, and what kind of criminals we'd be going up against. He said that he needed your approval before he allowed me to join the pack."

She waited for me to speak. Even energized, I was still a little slow. "Pack?" I asked with a frown.

"That's what he called it. A Band of Brothers kinda' thing. Or sisters, in my case. Is it like the He-Man Woman Hater's Club? Because I don't want to crash your groove or anything." She grinned, making my testosterone respond. It was definitely a bedroom grin: dark, dirty, and full of improper yet enlightening insinuations. Or maybe I was still thinking of Indie from this morning. "Is there a reason that he needs your permission for my help? Are you in charge?" she asked politely, face neutral of any disrespect.

I shook my head, and began to speak, but Gunnar answered. "I trust Nate...Master Temple with my life, and now you've seen why. We all have secrets, as I showed you mine a few seconds ago, but he is one of the scariest men I have ever met, and if he says you aren't up for recruitment, then I'm sorry to say that I would have to agree. This is a hobby of his, and he's survived encounters that are even less believable than what you experienced today. *Many* encounters like this, in fact. And the dangers will only escalate, with probably even scarier bad guys. He has veto power on my recruits."

I watched Gunnar, surprised that he had told her his secret. Was it National *Come out of the Closet Day* for werewolves? "I didn't even want to be in your...pack, and now I have veto power? That is...so cool," I added sarcastically. Gunnar and Tory grinned. "I have to be honest, Tory. This harem of dragons is nothing to scoff at. Today was a close call, but she has sisters, and I have no idea how powerful they are. We can hope that the silver one was the strongest, but I doubt it. It's kind of like the Billy Goats Gruff. The next one is always bigger than the one before. I had thought dragons were extinct until a few days ago, when we were attacked at my bookstore." Tory waited respectfully for my answer. Damn. I was hoping I could scare her off. "Do you have kids, a family?" She shook her head. "Boyfriend?" Again, she shook her head. "Manfriend?"

She laughed at that, the sound tickling the sensitive parts of my neck like a kiss. "I know my way around a bedroom," she spoke lasciviously, "but have yet to find a lover who could accommodate my...lifestyle." Before today it had just been me helping Gunnar, but now we had two new pups to take care of, and I didn't know if either were strong enough to benefit our cause or if I was simply setting them up to die a horrible death like pawns in a game of chess.

"One thing that's essential is absolute honesty on the team. Everyone needs to know the other's strengths and weaknesses in order to play to those strengths in a life or death situation. You've seen what I can do, well, some of it. I'm a wizard. I can harness, control, and manipulate energy to my will, but I'm no archangel. I use magic." I shrugged. "Like you use a gun. It's just a part of me. I was born into it. But it can be dangerous to be around me." I waited for her to run screaming, but if anything, she looked more content than before, relieved, as if finding a new home. *Damn it, damn it, damn it.*

"What else can you do, Tory? Is bending metal the extent of your power? Try and explain whatever you can. We need to know in order to see if it will help us."

Gunnar nodded approval, waiting for Tory to speak. "My whole life I've been strong. I never realized how much stronger until I was involved in a fatal car accident on a date." Her voice grew distant. "My date was trapped under the car on an old country road, dying of severe blood loss due to several deadly wounds. I was scratched up, but fine. Kind of like now. I climbed out of the car, looked down at him, and knew that he was going to die. It shouldn't have been possible, but I knew if I didn't help, he would die. I grabbed the car, and lifted it off his legs. It wasn't adrenaline. I know that now, because adrenaline can make me...scary strong. I managed to drag him out from underneath the car, and then the cops and medics arrived. A Good Samaritan must have called them. My date was too delirious from blood loss to remember what happened accurately, so no one ever knew about it. I decided to become a cop the next week."

She stared inward at her own memories, and I struggled not to drop my jaw. One handed car curl? Jesus. That might help out in a pinch. Tory's eyes refocused. "I wanted to use that strength to help people, and I've been careful about stepping too much out of bounds for others to notice, but anything to do with my muscles is simply superior to others. Running, lifting weights, punching bags. You name it. It's almost as if I have extra fuel inside me waiting to ignite my muscles...like Nitrous in a car. It's just there."

Gunnar was quiet for a spell, as if deciding if this petite cop was worthy of the club. I nodded at him to proceed. "I vote for her, Gunnar," I said confidently. "We can't have a gang without the token cool girl. We need some estrogen on the team," I added with a smile. "Even if she can arm wrestle better than us."

"Everything is better with a girl around," she added with a mischievous smirk.

I frowned at that. "This isn't like your usual beat as a police officer. This will be..." I struggled for a word, finally saying the first thing that came to mind. "Black Ops."

Tory and Gunnar both stared at me as if I had spouted a prophecy. "Well, damn. That's exactly what it is, isn't it?" Gunnar said in surprise, nodding. "I'm not saying that it can be our official title or anything. We aren't spooks, but it does have to be hush-hush from the traditional police force, so that's a pretty appropriate name."

Tory spoke conspiratorially. "Let's go hunt some dragons then, shall we?"

I smiled back. "Soon. I have to go beat up the Minotaur first, and then we can go hunt dragons. Well, after I swing by Temple Industries."

Her eyes widened in disbelief for a moment, but Gunnar spoke up. "He's being literal. We'll get in touch with you after the fight, and the meeting at his company, and then we'll figure out a plan." Tory simply shook her head, mouthing *Minotaur* to herself.

Thanks to the odd addition of their energy to mine, I was somehow refreshed, and I didn't even care how at the moment. Wizards needed nutrition to use their power: water, food, sleep, and vitamins. If I ever forgot to eat, or drink enough liquids, I found myself lethargic, and utterly useless in the magical department. Which meant I probably needed to grab some food and water stat, but for some reason none of that had hindered me today. In fact, I felt stronger than ever. As long as this odd recharge gave me strength against the Minotaur, all was just dandy. Without it, I wouldn't have been up to battle him, or even light a cigarette with my magic. At that thought, I beamed. I placed a cancer stick between my lips and lit the tip with a thought. "Well, driver, where's the car?"

Gunnar's eyes flicked away instinctively. "Expensive car go *Boom*." He mimed an explosion with his hands. I groaned in frustration as I suddenly remembered the bloom of fire where our car had been before I had passed out. Gunnar spoke fast. "But everyone survived," he added. "Oh, and I managed to get your man purse before it was destroyed." He held it up, smiling.

"Satchel, asshole. Indiana Jones carried one, and he called it a satchel."

Tory laughed, tossing him a set of keys. "Officially, you can commandeer a car when necessary. I think the police owe it to you. Just try not to scratch it up. I already destroyed one, and that will come back to bite me in the ass, no matter what the story. The bottom line is always money, ya' know?" she added with a grin.

"I bet you dress up nicely, Tory," I offered with a grin, hiding my anger at the totaled car.

She smiled carefully, studying me. "As a matter of fact, I do. Why?"

Gunnar rolled his eyes. "Come on! *Really*, Nate?"

I ignored him. "It might be handy to have a stunning piece of eye-candy accompany us to a gala tonight. You have something to wear?"

Gunnar looked unhappy, but resigned to the fact that she was now part of the group. "I don't know if I have anything nice enough for a VIP event." I peeled off a thick stack of hundreds from my wallet and handed them to her. "Get something. I don't know if you'll be going, but I want you to be prepared just in case." She backed away from the proffered cash with manicured hands up. "Stop. Just take it. It's for a good cause. I'm not trying to bribe you or anything. We need you to look convincing if you're to accompany us. We need to reek of money or they will think we don't belong. *Master Nate Temple can go anywhere*," I said mocking my own title. "But not with shabbily-dressed peasants." Gunnar grumbled at that.

She finally agreed, making sure I knew just how uncomfortable she was about it all. We exchanged numbers so that we could get a hold of her on short notice, and then we set off. Less than one day, and the beautiful Aston Martin had been destroyed. I wanted to beat Gunnar to a pulp, but that was risky in front of all the other frightened police officers. Oh, well. Nothing to be done about it.

Maybe I would get Gunnar a Hummer next. Or a tank.

23

Gunnar dropped me off at Plato's Cave, with me telling him I would call him when I was ready. I spotted Indie behind the counter, but no customers present. She was wiping off the counter with a focused gleam in her eyes. Spotting me, she straightened with a smile. "Evening, Cap'n."

"Indie," I breathed the word like a man dying of thirst. Her smile turned inappropriate, and her cheeks reddened.

"Well, you sure know how to pronounce a name. I don't think anyone has *ever* said my name like *that* before." She eyed me up and down, eyes tightening at the dust and debris all over my clothes. She plucked out a few pieces of windshield glass from my hair, her thumb brushing my temple in the process. "You're a mess, Nate..." she whispered softly, her eyes concerned.

"Yeah, and I have to head back out. The *company* requests my presence." I made the word *company* sound like a curse.

"Not like this, you can't. Come on." She grabbed my hand, and began weaving through the glass dividers, guiding me upstairs to my loft. One of my other employees watched us curiously. Indie noticed also. "Nate's run into a bit of trouble. I'm going to doctor him up a bit before he leaves again. Can you watch over things for a bit, Alex?"

Alex, a blonde-haired Greek med student nodded with a grin. "Doctor him up, eh? Sounds...*nice*. Can I watch?" His grin grew wider.

Indie glared. "Careful, Alex. Look at him, and tell me he doesn't need it." Alex looked me up and down for the first time.

"Shit, Cap'n. You all right? I'm the med student, maybe I should help you."

He took a step towards us. I held up a hand, grateful for his help, but knowing that I needed to say some things to Indie that no other ears were privy to. "Thanks, Alex, but it looks worse than it is. She'll be fine. Her *doctoring* probably means something more like 'Chew Nate up and down for his poor safety choices this afternoon.' My pride would appreciate it if no other males were present to witness my downfall. I've got a reputation to uphold."

He grinned again, nodding knowingly. "Ah, in that case, good luck. She's got a tongue like a razor. I'll watch over the ship for you. We managed to get it all cleaned up after the break-in. Whaddya' think?" He spread his arms at the shop proudly.

"It looks great. Thanks for taking care of everything today. And also, the premiere for Gods of Chaos IV last night. I'm glad you all made it out of here before the burglars stuck their noses in." He nodded agreement. "Good turn out?"

He laughed, shrugging. "Didn't take much convincing, I mean, Gods of Chaos IV? Seriously? Divorces have resulted from keeping a guy away from that franchise. It was fantastic. They really upped the visuals, and—" He realized he was babbling, and stopped. "It was great. I'll update you at the meeting next week. Go get doctored up. We can't have our fearless leader looking like a stray now, can we?" With that he turned away.

Indie mouthed *Thank you,* before leading me up the stairs. I spoke my thoughts before thinking. "I don't think you have a tongue like a razor, but I have wondered lately..." My implication was instinctual, still slightly dizzy from my new power high.

She stumbled up a step, turning a red face at me. "I've made my intentions clear, Nate. If we were at Chateau Falco right now, I might just have resorted to the kind of *doctoring* every man wants from a woman. I can be such a *good* nurse."

It was my turn to stumble. She laughed lightly, her hand squeezing mine as she led me into my loft. She closed the door behind us, and began to reach for the blinds to the windows overlooking the store. Instead, I snapped a finger, and they instantly closed. She turned to me, eyes moving slowly, dreamlike. "Makes a girl wonder what else a wizard can do."

I grinned back. "You have no idea..."

"Oh, but you are very wrong. I have many *ideas*, just no *facts*. Yet..." She winked, gliding towards the bathroom in that seductive sway that only girls can do—the grace of movement that could somehow make men physically hungry. She strode into my bathroom, and I heard the water turn on. My employees had even cleaned up my loft so that it was almost unnoticeable that anyone had broken into it last night. A few minutes later, she leaned out the door, smiling. "Here, boy." She patted her thigh as if calling a dog. I grinned, shaking my head, but complied. I did need a shower.

I entered the room, the mirror already fogged over. Candles were lit, and they filled the room with a warm glow, made more appealing by the steam from the shower. I didn't see her because it was a big bathroom, and the change in lighting slowed me down. The door closed behind me, and I felt Indie's fingers touch my coat. "Clothes off." She said softly from behind me.

"Indie..." I began, feeling worse for what I needed to say next.

Her fingers touched my lips, tasting sweet like strawberries. Must be her lotion.

"Trust me, Nate. You need help to get all the shards out of your hair." Her breath was like a breeze of fresh mint, not gum or candy, but the herb. Spicy. I complied, tugging off my coat and shirt, and tossing them on the floor. She hissed when she saw the wound on my forearm from Raven's attack. I waved off her concern with a smile.

"It's okay. It's already healing." She frowned, and moved behind me. Her arms encircled my bare waist, and I immediately flinched in pain. "What's wrong? That shy?" She asked softly, curiously fingering the leather thong with the dragon tooth.

"I think you brushed a bruise." I said, surprised that I hadn't noticed it earlier. She leaned to my side and inhaled sharply. I looked down to see three large black bruises around my sides where the red dragon had dangled me over the courthouse. Then I saw more from the net launcher. "It's okay. I just didn't notice it until now," I mumbled.

She was breathing heavily against my back, her cheek pressed against my shoulder blades, and I realized that I was sore there too, from one of the several fights I had been in. I peeled off the rest of my clothes until I was standing in only my *Superman* boxers. She circled me, hungrily looking me up and down. "Off," She said, motioning at my boxers before turning away with an amused grin. She sat down on the edge of the tub, and I realized that it wasn't a shower, but a eucalyptus-scented bubble bath that she had drawn for me.

She held out a hand, still looking away as I undressed. "I won't peek," she whispered. Dropping my boxers, I grasped her fingers, sensing the warmth under her skin, and just stood there for a minute. Her hand finally tugged at mine, so I obeyed, climbing into the steaming tub. I groaned. It was perfect. Not too hot, not too cold, and I had made sure to buy a tub that was big, wide, and comfortable enough to hold two people.

Once safely settled underneath the foam and bubbles, Indie turned back to me, snatching up a nearby pitcher. Her shirt stretched tight across her breasts. She leaned over me and scooped up some of the warm water, her hand dipping below the bubbles. The motion drew the shirt up a bit above the waist of her jeans, revealing a tanned expanse of hips and flat stomach, as well as a tiny ribbon of red panties.

She raised her hand, now coated in bubbles, and began pouring it through my hair, slowly, sensually, with her lips slightly open. She lathered some tea-tree shampoo in her palms, and then stretched her fingers through my hair like a cat pawing a soft blanket. Her manicured nails gently raked my scalp, making me shiver despite the heat as she plucked out several glass shards and tossed them into a trashcan. Huh. I had never experienced anything quite like this before.

"Keep your eyes closed, Nate." My mind went all sorts of adolescent on me, but I listened. The pitcher brushed my inner thigh, but she continued pouring the water over my head, washing out the shampoo without comment.

"Talk to me, Nate. I know you have a lot going on right now, but I'm here for you." She tugged on my shoulder, making me open my eyes, and sit upright. She had a washcloth in one hand, and began tenderly scrubbing my back as she waited. Macho man that I am, I managed to suppress grunts of pain when her cloth brushed any bruises.

I said the first thing that came to mind. "I got a call from the company. They discovered some video surveillance from the room where...my parents were found. It is password protected for me, so they haven't seen it yet."

"If it's password protected, do you even know the password?" she asked softly, her washcloth creeping lower down my spine.

"My parents gave me a list of potential passwords that I could use—depending on the severity of the need—in the event of a problem. I'll go through them, starting with the worst scenario first, I guess."

She murmured to herself as she leaned closer, one hand squeezing my shoulder for support as she reached even lower, cleaning the lowest of my back, and the top of another area entirely. I almost lost it when her breasts brushed my arm. "So strong," she whispered, massaging my shoulder unconsciously. Or consciously. Either way was fine with me. "You have scrapes on your back. Is that from this afternoon?" I shrugged.

"Or possibly yesterday. Before I picked you up I got in a bit of a tussle, but Mallory and Gunnar helped me out of it."

Her lips tightened, but she nodded. "What really happened today? I don't think your condition has to do with a business meeting at Temple Industries. Or the break in."

She climbed down from her perch on the edge of the tub, and knelt beside it to better reach my sides. I chose honesty. Somewhat. "I have to duel someone tonight. Someone strong, and I don't know if I can win. Then I have to confront another group of..." I hesitated, not wanting to scare her. "Bad guys who want something very badly. Enough that they might have even had something to do with my parents' deaths." Her hands paused at that, but quickly resumed their work, pressing me back against the tub so that she could move to my chest. Like an expert, she started high, saving the lower area for last.

I realized that as much as I cared about Indie, I didn't know if I could ever fully bring her into my life. It was just too dangerous. Even for me. But she was a Regular. She was defenseless. Well, she had martial arts and firearm training, and was damn good at both, but not enough training to jump into my weight class of bad guys. Dragons were out of her league. Hell, they were out of mine, too. I had to decide if I was going to keep allowing her to assume we were an item, or if I was going to shatter that potential outcome. Her washcloth came to my abs and I tensed instinctively.

She smiled at my reaction. "Well, if you were asking my advice, I would say that it's pretty damn important that you win your...duel?" She made the word a question. I nodded. "I didn't know people still used that word anymore. But I guess your life is not of our time, is it?" I shook my head, glad she had steered the conversation in this direction, but also hesitant to squash my feelings for her. Maybe once this fight was over I would be able to calm down. Slow down my life. Work for the company, and stop taking on such dangerous clients. Her advice was right though. I *had* to win tonight. Everyone depended on me surviving, so I could deal with the dragons afterwards.

"You're right, Indie. I *do* have to win tonight. I just don't know how. Some...strange things happened today. I fought some things that I had never dealt with before, and luckily, I came out on the right side. But I wasn't ready, and it could have cost others their lives. I can't be reckless when it comes to others. When it was just me, I didn't mind, but now..." I looked her in the eyes, placing my fingers atop hers. She stared back, eyes defiant. "My life is too dangerous, even for me. I couldn't bear having someone I care about hurt by something they could never defend themselves against. Like you. It's why I've always kept you at arm's-length. As good as you are, my enemies would make a game of hurting you, just so that they could see me hurt more, before they finished me off."

"I can't allow that. You've been my rock through some pretty rough parts, but I run two lives. I just can't seem to help it. I know it's dangerous, but it's a part of me that I can't give up. Those are the only moments where I truly feel alive. The other life is just a balance—safety and security for the dangerous half. Sometimes they overlap," she smirked at that, "But I must attempt to keep those I care about safe."

She waited, and then, as if I had said nothing, continued washing my abs, her delicate fingers massaging deep into my muscles through the soapy cloth. My blood was hot, seeming to melt the weariness from the muscles underneath her expert fingers.

She finished cleaning all the appropriate places. Her hand paused for a moment, and then she spoke softly. "I think you should handle the rest, Master Temple," she whispered with emphasis. She opened her eyes to stare at me, a feral, hungry gleam twinkling in the blue ice chips of her irises. "Alex might begin to wonder what kind of *doctoring* I am doing." I nodded dumbly.

She climbed to her feet, bending at the waist as she plucked up a stray piece of glass on the floor. Her face was close to mine, and her warm, soapy fingers caressed my temple. "I seem to remember you saying something about danger, but the steam must have made me forget. It must not have been that important. Teach me how to protect myself better, because I am not going anywhere unless you make me. Words are not enough to impede me from taking what I want, and what I know you *also* want. Danger is something I love just as much as I care for you, and it's why I am still around. Man up, Nate. I have."

She smiled to ease the sting of her words, then turned on the balls of her feet, and left me. I would hurt later. Any more cleaning, and I would have had to tip her. As it stood, I would remember this bath for a very long time. First pleasantly, and then with an ache that isn't entirely unpleasant in its own right. Guys are different from girls. Teasing can cause pain later if the teasing was good enough.

And yes, her teasing was glorious.

24

I stepped out of the bathroom in my robe, not wanting to leave the safety of my home. It wasn't just that I was scared, although I was terrified. Battling the Minotaur was not on my bucket list. This could be a very short day for the last Temple heir. And it wasn't just because I didn't want to go to Temple Industries and see whatever digital feed they had told me about, even though I didn't want to see that either. I couldn't imagine what kind of clip I would see, but if it was password protected from even their most trusted employee, Ashley Belmont, then it was not going to be pleasant.

No, it was more than that.

I could still feel Indie's touch on my skin. The whole process of her bathing me clung to my soul. I felt stronger, surer of myself, and I didn't want to leave that behind. I had experienced frequent dalliances with the fairer sex, but never before had I experienced such a strengthening as she had just shown me with a simple bath. I wanted to relish that feeling, and knew that the moment I stepped out the door, all hell would break loose, and the feeling would evaporate like the intensity of that first spray of cologne that leaves the skin somewhere during the middle of the night, when you want it on the most.

I sauntered over to my desk, the robe brushing my knees as I moved. I sat down in my chair, steepled my fingers, and glanced at my phone. I needed to make a call, a legally questionable call to an old college friend. To do that, I needed to use the scrambled sequence she had given me so that neither call could be traced to us. Paranoid?

Yes.

She was one of the most wanted cyber-criminals in the country. Possibly even the world. Her true identity was still a secret to the governmental agencies, but as I didn't know how close anyone was to catching her, or even if she was still being hunted, I couldn't use a social call to talk business with her. She would also be less than pleased if I did such a thing. I flipped open my iMac, and clicked the hidden icon on the desktop that she had sent me: An Encryption software that was years ahead of even most governmental branches. I typed in my cell number as prompted, and clicked *enter*.

The software began bouncing my cell phone number from one country to the next in five-second intervals, making triangulation impossible. I watched this all happen on a Google Maps image of the earth. Then it began switching my number at each location shift, until it revealed a temporary number for me to use, good for only the next seven-seconds. I hesitated. Did I want to do this? No.

But I had to.

Othello would probably relish the call. It had been a while since we'd spoken. I quickly typed in a number from memory. The system chimed, and then began tracing the number, the sequence of digits actually a code she had given me, and not necessarily a true phone number. But the system knew what to do with it. After a few seconds, her voice came to me through the speakers in Russian. I smiled at that, anxious to use the language after so long. That was, after all, where we had met in college. Taking Russian together. It was my fourth language, but I think it was her ninth. Ninth fluent language. Not counting any of the others she merely dabbled in.

"Привет, Фарос. Как дела?" I grinned. *Hello, Pharos. How are you?* Pharos was the nickname she had immediately given me upon discovering that I was a wizard. The Alexandrian Lighthouse, because she said that I shed light on shadows for a living, while she created shadows in the light so that she could work in concealment for a living.

"Очень хорошо, а ты?" I answered, already missing her, but knowing we wouldn't be able to talk personal matters over such a secure line. No breadcrumbs could be left behind for others to follow.

"Not bad. Very, very busy. As much as it pains me to shorten our conversation, keep it fewer than three minutes, if you please. What can I help such a dear flame with, this morning?" I could practically see the smile on her face as she said it. I realized that wherever she was, it must be morning. Or she was simply throwing false trails in the event someone had hacked into our conversation. One never knew with Othello. We were still speaking Russian, and it took me a few seconds to phrase my questions correctly.

I heard her chuckle once I was finished. "Your Russian is growing stale, Pharos. Perhaps you need to find a new Russian bedmate to fine tune that precious tongue of yours. You're beginning to sound rudimentary at best." That was one place we had frequented together, studying our…inflections between marathon bouts of, well, you know. She continued, conscious of our limited time frame. "Now, may I ask what Pharos finds so interesting in such an old book, and what it might have to do with the coming eclipse, or the…Minotaur?" She said the last word in English, but with a thick accent. I felt proud, realizing that I wasn't the only one who had trouble translating that particular word.

"You may not," I answered, smiling.

"No fun. You'll receive an encrypted email shortly with all the pertinent information. May I ask why the interest in this Tomas?" I watched the screen still bouncing our calls throughout the Google Maps image of the earth.

"Just a new face in the game I find myself playing. And I don't like new faces when my life is on the line."

Her voice grew clipped. "No one is allowed to hurt my Pharos. Want me to arrange an accident? I have new friends who specialize in such things." She spoke very softly. Was she asking if I wanted to place a hit on the dragon hunter?

I shook my head. "Not necessary. Yet. But thank you," I said quickly, very aware of the time ticking down. I asked her a few more questions, and she said she would include it all in the email within the hour. "You might need to expand your search to include myths. Anything might be helpful, even though it may not seem so to you. My... specialty finds useful tidbits where others would not."

"Oh, I don't doubt that. I know your...specialty very, *very* well," she purred with a thick Russian accent. My already testosterone-laden body responded, memories of tangled sheets filling my mind. She laughed at my silence. "No need to be a prude, Pharos. We shall chat soon. I may have need of your help in the future, but next time our conversation should be closer. I very much wish to witness your *specialty* firsthand, once again. Check your email soon." Then the line went dead, and the software shut down immediately. My computer rebooted of its own accord, running diagnostics that changed my IP address, and a slew of other safety precautions, basically erasing that my computer had even been running for the last twenty minutes. Pretty neat.

I leaned back in my chair, sighing. I hadn't thought about our bedroom tussles in years. That brought my thoughts back to Indie. Judging from my bath, I assumed she might even be able to top Othello's skills. Sensing something was out of place on my desk, I scanned its surface, and was shocked to see a satin red thong hanging from my lamp. I flinched, quickly snatching them away as if trying to hide them from any witnesses. I felt a piece of parchment folded around the elastic, and grinned. I unfolded it, reading the hastily scrawled lipstick note. The color matched the thong perfectly.

"*I have read that Warriors were usually dressed by their lovers before battle, but I hope that what I did will suffice. I have also read that Heroes carry a trophy into duels for good luck. So, I left you a trinket...Touch for touch, Nate. Your turn next...*"

A grin split my face as I stuffed the thong into my robe pocket. Good luck indeed, and also motivation to get my ass home as quickly and as intact as possible.

I dialed a phone number and waited.

"Mallory," he answered.

"Heya', Mallory," I said. "I was hoping you could pass on a message for Dean." Mallory grunted affirmatively. I made my request, listening to him scribble the note down on a pad of paper. "Repeat the address, if you don't mind," I asked at the end.

"I don't need to repeat the address, Laddie. We both went there the other night. Ye should have it within the hour. I believe yer father already paid for this specific beauty, and I hear it's just come out of surgery, so it's sitting there now. The trick is how to title it..." he paused. "Dean has Power of Attorney so will be able to complete the last request though, since he has Power of Attorney, and he wonna be none too pleased to leave Chateau Falco."

"It's important. I'll make it up to him."

Mallory grunted. "It will be done, Master Temple." Then he simply clicked off.

I nodded, wandering around the room for an appropriate change of clothes for the order of unusual events I would be facing tonight. I knew I would be back to meet with Peter this evening, so I could grab the last change of clothes then. If I was still in one piece after the Minotaur.

I realized I was thumbing the thong in my pocket and grinned to myself. They were still warm. Very warm.

25

Dressed and prepared for battle in my *Hugo Boss* suit, I picked up my phone and dialed the number Officer Marlin had left me. She answered on the second ring. "Officer Marlin."

"Master Temple," I quipped, following her terse response. She chuckled.

"You mean, Archangel, I'm sure. One should hear the scuttlebutt around the water cooler after the event at the bridge."

"I think I'll stick with Master Temple. It's catchier."

"Still, Archangel has a nice ring to it."

I made a disgusted sound. "You ready to entertain a less than deserving gentleman caller at an expo this evening?"

"Your...gift made my choices much easier than I was accustomed to. I found something rather flashy. I hope it won't be too much."

"No one would dare complain that a flower blooms."

I heard a surprised, but definitely pleased, intake of breath. "Well, *that* wasn't what I was fishing for, but thank you. How many times have you used that line?"

"Just this once, but if you vouch for its effect, I might keep it up my sleeve."

"It's definitely a keeper."

"Noted. I'll pick you up in an hour or so. Is that enough time?"

"More than enough. I've already been preparing, just in case."

"I'm sure you didn't have much difficulty. You were already more than halfway there when we met."

She sighed on the other end of the line. "From a near death experience to a ball. Young girls imagine stories about this sort of thing."

"But they imagine those stories with a gentleman or a prince. I am neither."

"Debatable," she answered with a demure chuckle.

"Gunnar has your address, so we'll see you then." I hung up.

My phone chirped back at me almost as soon as I set it down on my desk, Richard Wagner's *Ride of the Valkyries* blaring loudly. I let it play for a few seconds, enjoying the jingle, then answered. It was Gunnar. "Nate. There is a man outside my office adamantly waving car keys at me, declaring that I left them at a restaurant that I have never visited before. Do you have any idea why he's here?" I suppressed a grin.

"Not the foggiest." I paused. "Why don't you do one of your FBI things, like running the plates to see who the keys really belong to?"

"We're not supposed to use government resources for personal reasons," he answered, very textbook.

"Someone out there is looking for their keys, and someone happens to bring them to your attention, and you're not going to try to discover who they belong to?" I argued derisively. "And you wonder why bureaucracy doesn't work, why citizens are so concerned."

"Fine." I heard him fiddle with his keyboard, rapidly typing in commands. His voice was distant, speaking to someone else in the room. "License plate number." A shuffling of paper and then utter silence. "You're kidding me," he said in disbelief, voice full of disapproval to the agent in his office. I managed to tap the *mute* button on my phone before I burst out laughing into Gunnar's earpiece. A muffled argument took place as the agent vehemently defended his information. "Fine. *Fenrir*, it is," Gunnar snapped. I heard more keys tapping and then another deathly silence. It stretched on for a full minute. Then longer.

"Did you mean to hang up on me, Gunnar? You haven't spoken for a while," I said neutrally.

"Fuck you and the horse you rode in on," he growled.

"I take it you found the owner?" I asked.

I heard him dismiss the agent before speaking to me. "The report declares that a certain Gunnar Randulf and Nathin Temple have owned this 2012 Land Rover Defender Hard Top for the last three months. Funny, because I don't remember ever using my home as collateral for a..." I heard a few more clicks. "$80,000 SUV."

"I remember you having it, but you sent it off to Vilnar for customization, which added on close to $100,000, if I remember correctly."

"Hmmm...It's not as expensive as the Aston Martin," he said disappointedly.

"You destroyed the Aston Martin in less than 12 hours. This thing has bulletproof glass, and all sorts of other additions that would make it practically impossible to total. Unless you wanted to play chicken with an armored truck heading out of Fort Knox. That might be a different story. Then again, with as much as was spent on this guy, the armored truck might just die in shame."

"Nate, this is definitely crossing the line."

I argued back, ready. "It's registered to me with you as a co-owner. Should be fine. Just take the keys. Public transportation would cramp our style tonight."

"I will be fired for this. You ready for your chauffeur?" he asked, resigned.

"If you please."

"I don't."

"Then I'm afraid I must insist."

"Twenty minutes then, asshole."

"I love it when you talk dirty to me."

He hissed. "You do realize that this call is probably being recorded, right?"

"Of course. My company provided the tech, pro bono. See you soon."

He sighed on the other line. "Nate?"

"Yes." I answered carefully.

"Thanks." It sounded like he had been tortured into saying that single word.

"Men don't say 'thanks.' That's gushy girl talk. Just drive the shit out of it when necessary. It's really just an insurance policy for our survival. The way you drive anyway." I knew I was supposed to be staying out of the investigation into my parents' murder, as Turner Locke had informed me, but I couldn't just leave this on Gunnar's shoulders. It was my responsibility, too, and I knew shit would hit the fan soon, and he would need my help.

"Asshole," he muttered. "By the way, I've tried calling your dragon hunter a few times, but he hasn't answered. I also can't find a speck of dirt on him, let alone any hard facts. Think it's an alias? Have you heard anything?"

I began to speak when my phone beeped. I looked down. "Huh. Speak of the devil. I think that's him on the other line. Be here in twenty and I'll tell you what I find out." He grunted and I clicked over.

"The very magnificent Master Temple at your service. How can I assist you, you wicked dragon hunter, you?"

He growled back. "We haven't had much luck hunting any dragons, where it seems you've been doing nothing but that." He didn't sound pleased.

"Need me to train you on my extensive skills? So far, I count two, possibly three dead at my hand." I fudged the number a bit, because technically, Peter had killed Raven, but Tomas didn't need to know that. "And I haven't even been *trying*."

"Your survival skills are rather impressive, but I seem to remember a net launcher saving the city of St. Louis from having a wizard-shaped smear on her sidewalk yesterday," he said suggestively.

"So, it wasn't Spiderman. Damn."

"What?"

"Nothing. Listen, I'm kind of busy. Need the lesson or not?"

He grunted. "We're fine. But it seems they really have a hard-on for you. If we'd simply been following you around, our job could have been over by now."

"You mean your contract would be finished."

He was silent for a minute. "Perhaps."

"Who hired you? Because I'm sure that would give us one of those clues that seem to help one understand complicated situations."

"Not important," he answered immediately.

"Okay, fine. Does the eclipse have any significance to you?"

A longer silence. "Perhaps. Why do you ask?"

"I don't know if it's related, but shortly after we had our pleasant introduction, I found a note my father had left me, warning me of the eclipse."

"How cute. Your father left you a napkin note, and you think it's relevant. Typical—"

"It was written in his own blood..."

I felt him stiffen through the phone. "I apologize. I know what it's like to have a family like yours, and to suddenly lose the patriarch. My family is very old, tracing our lineage back to the crusades."

"Uh-huh," I answered, not hiding my boredom. My laptop chimed behind me.

"You don't sound surprised..."

"Hold on a minute," I answered, clicking the email open on my laptop. After a long password, I opened the encrypted file from Othello, and read quickly, catching the highlights. "Tomas Mullingsworth ...Ex RN. I thought you said you were from Brooklyn?" I added curiously. Silence answered me. "Served in Afghanistan. There's a lot of redaction. Hold on..." I made the false sounds of heavy typing and then came back. "There. Much better. Questionable operations: Three. Drunken bouts with superior officers: seven." I paused. "Really? That's quite impress—"

His voice was full of rage. "How dare you? That is personal information."

I let the silence build, his furious huffing the only sound between us. "My *life* is quite personal to *me*. And when it has been close to taken a handful of times in a span of days, shortly after meeting with your targets, I decided it wise to learn more about all the players involved. Was I wrong? Would you have done any differently?"

The silence built, and then he let out a breath. "You are a very dangerous man, Master Temple. I see why some have declared this city 'Poach-free.' Your research seems quite extensive. No one has ever been able to get that information, let alone remove the redactions. I made sure it was buried. Deep."

"Never deep enough for me, Tomas, and you should remember that. This is me being polite."

"Good to know. Now, what do you want?"

"The eclipse. Ring any bells?"

"Not directly, but I've heard stories. Legends, really. Some dark ritual the dragons have been searching for. But they've never found what they need to perform it. I don't know exactly what they need, what they seem to be missing."

"I think it's safe to say that they have discovered it somewhere near my city."

He grunted. "But I don't know what this has to do with my mark. I've heard neither hide nor hair of him since we arrived. Just a trail leading here, and then nothing."

"Tell me about him," I said carefully. "If you trust me. Perhaps we can help each other. I just want this all to stop, I don't care who gets credit for it."

"I was hired to take out a rogue black dragon. Sometimes he goes by the name Raego. Ever heard of him? Seen him?"

I shook my head, and realized he couldn't see me. "No." I searched Othello's documents for the name, but came up with nothing. "Why would your client want him dead? Or whatever it is you do."

"Questions aren't part of the job. Just the money for a head. I've never met a nice dragon, so it's pretty cut and dried. But this one is dangerous. Comes from an old family. Have you ever heard of a black dragon?" He asked very slowly.

I could sense the seriousness, so I kept my answer formal. "No, but I've recently seen a rainbow of others. Even silver."

"Yeah. I heard about that one on the news. Very dangerous. But nothing compared to the black."

"I was on the news?" I asked, surprised.

"Yep." He let the silence build, but I knew Gunnar was on the way, so forced the conversation forward.

"I've seen a red one spit fire," I added.

He growled, a familiar sound from Tomas, I was beginning to realize. "We almost had that one on the courthouse until that crazy old man harpooned her with a lightning stick. He one of yours?"

"Yes," I answered carefully.

"Damn. Maybe we *should* have you teach us a thing or two. You're mighty resourceful for a Noob dragon slayer."

"I'm *mighty resourceful* with anyone who tries to kill me. Whether I know dick about them, or not." He laughed deeply. "I saw the yellow one create oily fire. And the silver one could spit bullets in all sorts of shapes and sizes." I thought back. "And they all had some kind of mind control power. Is that common?"

He was quiet for a few seconds, and I realized he was taking a drink, obviously something stiff because his voice came back raspy. "Not common at all."

"You're telling me that the first dragons I've ever encountered are uber-dangerous? Cream of the crop murderers?"

"Seems that way."

Of course they were. "Okay, so what's so special about the black one?"

He took another drink, and then he spilled his words in a rush. "It's said, because I've never actually met someone who has survived one, that they can bend shadows, appearing and disappearing at whim. Their mind magic is so subtle and powerful that their victims won't realize until days later that they have acted any differently than normal. They can melt fire, petrify with a look, shape-shift into different people entirely, mind-fuck other dragons, et cetera, et cetera. Point being, the most dangerous of the bastards. Do you have any idea what kind of reputation a kill like that could make?"

"If he's guilty, of course."

"Right, I show up in town hunting rumors of the most badass dragon in centuries, and all of a sudden you have a reptile dysfunction in your city."

I began laughing. "Nice. I'm using that one."

Tomas grunted in pride before continuing. "A flock of lady dragons murdering and pillaging for no reason. Probably just a coincidence."

"Harem," I corrected.

"What?"

"I like to think of them as a harem. A bunch of females at your beck and call? Harem, definitely a harem."

"Fine, a harem," he chided, sounding upset he hadn't come up with it himself.

"But why would a book be so important to them?" I pondered aloud.

Tomas was quiet for the length of another drink. "A book? Is that what this is all about? Why they've been killing all you nerds?"

"See? Information trading is beneficial. And I am one rich, motherfucking nerd, thank you very much."

"Spill it, Temple."

"Each one I've encountered, or seen the aftermath of, was searching for a book. *The Sons of the Dying Sun*. Does that mean anything to your extensive knowledge on dragons?" I mocked.

"Can't say that it does. Do you think it's what they've been searching for all this time? For their ritual?"

"I haven't the foggiest," I admitted. "But it seems awfully important to them. Enough to risk losing a few of his flock to the local wizard billionaire."

"Billionaire?" he gasped. "Why in the hell aren't you in Bora Bora, fucking, drinking, and fucking your problems away?"

"Already done as much of both as I could before becoming a local nuisance."

"Damn. You do this for the fun of it, then?"

"To be honest, I didn't know what I was getting myself into. The first dragon just kinda stumbled into my lap." I remembered that first encounter and grew angrier. "She pissed me off by destroying a treasured tome. One of a kind type of book."

"Did you just say the word *tome*?" he asked, barely containing his laughter.

"It's what an educated man calls those flippy, heavy things with pieces of paper and strange symbols inside. They also have some with pictures, but those aren't usually called tomes."

"Alright, Merlin," he chuckled.

I scanned the email from Othello, catching Hermes' name a few times. Interesting. "I haven't been able to find much on this book. Barely that it even exists. Just mentions and vague references, but no hard facts. I didn't think I would be even that successful, or they would have undoubtedly found it by now."

"True."

I heard Indie shout my name from downstairs. "I gotta run, Tomas. I'll be visiting *Artemis' Garter* tonight, a club in the Central West End. Judging from my track record, no doubt I'll run into some interesting people there. You should have men there just in case, that way you aren't bitching at me tomorrow about stealing your glory and all that."

He laughed for a long time. "No way. You're picking *there* to hang out in the middle of all *this*? You really are a reckless bastard."

I frowned. "Never been there, but it has an open roof, which is good for quick escapes. And Artemis is the moon goddess, so it fits," I offered.

"Whatever. See you there, filthy bastard." He laughed again as he hung up.

Why did everyone laugh at that? Guess I'd find out later. I gathered up my things, pocketed my phone, and raced down the stairs. Indie was watching me curiously. I fingered her thong in my pocket and shot her a smile, revealing a bit of the thin satin so that only she could see. "I'll return them to you as soon as I am able, my lady."

"Such a gentleman," she cooed. "Like the note?"

I simply stared back, undressing her with my eyes. My look must have worked because her cheeks tinted the slightest red. I used a bit of magic to pinch her behind, and she squeaked. "I'll see you soon."

"Quite literally." She winked back seductively so that only I could see.

Alex looked back and forth between us, frowning. "Stop acting weird," he said, but appeared aloof to our true conversation. Indie intended for me to *see* quite a bit more of her soon. It sounded like a good idea to me.

"There's a monstrosity of a vehicle parked diagonally in front of our store. Just because he has a badge doesn't mean he gets to block your customers from the entrance," Indie grumped, very manager-like.

"Agreed. I'll file a complaint with the FBI." I bolted out the door and saw Gunnar pressing buttons on the dash, a look of pure joy on his face. He was early. The silver SUV gleamed in the sun, shiny rims, and military-grade tires lifting the body up high. I slid inside with aid of the 'oh-shit' bar just above the inside of the passenger door and smiled back at him.

"This is so cool!" He grinned.

"Glad you like it. The manager of Plato's Cave would like to file a complaint against the FBI for a terrible parking job that is blocking my front door from customers."

He smiled back. "Call Captain Kosage, I'll just run his little ass over with my shiny new tank." I laughed, nodding. "Temple Industries?" he asked loudly, pressing a button.

I began to answer when the Navigation unit spoke back. "Estimated trip duration, twenty minutes. Please buckle your seatbelts." Gunnar pounded the wheel like a child with his new favorite Christmas toy and took off.

26

My dress shoes clacked against the floors as I strode down the marble hallway of my new palace, Temple Industries. Receptionists, scientists, engineers, mail clerks, and lower peasants all, gawked openly as their new CEO meandered through the halls...

Hopelessly lost.

I'd been too stubborn to ask for help, and my minions had been too terrified to hurt my pride. So, we walked, Gunnar behind me, glancing here and there at different labs and offices.

I had no fucking idea where we were.

"So, is this the tour?" Gunnar teased.

I sighed, finally pointing a commanding finger at one of my new minions carrying a bundle of papers. "I need to speak with Ashley Belmont. Would you be so kind as to guide me to her office?"

He bumped into a copier, almost dropping his stack of papers. "Me?"

"No, the woman behind you." Bless his heart; he actually turned around to look. When he turned back he was blushing furiously.

"Um, follow me?" he said nervously, voice rising higher on the last word.

"Sure thing. But let me offer a word of advice. Don't incline your voice at the end of your sentences. Apologizing is a sign of weakness."

"Sorr—" He hesitated. "Right. This way then, Master Temple?" His face turned even darker as he did it again.

"Just think on it," I sighed reluctantly, motioning him onward.

He led us through the labyrinth of offices and labs, zigzagging this way and that until he finally came to a set of thick black doors and a desk. An aged receptionist glared at him, and then us. "Appointment?" she fired off in a no-nonsense tone.

"No," I answered, feigning frustration.

"Miss Belmont is rather busy, what with that rapscallion Temple son doing nothing around here. I swear. If he walked in right now, I'd give him a piece of my mind. It just isn't right to run a company like this." I nodded back. The tour-guide looked about ready to swallow his tongue, but remained silent out of corporate fear. "Be that as it may, you need an appointment. Honestly, I don't know how you got in here without beeping somebody." She arched her neck to study Gunnar. "He looks like a cop. Is that why you're here? A couple of upstart detectives looking for a case-breaker? Well, you can just leave like all the others. Appointments are like the Ten Commandments around here. Followed to a T." She leaned back, face smug with satisfaction.

I smiled, unable to help myself. "I hear all sorts of things about this Temple son. Is he as bad as all that? Have you never seen him before?" Gunnar and the tour guide stiffened as one, not wanting to be a part of the conversation.

"Off the record?" she asked, squinting her eyes. I nodded. "I hear he's into all sorts of depraved acts. Why, I hear he even..." she glanced around to be sure we were alone. She lowered her voice then, leaning forward. "Has premarital sex. Frequently. With all types of women. It isn't right. It just isn't. He needs a strong role model. He needs to be here running his company. I hear he even smokes and drinks. Bah. If he were my son, I'd grab him by the ear and teach him a thing or two. That's what I'd do. But who listens to old Greta? Nobody, that's who." She composed herself, patting her coiffured hair. "Now, names and identification, please. I will schedule an appointment at Miss Belmont's earliest convenience."

I strode forward, grinning like an idiot. The tour guide looked apoplectic, searching for an immediate escape. I handed over my driver's license with Gunnar's on top. She scanned his and opened her planner, flipping pages a few weeks ahead knowingly, speaking aloud. "There is an opening in three weeks on Wednesday. Shall that work, Agent Randulf, and..." Her eyes widened, looking up at me, horrified. "Master Temple!"

"The one and only." I grinned.

"Oh, bother! An old lady does have a loose tongue!"

"It's quite alrig—" I began.

"Oh, it certainly is *not*! Foolish, foolish, *foolish*! I'm terribly sorry. I'll just page Miss Belmont, and be packing up my box then." She was flustered, rearranging papers back and forth, utterly lost. I spotted a tear at the corner of one eye.

I opened my mouth to speak, and she leveled a gnarled finger at me. "Oh, no you don't. If I'm to be fired, I'll do it with all the dignity an old lady can muster."

"But—" She slapped her hand down onto her desk like a clap of thunder.

"*No!* You should be ashamed of yourself, letting me rattle on like that, digging my own grave. You are everything I heard about if you would do such a thing to an old woman. You don't need a *role* model. You need *Jesus!*" The last was a shriek.

The door to Ashley's office flew open then. Gunnar was pathetically trying to suppress a laugh, doubled over with his hands clasped around his knees. "What in the *hell* is going on out here?" She saw me, and blinked. "Master Temple. Is everything quite alright?"

I shrugged. "I was trying to tell Greta that all is well, and that I appreciate a little honesty now and then. Even a *lot* of honesty." I added with an appeasing grin. She scowled back. "Anyway, no harm done. Mind if we talk to Miss Belmont, Greta?"

Her eyes were twin coals, her cheeks reddening with embarrassment now. She waved a hand, shooing us on, but her gnarled finger locked onto our tour guide and her voice was low, dripping with venom as she proceeded to strip away his hide. Ashley looked bewildered, but stepped aside so that we could enter. The doors closed with a soft click behind us. "What happened?" Ashley asked carefully. "She's an old woman. I don't know how you managed to get her so worked up. I was outside just five minutes ago. How could you have possibly gotten such a reaction in so short a time?"

Gunnar spoke up between bouts of laughter. "He has a gift. Oh, god. My stomach," he wheezed. "It hurts. Laughing so hard. Sometimes I wish I had his charm, and then other times..." He waved a hand towards Greta in the other room, and began laughing all over again. Once he got a breath he continued. "I'm glad I don't."

Ashley looked at me and I shrugged. "She saw us, and began talking about *that rapscallion, Nate Temple.*" I mimicked her aged voice. "I should have stopped her sooner, but it was hard to get a word in. She's a tough old bag. I like her."

Ashley studied me, fighting a grin. "Me too. I'd like to keep her around for a while... without her having a heart attack on me."

That sobered me up. "Right. Sorry."

She nodded, motioning towards her desk. We followed, declining her offer of drinks. "So, you've come about the video feed?" she asked carefully, eyeing Gunnar a few times when he wasn't looking.

I nodded. She typed a series of commands on her iMac desktop.

"Well, I can't say I quite understand it. It seems to be a feed from a security camera that runs separate from the rest of the system. Nobody even knew of it until we had input your information into the system as an employee. As soon as your social security number hit the system we got a critical ping. Any time something important or dangerous happens at the company, the upper echelon of management gets a 911 email. This one came only to me and you." I leaned forward, interested. "I haven't been able to open the feed. It's encrypted, and I have no idea what the password could be. Your... parents gave me a list of potentials, but I regret to inform you that none of mine worked. I have been efficiently locked out. Our only hope is to see if you have access to it."

"May I?" I asked, pointing at her desktop. She nodded, getting out of her chair and holding it out for me.

"I already logged off." Gunnar leaned back in his chair, curiously watching the scene unfold, or possibly just watching Ashley. Puppy love. Did they even realize they were each checking the other out? She guided me through the logon process, and then helped me open my email, which in turn asked me a series of questions that only my parents could have arranged years before. Successfully answering the questions, my email finally opened. There at the top of the page—marked with a blinking exclamation mark—was the 911 email. I double clicked it, and a password warning popped up. I looked back at her and she grinned sheepishly, stepping back and turning her head.

I typed in the verse from Dante's Inferno that my father and I had frequently discussed through a tough semester in college. I flourished my finger dramatically, and asked her a question. "How many attempts did you have before it locked you out?"

"Three," she answered nervously.

"Here, we, *go*," I said, then pressed *enter*. The password box wiggled a wrong answer. "Hmmm." I mentally glanced at the list in my mind, wondering if any of the other passwords might work, depending on the severity level of my father's warning. I hadn't tried the last password yet, as I had been hoping that it might not be as serious as we all thought. I mean, how would the video feed know how important it was? It had to be something my father frequently monitored as a security precaution if it was automatically logged as such an important breach. Something others wouldn't have access to. Not even Ashley, judging by the fact that it had only appeared to her after my information was logged into the system.

I leaned back, thumbing my lip at the puzzle.

The room was as tense as a china cabinet in front of a live orchestra. Not thinking of a better idea, I typed the last password on my parents' list, realizing that the irony must be a coincidence. The title of a journal written by Isaac Newton about Nicolas Flamel, the Alchemist who supposedly discovered the philosopher's stone: *The Caduceus, the Dragons of Flammel.*

I typed *Caduceus*, remembering that the coin the Minotaur had given me depicted that very staff on one side. It was in my pocket now. Another discreet reference to Hermes. That bore looking into.

The password box shook again in angry denial. Ashley unbuttoned the top button of her blouse, breathing heavily. Gunnar tensed, noticing her movement very pointedly, but she didn't see that. "One more shot. I don't think it was one of the passwords on their list," she added respectfully.

I leaned back again, closing my eyes. She was right. It would have been too simple if it were the last password. I was letting my infatuation with dragons overwhelm my logic, but it had been the direst password on their list, so it had been worth a shot. I mentally zipped through memories of my father, trying to catch something, anything, that might give me a clue. An everyday password he would undoubtedly use. If it was to a secret video feed, then it was something he wanted kept separate. Something he could privately monitor at his own leisure. Which might mean a secret project. But why keep a project secret from his company? It must have been dangerous if he didn't deem it worthy of his employees' knowledge. I began to get a terrible feeling in my stomach. Was something here, in my new company, that he didn't trust any of his employees with, even his protégé, Ashley Belmont? My memory snagged on a brief conversation we had had while on a yacht in the middle of the ocean on my 21st birthday. Something I had only heard once. Something that *only* I had heard.

I slowly leaned forward one last time. Surely it couldn't be. That had been a night of hard drinking, a sharing of talk like we had never had before. An introduction into manhood, he had called it. We had talked until the sun came up, on everything from ancient alchemy to modern day particle theory at CERN; from Aristotle to Ayn Rand; from Greek myths to the Bible's Revelations; from one topic to another in almost every field of study. Then we had briefly discussed extremes. Extreme *measures* in particular.

My forearms pebbled as I remembered the two words that he had uttered as we had drifted off to sleep on the deck. He had repeated them three times, and then fallen asleep. I had merely assumed it was a disturbing thought from some vague mention of one of our topics, as we were both heavily intoxicated, but my eidetic memory was profound, and I had remembered these words despite the fact. Only now did I consciously dredge them up from the bottom of my memory, and the feeling of that wonderful night threatened to break me.

I hunched over the keyboard, shivering both in fear at the tone of voice he had used to utter the words, and also in profound loss, realizing all over again that I would never have the chance to speak with him again.

My fingers punched in each key, slowly, robotically. *Pandora Protocol*. I hoped my capitalization was correct, or that the password was even correct. It was a far-fetched idea, and to be honest, it didn't feel right. One drunken night, years ago? My father was much too methodical for that, right? But then again, it was such a specific statement to idly ramble about. It *had* to mean something.

I looked up at Gunnar. His eyes revealed how much it hurt him to see me so grief-stricken. I turned to Ashley. Her eagerness was gone as her eyes filled with empathy. She slowly reached over to place a hand on my shoulder. "If this isn't it, then it doesn't matter. He can't expect us to type in a password that we were never given. It's no one's fault but his own if he created an unbreakable encryption that was important enough for us to see, but not important enough to receive a hint. He couldn't expect that," she repeated.

"Oh, yes. Yes, he could. He would *demand* it," I whispered.

Without further preamble, I pressed my finger to the *enter* key the same way I would have pressed the lethal injection button at a sanctioned execution of an innocent man. The computer chimed above me, as my eyes were still locked on the *enter* key. Realizing the password had worked, my shoulders slumped further. *No, please not this. He couldn't have...*

My father had kept his promise then. His secret project had indeed been real. Was that why my parents had been killed? Had someone discovered his secret work? I slowly lifted my gaze to the screen. Ashley was shifting nervously from foot to foot behind me. I clicked *play*.

It flickered to life instantly. I read the timestamp on the recording as I waited for something to happen. It must have been a motion-activated camera, because it jumped ahead at random intervals, and only when someone was walking past a particular door. With each person, a name would materialize at the bottom of the feed. *Jenna Davis. Accountant. Regular.* I began to frown after seeing the first few people caught on film. Each time one passed, their name, title, and the word *Regular* would appear at the bottom of the screen.

I felt a chill at the back of my neck. Each person would walk by the door as if it didn't exist. One woman dropped a paper and it landed directly in front of the door. She glanced down at the ground, searching back and forth as if trying to see the paper that was barely two inches away from her toes. But she didn't seem to see anything. She checked a few papers in her hand, frowned, and then glanced at the floor again. With a sigh, she turned back the way she had come. Five minutes later, she reappeared on camera, walking briskly past the discarded piece of paper on the ground without a care in the world.

We looked at each other curiously. Gunnar had stepped behind the computer to watch. "Is she blind? It was right in front of her."

Ashley spoke up. "She has perfect vision. She also isn't a Regular." Sure enough, the word *Regular* hadn't appeared at the bottom of the screen, but no elaboration had been listed either.

We turned back to the camera to watch a few more people enter and leave the frame. Then, my parents came onto the screen. Their forms sparkled like radio disturbance on the feed, but all else was clear. They conversed casually, leaning against the wall beside the odd door, glancing out of the camera's view frequently. Then, in the middle of speaking, they both darted inside the door and then closed it behind them. A minute later, a man walked near the door, looked back and forth, searching, then turned away, as if he had been looking for my parents.

"Creepy," I said warily.

"Can you pause it?" Ashley asked.

I did, and turned to her. "That door doesn't exist," she said simply. I arched a brow at her. "Look at the symbol above the door. It's the Omega symbol. I recognize the hallway, and know I've walked past that stretch of camera at least two dozen times in the last week. But I have *never seen that door.*"

The silence stretched as we considered that.

"It's cloaked then," I told them. It was as if I spoke a foreign language. "Hidden. Secret. Hocus pocus." I waggled my fingers.

"Then how can we see it on this feed? And how does the camera know all the information about each passerby?" Gunnar asked.

I pondered that. "It must be why this camera is off the main system. It's unique. It can see anything, even through magic. I bet it could even sense—" I began, looking at Gunnar, and then stopped. I had been about to say that it would probably reveal his wolf form, but Ashley didn't know about that.

"You were going to say that it would probably show Gunnar's werewolf form," she said simply, as if reading my mind. "You're right. It would. I designed the software, but never thought of merging it with live cameras."

We each turned to her, eyes wide. "I know almost every Freak in town. Your parents kept tabs on everyone. You would be surprised at some of them, but your secret is safe with me, Agent Randulf. No one else here knows." She smiled, unabashed.

"Well, isn't that something," I added.

"You will be granted access to the Arcanum that your parents compiled whenever you wish," she told me as if it were nothing out of the ordinary. My thoughts were racing. My parents had indeed pursued their secret then. It couldn't be anything else.

"I'm going to keep playing the feed," I said. Everyone nodded, leaning closer.

The feed jumped forward seventeen minutes. Then my parents bolted out the door, each leaving in a different direction. Odd. Ten minutes later, a shadow blinked across the hallway, and a new figure stepped into view. A string of question marks appeared at the bottom of the screen. The figure didn't sparkle like my parents. He seemed to be cloaked in shadows, as if outlined by them. He looked each direction, and then slipped up to the door he shouldn't have been able to see. He fiddled with the handle a moment, and was then inside the room, the door closing behind him. The feed blinked red for a few seconds, the word *unidentified intruder* blinking instead of the string of question marks from before.

The feed jumped ahead seventeen minutes again, and then he slipped out of the room, darting down the hallway in the same direction my mother had left. Less than a minute later, my dad entered the feed, sparkling with his name at the bottom of the screen. He studied the door, seeming nervous. Then he lifted his eyes to the security camera and spoke silently. His face was haggard. I studied it carefully, reading his lips, and my blood turned to ice.

Then he set off in the same direction as the intruder. A steel door slammed down over the invisible door, securing it from any future tampering, and then the feed stopped. The video feed jumped ahead half an hour and then froze, blinking the date and time in large red letters. The only other letters on the screen were *Titan!*

Then it shut off, the whole computer shutting down, and rebooting.

I stood urgently, pacing back and forth. No one spoke. My mind scattered, rebelling against my futile attempts to control my fury. I felt my power rising up inside me like a tidal wave. I finally spoke, panting uncontrollably. "The feed stopped within one minute of the Time of Death announced by the coroner. That feed was somehow tied to my parents' heartbeat, stopping as soon as they died. That can't be possible," I said, exasperated.

Still, no one spoke. I rounded on Ashley. "Do you know anything, *anything*, about this?" I demanded.

She shook her head urgently. "Nothing. I swear."

Gunnar spoke softly. "You understood what he said to you." It wasn't a question.

I turned to him, slowly. "Oh, yes. I understood it perfectly." I continued pacing, trying to keep up with my fleeting thoughts.

"Care to share?" he asked sympathetically. I ignored him as the computer chimed back to life. I flew to the desk, logged back in, and signed into my email, but the video feed was gone. I logged off, and strode out of the room, Ashley and Gunnar barely keeping up.

Greta stood, looking horrified as she saw my face. A box was neatly packed on her desk. "You," I leveled an angry finger at her, my power leaking out enough to launch a flurry of papers from her desk into the air. She squeaked like a child, terror filling her eyes as the tempest of papers floated down around her like snow. "Are not leaving my company. Sit. Down." My voice was rough with emotion. She obeyed, collapsing into her chair with a faint squeak of hinges. Then I was off again. I called over my shoulder. "We'll be in touch, Miss Belmont. We will *definitely* be in touch." I turned my head to look her in the eyes over my shoulder. "Soon."

Gunnar followed in my wake like a good dog, as the Master Temple stormed out of his castle to pick a fight with a dragon, or the Minotaur, or some helpless bystander who happened to tick him off on the way.

Someone was going to die. Soon. By my hand. And I was going to relish every second of it. But first, we were headed to the expo center to try to learn something about the dragons' sudden interest in the eclipse tomorrow afternoon. Maybe I would get the chance to kill someone there.

One could dream.

27

We had picked up Tory and were headed into the parking lot at the *Eclipse Expo!* Or so the signs said. The hotel was vast, full of auditoriums designed for conferences and proms, loaded with luxurious restaurants, several spas, and a smattering of gift shops. I had been in a daze since leaving Temple Industries, pondering the implications of my father's last message to me. He had known it was the end, or at least seriously assumed it to be the case. He had relied so heavily on my eidetic memory, and skill of lip reading, and even the knowledge of a password that had mostly been a lucky guess. Now I had one answer, but it only led deeper into the rabbit hole, giving me countless more questions. When this was all over I would bury myself in solving their secret before it was too late. If it wasn't too late already...It was too volatile of a project to be left unattended. And it had already been over a week.

Being so distracted, I had barely noticed Tory joining us. She and Gunnar had made small talk while we drove, complimenting each other's clothing, but I had been mostly ignoring them. Not purposely, just so enveloped in my own thoughts that nothing else had mattered. My phone vibrated in my pocket. I plucked it out, glanced at the screen, and then answered the unknown number.

"Master Temple—" I instantly recognized the nasally voice.

"Go fuck yourself, Kosage." Then I hung up, calmly placing the phone back into my pocket. I didn't give one flying hell about the cops right now. The silence that ensued in the car was as delicate as brittle glass. Gunnar turned the car off and waited for me to compose myself. I blinked, looking around as if surprised. "You two ready?" I asked.

Gunnar nodded, and I heard Tory agree. I opened my door and hopped down to the pavement. I quickly unlatched Tory's door and opened it for her. Her hand was halfway raised to do it for herself. I held out a hand to help her since she was wearing bright blue heels. She stared at me, slightly surprised. "How did you move so fast?" she whispered very seriously.

I blinked back. "Pardon?"

Gunnar was watching me warily. "All I saw was a blur, and I'm a werewolf. You have never moved like that before..."

I looked from one to the other for a few moments and then shrugged uneasily. "My guard is down. You might see me do a few things tonight that are unusual. A wizard's life is all about control, and presently I seem to have none. I'll need you to be my compass between right and wrong, normal and irregular. Do you think you can do that for me?" I asked, unsure of myself for the first time in a very long time.

I never asked others to help me, but I honestly felt like my head was stuffed with wool, and yet somehow that I was thinking clearer than I ever had before.

"Perhaps you should wait in the car while Tory and I search the Expo Center," Gunnar offered. "And hanging up on Kosage probably wasn't your best idea."

I shook my head urgently. "A werewolf and the she-hulk might not be enough if we run into company. They could mind-fuck you without me there to protect you. Remember the Raven at my shop? She almost had you until I stomped all over her mind web." His face turned red, remembering all too well. "Just keep an eye out for me. I seem to have less restraint than usual, and I feel stronger. Which doesn't make sense. It almost feels the same as when I was first coming into my powers as a teenager. Perhaps I am reaching another plateau of strength." I didn't mention the oddity of the thief stumbling directly into the cops by the river. The less they knew the better. Plus, my distortion of chance might work to our advantage inside the Expo Center.

Gunnar's eyes widened at that. "Aren't you already stronger than most other wizards?" I nodded. "Is this spike normal?"

I chewed my lip for a moment. "I don't think so. At least not to this degree."

I reached further with my hand, offering it to Tory. She finally accepted, and allowed me to help her out of the SUV. I stepped back, eyeing her up and down speculatively. "Stunning. Simply stunning." Her cheeks warmed at the obvious interest. "And you call me Archangel. You look like Aphrodite." Her sleek white dress hugged her hips, leaving little to the imagination. It was slit at the side to reveal a thigh somehow still tanned from the summer. Either that or she carefully maintained a natural-looking fake tan. She looked classy, yet dangerously seductive. Like a James Bond girl.

I reached out a hand, but hesitated. "May I?"

After a glance to Gunnar, she nodded, obviously wary of my previous warning. "You two have nothing to fear from me. I don't think..." I delicately brushed her curled hair back to reveal her bare shoulder. I appraised her as if contemplating a purchase. Without asking, I unclasped the delicate chain necklace around her throat, and replaced it with a heavy diamond choker from my suit pocket. Not my intended purpose for the jewelry, but I had backups. Her eyes widened at the obvious quality of the necklace. I handed hers back and she tucked it into her purse. "This is better. It's flashier, and less likely to get in your way if you need to move," I said. I studied her face, admiring her skill with a brush. The makeup was definitely eye-catching, but it was missing something. "Do you have any bright red lipstick?"

She nodded, digging in her purse. I motioned for her to continue. She applied it expertly. Gunnar watched with apparent interest as she finished. It was as if she had suddenly found a spotlight, lips gleaming like fresh blood. She looked perfect. I glanced at Gunnar, looking him up and down, calculating. "I don't have any lipstick, Nate, so don't bother." I smiled back. He looked every inch the modern Viking. Nordic features flashed harshly in the afternoon light. I simply nodded approval and he rolled his eyes. "Who gets to judge you?" Gunnar grumped.

"How about our delicate Tory?"

"I can think of nothing that would make your outfit better." She appraised my tailored silver suit with more than approval. As if I was a dinner plate and she was starving. "I even like the James Dean look of the loose tie. You look very rat-pack. Rugged, yet refined. Is dress really that important to you?"

"Sartorial skill is a powerful weapon. Sometimes that is a huge advantage. Ever read Sherlock Holmes?" I asked.

She shook her head. "I saw the new movie."

"An adequate portrayal, but one should read Sir Arthur Conan Doyle in order to glimpse the full scope of how vital the right set of garments can be in a time of need. Disguises are a perfect sleight of hand. Think of a strip club. I assume you've visited one?" I asked without thinking. Her face turned a shade darker.

"Once or twice," she answered, guardedly.

"I just know that someone in law enforcement must see the darker shades of life in order to be competent at his or her career. Imagine a dancer wearing nothing at all." Her face flushed darker.

"Nate..." Gunnar warned. "Compass says, *no*."

"Point heard, but allow me to elaborate..." He finally nodded, protective of Tory. "Her natural curves..." I carefully brushed Tory's side, making her arms pebble, and her moist red lips opened instinctively as she took a breath. "Will no doubt catch the eye, but the surprise has already been given. There is not much more to see. Boring.

"Now imagine an extreme outfit on a dancer. A nurse, for example. Catches one's attention, but without the right circumstances, it's too flashy to keep your interest. She's flaunting herself too obviously. You know she's there to take it off. Again, boring.

"Now, lastly, imagine a stunning woman steps out onto the stage, fingers adoringly caressing the pole, eyes intent. She is wearing a flattering dress like Tory here." Tory's lips were still parted, her breathing deeper as she stared into my eyes. "Her hair is tied up with chop sticks. Then she stares straight into your eyes, and pulls the chopsticks out, her hair cascading down her shoulders like a waterfall." My fingers flipped Tory's hair before I trailed the back of my nails down from her shoulder to her elbow. She shivered again.

"You don't know what's about to happen next, or how long it will go on, but you can't turn away from her gaze. Then her hand carefully unzips the dress down the side, revealing an artfully tattooed ribcage, and then she begins to swing around the pole, masterfully, owning everything in the room. No one moves. Then she looks over her shoulder at you, and *clack*! She slams her stiletto down onto the stage, making you spill your drink slightly. You can't decide whether to meet her eyes or stare at the tease of flesh where the zipper dangles loose. She bends down at the hips, coming to hands and knees, and slowly crawls towards you with the grace of a predatory feline, eyes pinning you to your seat."

Tory was panting, and Gunnar looked stunned. Tory stepped back, resting a hand against the SUV for support. I didn't realize I had stepped closer to Tory. "Now, tell me which has a bigger impact?"

Neither spoke, so I continued. "That is the power of one's attitude and choice of dress. It ruled the European courts for centuries, power flashing from one to another with every change in fashion. There is a reason for every thread, every smile, and every flick of the hair. Everything matters. You live by this, or you can die by a smile that you didn't mean to give. The people we will be running into in the future, *live* by this. You better learn it, but until you do, I will be the group's...*fashionista*. If that's okay with you two?"

They nodded, regaining their breath. Tory looked at me as if she had never seen me before. "Was that magic?" she whispered.

I smiled back. "Yes." Her shoulders sagged in relief. "But not directly. Artfully choosing your attire and the attitude to match it is a very, very powerful magic. But it isn't magic like you saw on the bridge. I simply tapped into your imagination, feeding the flames of my point against your own personal experiences. What you felt was entirely genuine, and came from your own mind. I just helped reveal it to you." I leveled her with my eyes, smiled confidently, and then turned away. "Shall we?"

They followed me towards the entrance. I hoped I was right. I didn't *think* I had used magic in my example, but with as much power as was coursing through me, I honestly wasn't sure. As soon as I had met up with Gunnar, I had felt my strength bubble back up, my skin tingling. Then after seeing the video feed my power had threatened to burst out of me. It had taken a long meditative car ride to Tory's house before I was confident that I was in control. But once she climbed inside the car, it had gotten worse.

Something was happening to me, and I hadn't the slightest idea what it was. I had never heard of such a large jump in power around my age. Not without aid, but I hadn't done anything that would increase my power base. There were ways to measure it quantitatively, but I hadn't had any time to sit down and do so with my usual spells. It was like weight lifting. I knew I *felt* stronger, but without pushing myself to max out on the bench press, I had no way to know exactly *how much* stronger I truly was. I would have to keep it under tight control for the time being.

Power could be good, but it could also be bad. It was up to the user, and as power increased, it sometimes had a tendency to change an individual.

Here's to me not becoming an all-powerful sociopathic wizard over the next few hours. Huzzah!

28

Originally, I had been surprised that the expo was taking place during the day, but after further contemplation, it made perfect sense. A solar eclipse couldn't be experienced at night, hence the word *solar*. Sometimes I can be thick, but I blamed it on the rough few days before me. There were a surprising number of people at the expo, wandering from table to table in the main atrium, accepting fliers, drink samples, and various other marketing ploys hoping to cash in on the tourists. And there were tourists aplenty.

I heard a speaker from behind the closed doors of an auditorium, but ignored it. We each had accepted stickers for our names upon arrival, and Gunnar and Tory chuckled at my choice of names. "Discreet, very discreet." Gunnar laughed.

I spied a police officer near the entrance, and his face visibly paled upon seeing me. I grinned back, showing teeth. Gunnar shook his head. The police officer began urgently speaking into the radio attached to his shoulder—no doubt informing my good friend, Captain Kosage, of my whereabouts. Gunnar and Tory were stunned at the cost of tickets at the front door, but then relieved to find that I had already paid for them in advance. Tory tried to pay me back for hers, but Gunnar knew better after years of friendship. "Please, your money is no good here," I answered softly, hiding her offer of cash from any casual passerby.

I was buzzing with power, and I had to find an outlet. Flirting helped. There was magic in flirting. That rush of endorphins when it's win or lose, and you're trying to impress the fairer sex. I just wanted to make it out of here intact, and I needed Gunnar and Tory to be on their game to accomplish that. Before Kosage found a reason to drag me downtown.

I whispered, leaning close to Tory as if for a kiss. Gunnar took his cue, and snatched us each a flute of champagne as if he had been waiting too long for the waiter to make his rounds. "I need you to play the part. *Expect* me to pay for you. You are a treasured gem on my arm, nothing more. A casual dalliance for the evening. A flower on my lapel." I traced the backs of my fingers down her neck in a very, very intimate way as I sensed her shoulders tightening at my words. "*Doucement*, my precious orchid..." I said a pitch louder as the Mayor and his wife walked past us.

The Mayor winked knowingly at me, nodding approval before his wife elbowed him sharply in the ribs. I continued on with a knowing grin to the Mayor as he frowned at my nametag. Misogyny was mixed with the water in the upper circles of power. Sometimes one just had to use that to one's advantage, rather than railing against it. Disguise. Sleight of hand.

"Remember, this is a charade, a play, and we are the leads. I need you to watch my back, because *here there be monsters*." I breathed, pulling away with a dark smile. Her eyes dilated as she studied me, and then gave a brief nod.

I placed my other hand on her waist, looking to the entire world like a man staking a claim on his prize. "The less others think of you here, the better. It makes any change of character all the scarier." I gently pressed my lips against the carotid artery on her neck and then leaned back. I held out a blind hand expectantly, and Gunnar placed a flute of champagne in my fingertips. I raised it to Tory's lips. "Drink, my sweet."

She nodded weakly, accepting the drink with shaky fingers. I noticed her knees were quivering, so kept my hand on her waist. Gunnar offered me my drink and I took a long pull, savoring the pricey bouquet. Cakebread, if I had to guess. Palatable. Tory leaned in close to me. "Are you a vampire?" She asked, face smiling in a passable mask.

I shook my head, curious. "Why would you ask such a thing?"

She trembled. "Because I can't help but listen to you. You're just so *adorable*. It's like *Twilight* is happening to me!" I blinked at her sudden change of character. She didn't seem like the *Twilight* kind of gal. "Do you have this effect on all girls? If *that* isn't magic, I don't know what is?" She giggled oddly, a sound that seemed out of countenance for her. Then her eyes widened in sudden delight. "Oh, I'm going to go freshen up!" She took off like a rocket to the restroom. I turned to Gunnar, but he just smiled, amused. I took a swallow of my drink, barely keeping the shock from my face.

I had always been good with women. In fact, I was very good, but never *this* good. I groaned. She was right. It was as if my power was oozing out of everything I did. Without an outlet, it was making its own release. That meant that I had gained even more power than I realized after the attack on the bridge. But why?

I frowned thoughtfully. "It seems we might be in a bit of a pickle, Gunnar."

I noticed that one of his cuffs was loose, allowing him easy access to his tattoo. His eyes roamed the room like a lion, lazy, but hungry. "Why?"

"I'm leaking power on you two."

He arched a brow. "So?"

I blinked. "Have you noticed anything out of the norm? You are unusually copacetic towards me. You usually disagree and make everything more difficult. You're good at acting, but without question, you wandered off to grab us drinks. That's something

Dean would do, but never you. Something's wrong. I think my power is drawing whatever attitude I want out of you two."

He sipped his drink. "I just feel peaceful. But now that you mention it, I don't think I've ever felt this mellow before. Calm. I mean, we're here to hunt murderers, or find why your father left you that note, but I'm not stressed out at all." He thought about that for a minute. "I'm not even worried that I am not stressed." He shrugged, sipping his drink, looking bored.

"See. I was worried about myself needing a compass, but it seems that I've gained control of myself at the expense of you two."

"So, what's different about Tory? You barely know her, so why do you think she's acting differently?" He didn't sound that interested. Just conversational. Polite.

"I think she took my eye-candy advice literally, and has lost all common sense. She called me *adorable*. And apparently, she has a thing for *Twilight*."

"Despicable movie. Werewolves get shafted the whole time. Jacob totally kicks more ass than Edward." I wanted to slap the shit out of him, but he continued. "Adorable, eh? Man, I hate being the third wheel," he grumbled. "But it's cool, I guess," he said, already falling back into his easygoing manner. I groaned inwardly.

Tory was walking out of the bathroom, eyes dancing with joy as she smiled at both of us. "Right. We need to hurry this up. I'll try to guard you two, but I don't know how well I can manage it," I said for our ears only.

"Whatever, Nate. I'm fine," Gunnar said casually.

"He's cute when he pouts." Tory giggled, snatching up a second flute from a waiter. She guzzled the majority of it. "I love this necklace. Does it look pretty on me?"

I nodded, studying her acutely. Gunnar frowned, snatching up his own refill of champagne. "I am not cute." He took a pull from his drink. "And I'm not pouting." I wanted to scream, but we had to maintain our profile for the guests. Any one of them could be my parents' murderer, or they might know something that could help me with the dragons. I placed my palm on Tory's wrist, and concentrated. My mind finally quiet, I suddenly noticed the creeping tendrils of power oozing from me to my two companions. Now that I was aware of them, I could physically see them.

I quickly withdrew them, but a dozen more tendrils shot out into the people around us. The attendees had been studying us a moment ago, but now they each looked around, confused for a moment before turning away from us as if we didn't exist. I groaned. Tory shook her head with a frown, and then blushed furiously. Gunnar was instantly alert. Tension knotting his brow.

"I am so embarrassed," Tory began, trying to tug her arm away.

I held her hand tight, feeling slightly off balance. "No, it was flattering. Please don't be embarrassed. Remember how I told you I needed you to be my compass and keep me in line?" She nodded. "Well, I seem to have temporarily passed off my lack of control onto you two. It's my fault."

"I *despise* bimbos. I never act like that! And I *hate Twilight!*" She adamantly whispered. Then her pupils began dilating wider. "Do you think this dress looks good on me? Because I think *hers* looks like trash." She pointed at the mayor's wife, and the woman gasped, hearing her. Shit.

"Can we check out some of the souvenir tables?" Gunnar asked calmly.

The power was hitting everyone now. I hastily drew it all in to myself, and my eyes grew dazed, flecks of sparkling white flickering here and there as I steadied myself. The power tendrils were diminished, but several still latched onto my companions. Tory and Gunnar were more alert again, studying me. "I'm confused." Tory mumbled, rubbing at her temples. This was crazy. I had no idea what was happening to me. Was it the dragons messing with me? I mentally examined myself, but realized that it was all me.

"Let's just get this over with. Follow me," I commanded sharply. They each shrugged, Tory quickly snatching my hand. I was unable to fully block them from my leaking power, but it was a bit better than before. I used a brisk pace to help distract us. Just keep everyone moving. Maybe that would help.

As we slipped through the crowd, I allowed several tendrils to leak out of me whenever a group of people I didn't want to talk to would attempt to move towards us. I was, after all, a celebrity in town. Everyone wanted to be seen conversing with the Master Temple. Photographers mingled here and there. I pointedly used my power to guide them away from me. I didn't want a swarm of paparazzi following us. I wanted to find out anything that might help us, and then get the hell out of here. I had, perhaps, two hours until sunset when I would have to fight Asterion. We needed to hurry.

Without warning, a thick tendril shot out of my control, darting through the crowd to latch onto a curvy, tall woman in a red dress. As if in slow motion, she turned to stare at me over her shoulder. I saw a grin split her cheeks. It was the jogger I had seen outside the courthouse with Gunnar. The one who had given me a number, but no name. Gunnar grumbled about the world being unfair, then *gold digger*.

Tory's hand tightened in mine, her nails pressing into my palms. My control slipped a bit as the jogger approached. "Well, well, well. I've been waiting for you to call me, but it seems like you found a different piece of candy for the evening. Perhaps later?" she purred. She studied Tory from head to toe, nodding her approval. "Nice choice." Her eyes focused on my chest, exactly where the dragon tooth lay. I shivered, imagining that she could see it.

Gunnar laughed loudly. "I need a stiffer drink." Then he stared at me, and began laughing harder. "Stiff, heh."

Tory's hand squeezed tighter, and I knew my control was slipping even further. "She's really pretty, but am I prettier?" she asked softly.

The jogger stepped in closer, and her body heat hit me like a wave of power. Her hips brushed mine as her warm palm touched my chest, her pupils dilating. Something slid across the iris of one eye, revealing a glimpse of a horizontal black bar, and I blinked. Contacts?

Shit.

I jumped back, slamming my lack of restraint solely into the jogger. She stumbled, and then shook her head as if dazed. "Dragon," I whispered.

She nodded, happy that she could please me with an affirmative answer.

Gunnar and Tory both started at that, momentarily refocusing.

Without a thought, I simply commanded her, and she obeyed.

"Who are you?"

"Misha."

"What color are you?" I asked, terrified that other dragons were possibly surrounding us. She tapped her finger against the fabric of her dress in answer. "Red?" A nod. "You tried to kill me on the roof of the courthouse. Then gave me your number after. Were you wearing contacts then too?" I asked, disgusted at my own stupidity.

She nodded; her edgy blonde bangs brushing her thin jaw. "It wasn't very nice of me to do what I did, but I can make it up to you..." Her eyes promised a darkly appealing payment. Sex.

"Um, perhaps another time," I muttered.

"I'll go check out those tables, I guess." Gunnar offered, not seeming to care one way or another.

"Can you grab me one of those cute telescopes?" Tory clapped her hands delightedly.

"No, none of us are going anywhere." The girls sagged, frowning. Gunnar shrugged. "Misha, I want you to take me to your leader."

"But you are my leader," she answered simply.

Huh. That was...helpful. "No, before me, you were following the orders of someone else. Is he here?" She looked genuinely puzzled for a few seconds, and then understanding dawned on her. She nodded. "Can you introduce me to him?"

She squeaked in excitement and snatched up my hand, drawing Tory and me off bodily into a secluded hallway. "The Dragon Father is this way." Gunnar followed behind us, glancing unconcernedly at paintings decorating the wall. I was leading a pack of fumbling idiots, so what did that make me?

Tory whispered into my ear. "She works out, but her butt needs attention." She pointed at Misha's rear end. My face flushed, but luckily, Misha didn't appear to notice. "That one looks like you, Gunnie!" Tory giggled, pointing at a painting of Vikings.

Gunnar's chest swelled with pride as he nodded, not even hearing the pet name. What had I just gotten myself into? Meeting the Dragon Father? The one who had been trying to kill me for the last few days? *Hey, Dragon Father. I noticed that you've been trying to kill me lately, so just wanted to swing by and say, 'Hello.'*

Right, and I wondered why I always found myself in dangerous situations.

Gunnar began whistling lazily behind us, totally useless as a guardian. I struggled to withdraw a heavy tendril that was affixed to him, and his eyes immediately began to clear. He looked from me to the two stunning women pulling me down the hallway. "Is this a good idea?" he asked with a frown.

"Probably not. Try something for me. Touch your tattoo and keep your finger there."

He frowned, but did so. "Alright, I'm going to release my restraint for a second." He nodded, and I let go of my precarious grip. Gunnar flinched for a second, and then growled at the air in front of him as if he could see the tendrils trying to latch onto him. His awareness was simply too strong for my careless tendrils to overcome him while he touched his tattoo. I almost clapped my hands, but of course, each was firmly trapped in a different girl's hand. "Keep touching it. It's the only way for you to stay focused." He nodded, now studying the hallway like a caged tiger as he followed us.

I let go of Misha's hand, smiling at her curious glance back, and motioned her on. Her dress was open to the top of her tailbone, revealing a flat, muscled back, and the gentle curve as it crept lower to her rear. I didn't at all agree with Tory's claim.

"Tory," I whispered. She beamed up at me. "I need you to focus on your strength, your unique ability. Can you do that?" She looked puzzled. "I think it's cute," I added.

"Really? You think it's cute?" I nodded, forcing a smile. "Okay then." Her eyes strained for a minute, struggling against my power seepage. I didn't want to risk pulling it away from her in case it affected Misha too. She took a quick breath, and then stared up at me, eyes clear but wide. "Wow. The stupidity is gone," she stated bluntly.

"I'm so sorry that I put you through that. Can you control yourself now?"

She nodded, face set in determination. "I want to make something very clear though, Nate. You scare me. Do you normally have more control than this?" I nodded. "Good. You just made me look like an idiot. I had no filter for my thoughts, and that is flat out embarrassing."

I felt guilty as hell. "How about we just pretend this didn't happen." I offered.

"Please." She answered, cheeks rosy. We continued on in silence before she spoke again. "Do you think she's cute?"

I blinked back. "Um. Am I still leaking power on you?"

Tory shook her head. "No, I just think she's cute."

I looked at her. "Sure, but she's a dragon, and she tried to kill me."

"There is that..." There was a longer silence. "Do you think when this is all finished —if she switches sides, of course—she'll go out for a drink with me?"

I didn't have the slightest clue how to answer Tory. "Sure. You're beautiful." She smiled at that, so I chose subtlety next. "I take it you like girls?"

"I'm bisexual, but my tendencies lean more towards women most of the time."

I was quiet for a few moments before answering. "I'm pretty sure that if I was born a girl I'd be a lesbian, too. You girls are just so damned *adorable*." She turned to look at me, and then began laughing loud enough for Gunnar to grumble unpleasant things behind me.

My life.

29

Misha stopped in front of a large single door. The number 901 stood above it, marking it as one of the priciest suites in the hotel. Two women—dragons, I assumed—stood outside the door, guarding their Dragon Father. They also wore contacts, hiding the horizontal slits of their eyes. I couldn't believe I hadn't thought of that sooner.

"Misha, what have you brought us, and why can I not feel you?" An African American dragon hissed. Her eyes were a bright green, but I didn't know if that was the contacts or her real eyes. "Snacks? A..." She sniffed the air in our general direction. "Wizard, a werewolf, and an appetizer..." She smiled at Tory.

Tory simply smiled back, maintaining her bimbo disguise. I spoke. "I wish to declare the Accords in effect. We chose to come in peace, and you will abide by that or the Dragon Nation will be destroyed by the Academy." I had absolutely no authority to command such a thing on behalf of the ruling body of wizards, but they didn't know that. The dragons tensed, grimacing as if tasting something displeasing.

"Then where is your gold? Your diamonds? A gift befitting the Dragon Lord must be offered, lest he feel slighted." The second dragon argued, her orange eyes smoldering. "Or is this appetizer our diamond? She does have a fine collar on. Perhaps she's an obedient little kitty cat."

Having already given Tory the diamond necklace, I produced a gold bar from my pocket instead. Gunnar and Tory's eyes widened. My suit had been reinforced and tailored to hold heavy objects without dragging the entire suit down in a noticeable way. I liked to carry odd things on my person every now and then. "I bring gifts. Even for the guard dogs." I tossed the bar to the first dragon, and she practically quivered at the slight. "Open the door, Misha. I won't be kept waiting."

Misha complied, still pleasantly grinning at the apparent promise I had made of sex later. We walked inside, and there he was. I idly wondered whether I should address him as Dragon Lord, or Dragon Father since I had heard both titles, but didn't really care if I ended up using the wrong one. I already had enough friends.

He was older, but looked to be in the prime of his life. Silver streaks jetted back from his temples, fading into his golden blonde hair. He was built like a football player, and wearing a tan custom-made suit. He reeked of money. He stood before us, curiously watching us enter, and then he smiled. "Greetings, Master Temple." He grimaced at my nametag. "Or should I call you by your politically incorrect nametag, *Archangel*? I had hoped to meet you soon." He looked at Misha. "I assumed she had been killed when I could no longer sense her, but I see that she has simply found a new master. Good luck. She is quite unruly. And obviously incompetent since she couldn't even kill you at the courthouse."

Then he turned his back on us, and walked into a vast sitting room with a fireplace roaring near one wall. I gambled. "So, what are you doing here, Raego?" I demanded, remembering the name Tomas had used.

He frowned, looking momentarily confused at my knowledge of his name. "First things first," he answered instead. "I believe you announced the Academy Accords." I nodded. "Then we must exchange gifts." He clapped his hands and three more women entered the room, completely nude. I couldn't make out their eye color, but they probably wore contacts as well. They carried a chest between them, setting it on the ground before their master. He flicked a finger, and the dragons moved about the room to what seemed like pre-arranged positions.

Two of them stood near my party. One of them stared at Tory a bit longer than the other, and then sized me up and down hungrily. Hungry for eating me or sexing me, I wasn't sure. It looked like it could have been either. "Since you have requested my hospitality, it's only fair that you present your gift first. But I can't imagine what else you could possibly be hiding on your perfectly tailored frame. One gold bar was impressive, but I do not sense another on you. Perhaps the girl really is the gift?" He smiled politely.

I smiled back icily. "No, she is not. She is my snack to nibble, as I please." I sensed absolutely nothing from Tory.

I noticed my power was still draining out of me, drifting around the room for a target. The Dragon Lord scowled. "You are leaking, wizard. That is not wise. I have already taken precautions lest you take any more of my harem."

"I *knew* it was called a harem!" I exclaimed, grinning. Gunnar shrugged as if losing a bet. "Speaking of your little harem, what's up with all the different colored dragons? It's like a bag of skittles in here." I motioned at the array of dragons around us.

The Dragon Lord nodded. "There is a uniqueness to our genetics that doesn't guarantee a child will end up the same color as his or her parents. Just because I am a golden dragon does not mean that I will have a golden heir. I collect as many colors as I can in hopes of increasing my chances of getting the color I desire. But that really isn't why we're here, is it?"

I nodded, contemplating his words, and idly wondered what color dragon he was hoping for as his heir. He had said he was a golden dragon, but the dragon hunters had said Raego was a black dragon. Maybe he was lying about being gold. I knew I was missing something. I reached into my pocket to withdraw a heavy piece of paper. "Title to a small diamond mine in Africa, ready to be signed over to you at your leisure. I dare say that this is better than whipping out a bag of uncut diamonds, or another bar of gold." I added sarcastically.

The Dragon Lord seemed surprised. "How very thoughtful of you. How long has it been in your family?" He asked, growing interested.

"Since 1631, but we have never mined it. Some of my ancestors searched for their engagement stones in the mines, but it has never seen a commercial mining operation or work force since our ownership. It was estimated to be quite a promising mine, and my ancestors never had problems finding precious stones there when they chose to. I myself have five stones from the mine, ranging from two carats, to an impressive five carats. Of course, that is after it was cut. It was bigger when I found it," I added nonchalantly.

The Dragon Lord practically salivated. "I hope my gift can compare." I handed the deed to the closest dragon and she delivered it to her master without a word, and then came back to stand before me. Without preamble, she grabbed my wrist. Before I could even react, Tory slammed her hand down in a chopping motion against the dragon's forearm. The sound of bone snapping was louder than expected, and I felt my stomach shift as blood sprayed across both Tory and me from the dragon's bone tearing through the thin flesh and muscle of her arm. She shrieked, leaping back in surprise and pain. Then she took a step towards Tory, face contorted in rage as her arm dangled loosely at her side. "Stop!" the Dragon Lord commanded.

Tory wiped a bit of blood from her face, glanced down at her glistening fingertips and then the fine crimson arc across her white dress. She smiled. "My favorite color." Misha beamed approval as if it were a direct compliment to her.

"Oh, I *do* like her. You are quite right, Master Temple. She is no light snack. Nibbling would be the only way to taste such a bounty." The Dragon Lord chuckled. "But Aria was merely going to guide you to the chest. She really should have asked permission to touch you first. I believe her punishment will suffice?" he asked. I nodded. "She should be healed by tomorrow or the day after, at any rate," he said casually.

"What?" I asked.

"We heal rather fast, Master Temple. Take Misha for example. Took a lightning stick through the thigh last night, yet here she is." Misha nodded as she lifted her dress rather high to show me a bare expanse of thigh, as well as a quick glimpse of a red satin garter belt. Tory's eyes went hungry for a moment before she regained her control.

I strode over to the chest, wary of the prearranged gift. I undid the clasp and heaved the lid back. Inside sat a delicately worked music box. Tiny, really. Especially for such a large chest. I looked up at him, frowning. "This is a gift fit for a young girl, not a grown wizard. Perhaps I should give you a vending machine ring in exchange," I snapped.

He raised a finger. "The story is what is important." I waited, tapping my foot impatiently. "This was supposedly lifted from Temple Industries the day your parents died. In a mysterious room warded with magic. I reclaimed it from the perpetrator when he tried to flip it for cash. I paid heavily for it, assuming it to be quite valuable, but I have been unable to discover its purpose. No music. No magic. Nothing. Just a shiny box."

"Why shouldn't I believe that you just took it yourself?" I growled, power coursing through my veins as I remembered the video I had just seen in Ashley's office. I hadn't seen anything in the shadow-man's hands, but apparently, he had been a thief as well as a murderer. Gunnar and Tory took a step forward, unsure what to do. I held up a hand. "The Accords," I warned.

The Dragon Lord nodded. "I swear it on my power," he answered solemnly, drawing a sudden golden dragon talon down his forearm and touching the blood to his forehead. So, he really *was* a golden dragon. The circle of power immediately thrummed around him, and his golden claw was back to human form before I could even study it. Well, shit. He had to be telling the truth or he would have simply fallen over dead. The magic was legit; any wizard would know that.

"Then who?" I asked, furious. "Give him to me. He is mine by right."

The Dragon Lord studied me. "Two gifts for one? That's not fair."

"I gave your guards a 1 lb. gold bar worth at least $17,000."

"True." He rubbed his lips, contemplating. "Come to hear my speech tomorrow afternoon, and I will give you the thief."

I pondered that. "Your speech is during the eclipse?"

"Of course. That is why we are all here." He smiled.

"That's what I don't understand. The eclipse is why your dragons are running amok, killing citizens in search of some old book. As a native, I take offense to that. You never asked to enter my territory, and you have murdered several people rather than simply asking someone for what you seek. As an arcane book dealer, I could have helped you, but you never asked. You chose threats instead. Breaking into my bookstore not once, but *twice*, is a death wish." His eyes tightened, looking surprised to hear about the second break-in. But if it hadn't been him, then who? I pressed on. "Foolish for a leader of any kind. It's no wonder you couldn't keep Misha from my control. You are weak."

His face grew tight. "Be careful. I can be a generous friend, or a terrible enemy."

"I'll take my chances," I answered with a disdainful shrug.

He prickled. "The book is a family heirloom, and does not belong in the hands of thieves."

"The people who are dead were not thieves, obviously, or you would have your precious bedtime story by now. Fucking idiot." I looked back at Gunnar. "Can you believe this guy? Dragon *Lord*? What a crock! Can't even get an old family book back."

He growled then. "You would dare mock me?" His face was scarlet.

"There is a difference between fact and mockery. Stating the truth is not punishable. If it offends, it's because it's true, and you have no grounds for retaliation against stating a fact."

"I will strip the flesh from your bones..." he began.

I brought my arms down with a snap, and whips of power suddenly exploded from each wrist: one made of dripping fire, the other of dripping ice, even though they technically looked to be made of crystals, rather than liquid, and each fragment of crystal looked razor sharp. The whips extended six feet to either side of me, shattering a table and a clay vase. The rug caught fire at the edges where the fiery whip rested, and a quick flick of my other wrist shattered a huge fish tank, instantly turning the water and everything inside it into a solid block of ice. My body reacted to the sudden release of power, pleased beyond measure.

"Try me, *Raego*. I fucking *dare* you," I hissed back, smiling through my teeth. Gunnar was in half wolf form, perched on his toes, and Tory had one of the dragons pinned against the wall with her hand squeezing the delicate throat, the dragon's legs kicking feebly as she tried to escape. Tory squeezed tighter and the dragon slumped with a final exhale, unconscious, I hoped. Misha clapped her hands, giggling. My rage was passing through them like extension cords of my power, overriding their own conscious thought process. Creepy, but probably life-saving in this case.

The Dragon Lord blinked back, eyebrows furrowing. "I am not Raego, but I am very interested to hear how you discovered his name. My name is Alaric Slate. Why are you so fixated on Raego? Is he in St. Louis?" The man's eyes were anxious. "You can put away your weapons. I mean you no harm...this night. I stand by my word. As much as it displeases me not to kill you."

Sensing the truth, I drew back my power, motioning my friends to do the same. My whips of power snapped out of existence, but my thoughts raced. If he wasn't Raego, then that meant there *was* a third player out there somewhere. Not good. Perhaps the third player had broken into my shop. "The feeling is mutual, but know that I will see every murderer dead before you leave town."

"Well, we won't be leaving any time soon, Master Temple, so I propose a truce."

"I give you until this formal conversation is over."

He pondered that for a minute, and then nodded. "Agreed. Bring me the book tomorrow, and I will let you see the thief." I began to argue, but he held up a finger. "I carry bargaining power. The thief is not all that I have that might tempt you. I have obtained one of your friends, and their limited existence depends on your cooperation."

I instantly thought of Indie. "Who?" I whispered, the whips of power immediately flaring out again. Even I was surprised at my creation, because the more I thought about it, the surer I was that I had never created such a weapon as them before.

"You shall see when you accompany me at my short speech tomorrow afternoon."

"What is so important about this book? Or the eclipse for that matter?"

His smile grew distant, nostalgic. "The book is similar to the Old Testament of the Christian Bible. It explains much of our direct lineage from that first dragon. It is said that somewhere in that story is a hidden ritual to awaken a true Dragon Lord—the Obsidian Son—granting him the powers of our very distant, first ancestor. He will receive incalculable powers, and lead us into an era where we are respected, and feared. We have pieced much together from that ritual, but I would like to verify as much as possible before I attempt it. The eclipse is like the Solstices for the Faerie: A day of balance and power, where one reclaims control over the other. Alas, we will not be taking power from anyone, but rather reclaiming the power and control that was lost to us over the years."

He turned back to me, smiling. "It is very...*dear* to me."

"So, you think that you are powerful enough to be this leader?" A nod. "A leader is more than power. A leader has a sharp mind, where you have the mind of a brute if you can think of no other way to obtain this book than by shedding innocent blood."

His eyes laughed at my childlike naivety. "We are *monsters*, Master Temple. We don't play by the traditional rules of your precious humans. They are all *food* for us, not worthy of existing, but for our appetites. Check the guest list for tomorrow. You will see numerous aliases from all walks of life, but I guarantee that I will have *hundreds* of dragons to answer my call, from all over the world. If that isn't good leadership, then I don't know what is. Now, it is time for you and your friends to leave. Perhaps tomorrow I will discover how you gained your mind control powers. I must admit that I hadn't anticipated this ability of yours. It makes things...more complicated, but I could still have use for you when I take the city. Until tomorrow..." Then he bowed, and turned his back on us. He pointed at two particularly dazzling women, snapped his fingers, and pointed at a distant bedroom. He began undressing as he walked. "I trust you can let yourself out like good dogs?" He mocked over his shoulder.

We did. Fuming, I snatched up the music box, and we left.

Next batter up, Asterion, the Minotaur.

30

I stepped out of the SUV, feet crunching on the frosted grass. "You sure you don't want different backup? I would feel terrible if I helped kill the Minotaur," Gunnar added. I rolled my eyes. Some help he was. Misha and Tory sat in the backseat, looking anxious to join me. I didn't believe that I had permanently mind-fucked Misha, but she had switched sides at some point, and was proud of it.

"You two mind waiting here for us?" I asked the two women with a grin through the open rear window. They nodded, smiling coyly at each other. Maybe Tory would get her chance at that drink after all.

I began walking away from the car, speaking to Gunnar. "I doubt I'll need your help, but you must obey my commands if you come. This is between us. No participation unless I say so." Gunnar looked relieved that he wouldn't have to get his paws dirty. Since when did minions become so useless? In all the stories I had read, they looked after their master's best interests, even when warned to stay out of it. Maybe I was a crock leader also. I sighed, pushing the thought away.

We left the SUV running. The falling sun sat heavy and cold in the sky. We walked for a few minutes, past the point where I had conversed with Asterion two days ago. I began to grow nervous, wondering if I was too late, or at the wrong place. We finally stepped out of the proximity of the Land Rover's Xenon headlights and into darker pasture, the metaphor not lost on me.

I felt a tingle of power and we were suddenly in a different place entirely. Torches surrounded us in a wide circle, wicks crepitating loudly in the silence. Trees climbed high beyond the torches, allowing only a bit of the sunset to hit us. It felt old, ritualistic. In the center of the ring, limned by the firelight, sat a table, and before the table sat the Minotaur. Shadows wavered around the ring of firelight, swaying back and forth like dancers. I heard a snickering neigh from outside the light, but saw nothing except more shadows. There had been no visible sign that we were sharing the pasture with anyone while we had been walking through the empty field, yet here we were.

I looked up, and noticed that the sun had dropped significantly, resting just above the horizon, blazing with fire and warmth like it was the height of summer. Then I realized that I was warm, no, hot. As if it really was summer. I blinked at that. The grass wasn't frosted, but budding with life. Asterion was watching us, amused. "No wonder you convince all the heifers to bed you. You have the coolest digs in the pasture."

He smiled back, shaking his head. "None of my partners have seen this place. It wouldn't be appropriate. It is always warm and sunset at the Dueling Grounds," he said.

The Dueling Grounds.

"You mean that this place is set aside just for dueling? Where *are* we?"

He studied us for a moment, face pensive. "You are between worlds, wizard. Not part of your world, completely, and not part of mine, completely. It is a rift between the two, just like sunset, stuck between two stark realities: day and night; myth and your world." As if that were answer enough, he continued. "I see you have brought a friend. That is, I suppose, in agreement with the Accords, but still…"

"He's a huge fan of yours. In fact, I doubt he'll help me kill one of his mythological heroes if he has any say." Gunnar nodded simply, glad that I had made his stance clear. He still thought that a simple discussion could solve things—how terribly naïve. I, on the other hand, was more certain of a different outcome for the night. One of us must die, or be severely injured, maimed, or incapacitated to win the duel.

"Kill? I have informed you that I am now enlightened, or attempting to achieve such a state. Why talk of killing, Master Temple?" Asterion snorted.

"That's kind of the definition of a duel. And you did say that this was according to the old traditions, not your New Age protocol. *Promises made, promises kept* were the words you used, if I am not mistaken. And I am never mistaken when it comes to my memory."

"There are numerous ways to win a duel, Master Temple. Come, sit, we must converse like gentlemen." I heard another neigh beyond the flames, and then the scream of a dying animal.

"Um, do we have company that I should know about?" I asked. Gunnar looked uneasy.

"Grimm must have grown hungry…" Asterion said thoughtfully. He appraised me as I walked closer. "Your power has increased since last we met." I shrugged. He touched the air around me, feeling the tendrils that I thought only I could see. "Yet you leak all around you. Why do you waste your power?" he asked with a frown.

"It's kind of new, and when I don't leak, I become kind of reckless." I answered honestly. This was not the kind of duel I had expected, but the night was still young, so I remained guarded.

Asterion stroked his thin beard. "Your new power is seeking to fill you up, yet your cup—at the moment—is too small to hold it all in, so you spill over to those near you."

He studied me contemplatively. "You must deepen your cup," he finally said as if it was the most obvious answer in the world.

"Thanks, Confucius, but I don't know what that means or how to do it."

Asterion tilted his bull-like head. "You must learn. Soon. It is not finished growing." I blinked. "In fact, I think it is only just beginning. But come, we shall discuss other things this night."

Armed with that assurance, I sat down across the table from him. Most of my newfound power was centered in my chest, eager to jump out into whatever form I would allow, but the rest flowed loosely about me. "So, how does this work if we aren't going to bash each other's brains in?"

Asterion turned to Gunnar. "Does he always speak so boorishly, *Wulfric*?"

Gunnar nodded with a proud smile at the title. "He either talks like this, or like a man stepping out of a Dickens novel. No one really knows why he switches back and forth so much. Sometimes he acts like the perfect gentleman, but then others..." He waved a hand at me as if in explanation. Asterion pondered me with another stroke of his beard. I ignored it, but was surprised at Gunnar's perception.

A game board sat in front of us, black and white stones patiently waiting for our fingers to command. "Do you know the game? There are many different versions, but this one is quite unique, of that I can assure you..." Asterion smiled darkly, rattling a leather dice cup in one meaty fist.

"We're going to play a board game?" I asked in disbelief.

He nodded. "The game of the gods."

"*Oi chusoi Dios aei enpiptousi...*" I muttered to myself, remembering a phrase from my father.

Asterion arched a stunned brow. "The dice of god are indeed always loaded. I'm surprised at your languages, Master Temple. You are truly your father's son." He sounded sad.

"You were close with my father?" I asked softly, not even mad at the mention of them. It was almost pleasing to be able to talk to someone who knew my parents for who they really were.

"Occasionally. He would come to play now and again. Did he teach you the game?" I nodded. "Ah, then hopefully I will have a skilled opponent to battle this evening." His face lit up at the prospect.

I hadn't played it much, but my father had taught it to me, enjoying the complexity of the simple-looking board game. Even with only two colors of stones, the possibilities were endless. I had seen many remakes of the game: *Reversi*, and *Go*, among others, but I had never seen one meet the difficulty of the original. They were like the children of this game—each merely a shade of the former glory of the original. I couldn't help but feel the same about myself. Would I ever step out of my father's shadow?

Asterion spread his sausage-sized fingers imploringly. "We shall roll for first turn. Abandon your power for the duration of the game."

"No," I immediately answered. "We are dueling, and for that I need whatever magic I have to be at my beck and call."

Asterion eyed me for a moment. "Then at least do not cheat. The game does not appreciate...manipulations." I furrowed my eyebrows at that so Asterion explained. "The game is powerful, and will punish any direct manipulation with force."

I withdrew my own dice cup, packed especially for this unlikely possibility, and plucked out the correct five dice. They were ivory, real ivory. Asterion scrutinized them, eyes widening. "Those are quite...spectacular. Which animal lost his life for you to play such a game with them?"

"Mammoth," I answered honestly, or at least as honestly as I knew. They could of course have belonged to some other creature, but that was what I had been told when my father had given them to me.

"Hmmm...They are not imbued with any devious magic, correct?"

I shook my head, offering them to him for inspection. "No, but yours are."

His fingers hesitated as they were reaching out for my dice. "Pardon?"

"Your dice are loaded. Weighted opposite the five's if I judge correctly, but not enough to always roll a five." Honestly, I didn't know where the words came from, but I could feel the extra weight that would throw them off balance.

"I would never do such a thing," he said, glaring at me.

"You cannot fault something for acting in accordance to its nature. The nature of those particular dice is to cheat. Nothing in your new philosophy could possibly blame you for using them. Unless *you* made them to cheat, or are using them because you wish to cheat in order to win," I added, face devoid of accusation.

He watched me for a moment, and then snorted, slamming a head-sized fist on the stone table, and I jumped up to my feet. "I do not feel the mood for a game anymore."

"As you wish. Shall we have a dance-off then?" I threw down a quick dance move I had once seen a competitive break-dancer do to challenge his opponent. I thought it looked rather impressive, as I had practiced it quite a bit, but Gunnar burst out laughing.

"What was that? You looked as if you were having a fit." Asterion frowned.

"It's a perfectly good challenge move," I argued. Gunnar laughed harder.

"Do not mock me, wizard. I am not pleased to discover that these dice are loaded. Your father gave them to me. I always wondered why we played such an even game, attributing it to our sharp minds. But now I realize it was because we used the same loaded dice."

Interesting.

My father was a dirty cheat when necessary. Huh. Who knew?

"We could play with my dice." I offered.

"Like father like son. Yours are probably also loaded." He grumbled.

I squeezed my power tight, withdrawing all the tendrils to myself. Then I threw the dice on the table. *Five, three, six.* I scooped them up and did it again. *One, four, six.* I did it several more times, proving no consistent tosses. "Satisfied?"

After a moment, he nodded skeptically.

Then we began to play. It was a game of both luck and skill. Luck with the numbers rolled, and skill with how the player chose to use those numbers to move his stones. It symbolized life. One must make the best out of the cards they are dealt. I played rakishly in the beginning, but noticed a quick difference in this version of the game. Whenever I lost a piece to Asterion, I felt a sharp prick in my finger. After a few poor plays, the pricks grew more intense, one even drawing blood. Asterion had thicker skin than me, but he had also known about the consequences to the game beforehand. Gunnar inched forward as he noticed one of my flinches, watching us with both concern and interest mingling together.

After successfully goading Asterion into trusting me, I began to relax. He was leaning forward with excitement now as he watched the board, choosing where to place his stones. The board was heavily in his favor, as he had been playing more carefully, cautious of his new opponent.

Little by little, I released the restraint I held on my power, so that with each throw I was less and less in control of my power leakage. Asterion could sense magic, but I wasn't directly *doing* anything with my magic, merely releasing my hold on it. That's when the tables began to turn. I was hopelessly behind and it was his turn. He could have rolled almost anything and won.

But he didn't.

He sat staring at the dice on the table. Three one's, also known as the *Sisters of Fate* to the Greeks. It wasn't even enough of a roll for him to actually take the turn.

I scooped up the dice and tossed them disinterestedly, not thinking, not worrying. As they hit the table, I felt reality shift. It wasn't purposeful, and it was so discreet and natural that even Asterion didn't notice it. It was identical to when the thief had blundered into the cops by the river earlier. Odds running wild.

As a teen, when I had hit my first new power plateau, strange things had happened. My parents had been baffled by it, saying they had never heard of such a thing happening, but over the next week or so the things that happened around me became too random to ignore: a phone call from a girl who had never before shown interest in me; a cop suddenly deciding not to give me a ticket when I had been doubling the speed limit; a fellow student deciding to apologize to me for being so cruel when we had been children; and even a fire starting in a chemistry lab where I was supposed to give a report that I hadn't yet written. Then they had ceased, and life had returned to normal.

And they had all happened after such a sensation as had happened on the bridge. The sensation that was happening again, right now.

I rolled three sixes. Asterion grunted, and I moved my pieces, slashing a third of his pieces from the board. He actually grimaced at the physical pain of losing so many at once, probably drawing blood on one of his beefy fingers. My luck had taken over. He had already lost. He just didn't know it yet.

He rolled again, and although it was a better roll, it wasn't anything that helped him. Within three moves, I sat staring at the board full of my pieces, only one of his stones left. He scowled up at me, and then flipped the board over in frustration at his loss. Gunnar hid his smile well. I didn't.

"The first part of our duel is in your favor. We shall have a discussion next." I nodded, rolling my shoulders for circulation, glad that he hadn't noticed the change in odds as anything unnatural. What bothered me most was that I knew he wanted to hand over the book, but he had to fulfill the necessary obligations that Hermes had bestowed upon him.

Now, I knew that compared to all the other problems I was facing, finding a book for a client was not that important. But I had given my word that it would be done. And that is something I do not give lightly. But Asterion had also mentioned that the book had *something* to do with dragons, which I was neck-deep in at the moment. So, here I was, playing a board game and risking my life in order to figure out what the fuck, exactly, was going on in my city.

Asterion's voice was harsh as he spoke next. "Explain these three weaknesses to me. Life, death, and love." I blinked, waiting for more.

"I don't understand," I finally answered.

"How so?" he asked, heavy eyebrows lifting slightly.

"I don't know how love could be a weakness," I gave as an example.

Asterion leaned forward, folding his arms before him across the table to support his bulk. His gold nose ring glinted in the firelight. I heard the stamp of hooves outside the circle, and shivered as I remembered the scream from earlier. "Answering one answers them all. You *love* to deal *death*, yet *love* to promote *life*. You would *end* the lives of a few wicked to *promote* the lives of others. Yet you relish in the act. You kill too easily, and no executioner can be allowed to roam the streets without a check to that power. And finally, like the hummingbird, you *love* to flit from one pretty flower—a woman—to the next, tasting each, but never filling yourself. With humans, this hurts the woman, even if they presently do not understand it. Eventually they will. But by then it will be too late for them."

I thought hard about his words, because they were true, but I still felt I was right. On some of it. "The last is true. Something I was beginning to realize just recently."

"Oh?" He motioned for me to continue.

"Love is precious, and shouldn't be wasted on every passing whim, or it will mean nothing by the time you truly wish to share it with someone who matters," I said softly.

Gunnar grunted in surprise. Asterion smiled in approval. "And the rest?"

"I seem to link them all to justice. I do not relish the *act* of killing, but what it signifies."

"But who are you to judge right from wrong? Is it because you have power?"

"Yes," I answered without thinking.

"Socrates would roll over in his grave..." Asterion began.

I understood where he was going. "Okay, hold on. Not because I have the *power*, but because I have the *ability*. I do not judge who is naughty or nice. If someone harms an innocent, then they are wrong. Especially if they do so to gain power. I *am* an executioner, but only on behalf of those who cannot protect themselves. I relish the act of delivering *justice*, but not in the act of delivering *harm*. There is a significant difference."

Asterion weighed me contemplatively and then smiled. "Then it seems I owe you a token of my gratitude." My shoulders relaxed. It was over.

"Does this mean I won? Can I tell people I defeated the Minotaur in a duel?"

He snorted disdainfully. "You *beat* me at a childish board game. But you *passed* a test." He smiled eagerly. "*Now*, we duel."

31

Asterion stood. "Step away from the table, if you please. You may embrace your gift now." I did, and he led me away from the table, but still within the circle of firelight. I whipped up a hasty bit of magic behind his back, but he was too excited about the duel to notice. He turned to face me, and then bowed with hands formally folded together like a martial arts bout. Despite proclaiming to be a Buddhist, he looked particularly murderous and hungry at the moment. The addictive taste of violence had returned to the once-bloodthirsty Greek legend.

Then he was rushing at me, head down. His horns gleamed in the flickering firelight. They pierced me below the stomach, and I screamed out in agony as I fell down to the ground. But as soon as my form touched the grass, it disappeared.

Asterion blinked, suddenly wary as his eyes darted about, searching for my wounded body. From the comfort of the table, I spun my spell a second time, creating a second visual replication of myself to stand off to Asterion's right. He turned, nostrils flaring as he saw the image of me flicker, bloody hands clutching the wound. The Minotaur darted forward again, flicking his head at the last moment to send me up into the air, but then I disappeared again.

I smiled from my front row seat atop the table, invisible to everyone. I crossed my ankles as I wove three more visual replications of myself, placing them evenly apart before him. He leaned back, face angry, attempting to judge which version of me was real. One had no injury, one had only the stomach wound, and the other had both wounds. I made them flicker in and out of existence, but not the uninjured form, luring him. He charged, tearing up the grass in his rage. As his horns struck the resemblance, gossamer ropes as strong as Kevlar snapped around him, limiting his mobility. He roared in fury, lunging at the second replication of me.

Although I found myself horrified at his passion for violence, I smiled, pleased at my work, and also the raw fear on Gunnar's face as he watched the Minotaur maim me. Asterion pierced the second form as it turned to run away in mock fear. This time, the gossamer ropes of power latched around his arms even tighter, pulling them back to his sides, while several others restricted his thighs. Asterion bellowed triumphantly as he struck the last form hard enough to kill. I let the spectral image vanish on contact, and the last of my gossamer ropes wrapped firmly around his boots, snapping tight as he fell to the ground, completely immobilizing him.

I withdrew the cocoon of magic around me, clapping my hands as I stepped down from the table, now visible to all. Gunnar and Asterion both flinched to stare back in disbelief, realizing that I had never left the table. My voice was soft. "You question me on life and death, and you were so ready to kill me just now. I saw you mortally wound me five times. Bad Buddhist. Bad, *bad* Buddhist." I waggled a finger at him. "I have not harmed you in the slightest, yet I have incapacitated you. How do you suppose this is, if I am so intent on killing everyone who crosses me?"

He smiled as he spoke three words. "Your turn, Grimm." The torches around us evaporated with a puff and I heard the strange horse-like neigh again. Then the sound of galloping hooves raced towards me from the sunset shadows. I heard Gunnar grunt as something slammed into him, knocking him completely across the clearing. But in the sudden lack of firelight, it was difficult for me to see clearly, even with the fading sunset, because the surrounding trees cast an army of shadows around us, and they still moved back and forth as if alive.

A place between worlds, the Minotaur had said. What was out there, and what were the shadows? A dark blur moved before me, and I leapt back onto the table, just missing a single gnarled horn from stabbing my thigh. Silky black feathers brushed my arm, and I leapt backwards off the table. I heard a heavy flap of wings as a huge silhouette rose up before me, and then it disappeared again. It was toying with me. I called Stone Skin around me before I consciously thought about it, just like I had against the gargoyles.

Panicked—but better protected—I swept the clearing with my eyes, trying to use my power to light up the clearing with fire so that I could see what the hell was attacking us. But my fire quickly flickered out, as if the darkness had simply swallowed it up. Before the light disappeared, I spotted Gunnar lying on his back, staring up at the sky, but he was breathing. I hissed at the Minotaur, not looking at him as the world plunged back into darkness. "This wasn't part of the duel."

"We each brought a pet. Don't you like him? He's rather territorial though, I must admit." I heard something behind me only a second before I felt the impact knock me forward enough to blow the air out of me in a rush, the sound of crunching stone armor filling the clearing. I landed on my chest and rolled. I remained kneeling, hoping to use the sunset to outline my assailant while hiding my own silhouette from view. I hoped it had been using my silhouette to find me, and not that it had some seriously kickass night vision.

Then it suddenly appeared in front of me.

A horse the size of a Clydesdale pawed at the earth with a silver front hoof, fire tracing away from the ground in a smoky burn, helping me see it clearly for the first time. Its eyes were like blazing orange embers, and it was mostly covered in feathers like a peacock, but black with fiery red circles on the tips instead of the usual pretty turquoise. Similarly-feathered, monstrous, black and red-tipped wings flared out behind it, tripling its size, and more feathers flared out around its entire neck in a lion-like mane, quivering as it snorted at me.

One massively thick barbed-horn spiraled up from its forehead, looking more like a trio of horns braided together with tiny spikes curling off the sides like thorns on a rose-bush. Then it surged forward. To say it was graceful was an understatement. It was so beautiful that I was frozen still in admiration as I watched the red-rimmed mane of feathers tug back against the force of its sudden movement. Its horn struck my chest, and my Stone Skin crunched before the aged bone. The pressure was immense, but just as suddenly, it stopped.

I opened my very brave eyes, which had somehow closed as it hit me, and stared into a silky smooth-haired face. The beast neighed at me, stomping an angry hoof, but didn't bolt. Stupidly, I reached out a hand to pet the magnificent creature. Asterion and Gunnar both began to shout a warning, but stopped as my fingers brushed the snout. The feathers were just as smooth as they looked, but there was also regular velvety hair on its face. The eyes calmed as they watched me, and then it pulled its head away from my chest—as if apologizing—and snapped closed the red-tipped mane surrounding its head. I blinked, letting the stone slide away from my skin in sheets.

Asterion spoke. "It is finished. The book is yours." He was somehow standing up, my restraining cords of power gone. And he sounded shaken.

I blinked at him, lost in the feel of the creature's fur beneath my fingers. "That wasn't so bad."

"Granted, I should have taken into account the myths involving unicorns," Asterion muttered. "I should have remembered that they couldn't harm virgins."

I adamantly began to protest as Gunnar burst out laughing. "I am in *no* way a virgin! Of that I can assure you. Tell him, Gunnar"

The Minotaur smiled, reaching out a hand to help the werewolf stand. Instead of backing up my claim, Gunnar accepted Asterion's assistance with an awed gaze as he stared upon the myth towering over him.

For future reference, I mentally noted that Gunnar was useless in a duel.

Asterion clasped a meaty arm around Gunnar's shoulders. "That is where myth deviates from truth. You see, it's not just a virgin that is immune to a unicorn's wrath. It is also the last of a bloodline. It is just a coincidence that all of the documented survivors happened to be either a virgin, or both the last of their line *and* a virgin. It seems Grimm likes you."

Grimm knelt before me like a servant to a king. I stepped back, unsure. "This isn't really what I imagined a unicorn would look like." I said.

Asterion chuckled. "No, but you are imagining the adapted stories of Pegasus. This is his brother, Grimm. Perseus never met him...lucky for him, I should say." Until that moment, I had thought the unicorn and Pegasus were two different beasts, but didn't want to flaunt my lack of knowledge. I had a reputation to uphold after all.

Asterion judged Grimm as he knelt with head bowed before me. "Grimm is obedient, and takes care of himself. All one must do is call him when in need, and he will appear out of any nearby shadow to help." Just as quickly, Grimm suddenly disappeared. A single feather drifted down to the ground in his place. I picked it up, admiring the blazing red orb at the tip before carefully placing it in my pocket.

"What am I supposed to do with a horse?"

Asterion frowned. "You would be well advised not to demean his help. He is far more than a *horse*, as you just saw." I nodded back, swallowing reflexively. "You beat me fairly, Master Temple. But why didn't you simply battle me directly?"

"Sheer confidence in your superior ability to maim and murder, I assure you," I replied grinning. "I have friends that need my help, and I couldn't do that if I spent all my energy battling you directly. It was the path of the least consequences." The Minotaur smiled at the compliment.

"One can't die at the Dueling Grounds. You would have recovered from any injury in a day or so. At most. *Any* injury..." He added with a grin.

I stared back in surprise. "Truly?" I asked, astounded.

"Truly." Asterion smiled.

With knowledge like that, I wouldn't have been so fucking stressed out about tonight, but I let it go with a heavy breath. *Woo-sah*, I rubbed my earlobe meditatively. "I would also like to add that your Karmic conversation with me hit a point that I couldn't refute. So, I tried the path that would be the least offensive. I incapacitated you, but didn't hurt you directly. Hopefully Karma will remember that when it comes my way again."

Asterion appraised me studiously. "How appropriate. You are, of course, correct. You would make an excellent student."

I shook my head. "I would look terrible bald. Or fat. With both I would look positively ridiculous."

Gunnar rolled his eyes. "Here." Asterion handed me a book that I hadn't seen him grab. "This is what you seek." I accepted the aged leather tome from his hand without asking where he had grabbed it from, and tucked it away in my coat, noticing the picture I had drawn for him on the cover, and the faint smell of cold stone and snakes. Oddly familiar, but I couldn't place why.

"Thank you."

"Perhaps I should thank you, Master Temple. It has been in my care for so long now, and one can only hope that a better guardian was needed, and that is why I lost today." Gunnar was still staring from one of us to the other, a stupid grin on his face.

"We must be leaving now, Asterion. I have dragons to face."

"Of that I am certain," he answered cryptically. Again, I wondered what the book was about, and what it had to do with dragons. He had said it was an original, but an original what? He turned to Gunnar. "It is nice to make your acquaintance, *Wulfric*. Perhaps the next time will be under a less violent occasion."

Gunnar smiled back. "It would be my pleasure."

Then everything was suddenly gone, and we were left standing in the middle of a field, staring at each other. "You do lead the most interesting life, Nate," Gunnar said, glancing around in surprise.

"Tell me about it. Come on. We have a nightclub to visit, but I need to chat with Peter first. You can take Tory home to change, and pick me up after. We'll figure out something to do with Misha on the way." We walked towards the SUV, the headlights blinding as I realized it was suddenly night. How long had we been gone?

32

I stumbled inside my shop, shouldering the door open wearily. Some of the lights were on. Peter must already be here. I headed back into one of the projection rooms, following both the light and the sound of epic music and dying screams.

Ah, what a peaceful sound.

I nudged the door open to find Peter sitting before one of the screens, playing Gods of Chaos IV, leaning forward eagerly as if it would help against the dozen enemies he was battling. "Hey," I said, falling down onto the couch beside him.

He started, but didn't take his eyes off the game. "Sorry, didn't hear you come in." He gestured at the table to a full drink he had made. Another sat empty beside it. "Poured you one of your elixirs of life. Absinthe."

"You'll make a good wife someday, Peter."

"Yeah, give me a minute. Almost killed him." He continued playing, and I set down my satchel by the end of the couch, Asterion's book resounding with a heavy *thunk*. "Yes! Eat it, Minotaur!" Peter crowed.

I pondered the screen as I sipped my drink, warmth blossoming in my stomach and throat. "He doesn't really look like that, you know."

Peter finally turned to face me. His eyes were red-rimmed, and he looked tired, or extremely hung over. "I didn't even think about that. Here I was playing a video game against the Minotaur, and you fought him in real life tonight. I feel like an idiot. How did it go?"

I grunted, taking a deep gulp of my drink. "I survived, as you can see. I got what I wanted, and we parted on good terms. He was just fulfilling a promise he had made long ago." I leaned back, sighing. "Works for me, I suppose."

"Was it tough? I mean, he's tough in the game, and in real life you said that Theseus was the only one to ever defeat him."

"I didn't fight him directly. I played his philosophy against him. Gunnar saw it all."

"You took *Gunnar*? Why not me? I would have loved to see him! A real Minotaur!"

"*The* real Minotaur. And yes, I took Gunnar because I wanted backup." I let the silence build between us until I saw Peter squirm a bit. "Backup I could trust."

He looked at me then, cautious. "You don't trust me?"

I laughed. I couldn't help it. "*Trust*? *You*?" I spat. "I *used* to trust you. About two days ago. Then you just happened to whip out some magic like you had been doing it your whole life. And you never told me about it beforehand. How or why would I possibly trust you after that?"

He leaned back, resigned. "I was going to tell you. I swear. It just never came up. I wanted to be like you two for so long, and then I suddenly was, and I didn't want to be your weak-ass apprentice. I wanted to appear formidable, strong, dependable."

"Well, instead you just appeared untrustworthy. Satisfied?" I grouched. He shook his head, angry. "How did it happen? *When* did it happen? I would have known if you had an innate spark in you all these years. I sensed *nothing* of the sort though. What changed?"

He stood. "I need another drink first." He tried to step over my bag, but his foot got caught up in the strap and he stumbled before catching himself, spewing the book from the Minotaur onto the floor. Peter stared at it for a second, and then stooped down to pick it up.

"Don't, Peter."

He looked over at me, chastising eyes demeaning my warning. "It's just a book." Then it was in his fingers. I scratched my fingers through my hair. No harm in glancing at it. Besides, I hadn't had a chance to peruse it yet either. And I had risked my life for it. I watched Peter's face grow pale. He tried to speak twice, but no sound came out. When he cleared his throat, it was barely a whisper. "How did you find it?"

I squinted, taking another sip of my drink. "I already told you. I got it from the Minotaur. It's for a client."

He was shaking his head. "Is this some kind of a joke? This is the book I wanted you to get for *me*. The one my client *really* wanted. How did you know?" He looked hungry, and lost at the same time.

My forearms pebbled with sudden anxiety. "Alright, Peter. I don't know what you're talking about, but that book belongs to someone else. You look as if you've had enough to drink." I slowly stood, not wanting to spook him. He was ignoring me, reading the cover page. I leaned over enough to see, and read it myself. I somehow managed to keep my face neutral. *Sons of the Dying Sun* was written across an entire page. My skin pebbled even further. The book Raven had asked for. The one Alaric wanted.

"I thought that once that dragon lady asked for it, you wouldn't get it for me, thinking I was in league with her." He laughed nervously. "I ran upstairs to take away the note, but I guess that Jessie had written down the wrong title anyway, so I left it. Idiot kid."

"Who did you say your client was?" I asked, my mind suddenly racing.

"A rich old man who let me take over his portfolio. He said this was invaluable to him, and that I would be rewarded handsomely." He began idly fingering his bracelet with his thumb as he snapped the book closed. "I don't know how to thank you, Nate. I need to tell him right away! He will be thrilled! How much is it worth to you." He paused for a second. "Wait, did you say you got this from the Minotaur? Why would *he* have it?"

If my kid client had also asked Peter for the book, I'm sure he would have told me, but the brief description didn't sound like the creepy, secretive kid who had come to me a week ago. And the kid hadn't told me what the title was. He hadn't, for instance, told me that it was the same book a harem of dragons had been searching for, killing for. Alaric had said that there were many other dragons in town. Was there some kind of power play going on? If so, which side was I on? The kid didn't seem like he was working for anyone, if anything, he seemed to want everything on the hush.

I used the moment of confusion to strike, sensing the wildness in his eyes, and knowing something big was going on, even if I didn't have all the pieces. I snatched the book from his hands, and darted back a step. "I already told you, Peter. This book is bought and paid for by a client of mine. I work for myself first, others second, if at all. Your client has no right to this book."

"My client will triple what yours paid," he added, smiling.

"I don't change my mind after I promise something. My client asked me for the book, I obtained it, and he paid for it." The last was a lie, but I'd be damned if I was going to pass over such a high-demand book to a stranger when I had almost been killed several times to find it.

"Just hand it over, Nate. You'll have your money tomorrow. Enough to drown in Absinthe for the rest of your life," Peter added with a slimy smile.

I studied him for a moment, and realized something for the first time. "Perhaps you hadn't heard...I took over my parents' company yesterday. The money you offer for this book is a mere pittance to me. Quite literally. Money is no longer a motivator. Just my word." I clinked the ice cubes in my glass, swirling the jade liquid as I watched Peter's eyes widen in surprise. "I take on clients that I trust, and I haven't met yours. I do know that a harem of dragons wants this book mighty fiercely, enough to kill me for it. Perhaps I'll keep it for myself. After all, I did risk my life for it no less than an hour ago. The Minotaur was no easy meat."

Peter watched me. "Why would the Minotaur have it?"

I held up a finger. "He didn't have it, he obtained it for me," I lied, not wanting to drag the Minotaur into whatever this was. There was a loyalty factor between my clients and I. I wouldn't sell him out just to get myself out of some hot water. Well, scalding water.

"Come on, Nate. Just give it to me. We're friends."

I laughed. "Funny. Because I thought friends were honest with each other, and I distinctly remember telling you that you would get nothing from me until you explained your newfound powers. I promise you nothing in exchange, but you do owe me an explanation. So, start explaining."

He fiddled with his bracelet. Then I understood. "Your bracelet gives you the power?"

He nodded. "It's a gift on loan, for now. If I can obtain the book for him, the power is mine. If I can't get it, then I get a whole lot of pain. I thought, with you as a friend, I could find any book in the world, so I agreed. How hard could it be if my client was willing to pay anything for the book? And then I could be a wizard like you."

"Deals with the devil are usually like that."

His eyes darted to the book. "I don't want to be hurt by this guy, Nate. He's really strong..." He looked lost.

"Then let me help you."

He shook his head vehemently. "No. I can't. He'll kill me."

"Who is he? I can make him back off. I have a reputation for this kind of thing."

Peter's eyes squinted. "I don't need your protection. Just give me the book. Now."

My anger was an immediate response to his tone. "Not happening, Peter. I think it's time for you to go beg forgiveness from your client. You should never make a promise that you have no way of keeping. It's time for you to accept the consequences like a man." My voice was low, furious that he would dare threaten me so that he could keep a power that wasn't his.

Something deep inside his eyes snapped. Madness danced there, where nothing of the sort had ever belonged before. The power from the bracelet had somehow taken control. "Oh, I won't be begging anyone for forgiveness, Nate. You really should have heeded my advice and taken the offer."

He slammed his will against mine, sheer force against my hastily thrown shield. He was so *strong*. It was like a high school lineman trying to stop an NFL line, but I somehow managed to hold him back, and trip him up with a slash of fire at his ankles. As he lost his balance, his power lessened enough for me to regain my thoughts. Jesus, what the fuck *was* that bracelet, and where could I get one without the strings of servitude attached? I won't lie that it was an enticing offer from Peter's client. This was appealing even to me, and I had a considerable amount of power on my own. If he only had the finesse to match the power, he would be nearly invincible.

He regained his feet, lashing out with a rope of air to snatch the book. I tossed it behind me, cloaking it in shadows so that he couldn't see it anymore. He roared in anger. "I will have the book, Nate. Get out of my way."

"Peter, listen to yourself! You're willing to attack your best friend for a taste of power! What the fuck is *wrong* with you?" He didn't listen, but instead began tossing balls of fire at me in rapid succession. I swallowed them all with airtight pockets cast just before each, hoping to diminish the damage to my store as much as possible. Then my own power began calling out to me, that additional reservoir, and I used it. I cut directly through his attack, and slammed him into the wall, his head rebounding sharply.

He lashed out one last time, slicing a six-inch gash up my ribs with razor sharp air until I managed to shield him away from his power completely. I tied the knot around his core, allowing him to feel the power of the bracelet, but not tap into it. He slumped, arms hanging uselessly, and eyes rolling slightly. I was panting heavily. I didn't want him to keep the bracelet, but I was too scared to touch it, so I chose a different tack.

"The book is not yours. When you wake up, you will be home, and will have some time to think about all this. I doubt I'll ever trust you again, but I expect an apology, if you survive your encounter with your client. I no longer care what becomes of you, Peter. I don't tolerate betrayal." Then I slammed my power deep into his brain, shutting it down into a deep unconsciousness that would last until morning, a hibernated sleep of sorts.

I prodded him with a finger to see if it had worked, and smiled disgustedly at my success. Wizards weren't supposed to use dark magic like this, altering the brain directly, but who would ever find out? Then I used flows of air to carry him outside my shop, and hailed a nearby taxi. "My friend has had too much to drink. If it wouldn't inconvenience you, I would ask that you take him home." The driver nodded. I waved a hundred-dollar bill at him. "I have an eidetic memory," I glanced at his name placard on the dash, "Ivan Petranov. You will carry him to his room, lay him down on the couch, and lock up behind you. Leave his keys with the doorman and you'll have nothing to fear, and you'll make a few hundred bucks." I paused dramatically, and then hissed out the next words with a sound like a knife leaving a sheath. "If anything of his somehow disappears from his apartment, or if I hear that in any way you have deviated from my instructions, I'll hunt you down, take away your license, and make sure that the only thing you can eat from this day forward is Borscht, because you will have no teeth. Agreed?" The man's face went from angry to pale, but he nodded. I handed him two more hundreds. "Pleasure doing business with you."

It was only as I stepped back inside that I realized I'd been speaking in Russian. It was a perfect language for threats—full of harsh, angry syllables. Othello was rubbing off on me. I went back inside to ponder the book that had caused such a ruckus, waiting for Gunnar to pick me up so I could get the damned thing off my hands. Even though it was obviously dangerous, something about my client made me trust he wouldn't use it for harm. He was more concerned with keeping the book safe than anything else. He had even been making sure that no one else was asking after it, but of course, without the title, that had been impossible to relay to him. I hoped my instincts were right, and that I wasn't passing the book off to a psychopath. Oh well, we would see tonight.

At *Artemis' Garter*.

33

I had told Misha to spy on Alaric while I dealt with my client. Hopefully she found something useful on her haunt. We pulled up to *Artemis' Garter* around ten, and I cursed when I saw the line snaking around the front of the building, and then on, and on, into eternity. Heads turned as we cruised by, girls primping themselves, or proudly revealing their cleavage to our pimped-out SUV.

As we cruised by, I made eye contact with one of the valets and he froze for a second. Then he jumped into the street, urgently flagging us down. Gunnar stopped, looking confused. The valet ran up to our window and waited. Gunnar frowned at me when I shrugged, but rolled down his window. The valet was heavily muscled, wearing a fishnet Tee despite the cold, but he somehow pulled it off. His nametag said Clyde. His short, spiky hair looked like a weapon, and I wondered if it doubled as such. If security tossed him into the crowd, his hair would no doubt maim several people. He smiled. "Good to see you, Master Temple. If you would please park over there, I'll escort you and your party inside."

I looked where he had pointed. "That says reserved parking."

Clyde smiled again, amused. "Yes, reserved for distinguished guests and the VIP. Join me at the front when you're ready." He stepped away, satisfied, and I felt Tory and Gunnar's eyes on me.

"Have you been here a few times or something?"

I shook my head. "Never," I answered honestly.

Gunnar looked doubtful, but parked the beast of a vehicle into the designated spot, and we all got out. Gunnar wore a crisp white dress shirt, a heavy gold medallion hanging in a nest of blonde chest hair, and dark expensive jeans. His boots were mid-calf under the hem of his jeans, but they also looked expensive. I should know. I had bought it all. Tory was wearing a single-piece white cashmere sweater that dipped low, wide-open almost to mid-stomach, allowing her breasts to hang free without a bra, and revealing quite a nice expanse of cleavage. Her long brown hair flipped down over her shoulders, the tips curling up just underneath her breasts.

A wide leather belt helped her appear taller, and the fabric continued down into a mid-thigh skirt, which when she was facing the other way, hugged her rear like a glove. She wore black knee-high boots, laced up in the back with red ribbon laces like a Christmas present. Oh, how anyone would love to unwrap that gift. Several of the women in line snorted in jealousy as they spotted her with us.

I wore a starched black dress shirt with white cuffs, and white jeans. My black boots were even more expensive than Gunnar's. All in all, we did look like VIPs. We skirted the line and found Clyde waiting for us, an eager smile on his face as he handed each of us a small paper bag with a silver ribbon around the top. "Won't the rest of your guests be upset that we cut in line?" I asked.

Clyde shook his head. "A VIP can do whatever they wish. The others will just want to get inside even faster now that Master Temple is in the same club. It will be the talk of the town," he admitted unashamedly.

"Right. How did you know we were going to be here tonight?" I asked, fiddling with the bag to see what was inside.

"I didn't. I just recognized you in the car. Almost every club in town awaits your arrival, Master Temple. Most of us have codes to follow that if you arrive, you are to be instantly treated as a VIP. Free marketing." He motioned us inside the first door to a bouncer. The beefy man's eyes widened upon seeing me, and then quickly shuffled us through. Clyde continued. "Our patron sponsor for this evening requests that everyone don contacts for the night's festivities. And, since drinks are covered at his expense tonight, we expect all guests to follow such a simple request. Even VIPs." He smiled. "Now, if you will please put on your contacts."

Gunnar piped up. "I don't wear contacts. I have perfect vision." He was frowning as he held up a disposable contact case from inside the pretty paper bag.

"Already accounted for, Agent Randulf. None of the contacts are prescription strength. Well, we have a dozen or so different prescriptions in case the guests actually need corrective contacts and are already wearing some. But most are just for decoration. They're merely part of the event."

We must have looked startled at his knowledge of Gunnar's name because he smiled wider. "As I said, we follow news of you, and any of your known acquaintances." He frowned at Tory. "But she is not familiar to me." He smiled very politely as he reached out a hand. "Miss..."

"Officer Tory Marlin," She answered after a look my direction. "And yes, that works perfectly fine, but I do not understand why we should waste time putting on non-prescription contacts," she argued.

Her last comment rolled off his shoulders. "Pleasure to meet you, Miss Marlin. Now, if you will please follow me I will show you the reason for the contacts." His eyes sparkled with anticipation. He led us up a flight of stairs, and I could feel the bass thumping from deep inside the building like the erratic heartbeat of some monstrous beast.

He led us up to the second floor, past two sets of security guards, and then stopped at a bar. He beckoned the bartender. The man jumped to comply. As he neared, I abruptly halted, instinctively grasping at my core of power to restrain him with cords of magic so he couldn't move. My eyes darted around, making sure no one had noticed. The bartender looked terrified, suddenly unable to move. I leaned over the counter. "Who are you?" I growled, staring into his horizontal pupils. The pupils of a dragon.

The man looked about to soil himself. "I can't move! Why can't I move?"

"I'm a wizard, and I am holding you still." I smiled back, pleased at the fear that I had caused the sneaky dragon. I wouldn't give him the chance to even attempt mind-games on me tonight.

His face paled, and Clyde looked mortified, as if suddenly realizing that he had done something to risk his job, but not knowing exactly what I had done to immobilize his bartender. "It's the contacts, Master Temple. That's what I was trying to show you. Everyone is wearing them. It's required by the wishes of the patron sponsor for tonight's dance competition." I blinked, and then looked around. One by one, I realized that Clyde was right. Everyone had the same horizontal dragon-eyed pupils. I shivered, understanding now how dangerous this situation had become—that we could very easily be outnumbered if everyone looked like a dragon. We wouldn't be able to tell Regulars from Freaks. And that was probably the fucking point. I was suddenly interested in who this patron was, fearing that the Dragon Lord had been working one step ahead of me.

I let the bartender go, waving him away. Instead of resuming work, he darted towards the restroom, holding the rear of his pants without embarrassment. I shook my head. I guess I had literally scared him shitless. That was a first.

A lingerie-clad hostess glided up beside Tory and Gunnar, her dragon-eyed contacts shining an icy blue, leaning in close to help them put on their contacts. A minute later, Tory and Gunnar had each donned their disguise, and were studying the crowd, ready for anything. Gunnar shrugged at my look, fiery-red dragon-eyes turning to me. "If we're the only ones without the contacts, it will be pretty easy to pick us out in the crowd." I nodded, but was still angry. I hated being one step behind.

"Who is this patron, and where are your contacts?" I asked Clyde as I slid on my own pair. They looked bright green in the case. I had worn contacts before in several Halloween costume contests, so knew how to do it fairly easily.

"Since I am normally outside, I wasn't wearing them. Same with the bouncer downstairs. Didn't want to ruin the surprise for the guests," he answered. "The patron, although I'm sure it's just a nickname, goes by Raego. Perhaps he's a DJ, or a rising Rap star hoping to gain favor from the city. He is running a bit late, but said he would be here soon. He requested that if the Master Temple should arrive, he might be granted a few moments of your time. If it wasn't too much trouble, of course. It seems you caused quite the stir at the Eads Bridge this afternoon. It's all over the news. Archangel, they're calling you," Clyde said neutrally, no doubt itching to ask more. I said nothing, letting him think what he wished. The fucking news again. My secret was no more. Oh well, nothing to be done for it now.

But Raego? That was the name of the black dragon the dragon hunters warned me about. They would owe me big time if they were somehow able to bag him tonight after I tipped them off to this location. But how had he known I would be here? Had the Dragon Lord been lying to me? Was the Dragon Lord really Raego? Had someone followed us here? Or were the two working together?

"I was on the news?" I asked. Clyde nodded slowly, as if I were daft.

"Did you really slay a...dragon? They say you're a wizard," he asked as if embarrassed at the question. Then his eyes trailed back to the bartender who had run to the bathroom, and his shoulders tightened, as if suddenly reconsidering what he had seen.

"More than one, but the news only heard about the one on the bridge." I basked in the shock on his face. "Perhaps I could spare a moment or so. I am meeting a client here myself, but if Raego arrives before I leave, then I might say hello."

"Great. I'll direct him your way when he arrives. It's been a real pleasure meeting you, but I need to get back to the front. If you need anything, anything at all, just tell the waitress *Archangel*," he grinned, "and she will supply...*whatever* you or your party desires." The implication was heavy, and for the first time, I wondered what kind of club this was. Or was I reading too deep into things? Maybe I should have researched the place before telling my client I would meet him here. I had heard the name of the club through passing conversation and advertisements around town, and it had simply been the first place I thought of. Plus, I knew it had a rooftop bar. Always good to have a secondary escape option.

Maybe a little more research would have been smart.

Tory and Gunnar had moved over towards a balcony that overlooked the main floor below, and I saw their dragon contacts wide and clear as they watched the show below them in stunned amazement. As I saw what had caught their attention, my eyes widened, too. It was like Cirque De Soleil meets Hustler magazine. Three separate stages stood below us, with shiny steel poles climbing up to the ceiling above my head. As I followed the pole up, I realized that a nude woman was hanging by her thighs, arms outstretched, breasts hanging freely, and kissing the neck of a guest on the same level as me. She was thirty feet above the first-floor stage, barely holding on to the pole, and still seducing people on the floor above. The guest folded a twenty-dollar bill and tucked it inside a feather collar around the stripper's neck.

I shook my head, and noticed that Tory looked downright ravenous as she watched. I pinched her arm and she gasped, flushing red as she met my eyes. "Sorry, just incredibly...impressed," she said, lamely. I shook my head with an amused grin. Glancing back down, I saw a dance floor full of bodies writhing and thrashing to the music. Dragon eyes everywhere. I noticed a few strippers here and there, enticing couples into better positions, fueling their libido, but remaining just out of the grasp of too-eager hands.

Bouncers stood positioned through the room, ready to be anywhere at a moment's notice. I saw one stripper leading a young couple off to a back room, and shook my head in disbelief. A dance club, *and* a strip club. Who knew?

I pulled Tory and Gunnar's sleeves, drawing them away from the railing. "So, I guess I didn't research the locale very well. I had no idea it was a strip club, I swear." Gunnar frowned at me, not believing a word. "Seriously. But let's go up onto the roof. Perhaps it's more G-rated up there. That's where I'm meeting my client anyway." They nodded, following me as I searched for the roof access to the top floor of the club, where hopefully nudity would be frowned upon by neighbors across the street, if not discouraged outright by the cold weather.

I found the door, and climbed up a narrow set of wooden stairs, my posse in tow behind me. We exited onto a wooden dance floor sheltered by a glass-ceilinged area with couches and divans around the perimeter where couples cuddled up beside each other or strippers performed lap dances in public view. Space heaters surrounded the area, likely enough for a fire code violation.

Jesus. I felt like a prude. Don't get me wrong, I *love* the female body, and I may have even visited a strip club or dozen, but I was focused on business tonight, and I had a female guest with me, making everything slightly more uncomfortable, even though Tory seemed to be enjoying herself just fine as she studied several of the dancers acutely.

The heat lamps dotting the roof kept the cold at bay, and hidden speakers thumped loudly with different music from downstairs. I scanned the tangle of bodies, even peering around the shoulder of a dancer writhing upon a black-clothed man in one of the plush chairs. Her breasts almost hit me in the face as she turned into me, startled at my cold-fingered touch. Her dragon eyes instinctively shocked me as she looked me up and down. "Care for a dance, love?" she purred.

I shook my head. "No, I was just looking for someone."

"I could be *someone*," she whispered sensually. I shook my head again and strode away. Scanning the dragon-eyed people around us, I began to feel nervous. This was bad. Very, very bad. There was no way for me to spot a real dragon before it was too late. And with Raego picking the dress code, odds were that he wouldn't be alone, and that he had probably sent some dragons here ahead of time. Or why else require the disguises?

We grabbed drinks, asking the bartender if he had seen anyone that might fit my client's description. He shook his head, and offered us a free dance with anyone we chose as soon as he realized who I was. I declined, although Tory looked disappointed at my choice, arguing that we might fit in better if we looked like we were having a good time.

"So good a time that we won't see a real dragon come up behind us and snap our necks?" I retorted, quietly but severely. She sighed, nodding agreement, and we continued searching the roof for my client. I began to feel stupid that I had never pressed him harder for a name. I mean, he was paying me a lot of money, and I had procured a book for him; a very, very dangerous book, apparently. But I had let him get away with not answering the question.

In the future, I would have to remedy that. It would have made things easier if we could have passed out a name to the over-eager waitresses who never seemed to be too far away to suggest luxuries we might enjoy while we wait. Some of those luxuries promised to be quite strenuous. "Would you care to take your pick of two dancers to one of the private rooms?" One asked. I shook my head, the pain from not getting a release from Indie's affections earlier threatening to cripple me like a fist in the gut. "How about three, Master Temple?" Again, I somehow managed to say no, and we found seats on some of the couches.

We chatted idly, eyes searching the crowd. It was unsettling to see so many dragon eyes around me. Even when I glanced at Gunnar and Tory I would flinch instinctively. After a while, we finally began to relax.

And that was when Aphrodite and her sisters came to play with the mortals.

34

The five goddesses swayed our way, their eyes ignoring everyone but us. Two sat down beside Gunnar after scooting him over to a separate chair wide enough for three. One sat on either side of me, and the last sat directly in Tory's lap.

It happened so fast that none of us could even protest. They were experts. Super strippers. And only prior knowledge let me realize that they weren't *actual* goddesses, but just extremely talented dancers. They wore just enough to tease—little enough to steal your attention and make you search for the unseen straps or buttons that magically seemed to hold the sparse fabric in place.

Tory's eyes were wide as the dancer leaned down and licked the hollow of her throat, but that was all I had time to notice before my own strippers dove upon me with abandon. One leaned in, her rose-scented hair cloying my nostrils as she licked my earlobe. Her lacy top brushed against my cold drink and she moaned at the contact, the sound muddling my brain.

"Mmmm...*Archangel* is here to take care of us. Whatever shall we do?" she asked the other, wrapping her arms around my neck as she settled herself firmly in my lap. She used one hand to place my own upon her smooth rear end, able to cup the entire naked cheek in one palm.

That was it. The wizard was officially useless.

The blue dragon-eyes of the woman straddling me made it all the more alluring as she arched her back, leaning backwards to the second woman, who promptly reached out and gently grabbed a pleasant handful of breast. Her green dragon-eyes met mine as she did so—sexual hunger filling her gaze. Then they considered each other hungrily. "I say that we should do *whatever* the *Master* wishes of us." They turned to face me, as the one on my lap slowly continued to lean back until her spine rested on my knees, gravity pulling her breasts slightly to the side as her hands gripped my ankles and she ground her panties into my abdomen.

We had attracted quite a crowd. I managed to notice the dancers with Gunnar in various Chinese acrobatic positions across his body, and I saw one dancer fiddling with a fuzzy handcuff type bracelet in her hands as the other smothered his face with her chest, throwing her head back with a laugh. Gunnar was surprisingly enjoying himself, which was totally out of character for him. The thought scattered to nothing as my own duo regained my attention with well-placed bite-marks on my thigh.

One of the green-eyed dancer's hands found the book in my back pocket. "Hmm...a librarian. I have always wanted to play with a librarian. Do you like games, librarian? We know a game involving handcuffs..." Her eyes sparkled down at me as she withdrew a pair of handcuffs from out of nowhere. "I think this book is getting in the way. Perhaps we should remove it to reach what is underneath...Which one of us would you choose?" The green-eyed dancer moaned, her horizontal pupils dilating to a thicker, solid bar across her eyes. My haze evaporated in a blink, but I didn't show it.

"I'll have to flip a coin to decide..." I pulled the coin Asterion had given me from my pocket, hoping for the best, and flipped it up into the air. The coin instantly turned into a shield, slamming into the green-eyed dragon's—because that is what she truly was—jaw. I felt blood spray across my face, and one of her teeth landed on my shirt as she flew across the dance floor. I drew my power, embracing it to its fullest, and felt the telltale signs of mind control that had been clouding us. I grabbed the blue-eyed dragon by the throat, carefully plucking the book from her fingers. Then I shoved with all my strength, fueled by a riptide of magic, and launched her into a wall. She struck the wall with a solid smack, immediately silencing the music in an explosive shower of sparks near a couch, and fell to the ground in a crumpled heap, spine broken.

Dead was good.

I heard the snap of metal and turned to see the dragons with Gunnar smiling as their handcuff clasped around his wrist. His eyes immediately changed—even behind the contacts—glazing over. He was no longer home. Tory was oblivious, making out with her red-haired dancer. I grabbed the bitch by the hair, yanked, and threw her a dozen feet behind me with an added boost of air. Her bare skin screeched in a horrendous wood burn as she skidded across the dance floor. Tory's eyes widened as she saw me looming over her, her shirt tugged down over her stomach so that she was naked from the waist up. I saw the handcuff on her wrist, but thankfully it was unclasped. Feeling something on my own wrist, I glanced down and saw a similar handcuff dangling, unclasped. I shivered, flinging it off into the night out over the railing of the roof.

Tory bound to her feet, pulling her top back up into a semblance of decency. My own fly was unzipped. Damn. Aphrodite had *nothing* on them. I hadn't even noticed their power. The dragons stood from various positions around the floor where I had thrown them, but the two with Gunnar continued smiling up at me, one holding a thin chain attached to the bracelet in her fingers. "Good, wolfie..." The blue-eyed, red haired dragon cooed in his ear. Gunnar's shoulders relaxed at the praise.

"Gunnar, get away from them. Now," I demanded.

"Don't want to," he said, struggling with the words. "I'm happy here. So happy. They love me..." I slammed my power into him, but it struck an invisible dome emanating from the handcuffs, bouncing harmlessly away. Shit. One down. I had to kill these bitches now, or I had no idea what would happen to Gunnar.

The Regulars around the dance floor watched drunkenly, several shooting angry glares my way as they had just seen me hurt three strippers. Good men, but they had no idea of the truth. I wouldn't have time to differentiate between Regulars and dragons if it came to a fight, and if a couple of these drunken men thought they were protecting an innocent woman, they might wake up in a hospital tomorrow morning. *Shit, shit, shit.*

A cop appeared out of nowhere, brandishing his pistol, and aiming it in my general direction, yelling at me to stop hurting the women, his eyes wide as his overweight frame sloshed back and forth at any sign of movement. The green-eyed dragon dancer strode up to him, blood dripping from her mouth, eyes innocent and afraid. "He hurt me. Do something, officer. Please! Help me!" She was holding his arm in mock fear. His eyes turned on me, rage blinding him.

"Don't!" I yelled, as he began to raise his gun.

Her hand moved quicker than I had ever seen, tearing his throat completely from his neck to reveal a purplish white spine beneath the gore. Blood spurted into the air, painting the green-eyed dragon's face. Then she shifted into her true form, her legs kicking out a couch that had been too close. She wasn't as big as Misha or the silver dragon I had killed, but she was easily twice as long as a man from rump to snout, and green like a forest in summer.

Then mass chaos erupted. People ran, eyes wide, not even realizing where they were running, abandoning all ties with either their loved ones, dates, strippers, or friends. Screaming tore at my ears, making it hard to notice anything else, but I kept my eyes on the dragons, ready for the fight of my life. Four versus two. A sudden blast of fire ignited a nearby couch, and four more dragons emerged from the flames.

Okay. Now we were really screwed.

I realized I had the book in my pocket and groaned. The book they had been tearing up my city to find. If they turned Gunnar against us we were in serious trouble, because I couldn't see myself hurting my best friend. He wouldn't know what he was doing, but he was one of the most dangerous things I had ever seen when in werewolf form. It would also ruin his career if they made him shift.

Tory tugged at my arm, letting me know she was ready for battle. I waved a hand at the cop, but she shook her head, lifting up hands stained with blood. "He's gone." Crap, a dead cop. Kosage was going to be furious, and once again, I was present at the crime. What would that make him think? But I didn't have time to worry about that now. Fire from the sparks by the demolished speaker had caught the couch ablaze, and was now spreading to the beams that held up the glass ceiling. Thick dark smoke cloyed the air. The years of alcohol spillage had apparently made everything hyper flammable.

"Well then. I think it's time for you to earn your own nickname," I murmured, unleashing the same whips of fire and ice I had used at Alaric's hotel room earlier. Another couch burst into flame as my whip licked it with the faintest brush. "Come on down, bitches. Let me show you what I did to your big sisters." I grinned, flashing teeth, and then I began to cackle.

I think the non-masculine sound had to do with the suddenly power-drunk status of my body trying to figure out what to make of the new reservoir of magic I had been given earlier in the day. Regardless, it made the dragons hesitate.

Then they began to move, freaky fast, like, well...snakes.

I slung the liquid ice whip around the green dragon's throat, and her eyes went wide enough that I was curious if they might just pop out. Then, as I tugged back, her neck simply shattered into fragments of frozen dragon-meat cubes. Her body crashed to the dance floor, twitching. I slung the fiery whip over Tory's head as she darted low, and managed to latch onto the back legs of another dragon mid-shift. It knocked her completely off her feet, and sent her tearing through the protective railing bordering the roof, cloaked in flames, screaming as she fell.

"Stop!" a voice bellowed over the crowd, somehow penetrating the din of screams. I smelled that odd smell of cold rocks and snakes again, and froze. No, not snakes. Reptiles. How had I not recognized it earlier?

I realized that all the Regulars were gone, except for the now terrified, wide-eyed bartender holding a broken bottle in one hand, looking like a very scary person—the kind of person whose actions are completely unpredictable; a potential spark for the powder keg around us. Everyone froze, except Tory. She sequentially broke a dragon's forearm, her reptilian kneecap, and then a heel-kick sent her adversary screaming off into the black night, snapping out her wings as she fell off the side of the building, luckier than her sister who had fallen in a wash of flames. I turned, along with the remaining five dragons and Tory, to the new voice that emanated near a particularly dark part of the roof beside a dead fire pit.

A familiar figure stepped out of the shadows, and I blinked. My client.

"What are you doing here, *Rogue*?" The blue-eyed, red-haired dragon hissed, still clutching Gunnar's makeshift leash in a possessive claw.

"The name is Raego, despite its definition. You would be wise to remember it, Tatiana," my client growled back, shadows shifting and eddying about him menacingly.

"The book is ours, *Raego*," Tatiana spat. "You have no claim in this city. You forsook your titles long ago."

He nodded, taking a step closer, and I swear the shadows moved with him. "I seek no claim, only the safety of the humans. I will not allow him to do this." They obviously knew who *him* was, but not me.

So...

I raised my hand.

Raego turned to me, and blinked at my upraised hand. Then, not knowing what else to do, he nodded. "Thanks," I said. "But who is this elusive *him*?"

"Close thy lips, wizard. This is none of your concern, and neither is the book. Hand it over, and we will give you back your wolf. If not, you and everyone you care about will die."

Raego was silent, watching me. "Can I kill her without offending you?" I asked.

He laughed, a deep, calming sound. "It wouldn't offend me, but it might not be wise to attempt it. We're kind of outnumbered, if you hadn't noticed."

I wanted to ask so many questions, but there were too many people present, and I knew that knowledge was strength. If anyone thought I had no clue what was going on, I was screwed. So, I put on my mask. "Later, then. I guess I'll just have to kill her later, then," I mumbled disappointedly.

She took a step towards me, but Raego's voice boomed again. "Don't even think it, Tatiana. You may already have a master, but you don't want to tempt me into breaking you here and now. I can do it without a sweat, and you know it. It's why I was banished. Competition doesn't work well in our family." Tatiana took another step forward, and then Raego shifted. One moment he was the tall unobtrusive kid I had seen in the alley, and the next he was a black dragon, easily over nine feet long. He was heavily muscled, and he slammed a claw down onto the ground, making everyone freeze.

"I dare you…" The voice was lower now, throatier, and full of a raw power I had never heard from him before. The fire continued to spread, and I could hear sirens in the distance.

Tatiana immediately turned to the roof entrance, eyes angry as she sniffed the air. Then she leapt off the roof, her ocean-blue wings unfurling with a loud snap. Her heavily muscled reptilian forearms cradled Gunnar like a toy as the remaining dragons followed suit. I caught myself absently humming the song from *Monty Python* about Brave Sir Robin bravely running away, so stopped. Tory chuckled lightly.

Raego was still in dragon form, staring off into the night. "They have gone back to roost." He looked at me then, his huge black eyes showing no horizontal bar since they were so dark. "We'll get your friend back. But first, I assume you brought the book with you?" I nodded. "Good. Hold onto it. Everything depends on keeping it out of their hands."

My patience snapped. "You know what?" I began to yell, stalking towards him near the edge of the roof. "God Damnit. I am sick, and fucking *tired* of this book."

"You do know that God's last name is not *Damnit*, right?" I flipped him off.

"I risked my life to get it, not even knowing it was the same one those bitches were razing my city for, and now you want me to just *hold onto it*? I could have left it with—" I wisely kept myself from uttering the Minotaur's name. "With the person that I obtained it from if you just wanted it kept safe." Raego took a step away from me, holding up his massive claws as if he didn't want to get one step closer to either the book or me. "I don't know what is so fucking important about this book, or why so many people want it, but the one person who has it wants nothing to fucking do with it. Me. I am not holding onto this thing one second longe—"

Something suddenly punched into my kidneys, knocking my breath away as my entire back clenched up in unbelievable pain. I tripped, stumbling over the railing as I heard a familiar man's voice yell behind me. "Not him, you idiot!" The book flew out of my fingers as I fell. I saw an orange blur leap off the building opposite us, snatching the book in her talons before the dragon sped off into the night, her rust-colored wings pummeling the air as she increased her speed.

As I neared the beautiful street below, I felt something suddenly latch around my stomach, painfully halting my descent, and then I was flying. I glanced up to see Raego holding me tightly against his warm, scaly stomach, his wings beating in wide thumps like helicopter blades starting up. Flames were flicking all over the roof of the club now, and I saw a group of people staring at us as we escaped. One was Tory. I hoped she would be okay. The pain from the initial blow made me curl up in his grip. I wondered if I had broken my back as I struggled for breath.

I knew I would have the always-pleasant experience of pissing blood in the morning, if I was still alive by then, that is.

35

As it turned out, I didn't even have to wait until morning to piss blood.

In fact, I barely had time to make it to Raego's bathroom after we touched down from our flight. Instant gratification. It's the little things that make the world a joyous place, folks.

After painfully relieving myself, I had the honor of seeing the infamous black dragon's digs. Raego's pad was questionably hygienic. By this, I mean that insects chose their food carefully when rummaging through his fridge, counter, sink, or even couch. I decided that sitting down was not conducive to a longer life, so remained standing. He had flown me here, declaring my shop unsafe. "No one knows where I live. That's a bonus right now."

I carefully adjusted the bag of frozen peas pressed against my genitals—since the pain kept migrating back and forth from my kidneys to my goods—groaning at the Chinese water torture that would eventually, possibly, hopefully, relieve some of my pain from the kidney blow at *Artemis' Garter*, which had apparently not been a fist, or even a well-aimed liquor bottle thrown by that crazy bartender. No, it had been a fucking crossbow bolt shot by my well-intentioned friends the dragon hunters. Luckily, it had only been a blunt-tipped bolt, meant to stun so that they could catch Raego alive.

They hadn't wanted to risk bringing in live ammunition with so many civilians around. I was impressed that they had managed to get in at all, but I was sure that the bouncers had had their hands full, what with all the stampeding customers rapidly evacuating their club, raving stories about some crazy Archangel lighting dragons afire on their roof, or so I assumed.

"You should probably get that checked out," Raego muttered from his stained couch, reclining as if it was a throne. The smell of cold stone and snakes struck me again, but now I thought I knew why. It had to do with his flavor of dragon.

"Nah, I've been hit in the kidneys this hard before. I would know if it was anything life threatening. It feels the same as the other time. It was gone after a few hours, but I'll have a spectacular bruise." I scowled at him. "You owe me. I inadvertently saved your life."

He gave me a disgusted look. "You think something like that would have even made me blink in dragon form? It would have just pissed me off."

"Which is when, I'm assuming, they would have hit you with their true weapon. These guys aren't amateurs. They pack some heavy firepower. It was *supposed* to be a distraction, you dolt."

He shrugged. "Whatever. I can't believe you lost the book. Do you have any idea how much shit we are in now?"

I tried to scowl back, but groaned in agony as I pressed the peas too hard into my groin. When I got my breath back, I resumed my scowl. "As a matter of fact, I *don't* know how much shit we're in, because I have no idea why the book is so important to everyone." I leveled an angry wizard finger at him. "*You* didn't even tell me what it was called. If you had, I would have been able to prevent at least *some* of this from happening."

Raego sighed. "Can you at least sit down? You're making me uncomfortable."

I swept my gaze around the litter-strewn room. "I'll take my chances on my feet. I'm fairly certain that a biologist would pay top dollar to quarantine this place and study the unique strains of bacteria found here."

Raego's eyes swept the room. "Yeah, but it's the only place I could find on such short notice, and I've been running around a lot, trying to keep tabs on my family without them finding out I'm in town."

"See, that's another tiny detail. Your *family*? Maybe you could explain that. Did I just kill some of your sisters? Your mother? Aunt?" My voice grew softer at a new thought. "Daughter?"

He smiled, shaking his head. "They exiled me, so I couldn't care less who they used to be, but no, none of them were daughters. I'm still young and spry. I just *practice* procreating at the moment."

I laughed at that, shaking my head. "You and me both. You and me both…"

I chose the cleanest spot I could find, and sat carefully on the armrest of the couch. Raego turned on the TV as if needing it on so that he wouldn't fidget. I watched him. He was a curious man, always playing with something, or looking over my shoulder, or out a window, cocking his head as he listened to things I could only imagine. The paranoia of a man on the run.

A few minutes ago, I had watched as he tensed, darted to the side of the couch, waited motionless, and then after an excruciatingly long period of silence, slammed his foot down on a cockroach as it exited the underside of the couch. He had laughed madly, and then promptly snagged a piece of pizza from the counter. Flies dominated the apartment, but he paid them no heed, eating his pizza as if they didn't exist.

More than once, I wondered if he had lost his mind at some point in his life. Either that, or he had severe Attention Deficit Disorder. Or maybe living a life on the run for so long had cracked part of his psyche. They seemed the same to me, at the moment. Equally dangerous to me.

"So, the book," I began, but he anxiously turned up the volume, leaning forward suddenly. I almost decided right then to take my chances without him, but then I heard my name on the TV.

"Nathin Temple, billionaire playboy, and minor felon?" A petite TV anchor chimed with a smile. *"Should we call him God's child, or Satan's Angel? In one day, he has purchased two six-figure cars, harassed a judge at the courthouse, has been connected to several crime scenes, been involved in a high-speed car chase on the Eads Bridge where he allegedly battled a 'demon', and was seen tonight at a premier nightclub in St. Louis, fraternizing with two alleged call girls. We have video footage here."* They played a clip of the two dancers on my lap, much of the image blurred except for my face. I groaned.

"Eyewitnesses state that the party got 'crazy' shortly after he arrived, and then the entire club suddenly evacuated as the party upstairs became too intense for them, meaning the roof caught fire. Upon investigation, the local police found the charred body of one of their own officers, brutally murdered before being burned up in the fire. Further details have yet to be released to the press.

Information states that the FBI was supposedly involved; with one Agent Gunnar Randulf even reported cavorting at the scene of the crime with his long-time friend, Master Temple. No word from Mr. Randulf or Master Temple at this time. The owner of the club has refused to comment on the matter. Is this who we want running the largest company in St. Louis? With the solar eclipse tomorrow afternoon, who is to say what drunken debauchery he will resort to as his next method of celebration?"

The news continued, but Raego tapped the mute button and turned to look at me. "I'm not that guy. They distracted me," I said softly.

Raego smiled sadly. "They're quite good at it."

I glared back. I realized, now, why I had never noticed his horizontal pupils before. The black of his irises blended so perfectly with his pupils that it was simply impossible to notice. "You mean that *you* are quite good at it. *You* are one of them, too! And you didn't tell me!"

Raego frowned. "Along that logic, I could state that you are no different than Jeffrey Dahmer, as you are both human and share almost identical strands of DNA. But it doesn't make you the same, does it? Ever changing, ever evolving. That's what you preach. That each of you has a soul that separates you from the beasts, but you are no different from us. You can be just as evil when you want to." It wasn't accusatory, and that more than anything made me finally nod back in agreement.

"Touché," I muttered. "The dragon hunters warned me about black dragons," I added carefully.

He shrugged back. "I'm rare. My father no doubt put a price on my head after he exiled me years ago. They've been hounding me on and off for years."

"Why did he exile you?"

"Because I wouldn't submit, and when male sons don't submit, we're exiled or killed. Competition for the women, and all that." He gestured emphatically. "But black dragons are unique. I've never met another, but we do tend to keep a pretty low profile." He jumped to his feet without warning. "I need a beer."

I blinked. No sudden movement around crazies. It's safer. "I'll take one, too."

He grunted over his shoulder, plucking two from the fridge. He handed me one and sat back down on the couch, popping the top off onto one of the cleaner sections of the floor. He took a long pull, and then looked at me expectantly. "Oh, did you want me to open it for you or something?" He asked, looking at my face.

I gestured at my bag of peas. "It would be very courteous of you."

He obliged, sloshing a good portion of the beer into the couch before handing it over. I guzzled it greedily, savoring the alcohol, but not daring to look at the Born-On date, afraid that I would simply see a skull-and-crossbones etched into the label. "So, what's your stake in all this?" I asked.

He ticked off a finger. "No more deaths. Which means we have to get that book back before tomorrow afternoon. We can't let him use it." I frowned a question. "There's a lot of dragons in the city right now, from all corners of the world. Up until now, we've remained silent, hiding in the shadows since we used to inspire such avid hunters. For the last few hundred years we haven't been unified. The book which you found for me, and then lost, gives details on how to tap into the power of the eclipse, uniting all the dragons under a single leader, an all-powerful dragon: The Son of the Dying Sun, as in The Son of the Eclipse.

"The solar eclipse resembles a black egg on fire—the legendary dragon egg." I didn't even want to ask if they actually hatched from eggs. Gross. "Once the eclipse passes—if the ritual has been performed—that power is absorbed by the most powerful dragon in the room, the one who performs the blood sacrifice. My father will attempt to gain that great power, and unite the dragons under his call." His eyes met mine for a tense moment, and I saw fear in those black orbs. "Which won't be good. He could reveal our existence to the world, bringing back the fear of the dark ages, making all the mythical stories about dragons become actual fact for the very first time in history. Could you imagine the panic that would create? If Regulars knew we were real?"

I sighed, shoulders slumping. "I know exactly what you mean. All Freaks teeter on that line at the moment. I know I did my fair part of revealing that today when I killed the silver dragon on the bridge. Then tonight at the strip club. Sooner or later people will begin to put it all together, and there will be no more hiding from the truth." We each pondered that for a time, sipping our beer. Then another question came to mind, but I murmured it practically to myself between sips. "What I want to know is why my friend, Peter, was searching for the same book as you."

Raego perked up, smiling. "I'll be right back." I waved a hand, no longer concerned with his peculiarities as I pondered my question. Raego stepped into the other room, leaving me in silence. Tomorrow morning, I would need to head back to the expo. Doubly so now that they had Gunnar, and that he was persona non-grata in St. Louis after the news had so expertly smeared his name.

Without Gunnar at my back, I felt vulnerable. One friend had betrayed me for power, and the other was powerless at the hands of a mad man. And I had no bargaining chip to get him out. Just Alaric's warped son as a sidekick. But that wasn't true. I had Tory, if I wanted to risk taking her, and Jeffries, although I doubted that he would be much help in a fight. He was also standing in for Gunnar as spokesperson for their new team since Gunnar was on hiatus. Then I remembered Misha. Perhaps she could help.

I saw Raego's silhouette enter the living room again so I looked up. But it wasn't him. I jumped back in alarm, dropping the bag of frozen peas and my beer as I prepared a web of offensive magic for protection. "Aye, Aye, Cap'n!" The strange man said in a familiar voice. I blinked, my kidneys throbbing painfully at my sudden movement.

"I don't...understand," I finally said, studying the strange man before me.

"It's a disguise!" Raego's voice laughed triumphantly. "A black dragon thing. I've been working for you for weeks now. Jessie at your service, Master Temple." My mind reeled at the thought. Was it possible? The employee Indie had hired stood before me: long blonde hair, a heavily muscled frame, and a cinder-block jaw. As I studied Raego's disguise with my eyes acutely attuned to the magical forces of the world, black tendrils of smoke suddenly swarmed around him like a tornado.

After a few seconds, the smoke dissipated to reveal my dark-haired, lanky client again. I shook my head in wonder. Tomas' accusation of shape shifting into entirely different people was true. I had been too wrapped up in my grief to have much to do with the store in the last week. Jessie and Raego...the same guy. It all clicked in my head.

"You switched the title of the book Peter asked for!" I practically yelled.

Raego gave a formal bow. "I must have written the wrong title down when he asked me to leave you a message. Jessie isn't too bright. An honest mistake, really. Although Indie didn't see it that way." He paused, studying me carefully. "She's head over heels for you, Nate. The real deal. She'd take a bullet for you if she had to." His voice grew softer. "You can't ask for more than that." I nodded, suddenly emotional.

"She's just a Regular, Raego. You know how dangerous our lives are. She'd be helpless." He nodded agreement but also shrugged, as if asking why that mattered. I changed the subject. Girl-talk later. Guy-talk now. "Thanks for the help, Raego, but it would've been easier if you'd simply told me about Peter. I could have dealt with him directly. As it turns out, he attacked me for the book just before we went to the club. It fell out of my bag and he saw it."

Raego slapped his forehead, groaning. "That must be how they knew you had it on you tonight. They followed you. Peter must have called them. He's been working for Alaric." I stared, random events slowly joining into one bigger picture in my mind, mentally erasing questions from my list as the answers became apparent. Peter's rich investor was Alaric. I began to shake my head, arguing that Peter would have been unconscious, but then I remembered the power the bracelet had given him. Maybe the dragons had been waiting for him when he got home, and woken him up to get the information.

Or maybe my spell hadn't been enough to fight his newfound power. Either way, what Raego said made a lot of sense. It was really the only logical deduction. The dragons had found me at the club, and knew I had the book. Peter could have told them anything. That I was meeting up with a client for the exchange, for example.

"You're right," I grumbled. "By the way, you're a terrible employee from what I hear. Indie deserved a heavy-handed approach. I can't believe that all this time you were working for me."

"I had to see if you were trustworthy before I asked you to find the book."

"You're fired. Officially. Immediately."

"Can I keep the gun? It's pretty sweet," he said with a smile.

"Did you pass your firing accuracy tests?" He nodded, crossing his fingers in hopes of my affirmative answer. "Then, sure." He clapped his hands together in delight. "How long has Peter worked for Alaric?"

"Weeks. Where do you think he got his sudden power? Some of the older dragons can bestow gifts upon their servants, but there's always a price. Finding a book in exchange for becoming a wizard? Of course he would agree. Which is why I stepped in. As soon as I figured out he was your friend, I knew he'd ask you for it. So, I asked instead, and then switched the title he asked for. It seemed wise at the time. Sorry it didn't work out," he said, looking genuinely guilty as he averted his gaze.

After a minute, he looked back at me, eyes wary. "How did you hurt them with that coin? As soon as I saw it I knew it was old."

I reached into my pocket and dug out the coin. I had no idea how it had ended up back in my pocket after smashing into the dragon's face—or how it had turned into a lethal projectile—but it had been there as soon as I checked. "A gift from the Minotaur. He said he got it from Hermes. AKA: the messenger god; guide of the lavish Underworld; god of thieves, commerce, sports, and—"

"I get it." Raego shivered, motioning for me to put it away. "Scary guy. Did you know that he enslaved two of the eldest dragons back in his day, cloaking his Caduceus with their carcasses?" He stopped then, eyes glittering. "Say *that* five times fast!" He chuckled. I shook my head. Who would have connected the two snakes on the immortal healing staff to dragons? Not me. Raego continued. "He knew a thing or two about dragons. How did you get his help?" Raego glanced out the window, as if expecting to see the god hovering outside, ready to drape Raego on his staff as a third adornment.

"We all have our secrets, kid. We need to get some rest before we confront your dad tomorrow at the expo. He's expecting me, and after tonight I would say that he's expecting you, too." Raego nodded, face growing harder. "Are you the youngest of your siblings, Raego?"

Raego grew stiff. "What, you think because I'm the youngest that I can't hold my own? I'll have you know that—" I waved a hand, calming him down.

"No, it's not that. I'm just thinking of something." I winked at him, suddenly a shade happier as a plan began to unfold in my head. "Let's get some shut eye. I'll need to make a few calls in the morning so that we're ready for the family reunion. Until then, I bid you good night." Raego studied me curiously for a few moments before nodding, and clearing out a space in a guest bedroom that was remarkably clean, and even had a small bed to sleep in. Surprise, surprise. I was asleep as soon as my head hit the pillow.

36

I ignored the three missed calls from Captain Kosage on my screen and dialed a different number. Jeffries picked up on the second ring, despite the early hour. "Agent Jeffries."

"It's me, Civilian Temple," I answered drily, feeling *Master Temple* would be rather vain, but it irked me that others could answer with a title without sounding pompous. I heard the phone shift in apparent excitement.

"Let me call you on a different line. Be available." Then he hung up. I sighed, waiting. Jeffries didn't want to speak on a public line, which meant that the shit storm was bad.

My phone chirped in my hand, an unknown number displaying on the screen. "Hello?" I answered, just in case it was someone else.

"No names. This is White Lie. You're Merlin. What happened to the wolf?"

I recognized the voice, and smiled. "This is cool. It's like a movie or something."

"It's called Covering Your Ass. How bad is it?"

I pondered that simple question, but knew I couldn't reveal too much. "Bad." I answered finally. "But I've got backup. We're moving in this afternoon to extract the wolf, but I'll need you to stay behind to hold up the fort."

"What do you think I've been doing? What the hell happened last night? The news was pretty clear. A cop dead, and the wolf missing. It doesn't look good. He might lose his silver pin for this." His words were heavy with emphasis, and I knew we were talking about Gunnar's badge, because werewolves couldn't wear silver.

"Fuck. That's his life. It's more than his life."

"I know. There's a BOLO on his new Land Rover, because it wasn't found at the club last night. I just wanted to make sure you knew the stakes. Shit rolls downhill, and he's at the bottom right now. He'll take all the blame for this, despite the truth." I suddenly felt guilty. Was this my fault? Had I dragged him into something that he couldn't get out of? But no, they had been looking into the murders themselves. I had merely provided a link, a lead they could follow. Then I remembered that my name had been slandered too, and that Gunnar was a close friend of mine, and that I had purchased two cars for him in the last few days. It looked terrible. Bribery wouldn't make this look any prettier.

"Alright, White Lie. I'll get him back."

"You're telling the truth, Merlin. At least what you believe to be the truth. Keep in touch." I clicked off after that.

I stared at my phone for a long while, debating on whether I should call Tory or not. I had already almost cost Gunnar his badge, what sense was there in risking Tory's career as well? I already had Raego for backup. Did I really need Tory? I decided that I did, and that she would want in on this, if for nothing else than to save Gunnar. Plus, she probably had no idea where I was, or even if I was alive.

"Nate!" she answered on the first ring, voice shaken. "Where the hell are you? I thought you were dead, but the police didn't find your body."

She sounded as if she had been crying. "I'm alive. Raego took me to his place."

"Good. I'm ready for you to pick me up. We're ending this. Today. No one fucks with my boys if I can help it. You're untouchable." I smiled at that. My very own pocket-sized bodyguard.

"You sure you want in on this? It's—" she cut me off.

"Of course I want in on this! The news is all but stating that Gunnar is guilty of everything, and only you and I can prevent that. I'm already on leave for my injuries at the bridge and my...proximity to you. I'm under review. Not sure how long that axe will hang before it drops, but probably not too long. I might have to become a Wal-Mart greeter next week." She sounded sad, but quickly regained her composure. "But it's the right thing to do. So, I'm doing it."

"I'll pick you up soon, then. Be armed for bear, but wear something classy since we'll be going back to the Expo."

She agreed and we hung up. Raego saw that I was finished so opened his front door for us to leave, locking up behind us. "I'll meet you there. I can't go to the Expo with you, but I'll see you at the ritual."

I stared back, curious. "How do you know where we will be?"

"I'll be watching you, but I already have a good idea where it will happen. I called a cab to pick you up and take you back to Plato's Cave. You'll need your car, I assume." I nodded. "Until then." And then he left, long black trench coat billowing out behind him as he strode down the sidewalk. I saw the cab on the corner, and pulled out my phone. As I dialed a few last-minute people, I anxiously fiddled with Hermes' coin in my pocket. Here's to hoping it worked a second time.

37

We stepped out of the car Mallory had picked us up in—a vintage Rolls Royce Silver Wraith—and into a sunrise of flashes and noise from both cameras and questions. I smiled my best billionaire playboy smile, twirling the suit coat Mallory had brought me, and strode down the red carpet into the *Eclipse Expo!* Tory on one arm and Misha on the other. Misha wore her same red cocktail dress, but Tory wore a sleek black dress with an extravagant white fur over her shoulders. My smile grew wider as I relished how this would look; a publicity hound's wet dream. I didn't answer any questions about who the women were, what had happened last night, or what was going to happen with Temple Industries. I merely smiled, moving forward as if this was simply the way of the world. It was definitely doing what Turner Locke had advised me not to do, but I couldn't help myself.

The women on my arm looked ravishing, and several reporters tried to get answers from them, but they merely flashed shy, sultry smiles back, looking up at me with adoring eyes. The reporters smiled knowingly, turning back to me. "Why are you at such a public event after last night, Master Temple? Don't you think it might be taken the wrong way? That you're ignoring your responsibilities?" One reporter shouted above the rest.

I paused, turned to him, and smiled for the camera. "I wouldn't miss an eclipse for the world. Last night was only the *pre-game* to this afternoon." Then we were moving again. We entered the building and quickly found our seats for what I assumed to be a speech about astronomy or a detailed description of the upcoming eclipse at noon.

We were some of the last to enter, and soon the auditorium was left in silence as the lights dimmed and a finely dressed gentleman strode up to the podium before the several thousand guests in attendance. Alaric, the Dragon Lord. I grimaced.

"Friends and citizens. My name is Alaric Slate, as many of you already know. I am new to this fine city, but I feel no guilt at already calling it *my home*." I grimaced at his double connotation. "St. Louis is full of a quality of life not found in many other places around the world.

"We are all here to witness the coming eclipse, as such a display is a gift to be shared with those dear to you. This eclipse is special in that it will be almost uninterrupted for a full half-hour. A half hour where darkness will battle the light, and eventually the light will prevail...*hopefully*," he added with a mischievous grin. The audience chuckled as if on cue. Again, the double-entendre was not lost on me. "We have numerous scholars present ready to dazzle you with their years of expertise on this very subject, but allow me to take a moment to relate it in a very Plebian way for those of us who are not as intelligent as them, myself included." He laughed at himself, and the audience leaned forward, won over by his dripping charisma.

But all I could imagine was his dripping fangs.

"We are about to share an experience that our ancestors feared. The infamous battle between light and dark. In recent months and years, our world has been confronted with stories, legends, and myths that seem to have leapt right out of a storybook. Take our infamous Master Nathin Temple, for example." He pointed a finger at me without looking, and I barely hid my surprise. As one, the audience turned to follow his finger until I fought not to squirm in my seat. Tory and Misha beamed at the sudden attention, latching onto me tighter. "Some have taken to calling him Archangel as he battled *a dragon* over the Eads Bridge. But dragons are just a children's story, right?" He grinned hungrily at the audience, many women leaning away from the gleam in his eyes. "As are *wizards*, yet here we are, one battling another the same as others might argue over a prized painting for sale. Whether the stories prove true or not, many are starting to believe them, and in that is power. Light versus dark.

"But power like that cannot be allowed to be one-sided. There are obviously unbelievable abilities in our world, and thanks to the advances in technology, more of those inexplicable things are being caught on film for all to see, immortalized as fact, no matter what *some* would have you think." He expertly emphasized the last words, causing a hubbub of whispering throughout the audience. He let it go on for a moment before holding up a hand, commanding silence.

"But there are those who want you to *see* the truth rather than *hide* from it. Old, dark, dangerous powers are manifesting the world over. But where there is darkness, there is also light, like the coming eclipse. I urge our fellow citizens to come forth with their secret powers, because we all know that the darker powers will do so in order to take advantage of the weak. We must be unified against them. No more *Freaks* and *Regulars*. We are all one family. One race.

"I ask all of you to take a step forward as Master Temple has, and embrace your ability for all to see. Stand to fight against the darkness with Master Temple and me for the benefit of all, so that our children can have a safer future. Now, I humbly ask that you allow Master Temple and me to step aside to discuss our future plans for this coalition." With that, he smiled, stepped away from the podium, and motioned for me to follow him.

The crowd went wild as I stood. What was the meaning of this? What ulterior motives did Alaric have? Why did he want to seem to all these people as my friend? Was it a simple publicity stunt? Misha and Tory followed close behind me, Misha's face blank. Alaric had just blatantly admitted to all that I was a wizard, and that he knew it, and that I should be a spokesperson for all the Freaks out there since I had been brave enough to step out. Several in the crowd wept as I passed them by, reaching out to touch my arm as if I was an angel sent down from heaven by god himself. Others shied away or shot me dirty looks thanks to my recent media appearances. I kept my face neutral, my mind racing. What was Alaric's game? What did he have to gain from this? Chaos?

Alaric waited for me beside the stage as the next speaker approached the podium, looking displeased that he had drawn the straw to follow the charismatic dragon. He was doomed, especially if it was a scientific speech. "What was that about, Alaric?" I whispered angrily once we were close enough, the next speaker preparing to bore the audience with the general astronomy of eclipses in the background. Alaric reached out to grasp my forearm cordially so that the audience wouldn't think anything amiss. I tensed.

"I just saved your name, Master Temple. Last evening's news didn't paint a very pleasant picture of you and your ...well, my wolf now, I suppose. Everyone was focused on what new catastrophe you would cause this afternoon, and now they see you as the savior of their city. I have congressmen ready to back your demands with legal documents in order to promote your decrees into bills for congress to peruse. Bills that will pass. Wouldn't you like to see the Freaks as equals to Regular citizens? All this I give you, in exchange for your simple servitude, so that we may have a working relationship when I rule. After all, you did find my book. I owed you *something* in exchange."

I winced at his smile, letting go of his hand with more force than necessary. I managed to smile back after a second. "How is our partnership going to last after I kill you this afternoon?" His smile wavered this time. "What is your real reason for doing this? You know what would happen if it became fact that we exist. It would be the Salem Witch Trials all over again. Your kind would be hunted down, too."

Alaric held up a finger. "Ah, but not if they saw me as the one trying to promote harmony between the factions. They would see you and me as the lesser of the two evils. Come now, Master Temple. You know that it is only a matter of time before our secret is out. Yours, sooner than mine. And what will happen then? We will become Public Enemy Number One. I do not wish that."

"I'm sure you don't. But it still doesn't make sense."

"I have opened the gates a day earlier than they would have on their own, and by doing so, have gained us a notoriety of sorts that will allow us to not appear as the enemy. You should thank me."

"I would rather damn you, because it's all a ruse. I've peeked behind the curtain," I said with a menacing smile.

"Well, that is rather uncouth, Master Temple." There was that word being used to describe me again. He pondered for a moment, smiling and nodding at a guest over my shoulder before continuing in almost a whisper. "Some people delight in creating things, building cities, painting masterpieces, and then there are those others...the ones who love to walk up and flick that first domino...the domino that sets off a chain reaction of unstoppable chaos, destroying something that was most beautiful." He paused for emphasis. "That would be me. I would rather set off the chain reaction than be the domino stuck in the chaos." He glanced over as two women approached. I could tell by the way they moved that they were dragons, but they must have been wearing contacts because their eyes were quite normal.

"We must vacate this place for loftier heights," he said softly. "We wouldn't want to leave the wolf locked up all day, would we? He probably needs to be let outside. And there is the promise of the thief you wished to meet," he added with a sad smile.

Tory squeezed my arm. "Shall we?" she asked, eyes flaming.

"Oh, yes, shall we?" Misha purred beside her.

"I wouldn't be much of a gentleman if I didn't succumb to such beauties as the two of you," I said with a smile as an elderly couple walked past us, staring at us as if we were rock stars from their youth. I kind of liked the attention. I just hated its cause.

Alaric leaned closer. "I must insist on my own transportation if you wish to visit my home. We wouldn't want any strange vehicles left on the property if you decided to stay indefinitely." The words dripped with the promise that if I crossed him, my body would never leave the property. I nodded back, having expected it. "Good. I will be along shortly. Make yourself at home, of course." We followed the two female dragons away from the Expo, Alaric speaking briefly with two older gentlemen behind us.

I recognized them as congressmen.

Fuck.

38

We pulled up to Alaric's mansion half an hour later, granted entrance by a small intercom at the wide iron gates a mile down the driveway. The dragons had tried talking to Misha several times, but her face had remained stony, giving them no false understanding of whose side she was now on. Neat. I guess my mind control on her had been permanent. I felt slightly guilty about that, but didn't have the time to worry about it just yet. I felt odd as I noticed her repeatedly glancing at my chest where her dragon tooth hung around my neck. Could she sense it? But I remained silent.

I hoped Raego showed up, because if there were as many dragons as he feared nearby, then I would never make it out alive. And neither would Tory or Gunnar.

Alaric's Bentley stopped, and we were encouraged to get out by a sultry brown-eyed woman, her eyes so deep a mahogany that I almost didn't notice the horizontal slits. We followed her inside a home that seemed every bit as impressive as Chateau Falco, and I wondered how they had acquired such a nice home on such short notice if they were so new to town. Or had they been here longer than I thought? How long had Peter really been working for them? My gut lurched at thoughts of Peter's betrayal. I was pretty sure he would be here. He might have even convinced Alaric to let him keep his new bracelet.

Then I remembered that I would get to see the thief soon, the shadowy silhouette I had watched sneak into Temple Industries on the video feed, the person who even the high-tech camera hadn't been able to identify. That brought my thoughts back to the odd music box that I had stowed away in my secret vault at Plato's Cave.

Tory stumbled as one of the dragons forcefully encouraged her to move faster. Her resulting scowl was frightening if one knew her, but comical if not. She was just so tiny. The dragon didn't seem to care.

We strode past a wide-open room with a ceiling made completely of glass, construction work still apparent in some corners, and I stopped for a second. The floor and walls were rich sandstone, with massive boulders and slabs placed lovingly around the room like others would place chairs and couches. Then I saw a flicker of movement and realized that three full sized dragons were lounging on the rocks, lazily bathing in the sun. I saw the heating coils that spread throughout the room and blinked at the expense. The rocks were heated. Almost like a huge reptile cage that a child would have for a pet iguana. I shivered, and continued on.

We passed many more rooms, but finally headed into a more private area of the house, less glamorous and more dated; rougher stone walls and less decoration. Torches lit the halls. A heavy set of oak wooden doors stood closed at the end of the hall, an Italian phrase engraved into a monolith above them: *Lasciate ogni speranza, voi ch'entrate!*

Abandon all hope, ye who enter here.

Misha shivered. "Not here. Anywhere but here," she whispered. I placed a comforting hand on her soft skin and my power spiked. She blinked watery eyes in appreciation, not feeling the power surge like I had. Our guards opened the large double doors and ushered us into another cavernous glass-ceilinged room. Several dragons leaned against the wall around the room, but our guides remained close to the door like guards.

My two best friends stood before me.

Peter and Gunnar seemed to sparkle in the rays of sunlight that speared down through the clear ceiling. Gunnar sat in full werewolf form, but was without his characteristic *Underdog* underwear. He was attached to a leash held loosely in Peter's hand. The moon hovered beside the sun in the sky above us. It was almost time.

Peter smiled at us. "So nice of you to join us, Nate. Your *friends* are already here waiting." He motioned a finger at Gunnar, and then at an altar behind him. Raego was chained up with iron manacles, looking dazed. I blinked away the tinge of red from my vision, trying to maintain my composure. Tory touched my arm, and my power jumped again. I knew that I could incinerate everyone in the room as easily as breathing, but that wouldn't solve anything. I needed to kill Alaric, and I didn't know how many other dragons were present. I also didn't know the particulars of the spell. Had he already started the necessary steps? Would killing everyone somehow ignite it?

I took a deep breath, and Peter frowned. "No witty comment? No clever repartee? It seems might *is* right after all." If Raego hadn't told me Peter was involved, I might have had a heart attack upon seeing him here, but now it just made me furious at the betrayal. Defcon 1, furious.

"Why is he here?" I pointed at Raego.

"Alaric needs the blood of a traitor to fuel his ritual. His own son was almost too much to pass up once we found him snooping around. I have to admit that I was surprised to later discover that he was none other than your employee, Jessie, but now I see how my book request went sour." He backhanded Raego, spittle flying from the dragon's lips. His wrists were bloody around the manacles, proving he had struggled. He opened his mouth in a curse, looking furious, but there was no sound. A spell.

I took a threatening step closer.

Gunnar's white hackles lifted and he growled a warning at my advance. "Ah, ah, ah. I wouldn't do that if I were you." Peter smiled. "Your reputation has increased over the last few days, killing those dragons, but I must admit that I played a small part in the ruckus as well." I stared back, not comprehending. "The break-in at Plato's Cave, and the gargoyles for example. Even though they seemed to merely inconvenience you, one had to try after you so wisely told me *exactly where you were*."

I almost killed him. Right there. With my untapped reservoir of new power, I knew I could, but there were also a handful of dragons in the room watching me, no doubt ready to squish the weak humans before them, and Alaric was still absent. If Peter continued his banter, I didn't know if I would be able to control myself much longer. Which was probably the point.

"Who would have known that this renegade whelp was your client the whole time? Well, I put a stop to that, didn't I, Raego?" Peter backhanded him again.

I threw a sledgehammer bar of air at him before I even thought about it. The dragons tensed in the room, but Peter merely flicked his wrist at it as if swatting away a child's tantrum. The energy slammed back into me, stinging my arm all the way up to my shoulder. For every action, there is an equal and opposite reaction. I began to massage my shoulder, but stopped at Peter's smirk. "Pitiful, Nate. Just pitiful. But I wouldn't try that again if I were you."

"You weren't too hard to take down last night, Peter. We both know who would win if I really tried to hurt you," I sneered. He snarled back angrily. Something was…off in his eyes. I had seen it at my shop, but it had progressed since then, as if a madness was creeping in to reveal an entirely different person than my childhood friend. The bracelet wasn't just giving him power. It was changing him. Polishing those darker parts of his psyche until they obscured the rest of him.

"I could have taught you all this, and without the chains!" I yelled.

"Who is wearing chains now, Nate?" He glanced pointedly at Raego. "I made new friends—friends that share my same opinions on justice. Might *is* right. As you shall soon see. This bracelet has granted me what I have wanted my entire life. *Power*." A psychotic gleam twinkled in his eyes. "The only price was servitude. And after seeing what will happen when Alaric arrives, you will understand why that wasn't such a thing to give up. The justice of the strong will prevail. Thrasymachus was correct after all, damn Plato and Socrates."

"Peter, don't do this. I beg you. It's a line you cannot re-cross."

"Oh, I know the lines, Nate. Perhaps it's you who doesn't. I have lived on the other side of your precious line, and it wasn't favorable. Now I'm on the side of power, but I do not whine and cower like you. I embrace the gift, and will put it to good use under Alaric. I would be a god under a Titan." His eyes danced with hungry greed.

"I am with *him*." He whispered, pointing a finger towards the door. As if it were a cue, the heavy doors creaked open and Alaric strode into the room, three more dragons trailing him.

"Ah, our guests have arrived. Let the festivities commence!" Alaric's voice boomed into the cavernous room.

39

I recognized Tatiana—fully nude and in human form—with her fiery red hair and glacial blue eyes, but the other two were smaller red dragons in full dragon form, perhaps the size of two Great Danes mashed together. Misha tensed beside me, her hand rising as if to caress them. They shot her icy, hateful stares but remained beside Alaric.

I heard the faintest of whispers from Misha, raw with grief. "My babies..."

My heart broke. "You die first, Tatiana. I promised, and I meant it."

She smirked back, eyes daring me.

Peter was staring at Alaric like a loyal dog. There was nothing left of the man I had grown up with. Power had corrupted him entirely. I risked a glance at Gunnar, and saw a hopeless fight in his eyes. He was still inside there, but had no way to overcome the leash Peter was holding. It was up to me. To us.

Tory was breathing heavily as she glared at Alaric. Another nude woman stepped closer to her master, and I smiled in recognition. Aria. Tory had broken her arm yesterday in Alaric's suite at the Expo. Then my smile wavered. She lifted up a perfectly healed arm to inspect in the sunlight, twisting it back and forth with a grin. "I can do a better job of it today, if you're unsatisfied," Tory offered, smiling.

Aria hissed back, but Alaric raised a commanding hand, amusement on his face. "Oh, I really like her."

"Do you *like* me, like me?" Tory teased seductively, taking an aggressive step forward. I managed to hold her back, but it was like grabbing onto a moving car.

Alaric laughed at that. "What spunk!" He turned to me. "Do you like the reference?" He motioned at the epitaph above the entrance to the room.

"*Through me you pass into the city of woe: Through me you pass into eternal pain...*

Abandon all hope ye who enter here," I quoted easily. "But I doubt Dante would think this room worthy of comparison to the nine circles of Hell," I said, disinterested.

Alaric blinked back. "That is quite a memory."

I waggled a hand. "Eidetic. Kinda' neat, I know."

"Did you know that Dante encountered Wyverns—an arcane term for dragons—while traipsing with Virgil through hell?" I rolled my eyes, nodding. "So, I would argue that the inscription is indeed *worthy of comparison*."

"Toe-may-toes, toe-mah-toes," I murmured.

He frowned. "I hope that you now see how beneficial our collaboration could be, Master Temple. One mustn't be foolish or make hasty decisions. Our coalition will benefit all." Peter's eyes tightened at the prospect of me joining them.

"But I just can't *stand* the idea of my city being overrun by a reptile dysfunction. It's just not right." There was a long silence, and then Tory bent over laughing, but she was the only one, as the rest of the guests were all dragons, and had no taste for my wit.

Alaric shook his head in disapproval and turned to Peter, appraising him thoughtfully. "I hear congratulations are in order…" Raego struggled hopelessly against the sharp manacles, still oddly silent as his mouth opened wide in a yell of soundless pain.

Peter beamed. "I captured the traitor, Master."

"Only with our aid, human. Don't overstep yourself," Tatiana warned.

Peter shrugged. "Neither of us could have done it on our own, true, but it *is* done, thanks to *my* aid."

She began to argue, but Alaric interrupted her. "Pride *can* be agreeable…at times." Peter smiled wider. "Come to me. Your pet will be fine where he is for now." He dropped the leash obediently.

"You gave him a pet? He can barely take care of himself, and you give him responsibility over another person?" I blurted, laughing.

Peter scowled, but Alaric spoke. "The werewolf is quite securely under my command. Peter as his guardian is not as risky as you might think." Gunnar's eyes had lost their hopeful spark. I wondered what the leash had done to him. Was it permanent, like my control over Misha?

Alaric began talking to Peter in a low voice, and I leaned over to Tory and Misha.

"Be ready." I whispered, feeding my words through the link with them so that no one else could hear what was said.

Tory gave a barely discernable shake of her head. "I hope you two can be extra scary today, or we are all fucked," she breathed.

"Scary is my forte…" I breathed back hungrily. Misha smiled faintly, still glancing with concern at her dragon children. I turned back to Alaric, ready to lay my cards on the table. Part of me died at what I was about to do, a lifetime of memories flashing through my mind as I remembered all my childhood experiences with my two best friends: Peter and Gunnar. But that was all it was now. Memories. Peter was lost. He had chosen the wrong side. Still, I didn't know if I would ever be able to sleep again after this. It would haunt me forever.

But it was right.

"It seems Peter has found a new home with you here," I said. Alaric glanced over. "That's good. From what you say, loyalty is fairly important to your harem." He watched me more intently now, and I saw Peter's face turn stony, apprehensive. "I just find it interesting, curious really, that you're buddy, buddy with a man who happened to kill one of your..." I frowned dramatically. "I honestly don't know what to call her. Your daughter? Lover?" I waved a hand in dismissal. "But I digress. The yellow one. Oily fire dragon?" Alaric's face went blank in recognition. "Yep. Her. She sure didn't like a glacier bullet to the chest from your newest minion. But who would, right?" I laughed lightly, but the tension in the room spiked. Dragons hissed, and Peter opened his mouth to argue.

Alaric reached out and placed a suddenly golden-scaled hand on Peter's shoulder, the black talons piercing the flesh hard enough for Peter to cry out. "It seems my congratulations are unnecessary, and punishment is in order. She was one of my favorites...You told me that Master Temple was responsible for her untimely death."

Peter began to answer, but Alaric squeezed his shoulder tighter. Without a word spoken by Alaric, Tatiana grabbed Peter's arm and led him over beside Raego, chaining him up. "For this information alone I would have given you anything you wished, but as this is something I already promised it seems I will be in your debt," Alaric sighed to me.

I blinked, not understanding. Tatiana stepped away from Peter's bound body with a satisfied smile, but not before licking his neck hungrily. "I give you your thief, Master Temple. This is the man who stole the curious music box from Temple Industries... Your best friend." I stared, having momentarily forgotten about the odd box. I was dumbfounded, but suddenly even less concerned about what I was committing Peter to. Not only had he betrayed me, but he had also betrayed my parents.

Un-fucking-forgivable.

My vision pulsed with the blood behind my eyes as I stared into his soul, and I knew that even with his newfound power, part of him stilled in unbridled fear—a delicious fuel for my revenge.

It was a start.

"I see," I managed to say as the room steadily darkened. I glanced up to see that the moon was slowly merging with the sun, blocking out a quarter of the natural light.

"So, it seems we each have a traitor in our midst. Yours, a dear friend from childhood who would betray anything for power...even biting the hand that feeds him." Alaric added the last with a growl. "And mine, my own son who chose to abandon his familial duties." He turned away from the two traitors, and looked me in the eye. "So, who dies first?" He grinned; anxious at the pain the choice would cause me.

No one could ask for a better opening.

"Thought you would never ask." I drew the pistol at the back of my waist, and shot Tatiana directly in the forehead, the explosive sound was deafening in the cavernous room. Remembering Raego's warning about blood and the ritual, I quickly lashed out with a blinding bar of white-hot fire, decapitating her at the shoulders and burning her head to ashes in a single second. My fire even incinerated the gore from the blowback of the bullet wound before it had a chance to touch the ground, and then it scored a charred streak in the rock wall on the other side of the room before I released my power. Alaric leapt back at the first sight of the gun. Tatiana's wound was instantly cauterized, so no blood stained the floor. Her body struck the ground a moment later, breasts wiggling on impact. The room was silent as a tomb as I casually re-holstered my weapon. Alaric finally turned to me, face utterly blank. "I already told you. *She* dies first," I said with a cool smirk.

Tory looked sick to her stomach. "Scary is *definitely* your forte," she whispered.

40

Alaric's fury was palpable. "Perhaps our coalition will not work after all. You will pay for that, *Archangel*. She was my...most precious." His eyes glinted with rage and sadness as he avoided glancing at Tatiana's corpse. "I shall have fun with you later." His gaze almost made me shiver. "But back to business..." He pointed at the two bound men, the room slowly growing darker as the moon enveloped the sun by degrees. One of the dragon guards began lighting several torches around the room.

"Both shall be punished, of that I can assure you, but I only need one to fuel the ritual. Only one's blood must flow to make me the Obsidian Son the dragons have needed for so long." He brandished the book from a pocket, tossing back his robe so that he stood nude from the waist up, baggy pants covering his lower half with a wide silken sash. "Thanks for this, by the way." He caressed the book. "I've had the morning to study her secrets, relishing in our long history of power. The passage you will experience is rather short, but quite...impacting. Now, decide who dies. I'll even let you kill your dear friend yourself, if you wish."

I stared at Peter, my rage even more powerful than when I had first heard of my parents' murder. As agreeable as it sounded, I couldn't do it. It would forever break me. Tory didn't seem to know me well enough, anxiously shaking her head at me not to do it. My power began coursing down my skin almost as if preparing to form Stone Skin for protection, but it was slightly different. I couldn't stop it from happening. Alaric pointed a finger at me, commanding me to stop, but I couldn't.

The power washed out of me like a retreating tide, spilling over everyone in the room. Each of Alaric's minions instantaneously exploded into dragon form as it hit them. I tried to hold it in, knowing that it had only made matters worse for us. With extreme effort, I managed to regain control of it, fearing what would happen if I didn't. I was sure I'd just made matters worse for the home team since the dragons were stronger in their true monstrous form. Shit. Misha purred beside me as the huge red dragon I had met above the courthouse, her tail swishing back and forth. I appreciated how large the room was now. Even with this many dragons, there was still plenty of room to jog laps around the perimeter for a workout. Alaric had only shifted his arms, but he didn't look pleased at even that lack of self-control.

I spoke before he could. "Why must I decide? You, who resorted to a level of violence I have never before seen in my city for a book that I obtained so easily, are not even man enough to condemn your own son? Do you hold such little value for life that you would murder before all else? Yet now you cannot take even one life?" I laughed into the cavernous room, my voice full of scorn as it echoed off the walls. "You're a crock."

Alaric stared. "I am merely extending a courtesy to a guest. If your stomach cannot handle that, then I will make the decision. But I would never pay a thief to give back what is mine by right," he hissed.

"Then you could have gone to duel Asterion yourself!" I yelled back.

His face slackened in shock. "You slew the Minotaur?" He asked, suddenly wary. I remained silent, letting him assume what he would. "I must hand it to you, Master Temple. You are quite a formidable adversary. To slay the Minotaur—the bane of every dragon's existence—is no easy feat. A battle between him and a dragon would be muscle against muscle, as he is immune to our powers. And I would not wager on my best ten dragons succeeding...myself included." He added the last in a reverential whisper. "We shall discuss your conquest afterwards, but I must admit that I sincerely am in your debt now. It will be a shame to kill you once the city is mine. You would have been a great hound, once properly leashed."

I took a deep breath as Alaric stepped closer to Raego, who was rattling his chains in fury now. The chains must have kept him from shifting when my power leaked out, but I could see the fear in his eyes—not the fear of death—but the fear of what would happen to everyone else if his father succeeded. "I am no one's hound. I wear no leash." I took a step closer. Misha crouched low, spitting a warning stream of fire towards the row of dragons at the side of the room. They hesitated. She was at least twice as big as any of them.

"That's humorous. I recall your werewolf saying the same thing. But he seems to rather enjoy his captivity now, don't you, Gunnar?" The werewolf hunched lower, tail wagging as he licked his massive canines.

I tried to stall Alaric as his long, black claws reached out to Raego. The room suddenly grew darker as the moon eclipsed the sun. I was now on borrowed time. I had to do something. Quick. "What did my parents have to do with all of this? Why did they have to die?"

He looked over his shoulder, and I saw the faintest hesitation. But he didn't answer the question. That didn't make any sense. He looked like he genuinely didn't know the answer. "Gunnar, be a good boy and keep Master Temple entertained."

Gunnar growled, and slowly padded towards me, drooling. Then Alaric began to read from the book. Misha abruptly darted into the ring of dragons, bowling some of them over, but a ring of energy surrounded Alaric so that she couldn't cross. The room grew darker, and I had a second to glance up at my timeline. The moon was almost completely covering the sun now. Crap. I dodged a sailing body of a smaller dragon as Misha launched her back. Tory leapt after her, shattering the dragon's snout with one blow. I crouched, unsure of what the hell I could do to keep Gunnar away from me without hurting him too badly. He launched himself at me, and I swung a club of air at him, knocking him clear to the side of the room with a satisfying yelp. But he didn't stay down.

I listened to Alaric's speech as I kept my eyes on Gunnar struggling back to his feet. The recital was surprisingly short, only a page, really. His words mingled with the carnage just as I was sure Dante's *Divine Comedy* must have sounded as two poets sauntered through the depths of Hell, conversing amicably as millions of souls were tortured for eternity. Ironically appropriate, hence the title, *The Divine Comedy*.

Tory switched places with me, keeping Gunnar busy so that I could do what I do best. Destroy shit. I was ankle deep in a war: dragons, a werewolf, and the She-Hulk fighting for all they were worth. Spouts of fire, smoke, ice, stone, and other elements peppered the room as the *Skittles* bag of dragons used whatever weapons were theirs to control. Part of me wanted to catalog all the different types and colors of the species, but the larger part of me just wanted to survive the next five minutes intact. I heard Tory groan as Gunnar bit her arm hard enough for bone to snap, but her fist to his snout crunched enough for him to jump away, shaking his head. They circled each other warily. "Do something scary any time now," she complained, face tight with pain.

Alaric's voice boomed a conclusion. "I prepare the path for the dragons to thrive. I am the first, the father, and the Son of the Dying Sun!" His words tore through the room, a whirlwind of air swirling around him like a vortex of power fueled by the screams of the dying. A promise of what was to come. His clawed hand reached out towards Raego, inching closer to his son's vulnerable throat. Gunnar leapt at Tory again, and she screamed in pain. I reacted without thinking, instantly making a choice between two terrible options.

Tory or Raego.

I pulled Asterion's coin from my pocket and threw it like a baseball. I'm sure it looked pathetic at first, but then it transformed into an icy spear in midair, slicing Alaric's claw off at mid-forearm, and slamming into the lock holding Raego's chains. Alaric's scream tore through the room, momentarily halting the fighting. Raego's voice finally came out in a roar of such intensity that the hair on my neck stood on end as he freed himself from bondage with an explosion of iron fragments that pelted Alaric like a shotgun blast.

Then Alaric let his control go, and he was suddenly a pure gold dragon, scales gleaming like a pile of moving treasure. He was huge, bigger than any dragon I had seen yet, but he still had plenty of room to maneuver as he lunged at Raego. Ridges and scales covered his golden form like heavenly armor. "I will drink your blood like a fine bouquet of wine, my son," he promised with a toothy grin. Even with an arm missing, he still moved with an unmatched fluid grace. He swiped his good claw at Raego, who managed to duck underneath while shifting into his own impressive ebony dragon form, not quite as big, but big enough to battle his father. He speared Alaric in the chest, tackling him towards me in a rolling tumble of claws and scales and fire. Raego jumped away at the last minute, as did I.

I reached deep inside my power, and called my ace. I whispered the name with every ounce of my will, and he answered the call.

Black lightning struck the edge of the room, incinerating one of the dragon guards posted there, and the thunderous explosion of hell's gates opening up filled the room as the doors to the room kicked in, slamming two more unsuspecting dragons into the stone with a sickening *splat*. Thick, black smoke billowed into the room like fog, but pinpoint silver hooves emerged from the blackness, as well as a set of blazing, fiery eyes. Silver blue fire traced the *clip-clop* of horse hooves as he slowly entered the room, and he snorted a neigh that sounded both feral and hungry, freezing the marrow in my bones. His pearlescent horn seemed to glow in anticipation of the blood he sought. Everyone stopped to look, confused and frightened.

My little pony knew how to make an entrance.

Grimm launched out of the shadows like one of the Four Horsemen of the Apocalypse, ripping the throat out of a dragon with his gleaming horn. He neighed again, a chilling, crawling, bestial noise cast into the room, and all the dragons watched in surprise, and then pure fear. So, they were acquainted. It would save me the triviality of introductions. I had asked Raego if he was the youngest of his siblings for a reason.

It made him immune to Grimm's wrath. I hoped.

The unicorn's feathers snapped out in a rattling mane of black and red, and the dragons hesitated as he pawed a fiery hoof at the stone. "Good pony!" I bellowed, but as I turned away, I saw Alaric storming towards me. I quickly launched two balls of liquid fire at his chest, where they splattered over his torso in a wash of oily flame against his scales. He opened his jaws wide and roared, his own stream of fire singeing my suit as I dove to safety. I rolled on the ground, trying to extinguish any flames on my clothes before I lurched back to my feet. Dry cleaning could only fix so much, after all.

I instantly threw out a net of icy steel, tripping up Alaric as he reared up for a second attack. He collapsed, his momentum sending him sliding into the pile of dragons. Then Gunnar slammed into me, knocking me from my feet, and I crumpled to the ground, barely dodging his snapping teeth as my best friend tried to eat my face. His eyes looked crazed, as if he were watching a nightmare of his own making, unable to stop it from happening. My head rang as it struck the cold ground, and stars exploded across my vision as I managed to wrestle his jaws from my face by grabbing hold of his ears.

But the problem with grabbing a wolf by the ears was that, eventually, you had to let go. Tory saved me from that decision.

She grabbed him by the scruff of his neck, tossing him back into a candleholder on the opposite side of the room. He let out a sad, puppy-like squeal on impact. Misha was down, bleeding from numerous wounds, but so were many of her sisters. I saw her eyes darting about wildly, no doubt searching for her babies in the chaos. Grimm tore through the dragons like a scythe, ending lives as surely as a scythe cut wheat at harvest in days of old. Gunnar took a few seconds to get up, and I had time to glance at Raego.

He was standing near Peter, but staring at me with his huge dragon eyes. And in those eyes, was the ultimate question. Raego had heard the conversation while he was bound, and heard that I had condemned Peter to death, but here he was, asking my permission. His words somehow whispered into my ear, one of his abilities perhaps? *It's the only way. One must die to stop this, or we will all burn before his power. There isn't much time before the eclipse is over.* I stared back for an eternity, staring into Peter's pleading eyes.

And I nodded, my soul burning away forever.

41

Raego didn't even hesitate. He gripped Peter's hair and drew a talon across his pale throat. Blood spurted across the ground instantly, sizzling as it struck the ground. Then Raego breathed onto his face. My childhood friend instantly turned into an obsidian statue, mouth and eyes wide open in surprise. The power in the room coalesced as he died, spiraling into Raego as the moon overshadowed the sun for a few seconds longer. Everything was silent for a breath, and then a concussive ring of shadows exploded out of him. The ceiling shattered into a downpour of raining glass shards, some much bigger than others.

One of the latter slammed straight into my side, piercing me like a sword. I screamed in pain, feeling the hot fire of blood instantly escaping my body, and the sound of my voice was eerily alone as I stared transfixed at the explosion, one hand gripping my gun and the other clutching my cell phone.

Every dragon in the room instantly turned into an obsidian statue except Misha, Raego, and Alaric, who lay panting on the ground, struggling to climb to his feet. The other dragons were frozen in the pain and rage of battle, filling the room like lawn ornaments from a nightmare. I finally spotted Misha's babies, curled up in the corner as far from the fighting as they could get, eyes wide with fear as they held each other, forever frozen in their obsidian embrace. I felt a lump form in my throat at that. Seeing Alaric still alive and unaffected by Raego's blast of power, I hit *send* on the pre-typed text message on my phone, and then sighed, exhaustion and blood loss threatening to consume my dwindling strength. Grimm eyed Raego cautiously, but made no move against him, instead neighing anxiously in my direction as he swished his tail. His wings flared out protectively over Misha as she smiled up at him, ignoring the crimson drops that dripped from Grimm's wings and snout. Fresh blood. On a horse.

Gross.

"Nooo!" Alaric's voice boomed. "This cannot be! I will tear the flesh from your bones, wizard!" Then he was running at me, claws tearing into the stone. I raised the gun, fighting my dizziness, and unloaded the rest of the clip at his face. I'm a good shot, but he was just so big and strong, and his scaly, golden skin really was like armor. Several teeth shattered as my aim hit true, and blood exploded from his skull as first his eye was torn out, and then another bullet went straight up his nostril. Flaps of skin hung from his face, blood pouring over his long, glittering shattered teeth as he continued towards me, unperturbed. The gun clicked empty and I groaned, unable to get to my feet with the spear of glass still embedded in my body.

Then three sizzling spears of light slammed into his ribs from the side of the room, and I heard shouting as another swarm of projectiles peppered him, nets tripping up his feet, and more electric spears hammering his frame. He finally went down, sliding just past me as his claws reached out to catch me as he did. His claw scratched my cheek in a blaze of agony, but not enough to decapitate me before he was safely out of reach. I looked up to see Mallory and the dragon hunters leap onto his body, stabbing him over and over again. Several screamed as they were consumed by his fiery breath or were disemboweled by a stray claw in his last throes of self-defense. So many dead. It all happened so fast that none of my other friends had even moved, if they would have even been able to, that is. Finally, the Dragon Lord was still.

Between one moment and the next, Gunnar collapsed to the ground, shifting back to his very naked human form. Wounds crossed his body, his nose a broken ruin, and several hideous bruises painted his ribs. He breathed, but didn't move. Tory fell to her knees, cradling her broken arm and weeping. Gunnar lifted his head to look at me, smiled, and then closed them again. "Thanks," he wheezed. "Couldn't disobey…"

Misha ran over to Tory, her nude body curling around the little sobbing cop affectionately, smoothing her hair with a bloody hand. Tory smiled up at her new friend with a nod that she would be fine. I hissed as I glanced down at my own wounds, glad to realize that they weren't fatal. One was serious, but as long as I got medical attention soon, I would survive. Tory and Misha finally crawled over to my side, eyes widening as they saw the wound. One-armed, Tory helped prop me up and take off my coat as I struggled not to scream again. With a sharp breath, I withdrew the shard, slicing my fingers in my haste. Tory and I quickly tied my coat around my waist with a sharp pull, making me grunt. I panted, leaning back. "That should hold for now, but I think you should be fired as the group's *fashionista*. No respectable man would ever tie a coat around his waist like that." Tory smiled. I chuckled and she leaned in close, squeezing my upper body with her one good arm. "Thank you, Nate," she whispered into my ear.

We helped each other up. I felt dizzy, but mobile. Blood instantly seeped through the coat, but it didn't spread too fast, which was good. I closed off my perception of the pain like my parents had taught me so long ago. Mallory and the dragon hunters watched, maintaining a safe distance as their lips grimaced at Raego and Misha with distaste. Tory looked at my side, concerned.

"It's alright, but we need to get you checked out, too." I said, to her as she continued to watch me. She nodded, cradling her useless arm, her face tight.

Raego was back in human form, glancing at the statues and the hunters, looking impressed and cautious.

"How did they know where to find us?" He waggled a hand at the men.

I shot him a weak grin. "I texted Mallory. He was waiting with Tomas and the Dragon Hunters for my call." Raego shook his head.

"You definitely come prepared for the worst."

"I was a good Boy Scout," I said tiredly, looking around the room at the frightening dragon statues. "What are you going to do with them now?" I asked.

He pondered that for a minute. "Lawn ornaments?" he offered, face questioning.

Tory began to laugh between sobs of pain, struggling to catch her breath. I couldn't help it. I joined in, and soon we were all laughing between pants of pain. Grimm nuzzled Misha affectionately with his bloodstained muzzle and then clopped over to me to do the same. Just a friendly, blood covered, red and black peacock-feathered, death-unicorn. Cuddling. No big deal. Misha glanced at her babies in the corner, their faces contorted in pain, and I heard her sob lightly. Raego touched her shoulder and whispered a few words to her that seemed to cheer her up, her eyes widening with hope. I didn't want to ask. I just wanted to get the hell out of here.

Raego plucked the book from the ground, looking over at me. "Mind if I peruse this before returning it? It really is a family tome. I would like to study it before returning it to your guardianship. I don't want any surprises cropping up when I meet up with my brethren…" he frowned, "subjects," he corrected. "Of the Dragon Nation."

I nodded. "As long as Tomas doesn't diminish your flock in the meantime." Raego nodded seriously, glancing at the dragon hunters pointedly. "But I still expect the payment you promised." He laughed, but agreed.

Mallory approached, checking me quickly to assess the damage. Satisfied, he shook his head, grinning. "Ye were right, Laddie. You do know how to have a good time. Want me to start the car?" I nodded, too tired to speak. "I'll take Tomas and the rest with me. Dinna' want any more trouble with your other friend there. Old habits die hard." With a flick of his head, he indicated the dragon hunters and Raego eyeing each other warily. I nodded again. After a few words between the two men, Tomas met my eyes, promising a long talk later, and then rounded up his men to leave, grimly lugging away the bodies of his fallen comrades. I felt sick.

Once they were all gone, Gunnar climbed to his feet, looking drunk, but remained silent, eyes downcast. He had probably found a way to blame himself for everything. He usually did. Drama queen. But there was nothing to do about that now. I felt dizzy from both how much power I had used in the fight, and my wound. I was stunned that we were all alive. Well, all of us except for Peter. Oddly, I didn't even feel bad about that as I looked at his frozen fear-stricken obsidian face. "And how exactly did you come to command the unicorn?" Raego asked softly as he helped Misha—now in her impressively nude human form—into her dress.

"A favor," I answered simply. Grimm neighed one more time, and then flew into a shadow and disappeared. No one spoke as they watched me. At that moment, the room brightened significantly as the moon finally lost its control over the eclipse.

"I owe you, Nate. You could have used that coin to protect your friend, Tory, but you used it to save me instead. I'll never be able to thank you enough."

"It was a gamble, kid. Sometimes gambles work, and sometimes you go belly up. I was just lucky." I looked around the room. "We were all lucky."

"Son of the Dying Sun, or Obsidian Son, but not kid. Not ever again," Raego said softly.

"Maybe, but that's a mouthful. I'll stick with *kid*."

Raego shook his head, smiling. He motioned for us to leave the room, supporting Misha as we left. The rest of us supported each other. The house was mostly empty, few of the dragons from earlier visible. I wondered why, but Raego shook his head as I opened my mouth. "They can feel my power. Any loyal to my father were turned to stone, but the others have fled to no doubt spread word." As if verifying that claim, we did see several more dragons frozen into statues as we left. Creepy. "I will receive dignitaries soon, especially since all the big names are already in town. Everyone is covering their ass right now, no doubt preparing gifts appropriate for their new Lord."

We were quiet for a few hallways as we all recovered, regaining our strength. Gunnar finally piped up as he and Tory carried each other. "I am not fit to lead a team if I can't even protect myself from two dragons' seductive wiles," he said guiltily. "She took me too easily at the night club. I was useless."

I waited a moment and then smiled at him. "But they did have huge racks, Gunnar. I mean, they were beyond glorious. Many men have fallen for less."

Tory grinned darkly. "Hell, I would have done anything to see those up close. I could rule the world with a pair like that blonde one was blessed with." We each looked at her, surprised. She blushed, and began to laugh, but was cut short by a jolt of pain in her arm. Misha was there in an instant, supporting her weight. Tory nuzzled her head into Misha's neck.

"So, what happened after I was captured?" Gunnar asked carefully, face hard.

Tory and I told him the story, the full story about the media and the dead cop. His shoulders sagged further with each word. I even told him what Jeffries had said about the very likely possibility of him losing his job. He was quiet after that. We exited the house, stepping out into the large circular drive before he spoke again. The dragon hunters had apparently all left, but I spotted Mallory at the wheel of Gunnar's Land Rover, patiently waiting for us. He must have had a spare key on him. Gunnar finally spoke, "That was my life. Without it I have nothing. The FBI won't be able to stand up to the Freaks if they continue to crawl out of the woodwork. Even though I was under their control, I heard everything. I saw him talking to congressmen. He was giving them…gifts. Bribes. His dragons were seducing them in a back room. He owned them as much as he owned me. I don't think people are going to stand for his coalition, despite support in political channels. I think a revolt is coming. At least major ripples in the pond anyway. The Regulars don't want to accept us as humans with equal rights, and I don't blame them after the crimes I've seen."

Everyone turned to me as if waiting for the axe to drop. My name had been smeared across the media the most, and my secret was out, completely, stark naked for all to see. I looked them each in the eye. "Well, I've been thinking." Gunnar immediately groaned and Tory smiled. "As I was saying..." I continued, frowning at Gunnar's grin. "I *am* a billionaire who has no chance of spending all the money at my disposal. What do you say to me privatizing our little club here?"

Everyone's eyes widened at that, and I smiled, proud of the shocked reactions. Misha looked anxious, but the others hadn't overcome their shock.

"Like Vigilantes?" Gunnar blurted, face full of disapproval.

"No, no. That's illegal...But kind of." I flashed a guilty grin. Tory watched me curiously. "Perhaps consultants would be a better term?"

Raego remained silent, but was smiling alongside Misha. Tory turned to Gunnar, arching a brow. Finally, Gunnar nodded. "That sounds legal. Kind of." He grew more enthusiastic as he realized that perhaps his life wasn't over. "I like it. Black Ops Mythical Freaks Assemble!" he cheered, smiling like a child.

"Again, kind of a mouthful. How about Black Ops Wizards?"

"But I'm not a wizard." Gunnar argued.

"Neither is the she-hulk or Obsidian Son, but it sounds much catchier, and there is that Kentucky Senator who declared all Freaks were the spawn of wizards anyway. We'll talk about it." Everyone quickly agreed to that, nodding enthusiastically.

"We'll need to discuss pay though since we aren't all billionaires." Gunnar began. "For instance, we'll need enough to pay bills, healthcare, and—"

"Six figures work for everyone who wants to do this full time?"

My words cut like a knife. Tory blinked at me. "That..." She cleared her throat. "That is enough to buy me as your sex slave for eternity." She said before catching herself with a fierce blush. I realized I was focusing so much on my stomach pain that my power was leaking out again. I struggled to juggle the two so that she could answer honestly. She scowled at me, glancing at Misha first in apology. Misha grinned hungrily. "What I *meant* to say is that I come from a very poor family, and that is more than I have ever hoped to make in law enforcement."

"The job will be tough, and as you saw today, very dangerous. I will pay accordingly." I glanced at Gunnar. "With full health expenses covered outside of that, of course." I raised a hand for silence as Gunnar guffawed. "With no deductible."

The silence was thick, and then Tory spoke. "Nate Temple for president?"

Everyone laughed at that. I looked over to Misha. "I assume Raego will be needing you. I release you from my power." She blinked at me.

"It wasn't your power that kept me around. You wear my tooth." I blinked, but she continued. "And you promised sex once this was all finished." It was my turn to be embarrassed, and that was no easy feat. Everyone else joined in on razzing me after that. Misha looked from face to face. "I was serious. He promised." They laughed harder.

Gunnar's conscience had a say. "This still sounds shady. I stand by my pledge as a federal agent, and don't want to do anything illegal."

"We will be dancing on the fringes of the law, hence the term Black Ops. But the government will be hiring *us* if this coalition nonsense gains traction, so that should appease you. Otherwise we'll freelance into cases of our own choosing."

"They aren't going to like it..." Gunnar said carefully.

"Of that, I'm sure. But that's also the fun of it. No more red tape strangling innocents to death. You will have the agility to act swiftly. Think about it. People will cease to care once they realize who allows them to tuck their kids in safely at night." I paused to let that sink in. "Now, who wants to be Robin to my Bruce Wayne?"

Gunnar growled. "No fucking way. You went there."

Tory beamed. "I'm Catwoman!"

Raego rolled his eyes. "You can't be Batman. You don't even have any cool gadgets."

"I can make some," I argued.

We approached the Land Rover as Raego said his goodbyes to everyone. Misha agreed to stay with Raego for a little while, but made me promise her a date first. My mind was already working on a way to substitute Tory for myself, and I didn't think that would bother Misha.

We climbed into the car with Mallory at the wheel. He waited for my instruction. I reached into my pocket and felt a tiny slip of satin. I grinned from ear-to-ear. "Now, I think we all need to visit a doctor. Shall we drop you off at the hospital?" I asked.

"What about you?"

I grinned wickedly. "I have my very own doctor. Don't worry about me. I'll be fine." Tory and Gunnar gave me odd looks, but finally shrugged at my silence. "We can discuss details of our team later."

"So, it's official. I bet we'll even have Paparazzi soon," Gunnar groaned.

"Welcome to the lifestyle of the rich and famous," I smiled, already thinking of my *good doctor*, Indie, as Mallory pulled out of Raego's driveway.

42

I leaned back in the bed of my master suite at Chateau Falco, twining a red silken strip of cloth about my fingers, pondering wizardly thoughts as I stared into the fireplace at the edge of the room. The smells from the tray of fresh fruit on the bedside table beckoned to me, but I stoically resisted, content to just relax until my nurse came back to check on my recovery from the battle at Alaric's home.

I glanced at the coin Asterion had given me, which sat on my nightstand, and pondered the god's involvement in the dragon mess. It was devoid of its power now, but was still a powerful relic that I had yet to study in depth. Later. So many things to study. I would meet the Minotaur to try and get some answers, both about his history with the dragons and my musings about Hermes.

I had put out a few fires since the eclipse, and was still recovering in—and getting used to—my new home at Chateau Falco. I missed Plato's Cave, but I couldn't complain too much. Here I had a Butler! And Indie had delegated duties to all the employees at Plato's Cave with ruthless efficiency. It was business as usual, just how I liked it.

I had managed to get a grip on my new power after an intense personal assessment. The distortion of chance was gone, which was good, as well as the leakage factor on those around me. Double good. Once I was fully healed I would have to look into it more specifically in an attempt to figure out why and how it had happened. I briefly wondered if my parents had done something to pass on their power to me upon their deaths, even though I thought the idea impossible. But it just wasn't important at the moment.

People and newspapers both discussed the topic of Alaric's *coalition* openly and fearfully, but seemed pleased that it seemed to fizzle into nothing at the man's disappearance from St. Louis' social scene. Raego had cleverly issued a statement about

Alaric moving back to Europe, complete with travel itineraries and everything. No one questioned it, thankfully.

Detective Kosage had been forced to make a public statement renouncing my involvement in the recent crimes after I had put some weight on the mayor about moving my company to a new city. Kosage had been none too pleased, but no love lost there. In fact, I had no intentions of moving the company, but no one else knew that. Even if I had wanted to move the company, I had too many things to do to even entertain the thought at present. I still had to figure out what the Pandora Protocol—my parents' secret project at Temple Industries—was, and what importance the mysterious music box held. Why had the thief stolen it?

My fingers flexed about the satin in a brief surge of anger. The thief…Peter. But had he also been my parents' murderer? The video feed had said *Titan!* at the moment of their deaths, and I had a hard time believing that Peter would have been strong enough to take them out. Even with his new power.

And he was definitely no Titan.

A small part of me missed my old friend. Not the psychopath he had become, but the boy who had been with me since childhood. Gunnar and I didn't talk about it, except to answer a few phone calls about him joining Alaric in Europe. Again, no one seemed to question it. Raego had come by to drop off the book that had started it all, and to discuss the topic of the break-in at my company. He had no real answers—even having met with all the dragons in town for a brief oath of fealty to their new leader—but was confident that Peter had been the thief, but not the murderer. Alaric had had no reason for their deaths, and Peter had been unable to act of his own volition without the charismatic Dragon Lord's approval. Which meant that the murderer was still at large. But there was no one left alive to question now, what with Alaric slain by the dragon hunters.

I sighed, running the material through my fingers again, therapeutically. The dragon hunters had met Raego at my home under a white flag, learning that Alaric had used them as pawns the entire time. Tomas had been disgusted at that. Their enemy had tricked them into inadvertently working for him to take out Raego. They had agreed to a truce of sorts, that is, until one of Raego's dragons broke a law or stuck his neck out too high. Raego had smiled, nodding his wholehearted agreement.

Tory and Gunnar had healed without complications, and then promptly been fired. Of course, that wasn't how it was worded, but the result was the same. Jeffries had been the one forced to give Gunnar the news—against his will—as Special Agent in Charge, Roger Reinhardt, leaned on him. Ah, bureaucracy.

Kosage didn't mind firing Tory. My friends didn't mind too much, what with the new pay-raise from a certain billionaire benefactor, although Gunnar's heart did seem to break a little at the situation. So, I had cleverly arranged a self-esteem boost by asking Ashley Belmont to meet me for a very important business discussion at one of the priciest and most romantic restaurants in town. Somehow, I had forgotten to put anything in my planner, despite the fact that I had double-booked Gunnar to meet me at the same time and place for an altogether different business discussion. Gunnar and Ashley both showed, but I stayed home. I hadn't heard much from either since, other than the brief text message from Gunnar hours after the appointed meeting time. *I owe you one, asshole.*

Raego had informed me that Tory had been spending quite a bit of time with Misha as well. He also told me he'd been able to release her two children from their obsidian prison, and after an oath of fealty to the Obsidian Son, they seemed to be recovering nicely, wrestling all around Raego's inherited house with Tory, of all people.

I smiled at all the happy endings, then hissed softly as I put too much weight on my healing wound. I adjusted myself, leaning back into the pillows more comfortably. Then the bathroom door opened, and a silhouette stood before me, limned by the candle light behind her and the fireplace before her. "Ready for your hourly check-up, Nate?" A sultry voice asked. Indie took a few steps closer, and my testosterone replied hungrily. She stood there in a nurse's outfit, smiling darkly.

"Of course, my *good nurse*. Of course…" Flesh, hands, and lips met in a sweaty jumble, which hours later, I couldn't quite remember accurately. But I did feel better, healed. Completely healed…Ready to soon dive back into the fray and discover the truths behind my parents' murder.

The world was a darker place without them, but I wasn't going anywhere, and I hoped my new team would be a benefit to society. Someone had to be there to keep everyone safe. It was our duty. We had the ability to protect the weak, so it was on our shoulders. I sympathized with the Titan, Atlas.

Indie breathed softly, asleep on my chest, her sweaty hair tickling my arms as our warm bodies melded together as one. Someone was going to pay for what they did to my parents. Dearly. But not tonight. No, not tonight.

Sleep soon pulled me under, glorious, peaceful sleep.

And that's when the night terrors started…

Turn the page to continue with Nate Temple in **BLOOD DEBTS***…*

BLOOD DEBTS (BOOK 2)

1

The gnarled oak desk quivered as a subsonic blast shook the entire room. I flinched involuntarily, my drink tinkling lightly between my long fingertips as the lights flickered. I blinked eyelids that suddenly seemed to weigh a ton. *What the hell was that?* Had I been asleep? I couldn't seem to remember the last few moments. Perhaps I had been drinking more than I thought. Indie must have already abandoned me for bed by now, because she wasn't here beside me. And where was Dean? Or Mallory, for that matter? Surely, they had heard the sound. *Felt* the sound. The hair on my arms was sticking straight up in response to my sudden adrenaline spike.

Then I heard the scream. Like someone was being skinned alive.

I bolted from the leather chair in my father's old office – now *my* office – at Chateau Falco. Another distant blast shook the foundation of the house as I darted out the door and onto the landing that overlooked the first floor. Before I could move any further, a fiery comet came screaming through the second-floor stained glass window, barely missing my skull before it crashed through the banister beside me and blazed on into an adjacent room. The furniture inside instantly caught fire with a hungry *whoomp*. Dust and debris filled the air as I looked up in time to see the remnants of the window crash down to the marble floor, shattering into a billion pieces that looked like a detonation of Fruity Pebbles. The cloying stench of smoke instantly filled my ancestral home as it began to burn.

Fast.

More screams and shouts raged through the night amidst a barrage of gunfire and explosions as I crouched, trying to ascertain from where the sounds originated. After all, it was a huge fucking house. Seventeen thousand square feet was a lot of space to search. The single scream I had first heard didn't give me any time to check on Indie,

Dean, or Mallory. Someone was dying, right now, his or her screams full of tortured anguish. My home was under assault, by what sounded to be the combined efforts of the Four Horsemen of the Apocalypse.

Unforgivable.

I briefly entertained what I would do to the prick that dared attack my ancestral home. Then I was running, formulating plans and discarding them just as fast, drawing the magical energy that constantly filled the air around me into a protective cloak. The energy that most people didn't believe existed.

But I was a wizard. Special. A *Freak*, as some called us.

I could *see* magical energy. Feel it. Taste it. Hold it.

And *use* it...

To dish out all sorts of hell when I felt so inclined.

And *oh*, did I feel so inclined right about now.

As I raced past empty room after empty room, aged paintings seemed to grimace in distaste at my lack of protection... as if I was the ultimate embodiment of failure for a once-powerful family. I grunted, shrugging off the pain of those looks. It was just my imagination. They weren't really disappointed in me. They weren't even *real*. After all, I had instantly reacted to the attack, right? *Or were you dozing through obvious signs of intrusion, awoken only by the sound of their victory in kidnapping one of your friends...*

My Freudian Id is not a pleasant person. I ignored the smug son of a bitch.

I heard the scream again, and determined that it was coming from outside... along with the incessant gunfire. What the hell was going on out there? I sprinted down more hallways, zigzagging back and forth in an effort to get outside faster. Who was screaming? The voice was either in so much pain or so much rage that I couldn't even determine if it was male or female, let alone human.

I finally reached the front entryway, grabbed the massive handle to the front door, and heaved hard enough to tear it from the frame as a surge of magic fueled my strength. I tossed it into the foyer behind me and launched myself into a scene straight from Hell. The icy wind struck my face like a finely woven blanket of cold steel, sobering me instantly.

I practically shit myself with my eyes wide open.

The night was chaos incarnate.

Dragons the size of utility vans stormed the skies, blasting fireballs at my home from every direction. The ancestral home of the Temples was on fire, and the centuries old construction wasn't faring well. The porte-cochere above me leaned drunkenly, one of the supports abruptly cracking in half. I immediately dove to safety before the roof collapsed, nearly dying before I even had time to fully comprehend the situation. I rolled onto the balls of my feet, scanning the darkness amidst the dust, explosions, shouting, and dying. The fountain in the center of the drive was now a pile of useless rubble, and bodies decorated the once elegantly-stained concrete. But now it was stained an altogether different color.

The color of fresh blood.

A dozen of my security guards lay in smoking... *pieces* throughout the manicured lawn – bodies still steaming, per my magically-enhanced vision. Energy quested hungrily through the air, the waves of power coursing like gossamer threads of colored smoke. Power was *everywhere*... I grinned darkly. I could use that to my advantage. I saw a dragon or two also littering the lawn, betraying the fact that my security hadn't been caught entirely off-guard, even if their Master had been dozing in his office over a glass of whisky. I shook the guilt from my head. Despite the truth of it, I didn't have the time to feel sorrow. My guards knew the risks in defending my home.

Right? Had *I* even expected an attack of this magnitude?

I shivered as the guilt of their deaths threatened to overpower me. I shoved it down harder. Later. Instead, I sprinted towards a small pocket of humans battling each other near the old horse stable – that my family had upgraded to a car garage – a hundred feet away. I didn't know friend from foe, but I was heartened to discover that at least *some* of my men had survived. Reality seemed to abruptly shift, my vision rippling for a second like I had seen a mirage in the desert. I shook my head, frantically searching for the attacker who was messing with my perception.

But there was no one nearby, and the group of humans was too busy fighting each other to bother with little old me. No dragons either. I was temporarily alone, so who was messing with me?

After a few tense seconds, I took off towards the fighting again, dodging a small, jeweled box lying discarded in the grass. Thievery? A horde of dragons seemed like overkill for a robbery. I growled to myself. I would figure out the *reason* for the attack later. Now was time for *action*. I instinctively made a choice, and launched a crested wave of ice at the most unsavory looking group of men. Some collapsed under the onslaught while others remained upright – now frozen solid – but all as dead as a doornail. The survivors rounded on me with a triumphant hiss.

Shit. Wrong group.

They launched themselves at me with a unified roar of bloodlust, casting battle magic at my face like I had just slapped their grandmother at a holiday dinner party.

Dragons *and* Wizards?

I managed to dodge the majority of the numerous elemental attacks, feeling only a single blast of fire sear my forearm, but I ignored that pain. I shattered a stray arm at the elbow as I came within physical reach, too close for all but the most skilled wizard to use his birthright. It was my only chance against so many foes. I quickly realized I needed backup. A smile tugged at my weathered cheeks.

I bellowed out a single name into the darkness, never ceasing the lethal swings of my arms as they both physically and magically pounded my enemies. A deafening peal of thunder shook the heavens, followed immediately by a crackling bolt of black lightning, which sliced an unlucky dragon neatly in half, causing reptilian blood to rain down upon me. In its wake, a lamenting neighing sound filled the air with a very noticeable physical vibration.

Grimm – a seemingly Demonic black-and-red-feathered unicorn the size of a

Clydesdale – entered the fray. The single pearlescent, gnarled, and thorned horn protruding from his skull instantly gored one of my attackers through the heart. I might have hesitated for a second as I saw the unicorn catch a quick swipe of blood with a hungry tongue. I might have also shuddered with unease.

Might.

But despite Grimm's insatiable penchant for violence, I was glad the Minotaur had introduced me to him. He had helped me battle dragons once before... to their detriment. I hoped we would do it again tonight. Flaming, orange eyes met mine in a brief, appreciative greeting before we both refocused on our enemies. I called out familiar whips of fire and ice, utilizing them like Indiana Jones on crystal meth to eliminate the crowd of wizards attacking me. I spun in circles of crackling volcanic and arctic fury, lashing a leg here and a face there, feeding off their dying screams as I lost myself in the mayhem.

A ribbon dance of death.

What could have been an hour later, I realized that all of them were dead. Grimm was staring at me with wide, concerned eyes. I was covered in gore, blood, and ash. And I realized that I was grinning maniacally.

Before I could prove to the unicorn that I hadn't lost my mind, a familiar cry split the night. "*NATE!*" The agonized scream grabbed and shattered my mind into a million tormented fragments.

My breathing came in ragged grunts as I slowly turned, recognizing the voice.

The dragons had Indie. My girlfriend. The love of my life.

My Kryptonite. My Achilles Heel.

I spotted her standing atop the garage, a giant golden dragon gripping her in his talons.

Alaric Slate, the leader of the dragon nation.

My mind went fuzzy for a moment, my vision again rippling like a desert mirage. But... *wasn't he dead?* No. He *couldn't* be dead. He was right in front of me. Holding the woman of my dreams in his razor-sharp claws. A swarm of dragons I hadn't noticed until now unfurled just above our heads, simultaneously striking Grimm from behind. The mythical creature was obliterated in a millisecond, shredded into organic matter like he had fallen into a pool of piranhas. I screamed with vengeful fury at the death of such a magnificent beast – my friend – and cast my power at the earth around me in a fifty-foot radius. The dirt and rock exploded skyward, dropping the dragons into a ten-foot deep hole. A second later, I slammed the earth back over them like a heavy quilt, burying them alive. Tucking the monsters in for bedtime.

Permanently.

An amused chuckle filled the night air. I could hear Indie struggling, but I knew it was futile. I slowly turned to face Alaric, my vision throbbing with rage. He stood like an angry god – half shifted into his dragon form – a single golden talon pressing into Indie's soft skin like a hot knife resting on a plate of butter. "Hand me the box, Temple," he growled greedily.

I... blinked.

Because I had absolutely no clue what he was talking about. If I did, I would have given it to him. Hell, I would have given him *anything* to save Indie. Even my own life.

Indie screamed. "Don't do it, Nate!"

He silenced her by shoving his talon straight through her gut, causing her to grunt in utter shock, and then agony. I realized that I was suddenly closer, having instinctively raced towards him with murderous intent. He held up a claw in warning and I froze with one foot still in the air. His other talon was still embedded inside my girlfriend's stomach. I was stunned, in shock, unable to think straight, but I slowly lowered my foot to the cold earth. How had it escalated so quickly? He'd barely warned me. I glanced down at my feet, trying to control my rapid breathing while frantically assessing the situation for a way – *any* way – to save Indie's life. Her wound was fatal, not superficial. Alaric was a hunter. He knew my plight. He knew my skills. He had effectively commanded my obedience. He knew I would do anything to save Indie. Give up anything.

"Please!" I begged. "Take whatever you want, just release her!"

He nodded. "Of course. The box. Bring it here. Now. She doesn't have long without medical attention." Several new dragons were suddenly pumping their vast wings above me, hovering hungrily, as an added threat. I followed his gaze and glanced to my side, only to see the same box from earlier sitting in the bloody, frosted grass. *Wait... that can't be right. I saw that near the fountain...*

In a confused daze, I reached down, my fingers numb, discarding the stray thought.

"Easy, Temple. No surprises. Bring it here." I hesitated, not with any rebellious intent, but with simple confusion about how the box could have appeared beside me when I had seen it a dozen feet away only minutes ago. Alaric shook his head with a sad smile, abruptly twisting his talon inside Indie with a violent, final jerk.

"Nate..." she whispered between tortured gasps.

My senses instantly shut down. I was suddenly numb with disbelief and impotent fury. My body began to quiver, rattling the forgotten jeweled box that I still held in my now numb hands. The lid began to pry loose from the box. I looked down curiously. *Yes, do it. Do it now...* a strange voice cooed in my ear. I listened to it, not even caring about its origin, and began to open the box, knowing that Indie was already dead. A part of me was now dead, too. Only ashes remained of my heart. The world could burn, and thank me for it.

I no longer cared.

"No!" Alaric's voice boomed as he tore his claw entirely through the love of my life, effectively slicing her in half. I felt the mass of dragons dive for me as one cohesive unit, a pack of claw and fang. As if in slow motion, I realized that my death would be a painful one, and I also realized that I was fresh out of fucks to give. I deserved it. I had inadvertently allowed this to happen. Allowed them to kill the woman I loved.

So, I opened the box.

A wail of despair from the very pits of Hell filled the night before my vision turned an amber-tinted urine color, tunneling out to a single point. Indie.

The dragons' claws tore into me, trying to prevent me from opening the box. But they were too late. The world ended in a climactic symphony of pain and sound as I embraced death.

I *became* death.

Then, nothingness.

2

I jolted awake, shattering a glass of liquor that was clutched tightly in my fist.

The other patrons of the bar sprang back from their stools with a shout. The man beside me was the only one to remain in his seat, casually raising a drink to his lips. I was panting heavily – as if I had just finished a marathon. Adrenaline coursed through my veins, my eyes darting back and forth, trying to make sense of my change in surroundings, desperately searching for Indie and the dragons. But I wasn't at Chateau Falco.

I was in a seedy bar.

What the hell?

Then it hit me. It had been another of the night terrors – now turned day terrors – that had plagued me since the aftermath of the dragon invasion a few months ago. They were happening more often, now. Escalating in their brutality. But I was getting used to them.

Kind of...

I began my usual mental process of rationally stating the facts in order to calm my racing heart. *The dragons are no longer a threat. Indie is safe. I'm not at Chateau Falco...* After a few repetitions and deep breaths, I began to calm down, and reality slowly began to emerge from the depths of my fractured mind. I glanced at my watch and scowled. *I'm in a seedy bar waiting for someone. The man who called me with information on my parents' murder. I had dozed off. Again.* By sluggish increments, my breathing returned to normal.

I had lost track of the numerous variations of my terrors, but the mysterious box was always center-stage, and the vision only ended when I opened it. But while in the dream, I knew nothing of the box on first sighting. It was always a random prop, like any other piece of furniture. But some time later, I would realize I needed to open it to escape the dream, the monster, the demon, the pain, the torture – whatever flavor of torment my dream chose that night. So, I would open it...

Then, nothing but pain.

I waved at the bartender who was watching me skeptically – likely wondering if it was past time he asked me to leave since I had obviously fallen asleep while drinking, even breaking one of his glasses in the process of waking. "I'll sport a round for the bar. Sorry, guys," I apologized. "Long couple of days." The bartender eyed me warily, no doubt wondering what would happen if he told me to leave. After all, I was the infamous *wizard* and local billionaire, Master Nate Temple – the *Archangel* – as some had taken to calling me. But I preferred the self-appointed moniker, the Notorious N.A.T.

Biggie Smalls had nothing on me.

"I'm fine. Really. Let me make it up to everyone. And get me another one while you're at it," I muttered, plucking a few pieces of glass out of my now bleeding palm. I squeezed a napkin in my fist to staunch the blood flow. After a few moments, the bartender finally conceded. Several of the other patrons shook their heads and decided to drink elsewhere. I couldn't blame them. The calm man next to me still hadn't moved.

The bartender placed a new glass of cheap, gasoline-spiked whisky onto the warped, sticky, wooden counter. I scanned the room with a frown – of both anger and disgust. It had been many years since I had been in a *Kill* – a bar where violence was commonplace, even encouraged, and the hygiene equally dangerous – and was eager to pay my tab and get the hell out. But only *after* I got the supposed information about my parents' murder from the cryptic caller who had asked me to meet him here. If not for that fucking caller being late, I could have been home already.

I sighed. No use. I was already here. Might as well wait a bit longer. My notoriety was apparent, judging from the hateful glares cast my way from various men filling the bar. Which might say something about me. After all, a Kill was where only the most nefarious of supernaturals – or Freaks, as we were discreetly named – hung out. My reputation had really jumped after the Solar Eclipse Expo a few months back, when a harem of weredragons had decided St. Louis was the ideal place to host a ritual spell that would ignite the rebirth of the ultimate god of all dragons, as well as being a convenient locale to announce to the world that magic was, in fact, very real.

I hadn't agreed.

And they hadn't survived.

Now, even the locals were apparently terrified of me. And when I say *locals*, I'm referring to the *magical* locals. *My* people. Where I arrived, death and destruction was now expected to follow. That dragon event was what led me here tonight to *Achilles Heel* – the deadliest bar in town – waiting to meet a stranger who might know something about my parents.

I swiveled a bit on the squeaky wooden stool, scouting the seedy bar in a way that I hoped seemed nonchalant, doing my best to look inconspicuously lethal...

And my clumsy, bleeding fist knocked the drink straight out of the hand that belonged to the older gentleman sitting beside me. Some of the liquor splashed onto my open wound, causing me to hiss in pain. I instinctively called on my gift, filling myself with magic in order to defend myself from the octogenarian, doing my best to ignore my stinging palm.

Sure, he might *look* like a frail old man, but you never knew in a Kill. Plus, he hadn't freaked the fuck out when I had my conniption a few minutes ago. He had steel nerves. Which usually resulted from having a severe case of badass-itis.

The man smiled amiably at me, waving me off with a forgiving motion of his hand. "It happens. No worries." His eyes twinkled like arctic ice, seeming to glow. The silence stretched as I waited for him to make his move. His smile grew wider. "You can release your power now. It was just a drink." I let loose the breath I hadn't known I'd been holding, and then, slowly, my magic.

This was when he would attack. I knew it. *Wait for it...* I was ready for anything. I would never let my epitaph say: *The dragon slayer that was slain by a nursing home patient.*

He shook his head as if amused at a child's antics, and turned back to the bar, for all intents and purposes, seeming to dismiss my lack of trust. I finally swiveled back in my stool, still tense as a spring. *What the hell? Courtesy?* Ever so slowly, I began to relax. "Huh. Paint my lips and call me Suzie. You meant it."

The man turned his mercurial gaze my way, and I briefly noticed purple flecks in his icy blue eyes. "Why would I call you Suzie? You're Nathin Laurent Temple, of course. Kind of a big deal." He seemed amused at that. "And why would I say something and act otherwise? Is this a riddle? Or one of those New Age ideas that don't seem to make a lick of sense? Are you a... Hipster?"

The word sounded unfamiliar on his lips, but I could see that he was proud to have used it, as if it was one less thing pulling him from the grave, a last clutch at his youth. But as I appraised him, I began to wonder if he was really as old as I had originally thought. He had a youthful... vibrancy to him. I managed to stammer a response. "No, never mind. I thought... you know... this *is* a Kill," I finally grumbled, as if he were the one being strange. He shrugged and promptly ignored me as he studied the bottles of liquor behind the bar, apparently deciding on his next drink.

Which was extremely odd. See, my reaction was an important stance in a place like this. I compared a Kill to an African watering hole – where you went to do your business, grab a drink of water, and then efficiently retreat to your hidey hole – all the while watching your back for any threats. The place wasn't full – big surprise, with it being cold as balls outside and a weeknight to boot – but enough patrons lingered here and there to justify the sultry guitarist idly strumming cover band music in the corner. Because it was vitally important to keep this crowd entertained.

For they were primarily Freaks, as the *Regular* folk called them, or supernaturals.

Even though my new glass was a few inches from my hand, a distinct chime overrode the guitarist in the corner, as if I had tapped my glass with a fork. "Get him a replacement, please," I mumbled to the bartender, and then reached out to down my drink. "Me, too. But not this swill. Get me a decent whisky." The grizzled barkeep grunted, and I received a new glass of Johnnie Walker.

I lightly sipped the new drink in an effort to fuel my lidded eyes from drooping further. *Mustn't fall asleep again.* I visibly shook myself, noticing a pair of men down the bar whispering to themselves and pointedly glancing at me. I shrugged to myself. "I have enough friends," I muttered under my breath. I wasn't in the market for new ones.

The older gentleman rapped idly on the gnarled wooden counter with a bony hand as he spoke out of the side of his mouth for my ears only. "You can never have enough friends. *Never.* Also, this doesn't seem like an ideal place for sleeping." No one else had heard him. I was sure of it. "I'll take a *Death in the Afternoon*, Barkeep," he requested in a louder voice to the bartender, who seemed to be respectfully waiting for the man's order. *Absinthe and champagne*, I mused, immediately interested, and a little alarmed at what quality of champagne they might have behind the bar. If any at all.

"Nice choice," I mumbled, suddenly aware that this might be my contact. The man had been here before I arrived. Had he been quietly assessing me before deciding to follow through with passing on his information? I was suddenly glad I hadn't stormed out.

The man glanced over at me, his unique frosty blue eyes twinkling in amusement. He was gaunt, skeletal even, but wiry with a resilient strength underneath, and he sported long, straw-colored blonde hair in a man-bun. He was dressed sharply; formal even, and seemed to fairly reek of money, looking like Don Draper from *Mad Men*. I concluded that he definitely wasn't as old as I had originally thought. Just frail. He plucked a cigarette from an ornate silver case, casting me a curious brow as if asking my permission. "Coffin nail?" He offered me one. With a Herculean effort, I managed to decline, waving him to go ahead. He lit up, speaking softly between pulls. "I became infatuated with the drink many years ago. It's the color, I think. Silly reason, but there it is."

I nodded distractedly, trying to catch a whiff of the second-hand smoke. I had recently quit, but still craved a drag. "It's an inspiring drink." I dredged through my exhausted eidetic memory. "*Anything capable of arousing passion in its favor will surely raise as much passion against it.*"

The man grunted in recognition. "Hemingway was a great man, even though bull-fighting is slightly antiquated." He appraised me with a sideways glance. "Shouldn't you be attending some high society function or ritzy ball rather than entertaining a barfly in a Kill?" he asked with a refined degree of politeness, as if only making idle conversation.

"*The public has always expected me to be a playboy, and a decent chap never lets his public down.*" I winked, trying to flummox him with a different quote.

"Not many have read Errol Flynn. Learn that at one of your fancy dinner parties?" he drawled, unimpressed.

I leaned back, momentarily surprised at his literary knowledge. I finally nodded. "Sociability is just a big smile, and a big smile is nothing but teeth. I didn't feel like entertaining the crowd again tonight." I decided, for simplicity's sake, to refer to this stranger as *Hemingway*, after his drink of choice.

Before I could ask if he was my contact, I felt a forceful finger jab my shoulder, sending a jolt of power all the way down to my toes. Hemingway chuckled in amusement at the stranger looming behind me. I lifted my gaze to the bartender and realized he was not moving.

At all. Not even to blink. Then I realized that *no one* else in the bar was moving. No one but Hemingway, the stranger, and myself. In the blink of an eye, my sense of alarm reached a crescendo.

The sizzle of power still tingled in my feet from the stranger's touch. This person was juiced up to a level I hadn't seen in a while. And he had apparently gone to the trouble of stopping the flow of time in order to speak with the notorious N.A.T.

Knowing my luck, the night was about to get... *interesting*. And I had allowed myself to become distracted by Hemingway.

Who apparently *wasn't* my contact.

3

I lazily swiveled on my creaky stool to face the man. Time seemed to move slowly to me as well, whether a result of the stranger's power or my sleep deprivation, I wasn't sure. Delicious tobacco smoke drifted through the air in lazy tendrils, now motionless. Every surface of the room was wooden, splinter-laden, and filthy – coated with decades of blood, smoke, and various assortments of dried booze – an arsonist's wet dream. When fistfights and worse were frequent, why spend the money to spruce things up? Especially when the owner was Achilles, the legendary Greek Myrmidon, and sacker of Troy. No one dared challenge his aesthetic vision. Or lack thereof. Unless they liked having pointy things shoved through their jugular.

The man before me stood out as if the Queen of England had entered the Kill. He was dressed too nicely. And when I say *nicely*, I mean nicely as in formal wear a few hundred years or more out of date. He had a pompous air about him, as if about to check his shoes for filth. He sniffed idly, as if smelling something that personally offended him. He scowled at Hemingway's polite grin with equally polite disdain before returning his fiery eyes to mine. His long, black hair was pulled back into wavy order like a Prince. "This is a courtesy call. I apologize for my tardiness, but your methods of travel are unreliable." His gaze assessed me as I pondered his odd statement. "Stop digging into the murder. Nothing good can come of it. Accept that fact like the rest of them have."

My rage spiked at his tone alone, not even taking the time to get angry at his message. "Them?" I asked in a snarl, surprised that this person was my contact.

"Yes. The humans. Do try to keep up," he answered, sounding annoyed.

I didn't dare risk asking him what he was, in an effort to not appear ignorant, but I noticed a faint glow around the man, something that would be visible only to wizards.

Odd, because he was definitely not a wizard. I just didn't know exactly *what* he was. He was wearing a bulky 1980's era trench coat that clashed with the practically archaic dress clothes underneath, and he was much taller than me. He sported a clean-shaven, baby face, and moved with the grace of an underwear model. My wizard senses picked up the smell of frost and burning gravel. Which was an odd combination... I had never seen anyone quite like him. And the fact that he didn't know how to dress to fit in with the modern-day humans was unnerving. It meant he didn't belong here. On Earth. No doubt a smart person to avoid.

But the cheap liquor and his unexpected warning had me wanting to vent off some steam.

"Am I to understand that you arranged a meeting with me – to which you arrived abhorrently late – in order to tell me to stop meeting people with information about my parents' murder?" He nodded. "A phone call would have sufficed. Otherwise, I might be inclined to think that you were *deliberately* wasting my time. And very few people would consider doing that to me." The man shrugged, unperturbed. "What if I keep digging?" I pressed, idly assessing my surroundings for collateral damage, shivering as I remembered that everyone was frozen and unable to escape. That changed things. Hemingway took a sip of his drink, watching the exchange with undisguised interest. Why was *he* not immobilized like everyone else?

My contact assessed me up and down, not with overt disrespect, but merely as if wondering what form of creature sat before him. "This is a Heavenly affair, not your... jurisdiction. But it's your funeral." Hemingway immediately burst out laughing. I frowned at him. Was he drunk? My appointment was obviously powerful, and Hemingway looked as if a strong wind would blow him away like a kite. Something the man had said drew me back away from the frozen patrons of the bar. The man had casually said *Heavenly*. Was he being literal?

"This is none of your concern," the man hissed at Hemingway, causing my drinking partner's grin to stretch even wider, revealing dazzlingly white teeth.

Him threatening my brand-new drinking buddy pissed me right the fuck off for some reason. "Are you," I began, giving the stranger a mocking head-to-toe appraisal, "threatening me?" The man... blinked, as if seeing a kitten suddenly sprout horns. It fueled my anger even more. I mean, I wasn't the scariest kid on the block, but I was formidable.

Wasn't I?

"I don't need to threaten a man hunting for death." The stranger shared his glare with Hemingway and gave a faint grunt. "Just a polite warning." He began to turn away, his business obviously concluded.

But I wasn't finished. Not at all. He needed a lesson in manners. Since Hemingway seemed content to merely watch, and the other patrons of the bar were immobilized, that left me as the tutor.

I pulled the ever-present energy that filled the room deep into my soul in a cocoon of raw power. Enough that my vision began to twinkle with black flecks, and then I let loose a wallop of pure power straight into the stranger's stomach, before he had finished turning away. It punched him about as hard as a Mack Truck, and he went sailing out the front door, taking half of the frame with him. I grunted, nodding in satisfaction. Hemingway's eyes shot wide open in stunned disbelief.

And then alarm.

I was instantly surrounded by shiny, pointy things, all resting at my throat. I hadn't even seen anyone move. Wasn't everyone in the bar frozen? I swallowed. Carefully. Apparently, I had misread the situation.

I very cautiously glanced at one of my assailants, my gaze cool despite the uneasiness squirming in my belly. "I don't take kindly to pointless meetings, pointy things at my throat, or threats."

"Don't speak, mortal, or I will carve out your jugular," the pompous ass threatened.

I shrugged slowly, trying to appear unconcerned as I studied the gang of swords. They were professional. Not a single wrist quivered, and eyes of cold, merciless justice met mine. And they each wielded Crusade Era swords. The creature I had sucker-punched strode back into the bar a minute later, shaking off dust and debris from his trench coat, his face a thunderhead. For the amount of force I had dished out, he looked perfectly... unaffected. "Did you need some fresh air?" I sneered.

He halted before me, and his gang slowly lowered their weapons. "Do you have any inkling of what you just did, and who you did it to?"

"Man, if I had a nickel for every time I heard that line," I muttered.

"Don't be coy, wizard. You just struck an Agent of Heaven. I have every right to carve out your eyes."

"But then that would make me the holey one, and I was under the impression that was your shtick."

The man scowled at me with disgust, not amused by my blasphemy. I could take any number of insults, but *disgust*? That was just... confusing. Who had the balls to feel disgust for wizards? I mean, we were some pretty heavy hitters in the supernatural community.

He stared me dead in the eyes as I somehow managed to formulate a parting threat in retaliation to his disgusted look. "Words have consequences. You should be careful how you speak to one such as me."

He met my gaze, shaking his head with arrogant disdain. "One such as you..." he repeated with amusement, as if at a child. My anger was only growing stronger at the lack of respect he was showing my kind. He didn't acknowledge my threat, but sniffed the air curiously. "You stink like Demons. This whole town does." He leaned closer, taking in a big whiff of all the glory that is my aroma. "But you practically *reek* of it," he added. His mob of thugs inched closer as if to protect him, despite the fact that I had just laid him out with my best punch, and he had merely shrugged it off.

I blinked at the change of topic, uncomfortable with a strange man smelling me so deliberately. "Do dragons count as Demons?" I asked, feeling the weight of the new bracelet against my forearm. The bracelet that held the late Dragon Lord's teeth.

The stranger cocked his head. "It's not your trophy. It's *you*. Have you been consorting with Demons in your search for the murderer?" he accused, somehow seeming to gain a few inches of both height and width. His thugs grew tense, swords slowly rising again, ready to stab on command.

"No," I answered honestly, too surprised to take offense. "Listen, you probably shouldn't hulk out here. Achilles wouldn't like it. He's territorial like that." My mouth just wouldn't stay closed. Chalk it up to sleep deprivation, or whatever floats your boat.

He grunted, slowly returning back to his normal size. "It would behoove you to wash the smell away, lest it offend your betters. We believe that your parents' murder was directly caused by Demons, which you stink of. We have people on the case, but these people..." he said with a proud smile, holding out a hand to his gang of backup dancers, "are the kind to stab and exorcise first, saving questions for later. We wouldn't want any damage of the... *collateral* nature now, would we?"

"Okay. If you want me out of it, that's fine. But I demand progress reports."

The man blinked. "Only *One* commands us, and you are not H—"

"Daily," I continued, as if he hadn't spoken. "Yes. Daily progress reports should suffice."

The man actually let out a stutter of disbelief, followed by a momentous silence. I managed to control the urge to fidget. Barely. Then he finally spoke. "I would be cautious if I were you, mortal. Everyone has limits. Everyone should know their place in the world."

"Hmm. I'll take that as a *No* on the progress reports then. If that's the case, I won't be able to drop my investigation." I leaned forward. "I need answers to this. There's more at stake than my own grief. Although that's reason enough." I leaned back into the bar, reaching out for my drink. I took a sip as I considered my next words. *Why not poke the bear a bit more?* the insane Id of mine whispered. I – very stupidly – listened. "I'm sure you know what it's like to lose a father figure without explanation." I had time to smile before I was suddenly slammed up against the bar. Although the man hadn't moved, he was fairly tingling with blue power, and his shoulders were quivering as if threatening to bust out of his trench coat. Was he sporting a pair of wings under there?

Hemingway sputtered out his drink, but the hulk of a man dropped me immediately, holding up his hands, placating... to Hemingway.

Huh.

"Peace!" the man commanded. Still, his tone was nothing but threatening. "Be careful to whom you blaspheme. My Brothers are not so tolerant. And my sons have no compunctions against violence in *His* name. That is their purpose, after all." His smile was ice. "You've been warned. Consider yourself lucky."

I let out a nervous breath. "And you've been given your answer as to my next move, pigeon." I was playing a wild card, assuming by his words that he was an Angel, but the drinks had me feeling irrationally courageous. And I was pissed that he had slammed me into the bar without even a reaction on my part. A heavy hitter, for sure. I'd need to be on my A game if I wanted to tussle against him and his brothers. I was sure that

Angels couldn't simply *off* someone. Which was why he had immediately backed off when Hemingway reacted. Hemingway knew what he was, and knew that he had crossed a line. Apparently, there were rules. There were always rules. There had to be rules...

I hoped there were rules...

"Out of respect for what you are going through, I will let this minor annoyance slide, with a warning. If you ever strike a Knight of Heaven again, you won't even have time to apologize. We will smite you out of existence. If our nephews and nieces – the Nephilim, here – don't find you first. They have less scrutiny about their daily duties than we Angels." With that, he turned on a proud heel, nodded to his gang of warriors, and they all left the bar. His shoulders fluttered anxiously underneath his coat, as if alive. Then he was gone, ducking slightly through the broken door.

I sat down, breathing heavily.

I had sucker-punched an Angel, and I was still kicking.

I noticed that a man down the bar was appraising me thoughtfully. Somehow, he also hadn't been affected by the Angel's manipulation of time. He didn't look impressed at my bravery.

Or maybe stupidity.

Time jolted, and everyone in the bar seemed suddenly surprised at his or her abrupt locomotion, as if wondering whether or not anything odd had happened or if they had simply drunk too much. Even the Freaks hadn't sensed the Angel's ability to stop time. I heard the bartender begin shouting about the broken door. His eyes quickly flicked towards me but I was still at the bar, obviously nowhere near the damage. His brow furrowed in thought, no doubt wondering how I had done it. Hemingway finally belted out, "Balls! You've got a titanic pair of balls. Or you have a death wish," he exclaimed between bouts of laughter.

"Shut up and drink, Hemingway."

Hemingway smiled at my nickname, lifted his glass in salute, and downed his drink, shaking his head as he continued to mutter to himself.

What had I gotten myself into?

4

I continued to stare at the broken doorway with a frown of concentration, noticing that the chill air from outside was sucking out a good portion of the bar's heat. Thanks to me. People began putting on their coats, but remained inside.

I was too tired to connect the dots. I needed to clear my head. I stood and strolled outside, hoping to catch a glimpse of the Angel again. I checked up and down the street but saw no sign of him or his thugs. Just the typical *Mardi Gras* revelers.

I scratched my jaw thoughtfully.

Apparently, someone sent from *upstairs* wanted me to stay out of my parents' murder investigation. I just wanted justice. Nothing more. But someone was watching me. Did that mean I was close to the answer? Why were freaking Angels investigating their murder? And to top it all off, I reeked of Demons? But... *why*?

I had no idea. Shivering, I stormed back inside, ready to pay my tab and leave.

As I sauntered over to the bar, the TV caught my attention. Someone had turned up the volume. As the words reached my ears, I groaned inwardly. Hemingway seemed to be listening with rapt attention. It was the now familiar news rehash about me from the last few months.

"*Master Temple is still refusing to comment, so the world is full of speculation. As everyone is aware, a few months ago, our beloved benefactor, Nate Temple – recently nicknamed the Archangel – and heir of Temple Industries after his parents' murder, was allegedly involved as a person-of-interest in a murder spree the likes of which St. Louis has never seen before. At this time, he is not considered a suspect.*" Her tone said otherwise. "*Alaric Slate – Master Temple's business partner in a so-called coalition of* supernaturals *– is apparently missing, so no interviews with him are expected.*" The news reporter then went on to declare that the high-speed car chase over the Eads Bridge involving a *Demon* was no doubt a monstrous hoax. A woman *had* been found at the bottom of the river, but it was determined that she was most likely just an innocent crash victim. They had yet to determine her identity. I scowled. She hadn't been an innocent bystander. She had been a silver-scaled dragon intent on mutilating me. My best friend – werewolf, and now *ex*-FBI agent – Gunnar Randulf had barely helped me out of that one. Literally. Silver and werewolves were not cuddle-buddies.

I idly fingered the bracelet of misshapen teeth on my wrist. Dragon teeth. Acquired from the late Dragon Lord, Alaric Slate. I had killed him, and used his dental palate to make a fashionable bracelet. It had made me feel marginally better. When Alaric's ritual had backfired, thanks to yours truly, the spell had then transferred the power and designation of *Obsidian Son* to his offspring, Raego, making him the new de-facto leader of the dragon nation.

A two-fer if I ever heard one.

Raego, always savvy, chose to break the morbid news to his fellow dragons by making my bracelet an award, like a goddamned Purple Heart, declaring me a friend of dragons everywhere. One phrase in particular stuck out in my eidetic memory. *"He is the ultimate death for us. Our very own Grim Reaper for those who wish to act terrible to humans... or those who disappoint me."* I fingered the bracelet angrily. "I won't be Raego's fucking hit man," I growled.

I felt Hemingway turn to study me acutely. "What?" I snapped, nervous at both the attention the news story might have caused in the bar, and his reaction to my last comment.

But he didn't acknowledge my statement. "I'll rephrase. *Grandma, what great big balls you have!*" he chimed in a falsetto voice, grinning widely.

I grunted, which only made him laugh. I pondered my recent encounter. "You really think so? He didn't look too tough. Although he walked off my sucker-punch pretty well," I added, thinking back on the strange man.

"Well, does it take more guts to twice traverse a staircase in a burning building or to make a one-time leap into a volcano? Damned if I know, Kemosabe. All I know is when you're making those kinds of calls, you're up in the high country."

I chuckled. "Never heard that before."

Hemingway nodded. "One of the Greats. S. H. Graynamore. Interesting character." He took a deep pull from his drink. "I hate those amoral ass-hats."

I choked a bit on my drink, biting back a laugh. "Pardon?"

"That was Eae, the Demon thwarter. But he's nothing compared to the Archangels." He looked me up and down. "The *real* Archangels..." His eyes twinkled, referring to the nickname the media had granted me.

I felt an icy shiver crawl down my spine. "That really *was* an Angel? I thought he might have just been a temp employee. *Eae?* For an Angel, that name's pretty... lame."

Hemingway simply stared at me. Like, *really* stared at me. I began to fidget after what felt like a full minute of silence.

"Okay. It's a badass name. Terrifying. The Demon thwarter... interesting job description." He continued to stare. I decided to change the topic to deter his gaze. "Why didn't you stop me from pissing him off? He could have smote me... smited me... no, that's not right either..." I mumbled, having no idea how to conjugate the word. "Anyway, I could have used a warning."

Hemingway's intense scrutiny finally broke with another amused grin. "You handled yourself well. Except for launching him into the street. You shouldn't make that a habit. You wouldn't look good as a pillar of salt. Then you called him a *pigeon!* In front of the *Nephilim!*" He roared in laughter. "*Pigeon...*" he muttered again before taking another sip. "He was right, you know," he added, almost as an afterthought.

"About what?" I grumbled, still trying to wrap my head around the fact that I had just sucker-punched a freaking Angel. And then mocked him. And in front of his crew no less. I pondered his thugs. Nephilim – the offspring of Angels and humans. Supposedly powerful soldiers of Heaven, although I had never crossed swords with any of them before tonight. I hadn't even believed they were actually real.

Boy, was I damned.

Hemingway scouted the bar carefully. Having already scoped the place out myself several times – keeping track of the people who had entered and exited – I again noticed the other man who hadn't been affected by the Angel's time manipulation. He was several chairs away from us at the bar, and was currently glaring pure frustration at Hemingway. I briefly turned back to Hemingway and watched him nod amiably at the scarred man. The Irish-looking man just continued to scowl back, but finally gave a dismissive nod in return, swiveling to instead watch a pair of particularly cute vampires playing pool. I assumed the man was one of Achilles' generals. Playing bouncer 2,000 years later must suck after such a glorious feat as starring in *The Iliad*. Hemingway didn't seem concerned with the stranger, so I let it go. Well, put it on the back burner, anyway.

Maybe I was reading too much into things. I mean, it's not often that an Angel arrives in a bar to politely tell you to *cut it out*. How many other Angels were in the bar? Or Nephilim? Jesus. I had never considered tussling with an Angel. I hadn't even known they were real, let alone on our plane of existence. Thankfully, no one was close enough to overhear us as Hemingway took a long pull from a fresh cigarette.

My nervous fingers ached to reach out for the cancer stick, but I managed to compose myself. I had successfully remained smoke-free for a few days now, and was proud of my discipline. But I had just survived a smiting. Perhaps I deserved one. Just one. I shook my head defiantly. *No.* "So, what was the Angel right about?" I asked instead.

"You smell like Brimstone. It's a pungent odor, and it could get you dead quick if some of his more blade-happy brethren caught you unprotected." I sniffed myself, picking up the light sulfuric smell, surprised that I hadn't noticed it earlier.

"I don't know why I smell like that. I haven't summoned any Demons. Lately." Hemingway blinked at me with those eyes that seemed able to weigh my soul and judge my guilt. Was he an Angel too? Eae *had* seemed nervous of him. "Honestly," I said, holding up my hands.

Hemingway shook his head. "I believe you. But regardless, this town reeks of it. *You*, specifically. The rumor mill does hint at Demons being involved in your parents' murder." I blinked, suddenly pissed. This mysterious stranger, among several others, seemed to know more information about my parents' murder than I did. Hemingway continued, unaware of my frustration. "Get rid of the odor as soon as possible. It will only attract the wrong kinds of attention, as you just noticed. Angels don't make a habit of appearing to mortals, but when they do..." his voice and gaze grew distant. "Nothing good comes of it," he finally finished in a soft voice.

He studied me for a moment before deciding to continue. "I once heard a story from a down-and-out farmer about Angels and Demons. It might put things into perspective for you, as it did me. Especially since you're not bright enough to leave well enough alone." He winked. "It shook me to my core. But I was a different man, then. A virgin to the true ways of the world. Perhaps wiser. Perhaps less." His eyes grew far away.

He shook his head after a moment. "Anyway, the man was distraught, filled with grief. And despite offering him a ride the following morning, I never heard from him again. He fled in the middle of the night. I've thought of him often as the years have passed me by, curiosity getting the best of me. Perhaps he was telling me *his* story." Hemingway winked again, face mischievous. "Alas, I never discovered his identity..." He took a sip of his drink, gathering his thoughts. I nodded for him to continue and hunkered down, ready to listen. I would stay a little longer to hear this. Because I knew next to squat about Angels.

His words enveloped me like a warm blanket. Stories from an experienced raconteur could do that. "I'll tell it to you like it was told to me." I nodded. He cleared his throat again, his voice changing slightly as he began to tell me a tale.

An exhausted local farmer was on his way home from selling his wheat at the market a day's ride away. It was drizzling, but a true rain would fall soon. He knew these kinds of things after farming for so many years. He didn't know how he knew, but he was right more often than not. He was eager to get home and see his family after a long day, eager to share his success, and eager to revel in the more important joys life had to offer... family. He wasn't an established farmer, with vast fields and many clients. No. He worked only for himself and his family.

A prideful, peaceful, god-fearing man.

He trotted beside his horse and cart up the final hill to his home... only to discover his son's broken body on the lawn that led to the front porch. The farmer froze, unable to even blink. His boy was not even ten years old. His beautiful, daring, carefree son had been left to suffer, the long smear of blood trailing from the porch and down the freshly painted steps to the lawn was a statement of his tenacity to escape. But escape from what? What could so terrify his bold, courageous son in such a way? Especially while mortally wounded? The farmer could not even begin to fathom, let alone truly accept the death before him.

His heart was a hollow shell of ice, liable to shatter at the slightest breeze. The wind began to howl, heralding the approaching storm, but it was a distant, solemn sound in his ears. He carelessly dropped the reins to the horse and crouched over his son's broken body. He brushed the boy's icy-blue eyes closed with shaking fingers, too pained to do more for his fallen, innocent offspring. But what he would see next would make him realize that his son had been the lucky one. The farmer managed to stand, stumbling only slightly against the growling, suddenly fierce wind, and entered the small, humble foyer of his home. Like so many times before, his wife immediately greeted him, although those past circumstances were never as abhorrent as this.

His wife had been tied down to face the open doorway. Her dress lay in tatters beside her nude, marble-like form. There were many empty wine bottles on the ground, and several piles of ash from tobacco pipes. Enough ash to signify that several men had bided their time in this room while he had been away at market, bartering higher prices for his wheat. The house reeked of tobacco. And he wasn't a smoker. He subconsciously knew that his future path would now lead him to darker places than he could ever imagine. His life would be forever changed.

I shivered, feeling the dark story touch a part of me that I had to fight to squash down. I had enough frightening memories to fuel my recent night terrors. I didn't need another. But I knew Hemingway would tell this story only once. Also, this story would be my only knowledge about Angels and Demons outside of the Bible. If Angels were watching my movements, I needed the information. I waited for him to continue, signaling the bartender to refill Hemingway's glass. The storyteller nodded in appreciation.

Upon seeing that his dearly beloved wife had been brutally tortured and then murdered, the farmer crashed to his knees, the forgotten purse of money that was clutched in his fist dropping to the floor like... a sack of wheat. The coins spilled across the gnarled wooden planks, one coin rolling toward the tear-filled, terror-laden gaze of his wife, before briefly brushing her long lashes and settling flat against the floor in a rattle that seemed to echo for eternity. That and the desperate panting of the farmer's breath were the only sounds in the haunted house. But they were enough to fill it completely. He had been anxious to see the look of joy in her eyes at his successful accumulation of coins.

The sensation of pride from her had meant everything to him. It lent him his own pride. Instead, he received this glassy, empty stare that would forever haunt his dreams. The woman who had made his life worth living, the woman who had saved him from his own darkness, the mother of his beautiful son, the woman who had made the endless hours of toil in the fields worth it... now lay before him, filling his vision like a never-ending scream that tore at the very fabric of reality. Thunder rumbled outside as if an extension of his grief. He would never be able to look at a coin again without remembering this scene. He had been proud to come home. Proud of his success at market. Proud of what the money would mean to his family. The prideful, peaceful, god-fearing farmer felt a scalding tear sear his weathered cheeks.

He distantly realized that he was no longer a prideful man.

A cold, amused voice emanated from the shadows. "Do you seek justice, farmer?"

The farmer jolted, hands shaking with fear... and something else. A feeling he had not experienced in many years. White-hot rage. He stared into the shadows, only able to see a hazy silhouette, wondering if it was one of his wife's rapists mocking him. If it was, so be it.

Everything that mattered in his life lay dead before him. He would welcome the cold, merciless slumber of death in order to escape this haunting grief. Or he would avenge his grief on this wretched soul. It was a long time before the farmer answered, knowing that farming held no interest to him anymore. Nothing held any interest for him anymore. Well, one thing did...

Vengeance. The sight of their blood on his weathered knuckles, the scent of their fear filling his nostrils, the feel of their dying struggle under his blade. The sound of their endless, tortured screams was the only sensation that would appease this once prideful, peaceful, god-fearing man.

"I do." The farmer rasped, realizing he was no longer a peaceful man.

Lightning flashed, the thunderous crack instantaneous, rattling the open windowpanes, and billowing the curtains. With it came the downpour of rain that had been biding its time in the dark skies above. A new voice entered the conversation from another shadowed corner of the room.

"Together, then. We must each give him a gift. To represent both worlds. He must agree to neutrality. To live in a world of grays, as the final arbiter of truth." *This voice was deeper, more authoritative, and obviously hesitant at the situation, judging by his tone. The voice addressed the farmer again.* "After your vengeance is complete, do you agree to forget this past life, and embrace your new vocation? I cannot tell you what it might entail, but you shall never be able to deviate once the choice is made. I can promise that you will not be alone. You will have Brothers to aid you in your cause."

The farmer nodded. "If I can obtain justice first, I agree. I have nothing else left to me."

The first voice grunted his agreement with a puff of stale sulfur that the farmer could taste even from across the foyer. What could only be described as a Demon slowly uncoiled into the light, red eyes blazing with anticipation, his leathery, scaly skin covering an almost human-like frame. The horned, shadowy creature, pulsing with physical shadows of molten fire and ash, handed the farmer a gift, placing it over the man's face, which instantly illuminated the approaching darkness into a hazy green glow, the shadows evaporating under his newfound night-vision. The Demon stepped back, appraising the man before him with satisfaction and uncertainty... even fear, before waving a hand in the direction of the other voice. The farmer turned to assess the second creature, eyes no longer able to show surprise. The man-like being that stood before him crackled with blue power, like lightning given form. An Angel. Wings of smoking ice and burning embers arced out from the creature's back, sparks drifting lazily down to the wooden floor, dying away before contact. The Angel extended a marble hand, offering up a gleaming silver gift. The farmer took it, the item familiar in his hands.

The two creatures spoke as one. "Gifts given. Contract made. He shall be the first. Now, ride forth into your new life. You shall find a new horse befitting your station waiting outside." Twin peaks of thunder cracked the night, and the once peaceful, prideful, god-fearing farmer was alone again.

The farmer stood in the empty house, and realized he was no longer a god-fearing man.

Over the coming year, he found every last culprit in the crime that had destroyed his life. Their screams unsuccessfully attempted to fill the empty void in his soul, and he reveled in every sensation he created from their broken, mangled, twisted bodies. Immensely. But it was never enough. Then he faded from this world, to fulfill his new responsibilities, forever regretful of his decision to accept those cursed gifts.

5

I blinked at Hemingway. I could sense that he needed a moment to collect himself, so I downed my drink, waving at the bartender to fill us back up. I tried to comprehend the dark tale, leaning forward over the bar. "Wow. That was... dark. Really, *really* dark. Have you heard of Christopher Nolan?"

Hemingway glanced my way, ignoring my last question. "Most true stories are. I didn't do it justice. The pain in this man's voice was something... something I'd never experienced before. Or since." His eyes were lost to his past for a silent moment. "Desperation can lead men to do stupid, but necessary things. Or at least it might seem necessary at the time. I don't know what became of the farmer, but be cautious of folly, lest you face the same choice as he."

I pondered that in silence, considering how to respond. "You couldn't have done anything. I know what it's like to lose someone dear to me. If a survivor wants to disappear for a while, he'll disappear for a while. Solitude is sometimes the only true solace available for that level of grief. Perhaps this guy knew the farmer. A relative or something. Had too much to drink and shared his story. Felt guilty in the middle of the night, then left."

It sounded hollow even to me. "Perhaps," Hemingway muttered. "All that to say that Angels are bad news. Demons are bad news. Both together are worse than bad news. Advice given."

"So... the moral is not to make deals with Angels and Demons?"

"No. The moral is not to deal in any way whatsoever, with Angels or Demons."

I leaned back, considering. "What did they give him?"

He shrugged. "I told you the story as I heard it. The best stories are mysteries."

"I guess," I answered.

He made a dismissive gesture with his hands. "So, what really brings you here?" he asked, seeming eager to change the subject.

My mouth began moving without thinking, and I was suddenly telling him my story. I told him everything. I felt like the man who had shared that dark story with Hemingway so many years ago. Something about his presence pulled out the darkest part of my life like a moth to a flame. Perhaps he had an empathic ability to draw out the poison in one's soul. I finished speaking and felt about as limp as the damp rag near the bartender. But the invisible weight around my shoulders also felt lighter. More manageable.

"I've heard the tales regarding your parents," he finally said, lifting his glass. "To Pillars of Society." We drank deeply. "They truly were great people. Don't ever let anyone tell you differently."

I blinked. "Did you know them?"

"I met them once." He studied my face. "One time, and one time only. They made a distinct... impression on me. Between black and white is not a gray area, but a quicksilver, honey shade; a shiny, enticing, and altogether beautiful dividing line. If employed correctly, that is. That was your parents. Take the *pigeon*. His kind are as white as white can be. Now, there are varying degrees of white, yet for the most part, they're *White*. Capital W. Then there are their brothers. The Fallen. Now, they're considered as black as black can be, and for the most part, they are. But they didn't start out that way. They just wanted more of a father figure. God upped and favored humans over them, and it rightly pissed them off. Now, end of story, right?" I shrugged uncertainly; curious of how this strange man was using the present tense to describe something that had supposedly happened thousands of years ago. "Then there are the *Others*. The Policemen. The ones with horses, if you know what I mean..." I visibly started in understanding, eyes widening.

"The Riders? Are you talking about the Horsemen? Of the *Apocalypse*?" I stammered.

Hemingway darted a cautious look about the bar, shushing me before finally nodding. "Them bastards have faces like justice. One look in their eyes, and you'll shit yourself with your mouth wide open. Trust me. You ever did anything wrong, they *know* it," he said, meeting my eyes. "However, they don't rightly *care*. You're just a speck of dust to them. Literally. Their concerns are the Angels and the Fallen. Light and Dark. Black and White. They're the policemen of your very existence, the Universe's Supreme Court. They are the Judge, Jury, and Executioner. And they take their jobs *very* fucking seriously."

I waited a moment, and then spoke. Softly. "Our." Hemingway's brows furrowed. "Policemen of *our* very existence," I clarified.

Hemingway frowned, and then downed his drink. "Yes, that's what I meant. *Our* very existence. Are you the grammar police or something?" he muttered something in an ancient middle-eastern language, but I knew enough to catch his gist. *It's hard getting grammar correct when you learned to speak a now-dead language.*

I agreed with him. In roughly the same language. I think. Either that or it was drunken gobbledygook. Same thing to my ears.

Hemingway started, slowly turning to face me with hawkish interest. "Well, I'll be goddamned." He began to laugh, a deep belly sound. The numerous drinks caused me to play a very dangerous hunch as Hemingway leaned over the bar.

"Aren't you already?" Time literally halted as I was slammed up against a warped wooden pillar for the second time tonight, my head smashing against the splintered surface with a resounding *crack*, hard enough for me to see stars. Again, my magic had been useless. Everyone around me stood still as statues, not even blinking, as if they had all been encased in Jell-O. Just like with the Angel, Eae.

Hemingway spoke with a gravelly voice. "No. I. Am. Not." I gulped, holding up my hands in surrender. I was way too drunk for this right now. "Easy, Wizard. Let's not cross that line. It's not nice to accuse a stranger of being one of the Fallen." Hemingway was crackling with a vibrant green energy, different than Eae, like a fairy in a cartoon. He stared into my eyes for a few intense moments before finally stepping back. "If I was one of them, do you think that Pigeon would have just walked away?" I slowly shook my head. "I've had enough to drink. Need another drinking partner sometime, here's my calling card. I might be bored enough to... *assist* you." He tossed a large, heavy card on the bar before scooping up a small set of motorcycle keys near his drink. Odd. He didn't look like a motorcycle kind of guy. The keys had a miniature, curved blade of some sort as a small adornment. I picked up the card through blurry, alcohol-filled eyes, but my drunken state just made the colors swim wildly, so I stuffed it into my back pocket.

When I looked back up, he was gone. The world snapped back into focus at normal speed, and everyone had a slightly confused look on their faces for a second, as if they again sensed something wrong. But they dismissed it just as quickly – as if they had briefly suffered another drunken spin moment – before carrying on. They were having a rough night, what with Eae and Hemingway distorting the flow of time twice in less than an hour. I shambled out of the bar again, but saw no sign of the man. I spotted several Mounted Patrol Units trotting down the street, scowling at the drunks exiting the bar, but I ignored them as I stood on my toes, searching the street for Hemingway, but I could only see more drunks parading around for their *pre-Mardi Gras* shenanigans. I drifted back inside to finish my drink and text my ride. It was fucking cold outside.

As I waited, I decided to do a little mental decluttering of recent events in order to see if I was missing something glaringly obvious. It had been that kind of night.

My parents had been murdered a few months ago, by an unknown assailant.

At the same time, someone else had broken into their company, stealing a debatably magical music box from a secret stash of dangerous items they allegedly kept under lock and key. The lock and key I had yet to penetrate. Their Pandora Protocol. Said thief had been one of my closest childhood friends, Peter, tempted into working for the group of dragons that had recently plagued my city in exchange for power. I had taken care of the thief, and discovered that he had coincidentally had nothing to do with my parents' murder.

I had hunted down, maimed, and murdered all known related dragons. With a little help from my friends. But I still had the bit in my mouth. I wanted the full story. Why had they been killed? Who had killed them? Why had Peter stolen the supposedly magical music box from my parents, who had looked upon him as a surrogate son? What *was* the music box, really? Was it maybe worth a pile of money? It sure wasn't magical, as I could attest to, after having experimented with it in every way imaginable. I sighed. One thing I did know was that it was nothing like the box from my dreams. It was just a plain, fucking music box.

It only takes one loose yarn to unravel a blanket, and I was searching high and low for that loose thread as if my life depended on it. And I had apparently found the right yarn, considering Eae's entrance into my life.

I rubbed my wounded palm idly, making sure no glass shards were embedded in my skin, and realized I was growing angrier and angrier.

You see, justice was important to me. It truly infuriated me that someone, somewhere, somehow had gotten away with murder, for some unknown purpose. I had even broken into Peter's office in order to find clues. Again, nothing relating to the murder. I *had* found an item I had created many years ago, that magically cloaked the owner, most likely used by Peter to sneak into the Armory – their mysterious *Pandora Protocol* project – but no other clues.

And now, apparently, Angels were investigating the murder and wanted me to back off.

No pun intended, but *what the hell?*

I decided that it was definitely time to go home and get some sleep. This wizard was tuckered out. Maybe Indie and I could go on a last-minute vacation to escape the madness.

Yep. I was booking a ticket out of town. Let the Angels do their digging. If they came up with nothing, I would pick back up where they left off when I got back. No harm, no foul. I had enough on my plate already.

6

Feeling better with a plan to escape to some secluded, hot, sandy beach with Indie, I let my mind wander. I had met two super-strong people today, neither of which was a flavor of supernatural I recognized. Knowing one was most likely an Angel, I considered that a lucky thing. What would Regular folk think if they discovered that not only was magic real, but actual Angels walked among us? Or maybe I was just special. Maybe he had made his visit specifically to tell me to stop digging. It didn't seem likely. It didn't seem worthy of calling a soldier down to earth all the way from Heaven. That meant they were here, walking among us day-to-day. Perhaps my trash guy was an Angel. It made me a tad bit anxious. That was a lot of pressure to be good at all times – a skill I didn't have. Yep. Beaches, here I come.

Waiting for my ride, I scanned the bar, watching the various Freaks in their natural habitat. The belief of most of the world was that magic didn't exist. We didn't necessarily want to correct them on that grievous assumption. It was easier to stay in the shadows. Think of the Salem Witch Trials. Every culture had purges of a sort where they tried to banish, maim, or outright murder the Freaks that stood out for their unique abilities. Although the world had progressed since those times, it was still a tough nut to swallow, and we liked it that way. We preferred it, actually.

However, recent events had blatantly smeared my name across the evening news as not only the well-known, corrupt, billionaire playboy, but also a dangerous wizard. Most took it in stride, assuming the media had been desperate to sell copy that day, coming up with outlandish stories to garner viewers, but many more wanted explanations. Explanations I wouldn't provide. I wasn't about to confirm their allegations. Do I look crazy to you?

I turned back to my drink – exhaustion threatening to overwhelm me as I took another sip – hoping the excessive amount of alcohol would help keep me awake. Any time I closed my eyes for more than a few seconds, it was even odds that I would be sucked into another of my night terrors. Maybe it was post-traumatic stress disorder from the dragon ordeal. I had never before experienced such a prolonged malady, and was starting to show signs of wear as a result. I shook my head clear of the twisted memories of my most recent nightmare, knowing Hemingway's story would find a nice, comfy spot in my subconscious for later nightmares.

Yippee.

The tumbler of whisky abruptly shattered in my fist, causing the blood to flow freely again from my previous wound. I hissed, sticking my palm to my mouth in irritation. I was systematically destroying all the glasses the bar had to offer. Before I consciously thought about it, I had slapped a crisp, new hundred-dollar bill – the kind that looked like monopoly money – on the warped bar, prepaying for a new round of drinks. It spent the same as the old bill, although I was willing to bet the bartender had never seen one before. Sometimes I forgot how others viewed money. I had been born into it, and couldn't fathom having to work my body to the bone in order to achieve it. My parents had created a multibillion-dollar company, Temple Industries, specializing in all forms of technology. I was no stranger to making money of my own, but I was a stranger to living on the line, never knowing how the next bill would be paid.

It was a humbling thought. What was I without my money?

Several patrons scowled at me. The bartender grunted as he poured me a fresh glass. "Try not to break this one," he grumbled. I nodded, pressing a fresh napkin into my palm before taking a sip of the fiery liquor. I didn't want any trouble, but I wanted everyone in the room to know that I wasn't an easy target. Trouble in a Kill ended in just that – Death.

I quickly realized that I was unashamedly hammered after talking to the mysterious Hemingway for so long. I hadn't realized how much I had been drinking. I had been so enamored by the man's story, and the man in his own right, that I hadn't minded my liquor. I realized this most obviously, as is most often the case, when I attempted to stand up, and consequently bumped the beer out of the hands of the man behind me. *Come on! Twice in one night?* The man's hackles rose. Great, a werewolf. I spotted the same scarred knuckled man from earlier chuckling down the bar, turning his stool to watch as he gripped his mug like he was watching the last two minutes of a good football game. The werewolf bucked up, slamming his empty can on a nearby table. "Pay attention, wizard! Master Temple or not. You're just another drunk here." He realized he had the crowd's attention. "Not safe without your pet guard dog, I see. Maybe I should show you what a real Alpha can do."

I looked at him, trying to duplicate the intensity of Hemingway's gaze, but most likely looking like a roaring drunk.

Which was truer.

"Okay." I peered past his shoulder, scanning the room. "And where is this elusive bitch you cower from?" Before I could react, the man literally growled as he violently grabbed me by the collar, lifting me high enough to catch a glance over his shoulder. Which is when I saw her.

A beautiful, tiny woman stood in the broken doorway, limned by the light outside. She was wearing a cute polka dot dress and giant red heels under a little fur coat. Stiletto-saurus Rex. Her eyes shone like lightning bolts as she spotted the man holding me up. Tory Marlin.

And she suddenly looked hungry. I nodded before glancing down at the large werewolf holding me up in the air. "Oh, goody. Girl fight!" I sneered. He squeezed tighter in white-hot rage, frowning momentarily at my comment, but no doubt still angry about my *bitch* reference. I struggled to draw in another breath before all hell broke loose.

"Release him now, *Bitch*," Tory hissed. I instinctively laughed while choking for air.

"Yip, yip, yip," I managed between gasps. The man continued to glare at me, ignoring Tory. Which wasn't smart. I could taste the Budweiser on his breath as he dropped me back to the ground. My bracelet of dragon teeth got caught on his sleeve and snapped, scattering dragon teeth across the floor. He took an aggressive step towards me. But Tory was suddenly in the way. The man reacted instinctively, shoving Tory hard in an effort to get back to me. She stumbled slightly, and her heel broke.

She looked down at the six-inch heel now dangling from her shoe. I whistled as I leaned down to swipe up a handful of the scattered teeth and the cord from my broken bracelet on the dirty floor. "You just fucked up your whole night, pal," I chuckled.

"Go back to your tea party, little girl. The adults have business to discuss," he growled dismissively.

Tory decided to show her displeasure at his words by unleashing unrequited hell.

She let loose an uppercut that slammed the man into the ceiling fan above our heads. It splintered amidst a crackling shower of sparks before crashing to the ground near Tory. On the werewolf's way down, Tory then unleashed a right cross to his angular, hairy jaw in order to politely break his fall. He flew across the bar, and struck the pool table with a *thud* that I felt in my boots. Tory was kind of a badass, way stronger than any three men I knew combined.

The werewolf didn't get up. The music had stopped and the crowd stared at Tory in disbelief.

"*My bitch bad*," I sang familiar rap lyrics into the stunned silence.

The crowd reacted like a fart had gone off in church, and an epic bar fight ensued.

Someone began to take a sucker-punch swing, and a sickly-looking man seemed to be in the wrong place at the wrong time. The swing wasn't intended for the fellow, but he was about to be laid out. I cold-cocked the attacker with the force only a drunken sailor could wield, sending the assailant clear over the bar, shattering all seventeen dollars' worth of quality liquor stored there. The sickly man looked up at me and chuckled with a dry raspy sound, but nodded appreciatively before moseying down the bar, carefree. The fight was suddenly everywhere. I realized that the scar-knuckled Irish guy from down the bar was not taking part, and no one was bothering him. The guy I had just saved from the Hail Mary was right back in the middle of the fray, but was also not being bothered. Huh. He must be one of the ancient Greek warriors with a free pass from Achilles. I hadn't seen the famous Greek warrior tonight, but hadn't been looking for him either. Good chance this fight would bring him out, and I needed to make sure Tory and I were gone before that happened.

The vampires at the pool table were beating the bejeezus out of two more werewolves with their pool cues. A couple of trolls were ganging up on a pair of fairy men that looked like Abercrombie models. It was mayhem. I realized I was cackling maniacally.

I felt someone forcefully pick me up so I took another drunken swing, connecting solidly with a triumphant shout. I heard a grunt. "Damn it, Nate. It's *me*," Tory snapped before lugging me out of the bar, not trusting me enough to let me go. I saw that the bar fight was escalating rapidly, but the Alpha werewolf was still incapacitated. Poor lil' guy. Moments later, the frigid night air hit me like a bucket of cold water. Tory carried me a good dozen paces away from the bar. She wasn't even breathing hard, but the uneven steps of her carrying me on a single heel didn't feel great, like I was riding in a broken elevator that went *up, down, up, down,* incessantly.

I spotted Gunnar perched inside an idling Mini Cooper, reminding me of a gorilla in a golf cart, looking angry, as per usual. Tory set me down and I stumbled, the world spinning wildly for a few seconds. I almost decided to throw up, but the feeling slowly passed. The passenger window rolled down. "You cause that?" he asked, pointing to the sounds of insanity pouring out the broken door of the bar. I shrugged, stumbling slightly again. "You're hammered!" he declared.

I scowled, leaning on the car's frame for support. "And you're a party pooper." That earned an amused chuckle from Tory. "Give me a straight line to walk! I'll show you that I'm as sober as a priest!" I bellowed. One of the St. Louis Mounted Patrol Units was watching my meltdown with mild curiosity, glancing from me to the loud bar fight, but wisely remaining on his horse. "You!" I pointed in his direction, kind of. He sighed, and then trotted over to us. Gunnar almost had an apoplectic seizure.

"Nate, this is a bad idea," he warned, his fingers momentarily transforming into inch-long, claws. Werewolf claws. They retracted after a glare from Tory. It was her car after all.

"How may I help you?" the dark-skinned officer asked, guardedly. "Did you cause that?" He pointed at the bar fight. I shook my head. "Are you harassing these two? Ma'am?" He turned to Tory.

She shook her head with a laugh. "We're his ride."

"Sorry to hear that," the officer stated in a neutral tone from his high horse.

"Oy! I'm right here."

The cop nodded at me. "So you are. What did you need? Xavier doesn't give pony rides. Especially to drunks," he stated blandly.

"Draw a line," I snapped.

"Excuse me?"

Gunnar groaned. I held up a righteous, wavering finger. "I want to show them my ability to walk a straight line."

"I don't have time for this. You have a ride. Get in, or I'll bust you for disturbing the peace." Ignoring him, I chose a long, straight crack in the sidewalk in front of a dark alley. And walked the shit out of it. Then backwards. The cop blinked. "Now, that *is* impressive, given your state of inebriation," he said, looking flabbergasted. He leaned closer to me. "Want to see if your luck extends to a Breathalyzer?" he asked with a wry grin.

"No. Everyone knows that test is rigged. I think I made my point. Thanks. Sorry your rider is a smartass, Xavier," I said empathetically to the horse. The beast neighed loudly in what I took for agreement. My head began to spin again so I leaned against the wall near the alley. The officer studied me thoughtfully, possibly recognizing me from the news, but finally turned back to Tory and Gunnar to verify that everything was all right, and that they were, in fact, taking me home.

No one saw the claw-like hands grab me by the short hairs of my soul, and yank me back into the shadows of the alley. The claws – although invisible – whisked me into oblivion like a cosmic toilet being flushed, and I was shat out into the very bowels of space.

It wasn't pleasant.

7

I re-materialized in a dusty, murky building. The sounds of the city were completely gone. Then I promptly threw up. On my captor's shoes. He danced back with a hiss, letting me go with a shove that threw me into a wall. I bounced off said wall, dizzy, banged my shins against a metal beam of some kind, and collapsed to my knees with a shout of blinding pain. My head was spinning crazily, and my body felt tingly from the apparent teleportation. And shin bumps were the worst form of torture.

When my vision steadied a bit, and I had recovered from the blunt force trauma to my shins, the first thing I saw was shoes.

A fuck-load of shoes, no doubt belonging to an equal fuck-load of assailants.

"Okay. Now you've done it. I hope you're all prepared for an ass-whooping. But first, throw-up shoes needs to tell me how to apparate."

I tried to stand, and was promptly kicked in the ribs by a steel-toed boot. I grunted in pain, the breath knocked out of me, ribs bruised but not broken, and remained on the ground. For reconnaissance purposes, only. I swear. After a minute, I managed to find my voice, walling away the fire in my ribs and shins. "Fine. I'll..." I gathered my breath. "I'll just have to beat it out of you," I wheezed.

I tried to stand and the boot reared back to kick me again. I feigned clumsiness, hoping I was agile enough to catch the boot before a commanding voice shouted, "Stop!" The boot listened. My vision was only just now able to distinguish that bodies belonged to the boots. I looked up and saw silver masks staring down at me. My heart stopped. Each mask was a depiction of a different human emotion, and continued past the jaw like a silver cloth to rest on their chests. This wasn't good. At all. "I see you recognize us, but given your state of intoxication, I'll speak as if to a small child. We are the Justices. The police of the Wizard Academy. And you have been found guilty of criminal actions on multiple counts. Your sentence is cooperation or annihilation. Which do you choose?"

I stared back; ready to unleash a snarky comment, but the retort abruptly froze on my tongue. I blinked. "I figured it out," I said, more to myself than to them.

His voice dripped sarcasm. "How very clever of you. You deciphered the riddle of who we are from the complicated words I used."

I scowled. "No, daft-wit. I figured out how to apparate. And I didn't even go to Hogwarts!"

And I *had* figured it out.

I didn't know how, but it was as if the very experience of teleporting had shown me exactly how to do it. Perhaps my subconscious had been paying more attention than my drunken conscious mind, but I had never learned something that fast before. Ever. Especially not while roaring drunk. It didn't make any sense. But I was confident I knew how to freaking teleport, now, thanks to these ass-hats kidnapping me.

"What is this *apparate* word you keep saying? And what is Hogwarts?" the leader asked, genuinely confused.

"Only the finest school of Witchcraft and Wizardry in the world," I mumbled, shambling to my feet. I swayed slightly, assessing my kidnappers.

"I've never heard of it. It must not be *that* great," someone spoke with a rough tone.

I ignored him. Anyone who couldn't get a Harry Potter reference was beyond help. "So, couldn't take the time to schedule an appointment with me over a cup of tea? Had to snatch me up while I'm hammered drunk? And what are these crimes I'm apparently guilty of, because they're news to me. I never even got a ticket!" I grumbled, discreetly counting my assailants.

The eight thugs didn't find it funny. Or maybe they did. It was hard to tell behind their masks. Paying closer attention, I saw the differences in each mask. There were smiles, frowns, scowls, tears, screams, and several other variations of human emotion. It made me think of Snow White and the Seven Dwarves. I turned to the leader again, the only man not wearing a mask. "That makes you Snow White."

"Jesus, he's *sloshed!*" one of them chuckled.

"And I still kicked your ass," I snapped back.

"Throwing up on my shoes hardly counts as kicking my ass. You only just managed to pick yourself up off the floor."

"Oh, that's right. The ass-kicking comes in thirty seconds. Sorry, my mistake." I took an aggressive step forward for a surprise attack I knew they would never see coming. Another masked man swiped my foot out from under me like a ninja. I crashed into a table, and then my nose hit a nearby chair, causing an orange explosion of light behind my eyelids.

Sweet darkness took hold of me, read me a bedtime story, fucked me gloriously, and tucked me in for a nice long nap.

What felt like an eternity – or a second – later, an icy bucket of water struck me in the face, ice cubes stinging my cheeks like a swarm of frozen bumblebees. I gasped, yelping as I leapt to my feet. My nose was on fire, and I tasted icy, bloody water pouring down my face. I swung my fists wildly in all directions. A pair of strong arms grasped me around the shoulders. "Easy, champ. We're only here to talk."

"The hell we are, Gavin. This man is a criminal. You forget your place," the leader growled.

"Of course, *Snow White*," the man holding me muttered so that only I could hear. I smiled. I had won at least one of them over to my side. Maybe.

"What was that, Gavin?" the leader demanded.

"Nothing, Jafar." A pause. "Sir," he added as an afterthought. So, I had a name. Snow White, AKA Jafar.

"I thought so. Now, where were we before we were almost overwhelmed by Master Temple's daring attack against the chair? Ah, yes. His crimes," Jafar grinned.

I knew this wasn't going to be good. The nameless leader had told me they were Justices of the Wizard Academy. That was a very politically-correct term for them. The honest description of their vocation was *legal hit men*. They snuffed out rogue wizards and other supernatural criminals like candles. They were notorious, the grim reapers of our world. Which also meant they were badasses, and they didn't typically show up *just to talk*. Usually the sentence had already been given, and they merely showed up to enforce the Academy's will.

The silence grew brittle. My face was on fire, but my chest and ears were shivering from the ice water. I turned from face to face. "Anyone going to elaborate for me, or am I supposed to guess?"

Snow White finally spoke. "We received your report on the events in your city a few months back," he began. I stared back, hiding an insolent smile. Smartass comments would do me no favors here. I needed to tread carefully. But I did despise authority, and this guy reeked of it. He also reeked of loyalty and duty, one of those men who follows orders first, then thinks later, if at all. Not the type to question his betters, even when necessary. "Care to elaborate?" he demanded.

"Well, I assume that you mean that you didn't just *receive* it, but that you also *read* it, or were the contents above your pay grade?" The man kept his face a cool mask, devoid of any emotion, not rising to my bait. But I could tell that inside he was practically ready to stomp his feet and throw a tantrum.

He nodded. "Obviously, I *read* it. Sarcasm is the lowest form of humor, by the way, but if I was facing my impending doom as you are, I might be flippant as well."

I shrugged. "Nothing else to say, then. As entertaining as this has been, I'm glad we got this all sorted out in a professional matter without me having to lay waste to your seven dwarves. So, can you be a good man and return me to the bar? I'm thirsty." I smiled.

He arched a brow at me in disbelief. "Only the guilty or disrespectful would refuse to elaborate on the report that you emailed us from the free email account hotmale17@hotmail.com."

I kept my face deadpan. "The other numbers were taken so I used seventeen. I had security issues, so set up the free account to get word to you and no one else. Seemed legit. My other choice was *naughtywizarddragonslayer@hotmail.com*."

Jafar quivered slightly. "We thought it was a prank until we saw the other reports. You should have come to explain yourself. For example, you didn't mention that black magic had been used on an acquaintance of yours. Peter. An old friend, if our intelligence is correct. Using dark magic on Peter to shut down his brain for a night is a crime punishable by death. That wasn't in your report. But I'm sure if you could produce Peter to tell us his side of the story, we could at least clear up *that* charge from your growing list of crimes. We have been unable to do so on our own. Almost as if he disappeared. Permanently. Which would also be a crime."

I hid a nervous gulp. How had they found *that* out? Worse, did they know it was me who had used the dark magic on Peter? "I never found out who did that, or else it would have been in my report."

Jafar studied me for a moment, a look of resignation on his face. "Anything else you forgot to mention?"

"No," I answered too quickly.

"Hmm. What of the bar fight tonight?"

Damn it. They had obviously been tailing me. "I didn't start it... on purpose. I spilled someone's drink. Then everyone freaked out. But it's okay. I *finished* it," I added with a dark grin. "Since when do bar fights concern the Academy?"

"Since it involved Nate Temple. The rumored author of the coalition of supernaturals here in St. Louis. Imagine our shock upon hearing that. One of our own was not only outing magic, but was forming a fan club with a renegade weredragon. At a national convention." I scratched my pathetic scruff of a beard.

"Well, that wasn't really my idea. I got bamboozled into it. I never said a word about it. To anyone. Check the records. I was declared an author of it, but nowhere will you find me talking about it to anyone. It was the Dragon Father's idea of putting me in a corner. And nobody puts baby in a corner." I glanced around the room waiting for a laugh. At least a chuckle. The mindless thugs stared back with their stupid silver masks. "Seriously? Nothing? Have you guys even heard of movies? Philistines!" I turned my back on them to face Jafar. "Regardless, it didn't work out too well for Alaric Slate."

"Yes. I'm glad you brought that up. We seem to have a new Dragon Father. A Black Dragon to be precise. A messiah of some kind to them. The Obsidian Son. And again, you were directly involved."

I shrugged. "St. Louis is a happening place."

"Enough. We have been requesting your debriefing about that whole ordeal for quite some time. Unsuccessfully. We demand an explanation of a great many things from you, young man." He paused, wrinkling his nose, suddenly distracted. Then his gaze locked onto me like a bird of prey spotting a field mouse. "What. Is. That. Smell?" I froze, not knowing what he was talking about, but all too aware that he literally had the authority to end me, right here, right now.

"Brimstone, Sir," another wizard hissed in surprise.

"What have you been up to, Master Temple?" Jafar asked, seeming cautious for the first time.

"Damn it! You're the second person to say that. Do they make Demon Febreze?" No one moved. "I was told that the whole city reeks of it, but that I smell the strongest of it. Test the truth of my words. I don't know why I smell like Brimstone. I swear it on my power."

The man studied me, finally nodding. I had sworn it on my power, so I literally couldn't lie about it. That was good... but it didn't mean I was safe. The smell wasn't why I had been kidnapped.

"Listen, I think we got off on the wrong foot. I don't even know this list of alleged crimes against me. My city went to hell a few months ago, and it was either stand and fight it by myself or let a group of weredragons run amok, murdering civilians. I never once saw the Academy show up to help." The thug who had kind of bonded with me shifted from one foot to another.

"Did you have something to add, Gavin?" The leader asked with menace.

The thug turned to his boss. "He's got a point. How can he be guilty if he was the only one here to fight the threat? Condemning a man for being a vigilante when it was the only course available to him isn't justice."

The leader watched his man for a few tense moments. "It seems Gavin's resolve is weak. Sympathy is not becoming in a Justice."

"Maybe it should be," he answered defiantly. I hid my smile. A partner in crime! I held out my hand for a fist bump. He ignored me, still staring at his boss. I scowled at the side of his head, lowering my hand.

The leader blinked. "We will discuss this later." He shot Gavin a scowl that brooked no further discussion. "Like Gavin already said, my name is Jafar, and I'm the Captain of the Academy Justices. Let's move our discussion to a topic of much interest to the Academy. The Armory your parents supposedly stashed away. The cache of supernatural weapons. This was the reason the dragons were here in the first place, correct?" I felt my faint glimmer of hope sizzle out and die like a bug colliding with a bug zapper. He seemed to enjoy the look of shock on my face, enjoying my mental backpedaling. "No need to deny it. We've all heard the stories of how they stole artifacts from other families over the years, robbing graves, or outright buying items that should have been handed over to us for safekeeping. Until now, we had presumed them to be rumors, but your actions, and those of the thieving dragons, prove otherwise. Now, you are going to hand it over to us, as should have happened in the first place. Where is it?"

I hesitated. Dare I hand it over to them? Especially since it was... mine? But was it? *Really*? Had my parents stolen the rumored items that filled this elusive Armory? I hadn't yet been able to prove that it was even real, despite everyone else seeming to know so much about it. But, assuming it was everything that everyone feared, did I have any right to hoard it? Did the Academy have any right to *take* it? Thinking of their wrinkly, power-hungry hands caressing those items hidden away by my parents made me cringe deep down inside... like a dragon hoarding his gold. These men hadn't been in St. Louis to help me with the dragons, but as soon as they heard about the booty to be gained, all of a sudden I was a liability, and they wasted no time in visiting my city to take the prize. But they hadn't given a damn about the lives that could have been taken if I hadn't stood up to fight back. And now they dared call the actions of my noble friends and myself a crime. Did the world need men like that with such potential weapons at their disposal? I decided right then that they didn't.

Jafar continued. "I can see your dilemma. Do you die a martyr in a vain effort to thwart me out of some ill-conceived notion of honor for your parents' murder? Get the last word in, so to speak? Or do you play it smart, and bow to your betters? The men who play the longer game. The Academy. The ones who make sure you can tuck your loved ones in at night?" His eyes twinkled as he watched me.

I looked from face to face, gathering strength, judging the Justices. Their silver faces were supposed to embody human emotion in an effort to prove their empathy for the greater good. But they weren't good. They were just another breed of political animals. "Do you sleep well at night?" I asked softly into the still silence of the room.

"Pardon?" Jafar asked.

"Do you sleep well at night? You know, when you climb into your jammies, drink a glass of warm milk in your impregnable castle that's guarded by hundreds of other wizards. Before you close your eyes, because you are tired from a long day of paperwork. Do you think about the people who were murdered in my city a few months back before sleep takes you? The ones who had no idea what was happening, what they were dying for, the ones who were brutally murdered by creatures out of a nightmare, creatures that even I didn't know existed. The innocents who lost their lives while you were safe in your ivory tower. The ones who died while you delayed coming to my aid. While you were playing the *long game*, as you put it, people were dying. You seemed to have no problem coming to St. Louis as soon as you heard about the Armory. So, where were you when my people needed someone to 'tuck them in safely,' someone to keep them safe from the monsters of the night?"

The other Justices fidgeted uncomfortably. Jafar sensed it. "That was your own doing. Without the Armory, your city would have been safe. If your parents had handed it over, as was their responsibility, none need have died. Which is why we're here, now. To prevent further bloodshed."

"Tell that to the slain. I didn't know about the Armory. How could the Regulars have known? Regardless, people died, and it had nothing to do with the Armory. The dragons were after a book, not the Armory. And you can sit there with a straight face and tell me that my parents *caused* the mayhem? No one even knew why they were being attacked. Two of our own, my parents, were *murdered*, and yet you did *nothing*. Who was left to prove a point to, when they were already dead? After that, you should have been here to help. That is your fucking *job*. To protect the innocent. Yet you failed. And now you kidnap me, accuse me of being a criminal for saving innocent lives, and dare have the audacity to critique *how* I saved those lives? Go sip your warm milk and get bent, Jafar. My city has no need for cowardly thugs."

Jafar's face purpled. "You dare speak to—"

"You're still talking," I said smoothly, tapping into the innate confidence of the Master Temple, as my father had taught me. "What part of *get bent* did you not understand? I've never seen this Armory. I don't know a thing about it, despite spending months trying to find the truth of it. But even if I did, I wouldn't hand it over to the schoolyard bully."

The Justices loomed around me. Some looked confused, not knowing whether to attack me, arrest me, or cheer in agreement. Jafar snarled back, "Your parents were criminals to deprive the Academy of these stolen items. We don't tolerate vigilantes, especially ones who hoard stolen power. These things belong in the care of wiser, older wizards – those who've been appointed as a collective think tank to keep us all safe. Your parents had no right to take this into their own hands through thievery. The Hubris! Especially not to pass on these stolen goods to an irresponsible wizard like you. Does this have anything to do with the Brimstone smell permeating your business? Have you perhaps already made a deal with a Demon to bring your sweet parents back in exchange for the Armory?"

Power exploded out of me. An explosion of pure force buffeted the Justices off their feet. One managed to cross his arms in some kind of warding spell and was merely knocked into a table rather than over it, but the rest were blown back into the wall none too peacefully. My outburst had been purely instinctual. "Say that again and I'll have your head spiked to my front gate. Consequences be damned," I hissed as Jafar struggled back to his feet. Several other Justices were also scrambling to their feet, gathering power to subdue me. "Enough!" I commanded, slashing all power from the room and tying it into a neat knot within a foot of my chest. I didn't exactly know *how* I did that, but no one was able to touch their power without getting into my bubble. They stared at me in what appeared to be blank shock, several masks having fallen askew. "That was in no way an intentional attack. Think how you would have responded to be accused of Demoncraft when your parents are not even six months in the grave," I spoke softly, genuinely, letting them know I was not a loose cannon. "Your boss has a big fucking mouth to dare speak to me so callously, and he deserved much worse than getting his clothes a bit dusty from a fall. I mean no harm to anyone here." With that, I released my hold on the loose energy of the room. I wasn't sure I should have been able to do that, but it had apparently been effective.

"You will pay for that, Temple," Jafar began.

"Shut it, old man. I've had enough of your wobbling dentures. They're giving me a headache."

Everyone stiffened at that. I had just mocked their boss. Probably not smart. But after surviving an Angel and a gang of Nephilim tonight, his title didn't impress me much. One of the Justices spoke up, a female. "If what you say is true, how did you just manage to stall eight wizards while so obviously drunk? That is not... usual. Despite your rumored strength, we are all battle trained and you just swatted us down like insects. How do you think that looks to us?" she asked politely.

"Probably like I'm a big fat liar." I shrugged guiltily. She nodded, holding out a hand to show her point. "But I'm not. I noticed my power surge after my parents' deaths. Are you implying that it's not normal for parents to gift their strength to their offspring, upon death?"

"That... isn't even *possible*," the woman spluttered, turning to face Jafar with a curious brow. He nodded in agreement with her.

"Then I truly don't know," I answered honestly. "Now, if you are demanding I turn over the Armory, go ahead and arrest me. I don't know how to give you something I don't have. Next, you are the second person to mention Brimstone. I was led to believe that the whole city reeks of it, but that I specifically smell of it. What would cause this? I've had absolutely no contact with Demons. To be honest, it never even crossed my mind. I never thought to seek out a Demon for an answer when no Demon was involved with my parents or the dragons. If you have any answers, please give them now. Otherwise, I cannot help you." No one spoke for a long moment.

"Well, of course you would lie about consorting with Demons. It's against the law."

My gaze froze his scowl. "You said I already broke a gazillion laws. If that's true, what's one more crime when you make it sound like I torture kittens in my spare time? And I already swore on my power that I didn't consort with Demons." He merely glared back angrily. I could sense that I hadn't turned the tables. I was still the enemy, and they were eight. I had merely shuffled the deck a bit on a few points. It was a start. "Now, all I've been doing is investigating the same rumors you've apparently heard. I've never seen this Armory. I've just been following any leads I could dig up. As you well know, my parents were murdered the same night that a thief broke into Temple Industries. The thief was not the murderer. There was a third party. I saw the video of the attack. That's all I know. I'm simply investigating the why, how, and who. Like any responsible CEO and son would do."

"Let's assume you're telling the truth," Jafar began. "It is now time for you to hand over any information you have amassed on this Armory, and come with us to the Academy to answer for your crimes. You are in our crosshairs, Temple. You have repeatedly risked our secret to the Regulars. You never requested our assistance with the weredragons, you allegedly used black magic – even if in self-defense, and a long list of others crimes." *So, they did know it was me that had used black magic*, I cringed inwardly. "Your parents' actions were also unsanctioned, and therefore must be reviewed by us. Pass on this information and it will go a long way into removing you from closer... scrutiny. Hand over your knowledge of the Armory."

"I can't do that. I don't have anything to hand over. But even if I did, I'm not sure I disagree with my parents. You haven't exactly shown much discretion or restraint in this encounter. Imagine if you had nuclear launch codes and I accidentally bumped into you. You threatened me after I told the truth a few seconds ago. How can you say this alleged Armory is safe in your hands?"

"How about we just sniff around for the source of the Brimstone, then?" he asked with a hungry sneer.

"Please. Be my guests. I'm just as curious about it as you are. I'll set up an appointment."

Jafar smiled a dark smile. "No need for the appointment. Do you not recognize where we are?" His smile stretched wider.

I blinked, finally scanning the room we were in. It was a warehouse. No, a laboratory. Several orbs of light filled the room as one of the Justices cast them against the far walls to stick like giant lightning bugs. Then I saw the symbol on the wall. We were at Temple Industries.

Shit.

"We have sensed Demoncraft all over St. Louis, and think it might have something to do with you or possibly this Armory. The fact that you smell so strongly like Demons after admitting to researching this endeavor seals the deal. Now, show us the entrance to prove you are not consorting with Demons."

"I can't," I answered softly.

"Can't, or won't?" Jafar asked with a disgusted snarl. Before I could reply, he continued. "No problem. We will just follow the scent of Brimstone."

Huh. I hadn't thought of that. But then again, I also hadn't sensed the Brimstone before tonight. If it seemed to be centralized here, it made sense why I stunk of it so strongly. I had been here almost every day trying to get into the Armory. But why did my company smell like Demons? Were there Demons imprisoned in the Armory? I shivered. That was a sobering thought.

I had no choice but to follow them. The female Justice who had spoken earlier drifted out of the laboratory and down the hall like a dog on scent. Going straight for the door I had seen in the video footage. Could they be on to something? After a few minutes, we found ourselves in the fated hallway, staring at a blank wall. I bit back a smile. None of us could see anything unique about this section of hallway, as the room had apparently been spelled invisible by my parents. The first time I had realized anything was here was when I had seen the video footage of the attack, as the camera had shown through all magical energies, revealing the door behind the spell. The wizard waved a hand and a blast of hazy heat seared the protective spell from the air, revealing the giant *Omega* symbol above a worn, ancient door that hadn't been there a moment ago.

She smiled back at my surprise, and then placed a dainty hand on the door handle. After a deep breath, she yanked the door open, and instantly let out a yelp of surprise as a broom handle struck her in the mask where her eyebrow would be. I laughed. I couldn't help it.

Jafar strode forward, peering into the closet angrily. "This doesn't make any sense. This is where the Brimstone smell is the strongest. A mighty being manifested near here, and spent a great deal of time on this spot. Repeatedly, in order to be this pungent. This must have to do with the Armory." I laughed even harder.

"I don't know what you're talking about. I mean, that mop is kind of dangerous, but I doubt it's been spelled. You can have it for ten bucks." Even though we were standing directly in front of the alleged Armory's entrance, it was nothing but a broom closet. I didn't know whether to laugh or cry. I had, of course, already tried this. The broom must have been spelled because I had been armed for bear and had still been hit in the eye. I didn't know how it was possible, but the room was guarded somehow. It hadn't been when Peter had broken in, but perhaps the spells had been ignited upon my parents' murder. Without warning, Jafar slammed me up against the wall. "Give me the Key to the Armory. It belongs to *us*."

"I will tell you one time to let me go. Exactly once. Then I will knock those fucking dentures out of your ancient mouth," I warned in a soft tone. His grip tightened. "Don't think I can't. I've already shown you my strength. Do you really want to look a fool in front of your crew? If so, I'm your Huckleberry."

Jafar's arm quivered. He was strong for an old man, but he finally let go. He turned away and took a few deep breaths to calm down. Then he turned back to face me. "Hand over the Key to the Armory." I had no idea what he meant by a *Key*. He must have noticed this from my blank stare. "Magical crossroads like the one required to keep something like this secret for so long require a Key. You must have it. Your power is double what it should be, what it was last time you and your parents stood before the Academy on your Name Day." That brought back the terrifying memory of meeting the Academy for my first time. The Name Day was an initiation day for young inherent wizards to be accepted for training. I hadn't gone to their school as the majority of wizards did, having instead been 'home schooled' by my parents. They hadn't been too big of fans of the Academy, or the politics that were indelibly imprinted on her students.

"Give us your information on the Armory, and we will help you. Refuse, and we will take it by force. It belongs in our hands – where it is safe – not with one family. Until you see the errors of your ways, we are assigning you a caseworker. One of our best detectives. He will shadow you at all times. Gavin?" The Justice who had seemed to agree with me stepped forward. I merely stared at him, refusing to give them what they wanted. Jafar nodded after a few seconds. "You leave me no choice then. Akira?" I flinched, having anticipated an attack from Jafar or Gavin. They didn't move. Instead, I suddenly found myself set upon by the entire ring of wizards, simultaneously. I struggled for a moment, but they were too quick for my drunken reflexes. A warm blanket of energy began to settle over my shoulders, and then it turned to a tingling, icy pain as it was yanked away. I roared, feeling as if the skin was being torn from my bones. Darkness and a swirl of sparks filled my vision as I crashed to my knees.

When I came to, I was still on the floor, heaving through a raspy throat. Jafar's face appeared before me. "You brought this on yourself. You've been cursed. From this day forward, your power will no longer restore itself. As you use it up, it is gone... *permanently*. This curse will remain in place until you choose to comply. You have three days. Then I will come back to hear your answer. I'm interested to see what happens if you use up all your power between now and then. Logic leads me to believe that if you use up your magic, it will be gone for good, even if we remove the curse, but we've yet to test it out. Regardless, the longer the curse rests on your shoulders, the higher the risk that the power loss will be permanent. This is fitting, as the extra magic you briefly wielded was not truly yours, and could have only been granted through black magic or Demoncraft." His smile mocked my fear. Was this really happening? What was I without my magic? Who was I if not a wizard?

I was about to find out.

"The only way we will remove the spell is if you comply. Or beg Gavin's aid. It most likely won't replace what was already taken, but will halt the continuous deterioration of your magic. Again, all we demand is your compliance – your pledge to serve the Academy – and access to the Armory. It's past time for renegade wizards to do as they pleased, unchecked. I think we are done here, unless you have something to add?" he asked with a leering grin. The other Justices looked troubled, but resolute. This was all they knew. They didn't know me. They knew their indoctrination into the Academy, and wholeheartedly believed the creed enforced upon them from such a young age. This was why my parents hadn't let me train at the Academy. At least Gavin looked uncomfortable. That was a plus, right?

One fear plagued my thoughts. "How am I supposed to rid my city of Demons if my power is waning and you aren't helping? You told me I should have asked you for help a few months ago, well, now I'm asking."

Jafar looked at me with the cold eyes of a bureaucrat. "Of course... right after you give us what does not belong to you. Or when you come crawling back to us in three days, powerless. It's up to you. In the meantime, Gavin will be there to make sure you break no further laws. Despite his insolence earlier, he's a firm believer in order and justice. He's a tough task master."

I cursed under my breath. "I'll figure it out on my own, then. Like I usually do. You know, this is the kind of action that makes wizards rebel." The words hit me as doubly true after my conversation with Hemingway at the bar. He sympathized with the Fallen Angels... sort of.

With a rustle of fabric, everyone disappeared except Gavin and I. "So, this blows," I muttered. Gavin stared at me through the mask that resembled a frowning face, offering nothing. "Are you not allowed to talk to the criminal?" I asked him.

He cocked his head slightly, and then tore his mask away. It disappeared in a puff of vapor. Huh. Fairy made? "My job is to make sure you don't break the law. We aren't friends. I'm not here to *help* you, but to *watch* you. To make sure you don't cross any more lines. I'm not saying that I agree with the Captain, but I also don't believe that what you did was right." I simply stared at him, curious. Silence brought on the best answers, I had found, so I waited. "Order is important. Laws are in place to keep the greater good safe," he said, vehemently.

"I guess the greater good doesn't include Regulars, then," I said softly, watching his face. He looked torn.

"Apparently not," he answered with a sigh. "Look. The current system is broken. I agree, but without a system we are animals. Something is better than nothing. What can we do?" he asked with a helpless frown. "You want to find your parents' murderer. I understand. I won't stop you. But let's get one thing clear. I won't let you hurt anyone in your effort to do so. Jafar was right. You caused a lot of trouble with the dragons. The Academy should have helped you. But even though they didn't, it didn't give you the right to take the law into your own hands. If all it takes is an ideal and the power to enforce it, how is a vigilante any different than a criminal?" he asked me with all the passion of youth. I sighed.

"Fine. Stay out of my way, and we won't come to blows." His shoulders stiffened. "Easy, kid. That wasn't me picking a fight. You can tell by the fact that there isn't a Gavin-shaped dent in the drywall over there." I waved at the wall with a wry grin that seemed to diffuse the situation. I tried to ease the tension. "About that curse... Was he literal? If I use up my power between now and my trial date, will I become a Regular?"

He studied me for a few moments, judging how much to say. "Jafar doesn't joke. Or exaggerate. He's old school. Very old school. When he says something, he means it. But he was also right when he said he's interested in finding out what would happen. Theoretically, the effects would be permanent. It was either cast the spell or arrest you. He did give you an option, if you recall. Now he can justify his actions to his superiors on the Academy Council. He's a thug, but an efficient and necessary one. He genuinely believes everything spouted to him from on high. And he's in charge of the Justices, so they believe as he does. Most of them, anyway..." he offered with a shrug. "Enough to matter."

I nodded, turning back to the door. One problem at a time. I'd figure out the magic thing later. Perhaps I wouldn't need magic to fend off Demons and Angels while I tried to hunt down my parents' murderer. Yeah, right. I tried the handle and got bopped in the head with the damned broom, just like Akira. I bit back a curse as I heard Gavin muffle a chuckle. I turned abruptly, casting out a hand behind him as if we were suddenly under attack. He bought it, turning with his own hand cast out defensively.

That's when I gathered my power around me – like a cloak in a corny opera – cackling for good measure as I prepared to apparate back to the bar, using my memory of how the Justices had kidnapped me.

"Muah-ha-ha!" I pulled the room around me like a blanket, reaching for the darkness hidden in the air at all times, and grasped it like my life depended on it, all the while firmly imagining myself back outside the bar from earlier. I hoped I had gotten it right. I heard Gavin curse as he realized my ploy. Perhaps it was my evil magician stage laugh that gave me away.

The spell wrapped around me before I thought about how much magic it might use. What if it used up all my strength? But it was too late. I was hurtling through space at an alarming rate like a plate of Jell-O on a roller coaster.

8

My feet landed firmly on the concrete just outside the alley where I had been whisked away from not too long ago. Confident that I wasn't about to throw up again, I cheered. "Boo-ya!" I fist bumped the air in triumph. It had worked!

The chill hit me fast after the warmth of the warehouse at Temple Industries. I took a deep breath of the frigid air, trying to sober up a bit. The street was quiet. I scowled in the general direction of where Tory's Mini Cooper had been parked, but they were gone. Since Gunnar and Tory had rabbited, I would just have to call her back and ask her to pick me up. Again. Hopefully there wouldn't be any more bar fights. I dared not go back inside. Even though it was warmer. I was sure Achilles wouldn't be pleased to see me.

The alcohol sloshed uncomfortably in my belly as I began to walk, but I let out a deep laugh. It took me a few seconds to truly comprehend the fact that I had just teleported. How freaking cool was that? But I was too scared to try it again until I got a better grasp of the curse that had been placed on me. What if I burned myself out? I shivered, nothing to do with the cold this time. Right. Dwell later. Get home now. With the important decisions made, I reached into my pocket and whipped out my cell phone.

And saw that it was dead.

I blinked at it. Had I not charged it? I had been forgetting more and more of these simple tasks as my sleep deprivation increased, which probably wasn't a good sign for my mental well-being in the long haul. Like an elevator button, I pressed the power button repeatedly, confident that persistence would pay off. But, like the elevator, it didn't.

I looked up, judging how far I would need to walk to catch a cab. I wasn't necessarily in a spot many cabbies visited of their own choice. That was fine. Perhaps a walk among the *Mardi Gras* patrons would help sober me up a bit. Give me time to plan my vacation with Indie. Then I hesitated. But I couldn't go on a vacation now, not with this curse. I scowled at nothing in particular. Damn Jafar.

I began hoofing it, striding drunkenly along with angry stomps of my feet. Jafar would pay for that, but for now, I had to get home. And to do that, all I had to do was make it to a main thoroughfare. Simple. I quickly realized that there weren't many people on the street, but I could still hear them off in the distance. They had most likely congregated to a more *happening* place. A place with more bare breasts than Achilles Heel. After all, starving college girls needed beads for food, right? Someone had to provide for them. I realized I was idly searching my pocket for beads, which brought my thoughts back to Indie. She was no doubt at Chateau Falco, wondering why I wasn't back home yet. I wondered if Gunnar or Tory had called her, terrifying her with my abrupt disappearance. If so, I was in for a rough night.

I spotted a mounted patrol officer near a streetlight a hundred feet ahead of me and began to walk faster. He probably hadn't seen me clearly yet. After all, I was standing in a vast pool of darkness between the dim glows of the aged lights. Neighborhoods like this one didn't have too serious of a relationship with the city's maintenance crew. More like infrequent one-night-stands. I smiled as I sashayed in a mostly straight line towards him. I wasn't in that rough of a neighborhood if a mounted police officer was standing watch.

That's when I smelled it.

Brimstone.

The little hairs on the back of my neck jumped to attention as my eyes squinted, trying to retain any night vision I could. How had I missed the odor? Especially after being told repeatedly that I was doused in it. But this time it wasn't me. This was fresh. I shook the thought away as a dry, raspy voice seemed to whisper directly into my ear. "Does the Master Temple need a ride?"

I jumped, twisting like a cat in midair, swinging my arms wildly in a carefully orchestrated defensive maneuver. Lucky for him, I missed entirely. But I knew it had to have scared him a little. It was a ferocious display of the pure essence of manliness incarnate.

"Was that a seizure?" his voice crackled drily, pretending not to be terrified.

I didn't speak as I continued to stare in the general direction of the voice, hoping to get a solid glimpse of what I was up against. In the darkness, a shape materialized out of nothing, as if un-shedding the very night from his shoulders. A Demon. He looked similar to a man, but was covered in gravel-like skin. Rough and rigid. Not scales, but like hardened, hundred-year-old, weathered lava that had cooled off sometime before the ice age. Other than that, he was a beautiful specimen of the health benefits in Hell. I scowled. "No need to act tough. I know I scared you."

"Yes. Very frightening, mortal. Almost made me lose my appetite." With a puff of ash, he was gone. I took a step back, questing the darkness, and flinched as his voice whispered in my ear again. Behind me. "Almost..." he drawled. I whirled, trying to keep him in my sights, wondering how he had moved so stealthily. He chuckled, a sound like snakes slithering through dead leaves in the fall.

Fall. Fallen, my subconscious repeated, remembering my encounter at the bar.

I shook my head and briefly wondered exactly what Demons were. *Were* they all Fallen Angels? Or were some just damned souls? I raised my hand. The Demon coalesced again, cocking his head before nodding for me to proceed. "What exactly is a Demon? Are you just some poor bastard who made bad life decisions, or are you a Fallen Angel?"

He snarled in fury like a doused cat. "Do *not* blaspheme against my master. You are not worth the breath the Fallen take."

"You guys breathe?" I asked in disbelief. The Demon merely stared at me. "I mean, I guess I just thought that it was kind of hot and ashy down in hell, and that there wouldn't be much oxygen. I'm not much of a geography guy, so don't take offense. I honestly don't know what's down there. I've heard it's... less than ideal though, you know? But what about *you*? You've *been* there!" I slowly began walking as I talked, hoping to get closer to the cop I had seen a moment ago. The officer seemed to be watching me curiously, or at least squinting in my general direction, but I knew that if the Demon saw his attention, the man was as good as dead. "So, what's your opinion on hell? Good, bad, need a bit of a renovation? You obviously find it more desirable up here, or else you wouldn't be here." Another step. "Are you even allowed up here without a hall pass?" Another step. I was now only a few feet away from the edge of the streetlight's glow. "Or would a summoner do the trick? Yeah. That could work. Someone calls you up here, you answer. No harm in that, right?"

"Everything alright over here?" a deep baritone called out. "Who are you talking to?" It was the same cop from outside the bar earlier. "Master *Temple*?" the officer barked in disbelief, finally recognizing me. Tory or Gunnar must have told him who I was after my disappearance. "What happened to your face? And where did you run off to earlier? Were you mugged?" He began to reach for his radio to call in backup.

The Demon hissed in annoyance, having realized too late that he had missed his chance to take me out with ease. Then the Demon slowly relaxed. "This could have been so easy. I just wanted to introduce you to my master. But you had to involve the constabulary. Now I'll have to paint the sidewalk with his blood. Loose lips sink ships. Give me a moment. I'll be right back so we can continue our chat." He grinned, gravel crackling off his skin as he exploded into motion. That's when the cop finally saw what I had been talking to. Before then, the Demon had stayed in the shadows.

To the cop's credit, he reacted pretty fucking fast. He moved his hand from the radio to his holster like Clint Eastwood. His gun coughed four times in less than a few seconds as the Demon hurtled towards him and his horse, Xavier. The majority of his shots rang true, judging from the puffs of gravel exploding from the Demon's torso. The horse dodged the first swipe of the Demon by sheer luck, but the creature rebounded immediately, tackling the officer from the horse's back like an NFL linebacker going toe-to-toe against a high school freshman team. I was on top of the Demon in a blink, not sure how I had moved so fast, grabbing him by the throat with one hand, my magic flooding through my arm for strength as I slammed his body into the streetlight twice in quick succession. Things inside of him cracked at the impact, but he wasn't down for the count. Then the horse reared up, planting an iron hoof in the Demon's chest and sending him clear across the street to slam through a glass window in a tinkling shower of broken shards. The building trembled. "Alley-oop!" I crowed. "Good assist, Xavier!"

He snorted a nervous breath, eyes wide, but didn't bolt. The cop was out cold, but was breathing steadily. I had no time, and didn't want to risk duking it out with the Demon when I didn't know how much power I would need to use to win, and with a cop who could possibly wake up at any second. Only to be brutally murdered the moment the demon recovered.

I did the only logical thing my fuzzy brain could think of. I... *invisibled* him. I cast a weak illusion spell over the cop's body, hiding all trace that he was lying in the grass unconscious, and then I grabbed Xavier's reins. I mounted the horse as I heard the Demon cursing from deep inside the building with feral roars of anger. Then we were galloping away into the night towards the masses of humanity celebrating *Mardi Gras*.

The wind in my hair felt good, even if it was cold. Freedom and escape always tasted great. A few minutes later, we were far away from the Demon, and people were everywhere, many pointing up at me – a man who was definitely not a police officer riding what was definitely a police officer's horse. That sobered me up a bit. What if a cop saw me? It wasn't grand theft auto, but it was most definitely a crime. I couldn't just leave Xavier to wander around on his own, though. Some drunken idiot would no doubt find the courage to mount the horse, and then cause some mayhem...

Heh.

Pot. Kettle. Black. Yeah, I get there eventually.

The only way forward was to take the horse to Chateau Falco and find a way to discreetly return him in the morning. I didn't have time to debate with myself. I had fire in my belly, an unconscious cop hidden a quarter mile behind me, a fine steed between my legs, and a Demon on my heels. I leaned over to a group of gawking sorority co-eds. "Beads, please." A pretty redhead flashed me. "No, you've got it backwards," I said with a grin. I flashed her my chest instead.

"Oh, *right*," she giggled, obviously hammered, before handing me a fistful of beads.

"You're Master Temple!" one of her drunken friends chimed in loudly. I nodded with a smile. Her group of friends froze in awe. Then they all flashed me for good measure. I laughed like a maniac, tossing half the beads back before spurring Xavier on. Time to go talk to Indie.

9

It took me a while, but it was a pleasant way to sober up, after growing accustomed to the rhythmic gyration of the horse's stride. And even better, I hadn't been spotted. Well, I hadn't been *stopped*. Plenty of people spotted me on my way home, which only added to the thrill.

I wished I could have snapped a picture of my Butler's face when I pulled up to the gated drive of Chateau Falco atop Xavier. It was priceless. Of course, I didn't offer an explanation, and Dean never asked for one. Despite this being a first, he was too proper to question the Master Temple. He merely asked if either of us needed refreshment. I patted Xavier's head. "Horsey want an apple?" The horse snorted. I guessed that was a *yes*.

I tied Xavier off to one of the cars left outside the garage, near a patch of withered grass. A silver bowl of sliced apples had been placed on the doorstep. I grinned, picking it up and heading back to Xavier. I fed him a few slices, and then walked him inside the garage to stay warm, as it was climate controlled inside, and definitely *not* climate controlled outside. I placed the bowl beneath him, but left the saddle on, unsure how to take it off successfully. I would have to see about returning him tomorrow. How the hell that could be accomplished discreetly, I didn't know. I put it on my mental to-do list for tomorrow.

Return Xavier to the police. Secretly.
Find parents' murderer.
Avoid Angels and Demons.
Take a bath to wash off the sulfur smell.
Find a way to remove Academy's curse.

Gain access to the Armory.

Maybe get some milk.

That settled, I stumbled in through the front door of my mansion, locking up behind me before wandering through the house in search of Indie. I tried to be quiet in case she was asleep. I knew it was late, but with my phone dead, I wasn't quite sure of the exact time. I very disturbingly recalled the day-terror I had experienced at the bar – Indie being gutted in front of me. Familiar with the sensation, I managed to shake it off, but my brain felt like it was swimming in a little pool of alcohol.

I reached the stairs, and was immediately assaulted.

I was struck in the face by what felt like a hot iron shoved to the hilt up my nostril, right on the spot that had kissed the wooden chair at Temple Industries. Light flared as my mind shattered into a million blinding shards. I was knocked into a nearby vase, shattering the priceless clay. I lurched to my feet, letting loose an explosion of raw force at a nearby fluttering curtain. It shattered the window, which immediately set off the alarm. The sonic wail could be felt on a molecular level. I clasped my hands over my ears, eyes watering freely as I scanned my proximity for my attacker. And I found it.

My assailant was an overnight bag that had rebounded off my face and into the curtain. Of all the dumb luck. I had apparently overreacted. Fresh blood poured down my face and into my mouth, which was becoming a familiar taste. I clutched my head, awaiting the pool of sympathy in which I would soon be swimming.

Someone was about to feel downright guilty for launching luggage at my face from up the stairs.

Indie and Dean both appeared on the landing in a flurry of stomping feet. "I'm so sorry, Dean!" Indie was yelling over the blaring alarm. Dean was on the phone. I couldn't hear him over the screeching alarm, which was making my vision practically wobble. A few seconds later, the alarm shut off, and a buzzing whining sound filled my ears in the absence.

"Thank you, that will be all," Dean said into the phone before hanging up.

My ears continued ringing and my face throbbed. Indie was halfway down the stairs, crying hard. Here was my sympathy parade. Soft words, a soothing icepack, and a smoking hot Indie to tuck Nate into bed after a long day, but not before a full minute of apologies for injuring her boyfriend. "Nate! Are you okay? What *happened*?"

I braced for the attack. Her hug hit me like a train. I, being all that is man, survived it. But only just. "Shh... It's okay, Indie. It's just a window. No big deal. Don't cry," I said with an amused smile that she luckily couldn't see as she sobbed into my shoulder.

"It's not the window, Nate. It's... Wait, your face is covered in blood! From the bag?" I decided to let her think she had caused it. Easier than explaining my kidnapping. "And why do you smell like a farm?" she asked. My hopes for sympathy began to flicker and die. Surely any minute now...

"Is the horse taken care of? Did he appreciate his supper?" Dean asked wryly.

I nodded, impatient for the world to bow down to my desires for a nice bed with my feet propped up. "Horse?" Indie asked. "What is he talking about? You bought me a horse? What in the world would I do with a horse? I mean, the gesture is very sweet, and I appreciate it, but I don't know a thing about horses. And isn't it a bit late to buy a horse? I thought you were meeting up with a lead at the bar? I'm confused." She looked horrible. Don't get me wrong. Indie was a goddess. Beautiful on a level that was astounding, but she didn't cry well. The pretty ones never do.

"I had to borrow the horse to get home. Gunnar and Tory rabbited."

"Borrowed from the St. Louis Mounted Patrol Unit," Dean offered helpfully.

"The *police*?" Indie burst out. I glared at Dean. He was ruining my chances.

"I can explain. And I'm fine. The bag just caught me off guard." They stared at me blankly. I cleared my throat. "But first, please don't worry about the window. It's really not a big deal." Dean harrumphed, implying that to him it *was* a big deal, as he would be the one to arrange for it to be fixed.

Indie finally stepped back, mascara pouring down her face. "It's not the window—"

"I'm fine. I already told you." She shook her head. My hopes for sympathy began to die by crucifixion, now. I sighed. This just wasn't my night. "The vase then. We can always find another vase."

"*Ahem.* We most certainly can't. That was one of a kind. As are most of the furnishings of the home. Macedonian, if I recall correctly," he added, nudging a piece of clay with his foot.

"Nate, it's not the vase either. It's—"

"Jesus. I'm an idiot. I didn't even think about it. Tory and Gunnar probably scared you half to death with their phone call. It's fine. It was just a bar fight. Then someone..." I decided to play it safe, "wanted to talk to me about something. They were pretty mysterious and kidnapped me right from under Gunnar's nose, which is saying something. But I got it all squared away. I—" Indie placed a finger on my lips.

"Bar fight?" she asked with a frown. I began to backpedal furiously, knowing I might need to resort to my beach vacation idea in order to escape unscathed.

"Well, yeah. Kind of. But Tory broke it up. Or broke *him* up. You should have seen it. She laid him out flat. No problem. *Wham, bam*, no more werewolf." I chuckled. "But really, it's nothing to be concerned about. My phone died so I couldn't call you. I'm sorry I caused you to worry. I have an idea though. I—"

"Nate. Shut up for a second. Gunnar never called. Neither did Tory." She didn't sound pleased about that little detail. "It's... my mother. She fell and hit her head. She's in the hospital. I need to go see her. "

"Oh. Is she okay? We can leave right now. I'll pack a bag. I... crap. Can I erase the last few minutes from your memory and go back to before I mentioned my night?"

"No." She was tapping her foot angrily. If she had been a cat, her tail would have been twitching like mad.

"Right," I muttered. So, no sympathy and no vacation.

"Bar fight. Kidnapped. Stole a mounted patrol horse. Why don't you flesh that out while I finish packing?" I sighed as she turned on a heel and headed back upstairs. Dean coughed into a polite fist as he sauntered off into the house, leaving me to my fate. My life.

It took us a few minutes to get to our room where Indie had been packing. I threw myself onto the bed, careful of jarring my face. I fidgeted for a few moments, trying to get comfortable as Indie bent over one of the suitcases. I finally gave up on comfort.

"What is the point of this?" I fumed angrily, holding up a torturous, sparkly throw pillow. I was lying on the bed, my head propped up against another of the expensive decorative pillows that sported even more tassels and sequins. No matter how I shifted, they bore into my neck like needles.

"They look nice."

"Pillows are supposed to *feel* nice. These feel like torture devices. Do you think Martha Stewart designed them while in jail? Out of spite?"

She shook her head idly as she continued packing. "They aren't supposed to be used. Just to look nice."

I grunted, rearranging the death-shard pillow. "So, your mom... What happened?"

Indie shivered a bit. "I'm not sure. She doesn't remember, but it looks like she fell and couldn't get back up. Luckily, a friend came over when she didn't appear for their weekly book reading club. They took her to the hospital where she's undergoing tests to make sure she didn't injure her brain. She broke her hip after banging her head on the kitchen counter." The Life Alert commercial that many found humorous on a dark, sadistic level very briefly replayed in my mind, but I wisely kept it to myself, even though I thought that it might have actually been helpful in this instance. This comment, I was sure, wouldn't help me. "I need to go to her. She's confused, not remembering exactly what happened." Indie's eyes were far away, as if recalling the event clearly in her mind. I wondered if she was telling me the full story or not. But I wasn't about to press her on the details. Because I wasn't *entirely* stupid.

"I understand. Do you need money? Want me to arrange the jet to take you there?" I asked, feeling helpless to make her feel better.

"No. Dean already booked me a commercial flight. It leaves in a few hours. He's driving me to the airport." She wasn't looking at me, and began stuffing a few more shirts into her suitcase in a distracted manner. I knew how she felt, having recently lost my own parents. It was numbing to realize that the ones who raised you were, in fact, mortal. Frail.

"He didn't book two tickets?" I asked softly. She hesitated, still not turning to face me. I propped myself to see her better, suddenly understanding. "You... don't want me to go with you..."

She threw her hands up in frustration. "It's not that I don't want you to. It's... complicated. You have enough on your plate right now. You haven't slept in how many days now? You look like death, and I don't think I want death looking over my mom in the hospital." Well, that was harsh. "Plus, I saw the news today..." Her tone was suddenly icy, shifting as adroitly as a figure skater performing a... well, whatever type of move figure skaters performed. All that mattered was that anger replaced her concern in the blink of an eye.

"Oh?" I answered dumbly, hoping she wasn't referring to the blurb I had seen at the bar about my involvement with the dragon attack on the Eads Bridge a few months ago.

But hope abandoned me with a sadistic chuckle.

Indie slowly stood, leaning against the closet door as she began to tap her foot. This wasn't good. "I distinctly remember bathing your injuries around the time of that attack. You never mentioned it."

"Oh, you know how the news is. Always jiving for a story..." I answered lamely.

"No, I don't. You apparently didn't trust me. You didn't tell me you fought that dragon on the bridge."

I shrugged. "Allegedly. They never found the body, and the city thinks it was a hoax. They also think I killed a cop at Artemis' Garter. Or that Gunnar did. Everyone is fighting for their ten seconds of fame."

Her eyes weighed my soul. "Did. You. Fight. A. Dragon?"

I shifted uneasily, finally giving in. "Yes," I admitted.

She looked hurt, and I suddenly felt like crap all over again. But her next response surprised me.

"Thank you, Nate." I tensed, waiting for the trap to close. But nothing happened. I finally looked up at her. She looked pleased. "That wasn't so hard now, was it?" she asked softly. I felt my shoulders loosening. She was right. It felt good. Almost as if I was the one who had placed so much pressure on the topic in the first place. Which was true. I had wanted to keep her safe, away from the truth so that she couldn't become collateral damage later, but my answer hadn't scared her at all. She seemed happy, relieved. I let out a deep breath.

"It's dangerous to tell you these things—" I began.

"You could tell the truth, you know, to the media. Prove yourself," she answered, interrupting me.

"Yeah. I could." Her smile stretched, slowly, surprised that she had gotten through to me so quickly. Before she could pounce, I continued. "And confirm Alaric's very public speech about me being a wizard and starting a coalition of Freaks? No thanks. That would bring back another, more violent, remake of the Salem Witch Trials. Not even considering what the Academy would have done tonight if they had believed that the coalition talk was legitimate."

Indie watched me intently, no longer tapping her foot. "Tell me about this Academy."

I hesitated. "I really shouldn't." Her foot began tapping all over again, making up for lost time. "Indie, they're dangerous. There were a lot of them tonight. They're like the Russian secret police from back before the Iron Curtain fell. Immunity from almost anything they feel justified about. It was only quick thinking that got me out of their version of jail tonight." I didn't need to tell her about the curse they had put on me. Indie had enough to worry about. Then again, perhaps their curse would drain me of magic. I would become a Regular and none of this would matter anymore. No more secrets from Indie. I shivered at that. But what was I, if not a wizard? Then I shook my head. Who was I kidding? The Academy would never let me walk free with everything I knew. Even if I was a Regular.

"Fine. If you're not going to tell me, I need to leave."

"Indie..." I began, holding up an imploring hand. "These guys are heavy hitters. You don't understand. They have all the sympathy the Nazis showed the Jews." She began to shove things into her bag with more force than was necessary. "I just can't, Indie. Not right now. It's too dangerous. You don't know what you're asking me. It's an unnecessary danger."

"You don't think I can take care of myself? Is this how it's going to be? You keeping secrets from me? That's a great foundation for a relationship, Nate," she snapped.

I frowned, growing angry. How did she not understand that I was only trying to keep her *safe*? "There are things that I can't talk about, Indie. It's got nothing to do with me wanting to tell you or not. I just can't." *Without putting you in grave danger*, I didn't add.

She was silent for a few seconds, shoving and rearranging items into her luggage. She finally spoke, and I wished she hadn't, "I think you need a bit of time to yourself. To clear your head." She turned to look at me, mascara still running down her cheeks.

I wanted to hold her, comfort her, but I knew that was the last thing she wanted. We were going to be in for a long debate tonight. She never dropped things. Especially this topic.

Which was why I was surprised when she spoke. "You need to get some sleep. I'm worried about you. All you do is hit up the bars or tinker at your company, when you really need sleep. Uninterrupted peace. By the way, any news from the bar about what your parents were hiding? Or who killed them?" she asked, somehow able to bury the topic from a few seconds ago.

I shook my head in answer to her question about my parents.

She sighed sadly, as if having hoped I had finally found something to help soothe my grief. "Nate. I'm beyond pissed at you. But I know you have a lot on your plate, and it's not your choice to be in the situation you're in. I know you would drop everything to come with me, but it's not what *you* need. Despite your brave look, I can see that you are close to a meltdown. You're always working at the office, picking fights at shady bars, and you never sleep..."

I sighed. She was too good for me. The night terrors *had* forced me to dive headfirst into work, digging for information on my parents' murder, the Armory, and my growing magical boundaries. Well, they *had* been growing, up until tonight. Now I was on the opposite end of the spectrum. I was on borrowed power. How long would it last? What were the long-term effects of the curse? I shivered, not wanting to consider them. But I knew I would find myself back in the lab in the small hours of the morning, tinkering, building, making things... anything to keep my mind away from the night terrors. I would deal with it later.

All I'd wanted to do was to take Indie on a vacation, to get away from everything for a while. To smell the roses, so to speak. Indie was watching me sadly. "Nate... Maybe if you got some sleep you could look at it from a fresher perspective."

I sighed. "I'll try."

She smiled sadly. "We started dating during one of the most stressful times of your life, and that stress hasn't left. In fact, I think it's only grown more intense. Not that I blame you, but I don't think you gave yourself the time you needed to clear your head. I don't want our relationship to suffer because you were repressing what happened with your parents. Despite Raego trying to help by keeping the dragons in line after the murders, you're still far from the answers you thought you'd have by now. It's eating you alive. We barely talk. You wake in cold sweats, murmuring, fidgeting, and even shouting, during the little sleep you *do* get." That was news to me. "Perhaps you need to talk about it with someone. Maybe you're experiencing a wizard's version of post-traumatic stress disorder." Which was exactly what I had been wondering earlier. It wasn't every day you went up against a harem of weredragons and survived. "You keep me sheltered, and that's not okay. I hate to say it, but maybe this break is just what we need. I'll go take care of my mom for a few days, and you can focus on yourself for a bit."

I punched the pillow, scattering sequins over the bed. White-hot anger burned through my veins. Anger at myself. And... guilt. Damn it. She was right. I hadn't been there for her. She was great. Perfect for me, but I had been an ass. Between the night terrors, dealing with the new mantle of CEO of Temple Industries, and spending every waking minute – which had been a lot – trying to find the truth behind my parents' murder had put a large strain on Indie and myself. I needed to get some perspective. I was also still concerned about her... Regular-ness. How could I bring her into my life of danger? Werewolves, the Academy, dragons, magic, and now Angels and Demons. It wasn't fair for her. She had once told me that danger wouldn't keep her away, but I had. I had kept blinders on her, not allowing her to get closer than necessary to my oh-so-dangerous life. To keep her locked up in an ivory tower, not providing her the necessary training she would need to defend herself. And it had inadvertently hurt our relationship.

Indie looked pained as she watched my frustration. She climbed up onto the bed and placed a comforting palm on my thigh. "Nate, I'm not *too* angry with you, or disappointed in you, or even mad about everything, really. I understand. What you went through...well, no one should have to go through that. In my eagerness to be near you, I might have done you harm. I should have given you space, but I wanted so badly to be with you that I let my emotions get ahead of me. You needed space to figure things out, and I didn't give you that. I blame myself. Now, you keep things from me. You don't talk to me about anything meaningful. You're scared. Scared to let me get close to the *real* you. Well, I think it's time for you to put your big boy pants on. You've got three days to figure out what you want."

Her timeframe momentarily chilled my blood. The same timeframe as the Academy's curse.

"If you want me, then you'll remove the walls you've built around yourself, or... we will probably never see each other again." My heart stopped as I stared at her in disbelief, which started her tears again. "I'm not sure that I could go back to being a mere friend after knowing what we have, *could* have, together. So, while I'm in Colorado with my mom, you need to really think about what you want. When I get back you need to tell me what that is. If you want me, you will tell me... everything. No secrets. I deserve that."

"Indie..." I warned, ready to tell her how bad of an ultimatum that was, how dangerous.

"Can it. I've been training with Tory and Misha. They've been teaching me how to take care of myself. Like you should have done." That stung. "You'd be surprised what I'm capable of. Regardless, this is just something you'll have to accept... or not. It's all or nothing, Nate." She smiled sadly at me. "Just know that if you choose wrong, I will be using everything Tory and Misha have taught me to hunt you down and teach you the error of your ways. Your magic won't save you from my wrath. They say hell hath no fury like a woman scorned. Well, you don't have to scorn me to see my wrath, just piss me off." Her pearly white teeth shone in the dim room.

I placed a hand on hers, nodding with a faint smile at her threat.

"And now, Dean is going to take me to Plato's Cave to get some sleep. You're still drunk, and after your shenanigans tonight, you don't deserve to see Nurse Indie." She winked darkly. I groaned. "Shush. You brought this on yourself. Bar fights earn no sexy time. And you have a lot to think about while I'm gone. You can start tonight. Absence makes the heart grow fonder, right?"

"You're a cruel, cruel woman, Indie. I know I've been keeping you at a distance, and you know why I do, right or wrong is irrelevant at the moment. But maybe I can work on my communication skills with you while you're gone. Would that break your rules?"

She assessed me for a minute. "Perhaps I should use this tactic more often. Look how malleable my Master Temple has become. I tell you I'm leaving for a few days and you're already asking if we can talk on the phone. You're a teenaged girl," she teased, pinching my leg. My face turned beet red as I began to blurt out an argument, but her laughter overwhelmed my arguments. She tapped her lips playfully, enjoying this way too much. "I would like that." She leaned forward and kissed my brow for a long second, careful of my nose, and granting me an expansive view of her cleavage, which she definitely knew she was doing. She was sneaky like that. "Good night, Nate. Sweet dreams..."

Her hair tickled my neck as she trailed a kiss down to my ear, breathing huskily before she gave me a playful nip. My pants constricted as my subconscious threatened to take control and pin her to the mattress and sequined pillows. She placed a constraining hand on my chest, shaking her head as if she could read my thoughts. I closed my eyes, the alcohol dragging them closed as mercilessly as if she had spelled me. I sensed the lights flick off from behind my closed eyelids, and then she was gone, dragging her suitcase out of my room.

I was peaceful for perhaps ten minutes, rehashing everything she had said to me, realizing that she was right about it all. Then sleep dragged me under like a sack of potatoes, and the haunting night terrors waited anxiously to welcome me back to their domain like an old friend.

10

I stood alone in a field of fresh wheat beneath a purple sky. Humid air pressed down on me like a thick, wet blanket. I was physically sore. Exhausted even. Wisps of clouds scudded low in the sky, hovering over distant peaks like campfire smoke, and the air tasted like damp earth. I sniffed the air idly, catching a faint hint of wood smoke. It wasn't overpowering, and somehow made me feel relaxed. I spotted a house on a hill, a quaint, primitive place one might find in ancient Greece, mostly stone, and surrounded on all sides by more fields.

A farmer lives there.

Something tugged at my memory, but the thought was gone just as fast. My memory seemed to do that a lot of late. Why worry about the house, when I was merely out on an evening stroll in such a peaceful place? I decided to approach the house. Perhaps I would make a friend so that the next time I walked here I wouldn't be lonely.

Loneliness. The word tingled up my spine like the fingers of death. Now why had I thought that? I wasn't lonely. I had everything I needed. I had a woman, a steady life of farming, and a strong boy to teach my trade to. I shook my head as I began to walk back to my house.

My house... that wasn't right, was it? Then I was smiling as I imagined my wife greeting me at the front door, my son rushing out from between her legs to tackle me to the yard where we frequently wrestled. I dropped the reins to the horse behind me, as well as the tools I used to cut the wheat as I began to trot up the hill. The house loomed before me, both larger and smaller than it could be in real life, but this *was* real life, wasn't it?

"Hello?" I bellowed as I reached the front door. "Papa's home!"

Papa? I would never use that phrase. I was a *Dad* kind of guy, wasn't I?

No one answered me.

Then I smelled it. A sulfurous stink tinged with frozen stone – a cold, hard smell with a... coppery after-taste. That was odd. I had smelled that coppery flavor before, back when my horse had injured herself in a fall. Why would it smell like horse up here? No, not horse... blood. I looked back in confusion, expecting to see my horse injured. But I was utterly alone in the field. I blinked. *Hadn't I just left the horse behind me?* I shrugged after a moment. I must have worked harder than I remembered. Nothing that a good wine wouldn't resolve.

I stepped up the creaky wooden steps only to hear voices.

A jeweled box stood in the open doorway, all by itself. Beyond the box, my wife lay motionless on the floor. My son sat on his heels, rocking back and forth. "*Open the box, open the box, open thebox, open thebox, thebox, box, box...*" he muttered to himself over and over again, his eyes wild like a stray dog.

"Son, what's happened?" I demanded. He didn't seem to hear me, brushing his mother's hair out of her eyes as he continued his chant. I couldn't understand. All I had wanted to do was to sit down beside my wife with my son on my knees as we played a game and ate dinner together. I didn't want any violence, any problems, I had no enemies. I only wanted to be a good farmer. That was all.

I looked further on and saw a man standing between two creatures, speaking quietly. Now that I was inside the house, I noticed that it was storming outside. But... *hadn't it just been pleasant outside?* I was so confused.

I couldn't hear the words, but I saw my son look up at me, with a sharp rictus of a smile. "*You mustn't listen to them. Open the box, open the box, the box, box, box...*" he muttered over and over and over, his voice sounding like nails on a chalkboard. I cringed, tuning out the almost demonic chanting. Something about this seemed all too familiar, but I couldn't understand why. One of the creatures handed the man something and the world exploded in a green hue. My son screamed louder. "The box!" His words had a physical sensation to them now, like my very eardrum was the chalkboard. I grabbed my ears in pain, glancing up in time to see the other creature handing a tall tool to the man. The tip gleamed silver in the incessant flashing of lightning raging outside. The world seemed to be tearing itself apart – the house imploding in an explosion of sound, wind, and distant screams from the blackest pits of hell. My son huddled over his mother as if protecting her from the insanity. I glanced over at his frantically pointing hand to see that despite the strength of the wind, which was pushing even me back from the door, the box lay unmoving as if bolted down. I clawed my body closer to it, dodging flying planks of wood from the destroyed windowsills I had made last year. The box glittered encouragingly. I heard the snap as of great wings lifting a bird to flight, and a *crack* of sound as if the world itself had opened up. Not daring to look, I dove for the box, my son screaming over and over again. "*The box, box, box, box!*" my fingertips touched the box in a flash of scalding skin and I managed to flick the lid open with my thumbnail.

The world went white and I heard my son scream as my mind liquefied.

11

I woke up panting hoarsely. Another night terror. Had I screamed out loud again and woken Dean? Then I remembered that he was either dropping Indie off at Plato's Cave or taking her to the airport, depending on how long I had slept. Then he was out of town for a few days as well. I was entirely alone. Even Mallory was getting some sand in his hair and sun on his face for the next week. Pure bachelorhood. I growled, squashing my puny pity with my mighty willpower. I would be fine. I didn't need anyone to watch over me. I was a grown-ass man.

"Yeah. You're a grown-ass man," I cheered myself on with pure testicular fortitude. I tried to smile, but the constriction of my face muscles almost made me cry out like a small child. My nose sure felt like it was broken. I touched it gingerly and winced, realizing my hands were raw with several hundred thousand tiny cuts from the broken whisky glasses at the bar. Oh, well. Nothing for it. I glanced at my phone – which I had somehow remembered to plug in before I fell into a coma – through sandy eyes. Six in the morning. I had slept for several hours, despite having felt like I had only just closed my eyes. It might have been the longest I'd slept in weeks. Even catching some much-needed horizontal, I had the familiar sensation of being hung over. I groaned at the headache behind my eyelids as I rolled onto my back.

What the hell had my night terror been about? I realized after a few moments of deep breathing that I had dreamt about Hemingway's story from the bar... kind of. It was as if I had been the subject of the story, but also an outsider. Then there had been the cursed box. Always the box. Every night terror I had revolved around me opening a box. The boxes changed in appearance, but they were always there, and despite the chaos of the dream, the only way to escape was to open it. Which was always terrifying, and hurt like hell. I wondered idly, as I had a hundred times before, if the box was a subconscious replacement for the music box Peter had stolen from my parents' Armory during his brief sojourn inside. But I didn't understand how that could be true. I had tested the box. Again. And again. And again, to no avail. There was absolutely nothing special about the box. At all.

So why did I keep dreaming about it? Was it because it was all the evidence I had about the Armory?

And did I dream about Hemingway's story simply because the grim tale had been on my mind? Or was there some deeper meaning? I shook my head, kicking my shoes off the covers – which I had slept on top of – to place my feet on the ground. Of course, it had nothing to do with a deeper meaning. It was a dark fucking story, and I had heard it a few hours before passing out. And my dreams had incorporated it into their mad funhouse of horrors. That was just how lucky I was.

I was simply over-stressed. At some point in the past week, I had deduced another possible reason for dreaming about a box. My dad had once used a different phrase to refer to the Armory... Pandora Protocol. It was how I had heard about the Armory in the first place. One drunken night when he had said it a few times under his breath. He had been speaking about a secret project at the family company, Temple Industries.

I later found out that his Pandora Protocol had actually come to fruition. His goal of using extreme measures to hide dangerous items of power. An Armory. It was real. Real enough for the Justices of the Academy to hunt me down to take it. My father had called his project the Pandora Protocol as a subtle nod to the 'secrets' hidden away from mankind inside Pandora's Box. Thinking on it now, I was merely glad that no one else had heard his pet name for the project. If the Academy had heard Pandora Protocol, they would have no doubt killed me on the spot tonight for thinking it was literal, when my father had simply been grandiose with names.

I decided to go to the kitchen and scrounge up some food. Maybe snort a line of Tylenol for both my headache and what felt like a broken nose, even though the mirror showed me it wasn't. I prodded it gently and winced at the insomniac panda staring back at me. The day was starting off well.

If I had enough time, I wanted to run over to Temple Industries to catch up on some work before Ashley and Gunnar left for Bora Bora. That brought a smile to my face. Gunnar was going to propose to Ashley in a few days.

Silver lining.

Thirty minutes later, my phone began blaring from the nightstand while I was halfway through my pushup routine. I jumped to my feet, ignoring the pounding headache, and snatched up the device. "Gunnar," I answered, breathing heavily.

"Nate! What the hell happened last night? We tried calling you for an hour. The cop thought it was one of your drunk tricks and wouldn't take us seriously."

"Yeah. I talked to him about it after," I mumbled. If saving his ass from a Demon counted for 'talking about it,' we were golden. "I was picked up by some Academy... detectives." Gunnar was an ex-FBI agent. He could relate to the term *detectives*. Not so much, *Assassin squad*. "They wanted a de-briefing on the debacle a few months back."

"Didn't you send them a report already?" he asked, voice tight, as if doubting I had ever sent said report.

"Of course. It was all done up official and everything… via email." Gunnar sighed. I continued before he could butt in. "They wanted a face-to-face. I gave it to them and told them where to stick any further inquiries."

Gunnar was silent for a moment. "Which means they didn't take it very well."

"Relax. They understand the picture now."

"That's odd. Because I don't even understand the picture." He didn't sound happy. "Anyway, I'm glad you're alright. I didn't want to call Indie without solid news, and I heard her mother is in a bad way. I didn't want to add to it. Neither did Tory, or Ashley." His tone grew more responsible. "You put us in a tough situation last night. You continue to keep things from her, which makes the rest of us keep things from her, which makes a big fucking wall in the trust department. I would appreciate it if you would fix that. Pronto."

I rolled my eyes. "On it. We talked last night. She's going to Colorado to take care of her mom. She basically told me to get my shit together while she's gone so we can square up for round two. At least I'm still in the fight at the moment."

He sighed on the other end of the line. "Nate… I'm not the king of relationships or anything, but perhaps your love life would be simpler if you wouldn't relate your talks to boxing matches. If anything, they could be related to tag-team wrestling matches. You're supposed to be on the same side, not squaring off against each other."

"I know," I admitted. "But—"

"She's a Regular. Yeah, you told me. It's becoming less and less of an issue. Look at Ashley. She's doing fine, and she's dating a werewolf. You're just some schmuck wizard. Really not even in the same league." I could sense his shit-eating grin over the phone.

"Bad puppy. No treats for you."

He grunted. "Ashley and I are flying out at 2 pm. Need anything from her before we are incommunicado for a week?"

"Nervous?" I asked seriously.

"Fucking terrified. Square me off against a silver dragon any day, but this… man, it's a lot of pressure on a guy. What if she says *No*, or waffles about timing? Now I know why you stayed single for so long. This commitment thing has a lot of pitfalls."

I laughed. "Yeah. But this kind of opportunity comes along once in a lifetime. You have to grab it and assert your dominance. Hump the hell out of that leg, know what I mean?"

The line was silent for a few moments. "Nate. I'm a werewolf, not a schnauzer. I don't always think like a dog, nor do I need references made to relate human interactions to their animal equivalent to understand basic concepts."

"*Who's a smart puppy? Gunnie! Oh yes, Gunnie is.*"

"Nate, you need to stop talking. Right now."

"Oh? You're packing for the most terrifying moment of your life. Proposing to Ashley on a romantic vacation. We won't see each other for at least a wee—"

The door to my room suddenly imploded in a shower of splinters as a fucking mountain of white fur tackled me to the floor, jaws snapping amidst a flurry of drool and ivory canines. The phone flew out of my hands to slam into the wall behind me. We tumbled into the nightstand, and I barely remembered my curse as my instincts threatened to take over and incinerate the threat with magic. Instead, I rolled with my attacker and used my feet to launch him behind me into the dresser. The white-haired werewolf sailed into the mirror, shattering it with a heavy crunch before bouncing off the dresser and rolling to his feet. He sat down on his haunches with a panting doggy grin.

"Goddamn it, Gunnar!" I snapped, panting heavily as I tried to calm my racing heart and ease my pounding headache. I didn't know how I had restrained myself from using magic. It had been a near miss. But the fear of the curse being permanent had flown into my mind at the last second. Then I had noticed the white fur. Before I had consciously made a decision, I had used simple grappling techniques to toss him from my personal space, but if it had been a real threat, I wasn't sure I would have been so lucky.

He shifted from his hairy werewolf form to his usual self – a chiseled, blonde-haired, mountain of a man. His long blonde hair hung around his bearded face, framing his pearly white grin. And he was completely naked. I averted my eyes, which made him chuckle. "I warned you to watch your mouth," he said, glancing at the shredded fabric dotting the floor. "His werewolf form didn't tolerate human-sized clothes very well.

"How the fuck did you get in here?" I answered, pointing at my wardrobe so he could nab a change of clothes.

He nodded in appreciation, opening the dresser as he answered. "Dean gave me a key a while back. To keep an eye on you and Indie. He didn't know who or what might come looking for you two after the Dragon ordeal." He cocked his head for a second. "Hey, why didn't you Hogwarts my ass like you usually do? I mean, to be honest, you kind of just got your ass kicked. Like a little man bitc—"

Before I thought about it, I vaporized like I had learned last night, vanishing from Gunnar's view to appear directly behind him. Part of my shirt tugged at me, and I saw a piece flutter to the ground where I had been standing a moment before, having been caught in the void of the teleportation spell and not making the trip along with my body. I used the momentum of teleporting – as it felt like riding a rollercoaster – to cold-cock my best friend in the jaw. The resounding *crack* was satisfying as his head snapped to the side and into the dresser before he crumpled to the ground. It only took him a second to shamble to his feet, eyes wide as he blinked up at where I now stood and where I had stood only a second ago. He rubbed his jaw, stunned.

"Okay... give me a minute... that was pretty... I mean, *wow*. What the hell just happened?" he finally asked in genuine awe.

I grinned back at his astonishment, slowly walking back over to pick up the piece of fabric that had been left behind, hiding my fear of both using my limited power for no real reason, and what might have happened if that little piece had been a more permanent part of me. "I just *Hogwarts'd* your ass," I said drily.

He blinked at me. "Is that one of the things you've been tinkering with in your psychotic research experiments? I've never seen you do that before."

"Kind of." I shrugged. "Learned it from the Academy thugs last night. Apparently, it's a secret of theirs. They weren't pleased I picked it up so fast... or at all. And hangovers give me a short fuse. Sorry. You all right?"

He shook his head as if to clear it. "Yeah. Just didn't see it coming. How far can you do it? Just in close quarters like you did here?" he asked, curious.

"No. I teleported from Temple Industries to the Bar after my talk with the Academy last night. But that took considerably more power than what I just did," I said more to myself, realizing that it had barely cost me any of my dwindling magic to clock Gunnar.

"Wow. Well, consider myself all apologized. I was just giving you a hard time. I don't think you pulled that punch at all, did you? Rage issues much?" he teased. Werewolves could take a lot of pain and keep on ticking. Anyone else would have been out cold from my punch. But Gunnar was one tough son of a bitch, and I was glad to have him on my side.

I ignored the comment as he began to throw on a pair of slacks and a tee from the dresser. I kept clothes in his size throughout the house for events such as this when he needed to replace a destroyed wardrobe. "By the way, why did you send Tory into the bar last night instead of coming in yourself?" I asked.

"It was a powder keg in there, Nate. I can't believe you could stand it, what with how much loose energy was dancing around in there. I could even sense it from outside. I thought things like that messed with wizards."

"It does," I said, nodding, although I hadn't particularly noticed it last night. "I've just been so tired lately that it must have slipped my mind. I'm kind of off my game. I've been somewhat... reckless lately," I admitted.

Gunnar grunted. "That's why I sent Tory in there. My presence would have just instigated a territorial fight from the wolves. Also, Tory isn't necessarily an enemy of any of the creatures in the bar. She's just a woman with extraordinary strength. A supernatural Switzerland to the creatures inside the Kill." I was just glad it had all worked out. "Which leads me to wonder why you were in a Kill in the first place. You. Stupid. Bastard." He enunciated each word with tightly bottled frustration.

"Easy, swear-wolf. Virgin ears here."

Gunnar merely stared harder, if that was possible. "Looking for answers again," I finally explained, plucking my phone up from the carpet. The screen featured a spider web of cracks, eliciting a grumble of displeasure from my throat as I held it up to Gunnar, hoping to change the topic.

He shrugged. "You're good for it."

I pressed a button and saw that I could more or less still make out important details. I tossed it in my pocket as Gunnar continued. "Now, back to the important stuff. I thought you gave up searching for information after you were booted from several bars. For life."

"Nah. Can't sleep, so I hunt."

There was a long silence. "You're still having the nightmares?" I nodded slowly. He shook his head in disbelief, part concerned, part angry that he couldn't do anything to help. "Well? Did you discover anything helpful?"

I hesitated. Did I want to bring him into this? Angels were in a league of their own. I knew I could trust my friends, but I didn't want them in over their heads. I had no choice, but they did. "Nah," I lied. "But I've heard a lot of stories about my parents lately. Apparently, an impressive number of people considered them scoundrels. Not as many as praised them, but still... enough to make me reconsider."

"What do you mean? Why would they say anything bad about your parents? They were saints," Gunnar growled, instantly defensive and territorial. I smiled to myself, turning away.

Because my parents had helped Gunnar, and many, many others, with various magical maladies. Gunnar was no longer a slave to the cycles of the moon, thanks to them. They had given him a rune tattoo that allowed him to shift into a werewolf at will. Most other werewolves couldn't do such a thing. Unless they were super powerful or super old. Regardless of shifting at will or not, almost all werewolves had to shift during the full moon. But Gunnar didn't. All because my parents knew of an odd rune that allowed him to master his inner wolf.

Now that I thought about it, how the hell had they known how to do such a thing? If it were common knowledge to wizards, I would have heard of it at least a few times. Wizards would have sold that to trusted werewolves for a high price. Or maybe in exchange for an alliance. But I had *never* heard of a wizard doing a spell like that for a werewolf. Odd. Where had my parents learned it? And that wasn't the only uniquely magical cure my parents had given back to the community. In fact, it was one of *many* magical cures they had given out. Almost as if they had access to knowledge most wizards didn't. A shiver ran down my spine as the obvious answer came to me. The Pandora Protocol. The Armory.

I spoke over my shoulder. "They allegedly stole some things a time or two, always from old families. Random things. I've heard them described as heirlooms, paintings, and even ancient knick-knacks with no known nature or origin. Every story is different. But then other people denied those same accusations, admitting the items had been fairly purchased. Regardless, these stories are a decade old. Nothing useful to me, now. Still, it's an odd thing to hear. I think these informants all assumed that if they told me something juicy I could owe them a favor. I quickly discouraged that line of thought, which got me kicked out of the other bars. Everyone's just scared after Alaric's speech at the Eclipse Expo about outing magical creatures. They fear that if I give in, like Alaric told everyone I would, they would all be outed as Freaks, too. The world is crazy lately," I said, raking a hand through my hair.

It was almost as if the deeper I dug, the more I realized that I hadn't known my parents at all. They were public tech-tycoons during the day and devoted parents at night. All while being full-time wizards with secret agendas at their own company. And now I hear they were part-time thieves? But why? Had they amassed an armory of random weapons and artifacts in their Pandora Protocol? And what was the Titan warning on the video feed I had seen?

I could sense Gunnar still staring at me with concerned eyes. It ticked me off. I didn't ask my friends to look after me. I was fine. "Anyway. Enough psychoanalysis. How are you?"

"Great. Nervous about this whole proposal situation, though." I smiled, but he changed topics back to me. "It's probably a good time to get out of town, Nate. *Mardi Gras* is nuts in St. Louis. Maybe a vacation is what you need, too." I know what he really wanted was for me to stop digging into the darkness that was plaguing me lately. Maybe he was right. It would have been nice to get away, as I didn't want to get mixed up in Angel business. Or Demon business. But the Academy had put a stop to that with their curse.

I was being forced into a lonely stay-cation.

Gunnar continued. "Our new gig as black ops wizards – or supernaturals – could get dicey, so I'm taking a vacation while I can." He and Ashley weren't wizards, but since the world at large considered any Freak to be a wizard, our team's nickname had worked for me, although I wasn't betting on any government contracts in the near future, if ever. More just neighborhood vigilante jobs.

"I'm happy for you two." I was doubly glad I hadn't mentioned the Angel in the bar, or the Brimstone stench. If I told him what had happened in the bar, he would no doubt cancel his plans. And Ashley would agree. They were the best kind of friends. But I couldn't do that to them. I could handle this on my own.

Which reminded me...

"You have time to drop me off at Temple Industries before you leave, right? Dean is taking Indie to the airport, and then he's hopping on his own flight out of St. Louis. He hasn't left the Chateau in a while, so I gave him some time off. Mallory also left to get some sun and sand, so I don't have a ride. Plus, my headache will probably impair my vehicular control. I'd hate to start off the day with an accident."

"Yeah. Lately, with your temper and lack of sleep, an accident could easily turn into vehicular manslaughter." He paused, studying me. "You could always take your new horse," he added with a scowl of disapproval.

I blushed. "My horse?" I asked innocently.

"Yes. Xavier, if I remember correctly." He was tapping his foot. "That's a federal crime, you know. I don't even want to ask how it happened. Plausible deniability." He folded his arms.

I threw my hands up. "I didn't have a choice. I'll say this, though. My actions saved two lives. So, I'll take the consequences any day. But I'll have Dean return him as soon as possible."

Gunnar grunted for good measure. "Fine. I'm already packed and Ashley is at the company wrapping up a few loose ends. Workaholic," he said, rolling his eyes. "This actually saves me time. We can leave for the airport from there."

"Good. I have one more pit stop to make on the way."

He studied me skeptically. "Okay... where?" he asked warily.

"The church on the way to Temple Industries has a fountain outside, right?" Gunnar blinked before slowly nodding. "Good. Take me there. I fancy a dip. Care to partake in the morning's debauchery?"

He cocked his head. "Nate. You do know its seventeen degrees outside, right? I think I'll take a rain check."

"Seventeen..." That was the exact number of minutes Peter had been inside the Armory. "Of course," I mumbled to myself. "I'll be quick," I added hastily before he could question my comment.

Gunnar shook his head. "It's your funeral."

I smiled, preparing myself for the chill. "Not my funeral today, Gunnie."

This was one thing on my to-do list I could cross off... "How's the rest of the gang?" I asked idly, finishing up my pushup routine as he dressed.

"Raego is leaving for Europe to strengthen his rule. Tory and Misha are going with him to help, or maybe just so Misha can show Tory her homeland. It's cute. You should see Tory wrestle with Misha's... *dragonlings*." We hadn't known what else to call them. "Disturbing, but cute." He smiled. "I can't blame them." His gaze grew thoughtful. "With us all out of your hair, maybe you'll get time to clear your head. Get some real sleep." He assessed me like only a long-time friend could. "Or just get roaring drunk in a dangerous bar. I think they're both the same to you, lately."

I wrapped up my workout, feeling marginally better, grunting agreement with his comments. As I got dressed for the day, I found myself hoping that I wouldn't be attacked by one of my most recent enemies before lunch.

12

Greta smiled smugly. "You look like a raccoon," my secretary said, pointing at my rapidly forming black eyes. Then her eyes roamed with distaste down to the puddle at my feet, and continued back along the trail of wet boot prints I had left from the entrance. "A drowned raccoon. Or a slug."

I very carefully stifled my anger, not rising to the bait. "Don't change the subject, Greta. For the last time, I find it highly doubtful that this found its way to my mail cubby via regular mail. There's no stamp on it. This is junk mail. Or a solicitation, which is against company policy..." I warned.

"Well, if you consider your eternal soul to be junk, then you're technically correct," she answered drily. After a short silence, her eyes grew softer, motherly. "Just read it. You might learn a thing or two." With infinite tolerance, I pocketed the religious tract and didn't crumple it up to throw in her face. She meant well. Really. I just didn't take it well when people told me in a roundabout way that I wasn't a good person. The title read *Jesus and You, Your Only True Friend*. Gunnar very wisely kept a straight face.

We walked past Greta's desk and into my office. I instantly froze as my eyes settled on the room. A giant cross was nailed to the wall behind my desk, at least six feet tall and extravagantly detailed. On my desk sat a fresh cup of coffee inside a mug I had never seen before. A depiction of Christ adorned the coffee mug handle. "Greta?" I called out warningly.

She shuffled into the room on arthritic hips with a curious look on her face, not appearing to see anything amiss. "Yes, Master Temple?"

"It seems someone took the liberty to find me the actual cross that Jesus was crucified on, and then decided to hang it on my wall. And I seem to have a new coffee mug."

"Oh, goodness. I thought perhaps you had purchased the mug after reading the various pamphlets you had received. I don't know how the Cross got up there, but perhaps reflecting on his sacrifice might ease your stress. Touching Jesus daily might help also," she offered, pointing at my mug.

I stared at her in disbelief, then the handle of the coffee mug. "I'm sure palming his crotch would be a religious experience for some, but to me it's merely distasteful."

She prickled up indignantly. "Well, if I were in your shoes, I would take into consideration that someone must care for you very deeply, and I would cherish these gifts for that reason alone. Someone obviously holds a great deal of concern for your soul, despite your constant mockery of their faith." Her face was red, ready for me to command that the no-doubt expensive artifact be torn down and tossed in the trash. Religion was everything to her, and it seemed her sole purpose in life was to 'Save' all the lost souls around her. Namely, me. It was sweet... and annoying. Plus, I was sure she had expensed the extravagant purchase to Temple Industries, meaning I had paid for it myself.

I wanted to lash out on the old woman, but knew it would do no good. I sighed. She was right. It was done with the best of intentions. "That will be all, Greta," I answered in defeat. "Why don't you take the rest of the day off? Didn't you mention a charity event you were planning to attend after work? Why don't you go there early and help them set up? You deserve it," I said with a forced smile on my face.

Her beady eyes assessed me with distrust for a few seconds before slowly morphing in humble victory. She very wisely didn't press her luck, and instead turned to grab her purse and leave for the day. She called over a shoulder. "One of the interns found a broom closet he swears was not there last week. I set him straight, but you should look into it. He said it had an odd symbol carved above the door. Interns should be seen and not heard," she grumbled more to herself. My shoulders stiffened slightly, but she didn't notice.

"I'll check it out. Have a great rest of the day." She grunted back, not looking at me. Then she was off. As soon as she was out of sight, I instinctively reached to my magic to tear the cross down from the wall, but an icy chill of warning stopped me at the very last second. I couldn't waste my magic like that right now.

Instead, I called out to one of the minions in a nearby cubicle. "You." I pointed. It was the same man that I had terrified a few months ago, when I had first met Greta. The kid was as unconfident as I had ever seen. I needed to help him grow a backbone, but working for someone like Greta seemed to make that impossible. "Take down this monstrosity immediately. Then place it behind Greta's desk."

The kid stared at me, dumbfounded, before finally stammering an answer. "Um... you're my boss, but... she will literally kill me if I step foot into her Jesus-Zone. Then she will kill me again when she sees that I put the cross she gave you behind her chair. It's bigger than she is," he added nervously.

"Does she really call her workspace the Jesus-Zone?" I asked in disbelief. Surely, he was exaggerating. But he nodded, a sober look of fear on his pale face. "Tell her that you caught me trying to remove it and before I could throw it away you decided to put it in the only safe place on the floor – the Jesus-Zone." I winked at him. "This is a lesson in politics. Finding a way to work with conflicting orders to your best advantage. It's very useful information to know." The kid shivered, doubting his future as soon as I was not there to protect him from the saintly secretary.

"Gunnar, let's go find Ashley." He nodded, chuckling under his breath as we headed to her office. "Can it. It's really not that funny. It's not like I'm a horrible person or anything. Where does she get off passively telling me that I'm such a wreck that I need an intervention?"

"It's very... touching," he answered, his laughter fading. Great, he was siding with her. This was ridiculous. Why was everything turning against me lately? I didn't need to worry about religion when I had literal Angels scouting my trail. I was probably closer to Heavenly scrutiny than Greta would ever be... I pondered that for a few steps. Maybe she had a point.

Nah. I was probably fine.

I was here to study the Armory if I could find a way inside. That was all. Then I could be on my way. Wherever that was. I still shivered a bit from the dip I had taken in the fountain on the way here, but it gave me peace of mind to know that perhaps one problem was now gone. However, my damp clothes didn't feel very pleasant at the moment.

I began pondering the Armory as we walked in silence. I had spent practically all my time at Temple Industries trying to find some solid information on the secrets that were allegedly buried inside. But I had come up with nothing. Oh, sure, I had clarified a few points, but that was all.

Point one – Peter had broken inside the Armory the same night my parents were killed. The security camera that seemed omnipotent – able to detect the magical abilities and identities of almost everyone in town – hadn't known what to make of Peter, as he had been shrouded in living shadows, proving that he had used something to trick the camera and disguise himself. I had found proof of this after sneakily raiding his office once things had calmed down a bit. He had stolen a ring from my desk that helped one become forgettable, a spell of sorts I had been tinkering around with at one point in my life. It must have sat in my desk for years at Plato's Cave before Peter swiped it. After seeing the video, and after the chaos had died down, I realized that the distortion in the video had paralleled the forgotten spelled ring I had once made. I must have mentioned it to Peter at some point, as he had made it a priority to steal it from under my trusting nose.

So, Peter had broken into the Armory and returned with an apparently useless music box.

Point two – some unknown person had simultaneously broken into Temple Industries to kill my parents. I now knew that neither party had been affiliated with the dragons. That had merely been a coincidence that the late Alaric Slate, then leader of the dragon nation, had capitalized upon. Peter had immediately tried to sell his music box to Alaric in exchange for the gift of magical power. It hadn't worked out for anyone, and I had gotten the music box back.

So, now I knew that some third party had been after either my parents or the Armory. Immediately after Peter's intrusion, my father had locked down the room and then been killed by said third party, leaving behind a cryptic message on the security feed for my eyes only. Which made no sense to me. Even now. Then the word *Titan* had popped up on the feed, and the video ended. No one had been able to enter since, even after we removed the security door my father had activated. But if the additional security was now gone, and it was the same as it had been when Peter so easily opened the door, how could I not enter? It was baffling. Even more concerning was that now, thanks to the Justices, the illusion hiding the door was gone, leaving it visible to anyone.

Ashley appeared from around a corner, carrying a pile of paperwork in a manila folder. She smiled hungrily at seeing her beau, Gunnar, and then more professionally at me. Then she froze. "Jesus! Your face!" she blurted.

"Better not let Greta hear you talk like that or you'll get an avalanche of these on your desk." I tossed her the religious tract.

She caught it easily and then glanced around my shoulder, as if verifying Greta wasn't here, before deftly adding it to her manila folder. "Been trying to save you again, eh?" she smirked. I nodded. "So, did she hit you in the face with a Gutenberg or something?"

Gunnar lost it, his laughter filling the hallway. I scowled at the two of them. "It's not that funny, but yes, you could say Religion punched me in the nose."

She frowned at my choice of words, but let it go. "What brings you two rogues here?"

"Easy, you two," I muttered before Gunnar could say anything gooey and romantic. He didn't look pleased at my efficient slaughter of the mood.

"Why are your clothes wet?" Ashley was frowning at the trail of wet footprints I had left behind me. I had used a quick effortless spell to squeeze out the majority of the water from my wardrobe, but some still remained. Any stronger a spell than that would have used too much power.

Gunnar piped up in response to Ashley. "Don't ask. He's completely mental. Howard Hughes mental. He went for a swim in a holy fountain, but wouldn't tell me why."

They both turned to me, hoping I would elaborate. But I didn't feel like doing that. It would only bring about more questions.

I began walking down the hall, calling over my shoulder. "Shall we?"

Ashley and Gunnar shared a look before following me. I guided us to the door that had started it all. I was both excited and terrified to gain entrance to the Armory. I wanted, *needed*, to know what was inside, but wasn't sure if I was ready to handle it. *Anything* could be in there. It could in fact be the equivalent of nuclear warheads, as the Academy feared. What would I do if that were the case? I wanted to ask myself what my parents would do, but that was obvious. They had hidden it away, after all. I shook my head, noticing Gunnar and Ashley watching me discreetly as we meandered the halls.

Did the room have something to do with my night terrors, and their recent evolution into daymares? They had started immediately after the dragon attack. Was it some form of lingering effect of the dragons' mind-magic? But no, Raego had informed me that it wasn't. Unless... he was in on it. I shivered. If I couldn't trust my friends, whom could I turn to? I had even begun to look into the myth lore of Pandora – stretching for leads a bit since my father had named the project Pandora Protocol – but I had run into nothing substantial. Pandora had died, or disappeared, and no one had heard of her or the box – or urn as most stories elaborated – since. Maybe it was just an allegory – an example – of powers left best untouched that my father found fitting as a title for his secret project. A project that involved dangerous powers he wanted out of the hands of the community. What better name than Pandora? I had even pondered going to talk to Asterion – the Minotaur – to see if he knew anything about the myth. I mean, he would have been around during her origin. If anyone knew her story, he would.

Gunnar broke the silence. "So, made any new gadgets lately?" he asked me curiously.

I looked over at him, then away. I didn't feel like talking about it, as Indie's harsh words about me ignoring her for my 'tinkering' were still fresh in my mind. "No."

Which was a lie.

It was all I had been doing since the dragon attack. Every time I tried to sleep, the night terrors were there to welcome me. So, I tinkered. And I had managed to create some truly incredible things. It was as if my sleeplessness had awoken the Leonardo da Vinci hiding inside me.

Raego had provided me with a literal truckload of silver scales from the dragon I had killed over the Eads Bridge, and despite not knowing what I wanted to – or could – do with them, I had used them to create quite a few useful tools. The magical boost in power I had received after my parents' murder had fueled me to new heights of creativity I was sure no one had anticipated, but I needed to be careful with those secrets. If anyone found out what I had been making, they could use my friends against me to divulge those secrets. Very dangerous secrets. Secrets that might become necessary if my powers failed me and another Angel or Demon knocked on my door.

We entered the hallway that housed the now visible door to the Armory. A crude *Omega* symbol was etched into the stone over the frame, causing me to shiver. That symbol translated to *the end*. We were just down the hall from where I had been abducted by the Academy less than 12 hours ago.

"Um. Why is it out in the open like this?" Ashley asked nervously.

"I removed the spell hiding it, obviously," I muttered. Gunnar eyed me doubtfully, remembering my mention of the visit from the Academy Justices last night.

But, like a good minion, at least Ashley accepted my answer. "We still don't know how to enter, but your parents might have hidden their trail. They must have had some kind of key," she offered cautiously.

"The Academy goons mentioned something about a key, also. They seemed to think I had it on me, but I have no idea what or where it could be."

Ashley raised a brow. "Academy? As in, the secret wizard police?" she asked with growing alarm.

I nodded. Gunnar looked more concerned by the second.

"Maybe we need to stay in town for a while to help you, Nate," Ashley said, ever the corporate soldier. Gunnar's gaze crashed and burned with both the resigned weight of responsibility to a friend and the dying dreams of his impending proposal. I couldn't let that happen.

"No. You two need a break. They're just fact-finding at the moment. They want to know what happened here. And they took their sweet time coming to ask. I don't think they're in much of a rush or they would have come knocking on my door sooner. I think they're just trying to tie up loose ends for documentation purposes. They didn't really seem that concerned."

Gunnar's eyes weighed heavily on mine, but I could tell that as much as he wanted to stay and help me, he wanted to propose to this amazing woman even more. I couldn't blame him. He had spent his whole life looking for the perfect woman, never sleazing around, but merely waiting. This could literally be his once-in-a-lifetime chance at claiming true love. If I told them anything about the curse the Academy had placed on me, or my new parole officer, Gavin, I would never get rid of my friends, and Gunnar would never propose to Ashley. There are times when my life just really sucks. I could definitely use their help, but *my* problem did not constitute *their* problem.

Thinking of Gavin out there somewhere in my city, scouting me unseen, made me nervous all over again. Maybe he was using an Academy trick to watch me even now... I shrugged that one off as a bit excessive. They wouldn't have needed to confront me if they could do that. I hadn't noticed anyone trailing me on the way here with Gunnar, but *lack* of proof of being tailed was not proof that I *wasn't* being tailed. It's only paranoia when you're wrong.

I quickly realized that having asked to see Ashley might actually destroy Gunnar's big plan. I had to get rid of them. Now. I would have to figure this out on my own.

"Listen, guys. I'll be fine for a few days. Indie's out of town with her mother since the accident, and I could really use the *me*-time to clear my head. I know I've been impossible to be around lately, and to be honest, I'm not sure I dealt with my parents' murder the healthiest way."

"I don't know. Slaying a harem of weredragons felt very therapeutic to me." Gunnar grinned.

I smiled back weakly, nodding. "True, but I've got a lot of Demons, you know?" *No pun intended*, I thought to myself. "And I need to find a way to banish them before it costs me my friends, the company, or... Indie." Ashley's eyes glistened sympathetically as she laid a hand on my shoulder for support. I was definitely speaking literally *and* figuratively, but they didn't need to know that.

"Don't worry, Nate. You'll figure it out. You always do. Maybe you're right. No distractions for a few days. Clear your head. Tinker around a bit, and we'll be back to clean up the mess in no time." I scowled back and she smiled mischievously through still damp eyes. "You will barely even know we're gone." *Right,* I thought darkly. I would be too preoccupied with Angels, Demons, and the Academy to realize that my only allies were thousands of miles away, getting engaged. "If it wasn't for Gunnar winning those airline tickets online, we might not ever have decided to go. Admitted workaholics." She smiled, winking at Gunnar. I noticed Gunnar's gaze shifting to mild concern as he studied my face, reconsidering based on something he saw deep inside my eyes. I couldn't have that.

"Well, I'm glad he won the tickets," I said. "You guys really drag me down sometimes. An eagle needs to stretch his wings or else he becomes a chicken." Gunnar growled at that. I smirked back darkly. "Really, I'll be fine. Besides, I do have other friends, you know." A thought sparked at the words, but I kept my face straight. I hoped I sounded genuine. Gunnar was an ex-FBI Agent who could smell a lie a mile away, not even accounting for his werewolf sense of smell.

Gunnar's concern disappeared as Ashley reached up to caress the long scar on my jaw that had been caused by Alaric Slate's death throes. She hesitated near my nose, for which I was thankful. "No repeats of last time. We need you in tip-top shape." She spoke with concern.

Gunnar grunted. "Well played, Nate. I think we need to get out of here before he convinces you he's a decent guy," he warned Ashley, chuckling at my resulting sneer. Ashley punched him playfully on the arm, immediately flexing her fingers in discomfort afterwards. It wasn't fun to punch a werewolf. Gunnar kissed her knuckles sweetly before they waved a final time and left me alone in front of the door. I shot Gunnar a last second thumbs up out of Ashley's view. He scowled back with a shake of his head.

Great. I had gotten rid of any potential casualties.

Now what?

13

I hung up my cell phone with a marginal twinkle in my eyes. Perhaps I would actually get some help without risking anyone's life after all. It felt good to possibly be ahead of the bad guys for once.

With nothing else to do, I stepped closer to the mysterious door – or broom closet, as it now appeared to be – that led to the Armory. And I knocked.

Politely.

Hey, you never know when something is going to knock back, and it costs nothing to be polite. I felt more than a little ridiculous knocking on a broom closet door, but magic was funny like that. When I opened the door without permission, it was a broom closet, but if I knocked... things might be entirely different. I waited.

And waited.

And continued waiting a few moments longer.

But nothing happened.

I pounded the door with my fist. Nothing. So, I slapped it in a fit of rage with my open palm, immediately breaking open the wound caused by the broken bar glasses last night. I saw the hot blood splatter onto the door before the sting of pain registered. "Motherf—"

But I bit my tongue as the door began to suddenly open with a long, eerie creak, like the middle of every bad horror movie. A warm wind buffeted past me, ruffling my coat. Huh. It wasn't a *Key* after all. Maybe the password to open the door was an expletive. That sounded like just the kind of humor my father might use.

Then a chill went down my spine as I applied a sliver of brainpower to the situation. It wasn't a curse word. It had been my *blood*. My veins suddenly felt like lava as the long-term consequences of *that* thought entered my mind. That meant that whoever had my blood had the Armory.

I was the Key.

All one had to do was catch me, and they could use me whenever they wanted to open the door. That didn't sound good.

Not at all.

This made me a free agent for any baddie out there.

If anyone ever discovered my secret.

A lilting, feminine laugh drifted from beyond the now open doorway, chilling in its innocence. "It's about time, Nathin, my host." I shivered, trying to peer through the darkness without stepping a foot inside. Should I do this? Or should I wait for backup? But... I didn't *have* any backup. Everyone was gone. I guessed I could call that intern who was tearing down the crucifix in my office. *He would make good cannon fodder,* I thought idly. Then I blinked, surprised at my callousness. That wasn't a good sign. I had subconsciously decided to let the lowly intern risk his life in order to protect mine. Granted, it *was* part of the job description of interns everywhere – *five percent other duties as instructed...* but still, that wasn't like me to be so cold. Was it caused by my lack of sleep? Was I losing my empathy? I didn't have time for that train of thought, so I shrugged it off.

So.

Was I scared? That might sound like a dumb question. Of course I was scared, but that didn't usually slow me down. I always confronted my fears. But I always made sure I had backup somewhere or an ace up my sleeve, in case things got dicey. Now, I didn't have backup. I was entirely alone, and my magical reservoir was capped off. I would have to play this game differently than I was used to. Normally, I blew things up that scared me. Now I would have to think first, blow shit up later. If at all. To conserve my power.

"I didn't know men these days were so shy," the voice teased from the shadows.

I decided to answer back. "You're not a Demon, are you?"

The cute voice that answered had an entirely different tone this time. It now barely restrained eons of experience at fatal threats. "Never."

"Oh, okay. Well that's a start. Are you going to eat me if I come in there?" I asked, not knowing exactly what was on the other side of the door. That hiss could have been a monster. It sure didn't sound human.

"I am no beast. I'm a petite, curvaceous dream woman. No blades, fangs, or sticks. I swear. But I *detest* Demons," the voice called, sounding more human again, and slightly... amused.

"Um. Alright. I'm coming in now." I took a step and waited for the gates of hell to grab me by the short hairs. I realized my body was rigid, ready to flee at the drop of a hat. Listen, she *might* be a little girl, but she *also* might be a giant, dreadlock-clad, flying, gorilla-vampire hybrid. One never knew. Sensing no inhuman presence ready to gobble me up, I took another cautious step into the darkness. The door slammed shut behind me, bumping me forward a few inches. My butt cheeks were clenched tight enough to crack a walnut, not wanting to get pinched by a four-hundred-pound door.

In a blink, I realized the darkness was entirely gone, replaced by gold, crimson, and orange hues reflecting off thousands of metallic objects. Elaborate clothing, armor, and classic artwork from eras long extinct decorated the wall between literal piles of weapons and artifacts. The room I stood in had an open balcony with sturdy marble railings that ran right up to a sky that seemed afire from a vibrant sunset. A wide, long hallway stretched from the opposite end of the room, leading away for what seemed like forever.

And this was one room.

I could see dozens more openings spaced along the hallway.

The enticing voice floated to my ears from the balcony as I spotted a silky, lavender colored fabric fluttering in the wind. "Come out, come out, wherever you are," she teased.

I blinked. She was facing the opposite direction, but her thick auburn hair flowed in the breeze like a shampoo commercial's wet dream. She could be hiding razor-sharp Katanas in front of her, or she could have a gorilla-vampire hybrid's face after all. I had to be careful here. I didn't know the rules, but this obviously was not Temple Industries. I was somewhere else. It wasn't sunset in St. Louis, and it wasn't even remotely warm there. Here, it was almost toasty, as if I had stepped into a beach town near the equator. I didn't even know whether this place was real or a mental construct... or maybe even another daymare. My eyes suddenly darted back and forth eagerly, searching for a box, but I found nothing. Then again... I wouldn't even know to look for a box if this was a daymare, which meant that this *must* be real.

"Please turn to face me, if you don't mind," I called politely. Her amused laughter caused a pleasant tingle over my skin. It was captivating – the perfect mixture of amusement and darker, adult undertones. She turned to face me and my breath froze. Large almond eyes greeted me. Her face was oval and naturally tanned, with a sharp jaw and large, luscious lips, which were smiling up at me to reveal large, brilliantly white teeth. She was short, but a genuine goddess. And yes, she was definitely *curvaceous*. Was that my parents' secret? They had kidnapped a goddess? "You look... normal," I said bluntly.

She cocked her head curiously. "*Normal*? Well, you sure know how to woo a girl. I'm curious, were you *really* expecting a gorilla-vampire hybrid?" she asked, mischievously.

I blinked. *How the hell did she know that?* I opened my mouth after a few seconds of silent gawking. "If you knew my life, you might not think that so odd. Can you—"

She interrupted me. "Yes. I can read minds. Most of the time. It's my duty," she answered softly, curtsying like a princess out of a fairy tale. "I am at your service, if you will have me."

"I don't think I need any servicing." I realized how that sounded and instantly went on defense. "I mean, I'm all set in the servicing department. I've got this girl I really like, and she really likes me, too. She services me just f—"

Her laughter cut me off, and my teeth clicked sharply as my face flared beet red.

"Not *that* kind of servicing. I guess you could say that I *work* for you. Perhaps that is a more modern phrase."

I nodded, relieved. "Oh. Yeah. Of course. That makes more sense." I studied her curiously, the silence stretching as she met my gaze with infinite patience. "Why do you work for me again?"

"You could call me a librarian. Of sorts. I was created to be the ward of this place." Her eyes twinkled with excitement as she spread her dainty hands to encompass the room. "Here. Let me show you a few of my favorite things." She was suddenly directly in front of me, seemingly not having crossed the space between us. I didn't even have time to flinch before she eagerly grabbed my arm to lead me deeper into the room. I didn't have time to stop her, and I was caught up with her infectious glee at finally having someone to talk to about her toys. And I was damned curious about that, after having spent so long trying to gain entrance to this place.

We rapidly moved from pile to pile, weapon to weapon, rug to painting, all the while with her name-dropping ancient items of power that made my skin begin to crawl. I was flabbergasted as we darted from one astonishment to the next. Gems, jewels, art, weapons, maps, and hundreds of other things filled the vast room in every direction, and this was only one of many, many rooms. She had already pointed out a lamp with a genuine genie trapped inside, the Nemean Lion's skin that had adorned Hercules, and even a few journals written by the Brothers Grimm – the sociopathic hitmen of the supernatural world.

The artwork alone was worth millions of dollars, not even considering the jewelry.

But it wasn't just weapons. I spotted a collection of boxed action figures, signed baseballs, expensive antiques, and even vinyl records. It was a hoarder's paradise.

And it was all...

Mine.

It was slightly humbling. With only a handful of these items I would be practically unstoppable, and wouldn't need to worry about my curse at all.

A small part of me felt like Smaug hoarding his treasure, but another small part of me began to grow concerned. Was I worthy of being the Armory's caretaker? *Power corrupts, and absolute power corrupts... absolutely.* Lord Acton was right on that old phrase.

"You're like a playboy bunny version of Jiminy Cricket," I blurted after a time, perhaps too honestly. "The conscience for this place, like Jiminy was for Pinocchio." She smiled at my compliment, and released my hand. "Did my parents command you to keep watch over the Armory? Did they *create* you?" I studied her more carefully. I had felt her hand, so I knew she was a physical being, but where did she get her nourishment? Was she merely a construct created by my parents and this was all happening in my head?

"No. They didn't create me, and yes, I'm real." Her eyes threatened to suck me into their depths, so I quickly turned away. She laughed, patting me on the arm innocently. "This is but one of the world's armories. Albeit the most notorious. Your parents have transformed it into the greatest of all of them. But perhaps I say that only because I am here to help." I nodded politely, not knowing what to say. She eyed me up and down appraisingly. Then she took a slow step closer, brushing the scar on my face with a gentle touch. "How did you acquire... oh, a dragon." She had read my thoughts again. "You are a warrior then, a dragon slayer? Yes. I see it now. You're wearing war paint to terrorize your enemies." She pointed at my black eyes. "I like it. Who are we destroying today?" she said it with the tone and excitement a small child might use to declare we were about to play tea-party princesses. I shivered. "We have many weapons here if you so desire. You will never have to risk a scar again." I took a polite step back and cleared my throat. She smiled, respecting my distance without offense. "Your parents didn't tell me that they actually succeeded in granting you the power of a Maker, though."

She stared at me, waiting for me to speak. "A Maker?" I asked curiously, and with a small amount of alarm. She nodded, but her excitement slowly began to fade as she realized I had no idea what she was talking about.

"Have you noticed an increase in your power?" she asked instead. I nodded with excitement. Finally! Answers. "But they didn't warn you? They never explained why?" she asked with disbelief.

"They never had the chance. They were murdered," I answered softly, my hopes for answers crumbling to ashes.

She seemed to shrink a bit at the shoulders. "I know. I'm sorry. I didn't mean to bring that up. What I meant was that they took something from this place in order to give you a... parting gift, as it were. A workshop for your new gift to flourish."

I stared back at her blankly, a little mollified that my parents had experimented on me without my knowledge. "Gift?"

"You are the first Maker to walk the earth in hundreds of years."

I pondered her words. "Maker... That sounds kinda... silly," I finally answered.

She giggled. "It is in no way *silly*. It is how wizards came to be in the first place. It means that you can literally create new forms of magic the world has never before seen. Other wizards stick with the old tried and true spells, replicating what they have seen done before. They do not have the power to push the boundaries and create *new* magic. As a Maker, you can quite literally do whatever you can imagine. Whatever you dare attempt. Magic that your enemies could not counter, since they never would have experienced it before. It is a gift from the gods. Your parents wanted you to be strong enough to defend this place... and yourself."

Create magic? Unbelievable. My parents were pulling strings even from beyond the grave. "Well, it seems their hard work has only painted a bulls-eye on my back. The Academy wasn't too pleased to notice my jump in power."

She nodded sadly. "The world's thugs never are. They don't like things they cannot explain." She straightened her shoulders. "Well, I hope you made a right mess of those vipers at the Academy. You are, after all, limited only by your creativity and imagination."

"Well, I didn't make a *right mess* of them. They actually cursed me. My power is now fading, and will be gone in three days if I don't comply with their demands to give them the Armory. It will fade faster if I use my magic up before their deadline."

She locked eyes with me. "Then I must help you eliminate this wretched spell." She closed her eyes and lifted her arms to point in my general direction. I tensed, but nothing happened. After a few moments, she opened her eyes with a low growl. "Impossible! I can't even *touch* the curse. It repels my power like oil on water." She studied me for another second. "Even with your new abilities, it is too strong for you to remove on your own. They must have used a circle of wizards."

I nodded with frustration. "Eight of them, to be precise."

She growled. "Cowards!" I liked her already. The enemy of my enemy is my friend, after all. "It seems that the only solution is for you to find more power."

I blinked at her, not hiding my mounting frustration very well. "You and Asterion, both. Simple, but efficient with your fortune cookie answers."

She visibly started. "The Minotaur *lives*?"

I hesitated, not knowing if I had accidentally given up a State Secret. "Um. Yeah. We're kinda' bros." She watched me, uncomprehendingly. "Friends," I amended.

She continued to stare at me in silence, thoughts I couldn't even fathom churning behind those magical eyes of hers.

"Anyway," I continued, feeling uncomfortable. "How exactly do I find more power?"

She arched a brow, relaxing as she fought a growing smile. Finally, she sighed and lifted her arms at the Armory around us. I slapped my forehead in embarrassment, remembering at the last second to be gentle for my injured nose. Of course. Armory. Power. Duh.

"This is all *yours*. You can borrow items from here to aid you in your investigation. It's fitting, really. Use your parents' tools to discover their murderer. It wouldn't be the first time some of these items have reentered the world. After all, you've already been transformed into a Maker." I looked around, feeling slightly thick that I hadn't considered the idea immediately. But like earlier, my thoughts grew concerned. These things had been locked away for a reason. Surely, they shouldn't be wielded outside of the Armory. But... wasn't I already contradicting that statement? My parents had already done just that to transform me into a Maker. Supposedly. Did I trust this woman? Could she be lying about their gift? Then I thought about it for a few seconds.

I *had* made some remarkable discoveries lately. Tinkering had become a fiery passion where before it had been merely an interesting diversion. And I had learned to Apparate rather quickly, in a way that I had never learned anything before. Maybe she was right. It would explain the power spike that had so surprised the Justices.

I decided to change the subject, allow my mind to warm up to the idea slowly. "Why does everything I see remind me of the Greeks?" I asked curiously.

"Because they were brilliant marketers, of course. We have totems from practically every culture here. You just don't recognize them."

"You said there are more places like this in the world?"

"Yes, but they pale in comparison. Your parents quite outdid themselves bringing additional items of power here." She studied me as I scanned the room, fighting the selfish urge to arm myself for World War III. I could be all but invincible with even a handful of these items. I could take out the Justices, swat away the Angels, and banish the Demons with ease. No one could stand in my way.

But... and there was always a *but*.

My parents had locked them away for a reason. Power had a tendency to change a guy. And I liked myself the way I was. The urge was still persistent, but I squashed it. "Do as you will, but you are not without options," she said softly, reading my thoughts. "You are a Maker and must not give the Academy access to this storehouse," she warned.

"Is this Maker gift how I was able to learn how to teleport just by experiencing it one time?"

"Teleport? I don't know this word," she answered with a frown.

"You know. Moving from one place to another really fast."

"You learned how to run?" she teased with a grin.

I scowled. Of course she was a smartass. Why not? "Over great distances in the blink of an eye."

Her eyes sparkled. "Oh. You mean Shadow Walking." She tapped a lip, watching my pensive frown. "You mean this is not common knowledge among wizards?"

I stared at her for a few seconds before shaking my head. "No. Apparently, it's only known to a select few." I regarded her thoughtfully. This ability was nothing new to her, even though she had never heard the modern word *teleport*. Interesting. *Shadow Walking*. I wondered where I had been when between locations. An alternate reality? Was it dangerous? Most likely it was, or it would be common knowledge. Another fact hit me. The Academy was guilty of doing exactly what they accused me of – hiding power. Which instantly confirmed that I shouldn't trust them. They wanted the power for themselves. Not for the good of the supernatural community. They wanted control, weapons, and power. But why?

She had frowned in disapproval at mention of the Academy hiding knowledge like this from other wizards. She finally shrugged in answer to my original question. "Makers learn quickly. Their subconscious runs on overdrive. Always watching, cataloguing, learning." Her eyes were thoughtful as she watched the uncertainty on my face. She was obviously finished with that conversation because she moved to another topic after glancing at a nearby sundial. "Your situation could be worse..."

I blinked. "Losing my power? I'm helpless with this curse. It won't go away until I give them access to the Armory. To *you*. If even then."

"Then you must die, Maker." She didn't even look ashamed at the comment. Seeing my reaction, her eyes grew softer. "Some men aren't meant to find peace or happiness. They are meant to challenge Death. Fight Wars. They are meant to be *great*."

"Well, my death will put a damper on just about all of those things."

She shrugged, changing the topic again. "Now that you are my new master, how do you wish me to aid you?"

I could sense that she wanted me to formally acknowledge her assistance, but I was a tad nervous about what that might obligate me to do. My father had always taught me that there was no free lunch. "I just want to understand what this place is and why it was locked away."

She laughed. "Come now. Of course, your parents told you of this place," she said. I shook my head and she considered me, face slowly morphing to awe. "They never told you about this fortress? About... *me*?" I shook my head again, blushing slightly at her offended tone.

"Uh... nope."

"Well, I am here to serve... you, if you will have me. I keep record of the items of power stored here. What exactly do you wish to know?" Disappointment was clear in her voice.

"Just answers, I guess. I don't want to force you to tell me anything you don't want to tell," I said conversationally, looking over her shoulder at the vast array of items. As was typical for me, my gaze rested on a set of books that sat neatly on a table. I found myself wondering what their story was. Their spines were elaborately decorated, but they held not a speck of dust.

Her tone grew cold in the blink of an eye, arctic. Literally. Frost instantly coated the table and books. "But... you will if you must. Already you resort to threats. Against a slave, no less."

My mouth clicked shut, realization dawning too late. "No. No, that's not what I meant. That wasn't a threat. That was just a statement. I merely meant that I don't know the rules here. I am not like those you may have served before."

She chuckled sadly and the frost on the table simply disappeared, which was entirely creepy. Shouldn't it have melted rather than just disappear? "Never heard *that* before. I thought you might be different."

"Look, is there anything I can do to prove that I'm not here to hurt you? I didn't even know you existed ten minutes ago." Did this mean that my parents had abused her? Was that why she was so jaded?

She watched me curiously. "We shall see," was all she said. I was surprised that she hadn't asked me to free her, to beg for my help. I didn't think I would have said yes, but I wasn't sure. Perhaps I would have. Everyone deserved freedom. But I didn't know her story or the Armory's history. Not yet. I needed to be sure she wasn't dangerous first.

So, I let her assume what she would. Cold, but effective. I guarded my thoughts with a sudden wall of impenetrable power so that she couldn't read me. She squinted back, noticing my defense, and not seeming to be pleased.

Confident my thoughts were safe, I thought for a moment. It was obvious why my parents had been killed. Someone wanted access to this place. "But *who* killed them? Why am I having night terrors? Why does the door back there," I pointed behind me, "smell like Brimstone?"

Her sudden silence caused me to look up, realizing I had spoken aloud. Her eyes had changed to a milky lavender shade, gaze distant as if she could no longer see me.

The difference in her voice caused the hair on the back of my neck to rise, as it was totally different from when she had spoken before – older, wiser, and more lethal – like a completely different person. Like... an entity of knowledge *should* sound. "The doorway to death can truly be a hallway of opportunities. To tread the sharp edge of a sword – to run on smooth-frozen ice, one needs no footsteps to follow. Walk over the cliffs with hands free. Death will provide answers to thee." Then she blinked as if just waking up, unsure what had just transpired.

"Are you telling me that the only answers I can find will be through *death*?"

"Only the *ultimate* answer can be found through death," she answered distantly, her eyes slowly returning back to normal as she caught a hand on the table for balance. What the hell? Then she chuckled, as if amused at her own words.

"Very punny," I growled. "Now, what the hell did you mean, and what just happened? You almost fell over. And your eyes changed colors."

"I'm sorry, I don't know where the words came from... it happens sometimes. I'm not sure if it's the items here or something to do with me." Her eyes darted back to the sundial and widened in alarm. "Quickly. We haven't much time." I blinked at that, but she was already rushing to grab my hand and lead me around the room. I had all the time in the world to give her. She was the only one willing to give me answers. But I allowed her to drag me to a new room, smiling at her excitement to point out various items only read about in stories. A cold chill ran down my neck at some of them. Excalibur. Armor designed by literal gods. Vials of mysterious liquids and raw energy that she silently avoided. A blue phone booth... *no*, that couldn't be the *Tardis*... could it?

She finally looked content, having shown me some of the more dangerous items. Knowing this was one room of dozens – if not hundreds – I found myself again wary of my new hideout. "The Armory is a cache of magical items deemed too dangerous to fall into the wrong hands. Most things in here are deadly, but lethality is in the eye of the beholder. To the caveman, fire was dangerous, but one just needed to learn how to control it." She paused, no doubt reading the question on the tip of my tongue with her creepy mind-reading ability. "I don't know why you smelled Brimstone outside. Perhaps the thief from a few months ago resorted to using Demons in order to gain entrance. I don't know how that could be possible, but he ultimately failed. Knowing what he desired, and how powerful it was, I tricked him."

I felt myself lean forward eagerly. *Peter*. "What did he want?" This was it. An answer. Finally.

She appraised me wordlessly, judging me as surely as if I had been weighed to the ounce. "Power. He seemed fixated on the bathwater of Baby Achilles." She idly waved a hand at the array of vials we had bypassed.

"Well, as power goes, that seems kind of a poor choice." She arched a brow.

"That would be the water from the River Styx, which granted him his immortality on all but his ankle." I shuddered in comprehension.

"Oh. Well... thanks for not giving it to him then." She nodded. "It was as your parents would have wanted. Besides, why would I let him have what he wanted if he wasn't able to grant my freedom?" My mind worked furiously. So, she *did* want something.

"You could have asked him to take you with him in exchange for the water."

She frowned. "Don't think I hadn't thought about it... or tried it in the past. Only the custodian may grant my freedom."

She began studying the nearby weathered sundial nervously. "How can I find the man or Demons responsible for my parents' murder?" I asked, remembering her odd comment about limited time. She laughed, as if the question was too simple to waste her time on.

"That's easy." She immediately shimmered with power before casting a crimson haze of fog at a map of Eastern Europe on the wall beside us. "*Seek,*" she whispered. The fog condensed to several locations on the map, glowing faintly. "That shows current locations of Demonic presence."

The freaky part about it was that I knew I could replicate it, but it would cost me a ton of magic. "Um. With my curse, that spell would drain me really fast. I would have to use a lot of power, which would leave me useless to confront the Demons I had oh so cleverly discovered."

She nodded mumbling to herself as if reading a mental catalog of the items stored here, and then dove into a pile of items on the edge of a desk. After discarding several priceless artifacts, she held up a carved bone the size of a bird's egg. "Here. Take this. It works the same way, only doesn't require your own magic. It's instilled with the power itself. Merely think about what you want to find, say *Seek*, and hold it near a map." She handed me the bone egg and I grunted in surprise at its weight. It was so dense that it felt like a lump of pure lead. It was completely covered in continuous runes, not a single millimeter empty. I idly wondered what could have been sharp enough to carve it. It felt... ancient. Upon my touch, soothing whispers abruptly filled my ears, murmuring seductively, introducing themselves by the hundreds. The voices sounded seductive, and... grateful. Almost as if they were eager to partner with a new wizard after eons of silence. I quickly pocketed the totem and the whispers ceased. I managed not to flinch in fear, and the girl nodded in approval.

"Thanks," I finally said, glad for the silence, and not knowing quite what to make of the voices. I felt conflicted about borrowing anything from this place, but what choice did I really have?

She nodded matter-of-factly.

"I guess now I understand why it took you so long to answer my call. Your parents never told you about me. I thought you would have to develop insomnia before you realized I was reaching out to you."

That got me right in the stomach. The night terrors. "That was *you*?" I hissed, seething with sudden rage.

She began to chuckle, but her brow creased in confused alarm, not understanding my threatening tone. "Yes. I try to give all my hosts pleasant dreams," she finally answered, looking uncertain.

"Is this some kind of sick *joke*?" I bellowed, taking an aggressive step towards her. She squeaked, darting back a good dozen feet to the balcony. Then I took another step. Soon I was racing towards her, fury fueling my muscles.

She was as good as dead.

I *knew* this had sounded too good to be true, that she had *looked* too good to be true. She was the source of all my recent pain. Having visions of my loved ones being tortured and killed again and again and *again*. Some might say I was slightly unhinged.

"I think there might have been a misunderstanding," she spoke softly, suddenly standing just before me. I was panting with unspent energy, my muscles quivering to reach her dainty throat, but I was no longer running. I couldn't move a single muscle below my neck, so I snarled hungrily, ready to bite her throat if that was my only path. But I couldn't even turn my head. Her delicate hands reached up to touch my face, her soft fingertips gently caressing my scar and temples in a very doctor-like evaluation. I was ready to burst with rage, but my body wouldn't respond, and even my magic was tantalizingly out of reach. *What was happening*?

She flinched back with a gasp. "Oh. That makes much more sense. Someone has been tampering with your mind. Altering my sendings." She scrunched her face in thought, poking her tongue out the side of her full lips, Michael Jordan style, and stepped back up to me, grasping my skull more forcefully this time. I still couldn't move. I opened my mouth to threaten her to step back and stop, but even my voice wouldn't work. She was using some kind of magic to overwhelm me. Then, what felt like a bucket of warm oil slowly poured over my head, coaxing my neck, shoulders, and back into the equivalent of warm jelly. It was as if I had just stepped out of a hot bath after an exhausting spa day.

... Not that I had ever *partaken* in such a day. I could just imagine what it would have been like if I had.

My body shivered at the sudden release of tension I hadn't realized I'd been carrying, and the girl stepped back with a curious frown on her face. I collapsed to my knees, muscles too useless to support my weight. The slip of a girl stumbled up to a heavy table and sat down, turning to face me, looking physically drained and... concerned.

"Someone has been in your head," she spoke thoughtfully, lifting a shaky hand to tap her lips in thought.

"And you only just admitted to doing that very thing," I snapped, slowly regaining the use of my limbs.

She nodded distractedly. "My dreams were sent to tap into your subconscious mind and remind you of my presence. Your parents named this Armory their Pandora Protocol. A quotidian name for a place, but it fits." I frowned at her. Noticing this, she elaborated. "Your father was quite the one for elaborate names. He deemed the items in this location to be too dangerous for the Academy and other wizards to get their hands on. So, he named it after Pandora's Box – the legend that housed the world's worst horrors." She looked amused.

"But in the bottom of Pandora's Box was Hope," I said softly. She flinched, looking into my eyes with newfound respect. Her gaze was like a field of lavender on fire.

"That is true. Not many know that part of the story," she spoke softly.

I shrugged, relaxing. "Learning of their name for this place, I did a lot of research into the topic."

"My sending was to place a box into your dreams, reminding you of their pet name for the Armory. Opening it would cause you pleasure."

"Yeah, sure. If pleasure feels like your skin is melting."

Her eyes fairly smoldered. "That was not I. I wouldn't, and couldn't, do that to my host," she hissed. She sounded sincere. What the hell did *that* mean? Who else was in my head?

Instead of jumping down *that* rabbit hole, I looked around the room as my muscles slowly began to awaken, noticing a vast array of armor against one wall. One item in particular caught my attention. Between two shields was an aged section of sheepskin. *Golden* sheepskin. "Is that...?" I asked, my mouth wide open with disbelief.

She glanced behind her at the skin, but shook her head in reply. "No, but Jason's Golden Fleece is here. That is merely a replica your father liked, not realizing the authentic one was already here," she answered as if pointing out a can of tomato soup in a grocery store. I blinked in astonishment. The Golden Fleece! Able to repel any attack. What the hell? I had a brief daydream of me blazing into battle against a horde of Angels and Demons wearing the Fleece, stomping ass and taking names. She interrupted my reverie. "What I'm more concerned about is your dreams. Someone has been melding his or her will into my own projections. Locked away in this vault, it is very difficult for me to project dreams, but it is not impossible. The fact that someone was able to mutate my sending is alarming. It means someone is after you specifically, and trying to do you harm without letting you know who he or she is. Have your dreams been... particularly horrifying?" she asked in a very clinical way, not at all concerned with how much harm they had, in fact, caused me.

"You could say that," I said drily. "The city burning, my friends tortured and murdered, me helpless, but through it all was a box. The only way to escape the carnage was to open a box."

She nodded distractedly. "That part was mine. Just the box. It was agreed upon by your father and I that I would entice you with these visions of opening a box. He said anything more forceful than that would cause you to ignore the call. He called you a bit stubborn, to tell you the truth. At least that part of the dream was pleasant," she said softly.

I scowled back. "Opening the box caused me more pain than I've ever imagined. And each dream caused a new *type* of pain. Burning, freezing, being skinned, and even buried alive."

She looked crestfallen, and then... furious. "Opening the box was supposed to cause you pleasure, to lead you to me. Why would I cause you pain in order to lead you here?

Like I said, your father mentioned you had an issue with authority, so these sendings were to encourage you to come *to* me, not scare you *away*."

"True. But who could possibly know about your projections, and how the hell would they tap into them? Were they trying to discover something inside my head? Could it be a Demon?"

"That is a very good question," she answered slowly. "Why do you repeatedly fixate on Demons?"

"Because I was paid a visit by some... people, and they had the distinct impression that I and that door smelled like a severe whiff of Brimstone."

"I would never allow a Demon to enter this place. And you do not smell of Demons." So, my dip in the fountain of holy water *had* worked! "This is my sanctuary. My home."

Her tone sent a shiver down my spine. Even as small and young as she looked, she was obviously very, very powerful. I had been helpless in her hands. And her words had sounded like a queen talking about her castle. "Who are you, anyway?"

"I could answer that if you accepted my servitude. I could be of great help to you in the future, but you must allow me to serve you." Her tone sounded hopeful, desperate, almost.

And it sounded eerily like an unbreakable bond. And she had expressed her interest at freedom. "How about just a name for now." I could see the frustration in her eyes. I felt an uncomfortable twinge begin in my shoulders that was all the more noticeable after her therapeutic touch. *Get out, get out, get out...*

The girl continued, unaware of my predicament. "Fine. I was a wayward soul. One who wasted her life on earth, trying to help those who couldn't help themselves. One you would refer to as a witch. I was killed by my own people for what I was, and cast here to serve as a Guardian of sorts. You may call me—"

"Well, this has been great and all, but I really must be leaving," I interrupted. I was suddenly on my feet and striding purposefully back to the door. "See you soon, Hope." I don't know where the name came from, but it seemed to fit from the story I had shared with her about Pandora's Box.

The door back to Temple Industries opened before me and I stepped out. Before it closed again I heard Hope's voice. "Damn that spell!"

The door shut with a solid boom and the uncomfortable sensation evaporated. Why had I left? I turned on my heel, pounding on the door to be let back inside. Nothing happened. I reopened my wound and pressed it against the wood. Still nothing. *What the hell? I have more questions!* But it was useless. The room was closed again.

Then it hit me. I remembered the odd fact about the room. When my parents had entered – and then again when Peter had entered – they had been gone exactly seventeen minutes. I looked down at my watch. Huh.

Right on time.

Hope had mentioned a spell. That must be it. Perhaps Peter had hit the spell's time limit, and simply grabbed whatever he could before leaving, since Hope had been unwilling to assist him. Then he had 'sold' it to Alaric Slate, sealing his fate. I sighed. What a waste. He had been my friend for years, but I didn't tolerate betrayal.

So, this spell limited time allowed inside the vault. I wondered if there was a way around it. My parents had also been limited to the same window of opportunity – seventeen minutes.

Thinking of my parents made me recall the last time I had seen my father alive. On the video recording taken from directly outside this door. I looked down at my feet. Almost exactly where I currently stood. I might or might not have shivered at that thought. I remembered his last message to me, when he had mouthed his dying words to the security camera that was currently blinking at me. Luckily, I knew how to lip read. I had only been able to see the video a single time before it had been deleted, but I recalled his message perfectly. It made me angry, but some of it began to inch toward an inkling of sense after meeting Hope.

I let it go, thinking about the door. I heard footsteps coming down the hall, but they stopped, no doubt someone picking up papers from a printer before running back to their lab. I ignored the sound, pondering the Omega symbol over the door. Why that symbol? I could think of no real reason other than to scare someone. Then there was the door itself, and my blood was the Key. If anyone ever discovered that, I would become everyone's best friend. I couldn't ever let anyone figure that out or I would be locked in a cell forever to be used as a tool whenever necessary. "I am no one's tool," I promised myself.

A withered old voice responded from the hallway behind me. "You obviously didn't read the pamphlets I left you, for we are all God's tools." I sighed in frustration. Greta.

"I thought you left already," I grumbled. I heard no response, so turned around. No one was there. I instantly tensed. No footsteps. I cocked my head, listening. After a few moments, I relaxed. I was alone. Then I began to wonder if it really had been Greta or if someone *else* had been lurking behind me, using her voice. Or had I imagined it? How tired was I?

That's it. My paranoia was at an all-time high.

I scoured the hallways, searching for anyone, but found nothing. Not a soul. I gave it up as my imagination caused by sleep deprivation. After spending another hour at the door, trying everything in my power to open the Armory, I gave it up as fruitless and decided to leave. I was on borrowed time, with Demons hunting me down for the Key to the Armory. And the Academy's deadline was only two days away now. After that I would be a magic-less wizard. I couldn't stand still for too long.

I had things to kill and problems to solve.

14

I stormed out of Temple Industries, too distracted to be concerned with the brisk winter weather. It was the first time I had felt entirely relaxed in months, thanks to whatever Hope had done to quell my daymares. I was marginally dry from my brief stint in the Armory, and was ecstatic that I no longer sported the Demon's version of *Eau de Toilette*. I was also overjoyed that I'd finally be able to go get some real, uninterrupted sleep. Sure, I knew I needed to stop the Demons, but I suddenly felt practically comatose. I required sleep or I was likely to make mistakes. Also, thanks to Hope, I wasn't even sure I could make it home before falling asleep. I was that tired.

Indie was most likely already with her mom. I considered calling her when I got home. If I wasn't drooling and stumbling by the time I made it there. I was on borrowed time and I needed to figure out a way to appease the Academy while finding my parents' murderer before the curse ran its course. But... I deserved a quick nap before I faced any Biblical threats, especially after months of practical insomnia.

I dug in my pockets, searching for the keys to the emergency car I left here in the parking lot. I had learned pretty quickly that I usually found myself here after a few too many drinks, or being dropped off here by Mallory or one of my other friends, and rather than constantly waiting for someone to pick me up, I had set up a car to be left in the parking lot. It wasn't as flashy as my other cars, but it was really just a driver anyway.

I finally found the set of keys in my pocket and hit the remote start. The Xenon lights on the Vilner customized Mercedes G-Wagon pierced the night as the engine roared to life across the parking lot. I stood there for a few seconds, admiring her beauty.

As if the sound of her glorious purr had been a signal, a team of black SUVs suddenly swarmed into the parking lot on screeching tires, flashing lights in red, white, and blue. I froze. Was this a joke? The police? Then I frowned. Was this a ruse? Maybe some of the Demons had managed to possess a posse of officers to catch me off-guard. I waited as the cars skidded to a halt in a loose circle around me, closing off any chance of escape for the big, bad, scary wizard. I smiled at the unintended compliment.

The men – all wearing identical blue coats – launched themselves out of their cars in near perfect synchronization. "I smell Kosage," I sneered to the closest man, who was unashamedly pointing a gun at my face.

His was the only voice to answer, so I assumed he was in charge. "FBI! Freeze!"

I blinked. FBI? My concern began to escalate considerably. "I'm pretty sure my balls resemble two ice cubes at the moment, so I think we're set."

"Don't move!" the leader clarified, his cinderblock head swiveling on slabs of beef that remotely resembled human shoulders. He had no neck. As I scanned the men before me, I thought I saw a few familiar faces from the St. Louis Police Department mixed in amongst the unknown agents. What the hell had I done to get these two departments to join forces against me?

"Despite it looking like I'm moving really fast, I'm actually standing still. I know. Trippy, right?" I muttered. My exhaustion was making me angry.

He glared back. "Don't be a smartass. On the ground!" A few of the other men chuckled, but they didn't lower their weapons. I heard several murmurings about my face and the obvious black eyes. I scowled in their general direction until they grew silent.

"I'm actually quite content to stand until I hear a reason for this detainment, and I also require you to show me some identification." The man blinked. "You know, those flippy leather wallets you carry with a driver's license and your shield? The one with the agent number on it that I will memorize in order to ruin your career for eternity, if you don't provide a *damned* good reason for postponing my nap." I smiled through my teeth. This was it. If they didn't provide proof that they were in fact agents or police, I was Shadow Walking my happy ass out of here, consequences be damned.

Two other agents stepped forward with their shields out. I pretended to look at their badges, but studied their faces instead, clutching the artifact in my pocket. The one Hope had given me. If they were Demons, surely, I would sense some change in it. I should also smell Brimstone. I sniffed, and then blinked, which caused the officers to cock their heads in confusion. No Brimstone. No reaction from the stone.

Huh. I honestly didn't know what to do next. I'd been so prepared for supernatural problems that I hadn't considered what to do about the Regular old FBI or police.

That might say something about me.

"So, um... you're official. What can I help you with?"

"You're under arrest."

"For wh—" I began, but I unsuccessfully failed at suppressing a sudden massive, jaw-cracking yawn. I could have literally fallen asleep standing up. The agents pounced on my moment of weakness like a pride of lions on a gazelle. They violently tackled me to the ground, handcuffed me, and forcefully picked me up to press me against a nearby car door. I was so exhausted that I let them. I wasn't about to attack a squad of FBI Agents. They were supposed to be the good guys.

"What exactly am I being arrested for?" I wheezed, my anger beginning to wake me up a bit as the cuffs ground into my wrists.

"You're wanted as a person of interest in an ongoing investigation. Missing person. Alaric Slate. Among other things."

"Like?" I asked, barely restraining myself from unleashing my power on them. But it would do no good, and I needed my power for the Demons. Best to go along with them. For now.

He held up his phone, which showed a perfect image of me cold-cocking the stranger from the bar last night. Then he smirked as he studied my face. "Looks like it didn't end well for you."

"Goddamn it. How many people were keeping tabs on me last night?" I snapped, more to myself. "And for the record, I totally kicked some ass at that bar fight." I pointed to my face with pride. "This was from the fight afterwards with a totally different group of people, where I also kicked some major ass." He looked doubtful. "But I digress. Since when are bar fights part of your jurisdiction?"

The bulldog agent stared me down. "We're on a joint task force with the local police. This picture just gave us a chance to bring you in. We also have you on corruption of a fellow Agent, Gunnar Randulf. Your assets have been temporarily frozen until we get to the bottom of it all. Last time the police brought you in, you threatened to buy off a politician to make sure Kosage lost his badge. He took that personally. I mean... *professionally*," he corrected with a sadistic grin, shrugging his massive shoulders. His coat was barely able to contain his massive frame.

"Is that a s-medium sized coat? You know, the size between a medium and a small that some people use to feel manlier? You must pop your collar on your days off, too. Real studly."

His face began to grow a pleasant shade of purple as his fists flexed at his sides. Then my phone began to ring. The man held out a hand. One of his subordinates handed him my phone from my pocket, chuckling at the cracked screen. "Nice," he mocked me before answering the call on speaker. The other agents began patting me down. "*Master* Temple's phone," he answered in a polite drawl.

"Who is this?" Indie demanded. "Let me speak to Nate."

"This is the FBI, Miss. Master Temple is currently wanted for questioning and isn't able to answer the phone. Can I give him a message?"

There was an abrupt pause, then, "You can go fuck yourself, thank you very much. Give Nate his phone. This is an invasion of his privacy."

The Agent's face morphed back to that satisfying purple shade, but he kept his voice neutral. "I'm sorry. I can't do that. You should have just left a message. He won't be calling anyone for quite some time. Unless he uses you as his one free call. Good day." He hung up with more force than was necessary.

"Give me my goddamned phone you self-righteous, no-necked, son of a bitch. I've broken no laws. You can't arrest me." He merely glared back smugly. I took a calming breath. "I'm trying to work on my communication skills. At least let me put her at ease. Then I'm all yours for questions. After which, I will be leaving your tender loving care."

"Uh-huh. You can talk to her..." I nodded thankfully, glancing at my phone. "As soon as you *communicate* with *us*. It will be good practice. Put me at ease on a few topics. Like bribery of a fellow agent, for starters." He winked darkly. The other agents finished taking everything from my pockets, turning off my car when they found my keys, and grunting in surprise at the weight of the bone artifact Hope had given me. Then I was shoved into one of the SUVs.

One of the agents jangled the remnants of the dragon tooth bracelet that had been broken in the bar fight last night. "Cute. Did you get this from Panama City Beach during Spring Break or something? One of those cheap souvenir shops? Billionaire wearing cheap shit like this? Must be facing hard time."

"*Times*, you ignorant hick," I growled.

As if expecting this, he grinned wider. "Nah. *Hard Time*, as in, that is what you're facing right now."

I sneered back, not daring to use my magic to scare him. I used something else. "Those are the teeth of the Demon I killed on the Eads Bridge a few months ago. You guys must be very brave. I hear they even have footage of me killing it on YouTube. They call me something... what was it again...? Oh, that's it. *Archangel*. I knew it was something catchy..." I leaned forward with a grin that showed my teeth. "And true."

His smile evaporated as he turned back to the front of the car. A small victory worked for me. Still, I was fuming by the time we made it to the interrogation room of the local police precinct. Agent No-Neck had uncuffed me and brought me to his superior, Special Agent in Charge Wilson, who sat in silent stoicism, watching me with raptor-like eyes. I idly wondered if anyone knew about the horse I had stolen, but no one had mentioned it yet.

I didn't have to wait long before a familiar face entered the room. I laughed. Hard. For a good, long while. Tears were actually wetting my cheeks before I calmed down. "If it isn't my favorite hundred-pound hero." Wilson made a sound like a muffled cough, but his face remained stoic. Kosage merely stared at me, embodying a cold rage that was only mildly warmed with the satisfaction of having me under arrest and at his mercy. "*Confusion now hath made his masterpiece.*" I winked at Wilson, and not so discreetly pointed a finger at Kosage. The Agent managed to keep his face neutral, but I saw his eyes sparkle with amusement, recognizing Shakespeare's quote and seeming to silently agree. Then I turned to face the little firecracker himself. "Still toadying, Kosage?"

He scowled in response, his face slightly reddening, but kept his mouth shut.

"Go ahead, Kosage. I know you have something you would like to say to me. I'll even let you vent a bit before I put you back in your place. Like last time." I smiled, crossing my legs as I held out a hand for him to proceed. His red face grew darker.

Someone knocked on the door. Kosage and Wilson turned with a frown before the agent barked out a terse, "Enter."

Agent Jeffries, the human lie detector I had met a few months ago, stuck his head in, and I grinned. I wasn't sure what was about to happen, but he was a friendly. He nodded respectfully to his boss, ignoring Kosage entirely. "This hasn't been approved by the appropriate channels, Sir."

"Back off, Agent Jeffries. This is above your pay-grade. You're on my turf," Kosage snarled.

Jeffries didn't even acknowledge the vermin. I almost wished I had popcorn as I watched Kosage's fury practically steam out of his ears at being so blatantly ignored. "Permission to speak freely, Sir?" Jeffries asked his superior. Wilson nodded with carefully hidden amusement, so as not to further offend the already furious Kosage.

Jeffries slowly turned to address Detective Kosage, his eyes resting about a foot above his head – at the height most heads would reside. He gave a start, and then lowered his gaze to Kosage's much lower eye-level with a look of genuine surprise. I almost lost it. It was a total dick move to pick on a little guy's height. I liked it. He cleared his throat. "You're telling me that this is *above* a Federal Agent of the FBI's pay-grade, but still meets the pay-grade of a *lowly* curb-kicker on the St. Louis P.D.? You guys must have one hell of a benefits package. Perhaps you didn't spend a whole lot of time on criminal law over at the Police Academy. It's understandable. It's a *big* book. Lots of pages. I, on the other hand, being a *lowly* minion for the great cog that is the FBI, studied it quite profusely. I'll summarize for you. You can't arrest someone without probable cause. Even if you really don't like them. Even if – hypothetically, of course – they made you look like the *tiniest* little douche-bag idiot ever promoted to Detective that St. Louis has ever seen... Hypothetically." Kosage was quivering with each enunciated word referencing height or size. I was quivering, too... with barely restrained laughter. "Without solid evidence, detaining anyone – especially the wealthiest person in St. Louis – is enough to make said curb-kicker look like nothing more than a *little* Napoleon. *Over compensating*, even. Know what I mean?"

Kosage sputtered in wordless sentences, unable to speak through his anger, but I noticed that Agent Wilson was fighting a grin. "You should probably leave, Agent Jeffries." My only chance at a legitimate escape nodded before turning to me with a shrug as if to say, *Sorry*. Then he was gone.

Wilson spoke. "He's got a point, Kosage. Just ask your questions, and we'll move on from there." He turned to me, face composed again. "We do have surveillance of you at that bar last night. That should be enough for Kosage to hold you for 24 hours if he really wants to." The translation was obvious: *if we don't like your answers to our questions.*

Then Kosage laid into it, taking out his impotent aggression on me. Questioning me on everything that coincided with the dragon attack a few months ago – from the cow-tipping charge to the bribery of Gunnar. The alleged 'Demon' attack on the bridge. The cop killed at Artemis' Garter. Alaric Slate's disappearance. Then the *coup-de-gras*, "It seems that an officer lost his mount outside the bar you were caught fighting in last night. Know anything about that?"

I blinked, keeping my face neutral. I was so tired by this point that it was not that difficult. "You mean Xavier?" I asked with a frown.

Kosage leaned forward anxiously, slapping the table with a dainty palm as he finally heard something he liked. "How do you know the horse's name if you didn't kidnap him?" He accused triumphantly, turning to Agent Wilson with a victorious grin. Wilson was watching me, not acknowledging Kosage.

"Horsenap," I mumbled after yawning.

"Pardon?" Kosage breathed anxiously.

"I think you'd call it horsenapping. Calling it kidnapping seems disrespectful and... weird. If a horse is stolen, I think it's called horsenapping." I kept my face straight, speaking as I would at an academic debate, or to a small child.

"Fine. *Horsenapping* is against the law—"

I swiveled to Agent Wilson, not hiding my sudden excitement. "*Please* tell me you got that on the record. Me being accused of... horsenapping?" Wilson's eyes creased with an inner struggle not to laugh, but he nodded. "Great. That will be *excellent* in the courtroom later."

Kosage lunged at me, but Wilson barred his advance with a solid arm. Kosage knocked it away aggressively. I shrugged at Wilson. "Toddlers, right? You just can't win."

"Xavier is a mounted patrol officer for the City of St Louis. *That's* a felony. Where did you take him?" Kosage roared in retaliation.

I shrugged patiently. "I met him when I left the bar. His handler was a bit of a smart-ass, at first, but he ended up being cool in the end. He introduced me to his mount. Then I left. I was pretty drunk at the time, but I remember that much. Then I went home. He's probably eating an apple somewhere. I hear horses like apples."

Kosage scowled. "If you went home after that, why did the officer report some kind of attack less than an hour later by some sort of animal?"

I realized Kosage was actually waiting for me to answer that. "Perhaps it's because... *he was attacked less than an hour later by some sort of animal*?" I offered with a puzzled brow. I could tell it was infuriating Kosage, but I was loving it.

"The officer reported that someone else was involved."

I shrugged. "And? It's *Mardi Gras*. People are flooding the streets this time of year. This citizen must have helped him or your officer wouldn't have had a report to give you." I hoped, feeling slightly guilty, that the confusion of the attack might have allowed the officer to forget my presence. Fog of war. "What kind of animal attack?" I asked curiously.

Kosage drummed his fingers on the tabletop, realizing that he hadn't tripped me up at all. "He didn't know. I do find it curious that you were there less than an hour before he was attacked and his horse was stolen. You have a reputation for... unique events trailing you."

"Just my good fortune, I guess. Can I go now? Oh, I'll also need you to unfreeze my assets. I see no warrantable information to have done so, and I will definitely be speaking to the Mayor about this injustice. And about horsenapping," I shook my head, letting out a chuckle.

Kosage flashed me a sadistic smile. "Well, Nate. I'm so sorry to be the one to tell you, but you will be staying the night after all. Don't worry. I made a reservation under your name, on the house, of course, since you can't touch your money. I'll have more questions for you in the morning." I turned to Wilson. The man sighed, and then shrugged. "Resisting arrest. Verbal threats. Also, the missing horse is curious. You might have been the last one to see him. We'll need an alibi."

"Your no-neck detective hung up on my alibi when he arrested me. Call her back. Indiana Rippley."

The man nodded, writing down the name. "Kosage also has video footage of you tossing the cuffs back at him in the interrogation room a few months back. Then you left without being processed. He could make it stick. Tied to all the murders, it puts you in a funny spot. He just needed a little more mayhem from you to get a judge's permission. Last night was it." Wilson shrugged helplessly. He wasn't pleased with the situation, but also saw no way out of it. I nodded, actually coming to appreciate that the guy was just doing his job.

"Fine. I'll make sure you keep your job, but I predict that Kosage will be making balloon puppets for children's birthday parties next week." Kosage stood, snarled, and then stormed from the room.

They processed me, and placed me in a concrete cell. I passed out instantly, despite fearing the Demons finding me while I slept. I literally couldn't stay awake. Hell, I was lucky I hadn't nodded off during the interrogation.

Sleep found me on the rickety bench, and sent me into the equivalent of a mild coma. I was smiling as I drifted off.

15

I awoke as a drip of water struck me on the nose. It was warm. I blinked at my surroundings, trying to remember where I was. Nothing looked familiar. I was in a cold concrete room lying on a rusty bench that was bolted to the wall. Was this a night terror? Then I remembered. I was in the police station. Another thought hit me.

I had *slept*. And had no horrifying nightmare! I wanted to shout for joy. Hope's gift had helped me sleep in peace, after all!

Another drop of warm water struck my forehead this time, startling me from my reverie. I reached up to wipe it off, fearing what kind of diseased water was leaking through the pipes. When my fingers touched the water, they came back slippery. Like oil. Or blood.

I jumped up, glancing at my fingertips in the filtered light from the other room. The fluid was clear. My spine tightened in sudden alarm, but I managed to maintain my composure.

It was drool. I slowly arched my head to look at the ceiling, recognizing a smell for the first time.

Sulfur.

I had a cellmate.

"No one told me I would be sharing this cell," I muttered.

"The situation of sharing the cell is only temporary. It's about to be vacant again shortly, man-ling. Don't fret," a feminine reptilian voice hissed back in a low tone.

I let out a breath. "Well that's good. I was about to call dibs on the bench." I stared back at the Demon as she unpeeled from the ceiling like a lizard. She was naked and her body was covered in scales, but cloaked in shadows of some kind. She landed on huge, webbed talons like a dragon. But she wasn't a dragon. She was worse. The creature unfurled from her crouch, appraising me darkly, a shadowed cape billowing around her as if alive.

"We have something to discuss," she hissed.

"Really? Because I can think of absolutely *nothing* I want to talk to you about. I mean, literally nothing. In fact, it would be best if you just left. I was having a really raunchy dream about exorcising this scaly, ugly son of a bitch." I hesitated, appraising my cellmate more closely. "In fact, she looked a hell of a lot like you. Isn't that weird?" I shifted my stance in order to better react to any attack. The Demon blinked. Then she laughed.

"Exorcise? Me? You really are as arrogant as they say." She shook her head, wiping a jagged claw across her face as if to wipe away a tear. "They didn't tell me about your sense of humor! *Exorcise*! Ha!" She slapped her knees, laughing, the shadows swarming around as if alive. She was creepy, deadly, and I was scared out of my mind, but I briefly thought it would be pretty cool to have a coat that looked and acted like a shadow. I felt whispers in the corner of my mind, hypothesizing, analyzing, and mentally discarding ways to achieve just that.

It was as if I suddenly had a team of mad scientists in my brain working overtime for my subconscious. My thoughts briefly snagged on a way to possibly make a cloak of shadows and I froze for a second. "Well, shit. That wouldn't actually be that hard. How come no one else has figured that out?" I asked aloud. I was pretty sure I could make one. I had a mental image of my subconscious scientist doppelganger sporting horn-rimmed glasses and a comb-over as he fist-bumped me with a successful screech at figuring out the shadow cloak.

I hesitated, wondering again if this was another one of those dreams. The Demon was watching me as if doubting my sanity. "What in the bloody Heavens are you talking about, wizard?"

I shrugged. "I dig your threads," I said, pointing at the wavering shadows.

One of the tendrils reeled back and hissed at me in the shape of a cobra.

I jumped back in surprise. Well, maybe I hadn't figured it *all* out yet.

"Enough. I'm here to talk of my brother. You had a horse kick him. Through a building. That wasn't nice. He just wanted to take something from you. The Key. I'm here to accept your apology."

She waited.

I waited.

"Well, this is awkward. What did your brother look like again? I've taken out quite a few Demons lately."

She watched me. "Apologize, and I won't strip the flesh from your bones... as slowly as I originally intended. If you give me the Key now, I'll even grant you a clean death."

My muscles tightened. The Key again. What was with these guys? What could they want from the Armory, and how could I give them a Key that didn't exist? I knew I was in for a scrap, and without using magic, I would simply *become* a scrap... of discarded flesh and bone. I decided to stall as I set my mental team of mad scientists to finding a way for me to beat this Demon without magic. Which probably wasn't likely, but worth a shot. I would no doubt have to resort to tapping into my power or become a puddle of goo for the morning janitor. At least Kosage would enjoy my ending. In my head, I knew that any solution even remotely tied to me being a Maker would no doubt require a shitload of magic, which I couldn't afford to do, even though I wanted to see what kind of things I could actually accomplish. I silently encouraged my minions to go old school.

"What exactly do you want the Key for? I don't think Demons would last long in the Armory," I said honestly, remembering Hope's hatred of them.

"True. But the answer will not aid you."

"The Angels really don't want me talking to you."

"You've spoken with them?" she hissed in surprise. I nodded, hoping this would scare her off. "Ah, but the Angels can't really *do* anything in this realm, can they? There are rules, after all."

"Rules?" I asked, feeling slightly better… and worse. If the Angels couldn't directly act on this plane, then I might have a chance to survive being turned into a pillar of salt. It also meant that I would be killed sooner, like right about now.

The Demon smiled, revealing rotted, blackened, razor-sharp fangs. "Angels cannot act on earth. It would ignite Armageddon. If they acted overtly, the Demons could also act overtly. Which would start World War A." I blinked.

"World War A?"

"Yes. As in *Armageddon*." The Demon grinned wide, lips peeling back with excitement. "Everything must be in balance. If an Angel acts discreetly, a Demon can do something discreetly. This is why we use cat's paws."

I stared at her. "You mean possessions. Summonings." It wasn't a question.

The Demon nodded.

"Then how do Angels act? With the Nephilim?"

The Demon flinched at the word, watching me with renewed interest. But she didn't answer. "Enough. I'm bored. Time to give up the Key." I shook my head, trying to come up with a way to fight this soldier from Hell. "So be it. Say *hello* to your parents for me." She smiled.

Then she moved.

I juked to the side, causing her talons to dig into the concrete for a better purchase. I grasped the bench, and with a tiny boost of magic directed at the bolts securing it to the wall, I tore it away and swung it at her head. She raised an arm to block. It crumpled over her arm and shoulders, leaving a Demon shaped dent that she shrugged off after a moment. Then she began to laugh. I pointed at her hand.

"But I did break your nail. I bet a manicure for something like that isn't cheap. Do you use bolt-cutters or something?"

She looked down at her claw, and then used her fangs to forcefully rip the talon from her finger before she spat it out onto the floor. Drops of blood dripped freely from the wound, sizzling on the concrete floor like sulfuric acid.

She appraised me with a cocked head. "My turn." My mind went a million miles an hour, trying to find a way to fight her without draining my power. But there was nothing else in the room to use as a weapon or distraction. It was magic or death. Even with magic, it would be like…

Well, a prison brawl.

Demons were tough. After all, I had just hit a home run on her arm with an aluminum bench and it had only broken her nail. She darted at me, her shadow cloak whipping back and forth erratically so that I couldn't really see exactly where she was. The only way to kill a Demon was to hack them to pieces or exorcise them. Exorcising was out of the question because I had been stripped of any items that could possibly help me do so, and I didn't dare risk wasting the power necessary to do it without those items.

Then I had an idea. I waited, stock still, knowing it was reckless, but that it might be my only chance. I let her hit me, her claws latching onto my chest. Her talons began sinking into my flesh, and… I Shadow Walked. Kind of.

I teleported us a few feet away, releasing the hold on my magic almost the same instant we started to shift. I heard a gasp from her snarling fangs as they lunged closer, ready to eat my face. I twisted my head back to dodge the fangs and look where we had stood only a moment ago. The bottom half of her body had been cut off as I let go of the magic, essentially slicing her neatly in half. I had gotten the idea from the tiny piece of fabric I had seen when I cold-cocked Gunnar earlier today. It had been a piece of my shirt. Luckily, I had found out about the dangers of Shadow Walking on my tee, but it had come in handy just now. I shoved off the sudden weight of her upper body, careful not to get any of her blood on me. Her claws hadn't sunk in deep, but my chest still burned as I extracted them from my torso. She blinked up at me, stunned. "The Key isn't up for grabs. Tell your boss I said so." Blood pooled on the floor, hissing as it scorched the concrete. I sat in the corner of the room and hugged my knees, watching the life fade from her eyes.

I didn't have time for this. I could always Shadow Walk out of here, and hope that it didn't use up too much energy. But that would only freak out every cop in the building and put me on the most wanted list. And I knew the cops would have to release me tomorrow. They didn't have any solid evidence to hold me. And I *did* need the sleep. But apparently, I wasn't even safe in jail. They were taking great risks to get the Key to the Armory.

Time.

I didn't have any of it to waste. I needed to find a way to remove the curse from the Academy. It was going to get me killed if I was always hesitating. Maybe I could talk Gavin into releasing me. Yeah, right. The Demon's body disintegrated into a pile of ash with a puff, but the blood remained. That was odd. I watched as it slowly ate away at the concrete, edging closer and closer to me. I doubted it would actually reach me. It was already slowing down.

My thoughts went to Indie. I hoped she was okay, and that her mother was feeling better. I knew she had to be terrified after that son of a bitch officer had answered my phone. They had conveniently forgotten to grant me a phone call yet. My thoughts drifted to the cops and FBI. They had frozen my assets. I was essentially penniless. I had no idea how legal that was, but with someone as rich as myself, perhaps they had different rules. I could, after all, buy my way out of almost anything. Maybe they considered that a flight risk. Kind of like a weapon. Huh. I hadn't ever thought of it like that, but it was pretty smart on their part.

This was the second Demon to attack me in less than a day, and they had both wanted the Key. The Key that was actually my blood. They hadn't seemed too concerned about killing me, which let me know they had no idea how valuable I was. Which was good. If they killed me, they would never be able to get into the Armory. Hoorah! Temple wins by default! I remembered Hope's idle comment about answers being found through death. And I shivered.

I understood how Demons were able to interact on earth, but how did Angels sneak around? I mean, I had been directly manhandled in the bar by one of the feathery saints and his crew of Nephilim. How was that kosher? Did that mean that even now, a Demon had been granted the opportunity to act overtly? Had Eae's assault allowed the first Demon to appear only an hour later and attack me? Was that why the Nephilim had been with him?

Jesus. Had the Angel caused the war by coming to talk to me? I sensed the air with my powers, knowing that it didn't actually use any of my magic to do so. Everything felt more or less the same. The world didn't feel Armageddon-y. I shook my head. Regardless, I needed to find out how Angels were *supposed* to interact on earth – most likely through the Nephilim – lest I be surprised by a third party over the next few days. I couldn't afford a surprise attack. And I really didn't know how I felt about killing a soldier from Heaven. Even though the only Angel I had met so far had been kind of a dick, he was just doing his job. He saw me as a threat for some reason. Still, I thought there might have been a better way for him to handle it. Like with a group prayer or something. I sighed, frustrated. So far, I had managed to piss off an Angel, two Demons, three cops, a gaggle of Nephilim, and eight Academy members. Each of these groups had given me contradictory demands. Abiding by one set of commands made me *persona non-grata* for the other groups. Catch-22 to the third power. Even worse, I had limited power to fix the situation, and no friends to help me out. I felt my anger growing as I tried to think about what I could do to get out of this shit show.

Then the lights in the room abruptly winked out.

I scanned the darkness as I lurched to my feet, fearing another Demon was about to appear and jump me. I found my way to the bars and tried to peer outside my cell. I was pretty sure that the power to the entire building had just gone out. Emergency lights flickered to life, bathing me in a faint red glow. I began to get real nervous as I heard feet pounding down the stairs. I slowly backed up, ready to unleash hell. I had no idea who was here, but I had no doubt they were coming for me, and the only people coming for me were the biggest of the big hitters. Angels. Demons. Academy Justices. If

I was lucky, they might create a joint task force to take me out together, like a dark Justice League. My thoughts ran with that as I heard a door finally open and the footsteps quickly approach my cell.

I raised my hands, ready to vaporize the intruder. I spotted my foe across the room, slowly creeping closer and closer as if on all fours. A green glow emanated at its hip, which made me think of Hell. Then a *face* from Hell materialized as it crept closer. Horns, and war paint covering the upper half of its head. Then it sparkled in the green glow. I blinked. Glitter? Bedazzled Demons?

"Pharos?" I heard a familiar voice call out quietly.

My fear was instantly replaced by confusion and... hope. I raced back to the bars. "Othello?" I hissed in disbelief.

"The one and only." She said, sliding back her *Le Carnevale* mask to reveal her familiar face. I could have cried. She stepped up to the bars to touch my fingers. Pretty girls make graves, and Othello was breathtaking. Shorter than some, but stacked more than most, she sported a thick, wavy pony tail, and she had a small oval-shaped face, with plump cheeks just perfect for squeezing. I glanced at her *Le Carnevale* mask, shaking my head. "Like my disguise? I have one for you also," she cooed. "It's *Mardi Gras*, after all," she said with a grin.

"What are you *doing* here?"

"You didn't answer your phone." I blinked. "I guess you could call me clingy." She winked. I scowled back, shaking my head at her grin. "When you didn't answer your phone, I traced the embedded GPS and saw, to my surprise, your phone was here in this government building. Of course, I decided a face-to-face was necessary. Nobody takes my Pharos. Especially not the government."

I smiled. Othello *hated* the government. Any of them. That was why she was one of the world's most renowned cyber criminals. And they didn't even know who she really was. She was *good*. For her to risk breaking into a federal building to save me had put her at great risk, and it showed me how much she cared for me. Even after all this time. I wasn't quite sure how she spent her time outside of cyber stuff, but I had reason to believe that it wasn't *all* computer stuff. She had made several hints about having unsavory contacts in her debt.

Her glow stick illuminated my cell – revealing the Demon-shaped bench and the blood all over the floor. "Why is there... blood on the floor? Did they hurt you?" She looked suddenly murderous.

"I had a visitor. From my side of the park," I added, emphasizing that it hadn't been a human. "She wouldn't leave when I asked her to." Othello finally nodded after a moment.

"Good riddance," she muttered. "Now, stand back," she warned. Then she began fidgeting with the barred door. I did, still wondering how the hell she was here, what the hell she was doing, and how the hell we were going to get out. This was the freaking police station. For St. Louis. Not really a Barney Fife-type operation with only a single cop napping outside. These police had military grade weapons and a SWAT team for crying out loud. It seemed I was going to need to tap into my magic pretty soon.

I was kind of pissed about this. Here I was, about to be broken out of jail, which would only put me further in the cross-hairs of the police. When it was very likely they were going to release me tomorrow.

"Othello," I warned. "This is crazy. They're going to release me tomorrow. I don't have time to add *America's Most Wanted* to my resume. Just wait. I'll find you as soon as they release me so we can talk. But right now, you need to go. Please. They'll be here any second."

She halted, looking up at me. "No. They won't," she replied in a very cold tone.

My skin pebbled at that. She said it with such finality, as if there was no way the cops were going to come down here. As if... they were no longer a danger. At all. Or ever again.

"Othello... what do you mean? What did you do to them? They were only doing their jobs."

She blinked at me, and then laughed. "I didn't *kill* them. Jesus, Nate. They're *cops*. I called in a threat to empty the majority of the precinct." Her voice jumped an octave, sounding terrified as she mimicked a phone call. "Oh, my gawd! There's a bomb at Queenie's, the gay bar downtown. They're threatening to blow the place up to cleanse the way for God's Children! They said they would only surrender to a man named Kosage. I just came out here to dance, and now everyone's running and screaming! I already see a news crew setting up a block away! I have to go!" She flashed me a self-satisfied grin.

"You're telling me that you set up a bomb at a gay club to... bust me out of jail? I assume it's not going to explode in a shower of glitter and rainbows? You could hurt people!" I needed to get her out of here. And go save the people at the bar.

"There's no bomb, Nate. Although that glitter idea would have been great. When the cops arrive, they're going to see a poster-sized picture of your friend Kosage on a float wearing a pink unitard, with the song '*I'm coming out, I want the world to know...*' blaring on three sets of independently-wired speakers. I informed the patrons at the bar that a famous detective would be arriving tonight to come out of the closet and to support the gay community in St. Louis for *Mardi Gras*. His fellow officers were gathering to support him, with flashing lights for a celebration. The news was also in on it, so they needn't be alarmed." I blinked at her, my mouth opening wordlessly several times. And then I burst out laughing. "The float is titled *Napoleon comes Out*," she added softly. Apparently, Othello had been working on this for some time. There was no way she could have arranged this since my call to her earlier this afternoon.

"This wasn't a spur of the moment thing, was it? How did you Photoshop a picture of Kosage in a unitard, and... why?" I asked in genuine amazement.

She began to laugh, doubling over as she placed the last gadget on the cell door. "That's the best part." She enunciated the next words concisely. "*It. Wasn't. Photoshopped.* I'd intended to use the picture and the float at the Parade, but with what he did to you, the timing couldn't have been more perfect. It serves him right. I used sleeping gas to knock out the rest of the officers upstairs, so me and my team could bust in. I didn't *kill* anyone, Nate. But..." Her face grew troubled. "They aren't planning to release you tomorrow. I hacked into their phones. You weren't going anywhere. That's why I'm here. To bust you out. Something big is going down in St. Louis. And I think it has to do with your investigation into your parents' murder." She watched my face. "We'll talk about that later. Now, I need to get you out of here. Step back. I don't know exactly what's going to happen when I push this button."

"Then maybe you shouldn't—"

She pressed something and the metal at the door disintegrated in seconds, amidst a whining, grinding, and electrical sound like a thousand termites in fast-forward. It stopped after two seconds. The door let out a final groan before it fell into my cell with a resounding crash, barely missing my toes.

"Wow," she said, sounding surprised.

I blinked. I hadn't sensed any magic, and didn't smell any chemicals. And it hadn't been explosive, either. I stepped closer to her, staying on my side of the door, careful not to touch the gate that had fallen into the cell. "What in the hell was *that*?"

"Nano-bots." She grinned at the look on my face, and then shrugged. "Put this on." She handed me a *Le Carnevale* mask and a flannel shirt. I put them on. She adjusted it so that it was crooked, as if forced on me. "Good. I already grabbed your stuff from lockup, since the things you carry are usually dangerous to the uninitiated Regular. Now, come on." She grabbed my hand. Her fingers were feverish as we rushed out of the holding area. She hesitated at the last door, peering through the window. I could see several bodies slumbering on the floor, and several spent canisters lying here and there like discarded beer cans at a party. She nodded to herself, rearranging my mask again slightly. "Okay. I need you to follow me. Act like you're being kidnapped and that you're drugged from the gas. That way they can't suspect you in what happened, and what happens next." She grinned at that. "Don't speak. Building is wired. Just follow me like a victim. A scared puppy."

I began to protest when she suddenly kicked the door open and jerked me forward. I stumbled, playing the part she had requested, but inside I was fuming. What did she have planned that was any worse than what she'd already done? The mask scratched at my face, and ruined my peripheral vision, but I continued on, following her lead obediently, sluggishly.

Instead of heading for the front doors, or even a back door, we headed into the office area for the detectives. This couldn't be good.

Othello reached into her backpack and tossed an official looking folder on a nearby table.

She tossed another, different looking folder on a separate desk, then she jabbed me in the stomach, pulling her punch at the last second. I had instinctively tensed up for the hit, but quickly realized she was acting for the camera in the corner ceiling. She was good. I doubled over before allowing her to yank me the opposite direction. I followed on her heels, shuffling my feet as she led me out to a back alley where I discovered a limo idling for us.

"Here's our ride. Let's go." I followed her into the backseat and slammed into the leather as the driver floored the gas. With that, we were roaring through the city. Othello tore off her mask and hooted out the open sunroof.

I looked at her in amazement. "Wow. You're kind of awesome," I said after a few moments.

She grinned back, grabbing my hand. "You have no idea."

She continued holding my hand. After a few seconds, I politely pulled away and took off my mask.

"Your *face!*" she hissed.

"Not exactly one for bedside manner, are you?" I scowled. She smiled guiltily, shaking her head. "What exactly did you put on that desk?" I could see a calculating look in her eyes at both my black eyes and the fact that I hadn't resumed our handholding. But now wasn't the time to tell her about Indie. *Hey, thanks for risking your life to bust me out of jail, but I've got this kick-ass girlfriend. You two should meet. Maybe go shopping or something! It would be so much fun!*

Yeah, right.

Her smile came back in an instant. "More pictures of our friend, Kosage."

"What kind of pictures?" I asked carefully.

"BDSM." She caught my gaze. "Again, *not* Photoshopped."

I blinked at her. Then I hooted out the sunroof. Despite what happened next, Kosage's life had just gotten a whole lot shittier. Thanks to my little friend, Othello, cyber-criminal extraordinaire.

Life was good.

"I also included some photos of Kosage involved in some questionable extracurricular activities."

I shook my head, grinning. "Oh?"

Her eyes twinkled. "I didn't like how he treated you a few months back so I made a file for him. Currently, he's known to frequent Craigslist for Dominatrixes. The file has some pictures of him in some compromising gear. Pink gear. He will shortly be on the news for an altogether different reason." She didn't elaborate, but I could hardly wait. "I don't like people causing my Pharos trouble."

Picking up on her not-so-subtle words, I changed topics. "Who's driving us?" The divider was up, so I couldn't tell.

"Someone who owed me a favor. He repaid it with the extraction and the sleeping canisters. I think I about used up all my favors with this job. He's taking us to a safehouse since I assumed yours was not usable anymore." She leaned forward eagerly, squeezing my hand. "The other file I left was a ransom note for one Nathin Temple, by the way. Perfect cover for you. You can't be suspected in your own kidnapping!" She looked triumphant.

I shook my head, smiling at her. Oh well, I was technically broke, now, so I could use the money. If anyone paid. It wasn't like I could pay my own ransom. I mean, all my funds were frozen. Things were getting interesting. But she was right. At least I'd managed to escape without being an accomplice. "I guess we're about to find out how much the city likes me."

Othello grinned. "They can't afford you. I set it at One Hundred Million."

"Oh, well..." At least I was free for now. I would just have to make sure that the FBI didn't spot me in the next few days. Maybe I could call Jeffries to help me out. I didn't want to ruin his career though, so I would only do so as a last resort. I knew if I spoke with Jeffries, whether I told him the truth or not, he would *know*. It was his gift. He could sense lies. Talking to him at all would basically get him involved on a level that could ruin his career. I couldn't do that to a friend. Like I had with Gunnar.

And the party of one became two.

16

After several minutes of small talk, Othello reached into her bag and handed me my stuff from lockup. I eagerly turned on my cell phone and began shifting through the rest of my belongings as I waited for the phone to power up. Othello turned to watch the streets for signs of pursuit, but so far so good. I looked out my side of the car, wondering where Othello's safe house was as the number of graffiti-scarred ancient buildings began to increase. We were miles from the police station by now, and I felt my tension slowly evaporating with each passing block. The lights grew fewer and farther between as we headed through a more desolate section of the city. The air was cold, and the darkness of night reigned supreme, but at least we were police-free. I turned back to my goodies, pocketing some of them until only the most relevant items still sat in my hands. There was the Demon-sensing stone Hope had given me, my wallet with a little bit of cash in it – which would come in handy now that my accounts were frozen – and a few other magical knick-knacks. I texted Indie the moment the phone turned on. *Sorry about the confusion earlier with the FBI. Available to talk whenever you are. I didn't want to wake you up in case you were sleeping. Miss you!*

As I set my phone down, the Demon-sensing stone began to vibrate in my lap. I picked it up and stared at it for a few seconds, confused. I hadn't said anything to it, and I couldn't hear the creepy voices speaking to me.

I could feel Othello's tension rising as she watched out of the corner of her eye. "Why is it doing th—"

An incredible force suddenly slammed into the side of the limo, knocking us into a nearby building with a squeal of tires and crunching metal. The side of my head rebounded off the door, making my injured nose flare with heat, and my skull ring like a Looney Tunes character. Broken safety glass showered the inside of the car and brick dust clouded the windshield, eliminating our chances of seeing outside the car to discern what had caused the wreck. I grasped the door handle to try and get us out, but it was pointless. I was wedged up against the wall of the building.

Before I could speak, more glass exploded into the driver's seat as a giant claw entered the car, latched onto the driver's skull, and simply... extracted it like a berry from a bush. Blood splattered the windshield, front seats, and dashboard, even the glass divider that protected the driver from his passengers, painting everything a gooey, viscous red. As the blood and gore began to drip down the glass, something heavy landed on the hood with a *thunk*.

Through the blood and dust, I saw that it was the driver's head; eyes still wide with shock, staring at us in confusion. I hadn't even known his name.

Othello began to scream, lunging towards me as another clawed fist shattered the back window and latched onto her leg. I grabbed onto her hands and we were both promptly jerked from the car, my side slicing open as I was jerked over the remaining safety glass and through the tiny opening in the window. Othello's continued screams filled the night, but so did a malevolent, ancient laughter. Still attached to each other like the children's toy, *Barrel of Monkeys*, we were then unceremoniously tossed into the brick building. My head cracked against the brick hard enough for stars to explode across my vision.

Lucky for Othello, I had hit the wall first, so my body significantly cushioned her impact against the ancient brick, which didn't feel great for me in general, but especially didn't feel great over my freshly scraped sides. We hit the ground heavily, my head ringing from the two impacts in less than a minute. I felt like Humpty Dumpty. I heard Othello groan as I quickly assessed my injuries. She wasn't cut out for this, and she had stepped into a game against forces she couldn't even fathom, let alone survive.

I stumbled to my feet, still clutching the bone artifact in my fist. My phone lay in the center of the street by the smoking limo.

Directly in front of a towering Demon.

He was at least nine feet tall and covered in knotted dreadlocks with broken teeth and bones woven throughout his coarse body hair like a sinisterly-decorated Christmas tree. "They have people who do corn-rows in Hell?" I mumbled under my breath.

The Demon snarled back at me from beneath the wild mane of hair around his ginormous head, brushing the bones on his fur with a purring noise. There were enough bones woven into his hair that they might have even doubled as an armor, of sorts. Giant scarred fists flexed at his side as he let out another leonine roar, drool dripping off his fangs as he flexed his entire body, bulging with energy-filled muscle. A lot of it. "It speaks," the Demon growled.

"And *it* is about to whoop the living fuck out of you, Thundercat," I took a step forward and felt a warning wave of heat strike me like an oven door had just opened. The Demon's eyes flared like the burning embers at the center of a fire, halting my advance. There was no way in hell I was putting up with this right now. There was also no way we were surviving if I didn't dig deep into my magical reserves. I could sense the energy pouring out of this monster like a furnace. There was no running. Only fighting. I was fine with that. I was done pussyfooting around, even if it would drain a big chunk of my power. I held up my fist, and the offensive heat diverged around me. I held my fist out as I began to stride forward again.

My phone began to ring. It was pretty close to his foot. "Hold on, pal. I need to take this really quick." I began jogging towards the Demon, holding up a finger for patience.

The Demon stared at me in disbelief, and then lifted a giant clawed foot, ready to bring it smashing down onto my phone. "You won't be conversing with your metal Familiar."

My metal Familiar? He didn't know what a phone was? Rather than pondering that too long, I unleashed a hissing whip of purple darkness, the new power a result of the energy-manipulating experiments I had been tinkering on for months. It consisted of the coldest substance I had ever heard of, and once it grabbed onto something, it didn't let go until I commanded it, literally causing the worse freezer-burn ever. I lassoed the Demon's foot, the power of the substance burning straight to the bone in a second and a half, causing the stench of burnt hair to fill the street. The Demon roared in true pain. Then I swung the whip wide, hurtling the Demon straight into a lamppost across the street.

It bent into a ninety-degree angle.

The Demon crumpled to the street. I didn't even wait to see if he got up. That *had* to hurt him. At least a little bit. I needed to answer my phone or Indie was going to kill me.

I quickly snatched it up, answering the face-time call through the cracked screen. Indie's face filled the screen and I smiled at her. "Indie!" I shouted in relief. "Listen. I'm kind of tied up at the mom—"

"You don't listen very well, wizard." A fist grabbed me around the neck, lifting me high into the air and holding me there as I futilely kicked my feet. The air was slowly being choked from me and I couldn't even speak. The Demon warily plucked the phone from my fist, glancing down at the cracked screen with slight anxiety, as if nervous of the floating face that was cursing at him. Then he pointed it away from his face in apparent fear.

Indie's shriek filled the deserted street. "Nate? What *was* that? What's going on? Are you okay? I got your text. *Nate?* Say something. Stop breathing into the phone like a creep!" She sounded exhausted, and frustrated, like she had been up all night crying.

"I am a Greater Demon. On the pathway to becoming a true Knight of Hell after this brief sojourn. And I am about to skin your lover. Your assistance will not save him, Familiar," the lion Demon growled back at the phone, still fearful of directly facing the screen, despite his brave threat. He was on track to become a true Knight of Hell? What did that even mean? Was he, like, a recruit for Sir Lucifer's Knights of the Crooked Table or something? A sword-bearer for the Prince of Darkness? I mentally upgraded him from Thundercat to Hell's version of Lancelot. Sir Dreadsalot. Then he shattered the phone on the ground, stomped on it several times for good measure, and hooted in triumph. As I dangled there helplessly, my vision dwindling to a single point, I realized that this Demon honestly thought he had vanquished a great foe – my phone. He looked back up at me as if surprised to still see me dangling, choking to death in his fist. Then he tossed me over the limo, back into the brick building where I struck a bit harder than the first time, and then I landed on top of Othello in a heap of elbows and knees. It seemed to wake her up because she swung an elbow and clocked me in the ridge above my eye in self-defense. I gasped in pain as my nose flared with sudden heat. I blinked several times through the pounding headache. My breath came in through raw gasps. It felt like I had torn some important muscle or ligament in my throat, my breath making slight whistling noises. I could feel the bloody scratches from his claws on my neck burning slightly, frighteningly close to my femoral artery, or was it carotid artery? Regardless, it was one of my body's important blood tubes, but the wounds weren't deep.

I climbed to my feet and stumbled around the limo, noticing that the Demon eyed me more warily than before, the skin of his leg still smoking from my first attack. "Now I'm going to have to kick your ass, because she is going to kick mine for that."

"I destroyed your metal Familiar. It is no more." He pointed at the shattered device, quivering with a proud chuckle.

I blinked at him. Was he really that ignorant to the ways of the world? That was both a good thing and a bad thing. If he was really that ignorant, it meant that he hadn't spent much time on earth, which meant that he hadn't possessed anyone yet or else he would have had their knowledge at his disposal. Which meant that maybe he wasn't exaggerating when he said he was a Greater Demon. Which meant that he was *really* dangerous, and *really* old.

Goddamn it. I didn't even know if I had the juice to take on a run-of-the-mill possession, let alone a literal Demon that had been summoned here in the flesh.

Then I blinked as that dawned on me. The *only* way a real Demon was here on earth in the flesh was if someone had *summoned* him. That meant someone else was calling the shots. Someone I didn't know about. Before I could say anything brilliant, the Demon spoke, taking an aggressive step forward.

"You killed one of my daughters this night. I shall have my retribution by flossing my teeth with your flesh and adding your bones to my armor."

"Well that's uber-gross. But that's not how this is going to play out, Sir Dreadsalot."

The Demon chuckled. "You think you can defeat *me*? A Greater Demon?"

"We'll get to that in a minute. First of all, I have a question. Being a Greater Demon, how is it possible for you to be here? Is it because Eae interacted with me at the bar last night? I don't think even the baddest of wizards could summon a Greater Demon. Not without a whole bunch of people, and even then, there are rules. Certain times of the year, rituals, relics, certain number of people, and tons of other particular things that I really don't believe could have occurred."

The Demon blinked. "You know more than you should about the rules of Heaven and Hell. How?" he asked me, genuinely appearing threatened by my knowledge. Shit. I had stumbled across something I wasn't supposed to know.

"Your daughter told me," I answered.

His muscles bunched together, increasing his size. "She wouldn't."

I shrugged. "How else would I know? It's not like I summon many Demons. You should know the truth of that."

The Demon's eyes appraised me, and suddenly looked more than slightly afraid beneath all of that life-threatening muscle, teeth and claws. I was pretty sure that I had just been upgraded to a liability.

"Enough. I do not suffer liars. You attacked my son, and killed my daughter. For that, you shall die. You will give me the Key, and then I will let you and your plaything die."

"You see, Sir Dreadsalot, I don't think your boss would like that. You know, the wizard who summoned you," I clarified, not wanting him to take it as me talking about God, or Lucifer, or someone from his neighborhood. I really needed to brush up on my hierarchy of Angelic and Demonic beings. I honestly didn't know who worked for whom, and in what order, or if maybe some of them were free agents. "He wants the Key, which means that you have to *get* the Key. I can honestly tell you that killing me would get you nothing, and I know a bit about what powers a summoner would hold over a Demon they call to earth if said Demon fails. They take a bit of your power for themselves. I don't think you want that, do you?"

The Demon scowled back.

"Now, if you want me to help you, I need to know the who, what, and why of your situation. This is the third time I've been attacked by your kind about this Key, so it's obvious your boss wants it, and made it a condition to allow you to run free. I've been attacked by my own kind for this Key, and even the Angels have threatened me about it. I want—"

"The Angels have been in contact with you? How dare they interfere!"

"Yeah. Pot. Kettle. Black," I said. I didn't let on that I saw Othello creeping around a second parked car. She was holding something. Not good. If she entered the fight, there was no way I could protect her. "So, answers?" I demanded, attempting to distract him.

The Demon watched me thoughtfully. Then he pulled a freaking sword out of the Ether, straight from Hell. "We will do this my way." Then he charged me. I backed up against the limo, and felt blood wetting my back from the driver's corpse. It pissed me off. I held out my arms and cast a cloud of steam straight at the Demon's head. It instantly melted the flesh from his face, and he shrieked in agony, diving away from the cloud and swatting his face with a meaty paw. I began to feel good. Like I maybe had a chance at survival. "Bad kitty," I snarled.

The sword missed me by a millimeter, sinking into the limo by my shoulder like it was made of paper. I blinked. I hadn't even seen him move. He had freaking hurled it at me. Then he was charging me again, on all fours this time. I could see his skull through the dying skin on his face as it peeled back at the force of his speed. I jumped to the left just as he swiped at me, and unleashed a blast of white-hot fire directly onto his back. He roared in pain and swatted me onto the ground where I bounced, once, twice, and then struck another nearby parked car. I lay there, suddenly noticing the power I had been throwing around. It was a lot. As I delved into my reservoir, I noticed that it was significantly lower. I gulped. That wasn't good. I touched my head, noticed I was bleeding, and looked up to see the Demon slowly walking towards me. Then he hesitated, a new thought crossing his ugly melted face as he studied me on the ground.

"As much pleasure as I would get from skinning you, I believe I could cause you more agony by doing something else. I sense that your power is dwindling, but that you would use it all against me if necessary. Instead, I will allow you to live, and to keep what remains of your draining power. You will need it to choose who lives and who dies."

I blinked at him, confused. "Pardon?"

The Demon smiled through his scalded face. "Every day you delay in giving my brethren what they seek, I shall murder one of your fellow wizard-lings."

I stared at him. Wizard-lings. That was ancient terminology. It didn't mean wizards, it meant any number of magical creatures: wizards, werewolves, fairies, witches, and vampires. "What do you mean?"

"Every day you delay in giving me or my offspring the Key, I will arrange for one of your fellow supernaturals to be murdered in a very public way. I've enjoyed my jaunt into your realm, but I tire of servitude. Give me the Key and we both walk away happy, with less death on your shoulders, and less annoyance on mine."

I knew this was a tricky situation. Even if I wanted to save their lives, I couldn't give up the Key to the Armory... my blood. I *literally* couldn't. Then who would stand up to the summoner? No one would even find out who he was if I was dead. If I survived, others would think that I simply gave up the Key like a coward. The Angels would be after me. The Academy would be after me. Or if I were already dead, my friends would pay. They would shun my name to the entire magical world, and I would become the most hated being ever to walk the earth, depending on who wanted the Key and what they were intending to do with it. My guess was that if the summoner was using Demons to get it he didn't have noble intentions.

"Give me the Key to the Armory so I can give it to my master and be done with my servitude. I'll even let you live, wizard. No one needs die, and I will cast my Demons back to Hell. Win, win."

His offer chilled me. But I just couldn't give him the Key. Even if I wanted to. I was kind of... attached to it. I briefly remembered Hope's warning about Death being the ultimate answer and shivered. After a deep breath, I nodded, feeling something in my pocket that I had stashed away earlier. "On one condition. You tell me who murdered my parents."

The Demon watched me, considering. Then, a dark smile crept over his face. "Deal." I pulled the small object out of my pocket, looked at it once in defeat, and then tossed it to him. His eyes gleamed as he snatched it from the air. He began to examine the music box that Peter had stolen from the Armory. I had tried everything, testing it every way I could think, but had yet to find anything dangerous or powerful about it. It was simply a music box.

But the Demon didn't know that, and he seemed particularly aloof to the ways of my world, not even knowing what a cell phone was.

"*I* killed your parents."

Time seemed to slow, then stop entirely.

My vision turned red and my blood instantly boiled, making me feel like an inferno of fire, as if someone had just lit a fuse deep in my soul. My parents' murderer stood before me, and I was ready to burn away the last of my remaining strength to incinerate him so ultimately that even his cellmates in Hell would never recognize him.

He watched my impotent rage with an amused smile. "They stood between me and the Armory. Of course, back then there was no Key. But I knew they would prevent me from entering so I eliminated them. Then that thief snuck in while I was entertaining your parents, locking the entrance from me. Since then the room has been guarded by a Key. It all could have been so simple if it wasn't for him." He growled with minor frustration. Then he smiled at me. "But you know that already. If not for him, your parents may still be alive. Shame. He was your best friend after all. If that's what you do to your friends, I'd love to see what you do to your enemies." His fangs glittered in the moonlight. I could only see red. This was my parents' murderer. Right here. In front of me.

And I couldn't do a goddamned thing. I was tapped, magically speaking. If I fought this Demon here I wouldn't have enough juice for the summoner, and he was the real problem.

He watched me, enjoying my pain. "Easy, wizard. You might use up the last of your strength. Then who would save your friends? Now that I have the Key, we will depart this plane." He fidgeted with the box, and then frowned at it. He held it up to his ear. Scowling, he opened it to the effect of a tinny version of "You are my sunshine," filling the street. He roared in anger, throwing it on the ground. "What trickery is this? You thought you could fool me?"

I smiled. "Well, technically I *did* just fool you. Don't be offended. I do it to everyone."

The Demon moved. And when I say moved, I mean faster than even I could clearly see. He raised his arm, a nebulous dark ball of energy coursing around his fist. Then it came screaming at me. I raised my trembling arms to block it, but it bypassed my defenses easily, and a burning sensation struck me in the forehead like he had thrown a well-aimed, scalding rock. It instantly seared my skin like a brand. I found myself on the ground, staring up at the starry night. It had begun to snow, looking like the very stars were falling all around me.

Like Fallen Angels cast down from Heaven.

I didn't know how long I lay there, but it must have been only seconds, as I heard the Demon step up to me with a curious respect in his eyes.

"You shouldn't have tried to trick me. You have now been marked. The Angels will see you as an Agent of Hell. Even their sons will hunt you, and the Armory will be lost to everyone, for they will raze it, and possibly your entire city, to the ground. Also, my previous offer of your brethren dying upon each denied offer of the Key still stands. Each night you delay, we will murder a member of a different supernatural caste. Since you seem to care for the werewolves so much, we will begin with them. One will die before sunrise, unless you give me what I seek."

I briefly wondered how many of his brethren were enjoying their stay in my city. How many I needed to fight to protect my people. Sir Dreadsalot took a step closer, leaning so that I could see his scarred, melted face clearly. "I do applaud you on your trickery, and that lucky strike, though. Never seen anything like it. Do you make a habit of discovering new spells? Most wizards repeat the same old same old. Boring. But you, you're... *fun.*" He seemed genuinely appreciative. "Don't waste it here. Save it for our next encounter. I love anticipation. Foreplay. Mmmm... Just imagine how much fun the werewolf will have tonight."

My soul hurt. I was basically condemning an innocent werewolf to die. For some reason, all I could imagine was someone killing a puppy. No matter how badass the werewolf was, I'd just had my ass handed to me by this thing. No way a werewolf would fare any better. I shook my head. I couldn't pass the Key over to them. If I did, the Academy would kill me. Literally. If I didn't, the wolf would die. I had to find a way out of this before things got too out of hand. I was suddenly very happy my friends were all out of town. There was no way they could defend themselves from this thing.

The Demon smiled. "Thank you for the dinner. I love me some... *puppy chow*. Is that the right phrase?" he asked, grinning. "When you come to your senses and realize the forces against you, and are ready to discuss terms, ignite the Thirteenth Major Arcana in a confessional booth." My breath momentarily caught at his comment, but he continued. "Or when you are entirely out of options and tired of being hunted by the Nephilim. They exist to destroy agents of Hell, which you now appear to be." My blood chilled. The Fallen Angels had their minions – the Demons, whereas the Angels also had theirs – the Nephilim, the offspring of Angels and humans. Practically superheroes, if the rumors I had heard were correct. But I had yet to meet a person who had actually encountered one. I was almost 100% sure I had met an entire gang of them in the bar with Eae and Hemingway. "Both sides will now be hunting you. It's delicious, really. *Check*, as they say Master Temple. Your move." He turned to go, but slowed. "Unless, of course, you are ready to make a deal now... I specialize in these transactions, and a deal from one with your reputation would benefit both of us... I could eliminate your curse and give you new powers to make up for what you already lost..."

"Not a chance in Hell, Sir Dreadsalot."

He shook his head in disappointment. "Don't be so sure, mortal." I fumed, stumbling back to my feet. My legs wobbled and I fell back against the car. The Demon watched me pitilessly. "I would love to destroy you myself, but in your weakened state, it would feel like a cheap victory. Perhaps some other time, when you have full use of your power. I honestly don't see why you fight me so. Your own people have injured you, made you impotent. You continue to fight out of some mistaken creed. On the side of those who have shunned you. Even Demons have honor. Some of us, anyway. More than your allies, at least." He turned to walk away.

"What did my parents discover that warranted their deaths?"

He turned to face me. "That is none of your – or my – concern. Like I said, if not for Peter..." He winked.

Forget Peter. I knew the Demon would have killed them regardless of the horrible timing on Peter's part. The summoner. He was the *real* problem. I had to get to him. Also, I now had to watch out for the Angels' minions, the Nephilim...

He noticed my growing anger. "Easy, wizard. You might use up the last of your strength. Then who would save your friends? Who would save your friend over there?" He grinned, glancing over my shoulder at the limo. Then he noticed Othello wasn't there and began to frown.

"Hey, pussycat!" Othello called from across the street behind a trashcan. The Demon whirled, directly into an attack that even I hadn't expected. She shot something at the Demon, which he lifted his meaty paw to block. But whatever she shot at him stuck fast to his elbow. She shrugged. "That will have to do." I heard a click, and the next thing I knew, the Demon was on the ground, screaming as a thousand Nano-bots destroyed his arm from the elbow down, eating absolutely everything before falling to the ground, lifeless. His roar shook the windows, shattering several, before he disappeared in a cloud of smoke and ash.

I stared at Othello. "That was... incredible." She smiled weakly. "But you just made a very big, bad enemy. What were you *thinking*?" I demanded.

"You're either a meal or a monster in this world. I prefer to be a monster, or to at least have others think I am. It's safer." She helped me up, supporting my shoulder, glancing pointedly at my forehead before brushing my hair to cover it up with a shiver. I didn't care at the moment. I would check it in the mirror later. I had more pressing concerns at the moment. We glanced at the limo and stopped, staring sadly at the remains of its lone occupant. I studied our surroundings, shocked to realize that none of the fighting had attracted any attention. We were in a commercial district of some kind, but apparently, none of the businesses operated after traditional work hours. Lucky for us. I was, after all, a ransom victim.

"What the hell was he talking about at the end? Ignite the Thirteenth Major something. That sounds... ominous." I nodded, but didn't explain.

She studied me, waiting, but realizing I wasn't going to explain, she chose a different question. "What about the Nephilim? What are they? You looked concerned."

"Let's get somewhere safe, first. I'll tell you all about it."

17

We continued to assess the car in respectful silence, Othello nodding her head in agreement that it was time to leave. The driver was obviously dead. The side that wasn't slammed up against the building was covered in a mix of both a little of my blood and a lot of the driver's blood. Then, of course, there was his headless corpse in the seat, and his severed head on the hood. I shivered, glad that it wasn't facing me. I glanced down at my side, noticing a few shallow, but bloody gashes down my ribs. I had forgotten about them while being slammed into walls and such by the Demon. They weren't fatal.

"He might be on the surveillance footage with me, breaking you out of jail. This car will definitely be spotted. It's a burner anyway, but it could hold trace evidence. If they link this to you, it won't go well. Burn it all. No trace. He knew what he was getting himself into. He volunteered after hearing about you and the weredragons a few months ago. As did the others."

"Others?" I asked softly.

"I have some friends waiting for us at the safe-house. They have a few tools for us, but then their contract is up. Unless you have another twenty-thousand to pay them."

I blinked, not turning away from the dead man. I didn't realize I was such a celebrity with the supernatural mercenaries. "You paid them that much... to help *me*?" I asked softly, feeling both guilty and... appreciative. She nodded. "Using them over the next few days might not be a bad idea. I'll write them a check."

"Cash only," she answered.

That made sense. "Oh. Okay. That shouldn't be a prob—" Then I remembered that all my bank accounts were frozen. I scowled at life in general. "I guess we're on our own, then." She shrugged. Knowing my power was dwindling, I agreed with her assessment of the evidence. I felt cold, deep inside my soul. This stranger – who had helped me escape – was dead. The money Othello had paid him wouldn't ever be utilized. I didn't even know the man's name. I decided to honor the dead man by calling on the old Boatman. At least last respects would be granted.

I summoned up a storm of fire and incinerated the vehicle without a single movement. Othello jumped back in surprise. "It still gets me when you do things like that. You didn't even say anything. Or move. You used to have to do things like that to use your power." I looked at her thoughtfully. She was right. I normally had to perform some kind of physical action to use some of my larger spells. But with the power spike from my parents' deaths – transforming me into a Maker, as I now understood – I didn't need any assistance for spells that used to be difficult for me. Of course, none of that would matter in three days when my power disappeared entirely. I called Charon with a mental whisper.

The boatman hesitated when he saw me, sniffing the air. I frowned. The Boatman had never done that before. Maybe my Demon cologne wasn't entirely gone. Or maybe Sir Dreadsalot's smell filled the street. But the Boatman departed with his usual acceptance of the man's soul and a final wave of gratitude, sailing off into the curtain of falling snow before disappearing.

Othello waved back. I didn't. I turned us away and began to shamble down the street, letting Othello know it was time for us to leave. A voice called out behind me. "That was a crime." I froze. Othello jerked to the right, raising her Nano-bot gun. I slowly turned, and then held out my hand for Othello to stand down. She frowned, but complied. I scowled at Gavin, my parole officer.

"How long have you been watching me? I could have used some damned help."

Gavin watched me, looking angry. "It seems like plenty of *damned* people were here already," he spat. I frowned, and then understood that he was referring to the Demon as a *damned* Angel. A *Fallen* Angel.

"Why didn't you help?" I demanded, voice raspy with barely bottled anger.

"It is not my job to help you. It's my job to *prevent* you from performing any more crimes. Which you just did. Also, you seem to be out of jail, where you rightfully belong. I should deliver you back to them." He looked conflicted. "It would be the right thing to do."

I blinked back at him in disbelief. "*The right thing to do*? Arresting the only person who seems to give a shit about Demons running around my city, slaughtering innocents, and raising hell? That sounds like the *right thing to do*? You're one twisted bastard, you know that?" I spat back in disgust.

Gavin took an aggressive step forward. "Don't tempt me. I could justifiably end you. Right here, right now."

"*Tempt* you?" I snarled, quivering with anger. "I just fought a Demon in the middle of the street and you sat there and watched. Even the *Regular* jumped in to help me. What the hell is *wrong* with you? Are you honestly delusional enough to think you are wearing the White Hat here? The Academy has fallen a long way if that's the case. You guys are completely brainwashed if the right and wrong side of this situation is confusing to you. I used to be proud to be a member of the Academy. But your actions *disgust* me."

Gavin stared at me, trembling with rage and... doubt. In himself? But it didn't last long. He was back to his arrogant self a second later. "There were no innocents here to defend. Only a criminal and his sidekick," he argued.

"Now wait a damned minute. I am no sidekick. I just took out a Demon!" she hissed indignantly.

Othello was pissed. I looked from Gavin to her, and then shrugged. "Well, he has a point. It's kind of what sidekicks do. Save the day when the real superhero is down."

She slowly turned her fiery eyes to me and I took a step back in case she had any more ammunition for her death-eating, minion launcher. I turned back to Gavin. "Regardless, you were a disgrace. After seeing me fight a Demon, I'm pretty sure you can safely deduce that I'm not working with them. I nearly died trying to keep him from getting the Armory. And my power is fading. Fast. What the fuck more do you want from me?"

Gavin rolled his eyes. "The Key." I took an aggressive step forward. "As you were commanded. You were also commanded to end the Demons in St. Louis. I don't see how you believe this to be a noble reaction on your part when you are simply doing as commanded."

I wanted to rip his face off. Slowly. "No one *commands* me, Gavin. Fucking *no one*." I was literally shaking with rage and utter disbelief at his piety. "Especially a bunch of hypocritical little bitches sitting safely on the sidelines. I would rather slit my wrists than be associated with scum like you. You literally sat there and watched as a Demon fought me for your precious Key. Were you waiting for him to end me so that you could run to your boss, and get a promotion for how good a boy you'd been? Pathetic. I'm finished with the Academy. You're a stain to honor, everywhere."

Gavin slammed his fist into his thigh. A pulsing greenish light slammed into the ground and hurtled towards me, knocking me clear on my ass. I jumped to my feet ready to fight, but he still stood in the same spot, and looked... slightly embarrassed. "I'm sorry. I shouldn't have attacked you," he whispered.

I blinked.

He took a deep breath. "I don't appreciate anyone making a mockery of my life's work." He shifted from foot to foot. "However, I understand your frustrations. Working as a Justice hasn't been... exactly as I thought it would. I, too, sense... darkness in our purpose. It used to feel honorable, but now..." His eyes grew distant, confused, frustrated. "I'm not so sure. I see a lot of things happen, a lot of commands given, that I truly don't understand, nor agree with. But... if the good guys don't seem to be acting to the standards I expect; does that mean I am in some way unworthy? That I truly do not know the greater good? I can't seem to accept the fact that they are wrong or have bad intentions. They are the *Academy*, for Christ's sake. If I don't work for the good guys, what does that make me? I just want to do the right thing." He looked genuinely torn.

Huh. Was he really that naïve? Was he so brainwashed that he didn't know how to stand up to his superiors when they seemed to be making bad calls? Maybe that was how they had been trained. To never challenge their betters. In fact, it made sense. They wouldn't want insubordination in a life or death situation. Like the military. But this seemed like a huge chink in their armor. I could clearly see that Gavin truly wanted to be a good guy, but that he didn't know what that meant anymore.

"Gavin, listen to me. What were you commanded to do?" I asked, managing to relax my shoulders into an unthreatening posture. I noticed Othello's eyes darting back and forth between us, ready for anything, knowing me better than most.

"To watch over you and prevent you from making a deal with either party. The Key belongs to the Academy."

My fingers tingled. To make sure I didn't make any deals. Well, that was dicey. How could I use my trickery if I wasn't allowed to play one enemy against another? Making a deal was pretty much the only way I thought I could survive long enough to get to the summoner, which was the only way to end the Demon presence and keep the Armory safe. In fact, it was pretty much a guarantee that I would have to make a deal in order to get a face-to-face with the true enemy.

"And if I were to make a deal, but hadn't actually given over the Key yet, what were you commanded to do?"

He looked up at me with hard, but torn, eyes. "Kill you."

My head sagged. "You do understand that for me to get close enough to the bad guys to end this that I pretty much *have* to make a deal, right?"

He nodded, looking confused.

"Follow that thought to its rational conclusion, and tell me what you see," I said gently.

He did, and I watched his shoulders begin to sag, but he didn't speak.

"So, you realize that you were chosen to, pretty much, be my assassin. I am commanded to go after the Demons and end them, yet your boss bound my power so that I am not strong enough to accomplish the task. Which makes it 100% likely that I will have to use subterfuge and trickery to get close enough to finish this, meaning I would need to at least *pretend* to make a deal. You were hired to watch over me and make sure that I don't break any laws... but even if I *pretended* to make a deal, you were to *kill* me. So, the Academy has taken away my power to fight for myself, meaning I will be killed or lose my magic forever, but if I found another way to usurp them and made a deal, you would be there to kill me... to *end* me." I watched as his shoulders slumped further. "You were hired as a hit man, not a probation officer." I finally said. He wasn't looking at me. "*Look* at me, Gavin. Look at your *victim*. Your *target*. Your *mark*. You know you couldn't take me in a fair fight, so your boss helped you out, made your mark harmless." He flinched at each word, as if I was physically striking him, but he didn't look up. "LOOK AT ME!" I roared. Othello jumped in alarm. Finally, Gavin lifted his gaze. I stared him in the eyes for a long time. "Do you still think your boss is wearing a white hat?"

He finally shook his head. "But if I can't trust them, who can I trust?"

I sighed in resignation, rubbing my hands together for warmth. "Yourself, kid. Always yourself. You might not always be right, but at least you can rationalize all your actions and know why what you do is right or wrong, rather than blindly following some creed. It's never good when you blindly follow some belief system or group of people without consciously deducing whether what they do is right or wrong. The number one test is to wonder what would happen if you openly, but respectfully, questioned your commander's decision when you think it's wrong. If the answer in any way resembles punishment, pain, or ridicule, rather than an explanation, you're probably not working for the good guys."

Gavin nodded his head after a moment. "I want to do the right thing." My shoulders relaxed for a moment. "But I still do not trust you, Temple. You caused so much chaos here with the dragons, and you hold the launch codes to the Armory. I will give you a chance, but that doesn't mean I work for you. I work for myself... and possibly the Academy. I will not let their corruption get in your way, or the way of the innocents, but that does not make us friends. Understood?"

I nodded. "Thanks for hearing me out, Gavin."

"Don't thank me just yet. I won't mention anything to my superiors about what happened here tonight. But I'm still watching you." With a final nod, he Shadow Walked, disappearing with a faint *crack* in the air. The falling snow pulsed away from the void as if repelled, leaving a faint circle of bare street where he had been standing.

Othello watched me in surprise, several fat snowflakes settling on her eyelashes. "So, he's one of the good guys, eh?" I shrugged, letting her guide me in the direction of the safe house. Perhaps Gavin wasn't on my side, but at least I knew he wasn't a zealot for the Academy anymore. My thoughts drifted to the Demon's threats. How would I protect the werewolf? Who was he? Where was he?

At least I knew it wouldn't be Gunnar.

It's the little things that matter.

18

Since all of my known properties were most likely under surveillance, I trusted Othello's directions. The snow was still falling heavily, but at least the streets were empty. We were close, so we walked. Apparently, Othello had acquired Raego's old apartment from a few months back – the scarily unhygienic one. I have no idea how. Maybe there was a Craigslist page for dicey Black Ops hideouts. Othello had introduced me to her expensive 'friends,' the ones who had organized my escape. I hadn't been too responsive, focused on the imminent attack on the werewolf community. The men seemed like mercenaries, Tomas Mullingsworth types, but with sneakier spy traits. After several stunted conversational attempts and the stardom of meeting me began to fade, they got back to business, and offered us a whole mess of goodies. Disguises, weapons, fake ID's, and other things that I didn't pay attention to but that Othello seemed to appreciate. I did notice two men excitedly studying the soles of a few pairs of unique hiking boots, and waggled my finger at Othello to add them to the pile. I also made sure we had a whole pile of burner phones. Never knew when those would come in handy. She obeyed with a curious frown. The men finally left.

Othello guided me to the back room and set me down on the bed. "Nate. You need to get some sleep."

I shook my head stubbornly. "Can't. Werewolf's going to die. I need to save him. Or her."

She gripped my shoulders. "Nate. Listen to me. There is no way we could find him in time. You of all people know how big St. Louis is. We don't even know in what part of town to look. He could already be dead. In fact, I'm sure he is. We don't have enough information, and you forget this." She pointed at my head and pulled out a makeup mirror. I stared into it, watching as Othello brushed my hair back. There, burned into the side of my forehead near the hairline was a rune. An ugly, scarred, ancient rune. It emanated bad juju. And it looked like it was weeks old. Despite still hurting like a son of a bitch. "We don't know anything about this. He no doubt wanted you to run out there and try to save the day. This thing could even attract these Nephilim. Or any other number of bad guys ready to take you down. We were lucky Gavin didn't sense it. You're exhausted. We need a plan."

I lifted my tired eyes from the mirror. "We?"

She nodded, determined. "I'm not backing down from this. You're all alone, if you hadn't noticed. You need backup. And I can take care of myself. These guys left me some weapons that work on all sorts of supernaturals. I should be covered. I'm an excellent shot. Even for a *Regular*." She smiled. "There's a lot of talk on your end of the spectrum – with the supernatural community – about St. Louis experiencing a lot of weird events. That's why I came into town in the first place. As soon as I knew your friends had left, I knew you would need my help."

"You're tracking my friends?" I asked in disbelief.

She smiled coyly. "I spy on everyone I care about. And anyone involved in his safety." She licked her lips, not sensing how creepy that sounded. "Speaking of which, I haven't found out much about the Angel, Eae. He is known as the 'Demon thwarter', but other than that he apparently keeps his cards close." I had given her a small list of things to look up when I called her earlier in the day, thinking any additional information couldn't hurt. "Also, your parole officer, Gavin seems clean. Bit of a loner. Not a lot of friends. No social media accounts or email. After meeting him, I can see why. Are they all like that?" Which meant Gavin must have no friends. If Othello couldn't find dirt on someone, it didn't exist. Or he didn't have any kind of social presence, which wasn't out of the question for an Academy Justice. They were a mysterious bunch.

"Yeah. I guess they don't let them use social media. No *twatting* for the Academy."

Othello let out a cute laugh and shook her head. "I think they call it *tweeting*..."

"Oh. Well, I like *twatting* better. It's catchier," I said.

Othello laughed harder for a few seconds before finally coming back to the facts. "Tell me more about the Tarot card the Demon mentioned, and these Nephilim. What are they?"

I sat there quietly, not having a whole lot to tell her. I did need the help, and she was the only game in town. I couldn't go to Agent Jeffries, as the FBI was no doubt combing the city for me, and I couldn't risk him losing his job, too. "The thirteenth Major Arcana is a Tarot card with a picture of Death on the front. I guess he liked the irony of using it to make a deal." I shrugged. "And the Nephilim are the offspring of Angels and humans. They are the counterpart to Demons in the fact that they're the pawns the Angels are allowed to use to influence the world. Hell – has Demons. Heaven – has Nephilim. Other than that, I don't know much. I've never met one before last night. And I don't think I want to again. They seemed like hired thugs or soldiers. I'd feel bad killing one in self-defense. I don't think God would look kindly on that. Then again, if they're gunning to kill me, what choice do I really have?"

"Maybe they'll listen to reason and know that you aren't really aiding the Demons," Othello offered.

"I'm beginning to realize that *intentions* mean nothing. Not in my world. I'm pretty sure I'm fucked," I sighed, running my hands through my hair, careful to avoid the brand. I needed to find a way to cover it up before I went out into the city. At least it would attract less attention from Regulars. If things got out of hand and we had to fight someone, I didn't want a telltale mark of some kind to stick out in people's minds so that they gave the information to the police. Because the police might realize that the branded Freak was none other than the recently-kidnapped Nate Temple. I groaned, exhausted. "You're right, Othello. I need to hit the hay... but I can't. I need to be out there, helping my people. They didn't ask for this. I brought this on them. This is on me."

Othello sighed, nodding in resignation after a long moment. "How?"

I shrugged. "I have no idea. Drive around?" Othello looked disgusted.

"What about that rock?"

I slowly lifted my gaze to her. "Rock?"

"That thing that vibrated before the Demon showed up."

I slapped my forehead in response. A flash of red light struck my brain. Then I was floating in blackness. I woke up, lying on my side, to Othello shaking me in alarm. I batted her hands away after a few seconds. "What happened?" I whispered, my forehead a sheet of flame.

"You hit your head with your hand and immediately passed out. Your eyes rolled back in your head the second you touched it." She looked freaked out.

"It's okay. I'm fine, now. The stone detects Demons. I guess I really am tired. Forgot about the brand on my forehead." My head was pounding with the beginnings of a migraine from the repeated hits against buildings and the accidental slapping of my forehead. I wondered if I had a concussion.

"Maybe I was right," she began. "We should wait until the morning when you're thinking fresh." She looked very doctor-like at the moment. I shook my head and stood on shaky legs, ignoring my throbbing skull. My throat was still hoarse from the Demon choking me out. Then there was my new scar, which pulsed with a steady heat.

And my power was significantly depleted. I had used up a fair amount with the Demon. I realized that I hadn't warned Gavin that the Demon was actually a Greater Demon – not just a run-of-the-mill Demon possession. I was sure that information like that might convince him that the *only* way to stop the Demons was to arrange a deal in order to get the summoner. Next time I saw him I would tell him. Maybe. "Let's go."

Othello watched me doubtfully for a few moments before sighing and standing to her feet. "There's a car outside. What do you need me to do?"

I grinned. "Get a map."

She pulled one off of the nearby table and brought it over. "Now what?"

"You drive while I get my freak on."

She watched me. "Good pickup line. Not creepy at all." Then she walked out the door.

Pickup line? Then I realized the double connotation. I'd just meant that I would do my magic while she played my girl Friday. I sighed. No respect for the finer arts. Ignoring her comment, I pulled out the artifact, rubbing it against my thumb for warmth as Hope had shown me. Then I whispered a word. "Seek," I murmured. The bone began to vibrate. Swirls of inky crimson settled on two points of the map. I chose one at random, hoping it was the right one.

19

I cringed at the Lincoln Town Car's interior, feeling significantly poorer at being a passenger in such a vehicle. I wasn't snobby. It was just... *come on*. A Lincoln Town Car? Weren't they used exclusively in those old Private Investigator flicks? But since I was broke now, perhaps my taste needed an adjustment.

"You can stop looking so disgusted any minute now. It's not that bad, Daddy Warbucks. Discreet."

"Uh huh," I answered with a doubtful frown. But it wasn't like I could drive one of my flashier cars. I was sure that the FBI had a stack of BOLOs on my fleet of cars back at Chateau Falco. I resigned myself to the poverty of the Lincoln, idly remembering Matthew McConaughey's commercials – and Jim Carrey's SNL mockery of them – with an amused grin.

Othello rolled her eyes as she safely accelerated through the few inches of snow that had accumulated on the street; trying to hurry to the destination I had shown her on the map. We might already be too late. I slapped my cheeks – very carefully – a few times, trying to wake myself up without giving myself a compound concussion. Even with my own people against me, I was risking my life to assist those in need. That had to be worth something. After all, I very easily could have agreed with Othello to catch some sleep first. But I hadn't. I wouldn't have been able to sleep anyway. Maybe pass out, but not sleep. I was used to running on no sleep after living with night terrors for so long. I actually felt better than usual. Refreshed. I had actually managed to get some sleep while in jail. Before the Demon attacked me. Not many would qualify jail as a peaceful experience.

"So, why was it so important to make sure you had a phone? Are you planning on calling in backup?" Othello asked softly. "Am I not enough for you?" I cringed, sensing the words held a much deeper meaning that I definitely didn't want to touch. So, I did what men have done since time immemorial. I ignored it. You see, women spoke on many different levels. Men were snipers, focusing only on the one thing directly in front of us, where women were raging cyclones of a dozen assassins hidden inside a single person. Their conversations sliced and diced an innocent gentleman on several planes of existence... at the same time, and without him being aware of the fatality. I sensed that underneath her words was a plethora of dangers that I wouldn't have wanted to touch with a ten-foot pole. So, I listened to only the *actual* words she had said.

"Of course not. You're a certified badass. You Nano-botted Sir Dreadsalot. A Greater Demon. That will go down as a first in the history books, for sure." She smiled slightly, but I could tell she wasn't content with my answer. I opened my mouth to continue, but she eviscerated my attempt at peace before I could properly defend myself.

"Who called you earlier? When the Demon answered?" Her tone was crisp, professional even. I didn't buy it.

"Indie."

The temperature in the car suddenly felt frosty. "Indie?"

I fidgeted slightly, glancing at the map again to cover my unease. "Take a left here."

She hesitated a second before swerving the car, the vehicle sliding in the snow. Dawn would creep up on us soon, but it was still dark outside. Despite the hour, the snow gave the world a pristine glow. We were entering a low-income area, the kind of place that had recently experienced a jolt of rejuvenation, thanks to the rare tax-credit housing projects that sometimes found their way into major cities. Most of them seemed to occur in rural areas. I knew this because I was an investor in several. I think. I didn't really pay much attention to my various investments. I had a guy for that. I understood enough to verify that I wasn't being leeched, but other than that I was just a silent investor, primarily serving as the personal guarantee for about thirty million dollars' worth of apartment projects. Small potatoes for what I had inherited, but it made me feel good helping out the community. Any personal profits I received were even donated back to the community. I made my profits elsewhere.

"So, Indie?" Othello pressed as we continued driving.

I spoke before thinking, feeling uncomfortable about discussing my current girlfriend with my past collegiate fling, Othello. "She's the manager at my store, Plato's Cave."

Othello seemed to relax. "Oh, *Indiana* Rippley," she said, using her full name. I shrugged in agreement, not understanding why it mattered.

"Yeah."

"The Demon seemed downright terrified of looking at your phone. Is *Indiana* that hideous?" she asked, like a cat flexing her claws, enunciating Indie's full name.

"Um..." I didn't know how to respond to her tone. "No. I think he was unfamiliar with our technology. He seemed to think my phone was a witch's familiar. An entity bound to assist a witch in times of need."

"Oh." Was the air conditioning on? It felt downright frigid in the car.

"Turn right ahead. It should be a half mile away." But Othello continued driving, not heeding my advice. We passed the street. I rubbernecked the missed turn with the same despair as a stranded survivor on a remote island watching a cruise ship sail by without stopping. "Othello. You missed the turn. Take the next right."

She slammed on the brakes instead, sending the car into a complete spin, which didn't seem to concern her in the slightest. The seatbelt saved me from head butting the dash. As the car finally settled, the air inside the vehicle grew thick. "Why was it so important to make sure you had a cell phone from the gear my friends gave us?" she asked tersely.

I slowly turned to face her, but she didn't meet my eyes. Her body was tight, and she was breathing heavily. I didn't have time for whatever this was. "Indie tried to call me and instead she saw a Demon threatening to kill me. I wanted to make sure I allayed her fears, before she freaked out. Her mom's dying. She has enough on her plate without having to deal with whatever is going on here," I snapped. "Now, do you mind if we go save an innocent life?"

"Her mother. In Colorado," she said softly instead.

I blinked. She was keeping tabs on Indie, too? "Yeah," I answered.

"Okay. You just wanted to make sure she wasn't overstressed." I nodded as Othello finally looked into my eyes. What the hell was going on?

"Yep. If you were in her shoes wouldn't you want to know what the hell that was about?"

She nodded distractedly looking down at her lap. "Yes. I would. I couldn't take it if I thought you were in trouble. Especially with my mother's health on the line. Family first."

"Yeah. I just want to make sure she doesn't freak out and call the police or anything. Especially since I'm supposed to be in jail."

"Okay. That makes sense. You should call her. See how her mother is doing." Othello looked on the verge of tears.

"I texted her." Othello nodded, eyes far away and glistening slightly. "But right now, we need to focus on the werewolf that's about to be murdered." Othello's arms tightened on the steering wheel. "You good?" I asked her softly.

It took her a minute, but she finally lifted her gaze again, eyes growing harder as they dried up. "Sorry. Yeah. I'm good. Just... a lot to take in. This might be a normal day for you, but we Regular mortals don't have days like this," she mumbled. "Let's take care of your werewolf." With that, she released the brakes and drove back towards our turn. What the hell had that been about? But I didn't need to ask myself. I was pretty sure I knew *exactly* what it was about.

Othello still cared for me.

And that smug bastard, jealousy, had just made the first of many appearances to come.

Othello and I had frequented many bedroom study sessions back in college, and now... we were back together again. Like Bonnie and Clyde. All alone, taking on the world together. And I had yet to make a pass at her. In the past, even right before Indie and I had evolved, I would have hit on her immediately. I had no reason not to. Othello was beautiful, intelligent, and very... *very* experienced in coital adventures. We had always been casual, never needing more than the sexual foray every now and again, but tonight I was picking up something entirely different. I think Othello's opinion had changed. I think she actually felt possessive of me. I didn't have time for that kind of entanglement right now. I was pretty much up against the ledge on this one. My power was practically gone. I felt like I had been in the ring with Muhammad Ali for three rounds.

I had 99 problems, and – apparently – a girl *was* one.

Gunnar would be beside himself with laughter right now. Lucky for me I hadn't had a chance to call him. I briefly wondered if he had proposed yet. Then Othello slammed on the brakes again, this time a hundred yards away from a small, maybe fifty-unit, apartment complex. "Look," she whispered. Rather than scan the surroundings for danger, I merely stared open-mouthed at the familiar name on the sign out front. *Silver Gardens*.

This was a project I *knew* that I had invested in. It still looked new, especially with the clean snow, but... *rough*. As if the tenants weren't too keen on rules. Which made sense.

Werewolves lived here.

Shaking my head at the coincidence, I finally scanned the street and spotted three silhouettes sniffing the frosty air, patrolling the perimeter around the apartments. They moved on without noticing us, and I let out a breath. If I saw three, there had to be three more I hadn't seen. I glanced down at the bone artifact. It was vibrating violently, practically dancing in my lap. This was it. I opened the car door and jumped out into a snowbank, ready to blast a Demon back to Hell, or to let Othello do it with her arsenal of goodies. I sniffed the air, sensing the familiar faint sulfurous odor of Demonic presence.

Then I heard a lamenting howl from the center of the complex.

A lot of howls answered, causing me to shiver nervously. The three sentries reappeared for a moment, shared a look, and then bolted towards the first howl, still not noticing us.

I raced after them, my feet crunching too loudly in the snow as I ran parallel to their path with a building between us so as not to stumble into a dozen of the beasts by accident. Othello was hot on my heels, successfully keeping a low profile, but making just as much noise. Everything always sounded so much louder when it was snowing, as if the world had been temporarily muted, amplifying the sound of my steps like a Dolby Digital Surround Sound demonstration. I slowed as I neared the corner of the building, ducking behind a bush before peering around it. Othello knelt beside me, catching her breath. Snow was still falling heavily, adding to the several inches that had already accumulated on the ground. How long was this weather supposed to continue?

People were gathered around a single ground floor apartment, where I could hear a lot of agitated arguing from the men, and prayers from the women. It was like someone had kicked an anthill. But no one had noticed us yet. I held up a hand for Othello to stay still. I could see something on the apartment door, like a large wreath or decoration of some kind. Squinting, I saw a gap in the people surrounding the apartment, and I leaned back in surprise. A woman was nailed to the door. Crucified. One beast of a man was utterly silent, kneeling before the door, staring up at the woman he cherished above all others. The other figures fidgeted - both angrily and nervously – as if the man kneeling on the ground was someone important to them.

Then it hit me.

This must be their Alpha. The Demons had taken his mate. The mate of the most important werewolf in the area. I gulped. This wasn't going to end well. I was too late. There was nothing left for us to do, and entering the equation now to express our condolences would not be welcome, and might even be considered suspicious. Suspicion would get both Othello and I killed. I glanced around the complex and noticed several tenants glancing out the windows conspicuously. At first it confused me, but then I understood. Not everyone in this complex was a werewolf. I mean, how likely was it for fifty werewolf families to take over the same complex? That meant there were numerous Regulars living here, amidst a pack of murderous, vengeful werewolves.

Shit.

I turned to Othello and urgently motioned for her to discreetly get back to the car.

She frowned at me, but finally nodded and rose with the silence of a ninja before taking a step back. Right over a Power Wheel truck. She cartwheeled backwards with a crash, the sound echoing loudly. Several pairs of werewolf eyes turned our way but I managed to drop to the ground just in time. Still, these were werewolves. They would investigate. With something we couldn't mask. Smell.

Before I could move, a voice broke the peaceful night's silence like a thunderbolt in a clear sky. "Wolves! Tonight, you have faced a great calamity." The wolves forgot us in an instant, turning to locate the voice as they subconsciously formed a protective ring around their Alpha. I pointed for Othello's sake. There, standing on a nearby roof was a silhouette, glowing with white radiance. The wolves bristled with agitation. But part of me wanted to giggle with joy, glad that the voice had conveniently caused a distraction for our escape. Maybe it was Gavin finally giving me some support.

Without it, Othello and I would have most likely been chased back to our car like lame antelope fleeing a pride of starving lions. I motioned for Othello to get back to her feet and flee, before the wolves remembered the noise she had caused.

Karma chose that moment to metaphorically whip me in my family jewels.

"There, between those buildings lies the culprit. I am an Agent of Heaven, hunting a fugitive who has been working with Demons to cause harm to this fine city. *Your* city. Sensing the impending attack, I traveled here to this place only to find myself too late to save her. Yet fortune seems to favor us." I slowly glanced back to see several sets of fiery eyes staring directly at Othello and I. Feral howls filled the night.

So, not Gavin, then.

"Take vengeance on the wizard! He is marked. He currently works as an Agent of Hell, and murdered one of your own on behalf of his new Lords and Masters. Take him down like the animal he is. Hunt the cowardly murderer. Hunt Nathin Temple!"

One voice belted out. "How? He's a wizard. We hold no chance against the gifted."

"As a pack, you are all but invincible," the radiant Angelic voice answered with sublime confidence. The glow surrounding him made it impossible to get a clear look at him.

"Yes," a new, darker, more authoritative voice answered. It was the Alpha. And he sounded... familiar. "We are. Get the women and children inside. Tonight, the men hunt."

Every wolf in the area howled, making the air suddenly seem to vibrate. Every single curtain in the apartment complex slammed shut. No Regular was going to get involved in whatever was going on in the parking lot. Othello stared with utter confusion at the radiant apparition that had condemned us to death. I heard several explosions of fabric as the wolves shifted from their weaker human forms.

"You've gotta be fucking *kidding* me!" I hissed, finally recognizing where I had heard the voice before. It was the same werewolf from the bar the night before. The one Tory and I had made a fool of. "Click your heels, *now*!" Othello nodded in instinctual obedience, eyes wide with fear. I slammed my heels together, too, satisfied at the brief click I felt under my toes. "And now, we *run*!" I shouted. And we did, panting in fear. The sound of dozens of paws crunching through the snow was absolutely terrifying. Because I knew they were coming our way. Fast. We still had a building and numerous cars between us, but werewolves were distance runners. I knew that most of them couldn't shift at will, like Gunnar, but I also knew that they could shift during extremely emotional times. Like the death of their pack leader's mate.

And that was when they were the least rational. During times of war. Even vampires stepped carefully – or fled entirely – when the mangy mutts were working as a single unit.

I knew we had no chance of talking our way out of this. Especially while they were in wolf form. So, we hoofed it. Luckily, we had new scoots on our feet, thanks to Othello's mercenary buddies. I'd overheard two of the men whispering to each other about a unique feature of the hiking boots and, knowing what we were going to be facing tonight, I hadn't ignored serendipity's call. I had pointed at the gear, and Othello had added them to our pile. I still found it awkward to run in them, but they might just come in handy, given our current flight.

We rounded the building and I saw two werewolves scouting out our car. They were in human form, but they were sniffing the vehicle with too much interest. They let out a howl, triangulating our position. I quickly darted around the corner between the bushes and the building, racing towards the adjacent neighborhood. Unfortunately, a stealthy escape wasn't in the cards for us. The snow left a perfectly clear trail of boot prints wherever we went. I instinctively flung my hand back towards the car, casting our smell past the vehicle and racing a hundred yards further, not even considering my dwindling power. We would be dead if I didn't use my gift right now. Many of the wolves darted after the faint whiff as they rounded the building.

But many didn't. The Alpha hesitated as he rounded the corner, sniffing the air. He was huge, as black as midnight, and his predatory eyes and long teeth fairly glowed in the moonlight's reflection off the snow. Then two of the nearby wolves barked in our direction, still not seeing us, but sensing our presence. Othello followed my lead, staying low as we continued to run across the street. I launched myself over a backyard's chain link fence. Othello tried to duplicate the move behind me but her clumsy boots caught on the tip of the fence, causing the snow-covered metal to rattle loudly before she crashed into the yard. The wolves howled as they pinpointed our location, and then they loped after us with a fresh burst of speed. I cast balls of fire and ice blindly behind us, catching a few lucky strikes, bowling several groups of wolves over with yelps of pain.

But half-a-dozen more continued after us, unfazed.

Including the Alpha, who had seemed especially motivated after hearing the Angelic being say my name. But he had been the one to start the fight in the bar. Tory and I had merely ended it. More Tory than myself.

We were screwed. The wolves were almost upon us and there was no way we could outrun such a motivated pack. They were out for blood. "Click your heels again!" I hissed at Othello, low enough for only her to hear me. "Just a dozen more feet and then we make our stand." Othello nodded, clicking her heels right after I did. We stopped where I had indicated, breathing heavily and arming ourselves. She drew her gun, armed with silver bullets. I merely turned around, drawing my face into hard, tight lines, the face I wore when I was in a scrap. The wolves quickly surrounded us, but remained a safe distance away, yipping and growling in a rotating circle of claws and fangs. The Alpha approached us with slow, triumphant footsteps. He wasn't in full wolf form, but instead resembled a horrific beast of a man, part wolf and part human. Which was better... and worse. It meant he would be more rational than his pack, but also that he wanted to *rationally* cherish the violence to come.

One of his packmates suddenly shifted to human form, no doubt a lieutenant if he had that kind of control. "Sir, I spotted other paw prints in the area. Big ones."

"It was probably our own. Or a neighbor's dog wandering the streets," the Alpha responded in a growl, drooling as he stared me down, taking a step forward.

"Respectfully, it wasn't either of those," the lieutenant said, bowing his head. The Alpha snarled, backhanding his lieutenant in the face, sending him into the fence we had just jumped. Which was impressive. The lieutenant didn't get up. The growling ceased amongst the pack, suddenly leery of their Alpha's temper.

"Of course it was. Do you see or smell any other werewolves here?" He laughed, an odd, barking noise. The wolves yipped and whined in agreement as the Alpha stepped closer to me.

This was my moment. Use the chaos to my advantage.

In other words, it was time to fuck shit up.

"*Disrespectfully*, they belong to *my* pack," I said, lacing my voice with a heavy tone of authority.

The Alpha froze, cocking his wolf head at me, intelligence brimming behind cruel eyes.

"You are about to be eaten, slowly, by my entire pack." He looked amused. "I'll grant you this last farce."

I obliged him. "I have a pack of spirit wolves. They belong to the many wolves I have killed over the years. Having tasted my victory, they bowed down to my power and chose to follow me from the spirit realm. They are my constant companions." Without moving, I simultaneously cast several spells at once, all relatively small in power, but frighteningly effective nonetheless. No one noticed, which was the point. The spells drifted around the clearing like knives on velvet, patiently awaiting my next command. The snow continued, masking our confrontation from any nearby spectators, which was good. Things might get dicey.

The Alpha waited for a count of two, then he began to laugh. For a full minute. His pack slowly began to mimic him with anticipatory growls, but only after a few seconds of silent wariness. They were still leery. Of my words or their Alpha's instability? "You expect me to believe that you have a pack of spirit wolves protecting you? I've never heard of such a thing. You're just trying to scare my six bravest warriors, but it won't work." He held up a hand for silence. His pack complied.

But a sudden *yip* split the night and I smiled.

"Five," I said softly.

The Alpha turned to see who had caused the noise, then back to me. "What?"

"There seems to be only five of your warriors left."

The Alpha's shoulders tensed as he counted his remaining wolves through the now rapidly falling snow. One was indeed missing. "What is the meaning of this? Did he run away?" he snapped at the remaining wolves. One of them whined, as if fearful of telling his Alpha the truth, but also suddenly terrified of the night.

The Alpha pointed at Othello. "Take her!"

I activated another of the sentinel spells, allowing the whining wolf to scream in agony before my next spell camouflaged his now unconscious body. A gunshot filled the night and another wolf dropped, wounded in the rear leg, yowling pityingly in the falling snow. Everyone froze. Othello was a good shot. She smiled at the Alpha, licking her lips. "*Three* warriors."

He growled, taking a threatening step towards her. "Easy," I spoke soothingly. "You don't want a repeat of the bar last night. I didn't kill your mate. Look me in the eyes and see for yourself. We only just arrived."

The Alpha glared back, his mindless rage threatening to take control. I knew this wasn't about rationality anymore. His mate had been killed.

This was *absolution*.

For a loved one.

I get it. I had resided in that endless, eternal swamp for the past few months now.

"I swear on my power as a wizard that I didn't kill her. I came here to help. Having known it was *your* pack I might not have made the trip." I paused. "If I'm being perfectly honest."

The lieutenant came trotting back towards us from the fence where he had been lying since the Alpha had backhanded him. "Sir. It's true. The wizard only just arrived. I was on lookout at the street. Although having taken three of your wolves, I'd say it's only fair that we kill them anyway," he added with a growl, counting the rest of the pack.

The Alpha was panting heavily. Other than that sound, we stood in a vacuum of silence. I could even hear the snow hitting the ground. "Get out. Before I change my mind," he rasped.

I nodded politely at him, urging Othello to stick close. No sudden movements around bloodthirsty werewolves. "Thank you." Once safely out of the perimeter of wolves I hesitated near the Alpha, watching cautiously as his muscles quivered with impotent fury. Out of respect, I didn't meet his eyes, but I kept my spells handy just in case. "I don't work with Demons. I will find the monster responsible for this and make him pay. It seems no one else is willing to protect this city. Even my own kind." I spat into the snow, and reached out a hand. The Alpha appraised me in silence before finally reaching out a clawed hand. His grip was in no way friendly, but at least it was there.

"This doesn't make us friends, but I'll owe you one if you make him suffer."

I smiled darkly at him. "That's my specialty. Your packmates are alive and well. You'll find them after sunrise." I had set the camouflage and sleeping spells to dissipate at dawn. He nodded at me with unexpected relief and... respect, like a fencer acknowledging a worthy opponent.

Then Othello and I left.

20

Othello shook her head in disbelief as she carefully exited the snow-covered highway. "I thought you were bonkers when you had me add those boots to our gear. They're supposed to be for hiking, in order to deter lurking beasts or hunters from a campsite."

"It wasn't just the boots. The boots in combination with the inexplicable disappearance of their comrades is what did it. You'll find that the best way to survive is to cause doubt or fear in your enemy. If you can instill that emotion, it stays with them in the back of their minds, always ready to be the first answer to the next unexplainable event that goes wrong. People will believe anything if they are afraid that it might be true." *Thank you for that, Terry Goodkind*, I thought to myself with a tip of a mental hat. "You just have to cause the doubt."

"Yeah, but they were only rubber paw prints on the soles of our boots. You'd think a werewolf would know the difference. Or that they could smell the difference."

"That's why I told them they were from spirit wolves. It compounded their fear even more. They didn't know how to disprove it. Would a spirit wolf have a smell? Would spirit wolves steal a body entirely? Who knows? That's why I had us click off the paw print extensions before we stopped. It would have been pretty obvious if the prints ended exactly where we were standing, and then if we moved during the fight they would immediately realize it was a bluff."

She stared at me for a moment. We were at a red light. "You think that far in advance?"

I shrugged. "I guess so. Being a wizard means you have to think on the fly a lot, and make the best of the cards you're dealt. I didn't know the boots would be helpful at all. I heard your guys talking about their unique feature, and unique features can always be exploited." I waved her on as the light turned green. "Also, it's cold as balls outside and my sneakers wouldn't have kept me that warm in the snow, so I opted for us to change to boots."

She chuckled, mumbling to herself as she accelerated again. The car grew silent, the cheer slowly fading. We hadn't actually accomplished anything worth celebration. We had, in fact, failed to stop the Demon, and had in turn been framed by the Angel or whatever that thing had been. Had it been one of the Nephilim? My thoughts drifted as I tried to come up with a new game plan. "So. What happened to the wolves? Did you really kill them?"

I shook my head. "I knocked them out. When they wake up and reappear at dawn, it will make me look even more mysterious. Which is a good thing in my world. Mystery keeps enemies on their toes."

"Okay. That makes me feel better. I didn't want to kill mine either. I mean, I would have, but it didn't feel right. They thought we were murderers. Why would the Angel do that to us? Aren't they supposed to be the good guys?" she asked nervously.

I shrugged helplessly. "I'm beginning to find that there aren't really any good guys in this race. The Angels think I'm consorting with the Demons, so they figured they could get the wolves to take me out and keep their wings clean. The Demons just want the Key, as do my own people. No matter who I look at, everyone is making this harder than it needs to be."

"Well... *you're* a good guy, Nate." I didn't answer. The silence grew. "Right?"

"As good as I can be, I guess," I muttered, wondering exactly what I was. Was the Academy truly deserving of control over the Armory? Was I being petty? Greedy? Were my actions causing the equivalent of a nuclear arms race? Was *I* worthy of being in charge of the Armory? I didn't know. "I'm trying to be, anyway. I won't let anything happen to my people, or the people of my city."

That seemed to satisfy her, but she looked too thoughtful, as if gaining moral fortitude from my words. *Whatever helps her cope*, I thought to myself with a sigh.

We finally parked out back behind the safe house. The snow had finally stopped during our drive, but was still at least a few inches deep. We shambled upstairs and into the shabbier of the two bedrooms – mine – peeling out of our wet clothes before hanging them to dry. We got ready for bed and Othello sat beside me on the dirty old mattress that lay on the floor. "So, what's the plan for tomorrow?"

I had a vague idea, but I was too tired to discuss the Armory with her right now, anticipating the horde of obvious questions that would follow. "Maybe I'll come up with one after some rest. One thing I do know is that we're going to need to use that artifact to hunt down another Demon. Then use him to find the summoner. He's the one calling the shots. Shut him down, and we can shut the rest of the Demons down. Hopefully that will even get rid of this mark on my forehead. Then I kill the Greater Demon who killed my parents. That's all I ever wanted to do in the first place, to find my parents' murderer. The Greater Demon we met might have done the deed, but the summoner put him up to it. It had nothing to do with Peter's theft. I have to take the summoner out. Then I can confront the Academy and try to talk my way out of this curse. And if I can shut the summoner down, perhaps the Angels will realize I'm not a bad guy."

Othello frowned. "Explain that part for me. You've been cursed? By your own people? And that's supposed to encourage you to comply with their demands to give up a gift your parents left you? A gift that cost them their lives? Why would the Academy do that to you? And why would you even consider it?"

I nodded with a shrug. "They're scared. I've got..." I thought about it briefly, "Two more days before my magic is entirely gone. If not sooner. They want the Armory that my parents discovered. They think I'm reckless and a danger to society. So, they cursed me and told me that if I managed to wipe out the Demons and then hand over my parents' Armory, they would remove the curse. I'm not sure if I trust them with it, though. And the Demons want it, too. Well, maybe it's the summoner who wants it. It's why my parents were killed. What started this whole mess. And the Angels just want me to stay out of it entirely."

"Kill them," she growled.

I blinked. "Excuse me?"

"The Academy. Kill them. They deserve it. Taking your power away, and promising to give it back only if you can perform a miracle – taking out Angels and Demons *without* magic – and *then* that you must *also* agree to give them something *else* that's yours. The Armory. That's insanity. That Gavin guy seemed all right, but he's blindly following their orders. Men like that can't be trusted with what your parents discovered. Especially if it's dangerous. You should just kill them. All."

I sighed. "That would only increase my problems. Then I would be a fugitive from the Regular police as well as every other wizard in the world. You don't murder the police. That's what these guys are. That's why Gavin is keeping tabs on me, making sure I don't make a deal with the devil. I have to somehow prove that I'm not a bad guy."

"With your hands tied," she spat.

I nodded tiredly. "It's the only way, now. I wish it were different, too, but... It is what it is. There's no use whining about it. It's either sink or swim. *When you find yourself knee-deep in shit, don't sit there complaining about it. Start walking.*"

She chuckled softly before bending over to kiss my temple, careful of my scar. "We'll figure it out, Nate. Don't worry. I'm not leaving you." She looked torn, but perhaps that was simply because she still cared for me and I hadn't reciprocated her romance. I kept my face stoic, hating the pain it was causing her. I couldn't bring up Indie right now. Othello stood and walked away from the mattress, shutting the door quietly behind her.

"Good night," I said softly, before closing my eyes.

21

We entered the vast, office complex of Temple Industries. The heat blasted over us like a warm blanket as we walked through the front door. It felt pleasant after the weather outside. The snow hadn't picked back up, but it hadn't melted either, and the mass of humanity swarming St. Louis for *Mardi Gras* had put the snow plows in a bit of a pickle. We had slept the day away, utterly exhausted after fighting almost until dawn. It was afternoon, and I could almost feel the daylight slipping away.

I had wanted to make sure that our visit would be discreet in the event that the police or FBI was keeping tabs on the building. So, I had very sneakily dressed up like an accountant, wearing heavy framed glasses, khakis, and a short-sleeved dress shirt. With a pocket. The coat I wore was too small and only added to the ridiculous nerdy vibe I was putting off. I hated it, plucking at the threads as if they were a straitjacket.

"Stop fidgeting. You look nice." Othello nudged my shoulder with a grin.

"Yeah. As if I had never seen a girl before."

"Innocent. Just the way I like them." She winked suggestively.

"Not how I recall it," I answered instinctively, falling into our old flirtatious habits way too easily. I adjusted my dress shirt and then the glasses to cover up my knee-jerk reaction. Othello noticed with a contented grin. I ignored her. It felt odd walking into the impressive castle that was Temple Industries, knowing that all my assets were frozen and that I was more cash poor than anyone that currently worked for me. It was...

Humbling.

I had only the small assortment of bills buried in the back of my wallet, the pile of plastic cards utterly useless to me now. Was this what life was like for everyone else?

We encountered a guard who briefly touched his service piece before I took off the glasses and he recognized me. He did a double take, eyes widening in confusion, and then a scowl. I tapped my finger to my lips for silence, hoping he understood my meaning to keep my presence a secret from any outside curiosity – like the police. But his confusion only seemed to increase, as did his scowl. He muttered into his earpiece, no doubt to give a heads-up to the other guards in a hopefully discreet way. I couldn't afford to have the guards on alert. Othello looked highly uncomfortable. The guard nodded curtly and continued on his rounds. That was weird. Had I pissed him off at some point in the past? After a few minutes, we reached Greta's desk outside my office. She scowled at me with a no-nonsense look designed to deter outsiders.

"It's me, Greta," I said, watching her face morph into recognition. "We'll just be a few minutes."

Her eyes grew abruptly judgmental, no doubt assuming that I was cheating on Indie with the svelte woman beside me. "You were kidnapped," she said bluntly. "It's all over the news."

"Yeah. About that..." I began.

"Is this your kidnapper? Are you under duress?"

"Not yet," Othello quipped, to Greta's shock.

I held up a hand. "Everything is fine, Greta. I'm just showing an old friend around the company. She's an avid technology student. I was going to show her our drone program." I belted off the first thing I could think of. Greta appraised me, her arthritic hand on the telephone as if to call for backup. "I promise."

"The FBI froze the corporate accounts. Payroll was halted. You need to fix it. I was supposed to buy groceries tonight. What sinful acts have you committed to attract such attention?"

I blinked at her, ignoring the last question. The guard's scowl suddenly made more sense. No one had been paid. Then I arrive with a smoking hot girl beside me, as if nothing was wrong. And then I silently asked him to do me a favor. I hadn't truly considered the long-term consequences of them freezing my accounts. After all, my home, Chateau Falco, was held in trust, and the earned interest on the investments in that trust paid for any and all maintenance expenses she incurred – like taxes, utilities, food, etc. You know, the things that make a house a home. I'd never thought about what it might mean to my employees. "Um. I don't think the FBI is going to allow me to circumvent their freeze. Especially since I am being *ransomed*."

"You don't look like you're being ransomed," she said, folding her arms with a huff. "You look perfectly fine, although dressed more respectfully than normal. You look like a nice young boy, for once. A nice young boy who shouldn't be entertaining pretty women while you are considered missing, and while your girlfriend is out of town." Othello stiffened. "Should I be concerned? Is the company going to be shut down? Even if you don't need the money, we do. We consider this company a second home. It's how we pay our bills. You know, those pesky things that regular people have to concern themselves with. I wouldn't expect you to understand."

I stared at her. Really? Right now. "Greta. Everything is fine. Just a big misunderstanding. I'm trying to get it resolved as we speak. But I can't remove the freeze on the accounts. I'm supposed to be *missing*."

"Like I said, you look perfectly fine to me. Is your entertaining a pretty young woman more important than the welfare of your employees? Ashley wouldn't allow it if she was here."

"I know. I'm trying to get it fixed. Some bad people are after me, attacking the company to get to me."

"Yet here you stand, completely healthy, with a pretty young girl, walking into your own company, dressed respectfully for once, to show her our... *drone program*," Greta said, distrust obvious in her tone.

I groaned. "Greta..."

"I almost ripped our poor intern to shreds when I saw what he had done with our Savior's Cross. Move it back into your office or I'll call the police right now. Also, I think I'll make today a half day since the owner refuses to take care of his employees. Double pay."

I groaned. This was ridiculous. My own secretary was extorting me, too? But I didn't have time to argue. "Okay." I trotted over to the cross and hoisted it over a shoulder. It was surprisingly light. I heard Othello speaking with her as I set the cross against the wall inside my office.

"I think that's a great idea. How much do you need for groceries? I'm sure Nate will fix the issue as soon as possible, but in the meantime, let me help you."

Othello began to peel off a few hundreds out of her purse. Greta folded her arms in refusal. "I don't need your help. I need my boss to take care of his company."

Othello looked at me, siding with Greta. "She has a point."

I blinked, realizing I was suddenly outnumbered. I had no significant money on me, having spent the majority of my cash at the bar, *Achilles Heel*. Then a thought struck me. "Greta. How much is payroll this week?" She blinked at me before opening a document on her computer, no doubt checking her email for the amount that was denied. Rather than getting involved, I decided to trust her with a bit of responsibility. "Never mind. If I gave you a pile of cash, could you distribute it to everyone? Don't worry about the specific amounts. Just pay everyone three thousand dollars. If it's not enough, I'll take care of it with the FBI once everything has passed. If it's too much, they can consider it a bonus for the delay. Can you send out a mass email to make sure that I have record of it all?"

Greta blinked at me. "You have that kind of cash available? I thought they froze your accounts also?"

I nodded. "Ashley and I keep a rainy-day fund in my safe. No doubt she would have already resolved this, but since she's not here, and I had no idea you guys were impacted, I'm asking you to help me fix it. Immediately."

She folded her arms, leaning back in her chair, judging me. "You would trust me with all that cash? What if I just took it all? It would serve you right."

"I doubt our friend upstairs would think very highly of that." I pointed at the cross I had just moved to my office. Her frown grew steadier, not appreciating my comment. "Of course I trust you with this. There is at least two hundred thousand dollars in our safe. Write receipts for any money given out, since we don't want the IRS to audit us due to this confusion, but tell no one of the details. Deal?"

She finally nodded. I gave her the codes and she snorted as if dirtied by having to handle this duty. But she wrote the code down, and smiled at Othello. "At least he has one other respectable friend. Thanks for talking some sense into him. Honestly, he doesn't listen to anyone. He needs someone to keep him in line." Her matronly tone dropped. "Even if he already has a girlfriend."

"Greta," I warned. "Just take care of this for me. Please. I had no idea they froze the company accounts. I only just found out about my personal accounts being frozen. It's a big misunderstanding, but I'll get it fixed." I had no idea how, but she was right. I needed to take care of my own.

Greta finally nodded. "It will be taken care of. Be quick. If you're supposed to be missing and the FBI comes here asking questions I will have to provide them with anything they ask me for, including video surveillance."

"You wouldn't," I whispered in disbelief.

"I would. Jesus would demand it of me." She smiled back satisfactorily.

Othello saved me. "You're a saint, Greta. We'll be quick. I promise." Greta nodded once and headed into my office to gather the money. I would double check everything later. Make sure too much wasn't missing.

"Thanks for having my back," I muttered to Othello, leading her deeper into the building.

"It's easier to comply than confront women like her. It's a matronly thing."

I continued walking, hating that she was right.

"So, girlfriend, huh?" she asked, deadpan.

I nodded, spotting the hallway with the Armory entrance just ahead. "Yeah. Indie. She and I have been dating for a few months, now. I don't deserve someone as good as her, but she sticks around for some reason. She's been with me through some pretty rough patches. Like the dragons a few months back," I said.

"I see," she answered crisply. "If you recall, I was also *there for you* with the dragons. And busting you out of prison. Kosage's float. The Greater Demon. The werewolves."

"I know that, Othello," I said. I took her resulting silence as an end to the conversation. "We're here," I said, waving at the broom closet before us.

Othello looked at it suspiciously. "A closet? Did you take me here to have seven minutes in Heaven? You have a *girlfriend* now, Nate," she said in a dry tone.

"No. That's not what..." I shook my head as her eyes bore through me. "It's the Armory. My parents' secret project. It's just magically sealed right now. But I want to warn you, I don't fully understand what's behind that door. You might be surprised. I do know that we'll only have seventeen minutes to explore. And please don't ask why," I added before she could voice the obvious question. Her jaws clicked shut.

"Okay. How do we get in?" she asked, touching the door after a nod from me. She grasped the handle and pulled. A mop struck her in the forehead and I felt a moment of satisfaction as I let out a very small, respectable laugh. She scowled back.

"I need to use the Key. Turn around, please."

She looked hurt. "Really? After everything we've been through? You don't trust me?"

Some other emotion also flittered across her eyes, but I didn't have time to delve into it. I had already told her about Indie. I didn't want to poke the bear. "It has nothing to do with trust. Literally no one else knows about the Key, and I want to keep it that way. For *your* safety."

"Not even Indie knows?" I shook my head. She finally nodded, looking satisfied at the fact that I had kept this secret from my girlfriend. Then she turned around.

I pricked my wounded hand and touched the door. It groaned as it began to open, and I whipped my hand behind my back so Othello wouldn't see me bleeding. A wave of warm air rolled over us. "Shall we?" I asked, holding out an elbow like a gentleman at a ball.

She stared past me, dumbfounded, which was satisfying.

"You are back, my host. I feared it would be some time before I saw you again," Hope's familiar voice called from inside the doorway.

Othello gasped, taking an instinctive step back. Then she slowly turned to face me, a lecherous grin growing on her cheeks. "Nate... You *dog*. How many girls do you have tucked away for your pleasure?" She looked downright pleased to hear I had another woman locked away in a room. Women. I would never understand them.

"It's not like that. You'll see."

She grunted doubtfully, but she did accept my arm before we stepped into the Armory.

What was I getting myself into?

22

The sandstone walls emanated a soothing heat, like we had entered the tropics. The numerous artifacts lining the shelves, resting on the floor, sitting on tables, and hanging on the walls captivated my attention. I noticed Othello staring openly and smiled. "Beautiful, isn't it?" I asked.

She nodded. "Is that...?" She pointed at the fleece that I had asked Hope about.

"No. But the real one is here." I answered honestly, remembering Hope's answer to my exact same question. We continued on. I was here for one reason. I needed to find the summoner, and I was desperate – fearful even – of borrowing power from this room, but what choice did I have? I had no other friends for backup, and my most constant companion, my magic, had been taken from me, or would be soon enough not to make any difference. I had promised the Alpha werewolf I would make the Demon suffer for his crime, but I wondered if he truly believed in my innocence or not. It was mainly fear of my pack of 'spirit wolves' that had deterred them. The Nephilim were no doubt hunting me, despite not having run into them yet. Unless the creature egging the werewolves on had been one... I honestly didn't know, which was why I was here.

For answers. And possibly a weapon or two.

I wanted Othello here to act as my conscience. Another rational being to hopefully talk me out of doing anything too rash, like taking too much power from this place. But she seemed anything but rational at the moment. Talk of Indie had turned her into an ice queen.

We continued towards the balcony. A vast sunset cast a warm, reddish glow over a beautiful desert. I stopped, scanning the horizon. "Is this place real?" Othello asked beside me.

As if summoned, Hope stepped out of the shadows, looking just as beautiful as the last time I had seen her. "Yes. And no. The entrances are few, but this is a memory palace of a very real place."

Othello took a step back. "You're stunning," she said bluntly. Then she turned to me with a wry grin. "You're telling me Indie is better than *that*?" she asked, pointing a thumb.

Hope dipped her head in appreciation before turning to me with a questioning smile. "Just because she's beautiful doesn't mean she's mine for the taking. She's her own person," I grumbled.

Hope turned to Othello. "I offered him my services, but he told me he is being sufficiently serviced at the moment."

Othello burst out laughing.

"Can it," I muttered. "How are things, Hope? Sense any Demonic presence lately?"

"I adore the pet name you've given me, my host. I have seen no sign of Demonic presence, but..." she appraised me curiously, "I notice your power has drastically dropped since we last met. Because of your curse. Have you come to inherit your birthright? I have power here like the world hasn't seen in thousands of years. All yours now, in exchange for your acceptance of my servitude. Is that why you are here?"

Othello slowly turned to me. "Is she serious?"

I shrugged. "I think she's a very literal person."

"You look sad, downtrodden, defeated," Hope said, sounding concerned.

I could only nod.

"Accept my service."

I stared at her for a good long while, debating. This was my last hand. After all, I didn't *have* to use anything here, but Hope *did* need a guardian. I think. "Okay."

She beamed. "Thank you, my host. Contract made." I felt gossamer threads of power briefly settle over my shoulders as she spoke, and then it faded away as if I had imagined it all. I shivered.

"Now, let me show you something," Hope offered.

"Will it hurt? I haven't decided to take anything from this place. I fear the ramifications. I came here only to speak with you."

She nodded in understanding. "That is your prerogative. I am here only to serve. But allow me to show you something. It will do you no harm."

I finally nodded. She approached me and I realized my shoulders were suddenly rigid, afraid. She was powerful. I had thought she was going to lead me deeper into the Armory, but apparently not. She gently laid a hand on my temple and I was immediately overwhelmed by what I could only call a *vision*.

Sand blasted my face, and the sun threatened to scald any normal person's skin, but I was no normal person. I was a Myrmidon, *the* Myrmidon, and this was *home*... kind of. I glanced down at my hand and realized I was holding a short bronze sword. My other fist held a trio of spears tucked beneath a bronze shield. I was covered from head to toe in bronze armor. *Greek* armor.

I looked up and saw giant city walls before me, lined with archers, all hesitantly aiming their arrows at me. Thirty-foot tall city gates barred my entry, and I was alone.

I turned to look, but saw no one behind me. No Hope, no Othello. *Who are Hope and Othello?* Part of me was aware that this was a vision, but part of me was confused by the sudden thought, wondering if the daymares were back. I squashed my inner dialogue in order to pay attention to the experience.

"HECTOR!" I heard myself roar in a leonine voice that was raw from constant shouting.

Apparently, the man was very responsive, or I had been here for a very long time, shouting for him to come out. Because the gates opened, revealing a lone warrior.

How crazy was I? I stood alone against an entire city, and I was demanding for a man to emerge from the safety of his walls. Then I recognized the setting. More specifically, *where* I was, and *when* I was. *Who* I was, and what I was *doing*.

I was Achilles.

At the gates of Troy.

At the infamous battle with Hector, seeking revenge for my dead cousin, Patroclus. I felt my rage bloom at the thought. This man, Hector, had killed my most beloved of cousins. And I was about to rectify that grievance.

The man striding towards me looked saddened, defeated, apologetic, but still a formidable adversary. I shook the thought away. It didn't matter. He had wronged me. Rage and absolution ruled my emotions. He finally settled a safe, but approachable, distance away.

"This is *your* war. In war, there are casualties on both sides," he said in a rough voice.

I nodded. "A fact I mean to display to your city today. I will show them the true definition of *casualty*. What hope will your people have left after they see me slay their precious prince before their very gates?" I sneered.

"It was not my intention to kill your cousin. He wore your armor. Fought beside your men. I should have known after such a quick fight that it *couldn't* have been you. The gods did not favor him."

This was the wrong answer. "Are you telling me my cousin fought like a babe? You dare make a mockery of the dead? I will show your city mockery like they have never seen before."

Hector dropped his head in defeat. "That is not what I meant, and you know it. I meant to honor your *prowess*, not to dishonor Patroclus. You see only vengeance before you. It is clouding your vision."

"Honor my prowess by drawing your sword, Princeling. I have other tasks to attend to at camp. I hope you have said goodbye to your loved ones. You will not see them for some time."

Hector's shoulders tightened in resolution. "I have. But there is no guarantee I will not see them again shortly."

"Oh, but there is. Do you not know of my story? I am the son of *Zeus*. I am immortal.

You stand no chance. I will deliver you to the gods – my *family* – this afternoon, and drink to your death in an hour," I leered. "Now, draw your spear." I drew mine as well.

The moment Hector complied, I hurled a spear at his face. He hadn't been ready, and only just managed to deflect the deadly throw. That was fine. I didn't want a quick fight. Hector would be the best I had ever fought.

The best I had ever killed, soon enough.

I raced towards him, eagerly launching my other two spears in quick succession before drawing my sword. I was hungry for face-to-face combat, not a killing blow from a dozen yards away. I wanted to taste his last moments from up close. Patroclus deserved it. Hector narrowly avoided being impaled, and dropped two of his spears, choosing to fight the old way – his spear against my blade. My sword struck the tip of his spear with a *clang* that echoed off the walls before us. I grinned. "You hear my sword? It's *hungry*. For Princeling blood. For my cousin's vengeance. It will be sated soon enough, Trojan."

Then I launched all my skills at him, seeing only the killing blow to come. Hector was well-trained, blocking everything I threw at him, but he was becoming weary from my berserker blows. I – on the other hand – was fueled by the gods, by my rage. Honor was on my side. I wouldn't tire before he lay before me, a rapidly cooling carcass. I wouldn't sleep until his body lay at my feet.

Hector finally began to attack, no longer defending, no doubt realizing that he could not halt or even slow my tirade of attacks. He was good, but not nearly good enough.

It finally ended in a flurry of metal. My sword slashed deeply into his calf, dropping him.

From the ground, he slashed at my ankles wearily and I jumped back in sudden alarm. "Easy. You might scratch my sandals," I spat, kicking his spear away, successfully hiding my anxiety. He had almost struck my heel. I lifted my sword, aiming for his heart, and scowled down at him. "Prepare to meet my uncle, Hades, and atone for your mistake."

This was it. My moment. My retribution. Everything would be well after this blow.

Hector stared into my soul as my sword plunged through his heart.

I stared down at him, satisfied as I watched his life bleed away. The archers on the wall gasped collectively. I waited for the gift of peace to fill me. The peace I deserved in exchange for the justice I had delivered.

But nothing happened.

His body struck the ground, sliding off my sword. Still... nothing. No sense of peace.

I finally screamed in rage. What was wrong? I had served justice. Why didn't I feel better? In a fit of rage, I strode back to my chariot, and bringing back a coil of leather rope, I hastily tied a knot around his ankles. He obviously hadn't been punished enough. The gods demanded more shame from this once great warrior. I could do that. Anything for inner peace.

I climbed into my chariot, blocking a lone arrow that sailed my way by a disgruntled archer. I scowled up at him and shook my head one time.

No more arrows came for me, but lamenting screams filled the air, begging forgiveness.

I raced back to my camp, willing to drag Hector's corpse to the four corners of the earth if that's what it took to honor the gods. For some reason, I couldn't help but feel that even this might not be enough to quell my pain...

What felt like a bucket of ice water abruptly showered my soul, and I snapped back to myself, no longer a part of the vision.

Despite being back in the room, my heart still pulsed with Achilles' anger. It had been infectious. Even now it was hard to release. He had been so *angry*. I could honestly say that I had never been that angry. Achilles had lost it, completely. There was no more hero in him after Patroclus' death. Just grief. Despite attaining his vengeance, it hadn't been enough, and he had then chosen to cross a line of respect that had existed for thousands of years. It was hard to even fathom, let alone believe.

My voice was raspy, and I glanced up to see that Othello's eyes were full of concern. "What... what was that?" I croaked.

Hope watched me. "The price for vengeance. And now it's time for you to leave," she added sadly.

I looked down at my watch, noticing the time and cursed under my breath. Sixteen minutes. Othello looked from me to Hope. "What? We haven't gotten what we came for. We haven't even discussed it with you." A faraway look abruptly replaced her agitation. "Yes, we're late. It's time for us to leave." I nodded, understanding her urgency to leave on a slightly different level than last time I had been booted out. I was semi-aware of not really wanting to leave yet, but I still found myself traipsing out of the mysterious Armory.

"I hope to see you soon, my host," Hope's soft voice carried through the vast hallways in a faint echo. The door slammed shut behind us with a resounding boom.

23

It had taken Othello a few minutes to calm down, pounding on the door in a fury. Now, she followed me out of Temple Industries, using a different path than we had used to enter. I didn't feel like running into Greta again, and I also wanted to use a different exit in an effort to thwart anyone who might have tailed us here. She was still grumbling as she followed me. "That was totally pointless. You watched a memory of a great hero. How does that help us? She knew we were on borrowed time. You knew we were on borrowed time. Why did you let her touch you?"

I glanced over my shoulder, just as frustrated as her. "She said she wanted to show me something. How was I supposed to know it would take as long as it did? I thought we would have plenty of time." But now we didn't, and night was rapidly approaching. Which meant that another flavor of supernatural in my city was about to be murdered by the Demons. Since I hadn't turned over the Key to the Armory, I would have to live with another death on my conscience.

And there wasn't a thing I could do about it.

I didn't even have a clue as to where to start. But I knew I could use the artifact Hope had first given me. At least that would let me pinpoint out a few locations, and then I could choose at random, hoping I was correct. It was life or death. If I didn't guess correctly, an innocent died. A gamble.

But the only way out of this mess was even worse. Let the Demons or their summoner – which was most likely worse – have access to potentially unlimited power. We sauntered out of the building via a side exit, which was actually closer to our car. I saw a pale slip of paper flapping in the chill wind and raced for it. It was tucked under her windshield wiper. I unfolded it as Othello shifted nervously from foot to foot.

"Vampire," I cursed.

Othello leaned in, reading the single word. "Subtle, aren't they?"

Instead of answering, I tossed her the keys and opened the passenger door. "I'm going to try to hone in on any Demonic activity in the city, see if we can find an exact location. If we aren't too late, like last time." Othello turned the key and revved the engine. I rubbed the artifact over the map and whispered the word *Seek* under my breath. Scarlet smoke settled on three locations. The mausoleum where my parents' bodies rested, Plato's Cave, and Chateau Falco. I sighed. The Demons were taunting me. First, it had been an apartment complex I had helped finance. Now they were going to murder a vampire – likely in the most gruesome of ways – at another location that led to me. To poke my rage. I recalled the memory of Achilles in a new light, feeling myself being pushed dangerously close to the same ledge he had stood on, where he had jumped off into an inferno of vengeance that ultimately led to his death.

I squinted, trying to think like a Demon. Which location? Othello was tapping the steering wheel, letting out a soft whistle as she saw my options. "Which would hurt more?" I asked myself. My ancestral home, Plato's Cave – my bookstore, my very own creation. Or the final resting place of my every ancestor. It seemed pretty obvious. They had killed my parents. Of course they would mock them in death.

"Bellefontaine Cemetery," I finally growled.

Othello nodded once, placing a calming hand on my thigh, and then shifted into gear, peeling out in the parking lot.

I cracked the window as we drove towards the cemetery, desiring to feel the brisk air in an effort to cool my fury. It didn't help, especially since about a million cars stood between us and the cemetery. I resigned myself to waiting, using the time to try and center myself. The Demons were about to desecrate my one place of peace, and the final place of peace for my parents. It seemed the obvious choice, but I honestly didn't know if I was right. All three places were vitally important to me for different reasons. What if I was wrong? I pondered this for what seemed like days, but was more likely an hour as we darted through traffic, willing to risk dinging the Lincoln if others didn't get out of our way fast enough. I felt my rage building upon itself as we drove, which wasn't good. I needed to be cool, calm, and collected. I had limited power and was about to go toe-to-toe with a big meanie. I couldn't afford emotions right now.

We finally arrived at the cemetery, and I used my fob to open the gates. Having helped them refinance some renovations, I had been given my own key. Also, so I could visit whenever I felt the need. I jumped out of the car the moment we parked. I could hear Othello's feet racing to keep up with me as I ran to the Temple Mausoleum, dodging headstones and piles of snow. The frosty winter landscape eliminated the need for light as the moon rose higher and the night crept closer.

I scanned the cemetery, searching, questing for Demonic presence as well as the more mundane footsteps in the snow. I smelled nothing, saw nothing, and the night was silent. Frustrated, I began stalking the perimeter of the mausoleum, ignoring the beautiful carvings and statues for once. Othello followed me, eyes scanning the horizon for any sign of danger. I circled the entire building, and then focused on the large locked entrance. No one had been inside. There were no tracks, and there was no way for anyone to bypass such modern technology – especially a Demon. The building was warded against it.

"This doesn't make sense. They should be here. It's the worst place they could kill someone. The cruelest." Othello stayed silent. I pulled out the artifact and the map in my pocket, activating its power. There was no Demonic presence at the cemetery. I blinked. Had I just imagined it, or was this some kind of diversion? Or were they already done killing the vampire? I sighed in defeat, knowing that I had to use my power to see if anything had happened here. I calmed my racing thoughts and quested out with magical feelers. Another spell I had developed recently was a way to detect any Freak's presence... and even a way to detect any recently dead presences. My magical feelers scouted the entire cemetery, and I could sense even that small amount of power burning away, being used up, never to return again.

But there was nothing. No recently murdered body. It had been a ruse.

"What are you two doing here?" an authoritative voice asked from only a few feet behind me. I released my feelers and turned to the voice, jumping slightly to the side in case they were about to attack. My spell hadn't picked up on the voice.

As I turned, I saw a familiar face. Gavin.

"I own this building. What the hell are you doing here?" I snapped.

Gavin appraised both of us before answering. "Following you, of course. Why did you come here? Was it because of the Demonic presence a short while ago?"

I continued to stare at him.

"They're long gone. They merely came to scout your family mausoleum, and then left. They did nothing other than look, or I would have exorcised them."

"Here's an idea. Perhaps, if you see Demons, you exorcise first and ask questions later," I snapped.

"Not in my job description," he answered coolly.

"Figures. Don't do anything to aid the guy you've crippled, that way you can look better when things go to hell."

Gavin's eyes lowered at that. "It's not like that."

"It *is exactly* like that. You see a fucking Demon, you exorcise it. It's really not that complicated. Demons are bad news. Help, or get the fuck out of my way." My vision was red. This was ri-god-damned-diculous. Here I was, trying to keep my city free of Demons while my parole officer was basically giving them free rein to do as they pleased, waiting for me to fail when said parole officer could have easily deterred them. But no, they wanted to be able to tell their superiors that I had failed. Not mentioning the small fact that they had taken away the necessary weapons I would need to prove my innocence. I knew *that* fact would never appear in the official report.

"You understand how crazy this is, right, Gavin? You took away my power, then expect me to banish all the Demons, while you sit safely on the sidelines ready to accuse me the moment I fail... the moment I fail as a direct result of you limiting my ability to stop the carnage." Gavin's eyes lowered... slightly. "You have literally set me up to fail. I am still out here risking my life despite the fact that you've taken away my only weapons... or severely limited them. How can you honestly say it's fair that I'm guilty if I fail, when the only reason I might fail is because I don't have the juice to keep fighting?"

"Then give up the Key," he snapped in exasperation, realizing how ridiculous his charge was. I hoped.

"Why would I give up the Key to a group of power-hungry old men who are actively allowing chaos to take over my city? You understand how ludicrous that sounds, right? It's called *extortion*."

Gavin stared daggers at me for a few moments before giving up and nodding a single time. "Yes." It sounded like he was pulling his own teeth to say so. "I know it seems ludicrous, but you're harboring a dangerous cache of weapons that belongs to the Academy. The only group able to support and protect mankind from annihilation." It sounded rehearsed, and I could tell he knew it.

"The same group that is allowing innocents to die in order to prove a point, right? The ones who set me up on a suicide mission to prove my innocence. I've even recruited a *Regular* to help me because I'm so desperate. Yet you and Jafar wait for me to fail rather than help. How is that *justice*?"

Gavin's gaze dropped lower, but he didn't voice his agreement. I knew Othello wouldn't take my comment personally. She was just as angry as I was, judging by the fact that she had commanded me to kill them all.

"If you're just going to sit on the sidelines and wait for me to fail, you might as well join me. It won't be long now. My power isn't lasting as long as I would have hoped. I'm spent. But I will press on because there isn't anyone else. Because you, sir, are a fucking coward."

His shoulders hitched, but I turned my back on him.

"Time to leave," I said to Othello. "Let this vulture do as he will. I'll be dead soon, and probably deemed guilty for all of this despite fighting until my last ounce of effort. Even *you* are more of a Knight than this... ignorant child."

I turned to go, Othello following me. But I was suddenly slammed into a headstone shoulder first, and then I flipped over it, landing painfully on the other side. "How *dare* you," Gavin growled. I grinned to myself as I climbed to my feet, rubbing my aching shoulder. I hadn't heard it crack. Othello immediately drew her pistol and fired. I didn't even flinch. I wonder what that says about me.

But then again, neither did Gavin. The bullet stopped a millimeter from his face. He didn't even blink, never moving his glare from the tombstone as I appeared over the side. I showed him my wolfish smile. "Perhaps you aren't as much of a little bitch as I thought, although your string is still showing." I pointed at his crotch. He didn't look, but Othello laughed darkly.

PMS jokes between men were the bestest.

"Now, if you're done being a pawn, it's time for us to go and stop the Demons."

Gavin's icy gaze remained frozen on me for a few moments before he gave me a slow nod. I began walking away, and he followed without flipping me over another tombstone. Baby steps.

Manly baby steps.

I rolled my shoulder discreetly, glad that it was only sore. It would have been super if he would have managed to dislocate it. But the risk had been worth it. Causing him to lose control again helped me prove a point. Hopefully made him doubt his creed just enough to assist me. And it seemed to have worked. Othello opened the door and I flicked my head at the other car that I assumed Gavin had driven since it hadn't been there when we parked. "We'll follow you," I told her. She shot me a calculating gaze as if asking if that was wise. "It's probably not my smartest move, but I need to talk to him on the way and I don't think he will stick around for very long." She nodded once. "To Plato's Cave. At least if I'm wrong I can grab a few things, check up on the place." I could sense Othello wasn't happy with the situation. At all. We'd just been duped by the Demons. Either they had lured me here to give them more time elsewhere, or I had been totally incorrect and the Demon had just coincidentally been scouting out the mausoleum at the same time another Demon was murdering a vampire. I wasn't a big fan of the fact that this was the second murder being committed on soil that would directly link to me. I wondered if there was a reason for that or if they were just trying to drive home a point.

Othello drove away angrily.

Gavin climbed into the driver's seat. It was a Crown Victoria. A typical police car. I grumbled about it as I climbed into the cesspool of mediocrity. "It's not that bad," he stated flatly, not agreeing with my vehicular taste. "And this doesn't mean we're on the same side."

"Hopefully, it means you're intelligent enough to realize that you're on the *wrong* side. Even if it's not my side, I hope you see that your current side is following the opinion of a bunch of fucking imbeciles."

Gavin chuckled, and then abruptly stopped, looking disappointed in himself for doing so. His eyes were lost in thought as he followed Othello through the darkening streets. "Maybe," he finally said.

"The Demons are going to kill a vampire. In a place that directly relates to me," I said, hoping it wouldn't end our current alliance.

He nodded, not exactly with any interest, but accepting of the fact.

I decided to play my card.

"What do you really know about my parents' project? This Armory?"

"Just that it was a cache of objects they deemed too dangerous to fall into the hands of the *all-powerful Academy*. The same Academy that provided them with safety for so many years. I find it hard to agree with your perception of the ruling body of wizards. I know they have room for improvement, but I do not believe the Academy to be evil."

I nodded. "I can understand that. I have to be honest, though. This Armory, as you call it, is news to me. I only recently discovered it. It seems to be the reason my parents were murdered. Coincidentally, the Academy showed up almost immediately, demanding access. You can see my cause for concern, right?"

Gavin nodded in resignation. "Timing. If they could show up when they did, why not sooner?"

I nodded. "Exactly my point. But it does make me wonder what, exactly, my parents were hiding. I understand the draw to power, but what does the Academy expect to find? Something specific? Or just power in general?"

Gavin shrugged. "Mayhap the Academy lost something once, and hope your parents managed to... *acquire* it?"

I shook my head. "I doubt it. My parents were not thieves."

Gavin looked uncomfortable. "May I speak... freely, Master Temple?" I could tell that it pained him to address me by my title. I nodded. "The brief time I met your parents, they seemed to imply that they did... *acquire* some of their objects questionably. I make no accusation. Just speak the truth. I know that they did purchase quite a few objects as well, but when they felt necessary, they did resort to more nefarious methods in order to... protect the masses." I shivered, remembering my father's conversation on my 21st birthday, the only time the Pandora Protocol had been mentioned. I sighed. Perhaps Gavin had a point.

"Maybe. But I'm grateful you offered to help with this small Demonic inconvenience."

"Will it be dangerous?" he asked, glancing at me curiously.

"Consider it your second interview..."

Gavin looked nervous but determined. "Okay."

I needed his help. My power was fading faster than I had thought. I was also a target to the mysterious Nephilim that Hemingway and the Demon had mentioned, of which I luckily hadn't directly tussled with yet. Even if they had tried to throw me to the wolves. I also didn't want to risk Othello. Screw it. Gavin seemed torn on his allegiances. Trial by fire then. I needed to test his mettle. If he wanted to find the good side and ease his conscience, then he needed to earn that trust.

"Do you have a safe word?" I asked him as we continued following Othello. Gavin looked really uncomfortable for a few moments.

"Um, what kind of second interview did you have in mind? Because I didn't mean to give you the wrong impression. I'm not into—"

I chuckled darkly. "Not that kind of safe word. Things might get, not to keep the pun going," I winked, "but... hairy. I was just curious on what kind of tolerance you have for fear." Gavin relaxed instantly.

"Ah. I'm sure I'll be fine. I've sought out plenty of danger in my days. Even met a werewolf once. Filthy beast tried to kill me. Showed him," he said proudly. I smiled guardedly.

"Well, my best friend is a werewolf, so be careful about your prejudices. But that's good to hear. Wouldn't want you freaking out in the middle of a... difficult situation."

"I'll be fine. I know how to subdue any who would do me harm."

"Not sure subduing is an option, but you're more than welcome to try. I'll just say this. With Demons, the rule book goes out the window." Gavin's face tightened, but he nodded.

We pulled up to the front of Plato's Cave, and then drove on by, cruising casually. I noticed a blacked-out Ford Explorer parked near the entrance with two neatly groomed men inside – wide-awake – watching the streets. My place was being observed. Gavin grunted, spotting them. Othello continued on ahead of us, obviously noticing the stakeout as well. We pulled around the block, made a lap to be sure that there were no other spotters, and then parked. My disguise was entirely complete with the fake horn-rim glasses, so I had no fear that they would recognize me. Unless I walked through the front door after regular business hours...

Othello casually exited the car, as if having no relation to Gavin and me, pretending to talk loudly into her phone to a girlfriend. They followed me as I entered through a side door that only the employees knew about, safe from prying eyes. I was ready for anything, not knowing if it would be like the werewolf community, that somehow an entire coven of vampires would be here ready to take me out. But nothing happened. We entered the darkened building... *my* darkened building. And it was empty, the employees long gone.

"It seems clean. No murder," I said, frowning.

Gavin grunted. "Perhaps this is also a false lead."

I looked at him, unable to contain my anger. "There are 1,013,900 words in the English language, and none of them accurately portray how badly I want to hit you over the head with a chair. A heavy Amish chair."

Gavin... blinked. "With all your power, you wish to hit me over the head with a chair? For stating a fact?"

"You took away *all my power*. So, yes. A chair will suffice."

Othello chuckled quietly. "Boys..."

Gavin shook his head, muttering. "A chair..."

"This doesn't make sense," I said after scanning the entire store. I turned for the stairs that led up to my old apartment. Now, it was merely unused living quarters above the shop. But it had once been an old projector room, because the place had been a theater. "Light, please," I said to Gavin. He cast his power out into a bluish dim glow so we could see without turning on the lights and alerting the FBI. They followed me, watching in silence as I gathered a few things and a change of clothes. I was done hiding and using disguises. I snatched up a unique feather stuffed into a jar of pens on my desk – a feather that looked like it had been torn from a Demonic peacock – with a smile on my face. *Grimm*. Might come in handy.

"And what's the escapade behind this?" Othello asked with a leer, pointing at the pair of panties hanging on the desk lamp.

"Indie."

Othello sniffed haughtily. "Classy."

"They did the job," I mumbled under my breath. Gavin watched with curiosity.

"Alright, I don't see any other reason to stick around," I said, changing the topic. I hefted the overnight bag over my shoulder. I quickly emptied my pockets to transfer my stuff to my new pants. When I pulled out my wallet, a card dropped to the floor and I truly saw it for the first time since Hemingway had given it to me. "Well I'll be goddamned..."

A large boom at the front door of Plato's Cave shook the building as the door burst into splinters. "I meant *gosh darned*," I snapped. Heavy boots stomped into the entrance below us. "Oh, come on! It was a slip of the tongue!" I bellowed, shoving the card into my pocket.

"Meet your demise, wizard," a cool voice commanded from below.

Gavin merely leaned towards a window to look down at the threat, not actively doing anything to help me. Othello cocked her pistol hungrily.

I quickly darted to the window to see what the hell was going on, hoping my accomplices wouldn't shoot first and ask questions later. I couldn't make out the details, but he looked human.

"Who goes there?" I called.

"The might of Heaven, mortal. Bow down."

"Ice Cube? Really?" I asked. He didn't respond. I held up a hand for my accomplices to hold off, but it seemed Gavin had no intention of assisting.

"I'm not fucking with Heaven," he stated bluntly, and then Shadow Walked his happy ass out of my shop with a resounding *crack*.

I sighed. I had managed to piss off God. And my ally had abandoned me at the first sign of mayhem.

24

I snarled at the sound, "Hold off on the smiting. I'll be down in just a second!"

Othello followed me closely as I descended the stairs. I really didn't have time for this. I had done nothing wrong. In fact, I believed I was the only one doing anything *right*.

The man hadn't moved from the entrance, but what remained of the door had been propped back in place. He was much younger than I had thought. The youth held a hand on the hilt of his righteous sword, and he looked like he had been plucked straight from the Crusades, decked out in genuine leather armor that was engraved in platinum curlicues and exquisite geometric shapes that made my skin crawl. They were functional, not just for decoration. Spells. And they were so ancient I could only recognize that they *were* spells, but not their purpose.

He was young, appearing twenty-something, but the hard gleam in his eyes let me know he was formidable with wisdom well beyond his years. I settled the bag gently on the ground beside me. "So, what's a nice guy like you doing in a dangerous place like this?" I asked. I kept my hands in a neutral place – for most people anyway, but not that neutral for a wizard – at my sides, hanging freely. He was smart enough to understand they were still a threat, glancing at them with quick, assessing eyes.

The boy watched me coldly. "You are aiding the Demons. I can sense it on you."

I blinked back. He seemed to have no concern for Othello. Apparently, only I was on his list. "If I'm such a naughty boy, explain why I've shut down several Demons in the last twelve hours," I answered coolly.

The boy continued to stare at me, unruffled. "I do not pretend to understand your murky motives, magic mortal."

"Say *that* five times fast."

He blinked like a cat on a fireplace, not amused, refusing to acknowledge my comment. "It is a fact. I know what I see."

"And what you see might be jaded by your righteousness," I quipped.

He quivered with pious judgment. "Do not blaspheme again. I will grow angry." The boy growled. Although he was young, his strength was obvious, and he looked like he had grown up through the school of hard knocks, judging by the faint scars on his face. I guessed battling Demons your entire life left you a little jaded. Or maybe he had been brainwashed at a young age. A lot of that going around lately. "What you do directly affects Heaven, and directly aids Hell," he continued quite calmly. "For that, you must be destroyed."

He drew his huge sword with finality, the whisper of it leaving the sheath a grisly promise of what was to come. Othello didn't waste any time. She lifted her pistol. "I fucking dare you."

The boy seemed to notice her for the first time. "Do not let his words sway you. This man is dangerous."

"Me?" I asked in amazement. "All I've done is fight Demons and my own people the last too many hours. What have I done to piss off *Heaven*?"

"You made a pact with a Greater Demon. I can sense it." He leaned closer, sword out, but not threatening... yet. "I can *see* it." *Then* he moved. He suddenly flicked the sword so fast that he could have taken my head right off. If he had wanted to. It was a warning. The tip rested just above my eye. To the damning mark on my forehead. I could hear the crackling energy of his heavenly power reacting to the rune, feel it tingling against my skull.

"I didn't ask for that. It was forced upon me. I'm not one for brands. Ask her." I pointed at Othello.

She nodded. "It's true. I was there when he fought the Demon. This mark was the Demon's last attack, in order to pit your kind against his cause. The Demons want us fighting each other, but there is a true enemy out there."

Her voice was soft, soothing, and compelling. The boy shook his head as if at a temptress. "I will not buy these lies. I see the mark. Eae warned you to stay out of it. I saw the aftermath of you killing that wolf. Despite their kind being an abomination, murder is not tolerable."

"People are murdered all the time and I've never heard of your kind getting involved." Too late, I realized that I hadn't argued the most important accusation.

"You see," he smiled. "You don't deny killing the wolf."

I groaned. "No, I didn't deny it. Because it's crazy. I arrived *after* she was killed, hoping to prevent it from happening. My best friend is a werewolf. But someone of your ilk pitted a whole pack of vengeful werewolves after me when I only showed up to help, so I'm more concerned with where your people come into the picture and why they have a hard-on for me."

He smiled. "Well, our part is simple enough." There was no warning whatsoever. He lunged at me. Othello let off a few shots, pinging the blade out of the Nephilim's hands.

He didn't miss a beat, and instead physically latched onto me with his hands, and threw me.

Like, *really* threw me.

I grunted with each impact as I sailed through what I counted as three glass-walled dividers before landing on a cushioned couch and knocking it over. "Huzzah!" I managed to cheer through the throbbing ache in my ribs, jumping to my feet, glad that the couch had somewhat broken my fall. Then I saw a blindingly white light whipping towards my face with a supersonic whine. I dropped like a sack of potatoes, not wanting to waste any more magic than necessary by deflecting whatever the Heaven it was. A freaking crucifix boomerang whizzed by overhead, spitting off electric currents of power as it tore through several hanging chandeliers, sending them to the ground in explosions of crystal and glass. The weapon crackled with lightning at each strike, seeming to deflect the sparks of electricity, before sailing back towards the Nephilim who caught it with ease. The energy danced over his frame as his glare pinned me to the couch.

Othello was nowhere to be found. Had he killed her?

The Nephilim strode over to the sword and picked it up off the ground. It was dented and bent in a wavy line from Othello's well-placed bullets. He knelt his head and began to mutter a prayer. His words filled the room, and a ring of liquid golden power began to build around his feet. After a few seconds, it began to rise, circling his body, and I began to feel a little uneasy at what it might mean. A shard of crystal from the chandelier fell towards his head, but when it came remotely near the golden light it disintegrated to powder, and I suddenly realized I might have met my match. Heavenly armor of some sort would make my attacks useless.

If this was a Nephilim... what could an Angel do?

I shivered at the thought, but readied myself for war. The ring rose to his head level, shrunk, and became a perfect halo of raw force around his head. I watched in disbelief as the blade suddenly reformed to perfection.

I grumbled. Heavenly armor *and* an unbreakable sword? That wasn't fair at all. The Nephilim took a single step, raised the sword high, and then with a roar of power he slammed it into the ground like it was Excalibur. The golden halo around his head fled through his body and into the sword, causing a low thrum like a tuning fork, and a blast of energy suddenly rang out in every direction, demolishing or knocking down every piece of furniture or bookshelf in its immediate proximity. Then the entire building began to tremble, louder and faster, with each passing second. Pictures and books from the surviving shelves and wall mounts began to rattle, dancing into a free fall to the floor, and the lights began to erratically flicker on and off. The espresso machine kicked on and began flinging coffee beans all over the place. A jagged crack suddenly split the wall behind me, and brick and mortar began collapsing into the room as the building groaned tiredly, giving up. The walls were coming down. Was this fucker crazy? He was going to kill us all!

I Shadow Walked without thinking, appearing right behind him. I noticed the only adornment on his back was a second sheath with a feather sticking out. Without thinking, I snatched it up and Shadow Walked back in front of him...

Where his fist was immediately introduced to my face. It broke my nose with a most indelicate *crack* of cartilage and my vision exploded in a sea of stars. I flew backwards into a bookshelf hard enough for it to shatter and rain its contents down upon me. One struck me in the already broken nose and I almost squealed like I had been electrocuted. I heard his steps approaching and frantically, blindly, began trying to dig my way out of the pile of buckram and paper. Then I heard a loud click amongst the falling debris. "Don't move. I don't want to hurt you, but I will. Even if it damns me for eternity. You are about to kill one of the only good guys left in this city."

Othello's voice was like an Angel singing a hymn. I hurriedly fell out of the pile of books to see a strange scene. Othello was holding her pistol to the back of the Nephilim's head, and the boy was letting her. Couldn't he magic his way out of that?

"You would damn your soul for him?"

"Yes." She didn't even hesitate, which surprised even me. "You're making a big mistake."

"Othello," I warned. "Step a few feet away from him please. It's not safe. He's a zealot."

"As much as I hate to admit it, she's as safe as a babe from me. She is righteous... to a degree," he added, sounding frustrated.

Othello blinked at him. "What? To a *degree*? Well... I guess I'll take it."

I frowned at him. "What do you mean?"

"She is only doing as she believes is right, and I have no command to punish her. I swear on Heaven." He sheathed his sword faster than anyone could move, and then dropped his hands to his sides. "I cannot harm her."

I blinked. "Huh. Imagine that. Glad you could be here, Othello," I muttered.

"Just doing my job," she answered quickly.

The Nephilim's face suddenly fell. "My Grace!" He was staring at the feather in my hand and took an aggressive step forward before halting at Othello's warning. His face fell, but he continued to stare frantically at the feather I had stolen.

"Grace?" I asked, looking down at it.

"A feather from my father's wings. It was entrusted to me. It gives me additional strength to fight Hell." He looked entirely different from before. More like a child fearful of his father's wrath when he discovered the family car missing on a Friday night.

I turned it over in my fingers. It was silver, and big, but it didn't look like anything that special. Just a gilded feather you might find at a high-end jewelry shop. "This belongs to an Angel?" I asked doubtfully.

He nodded anxiously. Another crack that seemed to come from the foundation interrupted my thoughts. The building rumbled ominously. "Why doesn't your father just come down here himself and take care of the Demons?"

"He can't. If the Angels act, the Fallen can act, and then the Riders will destroy us all. Eternally."

"*Jesus!* Talk about overkill," Othello whispered, sounding shaken.

"No, not him. The Riders." He looked genuinely confused. Othello blinked.

I sighed. "So why is this feather so important?"

"It's not just a *feather*. It's my father's *Grace*. It grants him the power of Heaven. My temporary possession of it grants me extra power to battle Hell. If that feather breaks it would kill my father."

I subconsciously made sure I was holding it with both hands. "Well that's reckless. Why would you carry it around so openly?"

"Only extreme power could destroy it. And even the Demons wouldn't risk it. It would be the same as killing an Angel directly."

"You mean that it would call the Riders?" I asked in astonishment.

He nodded. "Please, give me back the Grace. I'll inform my father of your words. Perhaps it will change Eae's mind." He didn't sound like he believed it.

"Eae is your father?" I asked curiously.

"Yes. He commands the Flight of Nephilim on my task force."

I wanted to give it back, latching onto the hope that his father, Eae, would realize we were on the same side and get off my back. Really. What if I somehow managed to break it and called the Riders? But I needed to teach these guys a lesson, let them know that I wasn't to be trifled with. After all, if they were scared to attack me in fear of harming the Grace, I wouldn't have to waste my diminishing power fighting them. "This isn't the playground, kid. You can lose your balls here." Othello frowned at me. I rolled my eyes. "You know what I mean." I turned back to the Nephilim. "You just tried to kill me. Without even telling me who you are!"

"I was told you were allied with the Demons. And you carry the… Greater Demon's mark." He seemed to dodge the Demon's name for some reason. No doubt to avoid his attention.

"I already explained the mark. Can we agree that I'm not the problem? The world is going nuts the last few days. Demons prowling around town in search of a project my parents worked on. Am I safe to assume that you won't attack me while I hold this?" I waved the feather. The Nephilim flinched, reaching out clawed fingers instinctively. "Swear it on this feather. I can burn it with a thought. I am a wizard. You lie, pillow stuffing goes *poof*."

The Nephilim looked visibly sickened, but nodded, clutching a fist to his heart symbolically. "Good. Let's get out of here. You caused quite a ruckus kicking down my door like that, and those police outside are bound to be on their way any second. Especially if the building collapses."

The man shook his head. "I runed them. They'll be asleep until morning."

"Oh. Well. Good. So… what do I have to do to show you guys I'm not on the dark side?"

"I'm not sure. End the threat, I guess." I blinked at him.

"You want me to cast a whole army of Demons back to Hell to prove I didn't bring them here? I've been fighting them, alongside you, ever since I discovered them. They directly threatened me. And branded me with this mark against my will."

He nodded stoically, seeming to slowly regain his confidence. "Yet your parents are the reason they have come. With them dead, it is now your issue. You cannot accept the gift of the Armory yet ignore the consequences of ownership. It's on you. Now, give me back the Grace."

His form visibly rippled with power. "Cool it, feathers. I'm not giving you anything until I understand the whole picture, and you promise that Eae and your brothers will also stay off my back."

The scent of burnt sulfur abruptly filled my nostrils, my only warning of a Demon's presence. Before I could react, a form suddenly materialized behind the Nephilim. "Sweet dreams, little Nephilim." The boy began to react, but without his Grace he was too slow. Inky black Demonic claws decapitated him right before my eyes, showering me in his half-holy blood, which I somehow had time to realize didn't look or feel any different than regular blood, which was slightly disappointing. Othello grabbed my shirt and yanked me backwards just as a second claw swiped at me, raking my torso. Her grab saved my chest from becoming sliced lunchmeat, but it still did a fair amount of damage, causing me to gasp in only near fatal pain. The Demon frowned at his misfortune. "Luckily, you have her to save your pathetic hide. Such a lovely hide. It will look splendid as a throw rug."

I ignored his threat, clutching the Grace against my lacerated chest, scared that I might touch something that was supposed to stay on my inside. Feathers covered his frame like a raven, and beady black eyes assessed me hungrily. He even sported a vibrant beak that was stained with blood from a recent meal. Or permanently stained from a life of feasting on blood. "You lied. There was no vampire. It was a trap to lure me into a confrontation with the Nephilim. Why? If he had killed me, how would you get your precious key?" I asked, confused.

The Demon blinked at me, a look of utter confusion painting his features for half a second. Then he shrugged it off and began to stalk closer, speaking very clearly out of his beak. "I grow tired of talking. I didn't spend eons in Hell to waste my parole on earth."

I had time to think, *Huh... he doesn't know about the Key,* before another party guest arrived.

The room abruptly pulsed with a bluish glow and every single window blew out as power filled the room. The scent of sulfur was obliterated in a blink, replaced with the smell of burnt gravel and frost. Oh, shit.

Eae, the Demon-thwarting Angel.

The bird-Demon's black eyes went wide as a sword pierced his heart from behind, a much-too-wide blade pointing in my direction through the feathers on the Demon's chest.

"Wait!" I began, then the sword gave a sickening twist, shattering the Demon's sternum, and the monster disintegrated to ash. As he fell, I saw the Angel from the bar, Eae, standing behind him, crackling with power. He gave one contemptuous flick of his sword, disbursing the Demon blood onto my floor where it sizzled.

"You killed my son, stole my Grace, and allowed it to be fractured." He was quivering with fury, his voice a series of rasps, totally unlike our first talk. "If it breaks entirely, Armageddon will officially ignite, which you no doubt desire. I finally see the truth. Now that your Demon is dead, there is no one here to save you." The Angel spoke through ground teeth. I glanced down at the feather in my hand, which also gave me a great view of my wounded chest from the Demon's claws. The feather was indeed broken, the two halves connected by only a thin thread of cartilage.

"*My* Demon? I had nothing to do with him. When will you people get the hint? I was having a peaceful chat with your son before the Demon attacked us and cut your stupid feather! I was trying to keep it safe! He had information I could have used. Information that could have guided me to the summoner! The *real* problem starter. What the hell is wrong with you guys?"

I didn't even see him move. I merely felt a fist strike me in the stomach like a moving truck, and I was suddenly slammed into the wooden staircase on the other side of the building. I heard Othello scream, but I was too shaken to get my bearings. The Angel was suddenly towering over me, wings snapping out with a whoosh of air, quadrupling his size. "I don't believe you. Jonathan was no novice. No Demon could have killed him so easily. You killed him after he let his guard down." I began to stammer an argument, but the look in his eyes stalled me. I knew that look. The look of someone with nothing to lose. When a rage so dark and overpowering controlled your every thought. The kind of look one got after their family had been murdered. I had lived with that look for a few months now.

"No one kills one of my sons, or causes them to be killed without retribution. I have skirted the line by striking you, but since Armageddon is practically imminent, I hold no long-term responsibility for my actions. Just know this. If that Grace breaks entirely, my brethren will hunt you down. If it doesn't, my sons will. Regardless, your death will be slow and painful for your sins. Heaven will not assist you, and will now actively seek your demise. I will not forget this." The last was a whisper that rang with such a deadly finality that I actually kept my mouth shut.

The building gave an ominous crack, and Eae was abruptly gone. Othello sprinted over to me only a second after the Angel had disappeared, looking angry that he had already left. "Nate! Are you okay?"

"I just got my ass smited. What do you think?" I wheezed.

"I think it's smote, but I wasn't much of a bible school kind of girl. I will say that I bet no one in history has been struck by a Demon and then less than a minute later been smote by a freaking Angel." She glanced down at my wound, eyes growing concerned. "Shit." She averted her gaze to my face and I saw her eyes widen at my broken nose. "Um. You look like a badass?" she offered encouragingly.

I managed to feebly throw a brick at her. She dodged it. Then she pulled me to my feet, causing me to hiss in pain. My torso was lacerated, bleeding freely, and I had an Angelic fist shape indented into my stomach. "I think he bruised my stomach. The actual organ." It took me a few moments to gather my breath, and Othello continued to dab at my wounds with a shirt from the bag I had packed. I winced when her hands gripped my ribs.

"Sorry." Her eyes dampened with fear at the number of wounds painting my body.

"Yeah, those bookshelves were sturdy. And the glass-walled dividers. I don't think any ribs are broken though. To be safe, I should probably take some aspirin. Not Extra Strength though. No need to take risks." The store groaned again, more alarmingly, and the stairs leading to my loft suddenly collapsed with a crash, filling the room with dust and debris. Othello began to cough lightly through the haze. I heard another deep crack that sent more dust into the air. I needed to call this one in. The building might collapse any minute. I grabbed a new shirt and Othello helped me put it on, wrapping up another clean tee into a makeshift bandage to wrap over my wounds. Several small fires dotted the floor, burning through my priceless inventory.

I sighed as she finished, grunting in pain when she pulled the knot tight. "Let's go." We exited the same door from earlier and headed towards her car. Gavin's car was nowhere to be seen. Othello merely scowled at that.

A low, vibrating hum suddenly split the night, a keening wail.

A Horn of War. I glanced up and spotted Eae on a nearby rooftop, glaring at us.

At me, specifically.

His voice boomed through the night. "The wizard has proven his crimes, consorting with Demons to kill Jonathan, your brother, who attempted to trust him. He has broken my grace, but not destroyed it, no doubt to use me as his pawn. Which will not happen. I would rather die in *His* name. Let Armageddon be on the wizard's shoulders. Permission to decimate at will." With a giant flap of his wings, he was off, and I heard hundreds of answering horns fill the night. I shivered. Armageddon? I hadn't broken the feather, it was the damned Demon! I would do whatever it took to keep that feather safe. My life, and the world, now literally depended on it.

We raced to the car and jumped in, eager to be away from the answering calls of the dozens of Nephilim. Othello started the car and we took off in a squeal of tires. After we turned the corner, I heard an earth-shattering *thump* behind me, and then a crash like the earth had cracked open. Othello swerved, shouting as the car was shoved ahead on screeching tires. Several fire hydrants exploded beside us, showering the street with fountains of cold water that quickly began to turn to ice. I turned to look behind, fearing some sort of Angelic attack, but saw only a black cloud of smoke rising from my shop. My shoulders sagged. "First my money's frozen, then I'm arrested, then framed a murderer, and then my shop is blown to smithereens by a gaggle of geese. Someone is going to pay for this." Othello nodded. The thing was, I didn't really have anyone to take out my pain on. The Demon was dead, the Nephilim, Jonathan, was dead, and I was on Heaven's Most Wanted list. My parole officer, Gavin, had abandoned me when I needed him the most, and the only one I had on my side was Othello, a Regular.

"Let's head to the apartment. I feel like resting my eyes. Not sleeping, but resting my eyelids. Either that or we need to find some caffeine to pour directly into my eyeballs. One hundred percent caffeine. Not that diluted coffee swill. The real stuff."

Othello sniffed beside me and I could tell she was crying. I didn't have anything to say to her, though. I just wanted it all to be over with. I leaned back in my seat and closed my eyes.

I grew silent as we drove to the apartment. The facts.

This was all about the Demons and their summoner. He had brought a Greater Demon up from Hell in order to kill my parents and take the Armory. As if that hadn't been enough, he had either summoned more Demons for back up or the Greater Demon had brought a gang of his friends up for company – some of which were privy to details on the Armory, and some that weren't. Which was curious. Maybe they thought a little additional chaos would help. It sure hadn't hurt their cause. I was beginning to think that this summoner was either supremely powerful, extremely clever, or that there was more than one summoner... I shivered at that.

The Angel, Eae, had warned me to back off in the bar. And then the first Demon had commanded me to give up the Armory shortly after. Something had happened to bring both parties out into the open, but I didn't know what that could have been. It had been months since the break in, but now everyone was suddenly moving like they were on a time frame. I had since pissed off both Biblical parties and was now actively being hunted or framed by both.

Othello had turned out to be quite the sidekick. Still, things were about to get a whole hell of a lot worse, and I was running out of juice. And I was still a fugitive from the police, meaning I couldn't even tap into my money or assets.

Then there was the greedy Academy, who considered it a simple to-do item for me to banish all the Demons without my magic, extorting me in a moment of drunken stupor to curse me into giving them the Armory. No matter what I chose to do I was going to piss off someone I really probably shouldn't be pissing off.

I leaned my head back into the worn headrest, barely surviving the dull throbbing agony that was my face. I would need to set my nose before I went to sleep. I could taste the fresh blood draining into the back of my throat, and my chest felt hot from the deep cuts of the Demon's claws. My entire torso felt like a giant bruise, and I was getting kind of sleepy, enjoying the heat blasting from the vents as Othello continued to drive in silence, taking the turns carefully so as not lose control of the car on the snowy streets.

I fueled my pain into anger. It wasn't hard. I had plenty of each already. I decided that I would find that Greater Demon again and ask him a few pointed questions. It felt good to finally have a direction for my anger. I was in a race to kill the Greater Demon before my power failed me entirely. Or before the Nephilim hunters found me. Perhaps I could get the Demon's attention by killing one of his brothers. It had worked last time.

Othello murmured softly and I realized that I had been dozing lightly. I agreed with her. We opted to go get sleep rather than pouring caffeine into my eyes.

Probably a good choice.

25

Radio commercials from the car stereo droned on in the background as we drove through town. A beam of sunlight abruptly struck my eyeball like a spear, causing me to wince, which caused my broken nose to flare with pain. I hissed instinctively. Even my pain was causing me pain. I felt Othello glance at me, fighting a smile. "We still haven't found the murdered vampire." I grumbled to her as she made a right turn. "Let's swing by Temple Industries while we wait for news of the murder since we struck out twice last night. I don't feel like running all around town to be framed for yet another death I'm trying to prevent. I don't see the Demons passing up an opportunity to kill when their boss gave them free rein to do so." She nodded in agreement, navigating towards my company. We had gone straight to sleep after the chaos at Plato's Cave, and woken up late. My ribs ached from the fight last night, and my face was a landscape of tenderness. Resetting my nose had felt less good than me sticking my fingers in a live electrical outlet.

I shook off my injuries. They weren't going to get better any time soon. Which meant that I needed to quit whining about them. In fact, I was almost certain that they would increase exponentially before this was all said and done.

Which wasn't too motivating.

Nothing to do about it, though, so I searched inwardly for a plan. I wanted to speak with Hope again so I could maybe get a second opinion on what the hell was going on. The spirit seemed to know quite a bit, and she had caused us to waste our last visit when she showed me the vision of Achilles' hollow vengeance, which I still didn't understand. I wasn't acting like him.

Was I?

I was doing the right thing. I angrily stepped out of the imaginary psychiatrist chair in my mind. Later.

Perhaps Hope would know if the summoner and his Demons were hunting for something specific. And she had called me a Maker. I hadn't had much time to think about that, and still didn't know what it meant, but it sounded like something I should know. After all, my parents had made me into one. With all the fighting and running around, I had apparently bottled that one away deep inside my mind. I didn't know how to feel about it – angry, curious, frustrated? Apparently, I was an experiment. One of the feared items from the Armory. Should I lock myself away? Did it even matter now that my power was practically gone?

The commercials on the radio ceased and the news returned. I turned it up and listened acutely as we drove. It was all about the random attacks in town. The Mayor was even considering declaring Martial Law until *Mardi Gras* was over. "Detective Kosage allegedly came out of the closet at a big affair downtown, complete with a float and music. A real boon to the LGBT movement," the reporter declared, managing to sound both amused and politically correct at the same time. I chuckled, shooting a smile at Othello as I shook my head. She grinned absently. Silver lining. "Master Temple is still at large after his apparent kidnapping from the Police station where he had been detained for questioning regarding the attacks from a few months ago. He was only a person of interest, but now he's been kidnapped. This happened while a large contingent of officers was absent in support of their fellow officer coming out of the closet. The resulting lack of security will no doubt be investigated shortly." The radio grew silent for a moment. "Newsflash. Apparently, Master Temple's arcane bookstore, Plato's Cave, was destroyed in an explosion last night. And, wait, a ransom has been declared on Master Temple! Imagine that. Who could afford to ransom one of the richest men in the country? One-hundred-million dollars from Temple Industries CEO, Ashley Belmont. No word from her at present, as it appears she is on vacation. Too bad for Master Temple."

The artifact Hope had given me began to vibrate in my pocket, and I groaned. When it vibrated on its own it meant a Demon was practically on top of us. "I haven't even had my coffee yet!" I grumbled, scanning our surroundings anxiously.

"What are you whining about now?" Othello asked, seeming distracted by a swarm of activity at a nearby warehouse. We were between the city proper and Temple Industries. The area was occupied by numerous warehouses, reminding me of the area where Gunnar and I had fought the gargoyles and the silver dragon a few months ago. I began to pull out the map, not noticing any impending attack in our immediate proximity. Before I could situate myself, Othello slammed on the brakes. "Nate…" Her tone and the flash of pain from my tightening seat belt against my wounded chest made me look up with wide eyes. She was pointing at the same warehouse she had been studying. I leaned back as far as possible, breathing hard as I tried to loosen the seat belt. I spotted a gaggle of parents hanging outside the warehouse, drinking a hot liquid of some kind from Styrofoam cups. The flash of pain beginning to subside, I began to turn back to the map when I saw the vilest of evil scramble out of the building. Followed by another, and another of the beasts, each moving very swiftly. The kind of evil that cannot be vanquished. These creatures had mind powers to an exponential degree.

"*Must not give in...*" I whispered with great determination, clutching my seat tightly.

Othello turned to me. "They're just Girl Scouts. They must be building a float."

I nodded soberly. Girl Scouts were anathema to every grown man in existence who innocently decided to answer the front door in his sweats and a dirty undershirt after a long day of work, only to discover a pig-tailed, buck-toothed princess who so sweetly asked if you would like to buy some cookies. See, they knew when to catch you at your weakest moment, for they were tiny, vicious predators. You had just started a diet, but that didn't matter. Their power was too strong for you to survive.

The Girl Scout had arrived to steal your soul.

Your dignity.

And you were going to pay her to do it.

You couldn't find your wallet fast enough, even if you had to cancel your cable bill the next month to pay for it.

If that wasn't mind control, I didn't know what was. "*Will not give them my money.*" I whispered in a strained voice. "*Thin mints are poisoned with mind magic...*" I continued, reaching for my wallet dramatically.

Othello slapped my hand, rolling her eyes. "Stop it."

"Right. This just validates my hypothesis that Girl Scouts wield Demonic power. The talisman goes off as soon as they're near. And look at all their servants. Like big dumb cows, unaware of the possessed little beasts' power."

Othello arched a brow at me. "Their parents?"

I nodded, folding my arms. "If you want to call them that." She rolled her eyes, turning back to the building. It seemed like there really were people inside building a float, judging by the several groups of adult minions standing outside. Sure, the parents *looked* happy, but being a wizard, I could see through the dark mind magic controlling them. Either they were building a float or we had found their secret lair, the place with the mind control ingredients that was added to their cookies.

Othello began to speak, her tone alarmed. "Why are they running—"

As if in answer to her question, the side of the building instantly exploded in a shower of aged brick, a balloon of fire belching out the side like a giant forge fire. Luckily, none of the mindless thralls had been standing on that side. Then the screaming began. Girl Scouts began pouring out the front doors like someone had kicked an anthill. Alleged fathers and mothers began scooping up their masters like football players before racing towards their cars. It was rather amazing how fast they vacated. Several of the girls looked sooty and terrified, but I didn't see any injuries. Filthy little liars, with their lying lies.

Another blast shook the building, and a freaking box of cookies the size of a minivan flew out the open wall, wafers of burning Thin Mints rolling into the street, leaving trails of fire in their wake, before the giant box of cookies crashed into the street a dozen feet away from us. Shit. The girl scouts *had* been making a float for the *Mardi*

Gras parade. Smoke filled the street as I heard dozens of cars turning over and peeling out of the parking lot, leaving us alone for the most part.

A Demon like a giant, winged, hairy spider exited the building on scuttling feet, looking disappointed that no bystanders remained. Then the creature's eight eyes locked onto our car. I instantly climbed out, and Othello put the car in park, killing the engine as she followed suit. The building crumpled on one side, another wave of bricks falling into the street as more clouds of dust cloyed the air.

I heard Othello cock her pistol, glancing around for any remaining parents or children, but we were all alone. I smiled. That was a plus.

The Demon launched into the air, and landed before us with a great sweep of his wings, buffeting my coat. I held up a hand to shield myself from the smoke and debris, and then lowered my arm to appraise the Demon. He was huge, and his eight arachnid legs sported dozens of pointy protrusions that sunk into the asphalt as if it were grass. My gaze wandered down and I blinked.

"You're a chick!"

Her massive love pillows were out on display for all the world to see, hanging freely under her body. I reached into my pocket eagerly, latched onto something, and then tossed it at her feet, clapping with approval. The leftover beads from my travels atop the stolen police horse, Xavier, the night at the bar settled near two of her legs, and both her and Othello's eyes moved from the beads to my face with hot glares of disapproval. They didn't notice the additional item I had snatched out of my pocket.

Which was the point.

"I don't desire trinkets. I was let out to play. My lucky day that you happened by, wizard. Any last words before I drink your blood?" The Demon asked with a sneer through dozens of clicking fangs. It reminded me of the Lord of the Rings.

"Shouldn't you be trying to find a way into the Armory or hurting one of my friends? Not that I'm complaining. This makes my work simpler. I can just kill you here instead of chasing you all over town." I lifted my palm, a ring of blue fire resting there threateningly. I wasn't going to waste time playing nice. I didn't have time for it. Or the patience. I needed to end this threat now. Before the Demon caused more harm.

The Demon blinked at me. "I know nothing of this Armory, but I really do have other things I would rather be killing... or is it doing? I get confused with your language. It's really much simpler just to kill everything rather than talking about it. More fun. More natural. Well, if you're done talking, I'll just finish up here and then move on to the slaughtering." It reared up on four legs, the other four clicking in the air, ready to pounce on us.

"You're lying! What do you want from the Armory? Who brought you here?"

My ring of blue fire pulsed in tune with my anger as I took an aggressive step forward. I was ready to decimate the entire block if necessary. There was no way this was a coincidence. The Greater Demon had to have planted this Demon. While the Demon was distracted by my accusation, I adjusted the throwing knife I had taken from my pocket when I had snatched up the beads. A throwing knife that had been dipped in blessed water. I flicked my wrist and released the blade. It sunk into the Demon's breast, right above the large dark nipple, with a burst of blue flame as holy water met Hellish flesh. The Demon yowled like a drowned cat, which made me smile. I then prepared a beam of white-hot flame to cast at her, knowing the dagger wouldn't be enough. Perhaps overkill, but I wasn't about to waste time trading punches. I didn't have the power for a drawn-out fight.

Then I felt a surge of power behind me, someone gathering a whole lot of magic. A wizard.

A look of surprise replaced the pain in the Demon's multifaceted eyes, and I saw a dull reflection of a blazing inferno of black flame racing towards her. I unleashed my power and dove to the side as my second jet of black fire tore through the street, melting the asphalt beneath it.

The two spells touched for a split second, and then the ground exploded around the Demon, casting my body into a nearby building. My head struck a rearview mirror on the way, which didn't feel great, causing a flurry of stars to fill my vision, but the whiplash prevented my skull from also striking the brick wall. Between the twinkling blossoms of light, I saw that the twin fires had struck the Demon square in the chest at the same time, causing her to disappear instantly with a wail of anguish, leaving a crater of earth where the two bars of fire had not mixed together well. I touched the back of my head and winced. My fingers were bloody.

Gavin's voice filled the silence. "I'm not sure what you just did, but when our beams of power touched, it was quite efficient."

"I guess we just crossed swords." Othello laughed aloud at my innuendo, knowing my immaturity, but Gavin didn't seem to understand. I sighed.

"Regardless, she's been banished back to Hell."

"What are you doing here? I had things under control." I grouched, scrambling to my feet.

"You asked me to assist, and now you complain. Which one is it?" Gavin rolled his eyes.

"Boys," Othello warned, very matronly.

"Ring a bell or something. I almost offed you!" I snapped, stumbling slightly as my vision wavered.

"Your power is almost gone, and you look like you've been on a weeklong bender, or the losing end of a car accident. Perhaps both. I doubt you almost 'offed' me."

I fumed. He was right, of course. "Where did you disappear to last night? We really could have used your help. Did the big bad Angel scare little old Gavin, fierce Justice of the Academy?"

Gavin scowled back. "Too much heat. I'm not supposed to be involved at all. Especially not to *aid* you. Toeing off against Heaven is a pretty good way to get fired. Jafar wouldn't see that as a good thing. Let alone, God."

"Pansy," I muttered, walking back towards the car. He and Othello followed. "Why did she lie about the Armory?" I asked, speaking more to myself.

Gavin, apparently, deemed himself important enough to answer my question.

"It must have been lying for some reason. Then again, maybe they aren't all here for the Armory. Maybe some were released to up the chaos factor and keep you distracted. Anyway, you're welcome."

"*Ordo ab chao...*" I muttered to myself.

Gavin grunted his agreement. "*Order from chaos.* Seems appropriate."

As much as I hated to admit it, he had come to the same conclusion as I had. And he had just solved a problem for me. Hopefully, his aid would let me conserve my magic for a bit longer. I guess I kind of trusted him. He didn't have to help. He could have let me battle the Demon and drain my power further before helping.

But he hadn't.

I turned to Othello. She looked both concerned with my presently injured state, and as if she didn't quite trust the Justice before me. I couldn't blame her. Othello wasn't the trusting type, and his people had put me in this position in the first place. She had even advised me to kill them all. Not trusting *or* forgiving.

I opened my mouth to speak, but instead collapsed to my knees, my vision tunneling to a single point on the asphalt as I threw up noisily.

Othello was at my side, rubbing my back with shaky fingers, no doubt scared for me. "Huh. Maybe I have a concussion," I mumbled, looking at the impressive display of regurgitated food and coffee.

"We need to get you to a doctor. This could be bad. No offense, but you've kind of gotten your ass kicked for a few days in a row now," she advised. Gavin laughed at that, but quieted under Othello's glare.

I shook my head slowly, careful not to throw up again. "Ain't nobody got time for that. We have somewhere to be," I said guardedly. Gavin rolled his eyes, but Othello sighed in resignation.

The sound of sirens began to wail in the distance, heading our way. The parents must have called the explosion in. I wasn't about to sit around and attempt to explain what had really happened, so I decided it was time to rabbit. I was fairly confident in the ability of Regulars to apply a totally logical, but incorrect, explanation for the explosion. Despite what some might have actually seen. No one wanted to admit they saw a Demon blow up the evil Girl Scout headquarters. The scorched ring in the pavement from a nearby Thin Mint tugged at my attention. Who knew what was in Thin Mints anyway. Perhaps it really was flammable. Or it was a gateway to another dimension.

The seventh circle of Hell, perhaps.

I was also allegedly kidnapped, and couldn't afford to be discovered wandering the streets with a concussion and a palette of fresh bruises. I motioned for Othello to start the car. She shook her head in resignation. Gavin threw up two fingers as if to say *Deuces*.

I flipped him the bird over my shoulder.

He chuckled, and then disappeared with a loud *crack*, Shadow Walking to wherever he spent his time when not tailing me. Maybe he hung out with the Girl Scouts.

26

The massive oaken door to the Armory opened on now familiar creaky hinges. We stepped inside, welcoming the exotic warmth of the place.

Hope's pleasant voice called from the balcony. "Your power is almost gone, my host." Othello gasped, not realizing how rapidly I had been burning through my reserves, and apparently not having taken Gavin's earlier words to heart. She must have thought he had been lying.

I waved Othello's concern away, nodding in resignation to Hope. It was bound to happen sooner or later. Othello knew the stakes I was playing for. "Yes."

"You have many gifts at your disposal that could... even the score. But know that the path you are on is a dangerous one. Before seeking out revenge, dig two graves. Yet you still wish to proceed." Although it hadn't been a question, I nodded. "Even after I have shown you what unchecked rage can do? I fear what happened to the brave Achilles may repeat itself through you." I didn't respond. She studied me thoughtfully, tapping her lip. "Like your *Mardi Gras* festival, there is magic in masks...." she finally continued cryptically.

"Not many choices, and fortune cookie answers don't help," I grumbled.

"Oh, I wouldn't be so sure of that." Seeing that I still didn't understand her implication, she continued. "If you are unwilling to arm yourself with your new arsenal, then death seems the only solution available. Yet, there are many ways to die. To die heroically is honorable. And despite what you may think, death is not always eternal... seeking death has been a favorite repast of many young heroes."

I shivered at that. I wasn't eager to die armed with nothing but a hope for what came next. I also didn't want to die without seeing Indie again. I might not get that option, though. I sensed Othello watching me brood, so I shrugged my shoulders. Despite the temptation, I declined Hope's offer. "It would be too dangerous. I don't know what I would be unleashing. The things in here are dangerous. They were put here for a reason."

She smiled, leaning forward, debating like a knowledgeable professor. "Need I remind you that you are now one of those... *things*. Now *you* could be considered dangerous."

I nodded wearily. "Yes. Without my magic, I'm downright terrifying. Speaking of that, what exactly is this Maker ability? Is it separate from my magic? Part of it? If my magic disappears, do I lose this new ability?"

Hope shrugged sadly. "I truly do not know."

I sighed, studying my little playboy Jiminy Cricket, and thinking about what I should do next. Hope met my gaze, refusing to blink, seeming to appreciate my scrutiny for some reason. A new thought struck me. I realized that if I failed, she was stuck here... forever. Since my blood was the Key, she would no longer have a means of escape. She truly wanted to help me, but if I couldn't figure this out, she would be locked up here for eternity. After everything she had done to help me, she was going to be stuck in this Armory. If I died, she would have no way of escaping. I made a decision I hoped I wouldn't regret. But then again, if I failed, the world would be facing Armageddon anyway. What harm could little old Hope cause? "If I die, you're free to go. That is all I can promise you right now, Hope." She continued to meet my gaze for what seemed like an eternity, and then shed a single tear as she bowed her head, overwhelmed with gratitude.

After a few moments, and a few sniffles, she spoke. "But you must meet death for your salvation, Master. It is the only way. Sadly, your death will grant me something I desire more than anything in this world, but know that it will be a bitter achievement. I do not wish you harm, my host, but it is the only way for you to win if you do not arm yourself. Just know that merely dying will not save you. You must meet death at the right time and in the right circumstances," she added sadly, a metaphorical iceberg of deeper meaning in her answer. I didn't know what that iceberg entailed, but I could see it behind her eyes.

So, I laughed.

I couldn't help it. The situation was so utterly ridiculous, I could think of nothing else to do. I knew Othello was growing more concerned by the moment, fearing long-term effects of my concussion, and that only made me laugh harder. I was facing my death. What did I care about a concussion? My laughter subsided after a few minutes and I wiped my eyes, careful not to touch my broken nose. I walked over to the railing and stared out at the harsh landscape stretching as far as the eye could see. I saw no signs of human habitation anywhere. I was alone. I pondered my life. All of it.

My friends. I hoped they were enjoying their vacations. I imagined Ashley's face when Gunnar proposed, and my tears of laughter turned to hot tears of happiness. And regret. I had hoped I would get to be Gunnar's Best Man. Not that I was really Best Man material, but I was confident I had earned it by default. By saving our lives from a silver dragon, at least. Also, I had introduced them. Despite all the chaos of the dragon war, I had inadvertently brought two people together, and they were about to commit to a lifetime together.

Because of me.

I thought of Tory and all the amazing sights she must be seeing with Misha and Raego. Being allowed to enter the home of the Dragon Nation was no small gift. What would it be like? How would she be received? It must have been an amazing experience for her. And she was doing it with the woman she loved. I smiled. I had hooked them up, too. In the middle of the dragon war.

I was a regular Cupid. My smile stretched wider as I imagined myself in boxers covered in hearts, wielding a tiny bow. It was so ridiculous that my smile stretched into a guffaw of laughter. What would Indie say if she saw me dressed like that? She would be beside herself with giggles. Her gorgeous dimples piercing her cheeks as her dazzling white teeth shone beneath her full red lips, just perfect for kissing.

Indie.

I had also managed to find love.

During one of the worst moments of my life.

She was my everything. The source of my strength. She had nursed me back to health after the fight with Alaric. She had encouraged me by giving me the strength to continue fighting when I was broken. She had accepted my demons, my past romances, my obvious flaws, my night terrors, and rather than run screaming, she had stuck it out. Not only that, but she had given me an ultimatum to remove my protective walls or lose her. She didn't want to *run*, she wanted to get *closer*. When everyone else fled, she darted into the thick of things. She was like one of those World War Nurses, diving into the chaos of battle in order to save a single life. She had also taken care of my friends. My shop. My life. She was a *fixer*. Wherever she went, restoration and order seemed to follow. Like her own special kind of magic.

And I would never get to see her again. I dropped my gaze, seriously considering my options. Accept weapons that had been locked away for a very important reason, potentially unleashing dangers that could threaten more innocent lives. Just so I could selfishly get more time with Indie and my friends. But how many would suffer for my decision? And perhaps the thing I took ended up changing me into a monster. I could end up squaring off with Gunnar. If the weapon changed me for the worst, my best friend's fangs and claws would be there to stop me. It was just who he was. I expected nothing else from him. Hell, I would do the same thing.

Or I could die, and let the world continue on as it was.

With a slow movement, I lifted my head and made my decision, suddenly feeling much better. My humor even began to return as I faced Othello and Hope, who were both watching me with curiosity and concern. I smiled softly to them, nodding my head to banish their concern.

"You have come to a conclusion," Hope said.

I nodded. "Quite literally, I'm afraid. I will not take any of the weapons."

Hope's head sagged, and Othello began to cry. "But you will *die*," she sobbed.

I shrugged. "Yes. And apparently, I'm not even allowed to die on my own *terms*. But why should I be given *that* option?" I continued in sarcastic amusement, realizing that the confidence of my decision had eliminated my fear of dying. I felt proud of myself. I would die honorably. "My death will *also* serve a greater good."

I turned to Hope with a smile, easing the pain on her stunningly beautiful face. She nodded with studious respect, like a scientist encountering a creature they've never seen before. But I still had questions for her. If I had to die, I wanted to make sure I took out as many of the bad guys as possible first. But one person above all others.

The summoner.

Before I could formulate a question, my lips moved of their own volition. "Well, I guess I'm finished here." Othello nodded without argument. We left quickly, having other very important things to do. I barely noticed any of our surroundings as we strode through the hallway and back to the large door that stood open before us. We exited hurriedly, stepping back into Temple Industries. Othello was still sobbing softly.

The door closed behind us before we had even realized the spell had forced us to leave. I had been too preoccupied with Hope's news about me dying at the right place and the right time to notice the spell. As the door sealed behind us, I groaned. "God—"

Othello coughed. "Let's hold off on cursing his name. Didn't pan out well last time."

I bit my tongue, nodding begrudgingly.

"So, you gave up." She looked both sad and disappointed at the same time.

I felt a wolfish smile split my face. "Oh, no. *Definitely* not. I've just accepted a very likely outcome. But I won't be going down without one hell of a fight. I'm going to cause such a ruckus dying that Death himself will shake my hand and send me back with a farewell party to get rid of me." Othello's face began to split into a hungry grin. "And I'm going to take as many sons of bitches with me as possible. Angels. Demons. Or Academy wizards. Everyone's on my naughty list. The Boatman is going to have a *very* busy day soon," I growled. She laughed, and I patted her arm reassuringly.

We began to wander towards the exit in silence, and ran into absolutely no one.

Which was odd. People were always working at my company, even on weekends. As the cold air hit me in the face on our way out of an employee side entrance, we realized why.

Helicopters filled the sky, and people were *everywhere*. Sound filled my ears after our peacefully quiet sojourn inside both the Armory and the building. My employees filled the parking lot in droves, some in lab-coats, others in suits. Then there were the cops. It was like the *Mardi Gras* parade was in my parking lot. I instantly hunched lower, hoping to disguise everything about my person, wondering if I should use any of my power to create a disguise so I wasn't caught. Were they here for *me*? Of course they were. Othello's eyes darted back and forth like a feral cat, making sure we hadn't been spotted. But we were relatively alone by the building. It didn't seem that the cops were organizing a raid or anything. In fact, they seemed to be barricading the front doors to the building in an attempt to keep people out, not in... like it was a crime scene. They simply hadn't gotten to our door yet. Or, they had missed it.

My tension at being caught slowly dissipated, my curiosity taking over as I edged closer to the tape, doing my best to remain inconspicuous. It wasn't difficult, thanks to the horde of bodies filling the parking lot.

Then I saw it. And smelled it. Burnt flesh. To me it was obvious, but to everyone else it just looked like a particularly violent hate crime. A vampire was staked to a light pole near the entrance to Temple Industries. I could see the fangs from where I stood, as well as the wooden stake through her heart. And she was smoking lightly. Vampires and sunlight went together as well as dogs and stray cats. One of the cops must have hosed her down at some point, because a puddle of watered down blood pooled at the base of the pole. An artsy, painted card seemed to be pinned underneath the stake. With the size and look of it from this distance, I could only assume it was a Tarot card. Several sets of speakers belted out newscasts, cameras whirling eagerly as each reporter fought to be first to drop the news.

"Another *Mardi Gras* prank, and at Temple Industries, of all places..." A voice boomed on a megaphone, heavy with enunciation on the location. The voice continued on, describing the scene for the world to hear, as well as rehashing my kidnapping and my bookstore being destroyed, her words heavy with curious implication in all the right places. Each call of my name felt like a hammer blow from Thor, the God of Thunder. I groaned, suddenly nervous about my proximity to so many people at such a high-profile event. I motioned Othello to quickly sneak back to our car as nonchalantly as possible. I couldn't be seen here. I saw Greta talking to a reporter and hoped she kept her sighting of me quiet. Why couldn't things ever be easy?

27

I decided that a meeting with Asterion, the Minotaur, was in order. I literally had no one else to turn to, and the Greek legend was privy to a lot of juicy and arcane information in the magical community. Othello seemed eager to meet the legend in the flesh. I wasn't. I typically didn't receive favorable information when chatting with the 'born again' monster of Greek tragedies.

You see, the Minotaur had recently become a card-carrying Buddhist.

He was obsessed with it. Like all 'saved' members of any flavor of religion.

But hey, At least it was a peaceful choice. He spouted off about Karma, and *blah, blah, blah* a lot, but he wasn't murdering and devouring innocents inside a labyrinth anymore. So, he had that going for him.

As soon as we left Othello's car and entered the pasture proper, I could sense tension in the air. I loosened my shoulders, prepping for a scrap. One never knew, and it wasn't fun to be attacked when your muscles were cold. I felt marginally better after Othello had doctored up my wounds again. None looked infected, but several were concerning. The gash on the back of my head was just a deep scratch. Head wounds always bled fast and hard, but both of us had been nervous about that one. Especially after giving me what I was sure had been a mild concussion. My face felt worse, but as long as I didn't move it too much it was manageable. We continued on, heading more or less to the center of the field where I had first cow-tipped the Minotaur a few months ago... and then dueled him a few days afterwards in exchange for the book on dragons.

We hadn't really dueled *here*. We had instead been teleported to The Dueling Grounds, a place between worlds. I wasn't sure if it was a place one could accidentally walk into, or if Asterion had booked it from the supernatural time-share community.

Either way, I wouldn't be pleased if I found myself there, now. I had enough on my plate.

A set of gleaming horns materialized out of nowhere, the only part of the creature visible. I instinctively shoved Othello into the grass and rolled away just as the ivory spears pierced the air where I had been standing. I heard grunts of disappointment from a heavy set of lungs, and clumps of grass and dirt flew into the air as it thundered past me. Then the horns and the hoof prints were gone again, leaving only a heavy silence behind.

"Calm down, you psychopath! Bad Buddhist!" I yelled, eyes darting about wildly. "It's me! Nate Temple!" I held up my hands in surrender, not daring to waste my magic, making sure Othello was out of the danger zone.

The Minotaur's form slowly coalesced into visibility. He towered over us, a full two feet taller or more, and heavily corded with muscle. A set of Buddhist prayer beads hung from an impressive set of hairy pectoral muscles. It was like he had been formed out of pure testosterone. "Ye' can't be Master Temple. He's a wizard, and ye' barely have a drip of magic about you."

"I cow-tipped you a few months ago. Then I beat you in a duel," I said with a dry smile, more confident that we weren't about to be suddenly skewered. Othello's ears seemed to be falling off her head in amazement as she climbed to her feet. Here I was, almost gored by a monster, and she was admiring him like a groupie. Luckily for her, she hadn't fallen into a cow patty. Would have served her right.

Asterion stiffened, then his shoulders bunched up arrogantly. He smirked at Othello. "Not how I remember it," he told her. "He beat me in a childish game. But he did earn my respect in the duel." Then he turned to me. "Gods be damned. Why are you practically without magic? Last time we met, you had too much and couldn't contain it all. Now you have almost none? Can't you find a middle ground like other wizards? Zen is the answer. Balance—" I cut him off with a rude gesture.

"Later. I don't want to have to kill you out of frustration."

"You wouldn't want that kind of Karma," he stated matter-of-factly.

See? I told you he did that. *Karma, karma, karma. Blah, blah, blah.*

I sighed in resignation. "Karma will just have to stand in line. I'm pretty sure God himself has damned me." Asterion's brow furrowed curiously. He remained silent, sensing my impatience. "I have questions for you. As you can see, I'm at the end of my rope. Oh, this is Othello. A great cyber warrior." The Minotaur appraised her with a newfound respect. Othello's eyes widened. She was blushing for crying out loud. "Groupie," I muttered.

She shot a brief scowl my way in answer. "Warrior, eh?" Asterion asked, studying her from head to toe.

"World famous," I elaborated.

The Minotaur smiled. "Honored to meet you, warrior. No disrespect, but I wouldn't have guessed it. Welcome to my domain. Now, why don't you start at the beginning, Temple?"

So, I told him. Everything. He would need all the details if he was going to help me. His eyes widened as I continued, shaking his massive head in disbelief. "So, to sum it up. If I do as the Academy commands, the Demons will obliterate me and kill more innocent supernatural citizens in the process. If I do as the Demons want, Heaven and the Academy will obliterate me. If I do as the Angels want, I'll never get revenge on my parents' murderer, the Greater Demon, Sir Dreadsalot. And the Demons or the Academy will still obliterate me. In summary, I will be obliterated. Unless I find the right time, place, and method to die, in which case I will somehow apparently have a chance to survive this whole mess, which makes no sense. I don't understand how dying grants me a chance at survival, let alone winning."

"Where did you hear such a ridiculous thing?" Asterion blurted.

"From Hope. In the Armory. She's some kind of memory construct or librarian. She's the one who told me that I'm a Maker." The Minotaur stiffened at the phrase, taking a cautious step away from me. Huh. I continued. "That my parents experimented on me. That's why I was juiced up on power last time we met. Apparently, you've heard of one before. That's good, because I haven't. Explain it to me, because no one else seems able or willing to do so."

"But your power is almost gone..." I nodded. The Minotaur grew a thoughtful expression, causing me to arch a brow with the obvious question to elaborate. "A Maker is limited only by his own creativity. His imagination is his palette. Magic is nothing compared to it. Used to be more common than a wizard, but *respected*." He emphasized the last word. "They've designed things for the most dangerous of creatures. Like a supernatural blacksmith, in crude terms. More respected than the vermin who carry the wizard title these days..."

I blinked as Othello burst out laughing. "Ha. Ha. So, how do I use it?"

Asterion shrugged. "Never met one, personally. Regardless, I wouldn't begin to know how to teach you to use it. I don't even know if it's possible without magic. Even though a Maker is something more than a wizard, I've never heard of a Maker *not* being a wizard. I think they *created* wizards."

Of course it wasn't that easy, I chided myself. I chose a different topic. "Angels and Demons are involved. I thought that was ... illegal or something."

Asterion smiled wickedly. "Seen any Heavenly glows? Wings saving the day? Gateways to Hell?" I shook my head in obvious frustration, having already told him the recent events. "They're using pawns. Demons, not the Fallen; Nephilim, not Angels, would be my guess."

"Well, that's not entirely true... I think I hurt an Angel pretty bad last night. Or they think I hurt him. It was really the Demon attacking me that almost shattered his Grace. I was holding it at the time. He told me that if his Grace were destroyed that I would kick off Armageddon. Then he called the Nephilim after me." I patted my pocket, where I had stowed the Grace in an unused pen case.

Asterion flinched, scanning the skies, as if searching for Angels, motioning for me to keep the Grace away from him. "A Demon could not destroy a Grace. They could harm it, but not destroy it. Remember, cat's paws. That would break the Covenants."

"The Covenants that keeps everyone in line? The Covenants that everyone seems to be ignoring lately?" Asterion nodded. I shrugged. "Well, the Angel didn't see it that way. He attacked me, thinking I was with the Demons and that I had killed his son, a Nephilim boy named Jonathan."

Asterion froze. "Wait a moment. An Angel *struck* you? Are you telling me that you just kicked off Armageddon?"

I frowned. "I don't think so. Possibly. I'm not sure."

"Funny, because if the Angels think you killed one of their Nephilim, and severely injured one of their brethren, then the first domino has been knocked over, and Armageddon is here. *Now*." I stared back, unable to speak for a few moments. "But it's not. Everything seems the same as yesterday." He said, considering the situation. "I would appreciate it if you protected that Grace. Strenuously." He warned with a meaningful gaze.

"Sure, but it's spilled milk at this point. Why wouldn't the big guy stop them?"

"He can't. He'll let the Riders sort it out if anyone crosses the line."

"The Riders," I growled. "You mean—"

"Yes. The Horsemen. Of the Apocalypse. They're black ops at the moment, not unlike your own unruly band of misfits, but when they make an appearance, I guarantee you the world will notice. They know how to make an entrance... or is it example?" He furrowed a caterpillar unibrow. "I guess either works."

"Are the Riders good or bad?"

Asterion pondered that, tapping a meaty thumb on his massive, runed nose ring. I winced. It looked painful. "Neither. Both. Who knows? Only one way to find out. The eternal way."

"Mention of the Riders keeps popping up, but I don't know much about them."

"Well, to wax poetic for a moment, there are four of them, obviously. Death, War, Famine, and Pestilence. Their ultimate job is to cast their powers onto the world, destroying life in vast swaths if the Covenants are ever broken. Until that time, they are considered judges. They keep a tight rein on both sides, Heaven and Hell. Whoever kicks off Armageddon loses a significant amount of potential power, which would hurt in the upcoming War, so neither wants to be the one to ignite it. That's why they use cat's paws, in an effort to toe the line and hopefully cause the other side to break the Covenants first. But you're telling me that you almost kicked off Armageddon, which would mean that neither side loses power. Interesting. A paranoid person would not think that a coincidence..." he added.

"Wouldn't their very involvement signal the end of days?"

The Minotaur shook his shaggy head. "Not exactly. Like I said, they are judges. If either party – Angel or Demon – breaks the Covenants they are tried by the Horsemen. If a resolution can be attained, then the world goes on. If not, then... it doesn't. There haven't been many needs for their judgment, if you know what I mean... Both parties stay well clear of that line, neither one wanting to take the first shot that ends up kicking off Armageddon. There have been instances, less than a handful, when Armageddon *almost* happened, but from what I hear, the Riders found a peaceful resolution. I guess that has to be true or we would not be, well... *existing* right now. There are always times when Demons get close to the line, or Angels swoop in and save someone they shouldn't have, but so far, those occurrences have been judged, and deemed wanting. The Riders dealt out the punishment, and life went on."

The silence grew, Othello watching me curiously. Asterion finally spoke, facing the night pensively. "I'm more curious about this elusive little librarian sprite who seems to live in the Armory. Who is she?"

"I think she's magically bonded to the Armory, in an effort to guard the cache of dangerous powers hidden away."

Asterion suddenly turned back to face me, his face tight. "What did she say her name was?"

I frowned. "She didn't say. I just called her Hope. My parents nicknamed the room Pandora Protocol, so I gave her a moniker. *Hope*, for the last gift inside Pandora's Box."

"Oh, shit in Zeus' beard. You've got to be *kidding* me. As if you didn't have enough on your plate. You're telling me that you've been talking to—" Asterion suddenly stopped talking, mouth opening wordlessly in a fruitless attempt to finish his sentence. He looked as if he had just been struck in the forehead. Like he wasn't *able* to finish his sentence. He finally regained use of his mouth, but his words sounded scripted. "I am terribly sorry, but you must leave. Now."

Sensing my frustration, Othello stood. I knew that if Asterion couldn't even speak, I was out of luck. He wanted to tell me. But he couldn't. Of course not. Why would the lonely wizard discover the one thing he needed out of this meeting? Asterion looked torn, but waved a goodbye, and disappeared, head hanging low.

Apparently, Hope was more than I had initially thought. Someone dangerous for some reason.

And... I had just promised her freedom after my death.

At least I hadn't told Asterion that part. Judging by his reaction to her very *existence*, he might have had a heart attack at discovering she would soon be *free*. What had I done? It wasn't like I could rescind my offer. I had already been to the Armory today, so wouldn't be able to go back until tomorrow, which would be too late. Tomorrow was day three. My power would be gone, and possibly my ability to even enter the Armory. I didn't even know if I would be alive or have any power left to give up when the Academy arrived. I might not even be able to give them the Armory if I wanted to. We made our way back to the car and drove back to the apartment in brittle silence. It was late, and I had a lot to think about.

28

As we pulled up to the apartment, I spotted a lot of party revelers in the street. We weren't in a ritzy part of town, so the neighborhood was a little hectic with *Mardi Gras* in full swing. Not as bad as it would be tomorrow, but a lot of pre-gaming going on. Our drive back had been silent, Othello sensing my need for silence as I tried to determine my next course of action. She found a parking spot and we climbed out.

As we were walking back to the apartment, I noticed something out of place and snatched Othello's hand, halting her. A Girl Scout stood before us, tapping her foot impatiently, holding out a box of cookies as she watched us from beside a parked car. Then I saw that her eyes were red. And a blade was sticking out of her chest. The dagger looked slightly familiar. This kid was already dead. The Demon had possessed the corpse of a Girl Scout. Jesus.

"You've got to be *kidding* me. A Girl Scout? I *told* you they consorted with Demons!"

Othello smacked my arm with a glare. "I was a Girl Scout, Nate."

The Demon child was smiling at me with buckteeth. "Isn't it past your bedtime?" I asked. Her smile evaporated as she crossed her arms. "I'll give you one chance to answer honestly before I exorcise your ugly ass from that child, Demon. *Why. Are. You. Here?*"

Her girly voice was disarming, but her actual words had the opposite effect. "Causing Chaos, of course. Death. Mayhem. It's what I do." She didn't mention the Armory at all. Which didn't make any sense. Was Gavin right? Were these Demons just pawns? A distraction?

"Your boss, Sir Dreadsalot, said he's here for a different reason. The Greater Demon's stink was all over my company. I know that's why you're really here. He told me so. Know anything about that or do I need to remind you what hanging in chains over the pits of Hell is like? It is past your curfew after all."

The Demon stomped her foot, and the asphalt crumbled to ash, the smell of sulfur permeating the street in a sickening wave. Well, she was juiced up. Not just a petty Demon, but something much more powerful. "You dare speak of the Great Lord and pretend to know what we have endured?! I already told you—" She bit her tongue suddenly, as if having said too much.

My arms pebbled. Wait... this was the same Demon from the warehouse earlier? I *knew* I had recognized the dagger. It was *mine*. I had cast it at her before Gavin had banished her. But... That meant Gavin hadn't banished her, or she had made the fastest return trip from Hell ever.

"Shall I show you just how weak you are, mortal? I can feel your power dripping away like the blood of a stuck pig. It pleases me... makes me thirsty. Let me show you what it feels like to exercise your baser instincts like we do. It's *fun*." Her eyes glittered with malevolent glee.

An orb of... dark nothingness in the shape of a giant Thin Mint slammed into my chest before I could react. I instantly realized that the Academy's curse had removed my innate ability to nullify a Demon's mind control. She wasn't able to possess me, but it was close enough.

Which was a tad alarming.

I sensed my well of ever-present rage building to a crescendo as the Demon fed it like gas over a flame. I wanted the Demons to burn. I wanted the Academy to burn. I wanted the Angels to burn. I wanted her boss, the summoner, to burn.

I wanted... the *world* to burn.

A nearby car had parked over the dividing line, taking up two spots. It suddenly exploded as I flung a boiling ball of fire at it, using my dwindling magic to ignite the fuel tank. The Demon chuckled, and Othello shouted in alarm. I scouted the street, searching for something else to destroy in order to sate my rage.

I blew off the side of a building with another ball of fire where flashing lights and loud music was bothering me. Some kind of house party. I was tired. How was I supposed to sleep with that racket next door? The music stopped instantly and I could hear screaming and shouting. All I could feel was *need*. *Sensation*. My baser instincts. The ones you have to constantly battle on a daily basis.

A small part of me, in the back of my mind, railed against the power of the Demon, furiously trying to escape, attempting to think my way out of my dilemma. This might not seem like a big deal, but when you have the power of a wizard, you can typically destroy anything that gets in your way. Regulars didn't have this kind of power. If a loud neighbor annoyed them, they would have to consider storming the house of partiers to silence the music by hand, no doubt igniting the wrath of the partiers, and starting a fight. They would have to call the cops about the illegally parked car and hope the police had nothing better to do.

But being a wizard? Those annoyances were somewhat... *easier* to solve.

Like just destroying them from a hundred feet away with balls of fire.

"See how pleasant impulsive instincts can be? No morality. No consequences. Just *desire*," the Girl Scout cooed, clutching her box of cookies and gingerly plucking one out to lick with an extremely long black tongue. That would haunt me forever. I just knew it.

I knew the only way to overwhelm the Demon's hold on me was to override my senses with a different emotion entirely, but I was fresh out of *nice* emotions. I had faced too much hardship lately, and I was full of anger and fury...

Like Achilles.

Othello was screaming something, which started to annoy me. I slowly turned to face her, ready to silence her, too. She was gripping my arm, shaking me, which was even *more* annoying. She saw the look in my eyes and paled. My brain threatened to shut down at the realization that I was about to murder a friend because she was bothering my destructive intentions, and that I couldn't stop myself from performing the deed. Then, she did something totally unexpected as I prepared to incinerate her forever.

She tackled me to the ground, briefly pressing her ample chest into my face. Then her tongue filled my mouth. My mind shattered.

I *needed* companionship, my baser instincts whispered to me. My brain, however, began to whisper a name. *Indie*. Over and over again.

The guilt made me begin to struggle, realizing this wasn't what I wanted, and that Othello was making me angry again. As if sensing my distraction, and that her ruse wasn't working, she ripped her freaking top off, and my hands instantly found her breasts in greedy handfuls. Then we began to make out.

Violently. Like we were possibly the last two people in existence. Mad Max style.

I lost all mental cognition for an indeterminable amount of time as passion fueled my veins. Memories of long nights and late mornings with Othello filled my mind. I could sense that Othello was enjoying her sacrifice. The Demon's frustrated hiss startled me out of my fantasy.

I heard cheering on the other side of the street and managed to dodge Othello's lips for a desperately-needed breath. Her starving lips found my earlobe instead, making my hands instinctively squeeze her rear end in a death grip, which she also didn't seem to mind, because she moaned encouragingly. I managed to spot the source of the chanting. The group from the building I had attacked was now in the street. Many were pointing at the building and crying, but a group of Frat boys were pointing at me and yelling enthusiastically. The Demon had disappeared, most likely fearing the attention of the mortals. It wasn't every day one saw a Girl Scout with a dagger protruding from her chest.

The group continued to hoot and holler me on, snapping pictures with their phones, and beads began pelting us like mortar shells. "Yeah! That is one hardcore make out session, white-collar man! Look at the car burning behind them. Tits like that would make me ignore a burning car too. Yeah! Ride her, man!" The words caused me to flinch for some reason, dousing my passion like a cold shower. I didn't know why, but the words scared the shit out of me, and without the Demon present, the mind control was gone. "Ride her!" A voice bellowed again.

I gently but forcefully pried Othello's arms from my neck. She was panting, and her eyes were slightly glazed over as if the Demon had been controlling her also. "Othello. Stop," I commanded. She managed to snap out of it with slow resignation, her eyes returning to normal. With a start at the crowd, she leaned back and pulled her shirt back over her head. It was torn, but she held it closed before her, looking embarrassed. I managed one last look at her glorious décolletage.

She began to stammer out a defense. "It was all I could think of. She kept talking about baser instincts, and I thought – I *hoped* – that I might be able to distract you with an altogether different instinct." She looked terribly guilty, but silently pleased at the same time. "I'm sorry."

I shook my head, climbing to my feet. "As guilty as I feel right now, I think you saved our lives." I told her softly. "I couldn't control myself." I didn't tell her what had my heart hammering out of my chest.

I had used up the last of my magic. I felt drained. Empty. Powerless. And I hadn't solved anything. The next time I saw the Academy I was going to castrate them. Individually. With a spoon. I had liked that way too much, which made me angrier. What the hell kind of boyfriend was I? Indie had been out of town for a few days and I had been *all over* Othello. Of course, I hadn't been able to control myself, and I *had* imagined it was Indie... hadn't I? I shook my head, storming off to the loft. Othello followed me in silence.

I tried to light a flame on my fingertips as I stormed away. All that happened was a searing pain stabbing my eyes. "Shit..." I gasped, grabbing the back of my head. Too late, I remembered my wound and flinched in pain all over again. I shook it off after a few steps, Othello watching me the entire way, but saying nothing. The words from the drunk kids still pressed on my mind, prodding for me to catch their relevance. Why had they caught my attention? "Ride her..." It must just be my guilt over Indie getting to me.

We entered the apartment, and collapsed into the same bed, each of us too tired to move. "Othello?"

"Yes?" she murmured tiredly.

"I'm in love with Indie. That won't change. I'm sorry about what happened, and I feel horrible. For both of you. I'm a crap guy."

I glanced at her, spotting a single tear as she nodded. "We had our time together, Pharos. Did you never wonder why I called you Pharos? Other than the magic reference about shedding light on darkness? A lighthouse does have a certain phallic reference, does it not?" She winked seductively, making me blush. I turned away, closing my eyes to escape the torment. Should I tell Indie? Should I keep it a secret? I had no idea. I opened my eyes long enough to text Indie and tell her I loved her. I set my phone on the table and closed my eyes again. My thoughts spiraled to nothing, not even caring what was going to happen tomorrow with my magic now gone.

My dreams were odd. Battles with Demons, being cast down to Hell, God judging me before all the citizens of Heaven. My parents were there, shaking their heads guiltily, as if ashamed to be related to me. In fact, I even had a dream about me sleeping next to Othello. In the dream, my phone rang. Othello answered it tiredly. "Mmmm? No, you don't have the wrong number. He's sleeping, love. We've had a long day and are both *reaaalllly* tired. You know how exhausting he can be. Call back in the morning when we've woken up." She hung up.

I started, realizing it hadn't been a dream. Othello put my phone on her side of the bed, rolling over to go back to sleep. "Who was that?" I asked.

"Gunnar," she murmured tiredly.

"Oh, I'll call him later. Wait. I need to call Indie!" I reached for the phone, but Othello shoved it under the covers. I instinctively reached for it and realized Othello was gloriously naked. When had *that* happened? My breath returned to normal when I realized that I was still clothed. She arched a brow at me. My hands jumped back as if bitten. She grinned in amusement. "It's all yours," she teased. I scowled and she rolled her eyes. "Joking. It's late, Nate. She will no doubt be pissed at such a late call. She's probably spent all day at the hospital and you'll do her no favors by bothering her at such a stressful time."

I nodded in resignation. "Yeah, you're right. First thing in the morning, then." I rolled back to my side and passed out. I didn't even know what I would say to her when we spoke, but I needed to be on my game, which meant sleep was paramount.

Othello felt very warm beside me...

29

I had woken up with my panties in a wad. The slow-motion replay of Othello and I making out in the street had repeated in my mind all night as I slept, filling me to the brim with guilt. After several hundred replays, I had fixated on the cheers from the frat guys on the sidelines. Listening to it again and again, feeling a punch of guilt to the gut with each repetition. *"Ride her. Ride her. Rideher. Rideher. Rider."* I had woken up with a start, the words filling my mind with a severe sensation of anxiety.

Rider.

Of *course!*

I slapped my forehead in frustration and almost shrieked out loud at the orchestra of pain it caused the rune branded there, and the resulting ripples of agony it caused my broken nose, alongside the pounding headache from the several cranial rebounds my head had taken lately.

I survived all of this in silence, careful not to wake Othello, because I'm courteous like that.

After regaining my sanity, I realized I was hungry. I couldn't remember the last time I had eaten. I had gotten used to my unique ability of not needing to eat as much as other wizards. We magical beings typically needed to maintain our nutrition pretty strictly, as it directly fueled our power. But thanks to my parents transferring their magic to me upon their deaths – or them granting the ability of a Maker into me – I hadn't needed to follow such a strict diet. But now that I was without magic entirely, I was *famished*. Seemed backwards to me, but I shrugged in resignation. Othello was still asleep, so I dressed quietly and went downstairs in search of some grub.

Today was day three, and my power was completely gone. I was, for all intents and purposes, a Regular. But other than a deep panic, I didn't feel any different. I mean, I had expected to maybe not sense as much as I usually did. As if I would suddenly enter a world that resembled a black and white television. But that wasn't the case. The world around me was more or less the same. *I* was the one who had changed. That made me feel marginally better, realizing that I wouldn't be facing the nostalgia of missing sensations every time I stepped outside from here on out. The world would keep on keeping on, more or less the same. I simply didn't have magic anymore. The world was still a beautiful, chaotic, little slice of craziness. I could live with that. Piles of snow lined the sidewalk, implying that someone had shoveled the path since the most recent flurries. It was still icy, slushy, and dirty, but it was mostly clear.

I still had the feather in a pen case in my pocket. I pulled it out, contemplating what lay inside before pocketing it again. An idea came to me, but I let it age a bit as I walked down the street in silence. Hardly anyone else was outside at the moment, and I had the street to myself. Like those harmless little old senior citizens that woke up before sunrise to go for a walk. Which wasn't too far away from describing my weakened state. A few days ago, I had been a wizard. A billionaire. A celebrity. But now I was just a penniless fugitive without any allies or power. I was about as dangerous as a duckling. That sobered me. As if on cue, I saw an octogenarian round the corner before me. He sported a World War II Veteran baseball cap and moved with the aid of a walker, complete with tennis balls on the legs nearest his feet. Feeling a kindred spirit in the squat, little old man, I spoke. "Thank you for your service, sir," I offered, smiling politely as he neared.

He slammed one leg of the walker on my toe in annoyance at my taking up too much space, and then shuffled past me with a grunt and a curse. It hadn't hurt me, but I realized I was frozen stiff, staring after the man in disbelief. Maybe he was hard of hearing.

I shrugged it off and continued on, tapping my lips in thought as I walked, enjoying the crisp smell of fresh snow on the ground. With nothing else to do, and not eager to be looking over my shoulder for threats all day, I decided to speed things up. Flick the first domino, so to speak.

So, I decided to summon Eae. Why not? I was powerless. I might as well let them know they didn't need to destroy a city block to kill the harmless wizard. Even little old men weren't too terribly afraid of me at the moment. I wanted to save the Nephilim the trouble of hunting me down.

It began to snow big fat flakes of heavy precipitation, and I suddenly wished I would have checked the weather before leaving the apartment. How hard was it supposed to snow today? I shrugged. Did it really matter? My fight wasn't the type to get snowed out. Gathering my coat about my shoulders, I ducked into an alley for shelter and privacy.

Since I had no magic, I simply prayed over the broken feather in a darkened alley. It was a unique experience for me, not being particularly religious before now. Oh well, what was one more blasphemy? Finished, I attempted to walk into a delicious looking deli and promptly head-butted the solid wooden door. I crumpled to the ground, seeing stars, panting heavily from the numerous ripples of pain caused by my skull striking the door, reminding me of my too many head injuries and more than likely concussion. Maybe I shouldn't be outside unsupervised. I sat there, feeling sorry for myself, allowing the pain to fade away naturally before I stood up. The *closed* sign hanging on the door mocked me as I sat there like a vagrant. After a few seconds, I shambled to my feet and managed to put one foot in front of the other until I was more or less walking again. Luckily, no one else was on the street. I found another deli, and much more carefully, read the sign before trying to barge in. It was a health food shop. They specialized in sandwiches and smoothies. I wasn't particularly picky at this point. My stomach grumbled loudly.

After looking at the menu for a few minutes, I smiled. Then I ordered a pork sandwich, just to spite the Angel. I was fresh out of fucks to give.

The waiter came to my table a few minutes later with a steaming sandwich and I grinned. I lifted the sandwich to my maw and took a huge bite. The restaurant instantly grew silent. I looked up to see that everyone was frozen solid. I sighed, thinking about setting my sandwich down, then shook my head. I took another huge bite of blasphemous deliciousness as Eae entered the building, spotted me, and approached the table. "Thish ish delishus. Want shum?" I held out the sandwich to him. He slapped it out of my hand. Where it fell open into a messy pile on the table.

I scowled at him, chewing even slower, taking my time as I carefully reassembled the sandwich.

"Give me the Grace, wizard," he threatened. I finished building my sandwich in silence and looked up at him, unconcerned. His eyes abruptly widened and he took a step back in disbelief. Then his face slowly morphed into a predatory smile. "Wait. You're *powerless*? Praise the Lord. How foolish are you?" he asked, genuinely stunned. "Do you not realize what you have done? You have called your executioner directly to your door when you hold no weapon."

"Oh, I've got a weapon. Put your hand in my pocket and see for yourself." I smiled innocently. "But be careful. It bites." I was referring to the Grace, but I loved toying with him.

His glare was indignant, but I'd already accepted my fate. I sat there watching him in silence. "You slew my son, and then dare summon me with my fractured Grace? I will destroy you." He looked noticeably weakened to my eyes, as if the fractured Grace had hurt him. Badly. Either that or he had gone on a twenty-four-hour bender.

"No, you won't. You're not allowed." I reached over and picked up my sandwich, taking another bite. "And for the last time. I didn't slay Jonathan. The Demon you killed did that all by himself. Before he was killed, Jonathan said my partner, Othello, was honorable. He believed her, and wouldn't turn a weapon against her. Ask her if you think I'm a liar."

Eae fumed. "There is a reason we command the Nephilim. They are not without their... flaws. They are half-human after all. Just because he trusted your associate does not mean I will make the same mistake. I see the Rune on your forehead, after I specifically warned you to stay out of it. Remember, when the trumpet sounds your final hour, that you brought this on yourself."

I continued chewing my sandwich unconcernedly. He cocked his head, studying me for a secret ploy of some kind. "I will dispatch more Nephilim to hunt you down. If you survive, the Riders will sort you out," he finally added. I still didn't let any concern show, taking another bite. I chewed it slowly before swallowing, licking my lips in satisfaction.

"You sure you don't want some? It's quite excellent." Eae's weathered face purpled, the hidden wings tucked under his coat twitching in agitation. I shrugged. "Perhaps there's an alternative. The Demons want me to hand over something that is too dangerous for me to provide. You commanded me to back off the investigation. Then you attacked me, without knowing all the facts. After sending your little children after a full-fledged badass. That didn't turn out so well for them, did it? I didn't want to hurt anyone. Hell, I didn't think I could! The Demons won't let me back off. Your people won't let me solve the problem. My own people seem eager to kill me either way. As you noticed, they cursed me, taking my power, because they also want the Armory, and now I have no way to help *any* party. I'm in a tight spot."

Eae merely stared at me. "None of that is our concern. As you so wisely said, I can't get directly involved. So, follow your orders if you value your life."

"You see, Eae, I'm not too good at following orders. I get confused easily." He shook his head in displeasure, preparing to stand and end the conversation. "Just curious, since I'm pretty much screwed anyway, what is the end game? What could the summoner want so badly that he'd resort to summoning Demons to get it? *I'm* not even sure of the inventory of the place, so how the hell does anyone else know?" He didn't answer me. "Someone told me that the only way out of the curse is for me to meet my death at a specific time and place. I fail to see how death would help me remove my curse. Because, you know, the whole *death* part. Maybe my heart just needs to stop for a few seconds, and then be revived again?" I thought out loud.

Eae scowled down at me with judging eyes, seeming curious, but also like he was holding something back from me. "From what I understand of magic, something so simple wouldn't meet the requirements. Where does this talk of death removing the curse come from?"

I ignored that last question, fearing I had given up too much. "I'm being boxed in on all sides because of you and your fallen brothers, Eae. At least call off your dogs. I'm on my last legs here. Surely you don't fear me that much. Let me die swinging. Or help me to understand the bigger picture."

He bristled righteously. "I won't do that without proof of your innocence. At this point, I doubt even I could think of sufficient proof that you are innocent. My brothers are... upset with you." He smiled. "Oh, and speaking of my *dogs*... you were warned. Here come my nephews to destroy you and collect my Grace." Then he simply disappeared.

The windows suddenly blew inwards, and three human-shaped blurs pounced on me, tackling me into the counter of the restaurant. My head struck the bar, and a lance of pain sunk into my side before I could even complete my whiplash.

I was positive the blade had been dipped in molten lava beforehand. Warmed up especially for me. I could smell burnt flesh and fresh blood.

Then another one slammed into my leg.

Then my arm.

Each stab seemed hotter than the first, and each too fast for me to even scream, but the pain struck deep into my soul as if driven by a spiritual hammer. I was shocked at the raw violence of the attack, my impotence, and the potential life-threatening nature of the wounds. Three stab wounds to major appendages and organs in less than thirty seconds was downright psychopathic. Or was meant to send a message. Godfather style.

Heh. Puns.

I had never been powerless before. It was sobering. Scratch that. *Horrifying*. And my mind threatened to shatter, running away screaming to the depths of my psyche in order to avoid the scalding explosion of pain. My pocket was abruptly and neatly sliced open, and the pen case with Eae's Grace was extracted. One of the Nephilim kicked me where I had been stabbed, then spat on me for good measure. I could barely even keep my eyes open, panting in staggering bouts of agony.

When I managed to open my eyes, they were gone.

I took a few minutes to press my shirt into the wounds on my side and arm, hoping to slow the blood flow. I clumsily untied my belt and tied a makeshift tourniquet. I almost screamed when I pulled it tight, my entire leg throbbing. After a few moments, I was able to slow my breathing and look down. It hadn't struck an artery. I sighed in relief.

They had beaten me, stabbed me, robbed me, and left me for dead in a health food deli. And these were the *good* guys. But I refused to die in a sandwich shop. No matter how good their pork was. I managed to climb to all fours, and began crawling towards the door. My injured leg more or less dragged uselessly behind me, and I had a brief vision of me pretending to be a zombie. I was careful not to bump into anything, fearful of how pleasant it would feel. The occupants of the room were still frozen so that I was the only somewhat mobile creature in a world of statues. It was probably for the best. I didn't know how the hell I would manage to get out of here if anyone had seen the attack, or worse, if they had realized who I was. The notorious Nate Temple. The Archangel. The local billionaire playboy. The alleged *wizard*. The man wanted by the FBI, who had reportedly been kidnapped for a ransom the likes St. Louis had never seen before. If only they could see the quivering mass of shame that was the true Nate Temple, now. I was thankful that they couldn't see my pitiful state. I almost made it to the door before a thought struck me. I slowly turned around and began crawling back to the table, realizing I had left a long bloody smear in my wake. Like a zombie slug.

I reached into a back pocket, pulled out my wallet, and left a twenty-dollar bill on the table. I had snagged it from Othello's purse before leaving the apartment. It was the only cash I had to my name. The waiter had been nice, and he would probably have a lot of explaining to do after this. What with the store in shambles, the windows shattered, and a trail of blood crisscrossing the floor. Maybe Karma would remember my act.

As I exited the building, I realized that the street was still empty, but more snow had fallen while I had been inside, which would make my trip back even more difficult than it was already going to be. I couldn't imagine crawling that far. I would simply give up halfway and lie down, only to be trampled by the grumpy old war veteran when he returned. I leaned against the doorframe and slowly pulled myself to my feet, placing all my weight on my one good leg. After a few agonizing moments of leaning back against the door, breathing heavily, and expecting another gang of Nephilim to come finish me off, I decided to begin moving. I took off my coat and held it in a clenched fist at my side and began to shuffle slowly back to the apartment. At least I had gotten a few bites out of the sandwich before getting my ass officially smited.

I was careful to scuff up my trail behind me with my coat dragging behind me, as I would have left a quite obvious bloody smear all the way back to the apartment otherwise. After a few minutes of painstakingly concealing my tracks, I heard the first screams from the deli as time returned to normal. Eae's spell had lifted, and any second a gang of Regulars would be fleeing the deli in terror. I rounded the corner and stumbled along as fast as possible. I needed to get gone.

To where, I had no idea. But I wasn't about to go to jail.

30

Othello ignored the tears streaming down her face as she used a medical kit left behind by her crew of shady mercenaries to doctor me up. Her hands were shaking as she suppressed sobs of concern, rage, and fear. "You just went to grab some food! Why didn't you wake me up? How the hell does a hit-squad of Nephilim find you in a deli?"

"I'm just lucky, I guess." I mumbled, trying to ignore the pain from her stitches. Her eyes weighed me. But she knew me too well.

"What did you do?"

I fidgeted. She poked me with the needle, a murderous gleam in her eyes. "Ow! What the hell? I'm injured!"

"Start talking. I can make this take a long time, each stitch could take a full twenty seconds if I really wanted to be careful." She poked me with the needle again.

"Fine! Fine! I summoned the Angel, Eae."

"*What?*" she roared, jumping to her feet, storming back into the kitchen and waving her hands around like a crazy person before finally rounding on me again. "Why in the *hell* would you do that?"

I sagged back into the couch, glad that she hadn't pricked me again. "I figured it was worth a shot. We need help. Answers. Regardless, it didn't pan out. He called his Nephilim on me. They beat me, stabbed me, and then took the Grace back. I'm not sure if that means they are out of the picture or not, but with my luck, probably not."

She came back over and resumed her stitching, more gently this time. "These look like they were partly cauterized." She said, studying the wound.

"Yeah. Felt like it, too. Not pleasant. Old Testament brutality with a hint of the New Testament love."

"But they're still bleeding. It would have been better if they had been completely cauterized."

I shivered. "I see what you're saying, but it hurt plenty enough without adding an extra two-hundred-degrees to what already felt like lava." She grunted noncommittally as she worked. I continued to talk, needing a sounding board. "I guess our next option is to see if Gavin will help us out. He doesn't seem like he's one hundred percent in cahoots with the Academy. Either that or summon Sir Dreadsalot to make a deal."

"I don't trust Gavin," Othello said instantly. I arched a brow, barely flinching as she poked me again to sew up my leg.

"You trust a Demon more than Gavin?" I asked in disbelief. The fire in her eyes made me back down. "Well, to be fair, I don't trust *anybody*." Her eyes twinkled angrily. "Except you. But it's not about trust anymore. We need *help*. I'm running on fumes," I lied. I couldn't tell her that I was helpless. Yet. "We have to stop this. I don't have a choice. It started out with me trying to find my parents' murderer, but now that I've entered the game, I can only leave by death. Hell, I can only *win* through my death, apparently," I growled.

Her eyes were sad, torn. "Still. Gavin's hiding something."

"Everyone is hiding something," I snapped. "At least he's helped us out a few times. Kind of. Like with that Demon yesterday." Before I could continue, Othello interrupted me.

"You mean the Demon that reappeared to attack us and turn you into a psychopath shortly after he supposedly banished it?"

I nodded. "I know. I'm as curious about that as you. Probably more. But it *is* possible that the summoner called the Girl Scout back from Hell to attack us again outside the apartment."

Othello rolled her eyes. "Sure, with your dagger still in her heart. She had a hard-on for you, Nate. I don't think the Fallen Angels would send her back up to earth with a major injury. It seems like our Gavin might not be such a White Hat..." she whispered the last words, looking curiously introspective for some reason. "This looks bad, Nate." She gestured at the wounds. "You need to get these checked out. By a professional."

"No time. Just doctor me up as best you can. I'm supposed to die anyway. Why not go out with a story like this? Would look good on my tombstone." Othello stood up, a storm of emotions crossing her face in the blink of an eye – guilt, sadness, anger, remorse, and determination. I gripped her hand reassuringly, which only seemed to make her feel worse.

"It wasn't supposed to be like this. I was supposed to come *save* you," she sobbed softly, seeming to break down. I patted her shoulder comfortingly in understanding.

"You did good, kid. Not your fault we're up against the heaviest of hitters."

She seemed to regain her composure after a few moments. "Well, I'm not giving up, even if you are. Rest. Contemplate how much of an idiot you are for trusting Gavin. I'm heading to Temple Industries with your Demon-sensing artifact. See if I can spot any of the foul bastards. Maybe find your new buddy, Gavin, lurking around so I can kill him. Slowly."

I halted her with a hand on the arm before she could storm out the door. I gave her one last request. Her cool eyes assessed me thoughtfully, but she nodded with a final sad smile, seeming reassured. She still looked torn, but resolute. "Oh, can you grab me the bottle of absinthe on the counter? I'm thirsty, and in need of some liquid courage." She rolled her eyes, but complied. I tipped an imaginary hat at her in gratitude as she handed me the bottle, and then she left. And I was alone.

The party of two had become one.

I sat on the couch, sipping straight from the bottle for a few minutes, contemplating my next move, trying to think of anything else I could do. "Ah, fuck it. Why not?" I looked at my watch and smiled. "But first, a nap. Might be my last chance." As if the words were a lullaby, I fell asleep.

31

I woke up after my nap, and instantly realized that I had been asleep for five hours. More like a mild coma. I twisted my legs off the couch, and as they struck the floor I was reminded of the stab wound from the holy blade this morning. When Heaven had officially smited me. Stars sparkled across my vision from apparent dehydration as I gritted my teeth against the sharp throb in my thigh. The ensuing rush of endorphins then invited my other wounds to the party. Right. Long walks weren't in the cards for me today. Which could become a problem. Normally I would use my power to help me ignore my injuries, but having no magic to rely on introduced me to a whole new world of pain.

And it sucked.

I didn't know how people did it.

Since I didn't have anyone to help me, I called a cab to pick me up in an hour and take me to Soulard, where the festival and parade was taking place. It was as good a place as any, since the parties against me might be more careful around Regulars. It was a unique experience for me to plan a battle without my magic. I had to think differently, apply different tactics. I grunted as I slowly climbed to my feet and began to test my legs, walking back and forth across the living room. I really wished Mallory were in town. I could use the additional muscle to back me up. I still didn't know his full story, but he was a certified badass. Too bad he was on vacation too.

Now that I thought about it, it was kind of odd that all my friends were gone at the same time, leaving me all alone. I hadn't really thought about it until now. I wasn't typically the guy who made sure I had backup. I usually just went in on my own, or knew that a quick phone call could provide any kind of backup I might need. I had never really thought about making sure I always had a Plan B. I didn't typically make myself available for so much trouble on a daily basis, so hadn't ever considered it. Well, if I survived this, I'd have to change that. Having a plan for the future helped give me a bit of confidence, even though I was one hundred percent certain that this was my last hand. I mean, I had *nothing* up my sleeve.

I didn't even know which way was right anymore. Even *Heaven* was against me.

I shook my head and began to get ready for my last hoorah. A hot shower would be nice. I wanted to look good before I died. And I needed to redress my wounds, which might take a while without Othello to help. Thinking of Othello, I checked my phone, but didn't see any messages from her. Odd. I figured she would have at least checked up on me by now. I called her but it went straight to voicemail. Maybe her phone was dead. Oh well. I didn't have time to worry about it. I had slept longer than anticipated. I thought about texting her, but didn't know exactly what I could type. I wasn't entirely sure of my plan yet. So, I decided I would wait until she called me.

I turned on the shower and waited for it to get warm. And waited.

And waited.

It remained just a hair above freezing.

I turned it all the way to hot, hoping it just needed a boost. But it stubbornly remained frigid. "Give me a break!" I yelled into the empty apartment. A neighbor stomped on the floor above me in complaint. With no divine intervention warming the water for me, I resigned myself to taking a cold shower, which brought back the guilt over making out with Othello the night before. What the hell was I going to do about that? Indie would forgive me, right? But it had been the only way to stop me from destroying the neighborhood. It had been a smart move on Othello's part. But would Indie see it that way? Then I began to laugh. I couldn't help it. It was simply too ridiculous not to laugh about.

Here I was, about to die, no magic, no friends, a fugitive of the law...

And I was worrying about what my girlfriend would think.

Man, was I hopeless. Not that I didn't feel terrible, but it literally wouldn't matter by tomorrow morning. My wounds were that bad. Thinking of that, I glanced down. I was bleeding noticeably, and I knew beyond a shadow of a doubt that I was on borrowed time. At least I wasn't bleeding as badly as I had been before. I wondered how bad the wounds might have been if they hadn't been partly cauterized. Would I have even made it out of the deli? I was lucky that I had even woken from my nap. I really should have been in the hospital. That sobered me up. But I had no time for hospitals. I would see this through to the end. My parents deserved it.

Shaking my head and rubbing my arms to prevent frostbite, I finished washing as quickly as possible, eager to get out and put some dry clothes on. Highly motivated to maintain my core temperature, I jumped out of the shower in an effort to escape the icy water faster. Which wasn't a wise move, given my wounds. My injured leg touched first and I collapsed into the sink, shattering the cheap porcelain to the linoleum floor and snapping a pipe in half. Icy water instantly arced up into the air, splashing the room and my already frozen torso with more cold water. "Motherfucker!" I roared, stuffing my old clothes into the broken pipe in an effort to halt the spraying water. The neighbor upstairs began banging on the floor again. I wiped the water from my eyes, assessing the damage. The sink was destroyed, now a pile of cheap porcelain rubble, and my leg was bleeding freely thanks to my sudden acrobatics. Then my arm and side decided to join the bandwagon. My vision began to tunnel. I left the bathroom in a drunken crawl in order to find the medical kit and tie off the wounds before I bled out. Numb fingers and dwindling strength fought my inexperienced medical attention every step of the way, but I finally managed it. Once finished, I leaned back against the dirty couch, naked, panting heavily, and feeling very sorry for myself.

I couldn't even call Dean to help fix the bathroom. I was literally helpless without my friends. I growled to myself. "Pick yourself up, Nate. Don't be a little man-bitch. Roll your sleeves up. People are depending on you."

Feeling marginally better, I snatched up my bag and began digging through it for a fresh set of clothes. Apparently, I had left a can of shoe polish in the bag at some point in my life, because every single item inside the bag was coated with a heavy layer of the oily, black goo. I blinked in disbelief, shaking out the bag. "You've got to be kidding me," I whispered to myself. I spotted the bottle of absinthe on the floor by the couch and decided I deserved a drink. I gulped it for a good five seconds, the fire helping me wake up a bit. I coughed heavily at the pleasant burn, feeling my body warm up a bit as the liquor hit my bloodstream.

Having exactly no concern for my sartorial savvy any longer, I picked the least offensive clothing and began to dress myself. It was a pair of black sweatpants and a tee that I had picked up to sleep in. It had a single word on the front, *Touchdown*, and sported a cartoon image of a baseball player hitting a homerun. Indie had gotten it for me, mocking my lack of sports knowledge. I sighed, tugging it on – accepting the cosmic karma for making out with Othello. The back was liberally coated with shoe polish, but at least a coat would cover that up.

The cabbie honked outside and I growled. I didn't see my coat anywhere, but I also remembered that it was covered in blood anyway. I groaned with frustration. No time. I finished dressing in a rush, shoved my various knick-knacks in my pockets, and flipped off the bathroom for good measure. I snatched up the bottle of absinth and stormed out of the apartment, not even bothering to lock up behind me. The cabbie was waiting, and eyed me dubiously as he realized that the drunk, dirty, wet man limping towards him wasn't a homeless vagrant, but his fare. I couldn't blame him. I looked like I had just escaped *Fight Club*, I didn't have a coat, I was dressed like a dirty derelict, and I was clutching a bottle of liquor like my life depended on it. But it was *Mardi Gras*. Maybe he was used to it this time of year. "Soulard. Near a church if possible." I added as an afterthought, realizing with a sinking feeling that I was officially out of options, and that I would have to summon the Greater Demon, Sir Dreadsalot, after all.

My parents' murderer.
I leaned back into the headrest and closed my eyes.
This was it. My last hoorah. And I didn't even look cool.
I began guzzling the absinthe.

32

Mardi Gras was in full swing as the cabbie stopped the car. We sat there in silence, the car idling. The cabbie finally turned to face me, announcing the cost of the ride, and holding out a hand for his money. I abruptly broke out in a sweat, realizing that I was broke and had no money to give him. I reached in my pocket instinctively and almost gasped in relief. I whipped out my hand to find a crumpled fifty-dollar bill. I could have cried. I hadn't even considered how I was going to pay for the fare, what with fighting to stay awake and not pass out from blood loss in the backseat. I handed him the whole thing, and muttered, "thanks," as I exited the vehicle. He stared back, stunned that his vagrant passenger had so much cash, and was willing to part with it.

I took a pull of the bottle of absinthe in my fist, swishing the liquid around my mouth, hoping to absorb the alcohol faster and alleviate some of my increasing aches. It wasn't helping too much, and I was feeling a bit tipsy. I decided to slow down. I hadn't eaten much after all, and I *was* severely injured. Not a good mix. But I knew the buzz was practically the only thing keeping me on my feet. Still, moderation.

I began to walk in order to maintain my body temperature. It was a little warmer today but still below freezing, and it looked like it might snow again soon. And I was only wearing a tee. I watched the parade for a few minutes, delaying the inevitable, and took a small sip from the bottle. An old church loomed ahead of me. They were serving hot cocoa at the door. That decided me. I shoved the large bottle in my sweatpants pocket and immediately felt a firm hand grasp my shoulder.

"No drinking out of glass bottles in public, sir. Even though it's *Mardi Gras*..." I turned to face him, probably faster than I should have. He had startled me though.

He lurched back, hand darting to his service piece. Great. A cop. At least he hadn't recog—

"Master Temple!" he shouted in disbelief.

I wanted to groan, but remained calm. I had been so close. All I had wanted to do was confront the Demon that had killed my parents so that I could die in peace. Or pieces, as was most likely the case. Then dumb luck had to intervene.

"Listen. I can explain," I began weakly.

"You were kidnapped! Are you under duress?" He abruptly scanned the crowd with cop eyes. People were beginning to notice. This wasn't good.

I shook my head. "No. I'm alone. I—"

"I think it's better for everyone if I placed you into my custody. We can sort everything out at the station. You look like death walking." He began to reach for his cuffs and my frustration spiked. That was it. He'd brought this on himself. I didn't want to hurt anyone, but I didn't have time for this. I called my magic to fix the problem.

And promptly collapsed to the icy street with a blazing migraine, barely able to breathe.

Oh. Yeah. I didn't have magic anymore.

The cop scooped me up in his beefy arms and began carrying me away, shouting into his radio for backup. I couldn't even raise my head to see where I was being taken. I tried to mumble an argument to him, but I was pretty sure it came out as "Mrghh mnnow." The world tilted back and forth crazily as if I had just stepped off a carnival ride. It was all I could do to not throw up on the cop. But throwing up straight absinthe would feel not good, so I stomached it like a man. People flashed by me, looks of concern and astonishment on their faces. This was it. I had hit a wall. No more magic, no friends, my wounds finally getting the best of me, and I was in police custody. I almost laughed at the fact that Detective Kosage wouldn't even have the chance to charge me.

Because, well... I would be dead by then.

My body was gently settled down onto an uncomfortable chair.

My vision steadied after a few minutes and I noticed two people staring at me with disbelief and concern. We were in a peaceful, warm room. The cop was nowhere to be found.

Apparently, he had brought me to the church.

Huh. That was convenient.

The two of them watched me for a beat, eyes flickering hesitantly from my bleeding wounds to my face, before moving closer. One was a Sister, and she was clutching a Styrofoam cup of hot cocoa. The other was the Father, and he was clutching his rosary, murmuring a soft prayer with his eyes now closed. I managed to signify with my eyes that I wanted me some hot cocoa. The Sister smiled and knelt next to me. I wasn't strong enough to hold it so she lifted it to my lips. "Careful, son. It's hot." Then the sugar hit my lips and I groaned in ecstasy, greedily drinking the entire cup. It didn't feel hot at all. But I was practically frozen by that point. My body began to shiver uncontrollably. From both the cold and my blood loss. I slowly touched the bandage on my leg and noticed that it was wet and sticky, leaking through my sweats. I hadn't done such a great job, after all. How long had I been slowly bleeding out?

The Sister slowly pulled the empty cup away, motioning for another Sister to replace it. The woman shuffled back to the front door with a nod. The saintly woman returned her warm brown eyes to me; pure concern and compassion filled her deep gaze. "Better?"

I nodded slowly. "Thanks," I rasped. "Where..." I was interrupted by a coughing fit.

"He's just outside. Waiting on the arrival of his partner." Her eyes slowly lowered to my obviously bleeding wounds. I noticed that I had a slight puddle beneath me. "Would you like to pray with me?" she asked softly.

I almost argued with her, but then had an idea.

"Do you think it would be a problem if I visit the confessional booth instead?" I pointedly glanced down at my wounds. "You know. A few things I would like to get off my chest before..."

I left the sentence open ended, hoping she would buy it.

Before she could answer, the Father stepped closer. "Of course, my son. I'll deal with the policeman if he has any issue. This is a House of God after all. The Big Man comes first, here." Then he was supporting my weight as he led me to the booth. He set me down inside and I managed to get my breathing back under control from the short trip. "Comfortable?" he asked.

"As good as. Considering..." I motioned to my leg.

His eyes tightened. "Everything will be well, my son. Do you need me to listen, or would you prefer privacy?" I was pretty sure confessions were a two-person job, but I appreciated his thought to ask my preference nonetheless. He wasn't sure how long I had left and wanted to grant the fugitive a bit of dignity.

My eyes grew a bit misty at his compassion, genuinely realizing that I was almost about to take my last breath. And no one was here to hold my hand. "I'd prefer the privacy if you don't mind." I whispered, my head sunk low so that the words were directed at my lap. He patted me gently on the uninjured thigh, and then hesitated as he felt the liquor bottle there. I looked up guiltily. He smiled softly, and then winked with an amused shake of the head. Then he left, gently closing the door behind him.

I sat there for a few moments, fully comprehending my situation. *These* two humans were the good guys. The Angels should take notes from them.

I knew I was on borrowed time so I shook my head softly. Did I feel bad for what I was about to do?

Yes.

I was about to make a deal with a Greater Demon in a House of God. After everything they had done for me in my time of need. And they had given me cocoa. I wondered what they would say if they knew their holy pals had done this to me in the first place.

But I could think of no other options available to me. The Angels had refused to help. Their Nephilim had – for all intents and purposes – killed me. Slowly. Just like

Eae had told me they would. And my own people had tied my hands and pushed me into the ocean.

I delayed in calling the Demon for a few moments.

I deserved some *me* time.

So, I pondered my sins, feeling like this was the appropriate place to do so.

I had cheated on Indie. Sure, I hadn't known I was doing it, and I hadn't consciously chosen to do so, but the action was there. Intent didn't matter. I abhorred cheating. If someone was unhappy with their romantic situation, they should simply end it before seeking other opportunities. That didn't really apply to my situation, but still...

Now, I was one of the cheaters.

I wondered if Indie would have been able to forgive me, if I wasn't about to die, that was. I sighed sadly. The best thing that had ever happened to me, and I wouldn't even get to say goodbye. I hissed as I felt one of my wounds break open, reminding me of my limited time. I hadn't let Othello know, but I had known that the wounds were fatal, not merely superficial. I was literally dying. I was lucky that my nap earlier hadn't been permanent.

Then again, going out in my sleep would have probably been better than what I was about to experience. I pondered the upcoming battle, if you wanted to call it that. Without my magic, it was hopeless. Not a battle. An execution. I was making a last stand with no Ace in the Hole.

Merely for the sake of my pride.

I knew that I wouldn't have been able to live with myself, if I gave up now. Not that I had the option of living with myself afterwards anyway. Hell, I didn't even know if I would make it to the *fight*. I shook that thought off. I was freely choosing to enter the ring for a confrontation, where I was hopelessly outmatched. After all, I had proven that without my magic, I was a joke. I was no hero. Apparently, the only special things about me were my magic, my money, and my friends. Without them, I had been a wreck. Indie deserved better. My friends would be safer without me around to get them in trouble. The Academy was too ignorant to help, and even the almighty Angels were too proud to stand beside me. I had thought we were on the same side.

But I had been wrong.

With a sigh of regret, I pulled out the Tarot card the Demon had told me to use.

I prepared to light the card on fire with my magic, and was rewarded with another blinding headache and a deep warning tingle in my spine. I groaned, breathing hard. *Of course, idiot.* I didn't have my magic anymore. How dense was I? To be fair, it's easy to know that my magic was gone, but it's an altogether different concept to remember that the everyday actions I took using magic were no longer available to me. My subconscious was so used to doing things a certain way that it took an effort to remember those abilities no longer applied to me. I could only relate it to losing a hand. A phantom presence, where the amputee still felt like they had fingers and tried to use them to grab a glass of water, only to knock the glass from the table.

I looked down at the card with a scowl. The Thirteenth Major Arcana, as it was called. I guess I needed a lighter. Too bad I didn't smoke anymore or else I would have had one in my pocket.

That brought a grin to my face. It had been almost a week now, and over the last three days I hadn't even *thought* about smoking. Go, me!

... Just in time to die. I sobered up at that thought. Then I shrugged, whipping out the liquor bottle, and taking several deep pulls. Why not?

As I studied the image of the skeleton gripping a scythe on the card I was reminded of my own impending death. Several decapitated bodies surrounded the skeleton. The words *La Morte* were printed below the grisly image. Despite the somewhat obvious depiction, scholars and Tarot experts academically debated the card's meaning. Many thought that it didn't represent a *physical* death, but that it typically implied an *end* instead, possibly of a relationship or interest, and therefore implied an increased sense of self-awareness – not to be confused with self-consciousness or any kind of self-diminishment. Meaning that one should live every moment as if it were their last. *Memento Mori*, or *remember that one day you too shall die*. It was a reminder to make the most of what was given to you.

I pondered that in silence for a few breaths. It was comforting... in a way. Then a thought began to slowly emerge from the murky depths of my sluggish mind. I had never considered obtaining the card the Demon had told me to use. It was as if...

As if I had subconsciously known all along that I already carried one.

But I didn't typically carry around Tarot cards, so why hadn't I been concerned about finding one to use? I tried to remember where I had gotten the card. I noticed a stain on the corner and lifted it to my nose. I took a big whiff and smelled anise.

Specifically, Absinthe.

It was from... Hemingway. The card he had left me to call if I ever wanted another drinking partner. His words whispered in my ear. *I may be bored enough to assist you.*

An odd, creepy sensation began to squirm up my spine. No way.

Goddamn it. *Cat's paws.*

Having given up all other options, I felt my gaze intensify and begin to pulse with anger, a brief flicker of blue seeming to shade the world around me as my fury grew. I had been used. I had no magic left to me.

But the card burned to ashes in an instant.

Then I was Shadow Walked to the exact opposite of a church.

33

Rather than sitting in the peaceful solitude of a confessional booth, I found myself suddenly gripped by the throat and held a few feet above the dirty floor of an empty biker bar. A pale, haunting skull was glaring at me, eyes afire with a green glow behind an authentic bone mask that was etched with ancient, powerful runes. His pale, bony hand clutched me by the jugular.

Not Hemingway.

Death.

One of the freaking Four Horsemen.

A *Rider*.

I gurgled between his fingers. "I'm here to see a man about a horse," I croaked.

The room was silent for a second, and then an all-too-familiar tone of laughter filled the room – Hemingway's laughter. "Took you long enough." He grinned, slowly releasing the pressure on my windpipe and lowering me to the ground, eyes twinkling behind the terrifying skeleton mask. "Bored yet? Ready for another nightcap?" He eyed my bottle, and then snatched it away happily. "Seems you've already started." I shook my head in bewilderment. He had released me, but hadn't taken a step back. I managed to remain standing on my own feet and stared at him. He seemed a lot... bigger, more menacing than the last time we had shared drinks in *Achilles Heel*.

He took a swig of the liquor straight from the bottle and then leaned in closer, way too close for my taste. You shared a drink in a *Kill* and thought you knew a guy. He whispered to me, the sound like crackling leaves in the fall. "I'll grant you a gift. You may be the first mortal to view the world through my eyes in thousands of years. It will change your perception of the world, but it is a gift worth the cost. Remove my mask if you agree to my terms. You will receive the answers to your parents' deaths." I reached for his mask without considering the terms he hadn't yet stated. I was dead anyway, and would do anything for that information. Anything. My fingers brushed the cool bone skull mask and my mind fragmented into a million pieces as I pulled it away from his face.

I found myself floating in a room, as if underwater, and everything was tinted in a greenish hue. I was at Temple Industries. In a familiar storage room. But this room was now off limits. Even for storage. It was the room where my parents had been murdered. I saw my father valiantly fighting a Demon, neither of them moving, the battle taking place solely in their minds. My mother lay motionless behind him, but he fought as if to keep her alive. His forearm was bleeding from the self-inflicted cut he had caused to write me his last message. Then there was a brilliant flash, and it was over. Sir Dreadsalot left the room, looking furious. I saw Charon approach my parents and felt a single tear spill down my cheek. No one had called him. But he had still appeared. It made me glad that I had always paid respects to the Boatman. Maybe he had appeared *because* I always paid him respects. The odd part, though? For some reason, I understood why their deaths were necessary, in the cool mathematical precision of an equation.

Next, I found myself in a brilliantly white room. I squinted against the glare, assessing my surroundings cautiously. It was elegant, luxurious, and had a feel of royalty. *Where was I?* A couch sat to my right, mirrored by twin accent chairs to my left. The wooden floor stretched off into deeper sections of the house or building, but I was transfixed enough by what lay immediately before me. I didn't need to go exploring. A bookshelf was tucked against the far wall, loaded with elaborately designed spines of ancient books. A vase sat on a coffee table between the two chairs – stuffed with flowers – and paintings decorated the walls.

Except...

Everything was cocaine white. And when I say *everything*, I don't mean different things were each a slightly different shade of light colors. I *literally* mean that *everything* was exactly the same hue of brilliant white – the wooden floors, the painted walls, the vase, the bookshelf, the books, the furniture, the flowers, and even the *stems* of the flowers. They rested in what appeared to be milk rather than water.

I stood in a cocaine castle.

Even the paintings were white. When I stepped closer, I could see the ridges in the design, the painting emphasized with *texture* rather than *color*, and it was done so masterfully that I could actually see what the artist had intended just as well as if he had used colored paint.

I glanced down and saw that I was wearing a silver suit, Miami Vice style, with gray gator-skin dress loafers. My creepiness factor went up a few notches as I walked up to a window, placing my hand on the sill.

I stared through the glass to see that I was in a vast forest on the edge of a cliff that overlooked a milky white ocean. And, wait for it... everything outside was also white. The trees, the house, the sky, and the grass.

I lifted my hands from the sill and flinched in shock as my eyes caught the only color I had seen in this strange world. A gray stain rested where my hands had been. I almost had a fit of panic, fearing that the apparently obsessive compulsive owner of the building was about to come introduce himself and see that his perfectly pristine world had been tarnished by his gray-clad guest. I stared down at my hands, wondering why they had been dirty in the first place... and then I found myself just staring, and staring, and staring some more in utter confusion.

My hands were spotless.

I turned back to the windowsill, but the stain was still there. I furiously began rubbing it with my sleeve, but this only smeared the stain, as if my suit fabric was only exacerbating the problem, dirtier than even my hands had been. Realizing I was only making things worse, I hurriedly stepped away. My gaze flickered over the bookshelf and my eyes furrowed in thought. *Surely...*

I strode over to the bookshelf and grabbed the nearest spine, pulling it out, and leaving an alarming gray smudge. I opened the book anyway, hoping to see the familiar color of black font. But the pages were blank. Entirely. Well, everywhere but where my fingers touched. Those pages were stained gray with obvious fingerprints. I glanced at the cover only to see a raised title, *Through the Looking-Glass*. But it was also white. I could only read it because the letters had been raised above the surface of the paper.

Then I heard footsteps approaching. Big, heavy ones. I began to panic, shoving the book back in place, leaving another large gray stain. I frantically spun, wondering if I could hide my tracks, but it was too obvious in this place. Smudged boot prints also marred the wooden floor, and the approaching steps were only getting louder.

A glowing white form began to step around the corner of one of the hallways, but the world shattered like a priceless vase before I got a chance to see a face.

I abruptly came back to myself, panting. I latched onto the bar with shaky fingers, feeling sick to my stomach and dizzy – both from the visions and my beat-up body. The mask lay on the bar beside my hands, and Hemingway's familiar face was visible. Although now I knew it wasn't his real face. Hemingway. Death. I shook my head, the connection only making me feel worse. Death handed the bottle back to me. I chugged gratefully, scalding my throat, not even caring about what kind of germs I might be sharing with the Horseman by drinking out of the same bottle as someone older than the Bible. I was dead soon anyway. If this didn't merit a drink, I didn't know what did.

"The effects are temporary, but know that what you saw is how I see the world. Past, future, and present."

"Where was that last place? The white room? And why was I—"

He held up a warning finger. "You were in a white room?" His voice was razor sharp.

I gulped cautiously at the look in his eyes, nodding once. "Yes."

"We'll discuss that later," he finally said under his breath, seeming nervous and... resigned. I watched him. What in the world could have terrified the Horseman of freaking Death?

I was briefly reminded of him mentioning something back in the bar where we had first met. *Between black and white is not a gray area, but a quicksilver, honey shade; a shiny,* enticing, and altogether dividing line. If employed correctly... "It sure looked to me like I was a big flashing, unappreciated gray line," I muttered.

"Silver. Not gray," Death corrected, apparently having heard me. I looked up at him sharply. He shrugged. "It's the color of the path you find yourself on. Silver for the path of walking the sword between black and white. Silver to remind you of the sword's edge you walk across. Because you must always fight tooth and claw to maintain the goddamned line." He was breathing heavily. But why the hell did he sound so angry about it?

Apparently, that wasn't for me to know. Yet. He composed himself, changing the topic. "Seeing the world through my eyes will change you. A storm is coming, Master Temple, and it has something to do with the little *box* your parents dared open. The world will need you in the days to come."

I couldn't help myself. I began to laugh. "I'm literally *dying*. I know fatal wounds well enough to know that I'm on borrowed time. I'm about to meet you on an *official* level. What could I possibly do to help? And for once, will someone please tell me what in blazes this has to do with the Armory?"

"You may have heard it by a different name." His smile turned wolfish, drawing out the moment. "Pandora's Box. Congratulations on being somewhat correct. Even though you didn't believe it. That was your father's point in naming it so obviously. Hide it in plain sight."

I blinked, too flabbergasted to speak for a few seconds. I took another longer pull of the liquor. "Well, if I'm still kicking around in a few hours, I'll deal with it. I'm out of juice, so I pretty much have zero chance of helping anyone, not even considering my fatal wounds. I'll let you deal with the Armory."

Death studied me, considering thoughts that – no doubt – only a Horseman could fathom, and then dropped a freaking bomb on me as I took another pull of the drink, no longer caring how drunk I became. "You have something of mine. I want it back."

I choked. "Um. What?"

"The bone artifact. In your pocket."

I reached inside and withdrew the bone Hope had given me to track Demons. The stone that had caused me to also hear millions of souls speaking into my ears when I commanded it to *Seek*. Death stiffened, staring at the bone with a look of such pain that I was suddenly concerned about my life's outcome over the next few *minutes*. I offered it to him.

He snatched it up. "This is all that remains of my son. Thank you. I thought it lost," he whispered. My hair tried to climb right off my head and run away screaming. His *son*? That was a bone from... but his next words saved me from responding. He had pocketed the bone and looked more or less the same as earlier. A nice older man. "The Greater Demon has your friend, the Regular girl. She's been working with the summoner from the start." My vision pulsed with a blue haze again, and before I knew what I was doing, I flung out my hand and slammed Hemingway over the bar in a blazing fit of rage. His body hammered into the mirrored wall of liquor bottles with a shattering crash.

I was heaving, shoulders hunched forward instinctively. "How *dare* you accuse the *only* person who has helped me during this clusterfuck," I snarled, instantly ready to burn the world to the foundations of Hell itself. Magic filled my veins, more power than I had ever wielded before, but... different.

Death climbed up from behind the bar and brushed his shoulders off, totally unharmed. He finally lifted his green eyed fiery gaze to me, as if to ask, *Really? You want to take on a Horseman?* He was grinning. The fury filling me began to wither and die as I considered his strength.

"With all due respect," I added sheepishly. "Sorry. It just sort of happened. My magic does that when—" I froze.

Wait a minute.

I didn't *have* any magic.

Then I remembered that I had lit the Tarot card on fire with... magic.

"I seem to be telling you this often, but *it took you long enough*," Death muttered with an amused smile. His form rippled below the chest and morphed into a fog of weeping souls that I was pretty sure made my ears bleed. I clapped my hands over them for protection. Then he walked *through* the wooden bar, appearing on my side as if it were an utterly normal means of locomotion. The keening wails halted as he solidified.

"So, you were saying something about being powerless?" Death answered, sipping a glass of absinthe. I hadn't seen him pour it.

I nodded, still trying to wrap my head around the subtle transformation that had allowed him to walk *through* the bar. And what had those sounds been? "How... did I do that? Is it the Maker thing?"

Death didn't answer my question. "What are you going to do about the Box?" he asked instead.

"Well, even though I somehow managed to use this new power, I don't really know how to do it again. And I'm still almost dead. I'm on borrowed time." I was silent for a few seconds, then, "And before I do anything for the world, I need to save a friend."

Death cocked his head. "You're more worried about your traitorous friend's life than the fate of the world?"

I thought about it for all of a second. "Do you have proof she betrayed me?"

"Would you believe me if I said *yes*? Or better yet, would it change your answer?"

I finally shook my head. "No. If she betrayed me, she must have had a good reason. I'm going after her. I need to talk to the Demon anyway. And the summoner. I've got a Blood Debt for what they've done."

Death nodded in approval. "Good for you. A man who stands by his oaths. I understand Blood Debts. If you recall, I fulfilled one myself." I frowned, not understanding. Then it hit me. The farmer's tale he had shared with me in the bar.

It was... *his* story.

I shivered, taking a quick pull of the liquor to mask my surprise. Hemingway continued, "I thought you would have picked up on that by now. The tale was my... *origin story*." He said with an amused smile. His face grew serious again. "Fulfilling Blood Debts... changes you. Revenge in itself can be a cataclysmic choice, but declaring it a *Blood Debt* applies *magic* to it, making it binding, permanently tying your soul to the act. But it's too late to call it anything else now. You've already declared it to an Angel. At the bar. Where we first met." I nodded, not sure what he was talking about with magical oaths. I had simply called it how I saw it. They killed my parents. I sought vengeance. Justice. So, a Blood Debt it was.

Death took another drink before speaking, "Just for the record, Othello had no choice. She was coerced into betraying you. The summoner kidnapped her nephew. Four-year-old boy. Blonde. Good looking. Might change the world someday. It's not his time... but that can always change." The way he spoke the last comment made an arctic chill run down my spine. Like an accountant talking ledgers. Harsh. Cold. Analytical. Precise. That was a tough way to live.

I felt marginally better that Othello hadn't betrayed me by choice. I had already dealt with betrayal once from Peter, and wasn't sure how long I could maintain my sanity if it happened again. I also found a calming swell of power building deep in my chest at the fact that the summoner had also threatened my friend, kidnapping her nephew.

The only person who had been there for me during this whole mess.

"Well, it's the only thing I know I can control, and it's my fault she's been taken. If the world is going to hell, I'm at least going to ease my conscience. I need to save her." I thought for a minute. "Like I said, I'm on borrowed time, and I don't know how to reliably use my new power. So, I'm going to borrow your mask. You'll get it back. I swear on my pow... no, on my soul, I guess, which you'll have complete control over once I'm gone. Which is going to happen in the next few hours, regardless of what happens next. One last hoorah."

For some reason, it never crossed my mind to ask his permission.

This, apparently, offended him.

And I was reminded – quite severely – of where I stood on the totem pole of power.

Death spun faster than I could blink, and suddenly a wicked, ancient scythe drew a fine line of fire across my throat. Where the hell had it even *come* from? Death was wearing tailored slacks, for crying out loud. It took me all of a second to realize that I wasn't headless, but I was sure the whites of my eyes were blazing like floodlights. Death used his right palm to wipe my blood off the magnificent, gleaming, silver scythe – the weapon granted to him the night he had accepted his new job – and the blade disappeared with a puff of silver smoke. His other hand shifted into a glowing green set of bone claws and he slashed the palm that held my blood. He reached out his bloody right hand to me politely. I accepted the handshake.

And an implosion of blue and green light filled the bar, buffering us on a molecular level as my apparent blue *Maker* power joined with his green... *Horseman-y* power. But the force didn't affect anything in the bar, as if it were only a spiritual implosion. Which was super scary to think about. I knew we were somehow bound now. He didn't say a word about the strobe light show of our powers melding together. Kind of like how action movie heroes never turned around to watch the explosion, but instead continued walking away from it in slow motion.

After a minute, I pinched my arm. "Huh. That wasn't so bad." Death watched me with a raised brow. "I'm going to borrow your scythe," I said, since it had seemed to work for the mask. Maybe my charm was working overdrive to make up for my run of bad luck.

Death threw his hands up, and the room abruptly filled with a cold so deep that my joints ached, and then the scream of dying souls filled my ear canals, shaking my brain like a bowl of Jell-O. "Okay! Okay! Fine. No scythe! *Jeezus*, drama queen. A simple *No* would have sufficed." He smirked, and took another sip of his drink. "But I *am* going to borrow your keys. No more of that freaky death vibe. I get it, you're a badass. But a man needs a ride. I can't walk very well right now. And I refuse to show up in an Uber to my final battle."

Death smirked again, rubbing his chin. "Fine. Don't scratch him. He won't like it." He tossed me a set of small keys.

I caught them with a frown. "Well, *he* can just bite me, then." Death burst out laughing. I frowned harder for good measure, not catching the joke. I picked up the mask, mentally preparing for a scrap with... well, *someone*. I wasn't sure exactly who yet. Eae? Sir Dreadsalot? The summoner? I didn't rightly care.

I just wanted to hurt someone. Any port in a storm, right?

"Is there anything else you can do to help? I don't think you want a summoner traipsing around town either, and my power's unreliable. This bastard has caused enough damage already. Hell, my own people want to serve me up on a platter, and I haven't done a fraction of what *he* has."

Death shook his head. "Your own people do seem to hold you in high esteem. But I believe you have everything you need to accomplish your task. Piece of advice, I was never involved. Other than the bar where we met. You must have stolen my keys. And made a shiny new mask... *Maker*." He winked for some unknown reason. "I'll watch over your body while you're gone," he added. Then a door closed in my mind and I found myself standing outside below a streetlamp. *My body?* What the hell did *that* mean? Had I died? Or had the mask done something to my physical body? I pinched myself for good measure. I *felt* corporeal. Which should tell you something about me, that I was relieved to find my body still squishy and fleshy after meeting one of the *Four Horsemen*. Priorities. Mine were obviously screwed up. I didn't know exactly where I was, but I recognized the general area. I was near the church where the cop held me in custody. I wondered what he would make of it when they opened the confessional booth and I was nowhere to be found.

I wasn't exactly sure what I was supposed to be doing. My body was apparently in a strange biker bar, I had death's mask in my hand, and a Harley. It sounded like a bad action flick. I spotted the Harley and instantly felt a small surge of anticipation. It had been a while since I'd ridden a bike. I appraised the machine, admiring her almost glow-in-the-dark green hue with interest. Unique color. I wouldn't have guessed at it in a million years. To each his own, I guess. I started the engine, and heard a horse neigh loudly down the street. I glanced around nervously, ready to see a SWAT Team rappelling down the surrounding buildings, guns all pointed at little old me. But I was alone. No mounted patrol units, either. I was safe. The police were the last thing I needed. I'd been given a second chance. Time to make the most of it.

Memento Mori, indeed.

I put on Death's mask, and watched as the world morphed into a soothing green hue like I had put on night vision goggles. It was almost identical to the color of the bike, now that I thought about it. I turned to a previously-darkened patch between streetlights, and gasped. It really *was* night vision. I could see perfectly in all directions. Better than any night vision I had ever tested. I guess it made sense, thinking back on Hemingway's story of when he received the gifts in the first place. I shrugged with a smile plastered to my face beneath the mask, realizing that it fit perfectly. I could barely even tell it was there. And, now that I thought about it, nothing was holding it in place. I touched it curiously, but it merely stayed in place. I tugged it off, suddenly fearful that it might be stuck to me, but it pulled away easily. I put it back on and I felt it latch onto my face like a second skin. *Interesting...*

I began thinking about how to make something like it, and then burst out laughing as I realized what I was doing. I wouldn't have time to duplicate anything after tonight. This was my last run. Instead, I revved the engine, causing the unseen nearby horse to scream again in response. I smiled, imagining Kosage riding the beast as he scoured the city for me, and the horse bucking him off.

One could dream.

34

I was getting closer to the crowds of humanity celebrating *Mardi Gras*. It was now evening, and the debauchery was in full swing. I couldn't count the number of times I had seen breasts of every size, shape, color, and age – and I didn't even have beads. They were everywhere. It was an adolescent's fantasy. All a boy had to do was simply walk the streets tonight and he would have a veritable buffet of visual stimuli to catalog for years. Revving the Harley helped clear the crowds when they got in my way. And watching breasts, *erm*, people jump back in surprised fright at the sudden sound pleased me.

Another perk of the night was that almost everyone was wearing Le Carnevale masks. This eased my primary concern, that I would be recognized prior to finding Sir Dreadsalot. I had already tried *calling* him with the Tarot card, but since Death had hijacked that phone call I wasn't sure if the Demon had ever heard it. As I was riding through a particularly dense crowd on the street – the sidewalks were at a standstill – my heart suddenly froze. Two Justices stood on a set of steps leading up to a building on the side of the street, eyes scanning the crowd like birds of prey. Maybe the fact that Gavin was my parole officer allowed only him to find me, because none of the other Justices seemed to be able to do so. Not yet, anyway.

In fact...

One glanced right over me, scanning the crowd eagerly. I shivered. Even this close, they didn't seem to be able to sense me. I carefully rode directly through the crowd, never attracting the Justices' attention. I wasn't the only bike in the crowd – there was even a unicycle wheeling around – but I was definitely the only *neon green* motorcycle. I let out a sigh of relief when I was a safe distance away. I had no idea what I would have done if they had attacked. I didn't know how to use the Maker ability effectively yet. It had just *happened*.

It was day three, and the Academy had shown up to collect their prize – like a schoolyard bully waiting to accept his lunch money from his smaller classmates at recess.

But they weren't getting their grubby hands on my Armory. Not on my watch. I *ate* bullies for *their* lunch money.

As long as I remained vertical long enough to stop them, that was.

Death's comment about Pandora's Box made me nervous, but I shut that line of thought down quickly. I didn't have time to think about that now. I had enough on my plate. Othello needed me. Right *now*. I had a fresh, steaming murder to deliver to the summoner, courtesy of your friendly neighborhood wiz... well, *Maker*, I guess. I grinned wide as another thought hit me. Not just a Maker, but also a temporary *Horseman*. Maybe I could just scare him to death by pretending to be a Rider.

All these thoughts flew through my mind as I frantically struggled to find a way to prevent any collateral damage. I glanced to the side, spotting a silver blur, assuming it was a Justice. But as my eyes focused, I realized that it was just a woman. Staring at me. *Really* staring. The silver glow had no doubt been caused by the streetlight shining down upon her.

I slowed down, glanced behind me to see if she was actually staring at someone behind me. But no one was there. I turned back and flinched. She was half the distance closer, despite the crowds and the impossible speed that such a movement would require. Then I noticed something odd.

She was floating. A foot off the ground, and the wind didn't seem to touch her. She also had no coat on. Then a creepy sensation came over me. She was a *spirit*. A ghost. A lost soul. And she was staring at her savior.

Death.

I waved guiltily. Not knowing what else to do, I spoke in a whisper, drawing on the power of Death's mask. "I'm only a temp-worker. Finish up any last-minute business you may have. The real reaper will help you tomorrow."

She could either read lips or had uncanny hearing for a dead lady. She smiled with a nod of acceptance, waved a frail hand, and faded away to nothingness. I realized that my shoulders were locked up with tension. I hoped I wasn't messing up some cosmic balance by making her wait. Or whether I even had the authority to choose to send her on her way to the afterlife or to allow her to stay behind for an extra day. I didn't want to mess anything up, so I figured erring on the side of caution was the safest bet. I would just tell any more wandering spirits that *business would resume as usual tomorrow. Our apologies for the delay – Management.* After all, Death hadn't given me a job description. Consequences would be his fault.

I continued on, but not before picking up a handful of discarded beads from the street, because, you know, *Mardi Gras*. When in Rome... it would help me to fit in better if I seemed to be enjoying the various flavors of ample bosom. I spotted another Justice a few minutes later, and although confident she wouldn't pick me out from the crowd, I grew anxious as I crept closer. Her silver mask resembled a laughing face, but she completely ignored the cheers and roars of the crowd. I crossed her line of sight with a wave of trepidation falling heavily on my shoulders. I was about to be made. Surely, they could at least *sense* me from this close. But as I passed, she looked right *through* me. I blinked in both relief and disbelief. How blind was she?

Then I thought about it. Death had said he would watch over my body. Was I not physically here? No, that wasn't true, because I had picked up those beads. Maybe they just couldn't sense me because of Death's mask. But then, shouldn't they have at least sensed a Rider of the Apocalypse among them? Then I thought about *that* a little bit. *I hadn't ever noticed a Rider, or an Angel, in all my years of existence. Maybe they were immune from that sort of thing.

Interrupting my reverie, several young drunks stumbled up to the Justice and waggled beads in front of her to get her attention, noticing that she didn't have any beads. That was nice of them. They wanted to share. Poor girl. What kind of woman deserves to walk around on *Mardi Gras* without any beads? It just wouldn't be right.

She pointedly ignored them, still studiously scanning the street. I heard a loud bark of a voice and spotted another Justice not too far away. The woman obediently turned to him, body tense. The man motioned for her to participate. I could imagine the words. "*We must fit in. Do as they ask.*" I grinned wider. Her head hung in resignation, and she quickly flipped up her top, displaying an impressive show, but just as quickly dropped it back down. The drunks seemed disappointed at the brief glimpse of heaven, but still fed the woman her beads so she wouldn't starve tonight. Very generous. I pelted her with my whole wad of beads. Neither of the Justices paid me any notice. This was awesome! One enemy out of the picture! Now, I didn't have to worry about any surprise visits from my own wizardly police force. The ones who had taken my power. I very seriously entertained teaching them a lesson, right here, right now. A breath later, I very responsibly chose not to do so. It was a tough choice. They deserved it. Well, Jafar did. The others were just doing their jobs, as Gavin had taught me. He actually hadn't been half bad after getting to know him a bit, and showing him the error of his ways.

I continued on, spotting several more souls hanging out, watching me expectantly. I motioned for them to come back later. They didn't seem too upset. Several of them nodded at me with gratitude, even bowing. It was enough to make a guy realize just whom he was impersonating.

Then I spotted an Angel on a rooftop. His Heavenly glare assessed the streets with disgust, but he was vigilant, eyes darting back and forth like a falcon, taking everything in like a gargoyle. Then his gaze met mine, and his jaw dropped in alarm. He began to lift a horn to his lips. I couldn't have that. With a thought, and the rapidly becoming familiar blue haze to my vision, I held up a hand and clenched my fist. The horn instantly crumbled to ashes. I opened my hand and imagined claws as I mocked grabbing a throat in front of me. I saw a large spirit hand grip the Angel by the throat and slam him to the ground. Not enough to hurt him, just shock him

"Fuck off, Feathers. I'm here on business that doesn't concern you," I muttered under my breath. The look of alarm on his face told me he had heard me just fine. As good as it felt to shut down an Angel with such ease, I didn't have time for petty vengeance against the pigeon. It seemed ironic that now that I had enough *power* to take revenge on all the parties against me, I had no *time* to do so. Specifically, *Othello* didn't have time for me to do so.

As if in answer to my blasphemous disrespect of the Angel, it began to rain. Fat, icy drops crashed down from the sky, drenching everyone. I was simply surprised that it wasn't snow. I found myself murmuring under my breath. "It's a good day to die. True rain washes the soul." The last sentence was something my father had always said at the first sign of rain.

Scanning my surroundings, I was surprised to see that the rain hadn't diminished the crowd in the slightest. But of course, the excessive amounts of alcohol in their veins convinced them that they were immortal and not already close to frostbite. They cheered with excitement instead. I rolled my eyes. The Angel had vanished, but I didn't hear any horns or other sounds of pursuit. Which made me feel better.

One perk from the rain was that it would make using magic almost impossible for the Justices. Cold rain was worse, as cold rain caused a sense of panic in your mind, and magic was all about mental clarity. But really, any type of rain would nullify magic to some extent. Running water was anathema to wizards. I wondered if it would affect my ability as a Maker. Then shrugged. I would just resort to the power of the freaking Horseman, Death, if that were the case. I was kind of nervous and anxious to test that out.

It was like test-driving a Ferrari. Of course, you *said* you wanted to drive it, but once you sat behind the wheel a sense of profound respect and fear often made you realize just how dangerous your desire could actually be. Did you *really* want to drive close to 200 miles an hour? Probably not. With only a strip of fabric holding back your body and a thin sheet of glass to protect your face? No thanks.

I sat there, revving the engine slightly, wondering where to go. I really had no game plan, having thought that burning the Tarot card would call the Greater Demon and I would die shortly after. The rumbling engine caused several mounted police officers' horses to rear back in alarm, but the cops themselves apparently couldn't see me either. Just the horses. They eyed me with wide, panicked eyes. Not me. The bike. That was weird. Surely, they weren't scared of a motorcycle. They must see them all the time, and the place wasn't exactly quiet. It wasn't like I had suddenly revved the engine on an empty street in the middle of the night. As my gaze swept past their hooves, I spotted something odd. Twin, quivering cords of energy trailed off into the night at ground level, piercing the crowds in different directions. One black, and one white. They glowed with untapped power.

Unlike Robert Frost, I chose the path *most* traveled, knowing it was easier for people to commit sin rather than adhere to righteousness. And I was Demon hunting after all.

As I began to idle after the black cord of power I began to hum to myself. *Back in Black, I hit the sack...*

In my mind, I was nailing it, on key and everything. Even the voice was spot on.

I pumped my fist in the air and roared off into the night, chasing the cord of power. I cackled loudly into the rainy night, relishing the icy drops of rain striking the bone mask with little puffs of steam.

I bet I looked really cool right now. Even in sweats and my *Touchdown* tee.

35

I had left the celebrations behind a while ago, and now found myself at the entrance of a gated scrap yard in a commercial district. The gate was wide open. Barely hesitating, I drove the Harley inside, following the black cord of pulsing energy to the center of the area, towers of salvage vehicles rising above me on either side, several stories high. I briefly remembered Greta one time saying something about salvaging my sinful soul and chuckled. If she only knew. I gently pressed the kickstand, and double-checked that the bike wasn't about to fall over if I climbed off. Then I sat there, studying my surroundings and the black cord of power thoughtfully. The pulsating cord led to a nearby tower of vehicles that was taller than the rest. More towers continued on in the distance, creating a giant-sized labyrinth built of the corpses of the once great auto industry. I rolled my gaze to scan the rest of my surroundings. Whomever I had followed must know I was here. The Harley wasn't exactly quiet, and I was just sitting there. I hoped I hadn't accidentally followed a completely different bad guy's icky slug trail, and that it indeed belonged to either the Demon or the summoner. I didn't even question what the cord was, assuming it had something to do with Death's mask. His vision of the world, as he called it. He had said it would affect me.

Weak floodlights attempted to illuminate the scrap yard, but it was still dark. Well, it would have been dark to anyone else. It was light enough for me, but dark enough to earn an ick factor of 10 for any *Regular* person's eyes.

A crackling, basso voice cooed from the darkness, making me upgrade the ick factor to a 12. "You don't call, you don't write, you don't make deals, and you don't burn the card. It's enough to hurt a Demon's feelings." The unseen Sir Dreadsalot launched from the top of the tower of broken vehicles and landed before me, back facing me. The knotted dreadlocks of broken teeth and bones even covered his back, making me decide that it truly was an armor of sorts. His mane of longer dreads hung low on his back, darker, thicker dreads than on the rest of his body. He was still missing an arm, and as he slowly turned to face me, I was pleased to see that the aftermath of the horrific steam burn I had thrown at his face during our first encounter still remained. Lifting his glowing red eyes to assess his prey, he instantly took a reflexive step back as he truly saw me for the first time. "No! You cannot be here. No laws have been broken, Rider."

I smiled, not speaking, but revved my engine a bit. The Demon jumped back as the piercing sound of a horse filled the night. I blinked. No way was a cop nearby. I turned to look and caught my reflection in one of the side mirrors of a crushed car.

And my heart stopped.

Where I stood was the most terrifying apparition I had ever seen.

A giant, shadowy cloaked figure with a wicked skull for a face stared back at me with eyes of green fire. And he was sitting atop a literal fiery-eyed, glowing green steed, not too unlike Grimm, my murderous pet unicorn. A distant cousin, maybe? I discarded that train of thought, assessing my reflection. I looked friggin' *Awesome*.

And now I knew for sure that the black cord led to the Demon.

"Why are you doing this?" I asked, not betraying my true identity, remaining atop the Harley. "Even *you* know the Covenants," I added, trying to sound pompous.

The Demon looked nervous. "We have broken no laws. I was summoned. My master required Temple's blood. His *lifeblood*, not just a vial from a wound, in order to gain access to something he desires. I merely obeyed my commands. I broke no laws, Rider. Call your brothers and question me if you must," he said the last in wary resignation.

I blinked. First off, when had they figured out my blood was the Key, and second of all, how had they gotten my blood in the first place? I mean, I had liberally gotten my ass beaten on an almost hourly basis over the last few days, but I didn't think any of the Demons were smart enough to – nor had I seen them – take the time to snatch up a sample of my blood.

That was wizardry 101. Never leave blood behind.

Only one person had been with me when I entered the Armory. And that's when I understood it all. *Of course...*

Othello.

She had also been a cat's paw. Death had tried to warn me. It was somewhat comforting to know that he hadn't been mistaken. Or lying. Othello was the only answer that made sense. She must have given them a sample of my blood from one of my various wounds.

To protect her innocent nephew.

Part of my heart broke. I wondered how they could have gotten to her nephew in the first place. Almost no one knew of our past relationship. And almost no one knew who she even *was*. Being a notorious cybercriminal kind of made that difficult.

I spoke in a clear, deep voice to the Demon. "The Armory."

The Demon nodded, looking anxious to depart. A *crack* split the night as another figure suddenly appeared beside the Demon. The summoner. The puppeteer. I felt my heart rate increase in anticipation of what I was about to do to him. The Demon flung out a claw in my direction. "This was not part of our bargain, *summoner*. Our pact is ended. You never mentioned the Riders. Our contract is through." The man nodded, not speaking, and the Demon sighed in relief, getting ready to vanish.

"Not so fast," I said. "You took something from me." The Demon blinked in confusion, then tilted his head curiously.

"I have only heard of your reputation, Rider. We have never crossed paths," he answered neutrally. Respectfully.

I smiled back, unsure whether he could see my pleasure or not. Oh well, this was solely for my enjoyment. I didn't necessarily need him to know how pleased I was. He would discover that indirectly in the next few minutes.

I somehow tapped into the mantle of Death. It was actually very easy to do, which made me nervous on a very distant level. I was too immersed in the rivers of power that were suddenly coursing through my soul. I wielded the power like I was born with it, and used it to give the Demon a gift.

I gave him empathy...

Sympathy...

And guilt.

Then I sent him deep inside the pits of his own immortal mind to relive his most personal losses, failures, and heartbreaks.

Over and over again for eternity.

And it *broke* him.

The sound that tore from his throat seemed to break the very fabric of reality. I smiled as he withered to dust. The summoner watched, eyes widening. I had a moment to wonder exactly how I knew how to use the power Death had lent to me. Was it something to do with me being a Maker? Similar to how I had learned to Shadow Walk? Since I had witnessed Death showing off a bit at the bar, perhaps? The summoner finally turned to me after toeing the ashes with a boot.

"Hello, Nate," a very familiar voice spoke from beneath the hood. My skin turned to ice.

"*Gavin*," I snarled. The Harley – Death's horse – roared all on its own this time. I jumped down to my feet and was surprised to see that my legs worked perfectly fine. In fact, I didn't feel *any* of my wounds. Which was good. They wouldn't slow me down as I faced off against the man behind my parents' murder. My Parole Officer from the Academy. The man who had been tasked with keeping innocent lives safe from me.

But *he* wasn't safe from *me*.

In fact, he was entirely *unsafe* from me.

This made me deliriously happy on a subconscious level.

"So, we come full circle. It's just you and me, chucklehead," I hissed excitedly as I killed the engine and pocketed the keys to the motorcycle, speaking with a voice that wasn't completely my own.

36

Gavin peeled back his hood and smiled. "Not entirely." He waved a hand and suddenly Othello was kneeling at his feet, tears streaming down her face. I didn't know how long she had been there, but she seemed relatively unharmed.

For now.

"It's good to see you again. Othello, here, was quite the assistant over the last few days, even though she didn't know who I was, or that she had met me several times as your parole officer. I do love using cat's paws. I got the whole idea from the Angels and Demons. Keeping your own hands clean while orchestrating everything. I rather enjoyed being the puppeteer. Not unlike how the Academy runs things." His gaze grew distant for a moment, a frown crossing his features. "But they've gotten full of themselves and have forgotten their true purpose. I'm here to remind them what that purpose is." Now, his gaze became feverish, as if imagining the chaos that he would rain down on the ancient ruling body of wizards. I couldn't wholeheartedly disagree with him. We did need a change. But maybe a nuclear reaction wasn't the best opening move. "We needn't be on opposite sides," he finally continued.

"I don't like the benefits package your side offers. Although I definitely agree that the Academy is a group of doddering old asshats, I think I'm happy where I am." I smiled brightly. "And where *you* are. It makes it easier to kill you. Now, stand still for a second. This will only take a moment." I took an aggressive step forward.

He held up a finger. "You do know it's an immediate death sentence for impersonating a Horseman. You can take off the costume any time now." I didn't move. He laughed. "Fine. If that's what you wish to wear to your funeral, so be it. I won't begrudge a man his fashion taste." He appraised me for a moment, and then a grin suddenly stretched from ear to ear, and he began to clap his hands in applause. "Oh, this is *deli-*

cious. It seems the Academy's curse worked exactly as intended. You're powerless!" I remained silent. "You had to know that this was their plan all along." He chuckled, shaking his head. "Those fools. But don't concern yourself. I'll deal with them next. In your name, even, if you prefer. Seeing as you won't be around to watch them fall." His calculating eyes grew distant for a moment. "Now that I think about it, you would make an excellent martyr. A death for all other wizards to rally behind. And I will champion the injustice shown to you. Yes, I can see it now. It's neat. Tidy. Simple."

I growled, tasting bile in the back of my throat. He began to circle Othello, idly toying with her hair. "You being so weak does take the fun out of this part. Like robbing candy from a child. How did you possibly hope to fight me?" he asked, waiting for a response. Again, I remained silent. I could tell that he liked to hear himself talk, but I also sensed that deep down, my silence was bothering him. Silence was a powerful weapon when utilized correctly. "Tell you what, you give me what I want, and I'll let the girl and her nephew live. I have no need for them, anymore. It's not like you can stop me anyway. You're dying. A few hours, tops." He was right, of course, but I didn't know how he knew. After all, I appeared wound-free at the moment. Then I understood. Othello must have told him. Maybe she had pleaded my case? Telling Gavin that I was already dead. To leave me alone.

One could hope.

One could also hope that she hadn't told him about me being a Maker.

He continued speaking since I had yet to give him the satisfaction of a response. "Your impotence is astounding. No money, no friends, no magic. Tsk, tsk." He pointed at Othello. "Save their lives. At least you can do that. After all, it took so much work to turn everyone against you. A few files leaked to the cops, a few hints to Jafar at the Academy. You know, paperwork." He brushed his hands theatrically.

I decided to play along. It wasn't really that hard. I was exhausted, and Othello was there. And I really didn't know how to reliably use any of my powers. One wrong move and Othello died.

My shoulders sagged as a new thought hit me, making me feel all sorts of guilty. It had been a rough couple of days, but that was no excuse. "Fine. You win. But allow me one thing," I finally said. He paused, considering, and then gave a slow, benevolent nod. "Let me make one phone call." His eyes flashed with suspicion. "Calm down. It's just my girlfriend. I haven't spoken with her for a few days. She's out of town."

"As are the rest of your friends," he said with a dark smile. I began to feel uneasy. "It made things so much easier knowing that I wouldn't have to deal with your friends assisting you. It was surprisingly easy to arrange for all of them to be out of town. You really should be more paranoid. Did you never think it odd that they all had occasions to be out of town at the exact same time?" He didn't even try to contain his laughter.

But... that meant a level of planning I could hardly conceive.

"You... sent my friends away from me?" I whispered, almost heaving with fury.

"Yes." His triumphant smile made me want to break something. "Free airline tickets for the werewolf and your other friends." He paused. "Well, to be honest, Indie was rather difficult. I thought the night terrors would be enough to send her running in horror. But they didn't work. They tossed in a wedge, sure, but since she didn't comply, I had to cause an... *accident* with her mother. It really was the only way." He said, shrugging.

"You son of a bitch!" I lunged forward instinctively, ready to destroy every shred of his soul.

He held up a single hand, and a razor thin line of fire suddenly pulsated to life a hair away from Othello's throat. She squirmed against the flash of heat. "Ah, ah, ah. One more step and she dies. Quite painfully, I would imagine."

I was quivering with anger as I slowly pulled the burner cell phone from my pocket. It didn't matter now. The facts hadn't changed. I was alone, and he would kill Othello if I didn't comply. I had to give him my lifeblood. Samples wouldn't work, so he needed all my blood. Voluntarily. I had assumed it would come to this, and that I was a dead man walking anyway. I had come here strictly to save Othello. This was the only option left to me. Time to be a man. But I would do it with all the dignity I could muster. He had me by the short hairs, so I did the only other thing that was left to me.

I called my girlfriend. To tell her that I loved her.

My gaze grew watery as I contemplated what I wanted to say to her. She was my everything. The one who had held my hand in the darkness. Helped me through the worst time of my life. Inspired me to be good. To forget the awful nightmares. The one who wouldn't let me be weak. My rock. My love. My life. I wanted to somehow tell her all of this. To thank her. To tell her I couldn't have survived without her. I wanted to hear her sweet, silken voice. I wanted to tell her I loved her. And I wanted to hear her say it back.

The call instantly went to voicemail.

I was totally unprepared as the device beeped in my ear. "Um, Indie. I was just... look, I don't really know how to say this on an answering machine," I said, struggling for words. "I wanted to hear your voice one last time. I'm in a tight spot and won't be able to see you again. Just know that—" The phone shattered beside my ear. I jumped back with a yell, pulling my fingers away to find fresh blood.

"I saved her from having to listen to the rest of your suicide note," Gavin said disgustedly. "Let her remember her infamous *Master Temple*, not the sorry excuse for a man you are now."

"If only I had my powers..." I cursed under my breath, my mind frantically trying to come up with a way out of this. I had no clue how to use the other powers, and couldn't risk indirectly killing Othello as a result. Gavin waved me off, looking bored. Othello very carefully lifted her red-rimmed eyes, trying not to brush the fiery death resting at her throat, and began to mouth a single word. I think it was *sorry*... But then she saw my appearance and flinched, eyes widening. That's right. She saw Death.

So, this was it. I wasn't really surprised, really, just frustrated that I hadn't been able to at least get a small taste of revenge, first. Oh well. Maybe I would get to see my parents again.

Nothing had really changed. I had already accepted my death earlier tonight.

If I'm not dead already, I thought to myself. After all, my body wasn't even here. It was with the Horseman at the bar.

Wait a minute...

I *was* the Horseman.

"Goodbye, Nate." And that was it. I didn't even have time to feel the pain or consider my latest revelation. A screaming ball of black flame struck me in the chest, and I immediately became one with the universe, little Nate-icles exploding out into the cosmos of existence at the speed of light.

37

I floated in nothingness. I *was* nothingness. *So, this is what it's like to be a Buddhist*, I thought to myself, having a better appreciation for Asterion's frequent rambling about balance, Zen, and Karma. It was... well, boring.

I began to reevaluate my life, wondering if my current state of being might help shed some light on those age-old questions. Who was I? What had been the purpose of my life? Was it just supposed to end like this? Nothingness? I blinked.

Then blinked again, my heart rate suddenly increasing. Nothingness couldn't blink, and it sure as hell didn't have a pulse. I wasn't *nothingness*. For the first time, I visually concentrated on my dark surroundings, and almost fell out of the boat.

Because I was sitting at the front of a small, rickety, one-man canoe on a river of inky black water, floating through the darkest of nights *towards* nothingness.

Okay, this probably didn't bode well.

Craaaack! The darkness muffled the sound, almost as if it had happened underwater, but I still jumped like a little girl, rocking the boat slightly. It sounded like someone had just popped open a beer behind me. Here I was, being all one with the universe-y, and someone was cracking open a cold one? Did they have no respect?

I turned, and then flinched as I realized I wasn't alone in the boat. Charon sat behind me.

The Boatman.

He was extremely... *creepy* up close, making me reconsider the wisdom in being friendly with him in my past life. A darkly stained, burlap robe covered his frame and continued in a shadowy hood over his head. He pulled the hood back and I instinctively leaned further away in alarm, trying not to hiss like a frightened cat. His skin was the color of aged ivory, and parched like old leather. His lips were sewn shut with a decidedly unhygienic, thick, knotted leather cord, and his eyes were glittering ebony gems. His hands were entirely bone, no flesh, and they were slowly rising towards me...

To offer me a fresh can of beer.

Not knowing what else to do, I hesitantly accepted it. He nodded, and opened one for himself. *Craaaack!* He wasn't rowing. Apparently, he wanted to take a booze break between carting souls to the afterlife. He lifted his can to me in salute then dumped it over his sewn-up mouth, maybe succeeding in absorbing ten percent of the beer. It was... messy, liberally coating his chest in the frothy 'Merican drink of choice.

"Good run," he hissed in a rattlesnake on sandpaper voice, almost making me release control of my bowels in pure terror. His lips, after all, were sewn up tight. Then I realized that he had spoken entirely in my mind.

Once relatively composed, I chose to reply out loud, not sure how good I was at the whole telepathy thing. "Uh, yeah. I guess." I looked around. "So, this is it? Kind of dreary for Elysium." He didn't say anything. I quickly pressed on. "Because I'm 99% sure that's where you're supposed to be taking me. Not the other place. I hear it's hot down there, and I'm not a huge fan of anything above 110 degrees." I was babbling. He continued to watch me in silence.

"Should you be drinking on the job? Don't you think you've had enough?" I asked.

"Just satisfying my appetite," he said directly to my mind. Then, a sound like a dusty leather bag being beaten by a piece of driftwood emanated from his sewn-up lips, and I realized he was... chuckling. Even his laughter was frightening. I seriously considered jumping out of the boat to fend for myself in the current of never-ending woe. The River Styx, the River of Souls.

This was the guy I had been so friendly to? He was downright *terrifying*. "Who's going to tell me not to drink on the job? It's not like anyone else wants to do this. It... what's the word? Ah, yes. Sucks. But I do have job security." His voice of crumbling ashes pierced my mind. I wasn't sure how long my sanity would be able to take the sound of Charon's voice if he decided that he preferred to have a long, drawn out conversation with the wizard who had been so friendly with him in the past.

"I guess so. You *are* taking me to Elysium, or whatever you guys call it these days, right?" He shook his head. "I think I was pretty clear. I don't think I'm supposed to go to the other place."

Instead of answering, he poured the rest of his beer over his sewn-up mouth, and then picked up his paddle. Glowing green runes flared to life as soon as his skeletal hands touched it.

"Charon. Really. Listen. I'm not supposed to go there."

He hesitated, considering thoughts that only the Boatman to the World of the Dead could fathom, and then turned his nightmare gaze back to me. His ebony eyes glittered in the green glow of the runes on his paddle. Then he spoke, face screwed up as if trying to remember something. "I had twelve fucks as of this morning. Now I have a dozen fucks. How many fucks did I give today?"

I... blinked.

The Boatman was... making a joke? He was staring at me with what I thought was supposed to be eagerness, but instead looked ghoulish. So, I answered, understanding that he probably didn't get many chances to exercise his humor. "You gave zero fucks today, Charon."

He slapped his knees excitedly and his face bunched up in what I guessed was a smile, the knotted cords over his mouth pulling tight, which made me wince with imagined pain. His smile would have made hardened soldiers run screaming in horror. "And I'm not about to start giving fucks now," he added. Then he appraised me. "That was funny, was it not?" he asked me curiously. I was kind of getting used to his voice. The way someone gets used to nails on a chalkboard.

"Sure. Hilarious, Charon," I answered with a sigh of resignation.

Then he began rowing the boat, aiming for a sudden vertical split in the river before us, a beam of glowing green light.

"It's not up to you. Or me," he hissed compassionately.

I groaned, my temper rising. "You've got to be *kidding* me. You know how many enemies I have down there?" I snapped.

He shrugged, continuing to paddle towards the light.

So, I drank my beer. It tasted good. Really good. Perhaps it was because I knew it would be my last.

We didn't move very fast. I guessed Charon wasn't really in much of a hurry. After all, it wasn't like he cared about anyone else's time schedule. His fares were dead. They weren't necessarily in a hurry to get anywhere. Most were likely *not* in a hurry to get to their final destination.

I finished the beer as we entered the light. A faint tingling sensation coursed down my arms, and I mentally prepared myself for the worst thing imaginable. What would Hell be like? Was it individually tailored to each person? What was my worst nightmare? I had experienced a plethora of them over the past few months. What could be worse than those? But as the light washed over me, a familiar scene surrounded us.

The salvage yard.

I turned to look at Charon with a scowl. Was this my hell? To relive my death over and over again?

I turned away from the bastard, staring helplessly down at the familiar scene. Then I noticed something odd. My body was lying on the ground, dead.

Othello still kneeled where she had been. But Gavin was nowhere to be seen. Charon waved a hand and a metaphysical window appeared, showing me the entrance to the Armory at Temple Industries, where Gavin was liberally, and furiously, throwing a dark, viscous liquid against the door. My blood. Nothing happened. His scream of frustration was a soothing balm to my soul. Then, totally unexpectedly, the freaking door *exploded*. Gavin barely escaped in time as I watched my company implode like a nuke had gone off in the lab. Huh. I hadn't seen *that* in the blueprints.

Gavin reappeared before Othello in the Salvage yard. He was not entirely unscathed, much to my satisfaction. His face was cut up in two places, bleeding freely, and his hands were covered in my blood. His clothes were singed from the explosion, and he faintly smoked in places from the embers that had nearly burned him alive. His hair also looked silly, like a toupee on a particularly windy day. No, not *like* a toupee, it *was* a toupee! Oh, that was rich.

Apparently, my Hell was not being able to make fun of him for it, which was abhorrently cruel in my opinion. Not even a chance for one wise crack. I sighed.

Gavin struck Othello across the face, screaming in rage. "The place was rigged to blow!" Then he began to torture her in earnest. Like a child plucking the wings off of a fly, and I suddenly knew that he was much worse than the Academy. He was of the school of thought that *Might was Right*. Just like Peter had been.

I was forced to watch Othello be beaten to death.

I slowly turned to Charon, sickened and enraged. "So, this is it, huh?" I accused. "You're leaving me here to watch her die? As punishment for my sins? What sins have I committed to deserve this?" I finally roared.

Charon calmly stared back at me. He was used to this, most likely. Then he spoke in my mind. "It was nice meeting you, Master Temple. Do better next time."

Without further ado, he flung a hand at my face, and reality... *collapsed*.

I came to, panting hoarsely, my fingers clutching gravel in tight fists. I squeezed the gravel tighter and a blue haze filled my vision as the gravel silently imploded into dust. Then nothingness.

What the...

I slowly looked up as I heard the sickening *thud* of fists striking flesh. Gavin was towering over Othello. "You lied to me! I will tear the skin from your nephew for this..." The rest was incoherent babble as I realized a very important thing.

I was back.

I began to hum to myself as I climbed to my feet, once again in perfect key.

Back in the saddle agaaaiiiin...

38

I climbed to my feet and called out Gavin's name. Softly. Gavin flinched, practically jumping in his skin as he turned to face me, a look of utter disbelief painting his features. It made me smile, but I realized I still wore Death's Mask, and wasn't sure if Gavin could see my pleasure or not. "You... can't be here. You're dead. I killed you. I used your blood on the door. The Armory is mine now. You wouldn't dare attack me."

"You didn't get into the Armory. I saw you fail."

He spluttered defensively, spittle flying from his lips. His knuckles were covered in Othello's blood. He went with his original threat, seeing that I had called his bluff about the Armory. "It's death to impersonate a Horseman! I'll call them and tell them what you've done! Nothing points to me. I made sure of it. It all points to you!"

I watched him squirm like a worm. It was immensely satisfying after thinking I had died and was going to Hell. This was almost like *Heaven* to me. Then *that* thought sunk in.

This wasn't... Heaven, *was it?*

I hoped this wasn't Heaven – granting me hallucinations of victory for eternity. Oh well. If it was, so be it. I was going to make the most of it. I spoke softly, with all the authority I could muster. "Who said anything about impersonating? I'm here to condemn you for your lack of proper toupee etiquette. It's downright embarrassing, like a hungover zombie squirrel took a nap on your dome."

Gavin's hands jumped to his hairpiece, straightening it instinctively before a scowl crossed his features. I smiled. *Yes! Toupee joke accomplished.* This really *was* Heaven. "You saw what I did to the Greater Demon. I think you've had this coming for quite a while, Gavin. Don't worry, I'll make sure it's slow enough for you to experience every moment of it. I want you to see the twinkle in my eyes that signifies my sublime satisfaction at every millisecond of your agony. But first, tell me why?"

He quivered with frustration, but it quickly turned to pleading his case. "The Academy is broken. They've forgotten their true purpose. It's all politics, now. Favors exchanged for more favors. Not true Justice." He sighed, his shoulders sagging. "I was going to reset the rulebook. Establish a new Academy with the power of the Armory at my back. Start fresh. Salt the earth. A New World Order of Wizards."

I let him finish, not entirely disagreeing with his cause, but utterly disagreeing with the means he had used to pursue it. I nodded once – both in appreciation of his answer and as an acknowledgment of hearing his last will and testament. And, because I would literally never have another legitimate chance to say it, I quoted *The Princess Bride* as his farewell conveyance.

"My name is Inigo Montoya, you killed my father. Prepare to die." I had always wanted to say that, and... *damn* did it feel good. Especially with the accent.

Gavin jerked his head around in a panic, searching for any way out.

And his gaze settled on Othello.

He smiled. "Well, if I'm going to die, I'll do it with finesse. You killed my Demon, now I'll kill your concubine." Before I could even blink, he slit Othello's throat with a whisper of magic, too fast for me to even consider stopping him, being completely unused to my new powers. She hadn't even raised her head to look at me before she died.

Othello's soul slowly rose from her broken body. She stared down at it in pity, crying. Then her soul looked up and saw me. Her form quivered in fear as she realized she was about to meet Death in his official capacity.

I had seen my reflection. I didn't blame her.

I smiled compassionately, hoping she could see through my mask to the human emotion beneath. "It's me, Othello. It's okay. I forgive you. Come to me." I encouraged softly in my mind. She apparently heard me, her eyes widening. A tear fell to my cheek beneath the cold bone mask. She hadn't deserved to go through this. But she had done it all to save her nephew's life.

Othello was golden, folks. If you ever meet someone like her, never let her go.

And I wasn't about to let her go out like this.

Time for some fucking absolution.

She blubbered in a whispery voice, her soul drifting beside me like smoke on the breeze. "I didn't have a choice. He kidnapped my nephew. He threatened to hand him over to the Demons if I didn't help." I nodded sadly, patting her ethereal hand in forgiveness. Gavin watched me with a frown, no doubt wondering if I was hallucinating. Then his eyes widened in realization as he glanced at Othello's dead body beside him, and then back to the air in front of me. He couldn't see her, but had surmised that Othello's soul was still present. And that I could see her. Which meant that I might actually be Death in the flesh.

"Thanks for not telling him about me being a Maker," I whispered.

She nodded sadly. "It was the only thing I managed to keep back from him," she whispered back, heartbroken with shame.

I nodded, and then winked at her. I turned away from Othello's shattered soul and faced my tormenter. "You see, Gavin, one of the handy things about this mask is that I'm a temp-worker for Death. So, I get the final say on who lives and who dies." I hoped that was true. If not, I would beg Death to take me in Othello's place.

Knowing he was backed into a corner, Gavin began to prepare a nasty bit of magic to fling at me in retaliation, but I didn't know how to use my magic, and I wasn't sure how helpful the mask would be since I had already 'died' once. I simply reacted, not concerning myself with the numerous wizardly ways of defending myself. I didn't consider using magic.

Instead, like a teenager in a street fight, I used the only thing I had in my pockets. The keys to Death's motorcycle.

Now, you may not know this, but if you want to see some serious damage, throw a wad of keys at a milk carton. It *obliterates* the thing.

It's incredible.

I aimed the keys for Gavin's face, hoping to throw off his spell for a second or two so I could figure out how to use my new power to stop him.

But the damnedest thing happened.

Midair, I saw the cute little scythe keychain turn into a real scythe. *The* real Scythe of Death – Horseman of the Apocalypse. And that thing was both glorious, and horrifying as... well, *Hell*.

Heh.

Wails from a million trapped souls screeched through the night, causing Gavin's ears to instantly bleed, and the temperature dropped by about a hundred degrees. Just like I had experienced in the bar an hour ago. The scythe made a *whump-whump* sound like helicopter blades as it raced towards the summoner. Then it sliced right through his delicate little neck like a hot knife through butter, cleanly decapitating him. Gavin's body stood upright for a few seconds before finally toppling over. His head bounced, and Karma came full circle as his toupee fell off. His soul slowly rose up from the steaming carcass, a look of sheer surprise as he stared down at his body.

Then he turned to face me. Death's temp-worker.

And *this* temp-worker was a tad bit vengeful, not overly concerned about becoming employee of the month.

His soul began racing towards me in what I assumed was a spiritual attack. I held up a hand and he froze before me. He stared back, fearful and angry. "Speak. Tell me everything, shade." And, seemingly against his will, he did.

"I wanted power. Pandora. I needed her assistance to help me overthrow the Academy. She *gave* all the magical beings in our world their power in the first place. All the tricks we know, she came up with first. And we only know about them because she *told* us. But she is rumored to have found a pathway far past simple magic, and discovered an answer that is truly unfathomable." His eyes danced with feral hunger as he spoke.

Even though he knew he was dead, he *still* wanted into the Armory. To Pandora. To steal that little slip of a girl I had freed upon the world.

I would probably need to look into that later. But not now.

Right now, I had a dish to prepare.

Vengeance.

And I was about to serve it pure, raw, merciless, non-GMO, and *cold*.

I couldn't think of anything else I really cared to discover from him. The second his lips stopped moving, I decided to let his soul burn. Right there. In front of me. Out of pure spite. Because I wanted to watch. I was cold, and a fire sounded nice. I didn't know if any of this was strictly allowed or not, but who the hell was going to stop me? Death could clean up my mess later. Or punish me later.

Because at the moment, I only had attention for the task at hand, and I really wanted to make it memorable.

Which is why I made sure Gavin's consciousness remained, so he could watch *me* watching *his* agony.

I stoked the eternal flames hotter, enjoying the fact that he couldn't actually burn away. When I made it hotter, his suffering was more intense, but he couldn't actually burn away. He simply... *burned hotter*.

I don't need to tell you that he screamed. That was implied. Sometimes soundlessly. Mostly not. And he hit every note, every pitch, and every volume – from sobs, to cries, to shouts, to shrieks, you name it.

For curiosity's sake, I made it colder. And I watched with way too much enjoyment as spirit-cicles began to grow on his eyelashes, his soul quivering from the sub-zero inferno. All with a thought. After a time, I switched back to heat, since that produced more satisfying screams.

The sound of his ragged wails was like a Beethoven concerto to my ears.

After enjoying his torment for a few satisfying moments, I idly began to think about food. I don't know why that was my first thought, but I was downright ravenous. My vision suddenly pulsed blue, and two sticks with marshmallows appeared in my clenched fist. I glanced down in surprise. Then I looked at Othello's soul to notice her watching me with a sickened expression, like she wasn't sure what kind of person could enjoy something so harsh. I averted my gaze to avoid the judgment in her eyes.

Then I looked at her body resting in the pool of blood.

Why not?

Charon's boat interrupted my thoughts, appearing before us. I held up a hand, smiling at the drunken Boatman. "Dick move, Charon. You could have told me."

He shrugged. "Not in my job description." Othello's soul flickered as if trying to escape the repulsive sound of the Boatman's voice. Or the continuing screams.

I shook my head, smiling to myself. Then I turned to Othello. She looked as if guilt was eating her alive, and her voice had a similar tone. "I don't understand what's going on, but please make it quick, Nate. I never meant to hurt you. I just couldn't let my innocent nephew die for the Armory. I thought I could do it all. Save him, protect you..." She trailed off, a spiritual tear splattering against her pale cheeks. "Don't let me suffer."

"Not today, kid."

She furrowed her eyebrows in confusion. I held up my hands, and the blue waves of power around them shifted to green. I sensed Charon and Othello both watching me, but I ignored them as I very ungracefully forced Othello's soul back into her body.

Charon grunted, impressed or disgusted, I didn't know.

After all, I didn't really have any idea how to use Death's power. I'm sure I could have been a little gentler, but I was forcing someone back to life! Surely, she could forgive me for giving her soul a few bumps and bruises along the way. Her spirit and her body melded together until only Othello's battered body remained. I waited, fearful I might have done something wrong. Then her body arced up with a spasm, and she gasped as if being given CPR after drowning.

"It's aliiiiiive," I cackled into the night. Charon rolled his eyes.

Othello panted, eyes wild as she turned from me to Charon, patting her legs and chest in profound disbelief. Her wounds were gone, but she still looked unsteady. Weakened. Then her gaze settled on me, and I almost felt like a hero from a storybook.

"Pharos..." she whispered softly, her word filled to bursting with emotion. It was all she needed to say. Then she slammed into me with a great big hug, and immediately began to cry. I let her, closing my eyes as I smiled.

After a long minute, I gently extricated myself, holding her shoulders and looking her in the eyes. "Bros," I said, and lifted a fist. She glanced down at it, then, with a twinkle in her eyes, she pounded it with her own delicate fist.

"Bros," she answered in a faint whisper. Something in her eyes let me know she understood me completely. We were friends. Nothing more. Nothing less. But what we had was solid, and would always be there. Dependable. Loyal. Unwavering.

Bros.

As a side note, *definitely* my hottest bro.

I gave her another big hug, enjoying the background music of Gavin's agonizing screams as his soul continued to roast. I stepped back and appraised Othello. She looked a mess, but her wounds were completely gone. Which was good. They hadn't looked promising. And I wasn't sure how fast I could have gotten her to the hospital. I realized another added benefit of her not needing immediate medical attention. It gave me just the time I needed.

I motioned for her and Charon to both sit down beside me on the gravel so that Gavin's soul twisted and shuddered immediately before us, writhing in the green flames. I set him on a slow spin for aesthetic reasons. And personal satisfaction. My friends complied, and we sat before Gavin's burning soul and roasted our marshmallows. "Want one, Charon?" I asked politely. He shook his head, pointing at his sewn-up lips. I hadn't really wanted to see him attempt to eat a marshmallow. Instead, he cracked another cold one from a fresh six-pack hanging at his rope belt. Othello blinked, then winced as he eagerly dumped it over his sewn-up lips. "Another minute and mine will be perfect," I said conversationally. "You see, it's about that perfect brown color. You can't let it catch fire, but you have to let it get close to burning..." Gavin's eyes watched me with pure agony as he continued to shriek – watching as his agony produced our delicious treats.

My marshmallow was profound. Probably the most perfect marshmallow I would ever taste. After some time, I quenched the green flame with a thought, and found myself rather enjoying the immediate sounds of Gavin's relieved whimpering. I turned to the Boatman, knowing that he typically took the entire body of supernaturals rather than just the soul. "Leave the body. I'll need it to clear my name... hopefully." Charon shrugged, and as he climbed to his feet, he gathered up the remains of Gavin's ragged soul with a flick of his hand. The once-dangerous summoner's soul was dragged across the ground behind the Boatman, too weak to float or stand, I guess. Charon forgot to help him climb in, so when he yanked his hand, Gavin head-butted the boat, hard. Charon wasn't looking at his passenger, and simply yanked his invisible leash again, banging Gavin's face back into the side of the boat.

Once. Twice. Three times. *Then* Charon grabbed him by the face with that skeletal hand, picked him up, and slammed him into the floor of his ride.

Charon waved at us one time as he departed. Much slower than he usually did. I heard another beer crack open as the boat slowed even further. Something unseen began striking Gavin from the front and the back, causing grunts and gasps of agony as his soul twitched to and fro, unable to anticipate the direction of the blows before they landed. I watched as the abuse continued. Then I began to laugh, putting an arm around Othello. She collapsed into my chest, sobbing all over again with exhaustion, apologizing, and generally leaking bodily fluids all over me, ruining my cool outfit with her blood, snot, and tears.

But it felt nice to hold her.

39

I heard a horse stomp his hoof, neighing like a Demonic Clydesdale. I turned to see that it was only Death's – obviously not a Harley – horse. I appraised the beast thoughtfully, studying the same glowing green sheen to his coat as the bike had sported. Then I recalled Asterion's description of the Pale Rider. "I wonder if he knows Grimm?" I murmured out loud.

The horse fucking *answered* me, causing Othello to gasp and jump behind me.

"Ah, it has been eons since we slaughtered and grazed together. I thought you smelled familiar." Othello peered around my shoulder like a small child, eyes wide as she realized the horse had, in fact, spoken. He had a refined British Accent like a James Bond actor.

"Um... that was kind of a rhetorical question. So, you can talk."

The horse grunted. "As can you, Maker." He rolled his eyes.

"Do I just call you *pale horse*?"

"I am known as Gruff," he answered proudly. I dipped my head politely.

"Pleased to meet you, Gruff. This is Othello, and I'm Nate." The creature bowed his head in response. Othello's eyes were about to pop out at this point, and her fingernails were beginning to dig into my skin. I patted my pocket as an idea suddenly hit me. I found it and pulled it out. Othello blinked at the odd black feather with the red orb at the tip. "Grimm. Come to me," I called into the night.

A peal of black lightning responded, and my little death unicorn, courtesy of Asterion, appeared before us. He stamped a hoof, spotted Gruff, and trotted up to him, rubbing the side of his feathered head against Gruff's glowing green mane. Gruff made a surprised sound, but responded in kind. The two of them walked away from the humans, no doubt to catch up on lost time. I smiled, wondering if Grimm could also talk. I didn't hear any voices though. I pocketed my feather, glad I had snatched it up from Plato's Cave before it burned down.

"That was courteous of you," a familiar voice said.

Hemingway – Death – strode out from behind a pillar of salvaged vehicles, assessing the two horses with a thoughtful gaze. Othello sat down in the dirt behind me, legs finally giving out. Her wild eyes darted from Death to me, and back again with confusion. I wondered how she saw Hemingway. Was he a doppelganger of me at the moment or did she see the guy I had met at the bar?

"So," he nudged Gavin's detached head with an unsympathetic boot, turning the summoner's eyes the opposite direction. "You caused quite a stir. Who would have known that a little manling wizard child would almost start the End of Days? What have you been up to?" Death looked at me, weighing my soul.

"Whoops?"

He chuckled. "I don't think you made any friends today. I believe you won't be too long in the land of the living. Every Knight of Heaven will be after you now. Using Cat's Paws, of course. They won't be satisfied until your blood paves the streets. Did you at least have fun borrowing my... accessories?" he asked.

"Uh, the Scythe was a nice touch. Especially after you threw a bitch fit about me borrowing it." Death grunted.

"Bitch fit, eh?" My arms pebbled at his tone, but he finally shrugged. "Intentional. You'll see."

I frowned, unsure what he meant. "I met Charon. Real charmer. Might have an attitude problem, or a drinking problem. Or both. Kind of a dick, actually. He didn't tell me where I was going. This was the last thing I expected."

Death laughed. "That was kind of the point."

"You probably want this back..." I began to lift my hand to the mask, but Death held up a hand, stalling me.

"Did you know that our masks were created by the first Maker?" He threw in conversationally. "He was actually known as The Mask Maker after that. He made four... One for each Horseman. You are the first Maker in hundreds of years. I wonder what toys you might create if you live long enough. Perhaps a new mask?" he asked, tone heavy with implications. I merely stared back at him in surprise. "Your kind was hunted down quite excessively. Too powerful, what with the rise of the wizards." He watched me, grinning distantly. "Something to look forward to, perhaps."

"That's... nice," I finally stated. Now I was the most wanted man alive? I'd had enough of this. "Here, I've caused enough problems. Take this thing away before I do something even stupider than I already have." I began to take it off.

"Wait." His eyes quested the salvage yard. "We aren't alone. This is still Act Two..."

With a big sigh, I began to rub my hands together for a scrap. Othello cowered behind me. Couldn't I get a break?

40

A rumble of thunder shook the ground, causing several of the towers of vehicles to groan.

Three men entered the clearing, two of them recognizable from the bar where I had first met Hemingway. One was the red-haired, scar-knuckled grouch who had been glaring at us. Another was the sickly, older gentleman I had saved from the Hail Mary knockout punch. The third was a stranger to me.

"Allow me to introduce my brothers, the Horsemen. War, Famine, and Pestilence. Brothers, Nate Temple. The... Rider of Hope?" he smiled in good fun. At least, I hoped this was just some kind of joke. "He already has a horse. Grimm." The other Horsemen turned to look at the two horses off to the side. And then they each burst out laughing. Rather than taking offense, I shook my head, chuckling nervously.

"No thanks. I would make a horrible Horseman."

"He also looks rather like you now, Brother. I wonder why that is?" The beefy, red-haired Horseman added, pointing at my mask. War, no doubt.

I began to pull it away from my face and saw Death shaking his head quickly. "Not yet. It still has one more part to play. Trust me." The other Horsemen shook their heads in amusement. What the fuck was he talking about? Hadn't I caused enough mayhem? I studied the legends more closely. Pestilence sported a mask on his belt that looked like it belonged on a Renaissance Doctor, complete with the long beak for a nose and everything. It was a blood red color. Famine had an aged scarecrow mask dangling from his belt, having been made from what looked like a burlap sack. And dark, oily stains marred its surface. War sported a mask of laughing flame. Literally. The mouth moved as it made the motion of laughter. While burning. I shivered. And a Maker had *created* them for these four wraiths. Someone like me.

Before I could think about that too much, Heaven and Hell arrived amidst more peals of thunder and general ruckus. If this continued, the salvage yard wouldn't survive. Couldn't they simply walk? As if on cue, they congregated to separate sides and watched us.

Watched *me* in particular. They looked curious, glancing from me to the Riders to the two horses and murmuring amongst themselves. After all, thanks to Death's insistence, I still wore the mask.

Then the seven remaining Academy members arrived with their damning silver masks as the familiar *Crack* of Shadow Walking broke the silence. Jafar then saw that he wasn't alone. His eyes widened at the Riders, the horses, then further at the Bible Thumpers. He stumbled backwards, as if searching for a safe place to turn, and promptly tripped over Gavin's severed balding head. Othello groaned in disgust. He fell on his ass most ungracefully. His eyes finally settled on Gavin's face and he flinched. I burst out laughing.

Jafar's eyes rose to meet mine, pure fear filling his face. He was the only one without a mask. I briefly wondered what I looked like to the Academy.

"You cannot be here. It is not time to Ride, Horsemen! No Covenants were broken, were they?" His eyes darted nervously to the Angels. Then the Demons, searching for an answer. "I'm here for Nate Temple. He is to be arrested for crimes against the Academy," Jafar demanded.

I turned to Death, silently asking if it was time yet. He nodded back.

I took off the mask. The Academy members gasped. The Angels and Demons merely chuckled as if at a good joke.

After a brief flash of confusion, Jafar pointed an accusatory finger at me. "You have consorted with Demons. It's the only way you could have survived. The Academy will make an example of you for what you've done. I promise you that."

Gruff stamped a hoof, causing the earth to crack beneath him. Grimm was also there, staring hungrily, but he did it well. The wizards flinched at the implied threat. Death spoke into the silence. "On the contrary, wizards. He was the only one with the stones to stand against your arrogance. This was *your* responsibility, and you are lucky I don't make an example of *you*. I might yet. Your own soldier, Gavin, caused this. Such an arrogant name, *Justices*. The presumption." He shook his head in distaste. "Nate, here, has saved this city. Despite your interference."

Several dark shadows from the Demon side grumbled. I guessed they were Fallen Angels. A step above the pitiful Greater Demon I had battled. A single voice spoke up, a hissed warning like a snake had spoken. He still had nothing on Charon. "Aye. He has no relations with us, although I would like to extend a job offer to him…"

Jafar's eyes creased in rage, assessing me for some accusation that might stick. I turned to the Fallen Angels. "Lot of that going around lately," I muttered. "Thanks, but no thanks, weird shadowy guy."

His answering voice crackled with power. "Call me by my rightful title, *mortal*. Knight of Hell or Fallen, if you must. Do not show disrespect to a being such as myself.

Continue at your own peril. Even with the mask, you dare not stand against our might."

I shook my head, showing my palms and the mask, placating. This only seemed to cause a stir among them, as if I was threatening them with the mask. "Okay, okay. Calm down."

"No one is about to calm down," Jafar turned an accusing glare to the gathered parties. "He wields the power of a Horseman. How can this be? Surely, this breaks the Covenants."

I cleared my throat, standing closer to Othello, who was still sitting on the ground, trying to avoid attention from our powerful audience. I wanted to be close in case anyone tried to take out his or her frustration on the only unprotected class here. "I borrowed it. Stole it, to be exact. Death had no idea. I used my Maker's ability. It was the only way I stood a chance, thanks to your curse. While you were lounging away at the Academy, sipping warm milk, I was fighting for my life and the lives of those innocents in my city. Without my birthright!" I roared. "Innocent people died while you schemed safely away in your ivory tower, hoping to get your hands on the Armory when all the cards fell. Everything could have been lost because of your arrogance!" I was heaving. My vision rippled with a blue haze, a warning that I was dangerously close to tapping into my new gift. War appraised me, nodding in approval.

The same Knight of Hell spoke up, still not offering a name. "Much to our regret, the mortal speaks the truth. It was almost in the summoner's grasp. We were all used here, Heaven and Hell both. But you Academy *Justices*, on the other hand, have no excuse. We of celestial origins were all forced to use cat's paws to fight here. Angels with their Nephilim, we with our Demons, and the mortal here decided to gain his own cat's paw. The Horseman."

Eae, on the Angel's side, chimed in. "And all without breaking any Covenants, apparently, despite our encouragement to leave well enough alone. He has saved this city from my brothers' children. We judged you wrongly, Maker. Although I am interested in how you duped the Horseman."

The Fallen Angels scowled from within the shadows, grunting affirmation that they too would like to hear the story. I wasn't about to share it, or the lie that I had stolen it and that Death had actually *assisted* me.

I shrugged my shoulders. "Maybe some other time…"

Jafar growled in defeat. "Fine. You have allies in high places, Temple. Who was this alleged summoner?"

I smiled. "You just missed him. Well, you tripped over his head, but other than that, you just missed him. We had a few marshmallows and then he hopped on a boat out of town. You remember him, right?"

Jafar blinked with doubtful eyes, briefly darting to the corpse at his feet. "You expect me to believe Gavin caused all of this?"

"Having witnessed firsthand your impressive ability to see the facts before you and still make a horrible mess of things, no. I don't." I watched him like a bug in a box, watched as his calculating eyes tried to go into damage control. Politics. Gavin had been right. He didn't care that they had a psychopath in their midst. He cared only about how to pass the buck. Lay the blame elsewhere, so that his reputation wouldn't be tarnished. "He seemed to have this crazy notion that the Academy was broken. Political animals, he called you. Did you, by chance, happen to start this whole mess, jumping into my life and cursing me, as a result of information he provided you? Incriminating evidence of some kind, perhaps?"

Jafar's mouth opened. Then closed. His scowl grew tight. Then he nodded. "What is this Maker appellation they mentioned?" He said instead. Several of his Justices shifted nervously from foot to foot. I wasn't sure if it was from Jafar's question, or my accusation.

"Not your concern," I muttered.

Jafar opened his mouth, but War cleared his throat, flexing his fists at his side in warning. Jafar quieted under the Horseman's gaze. War's mask hung at his belt, flames covering a roaring, gleeful face. How did it not burn his *clothes*? I shivered.

Eae spoke again. "As fascinating as this all is, I merely ask the Horsemen for my Grace to be restored as recompense for this... misunderstanding. And I recommend you also return what you have borrowed from the Rider," he added, turning to me.

I smiled. "Will do. As soon as our *guests* leave." I made a show of discreetly angling my head to indicate the Justices. "Courtesy must be extended to even the most unsavory types, after all." The Academy bristled.

"Watch your tone, Temple. You have no power. You are now a Regular. Give us the key or we will raze your home to the ground. The Armory belongs under our control."

I paused. They couldn't sense my power? Odd. It was coursing through my veins like my magic never had before. More violent, feral, and lethal. Hungry. The blue haze across my vision intensified. I liked it better than the odd green hue from Death's mask. I definitely needed to learn more about this. After all, it was my only power source now.

War took a step forward, a meaty, scarred finger cleaning out his ear. "I'm sorry, did you just demand access to the Armory? The one your fellow Justice almost ignited Armageddon for? After everything, you think you can just walk in here and take the candy? It belongs to the Maker, who is now safely out of your jurisdiction. He no longer wields the power of a wizard. He has..." He winked at me. "Transcended such petty claims."

I burst out laughing.

Jafar's hackles rose. "Petty?" he roared. The other Horsemen instantly grew more still, and power fairly crackled in the air. A warning. I almost wished I had a bag of popcorn. Jafar moderated his tone, sensing his impending demise. "Every wizard is commanded by the Acad—"

War spoke. "That's his point, impudent *child*. Listen, before I grow angry." His voice was raspy, and one hand rested casually on the mask at his side. "Thanks to you, he's no longer a wizard. He's a Maker. Without your curse, you would have had a Maker and wizard under your thumb. Now you have neither. You truly are fools."

Jafar bristled, but I held out an olive branch.

Kind of.

"I'll take you to the Armory for a quick view of what your insolence caused." I turned to the waiting crowd. "This will only take a moment." I offered Death his mask. He shook his head. "You wear it well, and it might keep them on their toes." He added the last under his breath with a smirk. I smiled, nodding back.

I Shadow Walked the Academy members to what remained of the Armory, and pointed at where the door once stood. It was different using my Maker power to Shadow Walk. More efficient even. It hadn't taken nearly so much power from me, and I had done it while lugging seven people with me. Jafar rounded on me in anger, unhappy at me taking them here without his permission. "How did you do that? I thought you had no magic?" He accused. I didn't answer, only adding to his anger. I shrugged instead, turning to the wreckage before us.

The concrete around the door was charred in a black circle one hundred feet in diameter, and the building was destroyed for hundreds of yards, as if a bomb had gone off right where we stood. It still smelled. A light patina of snow had begun to fall here, somewhat dousing the flames. I heard sirens in the distance.

"Witness what you have wrought. This happened when I died." Technically it had happened after Gavin had thrown my blood at the door, but... semantics.

Jafar appraised me curiously. "Died?"

"Yes. I died."

Jafar cast a doubting gaze back at me, eyebrows furrowing like a caterpillar taking a nap. "Surely, you are exaggerating."

"No, I died. I can even get you a signed affidavit from Death confirming this. The ... ultimate alibi, if you will." I smirked.

"Death?" I nodded. "How are they *really* involved? I command you to tell me the truth."

I decided not to rise to the bait. "They weren't involved. He can merely confirm that I died. So, thanks to your curse stealing my power, I was unable to protect myself, died, and apparently lost control of the Armory. But you knew the curse was permanent, didn't you? You designed it that way." Jafar merely stared back. I thought I caught a flicker of concern at my knowledge of his ruse, but he hid it well. And it didn't matter anymore anyway. I was now a free agent, as War had stated. "I didn't even know for sure that the Armory was here until you pointed it out. But of course, thanks to you falling for Gavin's lies, you knew all about it."

Jafar grimaced. "And what of Gavin? Why would he do such a thing?"

"You know as much as I do. He knew about the Armory. Tried to get in. Killed me, but died in the process. Othello killed him before he could get in. She's the hero. I don't know what was in there, but it's your fault what happens next. If War wasn't clear enough for you, I'll restate it. I hereby resign. Immediately. You want the magical world to work together, yet you cursed me for not complying with your extortion scheme. Two members of our own caste were killed. My parents. You never helped.

Like sniveling family members, you tried to come to the estate sale and take what you could. You wouldn't help solve the crime, but you wanted a share of the profits. Karma bit you in the ass. You not only lost your opportunity to work with me to keep the Armory safe, but you also allowed the door to be fucking blown off. Who knows what is now loose in the world because of your greed? I won't be a part of your club. And apparently, I'm a hot commodity. A Maker." I winked at him with amusement. "Now it's time for you to get the fuck out of my city." I sent out tendrils of my new power to latch onto each wizard nearby and yanked them all back to the salvage yard with a slightly rougher version of Shadow Walking than before. They weren't pleased, and apparently didn't feel me doing it ahead of time, judging by their squawks of surprise. I very unceremoniously dumped them onto the ground, which didn't make Jafar very happy.

Everyone else was waiting patiently for our return.

Jafar drew a freaking sword, taking an aggressive step toward me after he had composed himself. "You lost it all. You are hereby found guilty of unleashing a weapon of mass destruction upon the world. The sentence is immediate death."

I smiled, and then used my hungry Maker power to inch the sword closer to his face rather than mine, watching as his muscles rippled in protest. Everyone froze, listening to Jafar grunt in disbelief. "What power is this? It can only be Demon-craft!" he hissed. His minions extended hands towards me, and a single ball of white-hot flame abruptly screamed towards my face with a wailing shriek.

Before I could react, the fireball froze in midair as one of the Angels blocked it with a sizzling flash of blue light. Simultaneously, a sickening red bolt of lightning shot forth from the Demons' side of the yard, shattering the frozen flame into a muffled implosion of darkness, eating the flame in a puff of shadows. "Touch him and die, Academy. We may have use for him someday..." It was the Knight of Hell. I shivered. "He has done no Hellcraft. Or Angelcraft for that matter. Do you think him that reckless? A mortal to wield the power of God? In the presence of God's favored and disfavored children?" The Angel waved his hand around the room in agreement. The shadows of both sides hungrily watched the Academy, anticipating.

Jafar spoke with a quivering voice. I released my power and he sighed in relief. "How could we not sense anything if it's not from Heaven or Hell? It *must* be magic, but I sensed nothing."

Eae shook his head. "It is *old* magic. Not from Heaven or Hell. You cannot sense it because you do not have the imagination to comprehend what Master Temple wields. Perhaps it is because he truly is a Maker." His eyes grew pensive as he appraised little old me. "I must insist that you leave this place at once. Before your presence offends your betters. More than it already has. Take what Master Temple has so graciously offered you. Life. I dare say you are no match for his new power. Even without the aid of the Horsemen." Then he smiled, slowly counting the Justices. "Even with seven of you." They blinked at this in sheer disbelief, and then looked at me in an altogether new light. I shrugged innocently. As I dropped my hands to my sides, I felt Death's motorcycle keys resting in my pocket. I frowned. How the hell? But I didn't let any of my surprise show.

I grinned at Jafar, clutching the mask in my other hand. "The grown-ups have important things to discuss. Run along, now, children."

They disappeared instantly, but Jafar's eyes fairly smoldered with hatred. I knew it wasn't the last I would see of old Jafar.

Famine spoke up, clutching his scarecrow mask in a bony hand. "I'm famished. Let's eat."

War rolled his eyes. "It's *still* not as funny as you seem to think it is." Then, without my permission, I found my ass violently teleported to a strange dimension. Much less gracefully than Shadow Walking. It felt like we were momentarily ripped out of existence, making me think I had actually been attacked. Othello gripped my hand tightly as a brave new world opened around us.

41

I found myself in a fiery courtroom of sorts, with volcanoes and glaciers in the distance to either side of us. The skies roiled hungrily. I instantly realized that we were the only mortals in a very immortal world. I managed to peel my eyes away from the scenery after a few moments, and with a start, I noticed that I stood before a chair, clutching the mask in a forgotten hand, all by myself.

As the accused would stand in a trial.

I saw War leading Othello off to the side, as if she was a... witness.

He left her there, and then approached a long ebony table with his brothers. It looked like aged bone. The Four Horsemen sat behind the table facing me like judges, and I abruptly felt all sorts of nervous. The Angels sat on the left, the blue glow from the towering glaciers behind them limning their now-visible true Angelic forms. Which was terrifying. They had chosen not to reveal those forms earlier. Now things were more... formal. It was blinding to look at them with their glowing white wings outspread – each pulsing with natural, but different, sources of power – whether it was fire, stone, ice, glass, jewel, ether, or water. They began neatly tucking them back behind their shoulders as they organized themselves efficiently – by rank, I guessed. I looked to the other side to see the Demons also flaunting their true forms, flickering geysers of lava spewing into the air behind them like acne from the surface of the planet. They were all uniquely different, some lizard-like, animalistic, and yet others representing the various elements on earth with a darker emphasis than the Angels' elemental power. And they appeared to be restless rather than orderly, their black wings fidgeting as they snarled at each other for better seats.

Death cleared his throat, so I turned to face him, but he was interrupted almost instantly. An IHOP waitress was suddenly there, pushing a cart of... pancakes towards the Horsemen. Her face was blank, devoid of any humanity. But she had the right apron.

She set a plate before each Rider, flinched when Famine thanked her, and then she disappeared. They began to chow down as if they were the parents at a family dinner, and the Angels and Demons were the children.

But what did that make Othello and I?

After a few bites, Death cleared his throat again.

"We are here to determine this young Maker's fate. Ultimately, it is up to me, but since there are… extenuating circumstances that could possibly ignite Armageddon, I called you, my Brothers to stand Watch with me." They nodded between mouthfuls, looking disinterested, as if this kind of thing happened all the time. "Now, since we went over most of this in the salvage yard, this is really just a formality. Begin, Eae."

Several Demons snarled to themselves as the name rang out, most likely past victims of his various Demon thwarting excursions throughout history. Eae stepped forward, and I got a fresh whiff of his being. Frost and burning gravel. Then he told his version of the story. It sounded pretty straightforward. It seemed none of the Angels knew how I had managed to survive, or how I had damaged Eae's Grace, but he and his brothers seemed to agree that it was because I was a Maker. At least that's what Eae told the Court. I was pretty sure that they just didn't want to admit to everyone that the Demon had been strong enough to do it. Save face and prevent any particularly motivated Demons from trying it in the future. Which was smart. But it was a lie. Here I was, listening to an Angel flat-out lie. If I weren't sitting as the accused I would have run away screaming. Political intrigue was apparently not limited to the mortal world. These pigeons could lie with the best of them. Then again, maybe Eae simply had a free pass to lie when convenient in order to thwart the Demons. I shrugged, cataloging the thought away deep in my mind for later scrutiny. Overall, the lie suited my purposes. It only added to my mystery. And I was still trying to come to grips with the fact that I was still breathing. It kind of messed with a guy when he prepared for his impending death only to find out that at the penultimate moment, it wasn't going to happen the way he thought. Or at all. But I was still on trial. Maybe *this* was the right time, place, and way Hope had warned me I needed to die. After Eae's story, there was silence as The Horsemen considered.

"Nothing further to add?" Death asked between mouthfuls. My stomach began to growl as I watched them eat. Eae shook his head.

Death glanced at his brothers and they gave varying nods of understanding between mouthfuls of pancakes. "We will allow your Grace to be restored. If we don't, then this would be the end of days. As much fun as that might sound, it is not yet time. Agreed, Brothers?" They nodded absently. I stared open-mouthed. This was ridiculous. They didn't even seem to *care*. Were these trials that common? My reverie was interrupted as Death continued. "Then I shall restore the Angel, just as I have brought Othello and Master Temple back from the grave." The brief warning glance he shot my way could have been measured in nanoseconds, as if to say, *don't say a word*. After all, *he* hadn't brought us back. *I* had done that. Death's mercurial gaze let me know that he was impressed, offended, and seriously, seriously didn't want Armageddon to start. Funny. You would think that he of all people would want Armageddon to set off with a bang. Death was the *source* of his power, because, you know, he was the friggin *Horseman* of Death. That many souls would make him and his Brothers amazingly strong.

He continued. "Since the Demons inadvertently started all of this, they do not get this boon." There were a few grumbles from the Demons, but they remained seated, having expected this outcome. Death flicked a hand at Eae. The Angel visibly shuddered, and then a ragged set of tiny, wilted wings snapped out from his back, reaching only a few feet to either side of him. He looked rough, no longer like a Calvin Klein model, as if he had just been found at six in the morning outside a Vegas strip club with no recollection of the last few hours. Or days. Several Demons chuckled lightly at the sight, but lucky for them, no Angels noticed. They were entirely transfixed on their brother.

Without warning, jagged bolts of lightning from both the nearby volcanoes and glaciers simultaneously hammered into the Angel with twin explosions of light. As the initial flare of light faded, I saw him again. He grunted. Once.

Holy crap.

He set his shoulders defiantly, withstanding the raging flood of crackling energy pouring into him in a continuous stream – fire and ice, the children of the unforgiving, merciless Mother Earth – and was slowly imbued with the powers that God had once created in seven days. The torrent continued unabated, the bolts of power only growing thicker, and thicker, wilder and wilder. Sets of eyes – inky obsidian from the Demons and galactic ice chips from the Angels – watched the spectacle with intense interest. Eae's wings slowly began to flesh out, sprouting gleaming, pristine feathers over rapidly growing corded muscle, until they stretched a good six feet to either side of him, quivering with sizzling elemental energy. With a crack that split one of the volcanoes down the middle, the cord of fiery power from over the Demons' heads simply ceased, and a single feather rose above Eae's head, gathering light from the remaining cord of power emanating from the glacier. Lava began spewing wildly into the air, a dust cloud filling the already dark skies. The feather began to glow as it slowly rotated on its axis, faster and faster, brighter and brighter with each passing second. A shockwave built around the feather and then screamed outward in a sonic boom that shook my hair. The glacier calved, sounding like the earth beneath me had suddenly split in two. The bolt of power disappeared, leaving a purple haze in my vision. I blinked several times to clear my sight.

Eae stood before us, a veritable mountain of muscle, much larger than when I had first met him, and his newly remade body would have made the famous Renaissance artists envious. His Grace had been restored.

"I declare the murder of the Demons, the Nephilim, and injury of the Angel even. Both were misunderstandings or misguided actions caused by the summoner, who I will deal with in my own way." The last was a dark promise that caused several pleased nods from the Angels, and hungry, thoughtful looks from the Demons. "It's not a crime that Master Temple successfully defended himself from several Demon attacks. And it is not his fault that he found a way back to the land of the living. It's mine." No one argued, as Death's judgment was the final word on the matter. After all, the Horsemen were the judge and jury of Armageddon, and I *had* been acting in self-defense, having done nothing wrong in the first place. I nodded in appreciation, but held up a hand.

Famine clapped excitedly, pointing at me. I blushed. Was he for real?

"I have a last request, if it's not already clear."

Death nodded.

"The little boy, Othello's nephew. He is to be released." I did my best to sound confident.

The Demons began to grumble unhappily, but Death held up a hand. "Agreed."

I nodded. Othello's knees almost gave out but she managed to maintain her feet, shooting me a smile of such happiness that I couldn't help smiling back. Famine leaned closer to her and offered her a sip of his orange juice with a friendly smile. She accepted, with wildly terrified eyes, as if fearful of refusing his offer. He beamed as she took the faintest of sips. I chuckled to myself, feeling my tension begin to drain away.

It was... *neat.*

Clean. Orderly.

The Angels couldn't be pissed, and neither could the few surviving Demons. They had only been on earth thanks to the Greater Demon and the summoner. Sir Dreadsalot and Gavin, and I had sent them both packing. Everything important concluded, the Angels and Demons left. Somehow. I didn't exactly dare to watch where they left to, not sure if directly catching a glimpse of Heaven or Hell would permanently destroy my brain.

Death held out a hand and I nodded in understanding. I handed him the motorcycle keys and his mask. As soon as they touched his hand, I collapsed in pure agony, as if every single one of my recent wounds had suddenly happened for the first time.

Simultaneously.

I was whimpering on the ground. The torture slowly began to recede, leaving behind only the lingering effects I had felt prior to the church. Which was enough all by itself to leave me as a quivering puddle of throbbing pain. Several eons later, the pain began to subside enough for me to move. Barely. I still hurt. Everywhere. But it was somewhat tolerable. Death was speaking to me as I felt Othello lift me back to my feet, supporting my weight completely. I survived it, but scowled at her for good measure. Then I turned to Death.

He watched me, speaking slowly. "You can either have your original power back or allow Othello to remain alive," He said. I felt Othello go rigid beside me.

It took me a few seconds to trust my throat with identifiable speech. I looked from him to Othello. I managed to answer with several pauses for breath amidst spasms of pain. "Not that this is my deciding factor, but... you think I want to get my magic back and be under the purview of the Academy... after all I said to them?" I grunted at a particularly nasty shiver, glad Othello still held me upright. "No thanks. Othello is the true hero. I consider it a win-win. No more asshats in charge of me, and she gets to keep on ticking." I was definitely a crock wizard, and didn't deserve my old power back. It would be a reminder, the grueling years it would take me to learn my new Maker ability – the cost of arrogance.

And failure.

I slowly began to feel more or less human, able to withstand my injuries on my own two feet. But Othello was shaking slightly with barely-contained cries, so I kept my arm wrapped around her, squeezing her shoulder for comfort.

War came down from the table, but Famine and Pestilence continued eating their pancakes. "If you are still alive at the End of Days, I vote that you become a Rider with us. It seems you already have a horse, Grimm, and he will fit in splendidly with Gruff. The grumpy bastard is intolerable." Death scowled back, but War merely smiled before continuing. "You will be the Rider of Hope, as that is your most cherished value." I began to nod in respectful appreciation for the offer, and the fact that he had considered Hope to be a cherished value of mine. Then he continued. "You will pillage and rape all Hope from the world." My nod froze instantly. *What?* I hoped that this was just idle talk, and that I wasn't actually being bound to such a career path.

"I'm not even a Christian," I finally stammered.

Respectfully.

"That doesn't matter, *Maker*. Ragnarok, Armageddon, etc. are all the same to us. Christians got most of the facts right, so we lean towards that title."

Famine spoke up from the table, seeming interested in our conversation for the first time in a while. "You think any of us are *Christian*? That would be a... what do you humans call it? Ah, yes. A *Conflict of interest*. We are all non-believers, judges, pious," he said, laughing. "Perhaps not *pious*, but cast-out. You will fit in *excellently*." The last statement was said as the Rider leaned forward with a lethal grin. Apparently, I had impressed the Horsemen.

"I'll... consider it," I answered softly. Othello's face was pale, but she kept her thoughts to herself.

"So be it. You're a good man, Nathin Temple. You can borrow my mask any time." I shuddered at the thought. "Now, your body *did* literally die, so you must rest while I finish the paperwork. This will not go easy on your friends. Your death is all over the news. Your body was found in a bar near Soulard." Death smiled sadly, waved a hand over my head, and I promptly blacked out to the sensation of my forehead catching on fire.

42

I woke to the sensations of warm air gently caressing my eyelids, and soft conversation from several voices tickling my ears. Unsure of who was near me, I carefully cracked my crusty eyelids open. Someone must have superglued them together because it took me a mountain of effort.

I was in the Temple Mausoleum.

And my friends surrounded me. Gunnar comforted Ashley in a close hug several feet away, his eyes chips of cold stone, and Misha and Tory were holding hands, sobbing softly beside them. Othello stood off to the side, alone, staring up at the Temple family tree as if she knew she wasn't welcome in their grief. Then again, she knew I wasn't truly dead. Had she told them it was just a ruse? No, they wouldn't be so grief-stricken if she had.

Then I spotted Indie. She stood alone, staring blankly at nothing. I took a deep breath and sat up, causing a slight *creak* of flexing wood.

Indie stiffened at the sound, then slowly turned around. She saw me sitting up.

From inside a coffin.

She... blinked. I smiled back tiredly. Then she took a shuffled step backwards and gasped. Gunnar glanced over his shoulder and saw her staring at me. His forearms shifted to claws as he shoved Ashley away. Everyone turned to look at me, then, with varying degrees of horror and confusion on their faces. Rage immediately rolled over each face. Claws appeared from Misha's arms with a *snicker-snack*. Her eyes flared red, a feral gleam catching the soft light. Tory's hand shattered the table she was using for support as she suddenly clenched her fist. And Indie cocked a freaking pistol held in a shaking hand. Right, I probably needed to put them at their ease or something. Before they made me die for real. But I was still groggy.

"I'm not dead yet," I rasped in a Monty Python accent. Then I began coughing. My throat was bone dry.

Ashley and Tory passed out in unison, crumpling to the floor like wet laundry.

Indie just stared at me with glassy eyes – shock taking over. The gun clattered to the floor uselessly, causing me to flinch in case it went off. With my luck, I wouldn't have been surprised if it took out the leg of the coffin I rested in, sending me crashing to the ground where I would instantly be devoured by my best friends. No one else moved.

I began to feel guilty about putting them through this. No one spoke, adding to my guilt, but Gunnar was growling and sniffing the air hesitantly. Then he bent over Ashley, keeping one wary eye cast over his shoulder at me. "Uh. Did you get my message?" I asked Indie. She continued to stare blankly back at me. "I didn't do so hot on my communicating, did I? Also, it looks like you're unemployed, as Plato's Cave was smited while you were away..." I turned to Ashley, who had been violently shaken awake by Gunnar and was groggily getting to her feet. "Temple Industries has a big hole in it. Crater, to be exact. Not sure how much that is going to cost to fix, but we'll probably need to talk about it. Later. I'm kind of tired right now. And thirsty." Blinks answered me. "So, how were your vacations?"

Then Indie covered the distance between us like a ninja and pounced on top of me. She began poking, prodding, and kissing every square inch of my face. It felt glorious. I sighed, leaning back into my coffin on my palms, breathing in her scent.

"How?!" she demanded between angry kisses and hugs.

"It's a long story. I'm just—"

Pow!

She smacked the living daylights out of me with an open palm. Stars exploded across my vision. Othello burst out laughing as the stars ever so slowly began to fade away. I continued as if nothing had happened. "Glad you're alright. Is your mom okay?"

She stared back at me, heaving. "Yes. Mild concussion, but she's fine." Her next words were precise, clipped, and dripping with warning. "What the *hell* happened while we were gone? The whole city is abuzz with talk of murders, explosions, and attacks." She shook her head, focusing on the important question. "How are you *alive*? They found your body three days ago. This doesn't make any sense." She began to sob, unable to maintain her anger, let alone comprehend my revival.

Othello chimed in. "Oh, he just stole Death's mask!"

Indie's sobs silenced in a blink. She turned an icy gaze to Othello. "She finally decides to speak. Who might you be, mysterious stranger?" Her tone dripped venom, even more of a warning than she had used when speaking with me. "Your voice sounds vaguely familiar..." Indie's eyes were diamonds as they turned back to me. I realized that Indie knew exactly who she was, and that I was about to pay for it.

Unfortunately for me, I had been an open book on my past romances.

"She's a friend of mine. Othello, meet my friends. Friends, meet Othello. She helped me while you were out of town."

"And do you make a habit of sleeping with all of your friends?" Indie's voice was brittle.

Gunnar chimed in, still sporting his werewolf claws, as if unsure what to make of everything. "He tried once with me, but I was able to resist. Thank god."

"That was in the past. We were much younger then." Gunnar burst out laughing. "*Her*, not *you*, you damn dirty dog." I scowled at him, fighting a grin. I turned to Indie. "I didn't even know you back then," I said softly.

Indie's eyes were flame. "What about while I was in the hospital with my mother?" I blinked, and then Othello burst out laughing. I felt an icy shiver down my spine. Did she know about our make-out session? Me being a dirty cheater? I had completely forgotten about it, thinking I had been about to die.

Priorities.

"Um... what?" I answered politically instead.

"Don't you *what* me, Nathin Laurent Temple! She answered the phone when I called, and led me to believe..." She rounded on Othello.

Othello finally stopped laughing and held out a hand. "Relax. I swear. I don't poach. He wouldn't stop talking about you and it made me... jealous. But I understand now. What we had was in the past... where it will stay. He loves *you*. Not *me*. In fact, it was quite disgusting to be around him, what with all the *Indie this,* and *Indie that* commentary. I acted like an adolescent schoolgirl. And for that I apologize." Indie's metaphorical territorial fur flattened a bit at that.

Bros.

Othello was a true *Bro*.

I would have held up a fist, allowing the glorious bro-light of the bro-universe to imbue my arm with a bro-ish salute if I hadn't already been in enough hot water. But I knew Othello understood my glance and everything it entailed.

But then she ruined it. She began to babble on unnecessarily.

"Everything I told you on the phone was true. We were tired. We had just survived a big fight with things way out of *my* league. A Greater Demon. Girl Scouts. A pack of Werewolves. The Academy. We were sleeping in the same bed. I kept him safe while he was injured. That's all. I swear. I owe him my life. Literally. You wouldn't believe what he did while you were all gone. It was beyond impressive. Even to the Ange—" I interrupted quickly. This was getting out of control.

"Wait, *you* called? I thought that was Gunnar!" I practically shouted to overcome Othello's diarrhea of the mouth.

Gunnar shook his head and Indie nodded. Othello blushed, admitting her white lie from when I had caught her answering my phone that night. Right before she had hidden my phone under the covers. My face began to heat up at that memory, but luckily no one saw it. Indie spoke up. "And what about the FBI, or that... *Demon*? You said you were going to work on your communication!"

Gunnar cleared his throat, approaching my casket as he held up a clawed hand. "I think we should give him a minute. Maybe he can tell us all from the beginning." I nodded gratefully, staring at his claw pointedly. He smiled slightly, allowing it to shift back to normal. He still looked wary, as if not sure exactly what to make of all of this. After all, I had risen from the dead. Gunnar then literally lifted me out of the casket and set me on my feet. After stumbling on weak legs, he supported me over to a group of couches in a nearby alcove. Where a toasty fire was roaring. I fell down into the couch. Indie jealously, and very obviously, sat as close to me as possible. Othello sat in a chair in front of me, understanding Indie's territorial claim.

"It all began when a roaring drunk wizard," I pointed a thumb at my chest, "An Angel, and a Horseman of the Apocalypse walked into a bar..."

Their eyes widened and their jaws dropped further with each word, shaking their heads in disbelief and amazement as Othello backed up and clarified several points. Her version seemed to paint me as much more of a badass than my version did. Not how I saw it. I had been running from fire to fire with a leaky water bucket, trying to put out a raging inferno as someone else poured gasoline onto the flames.

I told them about the Academy stealing my powers, my parole officer, Gavin, working as a double agent and setting all my friends up to leave town. That elicited a dark growl from Gunnar, which was gently calmed by Ashley placing a soft hand on his knee. I told them how Gavin had even hurt Indie's mom when she wouldn't break up with me. Indie stiffened at that, a single tear spilling down her cheeks as she realized just how close to death her mother had been. I explained the source of my night terrors. The FBI arresting me. Othello busting me out. Gunnar grunted at that. Death, the Angels, the Demons, and of course, the Werewolves. Gunnar seemed particularly amused at mention of the wolves. Tory nodded with a grin, "He wasn't that tough. I slapped the shit out of him in the bar. Not even a challenge."

"I'd like to meet him." Gunnar said with a distant, menacing grin.

Indie was clutching my hand. "You make it sound so nonchalant, while Othello paints it as the scariest few days of her life."

A new, familiar voice spoke up from behind the couch. "Nate is too humble. He literally battled agents of Heaven and Hell after his own people stole his magic and tried to extort him to give up the Armory. And he *still* won. He's earned quite a reputation in certain circles."

Gunnar had jumped to his feet at the first word from the intruder's mouth, claws shifting entirely, and the threads on his clothes popping and snapping as his body began to mutate into partial wolf form. Everyone was glaring with lethal intent at the creature behind me. Misha sported red dragon claws and a hungry, eager smile. I held up a hand to calm everyone down, but was secretly proud of my friends. I didn't turn to look at him, speaking over my shoulder instead. "Shut up, Death. You're going to make me blush. Everyone, meet Death – the Horseman of the Apocalypse. A recent drinking buddy of mine, and generally a bad influence."

I then turned, gently applying pressure to Indie's hand in reassurance. She looked terrified. Everyone seemed to calm down a few notches as Death politely approached our gathering. "Don't worry. He's not on my list. His death was a ruse. Othello and I had to make it look legitimate." He waved a hand at our surroundings. Othello nodded guiltily, blushing slightly as Death smiled at her.

Hmm... *That* wasn't weird.

"My apologies for the discomfort this may have caused anyone." Indie grunted at the understatement. "This is merely a courtesy call. Checking up on my patient... and new friend." Death added the last with almost a questioning tone. I gave him a respectful nod.

The tension in the room slowly dissipated. But no one spoke, as if fearing what he or she was supposed to say or not say to such a feared legend. Death, with all the charm I had first seen in him from the guy at the bar, soothed everyone's concerns. Individually. He moved like a wraith from person to person, murmuring a private word or two to each of my friends. I don't know what was said, but he left each person as white as a ghost, yet also smiling at something only they knew. It was as if he had told them something that eased a hidden dam of emotions they had bottled up for years. As if he had given them peace of mind. The skin on my arms shivered as he approached Indie. She was close enough that I could hear. He also spent longer at her side than any of my other friends.

"As soon as I heard about Gavin's attack I rushed to your mother's side in the hospital in Colorado. She had been attacked by a Demon that he had sent. After seeing to her immediate safety, I decided that I needed to meet Nate, here. To judge his worth. To see what kind of enemy would push Gavin to cross such a line as attacking a peaceful, defenseless old woman. So, I went to the bar, Achilles Heel. I learned of his night terrors. His parents' murder. His bravery against the dragons. And much more that I'm sure he didn't realize he had shared. I have the gift of being able to draw out life stories from people. Then I was awed, as I watched him stand up to a very, *very* powerful bully. All because he found it necessary to find justice for his parents' murder. To fulfill a Blood Debt. He was a pillar of... righteousness, despite standing against a creature that hopelessly outmatched him. I wish I could have been half the man at his age... After that, I watched over your mother while she was in the hospital. Because Nate had impressed me... and *you* had impressed *him*. Be comforted in the fact that your mother will live to a ripe old age, dying of natural causes. In the distant future."

Then he stepped a polite distance back from all of us. I was dumbfounded. Indie's jaw was wide open. I touched her hand but she didn't respond, so I leaned closer. "I guess I'm as awesome as I think I am." Her eyes flashed towards me, as if just waking up. Then she leaned forward very aggressively and kissed me right on the mouth, wrapping her arms around me in a hug that hurt so bad it felt good. I patted her back as she rested her head on my shoulders, sobbing lightly, overwhelmed with joy at her mother's Guardian Angel – erm – *Horseman*.

Death cleared his throat. Everyone turned to face him, eyes filled with various flavors of appreciation and gratitude. "I hope that allayed any concerns you may have about me." Everyone nodded, so he continued. "As I just said, this is only a courtesy call. I received a request from a mutual friend." I squinted at Death, wondering what he was talking about. Then Charon appeared, nodding respectfully to me from his boat, drinking a beer. Luckily, he was keeping his face covered by his burlap hood. "He really thinks a lot of you," Death added.

"Well, I'd rather not meet him on official business any time soon. Again. Or you." I hoped Charon wasn't about to speak, or else all of my friends would find out what it was like to soil their pants. That voice was going to haunt my dreams. I just knew it.

Death nodded with a grin. "Agreed."

"How's Gruff?" I asked, curious about his horse.

"He's fine. He was... intrigued by you, and your connection to Grimm." Death arched a curious brow. "Is it merely a coincidence that..." he glanced to my friends, and then continued cryptically, "That you already have a horse to ride?" His emphasis on the last word made me shudder slightly, but I don't think anyone else understood his meaning. Except Othello, but her face was blank, giving nothing away. I was not going to become the Horseman of Hope. First off, it sounded cheesy. Second, it seemed like a horrible job to take Hope from the world at the End of Days. They had only been kidding with me, right? I shrugged, ignoring my friends' curious looks.

Death turned to my friends. "I have something to show all of you. Some people I would like to introduce you to." My shoulders tightened.

"That's probably not necessary—" I began nervously. My friends did *not* need to meet any of the other Horsemen.

Or Angels.

Or Demons.

"It was not a question," Death answered coolly, reminding me of my place.

Wow.

My friends nodded as one, intrigued. We climbed into Charon's boat, which seemed much larger than the first time I had ridden in it. I followed suit. "Just make sure you leave your hood up, Charon, and please don't speak. Your breath is literally fatal." He took another sip of his beer. I pointed at it frantically like a tattletale and looked at Death, who sat across from me. "You okay with our driver being drunk?" Death shrugged. Charon merely took another unconcerned drink as everyone climbed inside the boat. Then the world around us shifted between one blink of the eye and the next, and I found myself back on the River of Souls. My friends thought it really interesting. I merely felt tense.

Who wanted to meet my friends? Was this a trap of some kind? I mean, I really didn't know Death all that well. Was he kidnapping me and my friends? My unease began to build at an alarming rate as I thought of all the horrible things that might await us. After an indeterminable amount of time, my friends realized it was actually quite boring to float down the River of Souls. There were, after all, no sights. Just nothingness. Then a faint green haze abruptly appeared before our boat. I spotted towering statues on either side of the river, menacing creatures standing guard to what seemed like a large amphitheater.

They each depicted Cerberus, Hades' pet guard dog. The beast that both protected his realm and prevented a spiritual prison break. As I watched one of them, I was suddenly ninety-nine percent sure that it blinked. I flinched as I noticed a giant drop of drool fall to the river without a splash. My friends didn't notice, but Death shot me an amused smile.

As I turned back to strange sounds emanating from the amphitheater, I realized it was... *hopping*. Big band music blared from unseen speakers. And hundreds of people were dancing. I stared in curiosity as Charon rowed us up to an ornate pier. We came to a gentle stop and Death assisted the women out of the boat, but left Gunnar and me to fend for ourselves. He nodded respectfully at Othello, appraising her in a very hungry way. No way... She seemed to notice, blushing, but said nothing. I left *that* alone. It was none of my business.

Freak and let freak, I guess.

We entered what seemed like a banquet or dance hall. And I realized that it wasn't people dancing, but *souls*. And they were *everywhere*.

My mortal friends simply stared. The music quieted noticeably, but didn't stop, and the crowd of souls turned as one to watch the master of their domain and his guests enter the party. Talk about Red Carpet attention. Death cleared his throat. "I believe you said something to Othello about *not going down without one hell of a fight*. That you were going to *cause such a ruckus dying that Death himself will shake my hand and send me back with a farewell party to get rid of me*." I felt myself shrinking in embarrassment as I stared into the Horseman's eternal eyes.

Then he extended his hand. "Well, here's your party, and here's my handshake... friend," he said with a smile. I relaxed, and slowly reached out to shake it with a guilty grin, acknowledging the quote and his offer of friendship. Then the souls surrounding us bowed respectfully, some pointing at me with interest, before they began to step to the side to make room for us. They made an empty path across the length of the room between them, and at the end I saw two souls in particular facing the opposite direction. The crowd hushed and the two figures slowly turned.

My heart shuddered and then stopped.

"Mom, Dad..." I whispered.

Death caught me before I collapsed. Indie grabbed me by the shoulders, helping Death support me.

My mom and dad approached, slowly at first, my father looking proud, and my mother full of love and... concern. Glowing tears trailed her cheeks. "My son..." she whispered. Then they were floating towards me in a dizzying blur. They abruptly halted before me and I heard Indie sobbing softly as she continued to hold me up. My legs were jelly.

My dad gripped me by the shoulder, despite being a spirit. "It worked!" He exclaimed. I blinked, and then understood that he must be referring to my Maker ability. I held up a palm, and a ball of blue flame filled my palm as my vision was transformed with the familiar blue haze. My eyes were misty as I stared back with a weak smile. My dad grinned like only a scientist could. "We are so *proud* of you, my son." He turned to the crowd of souls. "MY SON!" He roared, lifting his hands. The resulting applause was deafening, shouts of glee rattling my brain. My throat was raw. My mother latched onto me, hugging me tightly, and I broke down, tears falling freely. My flame died and I hugged her back. Desperately.

You see, I never thought I would ever get the chance to do this again. Like all stubborn youths, I had rebelled against them, pushing them out of my life to pursue my own dreams with Plato's Cave. But it hadn't necessarily needed to be a mutually exclusive pursuit. I could have, and *should* have, pursued both. But you never discovered things like that until it was too late.

The *pain*.

The *guilt*.

The *sadness*.

The *joy*.

It *broke* my resolve.

"I'm so sorry," I whispered. "I almost lost it all. I wasn't there to help you. My own friend, Peter, betrayed me to rob the Armory. I don't know if that was why the Demon killed you, or if you would have been spared without him breaking in, but it's all my fault. I couldn't keep it safe. The Pandora Protocol is broken, and... whom you had stored inside is now free. I failed."

My mother leaned back with a curious frown. I looked at my dad, who also seemed nonplussed. "The Pandora Protocol?"

I nodded guiltily.

Then he shrugged. "That's not really a big deal. She's been free before."

I blinked. "*What?*"

"The Armory was just a ruse for the Academy's benefit. We needed something to attract their ire so they wouldn't notice what we were *truly* working on. We also needed a way to free you from their clutches. Hence, the gift we gave you. The power of a Maker. Without the traditional magic, they hold no sway over you, now."

I stared, dumbfounded, unable to speak, despite my mouth opening and closing several times. "You mean to tell me that all this was for *nothing*? The Armory wasn't *important*?" I was huffing, sudden rage coursing through my veins. Everything had been for nothing. The death, Othello being killed, Indie's mom being hurt.

For *nothing*.

They watched me, abashed. "It was the only way. Dark times are coming, my son. You need to be out of their control. We fear what the Academy may do in the years to come. We gave you the tools to stand on your own two feet as an independent. The world will need you in the years to come. My Maker," my mother added with a loving smile. "Oh, how I wish I could see Jafar's face right now." Her eyes gleamed maliciously.

My anger began to fade as I remembered that I was with my parents again. *Really* with them. And that was all that truly mattered. "Yeah, he wasn't too pleased about my power surge, or the fact that I'm now a Maker and not a wizard." I pondered that. How had they known that my magic would disappear? After all, if I gained the Maker ability yet kept my magic wouldn't I still have been under their control?

My dad seemed to sense my question. "The reason your power spiked upon our deaths is that the Maker seed needed to feed on magic in order to survive. A very large amount of magic. It was the only way to birth the gift inside you. How long did it take for the power to dissipate?" he asked, again, like a scientist.

"It didn't dissipate. The Academy cursed me."

My dad blinked, and then... well, he burst out laughing, clapping and hooting as he did a little jig of joy.

"What's so funny? I almost *died!*"

My dad merely wrapped me in a bear hug. "They had no *idea!*" he roared into my ear. "Cursing you caused your magic to deplete that much faster, making you immensely more powerful as a Maker than anything we could have done. Oh, I would *love* to hear Jafar explain this to his boss. Not only did he curse you, but he made your gift infinitely more powerful than we ever could have. He literally gave you an adrenaline shot for your Maker power. The seed had to feed on the magic much faster and intensely in order to survive, which made it grow exponentially faster than it should have on its own. You are now something that has never before walked the earth. A Maker far more powerful than any who has ever existed." He clapped in sheer joy again, pushing me away to arms-length and then pulling me back in with several slaps on the back. My mother finally shooed him away.

I managed to reply. "Yeah. If I can figure out how to use it reliably," I muttered. My friends were staring at me as if they had never seen me before. Death merely looked interested. I was now more powerful than he had thought. Which could be utilized by any who knew how to manipulate me. I instantly wondered how much I could trust the Rider, and again, whether he had been serious about me becoming a fifth Horseman of the Apocalypse. My resume had just beefed up considerably.

"Don't worry, my son. We left instructions at Chateau Falco. Everything we could discover on Makers. That was our real secret. What I said to the security camera after our death. You did see the video footage, right?" I nodded. "Good. Also, the entrance to the Armory at Temple Industries was only a secondary entrance. Which is why there was a seventeen-minute window. The primary entrance at Chateau Falco has no such restrictions. You should find the Armory, more or less, as you left it."

I couldn't believe it. "This... really was all for nothing, then. Me trying to protect the Armory from the summoner and his Demons." They nodded, their excitement slowly fading.

I turned away in an attempt to hide my rage.

I almost lost it.

Right there.

But I was a restrained, wise, utterly in control wiz... no, *Maker*.

Instead, I took a few deep breaths to regain my composure.

I was alive. I had a woman who loved me. Everyone was safe. And I had learned a lot about myself. I wasn't just a wielder of ancient arcane power. I was something else entirely now. When I had been pushed up against a wall without backup, magic, or money, I had persevered. Even as a penniless Regular. I found solace in that.

I suddenly realized what the most important thing in the world was.

It was something I'd never thought I'd have the chance to do.

I turned back to my parents, grabbed Indie's hand, and walked up to my mother. I scrubbed a tear from my cheeks. "Mother, Father, this is Indie. She is... very dear to me." Indie's eyes filled with tears, and even Gunnar grunted with overflowing emotions.

Life wasn't all bad. It was actually pretty *good*.

43

We had left the Underworld, or Hell, or wherever we had been taken, after a whole lot of story-telling. Death had shared his origin story with my friends. The same one I had heard in the bar. My mother ignored all of this and instead fussed over Indie like only a mother-in-law could. Giving her advice on managing my temperament. I rolled my eyes at some of her tips, but curiously found myself listening as some of it was actually quite insightful. I would have to stay on my toes from now on. Indie was gathering quite a bit of useful knowledge. My father slapped Gunnar on the shoulder and hugged Ashley upon hearing of their engagement. He also recognized the stone on the ring. It had come from one of the diamond mines I owned. The girls had all fawned over Ashley's rock, causing Gunnar to swell with pride. My father had been very interested to meet Misha and Tory, even more so at their abilities. He had never met either flavor of supernatural before. They remembered Othello, and looked slightly nervous at her inclusion in my club, no doubt remembering our past romantic dalliances. But everyone seemed more or less accepting of that particular past, and had moved on to more important topics. To my relief, even Indie seemed less concerned about Othello than before. She even thanked Othello for watching my back when everyone else had been absent.

Death and Othello had walked off to the side, speaking to each other silently as the rest of us continued to talk to my parents. *Curiouser and curiouser.* Othello had a slight spring to her step after that, but I left it alone. She would tell me if she wanted to. I had enough on my plate without sticking my nose in that beehive. But I guess they did have the whole *shared life experiences* thing going for them after Othello had died and come back. It was practically like meeting the in-laws. Indie seemed downright encouraging.

Before we left, I pulled Death aside. "Can you do me a favor?" He grinned in anticipation of what I might ask, nodding. "I need you to deliver something to a werewolf for me. You still have it? Like I asked?"

Death began to laugh. "*That's* why you wanted me to preserve Gavin's head. You're one cold bastard." He chuckled with approval. "You're *perfect* for our club." He clapped me on the back.

I neither agreed with nor denied his statement. "I promised the wolf I would avenge his mate. Seems a fitting way to give him absolution, and Gavin deserves it," I added with a growl.

"I'll take care of it."

"Oh, and put a ribbon on it."

He rolled his eyes. "Okay. You're welcome back anytime," he offered with a grin. Then he left us to say our farewells to my parents and the other souls.

We had then retreated to Chateau Falco, and were now sipping drinks before a large fireplace. Dean and Mallory had returned from their trips and joined us, as well as Raego, at Misha's insistence, and Agent Jeffries at Gunnar's insistence. After the shock of my death had been proven false, things went splendidly. We had shared tales back and forth, and I was informed of the latest developments in my city. Apparently, I had been dead for a few days now. Kosage had been caught lying his ass off to get me arrested in the first place, pulling strings he really shouldn't have tried to pull. No doubt influenced by Gavin, but no one seemed to believe his story of a concerned citizen providing him information on my guilt. Especially since said citizen could not be found. Jeffries had apparently found proof that Kosage had bribed a judge to get the warrant for my arrest, as well as blackmailing a few of the FBI Agents. All that in addition to the blackmail footage Othello had left in the file at the police station with him in drag and BDSM gear had basically shut down his career.

Even though no one could explain how I had escaped my cell and been kidnapped, they had no proof of anything else, and I hadn't been spotted at any of the recent crimes.

Also, I was allegedly *dead*. I couldn't wait to reappear at an upcoming Gala with Indie on my arm like nothing had ever happened. Jeffries finished his story of Kosage's downfall with a grin. "Sound good, Temple?"

"Oh, if anyone tries to pull me back into any of this again you can bet your ass I will hire every lawyer in town to eviscerate him. I would destroy every lawman's career... Except you, Jeffries. You're the only honest one I've met. Agent Wilson wasn't too shabby either."

Jeffries grinned, "I spoke with him. They won't continue their inquiry, even after you announce your resurrection, if anyone could even call it that anyway. They even pardoned you and Gunnar for the dragon ordeal a few months ago. Gunnar has been reinstated if he wants to be. If not, he will receive honors befitting his retirement."

I grinned at Gunnar's resulting smile. "I also need Agent Wilson to call and formally apologize to Indie for what his Agents did. Hanging up on her. Not letting me get my phone call."

Jeffries winked. "Done."

"Also, it seems a patrol horse found his way onto my property. Could you arrange for Xavier to be quietly and anonymously returned to the police force? No one needs to know what happened, and I will look down upon any negative consequences his handler receives."

Jeffries nodded, chuckling to himself. Everyone left. Except Indie.

We made up for lost time.

And more.

She seemed exceptionally motivated to remind me what a catch she was. She thoroughly exhausted me. As I lay in my bed, Indie sleeping peacefully beside me, I felt a tug at my soul. Curious, I got up and wandered the mansion.

After a while, I realized I was being drawn to my father's old study. I sat down in the chair, and spotted the note that I had already read. It had been found on my desk when we came back. It was from Achilles. *Come back any time. I want to talk to you about something.* I shivered at that. Maybe later. I began fiddling with a pen, wondering about the odd sensation that had drawn me here, and its sudden disappearance. Was this the primary entrance to the Armory my father had spoken of? Somewhere in this room? It made sense.

As if in response, a soft voice abruptly invaded my thoughts, sounding defeated and weakened. *I've returned, my host. Freedom wasn't what I thought it would be. So much pain and suffering in the world, and I fear more is yet to come. You will need me in the upcoming years. I have foreseen great devastation, and you stand at the forefront of it all. Your parents and I await your presence in the Armory whenever you are ready. I have granted them temporary access thanks to the Horseman's... encouragement. You will need training in your gift. Only we can teach you to become The Maker.*

Then the voice trailed off. I shivered. My parents resided in the Armory with Hope? No, not Hope. Pandora. Death had *encouraged* Pandora to grant them access?

Then another thought hit me.

Pandora hadn't elaborated if I was at the forefront of the impending storm because I was *fighting* it...

Or *causing* it...

I wandered back to bed, very, very concerned about both my new powers and the role I would play in the days to come...

*Turn the page to continue with Nate Temple in the prequel novella, **FAIRY TALE**—which also explains what Nate does to tick off the Brothers Grimm in book 3, **GRIMM**, so be sure not to skip it.*

FAIRY TALE (PREQUEL #0)

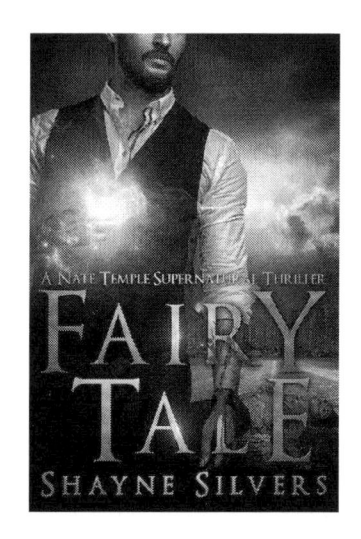

1

The chemical cocktail of hairspray and 1930's era musk cologne and perfume permeating the air of the old theater was enough to replicate the infamous Chernobyl reactor's explosion if anyone so much as *thought* about an open flame. The room was also notably warm and stuffy, transforming the flammable air into an almost physical entity despite the wheezing circulation of the aged air conditioning unit and ceiling fans weakly battling the noxious cloud. Not everyone in attendance was old, but it was fair to say that if the place did go *Kablooie* from the fumes, most relatives of the deceased would say *'Well, Gram and Gramps had a good run,'* and then carry on with their day.

But it wasn't just hairspray and perfume.

The air was also heavily laced with the recognizable scent of ink and paper.

Specifically, the pungent smell of freshly-minted Hundred Dollar bills.

Franklins.

C-Notes.

Cheddah.

You get it.

And there was enough to smell it, without seeing obvious pallets of cash lying out in the open, which meant it was a fair assumption that almost everyone had a fat stack in their pocket or resting in a nearby purse.

If one's nostrils were particularly acute, they might even smell the trace of aged money, the kind that was freshly dug up from the backyard or withdrawn from a dusty safe after a forty-year nap. Most of the elderly attendees trusted hard cash over the more modern methods of electronic financing also known as the nefarious wire transfer and its sneaky accomplice, the debit card.

The smell was comforting to me. Familiar.

I was no stranger to money myself, but I wasn't sporting a wad of cash.

The paddle in my hand spoke for itself.

Perfectly coiffed, industrial-grade hairpieces adorned the females in the crowd, interspersed with an equal number of shining bald heads that belonged to the gentlemen in attendance. The younger crowd of tech company billionaires, real estate moguls, and finance professionals made up the small change. No pun intended.

You could almost feel the raw hunger in the attendees' eyes as they leaned forward to stare at a rather small man in an ancient, wiry wool suit behind a podium on the stage. He stared back at us through coke-bottle thick glasses, politely barking numbers back at the crowd as this or that attendee waved a paddle to signify their interest in the item glistening from the center of the stage behind him.

I was at an auction house, and I was by far the youngest attendee here. Hell, I was fresh out of college a few years back. Practically a newborn in comparison.

I leaned back with a sigh, not interested in the current item.

The cool velvet chair felt pleasant in the sweltering humidity.

I took a slow meditative sip of the chilled wine I held in my hand, idly flicking the paddle back and forth in my other hand – out of view of the podium, of course. The hungry looking forty-something woman beside me caught my wandering gaze, and eyed me like a lion spotting a New York Strip on the African Savanna. I smiled back politely. Her grin morphed into a dark and promising invitation. I turned back to the stage, hiding my blush, hoping she understood my polite decline. My drink was probably the third one past what I should have consumed, but I was bored, it was a Tuesday, and I had nothing better to do for the evening. And the night was only halfway through.

My gaze continued to wander the room. It was an old movie theater that the auction house had rented for the occasion. The kind that had originally used reels and projectors. We were currently in one of three screening rooms. I looked up to see the old projector room overhead, currently retrofitted to shine light down on the stage. The building was entirely brick, both inside and out, and lent a quiet feeling of solidity – calmly and silently stating its age as a matter-of-fact, not to be outdone by whatever shiny new doodads were used in construction these days. It practically sniffed in disdain at its newly constructed brethren that were born on an almost daily basis. Those buildings screamed and yelled for attention.

Instead, this building sat stoic, confident in its superiority. It simply *Was*.

I liked it.

It was solid, and for some reason reminded me of home. My family was well-acquainted with age and old buildings in general. We were kind of an eccentric bunch, and had occupied St. Louis for quite some time, most of that as celebrities of one kind or another.

For better or worse.

The speaker interrupted my drifting thoughts.

"Our next item on the list is an old one. A book. But not just *any* book. The original

1812 first edition of *Kinder- und Hausmärchen*. Or better known in English as *Grimm's Fairy Tales*..." He stepped back to wave a liver-spotted hand at the book on display. It sat on a pedestal, limned by perfectly orchestrated ambient light. It looked holy. I stared at it intently, studying it with my magical senses. I couldn't get a good read on it from this far away, couldn't tell if it was glowing from the lighting or of its own power...

You see, I was a wizard. Came from a long line of them, in fact. But no one believed in magic these days. Which was just fine by me. Low profiles were key to our continued existence. Non-magical people – *Regulars* – and we supernatural folk – *Freaks* – had existed this way for quite some time now. And for the most part, it seemed to work out just fine.

Mostly.

Of course, there was the occasional Bigfoot sighting or demonic possession, but most Regulars shrugged these off as a trick of the light, too much to drink, or downright stress. Their denial was almost laughable. Except for the resulting murderers that got away scot-free as a result. That's actually where wizards typically stepped in. We were the unsanctioned police of the supernatural community. At least, it seemed to end up that way more often than not. It was more of a silent understanding among supernatural folks that wizards existed to slap the bogeyman on the wrist and say, *stop it.*

With extreme prejudice.

I could manipulate unseen energy from the world around me, tap into it, and use it as I saw fit. Whether to destroy or create. A lot of responsibility came with being a wizard. Having the power to destroy everything around you with a thought was pretty alarming, and older wizards spent the majority of their time making sure fledgling wizards were responsible with their abilities.

After all, with great power comes great responsibility. *Spiderman* taught us that. Young wizards spent years under a mentor – a family member if you were lucky, or a tutor assigned to you by the Academy if you weren't. The Academy was the bag of assholes generally in charge of wizards all over the world. They did things like making sure fledgling wizards were trained and deemed responsible enough to interact with the world without attracting attention, hurting innocents, or causing a war with any of the various other supernatural nations – werewolves, vampires, fairies, and other darker creatures of the night. They were firm in their version of justice and not known for their gentle, understanding nature. But like most groups of people with power, they weren't perfect. Politics was a magical power all in itself, and the Academy was not immune to its effects. Generally, I avoided any interaction whatsoever with the Academy.

It was safer that way. Stay under the radar. Don't rock the boat.

Regardless of wherever your training originated, all wizards had to learn mastery of themselves, their environment, and how to hide their abilities from the Regulars. Manipulating the very fabric of reality with your thoughts was freaking *cool*. But it was incredibly dangerous and had much larger consequences as a result. Being a wizard meant learning wisdom – when to use your power and when not to. To be a master of your mind and any emotions that may cloud your judgment. At one with the universe. Able to repel any and all distractions – no matter how compelling. The master of all sensory data—

A warm hand suddenly gripped my inner thigh, unabashedly saying *hello* to my naughty place.

I froze like a startled rabbit and almost squealed.

2

I instinctively glanced down and realized it belonged to the cougar sitting beside me. She was apparently done playing games. Not that I had known there *was* a game. Or that *I* was the game.

I downed my drink. "$250,000," I blurted, adjusting my leg so that her hand fell from my lap. She played it off expertly, chuckling as she shifted her grip to my arm in excitement – an act she put on for the crowd that had suddenly turned at my interruption of the speaker's explanation of the item.

I waved my paddle anxiously, not hiding the fact that I was beyond tipsy. I needed to keep this rapist off my jock, and the only way to do that was to keep everyone's eyes on me. And her. The number on my paddle did quite a bit to occupy everyone's disgust at my break in etiquette.

It was the number *1*.

Which meant that I was a highly respected and ancient member of the auction house. As in, their very first client. At least an *ancestor* of mine had been anyway. By default, that meant the number stayed with my family as long as we so desired. As long as we remained active.

Which my father did. Although this was my first solo trip, I typically tagged along with my parents on these excursions.

You could have heard a mouse let one rip. I doubted they did that sort of thing, but just imagine it. You would have heard it. Trust me.

I shrugged at the crowd, glad the attention was keeping me from being raped in public by the cougar. "Places to be. Debauchery to do." I elaborated in a higher-pitched voice than usual. The cougar's hand had squeezed my arm as if I was encouraging her.

"Arrogant prick," a gruff, younger voice growled.

"Shh. That's the Temple boy," the young girl on his arm chastised.

Murmurs filled the room. I ignored them, focused solely on silently and discreetly preventing the cougar from gripping my crotch again. She must have had an extra set of invisible hands that no one else could see.

Hey, it really wasn't that far-fetched in my world.

Before I could delve into my power to verify if she was a Regular or actually did have an invisible set of extra hands, the auctioneer cleared his throat in a disapproving response to my interruption. There were unspoken rules for places like this. Only heathens blurted out numbers. We weren't bidding on used cars. We collectively represented the 1% of society that everyone hated. I was only here by default, as my family had started one of the world's biggest tech companies within the city limits. But the glares I received very obviously informed me that even this was no excuse. Merely a look that categorized me as a worthless heir to a multibillion-dollar company.

Which would be true. Well, not the worthless part. At least in my biased opinion.

The auctioneer hadn't even gotten around to describing the book's history yet. "This is most unusual." He sighed in resignation at the frantic look in my eyes. "Alright. The bidding for the original *Grimm's Fairy Tales* opens at $250,000. Do I have a $255,000?" I remained active, fidgeting so that the cougar couldn't molest me further and flicking my paddle in order to stay at the top bid. Not many people were here for a book, but several men seemed intent to bleed me a bit, if for no other reason than to impress the women on their arms. I, on the other hand, was pretty-darned motivated to wrap up this purchase. The excitement of the crowd kept the cougar from anything too overt for the moment. I slapped her wrist away frantically, accidentally raising the bid. I groaned. Which only seemed to encourage her. Her hungry gaze met my panicked one, and I was surprised to see that she looked stone cold high. On something. I mouthed *later*, with heavy desperation. She grinned satisfactorily and her dozen hands stilled in victory. No longer playing defense, I focused on the item behind the speaker.

My parents had mentioned the book over dinner the night before. An old friend of theirs was putting it up at auction, and I had always been a heavy reader. Being the alleged original of *Grimm's Fairy Tales* had of course piqued my interest, but I was more interested in the previous owner deciding to get rid of it. He was a minor wizard, and wizards simply didn't get rid of old books. Ever. Unless it was to another wizard... but those transfers usually happened behind closed doors. You see, old books were like money to a wizard, and were most often not *entirely* what the cover depicted. It had been the original way to pass on information to other wizards before the invention of more efficient means of communication. Like texting. I was banking on this book being more than the cover depicted.

After ten minutes, I won the bid at a cool $300,000, and slapped the cougar's hands away again as I stood, deciding it was time to collect my book and leave. My eyes tracked the security guards carting my new book backstage. The cougar's inebriated eyes followed me hungrily, but I ignored her. As I approached the line to the table to settle the bill I felt a ripple in the air whisk past me, straight towards the backstage area as if someone had brushed up against me in passing. I glanced at the curtains, saw them shift, and then they fell back into place without anyone else noticing. I harnessed the power of my birthright out of instinct, probing the air around me but I sensed nothing within my immediate vicinity. I tensed, suddenly nervous for some reason. What had that been?

I blinked, waiting cautiously, but nothing else happened.

Maybe it was just an air vent kicking on. I relaxed, chuckling softly under my breath. I was jumping at shadows. How drunk was I?

As I waited in line I heard muffled conversation from behind the curtain. Then a grunt and the telltale smell of copper filled the air. Well, telltale to me since I was still holding my magic.

Hello, *wizard*.

I was about to dart through the curtain when a pair of familiar hands latched onto mine and yanked me past the curtains all on their own. I suddenly realized I had fallen for the con. It was dark backstage, and it took me a second for my eyes to adjust. I heard a surprised grunt but couldn't pinpoint the source. The cougar stood before me, giggling and panting. My eyes were wild as I stared at the cougar, trying to look behind her and gather my bearings. She apparently didn't like my wandering gaze.

She abruptly let go of my arm and tore open her blouse, exposing a very impressive set of knockers, sans bra. She reached out again, latched onto my shoulders, and tugged me closer as if she literally couldn't wait a second longer for me to ravage her. I shoved her away, fueled by the magical power coursing through my veins. What kind of half-assed robbery *was* this? She stumbled a few feet away and I had time to notice something. Two guards lay atop each other on the floor. The man on top was covered in blood and I watched as he let out his last breath. The man below was panting and weakly calling for help in panicked gibberish. I flicked my gaze up to see a silhouette nab the book I had just bought from the cart, turn to face me from over the cougar's shoulder, and then grin sadistically. Then he blurred – literally – into motion, and I felt a familiar rush of air zip past me, knocking me on my ass. I momentarily sensed power of some supernatural flavor but it was gone before I could react.

I rolled to my feet and tried to blindly lash out at where I thought the murderer's ankles might be, but missed. Instead, I caught a glimpse beyond the fluttering curtain to see my outburst hit an elderly lady standing in the line I had just vacated. She collapsed, shrieking in pain as she fell, most likely with a shattered hip or knee.

Then all hell broke loose.

I turned back to the cougar to verify she wasn't about to brain me. After all, she had tackled me back here. She had to be in on it. Or just experiencing a level of horny I had never known existed. She was holding her throat with a look of surprise and terror on her face. Then I saw why. A whole lot of blood leaked out from beneath her fingertips and had liberally painted her bare chest crimson. The second she pulled her fingers away arterial blood sprayed all over my coat and neck. I had turned my shoulder just in time to avoid my tank getting stained. I glanced over my shoulder, eyes wide, knowing it was too late to save her. I knew this was an image I would never be able to remove from my memory. She collapsed to her knees, and kicked a few times before lying still.

I could hear the auctioneer nervously trying to calm down the crowd outside the curtains, shouting for everyone to remain in their seats. It didn't sound like it was working, the crowd's volume steadily rising, amplified by the continued shrieking of the elderly woman on the ground. My sluggish brain suddenly informed me that I was standing over three dead bodies and I had just broken an older woman's hip a few feet away. She continued screaming, but no one had burst backstage yet. I rushed over to the dead security guards, shoving off the top body. It was just a kid. Now a dead kid. Amazingly, the man below wasn't dead, but he was getting his breath back and gearing up to roar in terror. I frantically cast my power deep into his mind, calming down the rush of adrenaline flooding his veins before he could alert anyone beyond the curtains.

He quieted instantly, eyes landing on my face in puzzlement. "What happened?" I whispered, knowing I didn't have a second to spare.

"The shadows came to life! Unfolded like the Grim Reaper himself and swallowed up Jake. It was his first day on the job, and now he's gone. It was a monster! A *monster!*"

"Monster?" I whispered feeling a slight chill down my spine. I had run into plenty of supernaturals, but hadn't been able to accurately identify the thief... no, *murderer*, I corrected, my gaze hardening. One who grinned sadistically after a double homicide.

The guard's eyes riveted on my face as I checked his head for wounds. He would be fine. "Yes! A demon of the night. It was the devil himself," he declared vehemently.

I met his eyes, locking gazes in an attempt to impart trust and honesty. The booze and adrenaline was beginning to make me spin a bit. "I believe you."

His brain seemed to kick back into security guard mode. "Who are you?" he whispered, thick eyebrows furrowing.

"A concerned bystander. Now, what did he want?"

He nodded in delirious acceptance of my vague answer. "The book. He spoke from the shadows. Said if we gave him the book we would live. Jacob hesitated and the creature... *laughed*. Then he exploded out of the shadows in a flash of blades, and the next thing I knew I was covered in blood and pinned on the ground. Jacob's body on top of me. Then... *Oh no!* What am I going to tell his parents? I *failed* him..." He sobbed.

I placed a palm on his chest and pushed a bit more of my pulsing magic into my fingertips before casting it deep down into his grieving heart. "Rest now, my friend. You did all you could. I'm sure of it." The man's eyes widened into a euphoric sensation of peace, eyes dilating. "You never saw me," I whispered. Then he shuddered as he passed out. Sounds from out front were growing more hectic, and I knew it was only a matter of time before they came backstage.

And I couldn't be seen. I had to get the book back. Avenge the murdered cougar and security guard.

I cast a spell around myself to make me unnoticeable – not invisible, I'm pretty sure that's impossible – and crept around to the other side of the room, remaining backstage to avoid the chance of detection. Then I exited the building, one destination on my mind.

3

I shambled down the street, keeping my eyes mostly open, and my magic ready. My adrenaline had died down a bit, but I was still on edge, which seemed to only increase the effects of the alcohol in my system. Still, the walk to my nearby destination from the auction house had helped out a bit. My coat and neck were still covered in blood, but it was dark so I felt safe from prying eyes. I wasn't too far from downtown and tonight's chaotic baseball game against the Cubs. But the night had remained fairly quiet so far; meaning people were still at the game.

Extra innings? Against the *Cubs*? I grunted in disgust.

I dazedly stumbled over a bit of trash that I briefly thought looked like a gorilla-vampire hybrid's tentacle, and almost let loose a panicked blast of fire, my pulse doubling in a second. I took a deep calming breath, slapped my cheeks to wake up a bit, then kept walking, glancing around to make sure no one had noticed. But I was blessedly alone. No one was tailing me. Then again, as long as they weren't flying a helicopter, I probably could have missed them.

I could think of only one thing to do in my mad escape from the auction house. Find out why the book was worth a double homicide, even though I was pretty sure the murders verified my original thoughts. The book was legit. But I needed more specific proof. A lead. Which meant I needed to pay the previous owner a visit. Maybe that would lead me to the murderer.

My parents had been friends with the prior owner of the book, Alistair Specter Silverstein.

Yep, the initials weren't lost on me. Must have been a rough childhood.

Alistair's conversation with my father was how I had heard about it going to auction in the first place. And I knew where he lived, having sat in the car once when my dad went to pick something up from his home. My eidetic memory came in handy like that. I remembered things. Practically *all* things. It annoyed my friends, Peter and Gunnar, to no end, which I exploited at every opportunity. After all, what were friends for if not to annoy?

As far as anyone else was concerned, this was just a rare book. Nothing dangerous about it. But it *was* an original edition, and original editions of books were known to sometimes have extra sections or secrets that the rest of the world knew nothing about.

After tonight, I was pretty damn sure this was the case.

I rounded a corner and saw the target brownstone a few doors down as I continued walking. A car was idling in the street, double-parked right in front of the house. That wasn't good. I was only fifty feet away when a silhouette abruptly exited the front door with a phone to his ear. It was too late for me to stop without looking too obvious, so I casually slowed my pace, fumbling for a cigarette. The person stood in the shadows for a second, speaking urgently, scanning the night. It seemed I had caught Alistair heading out for an evening stroll. The figure took a few more steps as I fumbled the cigarette out of my pack and tucked it into my lips, discreetly studying his silhouette. The figure's eyes locked on me as a lamplight struck his very young Nordic face, and highlighted his very powerfully built frame. Alistair was an old man. This guy wasn't.

He froze.

I froze.

Then I took a slow, sneaky step backwards. And tripped, landing on my ass.

"Don't even think about it, Nate," he called out as I climbed to my feet, readying for a rapid escape. I stopped.

"Nate?" I answered in a gruff voice, trying to sound confused as I lit my cigarette with a thought.

"What other billionaire would be walking around in a Captain America transition tank and a sports coat," he sniffed the air, "covered in blood, wearing a god-awful fedora?" I began to stammer an excuse in my sneaky stage voice. "And lighting a cigarette with magic?" He added like an uppercut. I winced. "Yep. *Fatality!*" He growled in a dramatic declaration, grinning.

I scowled back for good measure. "Damn it, Gunnar. What are you even doing here? Did you hear about the auction? How did you find his place so quickly?" I began shrugging out of my coat, suddenly reminded of all the blood, thanks to Gunnar's powerful sense of smell. What had I been thinking? I looked like Jack the freaking Ripper. I scrubbed my face and hands, careful to make sure I cleared away any trace of blood on my body. Gunnar was most likely not alone, and I doubted his partner would take well to me covered in blood. I tossed the coat into a nearby trashcan as we strolled towards each other. I didn't try to hide my annoyance as we gripped forearms. He was my childhood friend, practically my brother.

And he was a closet werewolf (so, of course he could smell the blood covering my coat) who currently worked for the FBI. He was one of the few people in the city who knew I was a wizard. We kept each other's secrets. Had for years.

He cocked his head. "Auction? I'm here about a noise complaint. And *please*, take a step back." I did. "Okay, another." I growled and stepped into his personal space instead. He rolled his eyes, waving a thick forearm in front of his face. "Your breath literally just made my eyes water. How drunk are you right now?"

I furrowed my brows haughtily. "Since when are noise complaints handled by the FBI? Is this a rookie hazing?"

Gunnar shrugged. "When noise complaints involve multiple gunshots. And when it's at the residence of a man who is currently being watched for allegedly trafficking illegal goods across state lines." He looked back at the house. "Well, *was* being watched for trafficking illicit goods. Looks like one of his customers wasn't satisfied. He went and got himself all dead. And here you are... obviously familiar with this now-dead, alleged criminal," he intoned, rubbing the stubble on his jaw thoughtfully.

"What?" I snapped haughtily, dropping my cigarette to the street in my drunken moment of melodrama. I quickly bent over to grab it and lost my balance, shifting to land sideways on my hip. Which didn't feel great.

But it had the added benefit of saving me from being neatly chewed in half by a dozen little bullets that abruptly whipped past my ear, like a swarm of ravenous mosquitoes. Gunnar dropped to his knees, grabbed me by the shirt, and tossed me behind one of the nearby trees lining the street. Splinters of wood shattered the trunk as more bullets rained down on us. Another agent came running around the side of Alistair's house, most likely Gunnar's partner. His chest was instantly pounded by a barrage of bullets, knocking him into a dumpster. He didn't get back up. Gunnar howled in fury – and when I say howled, I mean *Howled*, capital H – fists flexing into white, furry claws as he began to shift into his giant wolf form, ignoring the pistol on his hip. Werewolves were fast, deadly, and more resilient to pesky things like bullets. I grasped his forearm, trying to get his attention as a new noise filled the muggy night.

Tires squealed as a car rounded the corner from the nearby intersection at the other end of the street, flashing red and blue police lights as it barreled towards us. A form peeled itself from the shadows across the street blurring directly in front of the car faster than humanly possible. Well, that was that. Mr. Gunman had just become a vehicular manslaughter victim.

But it didn't play out that way. The man spun and slammed a fist down on the driver's side of the hood as the brakes locked up. The car instantly crunched down as if hit by a boulder from on high and flipped up into the air.

Straight towards us.

I threw up a last second sheet of dense air, angling it over my head as I used a second boost of power to haul the hulking werewolf out of harm's way. The car slammed right into Gunnar's idling car – which saved us from becoming pancakes – and careened off to slam off my shield and rebound into the neighbor's house just behind us. The car smashed through the front door, leaving the undercarriage facing the street as it rested on its side. Before it had even stopped moving, another tirade of bullets hammered into it, igniting the fuel tank. Then it exploded. The shield I had thrown quenched most of the flames, but the force of the explosion mercilessly tossed us into another tree, luckily keeping us out of the line of fire. I groaned at my bruised side, but Gunnar was already on his feet, still half-shifted into his werewolf form.

A car door slammed shut and then screeching tires filled the night. The super-fast super-villain was making his super-escape.

"Not today, bitch." I growled.

Gunnar's eyes were wide, claws somehow on his pistol. "He killed my partner. And I didn't even see anything to shoot! What the *hell* was that?" he literally growled.

I ignored the question. "We need wheels." I glanced at his car and scowled. It wasn't going anywhere. The doors were effectively welded into the frame. I spotted a moped by Alistair's front step. Without hesitating I ran up to it, sensing Gunnar behind me, still growling angrily under his breath the whole way. I saw the keys dangling in it and grinned, turning to Gunnar. He had returned to his human form, and was pulling out his radio to call for backup. I smacked it out of his hands and plumb forgot who and *what* I was dealing with.

A very pissed off werewolf FBI Agent who had just lost a partner. His eyes were smoking chips of glacial ice. "Easy, Lassie! We need to catch them!" I coaxed him down.

"I was calling in backup, you idiot!" He flexed his fingers, eyes roving the sidewalk for the radio.

"No. That was not human. This one's on us. Let's go. You're driving. I'm sloshed."

He hesitated for all of a second. "Fine, but... no one can ever know about this." He sounded resolute. The law was important to Gunnar. He was rigid with his rules and didn't tolerate vigilantism well.

"You can put it in your report that you lost your radio and pursuit was the wisest alternative. They'll be fine with it."

"Not that. The fact that we are about to pursue some freaky-fast monster on a moped." He smirked idly, but I knew that what we were about to do bothered him deep down.

"Oh. Right. Fine. Less talky. More drive-y."

He hopped on and revved all 5 horses of the moped's vigilante battle cry. I jumped on, hugged his back, and cringed at our piggyback ride of a pursuit car. Luckily, I could hear sirens in the distance, and I could still see the taillights of the fleeing car, which was apparently abiding by the speed limit to avoid detection. If we ever caught up to them, they would never see us coming.

Which would be their last mistake.

We tore after them at the intimidating speed of 25 miles per hour, straight into *Ballpark Village*.

4

Traffic and the nearby sirens were our saving grace. Despite our speed limitations, I was able to keep the attacker's vehicle in our sights, and it was actually beneficial to have a moped. We were able to bypass the bumper-to-bumper traffic caused by the mass exodus of Redbird gear leaving the Busch stadium. Drunken yuppies and college coeds filled the streets in every direction, completely halting traffic, despite the hundreds of horns wailing their frustrations.

The attacker quickly seemed to realize the flaw in his escape route as he was finally forced to slam on the brakes. The doors suddenly popped open and three forms darted out of the vehicle and into the crowd, moving together like a pack. *Three?* We chugged right up to the car and hopped off, sprinting after them as the moped crashed into the fender of their getaway car. *Take that, dastardly villains!* It was quite simple to chase them, because the attackers were the only ones not wearing red. Gunnar and I raced after them, slamming into the crowd of drunks.

"Easy, Bro!"

"Hey, you stupid fuck!"

"It's a Cubs' fan! Look at his shirt. Get him!"

I glanced down and quickly realized that my Captain America tank did indeed look similar to a Cubs logo at passing glance. Especially to this mob. Judging by their reaction, the game hadn't ended well for St. Louis. I picked up my pace, carefully using magic to forcefully clear a pocket of space around us as we tore after the attackers. This elicited more yells and growls of angry Cardinals fans. I heard a veritable lynch mob forming as we began to slow down due to the sheer number of people filling the crowded streets. The only good thing was that the attackers were slowing also, but Gunnar was almost near enough to grab one of them, having not drawn as much attention as me since he hadn't been pegged as a Cubs' fan. Through a gap in the crowd, I managed to spot a clear shot at one of the fleeing suspects. Without hesitating, I cast a quick non-lethal spell and threw it his way, beaning him good. He stumbled a bit but didn't slow. They momentarily disappeared from my view as the crowd swallowed me up.

Someone latched onto my arm but I managed to throw him off. I heard Gunnar snarling at the crowd, but at least he managed to gain a few more precious steps. Through a gap in the swarm of *Red Nation* gear, I saw him lash out with his claws and manage to brush the hoodie of one of the attackers. A gunshot cracked the night. The kid in the hoodie spun faster than humanly possible – a blur of shadows – and struck Gunnar in the jaw, knocking him back twenty feet. That's the last I saw of the chase.

A crowd of bodies moving like a hive mind pinned me to the ground, one or two fists striking me in the stomach, and then an explosive fist connected with my schnoz. My gaze flickered for a moment as my face erupted in fire, but my nose is made with cartilage of justice, and doesn't break easily. I tensed against more strikes as I heard bullhorns and cops swarming the crowd. Lucky for all of us, really. Otherwise I would have had to resort to using magic to avoid being beaten into a pulp, which wouldn't have lasted long for me. There were simply too many of them. As the bodies were torn free from my immediate vicinity, I managed to sluggishly assess my surroundings. Gunnar was nowhere to be found. I felt the cool click of handcuffs on my wrist, but didn't struggle. A platoon of police officers was handcuffing a dozen of the more drunken members in the crowd. I began arguing that I wasn't part of the problem.

"You're all part of the problem. Fucking hooligans. But don't worry. We've got lodging for the night covered." Then he wrestled me to my feet and slammed me into the backseat of a squad car. The door thudded closed in my face.

Gunnar was gone, hopefully unhurt.

The attackers were gone.

Alistair was dead.

The security guard, the handsy cougar, and FBI agents were all dead.

I didn't have my book.

And I was about to visit the hallowed halls of the St. Louis Drunk Tank.

5

The clanging of steel doors reverberated through my skull like a tightening vise.

I groaned, rolling over to my feet from lying on the steel bench. Other hungover groans mimicked mine as my roomies protested the loud noise. "He's right this way, Master Temple," a respectful voice offered. I groaned even louder at that, listening to the familiar *click-clack* of impeccably-polished dress shoes approaching the cell. They sounded like arrogance. Deserved arrogance. "Step back." The gruff voice snapped at us vagrants. More grunts ensued. I looked up, my skull throbbing, and met the very cold, hard, disappointed stare of my dear old dad. He snarled wordlessly before nodding at the guard and then turning on a heel. I stood on shaky legs and followed him out the open cell door. At least he had bailed me out ahead of my scheduled release. I paused to turn back to the cell as the officer slammed the door shut. I gripped the bars, searching for my new friend, and... found Jesus.

Heh.

I guess what they say is true. A lot of criminals find Jesus in jail. I met his gaze. "It's been real, Jesus." I pronounced his name with the *Hay-Zeus* Hispanic inflection. "Good luck with Trixie and your upcoming turf war." Jesus – one of my sleepover buddies from the cell – grunted in confused acknowledgement, no doubt wondering how I knew any of that information. He had spent an hour literally sobbing on my shoulder last night, telling me all about his problems. For a gangster, he was a surprisingly emotional cat.

Layers like an onion, that Jesus guy.

I signed some papers and accepted my stuff from lockup. My dad stood in the lobby, tapping his foot impatiently. At least mom wasn't here, too. I stepped up beside him. We both turned our shoulders instinctively, barring our words from the officers.

"Explain. It's all over the news, but I'd rather hear firsthand why one of my good friends is dead at the scene of what looks like a war-zone, the book we discussed the night before was stolen at an auction, and why you were arrested for starting a riot at the Cardinals' game only minutes away from his house. I have a feeling the news might have missed some connections. Which is the *only* good thing about this situation." His eyes roamed the room cautiously. "Especially when magical essence still taints the air at all three locations."

"Sounds like you got it all down pat. I'll just be leaving then."

"No. You. Will. Not." His arm barred my attempted exit, and I knew the cops subtly watching us would toss me back in the cell at even a murmur from St. Louis' most powerful industrial tycoon. Whether I was his son or not.

"I went to the auction. Bought the book. Things get hazy after that—"

"Because you were roaring drunk?" he asked, face tight with another helping of disapproval.

I rolled my eyes. "Yes. Prohibition's over. You can drink at 21 years old now. Though it all went to hell after we gave women the right to vote. Brave new world, Pops." I growled. His gaze smoldered. "Fine. After I won the bid, some... *thing* broke into the auction, killed a guard and a woman, and then stole the book."

"And the money used to purchase the book?" he asked, voice heavy with an altogether different question than the one spoken aloud. He didn't give a damn about the money. This was one of his *tests*. After an entire childhood of enduring his hidden underlying conversations and subliminal tests, I had already spent considerable time in the Drunk Tank considering this.

"I propose we get our legal counsel to... *encourage* the auction house to match my 'donation' amount and transfer it to the estates of the victims' families."

My dad closed his eyes and nodded slowly, letting out a satisfied breath. "That is good. Exactly right, Nate." I opened my mouth but he held up a finger. "But you couldn't leave it alone at that. You went to Alistair's house."

I nodded. "Yes. Couldn't find the murdering thief so I went to Alistair's home to question him about the book. And whom do I find? Gunnar. He was answering a report of gunshots. Alistair was already dead when we got there. But the killer was still alive and well. He started World War Three. Killed Gunnar's partner, a few other agents, and almost us too. We survived – barely. Then pursued them. We ended up at the Cards' game. Pursuit turned into a riot and we lost them, and I got arrested for being drunk in public and inciting a riot. Or at least being involved. They thought I was wearing a Cubs' shirt." I muttered, tapping my now-ripe Captain America tank top for emphasis.

"As if you would ever do something so stupid," he cracked his first faint smile. I couldn't help grinning slowly. My headache was fading, which was good, although I was still extremely hungover. I needed to shake it off. I had a lot to do today. "Gunnar told me the second half. I just needed the full picture. And now you will leave it alone to the authorities. It's past time for you to find something productive to do with your time." He took a breath before continuing. "Temple Industries needs—"

I held up my hands. "No. I've already told you. It's not happening. I'm not cut out for that kind of life."

His eyes squinted in quiet frustration, and I sensed him slowly gathering power about him, no doubt to teach me a quick lesson, but he released it a moment later. None of the cops seemed to notice, but my arms pebbled at the sudden surge of my father's power and its abrupt discharge. "Later. We'll speak of this later. When you've sobered up."

"Yeah. Much, much later. I've already told you Dad. I appreciate the offer, but it's not for me. You need someone who can do a credible job, someone who would enjoy it. That's not me." He held up a hand.

"Like I said, we'll discuss this later. Gunnar is waiting outside. For your mother's sake, please let this go. You've done enough. Leave it to the authorities."

I nodded. I sure would. I would leave it to Gunnar. And provide him pro bono assistance, as was my civic duty. My dear old Dad didn't need to know about the tracking spell I had managed to tag one of the thieves with last night. Gunnar would have to accept my help when he found out I was the only one who knew how to find the bastards.

My dad rolled his eyes, not believing me for a minute. After all, I was his flesh and blood, and he too had been a pretty rebellious young wizard at my age. "At least be careful. Gunnar might need your help on this one. But that doesn't mean you need to be reckless about it. Surely a barely-competent wizard and a werewolf with a badge can handle three punk kids." He muttered the challenge over a shoulder, striding out the front door to a gleaming black Aston Martin. A solidly muscled, silver-haired, old school sailor-type in a tailored grey suit opened the car door, closed it behind him, and then climbed into the driver's seat. I only caught a partial view of his weathered, bearded face, but I didn't recognize him. New guy? They pulled away, and I spotted Gunnar just outside. I exited the building and was struck in the retina by the sun, eliciting a pained grunt.

"No *Time-Out*? He didn't ground you?" Gunnar teased.

"Hilarious. I won't even comment on your finally learning the command to *Stay*."

"You just did. And he didn't command me. I'm not a guard dog, although if anyone needs one it's you." I grinned. "So what's next? Any wizardly leads you can give me?"

"Now I show you how to catch these fucks."

"I'm on leave after the fiasco last night. Three deaths is a big blow for the FBI." He looked haunted.

I patted him on the shoulder, suddenly reminded of the reality of our situation. "I'm sorry about your partner. We *will* avenge him."

"You know, as good as that sounds right about now, that's exactly the reason we have cops. Vigilantes are just another form of criminal," he recited as if reading a textbook.

I rolled my eyes as he led me to his vehicle. "At least give me a ride and I'll tell you why this one will require a bit of assistance outside their... *jurisdiction*." He complied and we piled into his government-issued vehicle. He pulled out into traffic and I directed him towards Alistair's house again. His grip on the wheel tightened as I told him about the tracking spell and the fact that at least one – if not all – of the thieves was some flavor of Freak. "You saw what he did to that car full of agents. He shut it down with a slap to the hood. You'll need me. And, if I have to hold their location for ransom, I'll do it. The consequences will be on your shoulders."

His grip on the steering wheel suddenly tightened further as white fur blossomed where his skin had been and a neat set of black razor-sharp claws punctured the leather. "What do you need me to do?"

"Drive, bitch." I smiled, feeling marginally better.

He did. A few moments later, my phone rang. I looked down at the screen and groaned, cursing my dad. "Hey, mom."

Gunnar almost lost it. I listened, waiting for her to rip me a new one. "Dinner plans. I'm making drumsticks!" She cheered, banging pots together in the background. This no doubt meant that our cook was making drumsticks and my mother was being a general nuisance in her proximity.

I blinked. "Tonight?"

"Yes," she answered happily. "Oh, I almost forgot. Your father told me you're spending the day with Gunnar. He's more than welcome. In fact, I insist."

"I don't know. I'm really busy."

"Nonsense. Your father told me you would have your project wrapped up by this evening and that you had already told him you would be here. Nice try. You can't surprise me. I'm smarter than you. I *made* you. You'll always be beneath me," she teased.

I grumbled several things under my breath that one should never say about their parents.

"It will have to be really late. I have an appointment."

"You don't have a job. I'll see you at nine. Gunnar too."

"Mom—" I began.

"Talk to you soon!" Then she hung up. Gunnar roared with laughter.

"Just drive, Scooby." I fumed, mentally rearranging my schedule to murder some murderers in time to make it to dinner with my parents.

Priorities. One doesn't cross their super-powerful wizard mother.

She could turn me into a toad out of spite.

6

I sat in a makeshift circle in the living room of Alistair's home. Luckily, the place was devoid of federal agents, the murder scene having already been processed the night before. Gunnar remained outside. I wanted to limit his exposure to what I was about to do next. I had the location of the thieves, but I still didn't know what flavor of supernatural they were. Or what the theft and murder was really all about.

Hence my circle…

You see, Alistair was a wizard with minor magical talents. He acquired items and then sold what he didn't want to keep for himself. Most of these items had a magical connection, which was how my father had met him. They had consummated several deals over the past few years. But someone with only minor magical talents like Alistair would need assistance to safely contain certain items he might stumble upon, let alone verify, some of the more dangerous items. He needed help. Which was why I had been sure he had some kind of assistant.

A Freak on a leash, to be more accurate.

And after a few minutes digging through his office I had hit pay dirt. A neatly-wrapped book lay carefully tucked inside a hidden alcove behind one of the bookshelves. Discarding the wrapping, I found it was a summoning book – complete with a bookmark on a certain page that showed how to call a librarian sprite in exchange for – *erm* – well, not to put too fine of a point on it, but *favors*… of the *coital* nature. Gross, but payment was payment.

Magic was frequently ritualistic. Like math. Perform a certain set of actions and get your result. It saved on energy, allowing wizards to tap into powers they might not personally be able to handle on their own. Which meant that they were also very dangerous. Anyone with the instructions could duplicate a ritual. Which was why we coveted – hoarded even – magical texts. This was what had set off the alarm bells in my head about Alistair selling a book in the first place. It was out of character. If the book had power, he would have sold it to another wizard. Unless it was so dangerous that he didn't want his name associated with it out of fear of what the Academy might think.

Or it was just a book. But given the unique nature of the title, and the fact that it was obviously selling at an auction, meant that it was indeed, an old book – which were typically Trojan horses for secret power or knowledge – leading me back to my first thought. It should have been given to the Academy or sold to another wizard.

I had prepared the spell more or less identical to the guidelines, but part of the page had been faded from frequent use, and no doubt Alistair had it memorized after so many years. So I improvised. I called out the True Name of the creature. Three times.

Now, names are a dime a dozen. You can mutter a different name at each bar if you were fishing for a wild night, but at birth everyone was given a very specific name from two people who loved you unconditionally. Your parents put a lot of thought into what they were going to call that burbling creature with the drunken stare. You. It meant something to them, and over the years, you learned it was yours. You associated with it. For better or worse. Grew into it. Made it your own. It's your True Name.

And it has Power. Capital P.

Give the right person your True Name and they could do all sorts of things. Mainly in Supernatural circles, but it worked with anyone. It bound things to listen when their True Name was called. Especially in a circle designed to trap them. They would hear it the first time, feel a pull the second time, and then be forcibly drawn the third time. After that, it was up to sheer strength of will, and the preparation of your circle to keep them there. If not, well, you might just annoy them a bit. Forcing them to stop their day by ringing their doorbell three times in a row tended to bother creatures of all dimensions.

The name struck the spell, and I snapped Alistair's existing circle to life with a small channeling of my will. And a hefty addition of magic.

You see, circles were vitally important. They acted as a containment field for magical power. Energy filled every particle of organic matter, including air, and could either amplify or nullify certain magical actions. So, when summoning something, you wanted to make very sure that you set up a limited environment. You didn't want to accidentally let loose on the world what you were summoning. Some of these creatures weren't all that nice, after all. Or more literally, they were perfectly *nice*, but their definition of *nice* meant 'neatly slicing up any and all organic matter in its immediate vicinity.'

To-may-toes, to-mah-toes.

Also, at this point you had effectively interrupted their perfectly pleasant day, so they weren't in the most conversational of moods.

I felt the energy around me tug my soul – a bit similar to mild indigestion – and then with a puff of sparkling fairy dust, a drop-dead bombshell appeared before me.

She was silver-skinned with long, straight white hair, and was stacked like a dreamy pinup girl.

And she was stark *nekkid*.

All twelve inches of her.

My brain went all sorts of adolescent on me at seeing the naked female anatomy in its entire glorious splendor. Even though she was only a foot tall, she was perfectly proportionate, and definitely an adult despite her height.

"Wow. You sure got the short end of the stick with Alistair." I paused. "No pun intended." I assessed her thoughtfully. "You let him... *hit that*? In exchange for verifying his collections?" Then a thought hit me. "How does that work, exactly? You're um... tiny."

Tact was not a gift of mine.

The spritely girl glared back, her full silver lips peeling back in a snarl of long needle-like teeth. I tensed. Well that certainly killed the sexy factor. She shimmered and was abruptly my height, her svelte proportions transitioning seamlessly to her new size. But without the needle teeth. Then she shifted back to her true twelve-inch form. "I adjust," she answered with a lilting voice.

"Oh. I guess that makes sense."

"Where is—" she froze, sniffing the air. Then her fangs reappeared between her silver lips. "You killed him."

Then she sucker-punched me.

Metaphysically. Which is worse.

She didn't even move her physical body. I came to my senses a few moments later spread-eagled on the ground, blinking back stars in my vision. Bars of solid light pinned my wrists and ankles to the ground. I began to struggle, but to no avail. Then I realized that I also couldn't speak. Something was gripping my jaw shut. A razor-thin beam of light neatly sliced my clothes away from groin to neck and peeled them back; expertly field-dressing the stupid, hungover wizard before her. She loomed over me, all twelve inches of her standing a few millimeters south of my exposed genitals. "You botched the summoning, by the way. Didn't use the bottle of quicksilver at the cardinal directions of the circle. And you drew the circle *deosil*, or clockwise as you call it. Backwards. Your loss. Your pain and agony will taste exquisite as I fuck you to death." Her voice was feral, and despite the lethality of her words my body responded to the *F-word* like a male college freshman at a sorority toga party. Entirely against my volition. This little sprite had *Power*.

Gunnar chose that exact moment to stride loudly into the room. "What's taking you so long, Nate?" He froze, looking down at me with shocked eyes. "Oh, wow. Is it getting a little phallic in here, or is it just you?" He smirked, not appreciating the severity of my situation. He turned and saw the look in the sprite's eyes, his demeanor morphing instantly. His claws popped out as he began to shift, taking an aggressive step closer.

The sprite curled a finger, beckoning him closer. "Mmmm... werewolf. I haven't tasted one of you in eons. Come closer, my pet. I will rock your world. She dropped a hand to her glistening crotch and Gunnar hesitated, whether in disgust or overtaken by her seductive power, I didn't care. With her distracted, I noticed that the spell pinning me down to the floor had dissipated enough for me to move my lips. I bellowed out her True Name three times in quick succession and she immediately went still, snarling angrily as her power evaporated. I held her strictly with my will now, understanding that the circle was worthless. I was powerful enough to do this on my own. Barely. It was taking everything I had to keep her constrained, but she didn't seem to be fighting me on it.

Still naked, I scooted back. "Okay, that's it." I wheezed, trying to hide my obvious erection underneath a heap of my shredded clothes. "No ethereal nookie for you. Bad sprite." Gunnar blinked.

"Nookie? *How*? She's *tiny!*"

"Spooky shapeshifting." I answered, climbing to my feet, still clutching the shredded clothes over my erection.

"That sounds like a made-up explanation. Utterly ridiculous sounding, if I'm being honest." He folded his arms.

I scowled back. "She can become whatever you need her to be. I would imagine even a werewolf." I cocked a questioning look at her. She shot back a single nod, but was presently unable to shift to that form in order to prove it.

"Creepy. But… cool. Like a pocket-sized magical sex doll."

I slowly turned to him, blinking in disbelief. "I strongly recommend you drop that thought."

"Right," he grumbled, face turning red in embarrassment.

I turned back to her. "Now. Alistair was murdered. I'm trying to avenge him. Who or what did it? I was hoping you could help."

She glared back, but seemed relieved to hear we hadn't killed him. "I can hardly find that out with you muting my power, wizardling," she growled. I hesitated, thinking about it for a few seconds.

"Okay. You have my permission to use your power only to do as I requested. Nothing more. Like killing us or sexing us up. Or both." I clarified. Sprites were very literal creatures, after all.

She rolled her eyes at me pointedly, waiting. I arched a brow.

She glanced down at the fistful of clothes covering my crotch, her eyes glittering. "You sure you don't want a quick—" I snapped a finger and she flinched as if struck. Her glittering eyes turned fiery. "Oh, you wretched little…" She took a deep breath, composing herself. "Fine. I agree." I nodded and released her, ready for anything this time. She closed her eyes, spun in a cute little pirouette, and then settled into a type of Tai Chi stance, squatting low as she brought her hands out wide, then drew them in closer to her body, moving as if under water. Her fingertips brushed her nipples and they stiffened into a pleasant military salute. She whimpered softly and then shot out her hands as if pushing the orgasmic sound out into the room. A wave of fog slammed into us, forcing me back a step and my gaze hardened, thinking she had broken her word. After a few seconds, I realized I was fine, and that the fog had morphed into a slightly-sparkly haze filling the entire room.

The haze settled into a silhouette sitting in the chair behind the desk, and I realized that we were essentially watching magical security footage of the previous night. The figure in the chair was Alistair.

Time moved faster than normal. We watched him stand and stride angrily towards the door to his office. Before he reached it, the door exploded inwards, striking him in the chest. A second darker form entered. All I could make out was shadows. A silent argument ensued. Then Alistair was struck a dozen times simultaneously amidst a swirl of shadow as the creature moved. A mist of blood filled the air. Then it was over. Time returned to normal and the haze evaporated.

"Can't you pick up the conversation?" I asked. Gunnar looked dumbfounded.

"No. Too many disgusting humans and their mechanical familiars came after. Distorted the calling. What you see is all that remains."

She meant all the cops and Scene of the Crime technicians with their cameras and other equipment.

"Do you have the Grimoire?" she asked suddenly.

"What?"

She looked at me sharply. "The book. I told him not to sell it. It's too dangerous. *They* can track it. It must be warded at all times. But he didn't trust himself with it."

"You mean the original edition of *Grimm's Fairy Tales*?"

"That's just a cover."

"Heh. Puns."

She didn't smile. "You don't understand. They are invincible. Immortal. They are *legion*. They never fail. Their prey never escapes."

"Who are *they*?"

She pursed her lips, not answering me immediately. "Do you think I'm foolish enough to call *their* name? You know nothing. You will die horribly," she answered sadly, crossing her arms stubbornly.

"We'll see about that. Whoever *they* are, they haven't met me and mine. Anyway, I don't have the book. I'm trying to recover it."

Her ancient eyes appraised me up and down thoughtfully before she spoke. "Promise me you will destroy it or lock it away. And that you will call me back if you require help. I will aid you for free on this. It is too dangerous to dicker over coital repayment for my services."

"Heh." Gunnar grunted. "Dicker..."

I rolled my eyes; mildly frustrated he had beaten me to the pun. "I'll think about it. I've got your digits, so I'll call you back if I can get it." She simply stared back. "What was that thing in the vision anyway? Was it one of them?"

She looked at me. "I will answer your question in exchange for my release and your oath to avenge my old... friend."

I thought about that. I really didn't need anything else from her, and it sounded fair. "Okay."

"He wasn't one of *them*, not yet, but rather a *cursed one*. Still dangerous, but even a toddler and a puppy should be able to handle him," her voice dripped venom. Then she disappeared in a puff of sparkling dust. I stood there for a second, wishing she hadn't gotten the last jibe. Then I sighed, pocketed Alistair's summoning book, and raided his closet for a new set of passable threads that fit me oddly. Jeans and a Ricky Martin tee. I sighed, tugging it on. Gunnar didn't comment, but hid a chuckle. Then we headed out the door without a word. Gunnar followed.

"So, *cursed one*. What exactly is that again?"

"I have no idea. But I propose we go find out. It's time to go meet our thieves."

Gunnar nodded and we climbed into the car. "You know, Nate. There's something I genuinely appreciate about you. I just never had words for it until now."

"Oh?" I answered absently, fumbling with my seat belt.

"Yeah. You're always *livin' la vida loca*," he said deadpan.

I murdered him slowly in the depths of my mind. He chuckled and set off down the road.

7

We sat in the idling car outside a gated entrance to Forest Park. The throbbing pull in my chest from the tracker spell practically shouted that the thief I had tagged was only a few hundred yards away from me. We had to be within sight of them, but it was just past sundown, and the night was dark, no moon to speak of, and it was a thick section of woods. A wall stood before us, the gates closed.

"So, they're in the park?" Gunnar asked.

I nodded, sensing their presence in a secluded, heavily-wooded area of the park just ahead.

"We should kil—" He took a deep breath, halting his previous vengeful statement. "*Apprehend* them," he corrected. "I don't know how I can pin it on them. I doubt they have the murder weapon anymore. Still. I can sweat it out of them. Maybe turn off the camera in the interrogation room and scare the living hell out of them." He was panting, practically drooling with anger. These little ass-hats had killed three of his fellow agents. I didn't blame him. But I did correct him.

"This one's not going to trial. They'll magic their way out of jail and disappear. This ends here and now. They've killed at least five people to get this Grimoire. And those last two never even stood a chance when the car blew up on the doorstep of that house. This one calls for retribution." I looked over at him. He was panting harder now, struggling with the options before him. "Can you handle that, Gunnar? If not, I'll see you tomorrow." I put a hand on the door handle as if to leave him behind.

My voice was hard. Alistair had been a family friend. Sure, I hadn't known him personally, but my father had. And that mattered to me. He had sold the book in order to avoid whatever temptations or dangers came with it. I still couldn't fully comprehend that, but I would deal with it after I had the book in my possession. I would even call back the sprite if I had to. But first I had to get the book.

"This is all because of a fairy tale." Gunnar muttered in disbelief, shaking his head.

"Apparently, it's much more than a fairy tale."

"So who are these guys? These *cursed ones*. Or the nameless evil that can track the book. Where are they? If they are so powerful and can track it so easily, why haven't we seen them? That sprite seemed to have some serious juice and she was terrified. She's not even on this plane of existence and she would have done whatever you asked if you would have promised to destroy this children's book."

I hesitated, debating whether or not to share my hypothesis. I didn't know if I was correct, but it felt right. The book was called *Grimm's Fairy Tales* after all. "I'm going to go out on a limb here and assume she's talking about the Brothers Grimm. They are supposedly a legendary gang of nigh-immortal murderers. Well, hit men in any case. They get paid to take out Freaks like us. Have done so since forever. Jacob and Wilhelm Grimm immortalized themselves by portraying characters that hunted down monsters as heroes. Nobody realized that it was basically their own personal documentary of their travels. But from what I hear, they didn't distinguish good Freaks from bad Freaks. They killed *all* Freaks. Innocent or not. Even the Freaks that hired them, if any Freaks were stupid enough to do that."

"I don't remember that from any of the fairy tales."

"It was alluded to. In the stories, some Hunter or Woodsman always seemed to show up and save the main character. This was a collection of stories gathered from all around Europe to introduce the idea to Regulars that Freaks did in fact exist. And none of them were to be trusted. It was more of a smear campaign against us than a historical text on the Grimms. To be honest, they're a pretty hardcore legend. I'm not even confident that they ever really existed. The Sexy sprite didn't seem to share that opinion, though. And she would be a nice trophy for a Grimm. It makes sense. There's the title of the book, and the fact that those are the only guys a sprite might be scared of. Also Alistair. He was terrified enough to sell the book at an auction rather than passing it along to another wizard. It's what I would have done if I wanted to get rid of an item so hot that it could potentially harm the buyer or myself. Or associate my name in any way whatsoever with the supernatural hit men."

"So, they're wizards? How else could they kill all types of Freaks?"

"Sheer testicular fortitude?" I said with a heavy breath. Gunnar merely stared back at me, waiting for a serious answer, which made me angry because... I didn't have the foggiest idea how to answer. They were considered to be myths by the mythological *community*, for crying out loud. And no, the irony was not lost on me. It was like the Illuminati having a conspiracy theory about secret societies.

I'd never met anyone who believed they were anything but a story. But the honest terror on the sprite's face had made me a believer. "Assuming they exist, they're almost certainly not wizards. I don't know if they have powers or not, but I'm guessing not since they hate Freaks. Like I said. This is all conjecture. I didn't even believe they were real until the sprite begged us to destroy the book. It's the only group I can think of that could instill so much fear in both the sprite and Alistair. I don't even know how destroying the book could stop them. Unless, like she said, it's more than just a book, complete with secrets better left untouched hidden somewhere in its pages. I just don't know how it remained out of the Grimms' hands for so long. It must have been hidden for a long time. Then maybe someone recently managed to steal it without knowing what it was beforehand. After they realized their mistake, it passed from unsuspecting hand to unsuspecting hand until Alistair managed to draw the short stick. Maybe the Academy originally had it. They wouldn't want something like that out in the world. And it would be a killer bargaining chip. *Stop killing us or we will kill all of you at one fell swoop by destroying your holy book.*"

The car was silent for a few beats as Gunnar pondered my dire words. "You in or out, wolf? I know this isn't really your thing. In fact, it's entirely the opposite of your thing. But your Federal Agent obligation will only get in the way and let the killers run free. And any future deaths would be on your shoulders."

Gunnar lifted bloodshot eyes to mine, snarling more at his personal dilemma than at my words. After all, the words were pure honesty.

"Shouldn't we call in the cavalry? Like your dad?"

"Not happening. I'm surprised my tracker has lasted this long. Any more delays could make it too weak to help. And my dad—"

"Would steal your glory. Rain on your parade. Make you sit in the car while the adults figured it all out."

I nodded. "Yes. He's powerful and you don't mess with him. But he's not emotionally involved. He doesn't know what we're up against, and the time he would take going back over everything we've already seen and heard would only waste time and let them get away. And he might make the wrong call. Plus, he's helping mom with dinner."

"And he would make you sit in the car." He grinned. I punched his shoulder.

"Yes," I admitted with an embarrassed grin. He shrugged.

"All right. I'm in. I'm not happy about it, but you're right. These pricks deserve it. They're carrying around a potential nuke and have killed three federal agents already. Agents just trying to do their jobs. Keeping an old man safe. Responding to a radio call for backup. And now they're dead. My boss, Special Agent in Charge Roger Reinhardt, wouldn't even know where to begin with this. Not that he would even believe me if I told him the truth."

"I'm going to be honest. It's more than likely that being my friend is not good for your moral character. This will most likely happen at least one more time throughout our lives. Possibly many more." I took a breath. "Or you could turn away. Be a white hat."

"Are you saying you are going to try to do something like this again? Are you calling yourself a... Black Hat?"

I thought about that. It wasn't a simple question. Of course I wasn't a black hat. But I also wasn't a white hat. I was a grey hat. No, a silver hat. I told him so.

"Are you subtly trying to compare yourself to Gandalf?" He kept a straight face. "Because that is something I will never let you live down."

I stepped out of the car rather than responding. My wingman was beside me.

And it was game time.

8

We entered the park, Gunnar following my lead, as the throbbing of the tracker grew more pronounced against my chest. The forest was silent. Up ahead I spotted a flicker of firelight and could hear faint voices murmuring to each other. I held out a hand for Gunnar to halt. I whispered so that only his enhanced werewolf senses could decipher my words. "Circle the camp. Make sure there are no traps. Keep them pinned. I'm going to approach from the front and see if I can subdue them before things turn ugly."

Gunnar nodded. He quickly unclothed rather than shifting in his clothes. The sound of fabric exploding into shreds was not quiet, and would also leave him naked when we tried to leave the park and get in our car.

Now, leaving the park undetected with three hostages would be difficult.

Leaving the park undetected with a naked Viking looking man *and* three hostages would be difficult-*er*.

Plus, I wasn't keen on the idea of some paparazzi or cell phone catching me leaving the park with a naked dude in tow. And leaving the park with a giant werewolf wouldn't go over well, either. Not even considering towing along the group of three criminals. But unless we killed them, I would have to work around that. Gunnar shifted silently. A pair of gleaming blue eyes met mine for a fraction of a second before he padded away on silent paws.

I took a deep breath, gathered up my will so I could cast magic without hesitation, and strode forward in a peaceful stride after giving Gunnar a few seconds' head start.

The voices around the campfire grew silent as I approached. Three sets of eyes followed me, looking leery. As I stepped into the clearing, I noticed that they were just kids. I blinked. *What the hell?*

One was a young girl, complete with the nerdy sexy librarian look and a university ID badge around her neck, and the boy beside her looked like her older football jock brother, complete with a varsity high school letterman's jacket. Which most likely meant he was younger or a new freshman in college, clinging to the past. The third was the loner of the group, dressed all in black, with a full, wiry red beard, and although still young, looked much older than the brother and sister. More calloused. He was the only one smiling. He was also liberally spray-tanned. Like, neon orange. A true soulless ginger. The other two non-gingers looked like they were about to bolt.

"Hey, kids." I said.

"Did you think I didn't notice the tracking spell, wizard?" The ginger stood, clutching a liquor bottle in his fist. He wore a dark, sadistic grin.

Shit.

Without hesitating, I bellowed. "Gobble up the gingersnap, Gunnar!"

A white-furred werewolf launched from out of the shadows, to my eyes looking like a slow-motion action movie segment, straight for the loner's back. The wolf's razor-sharp black claws flexed out and his jaws were wide, sporting glistening long ivory fangs as big as my fingers, and he looked hungry for vengeance.

The kid took a single step faster than I could blink. It still seemed like Gunnar was moving in slow motion but the kid was moving in fast forward. He cocked back and launched a fist at the side of Gunnar's snout. It connected with a sickening crunch and a tooth flew straight at a nearby tree, slamming into it point first and sinking in a good inch. Gunnar went flying from the clearing with a yelp of surprise and pain. But this little shit didn't know how much pain a werewolf could take. Gunnar would already be back on his paws, circling the camp like a wraith to catch the kid off-guard. Typical wolf tactics. Harrying their prey. Using fear like a warm blanket to tuck the bad guys in for bed one last time.

I almost felt bad for these little murderous bastards. Then I remembered what they had done. Five people were dead because of them.

"Alright. So, you're a super gingersnap. With sprinkles. But you just made a big mistake, pal." I warned. A roiling ball of golden fire began floating above my palm. "And now you're about to get a real fucking tan. Sunburn in fact."

He grinned. "Oh, I don't think so."

"Don't do it, Kyle! Let's just go!" The girl shrieked, sounding terrified. The ginger ignored her. I didn't hesitate.

I let loose, not sure where Gunnar was or why he was taking so long. The ball of liquid fire screamed and splashed towards him like a Molotov cocktail. He held up a hand and a vortex to... nowhere abruptly appeared before him. The fireball sailed into the void and disappeared from view. The gingersnap was clutching the book in his hand. And it was glowing.

And then a figure stepped out of the void. If Wes Craven and Stephen King's most horrific, most terrifying, personal nightmares met at a bar for a few drinks, ended up boinking at a cheap hotel, and producing a fledgling monster baby together, this figure would have terrified it. It was at least seven feet tall and *slightly* resembled a horse. If the horse had the head and tail of a demonic rooster, and instead of hooves had twelve-inch long by four-inch thick single talons so that it scuttled around on the tips like a spider. It let out a *cock-a-doodle-doo* that practically shattered my eardrums and rattled my chest.

Now, if you haven't heard the jarring sound of a real-life rooster belting one out, you won't know what I'm talking about. It literally hits you on a molecular level, screeching directly to your very soul.

And telling it to wake the fuck up.

This was worse.

It was telling me to *die the fuck down.*

And it almost worked. I felt my entire body tense in response, freezing me in place. Not with magic, but with instinctual terror.

The girl was standing too close, which seemed to pester the monster. One of its talons idly lashed out like a whip, piercing her in her center mass. She didn't even have time to scream. She dropped to the ground, and her brother roared incoherently. Before the brother could do anything he might regret, the gingersnap punched him in the jaw, knocking him instantly unconscious. The gingersnap blurred into motion again, and the next thing I knew he was fleeing the campfire like a comet, the brother slung over his shoulder like a weightless backpack, abandoning the girl to her fate. That was all I had time to see before the creature focused his rage on little old me, waking me from my catharsis in a heartbeat.

It scuttled towards me faster than a cockroach, rearing back on its back legs and slashing towards my chest with its front talons. It was too fast. I wasn't going to be able to dodge it. A freight train struck my side in a white blur and I was thrown out of the clearing. I struck the ground hard, rolling through mulch and twigs, gathering a mouthful of debris. But I was alive and well, more or less, thanks to Gunnar tackling me. But one of my arms wasn't working for some reason. I didn't feel pain, just numbness, so I knew it wasn't dislocated.

The creature let out another crow and tore after us. I ignored my useless arm and scrambled to my feet, realizing that Gunnar was already gone. I launched another haphazard ball of golden fire and darted to the side. The fire splashed the creature full in its open beak, causing it to shudder for a second, and then spit the damned thing back at me with a rooster belch. The regurgitated flame barely missed me.

"Well, *cock-a-doodle-doo* to you too!" I yelled over my shoulder, darting behind a nearby tree. It scuttled after me letting out another piercing avian shriek. I cast a swarm of foot long icicles into the air behind me, launching them out a millisecond later at various points on the monster's body. The air screamed at the speed of the icy projectiles as they came in contact with the humidity of the night. They struck the beast's shell hard but not hard enough to penetrate its tough skin. I had effectively thrown a handful of magic gravel at it.

So, I ran.

And not fast enough. Identical icicles sailed over my shoulder, one more than grazing my side in a gash that took my breath away before I managed to place another tree between us. I felt the blood begin to wet my side instantly, but I had no time to assess the damage. I focused my mind, settling into a light meditative state in order to clear my head and block my pain receptors. I needed a plan. The creature was copying me.

I took a deep breath and peeked around the corner quickly. My skin pebbled as I failed to see any sign of the monster. I was completely alone. I bolted instantly, and not a second too soon. A pair of talons tore through the tree I had been using for cover, like a hot knife through butter. As I ran I managed to glance over my shoulder, ducking, and weaving for my very life in case it sent more magic my way, and that's when I saw Gunnar dart out of the shadows and strike the beast a solid blow. It toppled sideways and the werewolf tore a nice chunk out of its side before disappearing back into the shadows. Apparently, it wasn't immune to Gunnar. It kicked its legs in an attempt to get back up and neatly severed two more waist-thick trees into stumps. I dove, barely missing one of the falling trees as it crashed to the forest floor. The other struck a clump of other trees and remained more or less upright with much groaning and raining of debris.

It came back to its feet and latched its beady black eyes directly onto the nearest threat.

Me.

I thought quickly. My magic wasn't helping. It could mimic me. I shivered instinctively at that, but buried the thought deep. Something about its legs had caught my attention when it had been lying on its side, kicking its talons to get back up. A thought came to mind and I didn't waste time second-guessing myself. I was not about to be killed by a magical rooster-horse. The wild, sadistic plan forming in my head would take a bit of finesse on my part.

I sprinted towards the fire, ignoring the fact that the girl was most likely already dead from blood loss or shock. I entered the clearing and rolled just as a pair of talons slammed into the ground where I had been standing. I had anticipated the speed of the attack this time, assuming the worst. I coalesced my thoughts and formed chains of crackling electrical power in my mind; my vision beginning to sparkle as I fed more power than was safe into my creation. Then I let out a defiant roar as I flung out my hands just before I would have blacked out. I wobbled for a second as my eyesight came back in a blast of sensation. My adrenaline was fueling my magic, diverting energy to protect and fuel my most vital asset – my mind – helping me recover faster than should have been humanly possible. My body was still physically spent, but my light meditative state had reprogrammed my bodily functions for my immediate survival – at the detriment of my long-term survival.

Hey, folks. Magic is dangerous. It plays for keeps.

The metaphysical chains struck the creature's front talons that were still embedded in the earth from when he had tried to squish me into a mist of atomic particles. The chains sizzled as they struck the creature's skin, eliciting a subsonic scream that made my ears pop. I delved deeper into my power, faint stars rapidly filling my vision again, and unleashed more of the chains to encircle all four feet. Then I yanked them tight.

Like you would subdue a chicken.

I stood toe to talon with the rooster-horse and grinned maniacally.

The chain collapsed on itself like a lasso around the rooster-horse's feet. Using every ounce of magical power I could safely wield at this point, I jerked the chain towards me and – thanks to my inhuman power – the laws of physics were ignored. I wasn't using my human muscles, but my very mind.

The mind of one severely pissed-off wizard.

I flipped the chains into the air, launching the creature up twenty feet into the night sky. The monster crowed again, not having time to duplicate my magic, and I could sense that the momentary surprise was working, and that the crackling electricity of my chains was practically acting like a Taser gun, stunning it.

Then I yanked that chicken nugget back to earth in tribute to Sir Isaac Newton.

Gravity is a bitch.

I mentally tipped my hat to Prometheus, the Greek God who had allegedly given mankind fire.

If gravity was a bitch, fire was a psychotic, vengeful ex-girlfriend.

Being a creature from another realm where magic was obviously common, I had hoped that real, authentic, mortal fire might do the trick. The rooster slammed into the campfire like a meteorite from the heavens, causing an explosion of embers and fire. Several pieces struck me, briefly flaring up on my jacket and hair but I ignored them.

Instead, I cast out a dozen weaker magical chains to the surrounding trees and built a web connecting the beast to the trees in every direction so that it couldn't move and was instead forced to sit and roast above the fire. I might or might not have cast a blast of air into the fire in order to stoke up the flames. I don't remember clearly.

The resulting crows of agony were most satisfying. I maintained my focus and cast a spike of raw mental energy into the monster's mind in case it tried to use any magic against me. I struck a wall of power, momentarily halted, before redoubling my efforts and finally breaking through. I can only surmise that I was able to do so because the normally fearless monster was facing fear for the first time in its life, and wasn't coping well. I definitely hadn't thought that I had enough juice left in me at this point to go toe-to-talon with this thing in the mental manipulation arena.

It let out another crow of raw pain and frustration, and then kept right on crowing, morphing into a forlorn wailing sound of despair. I watched and waited, as it was burned alive. I fell to my ass and just sat there, breathing heavily. I noticed Gunnar pad into the clearing and sit beside me just as the scent of drumsticks began to fill the air. The super rooster let out one final wheeze and then died. I let it keep burning but released my magic with a groan and fell back to just lie still for a few minutes.

I could have slept right there. I was exhausted. I felt a cold nose touch my side and shrieked in alarm. Gunnar grunted with a doggie pant.

"Gross. Dog drool just touched my open wound. I'm infected! Call the dog catcher!"

Gunnar shifted to human form as he too collapsed onto his back, completely naked, and put his arms above his head in a weary pose. I glanced over at him and saw blood trickling from his mouth where he had lost a tooth. I wasn't concerned. Werewolves had a great health package and typically grew back lost teeth for some reason.

Looking over at him I realized how this might look to a passerby.

Two dudes lying on their backs by an unsanctioned campfire in a closed park looking spent and exhausted. One of them stark naked. I bolted to my feet. Or tried to. My previously useless arm was now flashing with pins and needles as well as remaining completely useless. I fell directly on my face. Gunnar chuckled. I managed to stand, scraping up what was left of my dignity. "All right. The tabloids would have a field day with this scene."

"Nah. They wouldn't believe the chicken monster. We're set."

"No, not that, idiot. We're two dudes, one naked, lying next to each other beside a fire. Looking exhausted. In a closed park."

Gunnar peeled back an eye. "You mean to tell me that this... this feeling deep inside me, burning in my soul, tearing my heart apart with its secret isn't... reciprocated?" he asked deadpan. "I thought we were *livin' la vida loca?*"

I simply turned my back on him and began to scan the clearing, ignoring his laughter. I froze. The girl was gone. A mess of blood remained in the place I had last seen her. Gunnar stopped laughing as he noticed the same thing. I shook my head and began to walk back to the car. Gunnar caught up with me, snatching up his clothes along the way. "You hungry?" he asked, once fully clothed.

I thought about it. "Actually, yeah. Kinda disturbing, but that thing smelled delicious. Good thing mom's making drumsticks tonight."

"Heh."

I grinned. "Let's mosey on down to UMSL. We should have time to wrap this up before dinner."

"UMSL?" He asked curiously.

"Yeah. I saw a lanyard on the girl. It was a school ID badge. Didn't really matter at the time, what with dealing with the super-rooster back there. If two out of the three of them are students, you owe me a drink. Less, and I owe you."

"You're on." He grinned.

I scanned the parking lot as we emerged from the park. Then I frowned.

"Wasn't that super-dangerous summoning book in my car?" Gunnar asked.

I grunted.

"We should probably find it then. And my car." He offered lightly. I began walking away from the parking lot, hoping we could hail a taxi soon. We were on borrowed time. I felt queasy at the potential ramifications of those punks having possession of a deadly dangerous summoning spell book. A book that had directions to call up who knew what. The gingersnap obviously had some semblance of power if he had managed to tap into the Grimoire. Now he had *two* dangerous books.

And the city's youngest billionaire and resident werewolf FBI Agent were on foot. How were we going to make it to my family dinner now?

Some vigilantes we were.

"We're living the crazy life all right." I muttered.

9

Gunnar sighed. "Remind me why we're not up in their dorm room yet?"

"You're just mad that you lost the bet." I muttered softly, scouting the hallway for either people or cameras.

"No, I'm mad that these bastards stole my car and murdered another person. Right in front of us. But I'm also wondering why we're trying to break into the Chemistry department's storage room when the thieves are in a dorm. Or why you wouldn't let me call in an APB on my ride."

"I need to grab something. And I already explained, we can't afford to get the authorities involved by calling in an APB."

He relented on the car. It seemed to have been his only priority on our ride here in the dirty cab. "You need to grab something that's neatly locked up in a secure Chemistry storage room? Probably locked away for a very good reason, I bet."

"Yes." The coast was clear. If we could wrap this up quickly we could still make it to dinner. I motioned Gunnar to follow me, eating up the fact that I was going to – hopefully – finally try something I had wanted to test out for months. And the fact that Gunnar had no idea what that was and hated it. It was heaven.

I darted up to the door and cast out my power, questing blindly for the tumblers on the old-fashioned lock. Luckily it wasn't a magnetic reader. Then I would have been forced to break down the door. And I wasn't even sure if they had what I wanted. It took me a few seconds before the door clicked open and I ducked inside, Gunnar on my heels. I heard no alarm, but then again the good ones would be silent to a thief, instead sending a notification to campus security so they could swiftly, quietly, apprehend the thieves. We needed to hurry. The room was obviously dark so I cast a faint orb of light to hover over my shoulder as I made my way to the storage tanks I saw chained against the back wall. My excitement grew.

"Does this have anything to do with the balloons you just had to buy at that convenience store on the taxi ride over here?"

"Yes." I answered softly. "Now be quiet. I need to focus here."

"Wait. You're not going to make a bomb or anything are you? I know you have a copy of the *Anarchist Cookbook*. You better not be doing anything illegal."

"You mean like breaking into a locked room in a campus where we have no business being, let alone at night?" I answered drily. I was just glad there had been no classes in session.

"Fine. Anything dangerous then."

"Of course it's dangerous. Look at your accomplice."

"Why did you have to go and use that word?" he mumbled urgently under his breath. I quickly scanned the pressurized gas tanks along the wall, reading their contents. I almost gave up until I came to the last one. The label was facing the wall. I spun it around with my operational arm. My other arm was still more or less a pendulum. I almost yelled in delight at the label. "Yes! This is it!" I was practically dancing on my toes. "Give me the balloon."

Gunnar groaned in trepidation but complied, handing it over. "I can't even pronounce that so I'm not going to ask what it is. We should probably get your arm checked out soon. Still bothering you?" I nodded. "How about your side? Still bleeding?" I shook my head, motioning for him to shut up and help his handicapped, mad scientist accomplice.

I filled up the balloon with his help. Then another one just in case. I tucked them under my worthless arm and motioned him to follow me out of the room.

We locked up behind us and snuck out of the Chemistry lab, with none the wiser. Gunnar eyed the balloons nervously as we made our way down the sidewalk to the correct dormitory.

We passed a group of scantily clad college girls in heels and short skirts, no doubt on their way downtown. Once out of earshot, Gunnar spoke. "I can't believe your friend, Othello, was able to get the right information so quickly. Let alone that you were right."

"We're simply lucky I heard one of their names and saw the girl's last name on the ID card. Or that I saw the ID card at all. If not, we'd be sitting in the taxi doing nothing right now, and the thieves would escape scot-free."

"Still. It's kind of freaky how quickly she dug up their details."

"She isn't one of the world's best up-and-coming cyber criminals for nothing."

"Still. She used to be such a sweet girl when we were in school. Who would have known she was such a brilliant hacker. You guys used to be a thing, right? Why did you end it, and how did you remain friends after?" he asked, genuinely curious.

"It was more casual than it looked. Neither of us had long term plans together. We just had that Russian class together and we kind of clicked. Studied together." I blushed, remembering our nighttime 'study' sessions. A whole lot of *phonetic* practice, for sure. "Since neither of us were that attached, it just seemed to work out after."

Gunnar looked doubtful, shaking his head. After all, it wasn't common to remain friends after a breakup. Gunnar was also more of a one-girl kind of guy, not spending much time with the fairer sex if he didn't see marriage potential.

We entered the dorm, closely following a pair of guys stumbling out on their way to some late night study session by the looks of the book bags under their arms. It was almost Finals Week, after all.

"You going to tell me what the balloons are for, or am I going to shit my pants in surprise along with the thieves whenever you launch your Bill Nye science attack?"

"Soon." We made our way up the elevator, doing our best to look like college students, even though most students our age were not dorm material. We were a few years past our senior year. No one seemed to notice, although I did spot several girls I would like to get to know on a more personal level in the future. Perhaps I could come back and offer tutoring services of some kind. I shook off that testosterone-laden thought as we neared the correct door. We lounged outside, pretending to play with our phones as a swarm of freshmen darted past us and entered another dorm room a few doors down. One of the girls, a mousy California Ten if I've ever seen one, did a double take at me, looking mischievous. I winked back, causing her to duck into the room, blushing. The hall was momentarily empty.

"Alright. Here's my plan. Take a deep breath from one of the balloons."

Gunnar blinked. "Um. Hard pass."

"Look, it's perfectly safe. Like helium."

"You want me to suck in helium before we take down the thieves? Are we the Mickey Mouse brigade?"

"Just do it. Trust me. This is going to be awesome."

"Not going to happen. You can do your party trick without me."

"Fine. Watch." I let out my breath and bit a tiny hole into the balloon, sucking in a deep lungful of the gas I had nabbed from the Chemistry lab. It tasted like chemicals, of course, but wasn't overly unpleasant. I looked up at Gunnar with a manic grin. His eyes were wide and he was shaking his head, *No*. Then I felt a finger tap my shoulder. I flinched and spun; turning to face whoever was behind me, ready to unleash hell if it was one of the thieves.

But it wasn't.

It was the California Ten from a few minutes ago. She was much younger than I had thought. She shoved a piece of paper against my chest. "You should give me a call sometime. I like older guys."

By *older guys*, I assumed she meant drinking age. I clutched the paper and said "Thanks," in my most charming voice, forgetting that I had inhaled the gas.

What she heard was not even remotely a charming voice, but a demonic growl that sounded as if it were designed to announce the Commencement of the Apocalypse.

She shrieked and bolted away in terror. The background noise of the dorm instantly hushed as she slammed the door shut behind her. I heard the deadbolt slam home.

Gunnar was staring at me wide-eyed.

"What the hell?" he hissed.

I grinned with a full-blown nerd-on. "Sulfur hexafluoride. It has the opposite effect of helium. Makes you sound like the devil. It's six times denser than air." Then I remembered where we were. "Quick. We need to get in there before someone wonders why she screamed." Gunnar nodded frantically. I went to work on the door and had it unlocked in a few seconds using my magic.

Gunnar depressed the handle, and I kicked it in, going with the fairy tale motif. "I'll huff and I'll puff, and I'll blow your house down." I growled, sounding like Lucifer himself. Then I let out a deep, demonic, evil magician laugh, fueled by the gas I had inhaled. It sounded downright terrifying.

It was glorious.

I didn't even have time to be surprised at what we found. The previously dead girl screeched before I managed to reflexively gag her with a band of sticky air. Both boys jumped off their beds and launched themselves at us, the gingersnap moving faster than light. Gunnar managed to cold cock him at the last second, werewolf claws out. He gripped the gingersnap by the throat as I cast twin spells to subdue them all. It went off flawlessly. I gently kicked the door shut behind us.

I didn't know how, but the dead girl looked surprisingly similar to a non-dead girl, even if she did appear exhausted and terrified. "Now, it's time we had a chat." I glared at the gingersnap, pegging him for the leader of the trio. I used illusion to make my eyes glow red and my face waver like seen through heat waves. He paled, stammering under Gunnar's grip against his throat.

"Wh... Who are you?" he managed.

"Nate-Fucking-Temple. And I'm here to punch your card, shit-stain."

Gunnar glanced at me, still startled at the sound of my voice. It was beginning to wear off but still sounded frightening.

Of course, that's when the gingersnap made his move.

He had been playing us. I saw his canines stretch out into fangs and I reacted instantly. If the fangs were any sign, vampires were inhumanly strong and Gunnar wasn't ready for it. Hell, I almost hadn't been ready for it. I definitely hadn't expected the powers of a master vampire coming from the adolescent gingersnap – only a master vampire could move like that – but my battle reflexes kicked in before I could comprehend the situation.

So I sent a slice of molten hot air at his throat, hot enough to instantly cauterize the wound.

But it didn't play out like I had hoped.

A billowing cloud of black fog appeared where the gingersnap had been, and the room filled with his mocking laughter.

The book I hadn't seen clutched in his hands had begun to glow faintly like it had back at the park and was falling open as it fell from his now non-corporeal hands. I lurched forward to catch it, but my body responded too slowly, still filled with disbelief at the abrupt change in our situation. The book hit the floor with a loud slap, falling wide open, and a silent explosion of light filled my vision. Gunnar instantly shifted to full werewolf form, an explosion of cloth confetti filling the air as his clothes shredded to tatters. The electrical power abruptly went out of the building in an explosion of shattered bulbs and sparks from the sockets.

A dim glow from the book showed enough for me to faintly see the people in the room, but nothing else. Gunnar's snout darted left and right, tracking each body in the room out of instinct. His icy blue eyes settled on me and seemed to sparkle hungrily for a moment before he shook his head with a canine sneeze. When he looked back at me his eyes were wide, the universal face for *what the fuck* was easy to read even on a giant werewolf. I didn't have time to ask him the same thing, so I sent him the same face right back. We were outnumbered, and my vision was still screwed up from the flash of light, let alone the darkness of the room.

A screech like nails on a chalkboard filled the darkness and an inky black line split the air just to the side of the three thieves. The gingersnap now stood unharmed beside the siblings. The depth of darkness from the vertical sliver of power splitting the room was visible in the room's darkness only by being even *darker*. I could also feel it on an emotional level. *Despair, sadness, hate, sorrow, guilt...* I shook my head, closing my eyes for a second to gather my thoughts. I didn't feel those things. It was the line of power a few feet away. After a deep breath, I opened my eyes again and studied the line. The inky rip in reality was so dark that the rest of the room appeared illuminated in comparison.

I had never seen anything like it, and never wanted to again. The dark emotions pounded against my will power unsuccessfully, lucky for me.

As if in response, the line abruptly quivered and then expanded into the shape of a doorway. Impossibly, the doorway was even darker than the line of power had been, darkness so complete that it devoured light. I imagined that line from Genesis. *The earth was formless and void, and darkness was over the surface of the deep...* Then God said, *"Let there be light.* That was the darkness from this doorway. The *first* darkness. *True* darkness. The darkness of *nonexistence*. But something *did* exist in that darkness.

I could feel it.

And even now it was coming closer, wanting to eat the light of my life.

The little hairs on the back of my neck stuck straight out and then dove under my skin like a turtle hiding in his shell. This couldn't be good.

I tried to nudge the cover of the book closed, but a smoky dome of power suddenly appeared a few inches above its surface. As soon as my foot touched the dome, my world went white with pain as I was zapped by approximately a bajillion volts of electricity, most likely Genesis-level electricity.

The next thing I knew I was pulling myself to my feet from the other side of the room, my hair standing up in all directions, and – I realized with a moment of pure shock – my useless arm was somehow supporting my weight as I sat propped up on the floor. I switched arms and held up the previously worthless appendage in disbelief. The jolt of Genesis juice had apparently defibrillated it to usefulness again. "It's *alliiiiiive!*" I formed a claw as I lifted it into the air, and then slowly lowered all but my middle finger, and it was aimed in the direction of the doorway. No one laughed. The three kids were staring at us with wide vacant eyes. As if in a trance. Oh well. At least *I* knew I was funny.

From my position on the floor I cast out a ridiculously amped-up bolt of power, fully intending to pummel the kids out the window and into the night, consequences be damned. They deserved it. A smoky fist the size of my torso instantly darted out from the doorway, intercepting my power. The fist latched onto the invisible power and *squeezed*. My chest suddenly constricted as if the fist was squeezing my ribs rather than my magic. I couldn't breathe.

Gunnar growled, hunching down to launch himself at the metaphysical arm.

"Enough." An icy baritone voice, dripping authority, called from within the doorway.

The pressure released and I took a deep breath. The hand was gone. I took a second to shake my head and climb to my feet. Gunnar stepped up beside me but never took his eyes from the doorway. I thought furiously. Who had spoken? *What* had spoken? And why were the kids impersonating ventriloquist dummies?

"Before this gets out of hand, let me clear the air. That book and these three... *couriers* belong to me."

Gunnar stood motionless beside me, not making a sound. The voice still hadn't presented itself from out of the doorway. I didn't think it was because he couldn't pass through the threshold because his arm had crossed the barrier just a second ago. Something else then. I just needed to figure out how to get Gunnar and myself out of here before he decided to show his ugly mug. "Um. Possession is nine-tenths of the law, so... There's that. And people can't belong to people anymore. You can thank Honest Abe for that. So, *Check*, as they say, creepy-doorway-to-the-void guy."

The universe was completely silent for a few moments.

And yes, I do mean universe. I couldn't hear *anything*. No students screaming outside, no alarms, no horns honking from the nearby roads and parking lot, no birds chirping, no breathing. I mean, the power had cut off in an entire building. This usually caused mild freak-outs by everyone in the immediate vicinity. But there was nothing.

Dead.

Silence.

I fidgeted slightly.

Then I fidgeted a bit more just to verify that I still... you know, existed.

"Perhaps *belong* was the incorrect term. I have *need* of them." The voice spoke, tone polite, but with barely restrained rage.

Now, imagine a King being forced to converse with a peasant during a crowded banquet of fellow nobles. Not just speak, but *converse*. To have a *meaningful* conversation. Then imagine how said King might *sound* during this conversation, no doubt imagining the unheard mocking laughter from his fellow nobles the entire time.

This guy sounded more disgusted than that.

Having to converse with me literally disgusted him on a level I hadn't even known existed. Which kind of told me what I was dealing with right there. My mind began to work furiously as I tried to stall. My eyes caught the spine of another book only two feet away from me.

"Well, I guess that would be up to them." I answered. "Do you guys want to go hang out with creepy-doorway-to-the-void guy? He might have candy." I let their silence fill the room. They still stared out at nothing as if transformed into stone. "I think you heard their response loud and clear. How about you say *deuces*, cupcake? Don't let the door hit your metaphysical ass on the way out."

A roar of rage bellowed into the void on the other side of the opening. The backlash was felt on a physical level on our side of the doorway. It slammed into me like a heat wave, shoving me up against the wall. Then I saw a very physical, regular-sized boot extend from the void and into the dorm room.

I was out of options. I didn't even have time to verify our own safety. No circles or rituals this time. My next move was like a Wild West pistol duel at midnight; where void-guy was fully loaded with six shots, but I was only a quadriplegic with a Russian roulette rigged six-shooter.

I called out the True Name of Alistair's Nympho-Sprite. And I called that name out three times as quickly and as phonetically correct as I could. One slip up or mumble and I could practically guarantee that my one shot in the duel was an empty cartridge.

A crackling bolt of blinding silver lightning slammed into the doorway, and the body attached to the boot roared in surprised pain before disappearing. The now human-sized sprite stood in front of the doorway; silver fire dancing in her eyes, needle teeth bared in a snarl. I called out her name again. Her gaze flicked in my direction for the briefest of seconds and she saw me pointing at the book.

Grimm's Fairy Tales still sat open, protected by the smoky dome of power.

Her eyes darted back to the doorway and another crackling bolt of silver lightning hammered the doorframe. Without turning her gaze, several blazing bars of light hammered into the smoky dome surrounding the book. The same bars of pure light that had recently stripped me naked and then held me pinned to the office floor of Alistair's office. The exact *opposite* of the darkness this creature seemed able to wield.

I was banking on it being the key to dispersing the dome of shadowy energy protecting *Grimm's Fairy Tales*. I needed to close the book. Now.

The bolts pounded into the protective dome one after the other, and... I swear to God it sounded out the rhythm of *shave and a haircut, six bits*.

The dome of power dissipated in a poof at the last strike, and I launched my body at the book, hand extended to flip the cover closed as soon as it came in contact.

Time suddenly halted. I hovered in the air beside Gunnar, and had time to notice that he was still staring wild-eyed at the inky doorway. Unblinking. Just like the three kids. My mental processes seemed to be working a hundred times faster than my physical body. I wondered if everyone else was experiencing the same phenomenon. Able to mentally follow everything that had gone on for the last few minutes, but unable to act. It made me wonder how long Gunnar had been in the trance. I hadn't seen him move since the voice first spoke. But it hadn't affected *me* until just now.

Go Team Temple.

In fact, as I focused my thoughts, I could hear a conversation begin between the two creatures, despite the fact that my body hadn't moved a millimeter. I lay horizontal in the air like Pepe Le Pew riding the perfume cloud of the superhot Penelope Pussycat in those old Looney Tune cartoons.

"Begone, Grimm." The sprite spat furiously.

"But it has been so *long*." The voice whispered hungrily from beyond the door. "The quest was a lie." He growled the statement like an accusation. The sprite inclined her head in acknowledgment. "Clever. We won't make the same mistake twice. Our ancient journal has been found. Not only *found*, but *opened*, and by one with enough power to call out to us for the briefest of moments. But it was enough. Soon my brothers will walk your world again. *Our* world. We will finish what we started so long ago."

"You have no power here, Jacob." But the sprite sounded shaken.

Jacob laughed. A flick of smoky power exited the doorway and lightly struck the sprite in the face. "True. That is the extent of my power. At present. But thanks to the cursed one over there, my power will return. His life will fuel the bridge. Enough to bring us back. You aren't strong enough to both contain me and protect him at the same time."

The gingersnap, I thought furiously. He was the cursed one, whatever *that* was.

"Without the book, you're stuck," she snarled, furious at Jacob's light slap.

"Let us see," he spat.

Time abruptly returned to normal and I hit the book with my nose.

It was a solid spine. Iron-infused-oak, if I had to guess.

My vision flared red as I blindly lashed out with my hand. I found the book and fumbled the cover closed.

From beyond the door, Jacob screamed in frustration. The sprite crumpled to the ground as the door began to fold in on itself. "You will be my first victim upon my return, wizard. Return the book if you value your life. I could make use of you."

"Your rooster-horse tasted like chicken nuggets. Get bent, Jacob."

The jibe had the intended effect. His bloodthirsty scream lashed through the doorway and seemed to physically strike the gingersnap, vaporizing him instantly into a black fog. The fog zipped through the doorway just before it slammed shut, leaving the dorm room oddly silent. I managed to feel a bit concerned for my lifespan now that a Brother Grimm had personally promised to kill me.

10

The siblings collapsed into a tangled heap, breathing normally. Gunnar did the same, now back in his naked human form.

I seemed to be the only one conscious. I plucked *Grimm's Fairy Tales* up with a tendril of air, wrapped the air around it into an unbreakable knot so it couldn't accidentally or even purposely fall open, and then tucked it into a pocket. Then I strode over to check on the sprite.

She lay on the ground, eyes open, staring up at me. At least she was alive. Exhausted, but alive. I held out a hand to help her up. Her eyes registered me for a moment before she accepted my offer. She leaned heavily on me, gathering her strength.

"So, Jacob... as in Jacob *Grimm*. Is his brother, Wilhelm, kicking around in that dimension of happiness and rainbows too?"

She nodded. "Yes. It's a prison."

"What did he mean by, *the quest was a lie*?"

She took a deep, shaky breath. "The Grimms were sent into the void to hunt down the source of all supernatural power. It was a carefully-crafted rumor that the dark realm held the source of all supernatural power entering this world. Their blind righteousness caused them to chase after the opportunity without a second thought. It was too good an opportunity to pass up. Many innocent lives were lost starting that rumor. We had to make it look authentic. They went to destroy it. The doorway was closed behind them. We thought permanently." She glanced at the book through my pocket. "Apparently not."

My voice was soft. "How long until they come back?"

She shrugged. "Days. Years. Who knows? Now that he took the cursed one for power, I have no idea." Her shoulders slumped. "I must leave. I have to notify my people." I nodded. "He was right. You will be their first target. You offended him. But more importantly, you have his journal."

"I guess I'll just have to keep it safe. Like a needle in a haystack..." I muttered to myself as an idea began to form. I shelved the thought for later. "Thanks for saving our bacon. Hopefully you're not going to charge me for it..."

She chuckled and shook her head. "This one's on the house. Call on me when they come looking for you. If I hear first, I'll notify you. I will try to help you. We will *all* have to help..."

I shivered. *All* sounded ominously like *all* supernaturals. "Will do." She took a deep breath. "You sure you're fit to travel?"

We were saved the luxury of her answer.

I heard a gathering number of voices growing outside in the hall and realized it was the forgotten California Ten yelling about me frightening her. That wasn't good.

A fist began pounding on the door.

The sprite snapped her fingers and the siblings and Gunnar instantly awoke. Everyone lurched to his or her feet in panic. The sprite snapped her fingers again and a cloud of mist briefly settled around us. Everyone calmed instantly. "The wizard will take care of you. Be honest with him." Her eyes looked full of pain. "He's our only hope now." She turned to me. "They will have no recollection of what transpired. Unless you tell them." I blinked. Gunnar's eyes focused on me distantly and he frowned vaguely. Then he looked down at himself, realizing he was naked with a startled gasp.

Then the sprite disappeared.

I shivered. What had her last comment been about?

The pounding on the door grew louder. Gunnar quickly grabbed some sweats and a tee from the closet, clumsily getting dressed. No one objected, although the younger girl seemed highly interested.

I turned to the brother and sister. "I don't fully understand what the hell is going on, but I'm going to give you one chance to get, at least, this part right. We are friends from back home and are just hanging out with you. You are going to tell whoever is outside that door that everything is fine." I settled my gaze on the brother and sister, repeating the previous illusion of glowing red eyes and the heat waves before my face. "One wrong word and you're history. One wrong move and you're history. You saw what we've survived so far. Don't be a hero." I winked, pleased by their pale-faced responses.

"Room check. This is the RA! Open up. Now. Or I'm calling the cops."

I complied. "Just a second." I shouted. I fumbled with the door and pulled it open to find the Resident Assistant was not alone. Flashlight beams pierced the darkness of the room. The hallway was also dark. The power really had been cut from the entire building.

A crowd of students stood outside staring at us, worked up into a frenzy.

"That's him!" The California Ten shrieked, darting back to the safety of the crowd.

11

I feigned confusion, and did my best to mask my impatience. We didn't have time for this. "Yes. It's me. The guy you gave your number to a few minutes ago." I answered in a deep voice. Several males in the crowd chuckled.

"You... you don't sound the same. You sounded like a monster. You scared me."

"I'm getting over a cold. It's a good thing you didn't start a panic or anything. Oh. Wait." I muttered, pointedly crumpling her number up for all to see before tossing it into the waste bin. Someone cheered softly.

"What are you doing here?" The RA demanded, looking concerned. "The power to the building went out. Tammy, Ethan. Are you okay? Do you know these two?"

"Yes. We do. Friends... from back home," Ethan answered from behind me. I stepped out of the way so the RA could see the two siblings. The girl nodded numbly.

"They just stopped by to say hey. Catch up."

"You look distressed." The RA began, not sold on the story.

"They had some bad news about one of our friends back home. Shook her up is all. Then the power went out. Like a bad omen or something..." Ethan said distantly.

An empathic look filled the RA's face. "Oh. I'm sorry to hear that. Well, if everything is fine, we'll just leave you four alone. I need to get the power fixed."

We mumbled our agreement.

"Right. Okay everyone. Back to your rooms." She clapped her hands and the crowd dispersed. "I'm afraid visiting hours are over. I don't know how you got up here without an ID badge, but I'll let it slide on top of this mess. But still, you should probably leave. Maybe come back during the day tomorrow. When the power is back."

I nodded. "The news couldn't wait. I'm afraid we were in such a rush to tell them that we – *erm* – dodged the security desk. Sorry about that. We'll be out in five minutes.

If that's okay." I turned my charm on, hoping that admitting to a smaller offense might buy her belief. If I were willing to admit breaking a small rule, maybe she would buy the rest of the tale.

She blushed at my smile. "Yes. Of course. But don't let it happen again. Next time go through the proper channels. It's for everyone's safety."

I held a hand to my chest in agreement.

"You look familiar..." she began with a thoughtful frown.

"I guess I just have one of those faces," I answered with an embarrassed shrug, hiding my anxiety. After a few long seconds, she finally nodded back and then left. I was lucky she hadn't recognized me. I was kind of a celebrity in town. For all the wrong reasons. I closed the door behind me and waited a good minute before turning back to the siblings. I addressed Tammy.

"So, you're alive... I guess you're not allergic to chickens."

Gunnar stifled a laugh.

12

They told us everything.

Gunnar was pacing back and forth, no doubt confused about what had happened after I sent my magical attack at the gingersnap. I had to decide how much to share with him. And quickly. Gunnar was sharp. He knew something was hinky. My money was on telling him the entire truth. I could almost guarantee that Jacob Grimm would be back to kill everyone currently sitting in this room.

"So, you stole the book because you heard it had power over the Brothers Grimm and you wanted revenge against them for killing a friend of yours? Did he have powers similar to yours? Extreme healing, or whatever you call it?"

They nodded guiltily.

"Wait, let me guess. Kyle told you the book had power over the Grimms."

They blushed. They hadn't offered much of an explanation on their powers, and I hadn't bought it at first. So Ethan had demonstrated with a small knife, cutting his palm open deeply. He hissed in pain, but motioned for us to look closely. We watched it heal within moments. I was slightly jealous, now having a better idea why Jacob had been so interested in them. It was a unique power. I just didn't know what he would have been able to do with it.

I assessed them on a magical level, not wanting any more surprises. They definitely weren't wizards. I felt a headache forming. What exactly were they? It wasn't anything I was familiar with, but I could sense how terrified they were. They weren't predators, which was my primary concern. Just gullible college students, in over their heads. The next few minutes would decide whether I let them live or not. This didn't sit well with me, especially with them looking so helpless, but it was my duty, regardless of what

Gunnar might do to prevent me. It made me feel like a Grimm, sentencing a supernatural to death so callously.

I sighed. It wasn't the same. I would leave them with their secret. For now.

"Where does the gingersnap enter the picture?" I had told them he escaped during the blackout, but that I didn't anticipate him being a problem anymore. Gunnar had looked at me oddly curious, but the siblings seemed to accept it after gazing into my cold returning stare.

"He was the one who told us about the book. But he needed our help to get it from the auction house. He was going to handle the limited security with his... shadowy-stealth abilities while we nabbed the book."

"Master vampire. I think, anyway. It sounds less ridiculous than *shadowy-stealth abilities*," I offered, still not understanding how such a young kid had achieved such power. It meant he had to have killed a master vampire in a duel. With his bare hands. I shivered. We had really dodged a bullet with that one. I idly wondered how he had managed to find out about the book in the first place.

"Right. But when he heard *you* were in attendance, he spoke with an older lady, and all of a sudden she stuck to you like a fly to shit. But then when you won the bid for the book he panicked. So he... *improvised* to beat you to it. It wasn't our plan to kill anyone. But by then it was too late. He went rogue."

"Well, people died. The woman included." They looked sickened at the progression of events. Telling it in chronological order reemphasized how stupid their plan had been and how dangerous their compatriot had been.

"So, what are you going to... do to us," Tammy asked in a shaky voice.

I assessed them, glancing at Gunnar. He nodded, encouraging me to let them go. "Right now you're looking at accessory to murder charges. If I hadn't seen Kyle murder the woman with my very own eyes, I would have you taken into custody."

That sobered them up. "Murder? Us? That's ridiculous," the boy stammered.

"Listen, kid. You work with me on this and I think we can all walk away clean. I believe you. I've been around you several times and you never once tried to harm me. We'll need his gun though. To verify your story that you weren't the shooters."

The boy jumped off the bed and ducked into the bathroom. He came out with an Uzi, handing it over nervously. "I hate guns. I wouldn't even go shooting in the country back where we're from."

I handed it to Gunnar. He sniffed it for a few seconds and then turned to me, nodding. The kids were clean. They hadn't fired it. Gunnar would have said something.

I turned back to them. "Why go back to the old man's house? You already had the book," I asked. They had already handed over Alistair's summoning book, much to my relief. It didn't seem like any pages were missing, but only a closer analysis would verify that. Looks like I had homework. Which fit in neatly with my new Grimm problem.

Tammy spoke up this time. "Kyle said he visited the old man a few days earlier and might have made a bad impression. He wanted to scare the old man into silence in case the auction house came knocking. Especially after the murder and the theft."

"Well, he silenced him alright. Right to the grave."

"We were in the car the whole time. I swear. We would never kill anyone." That was true. We had seen the replay of the attack, thanks to the nymphomaniac sprite. Ethan hesitated. "Well, we might have killed a Grimm or two if we got the chance with that book, but no one else," he admitted. After a few seconds he added, "He also seemed ecstatic when we jacked your car and found the other book. It's possible that the book was his real reason for wanting to visit the old man..." He looked at me with questioning eyes. I fought the urge to shiver as I nodded at him in approval. His shoulders sagged in defeat, assuming this news had only sealed their fate further. I pondered that, wondering if the book held more secrets regarding the Grimms and possibly how to defeat them. I had to keep these books safe, and what better way to do so than in a bookstore filled with thousands of books? Looked like I had found a dadgum job. I would start a bookstore.

My dad would be so proud.

I let the kid stew on his words. The gingersnap had been well educated if he had known about Alistair's summoning book. I took a deep breath. We had been lucky. If the gingersnap had found Alistair's book in the office, we might have experienced quite a different welcoming party at the park.

"Well, I think you're guilty," I finally said. The color drained from their faces. "Of being colossal idiots. You should have gone to the cops the second things got out of control."

Ethan gained back a bit of color. "Kyle wouldn't let us. He threatened to *take care* of us if we tried. That we could choose to either be accomplices or be dead."

"Just a guess, but I'm pretty sure he was planning on killing you anyway." I decided a lie was necessary. "He tried to do so just before he left. I saved you and managed to take away his powers. Permanently." Gunnar's astounded stare seemed to physically hit the side of my face. He knew that wasn't possible. I continued, ignoring Gunnar's glare. "I think you two might want to leave town. Just friendly advice. He might have friends."

With a shared look, the siblings abruptly began packing up their belongings.

A distant thought hit me. Any time I had been around death before, I had run into Charon – the Boatman of wandering souls – so he could collect them and take them to the afterlife. But... when Jacob Grimm had vaporized Kyle, nothing had happened.

It seemed gingers really *didn't* have souls. I chuckled under my breath.

Gunnar and I made our exit, reminding the terrified kids that it would be better for everyone if this whole thing were forgotten. They didn't argue. I gathered up their contact information, knowing it would keep them vigilant, but also that the Grimms might go looking for them when they came back for their sequel.

The kids even tossed Gunnar his keys, telling him where the stolen car had been parked. He scowled at their blushing faces and stoically turned his back on them. I tucked Alistair's summoning book into my other pocket as I followed him out the door. I cast a quick ward over the unseen tomes to disguise them as textbooks to the casual eye if anyone stopped us to ask what the suspicious bulge in my pockets was, and then cast a stronger ward to conceal the magical contents from anyone but myself in case the Grimms really could trace it.

We found Gunnar's car and climbed inside in silence, having not run into any problems on our way back from the dorm. Gunnar started the engine, and spent some time fiddling with the seat and mirrors, murderous curses filling the enclosed space before he was finally satisfied and we pulled out into the street. "*Lucy, I think you have some 'splaining to do,*" Gunnar said in his best Ricky Ricardo voice.

"Later. I promise. Not tonight. Please."

Thankfully, Gunnar relented, and drove on in silence for a few more minutes, heading towards my parents' mansion, Chateau Falco, for dinner.

"Thanks," he muttered.

I shrugged.

"I wanted to rip your head off for whatever I'm imagining you really did to that kid, Kyle. But being forced to keep it inside for a few minutes helped me see the big picture. He had me dead to rights. I wasn't even looking at him. You... did something... Whatever it was saved my life. The next thing I know he's gone and the RA was knocking on the door." He was quiet for a few seconds. "You'll tell me when you're ready." I grunted an affirmative manly response. "You're okay in my book, Nate. Someone has to make the tough calls. It's hard for me to overlook that sometimes. I always try to stay within the lines, but then there are people like you who seem to be all over the place with their morals. It just takes people like me a second to see your true motives. And that you have our best interests at heart."

I smiled sadly. "I'm the surgeon."

He glanced over at me curiously.

"You know. The field medic that might have to amputate a fellow soldier's arm to save his life. It sucks, but that's the way of the world."

"I don't' know about being a field surgeon. I'll just stick with calling you Gandalf." He winked. I held up a fist. He punched it and mimicked an explosion with his fingers afterwards. I rolled my eyes.

"That balloon thing was pretty sweet. Their faces..." he began to laugh deeply, finally leaving the darkness of the night's events behind him. I joined him for a few minutes as we giggled like schoolgirls about our adventure. "*Cock-a-doodle-doo,*" he wheezed between deep belly laughs. My eyes were watery from laughing so hard.

Then my phone rang. I glanced down at the screen. It was my dad. Shit, we were a bit late.

I wasn't sure if I would share the night's true events with him or not. But I could spin a yarn when necessary. Or I could tell him the truth. See if he knew anything about the Grimms. But that might place him in danger too. I shivered. I would have to think about it. Tonight, I would just have to put a spin on certain parts of the story. I could tell the truth later, but once that cat was out of the bag, it was no takebacks.

"Hey." I answered.

"Nate. You're late. Your mom is upset. Which means my quality of life has lessened proportionally."

"We're on our way. What are you doing?"

"I'm just sitting in the office at Chateau Falco."

"Smoking a Gurkha Black Dragon and drinking Macallan, no doubt."

He chuckled. "True on all accounts. It's a good appetizer." He chuckled again.

"I'm sure mom doesn't agree," I smiled. He grunted in response, taking an audible puff through the phone.

"What your mom doesn't know won't hurt—"

"Doesn't know *what*?" I heard my mom call in the background. Then she began yelling at him in earnest. I put it on speaker for Gunnar's listening pleasure. I heard my dad clumsily put out the cigar and mutter a curse and an apology.

"We need to talk tonight. About Temple Industries." He finally said into the phone, having calmed the furious Mom beast.

"Not now, Dad. I've had a long night."

"We all have. It's imperative that you come work for the company. I think we have something right up your alley. No cubicle or stuffy office. I promise."

"No thanks."

After tonight, I would have to pursue a completely different vocation. My number one priority was locking these two books away where no one could ever find them.

He sounded irritated. "If not Temple Industries, what are you going to do with your life?" I thought about that for a second. I could tell him this much.

"Alistair's dead."

He sighed with regret. "Yes."

"I think I'm going to open up a bookstore. With a side focus on dangerous magical books."

Silence answered me. Then he began to laugh. "That's not a terrible idea, son."

"We'll be right over. Talk after dinner?" I asked.

"Sure," he answered cautiously.

"Mind if Gunnar and I tell you a... fairy tale?" Gunnar grinned silently.

"Does it have something to do with what I told you to leave alone?"

"Of course."

He chuckled. "Just like your dad. Get your ass over here. I'll have Dean prepare rooms, and then after dinner, I will hear your story about avenging old Alistair and taking up the mantle of St. Louis' arcane book salesman. And any other crimes you committed to come to this decision."

"Great. Be there in five. And dad?"

"Yes, son."

"You're an asshole sometimes. But you're *my* asshole. Thanks."

He chuckled. "Um... You're welcome... I think. Now get yourselves over here. Old men need their sleep. Or copious amounts of alcohol to stay awake this late."

"Better grab another bottle then. This story is a doozy. And I've already got big plans for Plato's Cave."

"So that's what you're going to call it, eh? Subtle."

"Yeah. It seems to fit. I even have the location picked out already," I added, thinking of the old theater-turned-auction-house. I was pretty sure they would be willing to sell after news of the murders got out. No one would want to attend an auction in the same place a double homicide had occurred. Especially when the murders took place at the auction's previous event. They would be *begging* to sell. And there wouldn't be many buyers.

"Well, looks like you're all set."

"Yes, I think I am," I answered with a smile, already envisioning the space in my mind. It would be so much more than a bookstore. It would have to be a fortress. "See you in a bit," I told him, hanging up.

Gunnar grinned, pressing the pedal to the floor. "Book nerd," he muttered.

"Federal K9 unit," I muttered back.

He barked out a laugh and we headed to dinner to tell my parents the story of Gandalf the Grey and his trusty sidekick, Underdog, sticking one to the Brothers Grimm. Or a variation of some sort I would come up with on the spot.

After all, the Grimms would be back, and with my luck it would be sooner rather than later...

Turn the page to continue with Nate Temple in **GRIMM**...

GRIMM (BOOK 3)

1

A lot can happen between *now* and *never*.

I once read that the phrase *it's now or never* was first coined to describe that moment that if one doesn't act upon right *now*, that they will never again get a second chance to do so. They would miss their one opportunity. Usually through their own fault, but sometimes that vindictive bitch named Karma could ninja flip out of a closet to give you a solid monkey fist to the stones.

You know...

Perhaps you had been facing a once in a lifetime opportunity – saying hello to the cute girl at the bar before anyone else; or maybe you had stood in silence for twenty seconds too long during your oral presentation in front of the classroom and desperately needed to formulate words that closely resembled anything intelligent.

Basically, you needed to do the thing *right freaking now*.

Carpe Diem.

Like me.

Right *now*, I was standing in the chilly sewers beneath the fine city of St. Louis in order to check off something on my to-do list. Something that was likely going to get my fancy new coat all smelly and icky in the process. Still, getting my coat smelly and icky was better than getting it bloody and hole-y. That's why I had brought backup. But the night was young. And I never counted my chickens before they hatched.

Especially when hunting vampires.

But I'll get to that in a minute.

Right *Now*, I was getting ready to do something marginally dangerous, and even with accomplices to watch my back, I wasn't quite ready to strap on my big boy pants. I was stalling.

I was here – hopefully – to save some lives. The victims didn't have Batman coming down to save them, or even the fine police persons of St. Louis. None of those upstanding people knew anyone was in danger down here, or would have even believed the intel that had led me here: a Greek hero gossiping at the bar over a beer. And all those victims had was one scraggly wizard, a disgraced werewolf FBI Agent, and a vanilla mortal to come save them.

Now was a brief period of time that was full of choices that would later result in more choices – harder ones – that would lead to penultimate consequences. The *now* part was pretty cut and dried for me. It was the consequences I was thinking about.

This whole mess had all started because of a favor I thought I owed Achilles.

Yes. *The* Achilles. The legendary Greek hero with – what some may call – vengeance issues.

And when one smashes up his place of business – allegedly – he could be known to display said vengeance issues by inflicting gratuitous amounts of pain upon the accused.

No thanks.

So, I wanted to make it up to him before the thought even crossed his mind. It wasn't like I could blame the Angel for fluttering into Achilles' bar and picking a fight with Death – one of the Horsemen of the Apocalypse – and I a few months back. Angels were Holy, above the law, beyond reproach, *blah, blah, blah ad nauseam.*

So. Rather than tattling on the pigeon, I had nervously waited months for the chance to gain his gratitude by doing him a solid.

Over drinks at his bar earlier tonight, Achilles had idly mentioned rumors about a vampire kidnapping young girls to bring them down to the sewers, after which they were never heard from again. The most recent disappearance was one of Achilles' own bartenders, and he feared the worst for her.

That was how I found myself in the sewer with my girlfriend and my childhood best friend on a perfectly cold November night. To possibly prevent my sad rear end from being dragged across St. Louis behind Achilles' chariot.

I glanced at my dismal surroundings. Maybe the vampire was just looking to Netflix and chill in his spacious tunnel home. I studied the slick, slimy walls with a look of disgust. No, not a home... a lair. Definitely a lair.

But this was par for the course in my experience. Find bad guy. Exterminate bad guy. Keep young, pretty girls safe.

Or avenge them.

It's what we wizards did for a living. Well, most of us. Even the ones who made millions of dollars per year on interest income from their daddy's technology company.

Ahem.

Maybe I was just doing it for the thrill. The challenge. Or maybe even to do the right thing. I grunted. *Who knows these things?* I asked myself with mild reproach. I shook my head before my inner Freud could psychoanalyze that too much further.

After the *Now* comes the *Never* part of the phrase. You know, the part where you won't be *here* anymore. The part where all of your family and loved ones have moved on and left you six feet under, while your soul is astral projected to the afterlife. Heaven. Hell. Atlantis. Nirvana. Or on a nice long boat ride with Charon – the chatty drunk Greek Boatman – who ferried souls on their trip to Hades in his Underworld funhouse.

Been there, done that. It didn't stick.

The point is, you're *dead*, so the consequences of your actions won't be your problem anymore. They will be felt by others, or by no one at all, leaving you with the peace of mind that you did all that you could, that it was worth it. That you made your move. Kissed the girl. Muttered something vaguely English in your speech class.

But you know what's in the middle of *now* and *never*?

Life.

Or in my case, annoying questions that interrupted my well thought out inner philosophical monologue.

"Remind me why we are standing in the literal filth of St. Louis in the middle of November, rather than back at *Chateau Falco* tipping one back before a roaring fire. Or why I'm here instead of curling up with my fiancé looking at wedding magazines and drinking a glass of wine," Gunnar complained. He lifted his boot with a disgusting squelch, emitting a whole new level of foulness to the brittle air. The dingy environment only seemed to amplify the stunningly royal bearing of my Viking friend. His golden hair was tucked up in a golden man bun, and his beard was impressively thicker than usual, as he had been growing it out for his upcoming wedding. Or so he had told me. I had recently had a nightmare where we were wrestling over a Monopoly argument involving my rapid construction of hotels, and I discovered that he was actually growing the beard out in order to hide a secret guardian inside – a leprechaun-sized werewolf willing and able to defend his master's honor in the event his master lost the wrestling match.

In my dream, I had lost to the violent little bastard.

So far, Gunnar's sniffer hadn't located any vampire scent at all, so I was appointed navigator based upon my eidetic memory of the scant information Achilles had provided.

"Well, if we're speaking of the latter, you should thank me," I muttered.

Indie punched me in the arm, scowling. I shook it off with an idle grin, glad that she had accepted my jibe at surface level. After all, I had been reading over every damn wedding magazine ever printed these past few weeks, which seemed to make my mother deliriously happy.

Yes, even a mother who recently died still went bonkers mad at the topic of gowns and weddings. You just had to find a way to talk to her spirit. Which I had. And she had commanded me to use her engagement ring when I asked Indie to share my life.

Which was the other reason I was down here, and the biggest reason I was stalling.

I was distracted. Conflicted. The vampire part of the trip was secondary in my mind. Which wasn't good.

But I couldn't seem to shake it. I was going to ask Indie to marry me!

My stomach made a little flip-flop motion at the thought. I shot her a discreet glance, but she was too busy fidgeting with her gear to notice. She was so god damned beautiful that I found myself simply staring at her at times. Like now. Her long golden hair fell past her shoulders to frame her perfectly shaped curvaceous upper body, but tonight it was tied up in a pony-tail and sticking out the back of a Chicago Cubs baseball cap.

The St. Louis Cardinal in me growled territorially at that.

She was about my height, a hair under six-feet tall, with legs for days, and curves that most men would drool over. Her face was narrow with a thin nose and icy blue eyes like sun-kissed sapphires. I averted my eyes as she glanced up, seeming to notice my attention.

I pretended to scout our path as I mentally ran over my proposal plan. I had made reservations at *Vin de Set*, her favorite French restaurant. Two days from now. I had cleverly used the excuse that we were past due for our regular date night where we usually 'recalibrated' our relationship. We typically did this once or twice per month, but so far it had stretched into month two now without either of us bringing it up.

It might or might not have started as a result of Othello's visit to town a few months back when Indie had been out of town caring for her injured mother. Injured because of my enemies, we later found out. Either way, several events from that visit had created a bit of friction between us. Not because I had been unfaithful – not by *choice*, anyway – but because Othello had openly admitted her ongoing infatuation with me. One that she had secretly harbored since our brief romantic relationship in college several years back.

She had admitted this to Indie. In front of me. Without giving me any warning at all.

Which had required some deft maneuvering on my part, let me tell you.

The two were amicable now, but boy oh boy it had been interesting for a time.

My thoughts drifted back to my dinner plans as Gunnar began sniffing down one of the halls, hoping to catch a whiff of fanger, AKA *eau de corpse*. Vampire. Indie was still fidgeting with her gear.

Before the dinner proposal, I wanted to see how she handled tonight, because, well, this was my *life*.

Hunting.

At least a big *part* of my life. And even though she had told me before that she could handle it, I needed to *know* that she could. There's a difference, folks. The proposal details were all set. The venue picked. Dinner dishes and wine already ordered. Her favorite dessert, strawberry shortcake, ordered from a local bakery.

Everything was set.

Well, *almost* everything… Which led me back to my *third* reason for jumping on tonight's opportunity.

Indie readjusted the contraption dominating her cranium, tightening one of the straps so that the headlamp mounted on top didn't jiggle around so much with each movement. Despite me being chock full of power, able to cast a ball of light to float beside us and illuminate the darkness, and Gunnar's near night vision thanks to his werewolf genes, a girl needed to accessorize to feel complete in this world. Practicality and logic be damned. And no man would ever get in the way of accessorizing.

Ever.

Indie looked grim at the unexplained dangers of tonight's extermination – seeing as how I hadn't yet explained it to either of them in depth – but was also conflictingly excited to be included in the boy's club. Even if she was completely mundane – as without magic as a boiled egg – it really didn't seem to bother her. Where Gunnar and I were at the opposite end of the spectrum. Dare I say that Gunnar and I were legen–

Wait for it...

Dary.

Indie and I had been binge-watching *How I Met Your Mother* lately. So, sue me.

I smiled to myself, which only made Gunnar's eyes tighten, as if it confirmed his sneaking suspicion that I was as mad as a hatter.

"We're all mad here," I whispered softly.

"What?" Indie asked, having successfully completed readjusting her straps.

I mumbled nothing in particular, putting my head back in the game. "Alright, gang. We're hunting an Alucard named Dracula," I answered distractedly, focusing my ears towards the two tunnels that branched off ahead of us. One of them led to our target. The other led to more smelly things and my third reason for entering the sewers tonight.

"Are you drunk?" Gunnar asked, very seriously. Indie blinked, having not been around me for the past few hours and realizing that it could very possibly be a valid question.

"What? No. I'm not... I had one drink with Achilles, but..."

"You just keep staring off into the distance as if distracted. And you're not making any sense. It's... unsettling." He folded his arms.

"Yeah, sorry about that. Few other things on my mind."

He waited. And I realized what else was bothering him as I replayed our conversation in my head. "Oh. I see what you're getting at. I meant to say *a Dracula named Alucard*." They stared at me, still not getting it. I rolled my eyes at Gunnar. "A vampire. The name *Alucard* is *Dracula* spelled backwards, you uneducated mutt," I turned to Indie, "and beautiful, intelligent lady."

Indie rolled her eyes. The silence grew before Gunnar finally let out a soft chuckle. "He seriously named himself *Alucard*? Does he have any idea how pretentious that is, or is it really his name?" He grinned hungrily. "I think I should ask him," he added, flexing his muscles. Or maybe he *hadn't* flexed. Regardless, his coat stretched along the seams of his arms and shoulders with a slight creaking sound.

"You're right. We should ask him. Word from Achilles is that he's kidnapped some girls. One of them was his. A bartender. I'm here to see if it's true. You two are here as witnesses. Especially you, Indie. No heroics. I'm serious. If he really is a vampire, stand back. Gunnar and I will handle it." She nodded her agreement, breath quickening slightly.

I consulted the mental map Achilles had shown me and took a left.

My posse followed me.

Which was good. Posses are supposed to do that sort of thing. It messed up the cool factor when they didn't.

We continued on for fifteen minutes or so until I began to hear faint whimpers coming from what sounded like only a dozen feet away. Still, with echoes it could be a mile. Gunnar took a big whiff of the air and nodded at me one time, looking suddenly relieved. Apparently, his sniffer was back on track. Or the vampire's apparent concealment spell didn't work this close up.

"Not far now. A few hundred feet at most," he whispered. "Won't they be able to sense us?"

I shook my head, mentally checking our map. "No. I masked our scent." There were two bends before any kind of opening that could house what might be used as living quarters.

I rolled my shoulders and patted my hip reassuringly.

Magic was suave and all, but I hadn't really mastered my new abilities yet. A few months back during *Mardi Gras* when my friends had been out of town, Othello and I had had a run in with Heaven. And Hell. And my previous governing institution, the Academy – which ruled and dictated the laws of the wizard nation. They had thought I was working for the demons. Heaven thought so too. I hadn't been, of course. But everyone and their mother wanted to get their grubby hands on the secret project my father had gifted to me prior to his death. An Armory of the deadliest supernatural weapons in recorded history.

During the struggle, my own people had taken away my magic, permanently, but my father had given me something else along with the Armory. A new, strange power that had historically been placed higher on the food chain than even a wizard's magic. To be honest, even months later, I was still struggling to wrap my head around it.

So, having not mastered my new abilities as a Maker, I liked to be reassured by the hundred-pound gun at my hip. Not really a hundred pounds, but the SIG Sauer X-Five Gunnar had given me a while back was definitely reassuring, and right now it really did feel like a hundred pounds of confidence.

"Alright, gang. It's now or never."

I lifted my foot to take a step, and a silver ball of light – I somehow had the presence of mind to notice that it resembled a stunningly attractive, anatomically correct, naked *Barbie* doll – struck me in the dome, knocking me clear on my ass and into a puddle of nastiness. I quickly scrambled to my feet, shivering, ready to obliterate the creature. She hovered where my head had been, staring directly at me. It *was* a naked Barbie.

And I recognized her.

"She looks familiar..." Gunnar murmured to Indie, who was staring wide-eyed at the silver sprite.

"What *is* she?" Indie asked bluntly, cocking her head sideways as she assessed the creature. "She's beautiful."

"A sprite. A fairy. A very dangerous fairy. Looks can be deceiving," I warned, shaking the cold sewage off my coat.

The sprite smiled in approval at the warning, flashing needle-like teeth at Indie, who flinched back a step. "He's back, and he's coming to murder you and all your friends." The glowing sprite hissed darkly to me, "it's time."

Like I said, a lot can happen between *now* and *never*.

2

I shook my coat off again with a growl, trying to detach, at least, the larger pieces of filth. Wet splashes marked my successes, adding to the fragrant stench filling my nose.

"Right before you sucker-punched me into that pile of defecation, we had been stealthily approaching the vermin in order to exterminate him. So, *shoo*, Barbie," I growled darkly. I didn't know what name she went by in casual circles, but I knew her True Name, the one able to compel her to obey if used three times in conjunction, which I was very tempted to use at the moment just to make a point. But I didn't. So, in my mind she was now *Barbie*, whereas before I had called her Nympho Sprite.

Nympho for nymphomaniac. Emphasis on *maniac*. I had met her before on an impromptu case that led to me opening my arcane bookstore, Plato's Cave – currently still under renovation from the gentle affections of a brawl involving a demon, an angel, and a Nephilim during *Mardi Gras* a few months back. This little light of mine had a thing for helping wizards in exchange for... well... *sexual favors*.

Look, I know, she looked all of twelve inches tall right *now*. But it's not as weird as it sounds. She could become *bigger* when she wanted to by shapeshifting to match her summoner's size. She had even hinted that she could shapeshift into other *creatures*, so being a werewolf for example wasn't an impediment to her, *erm*, bargaining price. I had also gotten the distinct impression that many didn't survive her affections, and that didn't seem to bother her in the least. If anything, it *pleased* her.

Creepy.

"Bah," she waved a hand at my comment. "Not the vampires, wiz–" She hesitated, eyes widening with sudden confusion. She stared at me more closely, assessing me on a deeper level than the mortal eye could, as if calculating a new equation in her mind.

She must have realized I was no longer a wizard, but I didn't know how. She continued on a few seconds later, shelving the topic of my abilities, and returning to her initial purpose. "Interesting development." She murmured to herself before continuing. "The Grimm. Jacob is back. And he brought his brothers. To kill you and all your friends. I warned you of this when we first met."

An icy fist seemed to suddenly clench my vertebrae. Indie gasped.

The Brothers Grimm. They were back. For me. And my friends. Because I had taken their book from them a few years ago, and rather than destroying it like the sprite had advised, I had hoarded it away. And now I was going to pay for it.

As were my friends, apparently.

"I *knew* I recognized her. She used to work for Alistair. The book guy," Gunnar hissed. "Remember, Nate? Back in the old days." He looked at me.

She turned suddenly arctic eyes onto the wolf. "If you ever refer to him again as *the book guy* I will feast on your sclera." She licked her lips eagerly.

"No offense," he offered genuinely, taking a step back as he held up his hands to idly touch his eyes, which she had casually mentioned eating.

"Too late, wolf pup." She bared needle-like fangs in a hungry snarl.

Indie chimed in before the sprite could do anything. "Did you say vampires? As in, *plural*?" Gunnar and I froze, turning to the sprite.

She merely stared back, shaking her head in disbelief at our obviously limited mental capacity. "Good thing you brought the Regular along. She actually has a brain."

Gunnar and I began to sputter angry responses, but Indie beat us to it. "That's why they pay me the big bucks," she grinned.

Then I noticed the change in our surroundings. A faint rustling. And no more whimpering. Damn it. The sprite grinned in anticipation, looking eagerly delighted at the likely violence to come. "You seem to have stumbled upon a nest," she smiled.

Before I could respond with a sarcastic retort, a blinding flurry of tattered robes struck me like a Mizzou lineman. I purposely let him. A surprise counterattack.

No, really. It was on purpose.

So was the next part, when I let him slam my head into the brick wall behind us, eliciting an explosion of stars to swim across my vision. I dropped the pistol clutched in my hand and heard it splash deep into the muck at our feet. "Attack!" I managed to groan. Now I had him right where I wanted him. I heard Gunnar grunt in surprise and then the sound of him being tackled into the sewage. I briefly managed to wonder why I hadn't heard the explosion of fabric that resulted from him shifting into wolf form from human clothes. His giant snow-white mountain wolf form was much better suited to fighting vampires. In fact, it was designed to do *just that*. I don't know how I managed to notice any of this, seeing as how I had a frothing mad vampire chomping down towards my necksicle, but I did. I also saw Indie's flashlight go sailing off into the darkness before landing in a puddle of ick.

Barbie's ambient glow was the only thing protecting us from the natural darkness of the tunnels. For which I was grateful, but she apparently didn't have the patience to wait for a little thing like the result of a life or death fight to conclude our conversation.

"All because you took their book. I told you to destroy it. Admit it."

She folded her arms. I managed to get a forearm against the vampire's neck, barely keeping him from gobbling up my tender throat. Despite still coming to grips with using my new power, I somehow managed to cast out a weak spell of air and bowled over the pair of vampires that had attacked Indie. She looked unharmed, but to be honest I couldn't see very clearly, what with the animated Disney birds and stars dancing across my vision and the strain against keeping the vampire from tasting my esophagus. Since it was now pointless to continue masking our scent, I dropped the small spell I had held to get us here undetected. Twin shots shattered the air as Indie let loose with her pistol.

Hollow-point, oak-tipped bullets worked like garlic cupcakes on a vampire. They dropped in a puff of dust. I heard fists striking flesh, and wondered again why I heard no howling or growling from Gunnar. Had they gotten him? My vision began to turn red in anger, and for the first time ever, the well of power that I presumed was available only to Makers called out to *me* rather than the other way around.

A river of molten lava flowing just beneath the surface of my mind invited me to play, and my vision pulsed from red to blue.

Before, as a wizard, I had essentially used the available elements around me to manipulate into magic. When the elements I needed were absent, I could draw from my own body for a limited time. But it was taxing.

The Maker power didn't quite work like that.

A constant pool of power resided just below the surface of the world around me, available to be manipulated into whatever the Maker saw fit to, well... *make*. To me, the well seemed bottomless in comparison to my old magic, but I was pretty sure it wasn't. It also wasn't as reliable, or I wasn't as gifted at using it as I had been with my magic. But then again, I had been a veritable force to be reckoned with as a wizard. Still, when the Maker power was harnessed, it could pack a punch that made a wizard look like a schoolyard bully. I began weaving the power together messily, still struggling against the vampire.

"Admit it, Temple," Barbie continued.

The vampire above me froze completely still. "Temple?" He hissed in alarm. I grunted an affirmative and he violently threw himself away before I could do anything. I fell into the muck at the sudden motion.

"The Maker!" One hissed from near Gunnar, who was holding a vampire's head under the filth, drowning him as he stared down the speaking vampire.

The one that had attacked me hissed again. "Retreat. None must harm the Maker."

I paused. *That* was never a good thing to hear. It usually implied worse, deadlier things were in store for you down the road. And they knew I was a Maker. Even though *I* didn't fully understand what that actually meant. Yet.

They disappeared back down the tunnel as fast as cockroaches when the lights were turned on. Vampires were *fast*. I took a deep breath, shook the stars from my eyes, and began to race after them, not wanting to give them a second longer than absolutely necessary with the victim I had heard whimpering earlier. I heard the clomping steps of my posse following me, and I felt Barbie latch onto my shoulder, getting a free ride.

Gunnar caught up to me easily so I shot him an angry glare. "You know, it would be really awesome if we had a werewolf to run them down right about now." Indie gamely let off a few pot shots as we ran.

He grunted in response. "Can't shift. Don't know why."

That dialed back my anger really quickly. What could prevent Gunnar from shifting? I hadn't even thought that was possible.

"Admit it, Temple. Admit you should have listened to me and I will take care of this... nuisance," Barbie spoke in my ear, interrupting our conversation.

I ignored her pointedly. We entered a cavernous space, and skidded to a stop. The vampires were scrabbling at a locked door, their fingers gouging at the wood to no effect.

"Rule number one, fangheads. Always have a back door ready."

They stopped, and then slowly turned to face me.

"We will leave you in peace," they offered, looking nervous.

"Not playing out that way," I muttered. The smell of blood and offal filled the space like a physical presence. My gaze swept the room quickly, searching for survivors.

But we were too late.

The girls were dead. I counted three bodies in direct sight. Two had been recently killed judging by the still-wet pools of blood around their crumpled bodies. Indie lifted her guns, pointing them at the vampires with a humorless grin on her beautiful face as Gunnar growled, taking a step forward. "Why can't I shift... fanghead?" He borrowed the nickname I had given them, somehow managing to tip an imaginary hat in my direction without averting his eyes from the vampires.

"Let us go and I will tell you. I'll even give it to you."

I laughed out loud. "Not too good at negotiating, are you? You just admitted that you have something that prevents my friend from letting his fur fly. That was your only bargaining chip. And you tossed it into the game without looking at your hand."

The vampires clammed up.

"We really do have more pressing matters, Temple," the sprite complained lazily. "Let's speed things up. They have a moonstone." She had drifted from my shoulders to float beside me. Most likely to avoid becoming collateral damage if they rushed me. I blinked at her. "Moonstone. A chunk of rock from the moon. It prevents a wolf from shifting," she elaborated. I exchanged a look with Gunnar. He shrugged with an arched brow. He hadn't heard of it either. I hated not knowing things.

"Why would you have something like that?" I asked them.

"Because he isn't the only wolf down here," the vampire snarled.

A piercing howl echoed throughout the tunnels. Followed by several answering calls.

The vampires tensed, arching up on the balls of their feet as if preparing to make a run for it. They weren't interested in tussling with us, let alone a pack of werewolves. The leader quickly reached into a pocket and pulled out a small stone. Before I could react, he slammed it into the wall, shattering it. Gunnar instantly sighed, his fists flexing into white furred claws.

"Admit it, Temple, and I will resolve this disagreement. You know you can't fight the vampires and the wolves at the same time. Time is wasting. They have your scent, and they will now be able to maintain their form when they get closer," the sprite whispered hungrily. I sighed.

"Okay, fine. I was right, you were wrong," I muttered. The howls grew closer, but silence still reigned supreme in our little alcove.

She shook her head, but didn't move. I saw the vampires tense up, ready to make their move.

"God damn it. *Fine. You* were right, and *I* was wrong." I shouted at her as the vamps took a step.

She beamed down at me for a few seconds, gloating, and the vampires were suddenly halfway out the room, escaping. But then Barbie snapped her dainty little toothpick fingers.

And a wave of pure silver light crashed down over the top of our heads like a heavy feather pillow. Not strong enough to knock me over, but enough to let me know it was definitely there. I heard an exclamation of surprise from my posse.

I stumbled a bit on wobbly legs, feeling oddly sensuous, as if all my senses were on high alert. I realized distantly that I was very definitely... in the *mood*. Like, instantly. I shook off the mental cloud and glared at the sprite. "If you hurt my friends, I'll roast you on a kabob." I took a threatening step towards her. "Or a toothpick, I guess."

"Tut, tut." She smiled, and I was knocked back on my ass, feeling dazed, and my pants just three sizes too small in the groin area. Indie let out a pleased whimper followed by a sharp exclamation of ecstasy. Then she folded to her feet with a dazed smile on her face. I blinked and turned my head to the sprite.

"That one was for free," she grinned.

"Did you just–"

"Granted, women are easier to please than men, if you know how we work. It just so happens that pleasure is my forte. Even *lethal* pleasure when the situation arises. But that's more for *my* enjoyment. This was just foreplay, a gift for your apology." She glanced at Indie, who was only now getting to her feet on shaky legs, looking excited and confused. She hadn't even commented on the filth covering her. "I think you may have an interesting night ahead of you, Temple," she smiled down at me. I shook the euphoria from my head, struggling to my feet. "You're welcome," she answered smugly.

Well, I didn't have anything to say to *that*. Thank you? A cigarette?

The vampires lay motionless on the cool stone floor. Their bodies slowly transformed into ash that was lighter than the air, before further disintegrating to nothing. Gunnar climbed to his feet, very obviously aroused, and even more obviously pleased at the situation. Great, everyone else seemed to get a happy ending, where I only got a case of metaphysical blue balls.

My life.

More howls punctuated my situation in a piercing lament.

3

"Alright. Time to scat."

"Where? If they don't have our scent yet they soon will," Gunnar answered, eyes darting back and forth anxiously.

"Follow me." I retraced our steps in a light jog back to the first intersection of tunnels, and veered down the other fork this time. The howls were coming from a different part of the sewer, which was a blessing, buying us a few minutes. The sprite whispered in my ear, having apparently hitched a ride on my shoulder again. Lazy freaking fairies.

"We have more pressing matters to discuss," she urged.

"I think survival is the most pressing issue," I argued. She grunted in disagreement. "Besides, I'm already working on the Grimms." She went silent, apparently satisfied at my answer and content to enjoy her free ride.

After several more turns we began to hear sounds above our heads.

"Is that a jackhammer?" Indie asked from my left shoulder, breathing heavily.

Gunnar tilted his head as we ran, remaining at my other shoulder. "It sounds like a construction site. Are we beneath roadwork?" He whispered softly, knowing how well werewolves could hear. "Is it safe for us to be down here?"

I grunted, spotting our next turn. They flowed with me. "Of course not. It's never safe down here. Remember all the signs I told you guys to ignore at the entrance?" Gunnar's eyes tightened, but he made no comment, focusing instead on our immediate survival.

We finally came to a gnarled iron door and I stopped. Water stains trailed down the brick-work surrounding the door, feeding a rather large patch of moss and algae of some kind. The construction sounds were louder now. I could imagine the familiar smells coming from the building above us. "It's louder now. It's definitely construction. Why did we stop?" A distant howl punctuated Gunnar's question.

"You're right. It does sound like construction. In fact, if I had to guess I would say we are directly underneath Plato's Cave." I reached into a pocket and nonchalantly withdrew an old-school iron key.

Gunnar muttered a curse. "This was your intention. You had this planned. No way we accidentally ended up underneath your bookstore." I smiled and shrugged innocently as I took a step forward and used the key to open the door to my hidey-hole.

Indie held up a hand, stalling Gunnar's impatience. "I got this. I speak Nate." She didn't try to hide her words. She turned to me, face deadpan. "Oh, Nate. You're so witty and clever. Why did you take us to your oh-so-secret underground lair? No, please, tell us. We can't take the suspense," she said, her voice monotone and dripping with sarcasm.

I scowled, and she winked, cracking a smile as she lifted her hands in a bow as if to tell Gunnar, *See*? She took all the fun out of it. I turned my back on them to address the door.

"No, really. Why are we here?" Indie asked seriously this time, peering over my shoulder with an affectionate squeeze as I struggled with the rusted lock on the door. I began to answer with the prearranged, carefully crafted lie on the tip of my tongue, but then I had a thought. Thanks to the sprite, I now had a justifiable excuse for wanting to stop by here. I didn't need to lie to cover the truth from her.

"I have a small vault down here as a precaution against the bookstore ever being robbed. I keep several things down here. The books the Grimms want are here. Lucky us, right?"

Gunnar studied me suspiciously, but didn't speak the question on his mind. If the sprite's visit was unplanned, why had I coincidentally known how to get to this place so quickly on a convenient vampire-hunting trip? I shrugged at him with a smile, silently urging him to drop it.

I finally wrestled the door open to loud screeching, which made me shiver.

The wolves had to have heard *that*.

I strode over to the hidden safe, the room comfortably illuminated by the sprite's presence on my shoulder. Several bookshelves lined two walls of the small storage room, filled with important-looking books, but they were just a front. I plucked a seemingly random loose brick free from the far wall to reveal a digital safe keypad. I heard grunts of surprise behind me but ignored them as I punched in the code. It beeped once, and a three-foot section of the brick wall swung silently towards me on well-oiled hinges, but the brick affixed to the small safe's door scratched the floor loudly. It had to be a tight fit to remain hidden, so there was nothing to do about it or else it would have been pretty obvious that it wasn't part of the wall.

I reached inside and plucked two books wrapped in silk from a jumble of random items. I also palmed a loose sapphire ring, glittering with a collection of tiny loose diamonds around its antique edges. The sprite – the only one close enough to see my hands and the contents of the vault – frowned at that, turning her gaze to the side of my face to regard me thoughtfully. I was too close to her physically to return the gesture so I merely pocketed the ring and lifted a finger to my lips, requesting her silence.

"Um, Nate? They're onto us. Did you get the books yet? If not, maybe we should come back later," Gunnar asked from out in the tunnel, speaking over his shoulder as he kept an eye out for us. Growling could be heard in the near distance, picking up on the sound of his voice and probably our scent too. They were close.

"Yes, I've got them." I tucked the books into my other coat pocket and shut the vault, carefully replacing the loose brick. The two books weren't particularly large, more journals than anything. Indie stepped closer to me, but hadn't seen the ring, thank god. It had belonged to my mother and I was going to use it when I proposed to her.

The growling suddenly ceased and I turned to find five figures facing Gunnar beyond the doorway.

"Wow, did I shake a bag of puppy chow or something?" I asked loud enough for everyone to hear as I stepped out of the room.

The leader stepped forward with a snarl. "Does he have it?" He asked one of his compatriots, staring past Gunnar and directly at me. He was a large specimen of a man, and sported a thick black beard that just touched his chest. They were dressed in casual clothes, grays and blacks, loose-fitting, and unremarkable. They all wore heavy hiking or combat boots, as if they had known they would be down here tonight. Which told me this wasn't a coincidence. The vampires had also been prepared for wolves. Blackbeard's eyes glittered expectantly in the darkness as he watched me.

One of the other wolves – a leaner, whip-thin scrapper, by the looks of it – took a deep whiff and nodded. "Yes. But he said nothing of the Maker being present. In fact, we are to avoid the Maker at all costs. Punishable by death," Scrappy warned Blackbeard.

I was more startled to discover that yet another flavor of Freaks knew about my new powers, but I didn't have time to ask about it. Things escalated rather quickly.

"I know what our fucking orders were, pup!" Blackbeard bellowed as he backhanded the lean wolf without taking his gaze from me, sending the skinny werewolf into the wall with a hard thud. The other wolves shifted their shoulders reflexively but didn't avert their gaze from our party. They were all different flavors of Hard Ass. *Blackbeard, Shorty, Rhino, Aryan, and Scrappy*, I silently nicknamed them in my head.

"Orders. Taking commands," I waved my hands to enunciate. "Wanting something of mine while tucking your tails between your legs in order to avoid a confrontation with me." I spoke softly but clearly. Gunnar grunted in agreement.

Indie piped up. "Gunnar, didn't you tell me werewolves were brave and honorable?"

He nodded. "I had thought so, but we're just people. Some good," he studied them each with a glare, "Some who shouldn't be let off their leashes." He yawned. Indie looked thoughtful, idly tapping a lip.

I nodded. "Not very impressive at all. In fact, you're boring me. Getting on my nerves, even. If you want to scrap, shed your human skin and let your fur fly, pups. We'll oblige. If not, Daddy's got important things to do. So, *shoo*," I flicked a dismissive hand.

Indie cocked her guns in the silence. Aryan took a step forward. "Our orders were not to kill you. I can handle that." He took another step.

Gunnar growled, fists shifting into long black claws sheathed in thick white fur. "One more step and you're a sack of meat," he warned, looking resolved but distantly sickened at the potential for upcoming murder. The wolf snickered in doubtful reproach and took another step.

Before his foot touched the ground, Gunnar shifted entirely to wolf form in an explosion of tattered fabric. All I saw in the dull illumination was Aryan, standing upright with his throat ripped out. Gunnar stood in his impressive wolf form, muscles bristling, on the other side of the pack, but still between the thieves and us. He growled a warning. The other wolves responded with menacing growls of their own.

Then the body thudded into the water.

Two of the others, Rhino and Shorty, instantly threw themselves forward and Indie's pistols *boomed*, sending Shorty back into the darkness with a cry. The other sailed right past Gunnar and Indie, straight for me. Of course, it was the bigger one, Rhino. I was fueled with plenty of rage at the moment, having anticipated a much calmer walk in the sewers than it had ended up being. The wolf's outstretched arms had been aimed at my feet, but since I had dropped to my knees, his fingertips managed to instead hit my side before time seemed to freeze. He was reaching for the books, but his hand got caught in the wrong pocket. The force of the burly werewolf's attack would have folded most people or slammed them to the ground. But I'm a wizard, and I had let him get close enough to touch me on purpose.

You may not know this, but wizards are dirty cheats.

I had needed him to make physical contact with me in order for me to add his momentum to my magic. My fingertips broke the surface of the frigid water. As time seemed to stand still, I exploded upwards, a single drop of frozen shit water resting in the air before my face. My sudden motion caused his hand to tear open the pocket of my coat, but luckily the books were in my other pocket. I flicked my finger and the wolf was abruptly engulfed in a vortex of icy, stinky water. I used the rotating momentum to cast him straight back the way he had come. The explosion of frosty air hit the tunnels like a snow blower, coating the walls and ground in icy hoarfrost, a shining surface that was as slick as quicksilver. The wolf hit it.

And kept right on going at warp speed, right past Blackbeard and the others, fueled by the maelstrom of my magic.

He disappeared from sight and slid down the tunnel quite a ways before the chill began to wear off and the friction increased, hopefully giving him one serious rug burn. I heard a final yelp and then a crumple as he struck a wall that was no longer slick, well out of sight.

I brushed off my hands and turned to the remaining wolves. Only Blackbeard and

Scrappy remained in sight, looking startled. "Stomach shots. It won't kill him, but it will slow him down," Indie spoke clinically, thrusting her jaw at Shorty's groaning body.

Blackbeard growled menacingly and turned to Gunnar. "You will pay for that, rogue. Every wolf needs a pack. It's time you learned your place. The night is dangerous for a lone wolf."

Gunnar responded by shifting back to his human form. He stood from the ground, looking like a Viking from the Norse legends, blood dripping from his mouth. The sprite murmured appreciatively.

He only smiled. "I'll take my chances." His pecs glistened with the victorious sweat of a Roman Gladiator.

Either that or icy shit water.

But that kind of killed the sexy factor.

Blackbeard's eyes were murderous. "Gather the wounded. This wasn't as we were told it would be. No one else needs to die." He assessed Gunnar hungrily. "Tonight." He promised.

Then they were gone. Well, except for the dead werewolf. I looked at Barbie and then at the body. She rolled her eyes at me and he was suddenly gone. Disappeared or destroyed. I shivered, not wanting to know the answer. Indie gasped too, and Barbie smiled darkly, licking her lips. I turned away from her. I had plenty of nightmare material already.

A few moments went by before Gunnar confirmed, "they're gone."

"Well," I sighed, "I don't know about you guys, but I'm exhausted from kicking ass all night. Let's head back. Gunnar, you're on point. Indie, in the middle. Barbie, watch our six."

"Oh, I'll definitely be watching *his* six." She pointed bluntly at Gunnar's prominent nakedness. He blushed. Indie burst out laughing.

"*Professionalism...*" I muttered, shaking my head as I took point instead—so as not to obstruct Barbie's view—and they began to follow in the order I'd suggested. I idly patted my pockets as we moved, my mind struggling to decipher why the sewers had been such a happening place tonight. And the coincidence that Achilles had sent us here, this night of all nights. Then I blinked, slowing my steps. I patted my pocket again more frantically as another second ticked by, feeling only the torn fabric hanging free. I halted, checking my other pocket now, turning it inside out.

I growled a curse as I came up empty handed. "Son of a bitch!"

The ring.

I searched the ground like a madman, scraping the puddles, ignoring everyone's incredulous faces and questions about what I was doing. I even cast out a bit of my new power, searching with magic for any traces of a small metal object under the filth, but I found nothing but a dented soda can. It was no use.

It was gone.

Rhino must have managed to swipe it when his hands got stuck in my pocket, tearing open the fabric.

I growled darkly as I climbed to my feet, glaring murder at the direction of the retreating werewolves.

Things can always get worse.

4

We sat in my BMW X5, Gunnar behind the driver's wheel and Indie in the passenger seat as we headed back to *Chateau Falco*. Gunnar had thrown on some loose sweats and a tee that he always carried around with him in case of needing to re-clothe after a shift. I had also changed into an old gym outfit buried in my trunk, but still stunk to high heaven. Barbie had stuck by our side and was now hovering beside me in the backseat, looking pleasantly naked. I turned my head in embarrassment, which elicited a small smile from her silver lips.

Having survived the night, I was ready for a drink and a long massage, especially after Indie's very obvious innuendos on our way back to the vehicle. It seemed the sprite's magic had definitely lit a match in her that I wanted to explore. I cleared my head with a gentle slap to my cheeks.

Later. Business first. Beneath the more life-threatening situation, all I could think about was the lost ring. Had Rhino managed to nab it before I sent him on his icy waterslide? It seemed unlikely, but the bottom line was that I had assumed I was quicker than the lycanthrope gene, and now the ring was gone. I was confident it hadn't fallen into the muck. I had silently tested the tunnel with magic to no avail. I shook my head. I would just have to ask Rhino about it before my dinner date with Indie in a few days.

He and his pack weren't likely to want to see me.

I wasn't likely to be too concerned about that. I would just have to ask nicely.

Also known as walking loudly and swinging a big stick.

"So… the Grimms," I began, desperately needing to distract myself with something other than the ring. Barbie watched me hungrily as if waiting for me to finally tear off my clothes and submit to her allure. Dark sex may be appealing to some, but that was taking it to a whole different level. I shivered at the thought. "I take it that they aren't too happy with me?" In hindsight, it was a good reason I was down in the sewers tonight. It hadn't been my intention, but it seemed awfully coincidental that things had gone to hell the very night I had decided to make a trip to my previously secret vault for personal reasons.

But now that was dashed all to hell. No ring.

Barbie answered my rhetorical question. "To put it mildly. They want their book back. But besides that, they've also accepted a contract on your head. And all known associates, guilty or not." The temperature in the car grew frigid as the implication sunk in. She nodded before continuing, "I think it's time you destroy the book. You will die either way, but at least they won't be able to summon the rest of their brothers into our world. Or their pets. I believe you were lucky enough to have met one of *them* once." I nodded, grimacing at the memory of the demonic rooster horse Gunnar and I had fought and destroyed several years back.

"The rest? How many are there?" I asked, dumbfounded. I had assumed only a handful. Unless Jacob and Wilhelm's mom had been particularly amorous in her day.

She smiled icily. "Hundreds. Why do you think we locked them away?"

I blinked in astonishment. *Hundreds?*

"How many are here already?" I asked softly.

"A dozen."

"Oh. Well that doesn't sound like too many. I've got a few friends who can help–"

"A dozen of the most dangerous, bloodthirsty, savage, supernatural hit men that ever existed. A dozen creatures who spent hundreds of years destroying supernatural citizens, regardless of their powers and joint collaboration efforts. Even Makers." The silence was deafening. She drifted closer and lifted my chin. "You had a good round, Temple, but you played your last card. You lost. You just don't know it yet. At least you can make sure that the rest of us don't die too. Bring me the book. Sooner rather than later. I will help you destroy it. And say goodbye to you. I wish we could have gotten to know each other better..." With that, she was abruptly gone.

Indie and Gunnar merely stared at me with wide eyes before clamoring over each other with demands for an explanation. So, I told them. Everything. I had first run into Jacob Grimm years before. Our introduction had been the true reason behind my career as a used bookstore owner. I had opened Plato's Cave to hide the two books now resting in the satchel at my feet. I had been warned that I should destroy them. I hadn't listened, instead wanting to study them. In the years since, the fear had worn off and I had put it on my rainy-day list. As well as a zillion other things that always seemed to take precedence. So, they had sat buried in a vault beneath my third projector room in Plato's Cave for years. Unopened. Untouched. And now a liability.

The Hubris of youth...

Sharing the story with my friends helped clear my head a bit and come up with a game plan. If there was a contract out on my life, I knew a guy who might have heard about it. I told Gunnar where to turn. He did so without complaint, slowly beginning to unravel his clouded memory from the particular night we had met Jacob Grimm. After the events that transpired that fateful night, Barbie had wiped his mind clean to keep the information compartmentalized. But now I had told him the truth, and he didn't look pleased at my deceit. Even though, technically, it hadn't been me, I had been complicit in essentially helping him believe a lie. Which didn't sit well with the werewolf.

I would have to make it up to him somehow.

To be fair, the sprite had wiped everyone's memories from that night. Well, except mine. Even Kyle and Tammy, the two innocent college kids with unique healing abilities who had found themselves unwittingly entwined in the scheme to steal the books in the first place. Their accomplice had been working for the Grimms, but he was long gone now. I idly wondered what had happened to the two kids. If they even remembered why they had suddenly left town and dropped out of college.

I stared off into the distance, lost in memory, until Gunnar reached our destination and parked in a vacant spot on the side of the road. "I need to make a call." Gunnar nodded. I picked up my phone and dialed a familiar number, waiting for an answer. I had thought tonight was going to be a quick trip.

But it now seemed like my *never* was approaching earlier than I had anticipated. This was really going to mess up my five-year plan.

A familiar agitated voice answered the phone. I listened to him for a few more seconds before responding. "Are you sure you don't have time to talk right now?" I asked softly, eyeing a Kinko's just down the street, mind already formulating a sinister plan. Gunnar watched me warily, recognizing the familiar tone I had used, and knowing that the only safe response would have been to comply with my request. He had been on the receiving end of that tone one too many times.

But the person on the phone didn't know me well enough to realize that.

"I shouldn't even be talking to you at all! Fine. Give me a few hours. I need to clear up a few things first." The phone muffled and I heard a female complaining in the background.

"I guess that will have to work. Unless you... *clear a few things up* earlier than expected. If so, I'll be waiting." He grunted noncommittally and hung up.

I opened the door and stepped outside. "I'll be right back," I told them. Indie darted out of the car to join me with a curious frown. Rather than arguing, I figured the safest place for her was in my sight. I reached out and held her hand as we walked through the frigid streets. "Isn't that Tomas' apartment?" She asked, pointing a thumb over her shoulder. "The dragon hunter that you ran into a year ago?"

I nodded, smirking lightly.

"Why don't we just head up there and talk to him really quick? That was him on the phone, right?"

I smiled at her, nodding. "Because he wouldn't be focused. At this point I think he would tell us anything to get us out of his hair." She frowned. "He's got a girl up there. I think they are going out for dinner." She rolled her eyes in understanding.

"Men. One whiff of 'tang and they're off like a rocket. No loyalty."

I chuckled. "It's in our DNA, and written in our Man Bible. We all must abide by it," I answered solemnly.

"Right." She rolled her eyes. "Makes you very predictable." She squeezed my palm.

I turned my head and noticed her cheeks were rosy from the cold. Snowflakes dotted her hair like ornaments, and her lips were a deep red shade like frozen raspberries. "We'll talk about predictable after you see my plan. I've been waiting a long time for something like this. The opportunity doesn't come up as often as you'd think."

I opened the door to the store and Indie studied me thoughtfully before entering first. I followed her and approached the register. "Good evening. I need you to do me a favor. I need some prints made," I addressed a matronly woman behind the counter with a dazzling array of badges and flair on her company vest. Her nametag read Nadine and she instantly noticed the smell suddenly permeating the room, but she didn't say anything about it. I handed her a flash drive I had swiped from my satchel, courtesy of Othello. I had held onto it for months, waiting for the perfect opportunity.

"Of course, how many would you two like?"

"Oh, quite a few. A hundred should suffice. You can pick your favorites." I told her. Indie managed to keep a straight face, even though she had no idea what I was doing.

"Well, that will take about an hour. Is that a problem?" She plugged in the flash drive as I answered, clicking buttons to get to the files. They were the only ones on the drive. It wouldn't take long for her to see them.

"No. But try to make it sooner. We can wait. We're parked just down the street. We'll also need a roll of packing tape and scissors."

She frowned. "Okay. Give me your number and I'll call you when it's all ready." Her frown was deepening at the items on the flash drive as the thumbnails pulled up on her screen. She glanced up at Indie thoughtfully, and then frowned. I barely managed to keep my face still.

"It's for a prank. Bachelor party. *Boys...*" Indie murmured, rolling her eyes in a *what can you do?* gesture. She deserved a Tony Award.

"O...Okay," Nadine finally responded.

"Perfect." I gave her three hundred-dollar bills, which she took gratefully as if it mitigated the questionable task I had just hired her to do, and then led Indie back outside. I spotted a coffee shop down the street and pointed at it. Indie squinted, and then grinned.

"Ooooh, hot chocolate!" She clapped her hands. We headed towards the coffee shop, Indie clutching my arm tightly while we crossed the street.

I could definitely get used to this.

She was forever material... as long as I could get my damn ring back from the fleabag werewolves.

"You know, even though I'm no longer in law enforcement, breaking and entering still doesn't sit well with me," Gunnar complained. I opened my mouth to defend myself but he held up a finger. "Even if you did Shadow Walk in there. Probably wasn't a good idea to take Indie along with you. Who knows what that kind of magic does to a *Regular*?" He spat the last word like a particularly foul-tasting racial slur.

Indie swatted his arm. "Easy, dog," she grinned. "Nate's done it with me dozens of times."

"Heh... heh," I chuckled huskily in my creepiest tone.

Indie rolled her eyes. "Men. I'm surrounded by an adolescent boy who laughs at the word *boobs*, and a senior citizen who wants to keep me locked away in a bubble-wrapped house." We both piped up at that, arguing vehemently but she cut us off, face pressed against the glass eagerly. "Shhh... Pay attention. He's coming back!" She pointed up the street, but a row of cars blocked my vision. "This is going to be film-worthy..." I grinned at seeing her excitement, mildly surprised that for once she wasn't sitting beside Gunnar chastising me. In fact, she was defending my irresponsible use of magic.

I loved this woman.

Here she was, out of her league, and totally stoked at a supernatural B&E. It made me feel more comfortable about my upcoming proposal. Even if I *was* enabling her criminal skills.

Which brought me back to thoughts of the missing ring. At some point, tomorrow or the next day, I needed to pay the were-mutts a visit. But I had enough on my plate tonight.

Gunnar was arguing with Indie. "Film-worthy, as in you two caught on film breaking into his apartment? Why are we sitting here, and what exactly did you two do in there?"

Indie made a surprised grunt and lowered her body deeper in the seats. Gunnar and I instinctively mimicked her, finally noticing our target walking down the street with a girl on his arm. She was clinging to him as if he was the only source of heat on the planet.

That, and possibly the only way she could remain upright without breaking her heels.

Apparently, they had shared a few drinks while at dinner. She wasn't sloppy drunk, but she definitely needed his support. I smiled to myself, wishing I had a bird's eye view inside the apartment. Then I remembered my new magic.

As a Maker, I was supposedly able to create things that had never been accomplished before: new magic, more powerful artifacts, and spells – basically able to work outside the limitations of traditional magic. Where other wizards were limited by their innate ability – their body and the elements immediately around them – a Maker was supposedly limited only by his imagination, implying that if they put their mind to it, a Maker could quite literally do whatever crazy idea popped into their heads.

Of course, I had a long way to go before I would be doing anything like that.

I was having a hard-enough time trying to figure out how to reliably use it to recreate similar spells I had used when I was a regular old wizard. When it worked at all, my new magic worked *differently*.

Entirely differently.

Before the Event, I would see the world around me in Technicolor, able to grab and utilize gossamer threads of power that floated in the air, weaving them into balls of fire, attack spells, tracking spells, utilize my body's own energy for rituals to summon... things. Essentially, I used my immediate vicinity – all of it – and reshaped it to my will.

But I had been severely limited by the elements around me.

I had been a pretty big hitter compared to most wizards, but still.

I had limits.

But now...

The Maker power was incredibly different. Instead of pulling energy from the environment, it felt more like delving deep into the earth to reach through a secret portal to grasp power out of the very cosmos. A river of power flowed through the universe, and a small tributary of that river seemed to course beneath my feet at all times. The tough part was tapping into it. It was like knowing you were thirsty and seeing a fire hydrant jettisoning hundreds of gallons a minute into the air at fifty miles per hour. You had to find a way to use it, but you couldn't just slap your cheeks into the stream and hope for a refreshing sip. You had to think. Use your mind. Grab a cup to catch the falling water, decrease the pressure of the hydrant, slow time so that the force decreased, you know, hard things to think about when you were in the thick of things.

Seeing as how I generally didn't get much time to sit there and think during a brawl, I had spent my time trying to relearn the equivalent of my favorite attack and defense spells as a wizard, with marginal success. I could always *feel* the river of power.

It was *harnessing* it that was not very often successful.

I could spend an hour and my attempt would pass through the river every time. The next day I could get it seventy percent of the time. Other times I had been angry and it had instinctively been waiting for me, ready to be cast in any way I saw fit. Like when the power had first hit me and I found myself in a tussle involving Angels, Demons, Academy Justices, and the Horsemen of the Apocalypse. I had simply *thought* of what I wanted, and it happened without question or effort. Easy as pie.

Absolutely every time since then had been a grueling battle of wills. It was almost like a relationship. *His Needs, Her Needs*. I needed to establish the proper code of conduct in order to impress the river of power enough to give me what I wanted. Like foreplay before sex. It required a bit more work.

So essentially, I had a new imaginary girlfriend rather than my usual wizard's magic. And my imaginary friend was an invisible, unquenchable river of power coursing beneath my feet at all times. A river that I was confident actually came from the cosmos, or the *Big Bang*. It didn't feel terrestrial. It felt... alien. There had been times in my experimentation where the force had done things that completely went against every Law of Physics that I knew. And doing those things had been easier than trying to make a ball of fire, for example.

My hired thug, chauffeur, and cook – Mallory – had spent quite a bit of time with me in an attempt to help me learn. We had met with marginal success. I had discussed it with my parents – who now resided in an Ancient Armory hidden in *Chateau Falco* – my ancestral home. The librarian of the Armory, Pandora (yep, that one) had also been of little help as a teacher. No one knew what to tell me.

The last Maker had died many, many years ago, leaving me no one to learn from.

My mind snapped back to focus as Indie squeezed my arm excitedly. I stared out the window to see the apartment in question now had its light on. Indie's breath was fogging up the back window as she watched, eyes twinkling with mischief and anticipation.

"Any second now. What do you think they've been doing for the last ten minutes? I had figured he would have made his move by now." She spoke softly.

I blinked. *Ten minutes?* I needed to get my head back in the game. The Grimms were out there somewhere. I would be pretty easy meat if I zoned out like that again.

"You sure it wasn't too much?" She whispered.

Gunnar's face twitched. "Sure *what* wasn't too much? *Nate... what did you two–*"

The front door of the building suddenly slammed open and the drunken girl came stumbling out, yelling angrily over her shoulder as she struggled to toss her coat back on. Only one of the straps on her shirt was attached correctly, and it seemed to be tangled up with her arm because she was having a hell of a time putting the coat on. Her bra was also openly on display, and it, too, wasn't completely attached, flashing a pale expanse of skin to the peeping toms in our car. Indie slapped my arm with an anxious laugh, one of the guys, making sure I zeroed in on the almost escaped boob.

I grinned.

A half-naked man appeared in the doorway to the building, pleading with her to come back so he could explain. We could hear it through the windows, so he had to be shouting. But she shambled on down the street, storming off into the night and forcefully flipping the man the middle finger. His bare chest didn't seem to register the cold.

Then again, with what he had planned for the night so suddenly imploding on him, I could understand his mindset with the no doubt near superhuman spike of adrenaline and testosterone blocking his cold receptors.

I watched as his face slowly began to darken in anger, his eyes scanning the street like only an assassin could. His eyes landed on our car for a second, but then flicked past. I called him on my new phone – one that managed to encrypt calls, texts, and emails – from both ends of the line. Only retailed for $17,000. A steal. I had gotten one for all my friends earlier this year. With us occasionally taking on questionable jobs – legally, that is – I wanted as much security and deniability as possible. It was also designed and built by my own company, Temple Industries, so R&D took on the expense for it.

I spoke casually, bubbling with enthusiasm. "Hey, man. I was driving in your neighborhood and wanted to see if your plans had chang–"

"You miserable son of a bitch," he growled. "That was low. Even for you."

"If I don't ruin someone's day I don't sleep very well. It's one of my gifts."

He grunted, still scanning the street. Gunnar rolled his eyes and finally flashed his lights once. The man acknowledged us with a fiery glare. He flipped us off, and then motioned for us to come inside before doing so himself, deciding not to wait at the door.

"See you in a minute, bastard. Keep a low profile on your way in," he said cryptically before he hung up.

Gunnar merely shook his head at me. "You are a real piece of work. How did you manage to get the girl to leave so fast?"

"Oh, you'll see." Indie burst out laughing as we opened the car doors to follow my friend, the dragon hunter, inside his apartment.

5

I wasn't sure what I had expected, but as we stood in the dingy hallway outside the apartment door, I guessed I could have summed it up in one word. *More.* Tomas was a dragon hunter, a hit man. Surely, he made better money than the building led me to believe.

Tomas opened the door, scowled at me for good measure, and then while leaning out of the doorway to glance both ways behind us, he swiftly darted in to plant a quick wet smooch on Indie's cheek. I instinctively tensed up, my inner alpha male growling at the challenge, but Indie burst out laughing, calming my beast. She jabbed him playfully in the ribs as she forced her way past him and inside the apartment, darting immediately to the back room to inspect the masterpiece we had recently erected. Well, if that hadn't given us away I didn't know what would.

He quickly let Gunnar and me in the door, grimacing at our stench before locking and dead-bolting the door behind us. But he didn't question our smell, just accepted it. I wasn't sure what that said about me. Or him.

Tomas seemed nervous underneath his calm demeanor. Perhaps I thought so because he had asked us to be discreet upon entering the building, or because he had scanned the hallway before letting us in. Or maybe it was because he was now hurriedly dashing to the windows to close the thick curtains. Regardless, he wasn't a nervous guy. Hit men were notoriously calm, cool, and collected. I was pretty sure it was part of their job description. I raised an eyebrow at him, but he didn't explain. "Phones," he growled, holding out a beefy palm. Which pretty much confirmed my suspicions.

We complied and he carried them over to the microwave, carefully tucking them inside and shutting the door. Gunnar frowned at me as if attempting to telepathically ask me if Tomas had lost his marbles at some point.

"Faraday cage. Blocks the UHF frequencies." Gunnar continued staring at me.

"I hear words coming out of your mouth, but I don't know what they mean."

"No one can use them to hear us," Tomas clarified, striding towards us.

Indie returned from gloating over her masterpiece, instantly catching onto the tension as she watched the men folk stare each other down. Tomas pointed at the kitchen.

Her face clouded over in a heartbeat. "You think that because I'm a woman I'm going to go make you men sandwiches? Fat chance, dragon hunter. I have half a mind to–"

"Indie, can you put your phone in the microwave, please?" I interrupted her tirade.

"Oh. Yeah. Sure," she answered sheepishly, but Tomas was barely repressing his laughter as she made her way to the kitchen.

"While you're at it, I'll take a BLT." He finally burst out, roaring with laughter. An apple sailed out of the kitchen and clucked him on the back of the head, abruptly halting his laughter. My laughter began the millisecond his ended.

He sat down into a worn leather recliner with a grunt, picking up the projectile in his scarred hands. "I suppose I asked for that," he murmured, grinning. I nodded, and the room slowly began to fill with idle banter as they caught up with each other. I merely watched, mind combing the facts as I planned out my next moves.

Indie, dancing on her toes with anticipation finally convinced Tomas to let her show Gunnar the artwork in the bedroom. We spent a few minutes chuckling over it, even Gunnar. A hundred pictures of the same girl, all taken from different angles, formed a serial stalker collage that took up a good six-foot tall by four-foot wide section of the wall. They had been taken from some random woman's social media account. It had no doubt made Tomas look, at best, like a crazy ex-boyfriend; and at worst, an obsessive stalker. Indie and I had efficiently *slaughtered* the mood. In my eyes, the elaborate joke made me feel that all was right with the world. Some good to balance the dire news I had learned today.

Pranks were soothing to the soul. They reminded you that if such an infinitesimal event like being cockblocked by an extremely well-thought-out master plan was the worst thing to happen to you that day, things were probably going to be more or less OK.

Also, my empathy factor was at an all time low at the moment. We had just survived a beating by two different supernatural groups in the sewers, but Tomas had been too busy planning on getting busy to spend five minutes of his time to talk with me. I had real world problems going on. I didn't have time for Tomas to get all twitter-pated for a few hours while I waited him out in a constant state of paranoia, anticipating a bullet to the head at any second.

Go Team Temple, crushing single guys' fantasies, one stalker collage at a time.

Tomas had taken a few minutes to truly calm down, but knowing who and what I was, he also likely knew there really wasn't anything he could do to me. *Hello, Maker.* Other than stealing a kiss from Indie's nonconsensual cheek. And accepting the fact that it really was quite an impressive prank, more than anything, seemed to cool him off. Also, seeing us all burst out laughing at the impromptu mural had finally allowed him to admit the humor in it.

He sighed in resignation. "Well, I definitely need a few drinks after that." He chuckled as he made his way into the kitchen. "Anyone else?" Everyone murmured agreement. He spoke over his shoulder as he began pouring drinks. "Bollocks! You should have seen her face. Hell, I'm sure mine looked just as shocked," he chuckled.

Gunnar pointed. "Where the hell did you get that many pictures of the same person? And who is she?" He asked me.

I shrugged. "Some girl. I have no idea who she is. I outsourced the job. Othello."

"Oh?" Indie said softly. Everyone knew about Othello and her *skills*... and our past relationship. The room grew brittle at Indie's tone. Then she let loose a dazzling smile. "Just kidding. She won't poach. We had a long... talk. Girl talk," she added as an afterthought. I shivered, wondering exactly what that meant. But I knew Indie had accepted my old college fling. Especially after *Mardi Gras* when Othello had literally died for me.

Othello loved me. But she also knew that it would never work out. And after a few 'talks' the girls seemed to get along splendidly, although I did always feel like I was walking on razor blades over a lava pit of fire-breathing ninja lemurs whenever I saw them spending time together. Especially when they grew quiet as soon as I entered the room, and then giggled loud enough for me to hear as I quickly walked away to do important man stuff like check the batteries in the remotes.

Freaking women.

"Anyway," I continued, "a few months ago, I told Othello to gather a slush pile of pictures of the same girl – any girl – so that I could do this to you or Raego the next time you got uppity." I smirked at Gunnar.

Tomas grunted, shaking his head in disbelief at my admitted depths of depravity. Gunnar merely scowled. "Well, I guess it's lucky for you it didn't work out like that..." he warned with a canine smile, letting his fangs lengthen as he partially shifted to his werewolf form. I rolled my eyes.

Tomas let out a belly laugh, watching Gunnar and I rib each other. "At least it's comforting to know that I'm not the only one on the receiving end of his stunts." He shook his head and took a deep drink of his wine. "I'm not going to lie. I played my cards right all night, told her suave stories, and made sure we both had plenty to drink. We got back to the apartment and I knew she was a sure thing." Indie shook her head and rolled her eyes in amusement. "We poured some drinks and took off to make some magic happen in the bedroom. I don't know who was more surprised to see my stalker collage. Linda certainly found zero humor in it," he muttered, shrugging his shoulders. "It was a good joke, even though it took me a few to realize it. I take it that this was your subtle way of telling me that your time was more important than my dating life?" He asked, risking a thoughtful look at me.

I smiled with my teeth. "Got it in one."

"Then I'm going to need another drink. We have some things we need to talk about. Quickly. In case anyone saw you come here," he spoke over his shoulder, heading back to the kitchen. We exchanged thoughtful looks as he left. He brought over the bottle and we all settled down around his rickety coffee table. My eyes idly roved the apartment and I was reminded again that being a hit man was apparently not a very lucrative career. Either that or Tomas was not a material girl. Or it was a front.

Bingo. That fit better. This was a disguise. A burner home in case he needed to flee.

"Out of respect, you go first, but then I have something important to tell you."

I didn't like the sound of that, but I rehashed our night's events. The vampires, the wolves, and their odd parting comments. As I took a second to wet my lips, he spoke.

"Promise you won't be upset..." he didn't make eye contact, looking ashamed.

"Don't tell me you know what's going on. Because that would mean I need to make a Tomas-sized smear on the wall," I growled, flexing my fists. Here he was, going on a date, all the while knowing I had been in danger.

"Possibly. This sounds similar to a strange contract I was offered a few weeks back. I didn't think it was related – and especially not that *you* were the mark – or I would have warned you sooner." Tomas was a mercenary, but he was loyal to me after the dragon ordeal a year back. I trusted him. "I didn't win the bid, and talk died down about it immediately. I had assumed it had been withdrawn. Then I got the update just tonight. I called you immediately, but your phone went straight to voicemail and I couldn't say anything sensitive on voicemail. I also couldn't say anything in front of Linda."

"Don't worry about that in the future. My phone is encrypted from both ends, so you can say whatever pleases you on my voicemail. Especially if it's important. Like a contract on my life." I stared daggers at him and watched him crumple a bit at the shoulders. Tomas was *good*. He and his crew were contacted for *all* the big hits. And when I say *hits*, I mean contracts involving an upcoming murder or kidnapping of a rogue Freak, or supernatural person. "So, spill," I demanded.

"No names were mentioned. Just a high-value target with strong defenses. A rogue wanted for punishment regarding unspecified crimes. No details on who the target was, who the employer was, or exactly what the mark had done. Just a lot of freaking money." I must have looked doubtful. "Enough money to make even *you* bat an eye." He amended, taking another drink. Which got my attention. "Then, a few hours ago, I was notified that the bidding for the contract was closed, and that the target must be avoided at all costs, except by the contracted team and their associates. Anyone interfering or getting involved in any way whatsoever with the target would be added to the hit list. They called it a Salted Earth Policy. All known acquaintances." He slowly lifted his gaze to meet mine. "And you are the primary target, Temple," he shivered.

I slowly relaxed. Then I began to laugh. Softly, but with great relief. I leaned back into the couch and took a long sip of my drink, crossing my feet on his coffee table. I had feared that Tomas would know more about the Grimms. Part of me was relieved to hear it wasn't so. Part of me wasn't. Gunnar and Indie looked just as confused, so I finally explained. "Well, if hiring a half-dozen werewolves to take me out is the extent of their genius, I'm not too worried. We already took care of them."

Tomas was shaking his head. "No. No. You don't understand. You didn't take care of anyone. Their first attack is always a probe to get to know their enemy. No one survives them. They are legion."

My shoulders went back to full anxiety mode.

I had heard of only one other group described as *legion*.

The Grimms.

Not only did they want to take me out for personal reasons, but also, they were now going to be paid a pile of money to do so. Oh, Capitalism. The thing that really got me was that no one should even know they were back in our world.

This smelled of the Academy. No one else was powerful enough, or ballsy enough, to risk contracting the Grimms. But I couldn't imagine even that being the case. That was blatantly illegal of the Academy. They literally couldn't touch me unless I openly attacked them. We had agreed that bygones were bygones. I had even attended a face-to-face meeting with the Grandmaster of the wizard nation after the events at *Mardi Gras*, accompanied by Death – a Horseman of the Apocalypse – and Eae, a freaking Angel of Heaven. If that wasn't a convincing team of people to have on your side, I didn't know what was.

The Academy had agreed, and written up a formal agreement that the past was behind us. I was a Maker, the sole member of my particular flavor of Freak, and thus outside their purview. Meaning they would leave me alone if I left them alone. We would be allies, with neither above the other.

So, what in the hell was going on?

"Just between us girls," Tomas continued, "chatter also says that this group is interested in acquiring a... *book* you may or may not have collected in your misspent youth." He glanced at me pointedly, eyes flicking to Gunnar and Indie with the silent question. I waved a hand, unconcerned.

"It's okay. They know what we're talking about. The Brothers Grimm, right?"

He frowned at me with his mouth open for a moment, and then regained his composure, letting out a single nod. "Aye. It was the book comment that made me think you might be the target. So, of course, I called you immediately."

Tomas polished off his drink and everyone sat in silence, pondering. A long minute later, he said a single word that sent a chill down my spine. "Run." He said it softly, but the emphasis made it a clarion call to my ears.

I was paranoid enough to actually jump to my feet, eyes darting to the windows, ready for an attack. But everything was safe and Tomas didn't look immediately concerned. I sat back down as Tomas chuckled.

"Not this *second*, Temple. But tonight. Or tomorrow. The earlier the better," he added, eyes darting to the windows instinctively. Which made sense now. He had said that anyone assisting or even interacting with me would be added to the list. I turned to see him watching me. He shrugged. "Yep. I'll be leaving town myself after your visit. Won't be returning here for quite some time. If that makes any difference or not. It was a burner house anyway. Temporary." He shrugged, not completely hiding the disappointment in his eyes at having to pack up and leave.

Because of me.

But he didn't say a word about me putting him in danger, which on a deeper level, meant a lot to me. I had shamed him in front of a lady friend, put his life in very real jeopardy, and instead of running to turn me in, he shrugged, laughed, gave me what information he could, and calmly told me that my visit had ruined his life in St. Louis and that he was leaving town – perhaps permanently. All without batting an eye.

Tomas was solid.

Indie chimed in, having been mostly silent up until now. "So, you said *Salted Earth Policy*. What exactly does that mean?"

"All known acquaintances, past and present," Tomas repeated softly, avoiding eye contact.

I spat on the ground in frustration, my mind racing. I doubted Tomas cared about getting his deposit back on the apartment. Gunnar's thoughts seemed to follow the same path, because his eyes suddenly widened and his hand went instinctively to his phone. But it was still in the microwave. Ashley was an acquaintance of mine. And she was his fiancé. Tomas clucked a warning, tapping his ears to signify the potential tapping of our phones.

"They're encrypted, remember?" I told him.

"Until you run into a hacker cleverer than your phone's engineer."

I folded my arms. "My company made them." Tomas merely stared back, unimpressed. "They cost $17,000. Each." His eyes widened a bit, but he shrugged anyway. "And Othello designed the encryption software." His face slowly morphed into a predatory smile.

"That one's a real piece of..." His eyes flashed to Indie, cheeks flushing, "Work," he clarified. Indie managed to grin and roll her eyes at the same time. "She's a real piece of *work*. Freaking cyber genius. I only got to speak with her for a few moments last time she was in town. Seems she helped me out on a few of my old contracts, not that I knew anything about it at the time, of course." Gunnar was already prowling to the microwave.

Tomas grew thoughtful. "Hey, when we first met you were able to dig up information on me that isn't available. To anyone." He watched me for a minute. "It was Othello, wasn't it?" I smiled and nodded. "Hot damn. You should arrange a more formal introduction sometime." He glanced back at his room. "Sans stalker collage..." His voice trailed off with a small smile. "Well, if there *is* a sometime in the future for any of us," he added. Gunnar was already shooting off a text, thumbs flying over the screen.

"The Brothers Grimm," Indie broke the tension slowly building in the room. "They wrote a collection of *fairy* tales. I still have a hard time believing they are the boogeymen of the supernatural community." She stated in disbelief.

Tomas shuddered. "You have no idea, little lady. No idea..." His eyes trailed off for a few moments before snapping back to me. "Wait a minute. How did you guys already know about them? Remember, if anyone talks, they get added to the hit list. You should probably warn them. Whoever they are," he probed.

I smiled, detecting his ploy. "We've all got people, Tomas. Just remember that I've always got more people than anyone else and you'll be betting safe." Tomas blinked, no doubt wanting to hear the story, but I was done telling stories. As far as Tomas knew, someone I had pissed off at some point had been willing to pay a lot of money to get me and my friends dead. This someone was also well-connected enough to know that the Brothers Grimm were back in play. Which made no sense to me. "How do *you* know about the Grimms?" I asked instead, not wanting to admit my ignorance.

Tomas shrugged. "People talk on the tougher hits. Stakeouts get boring. We do what soldiers have done since time immemorial. We tell stories. I won't lie. Some of their stories are downright legendary. *Impossible* hits. No evidence. No calling card. No bragging rights. Just a job well done." His voice trailed off. "Of course, there are also the stories about totally innocent people disappearing under similar circumstances, but we all tell ourselves it's just a coincidence."

I nodded. I hadn't ever heard any stories, but I could imagine. "But how does anyone know they are back? Or that they are even real?" I wondered aloud.

"They weren't secretive about announcing it. Flyers went up everywhere. Email notifications. Mailers. YouTube videos." He trailed off.

Indie and I turned to blink at him. "What?" We asked in disbelief.

He was nodding. "Yeah. Very odd. We all thought it was a prank. Looked like one of those *Anonymous* group's videos. Warning that they were back and they had some house cleaning to do. To stay out of their way until they came for you."

They had spent hundreds of years out of this world and their grand entrance includes a full social media blast? What the hell was going on? "How long ago was this?"

"Months," he answered. I blinked at him, my rage roaring to the surface. If I had only known sooner... But no, that wasn't Tomas' fault. No one had known that they had personal beef with me. Why would Tomas have even thought to tell me? He had no reason to do so. Other than as a professional courtesy. Hell, he probably assumed I saw the news like everyone else.

"Next time something like that happens, you get me on the phone immediately. I could have resolved this a long time ago without them having months to prepare." I warned. He swallowed guiltily, nodding.

My thoughts began to wander as I heard Gunnar speaking urgently into his phone. Indie was staring at me, but I didn't acknowledge her.

The Brothers Grimm were supernatural hit men – as in they killed *any* and *all* supernatural creatures, good or bad, naughty or not. Who ran in my circles that would be ballsy enough to hire a group of mad dogs to take me out? Mad dogs that would immediately turn around and kill them too? Who exactly had I pissed off?

Tomas spoke up. "The thing that gets me is why the wolves and fangers left you alone. Or why they were down there in the first place. If the wolves had orders not to kill you, why would they chance breaking into your vault when they could smell that you were down there?" I didn't tell him I had masked our scent from the vampires up until it had become obvious they were aware of our presence. Nor did I answer the unspoken question, *what are you hiding in a sewer vault that could attract a werewolf or vampire's attention?* Or the one he didn't know to ask. *How had they even known about the vault in the first place?*

I had enough problems on my mind, so I went along with the presumption that for now, it didn't matter how they learned about the vault. They simply knew.

So, next question.

I had no idea why they had been there, especially with conflicting orders. Rob from me, but don't kill me. They had to know that five wolves wouldn't have been enough for the job. Unless they hadn't planned on me being there. But then, how would they have broken into the vault in the first place? With me being a notorious wizard, my vault would undoubtedly be locked with *magic*. And why hadn't they tucked tail and run as soon as they discovered I was present? The wolves had scented us long before talking to us. Which meant they wanted something. Something they assumed I had hidden in a secret vault.

Questions piled on top of more questions. Maybe there was more than one thing going on here. I ran through the catalog of items in my vault, but couldn't think of anything particularly interesting to the supernatural community at large. Sure, there were nifty things in there, but all the super powerful and dangerous stuff was locked away in the Armory now. Maybe the wolves thought I had some kind of key to the Armory in my vault beneath Plato's Cave.

Still, these questions only led me back full circle to the most pressing issue.

No one knew about my vault.

I had *literally* told no one.

Not Gunnar. Not Indie. Not my parents. Not even my old traitorous friend, Peter.

No one.

And I couldn't remember the last time I had been down there, but it had been a long time. Which meant that someone must have followed me down there at some point, and then waited *years* until the perfect night to go get the goods. Tonight.

The same night I happened to be paying a visit.

Something smelled wrong about this whole thing, and I felt my face begin to scowl.

The only reason I had chosen tonight to visit could be summed up in one word.

Achilles.

6

The room filled with soft chatter between Indie and Tomas as Gunnar continued to talk into his cell phone, no doubt warning Ashley of the situation. I was apparently setting off the vibe that I needed a few minutes to myself. This would typically be a time when I would have lit a cigarette to calm my racing mind.

But I had quit eight months ago, during the *Mardi Gras* fiasco. I didn't miss the habit much on a daily basis. Not at all, in fact. But times like this?

Yeah, a cigarette would have been nice. Or a stiffer drink. Thanks to Tomas' warning about possible surveillance, I couldn't open the windows to smoke anyway, so I settled in to attempt to think without the aid of stimulants.

Achilles had asked me to go down to the sewers tonight. If not for that, it could have been a long time until I went down there. The only other reason I had gone down there was to get the engagement ring, and I could have done that any time in the next few days. But I hadn't told a single person about either the ring *or* the vault. Ever. I began running through all my interactions for the past few days but came up with no smoking guns.

So, Achilles just happened to have a damsel in distress who needed saving in the sewers tonight. I had planned on going to the sewers to get the engagement ring in the next few days anyway, so I had decided to combine the two into one trip. Vampires first, to test Indie's mettle, *which she had passed with flying colors*, I thought to myself proudly. Then the engagement ring. Simple. Efficient.

Right.

I glanced at Indie discreetly, amazed by her natural beauty and genuine smile. Tomas was eating it up. A naturally beautiful woman with glittering pearly whites could make any man feel eight feet tall and bulletproof. And Indie had those traits in spades. I focused back on my dilemma.

So, the wolves had shown up at a vault that they shouldn't have even known existed, wanting to take some old books... that they also shouldn't have ever known existed. The only person who knew of the books was Gunnar, but even he didn't know what they truly were. Barbie had wiped everyone's memory of my first encounter with Jacob Grimm.

Everyone except me.

I shivered at that memory. Jacob had been a heavy hitter for sure, even all by himself. Now he had his brothers to help him take out the trash... *me*. And my loved ones. I shook that thought away. It wouldn't help me now.

The wolves had been commanded not to harm me. By their Alpha, if I guessed correctly. If that was true, why pick tonight? Why not yesterday or tomorrow?

Because someone had tipped them off.

My main question was whether it was the same person who sent me down there tonight or if there was a third-party lurking in the shadows somewhere. Regardless, the Brothers Grimm had taken a contract on us. I was on borrowed time, and the best defense I had were the books in my satchel. If I called anyone for help they would be placed on the kill list too, so reinforcements were out. I had only my motley crew of supernaturals who were by default on the list. Gunnar and who else? Indie, Ashley, Dean... the list grew on and on. How many people were on the list? Were Raego and Death included? How extensive was the assassination contract?

"Tomas." The room grew silent at my tone. He glanced up at me, looking nervous. "I need you to find out exactly who is on the list."

"Um, everyone."

"A little more specific. I'm a local celebrity. Is the gas station attendant I say good morning to every day on the list? His name is Juan. Is the news reporter I've sat down with a dozen times on the list? My employees? My dry cleaner? Indie? There could potentially be hundreds of victims here."

He thought about it for a moment. "I'll see what I can dig up. If they know about our meeting tonight, then I'm a dead man anyway. If not, I'll have to be discreet about it. Seem hungry. Like I'm willing to nab a few for myself if the Grimms will let me. Otherwise they will assume I'm fishing for intel and add me to the list, which will help no one. Least of all me."

"Good idea."

He was silent for a few moments. "Perhaps only the supernatural associates. From what I've read, the Grimms don't kill vanilla mortals. Only Freaks. So maybe your lady friends are safe. And the gas station attendant, employees, whoever else. That would make the most sense. They are, after all, against anyone able to use magic of any kind. Mortals should be safe."

"Well, I've taken on this particular chucklehead before and sent him packing. I'm sure I can do so again."

Tomas fidgeted. "Not just one."

I turned to him, remembering Barbie's warning. "How many are we talking?"

"Um... more than one?" I scowled back. He threw up his hands. "I just know there is a team of 'em. *Team* implies more than one. And if I were a betting man I would say both Jacob and Wilhelm Grimm, at least. The founding fathers, if you will."

"Well, if the vamps and wolves in the sewer were related to the Grimms – as unlikely as that is – at least I sent them packing. They won't be back in the picture anytime soon."

Tomas was shaking his head urgently. "No way. The stories always start the same. Their first attack is *always* a probe. They treat their kills like hunts. They lead their prey right where they want them. I think that's why the wolves were commanded not to kill."

Gunnar chimed in, having ended his phone call. "Either that or it's because they don't want to incur the wrath of the only Maker in centuries. They did mention that title specifically. And I'm pretty sure they said their orders came from their Alpha."

I was glad he had confirmed my thoughts. The Alpha. Not the Grimms. Maybe it wasn't related. I mean, what kind of idiots would the werewolves be to team up with a hit squad of assassins who killed *all* Freaks? I had met the local Alpha, and although he was powerful, I didn't remember him being particularly smart. Then I remembered that someone had hired the Grimms. Maybe even the wolves, but I doubted they had any significant means to pay the kind of sum Tomas had hinted at. And other than the scuffle during the *Mardi Gras* fiasco, I didn't think they had reason enough to take such drastic measures to kill me dead.

Or a regular could have hired the Grimms, which seemed just as unlikely. They wouldn't even *know* about the supernatural community. Well, probably not anyway.

I could think of only one freak with the brass balls to do something so stupid, and he was definitely in a position of power, maybe even enough to insulate him from the backlash of hiring the Grimms.

And I had pissed him off something fierce. In fact, he was the reason my new Maker powers were so much stronger than my parents' experiment had originally intended.

Jafar, the Captain of the Justices – the secret wizard police for the Academy. I was no longer a wizard, out of their jurisdiction, as was made abundantly clear with the signed agreement between us. But even if they wanted to flake on me, Death and Eae had also signed as witnesses, and the Academy wouldn't dare renege on Heaven and Hell. That would cause fallout on a Biblical level.

I was a Maker, and that infuriated old Jafar, because it was essentially his fault I became such a nuisance. His fault that his boss had been forced to sign the agreement.

I stood and made a mental to-do list.

Step one, call Jafar. I needed to put a feeler out there. I couldn't let him know I was aware of the full picture. Just hint around the edges. Maybe something along the lines of bad magic was going on in my city and I wanted him to know about it ahead of time. A courtesy call. Like any good neighbor would do. But I was playing a dangerous game. They were either in on this Grimm business, or might know something about it. But to be completely honest, I was also just covering my ass. If they *weren't* involved, I *needed* to give them a heads-up as a token of good faith. It was part of our agreement. Even though I was no longer under their *jurisdiction*, that knife cut both ways. I was also out of their *protection*. I harbored no false belief that they would swoop in with a platoon to help me out, but figured they would instead likely find a political reason to declare my actions criminal when the dust settled – if I was still alive by then.

Step two, ask my parents for help. They were already dead, now residing in the Armory, so were in no danger by assisting me. I had to come clean with them about what Gunnar and I had really gotten into a few years ago, during our first encounter with Jacob Grimm. And the sole reason behind why I had opened Plato's Cave. To hide the deadly books now sitting a few feet away in my satchel.

After that, a chat with Achilles, who was legendary for his love of pointy things.

Gunnar and Indie followed me – saying their goodbyes on my behalf – as I wordlessly left the room. Tomas' advice echoed in my ears as I reached the door leading to the street.

Run...

As if that whispered word wasn't ominous enough, one sight of my parked car convinced me it was simply time to go home and hit the sheets.

I stopped on the steps, staring incredulously, first at the car – which had been beaten with a baseball bat, all the windows smashed out – and then at the street and rooftops for any hidden attackers.

The wind howled through the street, taunting my futile search.

They were gone, but they had left a poignant message.

Whoever they were.

7

"I don't like this," Gunnar growled, sniffing the remains of the car.

"It's not even your car. It's mine," I answered distractedly, eyeing the destruction clinically. The windows were shattered, the tires slashed, every section of metal dented, and a growing puddle of noxious liquids slowly grew from underneath the vehicle, inching towards our feet despite the cold weather. Which meant it was recent. The liquids hadn't had time to freeze. We probably should have heard something from Tomas' apartment. A car alarm at least.

But we hadn't heard a thing. Which was puzzling, and blatantly pointed towards a supernatural attack rather than a mundane crime of opportunity.

Now, *monetarily*, this was no big deal to me. But as a *message*, it was powerful indeed. Someone wanted me to know I was in their crosshairs, but I spotted no calling card or flashing neon sign stating his or her name. We were now stranded outside Tomas' apartment, so *someone* obviously knew we were here. The question was, did they already know Tomas lived here, or did they just happen to recognize my car and made a move? Regardless, if they didn't know yet, it was likely that they would soon connect the dots, realizing Tomas lived here, which explained what I was doing here. I had no other reason to be in this part of town. Which put him in danger. I shot him a text, warning him that he might already be compromised. Finished, I looked up to find Gunnar watching me.

"Call a cab. I need to make a quick call."

"Ashley's already on her way. She'll be here in ten minutes." He growled, still unsuccessfully trying to track the scent. Which was odd. A lot of sniffer problems for the werewolf lately. Maybe the thugs had another moonstone. Or maybe he was still feeling the effects from the vampire's moonstone in the sewer. It didn't matter now. I sensed no supernatural presence. At least I could reliably do *that* with my new powers.

"Good. I'm just going to step over here for a minute. We might want to walk a few blocks away. Let Ashley know to pick us up wherever you decide. As long as it's away from this." I waved a hand at the vehicle's remains.

Gunnar grunted, but began walking down the street, Indie hot on his heels, both of them giving me space. My phone vibrated, revealing a string of curse words from Tomas. I smiled at the screen as I followed a few steps behind Gunnar and Indie, scrolling through my contacts until I found the right name. *Arrogant prickface*. I clicked the name with a smile and readied myself for a cryptic, but not obviously so, conversation with a man who I hated and who hated me back even harder.

Jafar, Captain of the Justices.

"Who is this?" A scratchy, sleepy voice answered.

"It's your buddy. Your pal. Your BFF. Nate Temple. How you doing, sport?" I spoke, doing my best to sound overly positive and cheerful.

He growled back. "Do you know what time it is? What do you want?"

"To chat, of course. It's what friends… and *allies* do."

He waited a few seconds, gathering his sleepy thoughts together for an appropriate political response at the term *allies*. "I don't feel like chatting. What do you need?"

"Alright. No foreplay." I took a breath, forcing myself to sound confused and a little nervous. "Something is going on in town. I'm out of the loop, but everyone's acting… strange. Do you guys happen to know anything about it?" I waited a long second, replacing my fake anxiety with a harder tone. "If not, consider this a heads-up. When things get strange here, I usually end up taking out the trash, and I don't want you guys thinking I'm overstepping myself. You are more than welcome to come investigate, if you find it necessary."

I waited. The line was so quiet that I almost thought he had hung up. Then I heard faint rustling and some murmured words in the background. "Give me a minute," he muttered. He was apparently excusing himself to a more secure environment. "Okay. Strange how?" He finally asked.

I pondered how to answer that. If he was complicit, I didn't want to be sharing my movements with my hunters. If he wasn't, he needed a justifiable answer. He was a cop of sorts, after all, and even though I didn't personally like him, I was pretty sure he was good at his job.

Wizard of the month – or something like that – on the Academy's break room wall.

"I was jumped by a pack of wolves and then again by some fangs. In the same hour."

He grunted. "Sounds like a personal vendetta. You do have a reputation for making friends wherever you go." He sounded pleased at the snide comment.

I swallowed back a retort, taking a breath. This was to be a professional phone call. Even if it killed me. I needed to be able to claim deniability if things went downhill.

"They said they had orders not to harm me."

The line was quiet for a beat. "But you just said they jumped you."

"Exactly. Like I said, people are acting strange. It makes no sense. Vampires and wolves *hate* each other. So why would they have the same order not to harm me, but to jump me anyway?" I asked, not having to feign my confusion. "They were looking for something in my possession, but I'll be damned if I know what it was…" I teased, offering him something to bite. But he didn't take it.

"That *is* strange," he finally said. "What do you expect *me* to do about it? As you know, you aren't under our jurisdiction, much to my regret. So why should I send anyone to help you? It's obviously personal." He was quiet for a moment. *Then* he took my bait. "Unless… you wanted to make an exchange for our services. Say, unrestricted access to a certain Armory." I could practically hear him salivating.

"I'm not giving you the Armory."

"You don't have to give it to me. Or even the Academy. Just let us inventory it."

I laughed. "So you'll know exactly what you need to grab when you clowns finally make your move? Hard pass."

He growled. "Then I think we're finished here," he answered, sounding pompous. "Watch out for yourself, Temple. The night is dark and full of terrors." He roared in laughter at his own rapier wit.

"Fair warning. I'll put an end to whatever is going on, with or without you. If I do it without you, I don't want to hear the Academy crying *foul* when the dust settles, declaring me some kind of vigilante. Consider this my 911 call. Next move is on your shoulders. If you don't do anything I'll do what I do best. Maybe test out my new powers. Who knows what could happen? I'd be lying if I said I wasn't curious…"

The line was silent again. Not much of a talker, old Jafar.

"I'll run it up the flagpole. That's all I can do," he finally grumbled, realizing that he had to do so, no matter how badly he wanted to see me dangling in the wind. I had made it official by calling him. If he didn't follow the proper channels it could backfire on him.

"That's all I'm asking. Call me back and let me know what you guys decide."

He had hung up at some point during my last comment. I cursed at my phone and tucked it into a pocket, lengthening my stride a bit to catch up with Gunnar and Indie. They were only a dozen feet ahead of me. I recognized Ashley's car double-parked outside an apartment building just ahead of us. Indie glanced over her shoulder, looking concerned at the expression on my face. Gunnar had eyes only for Ashley, but Indie slowed down and placed an arm around my shoulders, idly scratching her long fingernails through my scalp. "Bad?"

"On the contrary. It's kind of comforting to know that he's the same flavor of asshole he always was." Indie nodded, massaging my shoulder with one hand as we walked.

"Perhaps you just need an outlet to clear your head. Release some tension," she murmured.

I nodded. "Maybe I'll go hit the bag for an hour when we get home."

She stopped, her hand turning into a warning claw as she gripped my shoulder, forcing me to stop or fall over. I arched a confused brow at the hurt look on her face. "I don't know how much more obvious I can be, Nate. I would hope you consider *this*," she waved a hand at her body, "a better form of release than a dusty old punching bag," she warned.

I blinked, realizing my mistake too late. I couldn't believe I had missed such an obvious pass. Granted, I had a lot on my mind, but still. When a pretty girl flirts with you, you damn well better pay attention, Apocalypse or not. "Wow," I sighed. "I'm an idiot."

She nodded curtly. "Yes. You are." She folded her arms, tapping a foot as she arched a brow. "So, what does a girl have to do around here to get some claw marks on her back?"

I grinned, suddenly focused on only her. "Say no more." She smiled back and gripped my hand. "Still a little high-strung after Barbie's psychic attack, eh?" I teased.

Her eyes were dark and captivating. "Only one way to find out..." Then she smacked my ass as we stepped up to Gunnar and Ashley, who were unabashedly hugging and kissing each other outside of her idling car. The sound caused them to jump apart and stare at us. Indie burst out laughing. So did Ashley. I simply turned to glare at Indie in disbelief. She shrugged, folding her arms before her.

Then she did it again as I was climbing into the backseat.

"I'm not just some piece of meat, you know." I grumbled, only mildly upset that my ass-smacking authority had been stolen.

"Tonight, you are," she grinned, climbing in after me. Gunnar rolled his eyes, but Ashley burst out laughing all over again.

"Looks like I missed a wild night." Ashley said, pulling out into traffic.

"Don't worry, we have a few more of them scheduled for the week." I grumbled.

"I'm guessing that's what the *car trouble* was really about?" She asked, glancing pointedly at Gunnar. His cheeks flushed slightly before he murmured an apology to her. I couldn't hear the words, but it looked like he was getting an earful.

He finally addressed me as we passed a row of commercial buildings. "*Chateau Falco?*" I nodded. "Might be a good idea for all of us to stick together for a few days. Until this, um, *car trouble* gets sorted out." He offered neutrally, giving me room to veto the idea if I wished. I glanced at Indie's hungry eyes and smiled. It was a big enough house. Plenty of rooms. I winked at her to let her know she still held priority of my attentions, guests be damned.

"Good idea. While you catch Ashley up I need to make another call."

They began talking softly together in the front seat while I made a call, feeling Indie's curious eyes on me the whole time. Even though I had warned Jafar on official channels, I wanted a more reliable insurance policy that was solely in my control rather than the shifting winds of political favor, and after events over the past year I had wisely planned for just such an event ahead of time. But it was risky. In fact, it was borderline *suicidal*.

"This can't be good," a familiar voice answered. I smiled.

"Consider this your answer. Commence *Operation White Knight*. Immediately. Then meet me at the ranch. Bring the family and anyone they care about." I hinted heavily, hoping he understood. "It's... bad." The line grew as cold as a grave.

"Are you *shitting* me? I thought that was just a doomsday plan. We only came up with it a few months ago, and you already need it?" I thought about it for a second, but I couldn't think of another option.

"Yes. Exercise extreme caution. Like we discussed. Don't harm them. Just hold them. If you *can*..." I added drily, knowing that his unique abilities made him the most capable of such a high-level operation.

The voice growled back defiantly. "Of course, I can hold them. Do you forget who you're talking to?" He challenged.

"Of course not. You're the Obsidian Son, *kid*." I teased.

"Damn right," Raego growled, the sound shifting to a deadlier timbre, that of a giant black dragon partially shifting into a menacing creature of the night.

And he was my pal.

"I'll feel safer at my home, no offense. Plus, if things are about to go FUBAR, spreading out the risk might be a good idea."

I grunted agreement.

We hung up without further words. Indie's eyes were wide. "What did you just do?"

"Hopefully something that won't *immediately* get me killed." That didn't appease the fear on her face. "It should be fine. I'm sure of it."

Instead of poking holes in my plan she merely sighed, gripping my hand in support.

Damn fine woman. I squeezed back in silent thanks.

8

I woke up with a start. Indie had moaned in her sleep, sending an explosion of adrenaline through my veins. My eyes widened and my breathing came fast as I bolted up to a sitting position. It took me a few moments of frantic searching to calm down.

We were alone. Safe.

I stood and took a drink from a bottle of water on the bedside table. My body was practically quivering with energy. Great. I wasn't going back to sleep anytime soon. I quickly glanced at the satchel beside the bed, verifying its contents were safe. I decided that I might as well lock them away now. Perhaps the brief walk would put me back at ease so I could get some shuteye. Check the wards, hide the books, and hit the hay. I had a long day tomorrow.

I climbed out from the covers and tossed the satchel over a shoulder before silently stealing from the room without waking Indie. I crept down the halls on the balls of my feet, pausing for a few seconds outside Gunnar and Ashley's room. Silence.

I continued on down the hallway, glancing idly over the balcony to the enormous sitting room below. A small fire burned lazily in the fireplace, casting a red soothing glow on the room. I watched it, trying to absorb the sense of tranquility.

A throat cleared behind me and I jumped out of my skin. I quickly spun, panting as I prepared to unleash hell. "Couldn't sleep either?" Gunnar whispered from the shadows.

"What the *hell*, man? Are you *trying* to give me a heart attack?"

He shrugged, smirking. His hands had shifted to his werewolf claws, long, obsidian talons against icy white fur. And they were idly scratching a steady line in the trim of a doorway. He'd been up for a while, judging by the curls of shavings at his feet. "Do you mind?" I growled, pointing at the damage to the woodwork.

He didn't meet my eyes, and continued scratching. "You're good for it."

"If you need to go outside to potty you don't need to scratch at the door." His eyes flashed an icy blue as his smirk widened.

"Figured it was easier to protect her from out here. In case anyone pays us a visit in the night," he answered softly. I nodded, stepping back up to lean on the banister. He approached on silent feet and copied me. We stood in silence, thinking dark protective thoughts. Our women were targets, and neither of us was powerful enough to defeat the Grimms. Hell, supernaturals didn't even have a good track record *surviving* them.

"I've got a pretty swanky security system. They're safer here than anywhere else."

He grunted. "Not good enough. You know who is after you. And me."

"Not just mundane security, wolf. I activated the *Guardians* tonight." He watched me curiously, having never heard me mention them before. I patted the beak of a stone griffin standing near my hip, using the motion to secretly tap my bracelet one time. The griffin was hidden in plain sight as a decoration. Stone creaked as it abruptly turned its head to assess the werewolf, sniffing. Then it cocked its neck, whipped its tail once to thump the floor in a warning thud, and then let out a soft caw. Gunnar's eyes widened.

After all, there were a few more gargoyles within throwing distance.

About three-dozen stone sentinels. Or gargoyles, as most knew them. Most depicted griffins, but there were a few other predatory creatures, including bears, wolves, lions, and even a few hybrid combinations as well.

They stretched the entire length of the impressive landing, a good hundred feet, give or take, and were spaced no more than ten feet apart. The bracelet on my wrist pulsed lightly to let me know everything was functional, but I avoided tapping into any of the live feeds, sensing no alarms. Doing so would have superimposed a visual sweep of each griffin's post over my own vision. A very disturbing sensation. Gunnar began to chuckle lightly. "Nice." I tapped my wrist in a quick double beat, reinitiating *sentinel* mode. The gargoyle cooed lightly and then shifted back to attention, appearing inanimate again.

"Puppy want to go for a walk?" I oozed in a high-pitched, animated voice. His face turned to stone. "I was planning on saying *hey* to my parents, see if they have any advice about the Grimms. Them or Pandora. I'd honestly take anything I can get right now."

Gunnar shrugged. "Why not?" He eyed the gargoyles again. "Sure they're enough?"

I smiled, nodding. "Yep. This is only one layer of protection. I'll know immediately if anyone shows up at the gate uninvited, giving us plenty of time to make it back here before anyone even gets near the front door of the house." He looked unconvinced.

"What if they can just Shadow Walk in here like you?"

"Warded. Only I can do that." It was one of the first things I figured out how to do with my new power. And the first thing I had tested against, much to Jafar's frustration.

"Okay. Let's be quick." He sighed, sounding resigned to leave his post to the *Guardians*. I rolled my eyes. Typical *Type A* personality trait.

Gunnar quickly matched my stride as I made my way towards the office. At times like this, it was still difficult for me to think of *Chateau Falco* as *mine*. I felt inadequate to the task of owning such an impressive and historic icon for a home. The grounds had been in the family since the 1700's. But now I was the last Temple. No other siblings or children to carry on the name. No one else to share the wandering halls with. A house deserved living bodies to fill it with laughter, cries, and life.

But it only had me. And my friends, I guess. Soon Indie would become a permanent staple of the rambling property, and I would get to show her all the Chateau's secrets. Gunnar knew quite a few of them, having practically grown up here with me, but he didn't know all of them. I wondered what it would be like to share my home with her, smiling distantly at the thought.

Gunnar spoke softly, "are you still planning on doing it this week?" He asked.

He was, of course, referring to my proposal. I nodded. "Yes."

He grunted. "Even with…" he waved a hand at, well, life in general, implying the Grimms. "All of this suddenly springing up on you?"

I thought about that for a few seconds and finally nodded. "Yeah. I guess I am. I can't let them take something like that away from me. I've got to keep on living, man."

He smiled over at me, nodding. "Good." We walked on a bit longer in silence, enjoying each other's company. "I'm assuming that is why you originally planned the stop underneath Plato's Cave. At your secret vault. The one even I didn't know about." He sounded hurt. Slightly.

"Yes. The engagement ring was down there," I answered. Then I offered an olive branch. "No one knew about that vault. No. One. Not you. Not Indie. Not my parents. No one."

He glanced at me, waving a hand to signify burying the hatchet. "Except someone found out."

I muttered under my breath, which caused him to look at me again. "Yeah. They did. Kind of fortuitous that the vault also held the books."

"Fortuitous. Right." He growled, not sounding pleased. "Or it was a setup."

I nodded, my attitude growing darker. "Or that." I agreed. I felt his eyes rest on me, then he nodded, glad that I was on the same page.

I was on the same letter.

We finally reached the office and I pulled open the massive wooden doors. The fire was burning softly, casting the room in an orange glow.

And we weren't alone.

Mallory sat before the fire in my father's old armchair. He didn't even hear us enter at first, but jolted as the door clicked shut. He lurched to his feet, a crackling spear of electricity in one hand, and a tumbler of whisky in the other. He was breathing heavy until he recognized us. "Master Temple…" He said, sounding guilty at his aggressive reaction. The power coursing over the weapon zapped out and he tossed it on the ground at his feet. "Dean told me something rather troubling…" He hadn't been around when we got home. He was kind of an enigma, disappearing at odd times. But he had always been that way. In fact, I hadn't even seen him more than one time in the years he had worked for my father. I guessed he was supposed to be an added layer of security. And security worked best when none knew it was present.

I nodded at him. "It's true. The Grimms are back in town and they want to take me out. And any acquaintances." I let him chew on that, no holding back for my crew.

"Aye. What do ya' need me to do, Laddie?"

I lowered my head in gratitude. *Laddie* was an affectionate name from Mallory. And I cherished it in my current mentality of despair. "You just did it, Mallory. Thanks."

"Aye." He eyed us curiously. "Paying yer' respects?"

I nodded.

"I'll make the rounds then. I don't trust the security system, even with the *Guardians* online, as much as my own eyes." Gunnar grunted his agreement. Mallory left the fire after picking up his spear and downing the last of his drink. On the way past us he offered me his scarred, iron-hard forearm, his eyes twinkling with anticipation and support as he nodded a single time. I clasped it, squeezing once.

He did the same with Gunnar and then left. The resulting quiet felt like a heavy blanket over the office. Aged paintings of my parents hung above the fireplace, staring stoically down at us. Two smaller paintings of Gunnar and me as children in ridiculous superhero poses framed the fireplace, lending life and humor to the hooded stares of my parents. My father had taken the photos, had them painted, and had chosen to place them here of all places. Gunnar was shaking his head slowly with an amused grin at the memory of that day.

It had been the day my parents gave him his shifting rune. The rune that allowed him to master his werewolf skin rather than becoming a raving psychopath once a month.

I approached the bookshelf and reached for the lever that opened the secret passageway. The house was rife with them. If it wasn't for Death allowing me to speak with my parents after they had died, I may never have discovered that the primary entrance to the Armory was here at *Chateau Falco*. My house. I had thought the only entrance was at Temple Industries, but that had been destroyed by a rogue Academy Justice who had been trying to break in and take the Armory for himself in order to ignite a new world order during *Mardi Gras* not too long ago.

It had been under Jafar's watch.

Yet another reason he hated me. As if it had been my fault his employee went bonkers and tried to use my inheritance to lay waste to the Academy.

I shifted the pressure release valve and watched as the fire suddenly roared brighter. This wasn't the Armory yet, just a secret access point to the area that *housed* the entrance to the Armory. See, I told you my digs had all sorts of cool secret passageways and whatnot. Some more dangerous than others, and I was entirely confident that I knew only a fraction of what lay hidden beneath *Chateau Falco*'s skirts. I couldn't wait to explore my home with Indie.

Gunnar glanced thoughtfully behind us to the doorway leading back to the hallway and our women as if about to change his mind, but then back to me. "Nervous?" I asked.

"I've just never been in there before," he admitted. "And I worry for them..."

I nodded. "Don't worry. They're safe. Mallory is prowling the halls too. With his crazy ass lightning spear." I smiled.

Gunnar chuckled. "Someday you'll have to tell me where he got it."

I shrugged helplessly. "No clue." Like I said, Mallory was sort of an enigma to me. "You ready?" I asked. He nodded after a pause.

"Okay. We're not there yet. This is a secondary security measure my dad installed. The entrance to the Armory is only one of the things he hid down in the crypts. Follow me exactly." And then I stepped into the burning fireplace, which should have roasted me into bacon, but didn't.

Instead, I fell. At least it *felt* like falling. Pandora had told me it was really just a form of Shadow Walking to another dimension, or at least the shortcut that existed between two locations on the map. I had told her it felt similar to my Maker power. She had laughed, patting me on the back. *Who do you think made the magic in the first place? Wizards just found a way to copy it. Even if only primitively.*

I landed lightly on my feet and waited for Gunnar to appear beside me. He did so with wide eyes, glancing about nervously before spotting me. He brushed off his pants and stepped closer. "This Hogwarts stuff creeps me out," he grumbled.

"Just wait." I teased.

We walked for a few minutes, turning down several halls, until we approached a ten-foot tall door made of living stone.

When I say *living*, I'm being literal. The door depicted a woodland scene, complete with foliage, nocturnal creatures, a small pond, stars, and a full moon. But the carvings on the door darted about as if alive. Fish darted about between reeds in the pond, and an energetic pair of small owls flitted from one thick branch to another. A lone wolf sat on his haunches at the bank of the pond, hungrily eyeing the owls. The trees swayed in an unseen wind, and then one of the owls abruptly dove down into the pond, razor sharp claws extended. He scored a hit, flapping back to the tree to savor his fresh fish. Knowing what was about to happen, I pointed down at the bottom of the pond for Gunnar to see. The lone wolf also watched, no obvious reaction in his hungry eyes.

When the unlucky fish broke the surface of the water clutched in the owl's talons, another was instantaneously born at the base of the pond. A fishling? A fish baby? I shook my head. I wasn't a biologist.

Look, people, a tiny freaking fish.

It was magical. Obviously, of course, but I'm referring more to the *beauty* of someone, at some point in time, investing their power to create a living mural for no other reason than that they wanted to. That was what magic meant to me. It wasn't all about cool explosions and Hollywood-level special effects. Magic, at its core, was about life. And death. And the beauty of those two forces comingling. At least to me.

I smiled distantly as I pulled out a small penknife to slice the pad of my thumb enough to cause blood to spill. Then I reached out to caress the lone wolf's fur. He growled, but it wasn't the familiar friendly sound I was used to hearing after visiting the Armory so many times.

Usually he growled in contentment, appreciation for his master's touch.

This time it was a warning growl, and he abruptly snapped his jaws at me before padding over to the opposite end of the pond, as if that would keep me away from touching a two-dimensional carving.

I stood there in disbelief. That had never happened before.

The entrance to the Armory usually opened at the touch of my blood to the wolf's fur.

But this time it hadn't.

Gunnar was watching me expectantly, no doubt waiting for a great revelation of some kind. I hefted the satchel on my shoulder nervously, only too aware that for whatever reason, I could no longer plan on storing the books in the Armory.

It was locked to me.

I really didn't have time for this sort of thing.

"Hey, wolf."

"Yes?" Gunnar answered drily.

"No, not you. Him." The wolf in the carving watched me silently. "What gives?" I asked him.

His mane of fur lifted in warning as he growled again.

"I'm locked out." I clarified, in case it wasn't obvious. The wolf barked once.

"Was that a yes, Lassie?" I asked sarcastically. He barked again.

Huh.

"Why?" The wolf merely stared back at me this time.

"Is it permanent?" I asked. The wolf barked twice. "No?" I asked. He barked once for *yes*. Unless I was batshit crazy, I was now speaking wolf. I turned to Gunnar for help. "You getting any of this?" He shook his head, eyes studying the wolf carving with sudden interest at the possibility of understanding him. I turned back to the door.

"You aren't allowed to let anyone in?" I concluded. He confirmed with a single bark.

I turned to eye Gunnar over my shoulder and then shrugged. "Well, that's a first. Not sure what to make of it." I idly wondered if it was locked down due to me activating the *Guardians*. "Must be some kind of security measure." The wolf barked once, which made me shiver. I hadn't been addressing him, which meant that he could understand general conversations in his vicinity. I idly wondered if I had said anything to offend him in the past.

I didn't want to piss off the bouncer at the door.

Even if the bouncer was a living stone carving. "Look, when I referred to you as a fleabag mutt the other day, I was just kidding." The wolf merely turned his head away from me haughtily.

"How long is the door locked down?" The wolf glanced over a shoulder, but that was it, so I clarified my question. "Will it be locked down for long?" The wolf continued to stare back, which made me shiver. It meant that there wasn't a *yes* or *no* answer to the question. Which meant other variables were involved that could alter his answer, rendering him unable to respond. *What the hell?*

Maybe Pandora was just taking a bath and wanted some privacy. Or my parents were having a romantic stay-cation, and didn't want to be disturbed – the equivalent of a sock on the doorknob in a college dorm room. But that didn't sound right to me.

I turned back to Gunnar, a feeling of dread creeping over my shoulders. "We should probably get back to the girls. I don't like this."

His posture instantly grew rigid as the situation dawned on him. If the Armory was on lockdown, something we probably wouldn't like was happening nearby.

Or, more likely, *had already happened.*

We began to run.

The wolf howled behind me, urging us on, the sound chilling as we raced back the way we had come, Gunnar hot on my heels.

9

Indie had been justifiably alarmed at being woken up by her paranoid boyfriend in the middle of the night, who was freaking out about an impending attack, yelling gibberish about the Armory being on lockdown, gargoyles, and a talkative wolf carving refusing to open a door.

Especially after a growling werewolf forcibly shoved Ashley into our room. Indie had shrieked, tugging the sheets up above her nakedness. We hadn't immediately gone to sleep after all, thanks to Barbie's gift.

I owed Barbie for *that* memory reel.

And the best part?

After I proposed to Indie, she was mine forever.

Which was awesome, yet terrifying...

In my mad dash from the office, I had deemed it prudent to nab the feather that Pegasus' brother, Grimm – no relation to the psycho brothers currently hunting me – had once given me. I had wanted to make sure I had my bloodthirsty pony on call to get us out of Dodge if we needed to flee on the spot. I spotted the black feather with the red orb on the tip – like a demonic peacock's coloring – poking out from my satchel now on the far wall of the tunnels where I stood.

It had taken me quite a few deep breaths to calm down and share the full story with the girls, by which time Gunnar and I had mostly downgraded from a Defcon 1 threat assessment level and had returned to merely believing in general conspiracy theories.

My drifting thoughts earned me a solid *thwack* from Mallory's quarterstaff.

"Ow!" I spat, shaking my thumb in the air by my side to ease the pain.

Mallory only looked determined. Then he attacked me again.

I calmly embraced the raging river of power that seemed to constantly reside beneath my feet, or more accurately, beneath the surface of the earth, which just so happened to be beneath my feet. No matter where I stood at any given moment – from the top of a ten-story building, to a hot tub, to the secluded basement halls of *Chateau Falco* – I could now at least *feel* the power every time.

Progress!

But it was the harnessing of that power that constantly eluded me.

I reached for the overwhelming force, hoping to eke out a small defense against Mallory's rapidly approaching quarterstaff, and my hands sailed right through it. Which earned me a thump on the head this time, knocking me from my feet to land on my backside. Even with padded ends, Mallory's quarterstaff packed a punch. I growled a warning at him, but he merely shrugged.

"Your enemies enna' gonna' give you an inch, Laddie. You asked me to train you, so I'll be a doin' it right. Like you want me to. Even though right now you wonna' admit it." He held out a hand to help me to my feet.

"I just can't seem to get a consistent feel for it. At least I can always sense it now, but I can't always tap into it."

"That's better than when you started training." He offered with a shrug. "Baby steps, my son."

The words hung heavy in the air, and I could tell that Mallory wished them back. A slip of the tongue. Still.

Instead of climbing to my feet I stayed on the ground, patting the dirt floor beside me for him to sit down. He complied, looking uncomfortable. We were in the crypts before the door that led to the Armory. We watched the wolf chasing the owls, yapping excitedly as he eagerly hunted for a quick snack. I smiled. Which didn't last long. The door was no longer a door, but an obstacle in my mind. It was all that stood between me and possible answers to the Brothers Grimm. So close, but so far away.

"Any luck after you deactivated the *Guardians*?" He asked. I shook my head. He stared at the door thoughtfully, but didn't speak.

I turned to him, feigning nonchalance. "Who are you, anyway? I've never asked. Just took you on faith after my parents passed."

His face turned stony.

"I saw you only once before, you know. That day at the police station when you were driving my dad to bail me out. That was years ago. Before I opened the bookstore."

His features slowly melted to their usual sunny demeanor as he grunted with a distant smile. "Aye. I remember it well." He chewed on his lip, idly plucking unseen things from his pants. "A lot happened that day. Maybe not all of it seemed important, but me thinks it was. Especially now."

I nodded thoughtfully. No one knew what really happened that night. Well, now they did since I had spilled the beans last night. But before that, I had told no one. Not even my parents. So how was Mallory aware that something big had happened that night?

"Why do you say that?" I asked softly.

He was silent for a few moments. "Intuition. I remember the air feeling tense that night. The sea was wild. Air thick with unseen lightning. The Perfect Storm..." he trailed off.

"The *river*." I said with a frown.

He chuckled. "Aye. The river," he corrected.

"Because claiming to know what the sea was like that night all the way from St. Louis would be crazy..."

"Well, I reckon I fit that bill, Laddie." He laughed lightly, squeezing his staff.

I let the silence calm me, focusing my mind. "You're not going to tell me."

"No." he finally answered with a sigh. But the word was apologetically firm.

"You know how that looks, right?"

He sighed. "Aye. I reckon I do."

"But that doesn't change anything."

"No. It doesna' change a thing." I let the tension in the air build, and was about to give him an ultimatum when he continued. "Your father swore that that was mine to keep. Even from you, his blood." He trailed off distantly. "I've done... things I'm enna' too proud of. I don't want to relive 'em. Or to have someone judge me by me past." He looked at me. "I'm sure you understand." He winked. I was about to press the issue, but found myself calmly admitting that he had a point. I briefly pondered a suspicion that perhaps his accent was another form of disguise, because I had caught him slipping out of it several times over the past months. His next words caused me to look up. "Trust me by my actions, Laddie. Can't go wrong with that, can ye'?" His eyes twinkled in the dim torchlight.

I shrugged. "You've done right by me. I was just curious. I don't like puzzles."

"I know." He climbed to his feet, offering me his hand. "We have enough time for another few rounds if you want. After that ye' need to get going. Big meeting today."

I groaned, accepting his scarred hand to help me to my feet. I didn't want to think about that. "Are you trying to rile me up? You know how I feel about today's meeting, despite what the Board of Directors says."

He nodded. "Riling you up seemed to work a few times. You tapped into this... *well* of power almost seven of ten times. And you were as angry as a fisherman coming home after a voyage to find his wife porking the local baker!" He burst out laughing.

I hadn't been *that* angry. But he had a point. "I don't get it. I can sense it all the time now. It's everywhere. And yet it feels... alien." He watched me thoughtfully.

"I'm sure the first wizard said the same thing about magic."

"Yes, but a Maker *gave* the ability to use magic to wizards in the first place. Just makes me wonder if I'm playing with toys better left untouched. Well, if I can ever figure out how to consistently touch it," I complained.

He was silent for a few seconds, turning his back to me.

"That won't work out too well for your lady friend..." he muttered. "Makes me wonder how much you really care about her. Down here in your batcave whining about this and that when you should be focusing."

My vision went blue in a blink. I don't really know how else to describe it. I used to see red when angry, but after my transition in power, the world seemed to turn an arctic blue tint whenever I grew angry now.

"You don't get to talk about Indie like that," I warned, instinctively.

"Call 'em like I see 'em. Whining down here about billion dollar meetings, probing into my past like a gossipmonger. Like any of that really matters. You're running." He called over his shoulder, not even looking at me, apparently disgusted. I must have struck a nerve with my questions.

Still, that gave him no right to bring Indie into this. I pointed a finger at him and unbidden power abruptly launched from my fingertips, slamming him into the far wall. He bounced off and hit the ground with a groan. Crackling blue cuffs sailed from my fingertips and lifted him from the ground, pinning him at my eye level, facing me now. "Take it back, *whoever you are.*" I snarled.

I noticed that a single tear leaked down his cheek. Then he smiled sadly. "Told you it would work." He spat blood onto the floor.

I blinked.

He had riled me up.

And I had tapped into the power instinctively. I focused on it now, feeling it settling around my feet in a seeming unending well, hungry to be used. I mentally dipped my fingers into the torrent and felt galactic frost, scalding lava, razor-blade air, moist earth full of life, and rock as dense as lead – all melded together into a single force.

And I was wielding it.

"Nate, you ready yet? We need to leave in ten minutes," a voice called from the distance.

Indie.

The power rushed out of me like water through a sieve, leaving me exhausted. Mallory slumped to the ground and took a deep breath. So did I.

"I'll be right up, mom," I muttered under my breath.

"I can hear you, Sir Echo. You're in a tunnel."

I muttered under my breath, softer this time. Mallory spat a bit more blood and saliva onto the dusty floor. "Sorry about that, Nate. Yer' easy to read. I needed ye' angry quick to see if ye' could do it on the fly."

I watched him, and his lone tear suddenly made much more sense. It had hurt him to hurt me. But he had done it anyway.

Trust my actions, he had said. Well, he had plum proven his character to me.

I thought about what he had done, and then began to laugh. "You taught me how to cheat." I finally said.

He grunted agreement, climbing to his feet. "If ye' can't consciously use your new power, at least ye' know how to cheat enough to keep yer' friends safe. One of yer' father's most valued lessons."

I lowered my head, nodding at the memory of my father. "Still, I'm sorry I reacted so strongly. You gave me a gift and I hurt you."

"The best gifts come at a cost. Now, it's time for you to get primped up. Big meeting today, whether ye' like it or not. Just don't get too angry with 'em." He winked, helping me to my feet again. "They're only doing their jobs, and they do work for you."

"Let's see what crazy scheme they have lined up for me this month," I muttered.

I made my way back to my room to rinse off and get ready to meet with Temple Industries' Board of Directors for an urgent meeting they had set up last minute.

Which was never a good thing.

I needed to be finished with this quickly. I had more important things to do than worry about my company right now.

The satchel with the books never left my sight.

Even from the shower.

10

I clicked the pen clutched in my fist, the sound surprisingly loud in the packed room.

Then I did it about a dozen more times in the space of a minute, while gazing lazily out the window of the twelve-story building. I shifted uncomfortably in the chair for a few seconds, and then finally lifted my feet up onto the table itself, letting out a soft contented sigh. That earned me a few thinly veiled looks of disapproval, but Mallory had beaten me up pretty good this morning, and my whole body seemed to throb with a dull, but constant pain, like a form of Chinese water torture.

I was waiting for the speaker to finish, ignoring the discreet glances of several more of my Board Members, who seemed more intent with my reaction to the speaker's words than the speech itself. Almost like they already knew the details... They seemed a tad concerned at my obvious display of disinterest, and I could feel their calculating eyes planning ahead for the next several days based on a million subtle clues they imagined they were cleverly deciphering from my body language.

It was enough to almost make me laugh aloud.

They thought they could read *me*? Every single move and reaction I made was deliberate, a disguise, purposely shown or hidden to lead them exactly where I wanted them to be. It was instinctual for me. These men and women thought they could out manipulate *me*? I was a *Temple*. I had attended dinner parties with more intrigue than they would experience in a lifetime.

But the thing about being known as a worthless, billionaire playboy was that people often forgot that I was eidetic, with a genius level IQ to boot. My cover persona was so blatant and obnoxious that many forgot this small fact. Which was purposeful, and I wielded this power like a razor in the night, quietly moving the chess pieces on the board to my desires, none the wiser.

I forced myself to take a soft, deep breath. But Mallory had been right. They didn't mean harm. Some of them were even ex-employees of the company while others had spent more than a decade serving on the Board for my parents. They thought they were doing the right thing. They just didn't know any better. We weren't enemies. They just needed... guidance. A firm hand. I glanced about the room. A *firmer* hand if they had thought this was going to fly with me.

They had worked very hard to broker this deal, without informing me ahead of time, which settled a threadbare cloak of barely constrained rage over my figurative shoulders.

Even if I hadn't been distracted with thoughts of the Brothers Grimm actively hunting me, I would have had the same response to the speaker's pitch.

Not *no*, but *hell no*.

Having already decided my response, I mentally began planning my day, idly tapping the satchel at my feet with my heavy winter boots. The satchel that held the two books that the Brothers Grimm wanted very badly. One was a book of summonings, and was how I had met Barbie the nympho-sprite in the first place. Some of the creatures in that book would be a fine catch indeed, for the Brothers Grimm. The book was essentially a free buffet menu to them. Open the cover, pick a page at random, perform the ritual depicted on the page, and a victim would be forced to answer the call – forced to appear against their will, trapped inside a nice summoning circle all neat and hogtied as you please for the Grimms to decapitate.

You see, with summoning rituals the creature called upon rarely had the power to stand up to the summoner – as long as they performed the ritual properly – and the pages in this book were very specific, leaving little room for error, and as a result, no way out for the victim. Well, Barbie's page had been smudged, causing a slight embarrassment for me when I first summoned her, but that is neither here nor there.

I shivered at that memory, and thought about the implications of the other creatures being called to their deaths. I had to keep the book out of the wrong hands or it would essentially be my fault when they were all killed.

The other book was the original edition of *Grimm's Fairy Tales*, or *Kinder- und Hausmärchen* in German. But it apparently was not only the first copy of the book, but actually held spells as well.

Of some kind or another.

I had flipped through the pages late last night, careful to make sure the protective ward remained intact so that the Grimms couldn't trace its location. Barbie had hinted at that being a likely possibility and I wasn't about to take any chances.

The first half of the book held the original stories: Snow White, the Princess and the Frog, and many, many more. Of course, these were the true, original tales, not the friendly *Disney* versions. For example, rather than kissing the frog, the Princess had dashed his body against a wall.

This was the *least* violent of the stories.

But then there was the second half of the book. It read more like a travel log, handwritten in big, loopy cursive German script. I wasn't fluent in German, but I caught enough recognizable words to get the main gist. It described creatures they had encountered while traveling the German countryside, and how they had murdered them.

Interspersed in the journal entries were sketches of supernatural creatures I had neither seen nor heard about before – likely long extinct thanks to the Grimms' hunting parties – and numerous depictions of diagrams, star positions, and plenty of vaguely alchemical or scientific calculations of some kind filling the margins. I shivered, glad that I couldn't read the language. The pictures had been gruesome enough.

I had scoured the text for one specific entry to no avail. I had been told that the book held the power to permanently lock away the Grimms or possibly kill them all. I didn't know if it was true or if it was in fact the opposite – a spell capable of drawing every Grimm in the universe to a single location in time and space. Cold fingers danced down my spine at the thought.

Whatever it was, the Grimms didn't want anyone else having access to the book. They had lost track of it at some point in recent history, and I had – completely by dumb luck – stumbled across it and decided to purchase it. Up until last night I hadn't really spent any time studying the tome, much to my embarrassment given the present circumstances. I had always told myself I would make time to study it... *tomorrow*. But, you know... *life* always seemed to get in the way.

After scarcely surviving my first encounter with a barely corporeal Jacob Grimm a few years ago, I had grown complacent, despite Barbie's persistent warning. I had thought he and his brothers safely locked away in a prison of sorts, and had been told that the book in my satchel was all they needed to escape. Perhaps that had been why I hadn't been too keen on reading it. I hadn't wanted to accidentally rub the proverbial lamp and let the genie out. Not that any of that mattered now. They had found their own way back, just like Jacob had told me he would. Perhaps if I could find out how he had accomplished this I could send him and his brothers back to the void. I grunted to myself, earning a few pointed looks from a Board Member sitting to my right. I ignored him.

And now Jakey and his brothers were coming for me. Not just to kill me for a personal offense, but now they were even going to get paid to do so! Talk about Karma. My arrogant pride had come full circle. The Minotaur would be hooting his nose ring off at the irony.

I was pretty sure I would need Barbie's help to either send them back or defeat them in battle.

Barbie had led me to believe that she had been involved in some capacity – a few hundred years ago – in imprisoning them in the first place. Or that she had at least witnessed it. I mean, she was powerful with a capital P, but I didn't really get an overwhelming combat vibe from her. Sure, she was sadistic, hyper violent, and savored murder by sex, but I hadn't ever really seen her Hulk out or anything, so wasn't sure what she could do in a battle. Which was sounding more and more likely.

I really could think of only one choice. I couldn't watch over and protect all my friends at once. I could only be in one place at a time. Which meant that I needed to bring the Grimms to me. I just needed to figure out how.

Someone cleared his throat, bringing me out of my reverie. I looked up to find everyone watching me expectantly. I put my worthless, billionaire playboy face in place, full of entitlement and general boredom at adult life. "Oh, thank God. Is he finished?" The gentleman beside me nodded, lips tight. "Good." I swept my gaze over each face for a few seconds, watching my Board squirm uncomfortably. "No." I took a casual sip of my bottled water, pretending not to notice the brittle tension in the room. "Now, is there anything else?" I asked, setting down my drink.

Ashley held a fist to her mouth and coughed lightly. She hadn't needed to mask it. The room suddenly roared with arguments, muffling her expulsion.

I let the sound build like a tidal wave for a handful of seconds. Then I held up a finger, breaking the sound wave like a cliff face suddenly rising out of the ocean, stopping it cold. I pointed at the man standing by the screen who was also taking a drink of water. "You've heard my answer. If you have anything to refute or add, I will give you thirty seconds to sell me. Give me the high points. I'm just a worthless heir after all, and you used a lot of big words."

He blinked, sputtered a bit, and then composed himself.

"We will pay ten times earnings for the last fiscal year. Your company's profits have plummeted since your father's... departure. We are offering you a golden parachute. An easy way out." That was an unheard-of offer. Easily double the industry standard.

"Now you're speaking my language." I finally answered, forcing myself to sound slightly interested. Several Board members seemed to relax in restrained triumph as the speaker babbled on a bit longer, biting onto my response hook, line, and sinker. I tuned him out, but still let on that I was completely focused on his words, nodding here and there convincingly.

But I was really assessing my Board with borderline murderous thoughts. They had set up this meeting behind my back. I could sense Ashley studying me, knowing I wasn't truly listening and that the other shoe was about to drop. I ignored her.

There would be repercussions for their actions.

Starting today.

No doubt the golden parachute would also be quite lucrative for each of the Board Members, seeing as how we collectively owned the majority of the publicly held company's shares. But I was the largest shareholder by far, and the heir to the company's founder, so my word was law. The speaker finally finished his spiel. I tapped my lip with a finger. "Thank you for your time... but my answer stands. Temple Industries won't be sold." A slip of rage escaped my carefully controlled façade as a sudden thought hit me. "Especially not to a German company."

The Grimms were German.

"We started here on US soil. I wouldn't be able to look myself in the mirror if I took those jobs away from American workers. *St. Louis* workers," I amended. "Some of them have been here for over twenty years."

"We would be inclined to leave your plant operational if that is a condition for your acceptance." He sounded eager.

I thought about that for a minute. But that wasn't truly my biggest problem with the pitch. Relocating the company would kill hundreds of jobs, which I of course wasn't okay with, but even if they kept the St. Louis plant operational, I didn't want to sell.

Temple Industries was *mine*. The last remnant of my parents' dynasty.

It wasn't for sale.

I shook my head. "No." The room imploded. I crossed my ankles and watched it play out. Sudden declarations of inattention on my part, no goal for the company's future growth or specific product lines to focus on, no plan for increasing or decreasing R&D, et cetera. I listened, nodding at the appropriate moments, remembering each comment, accusation, and face that dared speak.

"With this sale, you could focus on rebuilding your true passion, Plato's Cave. Especially after that explosion demolished your building earlier this year. That project requires a lot of focus on your part. Focus that you haven't given Temple Industries. Think about it, Nate. The company hasn't been a true focus for you, and it's suffered as a result." Of all the people who I had thought might challenge my authority, I hadn't anticipated Ashley.

My thirty pieces of silver. My Judas Iscariot with a kiss.

Her words were spoken softly, politely, but the voice swiftly cut through the outbursts of men ten years her senior like a hot knife through butter. The room grew silent, tension suddenly as thick as smoke.

I blinked, slowly swiveling to face her with barely masked shock. It was well known that she and I were more than just employer and employee. Everyone knew about her and Gunnar, and that he was my best friend, and that my parents had considered her a surrogate daughter.

And she had just sided against me. You could have heard a pin drop. My vision exploded blue and I couldn't contain myself.

"No." I growled savagely, slamming my fist onto the table enough to significantly crack it and send my water bottle splashing to the ground. Several Board members flinched at the impossible power of the strike, suddenly very, very nervous. After all, everyone had heard the news clips and general rumors about my exploits, even if they hadn't quite let themselves believe.

But that belief seemed to have changed in a microsecond.

I had fought a 'dragon' on the Eads Bridge, I had flown through a window to land on a Judge's lap – even though there was no possible explanation for how I had managed to jump through a third-story window with no balcony or stairway leading to it. I had started riots at *Mardi Gras* that ended with explosions at both my bookstore and Temple Industries. Brutally murdered bodies had been found at several of my properties throughout town. The police and FBI had held me in custody... several times.

Regarding both my parents' murder and other crimes that had gone unsolved. I had allegedly burned down a strip club where a cop's mutilated body had later been discovered. I had been announced as a firm supporter of magical creatures coming out of the closet at a nationally-televised solar eclipse convention, standing arm in arm with senators and politicians. I had even been referred to – several times, and all by respected persons in the community – as a *wizard*, of all things.

All of these wild accusations and unbelievable stories strolled across the newsfeed of their memory as they stared at the cracked table.

And a longtime friend of mine who had supported me through all of that had just stood against me. Openly. My response was to crack a solid oak table with my bare fist. Which shouldn't have been possible. Seeing as how the room was filled with ex-scientists and engineers, they knew better than anyone the limitations of the human body.

But there the broken table sat, loudly defying every Law of Physics known to man.

The room was completely still.

"Now that you are finished airing our dirty laundry in front of our guest," I pointed a finger at the potential buyer of my father's company, causing him to flinch in fear as his eyes tore away from the damaged table, "I think we are finished here. You may leave," I whispered darkly to the German. He nodded quickly, eagerly gathering up his possessions under an arm – not wanting to waste any time putting them away properly, and bolted from the room. I swiveled in my chair, facing the windows and the winter wonderland outside. I let the silence build for a solid minute. I didn't turn around as I spoke. "You bring up valid points." I admitted, resulting in a soft, relieved collective breath. "I task you with forming plans to resolve our current deficiencies. We will discuss this at our next... *scheduled* meeting." I emphasized the word, spinning the chair slowly to face them again, letting them know with my glare and tone that this cloak and dagger shit would not happen again.

Ever.

"That is all." And I rose from the table. Everyone else did the same, bowing their heads deferentially. Concerned Board Members instantly swarmed Ashley as I strode out of the room and made my way to the elevator.

I had a few murders to plan. A trap to set up.

I would leave the bureaucrats to... well, *bureaucrat-ing*.

Because if I'm being honest with myself, I didn't think I was very good at it.

11

I strode towards the elevator, grinning to myself as I spotted the man waiting outside the polished doors. The German turned at the sound of my heels on marble, and his face paled, looking panicked that he would have to share an elevator with me. I smiled wider at him and his face blanched further.

I jabbed the button several times to increase the speed, and let my smile slowly fade.

Then I waited. "You know that doesn't help..." he nervously teased, aiming for small talk. I didn't respond. "I... I wanted to thank you for your time. I understand your position, but ask that you respectfully consider the offer when your emotions have cooled." I slowly turned my eyes to him, face unyielding. His already weak resolve shattered. "I... I think I need to use the necessities before I leave." He stammered, clutching the messy collection of PowerPoint handouts to his chest. "Good day." He practically whimpered.

I turned back to the elevator, waiting. After a minute, I jabbed the button again impatiently.

"You know that doesn't help, right?"

I briefly entertained murder.

I turned a fiery glare to find Ashley standing beside me. I spotted several heads quickly ducking back into the Board Room upon seeing her confront me.

Ashley held out her hand. "Peace offering?" I looked down and almost had a panic attack to see her holding out my satchel. I snatched it away eagerly. "You left this in the Board Room," she said softly.

"What the hell is wrong with me today?" I checked inside for the books and sighed in relief.

"Just today?" She teased.

"Touché." I muttered as the doors finally slid open. We stepped inside and I pressed the lobby button, preparing myself to brave the horde of reporters and TV anchors no doubt waiting outside the lobby doors. I glanced pointedly at her and pressed the button again, making sure she noticed. Then two more times. She rolled her eyes with a tired smile. "So... mind telling me what the hell that was about?" I growled.

She sighed, shoulders relaxing into a neutral position. "Just doing my job, Nate. I took off the *friend* hat and put on the *Temple Industries* hat. It's what you pay me for. It's nothing personal. My job is to be honest with you at all times. Especially when you don't want to hear it... and that was about as honest as one could get," she replied, respectfully.

I grunted. "I'm not selling the company. It belonged to my parents." I said stubbornly.

"I get that. I cared for your parents too," she responded softly, eyes glistening. I didn't give her an inch, remaining silent. Crocodile tears wouldn't fool me. She had challenged me in front of my Board, and I had considered her in my corner. "If you want to keep the company, you need to become more active in our future. No offense. Just my very expensive business degree at work." She smiled softly.

"They should know how to run a company. They've done it for years. It's a cash cow."

She was already shaking her head. "Wrong. Your father was directly involved in almost every aspect of the company. He lived and breathed it. True, he spent a lot of time on side projects, but never at the detriment of the company at large." She didn't add that I had done exactly that. "Just take the offer into consideration. No emotion. It's true you don't have to sell. With a little guidance, the company could become a Tech Titan again, but we need a captain to steer the ship."

"That's what your very expensive business degree is for. Not blindsiding me in front of the masses." I muttered frostily.

She nodded. "That's true. I could turn things around. But if you want me to do that, I'll need a raise."

I blinked at her. And then I began to laugh. I wasn't against the idea – I just found her segue so unexpected that it made me laugh. She was pining for a raise while I was pining to stay alive over the next few days. She smiled. "Not like that. Of course, I wouldn't object if it came with a compensation bonus. What I mean is that I need more authority to act. There are a couple of bottlenecks in the decision-making process. We should talk about it if you are serious about keeping the company. We have a great team, but a lot of potential projects went dark after your parents passed. We need to breathe some life back into them, and kill a few others."

I shrugged. "Done."

She shook her head. "I know you have more important things on your mind right now, but you can't let this be an emotional decision. We will talk about it at length before I agree to help. If not, consider this my resignation..." I blinked at her, dumbfounded. She went on as if not noticing, emotionless. "Which will of course mean several other key members would likely leave. Possibly moving to Germany to work for Mr. PowerPoint back there." She finally looked up at me, adjusting her librarian glasses with a manicured finger.

"You wouldn't."

"That's kind of where we are right now, Nate. This is your company now, and it's time you treated it like more than a hobby. Or sell it. Our key people feel like they have no voice, and that feeling breeds discontent, which inflates turnover. They. Will. Leave. Especially after *this*." She softened the blow with a sad smile. "You didn't really show much respect in there. This is their *life*. When employees feel that they are more dedicated than the owner, bad things tend to follow. You can't be mad at them for it. You come in once a month and dash their plans to pieces. How do you think they should feel? You're a bull in a china shop in their eyes. Some of them have been here for decades. You haven't. Yet you have the power to destroy their passion with a single growl, phone call, or click of a pen." She arched a brow and my shoulders sank a bit. She had a point. Even though it infuriated me to admit it. She touched my shoulder lightly as we continued our descent. "You need to stop straddling the fence. You want to keep the company, fine, let go of the reins completely or jump in headfirst. One or the other. Not both. A company this size is like a plant. It needs room to breathe. It's a living being wrapped in a concrete building." she poked my chest hard. "You're smothering it."

The doors opened but I didn't move. My vision was slowly turning blue. Which wasn't good. It meant my anger was rising, and with it, the leviathan of power I now wielded. I assessed her words. She was right, of course. I held out my hand. She took it tentatively.

"You're right. When this is all over, we'll talk." She nodded her head once.

"That's all I ask."

"You're not allowed to quit. But a raise is definitely on the table. We should talk about that, too. As well as a list of other key personnel who you believe deserve a raise."

She nodded and then followed me into the posh lobby. The ceiling rested thirty feet above our heads, supported by thick marble columns. Several seating areas were present in case anyone needed to wait. I saw a small coffee shop in the corner, no customers present at the moment, leaving the two Rastafarian employees to thumb away on their cell phones.

Our heels clicked across the marble floor, two security guards tipping their hats our way as we approached the front doors. Ashley and I tugged on our coats, me wrapping the pea coat around my body tightly before buttoning it up and popping the collar to protect my neck from the wind and snow outside. Ashley wore a scarf, tucking it inside her coat.

Seeing as how the entire front of the building was glass, I could already see the frenzied horde waiting outside. News vans, and clusters of reporters filled the entryway, checking their recorders and microphones in eager anticipation to be the first to break the news – whatever it may be. They hadn't planned on the meeting ending early, and as soon as they saw me they began to scramble like a kicked anthill.

I wasn't quite sure how they even knew about the meeting in the first place. No doubt one of the Board Members had assumed a different ending to the meeting and had prepared accordingly, ready to steal the spotlight as soon as I agreed to sell. I wondered just how much money was riding on this deal for each Board Member and what it may have meant to their retirement plans. I would have to look into it. Because despite Ashley's advice, I was still pissed about how it had come to my attention. It would be a topic to discuss with Ashley in depth.

I was the freaking owner and I had found out via company email, which I checked only once a week. That would have to change if I was truly committed to following Ashley's advice.

Maybe I could negotiate up to twice a week. Max.

I took a deep breath, placing my hands on the door. Several people outside began eagerly pointing at me and raising their recording equipment. Ashley touched my shoulder in reassurance and support. "Your car ready?" I asked.

"I texted the driver from the Board Room." She pointed towards the street beyond the reporters.

"Good. Let's get you safely through the horde of vultures then. We'll talk later at the Chateau." She nodded and then followed me as I strode through the doors into the frenzy.

Camera flashes exploded across a sea of cold bodies, the tide of humanity practically frothing at the mouth to see that Nate Temple himself was the first to exit. I was a celebrity after all. For both good and bad reasons.

It began immediately, the crowd swarming us. "*Is it true that Temple Industries is selling to a German Industrial Company?*" One reporter shouted. What the hell was wrong with my Board? It seemed the media knew more than I myself, which meant someone had talked. Someone who had likely purchased *puts* – the right to sell at a fixed current price in case the stock crashed – or *calls* – the rights to buy my stock at a certain price in case the stock soared. Which, being insiders, would be illegal. Ashley's face went rigid, the same concern no doubt entering her mind. I forcibly continued to push us on through the crowd, tugging Ashley's hand firmly, forcing the crowd to part at a glacial pace. I may or may not have used subtle elbow strikes to speed things up.

"*How much are they buying the company for?*"

"*Will the factory remain on American soil?*" another shouted.

"*What do you have to say about this decision effectively killing hundreds of jobs in St. Louis, in an already precarious economy?*"

The cameras continued flashing and microphones dangled in front of me as I contemplated my response. My face remained expressionless out of experience, even though my mind was racing a million miles per hour. A gentle throb of warm energy seemed to abruptly fall over my shoulders, but I didn't have time to think about it.

Because that's when the *hit* went down.

Bullets began to fly.

12

The glass walls of the lobby shuddered under a barrage of machine gun fire, shattering into millions of glittering crystals that spilled across the icy concrete. Ashley and I dove behind the back of a parked van, trying to determine who was shooting at us and from what direction. My eyes scanned the scene in a blur, searching for the shooter, but the fender suddenly lit up with sparks as bullets hammered just to the right of my skull. I ducked back, but not before a tracer of fire nicked my ear. Which pissed me off. The world morphed into an azure glow as magic beckoned to me. Ashley yanked me back further, whipping a pair of pistols out of her purse with the skilled precision of a practiced student. I recognized them as the pair Gunnar had given her for Christmas.

I still hadn't discovered exactly where the shooter was, but something persistently nagged at me until I finally gave it a second of attention.

Something was off about this situation.

You see, shootings are *loud*.

Rifle bullets fire at thousands of feet per second from tiny explosions of a hammer striking a casing of gunpowder. These thunderous concussions cause your brain to dampen your eardrums in an effort to preserve your hearing. Cordite fills the air in puffs of pungent smoke that makes it difficult to breathe fresh air, which you are desperately gulping, as adrenaline kicks in to fuel your muscles in order to help you run away faster.

Hot chunks of lead either strike people, causing screams of agony or death and sending gouts of blood into the air, or they strike stationary objects, splintering wood, shattering glass, or ricocheting off concrete and metal until they strike yet *another* target.

Hopefully not *you*.

A tangible fear swamps the air as screams of panic fill the night, accompanied by the whine of bullets flying past your ears like a persistent cloud of mosquitoes, and each one of them could end your life. Right here, right now.

It's chaos.

Having said that, this time was different.

For example, there was no screaming.

At all.

No cries, shouts, or yelling. Now, all of the other sounds were still there – bullets hammering into walls, snow embankments, cars, and the other equipment from the news crew, but the crew themselves were as silent as ghosts. Ashley seemed to realize the same phenomenon and glanced back at the crowd of news reporters at the same time I did.

Every single one of them stood completely still. Not even blinking.

"Shit..." I muttered, still scanning the crowd for any signs of movement.

But it was a sea of statues.

That explained the sensation of power I had briefly experienced prior to the first gunshot. Someone was altering time, or at least everyone's perception of it, which never ended well for the people affected.

I had only seen two creatures with that kind of power.

One was an Angel of Heaven, and the other was Jacob Grimm.

My anger evaporated to be replaced by true fear. Panic. My magic withered and died like a guttering candle as the anger disappeared. The Grimms had come for me and I had been caught with my pants down around my ankles, and with a crowd of helpless mortal targets as leverage, and I had no one to help me. No one to back me up as Ashley – a mortal – and I took on the world's most feared assassins.

"Nate?" Ashley asked in alarm. I shook my head, trying desperately to kill my fear. I needed to be angry. Not scared. Otherwise I was just dead weight. I was a spellslinger, god damn it. Ashley needed me to start throwing around balls of fire and death if we were going to survive this. The pep talk helped slowly wear away my fear, but it didn't entirely fade, and my anger remained stubbornly out of reach. And with it, the link to my power.

I needed a few minutes to get my head back in the game, so I assessed the situation.

Apparently, we were the only ones unaffected by the spell. I heard a muffled barking cough, followed by the sound of more cascading glass striking the pavement at the entrance to the building. I quickly peered around the edge of the van and discovered that the attack was coming from *inside* the building.

The security guards. One of them grinned at me from behind a pillar, drawing down.

Noticing my attention, Ashley leaned out over my shoulder and opened fire at the lobby. "Get down!" I yelled, pushing her back to safety.

Bullets pounded the front and side of the van in retaliation. One of the tires blew out with a hiss, and the van lurched downwards with a sharp groan. After a few seconds of constant shooting, I sensed a pause in the exchange, which usually signified reloading. I glanced around the corner, careful to keep my torso behind the fender. But the other shooter had apparently been waiting for me to make that mistake. Shots immediately rang out, hammering into the van all over again, one striking the passenger side mirror.

Which immediately tore free and struck me in the temple.

I hit the ground in a sprawl, ears ringing, and vision swirling lazily. I struggled to get my bearings and find the van but I couldn't make up from down. I was supposed to be doing something. *Get angry*, a voice whispered at the edge of my subconscious, but I couldn't understand how that would help. A wizard's magic had nothing to do with emotion. Sure, being emotional could increase your output, but you didn't have to be emotional to use a wizard's power. You had to be in control of your mind.

Then a thought slowly limped into the forefront of my brain.

But you're not a wizard anymore...

Then it hit me, my mind suddenly lurching back into gear. I struggled to get pissed, but the blow to the head had rattled me good. I felt fingers grip my ankle and begin pulling me back to cover, but they weren't fast enough.

Something tugged at the flap of my jacket with a significant amount of force, and I was jerked out of Ashley's reach as a single gunshot coughed. A silencer. Then another blow hammered into my belly and I temporarily lost control of my limbs as my breath shot out of me in a whoosh. The sound of a gunshot came a millisecond after the blow. I glanced down to find a sizeable amount of blood oozing from my stomach. Then the pain struck me. A searing hot stomach cramp from hell.

Then the pain doubled. Then tripled.

I could hear Ashley screaming something before more shots from her twin pistols cracked the air in a steady rhythm. Her barrage apparently gave the gunmen pause because I didn't hear return fire. She grasped my leg and successfully pulled me to safety this time, which felt truly horrible, my stomach knotting up into a tight ball of pain that forced me to curl up into a defensive ball.

I slowly uncurled, leaning my weight against the fender of the van as Ashley quickly checked my wound, hissing as her eyes fell on my stomach. I had been shot. And not by an amateur. Two direct hits with two measured pulls of the trigger.

A marksman. If they could hit that accurately through a glass wall and a hundred feet, they very easily could have killed me dead. Ashley let off another volley of shots around the side of the van, aiming at the interior of the building.

I peered around the corner, unable to stand yet, and saw the gunmen using lobby furniture for cover as they methodically approached, one covering the other's advance before they switched. My anger slowly began to wake, grumbling in response at their skilled approach. Ashley was no soldier. Neither was I. We didn't stand a chance playing the game by their rules. These guys were professional hunters. And I wasn't about to sit here and die behind a news van like some lamed deer. Rage rose like a leviathan out of the deeps, illuminating the world in a dim blue glow as my power roared to life with single-minded purpose.

Self-preservation.

So, it was time for me to do magic and stuff.

I leaned out with a hungry smile, feeling useful again as I cast a shield of air to protect me from oncoming lead. Ashley's bullets struck an invisible dome in front of the advancing gunman but they disintegrated to dusty motes rather than piercing flesh. That was both cool and practical. If I survived, I would have to learn it.

So, like I suspected. Grimms.

We needed a plan. I glanced down only to realize that the satchel was gone. My eyes quested for it in a panic. *There!* I instantly spotted it only a few feet away where I had been shot. Even with access to my power back online, I knew we needed to call in backup, but first I needed to protect the satchel. I began scrambling towards it as I maintained my shield, slipping and sliding in the light smear of blood pooling beneath me, but then a thought hit me and I froze. If I grabbed the satchel, they would know of its importance if they caught me. I quickly managed to scramble back behind the van.

Taking a deep breath filled with pain at my brief foray into the kill zone, I had time to see a bullet enter the crowd, striking one man in the hip, which caused him to drop the microphone pole clutched in his gloved hands before he flew backwards. The pole struck a woman in the temple and she collapsed in frosty silence, but I had seen the explosion of blood from the camera guy and was sure the woman would also have a noticeable lump on her dome, if not a concussion. I couldn't let the Grimms cause any more collateral damage. The reporters were defenseless. And they would die. I took a deep breath and tapped into the well of power, seizing it forcefully rather than wasting time trying to coerce it.

The pool of viscous power rippled in response as if pleased. I didn't have time to analyze that, so I simply latched onto it and sent it coursing deep down into my body, numbing all sensory receptors so that I could move.

"Ashley, cover me!" She didn't hesitate. She unleashed a barrage of lead with both pistols as fast as she could. They disintegrated on impact with the Grimms' shield, but had the desired effect. They paused. I quickly cast a concealment spell on the satchel and used a gust of air to send it deep into the crowd where I hoped it would remain hidden. I then delved deep into the reservoir of power at my feet and imagined a duplicate copy of the satchel and fastened it to my hip. It was weightless, but I hoped it would do the trick. I didn't know if they knew about the satchel of books, but if they did and they saw me fleeing without it – when I had been toting it while exiting the elevator – they might turn back to search for it. But step one, I needed them to *follow* us.

I didn't have a step two for my plan.

I took a deep breath, turning to Ashley with a macabre grin. She was staring at me nervously, no doubt wondering how I was still upright. "Get ready to run."

Her responding nod was less than encouraging.

"Memento Mori," I muttered. Her eyes widened, and she made the sign of the cross over her chest.

Which did absolutely nothing for my morale. She had zero faith in the wounded wizard. Maker. Whatever I was now.

I sighed, hoping she wasn't right.

13

I lurched to my feet, the pain of my wounds now a dull, distant ache. It would have to be enough. I made sure the shield spell stood between us and prepared to hoof it.

I snatched the back of Ashley's coat and tugged her off to the right, away from the crowd. We ran for several paces with her firing over her shoulder before her guns clicked empty. She muttered a curse, but immediately focused all of her attention on running away, racing beside me with panicked eyes. We were beyond the crowd in a blink, tearing off into the snow-covered grass surrounding the building.

Pounding boots tore after us in hot pursuit, somehow sounding like they were gaining on us. Several rounds hammered into my shield but we kept moving, Ashley's eyes were wild, as she no doubt anticipated being gunned down any second. I heard the attackers' guns run dry and I really laid on the speed, hoping they would slow as they reloaded.

Instead I heard one of them laugh hungrily, and the clatter of his gun hit the pavement. He was eager to confront us without guns. Which usually meant the person was experienced with inflicting pain via fists or magic. He let out a howl that turned into a leonine roar, dripping with the anticipation of a proper hunt. I glanced over my shoulder at the terrifying sound, fearing the worst. But I was wrong.

It was worse-er than I could have imagined in my darkest nightmares, and I had spent some time on the receiving end of a true master of the art personally sending me night and day terrors.

For months.

Needless to say, what I saw earned an *A-plus* in the nightmare department.

I stumbled a step in utter disbelief, and immediately decided that the only chance of survival required me to run backwards, even if I did lose speed. Ashley soon began to outpace me, not having turned around to look.

Which was probably better for her sanity.

Because a freaking lion was chasing us. With eyes and mane of living fire.

And the top of the lion's back was about the height of a small horse, making him more akin to a freaking *liger* – yes, they're real – the hybrid offspring of a lion and a tiger. But this one looked to have fed on annoying wizards and an unhealthy dose of steroids for breakfast every morning for the past twenty years.

The other Grimm somehow managed to maintain the same speed as the liger, which just wasn't fair. We didn't stand a chance outrunning them.

Then the freaking scenery changed and I suddenly found myself racing through the equivalent of the African Savannah rather than snow covered grass. I spotted a herd of motionless gazelles where the reporters had been, and felt a faint whisper of an icy wind ruffle my shaggy hair. I didn't even slow down, well past my disbelief quota for the day. So, I rolled with it, but I heard Ashley let out a sharp exhale of surprise. Still, she didn't slow down either, apparently accepting our teleportation without breaking stride. Either that or the Grimms had simply made it *look* like we had been teleported to a new location.

Yeah, that jibed. *Fear*. They were trying to scare us. Now, being chased by a liger was terrifying. But being chased by a liger while suddenly being teleported to the African Savannah was a whole new level. Well, for most sane people anyway.

But Ashley and I were well beyond sane.

Without completely understanding how, I cast a cord of supercharged electricity behind us in a makeshift trip line. The spell crackled with purple energy across the ground, arcs of power sporadically zapping to ash anything it deemed alive. Then it disappeared from view. Invisible.

Huh.

I hadn't ever thought of doing anything like that before.

Without allowing myself to get caught up in the magic – *heh* – of my strange new powers, I copied the spell two more times, staggering their spacing in hopes that at least one would nab the liger, and switched the type of destructive power for each – one made of flowing lava and one of razor sharp crystals – both invisible. Remembering the size of the racing fire liger, I imagined that the height of the trip wires was a foot higher. Not being able to see it, I took it on faith that it was in fact higher than I had first seen it. I just hoped that the Grimms either hadn't seen it in their hunger for the chase, or at least didn't remember exactly where it had been.

Then the other Grimm decided he didn't want to be left out of the shapeshifting party, and shed his mortal skin midstride.

Again, it was really good that Ashley hadn't turned around. At least she wouldn't die with the shame of soiled pants. Even for me it was a close call as my eyes widened in further disbelief.

"Oh, come on!" I complained under my huffing breaths.

I managed to keep shuffling backwards in a clumsy run as I watched him shift into a freaking ape like Caesar from that new *Planet of the Apes* movie franchise, fully decked out in armor that covered his thickly muscled frame. He clutched a wicked looking bone-tipped spear in his stupid opposable thumbed fist. The twinkle in his eyes reminded me of how eerily intelligent Caesar had been in the movie.

But the Grimm looked smarter.

Proving this point, he launched himself onto the liger's back and they really began to pour on the speed, small craters of flame erupting with each strike of paw to sand.

The ape let out an ululating cry of glee from astride the liger as he pointed at my satchel with his spear.

The liger let out a roar of such ferocity I could practically feel it.

I opened my mouth to shout a defiant yell of my own, not wanting to feel left out, and immediately slammed into a warm body, my head cracking against another skull. My vision exploded in a supernova of stars. The sounds of pursuit rose in pitch. I managed to see Ashley lying beneath me, clutching her head with a groan. She had stopped for some reason, and since I had been running backwards I hadn't realized it until it was too late.

I managed to gain enough control over my body to look back and face our impending death. I realized my hand was resting on Ashley's rear end for support, which was firmer than I would have thought.

Gunnar and Indie would have killed me for that.

But I didn't have time to worry about Gunnar or Indie. It was over. Even as a Maker, I didn't have the juice to stand up to two of these things by myself, not while trying to keep an incapacitated Ashley safe. I murmured a goodbye to Indie under my breath, and pulled deep on the strange reservoir of power, clawing for something I could do to them as a final attack. I might die here, but at least I would go down fighting.

The liger jumped, fiery mane rippling in the wind as it sailed through the air in a parabolic arc that would end at my face. The ape reared back to launch his spear with a precision that had to have been rehearsed.

The motion drew my attention to a spot just below them a second before he loosed the spear.

A small purple flicker of hope among the desert brush.

I frantically imagined that the trip wire was higher. In fact, I imagined it was *exactly* where the Grimms were.

One second they were flying at my face, and the next thing I knew there was a purple implosion in the air. A wave of grit pelted us like a miniature sandstorm before I managed to shield my eyes with my sleeve.

I gagged, coughing up a mouthful of Grimm grit as I leaned to the side in case I retched. My head butted into a shaft of solid oak quivering in the earth beside me, directly between Ashley's legs. I looked up to see her staring at the spear that had almost killed her. Then her eyes rose to mine in wide-eyed disbelief. I'm sure my face was the same. The scenery abruptly snapped back to the chilly winter streets of St. Louis with a faint *pop*. She didn't even comment on *that*.

"A *liger*?" She whispered. "Why didn't you tell me there was a freaking liger chasing us?" She stammered in disbelief.

I shrugged, taking a shallow breath in case the air was still tainted with Grimm particles. I hadn't known she had seen any of it, assuming she had been down for the count. "That was nothing. Did you see the ape riding on his back?" She blinked at me. "That was his." I pointed at the spear. Her eyes darted to the spear, then back to me. "You can have it. I've already got one." I muttered woozily, clutching my stomach as a sharp burst of pain broke through my control. My fingers came back wet with blood, but I didn't let Ashley see.

And then she began to laugh, her brain unable to comprehend the situation in its entirety. After a few seconds, I joined her. I slowly climbed to my feet with a groan.

I glanced at the now snowy ground, idly wondering about the brief excursion into the Savannah and if it had merely been an illusion rather than a teleportation. Judging by its disappearance after the Grimms died I was betting so. Otherwise we would have been wandering around the desert right about now. "We probably need to get ba–"

"Your stomach!" Ashley jumped to her feet, gripping my shoulder as if I was about to fall down. "We need to get you to a hosp–"

"No," I gripped her arm to enunciate. She looked me in the eyes, frowning, ready to argue. "No way. No hospitals. I'm fine. For now, but we need to get back to the crowd and get my satchel. Now. Before it disappears or in case there were more of them."

I spotted a shiny item on the ground, and like all girls, squirrels, and toddlers, I made a move to grab it. I picked up a pair of ancient looking amulets right below where the Grimms had imploded in the air.

"What are they?" Ashley asked, peering over my shoulder curiously. I shoved them into my pocket for later.

"I have no idea. Let's go. Some of the reporters were injured."

We began to jog drunkenly back to the building, both our heads still a little woozy, but determined to retrieve the satchel and offer what help we could. We found the people milling about in a frenzied mass at the scene of the gunfight. Several Board Members stood apart, assessing the broken glass, and a small swarm surrounded the injured reporters, but the rest had turned on their cameras to document everything. Everyone froze at our approach.

And waited, unspeaking.

I cleared my throat, fighting my growing nausea. "The security guards tried to kill Ashley and me with machine guns." I mentally squirmed at the upcoming lie forming on my lips. "We chased them away, but they escaped in a waiting van and we lost them." I spotted the approximate location where the satchel should have been and sent out an invisible feeler to sweep the ground. I felt a slight resistance but when no one shrieked about someone grabbing their foot, I knew I had guessed right. I pulled it closer to hover beside me, still invisible. I could feel my power slowly fading, and the pain coming back.

"You chased them away..." One reporter murmured loud enough for all to hear. "Two men with machine guns." I nodded, trying to remain on my feet as the power began to leak out of me at a faster rate. The reporter met my eyes with a disbelieving look. "That none of us saw..."

I blinked sluggishly in response. Ashley swooped in to save me. "Yes. You'll find shell casings from my Glock 19's around here as well as those from the security guards."

"He's bleeding!" One of the reporters shouted, pointing at my stomach.

I glanced down and staggered at the sight. There was a lot of blood. Ashley suddenly gripped my arm, whispering in my ear. "We need to get you help, *now!*" She hissed. I nodded, feeling overwhelmingly dizzy as my magic went out with a weak puff, bringing back the pain like a surprise sledgehammer blow. My knees buckled at the agony, but Ashley held me, and immediately guided me towards a waiting taxi. I heard the sounds of her speaking to the driver, but couldn't understand the words. The world seemed muted by a fuzzy down blanket of lead, and a throbbing fire ate at my stomach.

I managed to mumble over my shoulder before Ashley was able to stop me. "I'm not selling Temple Industries." The crowd erupted with noise, before the car door slammed shut.

The car pulled out onto the icy streets and we fled, no doubt to avoid any authorities. I closed my eyes, and my breath began to increase in ragged pulls as I tried to remember the fight. Why hadn't the Grimms attacked in full force after the first salvo? Seeing a wounded wizard on the ground should have upped their bloodlust, but they hadn't come for me when they had held the best chance for success. Instead, their gaze had been fixated on my satchel. I had a leak somewhere. And only my inner circle knew what was inside the satchel. Unless it was just a lucky guess on their part.

I listened to the gentle lullaby of the tires on snow, trying to gather my thoughts. I glanced down and wished I hadn't. Apparently the Grimms had got me good and I had lost enough blood to convince my brain to do a hard reset. The darkness began to pull me under and I smiled, listening to Ashley yell something about a hospital to the driver.

"No, *Chateau Falco*." I murmured. Ashley shot me a nervous look, but I went *nighty-night* instead of waiting for her response.

14

I woke up a few subjective centuries later, instantly thrashing about wildly with my hands and breathing in short strangled gasps as I realized I didn't have-

"Easy, Nate. It's right here." Ashley offered the satchel to me. We were both in the back seat. I snatched it greedily from her hands, opening it to glance inside and verify the books were safe. I even risked lowering the wards for a moment to check that they weren't plants but the real books. We were driving, so I felt relatively safe that the Grimms would have a hard time tracking me while on the move. I hoped I wasn't underestimating them. I let out a sigh that sent a spasm of pain through my abdominal wall. I glanced down.

Oh yeah. Gut shot.

Curling my head to look at it caused the pain to flare again, but not as badly this time. My body had evidently grown used to the idea that the pain wasn't going anywhere anytime soon, so had welcomed the new wound to the numerous neighbors of older wounds I had accumulated over the years.

"So, how in the hell did we get back to St. Louis?" Ashley asked, noticing that I was fully awake.

"What?"

"I'm pretty sure we visited the desert for a while there."

I looked out the window, remembering the Grimm's transformation of their own bodies, and then the very reality around us. "What do you think of when you think of the African Savannah?"

She turned to look at me. "Danger. The hunt of predatory animals. Why?"

I nodded. "I don't think we actually changed locations. I think they just made the environment *look* like the Savannah. For the fear factor. To mess with us. Scared prey makes mistakes. I think it was a form of glamour." She blinked at me in disbelief. I could get that. I mean, on the fly they had managed to successfully alter every detail well enough to convince us we were on the Plains, running for our lives. "Did you see the gazelles?" She shook her head with furrowed eyebrows. "That was the reporters. Innocent, harmless, large group of creatures just standing there doing nothing." She blinked at me. Managing to make it look doubtful. "Look, a real herd of gazelles would have bolted at the first roar, right?" she looked thoughtful, nodding finally.

"Wow. That's... frightening. Is there a way to see through glamour? What if they do it again when we aren't expecting it? We think we're walking into *Chateau Falco* and really we're walking into their arms."

I shook my head. "It's not that easy. We were running for our lives. I'm pretty sure they would need us to be at least as keyed up as that in order to believe it. After all, they can't change every detail." At least these two Grimms hadn't been able to. "Did you feel the cool wind?"

She thought about it then shook her head.

"I did. It's what tipped me off. We just need to be hyper aware from now on. Look for inconsistencies in our environment."

She shivered. "Okay. I'll try. We need to warn the others. No wonder these guys have been so successful in killing off freaks. If they can trick their prey with glamour..."

I nodded morosely. She wasn't even bringing up the worst part. These two had shifted into uber-predator monsters. A fire-Liger and an intelligent cave-ape.

The driver made a left turn and I frowned. I hit the glass with a fist. "You're going the wrong way." The driver didn't acknowledge me and I felt a mild freak out coming on. Ashley noticed and began rattling the door handles and pushing the window buttons, but they were all locked up tight. She immediately pulled out one of her pistols and held it up to the window separating us from the driver. All I could see was a black, wiry beard and a *Fidel Castro* looking cap – or whatever they were called. Then she tapped the window in warning, staring into the rearview mirror. "Stop. The. Car."

The man lifted his eyes to meet mine and I frowned. He looked familiar. Then he tore off his hat and his fake beard. He pulled out two molded hunks of silly putty from inside his mouth, deflating his cheeks, and peeled off both a wart and a particularly nasty liver spot stuck to his cheek with adhesive. I began to laugh and waved for Ashley to withdraw the gun.

"Laddie," the man spoke with his usual Scottish brogue after rolling the dividing window down. "Thought you might need an extra set of eyes. One of my boys was on sniper duty outside the hotel, but his shots didn't seem to bother 'em too much. We'll upgrade our arsenal. Apparently, we needed big game ammunition and an elephant rifle after they shifted." He grunted. I was still reeling from the fact that Mallory had *boys* on the payroll. "Ye' did good. But I reckon we stop and get ye' patched up. Here. Now." He pulled over into a deserted church parking lot in a quiet section of town.

"Why? Let's go to *Chateau Falco*. I need to talk to everyone."

"That can wait," he mumbled, and then climbed out of the car. I began to open my now unlocked door, but Ashley gripped my hand.

"He's probably right."

I frowned at her.

"I wasn't asking for a vote. The others could be in danger. I need to get to them before the Grimms do."

"Not with a leaky stomach." Mallory grunted, opening my door and letting out all the hot air. He was clutching a familiar leather valise that belonged to Dean. He knelt on the slushy asphalt, giving me no room to climb out. "Stay in the car. We don't want a crowd seeing what we're doing."

I grunted. "Well this sure won't attract a nosy old lady's attention." I motioned at the sight of a man kneeling over the lap of another man in a parked car in a church parking lot.

Mallory chuckled. "Your car door is facing the church, which is empty. No one to see what looks like your everyday... *man on man action*." He laughed harder at Ashley's suddenly blushing cheeks. But instead of wimping out, Ashley held out her hands, inviting me to lean back so Mallory could get at my stomach. I sighed. Her chest did look rather comfortable – it came stocked with twin pillows that looked truly inviting – even if her werewolf fiancé would rip my eyes out for even teasing about it. Ashley shook her head and flicked my nose.

"I won't tell if you don't," she teased.

"Given your fiancé, that sounds almost as dire as you saying, *here, hold my beer for a second and watch this*! Usually never ends well." She laughed lightly and I turned my head before relaxing into her chest and lifting my shirt over my wound.

Yep.

Her pillows were great. In a strictly professional medical assessment. Better than any doctor's office bed I had sat in.

Mallory got to work instantly, cleaning the wound with iodine, which felt like slightly cooled lava and sulfuric acid had made a love child. I hissed a bit and Mallory rolled his eyes before continuing. I glanced down to see the wound and my guts did a nauseating little flip-flop. It wasn't pretty. The bullets had hit the side of my abdomen. I closed my eyes, not wanting to throw up on Ashley and ruin my very temporary pillows. Ashley sucked in a sharp breath as she saw the wound up close. Her hands instantly went to my scalp, fingers massaging idly.

"I'm so sorry, Nate. You should have had Gunnar or someone else here. Not me. I don't have a lick of power. This is my fault. If you hadn't been watching out for me, you could have laid waste to them without worrying about collateral damage."

I reached up and squeezed her hand, not immediately telling her the truth of the situation. I almost hadn't been able to tap into my power in time to do us any good. "You did great. Seriously. Great shooting skills. This had nothing to do with me being distracted. These guys are just that good. I'm lucky you were there." I hissed at a sharp pain from my stomach before admitting the truth aloud. "I'm not as formidable as I used to be. I'm still learning about my new powers. It will be a little while before I'm back to my old level. You saved us both, Annie Oakley."

She chuckled with a barely restrained sob, and then continued massaging my head. "I'm going to take the bullet out now."

"If the bullet broke into my stomach wall, mind shoving a protein bar in there for me? I'm starving."

"Fresh out. But I think it missed the organ anyway."

"Okay. Ready, I guess."

Then the wound was spread open further, twisted up, squeezed, and generally abused for a few excruciating seconds. Ashley groaned at the sight, increasing her massage reflexively. It didn't help me ignore the pain.

Mallory finally grunted and pulled something out with a wet sucking sound. I looked down to see him holding up a small piece of metal. "Huh. Small caliber." He looked up at my eyes. "They weren't trying to kill you," he said ominously.

I shivered, kind of hoping it had been the opposite. I didn't want to imagine why they wanted me incapacitated but alive.

"Now if the bullet had been anything larger caliber, your coat wouldn't have prevented it from entering 'yer stomach, which would have guaranteed a hospital trip, and likely death," he added soberly. I grunted.

"Maybe I should go buy a lottery ticket."

Mallory wordlessly began closing up the wound. I suddenly felt a gentle warmth pulsing from his fingers and my eyes shot wide open as I watched him. He glanced up once, a look of mild embarrassment flashing to a warning frown, calmly, harshly, commanding me to seal my lips. I watched in awe as the power dribbled from his fingertips, a golden glow like magic dust forming the shape of a knot before settling inside my wounds. Ashley didn't seem to notice. With the sensation came the realization that my power was roaring back into me, leaving me feeling refreshed and no longer exhausted. In fact, I felt downright chipper. He wiped it down when finished, and wrapped me up with gauze before Ashley helped me to sit up fully. Mallory shot me a look, shook his head once, and then packed up his bag, closed the door, and got back behind the wheel. I stared at the back of his head thoughtfully as he started the car and we began to pull out of the parking lot, the talking heads on the radio idly chattering in the background.

Looks like Mallory and I needed to have a chat soon. But he was right. Not now.

I felt a weight in my coat pocket and stuck my fist in there to see what it was. My fingers closed around an unfamiliar shape and I blinked. I pulled out a long, heavy chain with an amulet attached to the end. Another rested within the pocket but I left it alone.

I held it up to the light and watched a pendant swing by a thick, linked chain of an unfamiliar metal. An obsidian gem hung in the shape of a double crescent, like that of an axe, encased in a ring of blood red stone to hold it in place. Power ebbed from the amulet, and I felt a minor resonance deep within my own reservoir of power.

But I also felt a darkness. A hunger to consume. I shivered and shoved it in my pocket. I hoped it wouldn't contaminate me or anything sinister like that.

"*In last night's news, a local land owner woke up in the middle of the night to find his fields burning with a wildfire the likes of which St. Louis has never seen. Police have been on site trying to discover the source of the blaze, but have found no help from the land owner, Mr. Kingston.*"

My breath caught as the name rang a bell. "Stop the car."

Mallory did, looking around cautiously for an impending attack.

"We need to go to that farm."

"What farm, Laddie? We're in the middle of the city."

"The one on the radio. I know it. A friend lives there."

Ashley looked at me. "Do you really think you have time for that? They didn't say anything about any injuries. The landowner is fine. Just a fire."

"You're going to have to trust me on this. It's not the farmer I'm worried about."

Mallory eyed me in the rearview mirror. "If 'yer certain 'bout it..."

I nodded. "Drive."

I hoped Asterion, the Minotaur, was safe. His relationship with me had apparently made him a target too.

God damn the Grimms.

15

We pulled up to the farmer's house, which looked much... wealthier than I remembered, although I really hadn't spent any time in any place but his fields. But I did remember seeing it from a distance, and I recalled it looking like any farm you might find in any section of the Midwest. Nothing special. But the home in front of me wasn't similar to any farm I had ever seen in my life.

At all. I briefly wondered if we were at the right place, but the heavy scent of smoke made it pretty obvious. There wasn't another home for miles.

Mr. Kingston's farming operation looked *mysteriously* successful. Something was odd about the structure, but I was too busy scanning for threats and masking my dull pain to spot what exactly had caught my attention. Mallory's unspoken power had helped, but not eliminated my discomfort. Still, my magic was back, which was a plus.

No police presence was in sight, but I was still nervous. I didn't want my name attached as a person of interest to whatever had gone down here, especially after the Board meeting. I'd had enough of affiliating with crime scenes in the past. In fact, I had once been arrested in the very field adjacent to Kingston's house, and declared high on 'shrooms. All because my car had been spotted outside the field and the police had wanted to question me about my parents' murder. Poor timing to say the least.

The detective in charge of that particular investigation had suffered quite the career change as a result of my not so subtle retaliation. Something to do with pictures of him in bondage gear or some kind of deviant outfit appearing in a file on a policeman's desk, as well as documentation of his secret interest in certain dark Craigslist ads, which had immediately been publicized via the local news channel. I actually wasn't sure if he was even in police work anymore. The world was a better place for it. He had been an incompetent hack, and a danger to citizens everywhere he had jurisdiction. He was more interested in the collar than the crime. The fame more than the justice.

I had... *fixed* that.

Allegedly.

Heh.

I studied the house, the shadows, the barn, the garage, and every single tree within jumping distance of a liger or an intelligent ape. But I saw nothing. If the Grimms had truly been behind the blaze, I didn't want to be caught with my pants around my ankles again. Especially after taking down two of their brothers. How many did that make now? Ten? More? Could they call in reinforcements quickly or did they need the book first?

Mallory clicked off the engine.

We sat there for a few minutes, listening to the engine cycle down.

Then the scene before us abruptly folded in on itself like a mirage, and a very normal quaint looking farm briefly stood in its place. Mallory grunted, and Ashley gasped. The familiar farm I had seen in the past, complete with a worn-out barn and broken fence stood before us. Then another ripple to the air and the wealthy farm was back. The scene remained solidly on the wealthy farm for a good ten seconds before I shook my head. My friends were staring at me, waiting for an explanation, but I had none. Well, *that* was a first. I was beginning to realize that perhaps it wasn't a coincidence that the Minotaur resided nearby.

There was magic hinkyness afoot.

Before anyone could speak I opened my door. The front door to the house opened at the exact same time. I stayed in place, not wanting to appear threatening to an elderly farmer. They tended to shoot trespassers. I imagined him growling, *Get off my lawn*, like that Clint Eastwood movie, before whipping out a twelve-gauge exclamation mark.

Listen, farmers don't mess around. Welcome to the Midwest, folks. It's dangerous.

I studied the man, face neutral and unthreatening, peaceful even.

Unless I was grimacing. I *was* in pain after all, despite Mallory's mysterious magic. The spell I used to mask pain worked to some extent, but only to hide it, not eliminate it. My face could have been set in a perpetual scowl without my realizing it. An instinctive muscle formation. I would have to look in the mirror to know for sure, but thought that would only encourage the farmer's *City Slicker* impression of me. I waved a hand and then shoved them in my coat pockets, looking relaxed.

The farmer stared at me.

Not Mallory or Ashley.

Me.

His glittering eyes didn't blink. We were close enough for me to see the hard lines on his face. He wore a casual fitting dress shirt, sported golden hair that just brushed his shoulders, and wore what looked like designer jeans and expensive as hell gator cowboy boots with a fat, glittering belt buckle.

In fact, despite the boots and belt buckle, he didn't look like a farmer at all.

My eyes roved to his face to see that he was still staring at me. He had a weathered face, with piercing hawk-like eyes that seemed to calculate me down to the individual hairs on my head, and his sudden grin looked like he was confident that his estimation was as accurate as only my accountant – or my mother – could ascertain.

It was chilling.

"Please. Come in." He called out in a clear, authoritative voice. Then he turned back into the house, not waiting for us.

Mallory and Ashley blinked and then looked at me to silently gauge my response. I shrugged with a smirk and said, "Let's go talk to Mr. Not Farmer."

Mallory grunted in agreement.

There were, after all, no plants anywhere. Only cows in the field beside the house. Now, I didn't know cows very well, but one thing stuck out as odd to me. These beasts were spotless. As in, they looked to have never experienced a fleck of dirt or shit on their coats for more than a day. And the fields were also pristine. No gaping mud pits, and it seemed the patties were more or less centralized to one corner of the field, because the section they were standing in was green as green could be, not a single defecation crater in sight. As if to point out this fact, one of the beasts slowly began meandering towards that section of the field, just like a regular person would head to the restroom. She did her business, turned around, and reentered the herd, tail still spotless.

Huh.

Trained to shit in one spot? Some trick.

I also noticed that the odorous part of the field was as far as possible from the house.

Then there was the house itself.

It was no farmhouse.

It more resembled a stone castle dressed in modern clothing, like it had harbored a brief real estate identity crisis. Pillars supported a second-floor balcony that wrapped around the entire front of the house, and I spotted a wide sliding glass door that no doubt led to a living area or the master bedroom on the upper floor. Expensive shutters hung outside the windows, looking to be painted gold, and immaculate garden work had turned the property to the American equivalent of an English Lord's estate, with plenty of large trees that hunched over soothing seating areas complete with benches or swings. The pile had to be several thousand square feet, but I only saw one car.

A Bentley.

New.

Gleaming farm equipment stood in an open barn that looked more like a luxury Quonset Hut that those modernists seemed to recently love as a primary home. Windows, log siding, and a spotless cement floor. The equipment all looked new. Unused.

Weird.

"Yeah," I muttered. "My Spidey sense is tingling. This guy seems like runner up to the most interesting man in the world."

Mallory and Ashley had followed my gaze, seeming to come to the same conclusion.

I reached the expensive oak door, complete with a distinct set of scales burned into the wood. I knocked. It was partly open, but still, even though he had invited us in I didn't want to just enter. What if he was a Grimm? Or the Grimms had him under duress? I readied my anger, feeling the pleasant thrum of power at my feet, even though less than an hour ago, I had been drained. I definitely needed to drill Mallory on his past. But not now. I checked the pistol Mallory had handed me, tucked it back in my coat, and entered after I heard a distant, *come in.*

I gently pushed the door open and it stopped after a foot, catching on a rich Persian Rug. Rich as in far superior to anything I had decorating *Chateau Falco*. My eyes traveled up to the walls to find true works of art casually adorning the plaster without embellishment – Renaissance pieces, portraits, battles, and then a smattering of specifically chosen more modern work that I also noticed were expensive – not worth the cost in my taste, but to each his own.

The floors were made of a single sheet of polished marble, not sections of tile, and tables lined each wall of the seven-foot wide entrance hall, each holding figurines, clay vases and bowls, and other decorations that were both tasteful and a profound display of wealth in their own right. Gold and jewels glittered like nightlights. And this was only the entrance to his home.

It was like standing in the waiting room outside Smaug's cave.

Was his wife a billionaire interior decorator? Or did he inherit a pile of money at some point? None of it made sense to me, which put me on edge.

Mallory and Ashley were no strangers to being around money, having spent a considerable amount of time around my parents, myself, and at *Chateau Falco*, but that only seemed to make their awe more impressive. They looked dumbstruck at the contradiction of a wealthy farmer. I snapped my fingers. "Pick up your jaws. We'll discuss it after. Act casual, friendly, and polite. Extremely polite. It's like cocaine to rich people. They want you to know how much better than you they are, and that you openly acknowledge it. Don't act like bumpkins or they will lose respect for you. Thank him for his hospitality. Compliment him on his beautiful home and things. Then politely sit there and let me do the talking."

They nodded and followed me down the hall. We entered a spacious living area that looked like it belonged on the cover of *Log Cabins for the Stupidly Rich*. A massive six-foot wide by four-foot tall two-way fireplace centered the room, also made of some flavor of marble, and a hundred thousand dollars' worth of aged leather Chesterfields (plural) formed an arc around each side of the soothing fire, essentially creating two living areas, or two sections of one giant living area, like an Aspen Ski Resort.

A bar stood off to the side, fully stocked with a selection that only a single man would need. No fruity drinks. Just scotch, whisky, and a twenty-foot tall glass-fronted wine rack, complete with amber lighting and title placards with a brief paragraph neatly written underneath each bottle. Notes on the taste, vintage, and grading of each bottle were scribbled in a precise hand. Was he a sommelier? I noticed that the wine closet extended several feet back, telling me that he didn't just have what was visible to the room, but at least six backups of *each visible bottle*. The guy obviously liked his wine. A quick scan of the selection let me know that he collected nothing costing less than two hundred bucks a bottle.

More exquisite artwork decorated the walls, entirely out of place in a farmhouse. In fact, it was more fitting for a wealthy European Baron of some kind. I didn't even bother to further assess the value of the rest of the shiny artifacts and *objets d'art* surrounding us. Safe to say, none of it would ever be sold at *Ikea*.

Farmer Kingston sat in one of the Chesterfield chairs facing away from us, watching the fire contentedly. His shoulders were entirely relaxed, and if I had to guess, he seemed genuinely pleased at the occasional sounds coming from our throats, as if he didn't often get the chance to share his collection and was enjoying our honest reaction, and giving us the solitude to enjoy it without him watching us.

My cynical side reared his ugly head. Pretty trusting guy to turn his back on us with all this money lying around. Three of us against a lone senior citizen. It wouldn't have been difficult to rob him blind.

Which usually was a sign that we really, *really* shouldn't think of robbing him blind.

He slowly turned to face me, sensing my gaze, and took a sip of the drink clutched in his scarred fist. His hard gaze told me that he knew what I had been thinking, and that I had been spot on. Ashley and Mallory had finished their circuit and now stood beside me.

His eyes crinkled at the corners as he slowly cracked a polite smile. He motioned for us to sit and join him. A serving tray with an unopened bottle of *Johnnie Walker Blue Label* and three fresh glasses with crisp white napkins artfully rolled inside each sat on the artful coffee table between us. A meat and cheese tray piled high with rolls of salami, hard cured sausage, and small wheels of assorted cheeses rested on a wooden platter beside a large bowl of fat, juicy grapes, complete with stems. None of it looked like it would be available at the local grocery store, but more like it had been harvested fresh on the property. Which obviously couldn't be true this time of year. But I didn't voice my thoughts. Instead, I smiled politely and took a seat in the chair opposite Kingston. Ashley and Mallory sat on the adjacent couch eagerly eyeing the platter.

"So, been farming lon–" I began.

Kingston cleared his throat pointedly with a sharp glance my way. "Please, be my guests. Help yourselves." He motioned to the food and drink. A bucket of ice sat on the opposite side of the tray as the bowl of grapes. Mallory began to reach for the ice but Kingston made a grunt. We all looked up at him. He pointed a finger at me. "Serve them." I blinked.

"I like this guy." Ashley murmured with a light laugh. I dipped my head in acknowledgment of Kingston's game. It seemed pretty obvious that he knew who I was and that he thought forcing me to perform an act of servitude would bother me. In all fairness, it definitely would have bothered most billionaire heirs.

But he didn't seem to know that I had basically been a bachelor for the past few years. Rather than freeloading at my parents' mansion, swimming in piles of money *Scrooge McDuck* style, I had instead chosen to open and operate a successful bookstore. By a combination of my bootstraps and a loan from my father to help purchase the real estate – which I had repaid in full and on time – I had opened the trendiest and most exclusive supernatural bookstore for hundreds of miles, only hiring help once the operation grew beyond my scope to efficiently handle. I hadn't outsourced it like most heirs did with new business ventures. I understood all too well that a true leader served from the front, rather than whipping his people from behind. And that no one could get behind a man's cause if he wasn't behind it himself.

But...

Hadn't I done exactly that with Temple Industries? The thought hit me like a slap to the cheek and I stood motionless for a subjective minute, but likely only an objective second.

Perhaps I had something to learn after all. I shelved the thought for later, avoiding Ashley's eyes out of guilt at my revelation.

But Kingston couldn't know any of that. So, a test.

I decided to have some fun with it.

I carefully plucked each napkin from the glass, and – mimicking my Butler, Dean – unfurled them with two sharp snaps of my wrist before expertly placing one on both Mallory and Ashley's laps. I selected one of their glasses, picked up the ice tongs from the bucket, and asked, "How many cubes, Miss?"

Ashley was gobbling it up. "Four, please, good sir." She answered haughtily.

I did as requested. "And how many fingers do you prefer, Miss?" I asked, keeping my face professionally servile, fighting to hide my smile at her instantly blushing face. She also looked confused. Served her right.

"Apologize." Kingston murmured, not looking amused.

I nodded, feigning confusion. "My apologies, Miss. I didn't mean to offend. Scotch is often measured in fingers, like so." I held up two fingers parallel to the bottom of the glass, "Two fingers," I added another digit, "And three fingers. How many would you prefer, Miss?"

She scowled up at me, no longer enjoying the game as much. "Two. I'm not much of a scotch drinker."

"I'm confident that your opinion is about to change. This is an exceptionally smooth scotch with sweet undertones. Our Host has excellent taste." I nodded deferentially at Kingston. "Let the drink rest for one minute or so to give time for the melting ice to break down the scotch a bit." She nodded, taking the glass from my outstretched hand.

I turned to Mallory, but he didn't let me speak. "Four fingers, one whisky ball." I managed to hide my scowl and turned to Kingston. He pointed at the bar with a faint grin.

"In the freezer. Don't dawdle now, son."

I stood, hiding my growing impatience. I had just wanted to see if my friend, the Minotaur, was safe from the fire, but here I was playing Jeeves to assure an old man I wasn't a worthless heir. This was going beyond the pale. But it was a test. And I always passed tests. I used the brief walk to cool my heels. A little humility was good for one's moral character. As long as this guy had something worthwhile to tell us and wasn't simply fishing for a fun story to share with his pals.

I withdrew a fresh glass from the bar and opened the freezer. I instantly spotted the row of spherical ice cubes the size of small racquetballs. I set one gently inside the glass, closed the freezer, and returned to the table. Mallory looked ready to critique, but I knew better. Dean had been the best Butler I had ever seen, he had served hundreds of guests thousands of drinks at Temple functions, and I had paid close attention to his process.

I poured four fingers into the empty glass before Mallory, whisked the glass up with a spare napkin I had nabbed from the bar, and finally poured it over the top of the ice ball in the fresh glass from the bar. He settled back in his seat, looking disappointed he hadn't been able to correct me. I offered him the drink, tucking the other glass behind my back. "I hope the Gentleman enjoys the drink. Is there anything else I may do for you?" I asked, risking a glance at Kingston after my minions shook their heads and took sips of their drinks. Ashley looked impressed, while Mallory looked as if he had found a second home. Kingston nodded in approval and motioned me to sit down. "Any more tests–"

"I find that on a regular basis, it is beneficial to realize where your enjoyments come from, and how much work is done to bring them to you. To put yourself in their shoes once in a while." He spoke in a deep baritone to no one in particular. I nodded.

"You obviously recognize me."

He nodded, unimpressed. "Pour yourself a drink, sit back, be quiet, and listen, Temple. You might learn something." Then he turned to Ashley and Mallory, leaving me to stare back in surprise. "My name is Kingston. Welcome to my humble estate. I'm sure you're interested in the fire last night, but I want to hear more about you before we talk business." He didn't look in my direction, and I could feel Ashley's tension grow as it became apparent that she was the center of attention, not me.

I poured a few fingers of scotch, and after a moment's hesitation added two more. I scowled at nothing in particular as I realized I also wanted one of those damn ice balls. I began to stand.

Kingston lifted a hooded glare my way. That was all. Just a look.

I found myself sitting back down by reflex. He nodded once, returning his attention to Ashley. I sighed, adding a few ice cubes to my drink. Then I leaned back as Kingston peppered Ashley and Mallory with polite questions. He was relentless, wanting to know everything about them.

But it was the darndest thing.

He wasn't interested in anything, well... *important*.

Instead, he seemed only interested in mundane things. *What they did for a living and if they enjoyed it? Their fondest childhood memory and what made it so important to them? Who would they most like to meet, both alive and dead? What did they do for enjoyment and why? If they had family, and if those loved ones lived nearby or out of town?* We had each managed to polish off a plate of the delicious food during our talk. Time stretched on, and I found myself feeling rather sleepy, the ache in my stomach a gentle lullaby of faint discomfort, manageable and almost possible to completely ignore thanks to the spell and the pain-calluses I had obviously formed.

The room grew silent, drawing me out of my daze to see Kingston nodding in genuine appreciation. "Thank you for sharing your life with me." He smiled at Ashley, eyes crinkling at the corners in worn, often used lines. "I find it beneficial to understand the true nature of a man – or woman – prior to discussing business. Now that you have satisfied a lonely old man's curiosity, how may I be of assistance?"

He turned to me, waiting expectantly. I guessed it was finally my turn, although I found it curious he hadn't also peppered me with a background check. Perhaps he already knew enough about me, or more likely, all he had had left to learn about me was my character, which I hoped had been learned by watching me play servant earlier.

I must have passed his test, so I leaned forward to play word games with the mysterious old man, wondering what I may have gotten us into by stopping in to check on Asterion, the Minotaur.

16

I chose my words carefully. We still knew nothing about the man. I couldn't confidently answer whether or not he was clued in on the supernatural community at large. He could just be a wealthy old guy living out his days at the back end of nowhere.

Or he could be something else entirely.

Mallory had eagerly filled a second plate at some point and was now wolfing it down as if it were his last meal. My own now empty plate sat before me. Ashley was leaning back into the couch, legs tucked beneath her hips, looking stuffed and sleepy.

"I was concerned when I heard about the fire. As I'm sure you are aware, I was once arrested on your property a few years ago, by an upstart police detective looking to make a name for himself by single-handedly solving a celebrity murder investigation."

"Your parents." He answered, eyes distant.

I didn't pounce on the answer like I would have in the past, demanding to hear if he had known my parents before their murder. One, because I had already found the killer, punished him personally, claiming my rightful vengeance and burying the hatchet, so to speak. It still hurt to think about, but not many people had the option to speak with the spirits of their deceased relatives from beyond the grave. I had it better than most, but it was still a sucky situation. I would have given anything to have them back in the land of the living. I could really use their help right about now, which briefly brought my thoughts back to the suspiciously locked-down Armory. Kingston watched my eyes thoughtfully but didn't speak.

"You didn't press charges, for which I thank you." He nodded, more in appreciation of my thanks than in acknowledgment of his choice to not press charges. I took a sip of my drink, thinking. "May I ask why you chose not to do so? I was obviously trespassing, and you must wonder what I was doing on your proper–"

"You were visiting a friend." He answered simply. I blinked, not sure how to respond. Kingston saved me from over thinking it. "He told me afterwards. Asked if I would grant you access to visit from time to time." I blinked again.

Well.

"You know the M... that Asterion resides on your property?" I changed what I had been about to say, still uneasy about speaking so openly with a stranger.

He nodded. "We have a lease and everything. Even among old friends, I don't do much without documentation. I learned long ago to keep my business separate from my pleasure." He smiled. "Our friend wanted a break from his past, a safe space to clear his head, and I had the ability to assist him. He's set up on auto draft somehow." He winked.

I leaned back, thinking. *A friend from his past. Payments. Documentation. Obvious wealth.* Who was this guy? He didn't grant me the time to ask.

"The Grimms or their functionaries burned down Asterion's field late last night. The cops came. Found nothing. Left. Then you three arrive," he pointed at my stomach casually, "When, *at the very least*, you should be in a hospital bed. It's... intriguing." He drummed fingertips on his glass, waiting for an explanation.

I smiled in acknowledgement of his fatherly concern. "There was a piece on the radio about it. Is... is my friend okay?" I asked, suddenly heartsick. This was all because of me. He was an associate of mine. Which was now synonymous with the word *target*.

Salted Earth Policy.

Kingston watched me with hooded eyes for a few moments, as if debating his answer. He spoke after an eternity, drumming his fingertips on his glass again as if to find the right words. "The attack... tried his faith. He is safe. Gone now, but safe. He left. Won't be able to come back for some time. Not sure if he wants to come back after that."

"Oh." I replied softly, looking down. My eyes were watering. Ashley reached out a hand and touched my arm, which was shaking slightly. I looked up and smiled gratefully at her, then set my glass down on the table, taking a deep breath as I faced Kingston. "The Grimms are after me. It's my fault your property suffered damage. I will repay you."

The farmer watched me, and then his face stretched into a tired smile. "Thank you for accepting responsibility. I was more concerned with the admission than the money. It was just a field, after all." He lifted a hand at the house in general and let out a soft chuckle. Then he abruptly stood, looking resigned to end the discussion as his eyes darted towards the front door curiously. "It seems you have an unscheduled appointment waiting outside. We've kept him waiting long enough. Don't damage the house, if you please." He added as an afterthought.

"Um... what do you mean unscheduled appointment?" I asked in bewilderment as he reached out to shake my hand. I took it, surprised at the force in his grip. He turned to kiss Ashley's hand and then traded grips with Mallory.

"Appointment?" I reminded him.

"It has been a pleasure meeting you in person. One hears so many things. It's nice when they end up being close to the truth, *Nathin Laurent Temple.*" He winked.

I rocked back on my heels.

Wow.

He had gotten my name exactly right. And when I say *name*, I mean *True Name*. The dangerous kind. The one that could be used against you. For spells and dark intentions.

"Sure, Kingston..." I stammered, letting him politely lead us towards the front door. "Speaking of *names*," I enunciated the word, "What is your real name, if I may ask?"

He chuckled, reaching behind me to open the front door. "I suppose you've earned it." He turned to me with a faint grin, the opening door letting in a wash of frigid air that woke up the last vestige of my sleepiness. "My first name is Midas. I added the last bit to fit in with the age we now live in." Ashley and Mallory were studying the lawn warily. I blinked at the man before me. Midas Kingston... or was it *King Midas*?

He nodded in response to my unspoken question. "Now, you don't want to leave your guest waiting. Mind the rose bushes. They took forever to get right. Come back any time." He offered. I nodded numbly and stepped out the door, checking the pistol in my pocket as I scanned the front lawn.

I quested out with my power to locate the... *appointment* Midas had mentioned.

The door clicked softly behind us and I spotted a figure in black standing in the shade of a tree with an umbrella in one hand. He was tall, gaunt, and looked calmly menacing.

He didn't look familiar, but judging by his getup I was pretty sure I knew who he was. He waved lazily, motioning for me to approach him rather than the other way around. He couldn't come closer to the house uninvited. Either that, or it was the sunlight keeping him from attacking. An umbrella... yep, sunlight bothered this guy. Which meant... I scowled back at him, speaking over my shoulder to Ashley and Mallory. "Stay behind me. I think this is Alucard."

"Who?"

"The Vampire I thought I killed yesterday." And I trudged forward to stake a vampire.

One way or another, this would be over quickly.

For good this time.

17

I approached the stranger with caution. I was pretty sure he was a vampire, and not just any vampire, but the same conceited punk I thought we had killed yesterday in the sewers. The one who had led the kidnapping ring I had effectively shut down. The little shit that thought he was powerful enough to name himself *Dracula* spelled backwards – Alucard. But then again, he *was* in charge of the vampire coven, so it was a safe bet that he was at least marginally powerful, perhaps even a famed Master. With a name like his, he must have had something backing it up in order to prevent his metaphorical blood juice-box being taken away from him every day at vampire recess.

I needed to tread with caution.

My rage was steadily building as I realized I hadn't ended the problem last night, merely ending the operation – temporarily – by taking out his flunkies. Which tended to piss off the boss in most cases.

Which would make my upcoming conversation with Achilles – already a grim proposition since I was no doubt going to accuse him of setting me up – a tad bit harder. I hadn't taken out the leader, so the problem still existed. And his bartender was history.

I sighed, drawing in the power at my feet, glad that at least my anger was present. Thanks to Mallory, I felt strong enough for a scrap, but power like his usually had a cost. Typically spells like that laid the person out into a coma for a day or so, but so far, I was still going strong in the energy department. No time for half measures, I strode forward.

I reached the shade of the giant tree and stopped a few feet away from him. He didn't so much as shift his stance, remaining in a lazy lean against the trunk. Still, I kept my friends behind me with an outstretched arm as I nodded at him in greeting, my face set in a disgusted grimace. He tipped an imaginary hat back at me politely in greeting. His eyes were dark, distant, and lazily aware. Like a lion. Appearing bored and disinterested, but I would bet he didn't miss a thing going on around him.

Ever.

He wore trendy black slacks with the stereotypical loose-fitting white dress shirt of vampires from every movie ever made. A tailored coat hugged his torso before flaring out at the hips like a Steampunk piece, complete with oversized buttons and crisscrossing straps, reminding me of a 1700's era Colonial Pirate or Privateer. His hair was pulled back in a ponytail and a pair of heavy leather boots covered his feet, completing the look. His skin was naturally pale, but he had acquired a light tan somehow.

It seemed this vampire was willing to risk instant incineration along with sun cancer in order to obtain that perfect tan. Talk about priorities. He was also not one of the vampires from the sewer. Which was both good and bad.

"Aye aye, Captain." I sneered at his costume-like outfit.

He answered in a lazy New Orleans drawl. I noticed he was cleaning his teeth with some kind of toothpick. "Name's Alucard. You may have heard of me, Little Brother."

I didn't like vampires, but I *especially* didn't like one addressing me with an affectionate pet name. "Someone might have mentioned your name yesterday, but then they went and disappeared on me. Made quite the mess on their way out."

He nodded without taking immediate offense at me obliquely admitting to murdering his flunkies. "Yes. Glad you brought that up. Put me in a bit of a conundrum..."

He propped the umbrella against the tree beside him, but otherwise didn't shift his weight. He held up both hands, mimicking a scale as he left the toothpick in his mouth. "On one hand, you took care of some rogue associates of mine who had taken it upon themselves to open up a... snack bar without my express permission." He lowered one of his hands as if it were weighted down. "On the other hand, you killed my compatriots, Little Brother. Men – for better or worse – who were under my *Aegis*. My protection." His other hand shifted to more or less balance out the scales. I squinted, confused. Was he thanking me or threatening me?

"I came here for two reasons..." He waited patiently for me to speak. Instead I nodded, motioning with a wave of my hand for him to continue.

He tipped his imaginary hat again. I imagined it as a vintage Captain's hat for aesthetic reasons. "Obliged. First, to thank you for killing the vermin." He watched me, not speaking further.

I stared back in slight disbelief, waiting for a surprise attack of some kind, but nothing happened.

Apparently, I was quiet too long.

"Well, Little Brother. What do you say?"

"Um. You're welcome?"

He nodded, holding his hand to his stomach as he dipped his head politely. I found myself rather liking the guy, despite him being a blood-sucking parasite. I had dealt with many monsters over the years, and none of them had ever thanked me. Especially not for killing their men. "Next, I came here to kill you. For two offenses."

And my brief flicker of hope at gaining a new bestie died in a mental jet plane crash. He continued on, voice and tone even, despite the words that passed his lips. "One, because you slaughtered the several men that represented my entire St. Louis coven. Lowlife, greedy, treacherous bastards, but still. They were *mine*. And one must keep their... *street cred* intact. Now, I'm not particularly inclined to call in my other soldiers from down south to make your life a mess." He began ticking off fingers as he continued. "Logistics, required lodging, travel expenses, lot of additional death and collateral damage." He dropped his hand, meeting my eyes. He was very lucky that he hadn't glanced at Ashley and Mallory or I would have killed him on the spot. "My boys are a hungry sort, you see. I'd rather do it myself. One death. Clean. Neat. Professional. Respectful." He paused, plucking the toothpick out of his mouth with a wet *smacking* sound.

It was a finger bone.

He had been using a freaking metacarpal to clean his teeth. Yuck. And I had thought we could be friends. I really wasn't sure how to take this conversation. I mean, here he was threatening to kill me, yet he was being so freaking polite about it. It almost made me smile. It was a very old-school way of handling things. No shadowy revenge plots lurking over your shoulder for months or years, but an honorable, direct invitation to a duel. Brutal, yes. But also, honorable.

He continued speaking, satisfied his teeth were clean. "Second reason I came here to kill you is that I'm being coerced to do so. If I don't, a group that has some serious brass will raze my New Orleans coven to the ground. Reckon they been doing it for years. So. That about sums it up, Little Brother. Any last words?"

I stared back in masked disbelief. The Grimms? I turned my head to glance back at Mallory and Ashley. They looked just as surprised to hear that the Grimms had subcontracted my death, when the day before they had been adamant about leaving me unharmed.

A whir of fabric suddenly rustled past me and Ashley disappeared out from under my gaze. I spun with a snarl to find Alucard casually leaning against the tree in the same position as before except Ashley now knelt at his feet, and the tip of the umbrella – now a razor-sharp sword blade – was pressed gently into the back of her neck. "I asked you if you had anything to say and you turned your back on me. Can't really cry foul on that one, can ya', Little Brother? I stated my intent, no room for obfus... obfis..."

"Obfuscation," I offered in a snarl. He snapped his fingers together in agreement.

"That's the one, Little Brother. Obfuscation. So, you ready? Or does she die first? Either way we will fight. Here. Now. To the death."

I heard Mallory mutter a curse.

18

Alucard remained casually leaning against the tree, but I knew even a slight motion would kill Ashley. His glittering dark eyes watched me patiently, ready to react. I could sense that he didn't particularly want to kill Ashley, but that he would if I didn't give him the answer he sought.

"Leave her out of it and you have my word. We'll throw down within five minutes, Dracula."

He shivered at the name, shaking his head in amusement as he lowered the blade from her neck. I sighed in relief, but Ashley still knelt dangerously close to the blade for my comfort. She looked alert, ready to bolt at the first opening. But vampires were fast, so bad idea. I discreetly shook my head at her as Alucard continued. "Not my name. Parents thought it would keep the devil away to name me *Alucard*. Named my sister *Nevaeh*, of all things. *Heaven* spelled backwards. Now *she* was an evil little bint." He chuckled.

I didn't find anything funny. Threatening my friends did that to me for some reason. "Those are pretty elaborate names for little kids." I replied, thinking furiously.

He slapped his knees, shaking his head, which caused Ashley to flinch. "That's not even all of it! My middle name is Morningstar. *Morningstar*! It's almost like they *wanted* to set me up for failure. Not only was my first name associated with *Dracula*... my middle name was even *more* notorious! Bloody Lucifer's last name! Two men who fell from Greatness." He shook his head, chuckling harder now. "Parents meant well, I suppose, but they obviously hadn't ever heard the phrase, *curiosity killed the cat*. It only made me want to learn more, so I did some... *research*. Imagine what my eight-year-old-self discovered about those names, and what that did to my impressionable, naïve self-image! I felt like a *god*. I was already an odd boy, interested in all sorts of mystical whatnots. Living in New Orleans with *voodoo* on every corner will do that to you. And being terrorized by larger kids for the formative years of your life put what some might call a *chip* on my shoulder. So, I hunted the vamps down, earned their respect, and joined up. Slowly but surely, I realized that the fangers were rather lazy. Regulars had heard all the stories, but thanks to Hollywood, no one believed them to be true. We could pretty much feast openly, which made the top fangs fat, rich, and apathetic. I built my power-base, recruited new fangs, and used a little book to build a solid following behind me. The rest was inevitable."

"What book?" I asked, still formulating a plan to get Ashley to safety so we could conclude our duel without collateral damage.

"*The Prince*. Machiavelli," he grinned. "You like books, wizard?"

"A bit." I answered. This guy obviously didn't know much about me if he hadn't heard of *Plato's Cave*. It was mentioned in almost every news article about me. And that wasn't even considering the supernatural community to which I catered on a regular basis. "Alright, Alucard. Let her go and we'll settle this right now. I win – meaning you die – I get to put another set of fangs up on the fridge." His lips tightened a bit at that. After all, he had been exceedingly polite so far. But a thought was churning in my head as I realized where we stood. "You win, you owe me a favor, no questions asked." I folded my arms. He blinked in disbelief, opening his mouth to ask why I got something in return whether I won or lost, but I forestalled him. "I should correct you on one thing. Now that you told me your intention, I won't be letting you walk away without a fight. What kind of gentleman would I be to deny such an honest and polite duel? But I want you to know that I am no wizard." He frowned at both the threat and the statement, reading between the lines.

"Is that so, Little Brother?" He replied softly, like a dagger across velvet.

"Yep. I'm a Maker. Ever heard of that?"

His shoulders stiffened and his hand lifted up the umbrella faster than I could follow. It suddenly occupied the space between us, held in an upright defensive position. Ashley chose that moment to kick his ankle and roll away. Mallory snatched up her arm and yanked her to safety behind him, not letting her go even after she was safe. Alucard didn't even register the blow, other than a flicker of his eyes at her escape. He eyed me warily, thinking about my words.

"It's true?" He answered in a soft, curious voice.

I nodded.

He grunted. "Well, Little Brother. Can't claim as I believed that when I heard it. Thought it was a farce, a ruse, a legend spread by your own lips to keep your celebrity status going across the supernatural world. Heirs usually do such things."

I shook my head, sliced my mind with an imagined blade, tapping into the roaring torrent below, and spoke. "I swear on my power that I'm a Maker."

An invisible shockwave knocked everyone but me to a knee. Alucard was first to stand, assuming it had been an attack. But I stood neutrally with my arms hanging at my sides. He watched me for a few seconds. "Well, looks like you get something whether you win or lose, but I become a legend if I win. Agreed." He looked up at the sky and the bright ball of light that was the sun. Then at me. "Might have a bit of an advantage over me." He observed, not backing out, but simply stating a fact.

I looked up. Then back at him. Then off to the burnt-out field. Having him mention his disadvantage made what I had been about to propose even better. I smiled as I turned back to him, nodding. "I may have a solution. I'll give you at least a one-minute warning before I attack you. But until then I'm going to need you to trust me. Follow me step by step with no questions. I won't betray you or trap you anywhere. I know a place where the sun won't affect you. In fact, *you* will likely gain a slight advantage over *me*."

He frowned a bit at that. "Why would you do that? Why not take me here where I challenged you, Little Brother? Machiavelli would groan in his grave, he would."

I shrugged. "Usually I would do exactly that, but I'm not one for unfair fights when someone openly tells me exactly what they want to do. You've earned a fair... no, an *advantage* over me in a fair fight because of your honesty. Consider it a token of gratitude for not wasting my time with abductions and sneaky attacks over the next few days. I've got enough on my plate already."

He nodded in thoughtful thanks, and then motioned for me to lead on with a shrug.

Mallory quickly laid into me. "Just what the hell do ye' think 'yer doing? We have more important things to do! Now! You can't go throwing 'yer life around for every punk thug that wants a scrap, Laddie."

A veil of transparent blue silk seemed to settle over my vision as I tapped into my smoldering frustration and anger, using it to toss up a dome of power over my two friends, eliminating the possibility for sound to travel beyond us. Vampires had impeccable senses. I saw Alucard rub his arms idly as he watched me. I spoke to my friends. "Trust me. This is best. This way we aren't facing the Grimms while the vampire and his crew of bloodthirsty, hungry fangs sneaks up behind us. Remember, he also hinted that this was out of his hands, and that he was being extorted to kill me to save his coven from annihilation. Sounds like the Grimms. This way I can remove a player off the board. And I'm taking *no* risks to do so." They looked doubtful of that. "I want you two to leave. Now. Head to Chateau Falco. I'll be along shortly. Get Gunnar, Indie, and Raego to meet me there ready for war. I swear I will meet you there." It was hard not to gloat about my plan, but I didn't want to risk Alucard somehow overhearing. That was, if my crazy plan worked. "I'll explain later." I handed Ashley the satchel with the books, my eyes a silent warning to keep it safe. She nodded.

They blinked doubtfully despite the confident twinkle in my eyes. "You're up to something, boy." I nodded with a smile. Mallory shook his head and took Ashley by the arm. "Okay. Let's trust him and go. We're only dead weight here, at best. Collateral damage or leverage, at worst." I nodded my agreement. "You better be back, boy. I know where 'yer final resting place is. And I will make 'yer afterlife a living hell. Turn the family mausoleum into a museum. Maybe leave 'yer journal outside 'yer sarcophagus so everyone can read the true stories from 'yer youth." He winked darkly and I laughed aloud.

"You do that." I gripped forearms with him and hugged Ashley. Alucard watched us thoughtfully, but nodded his head in farewell to each of them as they swept past him. They didn't return the gesture, causing Alucard's lips to tighten in disapproval. Courtesy was a pretty big deal to this guy. I turned to look at him. "Alright. Just you and me. Come on. I've got an appointment in two hours, and I'd rather not be late."

Alucard blinked back incredulously. Almost as if bluntly stating that I couldn't possibly be that overconfident. That much ego simply couldn't fit into one person.

He didn't know me at all.

19

Alucard clutched the umbrella over his head to protect himself from the sun, careful to keep every millimeter of flesh hidden. Lucky for him it was the size of one of those golf umbrellas. I thought myself very mature for not teasing him about how ridiculous he looked walking around in November under an umbrella. In a burned-down cow pasture.

We both looked utterly ridiculous.

I was very eager for the duel.

Listen, I'm not crazy or anything. Sure, it was a duel to the death, but I had a plan…

And I was finally getting the chance to field test my new powers in a battle setting. It would be a great opportunity for me to actually cut loose, to both try and replicate my old wizard's spells using my new power, but to also see exactly what strange new abilities I could dream up on the fly.

Sure, practicing with Mallory and Gunnar had been immeasurably helpful, but I couldn't go all out, and most of the magic I had been used to throwing around had definitely been focused on going all out. Overwhelming aggression. I wasn't really a half measure guy in *any* area of my life. I ate the whole pizza. If I wanted to order a plate of hot wings at a restaurant, and someone asked politely if they could have one, I was more likely to order them their own appetizer rather than sharing. I overfilled my dinner plates. Over-committed on estimated arrival times. What I mean to say is that you probably would never find me trying to learn swordplay by looking for me in a park, expecting to see me swinging foam swords with other errant knights in a cosplay outfit. You'd have better luck searching in a seedy warehouse district where I would be getting bloodied against experienced swordsmen using blunted wooden practice swords to teach me the hard way.

I looked at the world as all or nothing. An extremist, I had once heard it called. It might have stemmed from missing the *sharing lesson* day at Kindergarten. Then out of pure spite, refusing to learn it after I got back.

Alucard followed me along the once familiar – but now ashen – trail through the cow pasture. Neither of us spoke, although I could sense Alucard growing impatient, which just broke my little heart.

Not too long now...

As if on cue, the bright sun-filled sky suddenly winked out like someone had thrown a light switch, and was replaced by a dark, imposing sunset. A line of fire traced the edge of the earth in the distance. We stood in an impromptu ring of crepitating torches, and beyond that was only an impenetrable void of mist and blackness. Creatures of the night could be heard fighting, mating, and hunting in the void, but none entered the circle of fiery torchlight. And no sunlight actually touched the ground. Alucard's shoulders hitched in alarm at both the scene and the sounds of violence, but seemed to slightly relax at my lack of reaction.

I turned to him to see that he was watching our surroundings as if fearing a trap. I grinned. "Welcome to the *Dueling Grounds*. The farm has seen too much heat lately." He grunted at my pun. "I don't want the owner to pay the consequences if you and I make a bit of a ruckus." I leaned forward conspiratorially. "*Spoiler alert*. Causing a ruckus is kind of my thing." My grin stretched wider, darker. "Consider this my one minute warning. Here are the rules," I took a deep breath as if preparing to recite a laundry list, "Anything goes."

He watched me, calculating. "Anything goes." He repeated flatly.

I nodded. "No holds barred. To the death." I began to turn away but hesitated, holding a finger up over my shoulder. "Almost forgot," I said, glancing back at him. "If the chance arises, I will let you speak last words before I destroy you. I expect you to do the same... in the unlikely event that you win. No trickery, just out of respect. Agreed?"

He listened, eyes narrowing at the threat, but finally nodded. "I'll give you your minute to get your affairs in order." He muttered, rolling his eyes.

"And remember. You'll owe me a favor if you win."

He merely shook his head in disbelief. "Fine."

I tossed my coat off, rolled up my sleeves, and stood in the center of the clearing taking deep, relaxing breaths. Alucard watched me, reading me, waiting for a trick, and counting down. I closed my eyes.

I wasn't afraid in the slightest. For one, it was only one vampire. And for the most part, a single vampire was not evenly matched against a wizard as long as the wizard had fair warning. Even though I was no longer a wizard, but a *Maker*, I liked my odds. Secondly, there was no chance for cops to see me throwing magic around, which was an ever-present paranoia of mine. Thirdly, there was no chance for collateral damage – biological or architectural. We were alone, and in a cow pasture, or another dimension of some kind, for all I knew. The Minotaur had never elaborated.

I opened my eyes slightly, squinting at him. "Go time. In thirty seconds," I murmured softly, relaxing my shoulders as I closed my eyes again, opening my fingers to caress the warm air around us.

I cleared my mind of entirely all emotion, removing the crutch of anger that let me cheat to use my new powers. Once eliminated, I quested about in my peaceful, tranquil mind, trying to find a more reliable and natural way to tap into my new abilities. A stubborn, instant gratification fueled part of me began to mutter lazily. *Why? You already know how to use it. Stop wasting our time. Destroy him already!* I tuned the voice out.

But it had a point. Kind of.

I just didn't like having to rely on anything or anyone. It was a weakness in my eyes. A crutch. And anger could definitely be a weakness.

It was fairly safe to say that I was often angry in a fight, so that was good. But I had also managed to survive too many times to count where I had been too terrified to be angry. Therefore, it made sense to nip that reliance in the butt while I had the chance. Especially when tip off time with the Grimms was rapidly approaching.

I peeled away even more of myself, silencing the impatient voice still nagging at me. *Kill the fanger, nooowwww...* the voice trailed away as if falling down a deep dark hole.

I delved into my mind, emotionless, detached, analyzing my core belief system and pondering how I had used to tap into my powers as a wizard. I could still feel the familiar space in my soul where my power had once resided. Now it was empty, but...

There. Faint, fluid tendrils of... *something* weakly latched here and there like the appendages of a stubborn octopus, the other end leading off into the darkness. I smiled, mentally following the cords, watching them grow thicker as they flowed through each section of my body. They looped back and forth several times, wider, stronger, and more resilient the further I traveled, until finally darting off to end at two specific points in my body.

My head.

And my heart.

The two throbbed in opposing rhythm.

Their pulsing combined into a steady beat, like a steady drum roll that began to fill me with confidence, power, and...

Peace.

Like my own miniature soundtrack.

I sunk deeper into myself, allowing the pattern of sound to fill my body, mind, and soul. And then I submitted to the glorious power, anticipating an explosion of euphoric magical light that would cause Alucard to surrender in tears of awe at the dreaded power of the first Maker in centuries.

But nothing happened.

I waited some more.

Some more nothing happened.

"Time's up, Temple," Alucard hissed, and I felt the air shift as he threw himself at me, fangs aimed at my moneymaker.

20

I needed more time. I dove to the side to protect my face and throat, fingers latching onto the pistol in my pocket. I managed to squeeze off a few shots at a nearby blur of fabric, and heard a soft grunt before the pistol was knocked from my hand, instantly numbing my fingers. I kicked out with a boot, connecting solidly with Alucard's torso, sending him into a nearby bench where he folded.

My anger pulsed instinctively, fueling me with enough power to stay alive and add a little bit of oomph to my kick. Which was slightly alarming. I hadn't consciously chosen to use my power to kick him. Yet another reason I needed to get a grip on my new power.

Alucard groaned from across the clearing and I frantically dove back into my mind.

I knew the tendrils hadn't been there before my magic had been taken from me. I had to be on to something. I knew it.

As I drew closer to the nexuses of power over my heart and mind I realized that the pulses of sound were actually not sound at all. That was merely how I had translated it in my mind. The pulses were oddly akin to the reservoir of power I now constantly felt beneath my feet. I heard Alucard stumbling to his feet in the distance and knew I only had a few seconds.

When using my anger to tap into the power, I had apparently been forcing the power to obey my command by sheer strength, rage, and will. Straight from the source. The never-ending river of power beneath the earth's crust. Which was a tad arrogant of me.

But apparently, I had a conduit right inside of me all along.

To use the river of power successfully, I had had to force it to my will, not submit.

Perhaps...

I opened my eyes in a squint, having lost track of time. Alucard was racing towards me, claws outstretched and a hungry gleam in his eyes. He launched himself at my throat again. "Gack!" I bellowed in challenge, diving away from his attack and rolling to safety. He didn't stop there. He landed in a skid, turned on a heel, and dove again. I reached out to the center of my heart and mind and instead of submitting to the power, I sent my essence out in a claw, clutching the cords of power in a metaphysical fist.

Then I squeezed.

Power exploded out of me in a torrent of wind and justice.

I felt like a god damned superhero.

A hot line of fire slashed across my throat, but the brief sensation of pain was instantly overwhelmed by magic so alien I could hardly comprehend it. My world suddenly exploded in a mushroom cloud of blue that resembled the color of the most ancient of arctic glaciers. Power ignited my veins like a lit fuse, flooding my body with raw, alien magic. A second shockwave shattered the night and I fell to my knees. I was sweating profusely around my neck and chest. I began to laugh in triumph, my voice sounding oddly raw.

I had done it.

I had learned how to use my power at will. All by myself. Which was important to me. It wouldn't have felt as good if I had accomplished it while training with Mallory. It had taken a real fight to break it out of me.

I began to feel very dizzy, but imagined a ball of fire, and it was suddenly there, although weak, sputtering. Then it died. I blinked. Tried it again, but all I saw was a spark before that too died.

I frowned and studied my surroundings, expecting to see a disheveled or disintegrated Alucard lying on the ground of a now dystopian world. The ground in a thirty-foot radius was completely clear of debris, and the torches all leaned away from me as if repelled. I looked up at a slight motion to see Alucard was hanging from a tree outside the clearing. He was staring at me in disbelief. He lifted up a bloody claw and I blinked. I touched my throat and it came away slick with blood, not sweat. I wasn't dizzy from the power. He had freaking cut my artery.

Sneaky bastard.

I fell to my back and heard Alucard land lightly on his feet. His footsteps approached closer as I struggled to breathe, my vision dwindling to a single point as a loud rushing sound began to fill my ears like ocean waves breaking over rocks.

I beckoned him closer. He watched me for a second, hesitating. "You made me promise to give you a chance to speak. No sucker punches, right?"

I nodded weakly. He shook his head, as if doubting his own sanity, but leaned over me, placing his ear near my lips. I whispered a few words. He leaned back with a frown, looking skeptical, but finally nodded. "Okay. I'll do it." He answered doubtfully. He watched me as I began to choke on my own blood. "Want me to make it clean?" I shook my head. I managed to speak louder than a whisper through another gurgle of blood.

"If I really die… bury me upside down," I gasped a short breath. "So the Grimms can kiss my ass." And I flashed him a peace sign before the world winked out to nothing.

21

I woke with a choked gasp, lurching into a coughing fit as my fingers instinctively flashed to my throat. I caressed the skin in a panic, practically hyperventilating as I tried to keep as much blood inside me as possible. I needed help. Immediately.

Then I paused as the pads of my fingers transmitted their observation to my brain.

My skin was perfectly smooth.

And not slick with blood.

Then I remembered. I had been at the *Dueling Grounds* with Alucard. And...

That polite southern bastard had killed me!

I managed to feel slightly betrayed and disappointed in him. He had displayed a level of genteel etiquette that was nonexistent these days. Just like my parents had tried to teach me. I had sensed potential camaraderie in him. A kindred spirit. A similar flavor of craziness.

But then I remembered seeing the beast in his eyes, the hunger for blood and vengeance. He was a *monster* first. *Human* last. I needed to remember that. People weren't always what they seemed. Or what we made them out to be. My breath had calmed down to the point where I merely felt like I had finished a brief jog, but my heart was still racing. I tried to let out a laugh, but it turned into a coughing rasp. I leaned back, contemplating my situation as I regained my breath.

The Minotaur had once told me that one couldn't truly die at the *Dueling Grounds*, but then again, he was also a monster. He could have been playing a long con on me.

I slowly stretched my neck, testing the motion, fearing that any second my head was going to just fall off. It felt like I had only just closed my eyes at the Dueling Grounds before abruptly waking here in my bed.

Wait, *my bed*. I was at Chateau Falco!

I lurched up to a sitting position, my eyes darting about wildly. I touched my throat again subconsciously, remembering the fiery slash of Alucard's claws and the sensation of drowning in my own blood. But now there wasn't even a tender scratch.

I jumped to my feet, testing my voice again.

"Tis' but a scratch!" I ran from the room, hooting and hollering as much as my throat would allow. "I'm invincib–" and I pummeled straight into Dean, tackling us both to the ground in an eruption of spilled cocktails, olives, and mint leaves. I sat up, coughing and wiping the booze from my face. "Where did *you* come from? Didn't you hear me yelling?"

He stood, brushing off his shoulders. "Yes, Master Temple. Of course. My apologies. I was just on my way to awaken the *Guardians* after I heard screaming and shouting erupting from a room that was empty when I passed by it less than three minutes ago, to gather refreshments for your guests. If you don't mind, I'll just be on my way now to activate them and exterminate the vermin."

"No one likes a wiseass, Dean. Unless it's me. I'm adorable. And apparently *invincible!*" He leaned to his right, peering at the side of my head as if checking for a head wound.

"Of course, Sir. Invincible. Quite right."

"I just *died!*"

"I'm sure it was most unpleasant. What would the Master Necromancer like to drink? Your undead servitors are waiting." He said, deadpan.

I scowled, not appreciating his lack of astonishment. "Water will suffice."

"Of course, Overlord. The Prince of Darkness may want to change. He's soiled himself." He plucked up the tray and turned on a heel, still brushing off his coat as he left. I didn't let his negative attitude kill my vibe.

But I did go change.

After a quick rinse, I headed to the office, anxious to share my plan with the team. I was sick of running. The Minotaur had been taken off the field, just for spending a bit of time with me over the past few years. Who would they go after next? I couldn't risk anyone else's life by waiting. It was time to bring the fight to the Grimms. It felt nice to finally have a plan. Once this was off my to-do list I could go visit the wolves to get my ring back. The way things were going my proposal would go off without a hitch after all.

My phone rang.

Achilles.

I groaned, sending it to voicemail with a nervous finger. One did not ignore a call from Achilles lightly. I waited for him to suddenly appear before me with a spear aimed at my throat, but nothing happened. I let out a sigh of relief. I would have to take care of him soon. He no doubt wanted an update on the vampire and bartender situation. Either that or he was checking to see if his ploy to have me killed had worked. I just didn't know whom to trust anymore, so I figured stalling was my best bet, short term.

Plus, the time on the screen told me we were running on a tight schedule.

Everyone turned to face me as I pocketed the phone and opened the office door. No one spoke, merely staring at me incredulously. Ah, they had heard about the vampire. Or the Grimms. Or both. I spotted my satchel on the ground near the door and picked it up, digging inside before letting out a sigh of relief. The amulet and books were safely tucked away inside. I nodded at Ashley as I approached. "What happened?" She asked carefully.

"I died. But it's okay. I was at the *Dueling Grounds*. You can't really die there. Vamp didn't know that though. Boy, is he going to be in for a surprise." Gunnar jumped to his feet, as did Indie. "What?!" They yelled in unison.

I waved them off. "No time. Drink up quickly. We're going on a field trip in ten minutes. I'll meet you outside by the stable." By now my friends knew *stable* meant *garage*. It was, after all, a converted stable. And it *had* temporarily housed a horse of the St. Louis Mounted Patrol Unit named Xavier in recent months. "I've got to round up a few things. Arm for bear." I thought about that for a second. "No. Liger. Arm for liger and intelligent apes." I nodded once to no one in particular, and then left the room without another word.

I made it a dozen feet before a hand latched onto me from behind, jerking me to a halt. Indie was breathing heavily. We didn't have time to stop and chat so I motioned for her to follow. She did, folding her arms and glaring at me.

"How have you been today?" I asked softly, wary of the apparent outburst forming behind her fiery glare. I knew I was treading on thin ice, but I needed to keep my head in the game if I was going to save everyone's lives. This was the biggest challenge I had ever encountered. I couldn't afford distractions.

"Oh, you know, I didn't die. You?" Her tone was arctic.

I gulped. "Yeah. It sounds worse saying it out loud. It really wasn't a big deal."

"What about the liger? Or the ape? Did they attend your meeting? Give a rousing presentation on the African Savannah?" Her words were clipped, precise, and full of venom. "You promised to call me after the meeting."

I groaned. It had completely slipped my mind after the attack, the gut shot, and then the race to Kingston's field. Then my duel with Alucard. "Listen, you're right. It's been kind of nonstop since the meeting. Some company from Germany wants to buy Temple Industrie–"

"I know. It's all over the news. I found out like that, rather than from my boyfriend, who attended the meeting, since, you know, it's *his company*." She sounded hurt.

"Right," I sighed in defeat, "Well, we were attacked on our way out the door by–"

"Shapeshifting Grimms. Yep. Heard that from Ashley. And Mallory, who I sent to look after you, by the way."

"Oh. Um. Thanks. I got scratched up a bit, but–"

"Nate..." She warned.

Crap. *Mallory, you loose-lipped bastard.* "Okay. I was shot. Mallory stitched me up." I patted my stomach by reflex and immediately froze. I tugged up my shirt...

And saw not a blemish. Nothing. "Huh..." I muttered lamely, thinking furiously.

Indie glanced down and frowned. "Are you saying Mallory lied? No, wait. You just said you were shot, too." Her face contorted in confusion and she rubbed her temples. "Nate, tell me what the hell is going on? My boyfriend is getting in fights anytime he leaves the house and I'm hearing about it from everyone but him. Then the dire wound I hear almost killed him suddenly disappears. Then you come in the office idly mentioning you died, but you're obviously not dead. *What. The. F?*" She folded her arms, scowling.

"I'm not really sure." I answered honestly.

And I wasn't.

Why was I healed? I mentally checked myself for all the scrapes and bruises from the last day, my astonishment continuing to grow. They were all gone. Did losing the fight at the *Dueling Grounds* ironically grant me a clean bill of health? I had bumped my shin two days ago, on our bedpost. I checked it. Still there. Huh. "I think dying at the Dueling Grounds carried an undisclosed perk. It healed me." I answered, amazed.

"Like twenty-four hours' worth, or one night to the next, or back up to a specific time?" She asked, thinking academically.

"I have no idea." I answered. I showed her my bruised shin. "Didn't cure this."

She pondered that. "We should probably find out." She grasped my hand. "Nate..."

I held up a hand to forestall her. "Indie, I'm going to be blunt. You mean the literal world to me, and I've kept you in the dark. I'm a big fat jerk." She nodded like a cat acknowledging their existence as the center of the universe, unimpressed. "Here's the thing. These guys are legendary. They never lose. And whoever hired them also ordered a hit on every one of my friends. That means I need you safe, but I have to be in the thick of battle on this one. Somewhere you can't be. I've been running around responding so far, trying to eliminate the problem before they come for *you*. That would..." I trailed off, my vision briefly flashing blue before I managed to calm my rage, "*End me*. I would let them do *anything* to me if it kept you safe." I paused. "Even let them kill me." I added softly.

She hissed. "Like hell you will." She growled, yanking me close into a hug. Her head tucked into my shoulder, the perfect height for a hug, just slightly shorter than me. I squeezed back with a sad smile. But I had been telling the truth.

I would do anything for this sweet, passionate, violent young woman.

I spoke into her hair. "That's why I've kept you back. I don't know what to do. Keep you locked away so you're safe until I can deal with them? But what if they take you while I'm away?" I shook my head in frustration, suddenly venting my impotent frustration with the only woman in the world I felt I could unconditionally trust. "I don't understand where they get their powers. Two could obviously shapeshift and use glamour, but that doesn't make any sense. They abhor freaks. So how can shifters also be Grimms?

"Or do I keep you close, stuck to my hip while bullets, fangs, blades, claws, and magic fills the night? You wouldn't survive." She began to argue, but I shook her gently. "Indiana Rippley. *Listen!*" I commanded, using her full name to get her attention. She blinked at me in surprise. "You *know* I'm right. That's not saying anything bad about you. Hell, I don't know how any of *us* can survive these guys. They never lose. Ever. It's why a whole nation of Freaks teamed up in secret to lock them away. Because they couldn't survive one by one. These groups *hated* each other," I paused for emphasis and she leaned back to stare at me through tear-filled eyes, frustrated at her helplessness. "*But they still teamed up to take the Grimms down.*" I finally said.

She was quiet, sobbing softly. After a second, she nodded, and gently tugged my arm until we were walking again, headed towards the stable. Her voice was a venomous hiss, like the words of an ancient prophecy come to life. "You gather an army then. You've done it before." She said resolutely. "You've helped enough people. They owe you. Call in the banners, and *destroy them*. Let them know their place. With extreme prejudice."

I shook my head. "Anyone I call in on this gets added to the naughty list, earning an immediate death sentence. I can't do that to people I saved in the past. It's selfish and cruel. Save them from one death only to be available to die for me at a later, more convenient time? I couldn't live with myself."

"You do have a few allies who are already well-known acquaintances of yours. They will already be on the hit list. Gather *them*."

"Why do you think I raced to the Minotaur's field so quickly? They targeted him. Burned his field down. He's alive, but gone, whatever *that* means." I spoke softly, the rage patiently purring deep inside me. "They're going after my allies first."

Indie shivered, squeezing my arm compassionately. "What's the vampire's story?"

"It was Alucard. He was never down in the sewers. Those were several members of his coven that went rogue. They impersonated him to scare everyone away from their new abduction and murder business franchise. He thanked me for killing them, but since they *were* his coven, he was still forced to challenge me to save face. I get it." I shrugged.

She nodded. She had killed a few of them herself. It looked like she wanted to remind me of that superhero act, to prove her strength and usefulness in battle. I stopped her before she could voice it. "You did good down there. Seriously. But the Grimms... they're on a level above even me. Above *any* of us. Perhaps *all* of us." I sighed at the defiant look in her eyes. "Look, I don't know how to beat them. But I do know that waiting for them to attack us is off the table. I can't let them stack the deck anymore. I need to *act* rather than *react*. I need to lure them out. And for that, I'll keep you by my side. Hopefully, we can end it tonight."

She was opening her mouth to argue at the beginning of my speech, but wisely clicked her teeth shut as soon as I said I was taking her along with me. I still didn't know if it was a good idea, but I truly couldn't think of a safer alternative. At least I could keep an eye on her.

She kissed me on the lips. Then darted away. "I'm going to go arm myself for liger. You have some hunting rifles and pistols in the gun safe, right?" I smiled and nodded. "Okay, I'll meet you outside. Oh, and don't forget about the Armory. We need to check it again and see what the deal was last night. Maybe it's fixed now." I nodded, silently reaching inwards to clutch the nexus of wires powering my magic, allowing the current to course through me. Then I imagined pinching her butt. She yelped and shot a hungry glare over her shoulder. Then stopped. "You figured it out!" I nodded. "Go Team Rippley!" She squealed as she took off with renewed vigor, leaving me no time to correct her. I really needed to get t-shirts or something. Make it official. *Team Temple*.

I sighed, patted my satchel, and mentally prepped myself for battle as I headed outside. I entered the stable and spotted an old rusty knife on the workbench. I had stashed it here as a small project to work on after finding it inside my dad's desk. Dean made a habit of fixing things before I had a chance to do so, which he knew infuriated me. So, I had decided that someday I was going to fix this little old knife, because it may have been important to my dad for some small reason. Maybe I would even gift it to him when I saw him next. I sighed, admitting that I hadn't really needed to collect anything for the upcoming fight, only my thoughts.

But Indie had seen to that better than I could have on my own.

I promised myself that once this was over I was going to make her weep uncontrollably when I proposed tomorrow. Messy, snotty, mascara-thwarting tears of joy.

"*Team Rippley*," I muttered under my breath.

She had it coming to her.

22

Naturally, we didn't drive. We Shadow Walked to our destination. I had wanted to make sure I still had the strength to do so. And it was more efficient. I had asked Mallory to stay behind and guard Chateau Falco with Dean. I didn't want to leave it unguarded. Especially with the Armory acting oddly. I also wanted Mallory to get a hold of Tomas, even though neither of us had had any luck with that over the past few hours.

But the rest of the gang was here. Gunnar, Ashley, and Indie.

If all worked out, I planned on having a few more in the next few minutes...

It was only an hour or so until sundown. We stood on the slushy streets just outside Alistair Specter Silverstein's old brownstone. Yes, his initials had been *ASS*. Poor guy.

But I didn't feel bad laughing at his initials. It was his fault I was even in this whole mess. He had listed an original 1812 edition of *Grimm's Fairy Tales* – known as *Kinder- und Hausmärchen* in German – at an auction house, which had ignited a murderous race to get the book first before ultimately leading me to the biggest bad I had ever faced, Jacob Grimm himself. And he hadn't liked me much afterwards.

It was a gift of mine. Annoying people to immeasurable levels of hatred.

It had been a while since I had been back to the old home. I had bought the place as a hidey-hole, and just in case ol' Alistair had secreted away any other potentially world-ending items in the walls or something. I didn't want a Regular couple to buy the place and accidentally uncover a weapon of mass destruction when renovating the bathroom.

Team Temple (not Rippley!) stood behind me, looking impressively foreboding. I was proud of them.

I glanced down at the prototype smart watch on my wrist. I had bullied the Board into funding the project, despite strong opposition, and was glad to have it today. After seeing the first test run they had quickly changed their tune and it was forecasted to sell extremely well upon release. I was ready to see a real-life field test. The weather wasn't optimal, which would make things difficult, but would also provide a plethora of information for the technicians to study later.

It also performed a truly magical action that many people took for granted these days.

It told the freaking time.

And we were on schedule. Now to see if a man was true to his word.

"Alucard," I called out in an inaudible whisper, knowing he could hear me. Vamps had supernatural hearing.

A man stepped out from behind a nearby tree, his predatory eyes quickly assessing each face in the group of thugs before him, searching for the man who had called his name. I stood behind my friends, biting back a laugh. He nodded at each face in recognition. His gaze finally met mine and he froze.

Like, literally.

I waved at him cheerily. "I see you wore the sunblock, like I asked."

He lunged backwards, his coat suddenly flaring out in the shape of giant black bat wings that propelled him a safer distance away. A dozen feet now stood between us. I grunted, eyeing Alucard's coat thoughtfully. Perhaps this guy was the real thing. Alucard stared at me, dark eyes skeptical. "You're dead. I killed you. Not an hour ago."

I turned to my friends. "See? I'm invincible."

They contemplated that, then shrugged, still not convinced. I scowled back.

I lifted my collar to display my throat, where no injury remained from his claws. "Listen, Alucard. I wasn't completely honest with you. I didn't have time to really die. Had a few things to do first. But I let you have your revenge, and I will gladly tell everyone that you killed me in a duel to save face with your people." I shot him a winning smile. And waited.

He pondered that, frown growing. "Yes, that would... wait," a thought crossed his face, and then his eyes widened as my words dawned on him.

He was... *undeadly* silent for a solid minute.

Then he began a slow clap of approval, letting out an impressed laugh as he shook his head in disbelief. He began walking closer as he spoke. "Well *played*, Temple. That would most *certainly* improve your reputation quite a bit, wouldn't it, Little Brother? You dying and then coming back to life an hour later." I nodded, still smiling. My friends stepped back, giving me room to approach Alucard.

"Sure would." I said. He had no idea how much. This story would spread like wildfire, which just might keep the Academy off my back for a while. This would be the second tale of me defying death. Only one time had been authentic, but that was my little secret. I knew the guy on the other side.

But then for people to hear about me returning from certain death *again*? They would lose their minds. I managed to bury my grin as I addressed Alucard. "I understand your position. Your people need to know you handled the situation appropriately. *An eye for an eye*. I needed to keep on ticking. So, I found a win-win solution." I had taken a few steps towards him as I spoke. Gunnar's shoulders inched up protectively, but I had warned him ahead of time. Alucard noticed the werewolf's movement, but didn't react. "And now you owe me." I stated solemnly, extending a hand in a gentleman's agreement.

He flung up his hands, stammering. "But... people will think..."

I nodded. "You tell everyone you killed me. I back up your story with an oath on my power so people know I'm not lying. Your people respect you. My reputation *explodes*." I winked. "Or, you do nothing and people see you traipsing around with the guy who slaughtered your coven." I added softly. "I'll play it however you want, but you did make me a promise. And I think your word actually means something to you."

He just stared back, and I felt the concerned looks of my friends doing the same, as if suddenly wondering what level of sociopath they had attached themselves to. I let them think what they would. This was a high stakes game, and Alucard had no cards left.

He knew I was right, but he was right as well. He just couldn't force the dots into a more beneficial picture. He threw his hands up in defeat. "Fine. I've either failed or double-crossed the Grimms – which won't make them happy – and now we're all going to die." He squinted at me. "Unless you're not really going to die. I still don't quite get that part, but a promise is a promise." He met my hand in a tight grip.

"Nice meeting a man of his word. Even if you are a fanger." He peeled his lips back.

"Careful, wiz... Maker." He corrected. "I killed you once. We aren't friends." He studied me thoughtfully. "Yet. But I am mighty impressed. The thought of an alliance is... intriguing. It's a shame that our maiden voyage is a suicide mission. Great things could have been ours, I reckon."

"Nothing is written in stone."

"The Ten Commandments are. And I think we both know that neither of us would pull off an *A* on that grading scale." He winked. Then he turned away to formally introduce himself to the peanut gallery who was watching the exchange with masked emotion. They didn't know what the hell was going on either. I didn't have time for an explanation of the *Dueling Grounds*. I had listed the facts, told them to believe it, and that I would clarify any confusion – like my death and the lack of fatal wounds that Mallory had treated only hours ago – after the Grimms were dead.

I had a different story to share with the class today.

A *Fairy Tale*.

About how one little old wizard had managed to piss off the deadliest of supernatural exterminators in recorded history. And for that, I had brought a prop. Well, I had brought a prop that would *summon* someone who could share the story in *Dolby Digital Surround Sound*.

I scanned the skies. It would be dark soon, which was good for innocent bystanders. Harder to see what was going on. Snowflakes settled on my nose before melting to droplets of water. I closed my eyes for a moment, taking a deep breath. Now that I knew how to access it, it was time to begin pushing boundaries. I wanted to see if I could tap into it without imagining the pulsing tendrils of power, and me clutching them in my fist. I attempted it, faced a brief struggle of conflicting challenge, but then broke through and was instantly flooded with power. I grinned, eyes still closed as I assessed my mind for strain. It had felt more like using the reservoir that time, except I hadn't had to be angry.

Baby steps.

Manly baby steps.

Not wanting to tempt fate, I left my experimenting for later. When I opened my eyes, the world resembled a snow globe, tinted with blue sparkling snowflakes, visible as if under a microscope as I honed in on each one. Like a bird of prey. Was that a perk I hadn't noticed, or had I just imagined my vision sharper? I couldn't wait to play with my new toys.

If things played out as I hoped, that would happen all too soon.

Everyone was waiting for me, watching me grinning at nothing. I let out a sharp whistle. Then I turned to address the group. "The door's unlocked. I'll be right in. Gunnar knows the way." Gunnar grunted, eyeing Alucard warily, not letting him near the girls. I liked that.

Then I waited for a response to my whistle, shrugging my shoulders a few times for warmth, scanning the skies as I ran through my plan one last time.

23

I listened as the last of my gang finally gained entrance to the brownstone. The second the door closed, I heard a sharp crack of wings snapping in close to a body, a rush of wind, and then a pair of boots landed softly beside me. I thought I heard a second click of boots, but it was faint, almost inaudible. I turned and held out my hand, neutrally studying the air beside Raego, thankful he had already accomplished his mission.

My insurance policy. Delivered by my trusty weredragon pal.

Raego gripped my hand. "We're secure. No willpower. Only able to observe."

"You're sure?" He nodded. "You didn't harm them, right? That's not the intention. I just need an impartial witness." I thought about that. "Well, as impartial as possible. They obviously aren't going to be happy about this, but hopefully they will understand by the end," I added. Raego grunted doubtfully.

"No harm. Just control." He studied me thoughtfully. "Ballsy move."

"You did as commanded." I warned in a growl. "I'll take responsibility." Raego watched me intently, wisely not saying anything, his face a mask.

With that, he turned and began walking towards the brownstone. I followed him, trying to ignore the queasy flip-flopping motion in my stomach. Misha was no doubt watching the building from the rooftops. Raego rarely went anywhere these days without his red weredragon for a bodyguard. Being the leader of the dragon nation – the Obsidian Son – and the only black dragon in existence made a lot of dragon hunters grow dollar signs in their eyes when they saw Raego. And if Misha was here, I could safely assume that my friend Tory was roaming the streets in plain clothes, watching out for *her*.

I smiled at the unlikely union. Not the girl on girl part. The dragon on human part.

Well, technically Tory was more than just a human – being able to crush cars like beer cans kind of eliminated her from the human crowd. And she was an ex-cop, meaning she wasn't what you would call a *people person*, so perhaps meeting Misha was a better fit for her in the long run anyway.

We walked through the front door, following the voices heard coming from the back room. I idly thumbed the satchel at my side, slightly nervous. I was figuratively turning on a giant bat symbol to illuminate the skies and taunt the Grimms. Only it wouldn't be a bat symbol. To them, it would feel more like a cloud-sized depiction of a wizard humping a Grimm from behind.

But I needed to bait them, so it was necessary.

I think.

I shook off my doubts. Anything was better than being drawn into a fight on ground where I wasn't ready. I found everyone in the office, and silently went to work, not even needing magic for this next part. It was a ritual. Even Indie could have done it as long as she could follow directions. That was the scary part about rituals. They were predesigned to perform a supernatural function, and as long as the ritual was performed correctly, *anyone* could use it. It was only if the ritual was botched – which I had done the first time, in this very room – that things went downhill, and it was good to have a wizard nearby.

I had already performed this ritual before, and had been not-so-gently informed of what I had done wrong, so I was able to correctly prepare everything in only a few minutes. Then, rather than letting everyone hear what I was about to say, I decided to say it only in my mind. I called out a True Name.

Three times.

The air beside Raego shifted unnaturally, a bit. I frowned but didn't say anything. Useful to know.

A silver comet slammed down into the center of the ring before me, instantly zipping around in circles, agitated at the confinement, moving too fast to get a clear look at the creature's shape other than to determine that it was made of blinding silver light. Everyone stared at the circle after taking a few steps back and shielding their eyes from the pearlescent light.

I folded my arms. "Are you quite finished yet?" I asked.

The figure halted, revealing a twelve-inch tall action figure of a quicksilver playboy bunny. My Barbie doll.

Her hair, teeth, skin, and even the irises of her eyes, all glowed with mercurial light.

Because she was entirely naked. Which let me know all was right with the world.

She glared up at me. "Maker," she spat. "Release me or die."

"Hi, Barbie. I just want to pick you up and squeeze your tiny face!" I clapped. I felt the murderous gaze of every feminine pair of eyes hit me like bolts of lightning, but I stoically ignored them.

"I will let you touch mine if I can touch yours," she cooed, grinning murderously.

I shivered. "No, thanks." My gaze pointedly rose to acknowledge the group. "Group, meet Barbie. Barbie, meet Group." The sprite whirled with a hiss, craning her neck to see the large number of people here.

"You dare let them hear my name?" She shrieked.

"No. I spoke it in my mind. That's just our little secret. Listen, you helped me out by telling me about the Grimms. Now I need your help."

"I know. I reminded you of this yesterday. You have come to die."

"So... oh," I stammered, realizing I didn't have to persuade her and that she was already on board. But I wasn't really on board with the dying part. I had a different plan. I fast-forwarded my sales pitch. "I'm going to need you to–"

"This is tiring," she mumbled, interrupting me. I scowled back. *If she would just let me finish my sentence...* Suddenly a six-foot tall pinup version of the same sprite now occupied the ring, causing my friends to jump back a step in surprise. She rolled her shoulders, which did very nice things to her unclothed frame, earning pleased sounds from the men present in the room and arctic stares from the women. She shot Gunnar and Alucard a dark wink, and then turned to face me. "Let me out and I will aid you."

"Just to clarify, I do not consider killing me to be an aid." She frowned, but nodded.

I didn't even hesitate. There was no room around that agreement. Sure, she had helped me out before, a few times even, but there was this one time she had also threatened to sex me to death.

It's really not as weird as it sounds. Sex was her thing. She fed off of it. Some kind of succubus. But I trusted her. So, I scuffed the ring with my foot and let her out of her cage.

She instantly crouched, flung her fists up, and what looked like life-sized duplicates of Wolverine's Adamantium claws shot out the back of her wrist. She let out a deadly hiss, preparing to pounce and *snicker-snack* me to pieces with a '*Hey, Bub*' thrown in for good measure. Shouts filled the room as I tensed to defend myself.

But nothing happened.

She suddenly cackled with unabashed glee as she sheathed the claws. "Your face..."

Listen, creatures like her don't giggle. They cackle. Trust me.

I had been ready to clobber her with a giant-sized fly swatter of magic, and was reconsidering my decision to hold back. I was panting, and every woman in the room seemed suddenly pleased with the sprite they had recently scowled at. Women.

She walked past me, patting me on the shoulder with a demure wink.

My pants tightened a bit by default. I didn't know if she exuded some kind of pheromone or what, but it was impossible to ignore. I expected Indie to start shooting me with her hunting pistol, but instead she seemed to be having a similar reaction. She wasn't even looking my way, eyes locked on the sprite. I wrapped my power about me like a cloak, feeling a sudden drop in the euphoria. But still...

A naked chick stood a few feet away, walking around with such a blatant disregard that it really should have been a crime. She stopped before my friends, who stood at attention like kids in front of a teacher at the first day of school, waiting to be picked as the favorite student. "What a delightful platter you have brought me to nibble on, Nathaniel..." She hummed erotically.

"Not platter. Friends. Warriors all." She eyed Raego, who stared back with obvious interest, but his faint grin looked like a totally natural response to a beautiful naked woman standing before him, not influenced by her magic. He was, after all, well acquainted with mind magic. Dragons used a similar power. He stared deep into her eyes, and nodded back with a hungry smile. The sprite of death-by-sex, one who had literally carried hundreds if not thousands of men to their deaths aboard the eternal train of climax, *blushed*.

Well.

Okay.

I was a regular matchmaker. They *were* both shapeshifters... I stopped that train of thought quickly.

I cleared my throat. "I need you to show them what happened to start all this. Who we are up against, and why. The story of a few years ago when we first met should help out, too. You can leave out certain... details that are irrelevant to the Grimms," I added, silently and very obviously hinting at what I thought should be left out.

"You should have placed that limit on me before you freed me," she murmured, shooting one last look at Raego, who was still smiling at her.

She turned back to my friends. "Alright, children. Sit. Let me show you a story..." My friends complied, sitting in couches, on the ground, against a wall, wherever was comfortable. The sprite bowed her head, closed her eyes, and breathed deeply for a moment, murmuring softly under her breath. Then she began to whirl in a slow ballet, or a martial arts form, and the air suddenly thickened with fog. Then the fog began to shift and sway, coalescing into shapes, forms, landscapes, seasons, and instruments of death.

It was a war.

She showed us a story. One I hadn't known.

Her words filled the air like the voice of an angel over the swirling world of fog before us. I couldn't see her, or my friends, or even the room. It was as if she took us some place up in the clouds. As she spoke, those clouds pantomimed her story with crude figures, most forms of life unfinished, mere shapes representing a concept. A werewolf was obviously a werewolf, but if you looked closely there were no defining characteristics to distinguish it from another wolf, unless the character was essential to the story. Then it gained a few more details – just enough to catch our attention. I sat back and listened. A part of me was amazed at the magic, but the majority was amazed by the story itself, watching the dancing fog as I listened to her words.

24

"During the Crusades, there existed a tight-knit band of holy warriors who participated wherever the battle was thickest. It was said these men were filled with Holy Fire, and were unstoppable. They considered themselves judge, jury, and executioner, and didn't fit well among the other Crusaders, especially their commanding officers. In hushed tones, their fellow warriors nicknamed them the *Decapitares*, or 'ones who decapitate.' Then, the morning after a particularly vocal disagreement with their captain, they were simply gone, having drifted away like smoke in the night. Not a single sentry saw them leave, and none could find so much as a hoofprint marking their departure." She paused for emphasis. "This was the first time in recorded history that the so-called *Grimms* entered the world stage on an official level.

"But their origins go back further. Before that they were merely a group of supernaturals gifted with the ability to see through glamour. Any kind of glamour. They could look at you," she pointed at Gunnar, "and recognize you as a werewolf, or you," she pointed at Alucard, "and see you were a Master Vampire. They couldn't control it. Even worse, they were defenseless people, with no offensive power to balance out their vision. When they saw through someone's glamour the supernatural person in their gaze saw their eyes turn entirely black as a warning.

"One of them wisely realized that this ability made them targets, and in order to survive with such a dangerous power they needed to watch out for each other. His last name was Grimm, and at some point, the others inevitably adopted his name as a tribute to that man who saved them from eradication. They hid their powers as best they could, banding together for protection.

"After a time, these new Grimms convinced themselves – and then preached to the masses – that the reason their eyes turned black was proof that the accused were demons. That the change of eye color was a direct result of these seemingly normal people seeing a reflection of their dark, stained souls shining back at them. And that the *Grimms* were the only warning readily available to reveal these monsters for what they truly were. People believed them.

"So, as history would have it, the supernaturals of the age typically murdered them on the spot in order to maintain their anonymity among the other villagers. Because anyone outed as having powers back then was instantly killed. To protect the masses, of course," she added drily. The swirling fog shifted, showing us murder after murder, monsters of the night killing humans with black eyes. I shivered, trying not to imagine living in such a time where you were hated and killed for things you couldn't control. For something you were born with. Then I realized that for some, that time was now. That sobered me up.

Barbie continued on, interrupting my thoughts. "So, it was a time of *kill* or *be killed*. The Grimms suffered cataclysmic loss, but a familiar figure took heart on these poor creatures..."

"Rumpelstiltskin." She paused as a figure loomed out of the fog, a twisted dwarf of a man with round lenses perched on his nose and a satchel over his shoulder. He handed the huddled Grimms something and the fog collapsed in on itself into a thick flat sheet.

"*What?*" I demanded.

"No questions until the end of the discussion, wizard." She admonished. "Now, Rumpelstiltskin, or someone very much like him, gave the Grimms an artifact that could absorb the power from a supernatural person, and allow the Grimm to wield it as their own. Then, if the Grimm was victorious the power permanently became theirs until they upgraded it to a new supernatural's power... by kidnapping or killing yet another supernatural. Rumpelstiltskin also showed them how to duplicate this artifact so that they could each have one someday."

"The Amulets." I exclaimed. Barbie nodded with a frown.

"So, they learned to defend themselves. Rather efficiently. Whatever flavor of supernatural they found themselves facing, they could match on even footing. A werewolf for a werewolf. Vampire for a vampire." That got my attention. It meant that whatever assistance I had on my side in the upcoming fight, the Grimms would be able to counter.

Well, *shit*.

"No longer in fear of being exterminated so easily, they sought training from experienced killers. And they each spent every moment learning these traits. Hunting, tracking, hiding, killing, escaping, and covering their tracks. Basically, espionage. They were the first super assassins. And being as how their eyes turned black upon seeing a supernatural, the opinion that this was a gift from god – the ability to see through the mists of hell to see the devils among us – took firmer root.

"Hard to blame them after a century of persecution, being on the run from any supernatural they happened to stumble across. Then they learned the study of law, seeing a perfect opportunity to sit in judgment of accused supernaturals. This was when they began to apply the definition of their adopted last name, Grimm, as a personal motto." She glanced around the room. "Grimm is German for *wrath*."

I shivered. Holy cow. Any time someone was accused of being a witch, wizard, or demon of some kind, with these guys on the panel as a judge they could *see* the truth and condemn as they saw fit. Which I assumed was usually an execution. The fog grew harder to watch at that point as I realized my own people were now being slaughtered at an alarming rate, and the Grimms seemed to grow taller, stronger, hungrier. Others seemed to have the same disgusted reaction to the story.

"Yes. Many died. Both good and bad people with supernatural abilities. The Grimms were ruthless. Then they decided to expand their business by becoming lawmen and hunting parties, actively pursuing the people who had murdered their ancestors for so many years. So, as you can see, our ancestors created their own worst enemy.

"I'm sure you can ascertain what happened to them after that. They entered government, the military, political offices, royal courts – any position that would give them the opportunity to expunge freaks from humanity. And they were good at it, assisting many of ancient history's most noted rulers. Every time a country went off in a ship to explore or take over new lands they typically had a secret Grimm or two in the party, willing to document, track, and kill any new creatures they might encounter.

"The American Colonies, Cortez' mission to South America, you name it. They took their family business global. Many of us in these undiscovered countries had no idea what hit us or where the Grimms' rage came from, but we soon found out. We were slaughtered for crimes we never committed. Until myself and hundreds of others collaborated to send them away." She grew quiet, remembering, and I suddenly realized that she was speaking first person. She had been there. Sure, I had heard her say that once already, but still, knowing the history now brought it into a whole new light.

"It was a big plan. Many died. We fed rumors into society that a meeting of freaks was organizing to take on the Grimms and also to coordinate the hiding of an artifact that could kill all supernatural persons if taken by the Grimms. Many died from the Grimms' torturous methods, many brave, brave souls. Men, women, and children. Totally harmless fairies, water spirits, woodland elves, and even a few of the more dangerous freaks, trolls, werewolves and vampires." She turned to me. "A *Master Temple* set up the plan. A distant ancestor of yours. It was his idea. A good one. A complicated one. And costly." I blinked in astonishment. My father had never told me *that*.

"How come I've never heard of it?" I asked.

She shook her head sadly. "Being a scribe of history, I'm almost confident that you have." She whispered. I waited, giving her a few seconds as silver tears filled her vision. "Roanoke."

I blinked. "The city in the American Colonies? Where everyone disappeared overnight?" I exclaimed in disbelief.

She nodded. "It was the location we led them to believe housed the artifact that could end us all for good."

I frowned. "But... that doesn't make any sense." Barbie smiled at me knowingly but didn't argue as she wiped away a lone tear. "Roanoke was abandoned around 1590, but *Grimm's Fairy Tales* was published in 1812..."

"You are correct, Temple. That's where the story gets *interesting*." I frowned again, but nodded, motioning for her to continue. "Now, it was around 1830 – my kind doesn't keep track of time like you mortals do – and Roanoke was now merely a shell of a town, having been abandoned long ago. The Grimms were full of bloodlust, hungry with the potential prize at their fingertips. Jacob and Wilhelm – who were actually related by blood to the real founding Grimm, not adopted to the name like others of the group – had managed to acquire the powers of a vampire so their lifespan went considerably longer than history states, and they were much more than mere German professors and authors. They were brilliant, ruthless, military leaders of a very literal army of assassins with one purpose. To end us all."

She paused, gathering her thoughts. "Master Temple, a *Maker*, in fact," she added, glancing at me, "Used his powers to create a doorway through time to Roanoke during the fateful disappearance hundreds of years in the past. The strain of such a mysterious historical event had left ripples, that he knew how to follow and pinpoint."

I blinked in astonishment, ready to pelt her with questions, but she continued on. "All of us leapt through the doorway to the past with the Grimms hot on our heels. We battled. Many died. Then he threw up a second portal leading into a void of darkness. He grabbed a bloodstained, weatherworn, fictitious map that supposedly held the directions to the artifact, and ran inside, leading the army away from our world. The Grimms followed. Most of them. Several more of us had to run into the gateway to convince all of them to follow. They sacrificed themselves for all of us.

"When they were all through, we carted the bodies into the dark void to eliminate any evidence and closed the gateway per Master Temple's instructions. Then we returned to our time. In a way, he banished the Grimms twice. Once in the folds of time, then again in the folds of the universe itself. Quite an accomplishment. He timed it perfectly so that our wholesale slaughter could be hidden in the pages of history." The silence was deafening. Ashley and Indie had tears in their eyes and were openly staring at me, seeming to empathize with the rollercoaster of emotions running through my mind. The Grimms had more than just one reason to kill me. My very ancestor had done this to them in the first place, sacrificing his life to save the world of magic. Gunnar slowly turned to me, but my vision was slightly blurry and I didn't acknowledge him.

"We carved the words *Roanoke* into every tree we could reach before fleeing. No one wanted to be found near the place when it was discovered by whatever authority happened to stumble upon the devastation and mystery that had housed a once thriving city on the fringes of the frontier. The event was hidden in history, a childhood mystery, the focus of many documentaries, but this is the true story. Perhaps the colony at Roanoke only disappeared *because* of what we did." Her eyes were distant, solemn, and almost regretful. "Without Master Temple back, we will never know the truth."

She turned to me. "Don't let them have died in vain. The Grimms must be ended, the bridge closed, and the rest of them prevented from coming over."

I had nothing to say to that.

It made me angry to realize that I didn't know if I could live up to the task of continuing or finishing what my ancestor had started. It was my fault they had found a way back. I just didn't know how to fix it.

This was well beyond me.

25

I sat in the corner, thinking furiously as I twirled the amulet in my fist, thinking of what needed to happen next. True, killing these asshats would give me immense satisfaction, but a small seed of empathy for their origin had also taken root. We had effectively *made* them. It didn't excuse their wholesale slaughter of Freaks, but I could understand a family feud that stretched over centuries. The supernatural community was rife with them. Even if they weren't all *technically* Grimms by *blood*. Even adopted family feuds could be violent, and as far as they saw it, they were true Grimms, blood or not.

I realized that the term *Grimm* was more accurately a sovereign nation of people with the unique ability to see through glamour. Not a last name, per se, but a *title*. And they took their jobs *very* seriously. But Jacob and Wilhelm were the real deal. Bloodline Grimms. Still, blood mattered little in this. Not at all, in fact.

And killing the ones already here would do nothing about the rest of them still waiting on the other side of the bridge. Somehow, some way, I needed to destroy this gateway or bridge or wormhole through time itself, and I didn't feel like visiting Roanoke to find it. To discover that my ancestor had been a Maker was astonishing. But to hear of the power he had wielded was even more inspiring. No wonder the world had crushed Makers. With power like that... I had never before heard of such a thing. I would have loved to quiz my father about it, but the Armory was locked down. And I didn't have time anyway. It was history. Not relevant to our current situation.

Closing the gate would require abilities I didn't quite yet understand. Which wasn't good at all.

The sprite had just shown my friends a 'video' of how this had all come back into the light. From the auction, a few years ago, where I had tried to buy the original copy of *Grimm's Fairy Tales*. My resulting trip to Alistair's house where I met Gunnar responding to a report of gunshots, my first encounter of almost being raped by Barbie after a botched summoning, and my ultimate introduction with Jacob Grimm, visible only on a metaphysical level through a gateway of superblack darkness, the depth of which had never been replicated by man. I tapped the book cover in my hands, annoyed by the group's laughter at my failed summoning. She spent entirely too much time on that section of the story for my taste, so I had left to a quieter section of the room, refusing to be the butt of a joke when we had very real problems to deal with.

Out of professionalism, not embarrassment.

The discovery of their book had led me to opening Plato's Cave. With Alistair – St. Louis' primary arcane book dealer – murdered, someone had needed to fill his spot, and I had been fresh out of things to do.

And I loved books.

I had needed a place to hide the edition of *Grimm's Fairy Tales*, which although small, was much thicker and more ancient-looking than any copy you could find on a store's bookshelf. I had also needed to hide the book of summoning spells that Alistair had owned. The book that had introduced me to Barbie in the first place. The Grimms had been very anxious to get their hands on it, as they could essentially summon defenseless supernaturals to their deaths. I had locked both books away underneath my store, underneath the third projector room that was used only for special occasions and was likely to be missed in the event of the store being attacked.

Like it had been earlier this year by a squad of vengeful Nephilim – the spawn of angels and humans – that had been sent to take me out. I had never told anyone about the vault beneath the store, but the very night I had gone down to pick up something entirely different from the books – the engagement ring I had been wanting to give Indie – no fewer than two groups of supernaturals had been waiting to nab the books from me. Someone knew my secret. Either I had an information leak or the spells I had used to conceal the books had faded and the Grimms could now sense it. Or my spells had never been strong enough. I had been a younger wizard back then. It was quite possible that my spells hadn't been strong enough to block it now that they were back in our world.

And I didn't even know *how* they were back in our world…

I looked down at the original edition of *Grimm's Fairy Tales* in my hands. It supposedly gave them the power to summon allies from the void of darkness where they had resided for a few centuries. I had met one of these lovely creatures already and barely survived. A demonic rooster horse I had turned into chicken nuggets. But it could also bring the rest of them back from the void. I had to keep it away from them. We needed more Grimms in St. Louis like we needed more Cubs fans in Ballpark Village.

At least I could try to even the scales a bit on the crew in my city.

This amulet thing made me nervous. Did it mean we were essentially evenly matched? I would have to change that.

Barbie had ended her story and everyone was now drifting my way. "You guys ready for a scrap?" I asked when they got closer. Their faces were grim, no pun intended, but they nodded as one, flexing fists and checking weapons. "Okay, it's now or never." I murmured, finally removing the warding spells from the books, hoping that would attract the Grimms like flies to shit. A greasy ball of acid wriggled its way into my stomach, but my magically enhanced gastrointestinal tract allowed me to hide the sensation.

I opened the book before me. It was filled with the traditional tales, all handwritten in German, but about halfway through the book morphed into a journal, complete with sketches, notes, and descriptions of various supernatural creatures no doubt encountered on their journey across the world. Power veritably throbbed from the pages, and I knew that my plan was a good one. This would attract them, all right.

I closed the book with a snap and tapped the screen of my watch a few times, setting the drone to watch the perimeter of the building. An added sentinel never hurt anyone. I wanted to know the second these punks showed up. I really hoped to see Jacob and Wilhelm. I also hoped that Misha and Tory would notice and respond quickly as a secret attack force.

"We should go outs–"

But I never got to finish that thought, because a freaking meteor hit the front door, sending it crashing inside the brownstone in an explosion of splinters and roaring sparks.

26

Everyone bolted to attack positions, racing for the door leading outside. No one wanted to be caught against a wall while fighting these guys. I led the gang, peering out the vacant hole in the wall where the door had been, staring into a winter wonderland. Snow was good. It would hide the battle. I turned to the sprite, "Mask the fight. I can't afford for the regulars to call the police when they see World War Three erupt on their front porches." She nodded, face tight, and cast a ball of condensed fog out the window that instantly expanded as it launched into the sky. I used the distraction to throw myself out the door, and also because I heard a monstrous roar of rage and an explosion of fire light up the sky.

I managed to glance at my watch's screen and my drone showed me a battle from the Apocalypse. A giant red dragon roared through the sky, casting jets of napalm flame down on a group of what appeared to be special-ops soldiers in all black outfits, complete with guns and night vision goggles. They scrambled, but didn't look afraid. They fled right into the waiting arms of Tory, who proceeded to Hulk Smash the first wave of Grimms with a city street trash can clutched in each manicured fist.

They didn't know what hit them.

Bodies went flying. Screams tore through the fog and snow.

The scent of blood struck me like a knife to the nose.

Then I was out the door entirely, using the diversion to cast familiar whips of molten fire and razor-sharp ice, using them like chains to harry a nearby group of ancient warriors as they opened fire on Misha and Tory. I tore them to shreds, watching their guns get slashed in half and their torsos explode in either flame or frost. I was cackling as my magic roared and hissed with unrestrained glee.

I heard a howl and Gunnar flew over my shoulder, tackling a black-eyed Grimm to the ground with his jaws snapping for a throat. Before he could kill him, the Grimm dropped his rifle and shifted to a wolf, rolling at the last second to land on his feet and twist out of Gunnar's jaws. He growled at Gunnar and then suddenly began packing on the pounds, doubling in size in a handful of seconds. Now, Gunnar was a huge freaking white werewolf. This one was now a twice-huge freaking white werewolf, and he gave Gunnar a lazy doggie grin before charging.

Gunnar barely paused, nothing but malice glittering in his eyes.

Twin shots retorted from out of a nearby window in Alistair's house and five-hundred-grain silver bullets hammered the Grimm Wolf to pulp. Gunnar looked over his shoulder and barked a complaint at Ashley who was leaning out the window with a defiant grin. But we didn't have time to revel in glory. There was the better part of a dozen more where these had come from.

Alucard was deep in the mix, tussling with two Grimms who had morphed into vampires and were trying to circle him as they lunged, swung, and bit empty air, razor sharp teeth clacking as loud as gunshots. Alucard whipped out his freaking umbrella again and withdrew a blade from the handle, spinning and whirling like a tornado as he threw himself at the nearest Grimm-pire.

Heh.

He was impressive. I wondered how old he was, because swordplay like that wasn't typically taught in school these days. But he sure knew how to party. His laughter filled the night as he moved in a blur, trails of blood painting the snow scarlet as he moved between the Grimms like a wraith.

I was kind of glad he had shown up.

As I picked out my next victim, preparing to face off with one who could duplicate my Maker abilities, I spotted a shady Grimm creeping among his own men, and silently slicing their throats with razor sharp claws. I watched in confusion, and then fascination, as I realized what I was seeing. It took the Grimms only a minute to realize what was going on and discover the traitor in their midst.

Raego, using his shapeshifting abilities to look like whatever he wanted, had disguised himself as a Grimm. Two Grimms immediately exploded into half-formed black dragons, glanced down at their arms in apparent surprise at the color, and then looked up at him with pleased grins. Raego smiled back and black dragon arms replaced his own in a violent explosion of scales and claws, his face partially shifting into a dragon snout and his body doubling in size.

Let me tell you something. A dragon's roar is *loud*. I expected windowpanes to shatter as the foreign vibration rattled the air, urging me to get further away from them.

The Grimms mimicked Raego and it was again two on one, but Raego was more familiar with his powers and used them to his advantage. Bodies struck bodies and razor-sharp claws slashed. One Grimm went down in a fountain of blood but no cry, and the other one redoubled his efforts. I could tell that the survivor was more talented.

I quickly glanced around, noticing another dragon racing through the sky chasing Misha, but overall it seemed like we were winning. I saw Tory swinging a car at another

Grimm, who took the hit like a champ, and then swung a bigger car at her, striking her in the shoulder and sending her into a nearby tree where she crumpled. I watched anxiously, but she got back to her feet with a glare and a slight limp. I sighed in relief, scanning the streets. There weren't many Grimms left standing. Perhaps we could pull this off after all!

But I didn't have time to watch as another Grimm slowly turned to face me, a smile forming on his face. His eyes were as black as the depths of hell. Like the void my ancestor had trapped him in. I instantly recognized him from the pictures in the book. "Wilhelm," I growled hungrily. "Heard you guys swung by for the book sale I set up."

His black eyes sparkled as he nodded. "Aye."

"We already ran out of milk and cookies. Shame. But I made sure to schedule some entertainment for you while you waited. Hope you don't mind." I sneered.

"Oh, not at all. I've been aching for a good scrap for ages. Thanks to your ancestor." He grinned teasingly, flexing his fists and rolling his shoulders in preparation for a fight.

I nodded. "It runs in our blood. We're a sneaky bunch. My ancestor bested you guys what, almost half a millennium ago? Don't learn well, eh? Or are you just a sore loser? Speaking of losers, where's your big brother? Had to send the sniveling younger sibling to take me on? Was he too scared or were you just an easy sacrifice for him to make?" I smiled as his features grew still. "That must sting. Knowing he cast you into a situation you weren't equipped to handle." I teased. He glared, obviously upset that I already knew of my ancestor's involvement, and my mocking tone only fueled his anger further. He watched my whips of elemental power with a hungry gleam, but he didn't seem to tap into any kind of Maker power. Not yet anyway. "You probably should have learned. We Temples pretty much piss excellence. I guess I'm going to have to show–"

Something struck my skull from behind and the world exploded in pain. The whips of power went out as I crashed face-first into the snow. I managed to turn my head, spitting out slush, and all I could do was watch as Wilhelm slowly walked my way with lazy, plodding steps. My mind was scrambled. I struggled to gather my power, but then Wilhelm stomped on my wrist, which pretty much shut me down right there. Thankfully, no bones seemed to break, but I did feel an alarming creak of joints. Which wasn't pleasant.

"Listen up, boy. You really don't get it. You don't even stand a fraction of a chance against us. Literally." He let that sink in, the sounds of battle punctuating his words. I heard a lot of screams, and they didn't sound like Grimms. "I see you managed to swipe up the vampire. No matter. He wasn't key to our plans anyway. Just like the Minotaur wasn't key to our plans. Just a fun excursion." He chuckled. "Now, you've got something that belongs to my family. I'll be taking it back now. I'll pay you, of course. I'm not a robber." He patted his pockets and pantomimed a frown. "Well, that's embarrassing. I guess I didn't bring my wallet. Looks like I'll be accepting your generosity after all." Hands forcibly pinned me to the snow as he patted down my back, quickly finding the books I had hidden there. I hadn't wanted to risk leaving them out of my sight so had attached them to my torso with a belt, using a small spell to keep them from weighing me down. He cut the belt and plucked away the books, giving me a quick kick in the ribs.

Once.

Twice.

Three times.

Then someone flipped me onto my back. "Shame it had to end this way." Wilhelm looked around us, scanning the streets, no doubt realizing how many of them we had taken down. I followed his gaze with a satisfactory smirk.

And blinked.

There were *way* too many Grimms standing. And all my friends were down. Were they all dead? No, they were alive. I let out a relieved breath. Even if we were about to die, at least I would get the chance to look them in the eyes one last time.

I saw Ashley on the ground between two hulking Grimms who were glaring at Gunnar. He lay on the snow; face bloody, scratches on one cheek, glaring back with his lips peeled into a frozen snarl. But he didn't move. Everyone knelt in a line under direct observation of a row of Grimms. Each guard seemed to mimic the power of their captive, ready to respond in a blink if necessary, but they didn't seem very alert. In fact, they seemed rather unconcerned about the whole thing; conversing softly with each other while my crew knelt in the cold, wet snow. Nothing moved in the windows of nearby buildings, and I could hear nothing from the outside world.

Just us.

I saw another Grimm stand wearily from kneeling over a body on the ground. His neck had been slashed wide open by claws of some flavor.

Then the dead Grimm stood, shook his head, and wiped his hands on his pants. He bowed in thanks to the lean Grimm, and resumed his position beside his brothers. The Grimm who had apparently healed him or brought him back to life had an iron collar across his throat, etched with deep, mysterious looking runes. A *necromancer*? Able to bring those back from the *dead*? Come on! I idly remembered the two kids with extraordinary healing powers I had met several years ago. The brother and sister that the Grimms had hoped to recruit or kill. Looks like they had been taken, judging by this Grimm's incredible healing powers.

Wilhelm chuckled. "Thanks, Ichabod." The man grunted in acknowledgement, tired eyes passing over me in what looked like quiet rage and calloused disgust. His eyes twinkled with power, but I didn't know what kind, and they weren't black. Perhaps he was the one duplicating my Maker ability, because I sure as shit couldn't think of another power that could do what he just did – not counting the two kids with healing powers the Grimms had no doubt taken. Unless I myself could have someday learned necromancy with my Maker ability. Well, that pipeline thought ended here and now. We were through. Caught. Kidnapped. Bested. My trap turned on itself. Ichabod walked away to stand a bit apart from the rest of the men. I idly wondered if his power came from the banded collar around his neck rather than the amulets I had seen everyone wearing so far.

Wilhelm turned back to me. "I have no further use for your people, but I do have use for you. I'll let you off with a warning this time. I have what we need for now, so get your affairs in order. We're back and we're going to end your reign of terror. I need you... *cooperative*," he smiled darkly. "So, I'll let your people go as long as–"

A thunderous crack interrupted him and his shoulder exploded in blood, which liberally sprayed me. Wilhelm howled, pointing a finger at the house. "Get the bitch!"

Men darted for the house, and I realized something I had missed in my first glance. Indie was nowhere to be found.

Ichabod approached on tired feet and placed his hands on Wilhelm. I felt a gentle thrum of power similar to mine as the flesh began to knit itself back together. She had hit him in the joint, destroying his cartilage and tendons with a five-hundred-grain silver bullet, the kind used for hunting big game. My crew hadn't taken my caution lightly after hearing about the liger.

But it didn't matter. In seconds, Wilhelm was back to normal. He turned on me with a murderous scowl, rolling his shoulder. "You'll pay for that. Luckily, we don't typically kill humans or she would be dead. Instead, I think I'll keep her. For myself. After we conclude our business." I began to shake, trying to break free. My head was still scrambled from the unseen blow that had taken me down. And I couldn't touch my power.

"Stop struggling. I've got Ichabod blocking you anyway, even if you managed to get up." I stopped, spitting out blood, hitting his boots. He kicked me in the face. I came back to consciousness what felt like a few million years later.

The Grimms from the house were talking with Wilhelm, who was looking more furious by the minute. "What do you mean you can't find her? She's a god damn human. You're telling me you can battle monsters and demons but you can't find a young girl?" He backhanded the Grimm, knocking the man to his feet. A single tooth sailed into a pile of snow, but the Grimm merely spat, stood, and bowed apologetically.

He nodded to Wilhelm. "Aye, Sir. My apologies. I offer my life as payment."

"Luckily for you, we don't have enough brothers left to punish you as you deserve. Just remember our goal. We need to get the rest of our brothers back." He scowled at the house, ignoring the nodding soldier. The man genuinely looked reprimanded. I shook my head in disbelief. These guys were true zealots. Wilhelm turned back to me, looking angry. "It seems I don't get my entertainment for tonight. Don't worry. You'll be hearing from us soon. She will be mine shortly thereafter. For now, we leave. I don't want to waste Ichabod's time bringing us back one by one if she decides to begin shooting again." He tipped an imaginary hat at me. "It's been a pleasure. Thanks for the... *book sale*. And also for masking the fight from the humans. We wouldn't want to show them your true colors, demon." He muttered, kicking me one more time for good measure.

Then, as one, they began trotting down the street, disappearing from view. Apparently, my people had been restrained, because none of them moved. They merely watched. None of it made sense to me. Why had Wilhelm let any of us live? The Grimms *hated* all freaks. I began to grow terrified as my mind stirred up all sorts of reasons for leaving any of us alive, and each was worse than the last.

As one, my friends suddenly jumped to their feet as if still in the thick of battle, glancing about frantically for enemies. I blinked at that. Then realized what had happened. The entire conversation had happened out of their time reference and I hadn't even realized it. As soon as Wilhelm began talking to me he must have frozen time, as I had seen his brothers do once before, so that our conversation remained private.

Raego exploded into his dragon form, snarling at the fog, droplets of fire splashing the snow in flashes of steam. After a few seconds, my friends saw me, no bad guys nearby, and bolted towards me to form a protective circle. They helped me to my feet, tossing questions back and forth and checking on each other. It seemed that more or less, everyone was okay. Flesh wounds all, but nothing requiring immediate attention. Other than rebuilding their dignity. I had brought a literal army to take on these clowns and it hadn't been enough. And Jacob hadn't even been here. He was apparently the bigger, badder brother. We had killed or injured plenty, but they had all been brought back by their spellslinger, Ichabod. He was the key to stopping them. I had to kill him next time we met. First. Fast. Without hesitation. Without his interference, we may have won.

"At least we still have the book. We lost the battle, but there is still the war." Gunnar was reminding Raego and Alucard, who looked as furious as it was likely to possibly get, having shifted back to their more or less human forms.

I cleared my throat, accepting Ashley's arm for support. "About that..." I said through pained breaths, sure my ribs had cracked or been broken from Wilhelm's well-placed kicks. My wrist throbbed. Everyone looked at me. "They took it." Faces turned white, lips setting in tight lines.

"Oh." Alucard mumbled. We absorbed that in silence as Ashley led me into the house. I had to find Indie. The rest of the world could burn for all I cared if Indie wasn't safe. The sprite appeared beside me, landing on my shoulder, now doll-sized again.

"She's okay. Don't worry. I led her to a safe place. She's in the office now. A nice shot." She murmured. I grunted, relief enveloping my shoulders. Indie was safe. I sighed as we entered the office. Indie stared at me, and her shoulders sank in relief. I gripped her in my arms, and then my legs gave out as the pain hit me. She fell along with me, cradling my head in her breasts. I began to cry.

I had been beaten, and I could think of no way to win. Soon they would bring over their brothers, and an already unbeatable crew of black ops mercenaries would get bigger. And badder.

I had thrown my best punch, setting the time, location, and we had been ready. We had been calmly swatted down like rueful puppies.

Mainly because of Ichabod. If we stood a chance of going back against them I needed to take him out first. Indie stroked my hair as the rest of my friends silently left,

Gunnar and Alucard taking charge of two smaller groups, leading them deeper into the house to give us some privacy.

"I failed you. I failed all of us. Who did I think I was to lead us into that? Without Wilhelm's mercy, we would all be dead now."

Indie continued to silently stroke my hair, letting me vent. "We were winning. We were beating them. Then my mouth got in the way and someone sucker-punched me. I didn't see what happened next, but when I looked up, everyone was suddenly down."

I felt Indie mutter under her breath. "That man, Ichabod, happened. He did... something and everyone dropped. Then he calmly went from body to body bringing everyone back to life. Misha landed on a car, totaling it. No one could move. As he brought them back, they broke off into groups and gathered up everyone, leading them back to kneel before you in a line. Taunting and mocking them before Ichabod gave them a look and they stopped. I think even they are scared of him. Or wary of him. Was there a third brother in the stories?" I shook my head. "I wonder why he's so much more powerful than they are?" She asked to herself.

"He was using the power of a Maker. I think." I felt her look down at me, her body shifting. I shrugged. "Each Grimm duplicated our powers. I felt him use his power to heal Wilhelm. It felt familiar. I think he was the one blocking me. Except he knew how to use the power. I don't. At least not nearly as well. Maybe these amulets of theirs let them understand how to use their powers completely. Makes sense. Of course, they would have no idea how to use the abilities they steal beforehand, so it makes sense that they gain not only the power but knowledge of the power as well."

She grunted. "Scary." We were silent for a time, me trying to breathe deeper and stretch out the injured ribs as Indie continued stroking my cheeks and head. "He needs to die first," she finally said.

"My thoughts exactly," I growled.

"Consider this a test run. *Veni, Vidi... we got our asses kicked.*" I burst out laughing as she improvised the saying, *we came, we saw, we conquered.* "We should learn from it. This doesn't sound over. They haven't brought anyone else over yet. And they let us live. That means that they need something else."

I nodded, hissing at the resulting shooting pain in my skull caused by the motion. "Wilhelm said the same. That we would meet again soon." Another thought hit me. "You can't see him again. He has plans for you. Especially after shooting him. And he wants to hurt me. He gets you, and I'll do whatever he wants. I won't be able to help it." Indie began to growl an argument but I interrupted her. "I can sit here and tell you whatever you want to hear, that I'll take the right path and do the right thing, but let's be honest. When it comes to you, I'll choose you every time." I didn't mean it to sound romantic. I was just being honest, showing my flaw as a leader, but Indie squeezed me in a loving hug that hurt me so much I wanted to scream. But I didn't complain.

I could hear her crying, as well as sirens in the background. The damage in the street had been noticed and reported to the authorities. And it was outside another property I owned. This wasn't going to end well.

"Nate..." She didn't say *what are we going to do*, but she must have thought it very loudly.

I nodded. "I know..." I answered her unspoken question. "We need to vamoose." She helped me to my feet and we headed towards the others to Shadow Walk back to *Chateau Falco*, the only safe place I knew. As I began to cast the familiar spell of Shadow Walking, a thought whispered in my subconscious. I modified the spell a bit, and instead of ripping us to a new location, a vertical ring of blue fire erupted before us, revealing the snowy steps leading up to the front door of *Chateau Falco*. A gateway. That was new...

The sprite appeared before me, not giving me time to analyze the unique power I had instinctively used. I would worry about it later. Barbie shot me a silent look that said *call me when you are ready...* I nodded back and continued through the ring of fire, wondering if I would ever be ready to sentence my friends to die in order to save the supernatural community at large from the Grimms. It looked like sacrifice was our only option.

27

We had managed to get everyone into his or her own rooms, and when I say 'we' I really mean Dean, my Butler. But he worked for me, so I gain credit by extension.

The task seemed to have filled Dean with a level of pride and energy I hadn't seen in him in a long time. This was his job, and he took it very seriously. Each guest's request was met with an eager smile and then promptly satisfied. Mallory was ever present to help Dean out, but when I caught his eye he shook his head discreetly, letting me know that no one had tried to break in, but that he also hadn't located Tomas either.

With Jacob being absent from the fight earlier, I had feared that he had attempted to break into the Armory or something while his brothers kept us distracted. But it looked like all was clear.

Alucard was very pleased, studying my house with acute interest. He had shed blood for me, and even though we had met under less than ideal circumstances – him attempting to separate my head from my shoulders – I realized that I trusted him. I hoped that wasn't a mistake, but then again, I noticed Gunnar studying him several times, looking wary but also impressed. It was nice to see him also approving of the vampire, a natural enemy of a werewolf, but I knew he would keep an eye on things, leaving me to focus on our bigger problem.

Bros.

A powerful word.

Gunnar had been beaten, knocked down, but seeing that Ashley was more or less unharmed had given him renewed vigor, and a personal stake in the matter. In fact, everyone was now personally involved. It was no longer about helping me out of my own mess. They had all kicked ass, and had their asses kicked by the Grimms, and all looked anxious – and terrified – for round two. But none looked as downtrodden as I felt. They looked full of purpose, so I put on a mask, like my father had taught me long ago. A leader couldn't show weakness.

A leader was more than just the guy giving commands. He was the candle in the dark, the little light of fire that kept the team focused.

I must have done a decent job, because only the women seemed to see the truth. As was always the case. Ashley and Indie had several silent conversations with only their eyes. Tory and Misha jumped in on a few of these exchanges, learning the same information by estrogenic osmosis, and each of them silently proceeded to take care of the men, encouraging us, congratulating us, and generally building our self-esteem for round two, fueling our fires rather than putting them out with doubts and fears.

It was kind of magical.

I didn't let on that I knew their superpower, but Indie saw me watching and shrugged. "It's what we do."

"Hey, don't belittle yourself. You also bake cakes and clean the kitchen." Her eyes turned playfully aggressive. I grinned.

"If you weren't injured..." she growled, jokingly.

My injuries had slowly faded after eating what felt like a cereal bowl of painkillers, but I knew they would come back to haunt me soon. Indie grabbed my hand and we began to walk the halls of *Chateau Falco*, simply enjoying each other's company as we made our way to my office. I was anxious to get to the Armory and verify that all was safe and that hopefully the mysterious ward was down. Everyone else had gone to bed, leaving Indie and me to secretly check on the Armory and hopefully gain some insight into the Grimms from Pandora and my parents. As long as the door would open this time. I hadn't had time to really ponder that but it bothered me. It had never happened before and I didn't like surprises, especially when those surprises coincided with the Grimms' arrival.

We passed a small reading room to find Tory and Misha snuggling together, fast asleep. I smiled, nodding to Indie. She grinned back in silence. As we took another step, Misha opened one eye to appraise us, no doubt making sure everything was safe for the woman in her arms. I wondered if she had even been asleep in the first place. Seeing it was just Indie and me, she winked and closed her eyes. Tory snuggled in closer to her chest with a sigh. Misha pulled a blanket over her shoulders and settled deeper into the couch, wrapping her arms around the ex-cop with a gentle kiss to the back of her head. I gently tugged Indie's hand, signaling for us to leave them in peace.

As we continued down the hall, I peppered Indie. "That's why I do this, Indie. To keep people like them safe from the Grimms." She nodded, eyes misty. We continued on for a few seconds in silence before I poked her playfully in the ribs. "You were saying something about me being injured...?" I teased, seeing the office just ahead.

She grinned mischievously. "I was saying that if you weren't injured, I'd have the sprite come over and remind me about the time you two met." My face turned red. "Then I would let her show me a few of her tricks for the next time you got out of hand." She winked darkly and I shook my head.

"I'd like to see you try that, woman. After you finish with the dishes, of course."

She lunged, chasing me, but I quickly darted into the office, pausing just past the threshold for her to catch me, so that I could possibly sneak in a kiss or two in private.

I had expected her to latch onto my shoulder, but nothing happened. I slowly turned and noticed that she was frozen in midair, arm outstretched to catch me. She was in the office, but completely immobile, still featuring a predator's grin as she reached out a playful hand, her eyes dancing with mischief. My good mood evaporated.

Indie was frozen, which could mean only one thing. Grimms.

I spun, fumbling to latch onto my power. We were under attack. And I hadn't activated the *Guardians*, fearing any misunderstandings with so many guests present.

I found the chair behind my desk slowly turning to face me. I didn't give him a chance to react. I launched a spear of ice directly at his cold, heartless chest, staring into his inky black eyes. I would finish what my ancestor started.

Here.

Now.

He waved a hand and the spear disappeared. He wiped off his hands with a smirk.

"Nate."

"Jacob." I acknowledged, forming another, more violent strike.

"I wouldn't."

"I would," I growled, tossing another lance of power, twice as strong.

The same thing happened. He wasn't even breathing hard. "We could do this all day. Or we could talk. I'm sure you've realized by now that I can duplicate all that you can do. Probably do it better, seeing as you don't yet know how to use your power, whereas I hold the knowledge of how to use it to its utmost potential." He held out a hand, palm up, waiting.

I grunted, flicking my head at Indie. "She's not a part of this." I warned.

"Why do you think I froze time?" He asked. His eyes slowly shifted from shiny black orbs to their normal blue shade as he stood. He shook his head. "Been a while since I had to deal with that." He approached me warily, not afraid, but as one would approach a skittish horse. It pissed me off. As if I needed to be calmed down. He was a murdering murderer. Of course, I was on edge. He carefully stepped to the side, studying Indie thoughtfully, not in a creepy way, but as if to see her for himself. "So, this is the one who shot my brother."

"Yep." I answered snidely. "And if Ichabod wouldn't have been there, boy, would his face have been red." I clapped a hand over my mouth and whispered pantomime. "Whoops. Too soon?"

He waved a hand, smirking. "Not at all. Wilhelm has always been... eager." He finally answered, face thoughtful. "It's why I lead. My younger brother can be very willful." He looked at me as if to give me inside information. "And he's very interested in taking your woman. As recompense." He watched me. "And that would be unpleasant for her."

"Yeah, well, that's not going to happen. I skipped class the day they taught *sharing*."

He blinked. "If he had his way, you wouldn't really have much say in the matter. Your body would be cold, providing sustenance for the worms." He added matter-of-fact.

"It wouldn't pan out like that," I said neutrally, letting him take what he would from my words. I was beginning to feel a little on edge. Why was he being so cordial? This was nothing like the monster I had first met several years ago.

He grunted. We studied each other. He was tall. Really tall. Well over six feet, and his hair was, *wait for it*, as white as snow, indicating his true age. Harnessing the powers of a vampire in his past had definitely agreed with his aging factor, because I spotted not a wrinkle. His features were long, harsh, and angular, as if he had recently vacated a sick bed, despite the healthy glow in his blue eyes. His long, bony fingers reached out from the sleeve of his black trench coat like a skeleton as he offered it to shake. I spat at it, hitting his palm with a satisfying *smack*. He frowned, shaking it off and then using a handkerchief to wipe it off. He tossed the soiled white kerchief on the ground.

"You surrendering?" I sneered.

He burst out laughing, patting his knees in amusement with those huge hands. They could very easily fit around my skull, which I wasn't interested in testing. "And why would I do such a thing? My... *B team* ate your lunch today, and you thought you were in *control* of the situation, setting a *trap* of all things. Cute. I see you've healed up a bit from my younger brother's... *ministrations*." He smiled in amusement, acknowledging the injuries Wilhelm had given me. "That's nice, but we can heal better." He tapped his knee with a finger. "So, I must ask. What more could you *possibly* throw at me? The Minotaur? The turncoat vampire?" He smiled, not necessarily mocking me but instead asking with genuine interest.

I studied him thoughtfully. "You seem less... *psychotic* this time."

He nodded, eyes growing distant at the memory of our first meeting. "You must remember. The first time we met, I had been spending centuries in darkness." He watched me for a moment. "*426 years* to be precise. You should remember that number." He added cryptically with a twinkle in his eyes.

Oh, I remembered. Thanks to my ancestor their prison sentence had been extended through time itself. Poor guys. I was mildly curious how he had figured it out though. Because for all he knew, they had never traveled through time, so if he was looking at time by merely counting years then it had only been *186* years. But I didn't want to press too many of his buttons. If he didn't know, that was his problem. Maybe he had counted tally marks on a wall or something.

He continued. "And the first thing my eyes saw of my lost world was an abomination. Sorry, a *Freak*, as society rightfully calls you creatures these days." He waved his hand. "And not just any Freak, but a *Temple*. Ho' boy! An descendent of the very man who put us in prison in the first place! I was a little... off my game." He smiled at the understatement. For all I knew, that first meeting was *on his game*, and this was merely a ruse. He waved his hand, motioning towards the fireplace, inviting me to sit. I complied, not knowing what else to do. I was essentially at his disposal; totally impotent to stop him from doing whatever it was he was trying to do. After all, if he had wanted to kill me he would have done so by now, and I didn't think I would have been able to stop him. He was right. He knew how to use the power of a Maker. I didn't.

Which blew.

So, I sat. With dignity. Realizing that with all my power and reputation, I was but a child to this legendary killer. My wrist ached. As did my ribs. Courtesy of his brother. I let none of it show. Let him think what he will.

He duplicated my motion, sitting across from me, steepling his fingers as he watched me like a bug in a box. "We have the book." He held up a finger. "We bested you in battle. Well, not *we*, but my brother." He held up another finger. "You and your motley crew of Freaks are injured, broken, and *you* don't even know how to properly use your power." He waited for me to argue, but I didn't. "There is a price on your head for me to take you out, which I had been planning on doing anyway." He held up a third finger, which was becoming damn annoying. "But you've done me a favor." He took a finger away. "And you have something else I want." He took away another finger. His gaze traveled to Indie, and he added as an afterthought, "And something my brother wants." He folded the last finger, and rested his palm in his lap. Then he waited.

"I don't understand."

He chuckled, nodding as he leaned forward. "I know."

I stared back, and decided to play my trump card. "You know I took out two of you single-handedly at the hotel." But he simply shrugged.

"A minor loss. They were hotheads, unworthy of life if they couldn't best you."

I hid a shiver at his callousness. "I have access to The Armory..." I stated, wondering if that name would mean anything to a man locked away for a few hundred years.

He clapped his hands. "Oh, you're not slow at *all*. That is *precisely* what I am speaking of!"

"And I could decimate you and your brothers with the weakest of toys from inside. Out of courtesy, I didn't bring them out to play today." I warned, smiling gently.

"Oh?" He asked, smiling.

I pressed on. "Yes. It really isn't even a question of the outcome. It's merely who you would like to sacrifice as cannon fodder." I said, tone neutral. "I'm willing to play. Are you willing to play, Jacob?"

He nodded eagerly, leaning further forward. "Oh, yes." Then he waited, watching me.

"Well, not this second." I finally said, growing frustrated.

"No, please. Go ahead. I will wait." He glanced at Indie thoughtfully, a frown growing on his face. "Oh, dear. I see now. You don't want to leave me with her. Wise choice." He tapped his lip thoughtfully before thrusting a finger in the air. "Ah! I could come with you and choose the weapon for you to slay me with." He offered.

I laughed. "Like I would show you where–"

He stood, leaned towards the mantle above the fireplace, and clicked a button I didn't even know existed. The fireplace roared like normal and he disappeared inside. I blinked, jumping to my feet a second later and rushing after him in a panic, torn between leaving Indie or leaving Jacob unattended. *How in the holy hell...*

And the bastard had moved so *fast*.

I landed in the familiar secret passageway ready to sprint and chase the fucker down, but found him casually leaning against the wall. "One hundred feet down, through the open room, second hallway on the right, last door on the first left hallway." He said laconically, smirking.

I blinked at him, not even attempting to hide my surprise. "How did you..."

"Yes, that is the proper sequence of words in the question, and ironically, my answer will start with the same three words." He maintained his smile as he continued. "How did you... *think we got here in the first place, Nathaniel Laurent Temple?*"

He strode past me with a whirl of his coat, rubbing his arms for warmth as he jumped back into the portal leading to the office. I blinked several times, then quickly followed, growing beyond agitated that he seemed to be one step ahead of me at every turn, but not wanting to leave him alone with Indie for one second.

When I appeared in the office he was already back in his chair, waiting.

I calmly sat down, checked on Indie, who remained frozen, and then stared into the fire. "What did you mean, Jacob?" I asked, voice dry as dust.

"The Armory. It was how we found our way back. Power calls power." He answered cryptically. Seeing my frown, he elaborated. "The fates would have it that you used it in recent months, and not just used it, but destroyed an existing gateway connected to it. Like all magic, power cannot be created nor destroyed, so the Armory sought out another gateway to connect to all on her own. Lucky for me, our calls coincided with her need and she let us link."

I blinked in astonishment. "She would never..."

He chuckled. "Oh, how delicious! I'm not speaking of your *librarian*." He emphasized quotes with his fingers, referring to Pandora. "I'm referring to the Arcanum itself, the Armory is a very literal being in its own right after so many years of housing the world's most deadly weapons. The items held in her clutches have tainted her – like magic does to everyone." He murmured with a bit of the zealot briefly peeking through his calm demeanor before he regained his composure. "The items have... awoken her. As any true guardian would know, if he had paid attention." His eyes looked me up and down with disappointment.

I shook my head in disbelief. "I'm kind of new to the position." I muttered defensively.

He reached out as if to touch my knee consolingly. I flinched away and he smiled. "I understand. Don't fret yourself, dear boy." That prickled up my spine, although I guessed he *was* several hundred years my senior. Technically. He watched me for a time before continuing. "Speaking of the Armory. Any luck trying to gain entrance lately?" His smile told me enough to know the awful truth.

Not only was he better than me in battle. He was also better than me at chess. I felt like I was in a philosophical debate with Gandhi, Aristotle, and Sun Tzu at the same time. "If you know enough to ask that you know the answer." I snarled in defeat.

"Yes. Well, you can blame me for that also. A few of us tried breaking in recently, but the Armory, or perhaps your *librarian*," he rolled his eyes. "Wouldn't let us in. Locked the door on us in fact." His eyes grew thoughtful as he studied me, no doubt pondering why he had failed. But I knew why. My blood was the key to the Armory. I kept my face blank as he watched me, but he finally sighed with an amused smile at my stubbornness. "No matter. It *is* quite the collection, I must say." My body tensed in alarm, wondering what devilish items he may have taken. He laughed at my bodily reaction. "Don't worry. I wasn't able to touch anything. Yet. Just a sight-seeing tour on our first time through." He watched me like a predator. "It was... enlightening. I saw..." his gaze trailed out the window, watching the snow fall for a few beats. "Vast potential for my brothers and I..." Silence stretched between us for a few moments longer before he resumed. "It will aid me immeasurably in the days to come. After I kill you, of course." He added as an afterthought, a slight crease in his forehead as if remembering he needed to take out the trash after dinner.

"Well, I'm not particularly fond of that plan." I was practically hyperventilating, but hiding it well. I hoped. He had taken a stroll through the Armory. Unaided. Had he hurt Pandora? Had she even known they were there? What about my parents? I buried those thoughts deep and faced him. "I'll take you on a tour myself if you wish. Why don't you and your brothers meet me here after I have a cup of coffee and I can show you my toys? And what they can do. Just me and your crew." I was almost whispering at the last, leaning forward with a hungry gleam in my eyes.

He watched me neutrally. "Tempting," he said, tapping his lips in thought, "But it will be mine soon enough. After you are expunged from this world."

"Well, I hate to ruin your plans, but killing me won't get you the Armory. It's keyed to my living blood." I answered honestly.

He nodded simply. "I know."

I felt smug with my small victory. I would win the war by losing the battle. Dying. Hoorah! Then he continued.

"But with my amulet, I'll absorb your very essence, able to do all that you can, be all that you are. Which means your powers will be mine, you will be dead, and the Armory will recognize me as her guardian." I began to shiver deep down in my soul. Would it really work out that way?

"Your amulet?" I asked, trying to stall for time.

He waved a hand at me, not even glancing my way. "Oh, come now. Don't act coy. I was waging wars before your Great ancestors were even a twinkle in another's eye. Judging by your reaction speed at the battle, you know all about our amulets and how they function. Else you would have shat yourself upon the first battle cry. I heard our old friend, Seraph, aided you in battle. I would so love to talk with her again. In private." His tone dripped venom, and I was pretty sure I knew whom he was talking about, even though I had never heard the name.

"Who?"

"The sprite that thwarted me when you and I first met." He amended. I managed to keep my face blank. I would have to warn her. At least she wasn't here. She was safe.

For now.

Jacob's forehead creased again as he continued to watch the snow fall outside. I was suddenly glad I had secreted away the amulets I had absconded from the liger and ape. I didn't know if he could have sensed them, but he likely would have taken them from me. And I wanted to study them. Jacob turned back to me. He looked supremely disappointed. "I grow weary of our talk. I had so hoped that you would be worth at least a little bit of banter."

He stood. "You know, I didn't even need to take the contract to want to kill you, but it was a large sum of money, and why do something for free when you can get paid? We have a lot to learn about this new world, and that costs money. We will kill you, my brother will play with your woman... for a time anyway, and then I will use my new Armory to bring back the rest of my brothers." He smiled in expectant euphoria. "Finally, to know that I avenged the fallen, taking down the very descendent of our captor. To free my brothers, my family... I won't tell you how sweet that first breath of fresh air was..." His voice grew with excitement. "We will cleanse the world of the filth of magic once and for all." His eyes were glazed.

"You know, speaking of your brothers, I'm kind of offended you didn't bring all of them to our reunion. There won't be enough to kill for me to feel well and truly sated. It's kind of like when you take the last bite of a meal and you're still pretty hungry, but that's it. No more. It's a living hell, you know? Knowing you have to wait a few hours to get what you want..." I looked at him, eyes opening in embarrassment. "Oh, I didn't even... of *course* you know what I'm talking about. My ancestor gave you that gift already. *For four hundred years...* And here I am, talking about having to wait a few *hours*." I shook my head in faux embarrassment. "Must sting a bit, eh, Jakey?" I smiled good-naturedly at him, enjoying the slight reddening of his face. Finally, I had been able to get a rise out of him.

Then he calmed, watching me with a slight frown. "I truly wish I could spill the beans and tell you what you are missing. It's particularly sad that you genuinely have no idea what is about to happen. What *has* happened. And who the instrument of your destruction is. I guess you will die ignorant. Unless I decide to whisper the answer in your ear before I slice. Off. Your. Head." He shrugged his shoulders, truly not concerned about casually mentioning decapitation. *These freaking guys*, I shivered. And I wondered about his comment. Wilhelm had said something similar.

"You know... you're here, I'm here, your douche bag brother is torturing innocent kittens somewhere nearby. Why don't we just start the party already? Why don't–"

I blinked, feeling as if a bucket of ice water had just been dumped down my back.

A diversion.

Jacob began a slow clap. "My, my, *my*. The hamster finally learns how to use the wheel sitting in his cage. You're quite astute when you need to be, but boy does it take you a while to gain some traction. In my day, you would have been dashed against the rocks before two years old, supernatural or not." He shook his head in disgust. "Don't worry. We'll be seeing each other very soon, *Temple*." He shivered to himself, smiling in anticipation. "Damn it feels good to say that word with satisfaction rather than a soul deep rage." He winked. "I might as well tell you, you can believe me or not, but your Armory is on lockdown for another thirty-six hours. Thanks to our little stroll through her halls. In the meantime, don't worry about an impending attack. You'll receive plenty of warning when we desire to meet again. We don't need to surprise a group of mewling children. This diversion was about something else entirely." He smiled, almost laughing at my face as I waited to hear what he had done. "I recommend the... *television*, I think you call it." He shook his head. "Wonder of wonders what mortals have discovered without the use of magic. Anyway, you should find the local news particularly interesting." Then he disappeared in a puff of black smoke and a laugh, the perfect evil overlord exit.

Damn it.

"You'll pay for that, Nate!" Indie hissed, laughing as she suddenly lurched into the room, claws outstretched to latch onto my shirt where she had last seen me.

But I was no longer there.

Indie stumbled and blinked, finally spotting me by the fire. Then she grinned. "Did you really just Shadow Walk to the fire in order to escape me? Wuss." She teased. Then she saw my face. "Nate?" she took an uncertain step closer. Rather than respond, I turned on the TV and sat in utter disbelief as the news report folded over me, numbing my brain.

"What in holy hell..." Indie began, collapsing into the other chair as a video played on the news.

28

I did what anyone would do when they find out their home has been frequented by a gang of monster killers.

I went exterminating.

Mallory and I had armed for bear, taking the West Wing of *Chateau Falco*, and I had kept my eyes open for any whisper of power emanating from the walls. Because, you know, Jacob seemed to know my house better than I did. Which made Mallory and Dean all sorts of offended. I hadn't told them that I hadn't known about the secret entrance, but simply that Jacob had *also* known about entrances he shouldn't have known about. It's called managing the chaos. I couldn't let them know how badly I had been outclassed.

Rage kept me warm as we traipsed through the halls, my power constantly beckoning to me. I almost *wanted* someone to jump out at me. We had left the girls with the other men, who had actively promised to guard them with their lives. Even Alucard. But I didn't think they needed any help. They were armed with a plethora of bullets, swords, and they had a Tory, a one-person wrecking crew. They needed no protection. Even if Alucard was handy in a scrap.

That small trusting part of me screamed at me not to be so foolish.

He was a vampire, and vampires couldn't be trusted.

Just like the Grimms thought that *none of us Freaks* could be trusted.

It sucks when your own arguments are thrown back at you. Unconditional bias towards a person or persons was a vicious poison.

As displayed by the Grimms.

It was time for me to open up my blinders a bit. A teeny bit. Vampires were after all murderers by default. That didn't mean that one couldn't rise above such little things.

Still, I would be on my guard. But I would also cut him a little slack. After all, he could have died several times today but he had been right there in the thick of battle.

But on the other hand, he had threatened, and actually killed me today.

I sighed, scanning the bookshelf before me, catching a newspaper clipping of my father and mother from several years before.

Standing in front of Temple Industries.

A part of me died with shame.

I had failed them. I had failed everyone. My friends. My company. Even the various Freaks of my city. They just didn't know it yet. I had given the Grimms access back to our world, and they were hungry to pick up where they had left off. The family business. Killing everything with even a drip of magic in their blood.

I realized I was growling when I saw the mirrored look on Mallory's face.

"We'll figure it out, son. Temple Industries will weather the storm." He trailed off, face distant, seeming as if even he didn't buy the words. "Somehow..."

I grunted.

We were back in the main living quarters. Raego and Misha were back from their section of the house, and they met us at the grand staircase, the obvious wealth of the marble balustrades and shining floors a blatant mockery of safety.

Chateau Falco had been invaded. Silently. Stealthily.

The Grimms had been in my home. And I hadn't known. I shivered. One night in the not too distant past I had been fast asleep beside Indie, and more than a dozen men had crept through my house.

And no one had noticed.

They could have even watched us for a time, unobserved, judging by Jacob's obvious knowledge of my floor plan. Just because he had entered through the Armory, that didn't explain how he knew of the secret entrance or how it had been activated. Unless his amulet did as he said, letting him know how to use his powers on a level so far above mine that I would snap my neck even trying to look up at him.

I knew the amulets could temporarily mirror whatever powers were thrown at it, but what was Jacob's *innate* power? The power permanently stored in the Amulet? Could the amulets store more than one type of power at a time? For how long? Centuries? And what had he meant by mentioning the *instrument of my destruction*? Was there a traitor in my midst? If so, I had no idea who it could be, although if I had to bet it would have been our newest member, Alucard. Or maybe that's what Jacob *wanted* me to think. To make me paranoid. I would just have to keep an eye on everyone. I shook my head as I silently began walking up the stairs. My friends followed me. No one spoke.

In one night, my whole world had collapsed. Every pillar that supported me shattered.

My own power was useless.

My friends were just as useless to defend themselves and had almost died trying.

I had unknowingly given a bus pass to history's baddest exterminators to come to St. Louis. And they were hungry to make up for lost time.

And my company...

I shook my head, glancing down at my phone. No missed calls. I angrily typed a text, demanding a response.

Now. Things needed to be done immediately if I stood a chance of surviving this.

Jacob had planned well. I just didn't know how he could have accomplished it. He had been locked away for centuries and had no idea how the world worked these days. I wouldn't have expected it of even the savviest of corporate lawyers – of which I had numerous on retainer, and not one had answered my calls – let alone a centuries-old assassin. It was almost worth an ovation, if I hadn't been on the receiving end.

I entered the office to find the television blaring, and my friends staring at the screen with ashen faces.

"In a late press release this evening, Nate Temple took to the camera to inform St. Louis of his resignation from Temple Industries." They played a clip of me standing there, in front of a gaggle of reporters, announcing my resignation, and then leaving with an insolent grin. Which was impossible. The reporter continued. "The stock value crashed as a result. This all happened in the hours leading up to the closing bell, allowing time for the stock to drop lower than it ever has since its Initial Public Offering. Temple Industries is the largest employer of our city, and one of the larger technology companies in the world. Following the death of the founders, Nate Temple's parents, the company has struggled to find its way. Some say as a direct result of an absentee owner. A meeting was held this afternoon with the Board of Directors and Nate Temple to discuss the sale of the company to a German firm. Nate Temple later informed the media, who had been anxiously waiting outside the hotel, that the company was not for sale. Then he left without another word.

"Police were called to assist several injured reporters at the scene of what appears to have been a gunfight. Nate Temple could not be reached regarding the obvious violence, and speculation abounds as to who caused the injuries. Sources report that Nate Temple did leave with a gunshot wound. Details are being investigated at this time and we will inform you of any updates regarding the attack and the future of Temple Industries." Venom was thick in the reporter's voice. I had heard this already, but I wasn't sure if all of my friends had.

The television suddenly elicited an eruption of sparks and the screen cracked in half.

My friends turned to face me, eyes questioning. Alucard watched me, face blank. Ashley looked livid, but not at me. She had been in the meeting after all. She knew it to be a lie.

"Nate..." Gunnar began.

I held up a finger. "It's a lie. All of it."

Ashley watched me, brain practically buzzing with questions. "I've been with you all day. I am almost one hundred percent certain that this isn't possible. No offense."

She answered my glare, speaking clinically. "Which means that this is corporate espionage, but who could have duplicated your every mannerism? I mean, that is *you*, Nate." She whispered. She began thumbing through her phone after a short vibration on the device.

I sighed, sitting down. "I have no idea. But to be honest, none of that matters. Stock values have plummeted. It almost doesn't matter now. Sure, we can fight it, saying it was fraudulent, and we will be in court for *years*. We will win, but will the company recover? Will anyone trust us long enough for the company to stay afloat?" I shook my head. "This almost *forces* us to sell in order to keep the doors open. I haven't been able to reach anyone, and you think my phone would be blowing up."

Ashley looked at me sharply. I nodded. "Which basically proves that this was set up by an insider. But who? And how are the Grimms involved? This is sophisticated stuff."

"We will be able to follow the money, sic a pack of angry lawyers at them. If it was an insider, someone had to profit off of it." I nodded, waving a hand to my previous point. "It looks like I'm going to have a busy day tomorrow."

"We all are. This was intentional. To keep me distracted. I just don't know why. We are obviously outclassed, why kick me while I'm down?"

Alucard piped up. "Because it's fun to dominate a victim."

We all turned to him, and Gunnar's hands rippled to claws. Alucard held out a placating hand. "I'm just telling the truth. I know a bit of how this works. I survived the vampire courts and excelled. You don't do that by collecting stamps. This is a calm, calculated full frontal attack from multiple directions. It was cleverly done. You can trace the money, sure, but Nate's point stands. Does that matter for tomorrow?" He shrugged. "I'm no CEO, but I think everyone is going to be very busy tomorrow. Lots of phone calls. Emails. Texts. Meetings. Then more meetings about *other* meetings. Bureaucracy. Busywork. Which will keep our hero occupied while something *else* happens."

I nodded, tipping an imaginary hat. "Regardless, we need to hit the hay. I had a run in with Jacob." The room erupted. Misha grasped Tory protectively, even though she didn't really need protection. She was tough cookies. I told them about my talk.

"He's going to let us know when we are going to die. That's... nice of him." Tory muttered, squeezing Misha's hand comfortingly. Misha looked as if she were in the middle of a war. Right here, right now. With enemies just around the corner. I was very glad Tory was trying to subtly calm her down.

I answered Tory. "He could have been lying, and a swarm of Grimms could already be outside my gates waiting to kill us all." My gaze settled on Misha, who nodded her approval. The room grew tense then. "But I don't think that's the case. He could have killed me tonight." I said softly.

Indie sobbed softly.

I regained my composure. "But he didn't. Which was a mistake. Now I'm ready for him. War Council time." I growled, motioning for them to gather round. I had some things to tell them, and we had some planning to do. I wasn't going down without a fight.

Hungry smiles met my words, and even if they didn't believe we stood a chance, at least they heard that it was going to be the most fun a failure ever had. Alucard laughed a few times, shaking his head in astonishment. Misha and Tory would return to Raego's compound to give him a heads-up. Because now more than ever, I needed to be sure that my insurance policy remained safe.

Also, Misha's daughters were with Raego, and the impending doom of battle had kicked on her Mom gene, flooding her with the need to protect her family at all costs.

I smiled, shooed them away with a last hug for each, and then the rest of us got ready to go back to bed. We needed our beauty sleep for tomorrow.

I did make sure to activate the *Guardians* before I followed Indie to our bedroom. I set them up to attack and destroy any living being attached to a Grimm's amulet. Which should be a nice surprise if Jacob thought to come back tonight.

I dreamt about Jacob's screams as a pack of *Guardians* tore him to shreds.

It was like a lullaby. A fairy tale.

29

"This is bad, Nate." I sipped my coffee, listening to my lawyer, Turner Locke, prepare to lay it out for me. I feared the worst, but knew it would be even worse than that.

"Proceed." I answered in a clipped voice, still unsatisfied with his response that he had been up all night putting out what fires he could, making phone calls, speaking with the mayor in my defense.

"As you surmised, several significant profits were made before closing bell." His voice trailed off. I waited. "Is there anything you want to tell me, Nate? You know I'm on your side, right? Anything we discuss is confidential."

I sighed. Sure, I could just tell him that a supernatural hit squad had physically attacked me outside the hotel after the meeting, and then again outside a brownstone near Cardinal Village. And then that this same group had hired my long-lost twin brother to do an official Press Release in order to announce my official resignation from Temple Industries. I could also just ask him to lock me up in a straightjacket now. Because he was a Regular. He *was* savvy to the world of magic, having worked for my father for years, but the story sounded far-fetched even to me. And I was the freaking *victim*.

"Nothing that would make a difference. Let's just say I was targeted."

The line was silent for a time. Then Turner began. "Documentation shows that you purchased one thousand married-put option contracts on Temple Industries stock, with the right to sell at five dollars below the previous day's closing value. Three months ago. The expiration date for these puts was tomorrow, but you exercised them yesterday, making you even richer than you already were. In an order of magnitude, thanks to the crash."

I dropped the coffee, causing Indie to gasp.

My vision flared blue, and the window exploded outwards. As did part of the wall.

"Nate?" Turner shouted into my ear. Indie had jumped to her feet with a shout and was now watching me as if having never seen me before. Her eyes darted from the explosion to me as if waiting for Grimms to appear out of the woodwork. Seeing me motionless seemed to calm her after a few seconds. Gunnar bounded into the room, already in his wolf form, Alucard hot on his heels. They swept outside into the frigid morning air, ready for war.

Still, I didn't move.

"*What?*" I whispered into the phone. Gunnar and Alucard reappeared, staring at me wild-eyed. I heard Indie speaking with them but didn't hear the words. A dull vibration filled my ears. I realized it was Turner talking.

"...what just happened? Is everything all right? Nate?" He sounded frantic.

"I... yes. Everything is... fine over here. Talk to me, Turner. I didn't have any put options on my stock. None. This was a setup."

"Well, I'm almost not sure it matters at this point." He responded after a beat. "Wait, you're on the news again. Let me catch this. I'll call you right back."

He hung up without waiting for an answer.

I pointed my remote at the TV and everyone turned to watch.

The reporter was animated.

"*This just in. Nate Temple has confirmed that his Press Release yesterday where he resigned from Temple Industries was some sort of prank. No further comment was given by Temple. New sources report that Master Temple sold options on his stocks, earning him a significant profit from the crash caused by his Press Release. The Board of Directors has stepped forth, issuing a unanimous statement voting Nate Temple out of the company for his reckless behavior. Ashley Belmont, CEO of Temple Industries, has not responded to numerous calls and it has come to the attention of our reporters that her stock portfolio also realized a substantial gain from the false press release, proving she was complicit in the fraud. Nate Temple has declined further comment on the matter, but effective immediately, he is no longer owner of Temple Industries. Having sold his majority share in the company, he is now only a minority owner, holding only 426 shares...*" I tuned out the rest of the report as the number struck a chord.

It was the exact number of years the Grimms had been imprisoned.

My phone vibrated. It was Turner.

"I couldn't have done this, Turner. Trust me. I haven't spoken to my broker in months."

"That was when the puts were ordered. The exact day you last spoke with him. It's all been recorded, and the broker has already met with the FBI." I blinked.

"Ashley has been with me. I know she isn't involved in this either." I tried to protect her a bit.

"Her puts were purchased at the same time as yours. Same day, in fact." Turner replied almost sadly. "And she's not answering her phone."

"That's... that's not possible. I saw her make over a dozen calls last night. She has been all *over* this."

"No one has heard from Ashley since the meeting with the German company. Tickets overseas were reported to the media. Even footage of her boarding the plane immediately after your Meeting."

That just wasn't... I growled to Gunnar. "Go. Get. Ashley. *Now*." I snarled. Gunnar didn't even respond, his giant werewolf form disappearing in a blink. I had seen her only fifteen minutes ago. And she had practically been stuck to my hip since the meeting. What the hell was going on?

"Nate, as your lawyer, you need to be up front with me." He began.

I didn't let him continue. "Listen closely, Turner. You worked for my father for years. You know how important Temple Industries is to me. And was to him. I would *never*..." I calmed my tone, realizing I was shouting. I took a breath. "I would never do such a thing. It's a setup." I whispered.

"I'm going to be honest with you, Nate. Your actions to date haven't been particularly flattering when it comes to company loyalty. You've professed to me personally that you leave it all to your employees. The Press Release from the Board Meeting even has audio sound bites of you stating this very thing. Among other, more incriminating statements – not even counting the video footage of you – that are going to take me months to argue–"

"Turner. Listen. Shut this *down*. Now. It's what you are paid to do. I'm telling you right now, Ashley and I had *nothing* to do with this. Now, I've got bigger issues to deal with at the moment. Don't let me down."

"But–" I hung up the phone as Ashley came sprinting into the kitchen, Gunnar loping along behind her.

"What's wrong, Nate? I was getting ready to make a call when I–"

"You and I have been framed. You are apparently overseas after having sold your entire portfolio at full price, right before the crash. As did I, allegedly. No one can reach either of us by phone. They have footage of each of us doing things we never actually did. I have now *officially* been fired, having sold all my shares. I have no voice with the company anymore. This was prepared months ago, and enacted yesterday before closing bell. My broker is a witness."

She sat down. "*What?*" Her face was confused. "I've sent at *least* a dozen emails, and not one person has answered a call or text." She shouted.

An icy chill trickled down my neck. Our phones had been hacked. It was the only logical explanation.

We had been hacked by the Brothers Grimm, which was impossible. They couldn't have had the sophistication to... "They outsourced it. It's the only logical explanation. They must have a crew of hackers working on this. Setting up the dominos for yesterday. Then they flicked it while we were fighting in the streets. Which explains why Jacob was absent. He was flicking the domino." I growled.

Gunnar snarled.

Alucard hissed.

And the *women*. Well, let me just say that one should never hear the sounds that ripped out of their throats. It hit me like a primal chorus of mama bears roaring.

The women were pissed. And no one messed with angry women. It was almost enough to give me a smile. Instead, I motioned everyone closer. "Alright. Our timetable has accelerated. We act *now*."

I idly realized that my engagement plans might have to be delayed. Which would mean I was going to lose my deposit. Maybe I could squeeze in a dinner at home instead. I realized now more than ever that I needed to ask this woman to marry me. Before it was too late.

The doorbell rang and we all looked at each other thoughtfully before racing towards the entrance. Dean stood before the door, scowling through the wood. "I'm not letting them in." He stated flatly. Then he turned on a heel and walked away.

My breathing slowed. The Grimms couldn't be here already.

I slowly leaned closer to the door and peered through. Three shady characters stood under the *Porte Cochère*, out of the sunlight, and I was suddenly shoved out of the way as Alucard let out a piercing hiss through his fangs. He flung open the door and his fingers abruptly elongated to lethal claws.

"What are you doing here?" He demanded of the people outside.

The closest figure leaned away from the door, almost looking as if he had been caught with his hand in the cookie jar. Then I realized how easy of a target I had made myself by peering through the keyhole. This son of a bitch had been ready to kill me through the wood. He smiled knowingly at me and then shrugged as if to say, *it's what I do.*

One of the others spoke. "We should ask the same of you... *Master*." They wore long coats with hoods pulled up around their faces.

"It is not your place to question *me*." Alucard warned.

The figures nodded as one, but the first figure continued. "The St. Louis Coven was murdered by this wizard," he pointed a claw at me, "and we hear you were to avenge them. Then we find you here. With him." His eyes flashed red. "So why is he breathing?"

The other two murmured their agreement.

Alucard swallowed as if eating something particularly vile before speaking. As he spoke, I understood why. He was being forced to comply with my demands from the *Dueling Grounds*, and to likely lose the support of his people. "I challenged Master Temple to a duel. I won. I killed him." One of the figures began to growl in protest, not pleased at the apparent mockery. Alucard held up his claw. "I swear it on my power. As does he." He pointed at me.

"Um. Yeah. What he said."

They stared at me.

Alucard turned a pained expression on me. "Perhaps you could elaborate that a bit. Prove your word." He offered, voice tight with frustration and embarrassment at my weak assistance.

"I swear it on my power that Alucard killed me." A slightly foreign – yet familiar – weight settled on my shoulders as I bound my new power to my words. I knew the vampires could feel it. "I used powers at my control to come back from the dead. I did this in order to prove to Alucard that we face a common enemy." They stared in disbelief. "And also, because I preferred not to die." I added drily. "Alucard avenged his people, as per your code, and now here we are."

The first vampire took a threatening step closer but Alucard was suddenly there.

"You expect me to believe this nonsense, *Master*?"

Alucard shook his head. "You felt his oath. I have nothing further to add. Other than to say that killing Master Temple, and seeing him come back from the grave altered my... perspective on the Grimm's contract."

The vampires turned to each other, staring at each other without speaking. Then I realized that they were likely conversing *mentally*. Creepy. The first figure broke away to address Alucard. "One does not break a contract with the Grimms lightly." He stated in warning. "You know the consequences of such an act."

Alucard nodded. "Not if we can beat them." He studied each face. "And after killing Nate here, only to see him come back, I have a good feeling about our chances."

The vampire stared at Alucard. "*Our...*" he repeated in disbelief. "Already you speak as his ally."

Alucard shrugged, and finally nodded.

"We cannot abide by this. I don't truly understand what happened here, but you can count on us holding our contract with the Grimms. The world must see that the vampires are no easy meat, and that attacks on them are met with extreme prejudice." Alucard's shoulders sagged ever so slightly. "Some would say that you are under his thrall."

"One does not enthrall a master vampire. A master vampire enthralls *others*."

The vampire merely shrugged. "We shall discuss this further. On the battlefield."

I cleared my throat. "By any chance, did you three trash my car last night?"

They stared at me as if witnessing a particularly slow-witted idiot declaring, "Chocolate ice cream! Trucks! Baseball!" I took their stares as a *no*.

And with a seemingly snide rustle of fabric, the vampires were simply gone.

Alucard turned to me, eyes pained. "Well, that could have gone better."

I patted him on the back. "You get used to it."

And I closed the door, mentally moving another chess piece to the Grimms side of the playing board.

30

I angrily shoved the new phone into my coat pocket. No answer. Which wasn't possible. Othello *always* answered. Thanks to the software we used to communicate – which was un-hackable according to her, and I believed it – she would have received the call and, unless she was dying, would have answered. This was my third phone call to her, which meant that I should have already received a response of some kind. Even a text saying, *on a date now, will call back in a minute.*

We had an agreement. I called. She answered or returned my call immediately.

Period.

But she hadn't.

Which made me all sorts of nervous. She had notifications set up on me, so anything on the Internet that involved *any* reference to my name would have instantly alerted her. And I would have received a call. Especially after the bombshell airing on the news right now. This had to be all over the Internet. Even with a new phone number, she would have been able to reach me.

But she hadn't.

As if in response to my thoughts, my phone suddenly vibrated and I jumped to answer, ready to unload in both anger and fear at my old fling, Othello, the internationally known – if only by an alias and an almost unflappable reputation – hacker. I needed her to fix this mess. Find out how it had happened and work with Turner to clear my – and Ashley's – name.

"Where are you?" A familiar voice spat.

But it wasn't Othello.

It was *Arrogant Prickface*, Jafar. I almost lost my bananas, succumbing to the full mental breakdown that had been growing in the back of my mind.

I managed to keep my tone dry, barely. "Oh, are you calling to offer your assistance to the situation I told you about? Because I never received the call that you promised."

"There will be no help," he snarled in pure rage. "Now, *where are you?*"

"Well, that's a shame. I'm at home, sipping a hot cocoa. Why?" I had expected this call, but the timing couldn't have been worse. I had known they wouldn't help, but I had expected a call telling me so. The car continued to move towards our destination, slush loudly smacking the undercarriage as Jafar replied, and his voice practically dripped with hatred. Gunnar's head leaned closer to me as he drove.

"Have you been here in the last twenty-four hours?" His voice was actually shaking he was so angry.

I laughed. "*What?* Did I happen to hop on a flight to *Egypt?* Are you kidding me? After you so bravely declined to help me by not calling me back? You guys aren't exactly on my Christmas card list. You know, for people who supposedly help others, you guys have a pretty strong track record of not showing up when the world is going to hell. Fucking pansies. If you recall, I'm also not one of you any longer, so get to your point." I didn't need to feign indignation. I also didn't have time to waste gabbing.

"I know your schemes, Temple. We refuse to help you out of a personal scuffle you no doubt brought upon yourself, and you retaliate by throwing a tantrum."

I kept my tone frosty, "I'm sure I don't know what you're talking about. If you need an alibi, I have a dozen. Things have gotten even *busier* for me since last we spoke." I paused significantly. "Know anything about that?"

"I already told you, *no*. Don't change the topic."

"Yeah, well. Funny thing about lying cowards is that I have trust issues with believing what they say when their lips move."

He grumbled in warning. "Your time is coming, Temple. I can only hope that I get to witness it."

"Get in line."

"Consider this fair warning," he snarled.

I hung up.

The car coasted to a stop. Gunnar and Indie remained silent. Ashley had decided to physically visit Temple Industries this morning, escorted by a very grim looking Mallory, who had received an earful and more from Gunnar about keeping her safe... or else. I had tried calling her a few times in the last hour but had heard no response, which also got under my skin. Mallory hadn't answered his phone either. Which made me angrier. I knew they were busy putting out fires, but now wasn't a good time to be ignoring their phones.

I kicked open the car door and approached the seedy bar, not waiting for my companions. I carefully pocketed the phone and stood in front of the entrance, staring at it angrily, a faint blue mist throbbing over my sight in tune with my heartbeat.

Then I blew the fucking door off its hinges.

I heard Gunnar grunt in surprise, jumping to shield Indie with his body. He hadn't needed to. I had made sure all the shrapnel went *inside* the building.

I strode into the dim bar to find two men sitting at a wooden table, calm as you please. The wooden door was leaning precariously against the bar, and then it crashed to the floor. The two men paid it no attention, staring at my silhouette in the doorway instead.

Achilles' skin was a burnished bronze, despite the season. The Greek Hero rippled with muscle, and was hauntingly handsome, golden hair tied back into a man bun, scalp buzzed on the sides. Like one of those CrossFit or UFC people. Death, one of the Four Horsemen of the Apocalypse, sat beside him, looking unimpressed. His skin was the exact opposite of Achilles, pale as fresh snow, or a skeleton, and he wore a heavy leather coat that hung to his knees. His gaze drifted to Indie, staring very intently, not speaking.

"Heard from Othello lately?" I asked him, pulling his attention from Indie. He frowned and shook his head, eyes distant at the question. He and Othello had shared a moment a few months back. I wasn't sure if they were an item or not, but figured it didn't hurt to ask. And he had been eyeing Indie too intently for my tastes. Jealousy?

Nah...

"Fine." I growled in frustration. I turned to Achilles. "Time to spill, Myrmidon," I demanded, pulling up a chair. I held a hand over my shoulder, signaling my friends. "Sit over there." I pointed at an empty table off to the side. "Rip his throat out if I so much as frown," I told Gunnar, pointing at the men.

"You haven't stopped frowning for days though," he answered.

"If my frown grows... *frownier* then." I turned to address the two legends before me. Then called back out over my shoulder. "The tan one. *His* throat, if I wasn't clear. I haven't yet decided about the pasty one." I heard Gunnar grunt his acknowledgment.

Achilles laughed. And Death peeled his stare from Indie to me. Any other time I would have rocked back on my heels at the intensity of the glare. Not today.

"Balls. You've got them in spades," Achilles chuckled.

I nodded. "My balls have nothing to do with this. Or with spades, for that matter." Indie coughed, unsuccessfully hiding a laugh.

"You think I'm scared of your wolf?" He asked incredulously, leaning back in his chair.

"No. You should be scared of *me*. He's just the cannon fodder." I leaned forward, glad Gunnar or Indie hadn't made a surprised sound at my callous words. "I don't care how badass you are. Or how many Trojans you killed. That was a long time ago. This is now." I growled. "I can obliterate you with a thought," I snapped my fingers. I turned to Death. "Just ask pasty here."

Death leaned back contemplating, and then he gave Achilles a single nod.

"If I give you the time to have a thought, that would matter," Achilles answered softly, voice tight with a controlled fury at my blatant disrespect. I didn't care. I would go all out, right here, right now, even though I was severely outclassed. Achilles was allegedly a demigod, and a legendary fighter to boot. I wasn't even confident that my magic could harm the son of Zeus, if that's what he really was. But I was already on borrowed time anyway. I just didn't have the patience to be scared, what with the Grimms breathing down my back and all. I could die here toeing off with Achilles or die later at Jacob's hand. It was really just about timing at this point.

"Your ball. Talk. You sent me into a trap. Was there even a girl?"

Achilles watched me, and then finally shook his head. I took a deep, barely restrained breath, almost letting loose right then. "Why?" I asked, voice like an executioner's axe.

"Let me be clear. This isn't me submitting. I am not afraid of you, Maker or not." I shrugged, unconcerned with his precious ego. "You will pay for this offense, but to be fair, I understand your position." I wagged my fingers, not hiding my impatience for him to get to his point. His glare hardened. "I got a tip that your place was going to be robbed. The place no one should know about. Only reason I thought to tell you was that it was underneath that comic book shop you own, and wizards are notorious for hiding their stuff in obvious places. It only made sense that if there was a robbery going down beneath your store, it was likely to steal your stuff. I couldn't interfere openly, so…" he held out a palm as if that explained everything.

I grunted. "Bookstore. Not comic book store."

He rolled his eyes. "You also sell comics there, right?" He grinned darkly. I squinted back and nodded.

"Let's pretend I'm not going to kill you right now. We can talk hypothetically. What if I told you that the Brothers Grimm are back to add me to their trophy collection, and that the supernatural community has been acting… odd lately. Strangely. Out of character."

"I would say that it took you long enough to catch on."

"You knew about the Grimms?" I all but shouted.

He chuckled. "Who didn't?" He watched my eyes, face stretching into a smile. "No. Tell me you're not that blind," he finally said, my apparent ignorance too impossible to believe. Then he began to laugh, whipping out a scarred fist to slap Death on the shoulder in amusement. Despite Achilles being incredibly strong, and possibly a demigod, Death didn't budge.

Not even a little.

"I've had a lot on my plate lately," I grumbled. Achilles' laughter slowly died away.

"Let's put the pissing contest on hold," his eyes hardened as he spoke, and I saw his shoulders flex beneath his tee. "Until later." I nodded at the unspoken threat. "Talk."

I nodded agreement. And then I told him about the werewolves and vampires. About the books. About the attack after the Board meeting. Alucard. Kingston – to which his face grew instantly closed off. The attack at Alistair's old house, the Armory, my meeting with Jacob. And Temple Industries tanking. I took a breath, and noticed that a glass of water now sat before me. I blinked. I hadn't seen a bartender. I met Death's gaze, and he shrugged with a wry smile. I drank the water.

"I don't believe in coincidences," Achilles finally replied, words heavy with undertones.

I agreed. "Maybe you could bring a few of your pals to join me when I meet up with them again." A flickering candle of hope wavered inside my soul.

Achilles' return glare snuffed it out, and then proceeded to dump a bucket of water over the wick. "No. You broke my door." He folded his arms. I blinked back.

"Fine. I'll buy you a new one."

"I doubt your cash position will be the same in the near future. But that's not the point. You *disrespected* me." The air grew brittle and my shoulders tightened instinctively, remembering the memory Pandora had once showed me. Of Achilles battling Hector to the death outside the gates of Troy. The tension slowly faded and he sighed. "Also, I can play no part in this battle. Against the rules."

I opened my mouth to ask what he was talking about, but Death cleared his throat, and shook his head a single time, warning me.

"But I am interested to hear how you plan to defeat them," Achilles said, drinking from a glass of water that suddenly sat before him. *What the hell?* Where were the drinks coming from?

I withdrew one of the Grimm's amulets from my coat, and *boy oh boy* did the two legends before me suddenly look interested. "Is that..." I nodded. "But that means you *killed* one," Death stated in disbelief, glancing at Indie again. I was getting sick and tired of his wandering eyes. I snapped my fingers and he turned my way, looking surprised.

"Eyes over here. I'm territorial."

He smiled, holding up his hands in mock surrender. Achilles reached out for the amulet and I handed it to him after a second's hesitation. I had another. I didn't need two. I also didn't find a need to tell them I had killed two. I tapped the screen on my watch while they fidgeted with the amulet. The screen blinked to life, showing a live feed of the car parked just outside the door. My drone rested on the roof above the bar. I wasn't about to make things easier for the Grimms by being caught by surprise.

Achilles noticed the view and began to growl. "Relax. It's a drone. On your roof. I didn't secretly install permanent surveillance on your bar." I didn't add that I had *thought* about doing just that.

All was clear on my screen.

The two legends began murmuring to each other softly, holding the amulet up to the light and inspecting it from all angles. My phone rang.

My hands dove into my pocket to answer it.

"Hello?"

"Master Temple. This is Joe with Candy Cakes." A pause, waiting for me to acknowledge. I said nothing.

"Yes, well, I'm not sure how to say this, but... several of our bakers called in sick and... well, we won't be able to meet your deadline." He stammered, sounding terrified.

A calm, quiet rage replaced my smoldering fight or flight anger, and it felt deadlier to me. Less restrained and more eager to be used. I needed that cake. Tonight. No matter what it cost. I needed at least *one thing* to go my way. "You must be mistaken.

Must have forgotten who I am. What I can do. Sure you want it to play out like this?" I spoke, voice dry as dust.

"Um, I don't think..."

"Exactly. *You. Don't. Think.*" I enunciated. The line grew silent. "You will have it ready at the contracted time, and I will come pick it up, as we agreed. Or... I foresee a rough year for you."

I carefully watched my words, all too aware that Indie sat only a few paces away.

"I'm sure that won't be possible. My boss was quite insistent." Then he threw in a doozy, and my vision practically wobbled. "Temple Industries is throwing a party of some kind, and have ordered a dozen specially designed cakes that we absolutely cannot refuse."

"You do realize who owns Temple Industries, you halfwit," I growled in disbelief.

"Yes, well... that would be the Board of Directors... not... not *you*," his voice was almost a whisper at the end.

"I will *destroy* you," I began to hyperventilate. "I'll burn–" Gunnar was suddenly beside me. He deftly reached over and grabbed the phone, terminating the call before I could say anything more. He handed it back to me, eyes wary of the manic look no doubt dancing in my eyes. *Burn it all*, a small voice teased in my ears. I squashed it quickly, taking a deep, calming breath.

"Might want to dial it back a bit. He's just doing his job." He placed a meaty hand on my shoulder, anchoring me back to reality.

I leaned forward, whispering so softly that I could barely even hear my own voice. "It was the baker. He can't make the cake! I need at least one freaking thing to go right, goddamnit!" Gunnar blinked back, looking amazed.

"You're still planning on..." He bit his tongue. I nodded.

"Now I'll have to get back to *Chateau Falco* and make my own." I sighed in resignation, realizing I had a better chance of sneaking up on a Grimm to pee on his leg than I did at making strawberry shortcake. I would have to make our go-to yellow cake with chocolate frosting. "There *will* be a cake, by seven hells!" I whispered violently.

"Do we really have time for that?" He asked softly.

I nodded. "That's really the only thing that matters to me. I want her to know that... in case... well..." He nodded sadly, understanding. "I'm probably going to need Dean's help. And yours. I need you to babysit her for me."

Gunnar's shoulders sagged. "I'm watching Ashley. I guess I can watch both. You doing it tonight?" I nodded. He sighed, gripped my shoulder as he stared deep into my eyes. "You're a good man, Nate. I'd say yes." His eyes twinkled in amusement.

I laughed. "Say yes to what?" Indie asked, sidling closer. "What's going on? Who did you just threaten?" She asked nervously, eyes assessing us, Gunnar's hand still gripping my shoulder. "Was it *them*?"

I opened my mouth, and then realized what it must have sounded like. "Kind of. An associate." I turned back to Achilles and Death. The Rider was watching Achilles fumble with the amulet. He set it down on the table and took a drink of his water, eyes peering over the rim of his glass, directly at me.

"I think it's time we leave." I snatched up the amulet, tucking it away inside my coat. I noted Death eyeing the amulet as I did so, looking thoughtful.

Achilles stood, so did Death. "We'll walk you out," he said under his breath.

I walked out the door, back into the cold. I began to turn around to say farewell and apologize when a fist latched onto my shoulder and I was suddenly sailing through the air, my ears whistling before my body slammed into the brick wall of the bar. I realized Achilles was holding me pinned against the stone, breathing heavily.

"Just so you understand. If you survive this mess, you and I are going to have a chat. A nice, long, *pointed* chat." His words were concise, clipped, and dripping with malice.

I used my power to sharply, but carefully pinch his Achilles tendon through his boots.

He yelped instinctively, dropping me as he darted back, fists up, ready to send an Olympian-sized fist at my delicate nose. I held up my hands. "I'm always up for a talk. But I don't take kindly to attacks when my back is turned." Achilles' face was red, heaving at the minor insult and obvious display of his only weakness. He was a hair away from Hulking out on me. "You want to talk? I love talks. To my face. Not as I'm walking out of a building. Your building. After we shared drinks with each other." My voice was low, dark, and imposing. Achilles eyes tightened, understanding, and looking slightly mollified at his action's lack of honor. One didn't attack a person they had just shared drinks with in their own place of business. Their *home*. "Just know. Next time you pull a stunt like that, Olympian or not, I will throw down without restraint. I'm awfully curious to see what a Maker can do when he really cuts loose." I was almost getting tired of using that threat. But the look in his eyes altered my opinion.

Perhaps I would use it a few more times.

Achilles took a step forward. I held up a hand. "Admit it. You sent me on a suicide mission. I survived, and came back pissed, as would anyone. I shouldn't have broken your door... but you shouldn't have tried to pull one over on me like that, good intentions or not." His shoulders sagged, and I happened to look over his shoulder for a millisecond. I stopped breathing for a second. A line of men stood on the opposite side of the street, watching us. They looked familiar. I began to growl, and Achilles whirled, knuckles cracking as he realized he had had his back to a gang of unsavory-looking individuals.

31

Then I realized who and what they were as Gunnar began to growl.

Werewolves.

And my heart skipped a beat as I realized *another* thing.

They held Ashley, bound and gagged, in a rough grip. She had a burlap sack over her head, but I remembered her outfit. Gunnar took a step closer, sniffing the air with a growl of recognition.

My mind scrambled. If they had Ashley, what had happened to Mallory? He had been the one watching her back. My anger was there instantly like a comforting blanket.

Well, I had needed to talk with these clowns anyway. One of them likely had my ring.

A thought struck me.

"Hey, Hector." I said jovially. "How was your vacation to Greece?" The lead werewolf looked back at me, losing a bit of his composure.

"Who..." he began to respond, but Achilles interrupted him.

"*What*... what did you say his name was, Temple?" Achilles asked in a very soft, very deadly voice. I grinned.

Achilles *really* hated that name...

"Hector, meet Achilles. Achilles, this is Hector." I turned to Death with a slight frown. "I'm sensing Déjà vu. Anyone else?" Indie's eyes were wide. "Huh. Damndest thing," I shrugged, turning back to the werewolves. Gunnar's claws were now out, and Achilles had effectively pinned the werewolves into place with only his eyes. A flicker of power danced over his frame, and I momentarily saw a much scarier Achilles. Dressed all in leather armor, clutching a shield in his left fist, a spear in his right, and a plumed,

Greek helmet over his dome, like those ones in *300*. Then it winked out and street-clothes-clad Achilles again stood in his place.

I shivered a bit.

"My name is *not* Hector." The lead werewolf answered, staring warily at Achilles. The Olympian grunted, nodding as his shoulders relaxed, obviously recognizing him on closer inspection. He shot a disapproving frown my way before approaching Death. I recognized the lead werewolf, the Alpha of the local pack, from a few months back when I had met him at this very bar. It had ended in an epic bar fight where Tory had laid him out cold. Then later I had a little skirmish with him and his pack. A rogue Justice of the Academy had framed me as his mate's murderer. I had cleared it up, sending the Alpha the Justice's head, but we weren't friends.

Things were about to get hairy. They weren't here to chat. And I was pretty sure they weren't here to sell me a magazine subscription. Especially not with Ashley under guard.

Indie was holding Gunnar's sleeve, tugging with all her might as she tried to keep him on our side of the street. He was panting – arms rippling with tension under his coat, fighting the urge to shift and destroy the threat before us. The threat holding his fiancé captive. I noticed Death leaning against the brick wall, smoking a clove cigarette, and watching the scene unfold. His eyes darted to Indie twice, eyes contemplating. I didn't like his obvious interest in Indie. Not at all. I just didn't have time to discuss it with him.

I returned my gaze to the wolves. There had to be a dozen of them. I hid my gulp. I saw a sign dangling in the wind in the background behind them, and burst out laughing.

The lead wolf glared at me, pulling his eyes from Gunnar. "What exactly do you find humorous about this situation, Temple?"

I pointed at the sign, immediately folding over as I clutched my stomach. "It's... I can't..." The werewolf turned to look. *Johnson's Dog Park* was just legible under the snow that had accumulated on the sign. He turned back, eyes flashing, not finding anything funny about the sign. Indie stifled a laugh and Achilles chuckled before stepping up beside Death to lean against the brick wall. Death offered him a clove cigarette but Achilles waved him away. They murmured softly to each other for a second, and then turned to watch the result of the showdown.

I sighed. Obviously, we were on our own. I idly wondered about Death's allusion to Achilles not being allowed to interact in a battle with the Grimms, and thought maybe the same restraint held him back here.

I mimed rolling up my sleeves as I shot a pointed glance at Death, flicking my head to Indie. Death nodded, called out to Indie, and patted the wall beside him and Achilles. If that wasn't safe, I didn't know what was. Indie shot a look at me, pained and concerned, but complied.

I turned back to the werewolves, stepping up beside Gunnar. "Looks like we've got all the tools necessary for a brawl, gents. Any last words?" I smiled. No one spoke.

"Okay. That works. Before I murder all of you, I think you should apologize for trashing my car last night after the sewer fiasco." The leader smiled, but didn't speak, the reaction basically admitting the crime. I continued. "Fine, I'll beat it out of you." They collectively growled at my threat, but I ignored them. "Also, one of your pups has something that belongs to me. Guy built like a rhino fancies himself a pickpocket." I didn't spot him in the crowd, but several of the wolves snickered. Death chuckled from behind me. "If you give it up now, I might not kill all of you," I shrugged out of my coat, folded it, and placed it on the hood of our car. "As slowly." I continued, turning back to them.

The lead werewolf scowled. "Before you get your panties in a twist, you should listen. The car was a warning. For him." He pointed at Gunnar. "We're not here for you. And your pack of spirit wolves is not permitted to participate." He added, shooting me a thoughtful scowl. I managed to hide my smile, remembering my second meeting with this guy. I had led him to believe I had a pack of spirit wolves at my beck and call. Apparently, he still believed it. He turned back to Gunnar. "You killed a member of my pack. I challenge you to a formal duel."

I blinked.

Well.

There was *that*.

I raised my hand. No one acknowledged me. "Hey, I might have killed one too, furface. Who do I get to fight?" I hopped up and down on my feet as if warming up. "I'm all dressed up with nowhere to go over here. And Rhino still has my property."

"*Rhino* survived. He's recovering. You're safe from repercussion." His eyes were cold, merciless. "For now. So. Please. Stop. Running. Your. Mouth." I stared back, incredulous. This was a first for me. I would have to let it play out and get my ring later. I turned to Death. He patted the wall beside him. Indie nodded furiously. My gaze tightened. But I couldn't leave Gunnar to fight the Alpha alone. What if he cheated and the pack swarmed him? But I thought about that. The leader had challenged him to a formal duel. Which meant...

If Gunnar won, he would become the de facto leader of the St. Louis werewolf pack. At least this guy's pack anyway. I wasn't sure how many packs were in St. Louis. It also meant that it would be a one-on-one fight. The pack wouldn't tolerate cheating. Even to help their Alpha. They valued strength and honor amongst themselves. Now, fighting another flavor of Freak was a different story. The victory was all that mattered there, but between wolves? Honor. Integrity. Duty. Responsibility.

So, Gunnar might actually have a chance here. I mean, Tory had taken this clown on. Then again, that had been a bar fight, not a no-holds-barred tooth and claw fight to the death. Still, Gunnar was downright scary when necessary.

And they had taken his girl, essentially forcing him to fight rather than submit. In their eyes, Gunnar had killed a packmate, and something needed to be done about it. Kind of like me having to fight Alucard yesterday.

Abruptly, a wolf stepped forward and spoke, eyes on the ground in submission. "Is this truly necessary, Ben? Surely you two can come to some sort of agreement. There are vampires in town, Grimms," he shivered slightly. "Other enemies. This will do nothing but divide us. I–"

The Alpha, Ben, turned on a heel and slammed a fist into the werewolf's stomach, causing him to fold to his knees. The Alpha stared down at him for a few silent seconds. "Anyone else?" No one moved. "I'm doing this to defend our pack's honor. It isn't a topic of conversation," he added. The injured werewolf took a shaky breath and climbed to his feet, keeping his eyes down, but I swear I saw murder in them. Perhaps this duel wouldn't be as professional as I hoped. The man nodded, and stepped back.

I kind of agreed with him. We were wasting time here, but I knew I would be outvoted. Even by Gunnar. Especially by Achilles, who was practically drooling at the chance to watch lethal violence outside the comfort of his own bar.

The Alpha turned back to Gunnar. "Your bitch hasn't been harmed. The one *protecting* her," he smiled wickedly, "was roughed up a bit, but should be fine." I almost used magic to kill him, duel be damned. They had beat up Mallory. That scarred old mystery man on my payroll with a murky past and a bit of secret magic. But *how?* I didn't have any time to think about it.

The Alpha waved a hand at Ashley. "She is merely... motivation. I've heard of your... distaste for battle when you didn't think it necessary." He glanced at Ashley. "She's here to convince you that this duel is indeed *necessary.*"

He stepped forward, claws suddenly appearing where his hands had been. Now, Gunnar had a rune on his wrist that allowed him to partially shift at will. The only other kind of werewolf that could partially shift at will was someone either very, *very* experienced with his or her power, or an Alpha. The primary purpose of Gunnar's rune was to prevent him from shifting into a raving psychopath on the full moon. All wolves were victim to this. Which was why they tended to live in packs, conveniently going on a long weekend trip or taking a few days off to go 'hunting,' far from civilization during these periods.

Alphas, on the other hand, were pretty similar to Gunnar. Not victim to the cycles of the moon, but *masters* of their beast.

Now that I thought about it, Gunnar's rune basically gave him the same abilities as an Alpha. He just didn't have a pack. But depending on the outcome of this fight, that story might change pretty damn quickly. And without a real job – having been fired from the FBI – maybe my friend *needed* a pack.

Then again, Ashley was a Regular, and would likely not be welcome in a pack. Possibly even seen as a sign of weakness or disrespect if their Alpha preferred a Regular to another wolf.

This political game was quite complicated now that I thought about it.

I turned to shoot Gunnar a questioning look. He shifted his eyes momentarily and gave me a single nod. I maintained eye contact, giving him a chance to change his mind. Instead, he shrugged out of his coat, set it on the hood, and tossed my coat back without actually looking at me. He stood in jeans and a white tee, muscles still rippling beneath as his beast struggled to break free.

I finally trotted over towards Indie. I glanced at Achilles. "Shouldn't we be worried about anyone seeing this?" I pointed at the windows.

Achilles shrugged. "No one looks. No one talks. Why do you think I chose this spot for my bar?" I didn't buy it, and my gaze must have relayed that. "It's mostly freaks in this part of town. They'll watch and leave it alone. The Regulars won't even notice. Not really a soft neighborhood, if you know what I mean. People usually duck and hide at the first sign of fighting in the streets." His gaze drifted to the wolves, conversation apparently over.

Indie smiled in relief that I wouldn't be fighting, and then shoved me lightly, noticing my distant gaze as my friend squared off with Ben.

"This really bothers you, doesn't it?"

I paused, thinking. "It's just... this is the first time the world hasn't revolved around me. It disproves years of scientific data. Did I not mock him enough?" She shook her head with a bemused sigh and we watched two werewolves get ready to claw the shit out of each other.

32

The pack formed a loose circle around the two wolves, blocking them from escape. I used the lull in action to shoot off a quick text to Mallory.

Stay strong, buddy. We have Ashley.

I pocketed my phone to watch the fight. This was to the death.

Speaking of which...

I shoved the Horseman out of my way to get between him and Indie. Or at least I tried to. Death didn't budge. Then he looked at me, gripped my coat with one idle hand, shook me a bit without any apparent effort, and then shoved me playfully, a gleam in his eyes as I stumbled a step, my coat caught in his fist. *Then* he let go. I glared back.

Freaking Horsemen.

He finally stepped aside, giving me enough room to take my space. I did so with a mutter, and turned to watch the fight. This was a new experience for me. Not being in the center of the chaos left me alone with my thoughts.

Standing next to the girl I wanted to propose to tonight. But I had no cake. And no ring. At least I still had the reservation at the French restaurant. As long as the Grimms didn't choose tonight to request my presence. If so, I would just have to propose in the car on the way to my death. Jacob had said something that had made me feel slightly better. They didn't typically harm mortals. Still, Indie had shot Wilhelm. I turned off those thoughts violently before they could escalate. Instead, I began running through scenarios, making sure I had enough time before our reservation to bake a freaking cake.

This was ridiculous.

I would have to get Indie out of my hair. I needed at least one part of my plan to go as scheduled. I had set everything up so meticulously and it had immediately begun to unravel with the arrival of the Grimms. I needed Gunnar to keep her busy while I *Cake Boss*'d my way through this proposal. Then I sobered a bit.

If, that is, Gunnar *won*.

My gaze swiveled to the impromptu fighting ring, and I settled back to watch. Two Alphas battling was rare. At least to non-werewolves.

Gunnar respectfully dipped his head, arms clad in fur with inch-long, razor sharp, inky black claws. They looked like they belonged on a freaking Polar Bear. Since he hadn't fully shifted they merely looked like an exceptionally muscular human's arm covered in fur, with wicked claws. It wasn't until he completed the shift that the joints popped into those more resembling a *steroid-infused* Arctic Wolf, the muscle mass shifting to the back, haunches, and jaws. But I idly began to wonder exactly *how* the transformation worked, on a magical or scientific level.

Then the leader snarled, and the fight was on.

Gunnar lurched back, barely dodging a fatal swipe of claws. It seemed this fight would take place in semi-shifted form, better able to take advantage of the mental cunning of humans rather than only the bloodlust of the wolf. A merging of the two forms. Perhaps that was normal. Not just showing brute strength but your humanity as well. I shrugged, wincing a bit as Gunnar dodged another swipe. He hadn't yet attacked. And it seemed he only moved enough to barely evade each attack. No more. No less.

I found myself fidgeting, impotent to help my friend.

As I watched, I noted that Gunnar was toying with him. After each failed attack, he took a step closer to his opponent, unapologetically, and unimpressed – face blank. Almost akin to how one allowed a toddler to throw his tantrum, and wear himself out, while the adult calmly watched, not feeding into the insanity. I grinned.

The Alpha lunged again, a flurry of claws. But Gunnar simply wasn't there. Then the leader fell over, grunting. Gunnar stood off to the side, holding a clawed hand in the air. It glistened crimson in the falling snow. He showed it to the pack, and then turned back to the Alpha, a questioning look on his face, "I'm finished if you are. Neither of us needs die today. I did what I had to do. I don't want to lead your pack. I was protecting a friend. That is all. Your wolves weren't following your orders. They stated you didn't want Temple harmed. But your soldiers didn't comply. They attacked anyway. After sufficient warning." He said softly, confidently, but voice still thick with menace. An olive branch. A chance to let both of them survive.

The Alpha roared in fury, pure carnage in his feral eyes. Gunnar sighed, and met him with a bodily impact I could practically feel. The wolves in the circle grew suddenly tense, fidgeting lightly from foot to foot. I heard a thickening crunch, and then watched as Gunnar lifted the Alpha over his head and tossed him into the nearby building. The werewolf slammed into the wall, brick crumbling slightly as his body crashed to the ground. He instantly climbed to his feet on shaky legs, eyes dancing with rage. Gunnar wasn't even breathing hard.

I told myself this was due to him sparring against a wizard on an almost daily basis for the past decade or so. But I was pretty sure I was witnessing Gunnar cut loose, and he was simply that *good*. It was pretty inspiring to see. After all, I had assumed he was just like every other wolf, that all of them were pretty much as skilled as he.

Apparently not.

I saw Ashley flinching with each sound, no doubt fearing that each was Gunnar receiving his last wound. With the bag over her head, she had no idea. "Go, Gunnar!" I cheered, clapping delightedly. More for Ashley's benefit than anything else. But it was like a shot of adrenaline for the Alpha. He launched himself at Gunnar in a blur and I heard a pained grunt from my friend, followed by a menacing growl. I darted forward without thinking, shoving wolves aside with a growl, eager to see what had happened. The wall of fidgety wolves had blocked whatever just happened. I heard a few responding snarls.

"Not interfering, just can't see, mutt. Calm down." This comment did not make me any new friends, but they did move out of my way, giving me ample space to see. Some weren't even paying attention, eyes locked on the two figures standing in the circle.

I blinked as the tableau unfolded, my stomach tightening in revulsion.

The Alpha had his claws *inside* Gunnar's chest.

Gunnar merely stared back at the Alpha, gripping the offending wrist with one hand, and the other held safely out to the side. The Alpha's arms quivered with tension, but didn't move, unable to overpower my friend. "Last... Chance." Gunnar managed with a grunt. The Alpha went into a frenzy, redoubling his efforts. His claws sunk a bit deeper into Gunnar's chest before my friend sighed in both pain and resignation. "Sorry about this, brother."

And his arms began to flex, slowly forcing the claws from his chest like a sluggish glacier. The Alpha was drooling, spittle bursting from his lips as he fought to sink his claws to the hilt.

But he couldn't.

A millimeter at a time, Gunnar slowly forced the claws from his chest, and the wound instantly began to soak his gleaming white undershirt, the fabric straining, popping, and ripping along the seams as Gunnar continued to force the Alpha's claws away. And he never broke eye contact.

In fact, his face never changed at all. No strain. No pain. No mercy.

The Alpha's face was incredulous as he was slowly but surely forced from a killing strike. Gunnar held him there, arms to the side, leaned forward, and snarled, "No one touches my girl." Then, faster than I could register, he was inside the Alpha's claws, right up against his chest. His massive hands clutched both sides of the Alpha's face. Time seemed to slow as I saw the Alpha's eyes widen in alarm, arms beginning to swing down towards Gunnar in a last second attempt to kill his opponent. Gunnar twisted his mighty arms with a roar that set off car alarms, and a *snap, crackle, pop* ended the duel like a tiny drum solo. The once Alpha dropped like a sack of bricks to the snow.

Gunnar's chest heaved as he glared down at the body. Then he tore off his blood-soaked tee, rounded on the surrounding pack in a menacing snarl, and slammed the bloodied rag to the earth.

Then he began to move, purposefully, confidently, and menacingly, towards the werewolf holding Ashley. The werewolf flinched, his allies suddenly a few feet back, leaving him to face the new Alpha alone, and clutching the woman Gunnar loved as a hostage. His hands instantly released her, and then hastily tore off the hood, taking an urgent step backwards. "Just doing as commanded, Alpha," he offered weakly.

Gunnar's chest heaved, still leaking blood from five very distinct and impossibly deep wounds over his right pectoral muscle. The muscle just might have been thick enough to protect him.

He didn't take his murderous gaze from the wolf to look at Ashley, merely extended a thick, blood-smeared claw out to her. Her eyes blinked for a few seconds, assessing her surroundings in confusion. She latched onto the claw, not even caring that it wasn't a human hand. Her eyes tightened as they settled on his wounds. Her hand fell into the pads of his paw, his claws instantly sheathing upon contact, and her skin disappeared from view as white, bloody fur swamped her dainty fingers. Her red hair stood out like a flame against his white furred arms, emphasizing the blood on the ground. "I'm fine." She murmured softly to him.

Gunnar's lips pulled back, and still, he didn't remove his gaze from the now-terrified werewolf guard. He silently moved Ashley behind him, shoulders rippling like giant slabs of steak had been tucked beneath the skin. The fur stopped mid bicep, transitioning to his human form at the shoulder, to ultimately reveal a hairy blonde chest. His six-pack had a six-pack.

Listen, you get it. Gunnar was *ripped*, folks. Like, really jacked and stuff.

His voice was gravel. "Listen up. I don't care if you believe me or not. I killed your Alpha because he asked for it, and wouldn't back down despite numerous chances to do so. I don't tolerate anyone harming, or threatening to harm, my friends. At all." He waited for a response. They nodded as one. Gunnar seemed to accept this. "Same as down in the sewers. I gave them a chance to back down. They didn't. I did what I had to do. I don't like it any more than you do, but it had to be done. And I always do what has to be done. Understood?" Again, they nodded, staring at him in awe. I idly wondered where the wolf leading the others in the sewer was. Blackbeard. And how I could find this Rhino wolf to get my ring back.

No one even glanced at the Alpha on the ground. Well, the werewolf who had been punched in the stomach seemed to smile momentarily before nodding along with the rest of the pack.

Gunnar's pack.

Huh. This could come in handy.

"Hey, Gunnar. This might just help us out a bit. We could really use some backup when the Grimms come back. And now you have your own army."

Gunnar was already shaking his head to himself. He turned to face me, and then pointed a finger at the brick wall.

Achilles burst out laughing. Several of the wolves smiled proudly.

I blinked, and studying the ice-cold nature of his glacier blue eyes, I wisely turned back to do as requested. I wasn't obeying an order. I was complying with a friend's wish. Seriously.

It wasn't like his Gladiator impersonation had rattled me a bit. I mean, I had known Gunnar his entire life and had never seen him like this. And I had put him in some pretty dire situations. But this time was different. I hadn't seen him resonate so much authority as he did now. It was almost as if his victory had granted him the ability to lead. And apparently, the pack seemed to agree. On the other hand, I realized him sending me away was a *very* wise move. His new pack would see him ordering a non-werewolf away rather than letting a friend jump into inner circle politics. This would earn their trust. Or solidify it. Just because he was my friend didn't mean I had any say whatsoever in future decisions regarding his pack.

I found myself smiling as I neared Indie. She was watching me incredulously. Achilles studied me, and nodded, realizing I had understood the underscored benefit of complying with Gunnar, even though I was used to ordering him around. Kind of.

In the *Nate and Gunnar* show, I was used to figuratively *wearing the pants*.

But in the *Gunnar and pack* show, I wasn't even a *consideration*.

I felt silently proud of my friend.

Then I saw a werewolf lunge at Gunnar's unsuspecting back, a wicked knife clutched in his fist as he closed in on Gunnar's neck. I didn't even have time to shout a warning.

33

The werewolf's dagger was less than a foot away when he was suddenly tackled to the ground with enough force to give the attacker whiplash. Then his head cracked solidly into the fender of the jeep on the street and his body went limp. The defending werewolf snatched the dagger from his unconscious hands, and slammed it hilt deep into the attacker's eye socket with a grunt. The body flinched and went still. It was the werewolf from the sewers. Blackbeard.

Gunnar had whirled, claws out, eyes dancing from body to body, realizing he was surrounded. Then he noticed the two wolves on the ground. One stood with a bloody knife clutched in his fist. It was the werewolf who had attempted to stop the duel.

Blackbeard sat in a pool of blood.

You could have heard a pin drop.

The savior tossed the knife to the ground and dipped his head in respect. Gunnar grunted, nodding after a few seconds as he stared down at the familiar werewolf who had started the whole mess down in the sewer. "Thanks," he finally said to his hero.

The man shrugged. "You're our Alpha now. It's kind of my job. I'm your Geri."

Gunnar was silent for a moment. I grunted, recognizing the word. "The *Ravenous*?" I translated the Norse word. "One of Odin's two wolves." I elaborated. The wolves simply stared at me with surprise, except for Gunnar. He continued to stare at the werewolf. "We'll see about that," he replied softly.

The man cocked his head for a moment, but didn't say anything.

Gunnar elaborated. "I'm not fit to lead a pack. I guess you could say that I led a *pack* of FBI Agents once. And failed spectacularly. You deserve better."

The crowd lit up in an uproar, arguing over each other in variations of, "he has to lead us!"

Geri studied the crowd until they grew silent. Then he spoke to Gunnar as if no one else was present. "They are right. Our pack will devolve into civil war as we fight for a new leader. This saves bloodshed. That is the point of the Alpha Duel," he said gently.

Gunnar grunted again. I knew after being fired from the FBI he had a sore spot in the confidence department. Surely this would nip that in the bud. Geri seemed to notice this. "It is for the best."

Gunnar finally let out a snarl. "How can I trust you? *Any* of you?" He rounded on the pack, eyes glittering like shards of ice. "Despite what you were commanded to do, none should have obeyed. Kidnapping a Regular," he said in disgust. "If I ever hear of anyone doing that again," he pointed a thumb back at the dead body, "You will beg for such a clean end. Regulars, all of them, are off limits." His tone dripped menace.

The pack dropped their heads, looking ashamed.

I recalled the drone to me, where it calmly latched onto my wrist, folding neatly into my watch. Death and Achilles watched the tiny technology thoughtfully, saying nothing. My phone rang.

I answered it, confident that Gunnar could handle himself for a few minutes without me. "Yes," I answered apprehensively, recognizing the number.

"Get the fuck over here! We're being overwhelmed. Operation White Knight has been compromised!" An explosion roared in the background, and gunshots almost made the words unintelligible. Then the line went dead.

Shit. Raego was under attack.

34

I let out a sharp whistle and Gunnar spun, claws out, scanning the streets. His eyes latched onto me. "Time to roll," I yelled. "Raego's under attack!"

Gunnar stared back in shock. He was aware of my secret mission, *Operation White Knight*, and the implications of Raego being under attack were not lost on him. He practically picked up Ashley and raced towards the car. Indie never strayed from my side. I rested my hand on the door and paused, realizing there was no way we could take the girls with us. It had sounded like a war zone. And I didn't even know who the attackers were, or whom they had with them. I assumed the Grimms, but given the alliances they had made so far, I could be facing off against a gang of Trolls or vampires or wizards or possibly more wolves. My stomach roiled a little at that. What difference were Gunnar and I going to make? My gaze slowly followed Gunnar and Ashley as they raced towards us. The pack remained behind, looking agitated, but Geri was hot on Gunnar's heels, eyes hungry with anticipation of a scrap.

Gunnar had made new friends. Perhaps...

He met my eyes, and knowing me too well, he shook his head resolutely. "No," he said simply, under his breath.

I scowled. "But–"

"I can't bring them into that five minutes after I killed their leader."

"But–"

"The Maker is right. We want to be there by your side. Our old Alpha was boring. Fresh leadership and a fresh fight go hand in hand," Geri spoke respectfully. Gunnar grumbled under his breath, not pleased.

"What are you doing over here?" He demanded in a low voice.

"Where you go, I follow. It is my duty to be a voice of reason for you and to watch your back," he answered simply. "Despite the consequences, as you saw earlier." He added drily, reminding us of the previous Alpha decking him for speaking out.

I smiled smugly to myself, careful not to let Gunnar see. "We can't take the girls." They, of course objected to this with much yelling and shirt grabbing. Well, arm grabbing in Gunnar's case. "You didn't hear what it sounded like. A war zone." I added. "We can't help Raego and watch over you two at the same time."

Death approached on silent feet. "I can take Indie to safety," he offered softly, dangling his motorcycle keys. Gunnar whirled.

"Take both of them," he demanded.

Death studied him with a squint. "I ride a *motorcycle*, not a *minivan*."

Geri spoke up. "Let the pack watch over Ashley." Gunnar's fists flexed as he slowly rounded on his second in command.

"You honestly believe I can trust you five minutes after you *kidnapped* her?"

Geri lifted a hand in understanding. "But was she harmed?"

Gunnar's eyes danced dangerously. Geri held up his hands. "I'm not excusing our actions. But we *were* commanded to do a distasteful thing, which we could not disobey, and we did it professionally and gently. How many kidnappers act in such a way?" He added. I didn't like it, but he had a point. Then he drove that point home with a sledgehammer that made me angry for not remembering sooner. "Don't forget that we quite literally cannot disobey you. Only an Alpha potential could do such a thing, and I assure you none of us are up to the task." He glanced back at the two dead bodies. "I just killed the only other threat to your authority. If you missed it."

"What about you?" I asked.

He chuckled. "As a Geri, I have immense power over other wolves, but I forfeit any rights to Alpha-ship in exchange." He turned to Gunnar, eyes contemplating. "You do not know of this?" He asked.

Gunnar grunted. "I've never been much of a team player. Never really spent any length of time around other wolves," he admitted.

Geri nodded. "Understandable. Then our intelligence was sound, but it is still surprising to hear that you know nothing of our rules. I'll tell you true. None of the wolves are strong enough to challenge your order. None are strong enough to challenge your authority. All must obey. Even your Geri. *Especially* your Geri. You can trust us with your lives. And we are quite good as a pack," he promised darkly.

Gunnar sized up Geri for a few long moments. "But you were, by extension, working for the Grimms. My enemies," he added in a soft, iron-weighted voice that sent his words crashing to the ground like a crystal vase.

Geri winced, nodding. "True. By command of our Alpha." He waggled his fingers, as if having already explained that part. "We had no choice. By killing him, you severed our... agreement with the vile creatures. We are all a bit... perturbed about having to work for them, even though it was indirectly. It didn't sit well. To be honest, we were all quite glad our Alpha challenged you. Having heard the stories of you two, we thought we finally stood a chance of gaining new leadership. Perhaps the wolves you slew in the sewers were in fact martyrs, knowing that their deaths would cause a chain of events that would lead to the only other Alpha potential in town going claw-to-claw with our Alpha..." His words trailed off, and the sewer exchange grew a little more significant in my mind. Geri looked thoughtful, as if only just now thinking of the possibility himself.

And as I thought about it... It kind of made sense. After all, they had stated their orders not to *kill* me, but their orders hadn't said anything about *hurting* me. Fine distinction, but enough to skate by.

Ashley spoke up. "Gunnar." He turned to her, the same hard-eyed gaze fixating on her until she took an instinctive step back. "They were completely respectful about my kidnapping. Honestly. Not a hair on my head was harmed. If you must fight, I won't hold you back. It terrifies me, but I know you have no choice. Let them take me to safety. The Chateau or wherever you want." She paused. "Just murder some Grimms for me and get back home." She winked.

Gunnar smiled for the first time in a long time. Still looking concerned, but resolved to the situation. The clock was ticking. I could Shadow Walk us there in a blink, as long as I knew the girls were safe. He nodded, so I turned to Indie and Death.

"You will keep her safe. No matter what. Stick by her side until I call you. No deviations. Keep her away from Chateau Falco. The Grimms know the place like it's their own home. I would feel safer knowing she was at one of your safe-houses or whatever biker bar you call home." I remembered the one time I had tried summoning him, when I had been transported to some kind of seedy bar. It was a safe bet that not many knew of the place. Death nodded, looking oddly intense as his gaze shifted to Indie. I remembered his thoughtful looks at her over the past hour and felt a little anxiety creep up my neck. What had his interest been all about? Had he sensed something in my future? Or maybe things were simply serious enough for even him to be concerned.

I mean, to be honest, I didn't really have an idea what he could do. I had seen him get mildly perturbed before, and it had been downright terrifying, but I had never seen him really let loose. I would need to look into the Horsemen a bit further. If I survived this. But I trusted him enough to keep Indie safe. I couldn't imagine anyone attempting to pull one over on one of the Four Horsemen.

I kept my smile in check. If all went well at Raego's I could run home to bake my cake without fear of Indie catching me. I had effectively just hired a babysitter.

"You ready, Alpha?" I grinned.

He nodded back and extended his still bloody arm. I noticed that his chest wasn't bleeding so much anymore, thanks to his slow but steady healing factor. I blew a kiss at Indie. Then thought, *what the hell?*

I blew a kiss at Geri and Ashley.

But not Death.

One does not simply blow a kiss at Death.

Then instead of taking Gunnar's arm and Shadow Walking, I tried out the gateway spell I had recently learned. A ring of blue fire erupted before me, tall enough for Gunnar and I to walk through. Death flinched, but the sound on the other side of the gateway immediately drew everyone's attention. Raego's mansion rose up in the distance, but a war plagued the lawn. We dove through and I pulled it closed before Geri or anyone else decided they wanted to join the fight.

I immediately screamed as the world erupted in chaos; screams, dragon fire, machine guns, and the steady roar of *magic* shattered the air, causing my ears to instantly pop. Gunnar instantly shifted to full on giant werewolf. "Welcome to the jungle," I yelled for encouragement, whips of liquid fire and ice snapping to existence as extensions of my fists.

35

Two smaller than usual red dragons abruptly swooped down over our heads, missing me by inches, and snatching a stealthy Justice whom I hadn't noticed sneaking up behind me. Misha's daughters had come out to play. I smiled, but it didn't last long as the image finally struck my rational mind.

Justices.

That meant we weren't fighting Grimms. And I wasn't sure my allies knew the distinction. I had to stop this. We didn't stand a chance if any Justices were murdered. The entire Academy would come back and destroy everyone. These were supposedly the *good* guys.

I summoned up my new power, growing a large quivering orb of it to coalesce in front of me. I wasn't even sure what I was doing, merely trying to duplicate spells I had used as a wizard. Once complete, I shouted into the rippling orb at the top of my lungs.

My new powers might have beefed it up too much.

"PEACE! Everyone stop! Jafar! Show yourself!"

A nearby tree branch exploded as if struck by lightning, as the amplified sound of my voice struck it. Then the force hammered into the house, shattering the windows.

Absolutely everyone halted. The dragons in the skies pumped their powerful wings to land lightly atop the mansion before us. Everyone turned to me, looking startled.

Well, the Justices, of course, stared back at me with their stupid silver masks that replicated various forms of human emotion. *Sadness, laughter, rage, compassion,* and *hatred*, even an *expressionless* mask stared back at me. But I told myself that deep down they were scared.

Yeah.

One person touched his mask and it disintegrated, revealing Jafar. He approached me slowly, wary of a trap. I honestly had none. My only interest in this was everyone walking away more or less satisfied. Or dissatisfied on an equal level. Which I had heard was the sign of a good compromise.

"What is the meaning of this, Temple?" His voice dripped raw fury.

"What we have here is a grievous misunderstanding, obviously. You show up, for whatever reason, attacking the Dragon Lord's home. What did you expect?"

"We got a distress call." My inner psyche screamed in panic to kill him before he spoke any further, or discovered the truth. But I calmed it. Barely.

"What kind of distress call would warrant an entire battalion of Justices?" I asked carefully. "There must be some kind of mistake."

"Distress calls are not typically made by mistake."

"Well, *who* called you? I'd like to hire them. I call you guys all the time and you never answer. This person sounds handy if they can get you guys to actually show up and do your jobs," I muttered.

He flexed his fists. "I'm not at liberty to specify. A friend. That's all you need to know." He answered cryptically.

"Well, how am I supposed to help you with knowledge like that? You want me to prove that this imaginary person is not here?" I waited a breath. "See the problem?"

He merely stared back. "Someone important to... *me* called for my help." His eyes grew thoughtful. "I think."

"We're down to *I think*, now?" I asked in astonishment.

"The transmission was garbled."

I let him stew on that. "You rounded up an army to attack the Dragon Lord's home? For a *maybe*? Really subtle, Jafar. It's amazing we... *you* people haven't caused a war recently. But then again, that could change," I muttered, shaking my head, trying to intimidate him with consequences and get them out of here. I saw Raego approaching in human form. He nodded discreetly. I took a gamble.

"Scan the area. If your *friend* is here, you should be able to sense them. And before you get too pushy, I know you could break through any wards preventing it." I rolled my eyes. "So, you get to do it from here. Outside."

"What if she's been moved?"

She, I thought to myself, suddenly wary about exactly what Raego had done for *Operation White Knight*. "I'm the only other person with the ability to Shadow Walk, and I only just arrived." I muttered. "Had a disagreement with the local werewolf pack that made me fashionably late. Speaking of which, he's the new Alpha." I pointed at Gunnar, now back in his nude human form after having briefly shifted to wolf and back again.

He was also still liberally painted with blood from his fight.

He didn't smile or move in any way whatsoever other than to stare down the Justice.

Jafar blinked. I smiled. "All that blood almost lets you imagine the screams of the recently deceased Alpha. Cool." I let that sink in for a second or two. "So now you have managed to piss off the only Maker in existence, the Dragon Lord, and the local Alpha of the St. Louis werewolf pack. Because you *think* you got a distress call from a... *friend*. And our response was to defend Raego's home, and then offer you the opportunity to take a look around." I added softly. "We could have done much worse. Still could." I added as an afterthought.

Jafar growled, snapping a finger at a nearby Justice. He instantly shook his head. "No sign of her, Sir."

Jafar's face purpled. "This isn't over." He promised. "I *know* you're involved."

I shrugged. "You keep saying that. One of these days I'll actually believe you." He took a threatening step closer and I smiled, holding out my arms in invitation. "You're not the scariest thing I've run across today, Jafar. Not even close."

Jafar watched me, and without another word, every single Justice Shadow Walked out of existence, leaving us all alone.

"Well, that could have gone worse. Thanks, Nate. Gunnar." Raego muttered.

"I'm just glad no one died." Blank faces stared back at me. "No one *died*, right?"

Raego shook his head, but still didn't look pleased. "They attacked my house, Nate." He growled. "For something I did for you."

"I know." I admitted, not hiding my guilt. "How did it happen?" I asked carefully.

"She's clever." He muttered under his breath. I stared at him, not pleased to hear his defensive answer. "It's been resolved. Tory's on duty now." He promised, pointing at the house, where apparently Tory was now watching over *Operation White Knight*.

I nodded. "Good." We didn't have time to get in a tussle with the Justices. Not yet.

"Let's part ways. I'll get back with you soon. Right now, I have a few things to take care of. I need to go bake a cake."

"A cake." Raego answered flatly.

"Yes. After dinner, things are likely to get... *interesting*." He didn't even respond.

I turned away, Gunnar stepping up beside me. I spotted Misha speaking sternly with her two daughters, now in human form. They looked efficiently chastised. Then Misha let out a dazzling smile and wrapped them up in a group hug, murmuring to their heads. Her eyes shone with pride despite her previous scolding. I smiled, preparing to open a gateway out of there when a dragon let out a ferocious roar behind me. I whirled to see every single dragon staring at the tree line.

Which was suddenly filled with ten Grimms.

Without a word, they began to advance.

Then advance faster. I glanced at Gunnar with a groan, but he had already shifted back to wolf form and was growling territorially. Raego's face drained. "You were saying something about after dinner, Nate?"

"How god damn hard can it be to bake a cake?" I muttered. Raego frowned at me, no doubt wondering if I was still sane. I didn't elaborate. "Let's do this." And we were suddenly running to meet the Grimms as the dragons on the roof launched into the sky with peals of dinosaur-volume cries.

It really was too bad that the Justices had already fled. We really could have used some cannon fodder about now, and them being attacked might have even forced them to team up with me.

But, it just wasn't meant to be.

And just maybe, neither was my survival.

Or my cake.

36

I heard a piercing howl as Gunnar entered the fray.

I tipped an imaginary hat at Misha – now a giant red dragon – as she swooped down to incinerate a lone Grimm sneaking up to the side of the house. His scream was most satisfying.

Then a black blur slammed into her side, hammering her onto the roof of the mansion just over my shoulder. Tile and concrete exploded from the force of the impact, and a billow of fire erupted like someone had let loose the largest Molotov cocktail ever.

But I didn't have time to watch.

The air abruptly throbbed, sending me, and all my people to their knees. The air felt thick, soupy, and then it was abruptly gone and everyone climbed back to his or her feet, glancing back at me like it was my fault. I shrugged, and my whips of controlled fire and ice manifested as extensions of my hands – and my mind.

I wasn't sure how many dragons were currently in town, but I did know that Raego's operation was global, so it was likely he had only a skeleton force here. Which wouldn't be good for our odds. Then again, these punks could duplicate anything we could do, so it was almost counter-productive to have too many Freaks available.

Grimms exploded into new forms – dragons, a few werewolves, and a true berserker of a man. The last plucked up a tree with one hand, tore it out of the ground like a weed, and threw it at the house where it shattered the front door.

Body met body in heavy impacts, claws, and scales.

It was chaos.

Bolts of fire filled the sky. But not just fire. Lightning, Ice, Earth, and metal spears of gleaming silver. All weapons of the various Skittles bag of dragons fighting to defend their territory. Each color of dragon had a unique specialty and flavor of power.

Lightning shattered from one blue dragon's snout, lancing another green dragon from the sky. As if on cue, several more dazzling bolts of lightning shot from two other blue dragons, aimed at the first. The Grimms were learning quickly, I just didn't know friend from foe. Two quicksilver spears tagged the two dragons in the wings, sending them down to the earth with roars like thunder. I noticed that the two downed dragons seemed to have large chains around their throats, and then it hit me.

The amulets.

I yelled into the night, using my power to amplify my voice. "Look for the amulets! Means they are a Grimm, and not a friendly." Obviously, no one answered me. And it wouldn't have mattered if they had.

A pair of humans suddenly appeared out of thin air on either side of me, lunging to grapple me to the ground. But they stepped in direct striking range of my whips. I twirled the whips in a circle, managing to catch one of them by the ankle and send him flying towards the second floor of the house with major freezer burn. He screamed, and his foot dropped a few paces away as the body sailed away. A dragon with a chain around his neck swooped down at the last second to catch him, helping him land gently. One Grimm waited for him, suddenly kneeling over the body. Fucking Ichabod, bringing them back to life.

But I was too busy at the moment to do anything about him.

The remaining Grimm duplicated my whips of power, sending one at my face. I blocked it with my own. A coruscation of sparks exploded on impact, blinding both of us. I reacted first, even as I sensed his other fiery whip crackling towards my face. I imagined a pulsing body of water – vaguely humanoid and flipping off the Grimm where I had been standing as I simultaneously Shadow Walked thirty yards away. I reappeared facing the Grimm's side from a safe distance. His face was morphed into a triumphant smile, too caught up in the moment to realize it was just a doppelganger made of water. His napalm whip – a duplicate of my own raced towards the watery figure, pulsating with several thousand degrees of heat. See, it was more like lava than fire, and since he was copying me blindly, he hadn't thought of cause and effect.

I smiled.

The tip of his whip connected with the water, instantly superheating it.

The explosion of steam instantly melted the front of his body and sent him sailing off into the lawn, a smoking, screaming, wet mess to cool in a snow bank. I didn't gloat, but turned to see Ichabod no longer kneeling over the body of the first attacker, but rather helping him to his feet instead.

I snarled.

I had to take him out or it didn't matter how many we took down.

A werewolf launched out from behind a bush, hungrily snapping his jaws at my neck. Two hundred pounds of white fur – previously camouflaged by the snow – hit him like a truck, eliciting a yelp of pain. Gunnar bobbed his head at me, and the two wolves squared off. I began to run towards Ichabod, intent on murdering him quickly.

War raged around me, but I tuned it out, focusing on the man who stood silently watching me with sad, resolute eyes. Which gave me pause, slowing my steps. He looked over my shoulder, a mere flicker of his eyes.

So quickly that no one else would have even noticed it unless they were staring at him like I had been. I whirled, rolling to the side as a set of jaws clamped down on the earth where I had been standing. A werewolf I hadn't seen yelped as he struck his snout into the earth and flipped ass over teakettle. A dozen more stood behind him, growling and snapping at each other, forming a loose line.

And...

Son of a bitch.

They had Ashley.

Gunnar tore the throat out of his opponent, and was just standing to full height again, nose sniffing the air, suddenly interested in something familiar. His glacier-like eyes discovered the werewolves, and Ashley, and he stilled for a heartbeat. Then he was suddenly by my side, pacing back and forth, snapping, snarling, whining, and quivering with barely restrained impatience, hackles lifted until they made him look twice his normal size. His lips were pulled back in a permanent curl, but he obviously noticed the same thing I did.

There was nothing we could do. One move on our part and Ashley died.

Because werewolves gripped each of her arms in powerful jaws.

A shaggy, wood-colored wolf stepped forward, chain gleaming around his throat.

He watched us, intelligent eyes waiting for us to make a move. We didn't. My eyes instantly darted to a fierce battle just beyond the werewolves.

Two small red dragons were battling on the ground with another larger red silver dragon wearing the familiar Amulet.

Misha's daughters.

The two adolescent dragons fought like a pack, harrowing, and darting in for quick slashes and bites while the other distracted the silver monstrosity, dodging his silver spray of molten metal. But after a few seconds, the silver dragon suddenly spun and latched onto the leg of one of the smaller red dragons, and I heard a scream the likes of which I never wanted to hear again.

Their mother, Misha, diving to rescue her babies.

The giant red comet of motherly rage slammed into the silver dragon, pummeling it into the ground and knocking her offspring free from the attacker's jaws. The wounded dragonling limped to safety, her sister jumping in front of her to keep her safe as two more blue dragons dove to help the silver dragon battle Misha.

The two assailants roared, and let loose bolts of lightning directly into Misha's side. Her body arced up with a million volts of power and I managed to meet her eyes.

My.

Heart.

Stopped.

For an eternity, we stared at each other, neither able to move or look away. I saw a single tear, and then her eyes closed, and her body crashed to the ground, twitching. The Grimm dragons launched themselves up into the air, unconcerned with the dragonlings now racing to their mother's side.

Raego appeared like a shadowy nightmare, ripping off the head of one of the attacking dragons, and swallowing it in a single gulp. His wings snapped out and the air imploded in a shockwave of force that catapulted the other dragon into the side of the house. Purple motes rained down around him as he dove to Misha and her daughters.

But he was too late.

I turned to the werewolf before me. My body quivered with the power threatening to overwhelm me in order to destroy everything within a hundred paces. The werewolf seemed to smile, if that was possible, but he didn't turn to look at Raego. The Dragon Lord landed on the ground with the thud of a monstrous tree falling to the earth, and the sudden roar that split the night told me everything I needed to know.

Misha was gone.

A female's scream seemed to shatter my eardrums and a Grimm went sailing over my head, slamming into a rock fountain, shattering it, and landing on his face, skidding across a good fifty paces of snow-packed earth before striking a tree. The tree trunk cracked, and began to fall.

It was a big tree.

Which told me Tory had just discovered her lover's fate. And was no doubt destroying anything between her and Misha's body.

What was left of my heart blew away to ashes.

And the bastard before me laughed as he suddenly shifted to his human form.

I saw the terror in Ashley's face instantly replaced with disgusted horror, as Tory's scream dawned on her. Her eyes instantly welled up, but she didn't move. Gunnar let out a howl of mourning to match Raego's, and he crouched, ready to lunge at the werewolves before us. I laid out a hand on his back and he flinched, but remained by my side.

Geri stood before us, a dark grin on his face. "Surprise..."

Gunnar's muscles locked under my arm, preparing to pounce. I squeezed. Hard. He yelped instinctively, which caused me to release my grip. I must have unknowingly used magic to squeeze him hard enough to actually hurt him. But he got the point.

"What is the meaning of this, Geri?" The werewolf merely stared at me, and then Gunnar. He waved his hand, imploring Gunnar to shift back to his human form. Gunnar hesitated for only a second before complying. He stood from a crouch, *Bowflex* body tight and steaming from exertion.

And covered in yet more blood.

His face was as pitiless as a gravestone. "I will floss my teeth with your tendons. As you watch." Gunnar whispered in a tone that made me cringe.

I had never before heard him speak such words, or in such a tone.

Ashley let out a sob, and then a gasp as another werewolf snorted down the back of her neck in warning. Drool liberally dripped down her shoulder. Gunnar's icy gaze merely looked at them, but their shoulders sunk a bit.

"It's about time our Alpha had a true mate." Geri said absently. Everything happened at once. Geri snapped his fingers and Gunnar lunged, but he was too late. He struck an invisible wall and bounced back, shaking his head. The werewolves gripping Ashley hesitated. I knew this because I was staring at her, dumbfounded as to why I could suddenly not use my magic.

Then they bit down.

I heard bone crunch.

Ashley screamed.

Blood dribbled from the wolves' jaws.

Then they let her go, heads down as they backed off, tails between their legs. The two wolves' eyes were wet, as if they were crying. I frowned at that, still hammering against the invisible walls blocking me from my magic. I glanced to the side to find Ichabod staring at me and I scowled. God damn it.

Ashley kept right on screaming as the werewolf gene hit her. The next few days would tell if her body accepted it at all or if she was to die a slow, painful death. And even if she *survived* the change, whether or not she was strong enough to control her beast or if she was doomed to become a mindless thrall to the change, hungry only for blood, more beast than human. It was a fifty-fifty chance. Gunnar hammered into the wall again, knowing how futile it was. But doing it anyway. Again. And again.

And again.

I did the same.

The pack shifted uneasily behind Geri, looking torn. How was this even possible? Gunnar was their Alpha. This shouldn't have been possible. Not even counting Geri's word, which was worthless. I knew quite a bit about werewolves, thanks to my father studying them before helping Gunnar. What Geri had said rang true. This shouldn't have been possible.

Unless... the man Gunnar had killed hadn't been the Alpha.

But that was impossible. I had met him before. Met his pack. He was definitely the Alpha.

My mind raced, suddenly alarmed about Indie. She had been with Death, and I severely doubted anyone could have pulled one over on him. It was impossible.

But there was a lot of that going around.

"You are no wolf. You wouldn't be able to go against your alpha's command so easily." And I said the only thing that made sense. "Wilhelm." I growled.

"You got me." Then he shifted to a doppelganger of *me*. A perfect copy, and my blood froze. "Whoops, wrong one." He shifted to his true form, the man I had fought at Alistair's house. His eyes as black as midnight.

Everything fell into place. The man I had seen on video – me – quitting Temple

Industries, and sending it into a freefall had been Wilhelm. Voice, looks, mannerisms, and dress all perfect. The only answer I could come up with was that at some point in his life he had encountered a skinwalker of some kind – one of those shifters that could change into *any* form. They were rare. And dangerous.

And Wilhelm had killed one.

Which meant that his amulet let him appear as the Geri. He had begun a chain of events leading Gunnar to kill the Alpha, but Geri had been no wolf, so his words had been a lie. But how were the wolves not forced to follow Gunnar? And whom else had he managed to copy lately? Had he been one of my friends the entire time? Maybe even listening in on my plans? No wonder we had never stood a chance.

"You and I are going to have a talk. A long one. At least, it will feel like a long talk to you. Pain and torture does that to one's perception of time."

"Oh, I know all about time perception... and manipulation. How do you think we got here so... *fast*?" His eyes glittered with humor. "I froze time as soon as you left. It took a bit of effort, canvassing that large of a place, and of course, the Academy stepping in helped. Gave me a few more minutes to get everyone here. We had to go by car. I am not familiar with your disappearing act. Yet."

My vision was steadily, solidly blue. Darker than I had ever seen. Almost black. But I couldn't touch my power.

It had been Wilhelm impersonating me, destroying my company. My father's company. This man had destroyed every facet of my life. No doubt behind the theft of my ring, destroying my company, turning supernatural groups against me. And he had been doing it for months, apparently. My stock options had been negotiated months ago. By me, speaking to my broker in person. Even then, Wilhelm had been setting this up.

This world of dominos.

And the first tile had been flicked.

It boggled the mind. Talk about your long con.

Wilhelm was grinning at us. "Now that that is settled." He turned to face me. "I wouldn't want you to feel left out, Nate. Your woman is with my brother, Jacob as we speak. And we have the... *gift* your dragons were guarding. Talk about silver lining!" He grinned excitedly. "Meet us at sunrise to finish this. I'll give you the chance to at least watch your woman die. I'll make it convenient for everyone. *Chateau Falco*. We'll be needing to gain access to the Armory after our... chat."

Then he disappeared. As did all the other Grimms. The wolves remained. My power flooded back into me like a tsunami, sending me crashing to my knees. Then again, a gentle breeze could have done so at that point.

Indie was taken.

Ashley had been turned.

They had the books.

Operation White Knight had failed miserably.

And they wanted my Armory.

Gunnar was suddenly at Ashley's side, picking her body up as it convulsed. He yelled into the sky, and Tory's instant cry was a perfect complement, the sounds melding together in a damning harmony.

I fell face first into the snow, crying, my vision pulsing from red to blue. Then to black as I pounded my fist repeatedly into the snow.

37

I finally lifted my head. After another second, I managed to climb to my feet. Every single werewolf was on his knees, but only one spoke, softly, to Gunnar's retreating back as he carried Ashley in his bulging arms.

"If it means anything, they told us that since your woman was a Regular, they wouldn't kill her. Just turn her. If we hadn't complied they promised to force one of us to kill her instead. Not that it matters to you." Gunnar's shoulders stiffened, and Ashley let out a soft whimper of pain, very much alive, as if punctuating the werewolf's words. He carried on, voice heavy with both guilt and the burden of accepting full responsibility. "I have a daughter. Two years old. They... took her. They took all of our children." Several answering sobs and growls responded to this comment. The man continued on.

"They killed my son. I... they let me choose which child would live." A soft sob escaped his dry lips, and I saw his eyes wet with unshed tears, but he wasn't begging. He spoke clinically, not asking for forgiveness from Gunnar. Just stating the facts to his Alpha. "If you want to take my life, I submit myself to you, Alpha. Just... just look after my girl. She's innocent... Even though her father is a coward... The choice to act was mine and mine alone. Don't punish the pack for my actions. Punish *me... please.*" He never lifted his gaze, just turned so that his throat was available for a quick strike. Now he was begging.

But not for his own life. He was begging to sacrifice his life for the pack.

Gunnar's chest heaved and the pack was silent.

My friend finally shook his head and continued on his way.

The man let out a breath, whether in regret or relief, I couldn't tell. I don't think anyone else could tell either. The pack looked at each other thoughtfully, guiltily, and then they began to round up, murmuring softly as they helped the pleading werewolf to his feet. He called out to Gunnar one last time. "Call on us when you need warm bodies ready to die. We owe at least *that* to you."

"You owe me nothing, because to me, you *are* nothing," Gunnar growled over his shoulder, almost too softly to be heard. But we were talking about werewolves here. Supernatural hearing. They caught it and the emotion under the surface. And their shoulders sagged even further, a pitiful sight. Then they nodded once to Gunnar and began to lope off in pairs.

I snagged the pleading werewolf's arm. He looked down at my hand, and then very calmly at my face. I wisely let go.

"What happened?" I asked softly.

"Our Alpha was forced to obey the Grimms after they took our offspring and women. Then Gunnar killed one of us in the sewers and sent our Alpha into a rage. He wanted a duel. Anything to show the pack that he wasn't defenseless. We didn't know that Geri was a Grimm. We had no idea. Not sure what happened to the real Geri. Probably dead somewhere." His eyes grew distant.

"That doesn't explain you guys here."

He nodded sadly. "When Gunnar refused to accept us, he left us without an Alpha. He didn't say the words. *You are mine.* The new Alpha has to say the words to the Geri. No one really thought about it until after you left. That's when Geri told us if we ever wanted to see our kids again we had to go with him. That's when we realized we had been played. But we couldn't do anything about it. Pack first. *Always* Pack first. And without an Alpha, our pack was our *family*, and the Grimms had them. We had no choice." He spat, not venomous with accusation, but with the fury of a man helplessly condemned.

I nodded, patted his shoulder, and spoke. "I'll talk with him. We will need you, despite what he said. Can you do that? As a favor? Without him saying the words?"

The man stared at me, and then shook his head. "Sorry, Master Temple. Pack first. Which means our families." His shoulders sagged. A thought crossed his features. "How come your spirit wolves didn't fight today?" I somehow managed a smile, and decided to be honest in hopes that it might gain both his respect and possibly his help.

"They never existed. It was just magic. And some cool boots." I admitted, smiling wider at his incredulous expression.

"Magic. And cool boots," he repeated, staring at me, a small smile slowly creeping over his face. "I can't believe that all this time we feared your invisible pack of wolves." He shook his head with a weak laugh. "Well played." I nodded in acknowledgment.

"Change anything?" I asked, voice hopeful.

He shook his head sadly. "Pack first." He recited. And then he loped away to rejoin his brethren. I couldn't blame him, but it sucked.

A nearby dragon watched to make sure the wolves left the property. I patted my pocket and frowned. One of the amulets was missing. When had *that* happened? I muttered a curse of frustration under my breath as I pulled out my cell phone, and dialed the only number in the world that mattered.

Death.

He answered on the second ring. "Is it finished?"

"Where is Indie?"

The line was silent for a moment, and then I heard a voice from Heaven. "Nate? Are you guys okay?" It was *her*. My heart seemed to shutter to a stop and then pick up double time.

"They didn't take you!"

"Um, no. What are you talking about?"

"The Grimms. Wilhelm. He said he had taken you."

"No, I don't really know where I am, but I'm with Death. He's reading a book," she paused. "*Through the Looking Glass*. Is everyone alright?"

I nodded, throat tight, then realized she couldn't see me. "Yes." I thought of Ashley. "More or less." Then I thought of Misha and Tory. "No. I guess we're not." Indie knew me well. She waited for me to speak rather than hammering me with questions. "Misha is gone." Indie gasped. "And Ashley was infected with the werewolf gene. We don't know how her body will react." I trailed off, and heard Indie let out a soft sob.

"I'll be right there. Death can get me there fast."

"Absolutely not." I snapped. For one thing, now more than ever, I realized how important my proposal was. I had to do it. Tonight. We had until tomorrow to confront the Grimms. And after that... well, I wasn't giving up, but odds seemed pretty likely I wasn't going to see the sun set. Perhaps I wouldn't propose, but I desperately needed Indie to know my intentions. But to do that, I needed to bake a cake first. With Dean's help, of course. Which meant that Indie needed to stay put.

After this fight, I didn't think I would have any problem encouraging everyone to recover in private for a few hours, to grieve, and prepare for tomorrow morning.

"The Grimms want you dead. They already kidnapped Ashley. Geri wasn't whom we thought, but was in fact, Wilhelm. He was also the reason Temple Industries folded. He can shapeshift into other people entirely. It was Wilhelm in front of the cameras announcing my resignation. It was Wilhelm impersonating Ashley to get on that flight. I'm going to make him pay in blood." I promised.

The voice on the other end went silent, not arguing. "How?" She asked softly. I began to answer, and then remembered how our unhackable phones had been hacked. And that anyone could be listening to us right now. Even with new phones, I wasn't taking any chances. The Grimms had known my every move so far. Time to change tactics.

"Somehow." I answered cryptically.

Indie got it. "When do I get to see you? When do we confront the Grimms? Why didn't they end it today?"

"They want the Armory. We have until tomorrow at sunrise. We meet at *Chateau Falco*."

"What about me?" She asked.

"You will prepare for a date. Tonight. I'm hungry."

"What! A dinner date? *Now*?"

"Pretty woman don't argue with man. Or man club pretty woman and drag her to cave," I grumbled in my best caveman voice.

"I'm open to that," she teased.

"Just get ready. Death can help if you need anything. He'll know where to take you. Hand the phone over to him?"

"I love you, Nate. See you at dinner, tiger." Her voice dripped promises that I wished I had time to explore.

"Yes?" Death answered. I told him where to take her and at what time. It would give me a few hours to bake the cake. Or cheat if I failed spectacularly, which wasn't out of the realm of possibility. He grunted acknowledgment. "And keep her safe. They already took Ashley from under our noses. Indie is my *everything*." I spoke harshly, remembering his wandering gaze earlier.

"I know. See you soon."

And he hung up. I glanced up to see I was entirely alone. Gunnar – carrying Ashley – and Tory – carrying Misha's now human corpse in her arms – entered the home, heads bowed. Raego approached me on silent feet, glancing here and there at the property to assess damage and verify that his dragons stood guard. He stepped up beside me, not speaking.

"I checked. They have your bargaining chip. Tory did her best to keep them away, but after Misha..." His eyes grew dangerous. "After that, well, she kind of lost it. That's when they took it." My shoulders sagged. *Operation White Knight*, my failsafe, had done failed. I couldn't blame Tory. This was on me. I shouldn't have left such a big responsibility to Raego and his crew. I shouldn't have let Raego out of my sight.

Dwelling on that wasn't going to solve the predicament though.

"We must rectify that. Or we're all dead." Raego merely arched a brow as if to say, *how is that any different than our current situation*? I grunted in response.

"Indie safe?" He asked. I nodded. "At least there's that." He muttered. "So... sunrise?"

"Yes."

"Good. I have a few things to say to these sons of bitches." His body rippled slightly, his dragon beast threatening to break free. I smiled sadly.

"Just make sure you speak loudly. I think they have hearing problems."

"Oh, I'll speak very loudly indeed." His eyes twinkled with malice.

"I need to run. Get everyone ready. I know this seems callous, but none of us stands a chance if we don't fight tomorrow. We must use our grief as armor. Or as a weapon." Raego nodded, eyes fiery. "*Chateau Falco* an hour before sunrise. I want to go over a few things before shit hits the fan."

He nodded. "We'll be there a few hours before sunrise then. Just to be sure they aren't setting up an ambush."

I grunted. "I really don't think they have any reason to do so. They already have almost everything they want. They just need my... *me* to show up." I changed my words. Raego studied me thoughtfully, but didn't press.

He extended his hand. I grasped it, squeezed hard, staring him in the eyes with a silent promise. "We'll make them pay for this, Raego. All of them."

He nodded, grinning expectantly. "Aye."

Then I made a gateway back to *Chateau Falco*, leaving my friends behind.

38

Once back in the comfort of my own home, I had made some cell phone calls. To Othello. Achilles. Tomas, the dragon hunter. Jeffries, the FBI Agent *slash* walking lie-detector.

No one answered.

Then I made a magical *call*. The Minotaur.

Nothing.

Which was probably for the best. At least for them. Then again, these people had been one-time allies and could have already been under threat of annihilation. Perhaps that was why they hadn't answered. Or, more likely, they had heard that I was persona non-grata and that any interaction with me would be bad for their health.

I hoped it was the latter.

Either way, it left us on our own. But we all had a vested interest in the Grimm problem.

People had died...

That hit me hard. It was essentially my fault. Putting myself at risk was one thing. I was willing to pay the price. But now my friends had paid the price. And my secret operation may have just made me the biggest threat to the Academy in recorded – and unrecorded – history.

I had been debating on whether or not to propose to Indie, but after the recent fight, and the deaths, I decided that timing be damned. I wanted her to know how I felt. She didn't have to *answer* me. But she *did* have to know how I felt. Some may call that cruel. Selfish.

So be it.

My death would hit her hard no matter whether I proposed or not, so I had made an executive decision that I wanted her to know my feelings. That we weren't just boyfriend and girlfriend.

We were *more*.

If that was only known for a few hours, so be it. I could carry it to my grave with a smile. A weight off my shoulders. No regrets.

Which meant I needed a baked good of some kind since the bakery had fallen through.

I stared at the mess that was now my kitchen. Egg shells, loose flour, and various other spills marred the counter. I was no baker. But it sure smelled good. I clutched the towel around my waist, my only garment as I was fresh from the shower, and strapped on the *Avengers Infinity Gauntlet* oven mitt Indie had gotten me as a small gift, knowing damn well I didn't cook.

Heh. I would show her...

The *Infinity Gauntlet* had almost given Thanos, the mad Titan, the power to overcome the Avengers.

Surely its power could help me bake a cake. I leaned down to the oven door, gazing inside to check on my masterpiece. The timer was almost up. I smiled to myself, lifting my *Infinity Glove* oven mitt into the air in a fist. "The world is mine!"

Which meant that I looked rather ridiculous when Dean entered the room and blinked at me, eyes widening, mouth opening to speak but no words coming to mind for a second. He wore neat slacks and a pressed shirt, impeccably tailored. He even wore a tie under his matching vest. The chain from a pocket watch glittered conspicuously.

He cleared his throat and tried again. "Does the Mad Titan need assistance baking his cake?" He was the King of Deadpan.

"Pfft. I already did the hard part. Icing it will be a cinch." I pondered that. "You do know how to ice a cake, right?" I asked, turning back to the oven and opening the door.

"Yes. I will return shortly with the icing. Need anything else while I'm out at the store?" I shook my head, reaching into the oven to clutch the cake and pull it out. "Okay. I will deliver the cake to the restaurant once finished." I grunted acknowledgment and heard the door close as he left.

I studied the cake with a proud whistle after setting it down on the counter. It needed to cool for a while, so I would go get ready while I waited. I went to the counter to pour myself a small glass of wine, needing to fortify my courage for the upcoming proposal.

Listen, I wasn't scared.

Per se...

More, I truly wanted this to be a momentous... moment. I wanted the gravity of my feelings to be expressed properly. I did better with winging these kinds of things rather than having a prepared speech. More heartfelt. Organic. Genuine.

Like Indie.

I was pouring the wine when I heard the door open. Likely Dean had forgotten something and had returned to grab it. I set down the bottle and turned to tease him. The towel dropped as I picked up the glass, exposing my danger zone. Before darting to pick it up in embarrassment, my eyes caught on the two figures standing in the doorway. And I stopped. They were smiling.

And neither of them was Dean.

Grimms.

They wore black leathers, looking like a cross between special ops gear and stealthy hunting garb. Like thieves in the night. It all looked new too; I could smell the freshly oiled leather. And here I was, all naked.

God damn it. I snatched up my towel. "Cold, Maker?" One asked in a honeyed drawl. His face was a cinderblock, complete with scars and a stubble blonde beard.

"Looks like it." The other answered. He was leaner, face drawn, and he wore a perfectly curled mustache. But he still looked tough. Just fashionably tough.

"What are you doing here? We have an appointment for tomorrow morning."

"Yes, about that." One, the beefier blonde one, answered.

Mustachio finished his sentence. *Tweedle Dumb* and *Tweedle Dumber*. "We wanted to talk to you about two of our brothers. It seems you accidentally killed them." He said. "Outside the hotel."

"No accident, I'm afraid."

"You should be. Afraid," he clarified. His hand twirled his mustache out of habit.

I kid you not.

I scowled. "Let me get this straight. You two clowns are here to get a little revenge on me for defending myself against two ill-prepared assassins who tried to punch my ticket the other day? Do you realize how idiotic that sounds?" I thought about setting my glass down, but wasn't sure if that would signal a reaction on their part. I took a controlled sip instead, trying to hide my nervousness. Being outnumbered was dicey. Being outnumbered and naked was worse. Especially in your own home. "Anyway, I spoke to Jacob and Wilhelm. They need me in one piece tomorrow morning. And he will probably need you two in one piece to be used as cannon fodder when I put an end to you guys for good. You know, take a few bullets for them so they can last a few seconds longer."

The beefier blonde shrugged. "We can leave you in one piece. One bloody and bruised piece, more or less functional." And he began to advance with slow heavy steps.

Unbelievable. Here I was, stark naked, still wearing the *Infinity Gauntlet* mitt, and a glass of wine in my hand, and these two chuckleheads wanted to scrap.

Fine. I'd had enough. I'd oblige.

I didn't even wait for the telltale pulse of blue to tint my vision. My power was now familiar to me, and I knew I could call it at will. Even though I wasn't as diverse in my use of it as I had been with my wizard power.

I launched a blast of air at the approaching Grimm.

But felt a familiar shield fall into place before I could strike.

Mustachio smiled, raising a finger to shake at me. "Ah, ah, ah. No power. Just a good old-fashioned ass whooping, Temple."

Well.

Two on one was never good odds.

So, I threw my wine glass at Mustachio. The glass shattered in his face, right in the eyes and his stupid mustache, causing him to roar in pain. The beefier Grimm yelled and began stomping towards me. I grabbed my towel and high tailed it out of the kitchen. I needed a weapon. These guys were strapped.

I tore through the hallways of Chateau Falco, trying to determine the closest weapon from the layout of the house in my mind. I hadn't had time to nab anything from the kitchen. The rapidly approaching footsteps told me I wouldn't have a chance at reaching any of the swords, guns, or axes in time. Then I had a thought. I veered abruptly to the right, racing through the dining room. I knocked over any piece of furniture within easy reach, lamps, chairs, tables, anything to slow them down. Then I hit the foyer, smiling at the sound of curses from the larger Grimm. At least the scrawnier, faster one was still plucking glass out of his mustache. I shivered at the imagined sensation of what was to come next, my fingers wrapping around the door handle leading outside. I threw myself through the door before I could think about it too much.

Icy cold hit my still damp hair and genitals like a knife. I pressed on, racing across the snow in bare feet, ignoring the stabs of pain from the gravel, and bolted straight towards the stable. I remembered the old rusty knife I had been meaning to fix sitting on the workbench.

The knife had surprised me by still holding an edge. It had once been a real specimen, long, full-tang, and bound with a sinister bone handle. An antique of some kind.

I tore through the door, which was luckily open, and sprinted for the workbench.

Or I tried to.

Something hanging just inside the doorway clipped me in the temple and I went sprawling, seeing stars. I heard heavily booted feet just outside the door as the beefy Grimm tried to close the gap. Having boots helped while running through snow. My feet were numb and no doubt bleeding from the gravel, and my head still spun woozily in the darkness of the stable. I lurched to my feet and stumbled to the workbench.

My hand closed around the hilt and I dove to the side, rolling to my feet quickly on the icy concrete as I anticipated the attack. A club slammed into the workbench a hairsbreadth away from clobbering me. I stood from my crouch with a manic grin. It was McBeefy Grimm. He took one look at my knife, smiled, and dropped his club. He withdrew a truly impressive knife from his belt, blade glittering in the filtered light coming through the windows. Luckily it was a wide-open space. Knife fights tended to require a lot of room.

I wrapped the towel around my left forearm – the one with the Infinity Gauntlet still covering my fist, and palmed the blade in the other hand. I felt naked.

Look, not just *literally*. I *was* naked in that department, which also wasn't good for a knife fight.

But naked without my *power*. I had grown used to having it, and knowing these punks were blocking me lent me a bit of paranoia. No backup. Just brawn against brawn.

And these guys knew brawn.

McBeefy approached on the balls of his elephant feet, surprisingly nimble, grinning as he shook his head at the ridiculous situation of getting into a knife fight in a garage with a nude, powerless wizard who was wearing an oven mitt and a towel for armor.

It would just make my victory more impressive.

Or my beating more embarrassing.

I lunged, swiping at his thigh like a snake. Mallory had taught me the ins and outs of knife fighting. I wasn't sure where he had learned it, but judging by his scarred forearms, he had practiced quite a bit in his youth. I scored a hit, a deep cut lashing his thigh, but he hammered my kidneys with his empty fist on my way by, and I grunted as the pain struck my groin, like only a true kidney punch could do.

He grunted at the strike, wiping a hand on the bloody smear and holding it up to the light. Then his brother, Mustachio, tore through the doorway, face bleeding and furious. His mustache was now lopsided, one side perfectly curled, the other a ragged protrusion of loose hair.

"Wardrobe malfunction?" I asked, motioning towards my upper lip.

He merely set his lips in a tight line, and pulled out his own knife. Then closed off any chance of escape as he nudged the door closed with a boot, eliminating the additional light from outside. They circled me like wolves.

Lucky me, I *knew* wolf. Gunnar had been my sparring partner for *years*.

I feinted left, watching with a distant grin as the larger Grimm fell for it. Mustachio yelled in warning but was too late. I slashed McBeefy's wrist. The one holding the knife. The blade clattered to the ground but he had instinctively reached to catch it, so caught my knee on his jaw instead, which sent him into a dazed twirl before he crumpled to the floor. I immediately jumped to the side rather than stomping on the Grimm for good measure.

Lucky me. Mustachio had lunged to catch me in the back, but missed. He growled, kicking his partner lightly in the ribs. "Get up." No response.

"I read him a bedtime story. Just you and me now." I smiled back, chuckling.

He snarled and lunged. I caught the blade on my towel-clad forearm, but it cut through the fabric easily. I felt fire lash my wrist and I tried to slice back, but he was fast. Not superhuman fast, which he no doubt could have been. Just experienced fast. Lucky me, these guys were staying true to their word and relying solely on their skills as humans.

For now.

I felt another slice graze my ribs – deep enough to draw blood – and my counter swing missed again. He was chuckling now. He was good. I needed to end this fast. Before Dean showed up and became collateral damage.

Or leverage. Which seemed to be a common tactic for the Grimms.

I threw myself at him in a savage flurry, missing with my first two strikes. I hit him two times out of four, one of them on his cheek. And that's when he began to change the rules. He used magic.

A force slammed into me, spinning me around, and his knife sliced my back. Hard. I fell, the bloody towel unraveling from my impromptu knot. The hand holding the knife hit the ground and the blade shattered. The Grimm began to chuckle.

"Aw, that's too bad," Mustachio called from over my shoulder. I turned to face him, lifting my *Infinity Gauntlet* to defend myself, calling on my power one last time, but to no avail. Apparently, Mustachio was the one blocking me, not McBeefy, or the shield would have evaporated. The knife raced towards me in a blur.

A crossbow bolt abruptly punched through his throat, sending him into a spin. His blade managed to slice the outside of my thigh in a deep cut as he fell, which hurt. Mustachio twitched once, and then a pool of blood began slowly growing around his body. I glanced back, grunting at the knife wound in my thigh. Dean stood in the doorway, holding a crossbow and a grocery bag. He hit a button on his key fob and his car alarm chirped on.

"Really, Master Temple. I told you about the crossbow on the wall by the door. Why did you grab that rusty old knife you so cleverly hid from me?" I blinked at him. Surprised at him saving my life, but also that he had known about the knife I had tried hiding from him. He calmly surveyed the scene. "Is that all of them?" He asked. I nodded. He hung the crossbow back on the wall and left without another word.

I blinked.

Then I used the towel to tie a makeshift tourniquet around my thigh. I used zip ties to bind McBeefy. Several of them on each arm and leg for good measure. Then I padlocked him to a fender of one of the late model cars parked in the stable. The kind made of all steel, no fiberglass. He groaned lightly as I did so, but didn't wake. I punched him in the nose and his head rocked back, striking the fender with a satisfying *clang*. I disarmed both bodies, threw a tarp over Mustachio, and made my way back inside *Chateau Falco*.

Dean was calmly plucking glass out of the cake. He turned to look at me with a frown of disapproval before pointedly glancing back at the cake. "You should shower again and bandage those wounds. You need to leave in thirty minutes to make your reservation."

I stared in utter disbelief for a few seconds as he silently began icing the cake. Then I left to follow his advice, muttering under my breath.

Goddamn Grimms.

Goddamn snarky Butlers.

39

I sat in the middle of the restaurant, trying not to fidget. My wounds were aching and burning in a steady, reliable rhythm, matching the uncomfortable feeling in my stomach. Dean had bandaged me up, and I was using my powers to block the insistent throbbing pain threatening to overwhelm me from the brief but violent knife fight, among other injuries over the past few days. I masked my grimace. It might send the wrong impression to Indie.

I, Nate Temple, life-long bachelor, was about to propose.

And then likely be murdered in the morning.

I signaled the waiter again impatiently. He danced over to my side, having been watching me out of the corner of his eye. "Yes, Master Temple." I had already ordered dinner for Indie and I, knowing what she generally liked and disliked, but also because she enjoyed the surprise. We always took turns. Sometimes she ordered, sometimes I did.

"Make sure to keep an eye out for–"

"Miss Indiana Rippley. Yes. Of course, Sir."

I grumbled dark things under my breath at his interruption. In his defense, I *had* reminded him three times already. "And you have everything you need to proceed as I ask–"

"Yes, Sir. Everything is ready, only awaiting your signal." He showed me the signal.

"And the–"

"Yes, the... *token of love* is ready and waiting. I'm sure she will adore the sentiment." His tone may or may not have held an undercurrent of sarcasm. I scowled for good measure, and then nodded. He left. I took a sip of my wine, waiting impatiently.

As if on cue, Indie entered the restaurant, and time seemed to slow. Everyone turned to look at her. She was very... *noticeable*, to say the least. She wore an ermine gown, slit at the thigh to reveal a small, tasteful slice of pale leg, and the fabric clung to her well-curved frame like a second skin. I smiled as I stood. She returned the smile as she spotted me and then approached. Many people continued to watch, some looking confused, and others shaking their heads before turning back to their meals. Perhaps they were still upset at me for the failure of Temple Industries, and my seeming blatant disregard in the interviews. But that had been Wilhelm, not me. Still, they didn't know that, and I didn't care about any of that tonight.

Indie stepped up to the table and the waiter was suddenly there holding the chair back, looking composed but slightly startled. Perhaps she had snuck in before they could guide her. I hadn't seen a waiter leading her to my table. And waiters in places like this could take those kinds of slights personally. I reminded myself to tip well.

The waiter arched a questioning brow at me and I nodded. His lips compressed into a thin line, but he continued on without Indie noticing. What the hell was wrong with this guy? Was he really that upset about not escorting her to my table?

I sat down after her, and all the weariness of the fighting and near-death experiences over the last few days slowly dissipated. I was still in pain and nervous as hell, but some of the weight had lifted from my shoulders upon seeing her dressed to the nines. I began to think about Misha, and Ashley, and quickly had to shake away the thoughts. Indie noticed, dropping her gaze in understanding.

The waiter spoke. "Shall I–"

"I'll have what he's having." She interrupted, staring at my drink. Which was not her typical drink. Then again, it was not a typical night. We were on edge. The waiter, still looking ruffled, nodded once, and then departed. Indie smiled at his back in amusement before turning to me, eyebrows arched. "Should we really be celebrating right now?" She asked softly. "It looks like many in this room would skewer you alive if they could." She added as an afterthought, glancing around the room.

Indeed, we were garnering many looks. Some hostile, some interested; all package and parcel for me. I was a celebrity in town, and was used to it. Indie would eventually get used to it also. She would have to.

"Of course, we should be celebrating. We are *alive*." I spoke softly.

Indie nodded, looking down.

"After what I saw today, I needed to remember what we are fighting for. What is truly important." And just like that, I found myself ready to spill my guts to her, not even waiting for our food.

Or Indie's drink.

The waiter was exiting the kitchen, and saw my pointed double blink. Our prearranged signal. He halted, glanced at Indie with a frown, and then back at me. I nodded discreetly and he disappeared behind the curtain. Why did he look surprised? I had told him more than a dozen times what I needed him to do. Even if I was jumping the gun a bit. But I couldn't help myself. Thinking of spending another hour in front of this woman and not asking her to marry me sounded horrible, and impossible.

Indie was watching me thoughtfully.

"But that's not the only reason I wanted to have dinner with you tonight," I began, noticing the owner of the store now standing by the curtain leading to the kitchen, barely hiding his interest in the upcoming action about to go down at my table. The waiter approached, set Indie's drink before her, and took a step back, waiting patiently. Indie frowned at him momentarily, but my words suddenly caught her full attention.

"Indiana Rippley. You are the most stunning woman I have ever encountered. Despite our... *differences*, I have thrived in your loving arms. We come from different worlds," she sighed at my words, eyes glittering as she smiled so deeply I thought she would burst out laughing. "But you have never been far from my side. I am not worthy to hold one such as you so close for so long, but I would ask that you let me do so a little bit longer... *forever*." My eyes met hers, and she glanced again at the waiter, who suddenly knelt at her feet.

The restaurant grew silent as a tomb, chairs creaking and scraping as everyone turned their heads to watch with disbelief. Her eyes flickered from me to the waiter and back again. I stood, approached her, and knelt at her other side, clutching her hand delicately. "Would you do me the great honor of becoming my wife?" She stared incredulously at me, and then her eyes darted to the waiter as he produced the kind of engagement ring only a once-billionaire could afford.

The *Infinity Gauntlet* oven mitt.

I accepted the mitt, nodding for him to leave, and then carefully, with great reverence, covered her hand with it. "No one else would propose with an *Infinity Gauntlet*. They would keep the power for themselves." I said solemnly. "But I want to share everything with you. The good. The bad. The ugly." I smiled at her, waiting for her response, my heart racing wildly. I had done it. All she had to do was say one little word.

Several customers left. In fact, I realized that quite a few customers had left. And the ones still in the process of leaving now had disgusted looks on their faces. The owner stared slack-jawed at me, then began to quietly but insistently berate the waiter whom had just left my table. But I didn't care. They could hate me all they wanted. I didn't blame them after what they had seen. After Wilhelm had impersonated me so perfectly to the local news channel, sending Temple Industries into a nosedive.

Then they got to see me at a posh restaurant, apparently unashamed, proposing to the woman I loved. Typical billionaire arrogance.

I realized Indie hadn't spoken yet, so I turned back to her, ignoring the increasing exodus of customers. "Well?"

She stared back at me, eyes staring at me with disbelief, and then they slowly began to transform into a smile.

But something was... *off*.

The smile was sinister. Wolfish. Mocking. Full of glee, but not for my intended reasons.

"Oh, this is likely the crowning moment of my existence." An entirely different voice spoke through her lips. Time momentarily froze with the familiar pulse of power I had come to fear, and the restaurant was instantly silent. Completely. People frozen in midstep. Then Indie's form began to twist and transform into a different being entirely.

Wilhelm suddenly sat before me, still wearing my engagement *Infinity Gauntlet*.

And I was clutching his hand like my life depended on it. I flung it away but couldn't manage to work my legs. My blood turned to ice. I didn't know how it was possible. How he knew to be here at this moment. The most important moment of my life. But it didn't matter. Here we were.

No... Not this, too.

He nodded, seemingly able to read my thoughts. "Oh, I'm afraid so. Your little wench is currently under lock and key, but on her behalf, I feel I must give you at least some kind of response." He caressed the oven mitt with pantomimed seriousness. Then his cold, dead eyes met mine, flashing black. "The answer is *No*. Indie is mine. But you will see her in the morning. Perhaps." He winked.

Then he was gone, leaving me kneeling beside an empty chair as time warped back to normal. Several customers suddenly tripped, clutching onto a chair or table for support. They glanced over their shoulders to see me standing beside an empty chair and frowned in confusion. The waiter and owner looked equally startled.

My vision pulsed blue and I began to hyperventilate. The waiter, noticing the look on my face, rushed over, urged on by the owner. "Master Temple? I didn't want to say it while he was here, but did I mishear your instructions? I thought you had said Indiana Rippley would be joining you this evening..."

I was growling, an unending string of dark curses pouring from my lips, trying to prevent myself from unleashing my power and burning the building to the ground. "What did you see?" I hissed.

The waiter's eyes widened. "Um, a rather scruffy gentleman in leathers sitting at the table. And then... well, you *proposed* to him." He looked as if his tongue was about to dry up and crawl out of his mouth. Not sure if my anger was at his failure or the apparent negative response I had been given by my dinner date.

I was going to kill Wilhelm. And then I was going to kill Death. I had spoken to Indie only hours before on his phone. Was he complicit in her abduction? Had he been lying to me even then? On the phone? Was he the source of the leak I suspected in my crew?

I stood, heaving, pinpoint flickers of light clouding my vision. I needed to get out of here. Fresh air. Cool wind. No people. Before I did something stupid.

"It's time I left." I managed to whisper. The other customers still present looked horrified and confused. I would have too if I had just seen the city's billionaire celebrity heir propose to a leather-armored man in one of the more exclusive restaurants in town.

The waiter nodded, turning as if to go grab the check. I tossed three one-hundred-dollar bills on the table and, without giving a flying fuck, Shadow Walked out of the restaurant and back into the kitchen of *Chateau Falco*, where I found Dean and Alucard waiting for me.

They blinked in astonishment, eyes slowly sparkling with eager smiles as if anxious to hear how everything went. Their stares slowly faded as they got a good look at my face, which was hard enough to grind rocks.

"We need Mallory up and running. Whatever it takes."

They blinked at me. "He should be fine in a few hours. That old bastard is beyond tough." Alucard sounded uncharacteristically impressed.

I nodded. "In the morning, we are going to murder every single one of those bastards. Slowly. I hope there are survivors. I want to make their remaining existence... *memorable*."

Alucard cleared his throat cautiously. "I take it the proposal didn't go as... planned?" He offered carefully.

I stared at him, eyes no doubt bloodshot, because they seemed as dry as dust to me. "They took her," I whispered, barely able to maintain my feet.

They leaned forward as if they hadn't heard me correctly. The granite countertop abruptly crumbled beneath Alucard's claws as he squeezed the stone at my words.

I also gripped the kitchen island with shaking fingertips, but didn't break it. "Indie's been..." I swallowed deeply, unable to finish as bile crept up into my throat. She was my responsibility. The love of my life. It was my fault she was taken. I had trusted Death, an immortal being with his own agendas, to look out for her, and I had been burned.

My world rocked, and Alucard lurched forward a step as if to catch me.

I held up a hand, took several deep breaths, and spoke in a snarl.

"Indie's been *taken*. Tomorrow their blood will feed my lawns. Their screams will be trapped inside *Chateau Falco* like a soothing lullaby. Their bones will lay buried deep under our maze. I will destroy everything they hold dear."

I paused, lifting my gaze to meet their eyes. "I have nothing else to give. So, I will just begin *taking* from them. They will not escape me. This I swear." I drew a bead of blood from my thumb, and uttered a spell, binding the promise to my soul. A Blood Debt. Alucard's eyes widened in disbelief, and Dean looked as if his heart had just been ripped from his chest. And then I left the kitchen, ready to arm myself for the biggest tussle of my career.

Wilhelm had warned me of his interest in her. And Jacob had all but admitted that she would be given to his brother. Why hadn't I seen this coming? I took another breath and strode through the house, stomping loudly without consciously deciding to do so.

I didn't even bother calling Death this time. I couldn't trust him anymore. If Indie were free, she would have been at the restaurant. So, she really was gone. This was not some ploy. Some trick. She had been taken. And Wilhelm had stepped into her place for the sole purpose of rubbing my face in it. The fact that I had been proposing was merely icing on the cake.

I began calling the crew, telling them to get here early. I was done playing games. My tactic for this battle was simple, but efficient.

Overkill.

Absolute, illogical overkill.

It was time for me to dig out the party favors I had secured over the last few months from Temple Industries. Several of my side projects that only some knew about.

The Grimms were history. They just didn't know it yet.

40

We stood outside the front door of *Chateau Falco*, the centuries-old monolith towering behind us as if in encouragement of our decision to fight. A calming giant backing us up. If only it could do more than look imposing. Inside her halls, maybe, but that wouldn't help me today.

Sunrise was in a few moments.

Leather creaked.

Fabric rustled.

Metal scraped and clicked, whether from gun, blade, or armor.

We had tried to go over plans a dozen times, but there were simply too many variables. We had killed several Grimms, but how many had truly died, and how many were left? McBeefy, my captive Grimm, knelt on the ground before me, struggling as if sensing my thoughts.

I didn't even look down as I lifted my boot and kicked the Grimm squarely in the back of the neck hard enough to give him whiplash and possibly crack one of his vertebrae. He grunted in agony and head butted the icy gravel.

Tory watched the violent blow without emotion, face devoid of any empathy whatsoever. I hadn't had the proper chance to talk to her. But she hadn't wanted to talk about anything anyway. She just wanted vengeance. I got that. Still, I wanted to wrap her up in a giant hug, help her carry some of those burdens. Even if she didn't want me to.

It's what friends did.

She was grieving. And I doubted that the Grimms would enjoy being on the receiving end of her fury. "You okay?" I asked her softly, our first direct communication since Misha had been killed.

Her eyes met mine. They were bloodshot, pained, and full of dancing, malevolent carnage. She looked away, not answering me right away. "I don't think it's a good idea for me to get in touch with my feelings right now. But soon I'll feel *much* better."

I nodded, and several others murmured their agreement.

Everyone shifted from foot to foot, the non-shifters trying to get used to the Kevlar vests I had provided. It wasn't perfect, but it would help. I hoped. Gunnar seemed especially uncomfortable, sniffing the air hungrily as he subconsciously adjusted the Kevlar vest covering his torso. He was the only shifter wearing one. I was anxious to see how it would hold up, seeing as how it had been made to hypothetically adjust on the fly, reforming to his new wolf form so that if all went well, I had a bulletproof werewolf on my side. I wasn't sure if the Grimms were packing silver bullets, or even whether they would use guns, but I wasn't taking any chances. I had told him of my conversation with the werewolf. He had listened silently, grunted, and then changed the topic.

It didn't matter anymore. He had more important things on his mind.

Like Ashley.

She was currently in a safe location under the protection of Gunnar's long-time friend, Agent Jeffries. He would use his FBI credentials to try and run interference if any police activity arose, which I highly suspected as a result of my alleged insider trading crime. Ashley was being held within a silver circle, watched and monitored at all times. I knew that more than almost anything, Gunnar wanted to be there by her side.

But this was the one place he would rather be, to exact revenge, just like everyone else here. Alucard stood like a statue beside him, idly thumbing his umbrella. He was liberally coated with sunscreen, and wore clothing meant to block the rays of the upcoming sunrise. You know, the kind of fabric you see on those pasty kids at the pool that get sunburns at even mention of the word *sunlight*. It was an odd pair, to see a werewolf and a vampire standing side by side, neither snarling at each other, but instead compatriots in the fight to come. Silent comrades, blood brothers of war, almost as if they had fought beside each other for decades, no further words necessary.

Raego and his dragons stood off to the side, speaking quietly, ready to shift in a blink, and far enough away to not take any of us out when they suddenly transformed to creatures ten times the size – or larger – of their human skin. But I wished we had more. Most of them were off on assignments overseas or protecting the Dragon Lord's American interests thanks to the arrival of the Grimms. And Raego had adamantly refused allowing Misha's daughters to participate.

I agreed.

The injured, but not down for the count, Mallory had finally gotten a hold of Tomas, who had been lying low after attracting too much attention to himself. The two were up on the roof at discreet points, armed with sniper rifles, relying on mortal means to aid in the battle. With Mallory already injured, his best support was being on the roof.

But to me, the world felt empty despite all my friends willing to die by my side.

Indie was gone.

Taken.

Captured.

Either Death had betrayed me, or the Grimms had overwhelmed him somehow, but I doubted the latter. Despite how badass the Grimms were, Death was a legendary warrior. At the Armageddon level. Which likely meant he had switched sides at some point. Made a deal with the Grimms. I realized I was growling, only noticing so as Tory placed a calming hand on my wrist. Her fiery eyes met mine. "Not yet," I nodded back, regaining some semblance of control.

After my head had cooled a bit, I had tried reaching out to Death to confirm my fear. But he hadn't answered.

No matter now.

Glancing at the skyline, I realized it was almost sunrise. Time to get to work.

I knelt down on the ground. My friends formed a loose circle around me, and I murmured a word, not bothering with the ritual. I wasn't here to protect myself, or make a bargain. I was here to do a single, all-encompassing action.

Raise holy hell.

On the third repetition of the word, I felt my friends stiffen as one, and three heavy thumps struck the earth strong enough for me to feel it in my knees. I rose, sniffing the air, which suddenly felt like a spring or summer morning in the woods, and saw two figures standing beside a silver-clad goddess. Well, what looked like a goddess. She and her companions were petite, despite the loud sound of their arrival. Alucard murmured appreciatively and the sprite noticed.

I wasn't sure if it was possible for silver skin to blush, but the skin of Barbie's cheeks did shift color a bit. Enough for me to smile faintly. The sprite turned to me. "So, it is time," she said simply.

"Yes. I needed some thugs, and your name came up." I looked at her two compatriots. "Brought friends to the party?" She smiled, and nodded.

Two women stood beside the sprite, also human-sized at the moment, and equally naked. One carried a small ebony stick, oozing the gravitas of age and power. Her mocha skin, almost black, seemed to shine, and her inky black eyes seemed to glimmer with undisclosed power. She was wrinkled, and aged like her stick, but you could tell that she had once commanded great attention from the opposite sex. If not from her looks, then from her seemingly raw power. It was elemental to my senses. Her cool gaze promised pain and pleasure in equal measure, and she didn't mind which one you preferred.

The other sprite was green. Like the green of fresh buds on a tree. In fact, her skin seemed made of grass and leaves. Gnarled vines formed a makeshift outfit that only emphasized her lean body. She wasn't curvaceous, but more of an innocent adolescent, a nubile maiden found by a pond in the middle of the woods.

The kind of young slip of a girl only read about in stories that usually ended with a disappearance of an innocent young boy. Her smile was cool, detached, and predatory. I averted my gaze as her eyes drifted to me.

Neither spoke. Not a word. "They have their own... *reasons* for joining me today. Old business with your... *guests*." Barbie offered with a humorless smirk. I shrugged.

Dean popped his head out the front door behind us. "Jeffries just phoned. Police have been served with a warrant for your arrest and are mobilizing now."

I nodded. "Is everything in order?"

"Yes, Master Temple," he responded, voice tight with stoic calm.

"Seek shelter then, Dean." The door began to close. "And thank you for your service." I added. The door remained open as I heard a sharp intake of breath, then he popped his head back out. "Movement discovered in the old gardens." The door closed, latching shut with a metallic snap. Several bolts slammed home, barring access to the mansion.

"It's party time, folks." And so I led the group of bloodthirsty Freaks to meet the equally bloodthirsty assassins. I used currents of power to shove my captive ahead of us so that he could be a meat shield against his brothers. I didn't need him for leverage. Just to prove a point. I masked his presence, so that the Grimms wouldn't see him at all. I didn't need them attacking on sight. I wanted to see Indie. Make sure she was safe.

Or even alive.

As we began to move, fanning out in an arch, I suddenly felt the now familiar throb of power that signified a time warp. We were used to it now, although I heard Barbie growl to her companions.

We were going to battle in our own cocoon of time, unaffected by the outside world. Which would prevent the approaching police from becoming collateral damage. I wondered if that fact was a conscious decision by the Grimms, since they preferred not to harm Regulars. Well, Regulars that weren't friends of mine. Apparently, being in the Nate Temple fan club revoked that mortal protection.

We walked for a few minutes in silence, braving the icy path that led down to the gardens. Tall trees suddenly stood before us as we crested a gentle rise, looking down upon the ancestral Temple Gardens. Benches, fountains, and statues dotted the pathways meandering through the once thriving greenery of the gardens. A small hedge maze stood in the center, surrounded by a soothing collection of perennial and floral arrangements that had been created to inspire peace and tranquility.

But like my current mood, the area was now barren, devoid of all life but the stone sentinels rising up like cresting waves over the brown shrubbery. And the towering trees that formed a circle of protection around the garden – casting an eternal shade over the life inside – only seemed to foreshadow the bloodshed about to take place.

The statues were all depictions of my various ancestors, and my father had hinted that no secrets could be shared within eyesight of any of them. Each statue had been erected using the cremated remains – if only a part – of the person in question to form either the statue itself or the base or the mortar. Regardless, each and every statue down there had a bit of the owner inside of it, and by extension, a form of immortal existence. I wasn't sure if it was possible to converse with them, but my dad never made idle warnings, and if he didn't want me spilling secrets near a statue, no matter how odd the advice, I damn well wasn't going to be uttering any secrets around them. A vast field of once perfectly manicured grass surrounded the gardens – now covered in a blanket of snow – gently rolling up to the foundation of the sprawling mansion itself, perched atop the hill like a living entity. From this angle, the house was foreboding, dark, threatening.

To everyone but my crew.

I noticed movement at the same time as Alucard and Gunnar. A dozen figures stood around a large statue at the edge of the gardens and trees. The *Gatekeeper* of the garden, my father had called him. No other description had been given to me, but I knew he was a distant ancestor of mine.

Indie was chained to the base of the statue with thick, heavy links of some kind of glittering metal. Thick enough to eliminate the chance of even most Freaks breaking free. I wondered if my magic would work against them. Perhaps that was the point. Indie stood no chance of escape on her own, and perhaps we didn't stand a chance of breaking her free either. At least not until the battle was concluded.

My blood began to boil at the sight. There she was. Helpless. Kidnapped. A Regular whose only crime was to love me.

And now she sat at the hands of monsters.

The Grimms turned to face us, eyes hard, glinting in the pre-dawn light.

We approached, and the Grimms waited, idly thumbing the weapons at their belts.

Well, all but Jacob and Wilhelm, who stood closest to the statue. Jacob's face was blank, but Wilhelm's was full of glee. I stopped before the two brothers, the other Grimms stepping a few paces out of my way to grant me unbroken sight of Indie and their Big Brothers.

My friends fanned out beside me, and the Grimms subtly squared off to match them, eliminating any holes in their formation, pairing off subconsciously. My eyes stayed on Indie for several long moments. She finally looked up and I practically felt the fear in her gaze. Her makeup ran down her cheeks, smearing her mascara, or whatever you called the stuff women smeared around their eyes. She was terrified, but seemed to have cried too much to have any more tears left. Seeing me seemed to rejuvenate her. She suddenly grew calm, confident, and resolved.

I didn't like that look. It gave me the Heebie-Jeebies for some reason.

Wilhelm tossed the *Infinity Gauntlet* oven mitt down on the ground between us with a smirk. "Looks like you won't be needing this any longer." Indie's eyes tracked the motion, locking onto the familiar glove, and her eyes grew sad as they rose to mine. She recognized it, and although not completely understanding the particular meaning of its presence, she seemed to at least understand its significance.

Perhaps she knew enough to realize it was a token of my love, and would only be in his hands if things had gone horribly wrong. She had no idea it was her engagement ring.

"Enough." Jacob murmured softly. Wilhelm grunted but complied, stepping back. Jacob nodded in thanks. "We have the book. We have your woman. We have shown you time and time again what happens to those who oppose us. It is time for you to end this pointless quest and accept your place in the new world. And that place would be six feet under the ground." He didn't sound menacing. He sounded clinical. Stating facts. Reading a report. I didn't respond. "The only thing left is to decide how painful you want your end to be. Give us the Armory, and we will make it swift. Painless. Or…" He held out a hand in invitation.

"They called you guys *Decapitares* during the Crusades, right?" I asked softly.

Jacob frowned thoughtfully, but nodded. In response, I shoved an unseen force ahead of me, and suddenly the beefy Grimm from my garage lay sprawled at my feet, shivering in pain and humiliation, abruptly visible where before he had been unseen. I withdrew the sword at my side – the confiscated weapon belonging to the Grimm – and decapitated him with one swift blow. His head thunked to the ground and I nudged it with a boot until it rested at Jacob's feet. Mustachio's head, which had been held by McBeefy on the way here, rolled towards Wilhelm's feet, touching his boot briefly before he angrily kicked it away. I dropped the sword. It clattered to the cold ground. Then I lifted my gaze to Jacob and shrugged, brushing off my hands. "His mustache offended me so I killed him, too."

I had their attention now.

Jacob's gaze smoldered with barely restrained rage. His brothers tensed, ready to destroy every last one of us. "Last chance, boy," I spotted Ichabod a few paces behind him. He looked sickened. I smiled back.

"But I gathered my crew and it would be such a waste to ruin a scrap when everyone's here to dance. No blocking my power. Let's see what you bitches can do without hiding behind that sad, old, pitiful wretch over there." I pointed at Ichabod.

Jacob nodded. Wilhelm looked anticipatory. Hungry.

"Good. Now, before we get started, I should probably warn you. You are trespassing." I said softly. "And we don't care for that 'round these parts." I did my best to sound like a Texan. I lifted a hand slowly, snapped my finger once, and one of the Grimms suddenly crumpled to the ground with an explosive exhale of breath and a bloody mist where his head had been. The crack of a distant gunshot echoed throughout the grounds a moment later. I snapped again. Jacob began to yell, but he was too late.

The same thing happened before anyone thought to seek cover, another Grimm collapsing in an explosion of blood. Two headshots. Most survivors threw up shields of power before them. Others rolled to safety behind a tree or bench or anything that would slow a bullet. Ichabod stared at the scene, unmoving. Jacob snarled at him to see to the men. Ichabod met my gaze… and winked.

I didn't have time to decipher what *that* meant, so launched a blast of power at him. It struck him true in the chest and he went cartwheeling into the statue, cracking it in half. I hurriedly sent another blast, knocking the collapsing statue to safety so that it didn't crush Indie. Ichabod landed in safety and didn't move. Indie shrieked as the stone titan crashed only inches away from her.

At least I thought that was why she screamed. My eyes met hers and I saw a spreading stain of blood surrounding an aged ivory knife handle buried in her stomach.

And there was Wilhelm, kneeling beside her, grinning at me.

I almost lost control right there, but managed to remember I was our only chance at survival. I tossed up my other hand in a prearranged signal as I used my other hand to cast an incomplete dome of power over my crew and a smaller complete one around Indie. A whistling scream shrieked past my shoulder and I instantly lifted the dome of protection the rest of the way. The ground where the Grimms had been standing exploded in a crater of fire and screams, sending rock, dirt, benches, and shrubbery in every direction.

Rockets were fun.

For some, more than others.

I wasn't sure how many Tomas had, or where he had gotten them, but I was thankful. I dropped the dome of power shielding my friends and let loose my restraints, leaving only enough power to keep Indie's dome up and running. My rage pulsed hungrily. She was dying. And the only way to save her was to end this quickly, and keep her safe from further harm with my shield. The rest of us were on our own for now.

On cue, my crew broke up in an explosion of shredded fabric as the shifters tore free of their mortal skins and raced after the regrouping Grimms, dragons and a werewolf already wreaking havoc. The Grimms answered in kind, barely hesitating as they met their foes with sickening thuds of flesh and claw and blood. I heard Raego's distinct bellow as he slammed into another black dragon. It reminded me of *How to Train Your Dragon*. Blue and purple fire slammed into each beast, but they didn't seem to notice the liquid fire splashing across their scales as they slammed into each other again.

Alucard was laughing as he danced between two Grimms, umbrella deftly swiping at their heavier swords. He moved like a wraith, cutting, slicing, stabbing, and biting. Their blood painted his face, and his ivory fangs glowed in the rising sun. Three familiar shapes suddenly swooped in from the darkness of the hedge maze, aiming straight for Alucard, fangs shining in the darkness.

Vampires. The ones who had stopped by my house to threaten Alucard.

Damn it. I had forgotten about them.

The two Grimms fled, leaving Alucard to fight his own subjects.

I tapped the bracelet on my wrist in a predetermined staccato. A distant wail instantly responded, the sound seeming to shred my eardrums, and then a freaking meteor shower of stone griffins slammed into the earth surrounding us, sending up geysers of rock and earth. *Chateau Falco's Guardians*. They immediately tore after anyone with an amulet, which was their only rule of engagement tonight, according to the command I had tapped out on my bracelet. It throbbed, letting me know all of them were active. Two exploded in a violent shower of gravel before they had a chance to enter the fray. I hoped they would even the odds a bit, but I didn't have time to worry about them now. They were effectively on autopilot until every amulet attached to a body was gone.

I looked up, but the vampires were gone. So was Alucard. I wished him well as my eyes quested the fight. A stone bench slammed squarely into Wilhelm, knocking him back a few paces before his boots planted themselves in the dirt. His face was a sheet of blood as he squared off against Tory.

She waved at him, flashing a teasing smile. Then she turned and ran.

Wilhelm pursued instantly.

Only to be met by my idea of the three Sisters of Fate, the sprites.

Trees and vines suddenly exploded out of the earth, wrapping around Wilhelm in a blink before morphing into obsidian, inky black tendrils of rock. Then a lance of pure silver light struck the trapped Grimm and the shockwave sent me flying backwards.

Roars of fury shattered the night as dragons slammed into each other in the skies, limned by the rising sun. I watched it all for a second from my vantage on the ground, trying to regain mobility. I finally scrambled to my feet to see Wilhelm standing in the same place, a steady ring of darkness surrounding him as he glared back at the sprites. Whatever he had done had protected him from the blast.

But not from a two-hundred-fifty-pound werewolf. Gunnar slammed into his side, actually managing to knock him out of one of his boots before the Grimm shifted into his own wolf form. Tory and the Sprites took off after a pair of Grimms racing to help a fallen brother who was struggling to his feet after being thrown from the skies by a dragon, judging by the claw marks on his chest. Crackling energy split the night as they did whatever mayhem they preferred. I didn't have time to watch.

Jacob stood before me. Waiting.

Gunshots cracked the air, which was already filled with the musky scent of beast and fire and dust. Neither Jacob nor I blinked. We just stared at each other, having a silent conversation. Howls, snarls, and the snapping of teeth surrounded us as Gunnar and Wilhelm fought to the death. I sensed that Gunnar was doing his best to at least keep Wilhelm from interfering with Jacob and I.

Mortals are off limits, you bastard, I snarled in my head.

He shrugged. *They are if they aren't aiding a wizard. Those that side with freaks are fair game. This all could have been avoided. All you needed to do was give me the book and die in silence.*

"Hey, Jakey?" I asked with a furrowed brow.

He frowned angrily. "My name is *Jacob*."

"Sure thing. Don't clench." I smiled.

Before he could react, I whipped out twin cords of purple fire and lightning-infused chains, sizzling and snapping hungrily as they latched onto his torso and legs, wrapping him up like a spider. I began to twirl in a circle, using my power to aid with his weight, and then launched him as hard as I could. He roared in fury, but just before he struck another set of trees, his body morphed into a dragon and he spread his wings, buffeting the air powerfully. He still struck the statues, pulverizing them, but his scaled skin was much tougher. He swooped down, racing straight towards me.

I dove and rolled as a blast of silver shards pelted the earth. I looked up to see that Gunnar wasn't watching, and was directly in the line of fire. I whipped out a blast of air and struck him in the back hard enough to give him whiplash. A second torrent of silver spikes slammed into the earth where he had been, and his body crashed into some bushes a dozen paces away. Wilhelm was already on top of him, swiping claws and fang at Gunnar's back as my friend tried to untangle himself from the brush with snarls of pain and rage.

Then he let out a terrifying bark of pain, instinctively jerking his head backwards. His jaws managed to clamp down on Wilhelm's foreleg, shattering the bone in powerful canine jaws. Wilhelm yelped and darted away, limping on three legs. Gunnar finally tore himself free from the shrubbery and slowly raised his gaze to glare unbridled rage at the Grimm.

His icy blue eye practically froze the Grimm in his place.

But the other eye socket was empty, a gaping, bloody, hole of mangled flesh.

My heart stopped in disbelief and shock. But Gunnar was having none of it. He took a single step, angling his head so that his one eye kept Wilhelm in his sight. Wilhelm crouched as if about to attack, then froze, whining as he stared over Gunnar's shoulders. I turned and saw a dozen wolves tucked low in the grass around the shrubbery behind Gunnar. Their growls filled the night, almost a cackling, bubbling snarl. Gunnar jumped ahead a step, so focused on Wilhelm that he hadn't noticed the pack was behind him. I didn't see any amulets, but perhaps they were still enthralled by the Grimms.

Gunnar erupted in an explosion of furious warning growls and barks that I could feel deep in my chest. His ears perked towards Wilhelm since he had only the one eye now.

One of the wolves crouched low and lifted his throat, baring it in submission. Gunnar blinked with his one good eye. The other wolves mimicked the motion, in complete silence. Gunnar seemed to grumble an acceptance, and snapped his teeth once at them in warning. "*You... are... mine...*" a truly monstrous voice growled from Gunnar's canine jaws. My neck instantly pebbled. I had never heard Gunnar speak when in full wolf form. I hadn't known that he *could*. Then he slowly turned to face Wilhelm. His one good eye seemed to dance with laughter.

Then he fucking *howled*.

And I almost believed that I could see the sound wave of it. It was so primal and aggressive that the goosebumps simply jumped off my arms and ran away, replaced by pure adrenaline. It was a reminder of when mankind huddled in caves and beasts ruled the night. It was a hunting cry. No, a hunting *command*.

And Gunnar's wolves obeyed.

The wolves launched over Gunnar like a cresting wave as they tore after Wilhelm. I had never seen a wolf run away so fast. Which only pushed the pack to faster speeds.

Gunnar chased after them, trying to become accustomed to his hampered vision. I smiled as Jacob landed beside me, now in human form, watching with a pensive frown.

"Looks like the wolves are mine again, Jakey." He didn't respond. "Just curious, but what do you think they're going to do to your brother? Disembowel him? Eat him? Or just kill–"

The blast of force should have been expected, but the *level* of power was not.

It slammed into my hastily prepared shield and I skidded back on my heels for ten feet or so. Sensing no other attack, I lowered my arms, brushed off my pant leg, and then smiled at Jacob. He was panting. The disgust flickering in his eyes almost hurt my feelings.

Now *this* was the man I had met several years ago. No more polite façade. This was the man who hated every single cell in my body. The polite, congenial, incredibly suave assassin had been so different from the beast of a man I had first met several years ago, that it was practically a Jekyll and Hyde persona. The man was mad. As mad as a hatter.

It was sort of a relief to see him back in his true form. Like Wilhelm. Now he was emotional.

And emotional people made mistakes.

The wolves were much faster than the injured Wilhelm, and they swarmed him, darting in for strike after strike, alternating and synchronizing with each other in a practiced, subconscious pattern. Tearing flesh here, snapping bone there, clawing a side here, and finally one wolf shattered the chain holding Wilhelm's amulet in an explosion of links. Wilhelm instantly transformed into his human form, broken, battered and bloody. The wolves stepped back, growling darkly as Gunnar approached on silent paws, head tilted to view the situation in his one eye.

Jacob instantly roared in defiance, morphing into his dragon form to defend his brother. I cast out a sizzling web of power that caught one of his wings, sending him crashing down to the earth, twitching and spitting in a furious snarl. Useless spikes of silver sailed off into the night as he tried to lock onto the wolves. Three of them broke off to harry the lamed dragon, but his skin was too tough for it to be too effective. Razor sharp silver talons practically ripped one wolf in half.

They seemed to realize all of a sudden that the dragon was *actually* silver, which was about as dangerous to a werewolf as one could get. They played defense, trying to instead wear him out and keep him distracted. I cast a few more spells at him, flashing lights and crackling explosions on either side of him, messing with his senses. Gunnar locked eyes with me, blinked, and then turned back to Wilhelm. He approached calmly, padding up to the wounded man, turned to glance at Jacob, snarled...

And then tore out Wilhelm's throat. He swallowed the meat, and then calmly strode off to find a new dance partner. The wolves slinked off to accompany their Alpha. Jacob writhed, roaring in pain, rage, and grief, eyes locked onto his fallen brother.

I had a moment or two to study my surroundings, the explosions, and fighting now more prevalent to my survival. My *Guardians* pelted the Grimms. Alucard slashed and bit at the other vampires – of which only two remained. Wolves harrowed. Tory physically *pummeled*. And the sprites, well, I'll let you imagine. I had a feeling that the stakes were about to rise a bit. We had just killed one of the infamous Grimms. Brother to the leader of them all.

And Gunnar had gobbled him up. No chaser.

I was sure repercussions would be severe.

41

It was one of those moments when time stretched. Not literally, but perhaps my heightened adrenaline merely sped up my brain. So, I got a clear view of the battle.

The war.

I spotted Tory squaring off against a Grimm who seemed to be matching her strength, judging by the fatal blows they were swinging at each other, and the fact that they kept getting right back up. It was like watching two bulls go at it. Unbelievable power. Direct hits that would shatter vertebrae to dust. Then another one. Then another. Tory was moving oddly, and I began to grow concerned that she wasn't going to be able to stand up to him.

Then I noticed why.

Her arm was missing at the elbow. Her left arm. I blinked, unable to process. *How was she still moving?*

She moved slightly off balance, but the make-shift tourniquet – made from pulsing green vines, no doubt courtesy of the green sprite – seemed to staunch the flow of blood, and was in fact growing inside of her arm socket in one place, as if giving her a transfusion. On closer inspection, I noticed that parts of her skin seemed bark-like, shattering off in splinters with each blow from the Grimm. He tried to duplicate her new power when the silver sprite appeared out from behind him and whispered into his ears.

He froze like a startled rabbit. So did Tory. And another Grimm I hadn't even noticed also froze in the act of creeping up on Tory's unsuspecting back from behind a low bush, clutching a knife in his fist. He stood from his crouch, dropped his knife, and began to approach the sprite openly.

The first Grimm turned to face the sprite, face quivering as he tried to fight her power.

His erection was quite obvious.

Then Barbie enveloped his face in an open-mouthed kiss. He began to ravage her, and a very sinister, joyful laugh pierced the night, creepily contradicting the sounds of battle. She grabbed the back of his head and held it before her... well... *that* was new.

Her eyes rolled back in her head as she moaned in rapture.

Tory tried to take a step closer, a jealous, envious dark look on her face. The vine keeping her alive pulsed brightly and she stopped, eyes suddenly clearing. I followed the vines to find the green sprite on the ground, staring up at Tory with determined, pained eyes. Then I realized why. She sported several slashes across her nude form that let me see *inside* her. I saw bone and a few organs before averting my gaze harshly.

She was dying.

And her last act was to keep Tory alive long enough to destroy the Grimm.

The second Grimm had reached the first Grimm and Barbie. The silver sprite opened her eyes, stared at the approaching Grimm, smiled, and then beckoned him closer with a seductive wiggle of her finger.

The second Grimm decapitated his brother, and then kicked his body away, standing before her curvaceous form all ready to be sexed up by a creature that was anathema to him. His excitement was also... *noticeable*, judging by the prominent bulge in his pants.

Another figure approached from out of nowhere, strolled up beside the Grimm and the silver sprite in a seductive sway. Her ebony skin shone brightly in the rising sun. Her hand reached down and clutched his manhood. He grunted in anticipation, his gaze darting from one stunning creature to the other, as if not believing his luck.

A crackling sound emanated from her fist, then she released him and walked away. In the place of his manhood now rose a lump of stone in vaguely the same shape as his previous appendage. Barbie reached down, swept her fingers in the blood of the first Grimm, and then wiped it down her face like war paint, swirling down around her breasts.

She gripped the surviving Grimm's head like a long-lost lover. He whimpered in agony. "Say *Please*." She cooed, gripping his hair tighter and tugging his body closer to her, enough for his chest to brush her nipples.

"Please..." He whispered in response. I didn't know whether it was in fear or expectation, but it was sickening how much he was in her thrall.

Without warning, she smiled, and squeezed her fist. His head simply ceased existing.

I stared, transfixed, forgetting Jacob was right behind me as I stared at the looping war paint covering her body. It was tribal, exotic, dark, seductive, and deadly.

I met her eyes, which instantly flew over my shoulder in alarm. I flinched, and my mind jolted back to my situation. Her warning saved my life. I felt the snick of a blade slide across my ribs, protected by my Kevlar vest, before a body slammed into me from behind. Even with my flinch and the Kevlar, it was a near thing, saved only by Barbie's warning.

I whirled, whipping up my hands while imagining a blade clutched in a defensive fist. Jacob's sword clanged into my metaphysical one in an explosion of sparks. I shoved him back with the aid of my Maker power, drinking in the quivering river of power beneath my feet.

And a vision of Indie filled my mind's eye.

These guys had stabbed Indie.

Gunnar had just eaten his brother's throat.

You could say that we were both more motivated than we had been at any point in our lives, and you would be underestimating our passion.

Our eyes met from a few paces away. Power erupted between us, sending up a cyclone of sparks that abruptly bloomed around us like a miniature big bang model.

I dove deep down into my mind, wading into the river of power that was so hungry to be utilized. I metaphorically dove in head first, allowing the power to roll and wash over me with violent, deadly, almost innocent glee. It crashed over me, rolled into me, fueled me, empowered me like an adrenaline shot to the groin. I reached out and introduced myself to the alien power. It recoiled, and then paused a few inches from my fist, as if smelling me. Like a dog with a new human.

It drifted closer, defying all laws of physics, and then slammed into my chest.

But there was no pain.

It was a high five.

Endorphins pummeled my mind and I somehow survived it. So much power coursed through me that the majority of it flowed right back out of me, having nowhere to take up residence. I studied my new roommate. It was pure emotion. Carnal. Beast-like. It wanted revenge for the Grimm's trespass and the harming of my woman. I sympathized, and allowed I knew not what inside of me, my mind beyond the realm of rationality.

It metaphorically beat me bloody, and I sighed in release. It felt right. No more thinking. Just emotion. Revenge. Make an example out of these killers. I almost let loose, but a small part of me was screaming defiance. I honed in on it and a flood of rational thought finally broke through, hammering me, slapping me in the face. Which woke me up just in the nick of time. I wasn't *just* emotion. I was *enlightened*. I had *thought*. *Rationality*. This presence did not. Sure, it was powerful beyond measure, but it needed a Captain.

I focused around that bubble of thought, forcing it back into the river like it had forced itself on me. I essentially slapped the shit out of it, and it calmed, startled.

Then waited, unmoving, the entire river of power completely still.

Good... I heard a voice whisper in my mind. *I can work with this one... But there will be a price.* I waited a beat, and then nodded my agreement. The voice laughed.

I felt a gentle, polite merging of the power with my soul this time, fortifying my resolve, strengthening my limbs, and whispering dark words of power that could be used to do *this*.

And to do *that*.

I opened my eyes to see only a second had passed, the sparks still falling around Jacob and I. He was glaring at me. I smiled back and unleashed some of those secret words.

The air exploded in a crackling wave that slammed into Jacob, forcing its way past his last second shield of power like a monsoon against a screen door.

He flew from his feet, body literally smoking. I noticed that the webs of sizzling energy I had first thrown at him had badly marred his body, leaving behind angry red welts, but they didn't seem to faze him.

He climbed to his feet, staring at me incredulously.

"What have you done?" He whispered, spitting out a tooth.

"I made a new friend." I whispered back, not fully understanding it myself.

And we fought.

He attempted to shift to dragon form, but I halted him midway, ripping the power out of him like gutting a deer. I don't know how I did it. It was instinctual. I merely told it *no*, and the power obeyed my wish, eager to be used by the world's last surviving Maker. Jacob coughed, instantly returning to human form, which had to hurt. Gunnar had once told me that abrupt shifts like that had broken the minds of many young shifters. One always had to be in control to shift like that, a master of their beast. Rapid shifts were often considered a sign of weakness.

Bullets rained down from the mansion, pelting the earth a few feet from Jacob. He snarled, rolling to cover, and began to flee.

Nope.

Again, without completely understanding what I was doing, I threw my hands up into the air. A purple vortex coalesced in the sky directly above me, growing larger as bolts of power emanated from its depths, forcing it to grow faster, wilder, and more erratic. I allowed emotion into the vortex then.

Fury.

Death.

Hope.

Absolution.

Then I threw my hands at Jacob. These monsters had a single purpose. An undying hope. To destroy the world of magic.

Fine. I would take away *their* hope. Not just that single hope for extermination.

But *all* hope. I would make their minds barren with any sense of motivation, replacing it with complacency and acceptance. I would neuter their souls by taking away their inner fuel. The necklaces would do no good being worn by broken warriors, terrified of their own shadows.

I remembered Death once teasing me about being the Rider of Hope.

So be it.

I embraced the moniker now, casting every particle of my being into the foreign spell.

The world seemed to groan, and then crack in two, and a blur of black flecks flew across my vision as Jacob was hammered by dozens of bolts of power within a second or two. Then all was still.

I realized I was lying on the ground. I sat up and my head swam. *Good...* the voice whispered approvingly in my head. Then it was gone. And so was the power. I was confident that I could still tap into it to do a basic spell, but the godlike power was gone.

I was myself again.

I decided to stay seated for a second, gather my wits. I looked around to find Tory running up to me, holding the green sprite over a shoulder in a fireman's carry. She set the body before the two surviving sprites. They didn't acknowledge their comrade, but instead stared at me with amazement... and horror.

Which should say something.

They were world-class sociopaths. What did that make me?

I shook off their looks as I noticed Gunnar pelting up to me with the pack close on his heels. They halted a dozen feet away and Gunnar continued on alone. He shifted back to human form, all naked manliness and scooped me up. Which was icky.

But I let him.

"Jacob." I pointed at the crater where I had last seen him. Gunnar grunted and carried me closer, the rest of the crew following. Alucard stepped out from behind a tree, clutching a vampire's head in one hand, eyes wild, and fangs out. He blinked a few times, composing himself, and then dropped the head before walking up to the crater. I noticed the two other vampires following him; head down as if in submission. That was good.

Gunnar reached the lip and we peered down. Jacob's battered body lay there unmoving. Then his body lurched suddenly and he gasped a labored breath. His eyes opened wildly, but he was too weak to do anything. I noticed the two surviving sprites suddenly dart off to equidistant points on either side of him. They pointed at Tory and then another spot, which would form a triangle. Tory blinked, frowned, but complied.

Once in their proper positions, Barbie spoke. "Just let us do the work, child. I only need you to be a conduit. You hold our sister's power for a short while. Let me use it. It will help you in healing. Consider it payment for the gift of life she gave you." Her voice was wrought with grief at the end. Tory nodded, looking guilty, and obeyed.

A ring of power suddenly rose from the ground, outlining the outside of the crater in a glowing azure light. Jacob's eyes darted to the sprites and he snarled, regaining some of his strength. His face began to morph into a scaly snout and Barbie belted out a foreign word. His amulet snapped free and flew to her hand, emitting sparks as it pierced the dome of power. Jacob collapsed with a groan and the dome fell, leaving only a broken, battered man behind.

I let him get his bearings, coming to his feet on shaky legs.

"I tried to warn you," I growled. Then I had Gunnar set me down and I began heading back towards the only thing that mattered to me.

Indie.

"Follow. Or die here, Grimm." I snarled. I heard the wolves spitting out warning growls as they shepherded my prisoner back to the entrance to the gardens.

"Oh, I've waited a long time to see this..." Barbie murmured darkly.

42

My eyes scanned the scene as I slowly began to trot, then run. Trees flew past me, broken, shattered, and uprooted. Benches, statues, the hedge maze, all were either broken, torn from the earth, or smoldering in flame, kept in check by the snow.

But I found no surviving Grimms. I saw several bodies. Grimms, dragons, and a few wolves, but none moved. It was a cemetery. Charon was about to have a busy day, but I hadn't seen him yet, which was odd.

I heard Gunnar lightly laughing off Tory's concern over his eye. "You're missing an arm." He said drily. She tried to laugh but only grunted in pain. I noticed that the green vines were growing weaker, but her wound looked better, not an immediate concern of bleeding out any longer. She murmured something to him that I didn't catch, but I did hear his response. "They were hiding on the grounds. When the Grimms left to fight us here, the pack was able to rescue their children. They apparently brought them to the mansion. Dean has them in a safe room inside *Chateau Falco*. The wolves wanted to make up for their disgrace. I accepted their offer as Alpha." His last words were dark, hungry, and a warning to the wolves trotting behind him. Tory wisely stayed silent. I idly wondered what he would ultimately decide to do with them.

But then I spotted Indie. She was lying on the earth, but no dome of power covered her any longer. A guardian fell from the sky and instantly dove to her side as if to protect her.

Then it opened its beak to rip her in half.

I began to panic.

No...

Then it hit me. When I had called upon the river of magic, I had directed all my power at Jacob. *But there will be a price...* the voice had said. And I had *agreed*.

Anything but this, I whispered to myself as I raced to her side. I didn't have a command to make the *Guardian* stop, not having planned on a need for it earlier. And I didn't have any power left.

But... the *Guardians* were *mine*.

Using my mind, I silently, frantically, commanded it to *stop*, hoping I wasn't too late.

It did, reverting back to a chipped stone statue, unmoving.

I let out a deep breath of relief. I didn't know what that had been all about, but I didn't care. Bloodlust, I guessed. She wasn't moving, and blood muddied the earth. She had fought, tried to escape. Maybe my power had prevented her from fleeing to get help from the house. Had I killed her by trying to protect her? My mind almost shut down with guilt, but I shoved it away. There might still be a chance to save her.

I gripped her shoulders, shaking her gently. "Indie, please. Wake up." My voice broke. Tears filled my eyes as I begged. "Please..." I shoved her chest several times, gripping her chin and forehead as I breathed air into her lungs. I lowered my head to her lips, listening for a breath.

Nothing.

I checked her throat for a pulse, my tears splattering her beautiful face.

Nothing.

I angrily slid an obstacle out of my way, not even looking to see what it was, as I checked her left wrist for a pulse, hoping for even a faint flicker of blood flow.

But found nothing.

My shoulders hunched as my watery gaze finally rested on the object that had impeded me. It covered the hand I had wanted to place my mother's ring on. To show her my undying love.

But that beautiful, delicate, hand was wearing the *Infinity Gauntlet* oven mitt, as if saying *yes* to the question she never got the chance to hear.

My heart shattered, then burst into flames, and I collapsed, body shaking. My mind flew, alternating between guilt, unbridled rage, sadness, and love at her wearing the ridiculous oven mitt.

"I love you, Indie..." I breathed as Gunnar rested a hand on my back, breathing heavily as he fought his own grief. A primal, beastlike scream shattered the night.

I didn't even realize that it was my own. Power raced out of me.

The earth cracked in a perfect circle around me, earth crumbling away to form a three-foot deep moat of living green fire that soared up a few feet above the ground. Screams and shouts of alarm filled the morning air. But I didn't have the energy to pay attention.

I was consumed with power. And it was beyond my control.

Energy poured out of me, deftly weaving to and fro at unseen commands by my subconscious mind, and the air abruptly formed a miniature tornado just inside the ring of fire, whipping our clothes and hair about with snapping cracks. My knees began to shake and my eyes instantly welled up. The ring of fire flared higher as a pillar of water waist-thick erupted into the sky, at least fifty yards high, originating near Indie's motionless body. A dozen bolts of lightning struck the top of the column of water in as many seconds, creating a dense fog to slowly fall to the ground like dry ice as the lightning effectively ate the excess water before it could rain down on us. The explosions abruptly stopped, causing my ears to ring, and gravity took hold, sending the water back down to the earth, the spigot abruptly ceasing. Jacob's eyes widened in disbelief, staring at me with shock.

Alucard suddenly darted out and latched onto a form hiding behind a bush. I heard fists striking flesh, and then a body landed on the ground at my feet. Without warning, I reached out and snapped open the collar around Ichabod's throat, not caring to discover what flavor of power he would use to retaliate. Then I stood and stomped on his back. I picked up a conveniently discarded nearby sword, ready to slice his throat.

Slowly.

Gunnar placed a restraining hand on my forearm, shaking his head defiantly. "Not like this. It will break you." His eye met mine in a blow of reality, bringing me back to myself. I was panting, muttering under my breath, feeling out of touch with reality, just a creature of emotion. Like a psychopath. Even the sprites were watching me cautiously.

I took a breath, closing my eyes for a moment. Then I opened them, and nudged the body, flipping him over so that I came face-to-face with their spell-slinger, Ichabod. His blue eyes were pained, momentarily stunned, but then they calmed, watching me in silence. I didn't spot one ounce of hatred at him losing the battle to a Freak. And his eyes weren't black.

Jacob sounded panicked, clutching his stomach in my peripheral vision. "He can heal..." He broke out into a fit of coughing, unable to finish. I had almost forgotten. I had seen Ichabod heal death.

I never broke eye contact with Ichabod. "You will heal my friends. Now. And owe me a favor later, no questions asked."

Jacob seemed to understand the implicit fact that to grant me a favor later they would have to be alive, which meant...

Jacob began to speak but I didn't look at him. "No questions asked." I growled.

He finally relented, realizing it was more than he deserved. "You took someone from the dragons." I told him, not breaking eye contact with Ichabod. "Where are they?"

Ichabod nodded at me, realizing Jacob no longer held any power over the situation.

A hazy silhouette became apparent off to the side, miraculously out of the danger zone and safe from the battle. They were wrapped in shadows, indiscernible other than as a vaguely human form. They turned to face us and I sighed in relief. The retaliation would have been profound if they had been harmed. I wasn't concerned for myself, but I was concerned for my friends. I was going to disappear after this. All I brought was harm to those near me.

My company was no more.

The threat was no more.

Indie was no more.

I had *nothing*.

Ichabod spoke in a dry voice. "They are unharmed." He mimicked my pronoun, not providing me an answer as to whether it was male or female. I wondered if he had done that subconsciously, or was it an effort to match my cloaked statement? Had he presumed that my choice not to name their sex was a subtle hint that those by my side shouldn't know? I pondered that, nodding finally at Ichabod.

Another thought hit me. He had used magic. But he was collarless...

He was a *Freak*.

On a leash. Well, he *had* been on a leash. Until I had broken it.

And I had seen him heal the dead. My heart began to beat faster at the potential. Perhaps Indie wasn't lost after all. I managed to keep my tone emotionless. "If you do this, I may let you two live." He met my gaze, unblinking, and then gave a single nod.

I pointed at Indie and he shook his head. "I need to... borrow some power from your friends to even have a hope at saving her. I'm spent." I didn't understand that, but waved him on to hurry. I didn't want to get my hopes up, but I also wanted to give him whatever chance he needed to bring her back.

He climbed to his feet, a hand slowly moving to his throat to reverently touch virgin skin, but eager to not make any sudden movements. He closed his eyes momentarily, and then approached Gunnar. My friend held up his hands, eye on fire with distrust. "No. I'll go last." The Grimm hesitated, and looked at me. I nodded. He bowed his head deferentially, and then moved on to Tory. He gripped her shoulders, which made me flinch, and her arm socket began to glow.

I saw the form of a new arm growing instantly, and then she gasped, collapsing to the earth with a groan. Everyone simply stared. The sprites were watching him with thoughtful, incredulous gazes. They began murmuring softly to one another in a language I couldn't understand. Ichabod smiled idly as if understanding them, but said nothing.

He approached Alucard, who was covered in scratches, some deep enough to sport muscle, gristle, and bone to the naked eye. But the wounds hadn't slowed him down at all. He made short work of my friends, healing a few broken limbs and gouges from claws, burns from dragon fire, and any other injury.

He slowly approached me, wobbling lightly on his feet before coming to a stop, hands at his sides. I pointed at Gunnar. My friend again shook his head, pointing at Indie.

Ichabod looked from Gunnar to Indie, then his head sagged.

"I cannot..." he all but whispered in defeat.

"Pardon?" I growled. "You told me you would power up with my friends' magic. I've seen you heal mortal wounds before. Do it. Now." The sword may or may not have risen in my quivering fist, ready to draw blood.

He held up a weak hand. "I do not have the strength to do so. Not after the fight and healing your friends. They were all weak. Expended. At their limits. They put everything into this fight, and there isn't enough for me to borrow from in order to heal her.

And..." he hesitated, "She is too far gone, and has no magic to aid me. Healing my... brothers was different. I could draw on their power to assist me. But everyone here is on their last legs." He lifted compassionate eyes to mine and shrugged in weariness, defeat, and resignation to his impending fate.

"Use mine, then." His head lifted.

"I cannot." He hesitated, as if debating to elaborate. "You should be dead right now." He looked at the still flickering green flames and the wet ground around Indie. "That shouldn't have been possible. You should be dead." He watched me thoughtfully. "Besides, I am barely standing. I have nothing left in me. Healing a dozen warriors without much remaining magic to aid me forced me to use my own reserves. I am depleted." He sighed, dropping his eyes, gaze locked onto the sword in my fist. "But even before healing your friends, I couldn't have helped her." He added, answering my fear.

I saw Gunnar shrug across from me, behind Ichabod now. He had circled him on silent feet. He wasn't going to be healed either. His pained expression let me know he shared my grief, relieving me of any responsibility or guilt I may have harbored on his behalf for sacrificing an eye.

Jacob began to wheeze in laughter. "You thought it would be that easy, Maker? Even *we* can't change fate."

I slowly turned to face him, confident that Gunnar could take out Ichabod if he tried to attack my defenseless back. "You look constipated, Jakey." I whispered.

"Wha–"

He abruptly cut off with a grunt as I slammed the sword into the earth all the way to the hilt. Bolts of green tracer fire instantly spider-webbed outside of the perimeter of the green fire, and I heard twin screams as they burned two unseen surviving Grimms to death. Jacob looked startled, sitting ramrod straight with wide eyes. Then he coughed, and blood bubbled out of his lips. Several took a weary step back, turning to me with confusion obvious on their faces.

I slowly withdrew the sword from the ground and it came out dripping crimson heart's blood. I wasn't sure how I had done it, but I had impaled him with the tip of the blade. From a dozen feet away. And it had killed two other Grimms I hadn't known survived. Hell of a way to go.

"There, now you should feel better." I muttered, turning away to face Ichabod again.

He was watching me. "You told him you would let us–"

"I lied." I answered bluntly.

He stared at me. Then he began to laugh. The motion actually seemed to wear him out because he fell to the ground and his eyes rolled back into his head. One of the sprites raced to his side and had him conscious again after a few moments. I didn't give him a chance to get his breath. My voice was cold, heartless. But I would at least do my duty. Keep my city safe.

"You are the last Grimm." The sprite made a choking sound, but Ichabod didn't flinch. "You will not bring your brothers back. You owe me a favor, and until then you are on a very, *very* tight leash. You so much as let out a fart without my permission and I will make your last days on this earth an eternity of pain." Alucard muffled a laugh, but Barbie looked agitated. I ignored her. Ichabod nodded once confident I was finished speaking. I flicked a hand dismissively and his body flew a dozen feet away, slamming into a tree trunk with a grunt of dispelled air. "Keep an eye on him." I muttered to no one in particular. I heard Gunnar begin coordinating some wolves to surround Ichabod, who very wisely hadn't moved.

I stared down at the love of my life, my cheeks dripping with unbidden tears. She was still sporting the *Infinity Gauntlet* oven mitt.

I smiled as I imagined a world where I had heard her shout, *Yes*, to my proposal.

A world where she had even heard the question in the first place.

43

I felt people beside me as I forestalled my next action.

Burying an innocent, beautiful, intelligent woman. A woman who had wanted to see my world.

My mouth tasted like ashes.

Well, she had gotten her wish. Gotten to see my world.

Gunnar stood on my left, unspeaking; his good eye closest to me. He held out a hand. I frowned, and finally found the muscles necessary to control my own hand to meet his. A cool metal object touched my skin, physically weighing practically nothing, but psychically weighing several tons. He murmured something about the wolves finding something, but I didn't catch it all as I opened my fingers and stared at my mother's engagement ring in my palm. Then I stared down at Indie, and the tears spilled faster.

Tory reached out from my other side and touched my arm briefly, and then she growled a curse and wrapped me in a bear hug. I stood motionless, accepting it the only way I could.

By surviving it.

I didn't have the energy to return the motion. It was all I could do not to run screaming for the nearest cliff.

She stepped back, face a mess, and gripped my chin.

She jerked it softly, attracting my attention to her own hands held out before her at waist level. She held my cherished feather, given to me by the Minotaur. It belonged, coincidentally to Grimm, Pegasus' brother, and grazing buddy to Death's own Horse, Gruff. The feather had been taken from me at some point, but I couldn't recall when. "One of them had it. He paid for his thievery." She whispered.

I murmured some form of thanks, which she apparently understood because she nodded, and then placed a large, bone white acorn in my palm. I frowned at it, lifting my eyes to hers. She shrugged. "It fell out of my wound after it was finished healing." I stared at it blankly. Then I shrugged, and bent down over Indie's body, resting on my heels as I shoved the feather into my pocket.

The ebony sprite was suddenly beside me, staring sadly at Indie's body. I almost growled at her to leave, but she calmly reached over and plucked the acorn from my palm before I could react. She placed it over Indie's chest, and then turned her sad eyes to mine. Their other worldliness seemed to pull at me momentarily, so I jerked my gaze away. After a moment, I nodded in thanks.

"Will you... I think she would have wanted you all to help me bury her." I rasped to no one and everyone. I heard several affirmative murmurs through emotional throats. The ebony sprite moved first, and a deep humming filled my ears. The ground began to respond, and suddenly began sinking down further into the earth, carrying Indie down into the ground at least a dozen feet before her motion slowed. She rested in a perfect curvature of smoothly rounded dirt.

I stared at her for a few moments, and then had a thought.

"Everyone... grab something important to you. Now."

I had meant to only talk to those immediately around me. But apparently, everyone involved in the fight was within earshot. I heard rustling all around. Then they began to step forward one by one.

Gunnar murmured a Norse funeral rite, and then bit his freaking wrist. Blood splashed into the earth. The sprites looked suddenly tense, and pleased.

Tory's face was blotchy, no doubt thinking of Misha. I promised myself that no matter what I did next I would at least go to her funeral. I could run away afterwards. Tory took a deep breath, and I watched her, not seeing anything in her hands. She took several breaths, closing her eyes for several eternal seconds.

Then she opened her eyes, and began to laugh. At first it was forced, tears wrecking her beautiful features. But the laughter soon infected her, and began to sound more genuine as memories flashed in her wet eyes.

And then they began to sparkle with pure joy. Soon the laughs were erupting from deep within her chest, and I noticed that it was affecting those around me. Everyone was smiling. Sadness was still predominant, but an undercurrent of joy now boosted their resolve. The laughter soon died away, and Tory knelt, kissing the earth, "I give you laughter, you dear thing. Carry it with you on your travels." Then she stood, head bowed in silence.

Barbie stepped forward and silently cast a tiny sphere of glowing light down into the grave. "May your path be ever lightened." The sphere touched her chest and erupted into a silvery dome, lighting the clearing. I noticed the vampires flinch protectively in my peripheral vision.

The ebony sprite stood and gave her a rippling black orb of power, the antithesis of Barbie's gift. "May this eat away any darkness your light cannot pierce." And the silvery dome of light evaporated, casting the scene back into the light of only the weak sunrise.

They then spoke in unison. "Our fallen sister gives you life, in the form of an acorn, a seed of hope for us to remember you both."

Everyone was silent until Raego stepped up. He calmly tossed a black dragon's scale into the pit. "To shield your soul from harm. You were a beautiful soul, Indiana Rippley. The world is now a darker place." He turned away, breathing heavily.

Alucard stepped up, looking uncomfortable. He looked torn. He met my eyes, kept my gaze for a few moments as he debated internally with himself. Then he tossed in his umbrella sword. "I didn't have the chance to know you, but anyone who commands such respect from such powerful people deserves my greatest possession. The blade has been in my family for centuries. Keep it safe and let it protect you from grief." He nodded at me and stepped back.

One of the wolves padded forward and silently dropped a mouthful of Grimm amulets into the hole. He whimpered at Gunnar, who nodded before interpreting. "He gives the trophies of the wolves. Those Grimms killed at their hands are pledged in honor to Indie." The wolf crept back out of the immediate vicinity.

Everyone turned to me. I debated. I too had nothing of value on me. Well, I did, but I didn't know what was more important.

The ring was the obvious choice, but I wasn't an obvious kind of guy. And I wanted to keep that for myself, as a reminder of the woman I loved more than life itself.

I withdrew Grimm's feather. The ability to call a fearsome beast for protection.

I let it fall from my fingertips. Everyone watched as it floated down to finally rest over her eyes. I knew that death wasn't always exactly an end, and I wanted to make sure she had a guardian. "To the woman who let me briefly see Heaven. She has gone home, and like Raego said, the world is a darker place for it. Let her passion be an example. She was the weakest of us, with no magic, but she was also the bravest of us. Whether she had been taken or not, she was going to be here to fight and help. Her courage was undisputable, and unparalleled. She was... my *everything*..."

And now I have nothing.

My breathing grew hoarse, deeper, faster, and pained. The blood of battle soaked the icy soil, as well as the dust of my long-dead ancestor's remains from the pulverized statue.

And the love of my life lay buried at the epicenter of the chaos. The restraint on my power crashed behind a torrent of raw power. I would create something beautiful out of this tragedy. It would be my last memorable act. Even if my world was now dead to me.

Even if it burned away all my power and killed me.

Indie deserved it.

I let out a yell, casting one fist into the sky and one down at her body – at the acorn – fusing *life* and *hope* into the seed. My broken dreams at a future life with Indie raged and screamed, producing the antithesis of my new reality.

Life.

Happiness.

Contentment.

My fists began to glow, one shining yellow as it pointed at the sky, and the other blue pointing down at Indie's body. Then they began to pulse, alternating, and I felt my soul washing away, power scouring away my existence. A bolt struck my fist from the heavens in a viridian explosion, and my eyes shot wide open. A heartbeat later, a purple blast slammed down into the earth in a web that halted a moment before striking Indie, coming to rest over her form like a blanket gently tucking a child in for bedtime.

The sprites were doing something, somehow complementing my power. Dirt began to fold in on itself and slowly cover up the purple blanket protecting the woman I loved. The ground quieted for a moment, now perfectly smooth and devoid of snow, and I realized that the sprites were singing in a haunting, angelic song of an unknown language. A language understood only through sensation, not words. Emotion given sound.

The entire earth began to rumble inside the ring I had made earlier, which was still guttering lightly with green fire. I stumbled, realizing that it was only growing stronger.

"Get back!" I roared, grabbing Tory's coat as I dove over the trench.

Moments later the ground rocked, and a sapling exploded out of the earth, growing in fast forward, widening, thickening, sprouting branches and leaves as it raced towards the heavens. I could feel and hear the roots screaming as they tore through icy soil and rock, but the tree didn't slow until it reached a height of at least a hundred feet at the entrance to the gardens.

And it was bone white, with pale silver leaves. Several fell from the force of the rapid growth, and lightly drifted to the ground. I reached out to catch one, sobbing openly at the beauty of the fallen sprite's gift of life from the acorn, and hissed as the leaf sliced through my fingertips like a razor.

I stared at my bleeding finger in disbelief and then began to laugh.

Just like Indie. *A mouth like a razor, that one...* I had once heard an employee describe Indie. I don't know how long we stared at the stunningly beautiful tree until a strange motion off to my right shattered the silent majestic safety of the sheltering branches.

I lurched to my feet, hungry to destroy something.

44

It was the shadowy figure kidnapped by the Grimms. She was shaking, railing against an invisible force, and I assumed she was shouting.

I turned to Ichabod, who was staring at the tree with wide eyes, mouth opening and closing wordlessly. "Conceal her. But leave her senses accessible." He did so with a wave of his hand. "Now, it's time to call in my favor." He waited obediently. "Make a call."

"I have no... *phone*." He said the word oddly, unfamiliar with such a device.

"You won't need one." I responded drily. His eyes squinted for a moment, and then he smiled in understanding.

He murmured several words and flung his hand out at the air between me and my friends, ripping a void in the fabric of reality.

A doorway.

Revealing Jafar.

He jumped to his feet from a chair, staring at me incredulously. Then at Ichabod. He began to shout over his shoulder. He was armed for battle. A dozen Academy Justices jumped through the opening ahead of their Captain, all strapped in battle leathers. That pretty much answered my question right there. They had been ready for this call. And had known it would happen around now. After my scheduled fight with the Grimms.

They had known it all.

Too bad they hadn't anticipated my success.

Or the fact that Ichabod had opened the gateway in the center of two aggressive fronts of Freaks who were a tad bit irrational at present. Several Justices let out a shout of surprise to see werewolves, vampires, sprites, and dragons surrounding them, and Ichabod the only Grimm in sight. And the last Maker in existence staring at them with cold, dead, heartless eyes. At least I was pretty sure I looked that way. It's how I felt, and I had no energy to put on a front.

I no longer cared.

"Well, I would love to hear you explain this one," I said drily, staring directly at Jafar.

He looked from me to Ichabod, no doubt wondering if I was under the man's control or if it was the other way around. As his eyes roved from face to face, he was bright enough to realize the Grimms were no more. He didn't look pleased, but he also didn't look disappointed. "Bravo." He muttered. "This was your little problem? This man?"

I didn't blink. "He had a friend or two. You can find bits and pieces of them around here somewhere. Well, *everywhere*, I guess." I pointed a finger at Jacob's body, which I suddenly noticed was very embarrassingly face down, exposing his rear end to the air. I decided to let imaginations run wild with the story of his demise. But I wasn't concerned with those stories, as entertaining as they may be. I was concerned with Jafar's reaction.

And he didn't disappoint.

There was a moment – a tiny, almost unnoticeable moment – where recognition flashed across his eyes. Then a flicker of disbelief. And then it was gone.

He turned to face me, poker face back in place. "This was approved through the proper channels? We don't condone murder," He growled authoritatively. Several Justices flexed fists at their sides, ready to throw down.

I began to laugh. No one moved. But Jafar's face darkened.

"Go right ahead," I chuckled. "Arrest us. There were no... *proper channels* involved. In fact, I killed this one with quite the *opposite* of the *proper channels*. I impaled him. A little out of fashion these days, but I found it quite satisfying." I straightened my face and enunciated each word, grinning openly. "I murdered this man in cold blood. He was defenseless at the time. I had hinted at letting him go. He was cooperating." Jafar's face looked victorious. "I killed him. Slowly. And I enjoyed every *second* of it." I shot him a wolfish smile, holding out my hands for imaginary handcuffs. "Do something about it, oh Noble Knight."

As if on cue, the dragons let out short puffs of fire and the wolves targeted individual Justices. Tory calmly picked up a stone pillar once belonging to a birdbath, calmly snapped off the bowl with her hand, and hefted the revised bludgeoning tool with a satisfied grunt. The sprites moved like wraiths, drifting closer to the action with predatory smiles.

The Justices, the most feared group of killers on the planet, *hesitated*.

Which seemed to infuriate old Jafar.

"I'm waiting, shit stain," I teased, using my grief to speak freely. I had no concern for my safety any longer. I was also *very* inclined to cut loose with my power again. I was slightly drunk off it from earlier.

Jafar quivered, but didn't make a motion to arrest me. I frowned, and lowered my hands. "So, how was this supposed to play out? You were obviously ready with a squad of thugs to go *somewhere*. And Ichabod here had a direct phone number to reach you. Almost as if you had worked together, or something."

He began to growl. "Very clever. It changes nothing. We hired assassins to take out a threat to our people. We were prepared to apprehend—"

I held up a finger, frowning thoughtfully as I blatantly interrupted him. "*We*? You're *sure* about that?" I asked softly. His eyes tightened. "As in, this was authorized via *proper channels*? You're telling me you had the backing of the Academy to take out a person who had signed a peace treaty with them in the presence of an Angel and a Horseman of the Apocalypse?" Even mentioning Death's name by proxy made my vision pulse blue. It was his fault Indie had been taken. I didn't know how or why, but he was going to pay. After that I would disappear.

Jafar threw up his hands. "Of course it was sanctioned. I'm the Captain of the Justices. Who do you think you are, questioning me? You are a *murderer*."

"Is it really murder when I defend myself from other murderers?" I smiled. "I don't see it that way. Neither do these guys. You're more than welcome to disagree." My eyes glittered hungrily, and I couldn't hide the interest in my voice. "*Please* disagree."

He did nothing. Just stared back at me, thinking furiously. Looking for a political loophole to weasel out of. But I didn't play politics. Neither had Indie.

"You hired the biggest threat in the world to take out little old me. A force so feared that they were locked away for hundreds of years to keep us all safe," I let the silence build, and then shrugged as I turned my back on him. "How did that work out for you?"

Several Justices moved, judging by the reactive snarls of my friends. I didn't turn around. It might have looked fearless and suave on my part, but to be honest, I welcomed someone to end me right here. The only thing I truly wanted to do was to kill the Horseman for letting Indie be kidnapped. After that I had nothing left to live for.

"How fucking stupid are you, Jafar? Did you honestly believe that they would act in good faith after they killed me? They are hungry to kill all of us. They don't even see us as human. We are pests in their eyes. We require extermination. *All of us*. Are you truly that arrogant?"

He snarled. "If you could beat them, so could I. You are nothing. You don't deserve to live after your blatant disrespect of the Academy. Your constant bending and shattering of the rules is a poison. You are a nuisance. An eyesore. A blemish that must be lanced. You are cancerous."

I turned to stare at him in surprise. "Do you truly believe all of that?" He nodded. "That's kind of... *mean*," I chuckled. "Anyway, you hired men who would kill us all to order a sanctioned..." I hesitated. "It *was* sanctioned, you said?" He nodded after a few seconds. "Right. To order a sanctioned hit on an ally of the Academy." I pretended to think for a minute, but I knew what it was really all about. The Armory.

"You really want the Armory that badly?" I shook my head in disbelief. "It's kind of amazing to me. To hunger after something so desperately. Not being given the toy must have really bothered you in grade school." I shook my head again.

"Well, this toy isn't up for grabs, like I told you last time. You're more than welcome to try and take it from me." I smiled, crossing my hands behind my back as I turned to face him. "Go ahead. Try."

Again, he didn't oblige. I sighed, shaking my head. "What do you think they would have done with the Armory after killing me?"

"It was to pass to our hands, of course." The, *you idiot*, was implied in his tone. "That's why we came prepared to fight. They wouldn't have stood a chance against us after your battle, and with the Armory at our disposal." He snapped, spittle flying.

I nodded, and then addressed one of the Justices. "You ever see an official order about this assassination contract?" He didn't answer. "Don't worry, you don't have to answer that. Answer this instead. Does this kind of subterfuge sound like it's official? And more importantly, do you agree with it... *Justice?*"

"Enough!" Jafar roared. "They answer to *me*, not *you*. Who cares if it was official? It was in the best interests of the Academy. When they hear how you slaughtered over a dozen humans, you will be finished. Friends helping you or not."

Which was actually a good point. Without the amulets, the Grimms were pure mortals. I would look kind of guilty.

Jafar's face looked victorious. I bowed my head in defeat for a few seconds, and listened as he commanded his Justices to arrest me. One took a single step, and I lifted my cold gaze to meet his. He rocked back a step, hands reflexively darting to the sword at his belt. I smiled, and held up a finger.

"Oh, I almost forgot..." I motioned to Ichabod. "Drop the veil on our guest. Entirely. Remove any hindrance on their senses. They were only placed there to protect everyone's safety until the proper moment." Ichabod smiled, and did as commanded.

To reveal the person Raego had kidnapped at the beginning of all this.

Operation White Knight.

I turned to Jafar, grinning like an idiot. I was going to enjoy this. His face paled, and a small part of my heart erupted in joy as he witnessed the person behind the veil. Then a surprising thing happened. Every single wizard dropped to his knees, and bowed their heads to the ground. Even Jafar. The Justices tore away their masks in a puff of fairy dust, which powered them. I frowned, turning in confusion. *What the...*

Then I froze, and might have made a small whimper.

A frail old woman stood only a few feet away; apparently having strode up to me in the few seconds I had been watching Jafar suffer. I held up my hands defensively.

"You've got to be kidding me! Raego! What the *hell* were you *thinking*? I didn't mean *her*! How am I supposed to regain their trust *now*?"

Her eyes were twin coals, and she seemed to be debating which one of us to skewer first. I couldn't attack *her*. I didn't think I stood a chance even if I tried. Even if all of us tried. Collectively.

Raego mumbled from the other side of Jafar. "You said an Academy Member. Someone of importance. She was the first one we saw. Easiest target." He turned to address her. "No offense. She must have mistaken me for one of her associates." He added sheepishly, hinting at his ability to shift into different people entirely. She didn't look amused, so he continued. "Why? Who is she?"

The old woman was tapping her foot angrily, glaring daggers at me, seeing as how I was the only person meeting her gaze. "Um, maybe because she's the *Grandmaster* of the Academy? You. Idiot." I swallowed, leaving my hands where she could see them. "This was a mistake. A very big mistake. I suspected Jafar's involvement and knew no other way to let the truth be known. With him as the detective, the Academy would only hear what he reported. Like last time." I lowered my hands slowly.

I wasn't concerned for my safety.

Okay, I *was* terrified to die, assuming that she could kill me in very creative, drawn out ways. But I was only terrified of the actual *experience* of dying slowly. I didn't care to live anymore, but that didn't mean I was going to go volunteer for the nearest torture house either.

But I *was* concerned for my friends. So, I assumed responsibility.

"This was all on me. These people did only as requested. They had nothing–"

She held up a gnarled hand. Despite her age, she moved with agility, authority, and the mantle of command. She had freaking *calluses* where the mantle of power rested on her shoulders. She was hundreds of years old, and the legends surrounding her life allegedly rivaled Merlin.

The first Merlin.

I didn't even know her real name. Just Grandmaster. Maybe *Madame* Grandmaster.

"You presumed he was acting outside his authority," I nodded. "But you had no proof when you kidnapped me. You weren't *sure*." I sagged my shoulders and nodded, not hiding my guilt.

"I only wanted one of the top dogs to see what their hound was doing behind their backs," I added honestly.

"Top dog?" She rasped in disbelief. "Yes, well, I believe you found your *top dog*." Her eyes could have frozen fire. "You will pay for your actions today. Even if you are outside my jurisdiction." She promised. And I shivered. When people like her made promises, they damn well kept them. I would have to run far, far away to escape her wrath. Then run *further*.

She turned to Jafar, and I relaxed a tiny bit. He seemed to sense her glare and lifted his face, looking guilty as guilty can be. She shook her head. "You have disappointed the Academy. You have disappointed *me*." She continued to watch him and each word struck him like a physical blow. "This man arranged for me to be kidnapped. But you betrayed morals for personal vengeance. Working with our greatest enemy, the Grimms. And you cloaked it with the Academy's stamp of approval. A nation that has spent hundreds of years to earn a reputation of trust – if not *peace* – from all supernatural persons. You abused that power and forced this *ally* to risk everything to prove his innocence."

Jafar crumpled in fear and submission.

She continued, addressing the Justices. *Her* Justices. "You are all on probation."

They shivered in response, but didn't raise their heads. I was guessing probation meant something akin to a long trip to Siberia. In the nude. While being squirted with super soakers. "Jafar," her voice was pure frost, and then I realized it was literal frost as the fires around us died instantly. "You are hereby under arrest."

My anger jumped back to the forefront of my mind.

"Nope." Everyone froze. My friends suddenly tensed, sensing the imminent fight.

"Excuse me?" She whispered, slowly turning to address me as if surprised.

"It's not going to happen that way. He's mine."

She blinked. "That is not how this works, young man."

I held up a finger. "I think you forget who you are talking to," I answered respectfully. "Don't take this the wrong way, but this man's actions caused the deaths of many people. *My* people. He was under your control when initiating this."

She snarled. "If I hadn't been *kidnapped*, I would have caught on before it escalated this far." I sensed her gathering her power.

"Remember our truce, wizard." I warned.

"You broke our truce." Her power continued to build.

I shook my head. "I didn't kidnap you. True, I ordered it, but were you harmed? Even remotely?" Her face grew victorious, no doubt remembering the Grimms abducting her. "Harm caused directly by me and mine," I quickly corrected.

"Semantics," she stated flatly.

"Yet that is exactly what our agreement states, yes?"

She flinched as if struck, lips tightening impotently. "You do not want to press me on this. He is *my* responsibility. *I* will deal with him."

"Like I already told you. That's not going to happen. He abandoned his position the moment he broke the law. Under normal circumstances I would agree with you. But you see that tree?" her eyes darted to it, knowing full well what lay beneath it. She had witnessed everything, after all. She didn't respond. "That can't be given back to me. He dies. Here. Now. By my hand." Her eyes glittered with malice. "Whether you want it that way or not." I promised. "There are witnesses here to see what you do. Do you really want the world to know what truly happened here? That the *Grandmaster* of the *Academy* was kidnapped? That your own *Captain* betrayed you? What do you think that is going to do to your precious reputation? What were you planning on telling the Academy members when they asked why you were holding a decorated veteran in your prison?" Her eyes grew thoughtful, and I felt her power finally diminish. I hid my sigh of relief. I would have thrown down, but some of us would have died.

Perhaps *all* of us.

I waited for her to respond. Her eyes darted from person to person. My friends stared back, ready to go to war. And she realized that she couldn't win cleanly. Whether she won or lost, word would get out. And the respect for the Academy would evaporate overnight. Their Grandmaster kidnapped. Their veteran Captain a traitor. Collaborating with the Brothers Grimm, whose hatred for *all* freaks was well-documented.

She was essentially politi-fucked.

She finally turned to me, frustration apparent on her features. I nodded coolly. "He's mine." She nodded, and flung a casual finger at Jafar as he opened his mouth to speak. His mouth clamped shut and he lurched to his feet against his will where he stood motionless, face turning crimson as he struggled against her bonds.

She turned to me. "Remember my generosity. Also, remember that I would not have been as gentle as you are about to be." She watched me for a moment, assessing. "You will pay for this," She promised.

I waved a hand, pointing at the scene of the battle and the fact that I had just killed the legendary Brothers Grimm. "I'm really not that concerned about it. St. Louis is off limits. You want to fight, call me. My friends were only defending themselves. They were targeted by the Grimms, thanks to your poor management structure."

Her face darkened, but she kept her calm. "You are amassing quite the arsenal." The Armory was left unspoken, but it was obvious. She was also subtly referring to my crew.

"Not by choice. By necessity. Your people obviously went rogue. You need to clean house. Then we can talk. Maybe. I might be busy." Her face darkened, but she didn't respond.

Then a subsonic scream tore the night as a gateway appeared before her. The sound wasn't necessary. More like a parting slap directed at me. She shooed the Justices through the gateway and we were suddenly free from their meddling. Jafar looked panicked. I smiled at him.

"Let's see how gentle I can be." I grinned.

And I sent a blast of power into him before he could retaliate. He slammed into the base of Indie's tree, head cracking into the wood in a red splatter. Then I let loose. Twin bolts of lightning slammed into him as I cast him up into the air in a vortex of power. He evaporated into nothing, and my vision rippled, more black flecks racing across my eyes. A coil of darkness overcame me for a few moments. I felt like I had swallowed rancid oil. And then I found myself somewhere else entirely.

Somewhere familiar.

And terrifying.

45

I stood in a blinding white room. White couches, white walls, white tables... listen, you get it.

My *existence* was a stain on this place.

And I had been here before.

Last time I had been here was only a few months ago. Ironically, it was also after a fight with Jafar and his Justices. A rogue Justice. A sprinkling of Horsemen, Angels, and Demons had also made an appearance.

But even having been here before, I still wasn't sure what this place *was*.

Death had told me not to talk about it. And had seemed alarmed that I knew of it. Last time when I had been here I had stained anything I touched. Out of curiosity, I tried it again on a hidden corner of a lampshade. As I withdrew my fingers, I saw the stain. Although this time the stain seemed darker. I began to panic at that. What did it mean? Where was I?

And what was that *noise*?

I froze.

Noise.

Footsteps approached from somewhere in the house, and they were rapidly drawing closer. I began panting, willing myself back to the gardens outside my home. But nothing happened.

And those footsteps kept right on coming.

They sounded like boots on hollow wood – like everyone's upstairs neighbor in the morning when you were trying to sleep in. In fact, the pictures on the wall began to shake slightly with each step.

Whatever was coming was *big*.

I clenched my eyes, willing, begging, to teleport myself out of here. I began to hear heavy breathing as the footsteps entered the room just outside mine.

Please, please, *please*...

I *really* didn't want to meet the owner of this house. Especially not after staining his lampshade. He seemed like the kind of guy who might notice. And might take offense. Anyone who lived in a white house was undoubtedly OCD about things like that.

My eyes quested the room for any possibility of escape. They briefly settled on a book resting on the coffee table and I froze. The book was obviously white, but stained with grey fingerprints. The cover was a pressed image and the words of the title were legible from a few feet away. *Through the Looking Glass*. I had touched this book last time I was here, and the fingerprints were all mine. My skin began to prickle. This book had been on the bookshelf last time I was here. Which meant that whoever lived here knew of my previous intrusion, and had left the book out as a warning... or a conversation starter. But I really didn't want to have a conversation.

At all.

The handle began to turn, and my stomach roiled as the door began to open.

I managed to see a gnarly red beard and a giant booted foot enter the room before my body evaporated to a cloud of mist and I found myself suddenly back in the gardens, panting wildly. Sirens filled the air, and I heard bullhorns, slamming car doors, and angry shouting.

My eyes danced about wildly, trying to make sense of the room and my sudden change in surroundings. How had the cops gotten here so fast? It had been quiet only a few minutes ago. How long had I been unconscious?

As my mind struggled to overcome my fear at escaping the strange room and make sense of the sudden riot of sound, my phone began to ring. I answered it instinctively, glancing at my friends. All were in the same position, and Gunnar was just now racing towards me, as if I had only just fallen. *What the hell?*

"Nate!" The voice belted directly into my ear canal.

My breath froze. "Othello?" I asked incredulously, feeling a deep anger building as I remembered she hadn't answered any of my calls when I needed her most.

"Yes!" She was crying heavily. "You're alright. Oh, thank *God*. I was so worried about you. I saw all your calls once I broke free–"

"Wait, what?" My anger sputtered.

"I was kidnapped. Held in a cell. I couldn't escape. They didn't harm me, just kept me in a cell. Really weird. Then last night I found that the door was unlocked and no one was guarding me so I fled. It was an abandoned building in Cairo. In fact, the whole street seemed deserted. I couldn't find anyone. Not even a taxi. I had to walk a mile before anyone helped me. Then I couldn't get a hold of you. What happened? You're all over the news."

"Yeah, I'm going to need to call you back. My lawyer is here." I said, spotting Turner Locke running towards me.

"I called him, you idiot. An hour ago."

I blinked. "Oh." Turner reached my side, puffing heavily, the police racing up the grounds a hundred yards behind him. Talk about good timing. "Thanks. I'll... I'll call you back soon." I lied, hanging up.

"Nate!" Turner shouted urgently. "Do I have your permission to prevent them from entering the grounds?"

I smiled. "Oh, yeah."

He turned and ran back, waving his hands like a crazy person, a sheaf of papers in his fist. The cars stopped, men jumping out with weapons drawn. "Stop!" He commanded before they could whip out their bullhorns. Several cars sat idling by the entrance, calling for everyone to come out with their hands up, but they were just far enough back to not see any bodies. As were the cops now talking to Turner. "I have a letter from the mayor, signed by three judges that this man is innocent and your warrant invalid," he declared.

I smiled, and walked towards the tree, tuning everyone out.

My mind raced as Gunnar stepped up beside me, turning to face the police, guarding me in case Turner failed, saying nothing. Othello had been kidnapped. It must have been the Grimms. They knew of her and didn't want her blowing the whistle on their attack on Temple Industries.

What blew my mind was that they had had the foresight to do any of it. Something was missing. How could they have become so interconnected? There was another player somewhere helping them, and I didn't think it had been Jafar. He was a thug. Not a planner. Not a schemer. This reeked of a schemer.

And the more I thought about it, I could think of only one other person who might know.

Death.

I had to go kill Death for failing Indie.

But I would make sure to ask him some questions first. I stood, ready to go take care of business. I looked up to see that the cops were mostly gone, the last of them making their escape. As if unaware of the cops, I saw a man climbing off of a motorcycle only a few feet away from me. I was sure I heard it neigh like a horse. But I hadn't heard him approach. I found myself growling, and then the world suddenly halted, except for us.

Snowflakes floated in the air, unmoving, and the last of the policemen stood outside their car, one foot inside the vehicle, one still on the ground. My friends stood in various positions, some pointing, some mouths open as if speaking.

All were still.

Good. I didn't even need to leave my house to take care of killing Death.

46

He began clapping, face serious, as he approached. "The Rider of Hope. I never thought you would be able to use it as a weapon so soon."

I didn't sense any magic other than the stillness of time. Which was odd. He normally reeked of magic, after you knew what to look for. "My hope is dead." I whispered, glancing over at the tree. "You saw to that." I finally lifted my eyes to meet his.

And he stopped.

Sure, I was kind of a badass and I had a reputation for being a hothead.

But this was Death.

And he had hesitated. Looking closer, I even noticed that he looked guilty, despite his next words. "I wouldn't be so sure..." he answered cryptically.

"You were supposed to keep her safe." My voice was a wreck, and my cheeks were wet with tears. "I thought that you of all people would understand that obligation. I trusted you." I let venom lace my words, alluding to the death of his family so many centuries ago. His face was tight, offended, but empathetic of my tone. "I have one question," he nodded. "Was it intentional?"

Death watched me in silence for a time, the world seeming to hold its breath. "You can speak freely. What you mean to ask is, *did I intentionally harm Indie in an attempt to hurt you*? Or, *did I intentionally allow her to be taken in an attempt to hurt you*?" He clarified. His face grew harder. "No. Neither of those. Never."

I waited for him to continue. "That wasn't my question."

His face grew pained. "I'll answer your *true* question. Was I manipulating events from the outside? Yes. Was it to aid the Grimms and overthrow you?" He stared up at the tree, a lone tear forming before he wiped it away. "I did not collaborate with the Grimms to aid them in any way, shape, or form. I swear it on my power. What they did, they did. I might have been able to stop it, but larger pieces are at play. It was... *necessary*."

"Necessary..." The word sounded foreign on my tongue. My fury bubbled over and I slammed my fist into the ground, causing a minor shockwave of power to roll outwards from me in a rippling ring. It struck an invisible force and the sound of a thousand bells crashed over us, and time lurched back to normal around us.

Death looked amazed, but not fearful as he turned from the previously unseen ward to me with thoughtful eyes. Gunnar caught a glance at me, and flinched, suddenly noticing I wasn't alone. He shouted and suddenly my crew was racing towards me. Most of them. Enough of them.

Although, I didn't need their help.

They skidded to a halt around Death, all too aware of my current opinion of the man. The place was silent as everyone watched me. I wanted to kill him. *Needed* to kill him. But... a nagging thought crept into my mind. I honestly wasn't sure what that would do to the world. Maybe we *needed* him. He was specifically tied to Armageddon. And I had met *actual* Angels and Demons.

They all walked cautiously around Death.

Not even considering his three brothers, War, Famine, and Pestilence.

I shook my head. Deciding that if at any point in my life I had needed a minute to clear my head, this was it. "Yeah. You should probably leave. I don't trust what I may do to you if I see you here for even one minute longer." He watched me, face looking torn with regret. He opened his mouth as if to speak, but shook his head.

He left.

On his motorcycle.

Again, I was confident I heard a neigh combined with the roar of the bike, but what caught me as odd was that he hadn't used any magic. He could have simply Shadow Walked – or whatever his version of it was – out of my garden.

But he hadn't.

A sign of respect? Not wanting to push the unstable Maker before him any further than necessary? Was I truly that dangerous in his eyes?

I didn't speak as I turned back to the tree, considering the conversation as I took deep meditative breaths. *Hope*. The Rider of Hope. A Fifth Horseman of the Apocalypse.

I chuckled, shaking my head.

Yeah, right.

They needed a new Human Resources department.

I couldn't even keep my girlfriend safe. Or my friends.

I had told Death that my hope was dead. And he had answered cryptically, as all ancient beings did, that maybe that wasn't the case. I watched the silver leaves swaying in the wind hundreds of feet above me. Thinking about it now, I had imbued the tree with my hope. My hope for Indie to have a pleasant passing onto whatever the next realm of existence was, if there was such a thing. Thoughts of the tree inevitably brought the memory of the White Room back into existence. I shivered, thinking about the giant ginger living there.

I would have to look into it.

Tomorrow.

After I decided what to do with Death.

After all, he had been in the room too. Or at least knew of it.

Regardless, the tree seemed to emanate a similar power as the gentle throbbing of the mysterious room. Also, it was a bleached bone-white shade. Pretty similar to the room.

Tory offered me her healed arm, face drawn in an attempt at a tired smile. I took it, and we slowly made our way back to the mansion. Gunnar was the first to speak.

"Ichabod is gone."

I halted, jarring Tory. His face was hard as we locked eyes. We had a silent conversation, where he promised to keep an eye out for him. I nodded, and continued on, strides more powerful now.

To be honest. I used my anger as a crutch. I wasn't angrily storming away to formulate plans to take out Ichabod and deliver the last dose of vengeance against the Grimms.

I was figuratively running. The towering tree seemed to chuckle at my cowardice as I fled. Laughing softly, silently, eerily familiar. I shivered, and blocked it away.

The conversation picked back up as we walked. I caught bits and pieces of the events after the battle, but to be honest, I didn't care. As long as they were safe, I was happy. They wouldn't have me around much longer to drag them into trouble anymore.

Small favors.

47

It had been a week since the battle, and the mansion was thankfully quiet again. Having a pack of werewolves and their pups in the residence had been stressful, but I had never seen Dean so lively. Every spill and broken artifact had been met with ultimate happiness at being able to perform his function.

A Butler.

I had let everyone stay at my place for a while to verify that their homes were safe and that we hadn't missed any of the Grimms. Other than Ichabod, that is. We had yet to find a trace of the man, no matter how hard we tried. It seemed that his experience off the grid was coming in handy for him. Not the other way around. I had hoped that his ignorance would allow him to be caught on camera, or to accidentally challenge someone to a duel for stealing the milk he himself wanted at the grocery store.

No such luck.

I had made sure to hide the books well, under dozens of protection spells so that they could never, *ever* be found. The sprites had been satisfied, barely. They still believed that at least *Grimm's Fairy Tales* should be destroyed, but I couldn't force myself to burn a book, no matter how dangerous.

I was a bookstore owner. Books were like children to me.

I had finally regained entrance to the Armory, checked in on everyone, let Gunnar give Pandora and my parents the cursory details, and then fled before the conversation could branch out to more painful subjects. They deserved more, but I didn't have it in me yet to talk about it.

About *her*.

I fingered the ring I constantly carried in my pocket now. An idle habit. The wind buffeted my overcoat as I sat on one of the repaired benches outside the garden, staring at the bark of the alien tree towering over my home. Thinking. Reminiscing. Trying to move on. I hadn't had time to reach out to Death, what with taking care of the dozens of werewolf pups secreted away at *Chateau Falco* during the fight. Like Gunnar had mentioned, the wolves had taken the opportunity to rescue them when all the Grimms left to fight me at dawn. They, having been suckered by Wilhelm, had been aware of the final meeting place, and had brought everyone here during the battle, secreting them away with Dean in one of the safe rooms. Then the parents had come to join us in battle.

Well, to join Gunnar.

I hadn't seen much of my friend. He had been preoccupied with watching over his new pack of werewolves, and their fledgling member.

His fiancé. Ashley. She had pulled through. Successfully surviving her first change. That was the last I had heard from my friend. An almost guilty, proud phone call that she had taken to it like a natural. I smiled, thinking about it. Working for my parents, she had spent the majority of her life around Freaks, so I wasn't too surprised.

Tory had flown to Scandinavia with Raego and the dragons for a brief mourning period. They had taken Misha's daughters along, in hopes that the countryside would do them some good. A place where there was less chance for collateral damage. Tory had stepped in as a surrogate mother to the dragonlings, much to Raego's pleasure and approval.

Agent Jeffries – the supernatural lie detector and FBI Agent I had nicknamed White Lie – and my lawyer, Turner Locke, had been in constant contact with me regarding Temple Industries. They – with Othello's help – had legally proven that my alibis held up, that I physically couldn't have been the one to cause all the mayhem and illegal short-selling of my own company, but it was too late. Trust in Temple Industries was at an all-time low, and for them to have any chance of surviving, Ashley and I had to stay out.

Temple Industries was no more. The best employees had already fled, joining the German firm. Part of me hated them for it, knowing that the Grimms had orchestrated it all, but part of me got it too. Despite my failed company, I knew the men in blue would be watching me even closer, now.

But I could live with that.

Money was my true concern. My mansion, *Chateau Falco* was actually owned in trust, with the funds held there sufficient to cover upkeep and maintenance in perpetuity, so I wouldn't have to worry about utilities or selling it any time soon. Still, I had no means of making income outside Plato's Cave, which was still undergoing renovations after a heavenly hit squad had disagreed with me a few months back.

I had lost billions of dollars, confiscated by my friends at the FBI, and it would take years and hundreds of millions of dollars, if not more, to get any of it back. So I had donated it equally to the families of those loyal employees. The ones who had stayed despite the news. St. Louis had an influx of *New Money* to contend with.

Which made me smile.

I thought of Greta, Ashley's assistant, the religious die-hard, and what she might do with all the money now at her disposal. Probably give it to a charity. Or make a charity specifically aimed at saving my everlasting soul. *That rapscallion, Nate Temple...* I grinned. Then my eyes fell back on the tree and it died slowly but completely as if it never were.

I heard a nicker nearby and glanced over to find Grimm grazing under the tree. He had become a permanent fixture on the grounds. I wasn't sure if it was a token of sorrow from Asterion, the Minotaur, or if Grimm sincerely wanted to be here, a shoulder for me to lean on. Or if he was drawn to his feather now resting over Indie's corpse deep underground. We had grown close over the last year; meeting up once a week or so, weather permitting, to go on a cross-country ride through Illinois or some other near locale. Of course, somewhere we wouldn't be seen. I had even taken Indie along once...

Grimm neighed as if in salute to my unspoken memory.

I wouldn't have been surprised to discover he really could read my thoughts.

Two ravens swooped down to stare at me, perching on one of the nearby trees. Their eyes were entirely too intelligent for my tastes as they studied me, but I just didn't have it in me to care too much. I ignored their presence.

It seemed the world had been holding its breath since the Grimms visit. The Academy was silent. In fact, I had been kind of expecting an invitation or threat from them every morning, but nothing had materialized. Perhaps I had finally made my point to them. I wasn't theirs. I wasn't to be bullied around. I was a free agent. The last Maker in existence. I had defeated the Brothers Grimm. With friends, true, but the stories never come out that way. They always seem to fixate upon one person, as if it was mere coincidence that anyone else helped at all.

I shook my head. To be honest, I had been a failure. Without my friends, and their sacrifices, we would all be dead right now. And I had lost the only thing that mattered.

Indie.

I stood, stomping my boots a bit for warmth, and approached the tree.

I had tried carving into it with a knife, but the tip of the knife had broken. I had even tried magic, but nothing seemed able to mar its bark. Which was puzzling. Grimm watched me as I placed a hand on the bark, closing my eyes in an effort to stop the lone tear forming.

What was I without Indie? A familiar flash of rage pulsed through me, thinking of Death, and yet again coming to no conclusion as to what to do with him. He had made a silent appearance several times over the last few days, staying in the shadows to watch me anytime I left the house. My very own Grim Reaper. We pretended each other didn't exist, and that it was a mere coincidence to run into each other here of all places. Like strangers on a sidewalk. Ships in the night.

I almost didn't care about him anymore. I didn't care that I had won. It didn't matter if he had betrayed me. Sure, I might try to avenge her, if such a thing were even possible. He was a freaking Horseman of the Apocalypse, after all. Pretty sure I didn't stand a chance, Maker or not.

The world tasted like ashes in my mouth.

My biggest fear had come true. I had warned her. She hadn't listened.

I crouched, murmuring to the universe. "I miss you so god damned much, Indie..." I rolled the ring in my fingers, the metal seeming to freeze my fingertips with accusations.

"*Nate...?*" a voice called from the depths of my mind, a taunting whisper, as if someone was messing with my mind. But it was most likely my own guilt. I ignored it, shaking my head sadly.

The bark grew warmer under my palm and I frowned.

"*Nate...*" The voice was louder now, closer, more corporeal, but weakened. Why was my subconscious so freaking twisted? Did it think I wasn't grieving enough already?

"Temple," a new voice commanded, sounding displeased. "It's rude to keep a lady waiting..." I jumped to my feet, whirling to find Death facing me.

He was smiling softly. His skeletal hand slowly rose to point over my shoulder. My body moved mechanically, heart hammering in my chest.

And then it stopped entirely.

Indie stood leaning against the tree, knees quivering, unable to fully support her weight. I froze, staring at her. She looked... different. A shade.

Death had brought Indie's shade to my home. Perhaps as a peace offering. I felt anger and desire building inside me in equal measure. Anger at Death, desire to gain even one more moment with Indie.

She began to fall, and before I could think about it, I was there, catching her.

And... a physical body hit my hands. I almost dropped her as my body went into shock, not understanding. I barely managed to prevent us from both collapsing, and groaned softly as my thighs flexed, my arms quivering as they clutched Indie's body to mine. My wounds screamed in protest, but I held her tightly.

"Nate..." her voice was barely a whisper, but gained strength with use. "I'm not that heavy... asshole." She finally managed. Then she smiled, and my soul exploded into a million fragments. I shook with laughter, squeezing her arms, her back, her face as my breathing quickened.

And then I was kissing her. Her forehead. Her cheeks. Her hair. Her eyelids.

And finally...

Her lips.

Ohmygod. My mouth exploded with tingles as flesh met flesh in a perfect fit. She was still weak, but gave the kiss her all, and I realized only afterwards that we were both crying.

Death cleared his throat behind us and we separated, smiling guiltily at each other. I turned to face him. He was smiling. My mind raced. "How..."

He smiled, opening his mouth to answer, but Indie beat him to it, struggling between exhausted breaths. The color was returning to her cheeks, and her eyes seemed brighter with each passing minute. I even sensed that her strength was returning as her muscles flexed now and again under my arms.

"It was a setup, Nate. Death *saw* me at *Achilles' Heel*. He *saw* my death in the near future. But even he can't stop Fate." I blinked at her, following, but not following. He hadn't said a word about any of it. Risking my hatred. My power. My fury.

My friendship.

All to save the woman I loved.

As if sensing my question, he spoke. "I am not at liberty to discuss Fate with those not directly affected by it," he answered softly. "The spell couldn't be broken until you chose to speak directly to her. Which you finally did today."

"Let me down, Nate. I'm fine now. Just a little shaky." I did, watching her like a hawk as I set her down on a bench one of the gardeners had repaired and moved closer to the tree. She sat down taking a deep breath, and rolling her neck. Then she withdrew a handful of amulets from her person, extending them towards Death. The metal was unfamiliar to me. The obsidian gem of each amulet hung suspended in the shape of a double crescent, surrounded by a ring of tiny rubies. I was reminded of the familiar power pulsing in time with my own Maker magic. But I ignored that for now, curious as to what was about to go down. Death stepped closer. "As agreed, Horseman." She said solemnly.

He held out a hand, took the amulets, but didn't do anything with them. They dangled by the chains from his fist. "Pick three." He murmured.

She blinked at him with a frown, but didn't argue, choosing three at random. He nodded, pocketed the rest, and then clapped his hands together. A green glow suddenly erupted from between his fingers, and the smell of burning metal filled my nostrils. His eyes were closed, and as the magic pulsed, I saw beneath his skin to see a fearsome skeleton in robes, with wings made of bone, and eyes made of fire staring down at his ten-inch long skeletal fingers. The power abruptly ceased and he stood before me as a human again, except now a single chain and amulet hung from his fist, thicker, wider, but still seemingly delicate.

Feminine.

He groaned with pleasure, muscles flexing underneath his coat. "Ah, I missed that." He murmured.

"Missed what?" I asked, frowning.

"My power. I lent it to Indie when I swiped your amulet at the bar." He winked. I stared back, shaking my head. How many freaking pickpockets was I friends with? I had assumed I lost it during the fight at Raego's house.

"Wait, when you offered to give her a ride, denying Ashley, it was all part of a... *plan*?" I asked incredulously.

He nodded. "I knew Ashley would go through trials and tribulations, but that she would ultimately survive, and *thrive* in the years to come. Indie, however... she was destined to die. All I could do was make it to happen at the right time. In the right way. Give you what you needed to bring her back. We worked together in secret after *Achilles Heel*. With her permission, I... *gave* her to the Grimms." He admitted softly.

My world rocked.

Indie had knowingly sacrificed herself to save me? To give me the chance to in turn save *her*?

Death used the silence to offer her the chain.

"Is this necessary? It's not really my style," she asked. He nodded once. She sighed and reached out for the chain. The moment her fingers touched the metal, a dozen bolts of black lightning slammed down in unison in a perfect circle around the tree. My skin instantly pebbled with gooseflesh, and my ears rang at the sudden lack of sound. That didn't make any sense. Something as large as the tree should have attracted every single one of those bolts. But instead, they had struck the ground in what I would guess was a perfect circle around Indie. She looked physically unfazed, but mentally startled.

Death was grinning as he spoke. "It is the bargain for your life. Indiana Rippley, the mortal, died. A Freak was born. Balance." He held his fingers out like a scale. His next words struck me like a hot knife to the heart. "You must not take this off. Ever. You are now the last Grimm. In this world, at least. I'm sure the others are still out there in their void, waiting for a chance to come back. As long as you hold this amulet you are powerful. Just like they were. Not invincible, but not helpless anymore. Use this power wisely, like you did with my gift." His eyes grew distant, and my mind raced. Indie was a *Grimm*? Death finally continued, as if having debated the words. "You chose Jacob's own amulet, which makes you the de facto leader of the Grimms should they ever come back."

"*WHAT*?!" We both roared in unison.

Death smiled. But didn't elaborate. Grimm began to approach, plodding on delicate feet, ice and snow melting beneath the miniature craters of fire left by his hooves. He dropped his horn to Indie's chest and nickered, flashing his tail and flaring out his peacock-like mane. She placed a hand on the barbed horn, careful not to cut herself, and the beast calmed even further. She smiled.

I didn't.

"You risked your own power to keep Indie alive?" I asked, but he was already turning away.

He halted a dozen paces away, and turned to face me, eyes smiling as he answered softly. "It's what friends do. What Brothers do..."

Without warning, I Shadow Walked directly in front of him, satisfied at the sudden look of alarm on his face.

I tackled him to the ground.

And kissed him right on the mouth, crying and laughing uncontrollably. I punched him in the arm and jumped to my feet.

He climbed to his feet, brushing off the snow, and rubbing his mouth as if to wipe away germs, but he was chuckling in amusement. "Be wary, Brother. Whether you accept it or not, you used powers yesterday that could anoint you as a Horseman. What started out as a joke from us to you is now very much a... *possibility*. Not mandatory, but interesting nevertheless." He glanced over a shoulder as he walked away. "Be wary of the White Room."

His bark of laughter echoed across the grounds as a vertical ring of green fire exploded into existence, revealing a murky bar on the other side. He stepped through and the fire winked out like a snuffed candle, leaving Indie and me alone.

Charon suddenly appeared on his boat, hovering above the ground. "Freaking overtime." He growled through his sewn-up lips, the sound equivalent to a dozen rattlesnakes crawling through a pile of ancient bones. My skin instantly pebbled at the sensation of his voice and his presence. He took a heavy swig of a beer as he paddled his boat over the graves we had dug for the victims of the battle. Indie watched, wide-eyed.

"What took you so long, Charon?" I asked curiously.

He turned to me, polished off his beer, and then threw it in the back of his boat as several souls rose from beneath the earth and drifted up to sit beside him. The spirits looked at us with distant eyes, as if not seeing us. Perhaps the delay had pushed them too far beyond the land of the living to remember why they had died. Which was sad to me.

Charon finally answered. "Death lent her his power. Gave me a mini vacation. But you ruined that now." He grumbled, scowling at us for good measure. Then he began murmuring dirty limericks under his breath as he went about his work collecting souls. He waved one time and drifted off, having carted off all the souls he could carry.

Or just the ones he wanted to carry.

I wasn't exactly sure what his job requirements were.

I heard him crack open another beer and then he was gone.

I shoved my hands in my pockets for warmth, and for something to do as I turned to see Indie staring at me, face flush with the desire of life after her brief trip to the Land of the Dead. I had been fidgety since Indie's death, finding myself constantly needing to fiddle with something to calm my racing mind.

My fingertips clutched the cool metal of my mother's ring and my heart stopped.

Hope is a powerful, dangerous thing.

She had been gone. Now she wasn't. I had thought our *now* would last forever. Then I had experienced the realization that I would *never* have the chance to hold her again.

But everything had changed, thanks to Death. That sneaky, slimy, beautiful, incredible Horseman. I was grinning like an idiot.

Indie was shaking her head in disbelief, staring off at nothing, fingers caressing the necklace she now wore. "I'm not powerless anymore, Nate." She said softly, eyes thoughtful. "I can protect myself now. Well, after you teach me how to use it. Do you think you could do that?" I managed to disguise my smile as she lifted her gaze to mine.

"Only one way to find out." I answered, fingers sweating as they clutched the ring.

I stepped closer, only a few feet away now.

"Good, because I feel funny. We should probably make it a priority. Or find someone who can help. Pandora?"

"Maybe. But for now, I'll give it a try." I was only a step away now.

A lot can happen between now and never...

"Indie...?" I asked, practically quivering with nerves.

"Mmm?" She answered, smiling up at me. I spotted Alucard's umbrella sword leaning against the tree. With all the surprises, its presence didn't even make me bat an eye. I pointed it out to Indie, using it to distract my approach. "Oh," she exclaimed, picking it up thoughtfully. "For me?"

I nodded. "Alucard's parting gift. From your funeral..." Her eyes grew thoughtful, but I didn't elaborate. We would talk about all that later. I was close enough now.

I more or less fell to both knees, and extended the ring to her. Her eyes widened. "Will you—"

"Yes!" She shrieked, tackling me into the snow and burying her tear-stained face into my shoulder for a second and squeezing me as hard as she could. Her hair fanned out around me like angel wings as she leaned back to stare into my eyes. "Yes..." she repeated softly. I placed the ring on her finger, her eyes watching the motion in rapture.

"It's no *Infinity Gauntlet*, but I don't know what happened to that after..."

Instead of answering, she kissed me like it was her last night on earth.

But in fact, it was just the opposite. This was technically her first night on earth.

Indie. My fiancée. Dead. And reborn as a Grimm. *The* Grimm, if Death was right.

Like I said, a lot can happen between *now* and *never...*

I was kind of anxious to see what the world had for us next...

DON'T FORGET! VIP's get early access to all sorts of Temple-Verse goodies, including signed copies, private giveaways, and advance notice of future projects. AND A FREE NOVELLA! Click the image or join here:
www.shaynesilvers.com/l/219800

*Nate Temple returns in **SILVER TONGUE**. Turn the page for a sample...*

Or get the book ONLINE! http://www.shaynesilvers.com/l/38703

TEASER: SILVER TONGUE (TEMPLE #4)

I was going to kill him. "Do we really need to talk about this right now? This isn't as easy as I'm making it look," I hissed, crouching in the shadows of an old brick warehouse, focusing intently on the illusion spell I'd wrapped around the both of us. I clutched a book tightly, a slight tingle vibrating my arm as I caressed the embossed black leather cover. The sensation was no doubt caused by the residual traces of magic that were warding it for safekeeping, but I was masking that from detection now. *Success*, I thought to myself as I tucked it into my satchel.

Alucard's fangs glistened in the moonlight. I looked up between the buildings at the glowing sliver of moon, and spotted a dark tide of hungry clouds rolling in. A big storm. One of those old Missouri Summer storms that pounded the city clean with a vengeance of rain and ear-splitting thunder and lightning.

As if a premonition of the storm to come, guttural howls of outrage, and an inhuman hunting cry pierced the air, and then the pounding of many thunderous feet filled the streets. I shivered. They were onto us.

My accomplice didn't catch my tone. Or prioritize our current predicament.

"It's just that... well, the job is *hard*."

I rolled my eyes, tracking the heavy footfalls that were racing about in a frantic search just around the corner. "It's a fucking bookstore, Alucard." I wanted to grab him by his canines and throttle him. Worthless vampires.

"Yeah, but—"

I held up a hand, silencing him instantly.

A throaty basso voice rumbled, "Clear," from just around the corner. It was a harsh sound, as if unused to speaking in anything other than consonants and growls. The thud of his calloused feet continued off into the distance. I took a deep breath and rounded on Alucard, careful to put as much venom into my tone as possible without breaking our masking spell. I was good, but not good enough to cover a shouting match.

"Get your head in the game. Ogres don't appreciate being robbed."

"Why don't you just *buy* it from them, then? You know, like you *told* them you were—"

A barbed arrow struck the brick wall right behind Alucard's ear, hammering deep into the stone. A frustrated curse rang out at the near miss, and all of a sudden I sensed many bodies changing direction to come directly at us.

"Goddamn it!" I hissed at Alucard, careful to not use his name now that they had found us. He tensed, as if about to launch himself at the archer on the roof that had nearly pierced his ear. Twenty vertical feet wasn't difficult for a vampire. I immediately grasped his forearm, squeezing hard to stress the importance of my warning. "Remember to stay in character!" His lips tightened briefly, and then slowly morphed into a grin. He suddenly belted out a pious clarion call for all to hear.

"Usurpers, fiends, abominations, all!" And then he ran *up* the side of the building against our backs, and laterally launched his body across the alley to tackle the goblin archer on the adjacent roof. The goblin simply stared at his impending demise in utter disbelief, the second arrow in his calloused hand hanging loosely, forgotten.

Alucard slammed into him and the weapons went clattering down the fire escape loud enough to pinpoint our exact location. *Damn it, Alucard.* I didn't have time to go after him. I tapped a few buttons on my watch, the screen depicting an aerial view of the city block around us. A swarm of glowing red forms were converging on my position in the dark alley at the bottom of the screen. I tapped a few options on the screen to send the drone home and covered my watch. I still had a warehouse of technological goodies I had, um, appropriated from my company, Temple Industries, before it had been sold to a German firm. The FBI frowned on insider trading, even though it had all really just been a setup: The Brothers Grimm complicating my life a few months back.

Seeing no other option, I sighed and stepped out into the open. A dozen or so gargantuan ogres skidded to a halt upon seeing me. They were covered in tan hides over their grey, warty, scarred skin. Primordial weapons of bone and flint hung in their meaty fists as they seethed with hatred upon seeing me. Their heads were bald, but some sported beards. Even a few of the Ogresses had faint mustaches. Ick. Several looked amazed that a lone, weaponless human stood calmly against their gang.

But if my illusion spell was working as intended – and the look on the archer's face had kind of confirmed it was working flawlessly – they saw something else entirely standing before them. Something to be feared... or at least acknowledged with no small amount of respect. Then again, ogres weren't too bright. So, I was ready for anything.

The leader gripped a club as big as my torso in his meaty fist. He let the tip thump to the ground as he challenged me with an aggressive glint in his eyes.

"Pretty birdboy going to die," he growled.

I smirked back in what I hope looked like pious disdain – in line with my character. I was still getting the hang of my powers, and wasn't entirely sure how adaptable my disguise was. For all I knew, I was standing there with a mentally deficient look on my face. Or no emotion at all. I guessed either would work fine with this disguise. I didn't speak, not wanting to risk giving my true nature away. Instead, I tapped my cane on the ground and it rang out like a bell. The lead ogre stared at the cane with trepidation, but of course, he didn't see a cane at all.

The ogres were all seeing a monstrous Crusades-era sword, and it was glowing with crackling blue-white light. Because standing before them was a Nephilim, a child of an Angel of Heaven and a mortal. And most avoided Nephilim like the plague, because they were rather... *Old Testament*, you could say. No forgive and forget with them.

Illusions kind of rock.

I wasn't sure how much action the illusion could handle, so I was banking on the fact that simply seeing a Heavenly Warrior might be enough to keep them at bay. That had been my plan anyway, before Alucard had stumbled into an empty trashcan while we were creeping out of their vault, alerting every ogre on the block. I couldn't risk my illusion failing if I threw down with them here and now, revealing my true identity. Especially if I used any overt magic. Nephilim were dangerous, but wizards they ain't. Magic would give me away faster than a cockroach skittering across the linoleum when the lights flicked on.

I felt the strain of my spell tugging at me as Alucard drew further away. Tiny droplets of sweat began to pop up on my forehead. My vision began to grow blue with the strain, as sometimes happened. If the spell broke, these guys would know exactly who had robbed them blind. Which wouldn't go over well. Not at all.

So, I was bluffing. And I hoped they didn't call me on it.

No elemental whips. No fire, no Shadow Walking. Just my shiny new cane.

"No God here..." The leader snarled, and then raced towards me like a charging rhinoceros. I waited until the last second, feinted left, then darted to the right, lashing out with my 'sword' at his feet. The cane traced a line of white fire across his flesh, and boy, did he howl!

I sneered contemptuously. The remaining ogres watched him writhing in pain as he bled out, none offering so much as to help him stand. They exchanged glances with each other, and I watched as their features began to darken in outrage.

"Oh, shit," I whispered, under my breath. They slowly turned back to me, hungry grins on their cheeks, and then surged forward with a murderous roar that seemed to make the pavement quake.

I thought about that outcome for all of a millisecond, and then turned and fled. I took two running steps up the wall and catapulted myself to the lower rungs of the fire escape. I used a tiny boost of power to give me the extra juice to reach, and latched on, quickly pulling myself to safety. One of the ogres pounded the wall below me with his hammer fist, the brick crumbling. Then his pals began to join in. The old building groaned. I raced up the metal stairs, gaining the roof to find Alucard ripping the throat out of his attacker. He leaned in as if to give the goblin a kiss.

"Stop!" I hissed. "Nephilim, *remember*?" I enunciated the words in low tones as I ran towards him. He shuddered, eyes lidded closed for a moment before dropping the body to the roof. He turned to me, eyes swimming with the bloodlust of his inner vampire, irises flashing a crimson red. The illusion didn't work on us. We saw our true forms. I grabbed his shoulder and shook him until his eyes cleared. I waggled a hand for us to hurry as the building quivered again, the pounding of hairy fist against mortal brick like a steady drumbeat. He nodded, looking slightly embarrassed. "We're out of here. I'm sending an illusion of us flying away like good little Nephilim."

Alucard nodded as I squinted in strained focus, gathering my power and wrapping it around a single thought. The literal belief that what I was making was real. That two Nephilim were throwing themselves off a perfectly good roof before unfolding their wings and fleeing the ogres' compound. Once confident of every minor detail, I let out my breath in a rush and flicked my hand. Power drained out of me and my knees shook as the illusion took form.

Two rather scrawny Nephilim hurtled themselves off the roof, anxiously checking over their shoulders as they flew to safety. I nodded to myself, redoubled the illusion spell that was no longer disguising us, but hiding our presence entirely, and ripped a hole through reality. A verdant spherical Gateway of fire flared into existence, revealing a quiet street several blocks away on the other side. The flames limning the door reached toward the calm street with hungry, dancing claws, stating the direction of the intended travel. As far as I knew, no one would be able to walk from the other side to my current location – they would be eaten alive by the flames.

As long as those flames pointed the direction you wanted to go, you were safe.

Sparks sailed off the flames, darting through the opening and into the street beyond.

Alucard's dark eyes glittered in the moonlight as he turned from the portal to me.

He looked impressed, but also thoughtful. I rolled my eyes at him. He was still getting used to how I handled things, but now wasn't the time. I shoved him through the opening, followed, and pulled it closed behind me as I heard the fire escape protesting under immense weight. A quick glance back revealed no pursuers, so I hoped no one had noticed our true getaway...

Get your copy of SILVER TONGUE online today! http://www.shaynesilvers.com/l/38703

MAKE A DIFFERENCE

Reviews are the most powerful tools in my arsenal when it comes to getting attention for my books. Much as I'd like to, I don't have the financial muscle of a New York publisher.

But I do have something much more powerful and effective than that, and it's something that those publishers would kill to get their hands on.

A committed and loyal bunch of readers.

Honest reviews of my books help bring them to the attention of other readers.

If you've enjoyed this book, I would be very grateful if you could spend just five minutes leaving a review (it can be as short as you like) on my book's Amazon page.

Thank you very much in advance.

I hope you enjoyed reading this first Boxset as much as I enjoyed writing it. Be sure to grab the second Boxset (30% OFF!) with books 4-6 on Amazon.

Be sure to check out the two crossover series in the Temple Verse: The **Feathers and Fire Series** and the **Phantom Queen Diaries**.

ACKNOWLEDGMENTS

First, I would like to thank my beta-readers, TEAM TEMPLE, those individuals who spent hours of their time to read, and re-re-read Nate's story. Your dark, twisted, cunning sense of humor makes me feel right at home...

I would also like to thank you, the reader. I hope you enjoyed reading this first Boxset as much as I enjoyed writing it.

Be sure to grab the second Boxset (30% OFF!) with books 4-6 HERE! http://www.shaynesilvers.com/l/57481

Be sure to check out the two crossover series in the Temple Verse: The **Feathers and Fire Series** and the **Phantom Queen Diaries**.

And last, but definitely not least, I thank my wife, Lexy. Without your support, none of this would have been possible.

ABOUT SHAYNE SILVERS

Shayne is a man of mystery and power, whose power is exceeded only by his mystery...

He currently writes the Amazon Bestselling **Nate Temple** Series, which features a foul-mouthed wizard from St. Louis. He rides a bloodthirsty unicorn, drinks with Achilles, and is pals with the Four Horsemen.

He also writes the Amazon Bestselling **Feathers and Fire** Series—a second series in the TempleVerse. The story follows a rookie spell-slinger named Callie Penrose who works for the Vatican in Kansas City. Her problem? Hell seems to know more about her past than she does.

He coauthors **The Phantom Queen Diaries**—a third series set in The TempleVerse—with Cameron O'Connell. The story follows Quinn MacKenna, a mouthy black magic arms dealer in Boston. All she wants? A round-trip ticket to the Fae realm...and maybe a drink on the house.

He also writes the **Shade of Devil Series**, which tells the story of Sorin Ambrogio—the world's FIRST vampire. He was put into a magical slumber by a Native American Medicine Man when the Americas were first discovered by Europeans. Sorin wakes up after five-hundred years to learn that his protege, Dracula, stole his reputation and that no one has ever even heard of Sorin Ambrogio. The streets of New York City will run with blood as Sorin reclaims his legend.

Shayne holds two high-ranking black belts, and can be found writing in a coffee shop, cackling madly into his computer screen while pounding shots of espresso. He's hard at work on the newest books in the TempleVerse—You can find updates on new releases or chronological reading order on the next page, his website, or any of his social media accounts. <u>**Follow him online for all sorts of groovy goodies, giveaways, and new release updates:**</u>

Get Down with Shayne Online
www.shaynesilvers.com
info@shaynesilvers.com

- facebook.com/shaynesilversfanpage
- amazon.com/author/shaynesilvers
- bookbub.com/profile/shayne-silvers
- instagram.com/shaynesilversofficial
- twitter.com/shaynesilvers
- goodreads.com/ShayneSilvers

BOOKS BY SHAYNE SILVERS

CHRONOLOGY: *All stories in the TempleVerse are shown in chronological order on the following page*

NATE TEMPLE SERIES
(Main series in the TempleVerse)
by Shayne Silvers

FAIRY TALE - FREE prequel novella #0 for my subscribers

OBSIDIAN SON

BLOOD DEBTS

GRIMM

SILVER TONGUE

BEAST MASTER

BEERLYMPIAN (Novella #5.5 in the 'LAST CALL' anthology)

TINY GODS

DADDY DUTY (Novella #6.5)

WILD SIDE

WAR HAMMER

NINE SOULS

HORSEMAN

LEGEND

KNIGHTMARE

ASCENSION

FEATHERS AND FIRE SERIES
(Also set in the TempleVerse)
by Shayne Silvers

UNCHAINED

RAGE

WHISPERS

ANGEL'S ROAR

MOTHERLUCKER (Novella #4.5 in the 'LAST CALL' anthology)

SINNER

BLACK SHEEP

GODLESS

PHANTOM QUEEN DIARIES

(Also set in the TempleVerse)

by Cameron O'Connell & Shayne Silvers

COLLINS (Prequel novella #0 in the 'LAST CALL' anthology)

WHISKEY GINGER

COSMOPOLITAN

OLD FASHIONED

MOTHERLUCKER (Novella #3.5 in the 'LAST CALL' anthology)

DARK AND STORMY

MOSCOW MULE

WITCHES BREW

SALTY DOG

SEA BREEZE

HURRICANE

CHRONOLOGICAL ORDER: TEMPLE VERSE

FAIRY TALE (TEMPLE PREQUEL)

OBSIDIAN SON (TEMPLE 1)

BLOOD DEBTS (TEMPLE 2)

GRIMM (TEMPLE 3)

SILVER TONGUE (TEMPLE 4)

BEAST MASTER (TEMPLE 5)

BEERLYMPIAN (TEMPLE 5.5)

TINY GODS (TEMPLE 6)

DADDY DUTY (TEMPLE NOVELLA 6.5)

UNCHAINED (FEATHERS... 1)

RAGE (FEATHERS... 2)

WILD SIDE (TEMPLE 7)

WAR HAMMER (TEMPLE 8)

WHISPERS (FEATHERS... 3)

COLLINS (PHANTOM 0)
WHISKEY GINGER (PHANTOM... 1)
NINE SOULS (TEMPLE 9)
COSMOPOLITAN (PHANTOM... 2)
ANGEL'S ROAR (FEATHERS... 4)
MOTHERLUCKER (FEATHERS 4.5, PHANTOM 3.5)
OLD FASHIONED (PHANTOM...3)
HORSEMAN (TEMPLE 10)
DARK AND STORMY (PHANTOM... 4)
MOSCOW MULE (PHANTOM...5)
SINNER (FEATHERS...5)
WITCHES BREW (PHANTOM...6)
LEGEND (TEMPLE...11)
SALTY DOG (PHANTOM...7)
BLACK SHEEP (FEATHERS...6)
GODLESS (FEATHERS...7)
KNIGHTMARE (TEMPLE 12)
ASCENSION (TEMPLE 13)
SEA BREEZE (PHANTOM...8)
HURRICANE (PHANTOM...9)

SHADE OF DEVIL SERIES

(Not part of the TempleVerse)

by Shayne Silvers

DEVIL'S DREAM
DEVIL'S CRY
DEVIL'S BLOOD

Printed in Great Britain
by Amazon